COMPLETE
SERIES

# KISSES

## DEBRA ST JAMES

# Kisses

## COMPLETE SERIES

### DEBRA ST JAMES

**Kisses | Complete Series**

© 2023 by Debra St James

No part of this publication may be reproduced, distributed, or transmitted in any form or by any means, including photocopying, recording, or other electronic or mechanical methods, without the prior written permission of the publisher, except in the case of brief quotations embodied in crucial reviews and certain other noncommercial uses permitted by copyright law.

This novel is a work of fiction. While references may be made to actual historical events or existing locations, the names, characters, places, and incidents are products of the author's imagination. Any resemblance to people either living or deceased, business establishments, events, or locales are purely coincidental and not intended by the author.

Any trademarks, service marks, product names, or named features are assumed to be the property of their respective owners and are only used for reference. There is no implied endorsement if any of these terms are used.

Website: www.debrastjamesbooks.com

Email: debrastjamesbooks@gmail.com

Published by: Debra St James Author

Edited by: Double AA Author Services and Cruel Ink Editing and Design

Formatted by: Debra St James Author

ISBN: 978-0-6454536-1-4 [Paperback]

ISBN: 978-0-6457395-6-5 [Discreet Edition Paperback]

ISBN: 978-0-6454536-0-7 [Ebook]

KISSES
*book one*

*stolen*
KISSES

DEBRA ST JAMES

*inspiration*

This story was inspired by the lyrics ...

—> *My Stupid Mouth by John Mayer* <—

# a note from debra

THIS BOOK IS DEDICATED TO THE WOMEN IN MY LIFE WHO HAVE FOUGHT and kicked breast cancer's butt. Jo and Di, you inspire me with your courage, poise, and positivity.

To all the women who have survived breast cancer
YOU ARE A LEGEND.
If you're in the middle of your own battle—
YOU'VE GOT THIS!

**To all the women and men who read this story ...
CHECK YOUR BOOBIES!**

Thank you, Di, for sharing your particular experience with me as I was working to ensure Emma's story reflected the reality of *Ductal Carcinoma In Situ*. I appreciate the candor with which you answered my numerous and personally invasive questions. You're the best, lady!

Everyone's journey with breast cancer is different. This story shows *one* woman's journey; her experiences and feelings are completely her own. What I would like you to take away from this story is that you must always be vigilant about your personal health.

# *playlist*

My Stupid Mouth … *John Mayer*
Tip of My Tongue … *Diesel*
Moves Like Jagger … *Maroon 5 with Christina Aguilera*
Happy … *Pharrell Williams*
All Woman … *Lisa Stansfield*
Scars to Your Beautiful … *Alessia Cara*
Can't Stop the Feeling … *Justin Timberlake*
Your Body is a Wonderland … *John Mayer*
Steal my Kisses … *Ben Harper and the Innocent Criminals*
Daughters … *John Mayer*

**You can check it out here:**
*https://tinyurl.com/stolenkisses-spotify*

# CHAPTER 1

## —emma—

I DON'T REALLY FEEL LIKE WORKING IN THE GARDEN TODAY, BUT I noticed the moving van pull up next door … and well, I'm a nosy parker. So here I am on the one day I could dress up and hang out at the mall uninterrupted, on my hands and knees, ass in the air, pulling weeds. When Nancy told me just over a month ago that she was selling, I didn't think I'd be getting new neighbors so quickly. The house is beautiful and recently renovated, so I completely understand why it sold so fast. If I was in a better financial position, I would have bought it myself. It's bigger than my place, which I think I'll need as the boys get bigger. I haven't laid eyes on the new owners yet because I'm doing my best not to be conspicuous, so I have my ass facing their house, which sort of inhibits my ability to spy.

"Hello, lady."

Sheet! I almost jump out of my skin. She certainly snuck up on me. Raising my head, I'm greeted by the most beautiful little girl I think I've ever seen. Stunning clear blue eyes the color of the sky, long honey-brown hair, which looks like it needs a good brush, a pouty mouth, and gorgeous olive skin.

"Uh, hello." I rest my ass on my feet, brushing my bangs out of my face. At a guess, she must be around four years old. I look around to see where her parents are. I would never let my boys speak to a stranger on their own. "Where's your mommy and daddy?"

"I dunno where my daddy is and my mommy's gone to heaven." *Oh!* My heart cracks for this little girl. She comes closer, squatting down to inspect the garden bed I'm working on. She points a chubby finger as she scrunches up her little button nose. "Is that a worm?"

I tear my eyes away from her to check what she's pointing at. "Uh, yeah. Looks like it. The soil must be pretty healthy for the worm to live here."

She giggles. "He's vewy wiggly."

"Yeah, he's pretty wriggly." I look back next door to see if I can spot her dad, but there's nobody in sight.

"Have you got kids?"

"Um, yeah, I do. Two boys."

"What's their names?"

"My oldest boy is Lachlan, and my youngest son is Austin. What's your name?"

"Kenny." Such an unusual name for a little girl, but I think it suits her. "Where are they?" She looks around as if they're playing close by and she's missed them somehow.

"Well, Kenny. They're visiting their nana and poppa today."

"When will they be home?"

"Not until tomorrow. They're having a sleepover."

She huffs out a sigh. "I wanted to play wiv someone."

"Sorry. Maybe you could ask your daddy if you could come back tomorrow afternoon?"

"I dunno where my daddy is. I'm wiv my uncle."

"Are you helping him move in?"

"I'm not weally much help. He says I'm too little." She drops down to sit on her bottom next to me. "Can I stay wiv you?"

"Won't your uncle be worried about where you are?"

She rolls her sparkling eyes. "He's busy in his workshop. He said I'm not allowed in there."

Well, I guess if he's too busy to watch his niece, at least I'll know she's safe if I'm watching her. "Sure. You wanna help pull the weeds out?"

"Okay."

I show her which plants are the weeds, then give her my small trowel so she can dig them out. I don't have any gloves small enough to fit her, so her hands will get dirty. Better than playing on the street unsupervised, though. I'll have to give her uncle a piece of my mind.

She gets to work and, for a short while; she focuses fully on her task. The sheer concentration on her face is adorable.

"What's your name?"

"My name's Emma."

"I'm four years old." She holds up five fingers and then uses her other hand to tuck her thumb down. "How old are you?"

Uhm, I'm pretty sure my eyebrows just hit my hairline. I shouldn't be surprised. Kids this age are inquisitive little characters.

"I'm thirty-seven." I cringe when I think about being closer to forty than thirty. The years are flying by and I feel as though I'm standing still with my life.

"My uncle's gonna be forty on Thursday." She brushes the dirt off her hands, stands up, and places them on her hips. "He told me he's not having a birthday this year."

If only we could do that and not age. I would certainly welcome the ability to skip out on birthdays. Kenny wanders around my garden, inspecting the various plants, holding her hands behind her back like an old man. She's quite the character.

"You've got some pwetty flowers. I like the purple ones best."

"Me too. I think purple flowers look lovely against the green leaves."

Kenny nods thoughtfully. "White flowers look nice, too."

"Yes, they do. What's your favorite color flower?" If she can ask questions, I'll ask a couple of my own.

"Mommy liked pink flowers best. They was her favowite. Now they're my favowite too."

There she goes, cracking my heart open again. I think it's sweet that she's taken on her mom's favored color. I don't have many pink flowers, maybe I'll get some more. They'll look nice with the purple and white flowers I already have.

She comes back and flops down next to me; laying on her back, she spreads out her arms and legs on the grass. Looking and pointing up at the sky, she asks, "See that cloud up there?"

Shielding my eyes, I look up to the sky. There's a single fluffy white cloud. "Yeah."

"Mommy's pwobably having a nap up there. She had a lot of naps before she went to heaven." Her cute little cheeks raise with a half-smile and my heart splits right down the middle.

I wonder how her mom died. Was it sudden? Or did she know she was going to be leaving her baby girl motherless? Boulders settle in my chest at the thought of something happening to me. My boys would be left with a father who's disinterested in them at best and no mother to show them the love they need to grow and thrive. I know

Mom, Dad, Max, and Sarah would look after them, but it's not the same.

She jumps up like a spring, brushing the loose grass from her shorts. "I better pull some more weeds out."

"I need to empty my bucket. You wanna help me?" I ask as I stand. "Okay."

Kenny takes one side of the bucket, while I carry the other, taking the bulk of the weight. We wander through my side gate and I take the opportunity to pop my head over the lower part of the fence to see if I can spot her uncle in his workshop, but I can't see anything from this vantage. Arriving at the bin, I grab the bucket and tip the weeds into it.

Heavy steps thunder on the other side of the fence. "Kennedy! Kennedy!" The deep, masculine voice is panicked. I look down at Kenny. I'm guessing her uncle's finally noticed she's missing and is now looking for her. She gives me a timid grin.

"I think your uncle's looking for you."

"Shhh. Let's hide." She holds her pointer finger up to her lips, which are tipped up, her eyes twinkling in mischief.

Oh, I don't think so. I don't want to cause her uncle any more worry, though it would serve him right. She's been with me for almost an hour. That's a long time for a four-year-old to get into all sorts of trouble. Where did he think she was?

"Kennedy Olivia Drivas!" Oh, he's played the triple-name card. "You come here right this instant," his thunderous tone echoes down the street.

I step through the gate and spot him. His broad back is facing me as he paces toward the street, hands on narrow hips, looking for his wayward niece. From the back, he's quite impressive.

"Hi." My voice cracks and my greeting doesn't quite make it out. I clear my throat. "Uh, hi," I say, louder and clearer this time.

He turns around and the wave I was about to offer dies in its tracks. All the saliva in my mouth dries up as I lay eyes on a mighty fine specimen of a man. He runs his hand through dark hair and steps toward me. Kenny's right behind me—hiding.

"Have you seen a little girl?" He holds out his hand at about hip height. "About this tall. Blue eyes, long light-brown hair." He wriggles his fingers down his body, showing the length of her hair, drawing my eyes to magnificent pecs.

I seem to have lost my voice, so I step to the side, exposing my new little friend. Do you remember all those words I was going to have with my new neighbor about looking after his niece? Well, they've all disappeared into the ether. I'm having a hard time trying to even think at this point. Striking blue eyes, dark scruff, and thick hair adorn a chiseled face that could easily be on the cover of GQ magazine.

His eyes wander downward, catching on to his niece. She's half hiding behind my leg, her head tilted down as though she's preparing to get into trouble. I'm not sure what their story is, but she seems a little scared of him.

"Kennedy, I told you to stay in the house." Ahhh, that name makes a little more sense. He steps forward, and she tucks herself further behind me, wrapping her arms around my thigh.

"Kenny," she whispers, poking her little head around my thigh.

"What?" He pauses mid-step, eyebrows drawn low.

"I told you, I wanna be called Kenny."

He looks up at me, raising his eyebrows, a ghost of a smile playing on his lips. "Sorry, I forgot." Holding out his hand to his niece, he coaxes. "I'll try to remember. Come on. It's time to come home."

*Home?* So she *must* be staying with him. She didn't mention an aunty. Is there a woman around to help him? Because he seems pretty clueless about caring for a young child. Her little arms tighten further around my thigh, and she's really digging in. I try to step to the side, but she steps with me.

Huffing out a sigh, my neighbor looks up at me and all I can offer is a shrug. *Some words would be helpful right about now.*

"Come on. I need to get back to work." He wriggles his fingers in her direction, his patience clearly wearing thin.

*What?* "You're not going to abandon her again, are you?"

His gorgeous blue eyes, which match his niece's, snap to mine. "No. She'll be in the house and I'll be in the workshop out back." He points his thumb over his shoulder toward the back of his house.

"You can't leave a four-year-old to her own devices while you do whatever it is you're doing out back," I snap, waving my arm in the direction of the workshop.

"Look, lady—"

"Emma. My name's Emma," I snap.

"Okay, Emma. Thanks for finding her, but she'll be fine. She can unpack her stuff while I try to get her bed sorted."

A four-year-old unpacking her 'stuff'. That's freaking laughable. "You can't expect a four-year-old to unpack their 'stuff', while you're not there to supervise. How much experience have you had with children?" I huff out, incredulous.

He raises his arm to scrub his fingers through his short bristles and my eyes are drawn—without permission, I might add—to the masculine bulge of his muscles. He looks at his watch. "Uh, about six and a half hours. Give or take."

*What the hell?* I'm pretty sure my chin's hit my paved driveway. I look down at Kenny. She said her mom's in heaven; surely it didn't just happen. He must read the confusion on my face because I'm terrible at hiding my reactions. Unfortunately for me, everything I think or feel is displayed clearly on my face for all the world to see.

"Today's the first time we've spent any time together since … her uh, her … mother, my sister, passed. Before that, I saw …" He tilts his head down toward his niece. "Kenny." He raises his eyebrows in a manner that says, *'see, I remembered'*. "When she was born."

I don't understand how that can be. Max and Sarah see my boys regularly. They want to be part of their lives growing up and the boys' lives are richer for it. Their relationship with my boys is an extension of our relationship as siblings. It's not my business, though. I don't even know this guy's name and it's incredibly rude to ask him all sorts of personal and invasive questions, even if I want to.

I place my hand on Kenny's back in reassurance. "She can hang out here while you get organized. I don't mind. She was helping me pull out the weeds before." I look down at Kenny. "She was doing a great job." I smile at her.

"Look. Thanks for the offer, but she needs to take some responsibility for her own things." He steps forward and attempts to pry her hands away from my thigh. His large hand is incredibly close to my lady parts as he peels her fingers away one by one. I suck in a breath at the tingles his touch elicits. "Come on, Kenny. Say bye to Emma. Let's go."

"I wanna stay wiv Emma. She's nice." She drops her bottom lip in a pout, as her eyebrows scrunch down over her eyes in defiance.

My neighbor pulls back as though he's been burned. "*I'm* nice."

"You're gwumpy and you won't play wiv me." I can't hold back my smile but manage to stifle my giggle at her statement.

He scratches his fingers through his beard again. "Because I have a sh— a lot to do. I don't have time to play with you," he huffs out.

"You know, Kenny. If you help your uncle …" I look up at him, hinting that he hasn't told me his name yet, but he's too caught up with his own agenda to notice my clue. "You'll get the work done quicker, and then he might have some time to play with you. There's a great park at the end of the street." I point in the direction of the park. I hope he takes the hint I'm putting down for him.

"I don't wanna unpack a million things. I wanna play." She stomps her little foot, dropping her bottom lip in a full-on pout. Anyone with a heart wouldn't be able to resist that little face. I'm certain he's going to cave, but he surprises me.

"You know that cookie dough ice cream I got just for you?"

"Yeah." A broad smile spreads quickly. She looks up at me. "It's Mommy's favowite flavor."

I swallow down the lump in my throat. "My boys love cookie dough ice cream, too."

"Yeah, well, if you don't come home, I'm gonna eat all of it. By myself." He finishes his statement with a lick of his lips, a shrug to his shoulders, and crosses his arms over his broad chest.

Mmhm. Those forearms are something else. I shake my head, drawing myself out of my drool-fest, and frown at him. He really has no idea.

"You wouldn't do that," Kenny retorts.

"Try me." He's smug in his confidence that this approach is going to work.

Her little hands peel away from my thigh and she takes a step away. Looking up at me, she says, "See ya, Emma."

Color me surprised. His technique actually worked. She takes his hand and they walk together back to the house next door. She turns back to look at me over her shoulder, offering a wave; he doesn't give me a second glance. I feel her departure acutely and give her a small wave in return. I can't help but worry about the gorgeous little girl and her handsome uncle. My need to stop him and check that he's going to be able to manage is strong, but I tamp it down. I'm going to have to keep busy for the rest of today and tonight to stop myself from constantly wanting to check in on them.

# CHAPTER 2

## *theo*

I'M GONNA HAVE TO GROW EYES IN THE BACK OF MY HEAD WITH THIS kid. I remember Mom used to say she had eyes in the back of her head and I'm already beginning to see why she needed them. Kennedy, *Kenny*, needs constant supervision. I can see why Dad couldn't care for her anymore with the amount of time he needs for the restaurant. When we lost my sister eight months ago to the same disease which took Mom, I wasn't sure how Dad would cope until I could move back to take over her guardianship at my sister's request. I realize now that taking care of Kenny would have kept him so busy, he wouldn't have had time to think. For such a tiny little thing, she certainly takes up a lot of mental space. Space I'm not used to being filled.

I'm ashamed to admit that Kenny and I don't even know each other. I'm a stranger to her and now, suddenly, I'm her primary care-giver. I know I was grumpy with her, but I'm not used to having to temper myself. I'm used to a life of solitude. Doing what I want, when I want, without interruption. I've never had anything to do with kids and the thought of raising this little girl, of being solely responsible for her, is fucking overwhelming.

I should have taken my sexy neighbor up on her offer to leave Kenny with her, so I could get shit done around here. Her conde-scending tone and look of disapproval were enough to have me on the defensive and determined to get my niece to come with me. It almost felt like a competition to get her to choose me rather than stay with the stunner next door.

What a knockout!

Those killer curves.

Her eyes; I couldn't quite tell if they were brown or green, but they were full of fire and incredibly beautiful.

The way Kenny clung onto her thick thigh—which I would love to have wrapped around my head—was enough to make me want to escape her presence before I did or said something to embarrass myself. I shake away the lustful thoughts which are completely inappropriate in the company of my four-year-old niece.

Kenny tugs on my shorts. "Uncle Theo, I'm hungwy."

I check the time. *Shit!* I've forgotten to feed the kid. I don't necessarily eat at the standard times, only when I'm hungry, but I guess little kids need food more often. Considering we ate breakfast at six this morning and it's now after one, she's been very forgiving.

"Sure, Kid. Let's get some lunch." We head into the kitchen and I unpack the bags of food we picked up on the way over from Dad's place. We only have basic supplies at this point. "What do you want on your sandwich? I have peanut butter, jelly, cheese, or turkey. I could do grilled cheese. You like grilled cheese?"

"Can I haf peanut butter and jelly, please?"

"Sure thing." She sits up at the counter, watching me make her sandwich. I slather jelly on one slice of bread and peanut butter on the other slice, then slap them together, chuck it on a plate, and slide it across to her.

Her little nose scrunches up. "You s'posed to cut it." She slides the plate back to me.

"Sorry. How do you want it cut?" I pick up the knife, ready to do her bidding.

"In four sqwares." She holds up five fingers and then uses her other hand to hold down her thumb. She's a cute kid and I think she's reasonably smart for her age, but I'm not sure since I haven't had much to do with kids before today. She tilts her head to the side, waiting for me to cut her sandwich and I'm lost in her expression; her mannerisms are so much like my sister's. A pang hits my chest and the regret of not being here for my sister throughout her battle strikes me hard.

It was too difficult for me to come home. I couldn't expose myself to my father's disappointment in me again, and I didn't want to relive the disease that stole our mother away from us when we were kids.

I cut the sandwich as requested and slide it across the counter. I make a sandwich for myself and fill two large glasses with milk. Maybe

I should give her some fruit as well? Kids need to eat a lot of fruit, don't they? I'm pretty sure that'd be the right thing to do. I slice an apple and put it in a bowl next to her.

As I sit down to eat, Kenny looks at her glass. "Mommy and Pappoús don't let me dwink fwom a glass."

Damn it! I've done the wrong thing again. "I don't have plastic cups. Can you be a big girl and be careful?"

She nods, a frown wrinkling her forehead. "I can do that."

"Use two hands, okay?"

"Okay." Carefully, she slides her plate to the side and then uses two hands to slide her milk closer. She raises up, but can't quite reach the top of the glass to take a drink. Maybe I should have put it in a smaller glass.

"Hang on, I'll get you a smaller glass." I tip some of the contents into a small scotch tumbler I have and hand it back.

We get through the remainder of lunch relatively smoothly and all I can think about is that I'll have to do this all over again for dinner. What in the hell do I feed a four-year-old?

"Come on. Let's get your bedroom set up."

"But you said my bed is bwoken." Her bottom lip wobbles. "Where I gonna sleep?"

"I fixed it. That's why I was in the workshop. I had to unpack my tools so I could put it back together." I stack our dishes in the sink for later, then help Kenny down from the stool.

She takes off for her bedroom, which is quite stark at the moment. I might need to think about painting it. "What's your favorite color?"

"Mommy's favowite color is pink. That's my favowite color now."

I huff out a sigh. I know pink was Anna's favorite color. Ever since she was little, everything had to be pink. She even dyed her hair pink occasionally. Scrubbing my fingers through my short beard, I look at my niece. "I know your mommy's favorite color was pink. But what's *your* favorite color?" I point at her to make my point.

"It used to be bwue, but now it's pink." She finishes with a wide smile.

I file away the information. "Okay. Let's get you set up."

I realize it's important for Kennedy ... damn it ... *Kenny*, to feel settled, so we spend the afternoon unpacking some of her things. I'm astounded at how much crap a four-year-old needs—we're not going to get through all of it this afternoon. I've only unpacked a few basics in the kitchen. I haven't even started on the rest of the house. I guess I'll be sleeping on my mattress on the floor tonight.

"Emma mentioned a park down the end of the street. You wanna go check it out with me for a little while before we start thinking about dinner?"

"Oh yeah!" She jumps up and down, her smile taking up all of her face. "I get my shoes."

I leave her to get ready as I get my shoes, phone, and keys before meeting my niece at the front door.

"You ready?"

"Yeah. Let's go."

As we step onto the front porch, I automatically look across to next door to check if Emma's still working in her garden. I can't see her, and I'm ... *disappointed*. I shake the wayward thoughts from my head. I can't be attracted to my neighbor, no matter how sexy she is—I doubt her husband would appreciate me drooling all over his gorgeous wife.

Kenny tears me from my thoughts as she slips her tiny hand into mine—my heart skips, then catches. She's so small, and she's trusting me, a stranger, to keep her safe. I look up to the sky, sending my thoughts up to my sister—*I hope I don't let you down (again), Sis*. Kennedy skips along beside me, swinging my arm back and forth as we make our way to the park. A large black dog that looks like a small horse frightens the hell out of Kenny as it jumps up, resting its paws on top of the front fence to bark at us. The deep tone of it vibrates right through my chest, as Kenny climbs up my body like a tree.

Wrapping my arms around her, I try my best to settle her. "It's okay. It's only a dog. He won't hurt you if you stay back out of his way."

I carry her the rest of the way to the park, her little heart beating rapidly against my chest, her head tucked into the crook of my neck. I find a bench in the middle of the playground and sit my ass down with Kenny in my lap. "You gonna go play?"

She pulls her head away from me, looking around the entire space before deciding it's safe enough to leave my lap. Running over to the playground, which seems a little small to me, she climbs up the ladder to the slide. Once I'm happy she's entertained, I pull out my phone to check my emails. I packed up my carpentry business to move back home, and it means I have to start from scratch in terms of clientele. Some of my happy clients from back east gave me glowing recommendations to family and friends over here, so I'm hoping those will lead to something to get me started. I generally rely on word of mouth from happy clients.

"Uncle Theo, push me, push me."

"In a minute. I need to check some things." I open my emails. I have a couple sitting in my inbox. Before I can open them, Kenny huffs out a heavy sigh as she sits on the bench next to me. "Why aren't you playing?"

"Got nobody to play wiv." She brushes her messy hair out of her face, then crosses her arms as she swings her legs back and forth. "It's no fun wivout fwiends."

Rolling my eyes, I reluctantly put my phone away. "Come on, I'll play with you. Where do you want to play?"

She jumps off the bench. "Yay! Swings first."

She sprints forward, and I follow behind. It doesn't take me long to catch up to her with my long strides. Helping her up onto the seat, I begin to push. She squeals and giggles as she moves through the air, swinging her little legs back and forth. My smile grows as I witness her happiness for such a simple thing.

I'm not sure how much Dad told her about our new living arrangement. I don't know if she understands that she's going to be living with me from now on. Dad'll still take her now and then, but I'm her legal guardian.

It's what Anna wanted.

I don't know why. She knew I'd never had anything to do with kids. I have no fucking clue what to do, but I'm getting the feeling that no matter what, Kenny must come first. I can't leave her to her own devices for very long. When I noticed she wasn't where I told her to stay earlier today, I almost had a heart attack.

We play at the park on the swings, slides, and climbing frames for almost an hour before heading home when Kenny's stomach grumbles. Now I have to think about what to make for dinner. I have some tinned soup—that'll have to do. I only picked up the basics to get us through today. I figured we can go shopping tomorrow after we work out what we're going to eat for the week.

As we step onto the front porch, I catch my neighbor out of the corner of my eye. She's carrying a casserole dish and is headed our way. I open the front door to let Kenny inside to wash up while I see what Emma wants.

"Uh hi …" She steps onto the first step, looking up at me, and I realize I didn't introduce myself earlier.

"Theo. Sorry, I should have introduced myself." I reach my hand forward to shake hers before realizing her hands are full, so I drop it back down by my side.

"Oh, that's okay. Nice to meet you, Theo." She raises the casserole like an offering. "I, uh, made my macaroni cheese for you guys, as a welcome to the neighborhood dinner."

I swallow my surprise at her kind gesture. I would never have expected her to welcome us in such a way after she basically chewed me out earlier today. I lean forward to lift the corner of the foil so I can see what's inside. The aroma hits me first, and it smells so damn good.

I catch Emma's eye. I think they might be a mossy green color, but I still can't be sure. "Smells delicious. Thank you. I was trying to figure out what to make for dinner. So I really appreciate it." If I plan it properly, this could possibly do us two meals.

"You're welcome." I move to take the casserole from her, but she pulls it closer to her body. "The dish is still hot. I'll carry it inside for you so you don't burn your hands."

"Sure, thanks." I open the screen door and stand to the side so she can enter. Her shoulder brushes against my chest with the lightest of touches, sending sparks through my body. "Excuse the mess. I still have a lot of work to do."

"Don't worry about it. I remember when the boys and I moved in next door. It took me months to get sorted. Between work and looking after the boys, it didn't leave a lot of time to unpack. I got there eventually."

I notice she didn't say 'husband'. Wonder if she's single? Not that I should care. She easily steps around the mess and heads straight to the kitchen; I guess she's familiar with the layout of this house. My eyes have a mind of their own, following the movement of her ass as she walks. What I wouldn't give to bite those luscious globes.

*Damn it, there I go again.*

By the time I shake myself out of my not-so-neighborly thoughts and catch up with her, she's placed the casserole on top of the stove and has started washing our dishes from lunch. Really? She's like a tornado at the rate she got to work.

"What in the hell are you doing?" I snap at her. As if she hasn't done enough by making our dinner, now she's also washing our lunch dishes.

She jumps at the harsh tone of my voice. "No need to be rude. I was only trying to help. I know what it's like to be in your position."

Placing my hands on my hips, I'm ready to go toe to toe with this woman. "And what position is that?" I snark.

"Moving into a new home. Having children that rely on you to do everything. Nobody around to help you out." She answers flippantly as she waves her soapy hands around the space, flinging bubbles all over the counters. "I remember Nancy coming over our first night with a casserole for me and my boys. I was so grateful that her thoughtfulness meant I had one less thing to worry about. I decided to pay it forward." She turns back to the sink and continues cleaning up our mess, mumbling something I can't make out under her breath.

Kenny comes running in. "Hello, Emma. You wanna see my new woom?"

"Hey, Kenny. Absolutely. Let me finish these dishes and you can show me everything."

"You don't need to finish the dishes. I'm more than capable of looking after us." I don't like feeling as though she thinks I'm incapable. I may not know what I'm doing with a kid, but I'm sure I can work it out. *How hard can it be?*

"It's okay. I'm almost done." She looks at me over her shoulder, giving me a timid smile. I can't believe she's still smiling at me when I've snarled at her since I walked into the kitchen. "There. All done. You can dry them and put them wherever they go."

"Yay!" Kenny rushes forward, taking Emma's hand to lead the woman to her bedroom.

I'm left standing in the kitchen—among boxes that need to be unpacked, dishes that need to be dried and put away, and dinner on the cooktop—wondering what the hell just happened.

# CHAPTER 3

## —*thea*—

THE EARLY RAYS OF THE DAY STREAM ACROSS MY FACE, WAKING ME FROM a restless sleep. I never sleep well in a new place; usually taking a week or two before I settle properly.

I may as well get up and enjoy the peace before the munchkin wakes up—the house is completely silent, unlike yesterday with the kid's constant chatter. As quietly as I can, I head downstairs, make myself a coffee, and climb back upstairs to enjoy the early morning on the deck outside of my bedroom. Leaning against the railing, I decide to make myself a rocking chair so I can enjoy the dawn in comfort. Surveying the view, my eyes wander next door, noticing the back grass could do with a cut. Emma's front yard is immaculate, the backyard— not so much. You'd think her boyfriend, if she has one, would cut the back grass every time he cuts the front. As I enjoy the fresh air, I take the first sip of my coffee. My eyes travel up toward the house next door —it certainly could do with some TLC. Maybe her partner isn't much of a handyman?

I catch movement in the upstairs corner window, but I can't be sure. Well, if someone was there, they'd certainly get an eye full, because I haven't bothered to get dressed. My preference will always be to sleep naked and enjoy the early morning the same way. I may need to reconsider my habits if Kenny's an early riser, though. It's probably not appropriate for her to see me naked. When she woke during the night, afraid of the dark, I made sure to pull on my boxers before going to her. My heart fucking broke to find her sobbing, her little body shuddering, her hair a sweaty mess.

The whole day yesterday, even when she talked about Anna, she had a smile on her face. To see her so distressed in the middle of the night was tough. Sitting with her tucked into a ball on my lap, snuggled against my body, she began to burrow deep inside as she gave me her unconditional trust to keep her safe. While holding her close, I decided to always put Kenny first—her heart, her needs, her wants. She's now my number one priority. It's what Anna would have wanted, and it's the least I can do for her after I let her down—like the asshole I am.

Finishing my coffee, I head inside to shower and dress for the day. I'm gonna wake my girl up with a serving of chocolate chip pancakes. Every kid loves pancakes. I can't go wrong!

*Huh.* My steps stall as it registers that I thought of Kenny as *my girl.* I guess that's exactly what she is. Dad and I are 'it' for her. I'm her guardian, which is the same as being her parent. I need to take this seriously. It's not a temporary situation; we're gonna be together through thick and thin. She's already lost so much, I refuse to allow her to experience any further pain. I want to make sure she gets to live her best life. Maybe that's why Anna requested for me to be her guardian. She knew I would take the role seriously and work my ass off to give her a good life. After all, I was always the one to come to my sister's aid when we were kids and into our teens.

I'm plating the last pancake when a sleepy-eyed little girl who's already stolen my heart wanders into the kitchen rubbing the sleep from her eyes.

"Morning, Munchkin," I call.

She stops in her tracks, drops her hands, tilts her head, and looks at me with eyebrows drawn down over blue eyes—just like her mom's, just like mine.

"Munchkin?" she questions in her sleepy little girl voice.

"Yep, I've given you a nickname, which means I like you." I point from her to the table. "Sit down. I have a treat for you."

With wide eyes and a ghost of a smile, she moves toward the table and takes a seat. I load the table with the pancakes and the limited topping items we have. Shopping is a must for today.

"I hope you're hungry."

"I'm starving." She licks her lips as she surveys the table.

I place a pancake on her plate and load the toppings on for her. Hmm. Should I cut them up for her? I'm not sure how much I'm supposed to do to help her out.

"Do you need me to cut it up for you, or can you manage?"

"I can do it." She works hard to manipulate her knife and fork, managing to tear pieces of pancake away. Good enough in my book. "This is yummy, Uncle Theo."

"Thanks. Yaya used to make these for your mommy and me when we were little."

"You was lucky. These are da best." She licks her lips. "Can we have them every day?" She looks at me with hopeful eyes.

"Ahh." I scratch my fingernails through my beard. "Probably not. Maybe just on Sundays." *Look at me being all parent-like.* I've got this, no problem. "Eat up. We need to get you dressed so we can go to the store."

# CHAPTER 4

## —emma—

OH, MY GAWD! THAT ASS. I'M PRETTY SURE I COULD BOUNCE QUARTERS off of it. The new addition to my Sunday morning quiet time certainly woke me up. I'm not sure if I moved away from my window quickly enough to not be seen, but I *was* caught completely off-guard.

Twice a month, if Preston doesn't skip out on the boys, I have from Saturday morning to Sunday lunchtime free. I normally wake at my regular time to enjoy a coffee on the cute window seat in my corner window. It's probably one of the few redeeming features of this house. I'm not lucky enough to have a deck out from my bedroom like next door, but the cozy seat that looks across my backyard isn't to be sneezed at. Sometimes I read, but today I was surveying my back garden. I need to get my mower repaired so I can cut the grass; it's grown so long. As I looked up at the house next door, I spotted a figure on the upper deck. I almost choked on my coffee when I realized my brand new sexy neighbor was stark naked while drinking his coffee. *Hot damn!* I wonder if that'll be a regular Sunday morning event. I certainly hope so.

I jump up after noticing the time on the clock next to my bed. I'd better get my chores done before I head over to pick up the boys from their sleepover with Mom and Dad. It's a godsend that they take the boys for me once a month. They stick to the same routine as I do, and with it being a regular occurrence, Lachlan has no trouble coping. I'm so thankful because it gives me the break I desperately need for my mental health. As much as I love my two sons, they can be a lot. Particularly Lachlan, with his needs and regular appointments each week after school.

I enjoy a longer shower, washing my hair, shaving, and scrubbing my body. Most days, I do the bare minimum because I don't have a minute to waste. This is a decadent luxury, standing under the warm water and letting myself be. Getting out, I put a mask in my hair, wrap it in plastic and follow with a charcoal mask on my face. Now to turn up my favorite music and get some tidying up done.

I'm putting my heart and soul into singing like a superstar about kissing until I'm drunk and dancing like Jagger when I look up, catching sight of my sexy new neighbor watching me through my living room window. I freeze in embarrassment. Gawd! Yesterday, I was a mess in the garden. Today, I have my hair wrapped in plastic, charcoal on my face, and I'm in my oldest T-shirt and yoga pants. I only have an old sports bra on while I'm bouncing around.

I'm finding all of my bras are becoming uncomfortable. I need to get new ones, but it takes me ages to find a bra I like for the size of my boobs. He's carrying my casserole dish from yesterday; his eyebrows are almost hitting his hairline, and he has a slight tilt to his lips.

He points to my front door and I can only nod; my head is the only part of my body able to move. Next thing I know, he's standing in the entry to my living room indicating I should turn down my music. I manage to collect myself and get my ass into gear to turn down the volume.

"You should lock your front door. It's fucking dangerous to have it unlocked like that. Especially with how loud you play your music. You won't hear anyone coming into the house," he snaps at me. Raising the dish he's holding, he places it on the entry table, turns, and leaves. The door slams behind him and I see him stomping across my grass to his house, shaking his head.

What the hell just happened? I've barely moved, still looking out of my front window.

Once he's out of sight, I blow out a long breath. Not sure what's up his nose, but I don't appreciate having my vibe smashed to pieces. I stomp my way upstairs to my bathroom. I angrily wash my hair and face, dry off, and get dressed—all of my calm vanishing into thin air.

# CHAPTER 5

## —emma—

Standing on Mom and Dad's front porch, I suck in a deep breath. Shaking out my body, I start with my fingers, moving up my arms, through my body, and finally, I roll my neck. Dropping my shoulders into a more relaxed position, I mentally prepare for the onslaught of my family. I love them all to pieces and they've stepped up over the past five years since my marriage fell apart, but they can be … *a lot*. I can't go in there feeling agitated; Lachlan will pick up on it and respond in kind.

Putting a smile on my face, I open the door to step into my childhood home. The smell of roast beef assaults my senses immediately and my mouth waters to taste Mom's roast vegetables. Sunday lunch has been a tradition in this house ever since we all moved out. It makes her happy to feed us all once a week and I'm happy to be fed by someone other than myself.

I have a routine when I arrive. I seek out my boys first; they're always my priority. As I walk down the hallway, Austin spots me. His cheeky smile lights up his face as he holds up his arms, running toward me. He leaps at my body for me to catch him. *My baby*. He wraps his arms and legs around my body like a monkey, giving me a sloppy kiss on my cheek.

"Hello, Mommy. I missed you." This boy overflows with affection and shares it often and freely. He gives the best hugs, and he's such a great little brother to Lachlan. He's so patient and empathetic to his big brother's needs.

"I missed you too, Baby. Were you a good boy for Nana and Poppa?" Not that I need to ask; he's usually a pretty good kid.

He screws up his little nose. "I'm always a good boy." I tickle his side in response, inciting giggles and wriggles in my arms. "Well, most of the time, anyway."

I tap his cute little button nose with my forefinger, pressing my forehead to his. "That sounds about right." I kiss his forehead before he wriggles to escape my hold. "Where's your brother?"

I'll know how well he's doing, depending on where he is. If he's in their bedroom, it means he's feeling overwhelmed.

"He's in the kitchen with Nana, Aunty Sarah, and Mona." He takes off with the energy of a five-year-old boy, before running out of the back door, probably to hang out with Max and Dad.

Standing in the kitchen doorway, I watch some of my most favorite people in the whole world. Lachlan is sitting at the kitchen table, headphones on, focused on his iPad. It looks as though he's using his *Magic Fluids* app. He uses it when he feels as though he needs to settle, but he can't be feeling too bad considering he's sitting in the kitchen and not in the bedroom. It took a lot of work with various therapists for Lachlan to identify when he's beginning to feel overwhelmed. When he notices the signs, he puts his headphones on to create quiet and focuses on the swirly patterns he can create within the app. I move forward and ever-so-lightly brush his hair with my hand. He won't acknowledge me right now because he's so focused, but he knows I'm here.

"Hey, Mom." I step over and hug her tight. "Thanks for taking the boys for me."

"Hi, Em. It's always our pleasure to have the boys." She nods across to my sister. "Your sister stayed over last night. So the boys had an extra adult to see to their every whim."

I kiss her cheek before moving over to my sister. "Hey, Sarah. Thanks for helping Mom and Dad last night." I wrap my arm around her shoulders, giving her a side hug, which she returns. I may be the eldest and she may be the baby of our family, but we've always been close. I used to practice braiding her hair when we were younger and we'd spend many a night talking about boys once she was old enough to notice they existed.

"No problem, Sis. I needed to get my nephew fix."

I lean my backside against the kitchen counter. "Hey, Mona. How are you?" She won't say hello of her own accord. She always waits until we acknowledge her first.

"Hello, Emma." Her eyes haven't strayed from her fingernails as she stands at the counter, painting them with some awful color that looks a lot like baby diarrhea with glitter. "I'm fine, I guess. Spending my Sunday afternoon here instead of at the mall."

Sarah and I look at each other, rolling our eyes. I don't understand what my brother sees in Mona. I mean, I get she's gorgeous, with her long platinum hair, big blue eyes, and model-worthy figure, but she's vapid. Max seems oblivious to her shallow demeanor. I'm thankful she doesn't come to Mom and Dad's every Sunday.

I move over next to Lachlan and crouch down beside his chair, carefully uncovering one of his ears. "Hey, Buddy. I missed you." I shift his hair out of his eyes with a gentle glide of my fingers.

"Missed you too." His eyes remain focused on his iPad as one of his arms reaches around my neck to squeeze me.

Standing up, I replace the headphone, kiss the top of his head, and then step outside to say 'hi' to Max and Dad. They're sitting on the back deck with a beer each, watching Austin play on the trampoline with Archie, Mom and Dad's chocolate and cream Dachshund. His little boy giggles along with doggy yaps and squeaky springs filling the backyard. Before my boys, it had been a long time since this yard hosted the play of children. I'm surprised Lachlan's not out here jumping on the trampoline. He loves jumping on his mini-indoor tramp after school most days.

"Hey, Dad. Hey, Max." I step into each of my favorite men, embracing them tightly as I kiss each of their cheeks.

"Hey, Sis." Max returns my hug, lifting me off of my feet.

"Hi, Em. How's your weekend been?" Dad asks as he wraps his arm around my shoulder, drawing me in close to his body, before kissing the side of my head. "I hope you managed to relax a little."

"It's been interesting. I met my new neighbors, did some gardening … Oh," I catch my brother's eye, "would you have time to stop by and take a look at my lawnmower? It broke down after I cut my front grass and the back needs doing."

"Sure. I'll check my schedule and let you know when I can stop by." I know Max is always busy with his business, which he runs on his own. I keep telling him he should hire an office manager at least, so they can handle the bookings, ordering, and account-keeping tasks, so he doesn't have to do it when he gets home at night.

"Thanks. I'd appreciate that. Maybe you could stay for dinner when you come?"

"Sounds good. I'll message you and set it up once I check what I have on the books this week."

We spend a few minutes catching up before Mom calls out that lunch is ready, and it's time to wash up. I collect Austin from the trampoline and we all head inside to stuff ourselves silly with a delicious roast lunch. Mom made a special effort with Lachlan's meal. His roast beef is sliced extra thin, and he has raw carrots, red peppers, and broccoli because he loves the crunchiness of the vegetables. Mom placed each item in a separate section of his plate, ensuring none of the foods touch each other—just the way he likes it.

All discussion ceases as we dig into Mom's delicious roast. Once we're about halfway through the meal, chatter starts up again as Austin asks Max about his latest car.

"I just got in a beautiful '64 Ford Falcon Sprint. I can't wait to get started on it. I'm taking it back to the original color, but I'll improve it with modern enhancements in the engine. Your mom will have to bring you boys to the workshop, so I can show it to you."

Austin looks at me, excitement in his eyes. "Can we go look, Mommy? Please?"

"Sure, I don't see why not. Maybe next Saturday morning? How does that sound?" I look at my brother for confirmation.

Mona sighs loudly, drawing our attention to her. "Another weekend, Max. Really? When do *I* get to do what I want on the weekend? Huh?" Her face twists up as though she's constipated.

"It'll only be half a day, then I'm all yours." He gives her a forced smile, which she doesn't bother to return.

"Yippee," she responds sarcastically, twirling her pointer finger in the air.

He ignores her, turning to Sarah. "How's work going?"

Sarah's boss has been hinting he's going to retire soon. She loves her boss, Eric. He's such an old sweetheart and treats Sarah more like a granddaughter than an employee.

Her shoulders slump forward and the sparkle leaves her eyes. "Eric hasn't come out with a date yet, but he's getting everything in order for his grandson to take the reins." She shrugs her shoulders. "I've never met his grandson, and I've worked with Eric for the past nine years. I'm not sure he'll be a good fit since he's never shown his face in the building."

"What makes you think Eric's grandson is going to take over?" Mom asks.

"Eric's always wanted Adam to take over. I'm pretty sure he'll get his way." She seems certain of the outcome.

"Mommy, can I have ice, please?" Lachlan asks.

"Sure, Buddy." I get up to fill a glass with ice chips and place it exactly at two o'clock in front of his plate.

"Thanks, Mommy."

"Anytime." I brush the top of his hair. "Anyone else want anything while I'm up?"

Mona holds her glass out to me. "I'll have a refill."

As usual, she doesn't bother herself with manners; that would be too much to ask. "Sure thing." I refill her glass and hand it back to her —still no thank you, but that's not a surprise. Max frowns, but doesn't say anything; he's not one for confrontation if he can avoid it—especially not in front of other people. I'm sure if something was really important to him, he'd speak up. He certainly never lets Sarah and I get away with anything like that.

Dad pauses eating. "You said you met your new neighbors. What are they like?"

Hmmm. Maybe I shouldn't have mentioned anything. "I only met them briefly, and I'm not really sure of the situation." I go on to tell them all about Kenny and how she surprised me in the garden and then proceeded to break my heart by telling me her mom died. Then I tell them that I think she's living with her uncle, but I'm not sure if there's anyone else living with the two of them. Austin's a social boy, so he's excited at the prospect of making a new friend.

Sarah's eyes light up. "Oh, what's *he* like?" She wriggles her eyebrows up and down. "Will he be good for eye candy?"

"Sarah!" Mom admonishes.

"What? I'm only asking." She giggles. Looking at me, she mouths, "Is he hot?"

I press my lips together to prevent my smile and nod slightly, raising one eyebrow. Her eyes widen in response and she gives me a knowing smile, finishing off with what she thinks is a saucy wink. I'm sure when she gets a spare minute, she'll be over to see if she can spot my new neighbor for herself. Wait until I tell her what he likes to do in the morning! *I wonder if that's a daily occurrence or just a weekend type of thing.*

"What was your favorite thing from the weekend?" I quietly ask my boys as I massage them both with sleepy time magnesium cream, preparing for bedtime.

Austin is quick with his response. "Uncle Max played tag with me and Archie. It was so funny. He kept pretending to fall over." He giggles as he retells the story.

"Uncle Max is always lots of fun." I agree. "What about you, Lachlan?"

He looks to the side of my face. "Can you please look at me, Lachlan?"

His eyes move to my face, not quite meeting my eyes, but better than before. "Poppa let me help him sand the railing of the back deck."

"Yeah? What did you like about sanding the railing?" Austin stops playing with his teddy to listen to Lachlan's answer.

He shrugs his shoulders. "I dunno."

I suspect it might be the repetitive nature of the task. He does like to do the same thing over and over. His focus on a task is second to none, especially when it's something he likes to do.

"Okay, boys. Time to brush your teeth and head to the toilet."

They do what they need to do, while I spray a few drops of lavender near their bedding. We settle down for a story or two. I make sure to use different voices for the characters, causing the boys to giggle. We talk about what's happening in the story and how the characters are responding to different situations. I always find talking through these types of social situations with the boys, using characters from the story, helps prepare Lachlan for similar situations in real life. It was a technique one of his therapists recommended and regularly uses in Lachlan's sessions.

I tuck Austin down for the night with a cuddle and kisses all over his face. "Kiss Teddy too, Mommy."

How can I resist? I kiss Teddy, his teddy bear—I know, such an original name, right? He snuggles down under his blankets and his sleepy eyes drop closed, as I whisper, "Love you more than all the waves in the ocean."

His little mouth curves up in a sleepy smile. "Love you too, Mommy."

I move across to Lachlan and spread out his weighted blanket, then lay next to him, half on top of him, supplying the additional pressure he needs to fall asleep. We lay together quietly for a long while before I whisper to him, "Love you more than all the waves in the ocean." That's his cue that I'm going to leave him to sleep on his own.

He sleepily whispers back to me, "Love you, Mommy. Night."

"Goodnight, Buddy." I kiss his forehead gently before carefully moving off of him. Turning on the overhead fan for white noise, I leave the boys' bedroom.

The bedtime routine we have has been fine-tuned to work out the best approach. It doesn't mean that Lachlan will sleep all night, but it does guarantee me at least four hours of uninterrupted sleep if I get my act together. I quickly make our lunches ready for school tomorrow, tidy up, and make sure the morning can run as smoothly as possible.

# CHAPTER 6

## —theo—

"HAPPY BIRTHDAY, SON." DAD'S VOICE IS SURE AND STRONG ON THE other end of the phone. "Why don't you bring Kennedy into the restaurant tonight so we can celebrate?"

"Thanks, Dad. That'd be great. We'll come around five-thirty if that's okay. I'm learning that Kenny needs to eat her dinner around six before she gets too tired to eat."

Rumbling laughter sounds across the phone. "Oh yes, she gets grumpy by six-thirty. I also fed her dinner early, followed by a nice, calming bath. Then we would read a story in bed together before I tucked her in for the night."

"Yeah, that's what we've been doing. It seems to work for her, then she's up at the ass-crack of dawn, ready to take on the world again." I scrub my fingers through my short beard—probably need to give it a trim. I don't know what I'm doing in terms of looking after a four-year-old girl. "I think we're doing okay."

We started as strangers last Saturday and over the past five days, Kenny's burrowed her way deep into my heart. I loved her purely because she's my sister's daughter, but getting to know her has changed and deepened my affection toward her. She's a sweet little girl with a heap of energy.

Actually, that reminds me. "Ah, Dad. I've gotta go. I haven't heard a sound from Kenny since I've been on the phone with you. I've learned that means trouble. The last time she went quiet, she decided to draw 'pwetty' flowers on one of her walls," I chuckle as I remember her little face when I caught her, "because it looked boring. I made her help me wash the wall while I explained it wasn't okay to draw on walls. Then we went out and bought a pile of scrapbooks so she could draw flowers to her heart's content. I plan to take her to choose some floral wallpaper to decorate one of her walls since she likes flowers so much."

The front screen door slams as Dad says his goodbye and little footsteps come running up the hallway. Kenny almost knocks me over as she barrels into me; something gripped in her hand. She pulls back from my body, thrusting her hand upward.

"Happy birthday, Uncle Theo." Her smile is wide, blue eyes twinkling in mischief. "I got you some flowers."

I pick her up to kiss her soft cheek. "Thanks, Munchkin." I kiss her other cheek. "Where did you get these flowers? We don't have anything like this in our garden." I have a sneaking suspicion about where she got them from, but I want her to tell me.

"I picked them from Emma's garden. She has the pwettiest flowers." She shoves them under my nose and I snap my head back out of the way to avoid them going up my nostrils. "Smell them."

I smell them and then shift her to my hip so I can take the posy from her. "Thank you for the birthday wish and flowers, Kenny. Let's go put them in a jar with water." I don't think I own a vase.

As I fill the jar with water, I think about how to explain to Kenny that she can't take flowers out of other people's gardens *or* leave the house without my knowledge. Picking the flowers for me was sweet and I don't want to be a grouch and ruin her thoughtful gesture.

As she helps me situate the flowers in the water, I decide now would be the best time. "These flowers are really pretty. Thank you." She smiles at me. "But … Kenny, it's not okay to pick flowers from our neighbor's garden without their permission."

"But Emma said I could. She even helped me." Her bottom lip's wobbling and my heart rate picks up speed as I prepare for her little girl tears. I could never handle it when my sister cried or was hurt; it's part of the reason I stayed away when she got sick. I'm a fucking coward because I couldn't stand by and watch my sister go through what my mother went through. The black hole of regret I feel for my selfish choice will forever swallow me. I shake myself out of my head so I can reassure my niece.

"Oh, well, that's okay then. I didn't realize Emma helped you." I kiss the top of her head. "I'll have to remember to thank her for the flowers when I see her next."

"She said she might see us this afternoon." Her eyes widen and her little cheeks rise. "I made a new fwiend."

This doesn't surprise me in the least. Every time I've taken her to the park at the end of the street, she strikes up a conversation with someone different. "Oh yeah. Where did you meet this friend?"

"Nex door. His name's Austin. Emma's his mommy. He said he would come to the park after school wiv me."

"That's great, Munchkin." *I wonder if that means Emma will come to the park too?* I muss Kenny's hair and she quickly pulls her head away.

"Don't mess up my hair." She frantically tries to smooth it back down, but it's a lost cause. I need to figure out how to tame this kid's hair. Maybe I can get online to search out some instructional videos.

I raise my hands to show my surrender. "Sorry." I place the jar of birthday flowers on the kitchen table. "Hey." I make sure I have her eyes on me. "It's really important that I know where you are. Please don't leave the house without telling me next time. Okay?"

She looks down at her feet. "Okay, Uncle Theo."

I smile at her and kiss the top of her head. "So, what are we going to do today?"

"Can we make my woom pwetty?"

"Sure. Let me make a list for the hardware store and then we'll go. You go put your shoes on." I grab a notepad and pencil as Kenny runs upstairs to get herself ready.

At the hardware store, I have Kenny sitting in the cart as we collect everything we'll need. I want to put some shelves up in her room and the living room, so she can have some photos of Anna on display. I don't ever want her to forget her mom. I've been telling her stories about Anna from our childhood every night before bed and she soaks up all the details, asking questions until she falls asleep.

The next stop is the paint and paper aisle. We browse the samples and Kenny falls in love with a wallpaper design of colorful flowers that looks like a wild garden. Flowers of all colors, shapes, and sizes grow about halfway up the sheet. It'll look bright and colorful; just what I was looking for. I collect some new white blinds and timber to make shelves to finish off her room. We choose a soft pink color from one of the flowers in the design to paint the remainder of her walls.

Then we stop at the store to get groceries before heading home to have lunch.

"I'm so excited. My woom's gonna look so pwetty."

After lunch, Kenny helps me to move everything out of her bedroom, so I have an empty space to work with. I should have thought about it *before* we unpacked her stuff and set her up. We put her mattress on the floor in the spare bedroom and I rig up a tent over the top to make it feel as though she's camping.

"It's gonna be so much fun to sleep in the tent tonight. Will you sleep in there with me?"

"Uhm, I'm not sure we'd both fit." It *is* only a single mattress and I've seen how Kenny sleeps. Sometimes she ends up lying diagonally across her bed. I don't fancy the idea of being poked in the ribs with her toes throughout the night.

A knock at the front door has Kenny running from her temporary bedroom. Following close behind her, I see we have company.

"Hi. We thought we'd stop by to see if Kenny wanted to come to the park with us." Emma's standing behind two boys, a hand on each of their shoulders. "Uh, this is Austin." She looks down at the smaller one with a look of pride on her face. "And this is Lachlan." She looks across at the taller boy, equally proud.

I open the screen door. "Hi. Nice to meet you, boys. I'm Theo and this is Kenny, though I think you may have already met this morning."

Austin nods. "Yeah, we met this morning. Can you still come to the park?" he asks Kenny directly.

Kenny tilts her head up with a hopeful look. "Sure. I'll just get our stuff. Kenny, go put your shoes on." I gesture for Emma and her boys to come inside, but they opt to wait on the front porch.

I lock the house, and we all head down the street toward the park. Emma's in the lead with her eldest boy by her side. Austin and Kenny are behind them, chatting away as I bring up the rear. My eyes automatically fall to Emma's delectable ass, wrapped like a gift in dark blue yoga pants which leave nothing to my imagination. Kenny moves closer to me as we pass the house with the huge dog, which I think may have been an anomaly because we haven't seen it since that first day.

When we arrive at the park, Austin and Kenny run off together to play, leaving Lachlan with me and Emma. He seems very quiet and shy compared to his younger brother.

"You wanna play in the sandpit, Buddy?" Emma guides the boy

over to the sandpit around the swings. It extends out quite a distance away from the swings, so if he stays toward the edge, he should be safe.

He sits down, begins to smooth out the sand, and then proceeds to draw swirly patterns with his fingers. Emma sits along the brick edge, which keeps the sand in place, so I figure I may as well sit next to her.

Emma looks across at me with a smile. "Did you like your flowers this morning?"

I smile, remembering how excited Kenny was to present the flowers to me for my birthday. "Yeah, I did. Thank you for letting her raid your garden."

She chuckles. "She was helping herself when I looked out of my living room window, so I figured I may as well help her out."

"Shit!" I realize I've sworn in front of her son. "Sorry. I shouldn't swear in front of the kids."

"That's okay. He hears worse when he's with his uncle." She finishes with a smile, reassuring me she's not upset with my faux pas.

"I'm sorry Kenny helped herself to your flowers. I told her that she shouldn't pick flowers from other people's gardens, but she assured me that she had your permission." I scrub my fingers through my beard. "Not to mention, she managed to sneak out of the house without telling me where she was again!" I huff out.

Emma chuckles. "She probably figured because I helped her, I was giving her permission. Please don't be mad at her. I didn't mind at all." She watches the kids for a few minutes. "Happy birthday, by the way."

"Thanks. I'd rather forget about it, to be honest."

"Yeah, it's getting to that point where I'd rather stop having birthdays."

"But Mommy, you have to have a birthday every year. You can't decide to stop having birthdays." Lachlan says, while still drawing his patterns in the sand. I thought he was so engrossed in his sand play that he wasn't listening to our conversation.

Emma reaches forward to brush the hair out of his eyes. "I know, Buddy. There's no stopping birthdays or getting older."

He nods in agreement with his mom and Emma looks back at me. "Have you had a good day?"

"Not bad, I guess. Kenny gave me flowers." We both laugh. "We spent the day working to empty her bedroom and bought some wallpaper and paint to make it pretty. Tonight, we're having dinner at my dad's restaurant."

"Why would she give you flowers? They are dead as soon as they are picked. I don't think that's a very good present." Lachlan interrupts.

Emma's head snaps toward me and she mouths, "I'm so sorry."

I mouth in return that it's okay.

"Buddy, people give flowers all the time as a present. They don't think about the flowers being dead, only that they look nice."

"Okay. I still don't get it." He shakes his head, then stands and walks over to join the other two kids. Austin says something, and he nods but doesn't join in, instead watching from the sidelines.

"Your boys are quite opposite in their personalities." I muse.

Emma's watching the kids closely. "Yeah, they are. Though, you're lucky. Lachlan actually joined in the conversation. He doesn't usually do that with strangers. It'll take him a little while to get used to Kenny, but once he does, he'll be more than happy to play with her."

My eyebrows lift in surprise. "Well, I'm honored."

She chuckles mildly. "So you should be." She finishes her statement with a wink. Her eyes look almost brown today. I want to look more closely, but I don't want to come across like a creep. A light breeze catches her hair and a strand catches on her plump lips. My hand begs to reach forward and brush it aside, tuck it behind her ear, and run my fingers along the smooth skin of her jaw—but I manage to fight the urge.

"We'd better head home then. You need to get Kenny organized for dinner. What type of food does your dad serve in his restaurant?"

It takes me a moment to shake out of my daydream. Looking at the time, I note she's right, we need to get moving. "It's a traditional Greek taverna."

"Oh, that sounds delicious."

"Yeah. Running a taverna has been part of our family for generations. Dad has the recipes perfected." I'm not sure what's going to happen to the restaurant now that Anna's gone. Guilt that I'm not interested in the family business wells up once again. It's a familiar feeling.

She fidgets with her ponytail. "Generations, hey? So do you work there too?"

"Nah, I'm the family disappointment," I say it as though it's a joke, but I've never felt comfortable there. "I didn't want to go into the restaurant business. That was my sister's forte. I chose to become a carpenter." I scratch the scruff on my face.

"I'm sure you're not a disappointment."

I know she's trying to make me feel better, but she wasn't on the receiving end of my father's scathing words and disapproving looks. We gather the kids to make the walk home. As we get closer, I notice a black Dodge sitting in Emma's driveway. Austin takes off running toward their house, excited to see their visitor.

"He didn't tell me he was coming over today," Emma mumbles beside me, but she doesn't seem too upset. We arrive at her driveway and she turns to me. "Enjoy your birthday dinner." Then she squats down to Kenny's level. "Be good for your uncle and have a nice dinner." She taps the end of her nose with her pointer finger.

"I will, Emma." Kenny reaches forward, wrapping her little arms around Emma's neck, giving her a tight squeeze. Emma looks up at me, her eyes glassy, a watery smile touching her lips.

Once Kenny releases her, Emma stands up, leading Lachlan toward their visitor. The guy rubs Lachlan's hair and picks Emma up off her feet, kissing her cheek. Placing her back on her feet, they walk together around to the back of the house. I can't stop the jealousy that rises in me that another man has the privilege of hugging and kissing her.

"C'mon, Munchkin. We need to get ready to visit Pappoús at the restaurant for dinner." I lift her onto my hip and carry her up to the porch. I try to steal a look over the back fence to see what's going on, but I can't see anything from this angle. I might be able to see if I stand on the deck from my bedroom. "Kenny, can you please put on that dress that we picked out this afternoon. I'll get changed and meet you back down here, ready to go."

"Okay, Uncle Theo."

Stepping out onto the deck from my bedroom, I stay back from the edge hoping to stay out of sight. The guy's looking at the lawnmower and they're all chatting while he works, but I can't hear what they're saying from here. He gets the mower started and Emma throws her arms around him, kissing him on the side of his face. Looking mighty proud of his achievement, he wipes his hands on his jeans, which look to be covered in grease already. It's not that fucking hard to fix a lawn-mower—they're a pretty basic motor. Lachlan has his hands over his ears, pacing away from the noise. Austin catches up to him and the boys head inside. Just as I think the guy's going to cut the grass, he sits on the porch steps and watches Emma do the work instead. *What in the actual fuck?*

I step inside to get changed for dinner, my blood boiling that he's sitting on his lazy ass while Emma does the work. I poke my head back out to check if he's gotten off of his ass, but he's still sitting there, but now he has a beer in his hand. I feel like the top of my head's gonna blow off.

Heading downstairs to meet Kenny, I try to think up some excuse to step out onto the back deck so I can see what's happening next door.

"Uncle Theo, I'm weady," Kenny calls out from near the front door as she puts on her shoes. She added blue fairy wings to her outfit and a unicorn headband to her head. She looks so fucking adorable.

"Okay, Munchkin. I'll just lock up the house and we'll get going. Are you hungry?" I ask as I check the back of the house is locked up, straining to see out of the windows as I do. I can't see for shit from here. Grabbing my wallet and keys, as well as the little backpack I keep packed near the door with all the stuff Kenny needs whenever we leave the house, we head out.

*Who knew someone so small needed so much stuff?*

## CHAPTER 7

### *—theo—*

THE MINUTE THE DOOR OPENS INTO DAD'S RESTAURANT, KENNY TAKES off through the main room to his office out back. I have to lengthen my strides to keep up with her. It's been a while since I've been here, but I remember the layout clearly after spending a lot of my youth hanging out here. While Anna helped out in the kitchen, I often spent my time repairing any wobbly chairs and tables. As I got older, I made some of the furniture, which I notice is still being used as I look around. One set, in particular, brings back unwelcome memories.

Dad steps out of his office, holding Kenny to him as she tells him all about her new friends—Austin, Lachlan, and Emma. He kisses the tip of her nose, his eyes sparkling with happiness, as she squeezes his cheeks with her tiny hands. I realize this would make a great photo, so I take out my phone and snap a pic. I might frame it and give it to him for Father's Day. I'm sure he'll love it.

"Theo!" Dad finally notices me. I've never felt like I fit in here. My passion is working with timber, creating custom furniture that's not only comfortable, but thoughtfully designed, and beautiful too. Stepping forward, he wraps his free arm around me, pulling me in for a hug. Kissing both cheeks, he pulls back with a smile. "You look good, Son."

"Thanks, Dad."

He winks at me. "For an old man."

"Ha ha ha. Always the freaking comedian." I tuck my hands in my pockets. Why is it that whenever I'm in my father's company, I revert to feeling like a damn kid?

It's great to see him with a sparkle in his eye as he looks at his granddaughter. Neither of us took losing Anna very well, but as her father, he took it worse. He felt powerless to help his baby girl. He couldn't 'fix' the problem and for a man, that's the hardest situation to deal with. It would have been tough for him to watch helplessly as the same disease that stole his wife ravaged his only daughter. It would have been better if it had been me. It *should* have been me.

"C'mon, let's go and eat. I've organized all your favorites for your birthday."

I wonder if he'll know my favorites. Everything was always all about Anna when she was still with us; which I understood as I got older. Their mutual love of cooking made them especially close. I was more of a momma's boy, so when we lost her, I felt adrift because I'd lost my person. While Dad and Anna grieved together, I turned inward; becoming withdrawn. I pulled away and at the first opportunity I had; I moved east—away from the pain and the memories.

Dad guides us to a private table in the back corner, hidden behind a screen. It's one of the first settings I made for the restaurant and I'm honestly surprised it's still here. I glide my hand over the smooth timber which I sanded to within an inch of its life. Memories of an extraordinarily lonely and painful time assault me. I'm thankful we're not sitting at the setting on the opposite side of the restaurant. The one that brings back memories of an even darker time.

"I remember you making this set for me in our garage. You spent many hours working to make it perfect. It's probably my favorite setting in the entire restaurant." My head snaps up to him and he gives me a ghost of a smile. The young adult that was always trying to impress his father puffs out his chest with pride. "Sit, sit. Let's enjoy some good food."

"I'm hungwy," Kenny informs us as she situates herself on a chair between the only two family members she has left.

"Good. I asked Thomas to make your favorite, *spanakotiropita*."

Kenny's eyes widen and her lips spread wide as she wriggles excitedly in her seat. "Yummy. I love the baby pies."

Dad taps the end of her nose and winks. "I know this. Now, have you been good for Uncle Theo?"

She looks across at me for confirmation, so I nod my head. "Yep." She nods as she speaks, confidence coloring her tone.

Dad looks at me with raised eyebrows. "She's been pretty good apart from disappearing on me twice and nearly giving me a heart attack. Then there was the time I caught her drawing flowers on her bedroom wall. Other than that, she's been great."

Dad covers his mouth with his hand, turning his head away from Kenny to hide his amusement. I'm glad the old man thinks it's funny that his only son nearly had a heart attack last Saturday.

I look at my niece, who looks as though butter wouldn't melt in her mouth. "We're working things out, aren't we, Munchkin?"

As seriously as she can for a four-year-old, she nods her agreement and I don't even try to hold back my smile.

"That's good to hear. When are you going to take Kenny back to pre-kindergarten?"

"I wanted to have a week together so we could get to know each other." I smile at Kenny and then ask her, "Are you happy to go back to pre-kindergarten next week?"

Her eyes light up as she jigs up and down. "Oh yeah. I missing all my fwiends."

I bet she has. She's a sociable little girl. "You made friends with the kids next door."

Dad's watching us closely, a small smile on his face. I know he was worried about how we'd get along. Whether I'd be able to cope with raising a little girl on my own. The plan is for him to take her on the first weekend of every month and for us all to catch up for dinner here every couple of weeks. He's always been close with Kenny because Anna moved in with him once she fell pregnant.

One of the servers arrives at the table with our meals. Small filo pies filled with spinach and feta for Kenny; I have the grilled lamb chops with lemon-oregano vinaigrette and lemon-flavored grilled potatoes; while Dad has the same potato dish with charcoal-grilled, dry-aged rib-eye and braised greens.

Dad introduces his employee to me. "Kathleen, this is my son, Theo. Theo, this is one of my best servers, Kathleen."

"Hi, Kathleen. Nice to meet you."

"Likewise." She smiles. "Happy birthday and enjoy your dinner." She leaves us to our dinner, returning to the kitchen.

We eagerly dig into our meals, enjoying the burst of flavors. I'm surprised and touched that he *did* know my favorite meal and that he went to the trouble of organizing it before we arrived. We talk about how the last week's gone and Kenny excitedly tells him all about how we're going to decorate her bedroom. I plan to get it done over the next couple of days, so she can be back in her newly decorated bedroom before pre-kindergarten on Monday; I'm pleased she's excited about her new space. She's had to experience things that a little girl her age should never have to experience. From here on out, she's only going to have happy, positive experiences if I can help it.

Once we've finished our meal, Kathleen returns to take our dishes and I feel full to bursting. Dad tells us about some of the celebrities that dine here on occasion, including local singer-songwriter, Toby Summer.

"Ah, Thomas, come and meet my son, Theo."

Thomas places three plates of what looks and smells a lot like my favorite dessert on the table in front of each of us, then reaches his hand forward. We shake in greeting.

"Hey, Theo. It's great to put a face to the name. Your father talks about you all the time."

"Nice to meet you too, Thomas. The meal was amazing."

"Thomas has been working here for the past five years. I think he's one of my best employees." Dad gushes. He clearly has a lot of respect for the man because he's not usually so forthcoming with compliments.

"I love working here. It's like being part of a family."

I'm glad he feels that way because I don't. Although, if I stop and think about our evening, I've felt relaxed and welcome throughout the entire meal. Dad's been more than interested in what's happening in my life, and I don't think it's just because I have Kenny to care for now. I get the distinct feeling he's happy to have me home.

"Your father asked me to make you a traditional honey cake for dessert. I hope you enjoy it."

"Thank you. It's my favorite dessert."

He nods slightly, then messes up Kenny's hair, knocking her unicorn headband off-center before excusing himself back to the kitchen. Kenny makes a big fuss about smoothing it out, but it's a lost cause.

"Thanks for all this, Dad. The meal's been delicious, and it's been nice to catch up properly." We haven't really had a chance to catch up over this last week. I've been trying to get Kenny and me settled as quickly as possible and I wanted time to get to know her without any interruptions.

"My pleasure, Son. It's great to have you home." His voice is watery as he reaches across the table to pat my hand, his eyes glossy.

"It's great to be home." And I realize for the first time in a long time that I've missed my family, my home. I think it'll be good to reconnect with Dad and create new memories with him and Kenny.

I take my first bite of honey cake in years and revel in the delicious cinnamon, orange, and honey flavors. "Mmmm, this is as good as I remember." Mom used to make this cake for me as a treat now and then, and it was always my pick for my birthday cake.

"Your Mom always made sure she had the ingredients on hand when it was coming up to your birthday because she knew without a doubt that you would request it." A pang hits my chest at the memory of Mom in the kitchen baking my favorite cake for me every year until she got too sick to even get out of bed.

Kenny's wriggling in her chair, playing with the salt and pepper shakers now the food's done. I take that as my cue to get us home for the night before she gets too bored and silly. We say our goodbyes to Dad and head home for the night, ready to paint and wallpaper at the crack of dawn tomorrow.

# CHAPTER 8

## —emma—

"THANKS FOR COMING OVER THIS AFTERNOON TO FIX MY LAWNMOWER. I really appreciate it." I embrace my brother in thanks. "And for helping to get the boys to bed."

"No problem. I enjoy spending time with my nephews."

"So, is it still okay to bring the boys around on Saturday to see your new project?" I want to check that our plans haven't changed. Mona wasn't happy about Max being in the workshop on Saturday morning.

"Of course. I'll be working just the same as I always do. Bring them by whenever you want." He gives me one last hug, then climbs into his car.

I move closer to the open door. "Okay. My friend, Kate, has her housewarming party in the afternoon, so we'll come over before that."

"Sure. Bye, Sis." He starts his car and pulls out just as my sexy neighbor pulls into his driveway.

I look down at myself, realizing I'm still in the same clothes I was wearing this afternoon. The same ones I was wearing when I cut my grass. I discreetly sniff my armpit and I realize it's not great. He gets out of his car and, as he comes around to my side; the streetlight illuminates him. Ripped jeans hug muscular thighs and a dark button-down shirt with rolled-up sleeves shows off a trim torso. I mean, I *have* seen him naked, even if it was from a distance; but in clothes, he looks sensational. He glances in the back window and then makes his way over to me, tucking his hands in his front pockets as he moves closer.

"How was your birthday dinner?" I step toward him before remembering that I don't smell all that great. There are only a few feet between us—it seems we gravitate toward each other without conscious thought. I noticed at the park this afternoon, we sat quite close together, as though we're attracted to each other like magnets.

"It was good, thanks." He pauses for a moment. "Actually, it was pretty great. It's been a long time since Dad and I sat and shared a meal."

"That's gotta be the best birthday present." I'm not sure why he's been estranged from his family, but it makes me happy to hear that he enjoyed his father's company.

"Yeah, it was." He rubs the bristles of his neat scruff. "How was your evening?"

"Well, I finally got my lawnmower fixed, so I was able to cut the jungle out the back." I laugh nervously because Theo's face looks like thunder at the mention of cutting my grass.

"You should consider getting yourself a *real* man. One who fixes the lawnmower *and* cuts the grass as well."

I feel as though I've just been slapped. His words are harsh and uncalled for. I don't need a 'real man' to cut my grass, because I'm capable of doing it for myself. Just like everything else I do around this place for myself and my boys. Max offered to cut my grass, but I chose to do it myself because that's what I do.

There's a knock on the back window, breaking me out of my internal tirade, and preventing the words from escaping. Kenny presses her adorable little face against the glass and my heart melts at the sight. Theo retrieves her from the car, holding her close to his body. Her little head resting on his shoulder. She smiles sleepily at me.

"Hello, Emma."

"Hey, Kenny. Did you enjoy your dinner?"

"Yep. My pappoús made my favowite dinner. It was so yummy."

Theo smoothes his hand down the back of her hair. "I need to get this munchkin to bed. See you later, Emma."

"Sure. Good night." I give a small wave to Kenny, which she returns with a sleepy grin.

He leaves me staring after him and I realize I didn't get the opportunity to put him in his place. He seems to think it's acceptable to comment on my life. I'm not usually one to stand silent when someone thinks they can have an opinion on me or my life, but he seems to catch me off-guard and on the back foot. Next time, I'll definitely give him a piece of my mind.

## CHAPTER 9

### —emma—

"WHEN I GROW UP, MOMMY, I'M GONNA BE JUST LIKE UNCLE MAX."
Austin's still in awe of Max's new project. "I'm gonna fix up old cars."

"Yeah. That'd be so cool. Maybe you could work with Uncle
Max."

"Oh yeah, I didn't think of that. Do you think he'd let me?" He's
so excited at the prospect, he's bouncing in his seat.

"I think once you're older, he would definitely let you."

"That'd be so cool."

Lachlan's staring out of the window, watching the other cars on the
road. "What did you think of Uncle Max's new project, Lachlan?"

"It was old and rusty."

"Yeah, it was, Buddy. That's why Uncle Max is gonna fix it. It'll
look just like new."

"But it won't be new. It will still be old."

"True, but some people like old cars that have been fixed up."

"I guess." He shrugs his shoulders.

We pull into the driveway of Kate's new home and I can't believe
what I'm seeing. I know her boyfriend, Oliver, has a load of money, but
this house is something else. Right on the riverfront, it's absolutely
stunning. It's an enormous home featuring red brick and large
windows surrounded by white trim. The garden and surrounds are
something from a *Home Beautiful* magazine shoot. Steps lead up to a
large porch that has beautiful furniture I can imagine Kate and Oliver
enjoying when they have spare time.

As we get out of the car, I give Austin and Lachlan the 'talk'.

"Don't touch anything in there. I don't want you to break anything because I probably can't afford to replace it. Okay?"

"Okay, Mommy." Austin rolls his eyes at me.

"And remember your manners."

"Yes, Mommy."

"Lachlan, Kate said she would have a quiet space for you to go to if you need it. Okay?"

"Okay."

We didn't bring a housewarming gift because Kate said they didn't need anything and I can understand why now. As we climb up the porch steps, Kate steps in, wrapping her arms around me.

"You never told me you were living in a McMansion," I whisper in my friend's ear.

"Oh, stop it! It's big, but I think we've made it pretty homey inside." She pulls away from me, ruffling Austin's hair. "Hey, Austin."

"Hello, Ms. Summer." Austin greets his teacher with a huge smile on his face.

She lowers her voice, speaking quietly to my big boy. "Hey, Lachlan."

Lachlan works hard to look at Kate's face as he gives a small wave. "Hello, Ms. Summer. How are you?"

"I'm great. Thank you for asking. Thanks for coming to my party."

"I didn't have a choice. Mommy decided for all of us."

Kate's eyes widen and her mouth presses into a tight line as she tries to hold back her laughter. "Well, I'm so glad you came."

"That's good," he responds.

More guests arrive, so I take that as our cue to leave Kate and Oliver to greet their friends. Stepping inside, Margie meets us in the foyer as my jaw drops to the timber floor. "Margie, this house is gorgeous."

"I know. Kate and Oliver have done a wonderful job to make it so homely." She pulls me into a tight hug. I haven't seen her since Oliver carried Kate out of the café on that fateful day. I'm so happy he didn't let her insecurities get in the way of their happily ever after. "You should see my place out the back. I can't believe they invited me to live with them."

"I'm not surprised. Kate thinks the world of you. There was no way they would have left you behind." I reassure her.

"I'm so touched. I was only her neighbor, you know."

"You were never *only* her neighbor, Margie. You're one of her closest friends. She loves you to pieces. They both do." I squeeze her in a side hug.

We wander out to the back deck, and the back garden is as spectacular as the rest of the home. It looks across the river to the city on the other side. Margie shows us the space which Kate has made available for Lachlan if he feels he needs a quiet place to go. He gives us a serious nod in acknowledgment. I'm not sure he'll need the space. He's becoming better at self-management the older he gets. He's able to read his body signals when he's had enough and quietly steps away to recalibrate himself. That's not to say he doesn't have his moments, because he certainly does.

A young, fair-haired guy, who could easily be a model, steps out onto the back deck, collecting a drink as he nods to me with a friendly smile. Kate's brother, Toby—did I mention—Toby Summer's here! He's so freaking good-looking and a nice guy to boot. If he wasn't a decade younger than me, I would consider jumping on that. Anyway, where was I? Yeah, that's right. Toby steps up onto the back deck and greets the young guy as though they're old friends. Together, the two of them could make women's panties disintegrate instantly. Two older couples step out onto the back deck, chatting animatedly among themselves, closely followed by half a dozen kids dressed in their swimwear. A giant of a man follows them closely, running his hand through his hair as he surveys the kids—this must be Roman. Kate and Oliver finally step out onto the back deck and Kate's smile is the biggest I've ever seen. I'm so freaking happy for my friend that she's found the love of her life.

"Emma, come meet Roman and the kids." She grabs my arm, dragging me forward. My boys diligently follow me over to the pool. Austin's been itching to go in from the instant he saw the swimming pool, but I told him he had to wait until everyone arrived. "Roman, this is Emma and her boys, Lachlan and Austin." She gestures to each of the boys in turn.

He reaches his hand forward, so I take it as we say hello. Kate's eyes ping-pong between us, waiting for cupid's arrow to hit its target. She's made it pretty obvious that she thinks we would be a good match. But when I shake his hand, there's nothing. Less than nothing. No spark, no interest. Sure, he's a great-looking guy and looks fit for his age, but he doesn't get my heart hammering like my new neighbor does. He steps away to deal with his charges and Austin takes the opportunity to remind me he's still waiting to get into the pool.

While Austin plays in the pool with most of the other kids, splashing about and having a great time, Lachlan seems to have made a friend of his own as they sit side-by-side on a lounge chair far enough away from the action that they won't get wet. As is the norm for Lachlan, he doesn't make eye contact with his new friend, which most kids find a little disconcerting, but Evelyn (if I remember correctly) seems to be okay with this quirk. I spend my time watching the kids in the pool and catching up with Margie, enjoying the warm spring sunshine on my skin along with the delicious food Kate organized for the afternoon.

As the afternoon wears on, shadows grow longer across the backyard. Roman gathers the kids out of the pool to dry off—and I can tell they're incredibly excited about something. Austin begrudgingly gets out of the pool. "It's no fun without friends." He pouts his blue lips. It's probably a good thing he got out.

"I know." I wipe him down with his towel, then wrap it around his body.

Oliver calls everyone's attention to the back deck, so we gather around to listen to whatever he needs to say. From what Kate's told me, he's an extremely successful businessman, but the man I see up on the deck is as nervous as anything. He wraps his arm around her shoulder, placing an incredibly sweet kiss on the top of Kate's head. It's very clear to everyone here how much he adores her. He thanks us all for coming as he holds Kate impossibly close.

Sigh, I would love to have that. To have someone who loves and adores me as much as Oliver loves my friend.

The kids all move forward with poster boards and I gasp at what I read! Oh my gosh, I can't believe I'm here to witness this. Looking back at my friend, I see the moment the words register for her. Oliver's down on one knee with his heart in his eyes and hope heavy on his shoulders. There's no way she'll say no. My chest feels tight as my heart rate picks up speed in excitement for my friend—she's nodding as her lips spread wide. I blow out the breath I was holding in anticipation of her answer, smiling for my friend.

"What's happening, Mommy?" Lachlan steps up beside me.

"Oliver just asked Ms. Summer to be his wife, and she said 'yes'."

Kate drops to her knees and they share a sacred moment as they seal their promise with a heated kiss. Watching their explicit display of affection, I feel my cheeks warm. Geez, no wonder she always has a smile on her face.

"Why are they kissing in front of everyone? That's gross. Do they know how many germs are in a person's mouth?" I giggle internally. Trust Lachlan to know something like that.

"They're kissing because they love each other and they don't mind sharing each other's germs."

"Well, it's disgusting. I'm never going to share mouth germs with anyone." He wanders away in disgust. I hope he shares mouth germs with someone special when he grows up. I want him to experience that all-encompassing love that's supposed to exist.

I'm brought out of my thoughts and back to the party as loud congratulations go up all around. The two people of the hour make the rounds so we can admire her engagement ring and pass on our good wishes individually.

When she finally gets to me, I can't hold back my excitement for her. "Oh my gawd, Kate. Congratulations." I lift her hand to admire her stunning engagement ring. "I'm so freaking happy for you, girl!"

"Thanks so much! I can't believe he surprised me. I was *not* expecting our afternoon to turn out like this." Her gorgeous cobalt eyes are sparkling with pure happiness, her lips spread wide as she admires the sparkling new addition to her finger.

The afternoon begins to wind down, and it's time to get the boys home. Lachlan's reached his threshold for the day if his pacing is anything to go by. We say our goodbyes, then head for our car.

"Austin, go straight inside and have a shower, please. Make sure you wash your hair to get all the pool chemicals off your body." I direct as soon as I park the car. I need a few minutes with Lachlan alone to check he's doing okay. He zoned out in the car on the way home; I think the afternoon was possibly a little overwhelming for him. I'm hoping the forty-minute drive gave him some time to gather himself. I unlock the front door for Austin and once he's disappeared inside, I turn to Lachlan. "How are you doing, Buddy?"

He stops next to me, looking past me, thinking. I can't rush his answer because he needs to evaluate himself thoroughly before he responds. If Lachlan has taught me anything, it's to be patient and not fill silences with compulsive talk. We stand, as though on pause, for what seems like forever.

"I feel okay. I'm tired, though."

"Do you need some quiet time in your room with your iPad?" I ask gently as I brush his hair away from his eyes.

"Yes." He steps, with purpose, toward the front door and I remain rooted to the spot with a relieved smile on my face. Collecting everything out of the car, I make my way inside to find Austin doing a nudie run through the house. His little boy chuckles sounding throughout the space. It's something else being a mom of boys, that's for sure, but those little boy giggles are the absolute best!

# CHAPTER 10

## —emma—

"YOU BOYS GO OUT TO PLAY WHILE I GET DINNER READY." NOW THAT the days are longer and warmer as we get closer to summer, the kids can play outside after school for longer, which means they don't get under my feet while I'm preparing dinner.

"Okay, Mommy. Let's go, Lachlan." Austin's already halfway out of the back door. He loves playing outside any chance he can get. Lachlan generally needs a bit of convincing.

"I don't want to play outside."

"You could play with your new parachute men. The ones you painted to look like *The Avengers*. Just make sure you stay far enough away from the house. I don't want them getting caught on the roof."

"Okay. I'll go outside. I need to make sure Austin doesn't get them stuck on the roof." I smile to myself. Lachlan often feels the need to ensure Austin's doing the 'right' thing, while Austin feels the need to keep an eye on his big brother. The way they look out for each other is really quite sweet.

I check on them from the kitchen window, which overlooks the backyard, and then continue with dinner prep. I may as well sort out the lunches for tomorrow while they're playing happily. With my head buried in my fridge, gathering the fruit and vegetables I need, I hear an almighty crash and a sharp cry from one of my boys. Dropping everything instantly, including my heart, I bolt outside to see what's happened.

Lachlan's pacing as he hits his head with his hand. Austin's on the ground, holding onto his arm, and half of my side gutter is hanging precariously from the roof. I drop to my knees next to Austin to investigate his arm. As I try to touch it, his cries become louder.

"Stop, Mommy!" Lachlan shouts at me.

"I need to check if your brother's okay, Buddy." I turn my attention back to my youngest son. "What hurts the most, Baby?" With a shuddering breath, he indicates his wrist hurts the most.

Theo comes racing through the side gate, Kenny hot on his heels. "What the hell happened? I heard a loud bang followed by a pained wail."

"I'm not sure. I just rushed out here myself." I snap.

"What do you mean? I thought you're supposed to watch kids twenty-four seven. How come you weren't watching yours?" he grumbles back at me as he investigates the hanging gutter. With a powerful wrench, he yanks it off completely.

I don't need this at the moment. "What in the actual truck do you think you're doing?"

"Making sure nobody else gets hurt. How's the kid?" he answers as he unceremoniously throws the piece of metal along my fence line.

I look back to Austin, who's calmed somewhat so long as we don't move his arm. "You're gonna be okay. Can you move it?"

He shakes his head, sobbing loudly. "I'm too scared."

"That's okay. We'll go to the hospital and get it checked out." I take off the scarf I was using to tie back my hair and wrap it around Austin's hand and forearm to stabilize his wrist, which is already beginning to swell, and then tie it up around his neck in a makeshift sling. Then I pick him up gently beneath his legs, ready to carry him inside. "Lachlan, come on, Buddy. We need to go to the hospital."

Lachlan follows me inside. I grab a bag of frozen peas, wrap them in a dishcloth, and gently place them on Austin's wrist to help with the swelling. Gathering the boys as well as my essentials, I lock the house and quickly get the boys in the car to make our way to *Mercy Vale Hospital*.

Once we're on the road, I decide to start my inquiries. "Can either of you tell me what happened?" I glance at the boys in the backseat as I ask the question. Austin's still whimpering, so I have to wait for Lachlan to gather his thoughts to tell me.

"My parachute man landed on the roof and Austin was trying to get it down for me. The gutter came loose, and he slipped. Then, he fell to the ground and hurt his arm. It's all my fault. It's all my fault."

He starts hitting his head again and if he wasn't strapped in, I'm certain he would be pacing.

"Lachlan. Please stop hitting your head. It's not your fault. It was an accident." I keep my voice calm and soothing. Austin's always been a climber. If I left the chair out at the table, he'd climb on it to get on top of the table. I had to have eyes in the back of my head once he learned he could get higher by climbing onto the furniture.

"You said not to let it go on the roof. I let my parachute man go on the roof. It *is* my fault," he shouts at me. I need him to calm down while I'm driving.

Austin butts in, trying to reason with his brother. "The wind blew it the wrong way, Lachlan. It wasn't your fault."

"I should have been more careful. It *is* my fault." At least he's stopped hitting himself and he's not shouting. I'll take that as a win.

Using my Bluetooth, I dial Mom. "Hey, Love. How're the boys?"

"Hey, Mom. That's why I'm calling. It's nothing major, but we're on our way to *Mercy Vale*." Mom's gasp comes across the line clearly, and I can imagine her hand flying up to her mouth. "Austin's had a fall. I think he's sprained his wrist. Would you mind meeting me there to take Lachlan back to your place? I don't know how long this will take, and I don't want Lachlan to be put in a situation that will be difficult for him to handle."

"Of course. I'm on my way. See you soon."

She disconnects the call before I can thank her.

"I'm sorry, Mommy," Austin whispers through his whimpers.

"You don't need to be sorry, Baby. It was an accident. Sometimes accidents happen." It's hard to console him properly while I'm driving. It's times like these I miss having a partner.

"But now Lachlan's upset and we have to go to the hospital and Nana has to come to get Lachlan and you don't know how long this is gonna take and I'm hungry." Half-watching him in the rear-view mirror, my heart breaks as his bottom lip trembles and tiny tears trickle down his chubby little cheeks.

"We can get something out of the machine to eat. It's all okay. I promise." I hope I can keep this promise. I work hard to keep my promises to my boys and I'll be most upset if I can't keep this one.

"But there won't be anything that Lachlan will eat," he whines. I'm so proud of how he's worried for his brother.

"Lachlan will be okay because he'll be going home with Nana. Remember?"

We pull into the parking lot at the hospital—thank goodness we're finally here. Lachlan follows me toward the entrance as I carry Austin to the front emergency doors. Mom's already standing there. She lives closer than we do, so I knew she would beat us. The relief is instantaneous. Knowing Lachlan will be taken care of and I can focus on Austin's care and comfort.

"Thanks for coming so quickly, Mom." She rushes forward, kissing Austin on his forehead and ruffling Lachlan's hair. He pulls away from her touch because he's already agitated.

"Of course, Love. You okay?" She studies my face closely. She knows me so well that she can see how well or how badly I'm doing just by studying my face. I have trouble hiding how I feel. I've always been that way.

"Yeah, I'm okay. Or I will be once I know what's wrong with Austin's wrist. I think it's a sprain, but I want to be certain."

"Better to get it checked out. Poor little guy. Okay, well, I thought it best if I take Lachlan back to your place."

"That'd be great, Mom. I really appreciate it. Lachlan's upset because he feels as though this was all his fault." Mom takes Austin from me so I can crouch down to speak with Lachlan.

"Hey, Buddy. Nana's gonna take you home. Okay?" He doesn't look at me as I speak, which is not unusual, but at this moment, *I need* eye contact to ensure he understands. "Look at me, please." I wait for his eyes to make contact with mine. "We'll be home as soon as Austin's arm is fixed up."

"Okay." He moves next to Mom, so I take that as his agreement. I kiss the top of his head and then take Austin inside, knowing that my big boy is in good hands.

We're greeted by a clerk at the front desk. "Good afternoon. What seems to be the problem?"

I go on to explain what I think the problem is with Austin's wrist and answer what seems like a million questions about health insurance and Austin's medical history.

"Okay. I'll get the triage nurse to take a look. Please take a seat in the green section." I guide Austin to a pair of seats out of the way and look around to see how many people are here before us. Surprisingly, it's not too busy. Maybe we won't be here all that long.

"I'm hungry, Mommy."

"I know, Baby. I'll get something for you from the machine. Stay here." The sandwiches are always a bit risky from these machines, so even though it pains me, I'll have to choose a not-so-healthy snack. I choose a giant cookie that's the size of my hand and a bottle of water. "Here you go, Baby." Opening the cookie, I place it on a tissue on my lap for him.

"Thank you, Mommy." He nibbles on the cookie, slowly working his way through it until it's all gone. I'm impressed—it was a big cookie.

A nurse wearing scrubs covered in baby sloths calls out, "Austin Miller." We both stand to make our way forward as she smiles in our direction. "Hello, Austin. I believe you've had a bit of a nasty fall."

"Yes, Ma'am."

"That's not good. That's a great sling, Mom." She looks up at me with a reassuring smile. "Let's take a look. Follow me, please."

We sit down in a small, sterile room and she works through what needs to be checked, asks the same million questions we were asked before, and then sends us back out into the waiting room. Even though she was as gentle as she could be, she still had to move Austin's wrist to investigate, which caused him more discomfort. His little body shakes as his tears return, but he's trying his best to be brave and hold them back. I snuggle with him on my lap, doing my best to distract him with a game of eye spy. Minutes tick by, the time seeming to drag. Our boredom is broken by a new text message.

MOM

Any news?

ME

Not yet. We've seen the triage nurse, just waiting to be seen by a doctor

MOM

Right. It always takes a while. I wanted to update you on Lachlan. He's calmed down, and he's had some vegetables to eat. He's now watching some TV

ME

Thanks Mom x

MOM

You're most welcome

Tucking my phone back in my purse, I brush Austin's hair away from his forehead, placing a tender kiss there. My boys are my world and I hate it when they're hurt or sick. It's the worst part of being a mom. His breaths have slowed and deepened, which is great. It's better for him to sleep.

After an hour and a half, a different nurse, wearing scrubs covered with cute little koalas, calls us through. I manage to pick up Austin and follow her without disturbing him. She gives me a sympathetic smile. "Poor cherub. We'll have him fixed up in no time, so you can get him home to bed. I'm Amy and I'll be coordinating Austin's treatment today."

"Thank you so much, Amy." Austin wakes as I place him on the stiff hospital bed. I sit beside him, wrapping my arm around his shoulders, carefully avoiding his injured wrist.

"No problem. Let's take a look." Amy gently unwraps the sling to observe Austin's wrist, the whole time making conversation with him about one of his favorite topics, *The Avengers*. "I'm pretty sure it's a moderate sprain, but the doctor will be in shortly to take a look. He may want an X-ray to confirm."

Amy leaves the room. Lying on the bed next to Austin, we talk quietly about school and what his injury will mean for him.

We're not waiting too long until an older gentleman, whom I assume is the doctor, enters our cubicle with a sunny smile. "Well, I hear we have an *Avengers* fan in our midst this evening."

Austin instantly perks up, a smile touching his lips. "Yeah, that's me. I love *The Avengers*, especially Spider-Man. He's my favorite!"

"Oh yeah. I'm a Hulk man myself. Been reading the comics since I was about your age."

Austin's face lights up. "Really? That's so cool." He looks at me. "Mom, can we get comics?"

"I'm not sure you can still buy comics, but if we can, sure thing." I'll do just about anything to get my boys interested in reading.

The doctor checks over Austin's wrist as he shares, "There's a great comic shop in the city. I'll write the address down for you." He smiles at me as he finishes.

"That'd be great. Thank you."

"Now, Austin. Did you hear any popping or snapping when you landed?"

"No, Doctor."

"Okay, I've dealt with many sprains over the years. I'm certain that we're dealing with a moderate sprain. We'll need to use ice on the injury for twenty to thirty minutes, then off for three to four hours.

Austin, you'll need to rest it for two whole days. Do you think you can do that? That means you can't use this hand to do anything."

With eyebrows drawn down low and a serious expression on his little face, Austin answers, "I can try."

"Great. You know, even superheroes have to rest sometimes." He looks at me. "We'll put a splint on it to keep it stable and, if possible, elevate the wrist tonight while he sleeps. A couple of pillows should do the trick. Some Advil to help with the pain and a good night's rest. It's important to keep it as still as possible for the first couple of days. Follow up with your GP in a few days. Any questions?"

# CHAPTER 11

## —theo—

"DO YOU THINK AUSTIN'S GOING TO BE OKAY?" KENNY'S BEEN worried about her new friend. I think she's asked me the same question half a dozen times.

"I'm sure he'll be fine, Munchkin." I follow the brush down the length of her long hair with my hand. I've been surprised to find brushing Kenny's hair quite therapeutic. "He probably just landed on his hand and bent it back. His mommy took him to the hospital and I'm sure they'll do everything they can to help him."

She's silent for long minutes as I follow the YouTube tutorial, showing me how to braid my niece's long hair. I'm slowly getting the hang of the basic braid, so I thought I'd try the French braid. It's not looking too bad. I've noticed some of the other girls have these fancy braids with ribbons woven through as well. I'm not sure I'm at that level yet, but I'm working my way up in skill. Kenny's hair is so silky that it glides through my fingers, making it difficult to keep the rest of the braid secure as I weave in a new lock. Finishing the braid, I tie off the end, feeling quite pleased with the result. Not bad for a guy who's only recently taken guardianship of his niece.

"Come on, Munchkin. Time for bed." I gently tug on the end of her braid.

"But Uncle Theo, I wanna see if Austin's okay."

"You can check on him tomorrow. It's late and you have school in the morning." I don't want to admit to Kenny that I'm just as keen to know if the kid's okay. She huffs out a disappointed breath but makes her way toward her bedroom.

We brush our teeth together, which has become a kind of ritual. One I find I like—*a lot*. We make funny faces in the mirror at each other and giggle when the toothpaste runs down our chins. *Who would have thought living with a girl could be so much fun?*

Kenny makes her last trip to the toilet for the night and then I tuck her into bed, ready for a bedtime story. "Would you like me to tell you a story about your mom?"

Her entire face lights up in excitement as she nods her head like one of the bobble dolls she likes so much. "Okay, well, she used to hate worms."

Kenny's face screws up tight. "Oh, she wouldn't like Emma's garden. She has lots of worms."

"Probably. I knew how much she hated them because she would get frightened whenever she saw them and scream really loud." I chuckle at the memory. "While she spent the day at the restaurant with Pappoús, I spent the day collecting as many worms as I could find. I kept them in a bucket until I knew she was coming home. I knew the first thing she would do would be to have a shower. So, when I thought she was getting ready for the shower, I covered the drain so they couldn't escape and tipped all the worms into the bottom of the shower." Kenny's eyes go comically wide and her mouth drops open as her hand comes up to cover it. "Then I went and hid in my bedroom and waited. And then I waited some more. Our mom decided we would have dinner first this one time."

"Uh oh!" Kenny's eyes twinkle with mischief.

"Yeah, uh oh! So it was about another thirty minutes or so by the time she went into the bathroom to have her shower. By this time, the worms had escaped the shower and were wriggling all over the bathroom. Her scream was so loud." I smile, thinking back to a simpler time. "I got into so much trouble. I had to collect every single worm, and then Yaya made me scrub the entire bathroom. Your mom didn't speak to me for three whole days."

"Oh, that's so funny, Uncle Theo."

"It *was* funny, but I missed your mom so much. I tried everything to get her to talk to me again."

"How did you get her to talk to you again?"

"I used my pocket money to buy her favorite treat. Do you remember what your mommy's favorite treat was?"

"Yeah, I do. Weece's Peanut Butter Cups!"

"Exactly. I knew she'd forgive me if I bought her some of those.

And it worked. I was so relieved when she started speaking to me again."

"You're funny, Uncle Theo. Why were you mean to Mommy if you didn't want her to stop speaking to you?"

"I dunno. It's what little brothers do sometimes." I tap the end of her cute button nose. "Okay, time for sleep, Munchkin!"

"Night, night, Uncle Theo."

"Sweet dreams, Sweet Kenny." I rub my nose against hers in a kiss and press my lips to her forehead. Soaking in her little girl shampoo smell.

She brings her little hands up to squish my cheeks. "I love you, Uncle Theo."

I freeze in place. My heart doubling in size at her words. Swallowing down the lump in my throat, I say the only words I can. "I love you, too, Sweet Kenny."

She snuggles down into her bed with a smile on her face, her eyelids heavy. I watch her from the doorway for long minutes, thinking about my sister and what she's missing. Thankful for what I'm now experiencing—it's a painful double-edged sword.

As I move through the house tidying up before I organize Kenny's lunch for tomorrow, I notice headlights from a car pull in next door. That must be Emma and Austin coming home from the hospital; I saw an older woman come back with Lachlan earlier. I know Kenny's out like a light, so I step outside to catch Emma before she heads inside. Quickly stepping out onto my porch, I jog down the steps to meet her just as she's about to open the back door.

"How's your boy?"

"Oh, hey. He's okay, just a sprain."

"That's good. It could have been so much worse with the state of your house."

She freezes in place, jutting out her curvaceous hip, and planting a fist on it. "What do you mean, 'the state of my house'?"

I throw my hand out in the direction of her place. "It needs a lot of work. Does your boyfriend ever do any maintenance?"

"What in the actual …" She huffs out a breath, blowing her bangs out of her eyes. "Who in the hell do you think you are?" she whisper-yells at me. "You always have something to say to me. I'm doing my damn best, okay?" Her voice is gradually increasing, her breaths coming out hard and fast. "I'm a single mom. I have two boys, one of which is on the spectrum. I work full-time to put a roof over our heads, food on the table, and clothes on my boys' backs! After school, I have to take Lachlan to appointments, do everything around here for everyone as well as prep for work! There's always so much to freaking do and I don't have anyone to help me keep up with everything that needs to be done inside and out." I can't stop my eyes from straying to her heaving breasts that jiggle every time she gesticulates toward her house with her hands. "And yeah, some things get ignored! But I'm doing my freaking best! I don't need you coming at me left and right about what I do or don't do! Keep your freaking opinions to yourself."

*Fuck, she's sexy when she's riled up!*

She turns her back on me and proceeds to retrieve Austin from the back seat. She's struggling to manage in her fury, but there's no way in hell she'll ask me for help after that tirade.

"Do you need some help?"

"Nope." She manages to get him out of the car, slamming the door closed with her hip and storming inside without a second glance at me. Through it all, I can't stop the smile from spreading across my face. Yeah, she's spectacular. Walking back inside, I go over the new information I have.

I have a spring in my step now that I know she's single.

# CHAPTER 12

## —theo—

"Hi, Son. How are things going with you and Kenny?"

"Hey, Dad. Good. We're getting into the routine of school and getting used to each other."

"That's great to hear. I was hoping to pop around this morning. I, uh, have something that Anna left for Kenny that I want to give to you." I swallow down the lump that immediately forms in my throat at the mention of my sister's name. "I would prefer to give it to you while Kenny's at school."

I wonder what it is? "Sure, Dad. I'm out at the moment. I should be home …" I check my watch, "by ten."

"Okay. See you then."

I make it home with minutes to spare. I wanted to get a new section of gutter to fix the portion Austin pulled down when he fell. I also had to buy matching paint. I'll probably end up painting all the gutters because the new paint will look slightly different from the rest and that'll annoy the shit outta me every time I look across at her house. As I'm climbing out of my truck, Dad pulls in behind me.

"That was good timing. Wanna come in for a coffee, or are you in a rush to get to the restaurant?"

"I have some time." He grabs a box from the passenger seat and follows me inside. It's the first time he's been here, so I give him the tour. I catch his smile as he looks into Kenny's newly decorated bedroom. We make our way into my kitchen, the dishes from this morning still in the sink.

I add two heaped teaspoons of finely ground coffee and two

teaspoons of sugar to the *briki*, stir, then add the right amount of cold, filtered water. As I put the traditional coffee pot on medium heat, I ask Dad, "So what did you bring over for Kenny?" I stir the mixture until all the coffee is dissolved, then stop.

"I'll show you once you sit down." The foam's beginning to form and the beautiful aroma of coffee fills my kitchen. I don't generally go to the trouble of making our traditional coffee, but I thought I'd show Dad I'm not completely useless in the kitchen. As the foam reaches the top of the pot, I turn off the heat and share the foam between the two cups, then make sure to share the coffee grains evenly without disturbing the foam.

Placing the cups on the table, one in front of my father, I realize my shoulders are stiff as I hold my breath, awaiting his approval. He studies the cup in front of him, takes a sip, then smiles at me. "A good brew, Son." He nods in approval, releasing the tension I was holding. He pushes the box he brought with him toward me. "Open it."

With trepidation, I drag the box forward. It's only the size of a shoebox, but whatever's inside is going to be important to Kenny. I take a sip of my coffee for fortitude and then, with trembling hands; I open the lid. The box is filled with dozens of letters. As I look through the first few envelopes, my breath seizes in my lungs at the sight of my sister's neat cursive script. Each letter is lovingly labeled with Kenny's birthdays. I look up at my father.

"How many did she write?"

"One for every birthday until she's twenty-one, graduations from school and university, first boyfriend, first heartbreak, first job, marriage, first baby." I flick through the sheets of paper, which undoubtedly hold words of wisdom only a mother can share with her daughter. My throat grows tight and I have to blink several times to hold back the stinging in my eyes. How fucking difficult would this have been for my sister to do? To know you won't be around for your baby for these milestones? I always knew Anna had a quiet strength about her, but this ... this is unbelievable, even for her. "She wanted Kenny to have something for every major event. Right at the bottom are some small gifts for graduation, her twenty-first, and her wedding day." *Fuck!*

Dad's bottom lip trembles as a tear escapes, tracking down his weathered cheek. The guilt I feel at not returning home to support him and my sister through her final months is overwhelming—suffocating me, drowning me. "I'm so sorry, Dad. Sorry for my selfishness! For leaving you to deal with everything. For not coming home when I should have. I … I just … couldn't go through it again! It was too much. But now I see how unfair, how cruel I was to you, to Anna, to Kenny. I'm so fucking sorry, Dad." My tears fall as if to punctuate my words, to highlight my pain.

My father, always stoic, stands and wraps me in his embrace. "It's okay, Son. We understood your reasons. You took your mother's death very hard. I understood."

"It's not fucking okay. It'll never be fucking okay that we lost the most important women in our lives to that fucking disease! That I let you down, *again*." I pull out of his embrace so I can stand and pace. I have so much anger and hate bubbling up inside of me, I don't know what to do with myself. "It's not fucking fair. They were good people, kind people. They didn't deserve to die so young. We didn't deserve to lose them! My sister shouldn't have had to write all of those letters to her daughter for moments she'll never be able to share. Kenny doesn't deserve to be motherless! I don't deserve to be motherless! You didn't deserve to lose your wife! Your daughter!" I stand in silence, my chest heaving as I look across my backyard to my workshop. Lost in thought, for I don't know how long, I jump when my father's hand makes contact with my shoulder.

"You're right, Theo. It isn't fair, but we can't change what's happened. We need to make sure that Anna remains a solid part of Kenny's life." He points at the opened box on the table. "Those letters and gifts will help do that. Us sharing stories about her mother will help do that. I'm so grateful that we have Kenny; she's part of Anna—her legacy. Just as you and Anna were your mother's legacy. I saw your mother in you and your sister every day. I see Anna in Kenny every time I look at her. Her quiet strength. Her kindness. Her friendliness. No matter where we went, Anna always came away making a new friend. Kenny is very much the same."

My shoulders slump forward and I tuck my hands in my pockets, contemplating his words. I'm having a tough time reconciling that our women were stolen from us too soon and as a result, two children grew up motherless. That history is repeating itself and another child is going to grow up motherless. "I am beyond grateful that we have Kenny, don't get me wrong. But I want Mom and Anna, too." I shrug my shoulders. "Call me selfish, but I want all of them. Here. With us. Where they belong." I point at the floor between us as if that will magically provide a space for their return.

"I know, Son. I wish for that too. But we can't spend our lives wishing for the impossible. We have to live for who we have left. She needs us. Now more than ever."

I nod, begrudgingly accepting his words as the truth they are. He pats me on the back. "I'll leave you to your day. There's a letter at the back of the pile for you. Read it when you're ready." I don't respond. I can't. I can't imagine what she wrote in those letters. Each and every one different for the special times in her daughter's life. The daughter she'll never see grow up.

I don't know if I'll ever be ready to read her letter to me. Will it be full of anger and hatred that I didn't come home in her final months, weeks, days?

The front door bangs behind my father and I'm alone with my thoughts. A fucking dangerous place to be. I head outside myself, needing to keep busy. I have the perfect task!

# CHAPTER 13

## —theo—

"UNCLE THEO, WHY ARE YOU PAINTING EMMA'S HOUSE?" KENNY asks from her position on the grass next to the ladder. As soon as I picked her up from school, we came over so I could finish the job I started this morning. It didn't take much to install the new gutter, which I suppose I could have painted tomorrow, but I wanted to get it started today. I need to put the primer on so I can paint all the gutters tomorrow.

Before I can answer, Emma's car pulls into her driveway. Damn, I was hoping to get this finished before she came home. She was so pissed at me last night; I figure she won't want to lay eyes on me for at least a couple of days. The engine turns off and I can see from here that she's watching me through the windscreen. She's probably still pissed at me. I decide it's best to just confront her head-on.

Climbing down the ladder, I prepare for battle. As I breach the side gate, she exits her car and I feel as though I need to approach her carefully with the kids around. Austin exits the car close behind Lachlan, and I notice he has a splint on his injured arm.

He races over to Kenny. "Hey, Kenny, see my splint. Isn't it cool?"

Kenny studies the splint as though it's a prized treasure. "So cool! Does your arm still hurt?"

He shrugs. "Eh, a little bit."

"You're so brave. You wanna play wiv me?"

"Yeah, come on. I'll show you our new parachute *Avengers*. Well, the ones we have left." He kicks the ground with the toe of his shoe.

I dig into my back pocket to pull out the one I rescued from the roof earlier and hold it out to him. "I think you might be missing this one."

His face lights up as he reaches forward to take it from me. "Thank you, Theo. I thought I'd lost it forever."

"No problem. No more climbing, though. Okay?" Emma still hasn't moved away from her car. I'm going to have to go to her.

"Okay, Theo. Come on, Kenny." He runs back toward his mom. "Can I have the key to get in?" She hands him the keys and the three kids move toward the house. Emma's leaning against the driver's door with her arms crossed, so I step forward, tucking my hands in my pockets so I don't reach out for her.

"What are you doing, Theo?" She raises her chin in the direction of the side of the house where I was working.

I look over my shoulder and back at her as though I need to check what she's talking about. "Fixing the gutter. I've replaced the section that broke away and I'm applying the primer so I can paint it tomorrow to match the rest." I shrug. "Look—"

"I need to—"

We speak at the same time, so I gesture for her to go first.

"I need to apologize for my outburst last night."

"Em—"

She holds up her hand. "No. Please let me finish." I nod and force myself to shut up to hear her out. "I was tired and upset before you even opened your mouth last night. But you didn't deserve my anger. I don't normally blow like that. I'm sorry." She lets out a long sigh. "Sometimes everything gets on top of me and I should manage my emotions and responses better."

"You finished?" She nods. "You don't need to apologize to me. I said the wrong thing. *Again*. I have a habit of words coming out the wrong way. I didn't mean to be so abrupt with you. I … uh … got frightened myself when I saw that Austin had fallen and I responded poorly to the situation. I'm the one who's sorry, Emma." I scratch my fingers through my short bristles. "For all the times I've said the wrong thing since we met. It's truly not intentional, and it always comes from a good place. I promise." A ghost of a smile crosses her lips, and she glances away from me.

"Shall we just forget about it and start again?" I don't actually want to forget about any of it. She looks fucking stunning in anger and I never want to forget those moments.

"Sure." I nod, then hold out my hand. "Hi. I'm your new neighbor,

Theo. Kenny, my niece, and I have just moved in." I gesture over my shoulder next door.

She smiles, taking my hand, sending sparks shooting up my arm. "Nice to meet you, Theo. I'm Emma and my two boys are Lachlan and Austin. Welcome to the neighborhood."

"Thanks. It's been great so far." I gesture over my shoulder. "If you don't mind, I just want to finish up the primer so I can paint tomorrow."

"Thank you so much for repairing my gutter. You really didn't need to do that, but it's greatly appreciated."

"No problem. It's the least I can do." I turn to head back to the task.

"Uh, how much do I owe you?" She nods toward the gutter.

"Nothing. It's my gift to you for welcoming me to the neighborhood." It feels good to do something to make things easier for her. I rub the tight feeling in the center of my chest as I walk away.

"Well, thank you. You're very kind. I'm just going to head inside to keep an eye on the kids."

"No worries. I'll collect Kenny when I'm finished here."

Emma turns to head inside and my eyes drop to her sexy ass wrapped in fitted pants that stop just above her ankles.

# CHAPTER 14

## —emma—

I'VE REALLY MISSED THE BOYS THIS WEEKEND. I'M ALWAYS RESTLESS when they're with their father, but this weekend has been particularly tough. Whenever the kids come home from his place, they're always ratty; Austin has an attitude that I don't appreciate, and Sunday night is generally spent with Lachlan having a meltdown. Thank goodness he only has them one weekend a month. I couldn't stand him having them any more often; partly because I don't trust him to have the patience required for Lachlan, but also because he never shows interest in the kids outside of his designated weekend. He never attends any parent/teacher meetings or therapy sessions, and if the boys' birthdays fall on a day outside of his designated weekend, he doesn't go out of his way to see them.

I'm pulled out of my musings by a small knock at my front door. If I wasn't cleaning up in the living room, I probably wouldn't have heard it. Poking my head around the corner, I spy the gorgeous little girl from next door, so I step out.

"Hey, Kenny. How are you today?"

She's joined the boys and me at the park after school a couple of times over the past week. Kenny and Austin have hit it off. Interestingly, Lachlan seems to enjoy her company, too. Since the first time we all went to the park together and Lachlan kept his distance; he's become more comfortable with Kenny, joining in with games.

"I'm good. Do Austin and Lachlan wanna go to the park wiv me?"

"They're not back from their dad's yet." I check the time. "They're due home in about an hour. You can come back then."

Her little face drops in disappointment. Looking down at her feet, she whispers, "But I'm lonely."

Her little forlorn face makes my heart break. "Where's your uncle?"

"He's too busy weading all the books he got from the libwawy."

That man has no freaking idea what he's doing. You can't ignore a four-year-old little girl. Mind you, it was *my* child that fell from the roof the other day. "How about we ask him if you can hang out with me?"

Her face snaps up to mine as a smile lights up her cherubic face, her eyes twinkling in excitement. "Weally?"

Stepping out of my front door, I take her tiny hand in mine and head over next door. Theo's sitting on a stunning rocking chair on the front porch, with a stack of books to his left and one in his hand. He doesn't notice our approach because he's studying as though he's going to be tested on the material. I catch the title, *Raising Girls*, and smile to myself. At least he's reading something worthwhile. Kenny drops my hand and runs up the few steps to reach him.

"Uncle Theo, can I play at Emma's house?"

His head snaps up as though he's surprised to be interrupted by his niece, his eyes catching on me and I realize I look a mess—*again!* His eyes start at my bare feet and travel up my yoga-clad legs to my ratty 'Friends' T-shirt, scanning my face thoroughly, before finishing at the messy top knot on my head. When his eyes make their way back to mine, there's a heat I'd recognize anywhere—a certain male appreciation.

*Wow!*

I haven't had anyone look at me like that in a very long time. My body heats under his gaze, and I'm concerned that sweat patches will begin to form underneath my armpits. Slowly, he pulls his eyes away from mine, giving his attention to Kenny.

"Did you go next door by yourself again, Munchkin?" He places the open book face down on the pile of parenting books next to him before leaning forward. His feet are bare like mine and he looks relaxed in gray sweats and a worn college T-shirt.

Kenny scoots closer to me, wrapping her arms around my thigh before being brave enough to answer him with a single nod. Automatically, I reach down and smooth my hand down her ratty hair, offering her support. "I wanted to go to the park with Austin and Lachlan."

"I get that, I do. But I told you that you weren't to go next door by yourself. You need to tell me that you're going next door to visit with the boys."

"Sowwy, Uncle Theo," she whispers, her head bowed low, looking at her bare feet. He drops to his knees in front of her and uses his pointer finger to tilt her chin up so he can catch her eyes—his face so close to my most intimate of places I have to consciously stop myself from rubbing my thighs together.

"I just want to make sure you're safe. Okay? Can you *please* try to remember?" His voice is gentle, soft—a marked difference from the first day I met these two.

"Okay." She looks up at me. "So, can I play at Emma's house?"

He looks up at me from his crouched position right next to my thigh, and my body tingles from the tips of my toes to the ends of my hair. "Is that okay with you?" He's still using that soft, gentle voice he used with Kenny.

I swallow down—*hard*. His eyes tracking the movement of my throat. "Of course. The boys will be home from their father's soon." I look down at Kenny. "Kenny and I can have some girl time. I never get any girl time."

"Me either," she states as though she's twenty years old. Her head swivels back to her uncle. "Can I please, Uncle Theo? Please."

"Sure. Remember your manners, though."

"I will. Pwomise." She tugs on my arm. "Come on, Emma. We need to get started." As we step down onto the path, I look back at Theo over my shoulder to offer him a smile, only to find him staring at my ass. There's certainly something about being appreciated by a hot guy that puts a spring in your step and a sway in your hips.

We spend the next hour painting our toenails while we wait for the boys to come home. Well, I paint Kenny's toenails. I think she got more nail polish on the skin around my toenails than what she got on my actual nails. She was excited to return to pre-kindergarten last Monday, telling me all about how she missed her friends. We only have four weeks left of the school year, and Kenny's excited for the last Monday of the year when she gets to meet her teacher for next year. Our school also does an orientation, helping the kids to transition from one school year to the next. It's a great way to help them settle more easily into their new class when they return after summer vacation. They already know which friends they'll be with and it eases any uncertainties they may have.

Our girl time is abruptly interrupted by the slam of my front door and stomping feet on my clean hardwood floors. Normally, they're so excited to see me that they, well, Austin mostly, almost knock me over with their hugs. They're too busy storming through to their bedroom to give Kenny or me a second thought. Kenny and I share a look, both of us raising our eyebrows.

"Can you stay here a minute?"

She nods in response. I look out of the front window to see my ex-husband making his way to the front door with the boys' gear, so I step out onto the porch to find out what's going on. Closing the door behind me to afford us some privacy, I ask, "What the hell's going on, Preston?"

"Jesus, you don't have to be a bitch the minute you see me." He turns to leave after dumping the bags on the front porch. No way, mister. You don't get to dump two angry boys on me and run. He makes it back to his car before I catch up with him.

# CHAPTER 15

## —thea—

MY SERENITY IS INTERRUPTED WHEN A WHITE CHEVROLET SS PULLS into Emma's driveway and her two boys immediately jump out of the car, slamming their doors. Only try-hard schmucks, who are trying to walk on the wild side, drive a car like that. The kids looked pissed at whoever's driving, and I already don't like whoever it is. The driver steps out of the car and I huff out a laugh when I finally lay eyes on him. Yep, definitely a schmuck!

He grabs some bags from the trunk and follows the same path as the boys, huffing and puffing, muttering something I can't quite hear from where I am. I turn my attention back to my book. I guess Kenny'll be happy now the boys are home to play. I'll give her an hour, then go over to collect her in time for dinner.

"Don't you walk away from me, Preston." *Yep, schmuck. What sort of name is Preston?* "I'm not being a bitch. I want to know why the boys are so upset." Emma sounds beyond livid, reminding me of the other night. "You don't get to dump and run without an explanation."

The guy, who I'm guessing is the boys' father, stops next to his car. He looks across the street and I almost feel a little guilty that I'm about to eavesdrop on a private conversation—not that they're speaking quietly. Anyone walking down the path would be able to hear them.

He looks down at the ground before he answers. "I told them they won't be able to come to my place next month."

"What the hell, Preston? You only have the boys one weekend a month. What's so freaking important that you can't do it on another weekend when you *don't* have the boys?"

"Stacey and I are getting married. I'll be busy." I lean forward in my chair so I can see Emma better. She rests her hands on her gorgeous hips, her face stunning in anger.

"What the hell. You trucking a-hole! You're excluding your sons from your wedding? What kind of father are you?" She crosses her arms, raising those beautiful breasts high. "How dare you hurt them like that. You selfish ass!"

"Enough!" Emma's head snaps back as though he's slapped her with the sharp crack of his voice. "Stacey doesn't want kids at the wedding, and I agree with her. They'll only get in the way. Besides, we both know Lachlan wouldn't cope, anyway!"

"She does realize that she's going to have to put up with the kids one weekend a month, right?" He grasps the back of his neck, looking down at the ground. "I wanted to talk to you about that. Maybe we can just make it for one Saturday afternoon a month, no sleepovers."

"Oh, my trucking God!" She drops her arms, slapping her thighs. "Do you hear yourself? Those boys are your children. You can't just pretend they don't exist because it doesn't suit your new wife. You have a responsibility to them."

"I'll still keep up my fucking payments, don't worry." *Oh yeah, he's a fucking schmuck!*

"It's not about the trucking money." I have to suppress my snicker at her cursing. "It's about your time and attention. They're boys. They need a father figure who's interested in them as people. A man who wants to help, support, and guide them in their growth. Not someone who only deems them worthy for one afternoon a freaking month!" *What did she ever see in this guy?*

They're both quiet for long moments and I think maybe that's the end of the argument.

"Be sure you don't knock her up." Her voice has changed from enraged to one dripping in hurt.

"What?" The schmuck seems genuinely confused by her statement.

"Well, her body will change once she falls pregnant, and even more so when she has a baby. We both know you don't like the effects of pregnancy and childbirth on your wife's body. Nor do you like the fact that children might just take the focus away from you." I see fucking red. *He what? What did I just hear, exactly?*

She turns, walking away a few steps, then turns back around. "Maybe you shouldn't bother coming around anymore. You only ever think of yourself, and they deserve more than that."

With that, she walks around the back of her house and he climbs into his schmuck car, driving away without a backward glance at the family he obviously walked away from. What a fucking idiot! I've not spent all that much time with Emma and her boys, but if I were lucky enough to have a woman like that, I certainly wouldn't be walking away. The side gate slams closed and then I hear a heart-wrenching sob.

I'm torn.

Do I go to her? Or leave her to her private breakdown? Everyone's entitled to have their moment in privacy. I don't know her well enough to offer support, so I leave her to have a quiet moment to express her pain and gather herself.

I take the three steps up to Emma's front porch, noticing the middle step is split. I noticed it the day I returned her casserole dish, but I was too pissed at her for not locking her door that I forgot all about it. It needs a new piece of timber before one of her boys hurts himself again. The porch area is quite large; she could do with a couple of rocking chairs with a coffee table out here.

I'm not sure if I've done the right thing, but I decided to invite Kenny and myself over for dinner with a few piping-hot pizzas. I figured Emma might not feel like cooking after her run-in with her ex.

Balancing the pizzas with one hand, my other hand freezes mid-knock as I hear a loud crash come from inside, followed by one of her boys shouting. I test the door handle and, sure enough, Emma hasn't locked it yet again. *What is it with this woman?* My feet quickly lead me to the source of the commotion to find chairs tipped over, Lachlan shouting at Emma as he hits his head, and Emma covered head to toe in milk. Kenny and Austin are nowhere in sight, so I place the pizzas on the counter, watching Emma watch Lachlan. I feel as though I'm walking into a war zone and that I need to place my steps carefully so as not to set off a bomb.

Keeping my voice low, I ask, "Everything okay in here?" I glance between Lachlan and Emma.

With wide eyes, Emma glances across at me, noticing me for the first time. Her body sags as she looks down at herself, around her kitchen area, then back to me.

Whispering, she responds, "Yeah, we're okay. Would you mind taking Kenny home? She's in the boys' bedroom. I don't want her to be frightened."

"I can stay and help if you like."

"No, thank you. I've got this."

I'm not sure what in the hell just happened, but Emma's level of calm puts me somewhat at ease and Lachlan's stopped shouting. She has a quiet steel beneath those sweet curves of hers. We all stand, frozen in place. I don't want to make a move and upset the calm. Lachlan wipes his hand under his nose and then steps forward to right one of the tipped-over chairs. I step forward to help him, but Emma gives a subtle shake of her head, so I remain locked in place. Once all the chairs are in their correct positions, Lachlan apologizes to Emma before leaving the kitchen. Her head drops between her shoulders, her posture one of defeat. I want to step into her, wrap her up, kiss her, give her comfort, but I hold myself back—she's clearly had a shit afternoon.

She brushes her hand through her hair, resting it on top of her head before looking at me. "Uhm. Kenny's in with Austin. Upstairs, down the hallway, last door on the right." She points in the direction she expects me to go, but I don't want to leave her like this. After the earlier confrontation with her ex and now this with her son, she's gotta be feeling like shit at this point.

"Will Lachlan be okay? Are you okay?"

The frown lines forming between her brows suggest she's surprised by my question. "Yeah. Thanks. Sorry about that. Kenny's been in the boys' room the whole time, so she was safe."

Shit! "I guess that should have been my first concern, but I seem to have an inherent trust that you would keep her safe." I awkwardly point to the pizza boxes I dropped on the counter. "I uh, brought dinner for all of us. I hope you don't mind, but I pretty much invited Kenny and myself for dinner."

She looks down at herself again, before looking back up at me with olive-colored eyes. "Thank you, but I don't think tonight will work. Lachlan takes a little while to come down and I need to get cleaned up." She looks away from me. "I need to check on Lachlan."

"If you're sure. Maybe another time?"

"I'm sure."

I collect Kenny and we head home sans pizza. It doesn't feel right to walk away, leaving Emma on her own to deal with whatever that was, but she didn't seem keen on Kenny and I staying. I notice she didn't offer up another time for us all to have dinner together, either.

# CHAPTER 16

## —theo—

Last week felt weird when I dropped Kenny at school for the first time since taking guardianship of her, and it doesn't feel any less strange this week. I'm not used to having to take care of someone else's every need—I barely manage to take care of myself most of the time—but I feel as though I'm getting the hang of it. As much as I'm not used to having someone around all the time, I've become used to her following me around, asking a million questions. I really missed her while she was at school, which was surprising. I'm happy I kept her home for the first week so I could have some time with her, giving us time to get to know one another. I would have kept her home longer, but she was keen to get back to her friends. All the books say kids need routine, so I guess it was for the best that she returned last week. There's only one month left until summer vacation, so she'll be back in my pocket before I know it—and doesn't the idea of that lift my spirits.

I open the large door to my workshop, eager to get stuck into a new project. I managed to get my workshop set up, but with Kenny home, I wasn't able to get started on any new projects. Last week, I knocked up a couple of simple but practical coffee tables and put up some notices at the local stores in an attempt to get some work. I had a couple of calls, so I'll follow up with the quotes tonight when Kenny's in bed. I find I need to use the time she's actually at school to build and the time when she's asleep to do the admin work that needs to be done.

Turning on the light, I head straight to the timber I purchased last week. I have the perfect project to keep me busy and my mind from wandering toward my sexy neighbor. Before I start that, though, I want to fix the middle step leading up to Emma's porch.

I wrap my tool belt around my waist, grab a stunning piece of redwood, and head next door to get to work. Studying the porch steps, I think it would be better to replace all three steps. The other two that aren't as damaged are pretty close to failing, and I would hate for Emma or the boys to get hurt on the steps. I head back to my workshop to pick up more timber, then head back to remove the existing steps before working to replace them with new redwood, which matches the rest of the porch. I'll seal them first thing tomorrow morning, so the solution has a good amount of time to dry. As I head back home, I notice her letterbox is unstable, so I quickly stabilize it.

Making myself a fresh coffee, I head back into the workshop to get started on a new pair of porch chairs. I get lost in the project; cutting lengths to approximate size before running each piece through the electric planer to cut down on sanding time later. I use my templates to trace the exact shapes I need before taking to them with my band saw. Before I know it, my phone alarm sounds, breaking me out of the zone. It's time to pick up my girl from school.

I've missed her today—I'm surprised at how quickly she's burrowed into my heart. It stuns me every night when she tells me that she loves me. It was so unexpected the first time and every time since— I thank my lucky stars that I'm the one who gets to put her to bed each night. With all the pieces cut to size, tomorrow I'll be able to add some details using the router before putting everything together.

Kenny comes running out of class with an enormous smile pressing her cheeks up high. "Uncle Theo!" she shouts as she jumps up into my open arms. "I missed you." The little girl who reminds me so much of my sister squishes my cheeks together and kisses the tip of my nose.

I can't hold in my laugh at her cuteness. "I missed you too, Munchkin." I jig her in my arms, rubbing my nose against hers. "You wanna get a milkshake and tell me all about your day?"

"Yay. Let's go!"

She collects her backpack and puts it on, then holding hands, we head out of the school building. As we breach the doors, Kenny tugs on my arm. "Look, it's Emma."

Looking in the direction Kenny's pointing, I spot Emma speaking with a woman with wild red hair. They look to be deep in conversation, but Kenny's bound and determined to say hello.

"Emma!" she calls out, waving wildly as we get closer.

Emma turns around, clearly surprised if her wide eyes are anything to go by. Today they look like grass in springtime and I'm mesmerized by their brightness. Her smile is instant the moment she lays eyes on Kenny. She looks gorgeous in wide navy pants and a white knitted top, strands of hair that have come loose from her ponytail falling around her face.

"Kenny, I didn't know you came to school here." She crouches down to Kenny's level as she speaks.

"Yeah, I'm a big girl. I go to pwe-kindergarten. Do Austin and Lachlan go to school here?" Kenny asks with excitement.

Emma laughs lightly, as does her friend. "Yes, they do. Austin is in Ms. Summer's class." She points to her friend. "And Lachlan is in Mr. Templeton's class."

Emma stands up. "Uh, hi, Theo." The way she's fidgeting as she greets me makes me think she's embarrassed for some reason. "This is a surprise." She tucks a loose lock of milk chocolate-colored hair behind her ear. "This is my friend and colleague, Kate Summer." She gestures to the woman next to her. "She teaches kindergarten."

Kenny bounces on her toes. "Will you be my teacher next year?"

Kate bends forward. "Maybe. Won't that be great?"

"Yeah. You're so pwetty. You have hair like a Disney Pwincess!" Kate and Emma laugh, and I'm relieved they have a sense of humor.

I hold my hand out to Kate in greeting. "Nice to meet you, Kate. I'm Theo, Emma's neighbor." Kate looks between Emma and me with a knowing smile on her face and wide eyes, her eyebrows almost reaching her hairline.

"Nice to meet you, Theo. Emma didn't mention that she had a new neighbor already." She looks at Emma with that look women get when they're not happy they've been kept in the dark.

"I was about to take Kenny for a milkshake. We'll see you later." I dip my chin to the ladies in goodbye.

"Bye, Emma. See ya, Ms. Summer." Kenny steps in close, hugging Emma around her legs.

"Bye, Kenny. Bye, Theo."

# CHAPTER 17

## —theo—

WE ENTER *COFFEE AND COOKIES* AND MAKE OUR WAY TO THE COUNTER. "So, what flavor milkshake would you like?"

Kenny studies the menu board with interest, though I'm pretty sure she can't read all that much yet. "Stwabewwy is my favowite."

"Okay, let's get you a strawberry milkshake, then."

I order our milkshakes along with a chocolate-chip cookie, the size of Kenny's head, for her and a muffin for me. Then we take a seat in a booth near the window.

"Did you have a fun day at school today?"

"Oh yeah. I missed my fwiends. It was so fun to see them again."

"But you just saw them last Friday."

"Yeah, but I miss them."

I sort of feel guilty that I kept Kenny away from her friends for that first week, but I wanted to get to know her better before life and routine got in the way. She must have *really* missed them over that week if she misses them only after a weekend.

A young woman with a bright smile delivers our food and drinks to the table. "Enjoy your treats."

I slide the strawberry milkshake toward Kenny, along with her cookie. Kenny takes a sip of her drink, then screws up her cute little face.

"What's wrong?"

"This tastes yuck!" She wipes her tongue with her fingers as though she can get rid of the taste.

"But you said strawberry was your favorite." I'm confused, so I take a drink for myself to check if it tastes as it should. It tastes like a freaking strawberry milkshake to me. I never liked strawberry myself, I'm a chocolate man. My sister always loved strawberry milkshakes … *and* … things click into place.

"Your mom loved strawberry milkshakes." Kenny nods with a smile. "Is that why you chose a strawberry milkshake? Because it was Mommy's favorite?"

She looks down at the table, then back up to me, her bottom lip wobbling. I reach across the table and take her little hand in mine. "You're not in trouble. I just want to know if that's why you chose it."

"It's Mommy's favowite. So now it has to be my favowite."

This little girl just broke what was left of my heart. Getting up from my side of the booth, I move into the seat next to my niece so I can wrap my arm around her and pull her in close to me. I kiss the top of her head. "Mommy wouldn't want you to change the things you like best for her. She would want you to still be Kenny." I squeeze her tight. "What is *your* favorite flavor milkshake?"

She looks up, eyes so much like my own looking back at me. "Chocolate." My cheeks rise slightly. I pull my milkshake forward and place it in front of my niece.

"Here, you have mine. I'll drink the strawberry one."

"Thank you, Uncle Theo."

"No problem. From now on though, when I ask you to choose something, I want you to choose what *you* like. Not what your mom liked. Okay?"

She nods. "Okay. I'm sowwy."

"You don't need to be sorry. You're not in trouble. I know you miss your mommy." I rub my chest. "I miss her too." We drink in silence for a few moments, side by side. "Maybe we could work out some things we can do to remember your mom."

She smiles up at me. "Okay."

# CHAPTER 18

## —emma—

KATE AND I WATCH THEO AND KENNY MAKE THEIR WAY TOWARD THE parking lot. As he climbs into his truck after securing Kenny, Kate turns to me. "Oh, my gosh! You've been holding out on me." Her eyes are comically wide as she fans her face.

"No, I haven't. There's nothing to tell!" I nudge her with my elbow.

"Nuh, uh, uh. You wouldn't let me get away with that when you found out about Oliver. Now spill!"

I tell her everything from the moment I met Kenny, to spying on Theo naked on his deck, to his verbal jabs at me and our argument the other night. Kate's heart breaks for Kenny and she oohs and aahs at the appropriate times, like the good friend she is.

"You need to jump on that whenever you get the chance. He's hot!"

"Oh yeah, like someone who looks like he does is going to go for me. I'm still carrying the baby weight from the boys and my youngest is five years old." I grab the extra pounds around my stomach to make my point.

"Stahp! Just stop it." She taps my hand away from my stomach. "You, my friend, are absolutely stunning. Besides, I saw him checking you out."

"Rubbish. I'm always a mess whenever he sees me, and today's no different." I point out my messy hair and the splash of red paint on my knitted top, thanks to Daniel gesticulating like it's an Olympic Sport while painting his favorite emergency vehicle.

Arriving home, the boys and I pile out of the car with our bags. Austin bounces up the steps just in front of me, Lachlan bringing up the rear.

"The timber is new," Lachlan states in his usual matter-of-fact manner.

Trying to balance everything as I slot the key into the lock, I turn around. "Huh?"

He points down at the step he's standing on. "This wood is new. It wasn't like this when we left this morning."

I open the door for Austin and then investigate the steps. Sure enough, the timber *is* new. The second step was starting to give out, but all three steps have been replaced. These steps have been on my list of things to do along with a million other things that need to be done around the house, but I have to budget carefully for renovations.

I don't remember organizing anyone to repair the steps. Heading inside, I continue to run through my mental filing cabinet but come up blank. I prepare an afternoon snack for the boys and then head out front to check the mailbox. As I close the latch after collecting my mail, I notice the lack of wobble. Gone is the old grayed-out wood, replaced with a fresh two-by-four of redwood, exactly like the new set of steps.

Sheet! How did I forget I had someone coming out today? Looking through the envelopes, I look for an invoice, but I come up empty.

I start to head back inside but change direction toward Theo and Kenny's house. It seems I'm always apologizing to him because I owe him another one for last night, especially since he left behind pizza— that reminds me, I owe him some money for that. I race back inside to grab my purse so I can pay him for the meal. I look down at the red paint on my top, wondering if I should take the extra couple of minutes to change. Shrugging my shoulders, I decide I don't care. He's already seen the mess, and he's seen me much worse. Just last night, I was covered head to toe in milk, courtesy of Lachlan's meltdown in reaction to his father's brush-off.

I take in a deep breath and knock on his screen door. I don't have to wait long before his silhouette comes into view. "Emma," he breathes out as he opens the screen door. "Hey."

"Hey." Now, what do I say? I mean, I know I owe him an apology for kicking him out minus his dinner, but where do I begin? "How was your milkshake?"

"It was great, thanks. Kenny and I had a good chat about some things."

"That's great. I'm so happy to hear that." I shuffle my feet. This is incredibly awkward. May as well get to the reason for my visit this afternoon. "Uh, sorry about last night."

Creases form across his forehead, and his dark brows slice down low over his eyes. "I'm not sure what you're apologizing for."

A nervous laugh escapes me. "For starters, I pretty much stole your dinner." His eyebrows shoot up toward his hairline as he tucks his hands into his pockets, a half-smile touching his kissable lips. *Oh God, stop looking at his lips!* "Uhm, Lachlan had a bad afternoon, and he wasn't able to regulate his response to the situation. I'm sorry it happened while Kenny was in my care, but at no time was she in any danger. Lachlan wouldn't hurt a fly, I promise." I pull out my purse. "So how much do I owe you for the pizza? Which was delicious, by the way." I point over my shoulder back home. "I still have two pizzas in my fridge. Did you want them back?" I need to shut my mouth to stop myself from rambling.

Theo rubs his hand across his mouth and, judging by the sparkle in his eyes, he's attempting to hold in a laugh. "Keep your money. It's all good, I promise. And no, you keep the pizza. Have them tonight or whenever." He leans casually against the doorframe. "So, you're a teacher." It's a statement more than a question.

"Yeah, I teach grade one. Used to be in corporate, but left after I had Lachlan and was pregnant with Austin. I wanted to be around more for the boys. Are you sure I can't reimburse you for dinner last night?" I don't want to get into all the ins and outs of my life with my neighbor. He doesn't need to know about my drama.

"I'm sure. Do you like it?"

"Pardon?"

"Do you like teaching?"

"Oh yeah, I do. I'm not sure why I didn't become a teacher to begin with. It's rewarding watching the kids learn and grow. That light-bulb moment when they finally understand what you're trying to explain." I realize I'm rambling again. "Well, thank you for dinner. It was a really kind gesture. Sorry it didn't work out last night."

I glance back toward my house. I don't suppose he fixed my steps, after all, he said he's a carpenter. "Did you happen to see anyone working on my porch steps and mailbox today?" I don't want to assume he did it. "We've come home to repaired porch steps and a stabilized mailbox. I don't remember hiring a contractor." I huff out an embarrassed laugh because this guy's going to think I'm a complete airhead.

He leans around his doorframe, looking across to my place as if he can see the porch steps from here. "Nah, I haven't seen anyone. I've been busy though, so I probably missed whoever it was." He runs his fingers through his scruff. "Anyway, I need to get back inside to Kenny. Have a nice night."

"Uh, you too." He steps inside without a backward glance. Well, that was an abrupt ending to our conversation. I discreetly sniff my armpit, because maybe I smell bad. Nope, still doing okay in that department. I turn on my heel and head back home.

# CHAPTER 19

## —emma—

"MOMMY, CAN WE GO TO THE PARK?" AUSTIN COMES BARRELING INTO the kitchen as I'm cleaning up after having Mom, Dad, Max, and Sarah over for Mother's Day breakfast. Thank goodness Mona couldn't make it. She was taking her mom out to some fancy champagne breakfast at some la-de-da restaurant overlooking the river.

"Sure. Should we make it a picnic?"

"Yeah! Can we invite Kenny, too?" Uhhh. That would mean Theo would probably come as well. "Please, Mommy."

"Okay. Take Lachlan with you to invite them. Tell them we'll be ready to go at twelve-thirty and I'll have all the food for everyone." It's the least I can do since he fed us for a couple of nights with the pizzas he left behind. He collects Lachlan and a few seconds later, the front screen door slams behind them.

I take deep breaths and decide to put some effort into my appearance, though I don't want to look like I'm trying too hard. I don't know him all that well, I only know that when he's near, my stomach flips and I'm tired of him always seeing me at my worst. I quickly change into a pair of navy capris and a pale pink babydoll blouse sans buttons. I always find it tricky getting blouses and shirts to fit across my bust properly, so I avoid them wherever possible. I can pair them with my Vans and look casual. Tying my hair up in a high ponytail, I swipe a light coat of mascara on my lashes and apply a slick of gloss to my lips.

I step back into the kitchen just as the boys come barging back inside to share the news that Kenny and Theo will be joining us for our picnic at the park. I prep enough sandwiches for everyone, fruit, sliced

vegetables for Lachlan in separate containers, drinks, and some chocolate cupcakes as a treat. Loading up the picnic basket, I grab the picnic
blanket and lead us all out of the house right on the dot of twelve-
thirty.

Kenny and Theo meet us out the front and Theo looks delectable
in ripped jeans and a Captain America T-shirt, which brings out the
gorgeous blue of his eyes. He has that perpetual dark shadow across his
masculine jaw. *Mmm, yummy.*

Kenny runs forward, wrapping her hands around my legs and
squeezing tightly. "Hi, Emma."

I laugh at her enthusiasm as I lower my basket to free up my hands
so I can squeeze her back. As Kenny and the boys greet each other as
though they haven't seen each other for days, Theo brings his arm out
from behind his back, presenting me with a gorgeous bouquet.

"Happy Mother's Day, Emma."

My heart literally skips a beat at his thoughtful gesture. The boys
each made me a cute card, but since splitting from Preston, I haven't
been given a gift on Mother's Day. This was completely unexpected,
but very much welcomed and appreciated.

"Thank you so much. They're gorgeous." I take the flowers,
pressing up on my toes to kiss him on the cheek in appreciation. The
soft bristles of his short beard tickle my lips. He sucks in a breath,
unexpectedly turning his head … our lips lightly connect for a brief
moment as I'm pulling away. Both of us startle a little at the lip-to-lip
contact. Heat rises to my face and I press my fingers to my lips to
temper the tingles.

"Uhm … I'll just take these inside and put them in a vase with
water." I gesture over my shoulder. "Back in a moment." I quickly step
away from Theo and the kids to head inside so I can put the gorgeous
blooms in a vase. I also need a moment to catch my breath and center
myself. I don't need to be getting turned on by my sexy neighbor
because he brings me flowers. Quickly, I arrange the flowers in a vase
with water and head back out to join our small group so we can walk
to the park for our picnic. The kids stroll in front of us, Austin and
Kenny holding hands, as Lachlan walks beside them. "Thanks again
for the flowers. They're beautiful."

"You're welcome. I figured your boys are probably too young to get
you anything. I remember Dad always gave Mom flowers on Mother's
Day. I think he even gave my sister flowers to acknowledge the day."
He rubs the scruff on his face as a ghost of a smile touches his lips.

"I'm sorry about your sister." I look back toward Kenny, motherless at such a young age.

"I took her to the cemetery this morning so she could visit with her." He scratches his fingers through his short beard. "It's the first time I've been. It was fucking hard. I can't believe my sister's gone. She was always so full of life." His voice has a shaky quality as he finishes. I watch his Adam's Apple bob as he swallows down his emotion.

I reach out, grasping his hand to give it a supportive squeeze. He surprises me by returning the gesture and then linking our fingers together as we walk, apparently not in any hurry to let go. To say I'm shocked by his gesture is an understatement. I'll admit it's nice to hold such a masculine hand, but I'm confused by the action. Arriving at the park, the kids take off toward the playground while Theo and I set up the picnic.

"Thanks for the invitation. I wasn't sure how I was going to entertain Kenny for the rest of the day." He laughs. "She has so much energy."

"How are things going for the two of you? Are you finding your way through the minefield of parenting?" I ask, remembering the stack of reading material on his outdoor table, as I empty the picnic basket, pulling out item after item.

"Wow, I'm not sure how you managed to fit all of this into that basket."

"You'd be amazed at what I can fit in my basket." Theo lets out a deep laugh and I stop pulling out items to look at him. It's then I realize how my words sounded. Flustered, I try to correct my statement, but have trouble getting the words out past my giggles. "I mean … that with careful packing, I can fit a lot of supplies into this particular basket." I push my bangs out of my eyes. "Sorry about that."

"No problem. It probably doesn't help that I have a perpetually dirty mind." He winks at me, causing my belly to do a complete three-sixty. I wouldn't mind being on the receiving end of his dirty mind. "And yeah, Kenny and I are finding our way. We've certainly had our moments, like the first day when she disappeared to your place and I couldn't find her." He huffs out a breath. "I was so goddamn scared that I'd already stuffed up and I hadn't even had her for twenty-four hours."

I rest my hand on his arm, tingles assaulting my palm. "So long as the two of you are working it out. That's the main thing. Not saying

I'm an expert or anything like that, 'cause you know I'm not, but if you need any help, I'm right next door."

His shoulders drop as he acknowledges my offer with a brief smile and a tip of his head. "I might take you up on that because I have no idea what the hell I'm doing with a four-year-old. Why my sister named me guardian in her will, I'll never understand." His eyes seek out Kenny and his lips tip up at the corners. "In saying that, I've fallen head over heels in love with my niece. I sometimes catch myself thinking of her as my daughter. We've only been together three weeks and I've already missed having her around while she's at school."

*Oh, how sweet.* "She's an adorable little girl; she would definitely burrow her way into anyone's heart easily." I think both of them could easily burrow their way into anyone's heart if I'm completely honest.

Theo pulls a Frisbee out of his backpack and tilts it this way and that with raised brows. "What do you think? You wanna play?"

Oh geez, I haven't played in ages, but I remember it always being so much fun. "Yeah, let's give it a shot. It's been a while for me, so I'll probably be rusty."

Theo wriggles his eyebrows up and down. "A while, hey?" He gives me a crooked smile. "I'm happy to refresh your memory." He wriggles his eyebrows some more, ensuring his innuendo hits home, making me giggle.

"Okay, Romeo, let's keep the conversation on track." I blow him a playful kiss, then turn to gather the kids for a game. *When did we start heading down this track of flirting?*

Theo gives us all tips on how to throw a Frisbee and then patiently works with each of the kids in turn until they're able to give it a good shot. I remind Austin to be careful of his wrist, even though it's not his dominant hand that got injured. Plenty of giggles and silly times ensue and it's great to see the kids having fun.

"Watch me, Uncle Theo!" Kenny puffs out her chest, ready to show off her newfound skills. With a fling of her arm, she releases the disc decorated to look like Captain America's shield, launching it toward the boys. I'm impressed by her throw and that she managed to actually release the disc in the right direction.

"Hmmph!" Austin drops to the ground, holding his stomach. I race over to my boy, dropping to my knees a split second after Theo.

"Are you okay, Buddy?" I ask him as I brush his hair away from his eyes to find a smile on his face as he 'fake' rolls around, groaning. "You little rat! You're okay."

"Of course, I'm okay. It didn't hit me *that* hard. I just thought it would be funny." He giggles and jumps to his feet.

Kenny gives him a playful whack on the arm. "You meanie. I got sad 'cause I thought I hurted you." Her bottom lip drops and she crosses her arms in a pout.

Austin wraps his arms around her, squeezing her tight. "I'm sorry, Kenny. I was joking around. I didn't mean it."

Kenny squeezes him back. "That's alwight. I'm glad you're okay."

"Alright, everyone. Time for lunch." We head over to our picnic blanket and get down to the important business of eating lunch. Theo watches me closely as I unpack everything from their containers and set Lachlan's plate to his particular requirements to maximize the chance of him eating.

"Thanks for the yummy sandwiches, Emma," Kenny mumbles around a mouthful of food.

She has great manners, which is not as common as it should be. "You're welcome. I'm so happy you could join us on our picnic today."

We enjoy our lunch, and before long, most of the food has been consumed. "Lachlan, you must have been hungry. You finished everything on your plate." I'm pleased with how much he ate. Oftentimes, when we're in a different situation from the norm, he won't eat his food, even though I prepare it in *exactly* the same way as I do when we're at home.

"I was really hungry." He rubs his tummy, looking at the remaining chocolate cupcakes.

"Let's go play some more." Austin pulls Kenny by the hand while Lachlan dutifully follows them, looking very forlorn at leaving the cupcakes behind.

Theo and I pack everything away, occasionally brushing our hands or bumping arms. Tingles erupt at every point of contact, which is getting harder and harder to ignore the more time I spend in his company. Watching him with the kids is such a turn-on. For someone who hadn't had anything to do with children until recently, he's amazing with them. The boys have had so much fun this afternoon. Even though they see my dad and Max every Sunday, they're still starved for that male attention. To be completely honest, I'm enjoying his attention myself.

# CHAPTER 20

## —theo—

WATCHING EMMA WITH THE KIDS IS SEXY AS FUCK! HER LAUGHTER AS we were playing with the Frisbee was proof of her sheer enjoyment of the simple activity. I don't know too many women who would be so uninhibited in their joy. The bonus, of course, was being able to watch her body move and shift. Her curves make my mouth water and my jeans tight. Visions of her chocolate hair spread across my pillow invade my mind, making the situation in my pants even worse.

*I've decided I'm going to make her mine.*

Our hands brush against each other as we pack away the picnic. Her gorgeous bright green orbs search out mine at the touch. My skin tingles and my heart races at the simple contact. I need more, so I take any opportunity I can to brush against her, touching her hand as well as her arm here and there. I take it as a positive sign when she doesn't seem to pull away or make moves to ensure we *don't* touch. I don't want the afternoon to end as she rounds up the kids for us to walk home.

"Thanks for joining us. I had a great afternoon. I need to get this lot sorted—" she gestures to the basket I'm carrying for her "—and settle the boys in front of a movie for the rest of the afternoon. I'm a little behind with my reports and prep for the week."

"I had no idea teachers had so much work to do in their own time." I'm not sure how she manages to do everything as a single mom and full-time teacher. No wonder her place looks a little run down and in need of some TLC. Luckily, I can help her out with all of that.

The kids walking in front of us allow us to chat without interruption. I squeeze Emma's soft hand to gain her attention. "You want me to take the boys for a couple of hours so you can get some work done?" Her head snaps toward me as she stops, pulling me to a stop by tightening her grip.

"Really? You'd do that for me?" The crinkles between her brows as she nibbles on her full bottom lip are adorable. Using my thumb, I tenderly smooth out the creases as I nod.

"Of course."

"What would you do with them?"

I shrug. "Dunno. I'll think of something. I could show them my workshop, and teach them some basic woodworking skills."

Her eyes narrow as she continues to nibble on her lip. "That's right, you're a carpenter. Were you the person who fixed …" She stops speaking and shakes her head.

I nudge her shoulder. I have a feeling she's perhaps put two and two together regarding the repairs of her front steps. "Go on."

She shrugs. "I'm probably being silly, but were you the one who replaced my stairs and fixed my mailbox?"

I don't know why I didn't tell her it was me the other day, but I didn't want her to offer to pay me for the work. She was already trying to pay me for a couple of pizzas. "I did. I hope you don't mind. I wanted to help you out a bit once I knew you were doing everything on your own." I tuck my hands in my pockets because I really want to pull her into me.

She moves forward, wrapping her arms around me and kissing my chin. "Thank you so very much. I can't tell you how grateful I am. How much do I owe you?"

"You're more than welcome, Em." I rub my nose against hers. "Nothing. I had the material lying around. It helped free up some space in my workshop."

She sighs, before whispering, "I would appreciate you taking the boys for a couple of hours. But you'll have to be careful with them in the workshop around all of your tools."

"I will. Don't worry, they'll be safe."

"Be sure to set strict rules." Oh yeah. She's put on what I assume is her teacher's voice. *Sexy!* Placing the basket on the ground, I wrap my arms around her, pulling her in tight to press my lips to her forehead. Her body's stiff in my arms, as though she's unaccustomed to being held. The feel of her soft breasts pressed up against my hard planes is magnificent—better than I could have imagined. The heat of her body seeps through our clothes, and I have to assume the sensation will be even better when we're finally skin against skin.

Leaning back, I lock eyes with hers, azure to dozens of different shades of green. "Have some faith. I promise I'll keep them safe." I lean forward to kiss her forehead again, my lips lingering against her warm flesh. Her warm breath heats my neck with a sigh; her body relaxes against mine as she nods her head against my lips. Reluctantly, I release her so we can keep walking to catch up with the kids, who are a little ahead of us now.

"Okay. I'd really appreciate it. But I have to warn you that Lachlan doesn't cope well with sudden loud noises." We lengthen our strides and pick up speed to catch up to the kids, who are already stopped in front of Emma's place.

"Not a problem. We won't use any of the machines today." We come to a stop next to the kids in front of Emma's home. "Boys, let's help your mom put this stuff away, and then you're coming to my place for a while."

Austin is the first to react. "Really? Can we help you make something?"

"Yay, you can color in wiv me!" Kenny cheers at the same time. She gives Austin a look that clearly telegraphs her displeasure at his suggestion.

Emma looks at me, awaiting my response. I appreciate that she's allowing me the space to lay the rules and boundaries down. "I *do* have a project you can help me with. No electric tools today, though. You have to listen to and follow my instructions. Deal?"

"Deal," he responds excitedly.

"Can I do sanding?" Lachlan asks eagerly.

"Absolutely, Buddy." I muss his hair and then pull my hand away quickly, worried I've done the wrong thing. I'm not exactly sure what Emma meant about him being on the spectrum, but my gut tells me he needs some tender handling.

We move inside to unpack from the picnic.

Handing the picnic blanket to Austin. "Can you put this away, please?"

"Okay." He takes it from me, heading in the opposite direction with Kenny hot on his heels.

This is my first opportunity to study the inside of Emma's home. You can definitely tell she has two boys living here with her. The amount of trucks and Lego constructions displayed on every available surface is a dead giveaway. It's clean and mostly tidy, apart from the boys' toys. The kitchen is immaculate, unlike my own. I'm not the best at cleaning up straight after a meal. I tend to save up all the dishes and do them once at the end of the day. I'm guessing Emma washes everything as she uses it.

After emptying the picnic basket, I hand it to Lachlan. "Would you mind putting this one away for your mom?"

"I can do that." He takes it from me and walks toward the room directly off of the kitchen. Once everything's packed away, we leave Emma to her work and I take the kids back to my place.

# CHAPTER 21

## —theo—

"Come on, I'll show you boys my workshop." Sliding open the large door, I flick on the light and both boys gasp at what they see. With wide eyes, they take a tentative step inside to investigate for themselves. There's nothing that can cause the kids any harm because I always unplug my machinery. My hand tools are all stored on hooks up high on the walls, out of reach. I'm certain they won't be able to get into any trouble while they're in here with me. The boys are frozen in place as they take in the large space. This is what sold me on the house. I needed a large space for my carpentry work and this workshop was perfect.

Austin is blatant in his appreciation. "Wow. This is awesome! Did you know I wanna be like my Uncle Max when I grow up and I'll get to work with big tools one day?"

"Oh yeah? What does your Uncle Max do?"

"He fixes up old cars, makes them like new again. He fixed our lawnmower, too. There's nothing he can't fix. I'm gonna be just like him."

Ahhh, so the dude that fixed the lawnmower is her brother. Still doesn't change the fact that he should have cut the grass after he fixed the machine. It hits me like a ton of bricks how hypocritical my thoughts are. At least *he* was here to help his sister. I left mine to die without any support from me—her only brother. The weight of that realization almost makes me collapse to my knees. I'm so fucking angry with myself. The worst part is that I can't go back and fix it, or change anything.

I'm stuck with the biggest fuck up of my life.

I snap myself out of that train of thought so I can focus on the here and now. "That's awesome. These machines are a little different from what your uncle uses and one day I'll show you what each of them can do, but not today." I look away from Austin to check on the other two. Kenny's sitting at the table and chairs I made for her in the corner with all the craft supplies she could possibly want. I figure it's okay for her to join me out here now and then when I'm hand sanding or carving delicate designs into the timber. Lachlan is running his hands over the two rocking chairs I made for their front porch. The tender attention he's paying to the timber reminds me a lot of my own appreciation for the material. Moving closer, I ask, "Do you like them?"

Without looking up at me, he nods slowly. "Yes, I do. They are very smooth except for a couple of small rough patches here." He points to a spot. "And here." He points to another area on the base. The pride I feel in his attention to minute details is inexplicable since my relationship with the boy has barely begun.

"Yeah. I thought we could smooth these out this afternoon. Then we'll put on the first coat of wax." He looks at me briefly, still avoiding eye contact, but it's the most I've gotten out of him, so I'll take it.

"Okay."

I quickly prepare my beeswax and turpentine mixture so it has time to cool down for us to use, explaining each step as I work. Grabbing the fine-grit sandpaper, I show the boys how to sand with the grain of the timber. I tried to show Kenny the week we spent together before she went back to school, but she wasn't interested—at all.

"Lachlan already knows how to sand. Poppa showed him when he was sanding at their house." Austin's clearly proud of his big brother's skills in this area.

My eyebrows rise in surprise, and I turn to Lachlan. "Really? What were you sanding?"

"Nana and Poppa's porch railing. He was getting the timber ready to repaint." The boy still hasn't removed his hands from the timber.

"That's great. Did you like the work?"

"Yes. I liked it a lot." He remains focused on his task throughout the conversation, but I can tell that he's enjoying what he's doing.

Austin's not so keen, so he leaves Lachlan and me to the task and joins Kenny at her craft table. She's certainly happy that he ditched me and joined her, as she rattles off instructions on how to use the various items she has available to her. Lachlan and I work quietly until both chairs are completely smooth on every single surface.

I hand Lachlan a soft cloth. "We need to make sure every surface is free of sawdust."

He nods, making eye contact with me. "Okay. I can do that."

I pat him on the shoulder and we both get to work. Once the chairs are free of dust, I grab the wax preparation to show Lachlan how to apply it. He's meticulous in his work, carefully applying the precise amount and working it into the timber exactly how I showed him. He's a quick study and I'm impressed with his diligence.

As we're finishing up, Lachlan asks, "Why were you kissing Mommy?"

Hmmm, I didn't think the kids noticed because they were in front of us, but maybe I shouldn't be surprised that Lachlan did. He seems quietly observant of the world around him. More so than Austin and Kenny, who are younger and not so aware of things around them.

"It was a thank-you kiss. For including Kenny and me in your picnic." I hope he buys it. I'm not sure what Emma's response would be.

He nods. "How many coats of wax do we need to put on the chairs?"

*Phew!* Subject dropped. For now, at least. "The chairs will need another two coats to ensure they're weather resistant. But we need to let them dry properly between coats. I'll probably do the next two coats tomorrow because it's getting late today."

"Can I help you do them after school?" Uh … I was going to do them while Kenny was at school and have them sitting on Emma's porch when she arrives home from work tomorrow. I suppose I can find something else to do instead while the kids are at school.

"Sure. We could do one coat tomorrow and the final coat the next day. How does that sound?"

"I don't think it has a sound. I didn't hear anything today while we were applying the wax." It takes me a minute to work out what he's saying and then I have to hold back my smile because he's very serious.

"You're right. It didn't make a sound when we applied the wax. I mean, does the plan suit you?"

"Oh, okay. Yes, the plan works for me." I smile and squeeze his shoulder in confirmation. He doesn't pull away, but I don't linger either.

"How about we order pizzas for dinner as a surprise for your mom?"

"That *will* be a surprise. I don't like pizza."

I wonder what he ate when I left the pizzas at their place last week? "Why's that?"

"Everything touches each other, and it's not crunchy. Sometimes, if the crust is crunchy, I'll eat the crust, but I won't eat the rest. I like eating crunchy foods. I have a crunchy apple with my breakfast and crunchy vegetables with my lunch and dinner. I even have crunchy vegetables with my afternoon snack."

"Right. So if you don't eat pizza, will you only have crunchy vegetables?"

"Yes, and Mommy makes me chicken nuggets too because they're crunchy on the outside."

"Alright. How about I order some thin-crust pizza, which will have a crunchy crust, *and* chicken nuggets? Would that be okay with you?"

"Of course."

Great. I order dinner to be delivered and get the kids cleaned up before heading back over to Emma's. I hope she doesn't mind that I've invited Kenny and myself over for dinner. Let's hope it works out this time.

# CHAPTER 22

## —theo—

My phone rings with an unknown number as I wait for Kenny to come out of class. "Hello, Theo Drivas speaking."

"Hello, Mr. Drivas. My name is Rosemary and I'm calling about the advertisement you put up at *Mal's Minimart*."

"Hi, Rosemary. What can I do for you?"

"Is it true? Will you really do any basic maintenance work for free if I'm over sixty-five? I'll only need to pay for materials?"

"Absolutely. What do you need done?"

"Uh, well, I'm not sure it will be considered basic maintenance. My husband recently had complications from a toe infection. The doctor had to amputate his leg above the knee and now he's wheelchair-bound. It was all so unexpected and sudden. We're going to need some adjustments made to our house to make it easier for him to get around with a wheelchair." The watery tone of her voice hints at her shock as she tells me what needs to be done. "Would that be asking too much?"

"Not at all. I'm currently picking up my niece from school, so I won't be able to come by until tomorrow morning. Would that suit you?"

"Oh, absolutely. He won't be home from the hospital for another two weeks yet. Oh, I'm so thankful to have seen your advertisement. I thought maybe it was too good to be true."

"I'm happy to help. I can be at your place tomorrow morning after I drop my niece at school. Please text me your address and I'll give you a call before I head over. I'll need a rundown of what you need and I'll take some measurements, so I can get the materials required for the job."

"Oh, thank you so very much! You're an angel. I'll send those details through now and I'll see you tomorrow."

"No problem, Rosemary. See you tomorrow."

I'm tucking my phone in my back pocket when the doors open and kids come rushing out. I look at every child as they come through the door until the doorway is empty. I don't see Kenny anywhere! My heart hammers and I panic that something's happened. Stepping through the classroom doors in a rush, I find Kenny sitting with her teacher. My girl's back is to me, but her teacher spots me, giving me a half-hearted smile. Five strides have me squatting next to the little girl who holds my heart in her tiny hands. When I see her face, I hope she's ready to catch all the broken fragments, as my heart shatters into a million pieces. Tears track down her cheeks as snot fills her little button nose. I've only seen her cry once in the whole time we've been together and seeing her like this hurts my fucking heart.

"What happened, Kenny-girl? What's wrong?" She wraps her little hands around my neck and crawls across to me, wrapping her little legs around me, latching on like a koala. She's sobbing too hard to tell me what happened, so I look at her teacher.

"Do you know what happened?"

She places her hand on Kenny's back and her eyes become glassy as she looks at my munchkin. "Uhm, there's a Daddy-Daughter dance on the last Friday of the school year. One of the kids commented—" she breaks off and mouths the next part to me, "—that Kenny didn't have a daddy or a mommy."

I see fucking red and squeeze my girl closer, kissing her forehead. "And what did you do about it?" Anger drips from my words.

"Ah, uh, I spoke to the child about being a good friend and asked them to apologize to Kenny. At this age, children really don't understand that words can hurt another person. It wasn't said with the intention to hurt her feelings, it was a statement of observation." She steps back away from the two of us. "At this age, it's important we guide our students in what's appropriate and what isn't."

My shoulders relax, some of the tension leaving me. I probably overreacted; the kids *are* only four-years-old. "Sorry. I didn't mean to snap at you. I was upset for Kenny."

"Understandable, Mr. Drivas. It's distressing to see your child so upset."

"Is there any information about this dance?"

"Of course. Kenny has the note in her backpack. It covers all the information you'll need."

"Okay. Thanks." Kenny's finally stopped crying. "Say bye to Mrs. Roberts, Kenny."

"Bye, Mrs. Roberts. See you tomowow."

"See you tomorrow, Kenny."

"Thank you."

"No problem." She finishes with a warm smile, and I carry Kenny and her backpack out to my truck. On the way down the hallway, I hear Lachlan's distinctive voice coming out of a classroom and slow to a stop at the door to see what's going on. The boys are shooting screwed-up paper into the trashcan and cheering as they make the shot. Emma's sitting at her desk, shuffling papers around. I take a moment to admire her, deep in thought. I wonder if she realizes how damn beautiful she is?

I clear my throat to let her know I'm here. "Hey." Kenny pulls her head out of the crook of my neck to look around. A small smile forms on her lips, but it's still plainly clear she's been crying.

Emma looks up from her papers, and the boys stop their game. "Hey, Theo. Hey, Kenny. How was school today?" She gets up and comes over to greet us, placing her hand on Kenny's back, her brows pinched. "What's up?"

"Hey, Kenny." Austin sings out as he comes over.

Lachlan moves closer, too. "Hello."

"Would you … uh … have time for a chat later?" I gesture with my head to Kenny, widening my eyes and hoping Emma catches on.

"Sure. No problem. We were getting ready to head home ourselves. Maybe we could all go to the park?"

That perks Kenny right up. "Weally?" She wriggles her way down my body to the floor, a smile on her face. "I love playing at the park." My eyebrows must almost hit my hairline at her sudden turnaround.

"Great, we'll see you at home." She turns back toward her desk and my eyes automatically drop to appreciate her sweet ass.

"See you in a while, boys." I take Kenny's hand and lead her outside to my truck.

When we arrive home, I check through Kenny's backpack looking for the note about the Daddy-Daughter dance. Apparently, it's an annual event organized to provide fathers the opportunity to spend special time with their little girls. I rub the tightness in my chest as I read on. Dress is formal attire, and the event includes a formal dinner followed by dancing. It sounds amazing and there's no way I'm going to let Kenny miss out on this experience. It's her first year at school and she deserves to participate with her friends. I may not be her biological father, but I'm her daddy in all the ways that count and I plan on showing her how a lady should be treated. I formulate a plan in my head, ready to share it with Emma when I get the chance.

"You want a snack, Munchkin?"

"Yes, please, Uncle Theo."

"Go wash up and I'll get it ready." I cut up an apple and some cheese, placing them on a plate along with some crackers. I'm pouring a cup of milk as Kenny comes back into the kitchen, looking a lot happier than she did when I picked her up from school. We sit at the kitchen table sharing the snack I prepared. "So, would you like to go to the Daddy-Daughter dance?"

She chews the food in her mouth slowly, and I can see her mind ticking over. She shrugs. "I don't have a daddy." She fiddles with a cracker. "That means I not allowed to go."

I think carefully about my words. "Well … your mommy asked me to look after you. That means she wanted me to be your daddy."

Kenny's face lights up instantly as she sits up straight. "Weally?"

"Really." I hold out my hand for hers. "Would you do me the honor of accompanying me to the Daddy-Daughter dance?" Kenny leaps from her seat into my arms, squeezing me tightly around my neck while placing kisses all over my face. I squeeze my eyes closed tight, absorbing her excited affection. This is the Kenny I know and love; it's great to have her back. She giggles and I laugh at her antics. "Is that a yes?"

"Yes, Uncle Theo. I would love to go to the dance wiv you. Thank you." She kisses my face some more. "You're gonna be the best daddy there." And now my heart melts into a puddle of goo on the kitchen floor as I squeeze her tight—our moment broken by a knock at the front door.

"Come on. I bet that's Emma and the boys ready to go to the park."

She quickly scrambles down from the table, catching up with me as I walk down the passage to the front door. Sure enough, the trio at our door consists of my gorgeous neighbor and her two boys.

"You guys ready for the park?" Emma asks.

Kenny cheers as I pick up the backpack I keep near the front door and we head to the park, the kids walking ahead of us. I take Emma's hand in mine, twining our fingers together, locking her to me. I've never been much for holding a woman's hand and considering I haven't even kissed Emma yet, I'm unused to the possessiveness I feel for her. We're not in a relationship. We haven't been intimate, yet I always feel the need to touch her in some way when she's near. If this is the only opportunity I'll get to touch her silky skin, then I'm not going to be backward in taking the opportunity. She's stiff at first, glancing down at our joined hands and then up to my face. I shrug and keep on moving as if it's something we always do. A small smile touches her lips, causing slight crinkles around her eyes as she relaxes.

# CHAPTER 23

## —emma—

HE'S DOING IT AGAIN. HOLDING MY HAND. I CAN'T REMEMBER HOW long it's been since a man has wanted to hold my hand for no reason other than to hold my hand. It took me by surprise on Mother's Day and it took me a moment to relax again today—but I like it. I like it an awful lot. His hand feels so big, warm, and safe. His grip is sure and strong. My stomach flips as he tugs me toward him and places a kiss on my temple as if it's the most natural thing to do. We make it to the park and I expect Theo to drop my hand, but he doesn't. He uses his hold to guide me to a bench seat. Allowing me to sit first, he positions himself so the entire side of his body is touching the entire side of mine, then he places his arm along the back of the seat.

Turning my head, so I can speak to him, my eyes instantly drop to his lips and pause there. Watching me, he whispers, "Don't look at me like that, Emma. I'm working hard to keep it PG in front of the kids. You studying my lips like they're a fucking dessert doesn't help my resolve."

I quickly look away, my cheeks heating at being caught out. Clearing my throat, I ask, "Why was Kenny upset this afternoon?"

"The Daddy-Daughter dance. Some kid said she couldn't go because she didn't have a daddy or a mommy." My head snaps back to Theo in time to catch him taking a deep swallow. "I was fucking pissed until I remembered they're only four."

My smile spreads unbidden. For a guy who's only recently taken on the responsibility of a child, he's settled into the role remarkably well. Better than some men who watch a baby growing in their wife's belly. I have to consciously push down the constant anger I have for my ex and his lack of desire to be a father to his sons. Placing my hand on his firm thigh, *oh my*, I squeeze. "Kids that age don't really understand that words can hurt someone's feelings."

"Yeah, that's what Mrs. Roberts said too."

"There's no reason you can't take her." I make a move to lift my hand, but he catches it with his free hand and replaces both of our hands on his thigh. The heat from his leg is scalding my palm.

"Oh, I plan to. But I'm gonna need some help." He looks at me pointedly.

"Sure, whatever you need."

"Would you be able to take her shopping for a party dress, new shoes, the works?"

"Of course, I'd love to. I don't get to shop for little girl dresses. It'll be so much fun." The excitement bubbling up inside me is something new. Whenever I shop for the boys' clothes, I always admire the cute clothes available for little girls and feel a little sad that I can't buy them.

"I'll take care of the boys for you while you girls shop."

"Oh, you don't have to do that. My sister or brother can come over to look after the boys."

"No, I want to." He looks at me as if he's uncertain. "If that's okay? They enjoyed helping me in the workshop and I enjoyed having them there." He looks hopeful that I'll agree to the deal. Why wouldn't I? The boys came back from his place smiling like loons, talking a mile a minute about how amazing Theo is with his tools.

*I wouldn't mind seeing him work with his tools.*

I nod. "Okay then. It sounds like a plan." He goes on to tell me what he has planned for the afternoon of the dance, melting my heart. I readily agree to help him. I can't wait to see the look on Kenny's face!

# CHAPTER 24

## —emma—

BRIGHT AND EARLY ON SATURDAY MORNING, MY CREW AND I KNOCK ON Theo's door so I can take Kenny shopping. I'm so freaking excited, I decided to invite my sister along as well to join in the fun. We're going to have manis and pedis, too. The front door's open and I spot Theo walking down the hallway as he pulls a T-shirt over his head.

*Mmmmhm! Yum!*

What I wouldn't give to lick those rock-hard abs of his. Sarah's eyes are almost bulging out of her head as her eyebrows rise halfway up her forehead. A sly grin touches her lips as she mouths, "wow" to me while fanning her face. *Could she be any more obvious?*

The screen door opens and my stomach flips as I lay eyes on Theo with shower-damp hair and smelling gloriously delicious. He hasn't noticed Sarah yet as he flashes me that panty-dropping smile of his. "Morning, Emma. Hey, boys."

"Hey, Theo. What are we gonna make today?" Austin's been talking non-stop about Theo's workshop.

He ruffles Austin's hair as Kenny comes running down the passage toward us. "Emma, Austin, Lachlan. I'm so happy to see you." This little girl is always so freaking happy, except for the other day, when she came out of school in tears. I could see her tears were difficult for Theo, and I knew he would do anything to make things better for his niece.

Theo finally notices Sarah. "Uh, this is my sister, Sarah. She's going to be joining us for our shopping excursion today."

Kenny jumps up and down in excitement as Theo offers his hand in greeting. "Hey, Sarah. Nice to meet you." He looks back at me. "Thank you for making today special for Kenny."

"My pleasure. We even have a special surprise planned for her! We need to get moving, though, if that's okay?" I look down at Kenny. "You ready?"

"Yeah! Let's go."

"Not so quick, Munchkin. You need to go to the bathroom first."

"Okay, Uncle Theo." Theo watches her race down the hallway. He leans backward, his T-shirt rising and showing off his defined v, to pick up Kenny's backpack before handing it to me. With his free hand, he gently grasps the back of my neck and presses his lips to my forehead for a brief moment; my eyes drop closed as I absorb his tenderness. Sarah's gasp rings out from the other side of the boys as my heart hammers against my ribs in an attempt to burst free. He tucks his hand in his pocket and then places a credit card in my hand, which makes me feel weird.

"Thank you again for this, Em," he whispers, capturing my eyes with his. The intense blue that I love so much has almost completely disappeared.

I can only swallow and nod. His tender kiss stealing my words.

He steps away from me, and I miss his proximity immediately. Gathering my composure, I address my boys, "Okay boys, listen to Theo and remember your manners." I turn to Theo. "I'm not sure how long we'll be, but if you have any issues, please call." I hand him a slip of paper with my phone number, in case he needs me.

He takes it from me, studies it for a moment, then tucks the slip of paper into his pocket. "Thanks for that, but I'm sure we'll be fine. Take your time. I've got us covered for the day." He looks across at the boys. "We're gonna have a great day. I have big plans for us." He rubs his hands together, giving my boys a wink.

Kenny comes racing back toward us. "Bye, Uncle Theo." She races past him without stopping.

"Uh, uh, uh. I need a goodbye kiss, Munchkin." He scoops her up, nuzzles her neck with his scruff, eliciting giggles from her, then kisses the tip of her nose. "Have fun. Be good for Emma and Sarah. Okay?"

"Okay, Uncle Theo. Bye, Austin. Bye, Lachlan."

I kiss each of my boys goodbye, then Sarah does the same and we're on our way.

Arriving right on time, we enter the *R&R Nail Salon*, ready for our manis and pedis. Phillipa and her ladies get straight to work fussing over Kenny. When I called Phillipa to tell her about Kenny and what we were hoping to do today, she was more than happy to help. She situates the little girl of the moment in a special chair as they discuss colors for her polish. I step in and suggest a pale pink polish because I'm not sure how Theo will take Kenny having a bold color on her nails. Phillipa gives Kenny a mocktail, then hands Sarah and me a Mimosa as they begin to work on our feet.

Kenny's busy chatting away with Mandy, so Sarah takes the opportunity to interrogate me about Theo.

"So, I just witnessed your sexy new neighbor plant a kiss on you that could melt the underwear off of a nun. Spill, Sis!" she whispers, her eyes wide. I was waiting to see how Theo would react to Sarah when he saw her because she's such a knockout, but he barely paid her any attention.

I feel my face heat at the memory of his touch. His grip on my neck was firm and direct, while his kiss was gentle and tender. "There's nothing to tell. We're neighbors and I'm helping him out with his niece. He was ... being grateful." I shrug.

She scoffs. "That's the most bullshittiest bullshit I've ever heard." She wriggles her fingers in a give it to me gesture.

I breathe out a heavy sigh. "Look, he was an asshole to me when he first moved in. Then we sort of had a big blow-up. He apologized and since then, he takes every opportunity he can to steal touches and small kisses like that whenever we're together. I'm not sure what it all means, but it's confusing as all hell."

"Why is it confusing? He's a good-looking single guy. You're a beautiful single woman. He obviously likes you more than just in a neighborly way." She wriggles her eyebrows up and down.

"Yeah, but why? Most times he's seen me; I've been an absolute mess." I go on to tell my dear sister about every interaction Theo and I have had since he moved in. Even the time I saw him naked on his back deck. She giggles at that tidbit of information.

"Is that a regular event?" She takes a sip of her mimosa.

I shake my head. "Even though I've been checking, I haven't been lucky enough to witness it again." We both sigh dreamily.

"Well, if you get the opportunity, which I'm sure you will at some point, you should jump on that!" I roll my eyes as we both burst into giggles.

We finish up at the salon and decide we need a coffee, so we head to the nearest coffee shop. "What would you like to drink, Kenny?"

Her wide eyes are taking in the quirkiness of the place. Various old-fashioned bird cages are hanging at all different heights from the ceiling. They're all empty, of course, but they're so interesting to look at. "Can I please have a chocolate milkshake?"

"Absolutely. Would you like a cookie, too?"

Her eyes widen while a smile touches her lips. "Weally?"

"Of course."

"Oooo, can I please have a chocolate chip cookie?" I nod.

"How about you?" I ask Sarah.

"My usual. Thanks, Sis."

"Coming right up," I order for the three of us as Sarah guides Kenny to a booth that looks out onto the street.

I take a seat with my sister and neighbor as they're admiring their manicures. "Thank you, Emma. My nails look so pwetty."

"You're welcome." I pull out the bottle of polish I bought to match. "We can retouch them before the dance." I give her a wink as she claps her hands together in excitement.

A young man brings our food and drinks to the table, causing the conversation to stall for a few moments as we all dig into our treats. I'm pretty sure Kenny gets more chocolate on her face than in her stomach.

"So, what type of dress are we looking for today?" Sarah asks Kenny.

Kenny looks at me for guidance, before answering, "A pwetty one that makes me a pwincess."

"Sounds perfect," I say as I wink.

After we've finished, we head into the main part of the mall. There are a few little boutique stores in this particular mall where I think we'll be able to find a pretty party dress for Kenny's dance. Sarah and I walk on either side of Kenny as she swings our hands back and forth. I'm not sure how long it's been since Kenny's been shopping with a woman, but she's so excited, she's almost vibrating.

Sarah shows Kenny a dress with layers and frills. "What about this one?" I'm not sure what she's thinking. It looks a little much to me.

Kenny screws up her button nose. "I don't like the fwills or how big it is."

Our first stop doesn't yield any results, which isn't surprising; the dresses were a little over the top. I can't believe parents would allow their young daughters to wear some of the outfits for sale. They seem more suited to a Vegas club than a party for young girls.

The second store is the winner; the dresses here appear to be more age-appropriate. After admiring and trying on a couple of party dresses, Kenny falls in love with a gorgeous floor-length party dress that has a sweet fitted halter top in white.

We step out of the changing room; her wearing a gigantic smile. "I love this dwess so much. It's so pwetty,"

She holds out the blue tulle gathered skirt, which falls to the floor, spinning around. The layers give it fullness, but not so much that it looks poofy.

"It's adorable, Kenny. You look gorgeous in it." Sarah swoons.

Kenny's such a cutie pie and this dress suits her down to the ground. We pair it with some silver ballet flats to enhance the silver glitter scattered through the tulle layers.

Sarah and I are possibly a little over the top with our fussing, but we're both heartbroken over the fact that she's motherless at such a young age. We're also loving the opportunity to do girly stuff with zero boys around. I love being a mom of boys. Even though they're young, they're quite protective of me and they do give the best cuddles. When Austin runs his little hands over my hair and tells me I'm pretty, my heart melts. And when Lachlan manages to look me in the eye as he tells me he loves me, well, that sends me into a puddle of goo. But, being able to fuss over a little girl and dress her up has been so much fun today.

Pulling into my driveway, I'm stunned at what greets us. Sarah's peering out of the windscreen with appreciation of the stunning view. My front porch has had a complete makeover. The railings have been repainted, something that I've wanted to do for some time, and sweet hanging baskets full of colorful flowers have been hung from the frieze beam. It totally transforms the front of my house. However, that's not what Sarah's admiring; no, she's admiring my handsome neighbor's bare torso as he works to attach a chain to a hook in the ceiling. His muscles tense and shift with his movements as he reaches up.

"My, my, my … what a welcome home!" With wide eyes, she looks across at me, wiggling her eyebrows up and down. I remind her with my own widened eyes along with a tilt of my head toward the back seat, that she needs to watch what she's about to say in our present company.

"Yay! Uncle Theo. I can't wait to show him my new dress and shoes." She's bouncing up and down in her car seat.

Sarah turns around in her seat to face Kenny. "You should keep it as a surprise. Don't show him until the dance. It'll be so much fun to surprise him. I'll even come over and help you get ready at Emma's house."

Kenny's eyes widen as a grin forms. "Oh yeah, let's do that. Is that okay, Emma? Can we do that? Can we surpwise Uncle Theo?"

"Absolutely, we can do that. It'll be fun." Kenny cheers as we exit the car to make our way toward the boys.

Austin comes running down the steps. "Do you like it, Mommy?" He takes my hand, dragging me the rest of the way. My eyes scan the entire area, not knowing what to look at first. There are two stunning rocking chairs, a table between them, and a porch swing ready to be installed.

"You guys did all this while we were out?" I can't believe how much they've done.

"Yeah. Well, not all of it. Theo made the chairs before, and we helped sand and wax them the other day." Lachlan looks up at me as I breach the top step. "Do you like it, Mommy?" My heart freezes in my chest at the look of pride on my eldest son's face.

"I love it. I can't believe you guys did all of this. You've been so busy." I look at each of my boys and Theo. "Thank you so much. It's beautiful." My hand comes up, pressing into my chest in an attempt to stop my heart from escaping.

Kenny comes running up the steps. "Uncle Theo, you should see my pwetty dress." She leaps at him with all the trust of a child who knows the man will catch her, no matter what.

"I can't wait to see it. I bet you look like a princess." He laughs, nudging her nose with his.

"Nuh-uh! It's gonna be a surpwise!" Theo looks across at Sarah and me with raised brows.

I tuck my loose hair behind my ear, then shove my hands in my back pockets to stop from fidgeting under Theo's scrutinizing gaze. "We, uh, we thought maybe Sarah and I could get Kenny ready for the dance and you can come over and pick her up from my place."

His features soften while a gentle smile touches his lips. I watch his Adam's Apple move up and down on a hard swallow. This guy is incredibly masculine and yet he's so gentle with his niece that I fear for the safety of my ovaries. "That'd be great. Thank you, ladies." He finishes with a tip of his head.

"C'mon, Mommy. We want to show you everything we did." The boys show me the work they've done and I'm drawn into their excitement as they point out, in detail, everything they've done.

# CHAPTER 25

## *—emma—*

AFTER RACING HOME FROM SCHOOL, I QUICKLY GIVE THE BOYS THEIR afternoon snack, then jump in the shower to wash my hair and get ready for the Daddy-Daughter dance that I'll be attending tonight. When I signed on to help out as waitstaff for the dinner, I had no idea my handsome neighbor would be attending with his adorable niece. Sarah's due any minute to stay with the boys for me tonight, so I work through my shower routine quickly. Being a single mom, I have my routine down to a fine art, so I take minimal time getting ready. Wrapping my hair in a towel, I dress in my underwear and cover myself with a wrap as my sister knocks on my front door.

"Come on in!" I call out to Sarah as I make my way downstairs to the front door. I'm not sure why she's knocking.

Standing there in all his glory, his niece tucked into his side, is Theo. I come to a screeching halt as I take in his face. He looks utterly pissed if the tightness in his jaw is anything to go by.

"Your door was f–," he pauses, looking down at his niece. "Unlocked. *Again!*" His anger is practically filling the room; even Kenny's attempting to put distance between her and her uncle, but he's holding her hand, so there's only so far she can go.

I smile at Kenny, then set my sights on Theo. "I *was* expecting my sister."

"But we're not your sister and we could have been any fu– ... one!" He scrubs his beard with his free hand.

"Well, you weren't just anyone. It's all good, so you can calm down." I widen my eyes, rolling them down toward Kenny to make my point.

His shoulders drop incrementally as a heavy sigh leaves his lips. "What have you got against keeping you and your boys safe?"

I can't believe the gall of this man. Who does he think he is? I work to temper my response in front of Kenny and my boys, as they step out of the kitchen at the sound of Theo's voice. Kenny manages to pull her hand free and runs to the boys with her usual level of excitement.

"Hello, Theo," the boys call out to him. They move back into the kitchen with Kenny, talking excitedly about what happened at school today, leaving the two of us alone in my foyer.

Crossing my arms, I dig in, ready to have words. "Stop it!"

He looks puzzled.

"Stop coming at me with your attitude like I'm some helpless woman who needs a man to tell her what to do." I drop my hands, slapping my thighs. "I don't need you or anyone else coming into my ho—" His hand grips the back of my neck, cutting off my diatribe as he steps into my body. Before I can take a breath, his mouth slams down onto mine. The suddenness of the action catches me off guard and I take a moment to realize what he's doing.

*He's kissing me.*

His soft lips, surrounded by soft bristles, move across my lips in an unexpected swipe. I open my mouth, ready to ask what the hell he's doing when his tongue darts inside. He presses his hard body into my softer one and groans into my mouth. I *should* push him away, but for some reason, I don't. His kiss is firm and as his tongue finds mine, I relax and kiss him back. The roughened palm of his hand slides up to the back of my head, releasing the towel. I feel the weight of it fall away, the wet strands of my hair falling free. He grasps a handful and uses his grip to direct my head exactly where he wants it, all the while stroking my tongue with his. This kiss is full of passion and fire, and I don't ever remember being kissed like this before.

*As though I'm his air.*

The scent of timber and something else fills my nose. His other hand glides around my waist, pulling me impossibly closer, eliminating all the space between us. The hardness behind his zipper is unmistakable as he grinds into my belly.

"My, my, my. What do we have here?"

My sister's voice interrupts our moment, dousing icy water on me.

I hastily remove myself from Theo's hold, stepping back to put some much-needed space between us. In my embarrassment, my foot catches on the discarded towel and I struggle to maintain my balance. Theo's hand shoots out, grasping my forearm to prevent my fall. I'm certain my face is on fire. My sister's smirk is unmistakable, and I know she's going to want all the details later.

"Hey, Sis. Hey, Theo," she says airily.

Theo moves to stand behind me, his hands on my hips. "Hey, Sarah." He clears his throat. "Nice to see you again."

She laughs as she moves further inside, banging the screen door behind her. "I'm sure it is, Handsome." She pats him on his shoulder as she strolls past, calling out to the kids.

My hunky neighbor edges his way around me, bending down to pick up my dropped towel before handing it to me. "I would say I'm sorry about that, but I'm really not. I'd better head home. I'll see you in a while when I come back to pick up my girl."

I stand, stunned in silence, watching his retreating form move across my porch and down the front steps. I'm not sure how long I remain rooted to the spot, trying to make sense of the last however long. I'm dragged out of my thoughts when Sarah bumps her hip into mine. A smile graces her face as she wiggles her eyebrows up and down.

"Sooooo …" She leaves the word hanging, expecting me to fill in the blank, but I can't. I have no words. He kissed them out of my mouth. Right as I was giving him what for, too. Her wide eyes are begging me to tell her something I can't make sense of. I shake my head to clear my thoughts and focus on what I need to do, rather than trying to work out the man next door. And he's *all* man, from what I could tell as he pressed up against me.

"C'mon, we need to get ready. Can you watch the kids while I get dressed, then we'll work on Kenny?" I hurry away before she responds.

I'm meant to look like a server tonight, so I'm wearing a black pencil skirt and white silk blouse, ensuring I engage the press button between my breasts to ensure it doesn't gape. Dressing quickly, I pull on my thigh highs and head into the bathroom to dry my hair and put on a little makeup. The school likes to treat the evening as though the fathers and daughters are dining at a ritzy restaurant. It's always so cute to see the girls in their party dresses and their fathers doting on them.

Stepping into the kitchen, Kenny rushes to me, wrapping her little arms around me. "Hello, Emma. You look so pwetty."

I giggle. "Thanks, Kenny. Are you ready to get dressed up? Your Uncle Theo will be here soon to pick you up for the dance."

"Oh yeah. Sarah said she could even curl my hair. Is that twue? I wanna look like a pwincess."

"Of course." I smile at her. "Are you boys okay while we get Kenny ready?"

"Yeah, Mommy." The boys go back to watching one of their favorite movies and Sarah and I take Kenny upstairs to my bathroom.

We wash her hair and dry it in preparation for Sarah to make the magic happen with the curling iron. Her hair is so silky soft, with natural caramel highlights scattered throughout. We tie the top half back, so her gorgeous new curls fall down her back to her waist. The blue of her dress highlights her wide azure eyes, which match her uncle's—she looks like an adorable little princess. We finish off her outfit with sparkly flats, then apply a little glitter to her eyelids and cheeks. She looks so freaking adorable. I pop on my shoes, buckling the strap across the top of each foot, and lastly giving my lips a final coat of gloss before we make our way back downstairs to the living room.

Austin jumps off the couch when he sees Kenny. "You look like a princess," he tells her. His voice is full of awe, his eyes full of wonder.

Lachlan glances away from the television to see what all the fuss is about. "You look nice, Kenny."

She curtsies like a princess, a wide smile on her face. "Thank you."

There are a hard series of knocks on my front door. My heart skips a beat. Theo's on the other side of that door. The man who kissed the words out of me just over an hour ago. Sarah gives me a knowing look and nudges me forward. I gather myself, looking down at Kenny. "That'll be your uncle. You ready to knock his socks off?"

"How do you knock someone's socks off?" Lachlan asks.

Sarah looks across at him. "You don't actually knock their socks off. It's a saying. It means to impress someone."

"Oh. Okay." He turns back to the television, satisfied with Sarah's explanation.

"Oh, yeah. I can't wait to show him my pwetty dwess."

"Okay, wait here. I'll bring him in." She nods and I turn toward the front door. Wiping my sweaty hands on my skirt, I suck in a deep breath to prepare for all that is Theo as I open the door.

All of my breath gushes out in a rush as my eyes land on him.

*In a suit.*

Holding flowers and a blue gift box. I'm not sure my heart can take it.

# CHAPTER 26

## *—theo—*

I ALMOST SWALLOW MY TONGUE WHEN EMMA OPENS HER DOOR. A sleek skirt resting just above her knees, molds to her luscious hips and thighs like a glove; black stockings ending in patent leather high heels make her legs look sexy as fuck. My eyes follow the path back up to a modest white silk blouse which shouldn't have my mouth watering but does. Her face has minimal makeup and her hair's tied up in a bun. She looks like a sexy waitress from a high-class gentlemen's club and I doubt she realizes how incredibly appealing she looks. This getup seems a bit much for hanging out at home with the boys, so she must be going out somewhere.

*Fuck!*

What if she has a date?

She'd better not be going on a date or I'll have to ruin my girl's special night spending it disposing of a body. I huff out a breath, working to put the thought out of my mind.

I was so pissed at her earlier when I found her door unlocked yet again. This woman has no sense of self-preservation. When she was giving me what for, I couldn't have stopped myself from kissing her if I'd tried and there was not one single fiber of my being that wanted to. Looking at her now, I want to start back up where I finished off earlier, but not stop at a simple kiss. I want to bury my face between her thick thighs and lose myself there for days.

"Where're you going in that outfit?" I demand. Just the thought of someone else touching her has my vision turning red.

Her head shoots back as though I physically struck her. I watch as her whole demeanor changes, her body going stiff, her eyes and lips narrowing. I've done it again.

Pissed her off! *Fuck, she's gorgeous when she gets riled up.*

This may just become my favorite pastime! Her hands land on her hips and her mouth opens …

"Uncle Theo, you comed to get me!" She spins around. "Do ya like my pwetty dwess?"

I crouch down so I'm at her level and lock eyes with my niece, noticing the light touch of glitter on her eyelids and cheeks. My heart melts at her expectant expression, waiting for my approval of her outfit. "Do *you* like *your* dress?"

"Oh, yeah! I love it so much," she responds, her voice full of pride.

"It doesn't matter what I think. You should always wear what makes *you* happy and what *you* like." I point to her heart. "You don't need to impress anyone but yourself, Munchkin."

"Okay. But do you think my dwess is pwetty?"

I look up at Emma, noting that her posture's more relaxed, less ready for battle, and she has a soft expression on her face. "Your dress is beautiful, but it's missing a little something." I hand her the gift I bought for her.

She takes the box from my hand. "Is this for me?" The excitement in her voice is contagious. I can't wait for her to see what I got for her.

"Yep. Open it." I stand to give Emma the flowers I bought for her as a thank you for doing this for Kenny. "These are for you. Thank you for taking care of Kenny and making this special for her."

Emma's eyes take on a glassy sheen as she accepts the flowers, swallowing hard. "Thank you. These are unnecessary because it was my pleasure to do this with Kenny."

Blue paper litters the floor as Kenny holds my gift over her head like a trophy. "I love it, Uncle Theo. Put it on me, put it on me."

Emma and I both laugh as I take the glittery tiara from Kenny's tiny hand to place it on her head. I look to Emma for guidance. Her nod puts my worry to rest that I'm putting it on incorrectly. "There. Now you look like a *real* princess!"

"I wanna see." She looks up at Emma. "Can I please use your bathwoom miwwor again?"

"Sure." Emma takes Kenny's hand to lead her to the bathroom, and I stay rooted to the spot, my eyes falling to her round ass. She looks over her shoulder, catching me in the act, but I don't care that she knows I was checking her out. "Are you coming?"

"Wasn't sure I'd be welcome in your bathroom." I move forward to follow them upstairs and through Emma's bedroom, which isn't overly feminine. Taking a quick look around, I spot the corner window I've often looked at from my upstairs deck. On several occasions, I've contemplated which room was situated on the back corner closest to my house. There's a cozy window seat, and I wonder if she ever gets the opportunity to relax there. Moving forward, because I don't want her to think I'm weird for checking out her bedroom too closely, I step into her bathroom. The vanity is littered with a hair dryer, some wand-looking thing, brushes, combs, and makeup. I'll never understand why women think they need all of that shit.

I pick Kenny up so she can see herself in the mirror. Gently, she touches her fingers to the small tiara. A smile forms on her lips as her eyes catch mine in the mirror. "I love it so much. Thank you." She wraps her little arm around my neck and kisses my bristly cheek.

I swallow hard. "You're welcome, Munchkin." I put her back on her own feet, taking her hand in mine. "C'mon, we need to get going."

Emma looks at her watch. "Me too. I don't want to be late."

She never did tell me where she's going, but I don't have time to get into it with her now. "Say thank you to Emma." I wriggle Kenny's hand to gain her attention.

"Thank you, Emma."

"You're welcome. Have fun at the dance."

"I will." Kenny leans forward, hugging Emma around her legs.

"Thank you, again. I truly appreciate all you've done for Kenny. We'd better get outta your hair so you can get on with your date." I can't help the snark that weaves its way into my tone. Her eyebrows draw down low as she tilts her head to the side, so I gesture to her outfit. "I assume you're going on a date tonight."

She looks down at herself as if she's forgotten the clothes she's wearing. Her shoulders drop and she lets out a huff of a laugh. "This. I wouldn't wear this on a date. This is for the Dinner-Dance. I'm a server tonight."

It's my turn to be confused. "Huh? You're going to be waiting on us tonight?"

She nods. "Yep. And I really must be on my way. I'm supposed to greet everyone as they come through the door. Sorry to have to rush you."

"We can all go together. Let's go." I step out of the bathroom, holding Kenny's hand. As we walk down the stairs and past the living room, Kenny calls out her goodbyes and I notice Sarah sitting on the couch.

"Hey, Sarah."

"Hey, Theo. Have a great night, you two!"

"Thank you, Sarah!" Kenny calls out.

"You're welcome, Gorgeous Girl."

We make it out of the house after Emma kisses her boys and gives Sarah instructions for dinner. I secure Kenny in her seat, then hold open the passenger door for Emma. "Uh, it's probably best if I take my own car. I don't know how late I'll be and I don't want you guys to have to wait around for me."

"Get in, Emma. There's no point taking two vehicles." I wait by the door until she gets the idea that I'm not going to give in. "C'mon, you're wasting time."

She huffs out a breath and steps toward me. "I can't work you out!" she snaps as she takes a seat in my truck."

Good. I'm glad I keep her as off-balance as she makes me feel.

Emma and Kenny chat on the way to the school as I concentrate on driving. I'm happy to listen to the girls bang on about girly stuff. My chest feels tight at the thought of Kenny not having her mom to talk with about that type of thing. I can try to be that person, but I have the wrong equipment and I struggle to understand the value of some of the stuff women seem to find important. Emma turns slightly in her seat to look at Kenny, allowing me a glimpse of a lace-covered thigh, which has my dick rising to attention.

Arriving at the school, Emma jumps out of the car as soon as I park. "See you two inside. Enjoy your evening." She waves as she moves toward the building.

I watch her hurry across the parking lot, marveling at the fact that she spends all day with these kids, then volunteers her personal time to wait on them.

"C'mon, Munchkin. Let's go have some fun!"

Walking toward the school gym, holding my girl's hand, I feel as proud as any father could be. Thinking of Kenny as my daughter and not just my niece that I'm caring for has become common for me. It struck out of the blue and shocked the hell out of me, but now it feels as natural as can be.

Emma and her friend, Kate, are standing on either side of the door greeting everyone with wide, friendly smiles.

"Oh my gosh, how pretty is your dress, Kenny?" Kate fusses. "And look at your shoes. Do you think they come in my size?" Kenny giggles as Kate reaches out, sliding a curl through her fingers. "Your hair looks gorgeous." With every compliment, Kenny seems to grow taller.

"Thank you, Ms. Summer." Kenny does a little curtsy. Nobody could call this kid shy; she loves the attention.

As we step into the room, I look down at Kenny, her wide eyes taking in everything. The decorations and the other girls with their fathers. Her little hand holds on to mine a little tighter, so I squeeze gently to reassure her I'm not going anywhere. I take a moment to look around the room; it looks like something out of a Disney movie. Large cardboard cutouts of Disney princes and princesses line the room, sheer curtains are draped from the center of the ceiling out to the walls, and chandeliers hang from the ceiling. A lot of effort has been made to make the room look like a ballroom that could be found in any castle. As I look at the other dads and their daughters, I decide Kenny's the prettiest little girl here—I may be biased, but I don't think I am.

We're stopped a few steps into the room by a little girl who is about a head taller than Kenny. Kenny freezes in place, her body tense, her little smile waning. The other girl looks up at me as though butter wouldn't melt in her mouth. "Hello, Kenny." She points to me. "Who's this? Because I *know* you don't have a daddy."

Kenny looks up at me, her bottom lip beginning to tremble. I squeeze her little hand. "*I'm* Kenny's daddy."

"But she doesn't have a daddy." The frown marring her face looks to be an expression she wears regularly.

"Her mommy asked me to look after her. That makes me her daddy." I look down at Kenny to make sure she hears my next words. "I'm lucky to be her daddy because she's the best little girl I know." Squeezing Kenny's hand gently, I step away from the little girl, taking my munchkin with me. "C'mon, let's go dance." We walk away, leaving the brat behind. So much attitude for a kid her age; I'd hate to meet her parents.

The smile that lights up my girl's face is contagious, and I return it easily. I've noticed I smile more since having Kenny in my life. We make it to the dance floor and immediately get swept up in a song all about being happy. I twirl my girl, inciting giggles from her, which makes my heart swell. I feel better when she smiles and laughs like she should.

The principal of the school takes to the stage, stepping up to the microphone. "Welcome to the annual Daddy-Daughter dance. We're so happy to see you all here enjoying this very special evening. Ladies, you look lovely and gentlemen, you look handsome. Please take your seats for the dinner service." It's all very formal, which I'm guessing is exactly what the school is aiming for.

Servers move between the tables with trolleys of food, and I can't stop myself from seeking Emma out. She's on the opposite side of the room, smiling and chatting with the people she's serving. My jealousy rises thinking about other men admiring her sweet curves, collecting her gorgeous smiles, or even thinking they have a chance with someone as stunning as her. I want to mark her as mine, so every other asshole knows to stay away from her.

The night moves along with dessert, dancing, and games. I was a little nervous about having to answer questions about Kenny for the quiz, but I think we did pretty well, considering we've only known each other for six short weeks. The questions about when she was a baby were the ones that stumped me but sent Kenny into a fit of giggles at my made-up answers.

The little girl who gave Kenny a hard time is sitting at the next table over, being ignored by her father in favor of checking social media on his phone. As it's getting close to the end of the night, we decide it's time to line up for the photo booth. Kenny doesn't look quite as put together as she did when we first arrived, but she looks more like my Kenny to me. We make silly faces for a couple of shots before having the photographer take a couple of formal photos for us. Our first photos together. I'll be sure to put them up on the photo shelves I installed in the living room.

Sitting at our table, Kenny's dozing off on my shoulder. I feel honored beyond measure that she trusts me enough to fall asleep on me. I try to remember my life before Kenny; it feels like it was such a long time ago now. Life was quiet, routine, and lonely without my girl. I gently brush a lock of loose, silky hair over her shoulder and study her cherubic face. I startle slightly when a hand gently touches my upper back. Raising my head, I find Emma watching us with a serene smile.

"I'm going to be a little longer. Kate said she didn't mind dropping me home. You should go. Take Kenny home to bed," she crouches down low as she whispers, allowing me a peek down her blouse to her lush breasts.

I'm already shaking my head in the negative. "No. We'll wait for you." She makes to speak again, but I cut her off with another head shake. "We'll wait. Don't rush. We're fine here," I whisper. My tone is firm as I run my knuckles gently along her jawline. The pulse point at the base of her neck picks up speed as she sucks in a sharp breath, but she doesn't pull away. In fact, her eyelids drop closed for a moment before opening again, showing almost brown irises. She gives me a nod before standing to return to her tasks.

# CHAPTER 27

## —theo—

EMMA RELEASES A HUGE SIGH AS HER BACKSIDE CONNECTS WITH THE passenger seat. Looking over to the back seat, a small smile touches her lips. "I love it when they're so tired, they'll sleep anywhere."

"Yeah. Wish I could do that." I start my truck as Emma pulls the seatbelt across her body. I take it from her and secure it in the buckle, ensuring it's locked in place. She drops her head back against the headrest, closing her eyes.

"My feet are killing me. I love these shoes so much, but they're really not designed to be worn when I'm gonna be on my feet for hours on end."

"Take 'em off. We have fifteen minutes until we're home," I suggest.

She rolls her head toward me. "If I take them off, I won't be able to get them back on when I get home. I don't want to ruin my stockings."

My suit pants start growing tight at the thought of peeling those stockings from her shapely legs. "Take 'em off, too."

Her eyes widen at my suggestion. "It's okay, I can wait." She rolls her head, so she's looking out of the windscreen. "Thanks for waiting for me. I'm sorry it took so long."

"No problem. I'm happy to wait for you." I hope she gets what I'm saying.

"You guys looked like you were having fun tonight." *Does that mean she was watching us as much as I was watching her?*

"Yeah. We had a great time." My jaw tenses. "I think I got to meet the kid that upset Kenny when the dance was first mentioned." Thinking back to the beginning of the night, I was proud of the way I reacted—like an actual adult!

"Really?"

"Yeah, she was a little rude toward Kenny when we first arrived. I think I worked out why she's the way she is, though."

"How'd you manage that?" Emma studies me as she waits for my answer and I like having her attention on me.

"I watched her with her dad. He pretty much ignored her all night in favor of checking his phone. I'd say she's a pretty lonely kid."

"Unfortunately, that happens a lot. Parents are too busy to spend quality time with their kids. Then the kids act up in an attempt to gain their attention." She lets out a heavy sigh. "I feel for the kids."

We pull into my driveway. "Wait there. I'll come around to you."

I help Emma out of the truck, like the gentleman my mom taught me to be, taking the opportunity to pin her against the back passenger door with my hips (maybe not so gentlemanly after all). My hard planes press against her softness; the fullness of her breasts elicits a low groan from me. Her breath hitches, her eyes snapping up to meet mine. Her warm breaths puff against the bottom of my chin as she looks up at me.

"What are you doing?" she whispers, her voice breathy.

"I'm gonna kiss you, Emma. You okay with that?" I whisper against the side of her face as I run my nose up from her jaw to her earlobe, taking a light nip when I get to my destination. Her breaths come faster as I trace upwards with my nose, placing a kiss on her forehead. Slowly, I drag my lips down her nose to the tip. I want to savor this moment where I don't have to worry about interruptions from kids. Yes, Kenny's asleep in the truck, but my experience so far with her is once she's out for the count, that's it until morning. I pull back slightly, checking Emma's eyes; lust and desire shine back at me. She gives a slight nod of her head and that's all I need. I lean in and slowly swipe my lips against hers; savoring the softness. Hands slide beneath my jacket to grip the sides of my shirt, tightening, pulling me ever closer. Pressing my lips firmer, I cup the back of her head, tilting her mouth to my liking. I pull back, my eyes tracing her face, her silky skin, the arch of her eyebrows.

"Kiss me already, Theo," she whispers; impatience coloring her tone as she leans up toward me.

Cradling her head in my hands, I swoop in to nip her bottom lip.

She opens with a gasp, allowing me to steal inside. We kiss with a familiarity born from kissing for years, but also like it's the first and last time. I want to kiss her forever, steal her kisses until my dying day. I just need to work out how to make it happen. Grinding my restrained cock against her in the heat of the moment, I can only imagine what it will be like to be buried inside her to the hilt.

I glide one hand down her body, finding the bottom of her skirt, and slide it up, allowing my hand to trace the inside of her thigh. The heat from her pussy is intense as my hand gets closer to her most intimate place. I brush my finger over her panties, feeling the wetness, applying pressure.

She returns my kiss with interest, pressing tighter against me and grinding into my fingers, which I relish—the rapid beat of her heart vibrating through me. I deepen the kiss further, massaging her tongue with mine, teeth clashing in desperation to give her everything I have. My fingers mirror the action against her folds.

"Oooh, Theo," she whispers against my lips. "Please don't stop."

"Never."

After long moments, I pull back slightly to study my girl's face. With her eyes closed, she moves forward, seeking my mouth to continue our kiss. My fingers slide between the fabric of her panties and her lips. I find her slit and thrust a finger inside her tight opening. She's so fucking wet. Her eyes open wide, colliding with mine as her mouth opens on an O. Pride swells in me at the sight of her swollen lips and the evidence of beard rash across her silky skin. I move back in to take up where I left off.

My body heats.

My heart hammers.

My soul connects with hers.

My fingers work in tandem with my mouth. Thrusting my fingers in and out of her channel, I mirror the action with my tongue in her mouth. She tastes so fucking sweet, and her pussy is like a furnace as it pulses around my fingers.

"Theo, please."

"I've gotcha." Increasing the intensity, I press my thumb against her clit, holding her up as she pulses around my fingers, releasing a long moan as she comes. "You look fucking beautiful coming around my fingers, Em." Slowing my movements, I kiss her gently, bringing her down from her high. My cock feels as though it's going to burst through the zipper of my pants. Pretty sure the head's caught behind my belt buckle. My heart's hammering so hard behind my ribs, I'm surprised she can't hear it in the silence of the night.

Carefully removing my fingers, I smooth her skirt down and reluctantly pull my body away from hers with Herculean effort. "Go inside, Em. Before I take this further than I should." I trace the shape of her jaw with my finger. "Make sure you lock your door."

She tilts her head to the side. "What is it with you and locking doors?"

I draw in a sharp breath. I don't want to break the spell, but maybe if I tell her, she'll be more careful. "When I was sixteen, we lived next door to Mr. and Mrs. O'Connor. They had a thirteen-year-old daughter. One afternoon, she was home alone when three young guys walked in off the street like they owned the place. Tied her up and ..." I swallow down the bile that always builds when I think back to the event. "Uh ... raped her. In her own fucking home." I scrub my fingers through my scruff. I felt so fucking guilty. "I was working on the table setting for Dad's restaurant in our garage when it happened. I didn't hear a fucking thing." I huff out a harsh breath. "She had a tough time dealing with it and she ... uh," I drop my voice to barely a whisper. It's still a tough pill to swallow all these years later. "She took her own life."

Emma leans forward, wrapping her arms around me. "I'm so sorry, Theo. That's beyond tragic." Her whispered words are dripping in sympathy. "Did the police catch the guys?" I wrap my arms around her, anchoring myself in the present rather than the past.

"Yeah, but it didn't make it any better for Stella. Apparently, she wasn't the only girl they attacked, but she's the only one that ended her life as a result."

Em's arms tighten around my body, her head resting against my heart. Even though we were only friends, she was yet another female I couldn't help. We were so young, and I didn't have the maturity to understand how badly she was affected by the attack. I didn't have the experience to be there for her. Looking back, I suspect she needed professional help, which she never received. We stand in each other's embrace for long moments before a shiver works its way through Emma's body.

"You should go inside. I need to get Kenny to bed." I press a tender kiss against the silky skin of Emma's neck, just below her ear.

"Are you going to be okay?" She looks up at me in the dim light.

"Yeah. It's been a long time. It's a memory I've pushed to the deepest recesses of my mind. I try not to think about it if I can help it."

She studies my face closely. "I promise to lock my door from now on."

I nod my head once, giving Em a tight smile. "Thank you."

She pulls out of my embrace and as I watch her make her way toward her front porch; I know there's no going back for me. I want to experience that level of intimacy over and over again for the remainder of my days on this earth, however long that may be.

## CHAPTER 28

## —emma—

WHEN THEO INVITED THE BOYS AND ME OVER FOR A BARBECUE HE WAS having for his dad's birthday; I was reluctant to accept. I don't know what's going on between us, but I'm not convinced we're at the stage of meeting parents or celebrating family events together. However, he insisted, and here we are. Standing on his doorstep, nerves as big as butterflies take over my stomach as I knock on the screen door.

My body heats at the memory of what I allowed Theo to do to me against his truck. It didn't take long for his masterful touch to set me flying into the stratosphere. His kisses caused a sensation overload on their own—I was powerless once he added his fingers. It's been an incredibly long stretch without that type of attention and I hadn't given much thought to having sex again. But since that night, it's all I can think about.

Last weekend, the boys were supposed to go to their father's, but he was getting married and didn't want them to attend. I was dreading the weekend, to be honest, because *I* even struggled to comprehend their father's decision to exclude his children from his wedding day— let alone how the kids would feel. It turned out that I didn't need to worry. Theo had the kids doing all sorts of carpentry work around our house and his. I don't think they stopped the entire weekend, and where Austin occasionally got bored and came to me looking for something different to do, Lachlan soaked up every new task, skill, and instruction. He adores Theo and working with timber; reveling in the attention to detail that's required.

My front fence has been restored to its former glory. I have new cupboard hinges and handles on all of my kitchen cabinetry, the boys' closets have new shelves, and I have some brand-spanking new bookshelves to display my signed paperbacks in my living room. While the boys were busy doing all of their manly activities, Kenny and I were busy keeping them sustained with delicious home-baked goods—I've been loving having a little girl around the house. The weekend spilled over to the first full week of summer vacation with the boys, particularly Lachlan, assisting Theo in completing some of his orders, while Kenny, Austin, and I pottered around having tea parties, playing in the backyard, and working in the garden.

It almost feels as though we're a family, which is utterly ridiculous, of course.

As our vacation routine became established, Theo and I managed to steal kisses here and there. Simple touches setting my body on fire at every available moment. He's not even shy about showing affection in front of the kids, whereas I'd rather keep it away from them until I'm sure this is something solid.

He *feels* solid, sturdy, reliable.

Everything I look for in a partner. Everything I thought I had with Preston, but didn't. The package that it all comes wrapped in is pretty spectacular, too.

The screen door opens, breaking me from my thoughts. The man at the door isn't Theo, but I would recognize the features anywhere. He has the same azure-colored eyes as his son and granddaughter. The creases around his eyes and mouth suggest he smiles a lot and his thick head of salt and pepper hair with more salt than pepper indicates a man of a certain age. His build is fit and strong, though he's not as tall as his son.

"You must be Theo's neighbor, Emma." He greets me, then turns to my boys, studying them closely. "And you must be Lachlan." He gestures toward my eldest son. "And you must be Austin." He gestures toward my smaller one. "Kenny and Theo have told me so much about you all. I feel as though I already know you. Come in, come in." He steps to the side of the doorway and the boys walk in, saying hello as they pass.

"Hi, Mr. Driv—" He waves his hand in the air, cutting my words short.

"Cristo, please."

I smile and nod. I was always brought up to refer to people older than myself as mister or missus. "Hi, Cristo. Happy birthday."

He takes my hand, pulling me forward, kissing each of my cheeks. Then he gently cups them in his hands. "Thank you, lovely." Maybe this is why Theo is always so demonstrative in his affection. He steps back from me, his smile wide and eyes crinkling around the corners, nodding his head to himself. "Yes, yes, this will work wonderfully." He takes each of my hands in his and holds them away from my body, studying me from the tips of my toes to the top of my head. "Yes. Very good. I'm very happy." To say I'm puzzled by his behavior and comments would be a gross understatement. I feel like stock that's being inspected by a prospective buyer. He drops one hand and uses his grip on the other to pull me inside. "Come, come."

Following him inside, amazing smells tickle my nose, and my stomach grumbles in response. *Oh my gosh, how embarrassing!* Theo's dad smiles at me, seemingly happy that I'm hungry. Theo told me not to bring anything this afternoon, which felt all kinds of wrong, so I brought my homemade rocky road as a pseudo dessert. I see Austin's left it on the kitchen bench, so I quickly stash it in the fridge to prevent the chocolate from melting before heading out onto the back deck to join Theo and the kids. Theo switched out the old glass sliding doors for beautiful bifold doors, opening up the kitchen/dining room to the outside deck, making it feel like one big space.

Theo's standing at the grill looking delicious in cargo shorts and a pale blue T-shirt. His outfit is nothing special, but I can see the flex and movement of his back muscles as he tends to the meat.

"Theo, look who's arrived!" Cristo announces.

The man who twists my stomach on the regular turns around with a wide smile that lights up his face. His eyes travel from the top of my head, pausing on my breasts, then my hips, continuing down to the tips of my toes. This is the second time in a matter of minutes I've been thoroughly inspected, though Theo's eyes on me heat my body. He takes the three steps into my space, cups the side of my face, and leans in to place a gentle welcome kiss on my lips.

ON. MY. LIPS.

In front of his dad! In front of the kids! Though to be honest, I think they're pretty used to seeing his displays of affection now. He glides his nose upwards along mine, then whispers, "You look gorgeous."

Heat rises from my chest, warming my cheeks. He makes me feel like a young girl, dating for the first time with the intensity of the attention he directs my way. Not that I'm saying we're dating, because I don't really know what we're doing. He makes me *feel* as though we're dating. His hand grasps mine as he pulls me toward the grill to keep an eye on the meat.

"Is there anything I can do to help? Set the table or anything?" I gesture toward the outdoor table.

Cristo answers, "I've got it. You keep Theo company." He steps inside and I turn to check on the kids. They're playing with the Frisbee, careful to keep it away from the house. I think Austin and Lachlan learned their lesson about climbing to rescue things from up high, so they're much more careful now.

Theo wraps his arm around my waist, pulling me close to his side. I've become more comfortable with his proprietary touches, but I'm unsure what it all means. We haven't talked about anything in terms of a relationship; we haven't even been on a date, but he acts as though we *are* a couple and the routine we've fallen into over the past few weeks suggests we are. All I know is that this is the longest form of foreplay I've ever experienced. Kisses and touches over clothes. Nothing more since the night of the dance. There's never an opportunity with the kids around. It's not like the two of us have had the opportunity to fall into bed together.

"What's going on up here?" Theo taps the side of my head, dragging me from my thoughts.

He always says what's on his mind, whether it comes across as intended or not. Maybe I should take a page out of his book? I look at his face; study it closely. Seeking any sign that he doesn't really want to know what I'm thinking. What I see is genuine interest in my thoughts. I take a deep breath, ready to ask him what's happening between us.

"Uncle Theo, I'm hungwy." Kenny steps onto the back deck, pushing her tangled hair away from her sweaty face. "Hi, Emma."

"Hey, Kenny. Are you having fun with the Frisbee?" I noticed her throw is becoming stronger since the first time we all played the game.

"Oh yeah. It's so much fun." Her smile is enormous, almost taking up half her face.

"Food's nearly ready, Munchkin. Go inside and wash up." He turns to my boys. "Boys, go inside and wash up ready for lunch."

The kids move inside, so I follow along. "C'mon, Kenny. I'll tie your hair back for you. It'll be cooler."

"Thanks, Emma. It's weally hot today."

The kids wash their hands, Lachlan paying extra attention to the spaces between his fingers. I tie Kenny's long hair up and we all traipse back outside, ready to eat the delicious-smelling food. I serve up for my boys and am delighted to find sliced crunchy vegetables on a serving plate with dividers, so the different vegetables don't touch. My stomach flips; a smile touching my lips at Theo's thoughtfulness for Lachlan's particular requirements.

"What would you like to eat, Munchkin?" Theo asks Kenny as he holds her plate, ready to do her bidding.

"Can I have some tomato, some potato, and some *dolmades* with my steak?" She points out each dish in turn.

"Sure thing." He scoops a small amount of each food onto her plate, cutting her steak into tiny bite-size pieces for her before serving himself.

Sitting around the large outdoor setting, silence descends over the table as we get stuck into the delicious food. "This table setting is beautiful." I run my hand across the timber. "Did you make this, Theo?"

Cristo looks across at Theo; the pride he holds for his son is written all over his face. "He did. Did you know when he was a teenager, he made some of the furniture for my restaurant? His settings are the most comfortable *and* the most stylish."

"Really? He mentioned something like that." I look across at Theo with raised brows. He told me he was the disappointment in the family. His father doesn't seem disappointed in him at all. "Did he tell you he renovated my front porch for me, complete with a swing bed, rocking chairs, and a table?" I wink at Theo. "He made a space that I never used into a place I want to spend time in every single day."

Cristo looks back at Theo. "No, he didn't. But it doesn't surprise me. He's always loved working with timber and making outdoor spaces more usable and appealing."

"Mommy, can we go play?" Austin pushes his empty plate away.

"Sure, Buddy. Carry your dishes inside to the kitchen sink, then you can play."

He pushes away from the table with his plate, cup, and silverware. Kenny follows suit so they can return to their Frisbee game. Lachlan finishes up with his food, takes his plate to the kitchen sink, then joins Austin and Kenny in their game. He smiles a lot when he's in Kenny's company, and I've noticed he's always keen to join in when she's around. She has a patience with him that mirrors Austin's, making Lachlan feel comfortable and accepted. It's like the kids have all grown up together, not that they met Kenny mere weeks ago.

Standing, I collect the remainder of the dishes to carry inside. As I scrape and rinse the plates, a hard, warm body presses up against mine, arms caging me in on either side. He runs his nose up the back of my neck before whispering, "Leave those. I'll do them later."

*Now, isn't that the hottest foreplay ever?*

Turning around within my cage, I face him. His eyes are the darkest blue I've ever seen on him, reminding me of the deepest ocean. "I feel like I didn't help with lunch, so I want to help with the cleanup. It'll only take a few minutes."

He moves forward, pressing a tender kiss against my lips. "I don't want you to do anything. Just enjoy the afternoon with us. The dishes can wait."

I press up on my toes, my breasts making contact with his chest, to return his gentle kiss. Though, this time, he's not as gentle. Cupping the back of my head, he takes over, swiping his warm tongue across my lips, encouraging me to open to him. I don't need a lot of encouragement, to be honest. I love his kisses. They take me to a whole different place. One I want to visit time and again.

"How come you're always kissing Mommy?" Lachlan's voice interrupts our moment.

Theo pulls away instantly, and I have to grasp onto the counter to maintain my balance. I look at Theo with raised brows, wondering how he's going to deal with Lachlan's question.

He scrapes his fingernails through his short beard, something I've noticed he does when he's thinking. "Well, when grownups like each other, sometimes they kiss." I have to cover my mouth to contain my giggle.

"You know there are around six million bacteria in the human mouth," Lachlan states matter-of-factly. "So that must mean you really like my mom if you're prepared to share that amount of bacteria." His eyebrows are drawn down low as he considers this possibility.

"Yeah. I like your mom a lot." He looks at me, giving me a wink. "I don't mind sharing some bacteria with her." He tucks his hands in his pockets as if he's waiting for further questions.

Lachlan nods. "Okay. Mommy, can I please have a drink of water?"

"Sure, Buddy." I push away from the counter, thankful for something to do.

We spend the remainder of the afternoon sitting around the outdoor table, drinking and snacking on Greek sweets and rocky road, watching the kids play, and listening to funny stories about some of the customers that dine at Cristo's restaurant. I adore the energy of Theo's dad. He has such a positive vibe about him; reminding me of Kenny.

"You really must give me the recipe for that rocky road, Emma. It was delicious." Cristo repeats. It must be the third time he's asked for the recipe, so I hand him the leftover rocky road to take home.

"Of course. I'll give it to Theo and he can pass it on to you."

He takes another piece of the sweet treat from the container, popping it into his mouth. "Thank you, Lovely. I can't wait."

# CHAPTER 29

## —theo—

Sitting on my porch with a beer, waiting for Emma to return home, I'm contemplating my feelings surrounding Emma and her boys. I'm not sure exactly when I fell, but I've fallen ... *hard*—for all three of them. Her friend, Kate, got married today and she was the attending bridesmaid. She left here with the boys yesterday afternoon and I haven't seen or heard from her since.

I've missed her.

Missed the boys.

I mentally run through the layout of this house, picturing where I could make changes and add an extension. I need to make this place big enough to comfortably house three more people. We could all fit as is. The renovations that were done before I bought the house were extensive. But I want to make certain this house is as appealing as possible to Em.

Emma pulls into her driveway, breaking me from my planning. Standing from my chair, I step to my porch railing and grip it to keep myself in place. In reality, I want to rip her car door open and then rip her clothes off. But she deserves more than that. *So much more.* I wait patiently for her to notice that I'm here.

That I'm waiting.

Waiting for her.

Finally, she looks across to my house and freezes in place. Her eyes lock with mine. The tension that's been building between us for weeks is about to boil over and I can't wait for it to fucking happen. This moment has been inevitable from the first moment I laid eyes on her.

Pushing away from the railing, I take in a calming breath, so I can greet her like the gentleman she deserves. Eyes locked, we watch each other as I take purposeful strides down the steps to the grass, then across to her car. I know what's about to happen; so does she. Stopping at her door, I get a closer look at my Emma. She's all made up and looks beyond stunning. Her throat bobs as she moves to release the door handle, but I have the door open before she gets the chance. Reaching inside, I release her seatbelt—my hand brushing against her breast, then take her hand in mine to assist her out of the car. Our eyes have not strayed from each other the entire time. The draw I feel toward her eclipses everything I've ever known.

Pulling her up to me, I band one arm around her waist, holding her tight to my body. Her soft curves press against my hard planes and I feel more settled than I have since she left yesterday afternoon—she's exactly where she belongs. I swipe my lips across hers, then follow with my tongue; tasting the sweetness of cake. She presses in closer, returning my kiss with one of her own, using her tongue to steal inside my mouth. Her familiar taste heightens my senses, my cock hardening further in my shorts. As I grind my erection against her to show what she does to me, we both groan at the sensation. We get lost in the power of this kiss, long moments of tasting, exploring, touching. She steals my breath with her tongue and her lips.

Lifting Emma into my arms, I pull away from her sedan, slamming the door closed with my foot. I carry her across to my place, still kissing, still tasting, still exploring. We manage to get inside, closing and locking the front door, before climbing the stairs to my bedroom. Pressing her back against the wall, I pull away slightly, locking eyes with the woman who's stolen my breath from the first moment I laid eyes on her. Panting to catch our breaths, we silently study each other. Her chameleon eyes hold me captive. The slim rings surrounding her dilated pupils are the deepest olive green I've ever seen. The warmth of her body heats mine, her breath puffing against my cheek.

This woman needs to be cherished.

She needs to be shown how beautiful she is.

I'm going to be the man to show her.

I run my nose along hers. "Hey."

She swallows, then gives me a genuine smile. "Hey." She looks around as if only now realizing we're no longer by her car. "This was quite the welcome home."

"I missed you. How was the wedding?" I ask as I glide my hand down her smooth arm, taking her hand in mine to lift it above her head.

She sighs, her eyes going soft. "It was beautiful. Simple, classy, and small. Kate and Oliver are so deeply in love. I felt blessed to be part of their day." I glide my free hand down her other arm, taking her hand in mine, also lifting it above her head. Her breasts push up into me with her hands up high like this, producing a magnificent cleavage for me to bury my face in.

Holding both of her hands in one of mine, I run the back of my free hand down the side of her face, using my knuckle to support her chin. "You look fucking stunning, Emma." I breathe in her scent—she never wears perfume, so it's all her—before running my tongue across her lips. Her panting breaths touch my tongue and I want them to coat my cock. "This dress looks beautiful on you, but I'm gonna need to take it off. You okay with that?"

Pulling back, so I can read her face, some of the lust that was in her gaze earlier has disappeared. Her brows slant down over her eyes, which are glancing all around my bedroom. I pull the rest of my body back from hers slightly. "You okay?"

Releasing a heavy breath, she looks back at me. "Uh, yeah." She presses forward, ensuring we're once again touching at every available point, then places a gentle kiss against my lips. It's a barely there touch, but I feel it all the way to my soul. "I'm …" She looks away from me, so I guide her eyes back to mine.

"Talk to me, Em." Maybe I've pushed her too soon. It's been difficult over the past couple of weeks, only being able to steal kisses and touches here and there. I thought I'd take this opportunity while both of us are kid-free to take our kisses further.

She swallows, then closes her eyes tightly. I release her hands and take a step back from her. The vibe she's giving off suggests this is too much, too soon for her. Her hands drop and clasp the side of my T-shirt, preventing my retreat. "I want this. Want you." She looks down, then back up at me with a sad smile on her face. "I'm just conscious of my body." Her words startle me as they rush out on a whispered breath.

I feel as though I've been punched in the gut. "What? Why?" I'm perplexed by her statement.

She rolls her gorgeous eyes, her grip on my T-shirt loosening. "Look at you." I look down at myself, though I'm more than familiar with my own body. Then look back to Em, waiting for her to continue. "Look at me."

Stepping back from her, I study her from the top of her rich choco-late-colored hair, running my eyes across her face, down her neck, across her collarbones, and everywhere in between until I get to the tips of her red-painted toes. I can't hold back the lust I feel for her as my dick grows exponentially harder behind my zipper. Tilting my chin down, I ask, "See what you do to me?"

I watch her eyes trail down my body to the obvious bulge trapped in my shorts. Her tongue makes an appearance to moisten those plump lips of hers, eliciting a groan from me. Her eyes are locked on my groin, so I click my fingers. "Up here, Em." Her eyes snap up to mine and a flush rises from her chest. "I asked you a question."

"Uh, what was it?" She swallows again.

I point to my dick. "See what you do to me?" I take her hand, pressing it to the front of my shorts. "All that stuff about your body running through your head. Get rid of it. There's no room for it here. When I look at you, I fucking love everything I see. I can't fucking wait to caress, lick, bite, and kiss every single curve."

Her eyes widen, a gasp leaving her lips. "But I carried two big babies. I have extra pounds and stretch marks … my boobs aren't per—"

I step in, covering her mouth with mine, cutting off her self-depre-cating words. Probably shit her ex told her if the conversation I over-heard was any indication. It takes her a moment to respond, but when I feel her arms slide up around my neck and tongue dance against mine, I sigh in relief. The kiss is everything and yet not enough. I need my skin against hers, my hands on her flesh, my cock encased in her heat. I kiss down to her neck and across her exposed collarbone. "Let me worship you. Let me put those demons to rest."

Her fingers sift through my hair. "O-okay."

I waste no time picking her up. I need to lay her down, but first I need her bare. I carry her closer to my bed, trying to slow myself down so this isn't over before it begins. Stepping behind her, I slowly glide the zipper down and untie the ribbon wrapped around her waist. The dress glides down her body, exposing her curves to me inch by magnifi-cent inch. The flare of her hips has me biting my tongue in antic-ipation.

My mouth waters, my heart hammers, my cock drips.

She's wearing pale blue lace panties with a matching strapless bra that is the exact same shade as her dress. I smooth my fingers over the lacy fabric, watching goosebumps break out over Emma's pale skin. Stepping around her body, stopping in front of her, I hold out my hand to support her as she steps out of the puddle of blue. I can't tear my eyes away from her, greedily scanning every inch. "You are fucking breathtaking, Em." I stroke down the front of her panties, feeling the heat radiating from her pussy. "Mind if I remove the rest?"

"Please," she breathes out.

I take her lips again because I need to have my mouth on hers, then kiss my way down her neck, to her breasts. Those magnificent tits that have captured my attention from day one. I can't believe how close I am to laying eyes on them. Kissing each one over the top of the lacy fabric, I reach behind to release the clasp. Moving back slightly, I allow the lace to fall away, then swipe my tongue over first one nipple, then the other. Groaning as her perfect peach-colored nipples bead under my attention. She sighs as her breasts drop free, finally landing in my waiting hands. Her hand presses my head harder against her breasts, holding me in place. Her chest rises then falls rapidly and I feel the vibration of her heart beating against my tongue. *Heaven!*

"Theo," she whispers, pressing into me harder. Desperation and lust drip from that single word.

"I know." Stepping back, I use my thumbs to glide her panties down her shapely legs until they land on the floor between her sexy, lace-up sandals. "Sit down." I guide her to sit on the edge of my bed. I know once I have her in here, I'll want her in my space all the time. Holding the back of her head for support, I kiss her, pressing her back until she's lying down. Moving away, I drop to my knees between her legs. Opening them as wide as possible, I lay eyes on her glistening pussy at long last. She's neatly groomed, but not bare. Thank God! I want to feel like I'm kissing a woman, not a prepubescent teen. "Fucking gorgeous!" I groan, then begin the slow torture of kissing up the inside of her thigh.

"Theo," she moans, widening her thighs further to accommodate my broad shoulders as goosebumps decorate her skin. *That's my girl.* I palm my cock through my shorts, rearranging myself for comfort; I'm gonna be here for a while. I kiss the crease between her thigh and pussy as I swipe my finger through her drenched pussy lips. Em tilts her hips up, trying to hurry me along, so I press down on her pelvis to keep her in place.

"I'll get there, Peaches."

I move in, spearing her entrance with my tongue, before swiping up to her clit. Her natural taste coats my tongue, urging me to take more. I'm a greedy bastard, so I'm going to take everything she can give me, and then I'm gonna come back for more. Using my fingers and tongue, I work her over until she can't keep quiet, her breathy cries and moans filling my bedroom. I store them in my memory banks, so I can draw on them during the nights we're not together. Her body synchronizes with my fingers, thrusting in time, encouraging me to go deeper, to pump harder. Finally, as I suck the bundle of nerves pulsing at the top of her pussy, she comes. Her walls gripping my fingers tight, her juices covering my stubble, her fingers pulling my hair, her legs crushing my head and I know … *I know* I'm gonna want to do this to her as often as she'll allow me the privilege. Looking up the length of her body, I'm blessed with the vision of her tits rising and falling with her rapid breaths, her body coated in a sheen of sweat, flushed pink with her orgasm.

"If I thought you were stunning before, you just eclipsed it." I carefully unlace and remove her sandals one at a time as she catches her breath.

"I have no words. That's the second time you've kissed the words right out of me." She giggles, causing her tits to jiggle. More cum leaks from the head of my cock.

"Oh yeah? When was the first time?"

Lifting her head, she looks down her body at me with a half-smile. "The first time you kissed me." She raises a finely sculpted brow.

Good to know the strategy worked. She looked sexy as fuck when she lost her cool, and I couldn't hold myself back any longer. Propping herself up on her elbows, she gives me a come-hither motion with her finger. She grasps my shirt, pulling me in for a scorching kiss. With one foot on the floor, my knee rests between her thighs, burning from the heat of her pussy. I make contact, applying pressure, and she instantly begins rubbing herself against me. *So fucking hot!* Her juices coat my leg and I groan my approval into her mouth.

She pulls back, eyes dazed and glassy, breaths short and heavy. "You need to get naked, Theo."

I don't want to separate from her, but I need my skin to be touching hers more. Standing up, I grasp the back of my T-shirt and pull it over my head. As my eyes make contact with Emma's, she groans. "Your body is a work of art," she states reverently. Running my hand down my abs, I throw my shirt to the floor and start on my button and zipper.

"I'm glad you like it, Peaches." At my new nickname for her, her lips quirk up. I drop my shorts and underwear at the same time, step out of them, and climb over my girl. We both groan at the sensation of our skin meeting for the first time. Her warm body welcomes mine; goosebumps cover my flesh as my heart picks up speed. If someone had told me when I first moved in that I'd find myself in this position with this beautiful woman, I would never have believed them.

Resting on my elbows, my groin lined up with hers, her tits pressing against my chest, I take her mouth again. Gently at first, but it doesn't take long for our lust to grow and take over. We're as explosive as I knew we would be.

I need to slow down, so I can cherish her. This isn't just a quick fuck for me. I push up and off the bed. "Move up the bed for me." I lift my chin, directing her where to go as I pull open the drawer in my nightstand to fish out a couple of condoms. She does my bidding quickly. "Open your legs for me. I want to see my pussy."

Her eyes go wide at my command, but she opens her legs for me. Not quite wide enough for my liking, but I'll fix that. Stepping to the end of the bed, her head follows my movements. She hasn't taken her eyes off my cock, which glistens with her pussy juices. I take it in hand and give it a couple of hard pulls, closing my eyes at the sensation of doing this in front of her. At her moan, I open my eyes to find her licking her lips, eyes glued to my groin. Her hand moves to her pussy, and she swipes her fingers through her delicate folds. I tear my eyes away from her pussy to watch her face. Lust fills her gaze, and as much as I'm enjoying the show, I want to be the one touching her.

A low growl escapes my throat. "Peaches." Her eyes snap up to mine and I shake my head. "I didn't say you could touch yourself."

I raise my eyebrows, waiting for her to remove her hand. She slowly moves it away, playing with her breasts on the way to her lips, where she proceeds to coat them with the cum on her fingers. I drop my head back on a groan and then bring it back to watch her, as I slowly glide my hand up her smooth leg. Climbing slowly onto the bed, I follow my hands with my tongue. Tasting every smooth inch of her. "Mmmmm." Kissing, licking, and nipping at her flesh, I make my way up to her pussy. Her hands immediately grip my head, directing it where she wants it to go. I'll let her think she's in charge for now. She lifts her pelvis off of the bed to meet my mouth and the contact sears my lips.

Her heat, her taste, her smell—an aphrodisiac like no other.

I groan.

She moans.

I kiss her like this will be my last opportunity, rubbing tight circles around her clit. If the pulsing is anything to go by, she's almost ready to explode again, so I plunge two fingers into her channel, massaging the spongy area on the front wall.

"Ooooooo, yeeeeaaaah." Her walls spasm around my fingers, holding on to them tight, strangling them within her tight channel.

"That's it. I'm starting my collection. Give 'em all to me." Slowing my fingers, I clean up her cum with my tongue before moving my way up her body, so I can pay some special attention to her phenomenal breasts. Cupping them in my hands, I press them together, nuzzling them. I've always been a boob and ass guy and Em has both in spades. I couldn't have created a more perfect woman for me if I'd put her together myself. Nudging my bare shaft against her pussy, I lick, kiss, massage, and pluck her breasts until they're peaked to my liking. Pushing back, I study my handiwork. Pride fills my chest at what I see. Beard rash surrounds her peach-colored areola. Her nipples point at me, begging me to taste them some more.

I reach across to the nightstand to grab a condom. Em intercepts me, grabbing it from me and tearing it open with her teeth. "Let me."

Resting back on my heels, I let her have at it. "Be my guest, Peaches."

With trembling hands, she carefully rolls the latex down my length. I have to suck in a breath to stop myself from coming too soon. "You have a great-looking dick, Theo." She looks up at me from beneath her bangs. Stroking it a couple of times, she guides me toward her entrance. I can feel the heat emanating from her and I hold my breath as she notches the head at her opening.

Slamming my mouth onto hers, I push her back down so I can slide home. Inch by glorious inch, her walls encase my dick, welcoming me.

She'll be lucky if I ever leave.

Emma tilts her hips up, encouraging me to slide in as far as I can go. Our eyes lock together as we both groan at the sensation. She presses up, takes my mouth, and slides her tongue deep inside. This moment is everything. I want to move, but moving will mean climaxing, and climaxing will mean it's all over, and I *never* want this to be over. She rocks her hips and wraps her legs around my waist, pressing her heels into my butt. "Please move," she sighs against my lips.

Pressing my forehead to hers, our eyes locked, mossy green to blue, I begin the slow glide out. Her walls hold me snug, not allowing me to pull all the way out, which I would never do. Sliding back in, I change our angle to ensure I rub against her g-spot and collect her clit as our pelvises connect. I move in the same fashion a couple of times before Emma picks up the rhythm, meeting me thrust for thrust.

I can't go slow.

My body's begging for release.

Begging me to pick up speed.

Demanding I lead us both to our release.

Sighs, groans, and moans fill my bedroom. Skin slaps against skin as our bodies become one in their desire to come. Squelching sounds permeate the air with each thrust into her wet channel.

This is an epic moment. Something not everyone is lucky enough to experience. One I'll remember and treasure for the rest of my days. The day I was fortunate enough to share my woman's body for the first time.

Our thrusts increase in speed and power, both of us chasing our orgasm. "My pussy." I groan in her ear. "Tell me this is my pussy."

"It's your pussy. O o o …" Her pussy walls flutter around my cock, massaging it, making it difficult to hold on to my release. I reach down and work her clit in the hopes of pushing her over the edge, so I can let go. "Ooooo, Theo." Her walls clamp down, trapping my cock inside. I slow my thrusts as her orgasm works through her body. Experiencing her orgasm like this feels completely decadent and is something I know I'm gonna become addicted to.

"Your pussy feels like a silk vice around my dick," I groan, picking up the pace again with my thrusts, chasing my release. Emma digs her short nails into my ass, encouraging me deeper. Her thighs tighten around my waist as she lifts her head off the pillow to bite my pulse point. It's enough to make me break. I press up into her as far as I can go, my cum filling the condom, and I have the strongest desire to knock her up. I want to fill her up with my cum. So much cum that it drips out of her body for hours.

Dropping down, so our bodies touch skin to skin again. I rest on my elbows so I don't squash her with my weight. Nuzzling her neck, I kiss and lick the perspiration there before making my way to her mouth. Sealing her mouth with mine, we kiss lazily for long moments. There's no need to rush. We're both feeling sated. The kiss continues languidly and I could do this for hours, but I really need to deal with the condom and clean up my pussy. Pulling away slowly, I swipe my nose back and forth across Emma's before kissing her forehead. Her eyes drop closed with a sigh. When I pull back to look, really look at her, my chest puffs up with pride.

Swollen lips, dazed eyes, and beard rash greet me, and she looks even more gorgeous.

"I don't want to get up, but I need to deal with this condom." I give her one more chaste kiss, then press away from her so I can get out of bed to deal with the latex. Sorting myself out, I wet a washcloth with warm water to tend to my girl.

Stepping out of my bathroom, I stop in my tracks and admire Emma. Her fancy hairdo is all messed up, the flowers crushed on the pillow. A serene smile graces her beautiful face, but it's the way she's lying with not a single ounce of self-consciousness about her body that is so damn sexy. I move forward to sit on the edge of the bed. I can't help myself, leaning down to take her lips in a gentle kiss. "Open your legs for me, Peaches," I whisper against her lips.

She follows my instruction, allowing me the space to gently wipe my pussy, noting the beard rash on her inner thighs. A half-smile touches my lips at the marks I've left on her.

"What are you smiling about?"

Running my finger up the inside of her thigh. I watch my nail leave a white line through the redness. "This."

She giggles. "You're weird."

I quickly drop back over her, pressing my groin to hers. Giving a gentle thrust, I rub my beard across the top of her breasts. "I like having my marks on you. If that makes me weird, then so be it." We get caught up in another scorching kiss. Which leads to another round of the hottest sex I've ever had the pleasure of enjoying.

DECLAN'S DINER IS THE QUINTESSENTIAL 1950S DINER, COMPLETE WITH black-and-white checkered floor tiles, laminate and chrome tables, and an atmosphere that is laid back and relaxed. Stepping through these doors for the first time in probably ten years, holding my girls' hands in each of mine, Emma's boys trailing alongside—it feels *different*. I'm a family man, not a young single guy seeking something greasy to eat after a big night out.

The pier and diner are busy. Plenty of people had the same idea as we did to spend Independence Day out and about before settling down to watch the fireworks. Unsurprisingly, red, white, and blue are the colors of choice among the hundreds of people making the most of the beautiful day.

Squeezing Em's hand, I ask, "What does everyone wanna eat?"

After studying the menu boards, we wait for our turn, then place our order. Each of us tells the young guy behind the counter what we want, then we choose a table outside on the pier so we can enjoy the weather and watch people as they pass.

"I can't believe we've already been on summer vacation for one month." Emma sighs. I pull her chair closer to mine so I can have some part of me touching her.

"I can't wait to start kindergarten." Kenny's enthusiasm shows in her entire body as she jigs up and down in her seat. "I love my pwincess teacher?"

Em and I laugh at her description of her teacher. "Her name's

Mrs. Stone now. She got married a couple of weeks ago. You're very lucky to have her as your teacher."

"Her hair is so pwetty." Kenny sighs with stars in her eyes.

A server brings out our order and I make sure everyone has the correct food and drink. Lachlan and Kenny are enjoying their chicken nuggets, while Austin eats his hotdog. Emma and I dig into our hamburgers and I love watching her eat with gusto—it's sexy watching my girl enjoy her food.

"I can't remember the last time I ate here," Emma moans around a bite, waking up my dick. We haven't been able to find time alone together since the day of Kate's wedding. Those hours spent cherishing her body are seared into my mind, making me impatient to do it all again. We steal kisses and touches whenever we can, which will have to be enough for another two weeks. I need her and the boys living under my roof, so I can have her beside me every day and in my bed every night. "These burgers are something else."

I nod in agreement as I shove another fry in my mouth. "They have that home-cooked taste, which separates them from all other burgers."

"Definitely." We continue eating in silence for a few more minutes.

Austin puts down his hotdog, his eyebrows drawn tight over his brown eyes, a thoughtful look on his face. "How come Daddy didn't come to get us today?" I was hoping this outing might have distracted him enough. That he wouldn't notice his dad had skipped out on him and his brother in favor of a weekend away with his new wife.

Emma swallows down the food in her mouth, tucking a lock of silky chocolate hair behind her ear. Her eyes briefly connect with mine before she answers her son. "Well, you know how it's a long weekend, right?"

He nods. "Yeah."

"Uh, well, he and Stacey wanted to go away for the weekend as a short holiday." She smiles as if that will take the sting out of the news for the boys. "You'll get to see him next month. Imagine all the news you'll have to share when you see him."

"Why couldn't he take us?" Lachlan asks. He may not say much, but he's very aware of everything that goes on around him and I've learned he feels everything deeply. "We like holidays, too."

Emma looks across at me, and I can almost see her heart breaking for her boys. I squeeze her thigh gently underneath the table in support.

"Did you notice anything new in my backyard this morning?" I ask the boys. I figure I'll try to distract them. They both answer in the negative. "Well, Kenny and I set up a tent early this morning." The boys' eyes light up as they look between Kenny and me.

"Yeah. It was so much fun. We're gonna sleep in it tonight!" Kenny almost shouts. "Like we're camping in the woods!"

"Really. Can we camp too?" Austin asks with hopeful eyes.

"Of course. That was the plan." Emma's eyes widen with surprise, so I gently squeeze her thigh again. I hadn't told her of my plan because I wanted to see how the boys went today. The plan had been for Kenny and me to camp, but I think she'll enjoy having the boys join us and it'll take their mind off not seeing their dad today.

Kenny turns to the boys. "You should see the tent. It's so cool, there are blow-up beds and sleeping bags. This is gonna be so much fun!" She claps her hands together with absolute glee.

"We have the ingredients to make s'mores over the fire pit, too. We'll make a big night of it." I'm doing my best to sell a night of camping in my backyard in an attempt to lift the boys' spirits.

"This is gonna be great. Can Mommy come too?" Austin asks, his voice full of hope.

A slow smile touches my lips. This may just work out in my favor. Even though nothing can happen, I can sleep with her in my arms. "She's more than welcome to join us if she wants to." I look across at Emma, raising my brows, awaiting her response.

With wide eyes, she looks like a deer caught in the headlights and I can't hold back my chuckle. She readjusts her position in her seat, flips her hair over her shoulder, then studies her boys' hopeful faces. I can see the moment she gives in when her shoulders drop and she huffs out a sigh. "Sure, sounds like heaps of fun."

The three kids cheer in delight at her agreement and I feel my shoulders relax, knowing I'll have her in my arms tonight. Well, my day has definitely taken an unexpected turn—one I like very much.

Wandering through the crowds enjoying the national holiday, I notice Lachlan's becoming more and more unsettled. Pulling Em close, I ask, "Should we head home? We can possibly see some of the fireworks from my upstairs deck."

"You and Kenny wouldn't mind?"

"Not at all. We can get organized for our campout." I tug her close, leaning forward to press a chaste kiss to her lips.

She nods in return with a relieved smile. "Thanks for under-standing."

"Anytime, Peaches."

"Why do you call our mommy Peaches? Her name is Emma."

Em looks at me with raised brows, challenging me to answer Lachlan's question.

I pull away from Emma so I can give Lachlan my attention. "Well, you see ... I love peaches. They're sweet, just like your mom." I pull Emma back in close to whisper for her ears only, "They both taste delicious, too." Emma chuckles, dropping her head to hide her face.

"But Mommy is nothing like a peach."

"It's a nickname. Like I call Kenny, Munchkin."

"What *is* a munchkin, anyway?" Lachlan seems quite puzzled by the whole nickname thing.

"It's a word used to describe a short person or a small child."

Kenny stops in her tracks, slamming her tiny fists to her hips. "Hey. I'm not short!" The incredulous look on her little face is enough to crack me up.

"You *are* short, Kenny. But that's partly because you're four years old. You'll grow taller." Lachlan states in his matter-of-fact way, without realizing he's added fuel to Kenny's fire. "You'll probably stop growing when you're between fifteen and seventeen years old."

I look at Emma, who shrugs at my unasked question. "I don't know how he knows the stuff he knows. He retains facts and figures like you wouldn't believe."

"Oh, I believe it. His recall of facts blows me away."

I pick Kenny up and land a smacking kiss on her cheek. "All the best things come in small packages, Munchkin."

She crosses her arms, pouting at me. "I don't wanna be called Munchkin anymore."

"Too bad. You're my one and only Munchkin. The name stays!" She smiles.

"I'm your one and only?" A hopeful expression on her face.

"Absolutely. Forever and always." I kiss her forehead. Her little body relaxes against mine as we make our way through the crowds back to the parking lot.

CHAPTER 31

*—emma—*

COULD I FALL FOR THIS GUY ANY MORE THAN I ALREADY HAVE? HE'S too sweet, and to think I thought he was an asshole when he first moved in. The boys are so excited to spend the night camping—even Lachlan, who values his set routine. The entire tent floor is covered in mattresses, pillows, and light cotton blankets—making one big bed for all of us to share. I know it's wrong, but I'm looking forward to being able to snuggle with Theo. It's been too long since we spent the afternoon and night together.

*What that man did to my body.*

The way he cherished me—every single inch of me. I've never experienced attention like that before in my whole life. He really loves my curves and the extra pounds seemed to turn him on, not off.

Standing on Theo's upper back deck, we manage to catch the higher fireworks. Every time I turn my head and catch sight of Theo's bed, my body heats remembering everything we did together. Lachlan's hand squeezing mine brings me back to where my mind should be. Looking down at him, he smiles at me before turning back to watch more of the display. Austin hasn't torn his eyes away from the fireworks at all and Kenny's equally mesmerized by the colorful explosions as she sits up high on Theo's shoulders; his hands holding her legs securely—keeping her safe. He's incredibly protective of her. There's no way he would ever put her in a situation where she may get hurt—physically or emotionally. He feels she's already suffered enough with the loss of her mom.

As the fireworks come to an end, Theo and I round up the kids so we can make s'mores over the fire pit. Something my boys have never done—Preston was never one to do outdoorsy-type stuff and the people-pleaser that I was, went along with whatever he liked and didn't like.

"C'mon kids, let's go downstairs to make our s'mores." Theo places Kenny on her feet and we all make our way downstairs.

"This is so exciting." Austin's almost bouncing down the stairs. "Mommy, what's a s'more?" he asks.

I ruffle his hair. "It's something that's yummy. You'll see."

On the way to the fire pit, we collect marshmallows, milk chocolate, and graham crackers. Austin and Kenny are almost bursting out of their skin with excitement. The small smile on Lachlan's face and the pace of his stride tells me he's equally excited about this new experience.

Theo works to set up the fire, showing the kids what to do: the best way to set up the kindling, and how to safely start the fire; as well as making sure the kids understand how dangerous fire can be.

"Lachlan, pass me the larger kindling, please."

"Okay." Lachlan gathers up the larger pieces and carries them over to the fire.

"Thanks, Buddy." Theo's a natural teacher, ensuring all three kids are involved in the process. He demonstrates how to make a s'more safely and then helps the kids to make one each. We work together to help them slide the sticky marshmallow onto the biscuit without burning their fingers. In between, Theo and I manage to make some s'mores for ourselves.

Kenny licks the stickiness from her fingers, leaving chocolate around the outside of her lips. "These are so yummy!" She smacks her lips together. "I wanna have them every day!"

Austin and Lachlan nod in agreement with the little firecracker.

I giggle. "You'd get tired of eating s'mores if you had them every day."

Kenny, Austin, and Lachlan each shake their head in the negative. "Nuh-uh. No, I wouldn't," Kenny states adamantly. It surprises me that Lachlan actually liked it, but maybe the crunchiness of the cracker appealed to him. We play a few games of snap, and then sleep starts to weave its magic.

Getting comfortable in the tent doesn't take long with all the cushions and light cotton blankets, making it feel cozy. Lachlan and I brought his weighted blanket to make sure he felt comfortable enough to get some sleep.

I read one of my favorite stories to the kids by torchlight, *The Lion, The Witch and The Wardrobe* by C.S. Lewis. I love the make-believe world he created, full of magical creatures, and I'm so happy to be sharing it with my boys and now, Kenny. I keep reading, using different voices for the characters, until they're all asleep; Theo laying on the other side of me and Kenny between her two best friends. Tucking the book out of the way, I roll over so I can snuggle into Theo's hard body. He kisses my forehead and I can't hold in my contented sigh.

He feels like home. It didn't take long to feel deeply for this man, and the speed at which my feelings have grown is downright scary.

"Thank you for a great day and for helping my boys deal with missing their dad." I lift my head to plant a chaste kiss against his lips in appreciation.

"You're welcome, Peaches. Kenny and I enjoy spending time with you and the boys. It's certainly no hardship for us." He punctuates his words with a kiss on my forehead, melting my heart.

"We'd better get some sleep while we can. Lachlan will inevitably wake during the night. I'll try to keep him quiet so he doesn't disturb you guys."

"Is that a regular thing?"

I sigh, whispering, "Yeah. There aren't too many nights that he'll sleep all the way through. It's part of life." I look up at Theo's eyes, not that I can see them clearly in the dark, but I can tell his brows are furrowed.

"How do you manage with such limited sleep? I turn into a grumpy bastard when I don't get enough sleep." He huffs out a quiet laugh.

Shrugging, I whisper, "I'm used to it, I guess."

He nods, kissing my forehead again. "Alright then. Roll over. I've got you."

I do as he says. Feeling secure in his arms, my butt tucked into his groin, his arms wrapped around me, cupping each breast, and I fall asleep.

# CHAPTER 32

## —emma—

I startle awake as the early dawn streams across my face. The first thing I realize is that I slept through the night. My eyes snap across to where Lachlan's sleeping and panic immediately fills me when I find his bed empty. My heart rate increases exponentially and the sweat under my armpits is out of control. Kenny and Austin are still sound asleep. As I move to get up, I realize Theo is also missing.

Oh, God!

What if something happened, and I slept right through it? I've been feeling tired lately, but I never sleep through Lachlan waking up. I get up as quietly as I can without disturbing the two sleeping beauties, trying to suck in deep breaths to ward off my panic—wincing as I push up from the ground. The side of my breast has been getting more and more annoying these past few weeks.

The zipper to the tent sounds deafening in the quiet morning and I wonder how I didn't hear it when Lachlan and Theo left the tent. I don't bother zipping the tent door closed, so I don't make any more noise than I need to.

Using the gate Theo installed in our common fence, I quickly head home to check if Lachlan decided to sleep in his bed. I left the back door unlocked last night, in case we needed to go home in a hurry. I slip inside quietly, so as not to wake him if he's still sleeping, heading straight for his bedroom.

He's not there.

My heart rate kicks up another notch, and I have to remind myself to keep breathing. I quickly move from room to room looking for him, but he's nowhere to be found!

Okay, calm down, think! Maybe he's next door with Theo.

Quickly stepping back through the gate, I move onto Theo's back deck, my heart hammering in my chest. It's taking all of my cohesive thought to put one foot in front of the other at this point. I couldn't bear it if something happened to one of my boys. My precious boys! I'm so trucking mad at myself that I slept through. Moving from room to room, I come up empty again. This is crazy.

Where could they have gone?

Moving outside to the back deck, the open door to Theo's work-shop catches my eye. There's a strip of light shining out through the opening. I can't believe I didn't notice it before. My bare feet are silent as they press into the soft grass. The blood in my body's pumping at a furious rate and I'm struggling to take in a deep breath. Reaching the open door, I hear low voices murmuring. Relief washes over me instantly and I suck in a much-needed breath to calm myself. My hand shoots up to my chest in a lame attempt to slow the beats, now that I know Lachlan's safe.

Leaning against the door frame, I fold my arms and watch in silence. Lachlan's obviously found his 'thing'. The thing that calms him and keeps him steady. He loves working with the timber and even manages to tolerate the noisy machinery required to do some of the work. Not that Theo's allowed him to use any of the machines, but Lachlan doesn't balk at the loud noises while wearing the ear protec-tion Theo insists the kids use whenever they're around. Lachlan's lips are spread in a genuine smile and I can see the glint of happiness in his eyes from here as he sands the outdoor table he's been helping Theo with.

Theo may be new to this parenting gig, but he does an awesome job with the kids. He takes the time to show and guide and teach the kids how to complete a task from start to finish. Explaining the reasons and finer points in just enough detail to keep their attention. My smile touches my lips as I watch the two of them work together. Theo glances up, catching me watching the two of them working together. He says something to Lachlan, then makes his way toward me with light in his eyes and a smile on his face. He moves straight into my personal space, cupping the back of my head before dropping his lips to mine in a gentle kiss. Combing his fingers through my bed-tousled hair, he pulls away, locking his eyes with mine.

"Good morning, Peaches," he whispers, then kisses me again. "How'd you sleep?"

"Too good." I swallow down the memory of my fear when I woke to find Lachlan gone. "I panicked when I woke to find Lachlan missing from his bed. How long have you guys been up?"

His forehead crinkles as he rubs his hands up and down my arms. The action comforts me mildly. "I'm sorry you were worried. I heard him rustling around and then he started huffing and puffing, so I told him we could get up quietly and get to work on sanding the table. We've probably been up for a couple of hours. I didn't even notice the sun coming up."

I place my hands on Theo's slim hips. "You didn't have to do that. I'm so sorry he woke you. He rarely sleeps through the night and last night he was out of his usual routine, which probably made it worse for him." I press up on my toes to kiss him in thanks. "Thank you. I must have been tired because I didn't hear anything."

He smiles down at me, and I can almost see his chest puffing up in pride. "That was the plan. I wanted you to get a good night's sleep." He takes my hand, pulling me into his workshop. The scent of timber and sawdust fills my nostrils; it's a smell that's become synonymous with Theo. "Come. Look at what we're working on."

It's a gorgeous hexagonal table made of redwood. As I run my hand across the surface, the mild spicy scent of the timber fills my nose. The slatted design on the tabletop is extremely intricate, adding interest to what would otherwise be a regular flat surface. "This is gorgeous, Theo. You're so very talented. Whoever ordered this piece is going to love it so much."

He scrubs his fingernails through his bristles then lifts his chin toward Lachlan, who's busy hand sanding the edge. "Couldn't have done it without my man, Lachlan's, help."

Lachlan looks up, eyes wide. "Really?"

"Really. You've helped me a lot. Your eye for detail, showing me the rough spots, really helped to make this a professional piece of furniture." He moves to Lachlan and musses his hair, and surprisingly, Lachlan seems to press his head into Theo's hand.

"Morning, Buddy. How did you sleep?" I wrap my arm around him, pulling him into me so I can kiss him good morning.

"I slept soundly for the time I was asleep, Mommy. I just woke up early." He shrugs as if it's no big deal. It *is* a big deal, though. He rarely sleeps soundly when he's asleep, he's always restless. I wonder if it was because we were all sleeping together.

"That's great. You look like you're doing a great job there, helping Theo."

He looks down at the wood where he's been working. "I like sanding the timber. I like making it smooth. Then I really like it when it's time to rub in the beeswax. I like to watch the wood change color."

I nod, a lump forming in my throat at his words.

"You were born to work with timber, Lachlan. You have a great eye for the cuts, grain, and the finer finishing-off details."

Two little arms wrap around my thigh, much like the very first day I met Kenny. My hand instantly goes to stroke her knotty hair. "Morning, Uncle Theo. Morning, Emma. Morning, Lachlan," Kenny says in a sleep-filled voice. I bend down to pick her up, nuzzling my nose into her neck, soaking in her little girl smell. Theo steps around the table to give her a good morning kiss as he rubs her back.

"How'd you sleep, Munchkin?" He keeps his deep voice low.

"Uhm, good. I think. I don't know. I was asleep." She reaches her little arms out toward her uncle, climbing across from me to him. "I'm hungwy."

"How about I go home and make breakfast for everyone, then I'll call you all over when it's ready?"

Kenny straightens in her uncle's arms. "Can I help?"

Even though we've been working together in the kitchen over the past few weeks, I look at Theo to check if it's okay with him. "Sure. I'll check on Austin. The boys and I will be over in thirty minutes. That okay?"

Kenny and I nod in unison. "Sounds perfect. Come on, Kenny, let's go."

We both go to the bathroom to do our morning business and wash our hands. Once we're in my kitchen, I pull out the ingredients we'll need to make the pancake batter along with bacon and maple syrup. Kenny and I work together to measure out the ingredients before I set the mixer to combine them.

"Uncle Theo mixes the pancake mix with a whisk," Kenny states as she watches the mixer do its thing.

"Well, you can do it like that. I do it like this so I can do other stuff while it's mixing. Plus, I find it makes them fluffier." I tap the end of her tiny nose.

Kenny's face lights up. "Oh, I like fluffy pancakes."

I tuck a lock of knotty hair behind her ear. "We all like fluffy pancakes the best." I grab an oven tray, baking paper, and bacon before turning on the oven. "Would you like to help me lay the bacon out on this tray?"

"Okay."

I turn off the mixer and line the tray with the baking paper. We work together to lay the bacon on the tray, making sure none of the pieces overlap, and sit the tray next to the oven so it's ready to go.

"We need to cut up some crunchy apples for Lachlan and juicy strawberries for our pancakes." I grab a couple of apples and a punnet of strawberries out of the fridge. Kenny and I talk about her favorite fruits as I slice the apples and rinse and cut the strawberries.

"I love bananas. They're my favowite." I have bananas, so I grab one to slice as a topping for our pancakes when we're ready to eat. "Okay, let's start making the pancakes. Then we can get that bacon into the oven."

"Uncle Theo cooks our bacon in a fwy pan on the stove." She tells me as she rests her chin on her closed fists, watching me pour the batter into the pan.

"A lot of people cook their bacon like that. I like to do it this way because I add a special surprise to the bacon. You wait, you're gonna love it!" It's so cute that she's comparing the way I cook to the way her uncle cooks.

Her eyebrows draw down low over her eyes. "How come you and my uncle are always kissing?"

Oh boy. Here we go.

"Well, when you're a loooooooot older, you may start to date a boy … or a man that you really like. Uhm … and sometimes when you really like that person, you … uh … kiss them to show them that … uh … you like them." I'm not sure why I said date. I don't know if Theo and I are actually dating. I still don't know what this is between us.

She nods thoughtfully, obviously processing my words. "So, like when I'm five soon, I could kiss Austin and Lachlan. I like them a lot." Her eyes widen and her eyebrows rise with her last sentence.

It takes me a moment to register her words as I pour more pancake batter into the pan. "Uh, no. Remember, I said a *lot* older. Like when you're thirty or something like that. And you definitely can't kiss brothers. That's not okay." I frown, wondering how this conversation turned to kissing brothers as I put the bacon in the oven.

The boys step through the back door. Austin is in Theo's arms, rubbing sleep from his eyes. "Morning, Mommy."

Theo brings him close to me, so I reach forward to kiss him. "Morning, Buddy. Sleep well?"

"I guess so."

"How about you boys go wash up. Then you can set the table." The three of them head to the bathroom as Kenny and I continue making pancakes. Pulling the bacon out of the oven, I coat each piece with maple syrup, then put it back in for another couple of minutes.

Kenny whispers, "You put maple sywup on the bacon?" Her eyes widen with mischief.

I nod and press my pointer finger to my lips with a grin. She licks her lips and nods with an excited smile. The boys set the table; I slice the banana, and we place all the food in the center so everyone can help themselves.

Theo makes a plate for Kenny, Lachlan organizes his own plate, exactly how he likes it, while I serve a pancake with a side of bacon for Austin. We're all quiet as we enjoy the first bites of food. I forgot the boys' milk and probiotics, so I get up to organize it. Naturally, I pour a glass of milk for Kenny, but I'm not sure if Theo would be happy for me to add probiotics to her drink. I hold up the container, catching his eye.

"You happy for me to add probiotics to Kenny's milk? My boys have it every day for gut health."

He shrugs. "Sure. I'll get some for Kenny at home if you think it's worthwhile."

I love that he didn't question my use of probiotics. It caused several arguments with Preston. I wanted him to have some at his house for when the boys visited, but he flat-out refused; said it was a waste of money. Just another way big companies are ripping off unsuspecting people. I gave up after a while. I figured they're with me most of the time. It didn't matter if they missed a day. Now they don't miss any days, because they don't spend the night with their dad anymore. My heart cracks at the thought. He's their trucking dad. He *should* want to spend as much time as possible with his sons regardless of our relationship. But he discarded me first and now he's slowly distancing himself from them. There'll come a time when they won't be bothered with their father because he couldn't be bothered with them. He'll be sorry when that day comes.

I return to the table with the kids' milk. "Here you go, guys. Drink up."

"Thank you, Emma," Kenny says before taking a huge drink.

"Thanks, Mommy," Austin and Lachlan say at the same time.

Nodding, I resume eating, feeling agitated at the thought of Preston neglecting his sons. Theo nudges my foot underneath the table, lifting his chin in a silent question. I sigh, nodding that I'm okay. I can't talk about it in front of the boys, anyway. I'm trying my best not to make a big deal about the change in their routine, even though my heart's quietly breaking on their behalf.

# CHAPTER 33

## —emma—

"So, what are our plans for the rest of today?" Theo asks, a bright tone to his voice.

Looking out of the window to my backyard, I note how long the grass has become. "I'll have to cut the grass today. I'll try to do it this morning before it gets too hot. Maybe we could head to the beach later? What do you think, boys?"

"I love the beach. Can we go too, Uncle Theo?" Kenny asks, eyes full of hope.

Theo looks at me. "Would you mind if we tagged along?"

I look at my boys with raised brows, waiting for them to make the decision. "Yeah, that'd be fun! I love the beach. I make the best sandcastles." Austin informs Kenny proudly.

Agreeing on a beach outing for the afternoon, we all work together to clean up from breakfast. Theo heads home with Kenny and I move upstairs to change into my gardening clothes. I realize I've been sitting opposite Theo without a bra on. Oops! I've never been able to sleep wearing a bra; these days, I'm battling to even wear one during the day. The wires are becoming painful along the side of my boob and causing a swollen lump. Maybe I need to get fitted properly for some new bras? I might see if Mom can look after the boys for me one afternoon, so I can go shopping.

My phone lights up with a message from my sister.

SARAH

Max and I are taking Mom and Dad to the beach this afternoon. Want to bring the boys?

ME

I'm already going to the beach this afternoon

SARAH

Awesome. Meet you there

I waffle back and forth for a few seconds. The sound of a lawnmower starting reminds me I have stuff to do before I can relax for the afternoon at the beach.

ME

We're going with Theo and Kenny

My phone rings immediately, my sister's face filling the screen. I press the button to accept the call to be greeted by my sister's shrill voice, "Oh my gawd! Is it like a date? Are you dating him now? Are you guys a couple? What's going on? Tell me everything."

I laugh at her barrage of questions. I haven't told her about the afternoon-slash-night we spent together. We usually talk about that sort of stuff, but … I don't know … it felt too special to share with anyone. I wanted to keep it sacred.

"We're just neighbors who spend some time together occasionally." I can't believe I just lied to my sister. We've done something with Theo and Kenny every day so far this vacation. It feels very much like we're a family. The noise of the lawnmower grows louder. Stepping over to my window, I investigate.

"Don't lie to me. Something's going on! Anyway, I can wait for this afternoon. I'll make my own judgment about the state—"

"Hey, I gotta go. I'll message you the time and place to meet." I press the end call button without waiting for a reply and race downstairs.

Bursting onto my back deck, which is a stark contrast to Theo's gorgeously appointed deck, I wave my arms in the air to gain Theo's attention. It doesn't work, so I quickly move toward him, stopping in front of his path, hands on hips.

He smiles at me, turns off the machine, then removes his ear protection. "Hey, Peaches." Leaning forward, he tries to kiss me, but I pull back quickly. Crinkles form across his forehead as he tilts his head to the side. "What's up?"

"What are you doing?" I'm fuming that he doesn't think I'm capable of maintaining my property. Helping out with the carpentry stuff, I can deal with, that's out of my wheelhouse, but this … *this* I can do.

He looks down at the lawnmower as if it's obvious. "I'm cutting your grass."

"I can see that. Why are you cutting my grass?"

He shrugs carelessly. "To help you out?" He poses it more as a question. The furrow between his brows and narrowed eyes suggests he's not sure.

"I can cut my grass. I'm more than capable of starting my mower and getting the job done. I've been doing it for the last … I don't know how many years." I used to cut the grass even when I was married to Preston. He didn't like getting dirty and sweaty from working in the garden.

He rests his hands on his hips. "I know you're more than capable of doing the job, but you don't have to anymore. I'll do it for you."

I know he's trying to be sweet and all, but I just can't let myself start relying on him for stuff like this. I sigh and drop my hands down by my side. "Thank you. It's really sweet and kind of you to offer, but I don't want to impose on you." I gesture to my house. "You've already done so much to help with the repairs and extra carpentry work. Which I really appreciate." I rush to add. "But I can't accept this. Cutting my grass is something I'm able to do myself. Please leave it. I was just coming down to do it when my sister called."

He takes a long moment to study my face. Nodding to himself, he steps out from behind the lawnmower. Cupping the side of my face, his bright blue eyes lock with mine. "I get that you're independent. I love that about you, I do. I get the feeling that you've had to do a lot of stuff yourself, even when you were married. No more." I open my mouth to interrupt, but he presses his thumb over my lips, shaking his head. "I know that we're in this era where men and women are equal and gender shouldn't define our roles. In saying that, I was brought up in a household where my dad took care of all this stuff. He looked after my mom and treated her like a princess." He shrugs, giving me a half-smile. "I don't know another way to be. Let me do this for you. Please?"

The fight falls away from me, my shoulders dropping in defeat. How can I say no when he puts it like that? Before I can get the words out, I nod my head in compliance. His entire face lights up with joy, and I don't understand why he's so happy to take on the task of cutting my grass. I get the feeling it's a whole lot more than just cutting the grass for me. "Okay. On one condition."

He presses his lips to mine briefly. "What's that?"

"You have to let me do something for you in return." His eyebrows almost shoot to his hairline as his lips widen, causing the crinkles around his eyes to deepen.

"What would you do for me in return?" There's a certain twinkle in his eye that warns me I'm going to get myself into a sticky situation here, but do you think I take heed? Nope.

"Any favor you want me to do that will make your life better." His smile widens considerably at my offer.

"Anything?"

My brows furrow. I sense a trap here. Narrowing my eyes, I reply slowly, "Yeah, I guess."

"Great, I have the perfect thing." He kisses me swiftly and replaces his earmuffs, starting the lawnmower.

I tap his shoulder. "What do you want me to do?" I shout over the noisy machine.

"I'll tell ya later." He winks at me, then continues to cut my grass.

# CHAPTER 34

## —emma—

THE BEACH IS PACKED, WHICH ISN'T A SURPRISE FOR THE INDEPENDENCE Day long weekend. I'm actually dreading Theo seeing me in my bathing suit compared to Sarah in hers. She's curvy like Mom and me, but her body hasn't been changed by carrying babies. I'm not even thinking about Mona in a bikini; hopefully, she won't want to come. Thank goodness for my coverup—I probably won't be brave enough to take it off. Theo looks delicious in board shorts and a T-shirt with a baseball cap. It doesn't matter what he wears, he always looks amazing.

We unload everything from the car and begin the trek toward the sand, keeping an eye out for my family. Theo didn't even balk a little bit at spending the afternoon with my entire family. I feel awkward having him spend time with them when I don't really know what we are yet.

Mom and Sarah are waving at us like crazy people from their prime spot. They have several umbrellas providing shade, coolers, beach chairs, and brightly colored towels delineating our space. I point in their direction. "There they are."

Theo looks across, a huff of a laugh escaping him. "They look happy to see you guys."

"I think it's more like they're happy to see you. Please ignore any and all matchmaking that will ensue from my mother and any innuendo which will inevitably come from my sister." My palms are sweating and it's not from the heat. I'm nervous as all get out.

He wraps his arm around my neck, pulling me into his body before kissing the top of my head. My eyes snap toward my family, catching them mid-gasp. Oh no! This isn't good. I try to extricate myself from Theo's hold, only to have him pull me in so tight, I almost lose my balance. "I'm sure it'll be fine. Stop worrying so much. They'll love me. I promise."

*That's not what I'm worried about.*

Austin runs toward Max, while Kenny makes her way to Sarah. They got along so well on our shopping excursion, then I think they fell a little in love with each other the day of the Daddy-Daughter dance. Dad steps forward, taking my beach bag off of my shoulder, while Mom moves in to hug me.

"Oh, it's so wonderful to see you and the boys enjoying a day at the beach with your new *friends*." The emphasis she places on the word 'friends' is excessive. Even for her. I feel the need to speak to her privately, so she doesn't scare Theo away. "Are you going to introduce us?"

"Sure, Mom. Would it be okay if we put our stuff down first?" I barely manage to suppress my eye roll.

She waves off my suggestion with a laugh. "Oh, silly me. Of course." She then proceeds to step across to Theo, thrusting her hand forward as she introduces herself. "Hi, it's so lovely to meet Emma's new friends. I'm Sally and this is John." She gestures back to Dad. "We're Emma's parents and Lachlan and Austin's grandparents." I can't stop my eyes from rolling this time. She half turns, pointing at everyone else. "This is our son, Max, and his girlfriend, Mona." Great. Theo's not even gonna look at me twice with her here as well as Sarah in a swimsuit. "And, I believe, you've already met our youngest daughter, Sarah."

Theo takes her hand. "Nice to meet you, Ma'am."

Mom interrupts. "Oh, please … call me Sally." She places her hand on her chest and giggles. Oh my God! Sometimes, she's too much.

He nods. "Okay, Sally. Nice to meet you. I'm Theo, Em's neighbor." He gestures across to Kenny, who's digging around in our things for her sand bucket and spade. "That's Kenny. My niece."

"Oh, she's such a gorgeous little thing."

Theo shakes Dad's hand as Max steps forward to greet Theo. The scowl on Theo's face as he greets my brother sends alarm bells ringing in the back of my head. Mona totters over with a full face of makeup in a barely there yellow polka dot bikini, which looks amazing with her platinum hair, and high-heel sandals. Really? High heels at the freaking beach. Who does that? I catch Sarah's eye and I know we're thinking the exact same thing. I almost can't suppress the giggle rising in my throat until I see her lick her lips as she looks at my man. Woah! Hang on a minute. He's *not* my man.

"Hey, Theo." Mona almost pushes my brother out of the way in her bid to get in front of Theo. "Nice to meet you," her words trickle out like honey as she touches his forearm.

In. Front. Of. My. Brother.

Theo steps back and to the side, reaching out for my waist, and pulling me in close to him.

"Nice to meet everyone. Thanks for letting Kenny and I tag along this afternoon." He tips his head to the other side of the area. "We'd better get set up, Peaches."

Everyone's head snaps in my direction, causing my body to heat— not from the sun either. I wonder if he realizes what he just did.

In. Front. Of. My. Family.

No less.

We move to get ourselves organized; Theo seemingly oblivious to the stir he's caused. First, the way he held me on the way from his truck to the beach, and now, holding me while using his nickname for me. Which I love, by the way. Mona looks slightly put out while Max is busy entertaining the three kids with his juggling skills, eliciting giggles from them.

"Mommy, can we go in the water now?"

"Sure thing, Austin. Let me check if Lachlan's ready."

# CHAPTER 35

## —theo—

EM'S BOYS ARE READY TO HIT THE WATER, SO I PUT KENNY'S WATER wings on. I'm surprised to find Lachlan seems quite relaxed at the beach, even though there's quite a crowd. Emma said he enjoys the beach—the sand and water calm him.

Holding Kenny's hand, we wait for Em to take off her coverup wrap. As she loosens the tie on the side, I catch a glimpse of a red halter strap. Her hair's tied up in some sort of knot all women seem to be able to do, making her neck appear longer. I just want to nuzzle my face in the crook of it and mark her with my beard. She pulls the rest of the fabric away from her body, revealing the sexiest damn bikini I've ever seen. I almost pass out as all the blood in my body rushes to my dick. *Shit!* I don't need a raging boner in front of her family.

"Have you got a T-shirt or something you can put on?" I snap as I gesture to her body. I don't want every asshole here to see what's mine.

She looks down at herself, adjusting the top, making her boobs jiggle—and my cock pulse. *Fuck!* "Uh, no." She twists so she can check out her ass and adjusts the top of her high-waisted navy and white polka-dot bottoms so they almost meet her red halter top, which spectacularly cups her tits. I grasp my T-shirt at the back of my collar and pull it off, holding it out to Emma.

"Here, put this on."

Sarah looks at me with fire in her eyes. Then turns to her sister. "You look gorgeous in that bikini, Sis." She looks back at me. "She doesn't *need* to cover herself." Stepping closer to me, she whispers, "Asshole."

Her entire family's looking at me like I'm a piece of shit, while Mona stands a little taller, pushing out her boobs as far as she possibly can in my direction. I detest sleazy women like her. It's then I realize how my words came out and how it must look that I offered her my T-shirt.

*Fuck!*

I've done it again … and in front of my future in-laws, to boot. Putting my hands up in the sign of surrender, I apologize. "I'm sorry. I didn't mean it like that. Em has a fu— … spectacular body that she should most definitely be proud of because … damn!" I gesture toward her. Her face is turning the color of a tomato, and she's trying to do something weird with her eyes. "I just don't want every other as— … man on the beach to see—"

"Theo!" Emma snaps. Her family looks between the two of us like they're at a tennis match. "Please. Stop. I don't have another coverup and I don't want to get his one wet." She gestures at the wrap she just removed. "I'm not wearing your T-shirt either. You'll just have to deal with it. There are women on this beach wearing a lot less than me." Her eyes slide toward Mona. "Come on boys, let's go." Taking each boy's hand in hers, she marches her fine ass down to the water's edge.

"Oh, this is wonderful." Emma's mom sings, holding her hands together in front of her chest, a wide smile gracing her face, which is similar to both of her daughters.

"Sally." Her husband admonishes, giving her a hard look. "Don't start."

Sarah giggles and Max looks me up and down as though he's sizing me up. *Come at me man, I'm not impressed by you.* Then I remember that I'd decided I was being a hypocrite in my dislike for him when he left Emma to cut her grass. At least he was there to help her. Emma probably reamed him out just like she did me this morning. This family seems close. I'm sure if Emma really needed something, they'd be there for her, unlike me with my sister. Sometimes I question whether or not I deserve to find happiness after what I did.

I grab Kenny's hand, gesturing over my shoulder. "I'm just gonna take Kenny for a swim." Turning, I head toward the water with my niece. Moving into the cool water until it's up to my knees, still holding Kenny's hand, I stand beside my future. "Munchkin, you can play in the water in the space between me and the beach. Okay?"

"Okay, Uncle Theo." She giggles as the wave splashes against her tummy, water droplets landing on her chubby cheeks.

Emma has her back to me, watching her boys who are out a little deeper. I move closer to her, still keeping my eyes on my munchkin. "I'm sorry, Em. I didn't mean it like that. You look so fucking sexy in that bikini. I got hard the instant you took off your coverup." Her head snaps to me as her mouth drops open. She looks down at my groin. "Don't look at me like that. I've just gotten myself back under control." I wrap one arm around the front of her and step in closer, so our bodies are touching. Kissing the top of her head, with my eyes fixed on Kenny, I whisper, "I need to have you under me again, Peaches."

"Uncle Theo, look at me!" Kenny calls out, interrupting our moment. Emma looks down, taking her chameleon eyes away from me.

"I'm watching, Munchkin. Show me your stuff."

She pushes off into the water, her hands out in front of her, kicking her feet. She holds her face under the water as she moves through the water a short distance. I hold my body still, trusting her to come up for air as she needs, but I'm ready to pounce if she takes too long. She pops back up, standing up in the shallow water, brushing her hair and excess water away from her face—a huge smile raising her cheeks.

"Did you see me? Did ya?" She points back to where she started. "I swimmed all that way."

"I saw you. Your kicks were nice and strong. Have you had lessons?"

"Nuh-uh." She stands tall, hands on her hips.

I widen my eyes in shocked surprise. "No kidding. Are you a mermaid?"

"Oh, Uncle Theo. You're so funny. Of course not." She gives me a look that telegraphs what an idiot I am, causing Emma to chuckle at my side. The boys come around in front of me, so they can play with Kenny in the water, allowing Emma and me to face the same direction back toward the beach.

The kids play as Emma and I stand side by side, holding hands. Being with her like this reinforces for me this is what I want. I need to have her and the boys with Kenny and me; living as one family.

*—emma—*

"Why aren't there any sexy bras for women with a fuller bust like us?"

Sarah sighs. "I know, right? It's so unfair." She holds out a gorgeous filmy lace bra with no underwires. "How cute is this one?"

Feeling the gorgeous soft lace between my fingers, I sigh. Fabric this delicate can't support boobs our size. My boobs seem to have grown bigger since I had the boys; they certainly sag more than they used to.

"I actually think I need to be measured properly. My boobs have changed a lot since I became pregnant and then breastfed the boys." I look down at the girls. "I think that's why I'm having so much trouble with my bras lately."

"Well, let's get you measured." She drags me over to the sales consultant. "Excuse me. Hello …" She looks at the assistant's name badge. "Dawn. Are you able to measure my sister for a bra today?"

Dawn smiles at us. "Sure. I'd be happy to help you out today." She looks at me. "When were you last fitted for a bra properly?"

"Hi, Dawn. Thank you." I stop, trying to remember. "Some time before I fell pregnant the first time. Hmmm … maybe nine, ten years ago." I can't believe it's been that long.

"Well, you're definitely due to be measured and properly fitted. We recommend getting it done every twelve months."

Sarah and I both gasp. "I had no idea we were supposed to do it so frequently." I'm shocked. I look down at my girls and silently apologize for my neglect.

"Not many people do. Did you know your bra size can change five times in your lifetime? So it's a good idea to do this." She gestures toward the back of the store. "If you would like to follow me, we can get started."

"I know we're here for you, but would you mind if I got measured, too?" Sarah whispers.

"Of course not. It's not just about me." I nudge her with my elbow. "Let's hope we can get something at least a little sexy."

She winks at me. "Trying to impress your new sexy neighbor? You *do* realize I'm not buying it that nothing's happened. The way he was always touching you at the beach. The way he wanted to cover you up so nobody else could see you in your bikini. I'm thinking he's your boyfriend!"

I swallow hard. "He's not my boyfriend. He's just affectionate, that's all."

She sniffs the air. "I smell bullshit!"

Dawn pulls back the curtain to the dressing room. "Please remove your top, leave your bra on, and let me know when you're ready for me."

I nod as she slides the curtain closed. Removing my top quickly, I adjust my bra, tie my hair up out of the way, and let her know I'm ready. She efficiently measures underneath my boobs, then across the fullest part of my breasts.

"Okay, so what size bra are you wearing today, if I may ask?"

"Uhm, I think it's a 32E. But it's been digging in here." I show her the area that's been causing me grief. "It's uncomfortable and a little painful, to be honest."

She runs her fingers gently over the area. As her brows furrow, she asks, "Have you been to see your doctor about this? I don't think this lump has been caused by your bra."

"Really? What do you think it could be?" I run my fingers over the painful area.

Her eyes widen. "Look, I just work in a lingerie store. I'm not a medical practitioner, so I really couldn't say. I'd just suggest you get yourself checked out."

"Oh, okay." I shrug.

"Right, so you said you're currently wearing size 32E. My measurements today indicate you need a 34F."

I'm shocked. "Really? No wonder my bras are feeling so uncomfortable. Do you even have anything remotely pretty or sexy in that size?"

Her face lights up, and a smile grows. "We sure do. When you're dressed, come out to me. I'll show you where we keep bras for women with fuller busts like yourself."

"Thanks. Maybe you can measure Sarah while I take a look."

Dawn directs me over to the section I need to look at, then heads back to the dressing room to measure Sarah.

As I'm looking through the bras on offer, my phone buzzes in my purse. The boys are at Mom and Dad's for the weekend. That's why Sarah and I thought we'd use the opportunity to do some shopping and have some girl time. I hope there's nothing wrong. When I pull it out of my purse, I'm surprised to find it's a message from Theo.

THEO

Kenny's staying at Dad's tonight

My heart thunders in my chest. Does this mean what I think it means? Another message comes through.

THEO

I hope you're ready for me, Peaches

Oh my gosh, I'm so ready. My thighs automatically press together at the thought of what he's going to do to me and my face heats.

"Nothing's going on my ass!" Sarah whisper-yells in my ear.

I jump, almost dropping my phone. I turn on my sister. "You scared the crap outta me. Don't sneak up on me like that."

"I wasn't sneaking up on you. You were so absorbed in your phone, you didn't hear me." My phone vibrates again and Sarah sees the message before I can hide it.

THEO

I still remember how your tight pussy felt wrapped around my dick

Sarah looks up at me with wide eyes, covering her mouth to hold back her laugh. "You've already slept with him! I *knew* it." She hits my arm with the back of her hand. "You lying liar!" Her smile fills her entire face. "Now spill."

I glance around the store. "Not here. Let's get our new bras and we'll go for coffee. I'll tell you some of it. I'm not sharing all the details. It's too personal."

Her eyes go soft and a dreamy look crosses her face. "You really like him. Don't you?"

"Come on. Look at these pretty bras. I don't want to be here all day."

"I bet you don't. You have a hot, sexy guy to get home to." She nudges me with a smirk as if she knows all of my secrets.

We both select a few bras to try on. I can't believe how much better they fit or how much more comfortable they feel. I wish I could afford to buy more than one. Maybe in a few months, I'll be able to buy another one.

# CHAPTER 37

## —emma—

My stomach's in knots and I'm a little light-headed from my nerves. It's not like I haven't already been naked in front of Theo before, but for some reason, I'm feeling incredibly self-conscious. Maybe it was the spontaneity of last time, whereas this time I *know* where tonight will lead. The butterflies in my stomach are going crazy as I shave the areas that need shaving and scrub every inch of my body until I'm smooth from head to toe. Drying and styling my hair, I moisturize everywhere, remembering how it felt when Theo ran his hands and mouth over every available inch of my skin. Goosebumps break out and I shiver at the memory.

My phone buzzes on the bedside table, breaking me from the memory. What is wrong with me? I'm about to see him. I don't need to get caught up in memories.

THEO

Are you ready for me, Peaches?

Before I can think to answer, there's a loud knock at my front door. I glance down at myself, only dressed in the brand-new bra and panty set I bought today. I quickly grab my wrap dress and put it on as I make my way downstairs. Knotting the ties, I pull my hair out of the back of my dress as I answer the door. Freezing in place, my eyes lock on a delectable-looking Theo in dark jeans and a dark blue button-up shirt that accentuates his muscular build. His stunning blue eyes light up when he sees me, while a gorgeous smile causes crinkles to form at the corners. His straight white teeth framed by his kissable lips and perfectly groomed beard set me alight. I remember how those bristles felt as he kissed his way up my body, purposely scraping them across my breasts to mark me.

"Oh, Peaches. You're trying to kill me," he breathes.

Stepping into me, he wraps one hand around my waist, the other cupping my head under the fall of my hair. His eyes track leisurely around my face before he leans in slowly to plant a chaste kiss on my lips. Try telling my body it's chaste, though. My heart's beating like crazy in response to his proximity. His hard body pressed against mine. His breaths touching my face. His woodsy scent surrounding me.

Leaning forward, I return the kiss, sliding my tongue across the seam of his mouth. He moans and opens for me. Our tongues reacquaint as he drags me impossibly closer. The heat of his body seeps through his clothes and mine, reminding me how intense this man is. Tugging my hair, he pulls back.

"I promised to feed you tonight. If we stay here like this, I can't promise we'll ever leave." Pressing his forehead to mine, he gives me a sheepish smile. Breathless, I nod in agreement because I'm so close to canceling our dinner plans and staying in.

"Let me finish getting ready. I'll be back down in ten." As I pull away, I press my fingers to my swollen lips. He smacks my ass when we're side by side, making me jump slightly.

Racing upstairs, I slick on a couple of coats of mascara and a touch of lip gloss, slide on my espadrilles and wrap the laces around my calves. Sucking in some deep breaths to settle my nerves, I grab my purse and head back downstairs toward the man who sets my heart racing.

He watches me from the bottom of the stairs. Our eyes connect and lock as I make my way down. He takes three steps at a time to meet me halfway.

"You look so fucking beautiful." His mouth smashes down on mine with a hunger I've come to expect from him. He's so very intense and it really comes out during these moments. His kisses take my breath away and make my mind go blank. Which is saying something because my mind is always filled with a million different things. I could get lost in his kisses for days on end and not come up for air. His hand slides down my arm, his fingers linking through mine as he pulls away from me. "Come on. I need to get you out of this house, so we can eat, then I can get you out of that dress."

I giggle. Like, actually giggle. As though I'm a high school girl getting chatted up by the hottest boy in school. I don't even know myself right now.

The sun sits low on the horizon as we make our way to the restaurant. The cab of the truck is filled with classic 80s tunes on low, along with the sexual tension hanging over us from the kisses we've already shared. We're quiet, both of us lost in our thoughts. I fold my hands together tightly in my lap to stop fidgeting with the edge of the light blue and polka dot fabric of my dress. Theo's strong hand lands on top of them, giving a squeeze that feels a lot like reassurance. He must have sensed my nervousness about tonight. I'm not surprised I've given away my anxiety with the way I've been fidgeting and squirming in my seat.

Theo parks behind a stunning restaurant, which is all stone and glass overlooking the beach. It's going to be spectacular to watch the sunset from this location.

"This place is gorgeous and I know it's booked out months in advance. How did you manage to get us a table at such short notice?"

He squeezes my hand as he smiles at me. "Dad's friend owns this place. They're always swapping favors." He winks as we make our way inside. Timber floors and uninterrupted views of the ocean greet us. The atmosphere is serene, the decor relaxed. A host politely greets us at the door, then seemingly glides between the tables, leading us to a setting at the far end of the large outdoor balcony area. Fairy lights wrap around the pillars and candles adorn the tables covered in white linen. The whole environment feels extraordinarily romantic and I wonder if, deep down, Theo is a romantic at heart.

"This is beautiful. Thank you for going to so much trouble." I don't want to forget to thank him for tonight, so I figure I may as well do it now.

"You're welcome. I wanted to take advantage of this opportunity to spoil you since our time without kids is limited." He pours water into my glass and his before setting the bottle back on the table. We spend a couple of minutes looking over the menu. A waiter takes our order, then leaves us alone. The warm breeze from the ocean caresses my skin and blows my hair. Theo leans forward, tucking a lock of hair behind my ear, his knuckles gliding down the side of my neck to my collarbone.

"How was your shopping excursion with your sister?"

I can't, nor do I want to hold back my smile as I remember my sister peppering me for information about Theo. "It was great. We don't get a lot of opportunities to hang out like that, so it was nice."

"I'm happy to hear you had a good time together." He gets a wistful look on his face, his eyes going slightly dull, and I get the feeling he's thinking about his own sister.

The waiter returns, filling our glasses with wine, and we both take a sip of the fruity beverage.

"What was your sister like?" I ask quietly, hoping I haven't crossed a line. He doesn't talk about her much, but he must have some good memories of her.

His eyes slowly make their way up to mine, returning to the bright blue that I love. "She was a lot like Kenny. Bubbly, friendly; always happy." His lips leisurely tip up in a smile. "I was telling Kenny a while ago about how scared she was of worms." He goes on to tell me about the prank he pulled on her when they were young, and I can't help the giggle that bubbles up. I can imagine a young Theo diligently collecting worms to use in his despicable plan to terrify his sister. "She always loved to help out in the kitchen. When we were small, she was always keen to help Dad cook. Then, as she grew older, she would help out in the restaurant. After high school, she went on to college to learn everything she could to help Dad in the restaurant. It was always going to be her thing." He takes a sip of his wine. "She loved feeding people. She loved that good food brought people together."

Reaching across, I take his hand in mine to squeeze it in comfort. I haven't asked how she died and he hasn't been forthcoming in telling me, so I leave it be. I imagine it's a difficult topic for him. "Do you mind if I ask a personal question, which is absolutely none of my business?"

"Sure. Go ahead."

I take a sip of wine just as the waiter brings our meals out. Both dishes look and smell divine. We're both quiet for a moment as we begin our meal. A rack of lamb for Theo along with puréed potatoes, char-grilled peaches, and a red wine jus. My grilled halloumi, chicken, and pear salad is a taste sensation with a pomegranate and honey dressing, and candied hazelnuts.

Theo swallows a bite of food. "What were you going to ask?"

I chew slowly, formulating the question in my head. "I was going to ask about Kenny's father. Why he's not involved in her life?" I rush to add. "But if it's too personal, I completely understand."

Wiping his mouth slowly, he places the napkin neatly next to his plate. "That's okay. It's a reasonable question given the situation. Anna felt she was running out of time to meet and fall in love with someone, but she desperately wanted to have a baby of her own." I nod. I can understand that feeling. "She actually, uh, she went through an agency and used donated sperm to fall pregnant. We don't know who Kenny's dad is. The agency assures their sperm donors the utmost discretion, so the women can never find out who they are."

My eyebrows must almost hit my hairline. "Wow. Good for her. Knowing what she wanted and going after it the way she did. I'm so impressed."

He nods. "She was determined to become a mom. By all accounts, she was a great mom, too." He sucks in a sharp breath. I need to direct the conversation to happier things.

"Do you remember the day we first met?"

His eyes widen at my change in topic. "Yeah. I do." He nods slowly. "I thought I'd lost my niece after only six hours of having her in my care."

I laugh. "We heard you running down the side of your house looking for her. The little character that she is wanted to hide from you in my backyard so you wouldn't find her."

His eyes widen comically. "She what?"

I can't stop the laugh that's bubbling up, so I don't even try. He shakes his head, a smile forming on his kissable lips. Pointing to the side of his head, he says, "See these?" I spot a couple of gray hairs at his temple, making me laugh harder. "I didn't have any of those until I started looking after my niece." He looks quite affronted at this recent development.

"Well, I think they make you look even sexier than you already do." I snap my mouth shut, realizing what I've said. I mean, I'm sure he knows he's sexy. He doesn't need to hear it from me.

One eyebrow rises as a ghost of a smile touches his lips. "You think I'm sexy?"

I wave away his question. "You know you are. You don't need me to tell you."

"It's always nice to hear it coming from your partner." *Partner?* Is that what we are?

"How about I show you how sexy I think you are later?" I wipe my sweaty palms on my dress. I don't even know who I am right now. This woman that offers such a thing to a man she doesn't know all that well is not me.

Theo moves forward in his chair, resting his elbows on the table, deleting the space between us. Excitement glistens in his eyes as he licks his lips. "Yeah?"

May as well go with this new me, so I lean forward, licking my tongue across the seam of his lips. Locking eyes, I whisper, "Yeah."

As quick as a flash, he pushes his chair back. Standing, he offers me his hand and I can't miss the unmistakable bulge at the front of his jeans. I stand and follow him to the cashier, where he pays quickly for our meals. Then he's on the move again. I almost have to run to keep up with him.

Giggling, I question, "Slow down. What's the hurry?"

He stops dead in his tracks; so fast that I almost run into the back of him. His hand goes to the back of my head, his body crashing into mine as his mouth slams down onto my lips. Nipping my bottom lip gently, he encourages me to open for him, which I eagerly do. I don't think there'll come a time when I won't want to kiss him. His kisses embolden me, empowering me to embrace my sexuality, my desires, my needs. He makes me feel sexy in this body of mine. Our kiss is hot, passionate, and all-consuming and I don't remember ever feeling so wanted.

Theo pulls away, grabbing my hand as he continues toward his truck. Even though he's clearly in a hurry, he still takes the time to open my door and help me up. Silence descends as Theo drives us home. One hand on the wheel, one resting on my thigh. The heat from his palm burning a brand onto my skin. I watch his forearm tense and move with each turn of the wheel.

What is it about masculine forearms that's such a turn-on?

The thick sexual tension building in the car has me rubbing my thighs together in a useless attempt to ease the throbbing at their apex.

# CHAPTER 38

## —emma—

I startle as we pull to a stop. Looking out of the windscreen, I'm surprised to find we're already home. Theo jumps down from the truck, moving swiftly around the front to open my door. I have my seatbelt off, ready to hop out—I'm so primed for what's about to happen. He almost drags me out of my seat, then presses me against the side of his truck with his hard body. I can't miss the erection trapped behind the zipper of his jeans as he presses his groin against my soft stomach.

A car races down the street and a group of young guys call out of the window, "Yeah, give it to her!" Breaking our moment. Forehead to forehead, we both groan at the interruption.

"Your place or mine?" Theo pants against my lips.

"We can go to mi—"

Locking his truck before I can finish my sentence, he almost drags me to my front door. Fumbling with the key, I manage to unlock the door and we fall inside as Theo grabs my ass. "I love your ass. I love the way it moves when I fuck you from behind."

My pussy clenches at his words. Moisture coats my pussy lips as butterflies take flight in my stomach the closer we get to my bedroom. Giggling as we trip up the stairs, I manage to get a couple of shirt buttons undone, one pinging on the timber stairs as it tears away from the fabric. I'll have to find it in the morning.

Crossing the threshold into my bedroom, we both move into action to remove each other's clothes. Another shirt button pings on the timber floor as Theo manages to untie the knot at my waist. My flesh pebbles as the air touches it, my nipples pressing against the delicate lacy fabric cupping them. My hands fly to Theo's belt and I fumble in my rush to get it undone; snapping a fingernail in the process. He pulls back out of my reach, his rough fingers gliding underneath the fabric still clutching my shoulders. I suck in my stomach the best I can. At least when I'm laying down, it looks somewhat flat.

"Don't do that. I told you there's no room for negative thoughts about your body between us. I love every single inch of you." I wonder if he realizes what he just said. I'm sure he didn't mean love as in 'love', but it's such a powerful word. Oblivious to my thoughts, he pulls the two sides of my dress apart. Slowly, he slides the flimsy fabric down my arms—his eyes full of appreciation for what he can now see. His gaze, like blue flames licking my body, sets me on fire; making me feel sexy.

He brushes his fingers delicately over a pebbled nipple. Reverently. Worshipfully. Bending forward slightly, he breathes over the point before landing a gentle kiss. Thrusting my breasts forward, I grip his shoulder for support. He's barely touched me, but he makes my knees weak, my heart race, and my breaths short.

"So fucking beautiful, Em." His eyes glance up at me, then focus back on my breasts. He gives my other breast the same treatment, then cups one in each hand, squeezing them firmly. Gathering my wits, I continue my quest to undo his jeans. Palming his dick on the outside of the stiff fabric, he groans into my cleavage. "You make me so fucking hard."

I moan at his words. If he were to slide his hand inside my panties, he would know how wet he makes me with his words and his kisses. As if hearing my thoughts, he drops to his knees in front of me. Running his nose along the outside of my new panties, which I'm certain are soaked, he follows the path with his fingers, then smiles up at me, one eyebrow raised. "Are you as ready as I am?"

I can only nod in answer, too far gone to form coherent words.

He nuzzles his nose back and forth across my covered clit, whispering, "Give me the words I need." His hot breaths heat the tops of my thighs. So caught up in not collapsing at the knees, I don't realize he's waiting for an answer until he lightly nips the same spot. "Answer me."

"I'm ready. Promise." I bite my lip to keep in my moan as his finger skims beneath the elastic of my panties to caress my opening.

"Oh, yeah. You're so fucking ready." His voice has developed a gravelly quality. So freaking sexy.

Sliding his fingers into the waistband, he slowly, torturously drags my underwear down my legs, tapping each calf for me to step out. Using my grip on his shoulders, I maintain my balance—just. Kneeling at my feet, he looks up, only a slim ring of blue surrounding dilated pupils as he winks. He runs his fingers tenderly up the backs of my calves, keeping his eyes on mine before widening my stance to his liking. A slow grin spreads as he moves his head closer to my thigh. Starting from my knee, he traces a path with his tongue, nipping and licking my inner thigh. Concentrating on first one, then the other, as if he has all night. I'm going to have to direct him where I want him if he doesn't put me out of my misery soon. The trembling in my legs seems to clue him into my situation, and he takes pity on me.

"Where do you want me, Peaches?" He kisses the crease between my thigh and pussy.

Sliding one hand into his hair, I gently guide his mouth where I want it most, pushing my hips forward to meet his lips. He huffs out a laugh, warm air caressing my tender lips before diving in like he didn't just eat an enormous meal. The first swipe of his tongue against my clit sends electricity shooting through my body—arcing and shimmering.

"Ooooh," I sigh on a breath. No longer able to hold my head up, I drop it back on my shoulders. Closing my eyes, I get lost in the sensation as Theo's tongue and fingers work me over. My fingers tighten their grip on his hair for purchase, my other hand squeezing his shoulder—hard. He thrusts a thick finger into my channel, and draws it out, replacing one with two, stretching me deliciously. My legs tremble with the sensations he's building as my heart pounds out a relentless beat. He presses thick fingers against my front wall as his tongue rubs and massages my clit in a beautiful rhythm. My pussy walls begin to tighten around his digits. Holding my breath, I let myself drop into oblivion, knowing Theo will catch me if I fall. My head spins and I have to remind myself to take a breath. Sucking in air, Theo's roughened hands glide up the side of my body, his heat warming my front, followed by his mouth on mine. I eagerly open for him, my taste-buds immediately assaulted by the muskiness of my cum on his tongue, and I moan into his mouth.

With tongues tangling, I get lost.

Lost in Theo.

Lost in his tenderness and attention.

It's something I'm not used to having directed at me.

Pulling back slightly, our lips still touching, he whispers, "I love making you come. Feeling your pussy tighten around me, trying to keep me inside." He punctuates his statement with a kiss as he deftly unfastens my bra. With fingers hooked into the straps, he steps back slightly to remove the lacy covering, releasing my breasts from their confinement. The temptation to cover them, to hide the stretch marks from his eyes is overwhelming; to support them so they don't droop quite so low. But Theo beats me to it. He drops my bra to the floor and immediately cups both breasts in his large, work-roughened hands.

He groans while I moan at the contact. I love having his hands on me, but it's more than that. It's the blatant desire that pours out of him for me, making me feel sexy. It's been a long time since anyone's made me feel even slightly desirable. Preston certainly made me feel extraordinarily self-conscious about my more pronounced curves since having the boys. Theo can't seem to get enough of my curvy shape. His hands and mouth are constantly in contact with my body at every opportunity. His appreciation is evident in his arousal, in his kisses, his touches.

He makes me feel more confident in my skin—it's a gift I'll cherish forever.

He still has too many clothes on. I shuck his shirt from his shoulders, tracing my hands down his biceps to his defined forearms as I slide the fabric away to reveal taut abs. I remember the first day I saw them; never in my wildest dreams did I ever think I'd have the opportunity to touch them like this.

Touch *him* like this.

To be able to trace each indent with my fingers. My desire to touch him is overwhelming, so I decide to follow my fingers with my tongue as I trace each defined muscle. His muscles quiver as his fingers slide into my hair, cupping my head.

So hard. So defined. He could easily be a fitness model.

Working my way down his body, I pay special attention to the top of those gorgeous v-lines that make women go stupid. I'm careful not to catch the head of his dick poking out the top of his boxer briefs as I undo his button and zipper. Pushing his jeans below his ass, I pull down his underwear just enough to get my hands and mouth on his penis. The upward curve and swollen head, sporting a bead of pre-cum greet me. Reversing our positions, I lower myself to my knees so I can return the favor, only he catches me under my arms, brushing the tender area at the side of my breast.

"As much as I appreciate the gesture, I want tonight to be about you. You give so much of yourself to your kids, to Kenny, and to me.

Let me spoil you the way you deserve." His words stop me in my tracks, and I take a moment to think. Looking at his face, I can see the sincerity of his words. He's serious about his offer, but I don't want this to be a one-sided experience.

I need him to hear what I'm about to say, so I make sure to hold his eyes with my own. "What would you say if I said I wanted to do this? That I get as much out of doing this for you as you get out of it?"

He swallows … hard, his eyes molten. He's studying me closely. Finally, he must see what he needs as he slowly nods, lowering me back to my knees. "I would say, knock yourself out. But I don't want to come in your mouth this time. Maybe another time, but not tonight. You okay with that?"

I nod and move forward, licking the moisture from the swollen head, making sure to run my tongue across the slit. Theo groans, tangling his fingers in my hair, pushing it away from my face. Looking up from this position, his sculpted body is the perfect landscape. We lock eyes as I lave his erection with my tongue, following with a firm squeeze around the base of his shaft in my fist. His jaw tenses, the veins in his neck becoming more pronounced as he moans. His hand tightens in my hair as he begins to thrust gently into my mouth. Using me for his pleasure. It feels powerful to be the one to make this man lose his control, but it's not enough. He's holding back, being too gentle with me. I *want* to feel him let go. This man who holds onto his control needs to let go occasionally. I slide my mouth off of him, waiting until I have his full attention. "Stop holding back."

He nods, and I return to my ministrations. Holding the base of his shaft with one hand, cupping his balls with the other, I get back to the task at hand—to make him lose control. With both hands, he grips my hair, guiding me to do his bidding. His thrusts come harder, deeper, and I relish in the burn on my scalp. I concentrate on relaxing my throat as I breathe through my nose. His deep moans fill my bedroom, causing my clit to throb for attention. I rub my thighs together to stifle the pressure building.

"Touch yourself."

It's a demand, but it also permits me to let go. It permits me to fulfill my own sexual fantasy, so I follow his direction. Sliding my hand between my legs, my fingers make contact with my wet folds. I moan around his shaft as he readjusts his hold on my hair, pulling back the loose strands that have fallen across my face. I'm struggling to keep my eyes on his, caught up in the sensations of his shaft in my mouth, the pressure on my hair, and my fingers massaging my needy clit. Using his hold on my hair, he pulls my head off of his dick, then helps me up.

"C'mon, Peaches. Get off the floor and onto the bed." His voice is gravelly, full of lust.

Stroking his cock, he directs me where he wants me. Balancing at the edge of my bed on my hands and knees. I watch him over my shoulder as he lines himself up with my opening. Holding his shaft, he strokes from the base of my folds to my clit and back again. We both moan at the sensation of intimate contact. Theo stops with the head of his dick at my opening.

"Fuck!" The frustration in that single whispered word is unmistakable. "I don't have any condoms here. They're in the drawer next to my bed." He moves back slightly and I feel the loss of his contact immediately. "I don't suppose you have any?"

Shaking my head in the negative, I twist around so I can face him properly. "Look." It's difficult to admit this because it's embarrassing. I haven't even told my family or Kate. "Uh, I haven't been with anyone since my ex-husband. I had to have tests done because I found out that Preston was cheating on me. The tests came back clean." I pull my hair over my shoulder like a shield, looking down at the floor. "I, um, I can't fall pregnant because I had my tubes tied after Austin was born."

He crouches down in front of me, using the roughened pads of his fingers to guide my face back to his. His lips touch mine tenderly before he whispers, "I'm sorry you had to deal with a cheating husband, Emma. You didn't deserve that level of disrespect."

My nose tingles, my eyes well, and as many times as I blink to hold back the emotions welling at his kind words, I can't. One tear, then another falls down my cheek. I swiftly wipe them away.

*What a mood killer.*

His lips whisper across my wet cheek, kissing away my tears.

"Nobody knows. I didn't want to add insult to injury with my family and friends." I implore him with my eyes. "Please keep it to yourself."

His jaw ticks as he glances away for a second. When he turns back, his blue eyes are blazing like the combustion zone of the fire. "I won't tell anyone, Em. Your secret is safe with me," he murmurs, cupping my cheek. "His loss is definitely my gain. For the record, I'm clean too. I had tests done as a matter of routine a year or so ago. I haven't been with anyone since then."

He kisses my lips before standing. Picking me up, he situates me in the center of my bed, coming down on top of me. The front of his body makes full contact with the front of mine. The pressure of his entire weight on me feels delicious and I revel in the physical contact, the smattering of chest hair tickling my chest. Staring into my eyes, he tenderly tucks my hair behind my ear, and I close my eyes to reduce some of the intensity of the moment. Lips land on each eyelid as light as a butterfly's touch. I have to swallow back the emotions welling up inside again as he undoes me with his gentle care.

Lips land on mine, his tongue licking across my seam. We both sigh into the kiss as I open willingly, allowing our tongues to mingle. This kiss is so damn sexy. Slow, sensual strokes. He maneuvers himself between my legs, cradling his erection against my mound, his fingers finding my clit. The pressure is perfect, his strokes firm and consistent, building my desire. The head of his dick notches at my opening before he slides in, one smooth inch at a time. Stretching, filling me in the only way he can.

Eyes locked, hazel to flaming blue, he settles his full length inside of me. Groaning at the sensation, I raise my head to kiss him. I need my mouth on his. I need my tongue tangling with his as we connect in this way. We kiss; our breaths mingling, as he begins to move with slow, steady glides in and out of my body.

Hearts beating wildly against each other.

Sweat slicking our skin.

Breaths in sync.

Our bodies move as though we've been together like this a million times before.

My hands find his tight ass as I raise my hips in time with his thrusts. He slowly picks up speed and power, shunting me up the bed until my head is hitting the headboard. He brings his hand up between the top of my head and the headboard—the action melting my heart. My bedroom fills with the sounds of skin slapping against skin, our moans, my bedsprings, and the headboard banging against the wall. I can't hold back my giggle at the symphony we've created.

"Oh fuck. Your giggles feel amazing around my cock!" His breaths puff across my face as he speaks. His words trigger fireworks and I shatter. From the tips of my toes to the top of my head, my body tenses for long moments, my breath seizing in my lungs. My vision grays around the edges as I moan out my release.

Theo's dick grows and pulses inside me before he pushes in as deep as he can and then groans through his own release. His cum releases inside my body and for the first time in five years, I wish I'd never had my tubes done. We find each other's lips and resume our kiss as he slowly, incrementally, begins to move again. Our connection is incredibly intense considering this is only the second time we've been intimate like this.

After a second orgasm, we finally pull away, Theo nuzzling into my neck. "I wanna do that all night." I feel his smile against my skin before he gently nips my pulse point. Pushing up away from my body, I mourn the loss of him instantly. He kisses each of my nipples, then rolls off the bed. I really should get up and clean myself up, but my legs feel like rubber—I'm not sure they'd hold me up for the short walk to the ensuite. I hear cupboard doors open and close, followed by the faucet turning on and off again. Psyching myself up to actually move my butt, I roll to my side in time to see Theo step out of the bathroom with a washcloth.

"Where do you think you're going?" He sits on the edge of my bed. "Lay down and open up. I need to look after my pussy."

I feel the heat of my flush rise from my breasts to my cheeks at his instruction, but I lay back down and follow his request. I can't believe the lack of embarrassment I'm experiencing. Having him look at me, albeit by moonlight, should make me feel completely exposed. Surprisingly, it doesn't. The heat burning in his eyes as he looks at my most private place erases every negative thought I have about my body. He wipes me tenderly, paying attention to each crease and fold, finishing with a chaste kiss on my mound.

While he takes the cloth back to my bathroom, I pull back the covers and climb under the sheet. Theo joins me after turning the ceiling fan on. "You mind if I stay?"

To say I'm shocked that he's asking is an understatement. I assumed he would, especially after saying he wanted to have sex all night. I nod. "Of course. You're welcome to stay until I need to pick up the boys tomorrow. I can make us breakfast."

Resting his knee on the edge of the bed, he drops forward, landing on his hands, his face a mere inch from mine. The smile that lights up his face takes years off of him, providing a lightness that I rarely see. Leaning forward, he kisses the tip of my nose, then takes my lips again, before pulling back. "Perfect."

He climbs in, rolls me over, and spoons me from behind. The hair covering his thighs tickles the backs of my legs. I can't help but notice how well we fit together with him wrapped around me like this. His hands cupping my stomach and breast as if he needs to hold me to him. He nuzzles into the crook of my neck, whispering, "Night, Peaches."

"Night." I wriggle back further into his body, falling asleep quickly with a smile on my face.

# CHAPTER 39

## —emma—

BRIGHT SUNLIGHT BEAMS ACROSS MY FACE, WAKING ME SLOWLY. MY cheek's stuck to Theo's firm chest, his steady heartbeat solid and strong. His chest rises and falls with slow, deep breaths. I wonder if he's worn out? He must have woken me at least three times during the night, keeping his promise to continue our lovemaking through the darkness. Closing my eyes, my cheeks rise as I remember his fingers and mouth on me. He certainly does have talented hands as he caressed and coaxed my body from one orgasm to another. As I rub my thighs together, the tenderness from a night of passion becomes apparent. Wincing, I think I may need to soak in a warm bath this morning.

I don't want to leave my bed, but I don't want to end up with a UTI either. As I work to extricate myself from his hold, his arms tighten around my body. His leg twists around mine to lock me in place. I look up at his face to find bright blue shining back at me. He kisses my forehead. "Morning, Peaches." A gorgeous smile graces his face.

"Morning, Stud!" I pat his hard stomach as he laughs at my nickname for him. "I need to have a warm bath this morning … to, uh, soak my sore muscles."

His eyebrows shoot up and his smile drops instantly. "Did I hurt you last night?"

I shake my head. "No, it's just, well … uhm, my lady garden hasn't seen that much action for a long time. I'm a little tender. Nothing a warm bath won't fix." I pat his firm stomach again to affirm my words.

"Stay here until I come and get you." He releases me and rolls out of bed, heading straight into my bathroom. I hear the faucets turn on and water splashing in the tub. He's such a sweetheart.

Gingerly, I roll out of bed to meet Theo in the bathroom. He stands from the edge of the bath, placing the box of bath salt on the counter.

"I told you to stay in bed. I wanted to carry you into the bath." Wrapping his arm around my shoulder, he pulls me in to meet his firm body.

"Sorry. I couldn't wait to get into the bath." Kissing my forehead, he nudges me forward to sit in the warm water. As soon as my vagina touches the warm salty water, I wince at the stinging sensation.

"I'm sorry. I was too greedy and too rough last night." The creases between his brows cue me in as to how worried he is that he's hurt me.

Reaching up, I grasp his hand and squeeze. "Everything was perfect last night. Please don't do that." I tug his hand. "Come and join me in here." Scooting forward, I make room for Theo to sit behind me. He slides into the tub, his long legs running down the side of me. I lean back against his body and sigh. "This feels perfect."

*I wonder what it would be like to wake up with Theo every day.*

"Yeah, it does." We sit, enjoying the peace for a long while, neither of us wanting to break the moment. The only movement, a few ripples in the water caused by our steady breaths. This bath was one of the reasons I fell in love with this house. It's so deep, I can sit in the water all the way up to my neck.

Slowly, Theo's hands begin to trail up the side of my body, his thumbs catching under my breasts, before sliding out to the side. He freezes as his hand makes contact with the raised area caused by my old bras. "What's this?" He manipulates me, turning me sideways, so he can have a proper look.

"My old bras have been rubbing me for months. It's nothing. It should clear up now that I bought a new bra that fits properly. I had no idea I'd been wearing the wrong size."

He rubs his thumb back and forth tenderly across the area. "I don't like how this looks. You should get it checked out by the doctor."

I drop my arm down. "It's nothing. I'm not going to the doctor about this. It'll clear up."

"How do you know it's nothing? It could be something and you're being stubborn by not getting it checked out." He huffs, pushing away from me to stand. He steps out of the bath, water trailing down his body, over those gorgeous abs that I licked from top to bottom last night. He roughly snatches a towel from the rail, drying himself as though his skin is the enemy.

I sigh, pulling the plug before standing. Stepping out of the bath, I grab a towel and begin drying myself. The angry energy radiating off of Theo fills the space around us. I'm not sure why the peace we were enjoying in the bath has turned into a space filled with quiet anger. I reach forward to lay my hand on Theo to calm him, but he steps away from my touch. Dropping my hand, I turn my back to him so he can't see the hurt on my face, drying my body in silence.

Theo's footsteps fill the quiet as he leaves the bathroom. I feel discombobulated at his sudden change in demeanor. Drying my body, I wrap my towel around me as a flimsy shield. I don't feel comfortable being so exposed, so I use the fluffy fabric as my armor before stepping back into my bedroom. Theo's already dressed, sliding his phone into his back pocket, half the buttons on his shirt missing.

Looking down at his feet, he strikes the final blow. "Dad messaged. He wants me to pick up Kenny." He scrubs his fingers through his bristles. Something I've noticed he does when he's thinking or feels uncomfortable. "I've gotta go. I'll … um … see you 'round, I guess."

My head snaps back as though he physically slapped me, and he may as well have. I recognize a brush-off when I hear one. What I don't understand is why. He makes for the door, still not making eye contact with me.

"Thanks for the orgasms," I snap. "Don't let the door hit your ass on the way out." I turn back to my bathroom. I can't watch him walk away from me like this.

Before I can make it two steps, he's in front of me. Eyes blazing. The pulse point at his throat is hammering a fast staccato. He looks ready to explode. "That's all I was good for, hey? The orgasms?"

Hurt radiates from him, bouncing between us. "You're the one in a hurry to leave. Something changed. I don't know what it was, but you can't even look at me." I blink quickly, trying to keep the stinging tears building at bay.

"I need to get to Kenny."

"Something happened before that." I throw my arm out. "But go. Go get Kenny and I'll see you 'round. I guess." I step around him, closing myself in my bathroom. Resting my head against the bathroom door, I hold my breath, listening for movement. The tears that I was working to hold back drop over my lashes. "God, I'm so stupid," I whisper to no one.

# CHAPTER 40

## —theo—

I HAVEN'T SEEN EMMA SINCE I LEFT HER LOCKED IN HER BATHROOM. I *know* I acted like a dick. I *know* I wasn't being rational or fair to her, but I couldn't be around her after finding that lump. The way she shrugged it off like it's nothing. Maybe it *is* nothing, but it might be something and she just brushed it off without a second thought. In the split second that I was looking at the raised area, my mind instantly went to Mom and Anna. The memories swamped me. Overwhelmed me. The need to protect myself and Kenny from yet another loss was all-encompassing. It was all I could think about, and I went into self-preservation mode.

I couldn't be next to her.

I couldn't even look at her.

With every second I remained in her presence, fissures began to form in my heart and I had to get away.

It's been tough not seeing her every day. Watching from my window, crippled by my anxiety as she cuts her grass, plays with her boys, and generally goes about her life as though I were never part of it. Kenny still sees her each day; Emma waits at the end of my driveway while the boys collect my girl to take her to the park.

It's not only her I've missed. I've missed the boys. Particularly working with Lachlan in the workshop. He loves working with timber, creating new pieces with me, and I enjoy having him work alongside me. I'm sure he's also missing working with the timber, so I dropped off a porch table a few days ago along with the sanding block he'd need.

"Uncle Theo!" Kenny runs into my room and jumps on top of me, forcing the air out of my lungs. "It's my birthday! I'm five!" She holds up one hand proudly, fingers spread wide.

I catch her around her waist, pulling her down so I can lay a kiss on her forehead. "Happy birthday, Munchkin."

I throw her up in the air a little and catch her, reveling in her little girl squeals of delight. As she drops down, I catch her as her little foot lands a kick to my groin. I squeeze my legs together to stifle the sharp pain, while stars form around the edge of my vision. I suck in a breath, collect myself, then proceed to tickle the birthday girl. I don't want her to realize she hurt me. She would want to kiss my boo-boo better and that wouldn't be appropriate.

"Come on. Get up. You need to give me presents." She scrambles off of my bed, making a run for the door.

"Presents?" I furrow my brow, making sure I look completely confused.

She freezes in place, then turns around to me, tilting her head to the side. "Yeah. You know you're s'posed to give me presents on my birthday. Right?" My heart jumps as she finally pronounces the letter 'R'. Emma did that. She's been working incidentally with Kenny on her speech. Kenny hasn't even realized that's what they've been doing, but it's finally worked. I'm gutted that she wasn't here to hear her hard work pay off for herself.

Climbing out of bed, I smile at my niece. I rub my beard, carrying on the charade. "About that. You know how I've been really busy? I haven't had time to get to the store." Her shoulders droop. "Maybe I can get you something next week?"

She looks at me, her brows furrowed down, her bottom lip jutting out. "I s'pose that's okay." She turns, leaving my room. I sort of feel bad for playing with her, but I guess the prankster in me never actually went away. I used to play pranks on Anna all the time. Now that I have Kenny, I can carry on the tradition.

I call out to her retreating back, "Go get dressed. I have a treat planned for breakfast." I throw on some clothes, grabbing the letter I pulled out of the box last night for Kenny. Running my fingers across Anna's feminine script, my heart hammers in my chest when I think of her writing whatever's inside. Stuffing the letter in my back pocket, I compose myself, meeting my girl in her bedroom as she's looking through the clothes in her drawers.

"What should I wear?"

"Wear your favorite dress. It's a special day, so you should wear your most special dress."

"Yeah. Good idea." She races across to her closet, moving her little dresses from one side to the other. "This one! Mommy bought this one for me. It was too big before."

I help her get it down, fighting the lump in my throat. I wonder if Anna bought it for Kenny to wear for her birthday. She seems to have thought of everything else. Kenny gets dressed and I brush her hair, tying the top half of it back, just the way Emma showed me. I wonder if Emma will still bring the boys over later for the small party we planned.

*Shit!* She was going to make the birthday cake. Maybe I should pick one up while we're out. Just in case.

"C'mon, Munchkin. Let's get this birthday started!" We high-five each other as we head downstairs.

## CHAPTER 41

### —theo—

Dad's already waiting in the parking lot when we arrive at *Pancake Paradise*. Kenny spots him immediately, wriggling in her seat with excitement. "Pappoús's here, too." She says it as though it's a coincidence that he's here, making me laugh.

Dad walks over, helping Kenny out of her booster seat. "Happy birthday, Kenny-girl!" He swings her up in the air, eliciting little girl giggles from her and a grin from me. I think he sometimes forgets he's sixty-seven.

He carries her, like the little monkey she is, into the restaurant. "Oh my gosh! Look at all the different pancakes." She changes her hold to one arm, twisting her body to look at the pictures on display. "I like all of them!"

I laugh, poking her stomach. "I think your eyes may be bigger than your belly."

There are so many options on offer for kids and adults alike. Green monster pancakes, blue ghost pancakes, multi-color unicorn pancakes, pink princess pancakes—there are just too many to name. There's even a range of *Avenger*-themed pancakes on offer which Lachlan and Austin would love. "What are you going to have, Munchkin?"

"Can I please have the unicorn pancakes?" She always has such great manners.

"Absolutely. What about a drink? Would you like a chocolate milkshake?"

She holds her hands together under her chin, almost as though she can't contain her excitement. "Yes, please."

"Dad, what are you having?"

"I'll have the apple cinnamon buckwheat pancakes and a cappuccino, thanks."

I nod toward a pink booth over by the window. "You guys go take a seat and I'll place our order."

Dad and Kenny make their way over to the table while I order and pay for our breakfast. When I join them, I catch the tail end of Dad asking Kenny what I gave her for her birthday. I wink at him for playing along with my plan today.

"He was too busy to go to the store. So I didn't get any presents for my birthday." She looks at me with wide, hopeful eyes. "You'll go to the store next week, won't you, Uncle Theo?"

"I'll see. It's a bit tricky if you're with me. I can't surprise you." Her shoulders drop in disappointment. Dad rubs a hand over his mouth to hold back his smile, but I can see the creases deepen around his eyes.

She looks at Dad. "Pappoús, did you get me a present for my birthday?"

He looks at me, and I tilt my head forward in a short nod. "I do have a present for you. Once we get to your house, I'll give it to you. Okay?"

"Yay, okay!" Kenny looks at me, giving me a 'see, *he* didn't forget' look.

Our pancakes are delivered. Kenny's bowl of multi-colored dollar-sized pancakes, with marshmallows, ice cream, and strawberry drizzle is almost as big as her head. "Can you take a photo? I wanna show Austin and Lachlan later."

My heart clenches as I take out my phone to photograph her pancake masterpiece. I hope Emma and her family are still coming over this afternoon. I haven't contacted her to check, because I don't know how to come back from the way I acted the other week. Kenny sorts her tiny pancakes into groups according to color before she begins to eat them in the same order as a rainbow—because why the hell not?

"I see you still like your chocolate, Theo." Dad uses his fork to point at my chocolate-flavored pancakes drizzled with chocolate sauce along with a complement of chocolate ice cream. As if that wasn't enough chocolate, I also went with a chocolate milkshake.

"Yeah. Can't seem to kick the habit." I cut off a portion and take a substantial bite to punctuate my sentence. Maybe that's why I can't get Emma out of my head. Her silky chocolate hair reminds me of my favorite treat. Dad laughs at me, shaking his head, before going back to his 'healthy' pancakes. "How are things going at the restaurant?"

He tilts a flat hand side to side in a so-so action. "It's tough finding employees who are as invested in the restaurant as I am, as Anna was. They seem to think it's okay to do a half-job instead of putting their best foot forward."

"Yeah, I tried having a couple of employees over east. It wasn't worth the hassle. They never paid attention to the small details and gave the jobs less than one hundred percent. I'd rather work by myself."

"Pappoús, I could help you in the restaurant. I'm a good helper. I help Uncle Theo all the time, and Emma showed me how to be safe in the kitchen." Her little legs kick back and forth underneath the booth seat as she rattles off her resumé.

Dad makes a big show of thinking it over. "You know, I could really do with your help, but I'd get into trouble if I hired you."

Kenny's eyebrows drop down over her eyes, so much like her mother's. "Why?"

He reaches across the table, pinching her nose. "Because you're too little, yet. But you keep practicing your skills, so when you're the right age, you can start helping at the restaurant straight away."

"But I'm five now. I'm a big girl. I start kindergarten soon!"

"Yes, you are. But you don't want to get Pappoús into trouble, do you?"

She shakes her head quickly. "Nuh-uh."

We finish up at *Pancake Paradise* and while Dad walks back to the parking lot with Kenny, I quickly jog down the street to *Blooms and Balloons* to get some flowers to take to Mom and Anna's grave. I make sure to get peonies and gardenias, their favorites. I find the scent of the gardenias too strong, but my sister loved them.

"Dad, did you want to come in the truck with us to visit Anna and Mom, or follow in your car?"

"Do you mind stopping back here to pick it up?"

"Not at all." He nods, then climbs into the passenger side of the truck.

"I can't wait to tell Mommy all about my unicorn pancakes. They were so yummy. Then I can tell her about my new friends, Austin and Lachlan. I won't be able to tell her about kindergarten yet, because I haven't started." Kenny rambles on about all the things she's going to share with her mom. Arriving at the cemetery, I unbuckle Kenny, grab the flowers with sweaty hands and we head in the direction of Mom and Anna's final resting places, side by side.

We wander along the winding pathway beneath the shady trees as Kenny skips alongside us. She spots the large Jacaranda tree that indicates the familiar location and sprints forward; Dad and I follow behind. My sweet niece drops to her knees while I collect the vases to fill with water for the flowers. Dad and Kenny chat with Anna and Mom, but I can't bring myself to do it. I'd rather keep myself busy; so while they chat, I pull the weeds around the headstones, clean them up, and arrange the flowers.

I catch the tail end of Kenny's conversation with Anna. "Uncle Theo said he'd go to the store this week to get my birthday present, but Pappoús has something for me today. I'm so excited to open my presents. I think Emma, Austin, and Lachlan will give me a birthday present when they come over later. You know how much I love getting presents."

I smile at Dad over the top of Kenny's head, which he returns. "Kenny, I have a letter your mom wrote for you to open today." I pull the envelope out of my back pocket. "Would you like me to read it to you?"

Her face lights up. "A letter for me?"

"Yep, just for you." I don't know how I'll manage to read her words, but I need to give her this. I was speaking with Dad about the best way to give Kenny the letters. He was the one who suggested we visit the cemetery and read them here.

"Can you read it to me now?"

I nod. Slowly, I slide my finger under the seal, then pull out a folded sheet of light-blue paper. I swallow and take in a deep breath to center myself.

"Are you ready?" I look at Kenny as I unfold the paper. She nods, eyes wide and waiting. I look toward my father for reassurance that I can do this.

He tilts his head to the side. "You've got this." He nods toward the paper. "Go ahead."

Kenny sits herself on my lap, and I secure her to me with one arm, holding the letter shakily in my other hand. I'm not sure if I'm holding her for her benefit or mine.

"Okay, here goes …

*Happy Birthday, Baby Girl*

*You're five today!*
*I hope today is so much fun for you and that your Uncle Theo and Pappoús*
*make your day special. Make sure you wear your best dress and eat loads*
*of cake!*
*I remember when I first brought you home from the hospital. You were so*
*tiny and I was so scared I'd mess something up. You looked up at me with*
*your big eyes, trusting me to care for you and to keep you safe. I knew I*
*would do anything for you, Kenny."*

I swallow down the lump in my throat.

*"When you first slept through the whole night, I think I must have gotten*
*up to check on you at least five times. I got less sleep those first few nights*
*than I did when you were waking up to be fed. But I wouldn't have had it*
*any other way. I loved being the one that gave you everything you needed.*
*You were such a beautiful baby, so happy and easy to please. So long as you*
*could see me and hear my voice, you would always settle. You would giggle*
*like crazy when I would tickle your tummy, kicking your little legs all over*
*the place. Your big smile would light up my days.*
*I loved holding you close and watching you when you were tiny. Even as you*
*grew bigger, I would sometimes watch you sleep—you were always so*
*peaceful. Your little eyelashes would flutter as you dreamed, and your lips*
*would turn up in a gentle smile. Always keep smiling, Kenny, my beautiful*
*girl.*
*I wish I was there with you to share this happy day. I'm sorry I'm not, but*
*I am watching over you—always! I'm in the sun, the stars, the wind, and*
*the rain. Look for me—I'll always be there."*

I have to pause. This is so fucking hard to do. To say these words
to Kenny. Words that her mother bravely wrote, knowing she
wouldn't be here today. I don't know how she did it. I draw in a
deep breath and let it out so I can get through the last part of the
letter. Blinking back the tears that are fighting to escape, I start
again.

*"I love you so much, Baby Girl. I want you to always remember that.*
*Have a happy day and a fun time at kindergarten.*
*Love you more than all the butterflies,*
*Mommy*
*kiss, kiss, hug, kiss, kiss, hug."*

Kenny takes the letter from my hand, her little fingers tracing over her mother's script, especially the kisses and hugs at the bottom of the page. "One day, I'll be able to read Mommy's letter all by myself. You'll see."

"Oh, I know you will, Munchkin." I run my hand down her long, silky hair. When I look across to Dad, I catch him wiping his finger beneath his eye. I may sound like an asshole, but I'm glad I'm not the only one who got choked up over Anna's words. We spend a little more time, then make our way back to the parking lot where Dad left his car.

"I just have to stop and pick up a birthday cake for Kenny's party this afternoon. See you back at my place."

"No problem. I need to quickly pop into the restaurant to check on some things."

We go our separate ways, Kenny and me picking up her birthday cake in case Emma's forgotten or chooses not to make one anymore— not that I'd blame her after the way I treated her. Kenny picks a multi-colored layered cake, reminding me of her unicorn pancakes from this morning. This kid's going to be hyped up on food coloring by the end of the day; she probably won't be able to sleep tonight.

Dad pulls in a few minutes behind us, carrying a couple of boxes wrapped in pretty blue paper with silver snowflakes. He winks at me as he places them on the kitchen table.

Kenny comes downstairs, spying the gifts on the table. "Yay, can I open my presents now?"

Dad picks her up. "In a minute, Uncle Theo has something he needs to show me in the workshop first."

Kenny huffs out a frustrated breath. "When am I ever gonna get to open my presents? It's not fair." She folds her arms, pouting. Dad and I give each other a half-smile, raising our eyebrows.

I unlock the workshop and turn on the lights, sucking in the familiar smell of raw timber, as Dad places Kenny on her feet. I pretend to show Dad some of my latest work. "Hey, Munchkin, can you pull that sheet off from over there for me, please?"

She throws her head back in a huff. "Okay." The sheet slides away, revealing her birthday present. As her eyes connect with what was hidden beneath the sheet, they grow impossibly wide. Her little mouth forms an O as she registers what it is. Dad and I move closer to her.

"Is this … is this for me?"

I crouch down in front of her. "Yeah. I made it for you. Do you like it?"

Kenny leaps at me. "I love it! I love it so much. Thank you. I always wanted a house for my dollies." Her little arms tighten around my neck as she kisses my face all over. I laugh at her excited appreciation.

"Do you want me to show you all the different parts?"

Kenny looks bewildered by the gift, but she still manages to nod. Dad runs his hand over the surface. "This is a beautiful piece, Son."

His words fill a place inside of me that's always wanted to make him proud. Something I could never do at the restaurant. It was never for me. I spend the next few minutes showing Kenny how the whole front of the house opens, so she has complete access to every room inside. Internal doors open and close, while the roof opens to allow for access to the top floor. I even attached battery-operated lights to the ceiling of each room.

"This is better than any of the houses I've seen at the toy store. Thank you, Uncle Theo. It's the best." She almost knocks me on my ass as she throws her little body at me.

"Let's take it up to the house." I built it on wheels, so it's easy to move around. She can play with it inside or on the back deck if it's a nice day.

We situate it on the back deck for today and Dad gives Kenny his gifts. She opens the larger boxes to find several smaller ones inside. As Kenny opens each one, she begins furnishing some of the rooms. She's in her element, designing the layouts of the different living spaces; moving between inside and the deck to draw pictures to hang on the walls, and finding odd bits and pieces she can use to add decorative touches to each room.

"Uncle Theo, Pappoús. Look how pretty my house looks!" She grasps my hand, pulling me closer to inspect her work. She has quite an eye for design.

"This looks great, Munchkin. Maybe you could help me choose some things to decorate inside our house."

Her little face lights up with a gorgeous smile. "Really? You'd let me help?"

"For sure. I like what you've done with your dolls' house. You could make our house look a lot better."

Kenny wraps her arms around my neck, squeezing me tight. "It will be so much fun! I can't wait. Can we go to the store now?"

"Not right now. Pappoús and I have to get ready for your party.

Remember, Austin and Lachlan are coming over to celebrate with you."

"Okay. Maybe tomorrow?"

"Maybe. We'll see how the day works out." I've learned that I shouldn't commit to something one hundred percent unless I'm sure I can follow through. "Now, I have to get organized. You play here with Pappoús for a while."

"Okay." She drags Dad closer to her house and I leave them to spend some time together, alone.

# CHAPTER 42

## —theo—

I'M PUTTING THE FINISHING TOUCHES ON THE CUPCAKES I BAKED WHEN there's a knock at the front door. I throw everything in the sink and make my way toward the front of the house. I draw in a deep breath, fortifying myself to lay eyes on Emma for the first time in two weeks. I'm not surprised she came this afternoon. She's a good person and I don't think she'd intentionally let Kenny down. I'll put the birthday cake I bought this morning in the freezer for another time.

Opening the door, I steady myself. My eyes land on Austin and Lachlan with huge grins standing on my front porch; no Emma. My heart sinks to my feet. Anger and hurt on Kenny's behalf overwhelm me and I have to swallow it down. It's not the boys' fault their mother's not here. The blame for that lands solely at my feet. I open the screen door wide and stand to the side. "Hiya, boys. Come in. Kenny's out the back on the deck."

"Hi, Theo. I have a present for Kenny." Austin tells me as he struts inside like he owns the place.

Lachlan locks eyes on my chest when I look at him. "Hello, Theo. Thank you for inviting us to Kenny's party. I have a present too." He holds it up for me to see. "I also finished sanding the table you left for me. It was too heavy for me to bring over today."

I ruffle his hair. "That's great, Buddy. Thanks for helping me out. I'll come to pick it up tomorrow. Come through."

Pulling the door closed, I glance up to find Emma carrying a birthday cake—her family following close behind. They all said they would come to Kenny's birthday before everything went to shit. My heart finds its way back to my chest, settling for the first time in two weeks. I take a deep breath. God, I've missed her.

She stops at the top of the steps, lifting the cake like an offering. Her eyes don't make it past my chin. "Uh, sorry I'm a little late, had a little trouble with the unicorn topper." She looks fucking beautiful in a light-blue sundress, but I need to see her chameleon eyes; they'll tell me exactly how she's feeling.

Her family is all smiles as they stand behind her—even Mona the leech came, but I don't think she came for Kenny.

"Hey, thanks for coming. You're not late at all." She still hasn't looked at my face. "That cake looks amazing. Kenny's gonna love it." I open the door wide. "Hi everyone, come in. Kenny's out on the back deck."

Emma's mom and dad say 'hi' as they pass, Sally pressing up on her toes to kiss me on the cheek. Clearly, Emma hasn't told them what an asshole I am.

"Hey, Theo. Nice to see you again." Sarah also presses up to kiss me on the cheek in a friendly greeting.

"Hey, Sarah. Are you keeping well?"

"Yeah, can't complain." She walks through to the back.

Max mumbles hello as he tips his head with Mona hot on his heels. She looks like she's dressed for clubbing rather than a birthday party for a five-year-old.

"Hi, Theo." Mona's saccharine voice drips in honey as she moves in to kiss my cheek like Sarah just did, but I pull back out of reach at the last minute. She actually pouts and I don't know whether Max doesn't notice or doesn't care about his girlfriend's behavior.

I collect drinks for everyone before making my way out to the back deck. I bought enough food in case everyone showed up, but I am truly surprised they did. Dad's speaking with Sally and John while Emma watches Kenny open the presents her boys brought over. I notice more gifts sitting on the table next to Kenny.

I move next to Emma because with her this close, I can't not be near her. Laying my hand on the small of her back, I lean in close, but she moves forward slightly, causing my hand to drop away from her body. I'm not sure why I thought I had the right to touch her; my only excuse is that it's become a habit. I push down my disappointment because this situation is my own doing; I have nobody to blame except myself. I had a good thing—no, a great thing—with Emma, and I threw it away because of my cowardice.

"Thank you for coming. I wasn't sure you would," I whisper. I don't want everyone to hear our conversation. I get the impression she hasn't told her family that things have gone south between us.

Without looking at me, she responds with carefully contained contempt. "I'm here for Kenny. I would never let that sweet little girl down. She's had enough heartache." She wraps her arms around her middle. "Austin and Lachlan love her like a little sister. It's important to all of us to maintain our friendship with her." She finally looks at me, her eyes full of hurt. "I hope that won't be a problem for you." She takes another step away from me as though she's only now realized that we were standing close together.

"Of course not. Look, I'm—"

"Uncle Theo, look at my dolls' house now! My dollies have everything they could ever want." Kenny's excitement bursts into my conversation with Emma.

Crouching down, I take a thorough look inside as Kenny points out all the different furniture, rugs, pictures, and decorations. "This looks fantastic, Munchkin. Did you say thank you to Emma and the boys?"

She jumps up from her kneeling position, wrapping her arms around Em's gorgeous hips. Emma's hand catches the back of Kenny's head in a familiar hold. "Thank you so much, Emma. I love everything."

Emma giggles. "You're welcome, Sweetie. I think my mom and dad have something for you, too."

Without shame, Kenny makes her way over to Emma's parents for her gift. Sarah and Max also have small items to add to Kenny's bounty. At this point, her excitement can't be contained. Dad sidles up next to me. "I don't think Kenny's ever had this many people celebrate her birthday. Even before Anna passed, it was only ever the three of us."

Cue the blade stabbing into my heart at Dad's words. I know he didn't say them for any other reason than to make a comparison, but I feel guilty as fuck. I should have been here. Plain and simple. I let Anna, Dad, and even Kenny down for no good reason. I was too caught up in old hurts to be here—where I should have been all along. I'll never forgive myself for not stepping up when I should have; for allowing the past to take away precious moments I could have spent with my sister.

*Moments I'll never get back.*

I can't take my eyes off Emma. Wherever she is, whoever she's talking to, my gaze naturally gravitates toward her. Not once does she look at me or even acknowledge I'm here and I'm man enough to admit that her dismissal fucking hurts. I want to apologize to her, but she's constantly engaged in conversation with someone.

I'm placing the candles on Kenny's birthday cake when a feminine arm slides around my stomach from behind. I immediately know it's not Emma from her sickly sweet perfume. No wonder Lachlan stays away from her. He probably has an aversion to her smell. She presses her body against me from behind, effectively trapping me against the counter. I try pushing my butt against her to provide me some space, but she pushes against me even harder, like it's an invitation.

"Do you mind backing the fuck up?" I growl.

She giggles. Fucking giggles. "Sure, big boy." Uh, I'm no fucking boy and I don't see what's so fucking funny about this scenario.

She moves back though, which is a relief, so I turn around. The hair at the nape of my neck stands on end as she presses up on her toes, connecting with my mouth before I realize what's happening. A gasp rings out from the back door, and I snap my head around in that direction. Catching a flash of pale blue fabric disappearing out the back door, I panic. Pushing Mona away, probably with more force than necessary to get to Emma, I catch her as she reaches the final step before the grass. Grabbing her wrist, I tug her around the side of my house before anyone notices.

"Let me go!" she hisses out, trying to pull her wrist free of my grip.

I use my hold to pull her around to face me. The tinge of red on her cheeks and heavy breaths causing her breasts to heave up and down capture my attention and I almost forget why I have her like this in the first place. Every molecule in my body wants to lean forward and kiss her. Kiss away the hurt and anger from before. Fill her up with my apology.

Pressing her up against the side of my house, I slam my mouth down onto hers out of desperation. She struggles, her small hands pushing on my chest. I catch them in mine but don't relent with my kiss.

"Ow." I pull back, wiping my lip to check for blood. The minx bit my lip.

She uses my shock to push against me, giving her space. "Don't you dare touch me like that again! You lost that right when you walked out of my bedroom and my house without a backward glance. With no thought about the impact your stepping out of my life and my boys' lives would have on us. No contact. No explanation," she spits at me, her voice full of venom.

"Ahem!"

Both of our heads snap toward the back of my house. Sarah's standing there, arms crossed under her breasts, eyebrows raised in question. Emma uses the opportunity to walk away from me, and all I can do is watch the sweet sway of her ass. Sarah wraps her arm around her sister, giving me the evil eye over her shoulder, then guides Em to the back deck.

With my hands on my hips, my head drops forward in shame. I take a couple of moments to gather myself, then head back inside to finish preparing the cake for Kenny. I collect everything I need and carry it to the table. Everyone comes in close to make a fuss over Kenny, singing her happy birthday. It takes every ounce of my being to be present in this moment for Kenny and not get lost in the taste of Emma's mouth beneath mine or the feel of her body as I pressed against her. Kenny's having a wonderful time, enjoying the attention of everyone.

"Blow out your candles and make a wish, Munchkin," I prompt.

She closes her eyes tight, sucking in a deep breath before blowing out the candles with exuberance—five-year-old spittle flies all over the cake. When all the candles extinguish, she pulls back with a proud smile on her face. "Wanna know what I wished for, Uncle Theo?"

"It's bad luck to tell anyone what you wished for. You need to keep it close to your heart so it comes true."

Her little face turns serious as she contemplates my words. With a serious nod, she replies, "Okay. I can do that."

Emma hands her a knife and helps her to cut through the cake. "Don't touch the bottom of the cake, or your wish won't come true."

"I won't. I really want my wish to come true." Emma smiles at Kenny, and I know it's because she noticed that Kenny pronounced her words correctly.

# CHAPTER 43

## —theo—

WE ALL ENJOY THE CHOCOLATE CAKE WHICH EMMA LOVINGLY MADE FOR my girl. It's getting late, so Emma and her family go home, leaving me alone with Kenny and Dad. The house suddenly feels too big and too quiet with everyone gone. We clean up and bring her new dollhouse, which is now completely furnished, inside.

"Can we look at my baby photos, please?" Kenny begs, so I dig them out.

Dad and I sit on either side of Kenny with her baby album on her lap. She carefully turns the pages and studies each photo. Dad comments on some of the images. When Kenny turns to the next page, it's filled with photos of me with Kenny when she was born.

"Uncle Theo, it's you!"

I ruffle her hair. "Yeah, it's me. I came to visit you and your mom when you were born."

When I look closely at the photographs, particularly at myself, I can see the love I had for my niece. I remember feeling incredibly protective of her and staying with Anna and Dad for a couple of weeks. I checked around the entire house, making sure it was baby proofed to my satisfaction; getting down on my hands and knees to see what was available for a baby to get into. Anna laughed at me. She said I was getting ahead of myself because it would be a while before Kenny would be moving around independently. I also remember how much I hated leaving them. For the first few weeks, Anna and I would FaceTime so I could see Kenny, but then schedules got in the way and those calls became fewer and fewer. Then Anna got sick and I couldn't bring myself to see her deteriorate, so the few calls became short text messages.

Somewhere along the way, I forgot how important these people were to me. I pull Kenny in closer, leaning down to kiss the top of her head, my chest feeling heavy.

Once we've looked through every single photo at least twice, I get Kenny ready for bed and say goodnight, so Dad can read her a story. When he eventually comes downstairs, I hand him a beer. "You wanna sit on the back deck? It's still nice out."

"Sure."

We sit quietly for a while, enjoying the sound of the cicadas in the evening, the darkening sky only littered by the starlight and an almost full moon. Dad takes a pull of his beer.

"So, how are things going with you and Emma? I sensed some tension there today."

Tension would be an understatement. "Things are over between us. I was … uh … surprised she showed up this afternoon after the way I left things between us."

He puts his beer on the table, leaning forward, giving me his full attention. "What happened?"

How do I tell my father I'm an asshole? To be fair, he probably already knows this about me. "I was a complete and utter asshole."

He nods, resigned. "Wanna tell me about it?"

Do I? My shoulders slump in defeat as I take in a deep breath, ready to tell my father what transpired between Emma and me. He sits, silently taking in my misdeeds. Once I finish my recount of the events, he reaches across, squeezing my shoulder firmly. He nods his head gently, almost to himself, a sadness filling his eyes. I can feel the disappointment radiating off of him. It's a familiar feeling.

"Theo." He waits until I'm looking at him. "I can understand where your reaction came from, but she didn't deserve that. This is the first time in your life that I'm disappointed with your behavior."

His words sink like lead in my gut, dragging me down, making me feel even worse than how I already feel about my behavior. I'm ashamed of myself, disappointed that I seem doomed to repeat the mistakes of my past. If I can't move past the hurt from losing Mom and Anna, I may lose my chance to have something long-lasting with the perfect woman next door—if I haven't already fucked that beyond repair. Then it registers that Dad said this was the 'first' time he's been disappointed in me.

"What do you mean, 'it's the first time you've been disappointed in me'? I've always disappointed you. I spent my entire life on the outer because I was such a disappointment," I whisper, my voice thick with childhood hurt. It's like being that seven-year-old boy all over again.

His head snaps back as though my words are swords. "Never. You were *never* a disappointment to me or your mother. We've always been so very proud of you and your talent. The fact that you managed to turn your passion into a thriving business is the cherry on top. My regulars know that the most sought-after location in my restaurant is the setting made by my son." He thumps his chest. "I've always been incredibly proud of you for following your dreams and not feeling obligated to follow in the footsteps of our ancestors. Unlike me." He shakes his head sadly. I can feel his sorrow and missed opportunity radiating off of him in waves.

"What do you mean? You love the restaurant."

"It was the family expectation that I would follow in my father's footsteps. When I was young, I wasn't allowed to follow my dreams. I *had* to go into the family business. I used to enjoy tinkering with machines, but it was considered a waste of time, so I gave it away. I moved into the role that I was expected to and left my dreams behind."

This is all news to me. I thought Dad happily took over the running of the restaurant from his parents. I had no idea it wasn't his passion. "What about now? You could sell the restaurant and do something you love. You still have time."

He shakes his head in the negative. "I've grown to love it. It's not so bad." He rubs the back of his neck. "I will have to think about selling soon. Anna was going to take it over. It actually *was* her passion." He shrugs. "Without her, there's nobody else to take it over. It needs to go."

"When are you thinking of selling?"

"Maybe three more years. Give or take."

"Fair enough." I rub my scruff. "I'm sorry it's come to that. The restaurant's been in your family for such a long time. Can we keep it in the family and get someone in to manage it?"

He shakes his head. "No. I think it's best to let it go."

We chat a little longer, then Dad gets ready to leave. We stop at the front door when he puts his hand on my shoulder. "I want you to try and work through your losses, Son. You don't want to miss out on a good woman like Emma. You owe her an apology." He nods to punctuate his sentence. "Make me proud." Squeezing my shoulder, he steps through the door and into the night, leaving me to my thoughts.

# CHAPTER 44

## —emma—

WINCING, I RAISE MY ARMS TO PIN UP THE FINAL LETTER OF THE alphabet for my display. The redness that was caused by my ill-fitting bras has cleared up, but the area is still causing me a dull pain whenever I lift my arm. It's freaking annoying. I think the underwires must have caused bruising at quite a deep level, so it's taking a while to heal.

I can't believe summer vacation is almost over. The students will be back on Monday; excited fresh faces to mold and shape. I know my boys are excited to start back at school. I'm finishing up for the day, admiring my freshly decorated classroom, when Kate pops her head in.

"Oh, your classroom looks fantastic. The kids are going to love it so much."

"Thanks. I love starting the new school year; seeing all of their fresh faces, ready and eager to learn."

Kate smiles at me, nodding. "It's the absolute best." She holds out some folders for me. "Here are the files for your students."

I grab them. "Thanks for bringing them down." Tucking them into my satchel, I throw the strap over my shoulder, grab my purse, and follow Kate out.

"How's married life treating you?" Her smile grows to a mile wide, her denim eyes lighting up.

She stops in her tracks, placing her hand on my arm, so I stop as well. "Oh my gosh, Emma. It's the best. Oliver's so ... well, you've met my husband. He totally fusses over me. I can't believe this is my life."

"I'm so happy for you, Kate. He's a great guy. There aren't too many guys like him around." I can't disguise the disappointment in my tone. Kate knows me so well, easily picking up on my dismay.

"Everything okay with you?" I don't want to burst her bubble. She's found a great guy who's devoted to her, so what if I haven't found my guy yet.

"Yeah, everything's great. Just thinking about everything I need to do when I get home." I force a smile, hoping it looks genuine.

Her eyes narrow. "I don't believe you. You know you can talk to me if you need to vent about anything." My shoulders drop. I should have known she'd see through my charade. She glances at her phone. "You got time for a coffee?" She indicates to *Coffee and Cookies* down the street.

"Sure. Why not? So long as you're not in a rush."

"Oliver won't be home for another couple of hours. I've missed you these past weeks." We drop our things at our respective cars and, arm in arm, we make our way over to the coffee shop.

We order our usual favorites, and Kate fills me in on the last few weeks of her vacation. She's practically glowing as she tells me all about her honeymoon and volunteer stint rebuilding and establishing a school in a remote community. She makes me feel like a lazy cow. Then I remind myself that I'm busy raising two gorgeous boys and I wouldn't have my life any other way.

"So, tell me, how's that handsome neighbor of yours? I see I have his niece in my class this year."

I release a heavy sigh and go on to tell Kate everything that's happened since her wedding. God, it feels like such a long time ago now, but it's been less than two months. I don't know how I became so attached to the man in such a short space of time. I mean, I know *how*—that gorgeous niece of his, the way he's learning to be a parent, his sexy smile, and grumpy but kind-hearted ways—he's all hard exterior, but a soft puppy on the inside.

Kate rests her chin on her hand. "Do you think there might be a reason for his behavior?"

"Do you think there could ever be an excuse good enough for the way he responded?" I brush my hand through my hair. "From the first time I met him, he came across as rude and overbearing. Maybe I got blinded by the orgasms?"

She huffs out a laugh. "Maybe. They must have been pretty great to blind you, though. I think deep down he's a decent guy, or you wouldn't have let him give you orgasms in the first place." She raises a sculpted eyebrow at me.

"You're right."

"Maybe you should give him a chance to apologize. I remember you giving me similar advice and look where I am now." She wriggles her eyebrows up and down.

"I'm not sure my relationship, or lack thereof, has the possibility to end up like yours. If he apologizes, though, I'll at least give him the courtesy of hearing him out."

"Great. Then see where things go from there." She finishes with a warm smile. "I want you to have what I have, Em. You deserve the best." She reaches across the table, squeezing my hand.

My heart melts at her kind-hearted wish for me. "I don't see a sexy billionaire banging down my door any time soon." I give a humorless laugh, glancing down at my phone. "Geez. I need to get going."

Kate looks at the time. "Oh, me too. Where did the time go?"

We gather our things and walk back toward our cars together, saying goodbye. We'll be back on Monday, but I doubt we'll see each other. The first week back at school is always crazy.

With the boys spending the weekend at Mom and Dad's, I have the opportunity to focus on my planning and prep work for the first few weeks of school, but I need to cut my grass. I'd like to get it done first thing before it gets too hot, so I check the time and decide it's not too early to be annoying for my neighbors. Changing out of my pajamas into my gardening clothes, I head outside to get started. I enjoy cutting my grass and working in the garden. I like the sense of satisfaction I feel at a job well done.

Every time I push the lawnmower back toward Theo's house, it takes great effort on my part to keep from looking for him outside. I should have never let things go as far as they did because I feel utterly awkward every time I step outside my front door now. I quickly trim the edges and pull the few weeds that have sprouted, then pack everything away and head inside to shower.

I only have the luxury of enjoying a long shower once a month while the boys are at Mom and Dad's, so I take full advantage today. I have nowhere to be, except to sit on my couch to finish off my planning and read through my student files, so I can make notes for individual education plans for students who may need one.

Making myself an iced coffee, I set my music playlist on low, get comfortable on the couch, and get to work. I'm only distracted a couple of times when I see Theo's truck leave and then come back sometime later. It's been a month since things went bad, yet I still wonder where he's going and what he's doing. Is he seeing someone new? I can't imagine a guy who looks like him would stay single for long. Add in Kenny and he's most women's kryptonite.

I ache at the memory of his hands and mouth on me. His attention in the bedroom was like nothing I'd ever experienced before. No man has ever been so devoted to my pleasure, to my curves.

I need to make a determined effort to stop thinking about him; it's unhealthy and unproductive.

It's not until the pages become hard to read in the fading light that I realize it's quite late in the day. My stomach growls, reminding me I completely missed lunch. Stretching my arms over my head, I wince at the sharp pain near my breast. Rubbing it gently, I notice the lump that had formed is less pronounced, but the pain when I raise my arms is getting worse. Maybe I *should* see my doctor about it.

My legs scream at me when I finally stand after being seated most of the day. I need to go for a walk. I haven't moved since my gardening this morning.

As my foot hits the final step from my front porch, Kenny calls out to me, waving madly. "Hello, Emma!"

"Hi, Kenny. Are you excited to start kindergarten on Monday?" I check that Theo isn't nearby and move closer to the little girl who's stolen my heart.

"Oh yeah. Uncle Theo got me a new backpack and everything. Wanna see?" She runs inside before I can answer, so I wait for her to return, hoping like hell her uncle stays wherever the hell he is—well, sort of. I wouldn't mind laying eyes on him from a distance. I know he's a jerk, but he's still nice to look at.

She returns, holding up her new backpack. All silver glitter with a unicorn in a rainbow of colors on the front. It's incredibly cute and very Kenny. Putting it on the ground, she opens it, pulling out a matching lunch bag and water bottle. "Isn't it so pretty?"

"It's gorgeous, Kenny. You are one lucky girl."

"I know." She tucks everything back into the bag carefully. "How come you don't come over anymore?"

I feel like telling her to ask her uncle, but that's not fair. "I always get busy before we go back to school, but we've still been going to the park together, right?" I work to keep my tone light.

"Yeah, I s'pose. I think Uncle Theo misses you, though. He's always looking out of the window at your house." Out of the mouths of babes. It's good to know I haven't been completely forgotten. She zips up the backpack, popping it onto her back as if she's going to school.

"Kenny!" Theo's deep voice comes from inside before the front screen door bursts open. Obviously, she went missing again. Maybe he should put a bell around her neck so he knows where she is at all times. He freezes when he sees she's speaking with me. "Uh … hi, Emma."

I wave like a pathetic schoolgirl with a crush. *What is wrong with me?* "Hi. I was just going for a walk." I indicate over my shoulder. "See ya, Kenny. Have a great first day at kindergarten."

"Bye." My hands automatically wrap around her as she hugs me tight. "You have fun at school, too."

"I will. Bye, Theo." I quickly wave, spinning on my heel to make my escape. Walking quickly down the street, I admonish myself for still being attracted to the man. I wonder if I would give him a second chance if he apologized and explained his behavior to me. I'm not sure if I would. I'm at the age where I know how I deserve to be treated and what I want.

# CHAPTER 45

## —theo—

WAKING UP AT THE ASS-CRACK OF DAWN, I ROLL OVER, MY EYES locking on the envelope sitting on my nightstand. I promised myself I would read Anna's letter on the first anniversary of her death.

Today is that day.

*September fifteen.*

The day I've been dreading.

I quietly head downstairs to make myself a coffee. I'm gonna need it. Once I've filled my cup with the steaming goodness, I make my way back upstairs, collect the letter, and sit out on my deck. My eyes automatically find Emma's window. I wonder how she's doing? Kenny still sees her most days when they catch up at the park because she always sends the boys over to collect her on their way. I inherently know I wouldn't be welcome, so I've stayed away, using work as an excuse.

I'm halfway through my coffee when I realize I've been procrastinating. I study the letter resting in my lap as though it's going to explode at any moment.

*What did my sister have to say to me?*

Placing my cup on the table, I take the plunge and tear open the envelope. Sucking in a deep breath, I unfold the paper and begin to read. I have to consciously release the tension that's built in my body since I woke up this morning.

*Theo,*

Well, that sounds curt and not at all friendly.

*I want to start by telling you how angry I am with you.*

I drop the letter back on my lap and look up at the sky as I blow out a long breath. This is exactly what I was expecting. I'm not sure I'm ready for her wrath from beyond the grave. I drink the rest of my coffee as I contemplate if I'm strong enough to read her words. I *know* I deserve her anger, but it's one thing to know I deserve it and another to actually see it in print.

*I needed you here with our family these past few months, but you never came. This battle has been hard on me and Dad—I wanted my brother to tell me things would be okay; Dad needed someone to share the load. You let me—us—down.*

*But I want to say that I understand your reasons for staying away and, after a lot of soul-searching, I forgive you. You already watched one woman you love die. I get you couldn't watch another.*

*As hurt as I am by your absence, I forgive you. Please remember that.*

I look out to my backyard, sucking in a harsh breath. She forgave me. I can't believe it and I certainly don't deserve it. I drop my eyes back to the sheet of paper with my sister's feminine script. The swirls and loops she spent hours practicing when she was young.

"I really want to have beautiful handwriting, Theo." She used to say when I'd ask her why she spent so much time writing and rewriting different phrases until she was happy with how they looked.

My lip kicks up on one side at the memory. It's funny, I've been sharing stories about Anna with Kenny, but I forget the little things, like how she practiced her handwriting.

*If I know you at all, I know you'll be beating yourself up over your decision to stay away. Don't. Don't do that to yourself. It's in the past and nothing can come from such destructive thoughts. It certainly won't change the outcome.*

*I need you to be strong and work your way through your grief and anger, so you'll be emotionally available for my little girl. She's going to need you.*

*I'm scared, Theo. Scared of what's to come. Scared for Kenny. For her future. Clearly, this disease is in our family and I'm terrified I've passed it on to my daughter. I need you to promise me that you'll make sure she gets checked for the gene when she's old enough. The doctor I'm seeing said that the best age is between 20 and 25. Please promise me you'll make sure she gets the tests done! I don't want her to experience this.*

*I know you're probably surprised I left Kenny in your care, but I know you're the best person to give her everything she needs. I remember how protective you used to be of me, and I want that for my baby girl. I trust you to keep her safe and to give her the love she deserves. I saw the way you looked at her when she was a baby—it was obvious how much love you had for her then. Theo, she's so incredibly easy to love and doesn't really need much else. Just love her as though she's your own—be her daddy. Make her childhood happy, fill it with memories of good times—happy times—and love. Give her the experiences I no longer can. It's such a beautiful privilege to give a child your unconditional love.*

*I also need you to look out for Dad. He's lost his wife and his daughter. It's a lot; too much. He's stoic and manages to push himself through each day, but he has deep wounds, too. He misses you, Theo, and doesn't understand why you left us to live on the other side of the continent. Mend your relationship with him—you both need it.*

*Do it for me. Do it for yourself. Do it for Kenny.*

*One last thing, Brother. I know losing Mom was tough. I felt it too. I know it shaped us, affected us both deeply, and colored our perspective on life. You were particularly close with Mom and I know losing her changed you in ways Dad and I could never comprehend. I'm worried about how you're going to cope when you lose me to the same disease. Please don't let past hurts prevent you from grabbing hold of future possibilities. If someone special captures your attention, grasp onto her with both hands and don't let go. Be happy!*

*Thank you for being my brother.*

*Love always,*

*your sister, Anna xxx*

A tear drops onto the page, followed by another and another. Her words ripped out my heart and then put it back into my chest, a little less mangled than it was before.

*She forgives me.*

In her darkest hours, she forgave me. I can't comprehend the strength it took for her to do that.

The sound of little feet padding across my bedroom floor breaks me from my thoughts. Quickly wiping away my tears laced in guilt and self-hate, I turn toward my door to find a sleepy Kenny rubbing her eyes.

"Uncle Theo, I'm hungry."

Getting up, I pick Kenny up, kissing her good morning. "Let's get you fed, then dressed for school. Okay?"

"Okay." She leans forward, laying a kiss on my cheek before snuggling into me, making my heart melt. I get what Anna was saying about Kenny being easy to love because it's been incredibly easy to fall for the little girl in my arms.

While she eats breakfast, I pull up the video I saved so I can braid her long hair into the fancy French braid she asked me to learn. It doesn't look exactly like the girl's hair in the video, but it's passable. I'm sure I'll get better at it with practice. We work through the rest of our morning routine, which we've fine-tuned down to the minute.

Each day as I drop Kenny at school, I'm always hopeful I'll catch sight of Emma, but I'm never that lucky. I haven't seen her since the weekend before school started back. I don't know how she manages to come and go without me seeing her—it's like she's a Ninja. I miss her terribly. I miss her boys, too. I loved having them around, helping me out in the workshop. They come over occasionally, but I think Kenny's picked up on the change of relationship between Em and me, so she doesn't invite them very often.

My days are routine. Drop Kenny at kindergarten, work from home filling orders for custom outdoor furniture, pick Kenny up from school, and spend my afternoon and evening caring for her. Once she's in bed, some nights I head back out to the workshop to sand or stain furniture. On other nights I do paperwork in my office.

Even though I have Kenny with me, I'm lonely. There are no chameleon eyes, gentle smiles, stolen kisses, and incidental touches bringing light to my days. There's no little boy laughter, no family. I know I have no one to blame but myself. I did this and I need to work out a way to fix it.

I don't know how to make it better and the more time that passes, the more certain I become that there's no possibility for reconciliation. My frustration with myself is at an all-time high, and I have to be careful to rein it in and not take it out on Kenny.

I need to make a plan.

# CHAPTER 46

## —emma—

"Hi, Emma. It's been a long time since I've seen you. What brings you into my office today?"

"Hello, Dr. Peterson. It *has* been a while. How's parenthood treating you?"

He smiles wide, his eyes lighting up. "Well, we don't get a lot of sleep, but neither of us would have it any other way." I update him about how the boys are doing while he shares his experiences as a new dad. "I'm sure you didn't come in to catch up on my life. How can I help you today?"

"Well, I've been experiencing some pain here." I show him the area at the side of my breast. "I found out a few months ago that I'd been wearing the wrong size bra. It caused quite a bit of redness and discomfort. I was hoping my new bra would sort out the issue, and it has to a degree. The redness is gone, but it still causes me a dull pain, especially toward the end of the day or if I do strenuous work. It feels as though there's a lump there, so I thought I should get it checked out since it's not going away."

He nods thoughtfully, eyebrows furrowed low as he makes notes on his computer. "Do you mind removing your shirt?" I nod. "Keep your bra on at this stage. Let's take a look."

He gets up to wash his hands in the small sink behind his desk. As he dries them, I remove my shirt with shaky hands—I'm sweating like anything. I'm a little scared that it's going to be something serious and I should have come sooner instead of ignoring it in the hopes it would sort itself out. Raising my arm, Dr. Peterson takes a closer look, moving the side of my bra out of the way. "Sorry, my fingers may be a little cold." He presses against the area, moving his fingers, and applying pressure in different areas. I wince slightly as he touches the most painful area. "Okay. You can put your shirt back on, thank you."

I get dressed, my hands still shaking, as he moves behind his desk. "Do you feel any heaviness in your breast or arm?"

"Yeah, this breast sometimes feels heavier than the other one. It's not a regular thing, though." My heart's starting to pick up speed the longer Dr. Peterson spends writing notes.

"How about when you lift your arm?"

"Yeah, if I do it a lot. I've been trying to be careful not to overdo it."

"What about the area behind your armpit?"

I have to stop and think. "No, nothing there."

"Good, good." He continues making notes. "Have you been feeling tired?"

I laugh. "I have two boys, one of which rarely sleeps through the night. I work full-time and am the only adult running the household. I'm always tired."

He gives me a polite smile. "Have you noticed if you're feeling more tired than usual since noticing the issue at the side of your breast?"

I shake my head. "No, not really." Fidgeting in my seat, my stomach rolls with nerves. "What do you think it might be?"

"I'm thinking you may have blocked lymph nodes. The lymphatic vessels are very thin and if you've been wearing an ill-fitting bra for a long period of time, the repeated pressure may have caused the vessels to close."

My hand flies up to my throat as the beats in my chest increase. This doesn't sound good. "What does that mean, exactly?"

"Our lymphatic system is responsible for removing waste from our body and helps in the fight against infections. Your bra has possibly blocked the lymph glands located in your armpit there." He indicates his armpit. "We can do an ultrasound and a mammogram to take a look at what's happening below the surface." He presses some buttons and his printer comes to life, spitting out a sheet of paper. "Here's a referral for an ultrasound and a mammogram. Once we get these results, we can move forward with the appropriate treatment." He hands the sheet of paper to me.

"Uh, is it treatable?" I'm surprised at how strong my voice sounds considering how discombobulated I feel right now. I honestly didn't expect it to be anything.

"Absolutely. Treatment will depend on how far along the *lymphedema* is." He gives me a list of locations where I'm able to go for the tests. "I can see that you're worried. I don't want you to worry. Get the scans and we'll take it from there. Okay?"

"Okay. Thank you." I stand on unsteady legs, a little shell-shocked that there's a possibility something may be wrong with me. I can't afford to get sick. I need to work and care for the boys; take Lachlan to his appointments. I hope this *lymphedema* isn't anything too serious.

"Please don't go Googling *lymphedema*. All sorts of things may come up in the search and I don't want your mind going to the worst-case scenarios." He raises a brow at me, knowing that's exactly what I planned to do when I got home. I've been seeing Dr. Peterson for a few years now and he knows me too well.

I nod. "Okay. I'll try, but I can't make any promises that I won't look." I attempt to smile, but I'm pretty sure it comes out more like a grimace.

Making it to my car, I sit for a few moments, digesting what my doctor just told me. Staring out of the windscreen, I decide to get the scans over and done with as soon as possible. That way, I can put all of this behind me. Checking the list of screening centers, I find the one closest to me and make an appointment for the Saturday after Veteran's Day. I managed to get the last appointment of the day. Programming the details into my phone calendar, I take a deep breath and decide to not overthink the possibilities at this stage. I'm sure it's going to be nothing and Dr. Peterson said it's treatable, so everything should be okay.

I need to calm myself down. I know I'm overreacting for nothing, but I worry about the boys. It's a lot of pressure being a single mom. Having the responsibility of being the only one there for the kids. Making sure they have everything they need and that all the bills get paid on time. I have sick leave, but I don't like to use it in case I need extra time off for my boys.

I decide to put it out of my mind for now. Starting the car, I head to the store to get groceries for dinner and lunches for the next few days.

Arriving home, Mom meets me at the door, the creases between her brows quite pronounced. "What did the doctor say?"

"Hello to you too, Mom." I laugh lightly, carrying the groceries past her into the kitchen. The smell of tuna bake hits my nostrils. I love Mom's tuna bake. "Thanks for making dinner, Mom. You didn't need to do that, though I'm thankful you did." I kiss her cheek, wrapping her in a grateful embrace.

"The boys helped." She kisses my cheek before pulling back, worrying the pendant at her throat as she waits patiently for me to spill. I decide to put her out of her misery and tell her what Dr. Peterson thinks it is and what I need to do next. "So, it's treatable then?"

"Yeah, absolutely." I'm trying to portray positivity, keeping my voice light. I must be doing a decent job because Mom's shoulders relax.

"Oh, that's good. When will you go for your scans?"

"The fourteenth. Would you mind watching the boys for me?"

"Of course. You know you don't need to ask. Just let me know what time and I'll pop over." She gives me a side hug. "I'd better head home to get dinner ready for your father." She grabs her jacket and purse. "See ya, boys."

Austin comes running out with Lachlan close behind. "Bye, Nana!" He wraps his little arms around her waist and she bends down to kiss the top of his head.

"Be good for your mom."

"We will."

"Goodbye, Nana." Mom gives Lachlan a side hug.

"Bye, Sweetie."

I settle the kids down and we get stuck into their homework. I prepare the lunches for tomorrow, then serve up Mom's tuna bake. I don't know why and I'm certainly not going to question it, but even Lachlan loves it.

# CHAPTER 47

## —emma—

I ARRIVE AT *BreastScreen* SEVERAL MINUTES EARLY—I WAS SO nervous about the appointment that I left home way too early. Sitting in my car, I decide to check social media. I'm giggling at the antics of the people in my favorite group on *Facebook*. They're all about leaving no 'bookwhore' behind. I can go in there and ask for recommendations about the smuttiest smut and someone always, *always* has a great recommendation. I'm so caught up in sharing my favorite books that I'm almost late for my appointment. Stepping inside, I introduce myself to the woman behind the desk.

"Welcome, Emma. Please complete this paperwork and hand it back to me. You can take a seat over there." She gestures to the waiting area across from her desk.

"Thanks." I take the clipboard and pen over to the seating area to begin completing the forms. They don't take long and before I know it, I'm handing them back to the woman. I'm so anxious, I can't keep still. I've never had my boobs scanned before, and I'm not sure what to expect.

"Emma Miller." A different woman calls out with a friendly smile, which I'm guessing puts no one at ease. I step toward her. "Hello, Emma."

"Um, hi."

"If you'll follow me, please." She shows me to a cubicle, directing me to take off my top and bra, replacing them with a loose cotton gown. She comes back to collect me, then takes me into a low-lit room for my scans. My heart's beating a million miles a minute and I'm worried the lack of deodorant will soon become obvious with the amount of nervous sweat pouring out of me.

"This is Naomi. She'll be doing your mammogram today." I nod my thanks, swallowing down my nerves as she leaves the room.

"Hi, Emma. Have you had a mammogram before?" She asks as she motions me toward the large machine. "Please remove your gown."

"No. Uh, this is my first time," I answer softly as I remove the gown.

"We try to make it as painless as possible. There will be some pressure applied to each breast as we take the images." She guides me forward. "Please place your breast on this bottom plate."

I do as she asks. Naomi handles my breast with tender care as she situates it on the bottom plate the way she needs, before lowering the top plate to take the X-ray. It's not really all that uncomfortable, and it's over and done with pretty quickly. I'm not sure what I was expecting, but this certainly wasn't it. She repeats the process with my other boob.

"Thank you. That wasn't half as bad as I was expecting."

Naomi chuckles. "You're welcome. I'm glad to hear that." She smiles at me. "Pop your gown back on and I'll take you through to the sonographer for your ultrasound."

I get dressed back in my stylish pink cotton gown and follow Naomi into another room, following her directions to position myself in the chair.

"Hi, I'm your sonographer today. My name's, Patricia. If you can remove your gown, we can get started."

I don't think I've ever shown my breasts to this many people in one day. Once I'm naked from the waist up again, Patricia holds up a tube. "Sorry, this'll be a little cold." She squirts the clear gel onto my breasts. I remember this from my ultrasounds when I was pregnant with Lachlan and Austin.

"That's okay." She uses the wand to spread it evenly over my breasts and then turns to the machine, moving the wand and pressing buttons. She presses in quite hard at the side of my breast, causing me to wince.

"Sorry, I have to press quite firmly to get a decent image."

"I understand. It's okay, just a little tender." Watching the screen, I can see parts of the image look different from the rest. That must be where the lymph vessels are blocked.

"While you're here, we'll scan the entirety of both breasts. It will help to give the technician a full picture of what is happening."

I nod. That makes sense, I guess. If they look at both breasts, they'll be able to identify the differences. She finishes up, then cleans the sticky goo from me, before allowing me to redress properly in private.

Patricia guides me to a small room. "If you wouldn't mind waiting here. The radiologist will take a look at both scans, then come out to speak to you about the results."

"Sure, thank you, Patricia."

I take a seat, willing my body to settle. The nervous energy running through my system makes it hard to keep still. I pull out my phone to check out social media again in an attempt to distract myself. I've been putting all of my stalking skills to the test, but do you think I can find Theo anywhere online? Nope. You'd think he'd have a website or something for his business, but nada! I don't know how he manages to find new clients. He once told me he mostly relies on word of mouth; happy clients who tell their friends and family.

Scrolling through my feed, I screenshot some interesting-looking reads and recommend a few books here and there. The time seems to drag and because I'm the last patient of the day, I'm alone in the room. I get up and walk around the small space for a bit, looking out of the windows to take up some of the time.

After what feels like forever, a different person steps into the doorway. "Emma?"

*Who else am I gonna be?* "Yes, that's me."

She holds out her hand, directing me where to go. "If you'll join me in my office, we'll go over the results of your scans today."

Silently, I walk toward the open office door, dread filling my gut. I have a bad feeling about my results. I don't know why, but I'm certain my life is about to change drastically.

"Please take a seat." I do as she asks.

"My name is Delta. I've been looking at your scans. Your doctor wanted us to look at your lymph vessels for blockages. There are some minor blockages, as your doctor suspected. You'll need to return to Dr. Peterson to discuss follow-up treatment."

I nod, acknowledging the results, releasing a heavy breath. This isn't a surprise. I had prepared myself for this news. "It's treatable, right?"

"Oh, most definitely." She looks down at her hands and I notice they're clenched tightly together. "Unfortunately, the scan picked up something else that will require further investigation." My stomach sinks to my feet. The blood rushing to my ears makes it hard to hear her next words. She turns her computer screen around, so we can both see it. Using her pen, she points to the screen. "Here, you can see the blockages on a couple of the vessels near this lymph node, which is causing your discomfort. You may find lymphatic drainage massage helps to treat this." She clears her throat, then points to the front part of my breast. "See these small irregular-shaped clusters here?" She moves her pen to the other breast. "And here?"

I nod slowly, my eyes locked on the screen. "These are what we call microcalcifications. These occur as a result of old cancer cells dying. Minuscule specks of calcium form within the dead cells." There seems to be a lot of them scattered throughout both breasts—more in the right than the left.

"What does that mean, exactly?" My voice is shaky. "Does that mean I had cancer, but the cancer cells died and now it's gone?"

"Not exactly. I believe we're looking at *ductal carcinoma in situ*. This is cancer that has formed *inside* your breast ducts. At this point, I don't believe it's spread outside of the duct, which is the best possible scenario. However, from these images, it looks as though nearly all of your ducts in both breasts are affected. I can't give you a definite diagnosis today."

Well, I'm glad she thinks me having cancer in my breasts is the best possible scenario.

*My stomach clenches and rolls.*

"I'm going to recommend you have a diagnostic mammogram, which may lead to a biopsy to confirm these results."

"Oh, okay." I'm honestly feeling shell-shocked. She said the word cancer. She's talking about my breasts having cancer. "Uhm … is this serious?"

What a stupid freaking question. Of course it's serious. It's freaking cancer. She said the word cancer when she's talking about my breasts.

My breasts have cancer in them!

I need to take a breath. My head is starting to spin and I can't afford to faint.

"Look. If it's as I suspect, it's easily treatable and the least serious of all the different forms of breast cancer. But … it's very early in the diagnostic process. The diagnostic mammogram will provide a more detailed image and give your doctor a more accurate diagnosis. Once you have this scan, we'll know whether you should go for a biopsy and be able to give you a formal diagnosis."

The steadiness of her voice and no-nonsense explanation is somewhat calming. Maybe I'm overreacting. The approach sounds sensible to me. I don't want them to miss anything. "Can you do that here?"

"Unfortunately, no. We do have a center about an hour away that I can book you into while you're here." She turns back to her computer.

"I'd appreciate it, thanks." My voice sounds robotic, my brain going in a million different directions. I need to slow it down and concentrate. We make the appointment and I put the details into my calendar app.

"I'm sure this is a shock for you. Do you have any questions?"

I rack my brain. I'm sure there's something I should ask. "Was it caused by something I did? Am I going to lose my breasts?"

Delta stands, coming around her desk to sit in the chair next to mine. "It was nothing you did. Researchers are still investigating, but it's believed to occur when DNA damage causes your healthy cells to reproduce at an uncontrollable rate. We don't yet know what causes the DNA damage." She pats my hand in comfort, giving me a gentle smile. "It's too early to discuss possible treatment until you get the results from the diagnostic mammogram and possibly a biopsy."

We both sit quietly for a moment when I remember I was the last patient, and Delta's probably waiting to go home. "Uhm, thanks, Delta. Sorry to have kept you late."

"You haven't kept me. I'm happy to answer any and all of your questions. Some things I can't answer at this point, because this is by no means a complete diagnosis." Her caring eyes and warm smile make me feel mildly better.

"I … I can't really think of anything at the moment." I huff out an uncomfortable laugh. "I think I'm in shock."

Her face softens further. "Understandable, Emma. Look, this *is* shocking news. But, in terms of cancer, this is possibly the least invasive of them all."

"Thank you. I guess." I stand, Delta standing with me.

She nods. "Good luck. See ya, Emma."

"Bye." I tug the strap of my purse over my shoulder, making my way out the door on shaky legs to my car. My hands tremble, and my legs feel like they're going to give out beneath me. Leaning against my car, I take in some deep breaths, attempting to calm myself down. I can't drive while I'm this upset.

Blinking my eyes, I work hard to keep the tears building up at bay. There are too many to contain and I lose the fight. One tear, followed by another, and another begins streaming down my cheeks. I have to remind myself that she said this is the least invasive form of breast cancer.

But it's not in *her* breasts, it's in *mine*. I have two boys who rely on me for everything. I have to be okay. There's no other option for me.

I look down at my boobs and I feel as though I'm looking at the enemy. I've always loved my breasts. They make me feel completely feminine. I love that I nourished both of my boys with my breast milk. I loved how much Theo loved them.

At this moment, though, I hate them.

# CHAPTER 48

## —theo—

THANKSGIVING WAS A QUIET AFFAIR—DAD, KENNY, AND ME. I couldn't help noticing that Emma and the boys left quite early and didn't come home until late. I wonder how they spent their day. I'm guessing they spent it with Emma's parents, sister, and brother. Emma's family knows how to make a celebration fun, so I bet it was a great day.

Dad is still pissed at me for what I did to Emma and the fact that I haven't gotten off my ass to fix it yet. It's been four months. At this point, we've been apart longer than we were together. The more time that passes, making amends feels impossible. I have no idea how to make it better, but I know I have to at some point.

I want her back.

I'm scared though—I'm man enough to admit it. What if something were to happen to her, and I lost her, too? How would I cope?

My phone buzzes on the workbench next to me.

"Hello, Theo Drivas speaking."

"Oh, hello, Mr. Drivas. I hope you don't mind me calling. A friend of mine gave me your number. Is it true that you work for free for seniors who need a hand?" The man's elderly voice comes across the line.

"Yes, that's true. You only need to pay for the materials and I'll do the labor for free." I enjoy giving some of my time to the elderly, whether it be simple maintenance or making modifications to their home to make it more suitable as their requirements change. "What do you need done?"

He releases a hefty sigh. "My wife recently had a severe stroke. We need a ramp installed at the front and back of the house, so she can come and go more easily in her wheelchair." His voice is shaky as he explains what he needs.

"I can do that. I can come around to take a look at the job now if you're home." I grab a pencil and my notebook to jot down the address when he tells me, then lock up my workshop to make my way to his place.

Pulling up in the driveway of a neat bungalow, the paved ruby-red pathway from the mailbox to the front steps catches my eye. There are only two steps, so the ramp can have quite a shallow rise, which is always the preference. The first problem I notice, though, is there is no pathway from the driveway to the front porch. How will they manage to push the wheelchair across the grass at their age? Not that there will be much grass once the ramp goes in, but they won't want to be tackling a wheelchair on grass.

An elderly man steps out of the front door as I exit my truck, grabbing my tape measure and notepad on the way. He meets me at the bottom of the steps, hand outstretched in welcome.

"Hello, Theo. Thank you for coming out so quickly. I'm Bruce."

"Bruce." I tip my head as I shake his hand. "Nice to meet you."

He shows me around to the back of his home. There's a three-step drop here, still not too bad. I record the measurements and calculate the timber I'll need. I normally purchase the materials, because I can get them at a discounted rate, then bill the client. I always have a rough idea of the cost, so I let Bruce know how much the materials will be.

He looks at his watch. "Have you got time for a cup of tea?"

"Definitely." I never hesitate to stop for a chat. The elderly are often lonely and miss company.

We head inside and Bruce gets busy making the tea. "My wife's due home early next week." He carries the cups to the table where I'm seated. "My girl, Elizabeth, is a fighter. This isn't the first time she's spent time in the hospital. She fought a tough battle with breast cancer when we were in our fifties."

My breath gets caught in my chest and I worry my lungs are going to burst at his mention of breast cancer. I'm sure tons of women survive the disease, just nobody that I know. "I lost my mom and sister to breast cancer. Can't say I'm a fan." I'm not sure what compelled me to tell a total stranger about Mom and Anna.

His eyes go soft. "I'm terribly sorry to hear that, Theo." I can only nod as I swallow down my despair. I have no words to follow up on my statement. I'm sure he can see the devastation written all over my face. "What were they like?" I'm surprised he asked. People usually pretend they don't exist when you tell them you lost your mom and sister.

I scratch my nails through my short beard. "They were both beautiful women. I was only young when we lost Mom, but I remember her always spending time in the kitchen cooking for her family. She gave the best hugs and was always smiling. Except for the one time I filled our shower with worms to scare my sister." I huff out a laugh at the memory. "She was so mad at me." Bruce laughs, too. "I always knew how much she loved me. She was so easy with her affection. Mom would always help me and my sister with our homework and bake my favorite cake for my birthday." I get lost in the myriad of memories I have of her. I realize I don't spend enough time remembering the good times. I'm always too caught up in my grief. "My favorite memory of all is of her cuddling up next to me each night to read me a story. It was the best part of my day and the part I looked forward to the most."

Bruce nods along. "She sounds a lot like my Lizzy. She always gave her all when our kids were little. Now she fusses over the grandkids." He chuckles to himself.

We finish our tea, Bruce telling me all about his grandchildren and showing me photos of them. We both have a good chuckle at some of their antics. As Bruce walks me back outside, I bring up my concern about the lack of a pathway from the driveway.

He rubs the back of his neck. "I hadn't thought about that."

"I can lay a little paving. It'll only be about two yards worth. If you order the bricks, I can come back and do it once they've been delivered."

His eyebrows shoot up to his hairline. "I can't ask you to do that. You're already helping so much by doing the ramps for us."

"You didn't ask. I offered. I'm more than happy to do it for you."

I measure the area to calculate how many bricks he'll need to order. It's a straightforward job.

"Thanks, Theo."

"No problem." We shake hands and I drive straight to the timber yard to get the materials I'll need. I promised Bruce I would be back first thing tomorrow to get the job done for him. I also make a stop at the hardware store to pick up some grab rails to install in the shower and toilet to make it safer for Elizabeth.

# CHAPTER 49

## —theo—

KENNY COMES RACING OUT OF SCHOOL AT THE END OF THE DAY, jumping into my waiting arms. Her smile contagious. "Hiya, Munchkin. Did you have a good day?"

"Yeah. I did." She kisses my cheek. "Mrs. Stone wants to see you about something."

"Did she say what it was about?" Kenny shakes her head. I place her on her feet, take her hand, and we head back inside together to see Kenny's teacher.

Standing at the doorway, I clear my throat as I knock to let the teacher know I'm here. She spins around, a friendly smile lighting up her face. "Mr. Drivas, thank you so much for coming in." She steps forward to shake my hand. "Please come in, take a seat." She turns to Kenny. "Would you mind tidying up the puzzles for me?"

"Okay, Mrs. Stone." Kenny darts off to the back of the classroom, dropping to the floor in front of a set of low shelves piled high with wooden puzzles.

"I'm sure you're wondering why I called you in today, Mr. Drivas." I nod. "I wanted to speak with you about Kenny's reading."

"Theo, please. What about Kenny's reading?" I read to her every day and I make sure whenever we're out and about that I read signs to her. Lately, she's started reading on her own, which I found surprising.

"Well, Theo." She stops and smiles at me. "She's doing really well with the basic decoding readers we've been using. I wanted to ask you if you'd be happy if we moved her on to some books with some more challenging words and concepts. I wouldn't normally extend a child this early, but Kenny has remarkable skills. She doesn't just read the text, she understands what's happening. Her comprehension skill is above the level I would exp—"

"Kaaaate, I'm so ex—" Emma barges into the room, looking beyond beautiful. When she notices me sitting with Kate, she freezes in place. "Sorry, I didn't realize you were speaking with a parent." She turns to leave, but I stand quickly, shoving my hands in my pockets so I don't reach out to touch her.

"Hi, Emma. How are you? How're the boys?" I move closer to her as I speak. It's an unconscious action on my part—I'm drawn to her like a magnet to metal.

"Hello, Mr. Drivas. I'm fine, thank you and the boys are well." She looks past me to Kate. "I'll see you tomorrow."

Kenny runs forward, throwing her little body at Emma's legs. "Emmmmmaa!"

Emma chuckles, smiling down at my niece. She cups the back of Kenny's head. "Hey, Kenny."

I've never felt jealous of a kid before, but I feel jealous of my niece. I want to throw myself at Emma; beg for her forgiveness. Wrap my arms around her and never let her go. I want her smiles and gentle touches.

I can't, though, because I'm an asshole.

"Are we going to the park today?" She looks up at Emma with wide blue eyes, which are almost impossible to deny.

"Sure. I'll send the boys to pick you up when we're ready. Okay?" Emma doesn't check if it's okay with me. She knows I won't stop Kenny's excursions to the park with her and her boys. Kenny loves them all so much and it brings her so much joy.

"Okay." Kenny's satisfied with her answer, so she goes back to the puzzle shelf.

Kate smiles at her. "I won't be too long. I'll pop in when I'm done here."

Emma nods, turning to leave without a backward glance at me. I've been completely dismissed from Emma's life and while I under-stand it's my own fault, I wish she would soften toward me. This is only the second time I've seen her since Kenny's birthday, and both times she's been ice-cold toward me.

I want to thaw that ice.

I want to see the warmth in her chameleon eyes when she looks at me.

I want to be able to wrap her in my arms.

Kate and I finish our meeting. I agree to support Kenny at home with the more difficult readers, as well as continuing our bedtime routine of reading different stories. It was something Mom always did for me and Kenny told me that Anna used to read to her every night, so it's a no-brainer for me to continue the tradition.

Kenny and I stop at the library after school to pick up some new reading material, but Kenny's in a hurry to get home so she doesn't miss out on playing at the park.

I drop Kenny at school, then head to Bruce's place to install the ramps for his wife. He's sitting on the front porch waiting for me. "Morning, Theo. You want a cuppa before you start?" He's a cheery guy, considering his wife's in the hospital recovering from a massive stroke.

"Morning, Bruce. I wouldn't say no. I'll unload while you're making it if that's okay?" I put on my gloves as Bruce waves over his shoulder. I neatly stack the timber near my work area, set up a couple of sawhorses, and wrap my tool belt around my waist. I place the grab rails on the porch for now, so I don't forget to install them before I leave.

Bruce brings out the tea, and he tells me how his visit went with his wife yesterday afternoon. "So, do you have any kids?"

I shake my head. "Not biological, no. I'm raising my sister's little girl. She recently turned five."

"How's that working out for you?" He takes another drink.

"It was tricky at first. I actually lost her on the first day I had her." I huff out a laugh. "Scared me half to death."

Bruce laughs. "Gotta have eyes in the back of your head with the little ones."

"Absolutely. I'd never had anything to do with kids before I took guardianship of Kenny. I've been learning on the job, reading as many books as I can, and YouTube is my best friend." I laugh. When I look back to how I was when I first started looking after Kenny to now, I realize I've come a long way.

"We all learn on the job when it comes to raising kids and parenting. The most important thing they need is your love. Oh, and consistency. They need those two things to thrive. So long as they have that, they'll do well." He pats me on the shoulder. "I'm certain you're doing a marvelous job."

He showed me photos of his kids yesterday, so I return the favor today, showing him the photos I have of Kenny on my phone. "She's a cute kid. You actually look as though you could be her father."

"She looks a lot like my sister and my sister and I looked a lot alike. We both take after our father." I finish up with my drink. "How did you go with ordering the bricks for the path?"

"Great, they're delivering them tomorrow."

"That was quick. I'll hopefully get most of the ramps finished today, then I can start on the paving once they arrive."

I get to work and Bruce leaves to visit with his wife. He generously leaves the door unlocked so I can use the bathroom while he's gone. I remove the existing banister on the steps, then work out the levels I need to start with, ensuring that the timber will sit flush with the existing levels to make it easy for the wheelchair. I measure, double-check the measurements, cut, drill, screw, and hammer my way through the construction of the frame, joists, decking, and railing. The last thing I need to do is concrete the posts into the ground. I'm happy with how it turned out. It has a gentle slope which I think the elderly couple will be able to manage with ease.

I always feel a sense of accomplishment when I complete a project. But none more so than when I help someone out; knowing I've made their life a little easier.

## CHAPTER 50

### —emma—

WHAT A WAY TO START MY THIRTY-NINTH YEAR OF LIFE. *Happy birthday, Emma!*

I couldn't even relax and enjoy my thirty-eighth birthday last night with my family. Standing in front of my mirror, I study my breasts, something I've done repeatedly since finding out I have breast cancer.

*I have breast cancer.*

Even in its least intrusive form, I feel as though my body has been invaded. I press and push, moving them this way and that. I can't see what's going on inside, so I have to trust the imaging and biopsy results that say there *are* cells in my body that need to be removed.

I work my way through the simple exercises I've been doing in preparation for my surgery. I study the side of my left breast. It's already feeling so much better as a result of the manual lymph drainage massage I've been having. I won't be able to have it again until after things settle down with my breasts, but that's okay. I need to concentrate on one thing at a time, anyway.

Carrying my overnight bag downstairs, I make sure everything is ready for my sister's stay while I'm in the hospital so she can look after my boys. Mom and Dad offered to have them stay there, but Sarah wanted to stay here with them so they could sleep in their own beds and maintain their routine. She's been such a terrific support for me these last few months. I don't know what I would have done without her shoulder to cry on. First over my stupidity with Theo and then finding out that I needed to have a bilateral mastectomy. I know they're just boobs and they'll be reconstructed … it's more the thought that I have cancer growing inside of me and I had no idea it was happening. It's scary to think and wonder about what's happening inside my body that I can't see. I'm still so mad at myself for not seeing the doctor sooner when I noticed what was happening at the side of my breast. Maybe if I'd done something sooner, it wouldn't have come to this. *I don't know.*

I kept the boys home with me today—I needed to have them close since I won't see them for a few days. I'm not sure I want them to visit me in the hospital. I'm not sure I want them to see me at my worst. I have to be at the hospital mid-morning because I need to have the sentinel node test before they operate late this afternoon. It's quite a lengthy procedure, but Mom and Dad are going to take me to the hospital and wait until I come out of surgery to make sure everything's okay.

While I'm in the hospital, they'll pick the boys up from school and stay with them until Sarah gets home from work. We worked out the logistics of everything the day I was booked in for surgery.

I don't know why I'm startled when there's a knock at the front door; I know it's Sarah with Mom and Dad. "Boys, Aunty Sarah's here with Nana and Poppa." I lay my hand across my stomach to quell the nervous butterflies as I open the door. I put on my best smile, but it's watery at best.

"Morning." Sarah breezes in, kissing me on the cheek before bending down, ready to catch Austin as he runs straight for her. They both giggle as their bodies collide.

Lachlan comes around the corner. "Hello, Aunty Sarah. Nana. Poppa. How are you today?" He gives each person a small wave as he greets them.

"We're good, Lachlan." They move inside, hugging and kissing me and my boys in our usual greeting. I look out of the closed screen door to see Max breaching the final step to my porch.

"I wasn't expecting you." Max hasn't said much since this whole situation started, but I'm guessing since he's here, he must be a little concerned. He tends to hold his feelings close to his chest.

He takes me in a bear hug, rocking us side to side. As he kisses the top of my head, I absorb his love for me and his quiet strength. "Where else would I be? I thought I could help Sarah look after the boys while you're in the hospital." It's then I notice the duffle at the bottom of the steps.

"Are you staying over as well?" I really shouldn't be surprised. He's always been there for me whenever I've needed him. I see today's no different. Warmth fills my body at his steady support.

"Yeah. That okay?" Creases form between his brows as he looks at me.

"Absolutely, but I'll need to make up the spare bed before I go and I don't think I made enough dinner for tonight and—"

He cuts me off. "Stop stressing. Sarah and I will work it all out." He squeezes me tight, then steps out to collect his bag.

"What about Mona?" She can't be happy to have him abandon her while he looks after my boys.

He shrugs. "What I do isn't her concern anymore. I broke it off with her last week."

I feel awful that I didn't know. I've been so caught up in my own drama that I missed something that had to have been huge for Max. I place my hand on his arm. "You okay?"

"Yeah. It hasn't been working between us for a while. I'm not what she wants anymore. I'm okay with it." He smiles at me. "I feel better than I have in a long time. So don't worry about me. Now, where are those boys of yours?"

My heart feels swollen from all the love and support my family's giving to me. "Thank you."

"Anything for you, Sis." He brushes by me, heading straight for the guest bedroom to dump his bag before finding everyone in the kitchen. I wipe down the counters for the five-millionth time, make sure everything's put away in the living room, then check the laundry room is tidy.

"Come on, Honey. We need to get moving." Mom finds me digging a stray sock out of the back of the dryer. Straightening up, she folds me into her, rubbing my back in a soothing motion. "Everything will be okay. You'll be back home before you know it."

I nod, sucking in a deep breath. "I know. I don't know why I'm so anxious. I've stayed in the hospital when I had the boys, but this feels different."

She brushes my bangs out of my eyes. "I know, Honey. Everything will be fine, though. You'll see." She smiles at me, but I can see the tension surrounding her eyes. "Come on. Say bye to the boys. We need to get moving."

I say my goodbyes, hugging both of my boys tight—even Lachlan understood it was important to let me hug him extra tight and hold on a little longer. It's not like he never allows me to hug him, he just allows it less often than Austin does. I generally don't compare my boys, because they're each so different, but sometimes it's hard not to.

Arriving at the hospital, my butterflies feel more like bats flying around at night looking for insects. It's crazy how churned up I feel. I kiss Mom and Dad goodbye as a nurse leads me away to get prepped for surgery. A radioactive tracer is injected into my breasts where there is evidence of the DCIS. Over the next couple of hours, I'm monitored as the medical team waits for the tracer to reach the first nodes in my lymph glands under my armpits. Even though I know the amount of radioactive material is minuscule, it feels strange to know that I have it in my body and that it will help the surgeon.

The surgeon does another ultrasound, using a felt-tip marker to draw on my breasts. He explains where he'll be cutting into my body to remove the affected tissue. It's already been decided that he'll take out all the breast tissue to be certain he gets every last bit of cancer. He's going to work to save my nipples so my breasts look as normal as possible after the surgery. I'm taken into a room where tubes are inserted into the back of my hand and before I know it, I'm drifting off to sleep.

# CHAPTER 51

## —*theo*—

TODAY'S THE DAY.

I'm going next door and I'm going to apologize and I'm going to grovel.

I'm gonna get my girl back. I can't go another day without seeing her smile, touching her, kissing her.

She's everything I want, everything I need.

When I told Dad my plan, he offered to take Kenny for the weekend to give me the time and space I need to win back the woman I love. I can't believe I didn't see what I was doing. It wasn't until I was talking with Bruce about his wife surviving breast cancer and I read Anna's letter for the third time that the penny finally dropped and I realized what I'd done.

I'd let the past steal my future. The very thing Anna told me *not* to do.

Stepping out of the shower, I dry off, trim my beard, and get dressed. I have her favorite treats and I'm ready to apologize. My stomach rolls at the thought of her rejecting my apology as I put on my jacket and shoes. Stepping out of my front door, I see Max and Sarah's cars parked behind Emma's. Damn it! Too bad if I have an audience, I need to do this today. Too much time has already passed. Too much time has been wasted.

Knocking on Emma's front door, my mouth goes dry as my heart hammers heavily in my chest. I've been running over what I want to say to her for the last couple of days. I only hope it comes out the right way. It seems to take ages for the door to open and when it does, I'm disappointed it's not Emma.

"Hey, Theo."

"Hiya, Austin. How are you, Buddy?"

"I'm good. Aunty Sarah and Uncle Max are playing games with us." He's clearly happy about that if his huge smile is anything to go by.

"Is your mommy around? I'd like to speak with her if I can."

"She's in the hospital having an op-er-a-tion!"

My heart lurches, the edge of my vision going blurry. I grab onto the door frame for support.

"Austin, who are you—" Sarah's words cut off when she lays eyes on me, her expression changing to one of disdain. I'm guessing she knows what an asshole I am. "You need to get back to your game. It's your turn. Uncle Max and Lachlan are waiting for you."

"Okay. Bye, Theo."

"Bye, Austin." He's gone before I finish saying his name.

Sarah steps outside, pulling the door closed behind her. Crossing her arms, she scowls at me. "What in the hell do *you* want?"

"Why is Emma in the hospital having an operation?" I need to know.

She drops her hands to her hips, eyes narrowing. "It's none of your business. Remember? You completely ghosted her. You were an asshole to her. What makes you think you have the right to know what's going on with my sister?"

As my heart hammers in my chest, I lamely hold up the three-and-a-half-pound tub of red vines I bought. "I was coming to apologize to her. I know I was an utter dick to her. I was going to explain and grovel like hell. I want her and the boys. I want them with Kenny and me for always." I scrub my beard. "Please tell me what's going on." I'm not above begging. I'll drop to my knees at her feet if I have to.

Sarah's shoulders drop as she huffs out a heavy sigh. For long moments, she looks out across Emma's front yard. Folding her arms again, she looks at me. "I'm not sure Emma would want you to know, Theo. I'm sorry."

"Can you at least tell me which hospital? I'll sit and wait there for as long as it takes," I implore. "Please, Sarah. Let me make things right."

She takes long moments. "Mom and Dad are at *Mercy Vale Hospital*, third floor." I move forward, wrapping my arms around her in gratitude. "Don't make me regret this, Theo. Or I'll cut your balls off."

My balls retract into my body at her threat. "Thank you." I kiss her cheek. "My balls will be safe, and I promise you won't be sorry. I'm going to spend the rest of my life making it up to her. You'll see."

"You'd better not disappoint me." She looks at her watch. "She'll be out of surgery in a couple of hours."

I give her my thanks and go home to collect my phone, wallet, and keys. While I'm driving toward the hospital, I run through all the possible scenarios. Why in the hell is my girl in the hospital? What happened? Has she been sick? How long? Why didn't she ever ask me for help? She's still been doing everything for herself, so it can't be anything too serious—*right?*

I barge into the waiting room on the third floor like the hounds of hell are on my tail. The chemical smell of the hospital assaults my nose, bringing back unwelcome memories from my childhood. I push them away as my eyes land on Emma's parents, my feet automatically moving in their direction. "Hi, Mr. and Mrs. Stanfield. Is there any news on Emma?" It seems to take them forever to respond to me, and I realize I have no right to ask anything about Emma. "I'm sorry. I have no right to ask. I'll just sit over there and wait." I point over my shoulder at the chairs on the opposite side of the room.

"No, no, please sit with us, Theo," Emma's mom responds, standing from her chair to engulf me in a warm embrace. "We were surprised to see you here. That's all." She looks at her husband. "We didn't realize you and Emma were together again."

Well, this is awkward. "Uh, well …" I scrub my short beard. "We're not *actually* together." I go on to explain how I came to be here and what my intentions are, hoping and praying they allow me to stay.

"Ah, I see," Mr. Stanfield responds, nodding thoughtfully. "You hurt our daughter and our grandsons deeply. I hope you've learned from your mistake." I nod emphatically. "Of course, it's entirely up to Emma whether or not she forgives you."

"I know. I'm prepared to put in the work to win her back, though."

Emma's mom smiles wide, and her dad gives me a nod. We sit together, in silence, for long moments. Pulling out my phone, I check my emails for something to do. I'm tempted to ask why Em's having surgery, but I'm holding back so I can have the discussion with Emma. I figure I owe her that much. Time seems to drag and I'm finding it difficult to sit still. Getting up, I pace around the room, stopping at the windows to watch people down on the street. The sun has dropped lower in the overcast sky, coating the buildings in a gray hue. The quiet is interrupted when a doctor steps through the double doors. My heart picks up speed and I wipe my palms on my jeans.

"Mr. and Mrs. Stanfield?"

They step forward as a solid unit. "That's us. How is she, Dr. Barnes?"

"She's out of surgery. Everything went smoothly and as we expected. Emma's currently being moved into a room, where she'll spend her time here recovering. A nurse will be down shortly to take you to see your daughter."

John wraps an arm around Sally's shoulder, the relief on both of their faces plainly evident. "Oh, thank you so much, Doctor." Sally smiles at the man.

"No problem. She'll be sore for a while, but we'll be able to manage that with pain relief while she's here. She needs to take it easy to allow her body to recover." He's all business.

"Thank you. We'll wait here until the nurse comes down."

"Sure. Bye for now." He smiles, and with a tilt of his head, he's gone.

I look across at Sally and John. I still have no clue what surgery Emma had, but at least I know whatever it was went well. It sounds like there'll be a recovery period. I mentally run through my projects over the next several weeks. Work is always quieter during winter. People aren't thinking about entertaining outdoors so much, so they're not thinking about outdoor furniture or decks. I should be able to spend a fair amount of time looking after her as she recovers.

We all sit together in silence until a nurse comes through the same doors the doctor did. "Mr. and Mrs. Stanfield?" She looks up from her clipboard expectantly. There are only the three of us here. They rise and I remain seated. After rushing here this afternoon, I've realized I don't have a place. They make it halfway to the nurse, who's still standing in the doorway when Mrs. Stanfield turns back toward me.

"Well, are you coming?" I stand up like lightning, appreciating her gesture to include me.

"I'm sorry, only family members are allowed past this point." The nurse directs my way.

Mr. Stanfield speaks on my behalf. "He's our daughter's boyfriend. I'm sure you can make an exception for him." His gesture goes well above anything I was expecting from Emma's family, but it gives me a sense of hope that if Emma accepts my apology, things will be okay between me and her parents. I know how much they mean to Emma, which means I need them to accept me back in her and the boys' lives.

She looks me up and down as if making sure that I am, in fact, Emma's boyfriend. "Sure. Follow me, please."

When we enter Emma's stark room, the beeping of the machines fills my ears. Stopping just inside the doorway, I allow her parents to go in first and have some time with their daughter. Emma's coming around, but she's still mostly out of it by the looks of it. They each take turns bending down, planting kisses on her forehead. She has tubes sticking out of her and wires attached to machines that are monitoring her heart and breathing.

Sally and John take a seat on the chairs on either side of the bed. Emma's mom brushes her daughter's bangs in a motherly fashion. Her dad says something quietly to her, making her smile slightly. Her eyes open for a short while before fluttering closed again. I feel like a creeper watching them like this, but they *did* say I could join them.

I wonder if I should wait for Emma to get home from the hospital before approaching her. This seems like a douche move to talk to her about my behavior when she's just come out of surgery. But then again, I *am* a douche. A douche of the highest level. I shrug internally. Leaning against the doorframe, I make myself as comfortable as I can while I wait for my turn to visit.

After what seems like an eternity, Emma opens her eyes properly, indicating that she's thirsty.

"Here, Honey. Have a sip." Her mom holds a glass with a straw close to her lips for Emma to have a drink. They chat quietly for a little while and I'm doing my best to be patient. As though Mrs. Stanfield suddenly remembers I'm here, she turns suddenly in her seat, waving me forward. I move in, stopping right beside Emma's bed. Her eyes widen as her mouth opens; probably to protest my presence.

Her mom speaks before Emma can get any words out. "Isn't it lovely that Theo came to visit? Now, your dad and I are going to head home. You're in good hands here." She stands, kissing Emma on the forehead. Mr. Stanfield's looking at his wife as though she's grown another head. I rub my hand across my mouth to hide my smile at his confused expression. "C'mon, Love. Let's go and let Theo have his visit."

He stands from his chair wordlessly, kisses his daughter before whispering something in her ear, then follows his wife out of the door. Mrs.

Stanfield winks at me as she approaches me. Tapping my forearm with her hand, she whispers, "Good luck."

John tips his head, giving me the universal sign that he's watching me by pointing two fingers at his eyes, then pointing them at me. Once they're gone, Emma turns her head away from me, so I take a seat in the chair.

"How are you feeling?" *What a stupid fucking question.* She's just had surgery. As if she's going to be feeling fantastic a couple of hours after.

She rolls her head on the pillow so she's facing me. Her face looks like thunder, her perfectly shaped eyebrow raised at me. "I feel trucking peachy." Her voice is husky. "Thanks for asking." She rolls her head away from me so she doesn't have to look at me any longer.

"I'm sorry. It was a stupid question. I realized after it was out of my mouth. You know what I'm like. I'm always saying the wrong thing." A deprecating laugh escapes unbidden.

Without looking at me, Em quietly asks, "What are you doing here, Theo?" Her scratchy voice is soft.

That's a fair question, I guess. "Can you please look at me and I'll explain?" I wait for her to turn her head toward me. Her eyes are almost a muddy brown today and she looks defeated. I want to take her hand in mine, but I don't think the gesture would be welcome at this point. "I came over this afternoon to apologize to you for my behavior all those months ago."

Her eyes widen at my words. "Took you long enough," she snaps out on a huff. "Why now?"

I scrub my fingernails through my scruff. "I realized something yesterday. Something huge and decided I needed to make amends and go after what I want."

"What did you realize after all these months, Theo?" she grumbles.

"First, I realized that I'm an asshole. But you already knew that. Second, that I'm allowing past hurts to steal away the possibility of an amazing future. A future with you and your boys. A future as a family. The five of us." I release a heavy breath. "I'm sorry my apology and subsequent explanation for my behavior have coincided with your surgery. I had no idea what was going on when I knocked on your door this afternoon."

"And what? You expect me to forgive you and go back to where we were before?" She rolls her gorgeous eyes. "Not happening any time soon."

"I don't expect you to forgive and forget any time soon. I'm prepared to put the work in, Em. Can I please explain? I think it may help you understand why I reacted the way I did. Not that there's any excuse for walking away from you the way I did."

She swallows and nods—that's all I need. I take in a much-needed deep breath to fortify myself for what I'm about to share. I still find it so hard to put my losses into words. "You know I lost my mom and sister." She nods again, her face softening a little. "I … *we* lost Mom when I was eight and Anna was ten." Emma gasps. "She was only thirty-three."

"Oh, Theo. I'm so sorry." She places her hand on my forearm in support. She probably doesn't even realize that she's done it, but it feels amazing to have Emma's touch again; I'll never take it for granted.

Covering her hand with my own, I continue. "I felt her loss deeply. Mom and I were close. Anna and Dad were always off at the restaurant together and I never really fit in there, so I would stay with Mom. She understood I was different; that my heart wasn't in the restaurant, even at a young age." I tangle my fingers with Emma's. "Then last year, we lost Anna."

When I look at Emma's face, tears gently track down her cheeks. Her bottom lip quivers as she whispers, "Theo." Just my name. So simple, yet so heartfelt. Using my thumb, I gently wipe her tears away. "How did they die?" she asks, her bottom lip trembling.

I can't look at her as I swallow the excess saliva in my mouth. "Breast cancer," I whisper, barely able to produce those villainous words.

She pulls her hand out from under mine, making my eyes snap up to hers. Her face hardens, and I can practically see her walls being constructed in front of my eyes. "I'm sorry you went through all of that, Theo. Truly I am."

I plow on because I get the distinct feeling she's going to shut me down. "When I felt the swollen area and saw the redness at the side of your breast—I panicked. Then when you brushed away my suggestion to get checked—I … I couldn't do it." I look deep into her eyes, my anguish pouring out of every part of me. "I can't lose another woman to that disease. I just can't, Em." I shake my head. "I can't do it to Kenny and I can't do it to me." She opens her mouth to speak, but I gently place my finger over her soft lips as more tears track down her face. "Anna wrote me a letter. She made me promise not to let past hurts stop me from future possibilities. I realized I pushed you away because I was scared of something that may never happen." I lock eyes with my future, clearing my throat to ensure these next words come out clearly. "Please forgive me." I take her hand in mine, kissing the back of it in apology. "I'm so fucking sorry, Emma. Please say you'll forgive me." Wetness tracks down my cheeks. Sharing something so deeply personal is so incredibly foreign to me. Being this vulnerable leaves me open to being hurt.

She pulls her hand from mine again. I realize this conversation was too heavy for the moment. She just woke up after surgery, for fuck's sake. Long, silent moments spread out between us, wider than any canyon. I fear I'm not going to get the answer I want today. But that's okay because I'm not going to give up this time. I'm going to fight for what I want.

"I'm really sorry for your losses, Theo. Truly. Nobody should have to go through what your family has been through." She draws in a deep breath. "I want you to know that I forgive you for the way you reacted. It makes complete sense that you would respond in such a way." She looks away from me for a few seconds, her eyes glassy, before locking her eyes on mine. "However, there is no future for us." I try to butt in, but she holds her hand up. "Please respect my wishes. Maybe sometime in the future, we can be friends. But we can't ever be anything more than that."

My heart drops to my feet. My hope shatters. Her tone is sure and strong. Her voice doesn't waver. I drop my head to my hands, releasing a long breath while blinking away the sting in my eyes.

"Goodbye, Theo."

I look up at her as she swipes angrily at a tear on her cheek. She turns her head away from me. Should I leave or sit here to keep her company? Even if we don't speak, at least neither of us will be alone.

I decide to stay.

Sitting back in the uncomfortable plastic chair, I stretch out my legs, folding my arms across my chest. Looking out of the window across the room, I see a couple of lights on in the top floors of nearby buildings. I focus my attention outside, away from the uncomfortable situation I now find myself in. I glance down at Emma occasionally, only to find she's dozed off. A nurse comes in to check on her and I tell her how long she's been asleep.

"Do you mind buzzing me when she wakes up? I need to check her pain level." She holds up the button I need to press and I nod in agreement.

The sky becomes completely dark, more lights turning on in the buildings across the street, and dishes clank down the hallway as the dinner service is delivered to the patients on the ward. My beautiful girl stirs. Her eyes flutter open slowly as she turns her head toward me. She attempts to sit up, crying out and wincing as she does. I jump out of my seat to help her, but she stops me dead in my tracks. "Go home, Theo. I don't want you here."

I press the buzzer as the nurse requested, then sit back down. "I'm not going anywhere, Peaches."

She grits her teeth, fire in her eyes. "Go home. Leave me alone."

Before I can respond, the nurse breezes in, giving Emma a warm smile. "Good evening, Mrs. Miller. How are you feeling after your nap?"

"Hi. I'm a bit sore, actually." She looks at me, then back at the nurse. "Uhm, I thought only family were allowed to visit?"

"Yes, that's right." The nurse slows, looking across at me with eyes full of accusation. My gut sinks because Emma's gonna have me kicked out of her room.

Emma looks at me, steely determination in her eyes. "He's not family. Can you please have him removed?"

The nurse looks at me, her features drawn tight. "You heard Mrs. Miller. Please leave, or I'll call security and have you escorted off the premises."

I nod once. Standing, I kiss Emma on the forehead, my lips lingering on her soft skin. "I'll see you at home, Peaches." I leave the room, knowing this will be the last time I walk away from her.

# CHAPTER 52

## —emma—

I BLOW OUT THE BREATH I WAS HOLDING.

Crinkles form between the nurse's brows as she looks me over. "I'm so sorry. Your parents told me he was your boyfriend, that's why I allowed him to stay." I'm not surprised my parents told her he's my boyfriend. Ever since Mom met Theo at the beach, she's been harping on about how wonderful he is and that I should forgive him. She was always reminding me that everyone makes mistakes and should be allowed second chances.

"That's okay. It's not your fault."

She nods, then does what she needs to do before leaving me alone with my thoughts. My heart broke for Theo. For the little boy who lost his mom. For the man who then lost his sister. His reaction to my sore breast was completely understandable, given his experiences. God, how would he react if he knew what surgery I'd just had done? He certainly wouldn't be asking for a second chance.

*Not with me.*

My breasts are scarred now. So different from before. I know I should be thankful that the cancer wasn't worse, but I'm not sure how I'll manage to look at myself in the mirror. I look down at the offending part of me. Tightly wrapped up, I can't tell there's any differ-ence, and the area feels numb at the moment. I'm sure I'll feel different over the coming weeks and months as I heal and the doctor recon-structs my breasts. He was going to operate in such a way as to save my nipples, so there's minimal visual impact.

Footsteps sound outside of my doorway, and I wonder if Theo's come back. Half of me hopes he has, the other half wants him to stay away. My stomach sinks and I'm disappointed when Dr. Barnes, my breast cancer surgeon, breaches the doorway with a smile.

"Hello, Mrs. Miller. Good to see you awake and alert. How is your level of pain?" he asks, coming to a stop at the edge of my bed.

"I think the pain medicine is doing its job. I'm okay at the moment. Feeling a bit sleepy, though."

"Good. Good. That's to be expected." He looks down at his tablet, then back at me. "Now, the surgery went well. As we discussed, we were able to perform a nipple-sparing bilateral mastectomy. We made sure to remove all the breast tissue. As you know, the results from the sentinel node test came back negative, so we didn't have to touch the lymph nodes. Dr. Corrigan has also put the expanders and drains in place while we wait for you to heal, then she'll go ahead with the reconstruction of the breasts for you."

"So you managed to get all the cancerous cells?"

"I'm confident that we have. The sections of breast tissue we removed have been sent to pathology. Once they take a look, we'll know for sure. The best-case scenario will be that the cancer was definitely contained within the ducts to ensure that you won't require any radiation or chemotherapy. You've been extraordinarily lucky, Mrs. Miller. I know you probably don't feel that way right now, but you are very lucky indeed."

"Thank you, Doctor." I give him what I hope is an appreciative smile.

"I'll be back to check on you again tomorrow. We'll unwrap those bandages and take a look." He tilts his head toward my breasts, then leaves me to my thoughts.

I'm going crazy cooped up in here. A girl can only read so much and I miss my boys terribly. I've never been away from them for this long. Even though the plan was to keep them away from the hospital, I caved and asked Mom and Dad to bring them up this afternoon after their afternoon snack. They should be here any minute. I carefully climb out of bed and step into the bathroom to brush my hair and tidy myself up.

As I step out of the bathroom, Mom, Dad, and the boys enter

through the doorway of my room. My heart instantly feels lighter as my eyes land on Lachlan and Austin. God, I've missed them so much. I step forward urgently. I need them in my arms. Carefully, both boys wrap their little arms around me, snuggling into my body. Moisture wells in my eyes, and I know I won't be able to hold the tears at bay. Bending forward, I kiss the top of each boy's head, mussing their hair. The surgery was tough, but being away from my boys is tougher. I breathe in their little boy smell and I feel brighter than I have in days. I've spoken to them over the phone and used FaceTime to communicate with them, but it's not the same.

"Hey, guys. I've missed you so much!" I tuck them in tight to my body, careful to avoid my breasts. Kissing them again, I close my eyes, absorbing them. They snuggle me back and it feels fantastic to have them with me again.

"Emmmmaaa!" My head snaps up at Kenny's sweet voice. I didn't notice her with my parents and now I understand why. She's here with her uncle. My hand automatically goes to my hair, smoothing it down. Why I still care how I look in front of him, I'll never know.

Lachlan moves out of the way to allow the little dynamo to get in close enough for a hug. I keep my eyes on the kids and Mom and Dad, doing my best to ignore Theo's presence, but it's hard. He looks so freaking good. After carefully hugging Mom and Dad, I sit on my bed, encouraging the kids to join me. Mom and Dad take the guest chairs while Theo stands in the corner, as though he has every right to be here.

"Hey, Emma. It's good to see you up and about." His deep voice catches me off-guard. I thought maybe he would stand in the corner and not participate in the visit.

"Thank you. I'm surprised to see you here, but I'm glad to see Kenny." I return with an arched brow. I know my dig at him is juvenile, but I couldn't help myself.

"Even though I've managed to keep up the visits to the park after school with the three kids, she's missed seeing you." He gives me a smirk when my eyes widen. The boys haven't mentioned going to the park with Theo. I assumed Mom and Dad had been taking them each day and including Kenny because that's what I do. I look at Mom and Dad, waiting for an explanation. Mom smiles innocently, which I know is so far from true. It isn't even funny.

"What's that, Mommy?" Lachlan points to one of the bulbs visible at the bottom of my shirt.

I've been honest with the boys. I told them that the doctor found cancer in my breasts and that I had to have surgery to get it taken out. I kept the explanation really simple for them. I keep my eyes on Theo as I answer Lachlan. "Uhm, it's to collect the fluid that builds up where the doctor took the cancer out of my body."

The color drains from Theo's face. Maybe now he'll stay away—as I asked.

I watch his Adam's Apple move up and down on a hard swallow. His eyes stay locked with mine as he stands a little taller. A little straighter. He tilts his head in acknowledgment and I focus my attention back on the kids.

"Is it working?" Lachlan asks.

"I think so. The nurse comes by every now and then to check on it. She seems pretty happy with how it's working."

"Cancer?" Kenny's eyes well, her bottom lip trembling. "Are you gonna go to heaven like my mommy did?" she whispers, breaking my heart.

"No, Kenny. I'm going to be just fine." I stroke down her long hair, attempting to comfort her. She leans into my right side, knocking my wound site accidentally. I suck in a sharp breath, my hand flying up to protect the area as a gasp escapes. I clench my teeth in pain and my vision goes a little fuzzy. Luckily, I'm sitting down.

"I'm sorry, Emma. I didn't mean to hurt you." Tears drop over her bottom lashes onto her sweet cheeks.

Theo steps forward quickly, lifting Kenny from the bed. "You need to be careful, Munchkin." He looks at me apologetically. "Sorry about that." His eyes drop to my breasts. My breasts are so swollen and with the expanders in place, it's not obvious that I've had surgery to remove the tissue. He smooths his hand down his niece's back, murmuring something to her I can't hear.

Now he knows it was breast cancer. Will that be enough to make him leave?

"Have you seen the surgeon, Honey?" Mom asks, interrupting my thoughts.

"Yeah. He's happy with how everything's turned out. Both of my surgeons have been checking in on me each day. I'll see the plastic surgeon when it's time to remove the drains and start increasing the size of my expanders."

"Dr. Barnes seemed like such a nice man." I roll my eyes. Mom thinks everyone's a nice man or a nice lady.

We spend the next hour catching up. The boys tell me all about school and how Aunty Sarah burned dinner. Lachlan informs me he didn't get upset about it because he already had his chicken nuggets and sliced vegetables. I can't help but laugh a little at how proud he is of himself, which, in turn, causes a sharp pain in my chest.

As much as I've missed seeing my family, I'm feeling suddenly tired and a rather large yawn escapes.

"Come on, we should let Mommy rest." Dad prompts everyone into action.

I hug the boys as tight as I can to get me through the last days of my hospital stay. "I love you guys. I'll be home soon. Okay?" I give them a bright smile. Brighter than I actually feel at the moment.

I carefully embrace Mom and Dad.

Dad whispers in my ear, "You should give Theo a chance to make things right."

He doesn't know. He doesn't know that I'm Theo's worst nightmare come to life. Not that I'm going to die from this disease, not even remotely. But I would be a constant reminder of what he's lost. That I survived when his mom and sister didn't. Every time he looks at my breasts, he'll be reminded of the battle I won and his mom and sister lost.

Kenny comes in for a gentle hug. "Bye, Emma. I'm sorry I hurted you."

I smile at her, running my hand down her unruly hair. "It was an accident. I'm okay. I've been missing you, so thank you for coming to visit me today."

She nods, stepping back to her uncle's side. He whispers something to Mom, then passes Kenny's hand to her and they leave. Leaving me alone with Theo.

"Thanks for bringing Kenny up to visit. I miss seeing her little smile." I don't know what else to say. I'm unsure why he's still here.

Tucking his hands in the pocket of his jeans, the ones that hug his muscular thighs, Theo steps closer to me. His sweater pulls across his broad chest as he invades my personal space. Surprising me, he plants a gentle kiss on my forehead, careful not to touch me anywhere else as he lingers.

"Why didn't you tell me?" he whispers. His lips still touching my skin, setting my body on fire at the memory of his lips caressing the length of my body, my breasts, my thighs.

"How could I tell you after you shared the history of your family with me?" I whisper in return. I blink, working to keep back the tears pricking at my eyes.

He brushes his fingers across my bangs, tucking loose hair behind my ear, then follows the line of my jaw with the back of his fingers. "I get that. But I need you to understand that I'm here." He crouches down slightly, ensuring my eyes are locked with his. "For better or for worse."

My hands reach out to grasp onto his slender hips, to keep my jelly legs from collapsing beneath me at his words.

He means them.

With every ounce of belief.

It's there, in his azure eyes. The honest truth. He guides me to sit back down on my bed, sitting gently beside me. "Will you tell me the prognosis?"

I swallow and nod slowly. "Dr. Barnes feels he got all the cancerous cells out. I had *ductal carcinoma in situ* in both breasts, which is the least invasive form of breast cancer. I'm incredibly lucky by all accounts. The surgeon removed the entirety of the breast tissue to ensure he got it all. I'll find out more at the follow-up appointment." I shrug, sending shooting pain through my chest.

I have to remember to stop doing stuff like that.

He rubs his hand up and down my back, careful not to disturb the drainage tubes coming out of my body. I wince as he catches the stitches on my back from where Dr. Corrigan shaved the muscle in my back to use around the front of my body to support my implants.

"Sorry. I didn't mean to hurt you." He snatches his hand away.

"It's okay. You didn't know I had stitches there."

"It's good news that they got all the cancerous cells. Will you need to have radiation or chemotherapy?"

"He didn't think so, but I'll know more once the pathology report comes back."

"Okay. Do you need me to bring you anything? I can come back tomorrow once I drop Kenny at school."

"Oh, you don't have to do that. Honestly. I'll be home in another two days." This feels incredibly intimate and I'm unsure how we got to this point so quickly. "I meant what I said the other day, Theo. There can't ever be anything more than friendship between us."

"Look, I know I fucked up. I fucked up big time. I get that. But I'm willing to put the work in to make it right." He scrapes his beard with his fingertips. "All I ask is that you give me a chance."

We sit, in silence, locked in each other's gaze for long moments. I'm working hard to portray that I don't want anything more from him, even though I would love something, make that plenty more with him.

But I can't put myself at risk again.

Theo was mesmerized by my boobs. They're different now and they will be smaller once I'm through with everything. When Dr. Barnes removed the bandages to check my wounds, my boobs looked like a war zone. I know the bruising will disappear and the scarring will heal and it won't look as bad as it does right now, but that's going to be a long way off.

How will he react to the changes?

Preston hated the way my body changed as a result of my pregnancies. I've only recently recovered my self-esteem as a result of his disparaging comments and rejection, thanks to Theo. I don't think I could go through having him do the same, especially when he used to make me feel so incredibly sexy in my skin.

How could he even look at my scarred breasts and not be thinking about his losses?

Why would he want to be in that situation, day in and day out?

He tilts his head, then leans forward, laying a gentle kiss against my forehead. "I'd better head out. Your parents are probably wondering where I am." He stands to his full height, running the back of his hand down the side of my face. I fight the urge to press into him. "I'll be back tomorrow and the next day, and the day after that. I'm not going anywhere, Peaches." Turning on his heel, he leaves my room before I can answer, taking his sexy scent with him.

# CHAPTER 53

## —theo—

I SPENT THE TIME EMMA WAS IN THE HOSPITAL CLEANING UP HER YARD, so she's not tempted to do anything when she gets home. It all looks pristine for her return later today. Despite her denial that she didn't want anything with me, I sensed she was scared. Scared for me and scared for herself. I can't blame her for not trusting me to stick around after the way I responded; especially since she just had cancer removed from her breasts.

*Fucking cancer. In her breasts!*

I thought my world was going to crash down around me when I finally learned why she was in the hospital. Of all the surgeries she could have had, it had to be fucking breast cancer—I couldn't believe what I was hearing. It's like the fucking universe wants me to suffer as much as humanly possible. I was so close to walking away, but Anna's words ran through my mind on repeat, bringing me back from the brink.

I came home that afternoon, spent time with Kenny, and then once she was in bed, I read Anna's letter again.

I did some deep soul-searching. Something I hadn't done before.

I needed to be sure I could stand by Emma through this challenge. I haven't had the best track record of supporting the women in my life. First, I was too young to help Mom, but I had no excuse for not returning home when Anna became ill—only my lack of backbone. I wanted to be completely certain I could be with Em through thick and thin because it's what she deserves. I Googled the shit out of her form of breast cancer, so I had a deep understanding of what we were going to be up against. But it seems Emma's already been through the worst of it.

I spoke to Dad the next morning—he gave me the best advice. He told me he would rather have had the short time he had with Mom than to have never had that time with her at all. That every day of pain and suffering since losing her was worth it for the days of happiness and sunshine he experienced by her side. I decided I wanted days of happiness and sunshine with Emma by my side, no matter the outcome. Live for the now and put off worrying about the future for another day.

Shit! Flowers. I need to get some flowers and more of the Red Vines that she loves. Grabbing my essentials, I head for the door.

I have a pep in my step as I walk into *Blooms and Balloons* for some welcome home flowers for my girl. I'm greeted by an elderly lady instead of the younger woman who's usually here.

"Hello, young man. How may I help you today?"

"Hi. My girlfriend's coming home from the hospital today, so I want to surprise her with some flowers throughout the house. I'd like to get …" I stop to think, maybe some in the kitchen/dining area, living room, and her bedroom. "Three floral arrangements for different rooms in her house, please."

Her hand comes up to her chest. "Oh my, how sweet of you. Any idea what type of flowers you would like for your arrangements?"

"Something bright and happy. She's going to be my everything."

"Okay. I have just the thing." She holds up a finger and wanders out the back.

As she works, we talk about the store. How it used to be hers before she passed it on to her granddaughter to run. She goes on to tell me she recently came out of retirement to fill in for a while because her granddaughter and her employee were attacked in the store just over a month ago. Shocked that such a thing could happen in such a serene space, I look around the store as if I can see evidence of the attack.

Something about Iris has me spilling everything that I rarely share or even acknowledge. I tell her all about Emma, the breast cancer, my history with it, and how badly I messed up with my girl. She sympathizes and wishes me luck in my quest to gain forgiveness and secure my future with the one woman who's perfect for me.

Forty-five minutes later, I walk out of the store with three stunning arrangements, which I hope Emma will love. Now to get home before she does. She wouldn't let me pick her up from the hospital, refusing to let me help her. I'm determined to help her out over the next several weeks as she heals. I don't want her worrying about getting stuff done around the house or looking after her boys. I've spoken to Sarah and Max and asked them to allow me to step in to help out. Max was hesitant at first until I explained my long-term aim was to be with his sister. Then, after he threatened my balls—*what is it with this family and my balls?*—he reluctantly agreed to take a step back so I could step up. She's not allowed to drive for a while, so I've appointed myself as her taxi service, whether she likes it or not. I'll be taking the kids to and from school and I'll drive her to all of her upcoming appointments.

Dad insisted on cooking up a storm for dinner tonight to welcome Emma home from the hospital. I told Sarah, so she's organized for the family to stay for an early dinner, then I'll have my girl all to myself—I hope!

Pulling into my driveway, my stomach drops as disappointment fills me when I see Sally and John's sedan in Emma's driveway. Jumping out of my truck, I head straight next door. Emma's sitting on her porch in one of the rocking chairs I made for her with a blanket covering her legs and her Kindle on the table beside her. She has her hands wrapped around a mug of something hot. Her eyes closed in appreciation.

"You look stunning sitting there," I say quietly as I approach her, three bunches of flowers in my arms. Her eyes snap open, and she almost spills her drink. "Sorry, didn't mean to startle you."

"That's okay. I was enjoying the fresh air after being cooped up inside for days."

I hold out the flowers. "These are for you. I wanted you to have flowers throughout your house, so I got a few bunches. You want me to take them inside and get them sorted?"

Em begins to stand, but I gesture for her to stay seated. I don't want her moving around any more than necessary. "Thank you. They're gorgeous, but you didn't need to go to so much trouble."

"It was no trouble. Where are your vases? I'll get them sorted for you." I head for her front door.

She leans back in the chair, getting comfortable again. "Mom's inside. She'll happily sort them out."

"I'll be back in a minute." I step inside, finding Sally near the front door, probably trying to listen to our conversation. She's made it pretty clear that she would be happy if Emma and I worked things out.

"Theo! I'm so happy to see you. Are those flowers for Emma?" She presses up on her toes to land a kiss on my cheek.

"Hi, Mrs. Stanfield."

She playfully hits my arm. "None of that Mrs. stuff. Call me Sally."

"Okay, Sally. These are for Emma. I wanted to put some in the kitchen/dining, the living room, and her bedroom. Do you know where she keeps her vases?"

"I'll sort these out. Do you want a coffee? I just made one for Emma." Sally busies herself in the kitchen before I can respond. Her husband comes through the back door from the deck.

"Theo. Good to see you, Son. You've done a great job with the yard work. There's nothing left for me to do."

"Mr. Stanfield." I tilt my head. "I didn't want Emma to feel she needed to do anything other than healing and spending time with her boys."

He steps closer, holding out his hand, and I take it without reservation. "Thank you for looking out for our girl. Please call me John. Okay?"

I nod. "Here, take your coffee and keep Emma company on the front porch."

"Thanks, Mrs.— uh, Sally."

I take the coffee and step onto the front porch. We sit in comfortable silence for a few moments, enjoying the quiet of the street, and sipping on hot coffee. "How are you feeling? Are you in any pain?"

Bright green irises meet mine. "I feel pretty good at the moment. They gave me some pain meds before I left the hospital and we picked up my prescription for more on the way home."

"That's good. If you need anything, please let me know."

She nods. "Thanks. You don't need to worry about me, though. I have my family to help me."

I don't respond, quietly drinking my coffee. I think actions will be more powerful than any words I can offer her at this point. She doesn't trust me to stick around, which is fair enough after what I did. I'll *show* her instead of giving her promises. Sitting next to her like this feels like a fucking privilege that I won't take for granted. Not now, not ever.

After a while, I notice Emma's hand slacken, threatening to drop her cup. Her eyes are closed and her chair's still. Carefully, I remove the cup from her hand, place it on the table between us, then situate my chair, so I can use my foot to keep rocking her gently as she sleeps. Watching her like this gives me peace and I know I'm prepared to do everything I can to show her I'm here for as long as she will allow.

# CHAPTER 54

## —emma—

I CAN'T BELIEVE I FELL ASLEEP IN MY ROCKING CHAIR WITH THEO sitting right there. I hope I didn't drool or talk in my sleep. I've been finding I'm so tired since my surgery. It seems I can't get through the day without a nap—it makes me feel so old. When we arrived home, Mom didn't even let me go inside my own home. She sat my ass down in my favorite rocking chair and brought out a hot cup of coffee for me. It felt like heaven to be sitting outside enjoying the fresh air. Then I thought I'd died and gone to heaven when Theo rocked up with not one, but three bunches of flowers, looking as delicious as ever in worn jeans and a sweater the color of the ocean.

"Sorry, I fell asleep. You must think I'm so rude." I sit forward too quickly, pulling my stitches and catching my drainage tubes. Theo leaps forward, eyebrows scrunched low over Caribbean-colored eyes, as I gasp at the jarring sensation.

"You okay?" he asks, the heat from his hand burning through the fabric of my sweater.

"Yeah. Just moved too quickly. I need to move like a trucking geriatric and I keep forgetting." The sun's disappeared behind the clouds and a chill has settled in the air, leaving goosebumps. "I think it might be time to move inside. What time is it?"

"It's just after two. You must be feeling hungry. Dad's preparing a Greek feast for everyone tonight, but I can make you a snack to tide you over until dinner." After two! Sheet, I must have slept longer than I thought.

*Hang on, what?*

"What do you mean, your dad's preparing a Greek feast for every-one?" I wanted to spend a quiet night alone with my boys. The disap-pointment at my plan being disrupted is overwhelming, and I sag back in the chair.

"Is that okay? He offered, and I thought you'd enjoy some decent food after eating hospital food all week. I checked with your family and they thought it was a good idea. It's an early dinner, so we can enjoy the rest of the night hanging out with the kids." *We?* Have I woken in the twilight zone?

Theo gets up from his chair to help me stand. I take careful steps inside with Theo at my side, ready to open the door for me as though I'm an invalid. He helps me lower to the couch, making sure I don't squash my drainage tubes. "I can cancel Dad if you would prefer."

He's probably already made half the food. It would be incredibly rude of me to cancel, and he's trying so hard to be sweet. I give him a smile I know is weak at best. "That's okay. It'll be nice to catch up with everyone at once. Plus, your dad's cooking is delicious."

He huffs out a laugh. "Would you like me to make you a sandwich? Or I can get you some cheese and crackers?"

"If we're having a big dinner, I'll just have some cheese and crackers for now. Thanks, Theo."

He disappears into the kitchen to make my snack. Working my body carefully, I manage to make myself a little more comfortable on the couch. The areas where the stitches are feel so freaking itchy, and now that he's out of the room I can scratch my boobs. Not that I can feel myself scratching, so I need to be careful not to get carried away. The nurse warned me to be gentle because I wouldn't be able to feel if I hurt myself.

"How are you feeling after your nap?" Dad sits on the cushion beside me.

"Better. I'm a little sore, though. I think I was in an awkward posi-tion when I fell asleep."

He pats my thigh. "When are you due for your next meds?"

I look at the time on my phone. "Probably now."

"I'll get them for you, Honey." He kisses the top of my head, moving into the kitchen to sort out my pain relief.

Dad and Theo step into the living room at the same time, Mom hot on their heels. "We need to go pick up the kids. Will you be okay here with your father for a little while until we get back?" Theo places my snack on my lap and Dad hands me a glass of water with my meds.

"Sure. That'd be great." I smile at Dad. He barely gets a word in when Mom's around.

Mom kisses my cheek as she leaves the room, bustling about as though she's in the middle of doing a million things. Theo bends forward, brushing my bangs out of my eyes before laying the gentlest of kisses on my forehead. I swear I melt every single time he does it. It's a kiss full of care and concern. It's a kiss that makes me feel warm inside. He's been so attentive, with little touches and kisses here and there. I secretly love it, but I can't let him back in. I would have to be an idiot to go down that road again.

"That man has something to prove." Dad points out once Theo and Mom leave. He gets comfortable on the cushion next to me. "He worked tirelessly tidying up your yard before you came home from the hospital."

My mouth drops open, and I'm sure my eyes are as wide as saucers. I assumed my family had done everything to make my yard look so good. "Really? I thought you guys did everything."

He shakes his head. "Nope. He's also arranged to be the person to drive you to your appointments, as well as dropping and picking up the kids from school with you starting next week."

"What!"

Dad nods, a smile slowly widening across his face. "He's bound and determined to win you back. Theo's made his intentions very clear to all of us. You may as well just give in."

I shake my head in disbelief, fighting the smile that wants to form. "You know he lost his mom and sister to breast cancer?"

Dad nods. "Yes, he explained everything to us. Broke your mother's heart in the process. She's pretty much already picking out wedding stationery."

An unbidden laugh escapes and I wince at the sudden movement —I'll be glad when I can move freely again. "How can he want to be with me now?" I look down at my missing breasts. "Why would he want the constant reminder of what he lost?"

Dad studies me for a moment, looking down at my chest and back again, his eyes becoming glassy. "Maybe it's more about what he's found, rather than what he's lost." He raises his eyebrows, clearly proud of his profoundly wise words.

"I don't know if I can be the one he looks at every day as a reminder that I survived while his mom and sister didn't. It's bound to cross his mind." I feel I'm completely justified in my concern.

Dad releases a heavy sigh. "Maybe you need to let him make that decision."

We sit in silence for a few minutes. "I'm scared, Dad," I whisper.

He shuffles closer to me, wrapping his arm carefully around my shoulder. "Of what, Honey?"

"That he'll reject me when he sees what my body looks like now. Preston was turned off by my body after I had the boys. I don't think I could bear to have that happen again, especially because of the scarring to my breasts." He kisses the top of my head.

"First, I have to acknowledge that I never thought I'd be having a discussion like this with my daughter. Second, I've seen the way Theo looks at you. It's exactly the same way I look at your mother. There is nothing, and I mean *nothing*, that would cause me to reject that woman. She could have both breasts and her arms removed and I would still think she's the most beautiful, sexiest woman on the face of the earth." He pulls away slightly, his cheeks tinged pink. "Maybe you need to give him a chance?" He stands, collecting the dishes. "I'll clean up before the troops arrive."

I'm alone with my thoughts—analyzing my feelings and past hurts.

Can I move forward?

Can I trust him?

I don't know.

The front door slams open—a whirlwind of arms and legs comes running toward me and I brace myself for impact. Thankfully, Theo's quicker than they are, catching Kenny under one arm and Austin under the other.

"Mommy!"

"Emmmmmmaaa!"

I put my inner assessment aside so I can enjoy seeing my kids for the first time in days. "Hey, you guys! I've missed you so much." I carefully pull each of my sons in for a hug, breathing in their little boy smell. Kenny's up next, being extra careful with me; she's such a sweet little girl. They sit with me, catching me up on their week as we all share a piece of chocolate cake, courtesy of Sarah. Austin and Kenny eventually get bored and head into Austin's room to play. Lachlan stays close to me. We don't speak, just hang out next to each other—me reading my latest book, him watching cartoons on TV. It feels … nice to be home.

Theo's dad arrives with a ton of hot dishes, which smell incredible. After putting the food in the kitchen, he comes straight toward me; grasping my face, he kisses both of my cheeks. "How are you, *to gennaío mou korítsi?*" I look over his shoulder at Theo for him to explain what his dad just said.

"He called you 'my brave girl'," Theo responds with a smirk. "He's not wrong."

I look back at Mr. Drivas with heat rising on my cheeks. "Thank you. I'm feeling much better. Still a little sore and a whole lot tired. But I'm feeling better each day."

"Good, good. That's what I like to hear. Now, I'll go get the dinner ready. You sit here." He taps my cheek gently before moving away to do whatever it is he needs to do. I hear the silverware clanking as someone sets the table and I count my blessings that I have so many people around me who love and care for me.

Sarah and Max walk in like they own the place. I guess they have been staying here for almost a week, so they probably feel like they do. They both come straight to me on the couch.

Sarah leans down to kiss me on the cheek first. She presses her forehead against mine, her eyes glassy as she whispers, "I'm so happy you're okay, Sis." Her words are soft but heartfelt. I know this has been tough on her and Mom. I guess as women, we have a different bond with each other. When one of us has to go through something tough, we all feel it. This is particularly personal for the three of us. Mom's been having mammograms for years, coming back clear every single time—thank goodness. Sarah's too young to have started with the annual screening, but she's promised to talk to her doctor about getting one done sooner rather than later.

Max is next to welcome me home with a kiss on my forehead. His rough hands cup my face as he studies my eyes. "You're a champ, Sis. But you look tired. Want me to kick everyone out?" Only Max. He never says much, but he sees everything (except maybe that his girlfriend was a leech).

I smile at him. "I'm okay. Thank you for asking, though."

He nods as he stands up. "Need me to get anything for you?"

Theo steps forward. "I've got it, Max. Thanks." The two men study each other for long moments. Max tilts his head forward, then steps out of the living room.

"What was that about?" I ask Theo.

He shoves his hands in his pockets. "Nothing." It didn't look like nothing to me.

Moments later, Theo assists me out of my seat so he can help me into the dining room. The arm he has wrapped around my back burns through my shirt, warming my body. Even though I know I shouldn't, I love being this close to him again after so long. Being surrounded by his scent fills up a piece of me I thought I'd lost forever.

There's a literal feast laid on the table for us to enjoy. It smells amazing and I don't think it's because I've been stuck eating very ordinary hospital food for the past several days. Every time I've eaten food prepared by the Drivas men, my taste buds feel completely and utterly spoiled.

Dishes are shared around the table as everyone piles their plates high with delicious food. I notice there are a couple of dishes with crunchy potatoes and crunchy chickpeas. Theo must notice me watching Lachlan. Leaning in closer, he whispers, "I have some of his favorite sliced vegetables ready in the fridge if he doesn't like anything here."

And just like that, my heart softens toward the man sitting beside me. That he thought to have food on standby for my son amidst everything else he's already done is so incredibly endearing. If he keeps this up, my walls won't stand a chance.

There's a lull in the conversation, so I look around the table, ready to express my gratitude. "Thank you, everyone, for stepping in to help me out this past little while. I really appreciate everything you've all done for me." I look at Sarah and Max. "Thanks for staying here with the boys. For looking after the two most precious people in my life." I look at Mom and Dad. "Thank you so much for taking care of the boys after school and visiting me in the hospital." I look at Theo and his dad. "Thank you for everything you've both done to welcome me home. I appreciate you taking the time out of your busy days." They all brush off my thanks like their support is no big deal, returning to their meal. "No. I really mean it." I swipe at the tears escaping. "I don't think you understand how your help reduced my stress and made the process a little easier to deal with."

"You're welcome, Honey. We'll always help you out in any way we can. You know that." Mom gives me her warmest smile, followed by a wink.

Dinner comes to an end, and everyone boots me out of the kitchen so they can clean up. Gradually, everyone heads home, leaving me alone with Theo and the kids. Theo makes a pillow fort on the floor for the kids while we sit on the couch. With a full belly, I get comfortable on my end of the couch, gradually relaxing against the arm of the chair.

# CHAPTER 55

## —emma—

ARMS SLIDE BENEATH MY LEGS AND BEHIND ME, JOSTLING ME AWAKE. I must have fallen asleep—again. All the lights are out and the kids are nowhere to be seen. Looking up, I get caught up in stunning pools the color of the ocean. "How long have I been asleep?"

He lifts me as though I weigh nothing. "A couple of hours."

"Why are you still here?" I shake my head. "I can walk. My legs still work fine, you know." I smirk at him.

"I'm here because this is where I need to be. I won't be going anywhere any time soon. I know your legs work fine, but I *want* to carry you." He kisses my forehead as he makes his way upstairs with me. "Let me help you. Please."

What can I say? *Nothing*. So I keep my mouth shut and let him carry me upstairs. He takes me into my bathroom, carefully placing me on my feet. "I'll just be on the other side of the door if you need me. Okay?"

"Okay." He closes the door with a gentle snick and I get busy doing what I need to do. Stripping off my clothes, ready to shower my hospital stay away, I realize I don't have anything to cover my dressings so they don't get wet. Wrapping a towel around my body, I step out of the bathroom to grab the *Saran Wrap* and shriek as my body jolts to a stop. Theo's sitting up in my bed. No shirt. As though he's meant to be there. "Uh, why are you sitting in my bed, naked?"

"This is where I need to be. You might need something during the night."

"Where are the kids?" I probably should have asked this before, but I was still half asleep when he left me in my bathroom.

"I set up a fort in the boys' bedroom. They're all sleeping in it just like they did when we camped in my backyard." He says it so matter-of-factly, but it immediately conjures a memory of a better time. A simpler time. I look at my bedroom door and back again.

"You can't sleep in here with me. I don't want my boys to see you in my bed. So you can put your clothes back on and get out of my bed. Kenny can stay the night, so you don't disturb her, but you need to leave." My heart's hammering like crazy in my chest. All that bronze skin on display, those sexy abs that I spent hours exploring, waking up my core.

He pulls the sheet back and I prepare to see his dick, but he has gray sweats on. The disappointment is profound, and I mentally kick myself for my reaction to him. "I promise to keep my hands to myself, Peaches. This is purely to make sure you're okay tonight. It's your first night home. Please humor me." He gives me his best puppy dog look and I begin to waver. Rising to his knees, he makes his way over to the side of the bed closest to me. His rough hands land on my hips and he closes the distance, placing a gentle kiss on my lips. The lightest of touches has me questioning whether he actually kissed me at all. "Please, Em. I won't get any sleep tonight if I'm not next to you. I need to know you're okay. I promise I won't touch you unless you ask me to."

How can I say no? He's being incredibly attentive.

I give a stiff nod, then head for the door to grab the plastic wrap I need to cover my dressings.

"Where are you going?" Turning around, I capture the creases forming between Theo's eyebrows.

Feeling exposed and vulnerable, I keep my explanation simple. "I need something from downstairs."

"I can get it for you. What do you need?" He begins to climb off of the bed, but I hold out my hand in the universal sign for stop.

"I'm okay, I'll get it." My feet move quickly, taking me downstairs. I grab what I need and head back upstairs. When he spots the box of *Saran Wrap* in my hands, he jumps out of bed.

"What's going on?"

"Nothing. I want to have a shower, which means I need this …" I wave the box around. "to cover my dressings and stitches. Even though it's okay to get the dressings wet, I don't want to sleep with them damp."

"You gonna need help with that?" He follows me as I walk back toward the bathroom. I grab my pajamas and step back inside.

"Nope." Closing the door with a snick, I lean against it heavily. Dropping my towel, I get to work, only to realize I can't do this by myself. Tears of frustration break free as I screw up another wasted ball of plastic. "Damn it!" I drop my head into my hands. I'm going to have to wipe the essential areas over with a wet cloth. I huff as I drop the box onto the vanity. I should have thought about this while Sarah and Mom were here. One of them could have helped me.

A quiet knock breaks me from my pity party. "You okay in there, Peaches?" His voice is thick with concern. What I wouldn't give to have a warm shower. "Em?"

Wiping my tears from my cheeks and wrapping myself in my towel, I open the door slightly. "I really wanted to have a shower." He nods. "I can't get the wrap around my body on my own." I look down at the floor because I can't bear to see the pity in his eyes. "I'm desperate to wash my hospital stay away. I ha—"

He pushes the door open carefully, stepping inside the bathroom. He grabs the wrap and gestures toward me, asking permission. I lower my towel to below my bust without words. Without looking down at my chest area, he locates the end of the *Saran Wrap* and begins carefully wrapping it around the top portion of my body while I hold the drains out of the way. His eyes leave mine only to ensure he's covering the entirety of my chest area carefully. I close my eyes as he makes his way around the front of my body. My bottom lip quivers as I work to keep my embarrassment at bay. He'll probably take off now that he's seen the physical evidence of my surgery. It's one thing to know something has happened. It's quite another to be confronted so blatantly with the evidence.

"There ya go," he whispers against my forehead, finishing with a gentle press of his lips.

I nod slightly. "Thank you," I whisper, my mouth dry.

As he backs out of the room, I glance up. What I see looking back at me steals my breath away. Eyes—full of desire that I find impossible to believe. Dropping my eyes to the floor in avoidance, I can't miss the unmistakable bulge of his impressive erection in his sweats. My eyes snap back up to his as my cheeks heat. He winks at me with a smirk, closing the door behind him.

Preston never looked at me like that after I had the boys. Once I gained a bit of extra weight as a result of my pregnancies, his dick was permanently flaccid in my presence. Don't get me started on my 'unsightly' stretch marks—his words—that he couldn't bring himself to touch. Here I am standing with all of that, plus scarred breasts and dirty hair, and he's still looking at me like I'm the sexiest woman on the face of the earth. My lips tilt up at the corners as I do a gentle shimmy.

Dropping my panties, I step under the warm water with a sigh, feeling completely indulgent. I let the warm water wash away the last week of hospital disinfectant, itchy gowns, and scratchy, stiff sheets. The warm water erases the touch of the surgeons and nurses. I *know* I'm one of the lucky ones. My logical mind knows this. It could have been so much worse. I almost feel like a fraud saying I had breast cancer when other women have more serious instances of the insidious disease.

My tears mingle with the warm water and a loud sob escapes unbidden. From the moment the doctor sent me for the scans, it's been a whirlwind of emotions. I've held it together pretty well … *until now.*

A cool draft brushes across my wet body as the shower door opens and closes.

"Turn around."

I can't.

I don't want to face the man who walked away from me. The man who made me feel like a fool. His calloused hands smooth up my arms until he reaches my shoulders. He massages me gently before guiding me around to face him, then slides his hands back down, taking each of my hands in his.

"Look at me, Em." His voice is raspy, full of emotion. Raising my head, I look to the side. I don't want him to see the evidence of my tears. It leaves me too vulnerable. His hands come up to cup my face, directing my eyes to his. "Talk to me."

Closing my eyes, I shake my head. "I can't." More tears escape; it's like the floodgates have opened and I can't stop them. He presses my face into the crook of his neck and we stand together in silence, under the warm spray of the shower.

He lets me cry.

Soothing me with kisses on top of my head, he caresses his hand up and down my spine. His hand moves higher, smoothing down my hair. After a few minutes, he stops and the sound of my shampoo bottle clicking open startles me. His capable hands go back into my hair, massaging my scalp, and I drop my head back in pleasure. His hands feel sensational in my hair, working the shampoo through the long strands. He turns my body slightly until my hair is directly under the warm stream. He repeats the process with the conditioner and I feel almost human again. His strong hands work miracles, soothing my frayed emotions, and treating me as though I'm something precious to be treasured.

Finally, I become brave enough to open my eyes. His heated gaze locks with mine. "Feel better?"

"Yeah," I sigh. "Thank you." I try my best to give him a grateful smile. "I almost feel human again." I look down at my feet, noticing that he's wearing his boxer briefs, from which his penis is doing its best to escape. A genuine smile touches my lips at the sight. I look back up at him with wide eyes.

"Don't ever think I won't be turned on by your body, Peaches." He smirks. "I'll never stop finding your body sexy, Em. But it's more than that. Your spirit and your fire are such a turn-on for me." He kisses my forehead. "The way you care for the people around you makes me want to be the one to care for *you*. It's everything. The way I feel when I'm with you …" He looks away, then back at me. "I missed you these last months. I've realized I don't want to be without you. I want …" He swallows, then whispers, "I want you. All of you. Plain and simple, Em." He presses forward, our lips connecting for the first time in months, and I feel as though I've arrived home. His heartfelt words fill up the cracks around my heart, and I know I shouldn't forgive so easily. I *know* I should make him work harder, but I've missed him, too. I'm just not sure I can trust him with my heart.

The water begins to cool, so we finish up. He dries me off first, helping me to unwrap the plastic from my body before inspecting my dressings to ensure they're all dry. I dress in my not-so-sexy after-surgery compression bra and pajamas as Theo drops his wet boxers to the floor, exposing himself without any sign of embarrassment. And why would he be embarrassed? He certainly doesn't have anything to be ashamed of and it's not like we haven't seen each other before.

"You want me to dry your hair for you? I can't imagine it'll be easy to raise your arm above your head." He asks as he pulls on his gray sweats, sans jocks. I could lift my hands if I wanted to, but I'm enjoying his pampering. The stitches pull a little when I lift my arms too high, and I can feel the drains pulling too, so I may as well take him up on his generous offer.

I grab my hairdryer and hand it to him. "I would appreciate it if you don't mind. I feel like I've already taken advantage of your generosity, though."

"It'd be my pleasure." Turning me around, he runs my wide comb through the strands, then sets about drying the saturated locks. I feel so much more human after showering and having my hair washed.

Turning around to face my dreamy neighbor, I rest my hands on his slim hips. "Thank you so much. It's amazing how much better I feel."

"You're welcome, Peaches. It was my absolute pleasure." He kisses my forehead. "I'll leave you to finish up." He leaves me alone in the bathroom; a gush of air escaping my lungs as I sag against the vanity. I can't believe what just happened. It's probably the most intimate experience of my life to date. Him caring for me in such a tender way that didn't involve sex was so unfamiliar, yet so beautiful.

I deal with my drains, emptying each one in turn into the measuring cup. It's a little tender where the drains enter my body. I make sure to keep the pressure consistent on the bulbs as I close each valve, then hook them back onto the strap under my compression bra. Checking the measure on the cup, I record twenty-five milliliters for my left side and twenty-one milliliters for my right side on my chart. That's about the same as this morning. Tipping the fluid that seems to be changing color day by day into the toilet, I flush it away before rinsing the cups.

I draw in a deep breath, turn out the light, and step out of the bathroom with my shoulders back. Theo looks at me, keeping his eyes locked with mine as he holds out his hand. With my heart hammering in my chest, I slowly slide my hand into his. His calloused palm glides against mine before his grip closes, slowly pulling me forward. Holding my breath, my knee makes contact with the edge of the bed and I carefully move forward. His tongue slides out between his lips as his eyes drop briefly to my mouth. My breath stalls in my lungs as the look in his eyes becomes heated, the blue disappearing, being swallowed by his dilated pupils.

"C'mon, Peaches. Relax." He kisses the back of my hand, his lips leaving an indelible mark on my skin and my heart. Theo's managed to wedge up the mattress and has arranged the bed pillows so I can sleep almost sitting up. I position my mastectomy pillows under my armpits and lay against the bed pillows carefully, trying to keep space between Theo's body and mine. "You okay?"

I turn my head on my pillow, facing him. "I think so. Thank you again for looking after me." He rolls onto his back, takes my hand in his, and turns out the light.

"Any time. Get some sleep."

"Okay."

I wake to sunlight streaming across my face, and the desperate need to pee. Looking across at the pillow next to mine, my heart sinks to find the space empty. I guess he left once he realized I didn't actually need him during the night. I know I made a big deal about him being in my bed and not wanting the boys to find him here, but I'm still disappointed he left. I get up and sort myself out, emptying my drains and recording the measurements, then dress for the day. Making my way down the hallway to the boys' bedroom, I find it empty—I can't believe they're up and they let me sleep.

My foot barely touches the floor at the bottom of the stairs when Austin comes out from the kitchen. "Mommy." He wraps his little arms around me, burying his head in my stomach.

Gliding my fingers through his silky hair, I bend down to kiss the top of his head. "Morning, Buddy."

He looks up at me, a sparkle in his eyes. The smell of bacon reaches my nose as Austin's words reach my ears. "Theo's making us breakfast." Grabbing my hand, he pulls me toward the kitchen and I'm grateful that I decided to dress. At least I look somewhat put together after my emotional breakdown last night.

Theo must have gone home to change because he's wearing jeans that hug his muscular thighs and a navy long-sleeve Henley, which complements his eyes. "Morning, Peaches. I'm making breakfast."

"Morning. I can see that." I move around the table to Lachlan and Kenny to say good morning, kissing the top of each of their heads. "How did you sleep, Lachlan?" Sarah said he'd been having trouble this week while I was away. I expected as much, despite Sarah knowing the routine. Lachlan would have had a hard time coping with the changes, even though he understood why they had to happen.

"Good, Mommy. I like sleeping in the fort with Kenny and Austin." My eyebrows almost shoot to my hairline in surprise. I knew he'd slept pretty well the night we camped in Theo's backyard. I assumed it was because we were all snuggled in tight in the tent; maybe there's something to him co-sleeping that helps him to settle better.

Digging into the delicious breakfast, I watch my boys interact with Kenny and Theo as though they're already a part of our family. Theo makes our plans for the day, and I'm happy enough to let him take the lead.

He and Kenny spend the weekend with us as though it's the way we spend all of our weekends, and I find I'm in no hurry for Monday to arrive.

# CHAPTER 56

## —*theo*—

WE'VE BASICALLY SPENT THE WEEK LIVING TOGETHER. I GET BREAKFAST, Em makes the school lunches, and we drive the kids to and from school together. I work in my workshop while she reads, naps, and potters around her house. We have our morning coffee and lunch together on her back porch, then I head back to my workshop until it's time to pick up the kids from school. It's given me a glimpse into our possible future together as a family, and I like it.

I like it a *lot*.

It's felt real and right and easy.

Even though I'm still sleeping in her bed, I haven't pushed for anything more than what she'll allow me and I don't want to at this stage. I *need* her to come to me. To show me she's ready to let me back in. That she trusts me with her heart. But I get the sense it's more than trusting me with her heart. She needs to trust me with her body, too. She's also still very sore, as I presume she will be for quite some time to come.

I remember overhearing her argument with her ex. She said something about him not being interested in her once her body changed after having the boys. I hope she got my message loud and clear that I'm not going to lose interest in her *or* her body. When she let me help her in the shower the first night she came home from the hospital, I couldn't stop my body from reacting to hers even though she was clearly bruised, swollen, and sore—both physically and emotionally. I don't understand any man who doesn't appreciate the miracle of their wife's body—that they can grow and nourish a human life inside of theirs. So what if her body changes? It *should* change. *She* is fundamentally different as a result of carrying a child, and *that* should be reflected, appreciated, and adored.

Sitting in the passenger seat of my truck on the way to her follow-up appointment with her breast cancer surgeon, her fingers are white as she squeezes her hands tightly together. Reaching across, I gently squeeze her thigh to gain her attention.

"You want me to come in with you?" *I desperately want her to say yes.* I want her to trust me enough to be there to support her when he delivers whatever news he has to deliver today. "Are you nervous about getting your pathology results?"

Her head snaps around to face me. "Why would you want to come in with me? What if the news from the pathology isn't so good? What if he tells me they didn't get it all? What if I have to go through radiation? Do you really want to sit in there with me while I learn my fate?" All of her questions come tumbling out, one after another.

I can understand her doubts. After all, I didn't support my sister through her battle. I know I'm an asshole for that and even though my sister said she forgave me; I'll *never* forgive myself. I don't deserve forgiveness for my selfish and unforgivable actions. For letting my sister, father, and niece down in such an epic way.

I can't go back in time to make different choices; I can only make different choices *now*.

Better choices.

The *right* choices.

My answer to her question is simple. "Yes, I do. I want to be with you every single step of the way throughout this process. I want to support you wherever I can."

She turns away, facing the passenger window, and my stomach sinks. The heavy silence that descends on us is stifling. We remain that way until we arrive at the surgery. Heading inside, Em tells the receptionist she's here for her appointment and we sit in the serviceable waiting room in silence—as though we're strangers. I don't like it. I refuse to allow it, so I take her hand between both of mine, pulling it across to rest on my thigh.

"Mrs. Miller?" My head snaps up at Emma's married name being called. I hate that she still has the asshole's name attached to her. Emma stands, moving toward the nurse, and I slouch back in my seat.

She turns around, raising a sculpted eyebrow at me. "You coming?"

It only takes me a split second to respond. Within three strides, I'm by her side and we're making our way toward the surgeon's office —*together*. The way I always want us to be. I take her hand, attempting to give her any support I can. Immediately, I recognize the surgeon who came out to speak to Sally and John after Em's surgery.

Stepping out from behind his desk, he holds out his hand to greet both of us in turn. Tipping his head forward slightly, he welcomes us, "Mr. and Mrs. Miller." The hackles on the back of my neck immediately rise, but I don't want to embarrass Emma, so I keep my mouth shut. Because we all know that words don't always come out of my mouth in the right way.

"Hi, Dr. Barnes. Uhm, this is my friend, Theo." She gestures toward me.

*'Friend'*. I hate it.

"Oh, sorry, I assumed. Please, take a seat." He gestures to the seats opposite his desk before looking at Emma. "Are you happy to discuss your results and what we need to do, moving forward, with your friend in the room?"

Emma looks at me as she answers, "Yeah."

I squeeze her hand.

To show how much I appreciate her trust.

To show her I'm here for it all.

To show her I love her.

Not that I've told her I love her. I don't think she would want to hear it at this point. She would assume it's out of sympathy or regret— which is ridiculous.

"Okay. As you know, your DCIS was spread throughout the ducts in both breasts, meaning we had to remove all the breast tissue. We discussed this before the surgery, so that shouldn't be a surprise." Emma already explained this to me, so I'm not shocked to hear this. "The pathology results show that we removed all the cancerous cells from your breasts. The sentinel nodes were clear, which is a great indication that the cancer hadn't spread any further. I am, however, recommending you get a second opinion from a medical oncologist due to the size of the mass we removed. I've booked you an appointment for three weeks. At this stage, if their results corroborate with mine, I don't see any need to follow up with radiotherapy." Emma's shoulders drop and the tightness around her eyes releases, while a small smile touches her lips.

She looks across at me; her smile widening as I squeeze her hand in relief, returning her grin. I can't imagine how relieved she must feel, because my relief is immense. For the first time since learning about Em's cancer, I can take a full breath.

"That's great news, Dr. Barnes." Em's voice is brighter than it's been since we first reconnected in the hospital. We finish up, then return to the waiting room for her follow-up appointment with her plastic surgeon. It's a great setup with all the breast care surgeons and nurses in one place, making it easier for the aftercare process.

"Emma Miller." We both stand, making our way toward her plastic surgeon.

"Hello, Dr. Corrigan." We follow the woman down a short hallway to her room.

"It's great to see you, Emma. You're looking as though you're doing well."

"Other than feeling tired, I feel as though my recovery is going smoothly."

"That's great to hear. How are the drains coming along?"

Emma hands her the records she's been keeping. "Down to twelve mils the last couple of days." They've been annoying the shit out of her. I know she's hoping the doctor will remove them today.

Dr. Corrigan nods. "That sounds great." She scans the paperwork. "Okay, can you hop up on the table over here, take off your shirt, and let's take a look."

I reluctantly release her hand as Em nods in confirmation, then stands to make her way over to the table. Removing her sweater and shirt, she raises her head, our eyes locking. I can read the worry in their depths. I haven't seen her scars. She changes her dressings privately, not allowing me to see everything. I tip my head forward, giving her a wink as the only way I can show her it'll be okay. She removes the final article of clothing, which is hiding her from me. When all of this is done, I'm taking her lingerie shopping. I don't want her thinking she needs to hide anything from me—*ever*. I want her to celebrate her success against this fucking insidious disease.

The doctor carefully peels away the dressings covering her scars. Red, angry lines from the side of each breast almost reaching the nipple are revealed. I don't know how to portray to her that the scars aren't ugly to me. They don't fucking matter. They don't lessen how beautiful she is, nor do they reduce how sexy I find her. They're a sign that she survived something that some women don't. I swallow hard at the thought.

*Did Mom and Anna have these scars?*

I have no idea if they went through surgery, but it was too late and the cancer had already spread, or was it too late and they didn't go down that path at all? I have no idea what battles they faced.

With the tips of her fingers, the doctor pokes and prods gently along the line of the scar, paying particular attention to each end.

"These incisions are looking fantastic. The bruising is on track, and so is the swelling. Your healing is coming along very nicely. Have you been following the high-protein diet I recommended?"

She smiles at me, then answers Dr. Corrigan. "I have. Theo's been cooking for me, making sure I follow the regime to the letter." My chest puffs up with pride that I was able to help my girl in some small way.

"Great. Your nipples are looking really good at this stage. Just keep an eye on them. We're not quite out of the woods with them yet." Emma nods in acknowledgment. "Let's remove these drains." Dr. Corrigan smiles at her. She must have some idea of what these women go through physically and emotionally after such significant surgery. She's been incredibly gentle and respectful with Em.

As Dr. Corrigan washes her hands and dons gloves, Em turns to me. "Yay," she whispers. Her smile is so wide. I want to snap a photo to remember this moment forever. She has a sparkle in her eyes, one I haven't seen since before I fucked up.

The clear covering is carefully peeled away, followed by the small white discs at the entry point. "I'm going to cut this stitch here and then I can remove the tube." She snips, removes the stitch, and then pulls the drain out. I follow its path as it slides beneath Em's breast before it comes free of her body. My eyes move up to her face to see if she's okay, but her smile hasn't changed at all.

Dr. Corrigan repeats the process with the other drain, before covering each opening with a band-aid. "These small holes will heal up on their own in a day or two. You can have a shower without any issues." She smiles at Em.

Em raises her arms, displaying a slightly pinkish patch where the clear adhesive was protecting the drains. "That feels so much better. Thanks, Doctor."

"You're welcome. That pinkness from the adhesive will also clear up in a day or two." She snaps off her gloves, washing her hands again after pushing the trolley of implements out of the way. "You can get redressed now."

We finish up with Dr. Corrigan and make our way out of the

surgery. Em's demeanor is significantly lighter than it was when she entered the building. I'm incredibly thankful I'm the one with her to share this moment. Holding hands, she swings them back and forward between us. "It feels so great to be rid of the drains."

"I bet." Arriving at my truck, I unlock her door and lock the seatbelt in place after my girl gets comfortable. Brushing my lips across her forehead, I ask, "How do you feel about stopping in at the restaurant for lunch?"

Her eyebrows slash down over her eyes, forming creases between them. "Don't you need to get back to your workshop?"

"Nope. I have time." Closing her in my truck, I make my way around to the driver's side and climb in. "Well?"

"I won't say no. I love your dad's food."

I put on a playful pout. "More than mine?"

She laughs. "It's pretty close. Don't make me choose." I love this lightness about her—it's been missing.

Putting the truck in drive, we head across town to Dad's restaurant. Em turns the stereo up and starts singing at the top of her voice about a feeling inside her bones going electric. I join in with her, sharing her joy. It certainly beats the heavy silence that filled the truck on the way to the surgery.

# CHAPTER 57

## —*theo*—

When we enter the restaurant, it takes a moment for my eyes to adjust. Once I can see properly, my eyes land on Dad standing near the greeting podium. His face lights up when he realizes who his new patrons are. He immediately engulfs Em in a hug, being careful not to squish her too close. "Emma. So great to see you. You must have lunch." He kisses each of her cheeks.

"Hello, Mr. Drivas. I hope you don't mind us dropping in."

"Of course not. Come through." He pulls back, taking Emma's hand to guide her through to the table at the back of the large room that he reserves for special guests. It's the setting I made when I was younger. "Hello, Son. Good to see you."

"You too, Dad." Nice to know I didn't get forgotten—I *was* starting to wonder.

"Sit, sit. I'll get some wine and bring out lunch." He pulls out Emma's chair and tucks her in, then moves toward the bar.

"I'm so sorry. I'm choosing not to drink wine anymore." She glances down at her lap, then back at us. "It's been recommended for me to avoid or at the very least limit my alcohol intake as it can increase my risk of cancer, and well, since I've already had it …" She swallows. "I'm already at an increased risk."

Dad smiles widely at her. "No problem. I have a lovely bottle of non-alcoholic sweet white wine that tastes just like its alcoholic sister." He heads off toward the bar with a bounce in his step.

Emma smiles at me with raised brows and wide eyes. We both burst into laughter at the same time. Dad returns with three glasses and the wine, which he pours, then heads into the kitchen. "I guess he's going to join us for lunch."

"I guess so." Emma laughs.

"When is your next appointment with the plastic surgeon?"

"Monday. Do you mind taking me to that appointment, too? I know I'm being a bo—"

I cut her off. "Absolutely. You know my days are flexible." I tip my head forward as though I'm tipping my hat. "I'm at your beck and call."

She leans forward, across the table. "My beck and call, huh?" That twinkle in her eye is sexy as fuck.

"Anything you need, Peaches. I'm there." We hold each other's gaze for a long moment, interrupted only when Dad returns with a spectacularly presented *Mezze* platter. Dips, feta, cucumbers, roasted peppers, marinated artichokes, pita, breadsticks, the works. It looks amazing. He takes his seat and we all take the opportunity to toast Emma's positive results today.

We spend the next few minutes indulging in the delicious flavors and textures which are so familiar to me. Emma points at the artichoke. "What's that?"

I use the fork to present a portion to her. "Marinated artichoke. Tastes a little like young asparagus. Would you like a taste?"

She leans forward, opening her mouth, and I slide the vegetable onto her tongue. Her eyes drop closed as she closes her mouth and all I can think about are the times her mouth closed around my dick and her throat swallowed around my shaft. Discreetly shifting in my seat, I adjust myself to prevent my zipper from digging into my cock.

"That's really tasty. Thank you." She looks at Dad. "Did you make all of this yourself?"

He shakes his head. "Unfortunately, no. I put it together on the platter, but my chef prepares all the different foods. I don't have so much time to spend in the kitchen with running the business side of things." He shrugs, disappointment radiating off of him.

Emma and I catch Dad up on the kids. It feels completely natural to refer to them as one unit; as though they're already siblings. They certainly act as though they are. There have been a couple of arguments this past week with us all living together. I'm sure there are bound to be some teething problems as we all adjust to the new living arrangements. Emma thinks it's a temporary situation while she recovers from surgery, but Kenny and I won't be moving out any time soon.

Once lunch is finished, we leave Dad and drive to the store to buy groceries. "We seem to be going through a lot of food," Emma mumbles as we fill the cart.

"There *are* five of us." I point out.

She looks at me as though she's only now realized we've been feeding five people. Granted, three of them are kids, but I've been trying to cook high-protein and vegetable-rich meals to help Emma's healing. I've also been slowly encouraging Lachlan to try eating some of the same foods as the rest of us. I always have his favorites on standby just in case, but it hasn't been needed for the last two nights. I think it helps him take the risk with the new foods, knowing his regular favorites are available to him.

Emma nods. "I guess so."

We move toward the milk, our last stop, before heading for the register. After the shop assistant scans our groceries, she looks at me. "That'll be ninety-three dollars and eighty-five cents."

I grab my wallet, pulling out my card at the same time as Emma, barely managing to scan my card through the machine first. "Why are you paying for our groceries? You're already helping us out so much."

"Kenny and I are eating the food as well. I like to pay my way. You can pick them up next time." I shrug and begin loading the bags into the cart. As far as I'm concerned, it's the end of the conversation. I hear her huff behind me and in my mind's eye, I can see her rolling her gorgeous eyes and crossing her arms in a pout. I smile to myself, knowing I've won this round.

# CHAPTER 58

## —emma—

I FEEL AS THOUGH I'M WRAPPED IN A FURNACE—THE BLANKETS TWISTED around my body make it difficult to throw them off. Working to disengage from the tangle, I realize it's not the blankets making me feel hot, it's the body wrapped around mine from behind.

I sigh in comfort.

Every night, since coming home from the hospital, Theo's been in my bed. His excuse is that he needs to make certain I'm alright, which has been completely unnecessary. The thing is, it feels good to have him here—it feels … *right*. I should put a stop to it, but I can't bring myself to give this up—whatever *this* is. Surprisingly, the boys haven't questioned Theo sleeping in my bed. Austin came in one morning and climbed in between us; Kenny did it yesterday. When Lachlan wakes in the early hours of the morning, Theo tells me to go back to sleep and he gets up to spend time with him; allowing me to rest. It's as though this is the way it's always been and the way it always will be.

*I like it*. Maybe too much.

Turning my head to look over my shoulder at him, I smile at the peaceful, almost boyish appearance of his face in slumber. His thick lashes rest on the tops of his cheeks. Studying his features, I'm reminded of Friday. How his forehead creased in contemplation when he asked to come into my appointment with me. I wasn't sure if it was a good idea at first. Then I thought, what the hell, maybe if he hears what the doctors have to say and sees the ugliness as a result of the surgery, he'll choose to walk away.

When I think about it now, I was definitely testing him at my appointments on Friday.

He stood strong and firm.

He was my support and encouragement.

When my scars were finally exposed, he didn't look at me any differently than all the times before. He didn't cringe or shy away. I felt acceptance in his presence. Support and strength in his grip as he held my hand. Heat in his gaze as he looked at me. There wasn't any sign of disgust or that he found me lacking in any way.

My bladder screams at me to get up, so I carefully remove Theo's arm and slide out of bed. He must be exhausted because he doesn't move a muscle. Making my way to the bathroom, I do my business and decide to have a shower, which is so much easier without the drains. Removing my clothes, I study my scarred, bruised, and still-swollen breasts. The expanders feel hard as rocks behind what little tissue I have left and I'm hoping the plastic surgeon is right, that the implants I'm due to get will feel less invasive.

Today, I'm getting my first injection to begin increasing their size. Carefully cupping the smaller mounds, I peer at them closely. Studying their flaws, tears form in my eyes, welling to the point they can no longer be contained. Splashes of pain land on my scars. I'm so caught up in my stupid, waste of time and energy self-pity party that I jump a little when Theo's hands come up to cover mine. With eyes locked together in the mirror, he bends down, placing the gentlest of kisses on my shoulder. The rasp of his beard reminds me of other places his bristles have touched.

"You wanna know what I see, Em?" he whispers roughly beside my ear. His breath sends goosebumps rising across my body. I nod slowly, swallowing down my doubts and fears in preparation for what he's about to say. "I see a strong woman who did what she had to do to ensure her survival for not only herself but her family." He lays a tender kiss on my shoulder. "I see scars that remind me you were brave enough to make tough choices." Another tender kiss lands in the crook of my neck. "I see power in the way you took control of the situation you found yourself in." Another tender, barely there kiss touches my ear. "I see a sexy woman with the most feminine of curves, dips, and valleys that I hope I will have the privilege of exploring again one day." Yet another kiss is pressed against my temple this time. "I see the woman I hope will allow me to share her life, her family, her mind, her body, and her bed for the rest of my days." He lands a light press of his lips against my cheek.

Turning in his arms, I press up, touching my lips to his. His hands move up to cup each side of my face, the roughened pads of his thumbs wiping my tears away from my cheeks. "Theo," I whisper against his lips.

"It'll be okay, Em. I promise," he breathes before sweeping his tongue across my lips, requesting entry, which I readily grant. Our kiss is full of life, fire, and affection. But it's more than that. It feels as though this kiss is branding my soul, marking me in a way that makes me undoubtedly his.

Slowly, our lips separate, breaths coming in short pants. Opening my eyes, I'm greeted by pupils that almost swallow the blue that I love so much. We both tilt our heads forward, pressing our foreheads together. "Do you mean it?"

"I do. Every single word and more. I understand that it'll take time for you to trust me. I promise, with everything I am, that I'm here with you for better or for worse, Em." He finishes his statement with another peck to my forehead. "Come on, we need to get ready to take the kids to school so you can get to your appointment this morning."

Stepping away, Theo starts the shower for me as I remove my panties and tie my hair up out of the way. The warm spray feels amazing on my skin. Closing my eyes, I enjoy the warmth of the water sluicing down my body. I feel more than see Theo enter the shower behind me, the click of the soap bottle my only warning before calloused hands begin gliding over my skin—heating me in ways the water can't.

I hope he understands that sex won't be on the horizon any time soon. As much as he turns me on, I'm not up for it. Not yet. I'm not sure when I will be.

"What's going on in that gorgeous head of yours?" He has a playful tone to his voice.

Turning to face him, I swallow down my nerves. "Uh, I was wondering if you were aware that I won't be ready for sex any time s—"

Placing a rough finger over my lips, he smirks at me. "Don't finish that sentence, Em." Raising his eyebrows, he continues. "Do I love having sex with you? Abso-fucking-lutely. Do I want to have sex with you again? The answer is unquestionably yes. Am I willing to wait until you're completely ready? Physically *and* emotionally ready. You can take it to the bank. I'll be here whenever you're ready—" He looks down at his erect dick. "—and waiting. Take your time, Peaches. I'm in it for the long haul." He finishes with a searing kiss, stealing my breath and making me dizzy. His dick pressing against my stomach is a reminder that this man has needs. Maybe not today, but soon, I'll help him out with those.

We finish in the shower, get dressed, and I head in to wake up the kids so they can get ready for school. Lachlan's lying quietly in bed with his iPad, creating swirly patterns. "Morning, Buddy. How are you doing?"

He looks up at me, noticing me for the first time. "Morning, Mommy. Look at this pattern I made. It has Kenny's favorite colors."

He tilts his iPad toward me, so I can see it clearly. "That looks great. You should take a screenshot to show Kenny."

"Good idea." He busies himself taking the shot while I open the curtains to let the sunlight in.

"Come downstairs when you're ready." I kiss the top of his head on the way out of the door.

As Theo prepares breakfast for everyone, we move around each other seamlessly in the kitchen while I make the kids' lunches. We make a great team; working together as though we've always done this. As I slice the apples to place in the lunchboxes, I can't suppress the spread of my lips as the kids settle around the table to be served by Theo without a second glance. They've become so used to him and Kenny being here, I'm not sure how they'll respond when Theo and Kenny aren't staying here anymore. My mood drops at the thought of them not being here. Not hearing Kenny's chatter and laughter, or the way she bosses the boys around to play dolls or have pretend cups of tea. Not having Theo's clothes draped on the chair in my bedroom or his work boots at the back door. Each day they bring across more of their things but never seem to take anything back to their place. Theo startles me with a kiss to the side of my neck as he passes with the kids' empty breakfast dishes.

"Okay, guys and gal. Go brush your teeth and get your school bags. It's time to get moving." He claps his hands together, ushering them out of the kitchen.

Kenny replies as she stands from her chair. "Okay, Daddy."

Theo freezes in place as his niece strolls out of the kitchen as though her words weren't life-changing. His head drops low between his shoulders as his hands come up to rest on his hips. His shoulders rise and fall with exaggerated breaths. I move around the kitchen counter, laying my hand gently between his shoulder blades.

Dropping my voice low, I ask, "You okay?"

His head turns toward me slowly, eyes glassy. "Yeah. That was … unexpected."

"I'm honestly not surprised. You two are extraordinarily close."

"Yeah," he breathes out.

"Are you mad?"

His entire body snaps into place. "Of course not. I … I fucking love that she called me 'daddy'. I'm not sure I'm deserving of the title, though." We both smile—mine reassuring, Theo's tight and unsure—and I lean forward, placing a kiss on his bristly cheek. "I don't think she actually realized what she just said, though."

I glance upstairs, where I can hear the kids in the bathroom. "Probably not. That makes it even better, don't you think?"

He nods before collecting more dishes. "Absolutely." We both get back to our tasks, managing to wrangle the kids out of the door in time to get to school.

I pop my head into Kate's class after dropping my boys off at their respective classrooms. Theo's still sitting with Kenny as she does her morning reading. I haven't seen my friend since she stopped in to visit me while I was in the hospital. She spots me straight away, walking directly to me.

"Emma! I'm so happy to see you. God, I miss you around here." She leans in to hug me but pulls away before we can make contact. "Sorry. I don't want to hurt you."

I wave away her concern. "That's okay." I lean forward, giving her a side hug. "How are things?"

"Don't worry about me. How are you? How is your recovery coming along?" Her denim eyes are soft as she studies me. "You look great."

"Thanks. I'm feeling okay. Tired. Extremely tired. Which I did not expect, but the doctor says it's completely normal."

"You need to make sure you're resting, Emma. Is there anything I can help you with, so you don't overdo it?" Of course she would ask if she can help. It's in her nature to help the people around her, but she has enough on her plate with Margie and the kids at the shelter. Not to mention her billionaire husband.

"I'm good. I promise I'm not overdoing it." Theo steps in behind me, wrapping his arm around my shoulder before kissing my temple. Looking between us, Kate's eyes widen comically.

"I'm making sure she rests. Don't worry about that." Our conversation is cut short by the ringing of the school bell.

As Kate hugs me goodbye, she whispers, "You and I have plenty to talk about at our next coffee."

*—emma—*

"Right. Come and sit up on the table over here. Please remove your shirt and bra. Let's take a look to see if we can start filling your expanders."

Dr. Corrigan is happy with my healing so far. She studies the scars closely, pressing against the swelling and bruising. "How does this feel?" she asks.

"I can feel pressure, but not much else."

"To be expected. I'm happy with the healing of your scars. When it's time to do the implants, I'll be opening your breasts at a small section along these same lines," she gently runs her finger across the angry red line, "so you won't have any additional scarring to your breasts." She applies gentle pressure to my back, encouraging me to lean forward. "How are these feeling here at the back?"

I shrug. "Okay, I guess. It feels a little weird when I use my hand to push myself up out of a chair. The muscle tightens at the front, which I'm not used to."

Dr. Corrigan smiles at me. "Yes, I've heard that takes a little time to get used to. How's the discomfort?"

"They actually cause me more discomfort than my breasts, to be honest. If it gets too bad, I take some pain relief." Theo's watching and listening to everything intently.

She nods. "Good. You know your body and what you can handle. Don't be afraid to use the pain relief we gave you at the hospital."

I look down at my scars. They're still pretty angry looking. "How long before the scarring settles down?"

"I wouldn't worry about them at the moment, because a small section will be opened again for the follow-up surgery. At that point, you'll be able to use an ointment to reduce the appearance of the scars once they've properly closed."

Theo's sitting on a chair on the opposite side of the room, watching the doctor closely as she completes her checks. "What ointment do you recommend, Doctor?"

Dr. Corrigan glances at Theo. "I always recommend starting with a product that prevents the skin from drying out straight out of surgery. Something like *Aquaphor* to keep the wound moist, then moving onto *Medihoney* for its antibacterial properties which supports the body's natural healing processes." She looks back at me. "We can do some fine needling as the healing progresses, which should help to reduce the scarring considerably. But that is entirely up to you."

I nod as Theo types something into his phone, then tucks it back into his pocket. "Can we start using that for the scars on Emma's back?"

"Sure. You can skip the *Aquaphor* at this point and start using the *Medihoney* any time you're ready. Though the earlier you begin the treatment, the better chance you have of minimizing the scarring." She steps over to the counter, collecting a marker and a small gadget, which she slides over the top of my breast. "This little gadget helps me to locate the valve in the expander, so I know where to inject the saline."

"Oh, that's pretty cool."

"Yeah, it is. There's a magnet inside at the location of the valve. This helps to locate it, so I can direct the needle to exactly the right position." She marks a dot on each breast where the valve must be. Then she puts on gloves and uses a swab to clean the area, followed by an alcohol wipe.

"I need to make sure the area's completely sterile. We don't want the needle transferring germs from the surface of the skin to the inside of your body. That may lead to an infection and delay the whole process, not to mention affect your scarring."

I'm glad she's explaining everything as she works because I had no idea what to expect today. I have to go through this process several times before I'll be ready for the actual permanent implants.

Dr. Corrigan picks up a syringe and carefully places the tip on my breast where she marked the skin. "I'm going to give you fifty CCs of saline in each expander today, taking you up to three hundred and fifty

CCs on each side. You still have a bit of swelling, so I don't want to increase the volume too much today. You'll notice pressure as we fill the expanders each week, until you reach six hundred and fifty CCs on each side, making you smaller than your original size, as you requested. They'll begin to feel quite heavy and hard, which is all normal. I've been told they become incredibly uncomfortable, so be prepared. Okay?"

"Okay." With all the information I've been given since I was first diagnosed, I have to concentrate hard to make sure I remember everything she's saying. Dr. Corrigan pulls out the syringe, picks up another one, and moves across to my other breast. Looking at Theo, I can't miss his wince as the doctor inserts the needle. "I can't feel a thing. This entire area is completely numb." I smile at him, trying to show him I'm okay.

"It takes several months for sensation to return after such a major disruption to the nerves, but it *will* come back." She finishes up, placing the needles in a sealed sterile container and removing her gloves. "All done. You can get dressed. Keep doing what you're doing and I'll see you in two weeks."

"Thanks, Doctor."

She leaves the room and Theo passes my clothes to me. I watch him carefully as I redress. He hasn't said much throughout both doctor's visits, but I can tell he's taking in every scrap of information. Guiding me out of the surgery, we climb into his truck.

"Do you mind if we stop at the drugstore to grab some of that *Medihoney*? I'll start rubbing the ointment on the scars on your back tonight." He starts his truck, pulling out of the parking lot.

My plan has always been to do whatever I could to minimize the scars. I don't want them to be hideous or a constant reminder of this time in my life. But I have to wonder why Theo's so eager to get started. Does it mean he can't stand looking at my scars? Are they the reminder I feared they'd be?

"Uh, sure. But I can manage the treatment on my own." I turn away, looking out of my window, so I don't have to look at him.

"Hey. Look at me, please." Theo's voice is firm, demanding. I turn to look at him without hesitation. "The scars don't bother me in the least. I saw the way *you* looked at them in the mirror." He grasps my hand. "I know you don't like them. That seeing the scars upsets you. I want to help you through the healing process, so you can look at yourself in the mirror and feel at least somewhat happy with what you see reflected. I want you to see the beautiful, sexy woman that I see. That I'll always see when I look at you."

My shoulders drop in relief as the truthfulness of his words is reflected in his eyes. Placing my other hand on top of his, I squeeze his hand. "Thank you."

We stop at the drugstore and then head home. Theo has an order he needs to work on. He won't admit it, but I think he's running behind with his work because he's been looking after me, driving me to and from my appointments, as well as looking after the kids when they finish school. Then he makes dinner for all of us, while I help the kids with their homework. It feels great to have his support at home; to work together as a team.

I've never had it before.

When I was married to Preston, we both worked the same hours, but I would be the one to come home and cook dinner, do the washing, and clean the house. I was lucky if he cut the freaking grass. Once the kids came along, I stopped working, and then I was expected to do absolutely everything. Including getting up all night for feeds as well as everything in the garden.

Once the kids are in bed, Theo sends me for a shower while he cleans up downstairs. Sitting on the side of the bed, I rub moisturizer onto my legs, which I finally got around to shaving. At least they'd gone past the spiky stage, so they weren't scratching Theo's legs to bits.

"How're you feeling, Peaches?" Theo's deep rumble comes from the doorway. Looking at him over my shoulder, I find him leaning against the door, looking as handsome as ever. I wonder how long he's been standing there?

"I feel great."

"Don't lie to me, Peaches." He presses away from the door frame, his long strides bringing him to me.

Tilting my head back, I lock eyes with the man I'm falling for. He stands patiently waiting for me. My shoulders drop, as does my fake smile. "I'm tired and sore tonight. Dr. Corrigan was right about the pressure."

He holds out his hand, opening his closed fist to present my painkillers to me. Grabbing the glass of water from the nightstand, I swallow down the pills with gratitude that he saved me another trip downstairs.

"Thank you."

He nods as he climbs onto the bed behind me. Lifting my pajama top over my head, he then reaches around to the front of my body, releasing the clasps holding my compression bra closed. Slowly his work-roughened fingers slide the straps from my shoulders, his hands gliding down each arm, following the path and sending electricity shooting through my body. Pressing the softest of kisses against the crook of my neck, he begins massaging the ointment onto each scar on my back. His hands on my body mesmerize me and I block out all other thoughts to concentrate on the sensations he's eliciting in me.

My body relaxes into his touch, and a sigh of epic proportions escapes me. His breath whispers across my skin as he chuckles softly. "That was a big sigh. You okay?"

The fact that I don't have to look at him as I speak gives me the space I need to answer honestly. "It's all been a *lot*. You know? From the first visit to my GP, to now. So many emotions ... the whole process has been a whirlwind. I've had to make so many decisions in a short space of time while coming to terms with having cancer—even in its least invasive form." I blink to hold back the tears building in my eyes, but all it does is send them falling over my bottom lashes onto my cheeks. "I almost feel like a fraud to say I had cancer because my form wasn't as serious as others. It was caught early enough." I slam my mouth shut.

*Oh, God. Stop it!* He lost his mom and sister to the worst, most aggressive form and here I am blabbing on about mine. I cover my face with my hands to stop the word vomit. Strong arms wrap around my body, pulling me into the safety of his embrace.

Warm lips surrounded by scruff press against my temple. "It's okay, Em. Let it all out. I'm here to catch you."

And just like that, the floodgates open—*again!* My shoulders shake with my sobs as he silently holds me. My tears soaking through his shirt, snot running out of my nose. I'm a freaking mess of epic proportions.

Goosebumps cover my exposed skin, and I reluctantly peel myself away. Keeping my head low so he can't see my face, I step into my bathroom, quietly closing the door behind me. I stand, leaning against the cold surface for long minutes. I can't believe I broke down like that and it's not the first time either. I can't believe Theo hasn't already run for the hills.

Maybe he does mean what he says; that he's here for the long haul.

# CHAPTER 60

## —emma—

THEO AND I HAVE FALLEN INTO A ROUTINE OF SORTS, A RHYTHM THAT feels comfortable, and feels right.

He's been my rock, while still keeping up with his business. Every single school drop-off and pickup—he's there. Every single appointment for me or Lachlan—he's there. Every night, he massages the ointment on the scars on my back, rubs my feet, and brushes my hair. Every night, I've been tempted to turn around and kiss him senseless, but I don't.

I'm still scared and I don't know why.

Sitting on my favorite rocking chair, I take another sip of hot coffee. Theo insisted I relax, setting me up with everything I need—coffee, a warm blanket, and my Kindle. I'm feeling all hot and bothered as I read about Josh McKinley. Kylie Kent certainly knows how to write a dark antihero! I'm reaching a particularly sexy scene when a familiar car pulls into my driveway.

My good mood evaporates with the slam of his car door.

My body deflates as his foot hits the first step.

When he looks up from his phone, his eyes land on me, then immediately drop to my breasts. I pull my sweater tighter around my body like a shield. I don't bother standing to greet my ex-husband. I'm not exactly sure why he's here. This would normally be his weekend to take the boys, but he stopped coming around once he got married. He stands at the top step, tucking his hands into his pockets.

"Hey, Emma."

"Hi." My reply is hard. I'm not giving him an inch; he doesn't deserve anything from me.

"Uhm, how are you feeling?" He tips his head down, gesturing toward my boobs. *Ugh, what a jerk!*

"Fine." I'm not sure how he found out about my surgery.

"Good. Great." He pauses, glancing around at my porch. "Uh, how're the boys?" *Here we go.*

"Great."

He nods to himself. "Great. That's great to hear." He reaches into his back pocket, pulling out an envelope. Stepping forward, he holds it out to me.

I reach forward, taking the envelope as though it may bite me. "What's this?"

"Open it."

I slide my finger beneath the seal, lifting the flap, revealing a thick wad of one hundred dollar notes. My head snaps up to Preston. "What's this for?" If he thinks he can buy himself out of the boys' life, he has another thing coming.

He tucks his hands back into his pockets. Looking around, he sighs heavily. "Can I sit for a minute?" He gestures to the other rocking chair with his chin. There's something different about him. He's less … arrogant. Almost defeated.

"Sure."

He sits, smoothing his fingers over the timber. "These are nice. Real nice. What sort of timber is this?" I roll my eyes. This is Preston's typical style when he's feeling out of his depth.

"Yep, they *are* nice." Silence falls between us for long moments. I'm not willing to offer up conversation to fill the space. If he came here for a purpose, he needs to be the one to start the conversation.

He huffs out a heavy breath. "Look. Em. I'm sorry. Okay?" The hackles on the back of my neck rise.

"What exactly are you sorry for, Preston?" I can't believe I used to think his name was sexy. Ugh!

"Sorry for bailing on the boys, on you, on our marriage." He gestures to my boobs again. "For what you're going through." His voice is full of genuine apology. His sorrow is written all over his face in the creases across his forehead and the furrow between his brows.

I take a moment to digest his words. "Where's all this coming from?"

He looks down at his hands, then sits back in the chair, looking up at the exposed roof, and then back out across the street. "I caught Stacey cheating on me." My gasp is audible, forcing him to look at me. The slump in his shoulders and the downturn of his mouth hint at his sadness and hurt. "I guess I got a taste of my own medicine. I've had a little time to do some serious soul-searching."

"And what did you discover during your *soul searching*?" I can't temper the sarcasm in my voice.

"I discovered I'm a dick." His comment catches me off-guard and I choke on a swallow. Covering my mouth, I try to stop the coughing fit that ensues. The front screen door opens, revealing Theo in all his glory. His posture automatically becomes stiff, his face hard.

"You okay out here, Peaches?" If it wasn't for my lingering cough, I would smile at his obvious display of familiarity in front of my ex. He passes my coffee to me, patting my back to help me.

"Yeah." I wink. "Thanks, Stud." His eyes widen at my nickname for him. Preston coughs, his face turning red.

I turn to Preston. "You haven't met my boyfriend, Theo? Have you?" I know it's petty, but I love that Theo's so much bigger than Preston. So much more masculine. And I know for a fact that Preston will be well aware of the differences between the two of them. Internally, I revel in his discomfort. After years of him chipping away at my body image, I love that he's feeling insecure about his masculinity at this moment. I know it's unfair of me to use Theo in this way, but by God, it feels so good to watch my ex-husband squirm.

Preston stands to his full height but still comes up short, in more ways than in the physical. He never would have stood by me through what I've been going through. Not like Theo has. Theo holds out his free hand to shake, squeezing Preston's a little tighter than necessary. "I don't believe I have. I'm, uh, I'm Preston. Lachlan and Austin's dad."

"I know who you are." Theo's deep baritone is strong and sure as he releases Preston's hand like it's covered in poop. I have to work hard to suppress a chuckle at the look on my man's face.

Huh! *My man.* When did that happen?

I mean, I introduced him as my boyfriend, but that was to make a point. Do I think of Theo as my boyfriend?

I think I do.

I care about him a lot. I appreciate how steadfast and true he's been since he's been back in my life. He hasn't pushed for anything more than a few hot kisses here and there. Every morning, I wake wrapped in his embrace. Every night I fall asleep to his steady breaths and heartbeat beneath my ear. He looks back at me, eyebrows raised. "You okay out here?"

I squeeze his hand, giving him a confident smile. "Yeah. I am. Thanks for checking on me." He gives me one last squeeze before bending down to lay a hot kiss on my lips before standing again. He eyes Preston as he walks back inside, closing the screen door quietly behind him.

"He's a bit intense." Preston gives a nervous chuckle.

I don't respond, just raise my brows, waiting for him to continue with what he was saying before.

"Uh, anyway, I thought I should apologize for being a dick and probably worse than that to you and the boys. You didn't deserve my mistreatment and disregard for your feelings throughout our marriage, particularly toward the end. I'm sorry for these last months, bailing on the boys. I, uh, I really miss them. More than I ever thought I would."

Tears prick at the back of my eyes for his genuine, heartfelt apology. His regret pours out of him in waves. "So, where do things stand with you and Stacey?"

"We're done. She was the catalyst for the wedge between the boys and me. *Not* that I'm blaming her completely, because *I* allowed it to happen." This is new. Preston's actually taking responsibility for his choices. "But she certainly made them feel unwelcome, and it was easier to keep the peace with her and go along with what she wanted. I'm sorry I was so weak. I'm sorry I let the boys down." He rubs his hands on his thighs. We sit quietly for a few moments. My mind is racing with his apology and everything he's said in the last few minutes. "I would like to have the opportunity to apologize to them. If that's alright with you?"

I nod. "Of course. It's never been my intention to keep them away from you." I pause and hold up the envelope filled with money. "What's this for?"

He swallows before looking at me. "I know you're going to need to take a fair amount of time off work. I also figured you probably don't have enough leave saved up to cover the whole period. The other thing I know is that insurance won't cover all of your expenses." He gestures with his head toward my boobs, and I roll my eyes. "So, I wanted to help you out as part of my apology for being a dick."

I'm glad I'm sitting down because this is completely unexpected. He has been a dick of epic proportions and his payments certainly don't cover all of my expenses raising our boys, as well as putting a roof over our heads. "When do you expect me to pay you back?"

His eyes scrunch up as his brows drop. "It's a gift—let's call it 'being a dick' tax." I burst into laughter, wincing at the pressure on my expanders. "Are you okay?" He sits forward, ready to help me if I need it.

"I'm okay. I have to be careful not to move so suddenly like that."

He looks at me and for the first time in a long time; I see compassion in his eyes. The protective walls I've built up over the years toward him begin to soften. "I don't expect you to pay it back—ever. I also intend to increase my monthly payment for the boys above what the court stipulated. I know what I've been paying you has been subpar."

I run my finger over my eyebrow, to check it's still on my face because I'm worried it just flew off in surprise. "Uh, this seems a bit much, Preston."

"It's not enough. Not really. I want to help you out." He looks as though his puppy just died. "Would I ... uh ... can I see the boys? Maybe take them out?" Well, today is all about surprises. "I mean, I know it wasn't planned, and I didn't let you know ahead of time, but would it be okay?"

"Sure. Let me go check with them. Wait here."

"Boys!" I call as soon as I step inside.

"In here, Mommy." They're sitting on the couch watching their favorite movie.

I turn off the television and crouch down in front of them. "Your dad's here. He would like to see you if that's okay." I look between each of my boys, gauging their reactions.

Lachlan's shoulders slump. "Is Stacey here too?"

"No, Buddy. Daddy's here by himself. Stacey and Daddy aren't together anymore." Both boys' faces light up with wide smiles. "So, would you like to see him?"

"Oh yeah!" They both jump up from the couch. They haven't seen him since May, the month before his wedding.

I laugh, caught up in their joy and excitement. "Hold on. You guys need to put on some warmer clothes."

The three of us head upstairs. I get them ready to spend some long-overdue time with their father, dressing them in layers. Kenny follows us back out to the front porch to say goodbye to the boys, Theo following close behind.

Preston immediately embraces them both, the release of tension from his shoulders obvious. Kissing both boys on the top of their heads, he glances up, spotting Kenny. "Who do we have here?"

Theo rests his hand on Kenny's shoulder. "This is Kennedy. My daughter."

My eyes widen at his statement, a smile touching my lips. Kenny looks up at Theo as though the sun rises and sets with him. He bends, scooping her up into his arms, landing a kiss on her cheek making my heart burst with his fatherly display of affection.

Preston holds out his hand to Kenny. As she places her hand in his, he bows slightly. "Very nice to meet you, Kennedy." Kenny giggles, tucking her face into Theo's neck. I've never seen her so shy before. "Okay, boys. Are you ready?"

Simultaneous 'yeses' ring out on the front porch from the boys. I kiss each of them goodbye. "Have fun and be good for your daddy."

"We will," they both answer in unison. I marvel at how in sync they are sometimes.

"What time would you like them home?" Preston asks as he places his hand on each of his son's shoulders, tugging them close.

This Preston is unfamiliar to me. I look at Theo for guidance, but he's no help, offering only a shrug. "Uh, in time for dinner? Unless you want to take them somewhere for dinner, too?"

"Would you mind if we see how we're going and I'll call you?"

"No problem." He smiles at me, tipping his head to Theo and Kenny as he takes his first step from the porch with our boys.

"Bye, Lachlan. Bye, Austin," Kenny calls as she waves them good-bye. She's going to miss them today. Maybe we can have some girl time this afternoon.

The boys disappear down the street with their father, leaving the three of us behind. I have to be honest—it feels weird. For so many months, he hasn't been part of their lives, and now he's back. The smiles on the boys' faces were priceless, their little bodies were vibrating with joy. I only hope Preston's learned his lesson and makes better choices from here on out.

# CHAPTER 61

## —theo—

"You go up for your shower. I'll be up soon." I wipe over the counter, ensuring the sticky residue from the ice cream we had for dessert is completely gone.

"Okay. See you upstairs, Stud!" Emma presses up on her toes, laying a soft kiss against my lips. Even that chaste touch wakes up my dick. I don't think my dick actually sleeps whenever I'm close to Em if I'm being completely honest. She winks as she sashays her fine ass out of the kitchen.

Sleeping next to her every night, massaging her body, showering together—it's been fantastic, but it's also been torturous in the sense that I can't touch her the way I want to. I don't want to push. I want more from Em than sex, though that would be great about now.

Switching off all the lights and locking up, I make my way upstairs. Poking my head into the kids' bedrooms, I'm happy to see they're all sound asleep. The overhead fan creates enough white noise to keep Lachlan happy.

As I breach the bedroom door, the soft sound of the shower still running brings a smile to my face. My girl's naked and wet in the room on the other side of the wall. Pulling my T-shirt over my head, I strip down to nothing so I can join her. It's one of my favorite things to do; shower with my girl. Running my hands over her slick skin under the guise of washing her is one of the highlights of my day.

I don't know if she's posing just for me, but she has her hands tangled in her wet hair, her breasts thrust forward, and the dip at her waist curved to perfection. Her eyes are closed, but they open, revealing irises the color of wet grass as her lips form a seductive smile.

"Let me do that." Judging by the bubbles disappearing down the drain, Em's ready for the conditioner. I dispense a generous amount into the palm of my hand, then share it with my other hand before starting at the ends of Em's gorgeous chocolate-colored hair. It looks almost black when it's wet like this, contrasting beautifully with her pale complexion. I make sure to press my fingers firmly into her scalp, massaging her head the way she likes.

"Mmmhm. It feels so good to have your fingers massaging me like that." Can someone please tell my dick it needs to behave? It's acting like a heat-seeking missile, knocking against Em's gorgeous ass. She giggles and my dick twitches. Settle down buddy, don't get too excited. She turns around, dislodging my fingers from her hair. Her sparkling eyes connect with mine, and a sly grin touches her lips. "You've been so incredibly patient as well as generous with your care and consideration. I want to thank you for everything you've done. The way you've been with me every step of the way. Supporting me emotionally and physically."

She drops to her knees, conditioner in her hair, a twinkle in her eye. She glides her hands up my thighs and if she does what I think she's about to do, I'm not sure I'll be able to remain standing. It's been a while and I've been willing my dick to behave for weeks now.

"Em?" I whisper, water tracking down my body, goosebumps covering my skin.

"Let me do this. It's the only way I can show you how much I appreciate you and everything you've done." Her hands continue their journey. One wrapping around my cock, the other cupping my heavy sac. Her breaths brush across the swollen head before her tongue passes across the slit.

Groaning in pleasure, I grasp Emma's hair gently, pulling her face away from my dick. "You don't have to do anything to thank me, Em. It's been my pleasure and privilege to help you. To be with you."

She smiles at me, then moves forward, engulfing my shaft in one take, almost dropping me to my knees. Her mouth. *Fuck!* It feels sensational around my cock. Not as good as her pussy does, but there's not much between them. "Fuck, Em. My dick in your mouth … I'm not sure I deserve the attention … mmhm." Unconsciously, my hips begin to move in time with her mouth sliding up and down my shaft as my heart attempts to hammer its way out of my chest.

Her cheeks hollow as she applies stronger suction, almost causing me to come. Squeezing the base of my shaft as her mouth pleasures the rest, her other hand fondles my balls as they begin to draw up tight.

She looks fucking beautiful with her mouth full of my cock.

That familiar tingling sensation starts building at the base of my spine, warning that my orgasm is imminent. She moans around my shaft as it pulses, ready to explode. Pulling her hair, I tug her off my cock and cum all over her gorgeous tits. The water washes some of it away as it lands. She looks down at her breasts, then back up at me with a proud smirk on her gorgeous face.

Catching my breath, I lean down, carefully grasping underneath her arms to pull her up to her feet. Running my hands tenderly over her flesh, I rub what's left of my orgasm into her skin. The firmness of the expanders under my touch reminds me of what's about to happen tomorrow. I press forward, sighing as our lips connect. She opens for me, welcoming me inside, and I thank the gods above that she's allowed me back into her life. That I get to share these private moments with her. That I'm privileged to know her; the private parts of her that nobody else gets to share. Our tongues move against one another in a dance that is so familiar to me now—one I want to experience for all of my days.

Slowing the kiss to light pecks, I whisper against her lips, "Thank you. I'm sorry I didn't last long. After being without you so long, it was never going to take much to tip me over the edge." I huff out a short laugh.

"I'm sorry it's been so long." Her face drops, stealing her eyes from mine.

I don't like it.

Using my fingers, I raise her chin. "Don't say sorry to me, Peaches. I would wait a thousand years for you. Don't feel guilty or that I'm not happy to spend time with you when sex is off the table. Okay?"

Her eyes study mine carefully before she nods slowly. "It's just that I don't want you to get to the point that you go looking for sex somewhere else because you're not getting it from me."

I see fucking red. "I'm not some kid who can't control his urges, Em. I don't have sex just for a fuck. I'm a grown-ass man who can wait until you're ready to have sex. Because, ultimately—and hear these words clearly, Emma—you're the only woman I want to have sex with." She blinks at me. I know my tone was aggressive, but I wanted to be completely transparent with her. I don't want her to ever worry that I'm looking elsewhere for that shit. I'm not like that. Never have been.

She huffs out a breath. "Okay. I think I finally get what you've been trying to show me. I didn't mean to suggest that you would cheat or anything like that. I think I inherently know you wouldn't do that to me." She presses her luscious lips against mine.

The tension in my body dissipates with her words. "You don't know how happy it makes me you realize that." I kiss her again because I can't not. "You're the only one for me, Em. I'm not going anywhere."

The water's beginning to cool and Em still has some conditioner in her hair, so I rinse it out for her and we step out of the shower to dry off. I blow dry her hair and then massage the ointment into the scars on her back, which are fading nicely.

"Go lay in the middle of the bed for me, spread those gorgeous thighs of yours." Her eyes widen as she opens her mouth to respond. I place my finger over her lips to stop her. "No arguments. Do as I say. I'll be there in a second; be ready." I smack her delectable ass as she leaves the bathroom.

I hang the towels up and put away the hairdryer before turning off the light. When I step into the bedroom, I stop in my tracks at the sight that greets me. Em's legs are spread wide, feet flat on the bed, knees up and open, allowing me to see her most private of places. I can see her excitement from here as she slowly rubs her clit.

"Did I say you could touch my pussy?" Her fingers freeze as she startles at the sound of my voice.

She raises her head slightly from the pillow to look at me. Her eyes drop to my hand stroking my cock. She raises a perfectly shaped eyebrow at me. "Did I say you could touch my cock?"

One side of my mouth tips up. I like this side of her. The confident side. The one that trusts my attraction to her. "Cheeky girl." Moving onto the bed, I position myself between her legs. "You ready for me, Peaches?"

She nods. "Mhm."

"You tell me if it's too much, okay?"

"Okay," she whispers.

It's all I need. Smoothing my hands up the inside of her thighs, I follow with delicate kisses until I reach the crease between her leg and her pussy. Running my nose from the base of her pussy to the top, I breathe in her delicious scent. "Mmm, delicious." Smiling against her pussy lips, I lock my eyes with her forest green ones as I take my first swipe in months. Her eyes roll upwards as she sighs, dropping her head back onto the pillow.

Starting slowly, I lick and kiss her pussy lips thoroughly. Treating myself to Em's delicious taste. I'm in no hurry. I could stay down here all night if she'd let me, but I know she needs to get a good night's rest before her surgery tomorrow. Hopefully, the orgasms I'm about to deliver will help her sleep. Sucking on her clit, I slide a finger into her tight channel, which squeezes me in welcome. She's so fucking responsive. "You like my fingers in your pussy, don't you, Em?"

"Mmhm, yeah, I do. I've missed you. Missed this so much," she whispers the last part.

"Me too, Peaches. Me too." I never thought I'd have this chance again. To be able to touch her in this way. I feel fucking privileged that she's allowing me to do this to her.

Swirling my tongue around her pulsing clit, I add another digit, making sure I rub against the spongy tissue on the front wall. I know I have the right spot when her hips fly up off the bed, pushing her pussy further into my mouth. *Oh yeah!*

"Oh my God! Theo!" she whispers hoarsely. "Theo, Theo, Theo," she repeats as her hips move in time with my ministrations. I love that I can do this to her. That I can bring her pleasure. Normally, I'd pinch her nipples about now, but I know she still lacks sensation and I don't want to break her out of the spell we've created.

Her walls flutter and tighten, holding my fingers inside as she breaks, her hips dropping to the bed, her legs tightening around my head as though she wants to lock me in place. I slow my fingers, drawing out her pleasure as long as I can. Smiling as she sucks in a long breath—my girl forgets to breathe as she builds to orgasm. I move back to tenderly kiss her pussy as she comes back into her body, a smile touching her lips.

I'm not finished with her, though. I want to take her there again. Just one more time tonight.

# CHAPTER 62

## —emma—

STANDING IN FRONT OF THE BATHROOM MIRROR, I STUDY MY BREASTS. Six weeks ago, I was in the same position, doing the very same thing. Warm, calloused hands come around my body to cup the heavy globes as soft lips surrounded by bristles press against my shoulder. I reach my hand up, running my fingers through his silky hair.

"You okay, Peaches?" His eyes connect with mine in the bathroom mirror.

"Yeah, I am. I'll be glad to get these expanders out. They're so freaking hard and heavy. Though I'm not looking forward to having the drains in again." I sigh. I just want this whole process over and done with.

Theo's hold is tender as he tests their weight. "They *do* feel heavy." Releasing them, he slides his hands across my beaded flesh around to my back, heating it as he goes. Running his fingers over my scars, he whispers, "These are looking really good."

"Yeah?" I'm surprised I could get the word out while he's touching me. I love having his hands and mouth on my body again. To feel him inside me, the way we were before. Last night was something else—he made me fly. I'm not sure if it's because it's been so long since we were intimate like that or if it's because I feel so much closer to him now.

"Yeah, they do." He kisses me again before stepping away. "I'm heading down to get breakfast sorted. Come down whenever you're ready."

He's gone, leaving me to my inspection. Once this part's over with, this ordeal will finally be behind me. I *know* I'm one of the lucky ones, but it's still been tough. The oncologist I saw for the second opinion requested by Dr. Barnes concurred with the initial pathology report. They both agreed that I could safely forego radiation treatment, which was a huge relief for me as well as for Theo. The sheer relief that swept over his features was plain for the oncologist and me to see; the tension I hadn't realized he'd been holding across his shoulders released. I've been so blessed to have Theo's support and attention these past weeks. He's made the entire process that much more bearable. The man still looks at me as though I'm a goddess, which has been fantastic for my bruised self-esteem.

I get dressed and grab my small overnight bag for my short hospital stay. It'll only be overnight this time if all goes well. Preston will pick the boys up from school today and keep them for the weekend to help me. He's been calling the boys every night to talk with them and he's stopped in after school to take them to the park. He even took Lachlan to his therapy appointment last Thursday. I think he's definitely making better choices than he has in a long time.

Mr. Drivas is picking Kenny up from school and he's going to keep her for the weekend, too. Theo wanted to be able to spend as much time as possible at the hospital with me and then allow me time to rest over the weekend.

Nervous butterflies assault me as my foot touches the floor at the bottom of the stairs, the kids' voices reaching me loud and clear.

"Mommy can't eat breakfast today because she's having surgery." Lachlan's memory for details astounds me sometimes.

"But I made Mommy these yummy strawberries." Austin's sweet little voice sounds so disappointed. I'm incredibly proud of his thoughtfulness, but I'm also brokenhearted that I can't eat the food he thoughtfully prepared for me.

Stepping into the kitchen, the kids notice me straight away. "Mommy." All three of them call at the same time. My head snaps across to Theo as he turns toward me. Our wide eyes locked on each other at Kenny calling me Mommy. Theo's lips tilt slightly, matching the sparkle in his eyes, which shows he's not bothered by this new development. I think it was a natural progression for Kenny after all the time she's spent here with the boys. With a full heart, I kiss each of the kids good morning and go about preparing each of their lunches for school while they eat breakfast. Then we all head out the door for school drop-off.

The closer we get to the hospital, the bigger my butterflies get. Theo reaches across, laying his large hand on my thigh. "You know you've got this. Right?" He sounds so certain.

"I guess so. I hate leaving the kids." I know it's only overnight this time, but it's a forced separation, as opposed to them staying with Mom and Dad for the weekend. "I missed them so much when I was in the hospital last time." I breathe out a heavy breath. "I'm also worried. I've had such a smooth run throughout this process. What if this part goes wrong?" I look across at the man who's very quickly become my mainstay as I chew my bottom lip.

Squeezing my thigh, he briefly glances away from the road to me. I watch his Adam's Apple bob up and down. "Mom and Anna know how important you are to me. I'm sure they're watching over you to make sure nothing happens."

My heart cracks at his words—the confidence behind them is strong and clear. He's lost so much and for him to be here with me through something so similar to his past experiences means so very much to me. Twisting in my seat, I turn my body toward him. "Thank you."

He gives me a quick smile, then turns back to the road. "No problem."

"No. I mean, thank *you*. You've been amazing throughout this entire process and I know it's had to be especially difficult for you." I swallow the excess saliva my nerves are producing for what I'm about to say. "I can't imagine how hard it's been to support me throughout this process. I'm surprised you stayed, to be honest."

He looks at me, huffing out a breath. His shoulders drop. "If we're being honest, there was a moment of doubt in the hospital when I first learned *why* you had surgery." He glances across to me, then back to the road. I guess I shouldn't feel hurt, but I do. "But I decided that even if I could only have one more day with you, I wanted it more than I wanted to preserve my heart."

What can I say? *He stayed.* Even though he knew this would be painful; could possibly even have a tragic ending. *He stayed.* That means more to me than he could ever possibly imagine. I want to jump all over him right now. "Thank you. For everything."

He squeezes my thigh in acknowledgment as he pulls into the

hospital parking lot. I suck in a deep lungful of air, hold it, then release it. I watch Theo jump out of his truck and walk around the front to my side. Opening my door, he holds my hips to help me down. Pulling me in close, he presses his warm lips against mine. Swiping his tongue across the seam, I sigh as I open for him. I can't see myself ever denying this man. He's been incredibly steadfast during a time when I've had nothing to offer him. He hasn't pushed, he's been patient, giving, and honorable. I think I've seen the real Theo these last few weeks. The man who's let go of his fear and is ready to commit to making the future he wants. Sliding our tongues against each other in a dance we've practiced many times in the last several weeks, our breaths combine as our hearts beat in sync. Pressing my body against his at every available point, I feel his cock harden behind his zipper. I'm reminded of my impending surgery as the hard expanders press into my ribs. Pulling away, Theo presses his forehead against mine. Our eyes locked. The blue of his as bright as the sky today.

"You don't need to thank me for anything. I love you, Emma." Even though my heart's already racing from our kiss, it picks up more speed as I suck in a startled breath. "You don't have to say it back. I just … I … wanted you to know before you went into surgery. I'm always gonna be here for you. I want to be the best man I can be for you, your boys, and Kennedy. I want you to know that you can rely on me. For always." He gives me a half-smile, grabs my overnight bag, and my hand, then guides me toward the building. "Come on. You don't want to be late."

I walk alongside him in a daze at his confession. As soon as we enter the hospital, it's almost as though I'm on a conveyor belt. Signing forms, getting prepped, talking with the plastic surgeon, then being taken through to surgery—Theo with me every single step of the way. He kisses my hand one last time as the orderly prepares to roll me away from him. Looking up at the orderly, I ask, "Can I have a couple of seconds, please?"

"Sure." He steps away, allowing Theo to move in closer.

I grasp his hand, pulling him down toward me. Kissing his lips gently, I whisper, "I love you, too, Theo." His eyes widen and his lips tilt upward as he shakes his head slightly.

"You love me?" It's sweet how confused he is at my confession.

"Yeah. I love you, Mr. Drivas." I kiss him quickly as the orderly returns.

"I'm sorry, we really must head up to the theater." I nod.

Theo presses one last kiss to my forehead, then I'm wheeled away.

# CHAPTER 63

## —theo—

SHE FUCKING *LOVES* ME.

I don't know what I did to deserve such a gift, but I've gotta be the luckiest man on the face of the earth. I plan on doing everything I can to keep her loving me for the rest of our lives. The first thing I need to do is contact the realtor. I have shit to organize.

After making plans, I make myself as comfortable as I can in the waiting room. It feels as though it wasn't all that long ago I was sitting here with Emma's parents, not knowing why she was in surgery, just knowing I *had* to be here.

I'm making my third lap of the waiting room when Sally and John step through the doors, coffees resting in a cardboard tray along with a paper bag. "Hi, Theo. We hope you don't mind that we wanted to come by, too."

"Of course not. She's your daughter. I can't imagine how difficult it's been for the both of you since you learned about her diagnosis." I step forward to shake John's hand as Sally's shoulders drop to a more relaxed position.

She offers me a smile. "Oh, I'm so glad you understand. We didn't want to intrude, you know?" She leans forward, giving me a one-armed hug. "We brought supplies." She raises the coffees she's balancing to make her point.

Thinking over everything I've said to them over the past few weeks, I'm worried I've given them the impression that I didn't want them around. I grab the coffee handed to me and take a welcome sip. "I'm sorry if I've ever given the impression that you were unwelcome or intruding when I spoke to you after Em's first surgery." Their eyes widen. "I just meant that I wanted to be part of her support network, not that you couldn't be."

"Oh, no. We knew what you meant. We were more than happy to allow you to support and care for Em during her recovery." I breathe a sigh of relief. I need to watch what I say and how it comes across. My stupid mouth is always getting me into trouble.

We settle in, drinking our coffees and snacking on the blueberry muffins the Stanfields brought with them. Sally keeps the conversation going and I'm doing my best to converse with her. Until I started living with Kenny, I pretty much lived in silence; only talking with clients and a couple of guys I met on different jobs over the years. I'm not sure I'd be able to cope with Sally's chatter if I hadn't spent these last months with the little firecracker I've started to call my daughter.

This surgery is so much shorter than her first one, but it seems like it's taking an age. I feel as though I'm going to come out of my skin while I wait to see my girl again. I only hope everything goes as smoothly as it has so far. We both know she's been incredibly lucky with her first procedure.

I'm staring up at the ceiling when Dr. Corrigan enters through the double doors with a wide smile on her face. She comes straight toward me. "Theo. Emma's done really well in surgery. She's being taken to recovery for a short while before she's settled in a room."

My body sags with overwhelming relief. Exhaustion from these last weeks settles over me. "Thanks, Doctor. These are Emma's parents." I gesture toward my companions. "Sally and John."

They shake hands. "Great to meet you. You should be able to go through to see Emma shortly."

"Thank you so much. Em's spoken very highly of you over the past few weeks."

Dr. Corrigan smiles at Sally. "Oh, that's lovely to hear. Thank you."

She says her goodbyes, taking her leave through the double doors where she entered. The three of us return to our seats, breathing easier as we wait for a nurse to collect us. This time, when the nurse comes through the doors, I'm the first one stepping up to him rather than lagging behind as though I don't belong. I *know* for certain the only place I belong is by Emma's side with Kenny, Lachlan, and Austin.

Stopping beside Emma's bed, I lean down slowly to press a gentle kiss on my girl's head. She's still not quite with us. I stand at the end of the bed, allowing Sally and John to have the chairs on either side.

Lifting the sheet and blanket, I begin to rub Em's feet and calves so I can have my hands on her; to reassure myself she's here, and she's okay. I've been giving her regular massages, mostly to help her, but also so I can justify having my hands on her again. It started when I was rubbing the cream into her scars, which then moved on to other parts of her body—her lower back, shoulders, legs, and feet. I would have loved to have massaged more intimate areas, but I didn't want to press her. I also felt her body and mind probably weren't ready. That's why I was so surprised last night when she dropped to her knees in the shower.

Sally and John speak quietly to Emma as she wakes slowly. As she listens to her parents, her eyes land on me, locking me in place. She gives me a tired smile as her eyes drop closed again. I can't believe what a jerk I was the last time she came out of surgery. She was barely conscious when I laid my personal grief at her feet, begging for her forgiveness.

Sally stands, coming closer to me. "We'll get going and leave her to rest." She hugs me. "You'll watch over our girl, won't you?"

"Of course. I don't plan on going anywhere. Dad has Kenny for the weekend and he'll keep her longer if I need."

They both kiss their sleeping daughter goodbye. "Tell her we love her." I nod as Sally hugs me again, followed by John taking my hand and pulling me into a manly hug.

"Thanks, Son." He slaps me on the back in much the same way as my father does.

I swallow down the emotion at their ready acceptance of me into their daughter and grandsons' lives. "No problem."

They leave, and I carefully cover Em's legs and feet with the sheet and blanket. I guess I may as well make myself as comfortable as possible in the rock-hard chair. Pulling it in close, I hold Emma's hand in mine as I check to see if I have any messages or emails. I answer a few inquiries one-handed because I'm not prepared to let go of my girl.

Finally, she stirs. Tilting her head in my direction, she licks her lips. "Hey," she whispers, her voice a little rough.

Grabbing her glass of water, I guide the straw to her lips. "Hey." I smile down at her and follow with a kiss on her forehead. "You need me to get the nurse for you?"

She nods carefully, as though it pains her to do so. "Feeling really sore." Those three whispered words are enough to move me into action. Standing, I release Emma's hand so I can get her the help she needs. Two steps into the hallway, I see the nurse that brought me to her room.

"Excuse me. Emma's just woken up, and she's in pain." I gesture over my shoulder to her room. "Can you please help her?" I feel helpless that I can't do anything for her. I have to rely on the staff here to look after my girl.

He nods. "Sure." I follow him as we both head back to Emma's room.

I step off to the side to message Emma's parents while the nurse checks on my girl.

ME

Hi Sally. Em's awake again. The nurse is with her now

It only takes a few moments before my phone alerts me of a response.

SALLY

Oh, thank you. Give her a careful hug from us.

ME

I will

SALLY

Thank you, Theo. X

Glancing across, I see Em's still busy with the nurse. I quickly call Dad, so I can speak with Kenny.

"Hello, Daddy." Kenny's sweet voice comes across the phone straight away.

"Hey, Munchkin. How was school today?" My heart swells and I can't stop the smile stretching my lips as she goes on to tell me about her day, in detail. Kenny likes to make sure she doesn't leave anything out.

"Can you hug Mommy for me? But don't hurt her, okay?"

"Of course, Munchkin. Be good for Pappoús and have sweet dreams."

"I will. Love you, Daddy."

"Love you, too, Munchkin. I'll talk to you in the morning."

"Okay, bye."

"Bye, Kenny." The line goes dead and I take my seat beside Em's bed as the nurse leaves the room.

Her almost-brown eyes are looking heavy again. "Sleep, Peaches. I'll be here when you wake up." I brush her bangs out of her eyes, running the backs of my fingers along her cheek to her jaw. "Rest. It's what your body needs." Kissing the back of her hand, I give her a wink.

"Why don't you go home? No point sitting here when I'm sleeping," she whispers, her voice hoarse from the breathing tube.

"I'm fine where I am." Holding her hand in mine, I rub my thumb slowly and steadily across the back of her hand, studying her closely as her eyes eventually close.

# CHAPTER 64

## —*thea*—

Déjà vu strikes as I pull into the driveway with three bunches of flowers for my girl along with the three kids sitting in the back seat. Dad and Preston dropped the kids off at school this morning with the understanding that I would collect them this afternoon. Preston's attitude has improved significantly since he apologized to Em and the boys. I know Emma's certainly appreciated the changes in him and I've noticed the boys are happier, too. Even though they hadn't said anything, I know they missed spending time with their dad.

Em's sitting in one of the rocking chairs on her porch, looking as though she's enjoying the fresh air. The boys climb out of my truck on their own, each grabbing a bunch of blooms before running over to their mother. Em's face lights up as she climbs to her feet.

"Hurry up, Daddy. I wanna see Mommy." Kenny wriggles in her booster seat, kicking her little feet.

"Okay, Munchkin. Settle down. I'm going as fast as I can." I finally release the buckle with a chuckle and hand Kenny the last bunch of flowers after placing her on her feet. She takes off straight for Emma and the boys. She knows to be careful with Emma this time around, so I don't have to catch her like I did last time.

Grabbing the bags of shopping out the back of my truck, I slowly make my way across Emma's front yard. "I bought ingredients for dinner. I'll take them inside and get everyone's afternoon snack ready."

She looks over the top of the kids' heads at me, then gives me the 'come here' motion with her finger. Moving closer, she points to her lips, letting me know she wants a kiss. I'm always happy to lay my lips on hers, so I eagerly oblige before leaving her to catch up with her favorite people. It's tough to keep it chaste; whenever I touch her in any way, I never want to stop.

I'm preparing cheese, crackers, hummus, and sliced vegetables when the screen door slams, followed by the sound of the kids.

"Gather 'round kids. Your snacks are ready." They each climb up on a stool at the kitchen counter and dig in. Lachlan goes directly for the crunchy carrot and bell pepper sticks.

The screen door slams. "Theo!" The worried tone in Emma's voice has me stepping out of the kitchen to make my way to her as quickly as possible. "Someone's putting a 'For Sale' sign in your front yard. I told him he has the wrong place, but he's still hammering the darn thing into your grass."

Geez, they work quickly. I only called them on Friday morning, met them on Saturday while Em napped in the hospital, and signed the contract with them immediately. "It's okay, Peaches. He's in the right place."

Wrinkles form across her forehead as her eyebrows scrunch together in confusion. "What do you mean? Are you moving out? Where are you going? You never said any—" I cut her off with a kiss. Nipping her bottom lip, followed by the top. I swipe my tongue across the plump pillows before sliding inside. She pushes me away, not so keen to continue. "What's going on, Theo? I'm confused. I thought we were starting something, and now I find you're moving away."

A single tear drops over her left bottom lash, breaking my heart. Maybe I should have spoken to her about my plan. "I'm not moving away. Kenny and I are moving in here." I point to the floor between us and her mouth drops open. "Permanently. I didn't see the point of having two houses." Cupping her face, I use the pad of my thumb to wipe the stray tear away.

"What? Moving in here?" She points to the floor between us. "Why would you sell your gorgeous house and move in here?" She carefully moves her arm, gesturing around us.

"Why wouldn't we move in here with you guys? This is where you are. It's easier to move the two of us rather than the three of you." I *was* trying to be thoughtful, but I'm guessing I've done the wrong thing. "I also thought it would be less disruptive and upsetting for Lachlan." Her face softens as her shoulders drop.

Holding onto my hips, she presses up to land a kiss on my lips. "You're so sweet to make our lives easier. But the thing is, your house is bigger than this one. It's in better condition, has a newer kitchen, *and* fancy bathrooms. And what about your workshop out the back? It's perfect for you."

"I know, but … well, I thought I was making the right choice for you and the boys. For all of us. I didn't want to disrupt you guys." I whisper against her lips.

She carefully wraps her arms around me, keeping space between our bodies, and I wrap mine around her, careful not to squeeze her tight. Looking up at me, she asks, "Is this your way of asking me to move in with you?" I know she's no longer mad or confused by the twinkle in her hazel eyes and the gentle smile touching her lips. She tips her head to the side.

"I wasn't gonna ask, Peaches. I didn't want to chance you turning me down. I was just going to move Kenny and me in." I press a kiss to her lips, which quickly becomes heated.

We're interrupted by a quick knock on the screen door before it opens and Max steps inside. He stops dead in his tracks and turns his back to us. "Uh, sorry for interrupting. I came by to check up on my sister, but I can see she's busy being mauled."

Em and I chuckle at her brother's embarrassment. Pulling away, Emma moves closer to him. "Hey, Max." He turns, reaching down to hug her carefully.

"How are you feeling?"

"Uncle Max!" The kids come running out of the kitchen. The worry lines between his eyebrows disappear as he smiles at his nephews. I notice Kenny also called him Uncle Max; she's already made herself part of Emma's family. The two younger kids leap at him at the same time, and the legend that he is, he manages to catch them both. Thank goodness Lachlan's more reserved or Max may well have ended up flat on his back.

"Hey, guys." He kisses the kids in his arms before placing them on their feet so he can do the same with Lachlan.

We all move into the living room. Max wraps his arm around his sister's shoulders. He kisses the top of her head and I feel a deep pang in my chest that I can no longer do that with my sister. That I forfeited the time we had left together by living on the opposite side of the country. I rub the area in the center of my chest as the pain of my loss hits me all over again. I wonder if it'll ever stop hurting.

Max looks at me once we're all settled. "I saw a 'For Sale' sign in your front yard. Are you selling?"

Emma looks at me, eyebrows raised. "Uh, yeah. Em and I were just talking about it."

"Theo wanted to sell his place so he and Kenny can move in here with us," Emma adds.

I don't think I've ever seen eyes widen as much as Max's do at Emma's statement. "You're moving in together?" He waves his finger between the two of us.

I look at Emma, waiting for her answer. She shrugs with a smile. "Well, we haven't discussed it with the kids, but yeah." I want to pull her into my body and kiss her senseless right now, but I'm pretty sure her brother wouldn't appreciate it. I don't need a mirror to know my smile takes up my entire face.

"But I thought we were already all living together?" Lachlan asks, confused.

"Well, we are, but I wanted to make it official. And we only need one house, so I thought we could sell mine." I clarify for everyone in the room.

"But I like your house better. It has all the cool tools in the workshop."

"Yeah, and you have that big back deck." Austin pipes in.

"I like our house, Daddy." Kenny's bottom lip trembles and I feel like the biggest failure as a parent. In my attempt to not disrupt Lachlan, I didn't consider what another move might do to Kenny.

"I like your house better, too, Kenny. So, if it's okay with everyone, I vote we move in with you guys. What do you think, boys?" Em suggests to everyone.

Austin throws his fist up in the air. "Yeah!"

Lachlan nods. "I agree with your vote, Mommy."

"Then it's settled. We're moving in with Theo and Kenny." The kids jump up and down with glee.

I wrap my arms around my girl, kissing her chastely in front of her brother. "Then it's settled. You've made me an incredibly happy man, Peaches." I kiss her again. I can't help myself. "I do have some plans I drew up a while ago to extend our house. I'll show you and maybe get started on them." I kiss the tip of her nose.

"Well, I guess congratulations are in order, guys." Max high-fives the kids, hugs Emma carefully, and slaps me on the back, pulling me in close. "You'd better look after my sister and nephews."

"That's a given, Max. You don't need to worry." I pull back, tipping my head in deference to the man. He nods mildly in return. I think he gets the depth of my feelings for his sister and nephews. I pull my phone out of my pocket. "I need to make a call to the real estate agent. Back in a minute."

"Ask him when he can come to value this house," Emma calls as I leave the room, her smile evident in her voice.

# CHAPTER 65

## —emma—

THEO'S UP TO HIS ARMPITS IN RENOVATIONS. HE'S BEEN WORKING DAY and night to get his house ready for us to move in. I'm worried about him, though, because he looks exhausted. This is our first weekend on our own since my scars have fully healed—the red lines no longer look as angry because of Theo's nightly diligence.

Now I want some sexy time with my man.

Theo's standing up on a ladder working on the architrave above the bi-fold doors leading out to the back deck, giving me a great view of his ass and legs. Leaning on the door frame, I take a moment to enjoy my boyfriend's sexy physique.

"Hey, Stud." Stepping forward, I hold up his coffee. "Come down here and kiss me already."

His tired eyes light up with his smile. Climbing down the ladder, he makes a beeline straight for me. Taking the coffee from my hand, he places it on the floor, then proceeds to stand to his full height, backing me up against the wall he hung. "Stud, huh?" He runs his nose up along my throat before nipping at my ear. "Where exactly do you wanna be kissed, Peaches?" His breath coats my skin with his gravelly whisper. His natural scent, enhanced by the timber he's been working with, fills my nose.

My heart pounds in my chest and I'm already raring and ready to go. My body doesn't need a lot of encouragement when Theo's close by. It's been a long time since we've had the house to ourselves and I'm feeling like my old self; ready to get down and dirty with my man.

He licks the crook of my neck, followed by a suck and bite, before placing a kiss. "Here?" His hand moves up to slide the collar of my T-shirt to the side where he repeats the process. "Here?" he whispers. Sliding his hands down to mine, he takes them in his, moving my arms above my head in a delicious stretch. He kisses the underside of my upper arm. "What about here?" Goosebumps break out over my skin as his hands press mine into the wall before he releases them, the tilt of his head asking me if I'll keep them in place on my own. I can only swallow in anticipation and offer him a nod. His roughened hands glide down my body, over my breasts, to the bottom of my T-shirt, which he swiftly lifts and twists around my raised hands.

His mischievous smile, along with the sparkle in his eyes, tells me he likes seeing me like this. Trussed up a little, waiting for his touch. My breasts heave with my shallow breaths, waiting to see what he'll do next. With only the tip of his finger, he scrapes his fingernail along the silky red lace of the bra he bought me last week for Mother's Day. "I do like this new bra on you, but it's in my way."

He licks his way slowly from the bottom of one breast, across the nipple all the way to the top, before repeating the process on the other side. Sliding his hands around my body, he releases the clasp and my breasts drop free. If I can take a positive from my recent medical experiences, my boobs don't hang quite so low since the surgery. Not that they're perky young adult, pre-breastfeeding boobs, but they're certainly better than they were.

Smoothing his hands reverently over the mounds, he cups them in each hand. "Beautiful." He looks up at me, our eyes locking. "I've always loved your boobs, Em. I loved them before and I love them now." He moves in, kissing across the scar line before laving one of my nipples with his tongue as his fingers caress and pluck at the other one. There's still no sensation, but Dr. Corrigan said it would come back slowly. He swaps to my other boob, treating it to the same teasing kisses and bites. My hand reaches up to grasp his silky hair, holding him in place. I need this. I need his mouth and hands on me. I need to know he's not going to shy away from the girls.

Grasping onto his head, I murmur my approval, "So good, Theo. Mmmmhm." His hands move down, cupping my ass as he lifts me easily from the floor. There's certainly something to be said for a guy who can lift a girl off of her feet. Wrapping my legs around his slim hips, I press my heated core against the hard wood in his shorts. He presses in, grinding against me in the most thrilling way. "Oh, God!"

Tilting my head back to expose my throat to him, he licks up the column to my ear, sending heat to my core.

"So fucking sexy, Em. I can feel the heat of your pussy against my cock." His hot breath sends a shiver down my spine and I move my hips to rub against his shaft. I'm incredibly horny; it's been so long since I've had him inside me. Breathing heavily, I drop my bound arms to his shoulders, wrapping them around him as best I can to pull him in tight. "It's okay, Peaches, I've got you."

Pulling away from the wall, he carefully lays me down on the drop sheet in the middle of our soon-to-be bedroom. Holding the back of my head as my body connects with the hardwood floor, he protects it from the hard surface. Leaning up, I swipe his lips with my tongue and he opens for me. Our tongues meet and I feel it throughout my body; from the top of my head to the tips of my toes. Sighing, I open further, deepening the kiss. We've kissed a *lot* since we reconnected, it's been absolute torture.

I want him inside me in every way.

I *need* him inside me in every way.

Pressing my hips up, I grind my pussy against his shaft. "Theo. I … I need …"

I need more. More of everything I know he can give me. Kissing his way down my body, he swiftly relieves me of my shorts and panties.

"You're so fucking beautiful, Em," he whispers, and I preen under his praise. No longer conscious of my curves because Theo loves them. *Every single inch of them.* Cellulite, scars, creases, and bulges—he loves and adores every inch of me.

He dives in between my legs, running his nose from the bottom of my seam to the top, his tongue spearing straight into my core. His shoulders push deeper into the space between my legs, as though he can't get close enough. Two rough fingers breach my opening, spearing into me as he bites my clit gently. *Oh my God!* My hips shoot up without warning at his invasion. As much as I want his mouth on me, I want him inside me more.

"Theo, give me what I want." Reaching down, I palm his dick through his shorts, which is pressing hard against the zipper. "Give it to me."

"But I want you to come on my tongue first." He almost sounds like a young boy bargaining for his favorite treat.

"Can I at least have your dick?"

He pushes away from me, removes his shorts, and lies on his back. "Come sit on my face."

I scramble into position, careful not to put all of my weight on his face, but he pulls me down, so I'm literally sitting on his face. He begins where he left off, teasing me. Turning me on as I get lost in the sensations. Leaning forward to change the angle, I remember that we're in this position because I wanted to get my hands and mouth on his dick. I wrap my hand around his shaft while using my other to grip his steely thigh for balance. It's difficult to concentrate on what I'm doing as I draw his cock into my mouth. His groan against my pussy feels amazing, the vibrations making my clit pulse. Once his fingers push their way into my channel, I explode. My walls press in tight around his fingers, squeezing, holding him in place. Moaning around his cock with my release, his dick jolts in my mouth, swelling, filling the limited available space.

He slides out from beneath me, stealing his shaft from my mouth. Rough hands come up around my waist, changing my position as he sits me upright. Theo's front makes contact with my back before he turns me around and situates me over his dick. Slowly, he pushes himself inside before I can gather my bearings.

It feels divine.

The slow push and slide.

In this position, our mouths are level. It's easy to meet, to join, to combine. To taste, to enjoy, to savor. Without moving an inch, we kiss for long moments. His kiss fills my heart and soul with his love for me and I hope he feels my love for him as deeply as I do. Our bodies heat, slick against the other. My breasts press tight against Theo's hard chest. Pulling back slightly from the kiss, I whisper against his lips, "I love being naked with you. Connected to you like this."

"Me too." He surges back in, taking my mouth in a hard kiss. Gone is the gentle, languid exploration. He's upped his game, taking me higher. I begin to move my hips, trying to rise to my knees so I can sink back down his dick, but his hold on my hips stops me.

Pressing his forehead to mine. "Don't move. Not yet. I want to feel you around me a little longer. I've missed you so fucking much, Em." Emotion colors his words, his eyes glassy as he shares his feelings with me.

"I've missed you, too." I kiss him gently. "So much." I blink back my emotions, but it's futile. It's too overwhelming and my tears drop over the bottom of my lashes. This man has been through everything with me these last months. Not once has he balked at anything. Not once has he let me down. He's been strong and true and steadfast. I pull back, locking my muddy eyes on his clear blue. "I love you so much, Theo." Creases bracket his mouth, and he presses it to mine.

I glide my hands down Theo's strong back, enjoying the feel of his muscles moving and tensing as his hands caress my back before coming around to massage my breasts and pinching my nipples. Our kiss lingers, neither of us is in any hurry to move things along.

Slowly, surely, Theo begins to grind up into me. The pressure against my clit, combined with the pressure of being filled by him, is divine. His hold on my hips tightens as he begins to guide me up and down his shaft, matching his movements. Our bodies glide against one another, adding to the friction. Sweat coats our skin as the potent scent of sex fills the air. My heart feels as though it's going to hammer its way out of my chest. My heart overflows with love and emotion for this man.

Our thrusts work in tandem to bring us both to the brink. "Let go, Emma. I've got you." He lowers his head to suck on my breasts, his thumb pressing against my clit.

My pussy spasms, sparks filling my vision as if on command. Tension fills my body as I break apart in Theo's strong arms, knowing he would never let me fall. "Ooooh, God! Theo," I moan.

"That's it, squeeze my dick." I manage to tighten my pelvic floor, squeezing as tight as I can. "Fuuuck! That feels amazing." He finishes with a long groan as he thrusts up into me one final time, holding onto my ass cheeks with his big hands. Holding still, I feel his length pulsing inside as he fills me with his release.

Our foreheads press together as we each catch our breath. Slow smiles form as we come back to ourselves after such a brilliant high.

I place my hand flat on his chest, over his heart. It's racing in a staccato to match mine. "I missed you so much, Theo. Even though you've been by my side, I've missed this connection we share. I never want to go that long without feeling you again."

"Never, Peaches. I promise. We're gonna do this …" Kiss. "Every." Kiss. "Single." Kiss. "Day." Kiss "For the rest of our lives." Kiss.

The muscles in my legs begin to twitch. I'm not really sex fit after such a long hiatus. "I need to try to stand up." I grimace as I work to find my feet. Theo's cum slides down the inside of my thigh after I disengage from him.

He stands quickly, helping me stagger to our new bathroom. "Sit down." He closes the lid on the toilet. "I'll clean you up." As I sit on the cool lid of the toilet, he wets a washcloth with warm water. Embarrassment fills my body as he spreads my legs open, studying my pussy closely as he uses his fingers to push the cum back into my vagina, then wipes around the area.

"What are you doing?" I giggle.

"I want my cum to stay inside you," he says matter-of-factly, as he pushes some more inside.

"You know I can't get pregnant, right?" *Sheet!* What if he wants a child of his own?

"Yeah, I know," he whispers. "Maybe there's something inherently wrong with me, but I like the thought of you filled with me. If it can't be my cock, then my cum is the next best thing." He winks at me, throwing the washcloth into the hamper. He pulls me up to his chest. "You okay?" He shifts so he can see my face, studying me closely. "I didn't hurt you? I wasn't too rough, was I?"

I hope my grin reassures him. "It was close to perfect."

His eyebrows draw down and I can tell he's running through what we just did to work out why I didn't say it was 'perfect'. "I think we should practice some more. Don't you?" I wink as I pull away. I walk him backward toward the door, pushing him through to the bedroom. "I need to pee. Then I'll make you a fresh cup of coffee."

Closing the door, I do what I need to do, then wash my hands. Studying myself in the mirror, I smile at the beard rash across my boobs and the hickey he left in the crook of my neck. Evidence of our lovemaking, our passion. I feel like a teenage girl who's just made out with my high school crush—I feel giddy.

I love it.

This feeling of excitement over a boy—not a boy, a man.

*My man!*

# CHAPTER 66

## —*theo*—

"I THOUGHT YOU MAY HAVE BEEN FURTHER ALONG AFTER HAVING THE weekend without the kids," Dad comments as I show him the renovation I've been working on since he left on Friday.

I probably would have been further along if I could keep my dick out of Emma's pussy. But it is what it is. I'm surprised we got anything done. I shrug. "Some things took longer than I anticipated." *Not a lie.*

Dad nods in understanding. "I guess so. When do you think you'll be finished?"

"The sale on Em's place closes in two weeks. I'll be ready." We move through to the kids' zone. "The boys' bedrooms are ready for them, with the shared bathroom. Kenny will move into my old room, which Em finished decorating for her this morning. Our bathroom's finished, so I only need to finish our bedroom and finalize the study." We decided to give the boys their own bedrooms because, as they grow older, they'll each need their own space.

"It all looks fabulous." He gives me a fatherly pat on the back, followed by a squeeze to my shoulder. "I'm proud of you, Theo. Proud that you made amends with a woman who is perfect for you. Proud of the way you stepped up with Kenny and the boys." He waves his arm around the room. "Proud of everything you've done here to make a beautiful home for your family." His eyes look glassy as he fills my soul with his praise.

Teenage me preens like a peacock at finally feeling like I have my father's approval. "Thanks, Dad. That means a lot to me."

Little footsteps come bounding up the stairs. "Daddy!" I catch

Kenny easily as she leaps for me. "I missed you." She kisses the tip of my nose, followed by each of my cheeks.

"I missed you too, Munchkin." I tickle her until she squirms with laughter. "Did you see your new room's all finished?"

Emma, Lachlan, Austin, and her parents breach the top of the stairs. Moving toward my family, I kiss the top of each boy's head, then hug Sally and shake John's hand. "Did you guys have a great weekend?"

"Oh, it was wonderful. We love having the boys so much. Maybe one weekend, Kenny might like to join us?" Sally looks across at Dad. "Though I know she enjoys time with her pappoús." She's highly maternal. She always seems so happy to be with her family. A lot like Mom.

I look at Dad, shrugging. "She would probably like that." He nods, tucking his hands in his pockets.

Kenny's smile is huge as she moves in to hug Sally. "Yeah, that would be heaps of fun. I could jump on the trampoline and play with Archie."

Em takes each of her son's hands. "I was about to show the kids their rooms. Shall we all do the tour?"

"Yeah!" they each call out.

The eight of us head down the hallway toward the boys' rooms first. Dad and I stand inside the doorway as the others explore every nook and cranny of their rooms. Even though the boys have their own rooms now, Em decided to keep them looking the same as their shared bedroom at her place. Everything works well, and the colors were selected based on what Austin and Lachlan like. I figure she knows them best, so I followed her lead. I have an electrician coming out during the week to install ceiling fans in each of the kid's rooms. Lachlan, in particular, needs it to help him sleep.

Austin's eyes are wide as he takes in the bathroom, which has doors opening into each of their rooms. "Is this bathroom ours?"

I move into the room, leaning against the bathroom doorway. "Yep, for you boys to share. You gotta keep it tidy, though." Emma looks at me, raising a perfect eyebrow as she tilts her head.

"Okay, Theo. We promise to keep it tidy," Lachlan answers on Austin's behalf.

Next is Kenny's room.

"This room's so big!" She runs in, squealing in delight. We bought more of the flower garden wallpaper and kept everything within the same color palette for her. We figured she loved it so much, we might as well stay with a winning combination. Em even set up a cozy reading nook for her in the corner.

She races into the bathroom, which will be solely hers. "I can't believe I get a whole bathroom to myself."

I wasn't sure it was a good idea, but Em assures me the boys and I will be thankful that she has her own bathroom as she gets older.

Wrapping my arm around Emma, I pull her into my body, kissing the top of her head. "I was thinking we could start moving some of your stuff across next weekend."

She wraps both arms around my waist, looking up at me. "Sounds perfect."

I can't resist. I lean down to kiss the tip of her nose. I can't wait to have them all living here with Kenny and me. The plans I drew up all those months ago were perfect for what we wanted. We made a few minor adjustments and then I got to work.

Looking at our parents, I ask, "Would you guys like to stay for dinner? I can get the grill going real quick."

Sally looks at John. I don't know why, because she'll decide for both of them, anyway. "That would be lovely. Is there anything we can do to help?"

"I'd love to, Son. I'll head down to get it started." He leaves to get the grill going and we all follow him downstairs.

# CHAPTER 67

## —emma—

IT'S STRANGE TO BE BACK AT SCHOOL. IT SEEMS LIKE FOREVER SINCE I last walked down this hallway as a teacher here and not as a parent, dropping off the boys and Kenny. The butterflies in my stomach are in full flight as I step into my classroom. It doesn't feel like my classroom; another teacher has put her mark here, making me feel like a foreigner. I feel fundamentally different as I stand inside the doorway of my classroom—so much has changed for me.

"Welcome back!" The entire staff calls out. So this is where everyone was. I thought it was strange when the ladies weren't in the front office and it seemed awfully quiet as I walked down the hallway. Thank goodness Theo's bringing the kids closer to the start of school, or Lachlan wouldn't have done too well with the sudden loud welcome. My smile must be as wide as the Grand Canyon—it feels amazing to be greeted so warmly by my colleagues and friends.

Kate's the first to break away from everyone. "I'm so happy you're back and that everything worked out so well for you." Wrapping our arms around each other, we sway from side to side in happiness. Blinking rapidly, I barely manage to keep my tears at bay. I feel incredibly blessed to have such an amazing friend in Kate; to work with such great people. Not to mention finding the perfect guy for me and moving in together to be one family. Things are really looking up for me.

Everyone takes their turn, welcoming me back before heading to their own classrooms to get ready for the day. Once I'm alone in my room, I notice the huge 'Welcome Back' banner secured across the board at the front of the class. My hand automatically comes up to my chest, as if I need to hold my heart in place. How sweet of my replacement teacher to work with the kids to make such a colorful banner. Brittany's been wonderful throughout this whole process; keeping me up-to-date with everything at the end of each week. Her emails were always so incredibly detailed and often made me laugh as she updated me on the students' progress and funny antics. I hope she manages to secure a full-time position here because she's an absolute gem; she would be a real asset to our school.

"Hey, Peaches." Theo's deep voice reaches me before he does.

"Mommy!" Kenny and the boys move forward as one to hug me. I saw them less than an hour ago, but they act like they haven't seen me for days, which always makes me feel special.

"Hey, guys." I laugh as we hug, Theo leaning over the top of the kids to plant a chaste kiss on my lips.

His eyes light up as they land on the banner. "That banner looks great."

"Yeah. I had the whole staff in here this morning welcoming me back. It feels a little weird to be here if I'm honest." He wraps his arm around me, pulling me in close, kissing the top of my head—something I love so much. His easy affection makes me feel incredibly safe and cherished.

"Well, if we're being honest. I'm gonna miss having you around all day. I loved our coffees on the porch, sharing lunch, and knowing I could see you whenever I wanted." His voice is soft as his words fill my heart—so sweet and beautiful.

I wrap my arms tight around him, just as the bell rings. "I'm gonna miss you, too. It's been so special to spend all of that time with you. Thank you so much for everything you've done for me throughout my recovery."

The sound of kids fills the hallway and I know my tranquility is about to come to an end, so I step back from the man I love with everything that I am. I feel as though I've known him forever, not for just over a year. All of those days he spoke of allowed us to get to know each other on such a deep level.

He lands a chaste kiss on my cheek. "See you at the end of the day, Peaches. Have a good one." He takes Kenny's hand. "Say bye to Mom, kids. We gotta go."

Hugs, kisses, and goodbyes surround me as my students come streaming through the classroom door. Huge smiles and happy hellos from the kids and their parents remind me why I love my job so much.

"Here are some flowers for you, Miss." Jack thrusts a bunch of daisies in my direction.

I take them from him. "Thank you, Jack. These are lovely." I head toward my desk to put the flowers down.

"Mrs. Miller, I made you a card." I turn to find Sue-Anne holding up a beautifully decorated handmade card.

Taking it from her, I study it closely, noticing the amount of detail she's included. "This looks gorgeous, Sue-Anne. Thank you so much."

She wraps her little arms around my hips. "I'm so glad you're back and you're okay."

Oh, my! "I'm glad I'm back, too. I missed you guys so much."

The second-morning bell sounds and we all settle in to get started for the day.

I'm freaking exhausted as the last child leaves for the day. Flopping down in my chair, I drop my head back, closing my eyes. Clearly, I need to build up my stamina. The surgeries left me feeling exhausted, and teaching grade one is an exhausting job. Maybe I should have waited a little longer to come back to work, as Theo suggested. The only problem with that is I've used up all of my paid leave along with a substantial amount of unpaid leave, which ate into my limited savings.

"Mommy!" I tilt my head back down, opening my eyes at the kids' sweet voices.

Standing, I open my arms wide. "Hey, guys. How was your day?" Austin and Kenny move into my embrace, one on each side of me. Lachlan comes forward once I release the younger two. I hug him, ruffling his hair as he pulls away.

"Hey, Peaches. How was your day?" Theo moves in to give me a quick kiss on the lips.

I blow my bangs out of my eyes. "It was great, but I'm shattered."

Creases form between his brows. "Let's get you home then. I'll run you a bath and you can relax while I deal with the kids."

My shoulders drop in gratitude. "That sounds divine. But I can help. You don't have to do everything. We're a team, remember?"

He takes my hand, pulling me to his side. "I remember. But I want to look after you while you get used to being back at work. You'll be back to your old self in no time, and then you can help." He punctuates his words with a kiss.

"How was your first day back?" Kate strolls into my classroom. "Oh, hi, Theo."

"Hey, Kate. My girl's a little tired after her first day." He pulls me in tighter against his body and I revel in the hard planes supporting my softer curves.

Kate's eyebrows tighten over her gorgeous denim eyes. "You didn't overdo it, did you?"

I look between my closest friend and my boyfriend. "I promise I took it easy. I sat when I could and the kids were so sweet. They helped me wherever they could."

Kate's face softens. "Awww, they're so sweet. You have some gorgeous kids in this class."

"I have, I'm incredibly lucky. I feel bad that I've messed them around this year with all the time I had to take off."

Kate brushes off the comment with a wave of her hand. "Kids are resilient at this age. They loved Brittany, and she was happy to fill in for you. So don't feel bad."

"You can't help what happened, Peaches. You can't feel guilty. I know you gave the kids your best before you left and you'll give them your best now you're back. It sounds like they were in good hands." He squeezes me in tighter, kissing the top of my head.

"You should go home. Refresh yourself; ready for tomorrow." Kate hugs me. "I'll see you in the morning."

"For sure. Bye, Kate."

Waving to the kids and Theo, she says her goodbyes.

"C'mon, Peaches. Get your things. Let's go."

# CHAPTER 68

## —theo—

I'VE MISSED EMMA MORE THAN I ANTICIPATED I WOULD. I KNEW I would miss being able to see her throughout the day on a whim, but I feel as though part of me is missing—the feeling is completely new to me. I've never felt the need to want to spend every waking minute with someone else, generally happy with my own company. But with Em—I do. I want to see her, touch her, kiss her constantly. It's almost become an addiction.

I've been working my ass off every day to get our place finished this week. I finished all the detailing, baseboards, painting, and shelving. I only need to clean the space up and then finish the hardwood floors. I want to move us across next week while Em's at work. I've organized both of our dads and Max to help me move the bigger stuff on Monday, so I can move the smaller stuff over the course of the week. Hopefully, by next weekend, it'll all be done and dusted.

"Why can't I see what you've done this week?" Em whines.

"I told you. I want you to be surprised when you see it all finished. Don't spoil my plan." She pouts, folding her arms beneath her glorious tits.

Sighing, her shoulders drop in defeat. "Okay." She blows her bangs out of her eyes as she looks around the living room. "I might pack a bit more, so we can move it across when we're ready next weekend."

"Sounds like a plan, Peaches." I look around. "I need to finish a few things off today. I can help you pack in between."

"That's okay. You do what you need to do. I'll work slowly. I promise I won't do too much." I smack her ass as I step past her.

"Take breaks."

"Hey, did you forget something?" she calls, pressing closed fists into her generous hips.

I run through the last few minutes and come up short. She taps her lips, raising her face. My feet move without instruction back to my girl. I can't believe I didn't think of it and was going to walk away without a goodbye kiss. Cupping the back of her head under the fall of her hair, I drop my mouth against hers. "Sorry, Peaches." My lips make contact with hers and I feel that instant spark ignite as it always does. Pulling away quickly so I don't get distracted—because damn, it's easy to do when Em's in the room. I step away from my girl. I can't afford distractions today. I've gotta get this done. I'm so close to finishing. "I'll be back in a couple of hours."

I clear everything out of our new bedroom and study, put all of my tools back into my workshop where they belong, then get to work sanding the new hardwood floors. If I can get this done, then I can put on the first coat of sealer this morning. It should dry in a couple of hours so I can put the second coat on later this afternoon. With ear muffs protecting my hearing, I get lost in the work, ensuring every single square inch is sanded to perfection. Even though the sander I hired has a built-in vacuum, I make sure to go over the area again to remove any dust. I want it pristine for the next step. Preparing the sealer, I get down on my hands and knees to cut in with a wide brush around the edges, then I grab my lambs' wool mop to coat the remainder of the floor evenly.

Standing in the doorway, I admire my work. My eyes wander over the room from the ceiling to the floor and everywhere in between. The sense of satisfaction from a job well done is such a high. To know I made this for *my* family fills me with pride. I always feel proud of the work I do. I love seeing my finished work being appreciated by the people who commission it, but it's always for someone else. It's not often I work on things for myself and this renovation has been bigger than anything I've worked on in a while. I've enjoyed every second of it.

Time to head back next door to help with the packing.

We opted to keep Emma's couch and get rid of mine. Hers was more comfortable and larger, which suited the size of our new family better. Carefully positioning the couch on the rug in the center of the living room, I release a long breath. "Thanks for all of your help today. I couldn't have gotten through it all this quickly on my own. Em's going to be surprised when she gets home from work to find we've moved everything across." And I mean everything. I only expected to move the larger items of furniture today, but the guys insisted on getting it all done.

"No problem. Happy to help." Max grabs a couple of cold beers for us. Both of our dads left when we only had a couple of things left to move. He cracks them open and hands one to me, tapping the neck of his bottle against mine before taking a long pull.

"I appreciate the time you've taken away from your own work today." I take a long pull, swallowing down the cool beverage. "What are you working on at the moment?"

"I'm close to finishing the bodywork on the sixty-four Ford Falcon Sprint." He sits, stretching out his long legs. "It's been tricky sourcing parts, so I've had to manufacture some of them. I enjoy that side of it, the challenge of making a component from scratch. I would imagine it's much the same for you in your carpentry work."

"Yeah. I do like the sense of achievement I get from making something from scratch. Seeing the different components come together to make a whole."

He sits forward in his chair. Resting his elbows on his thighs, the beer bottle dangling from one hand. "You won't let my sister and nephews down, will you?" He waves his hand around the room. "This isn't just a temporary thing until you get tired of playing happy families, right?"

I get where he's coming from. Em's been hurt in the past. Hell, one of the guys who hurt her was me. "It's not temporary for me. I plan on marrying your sister and tying her to me for good. I know she's too good for me, but I'm not letting her go. *Ever.*" I hope he realizes how serious I am.

He nods slowly, then takes another pull from his beer. "Good." Looking at his watch, he finishes his drink, then stands. "I'd better get going. I'm meeting some of the guys for a game of soccer later and I need to stop by the workshop first."

I walk him out as Emma pulls into her driveway with the kids. The first week back after such a long break really took it out of her, she was exhausted every day. Then she spent a lot of time over the weekend packing up her house, ready for the move. I'm worried she's overdoing it.

"Hey, Max. I didn't know you were coming over today." Emma walks over to her brother, embracing him as they always do.

"Uncle Max!" Austin calls out as he runs toward his favorite uncle. Well, to be fair, Max is his only uncle. But he really connects with Max, because he loves the work that Max does. Austin's always telling me that he wants to work with cars when he's a grown-up, just like his Uncle Max.

"Hey, guys. I stopped by to help Theo out with something. I was just leaving. Sorry, I can't stop any longer, but I need to check something at the workshop and then I'm meeting the guys for a game later." He picks Austin up, swinging him around in the air, then places him back on his feet. "Hey, Austin."

Kenny moves in to wrap her little arms around Max's legs. She looks up at him with her usual cheeky grin. "Hello, Uncle Max."

He picks her up, kissing her cheek. "Hey, Ken." I love how Em's family has welcomed Kenny into the family as though she's always been part of it.

They all catch up quickly before Max leaves. Emma grabs her school stuff out of the car, throwing the strap of her satchel over her shoulder. She's not carrying that when I'm around. I step up to her, transfer the strap to my shoulder, then take her files from her before landing a kiss on her soft lips. "Hey, Peaches. How're you feeling?"

Her shoulders slump forward. "Exhausted," she sighs. "I need a coffee." Walking toward the house, I let her go.

Lachlan comes running out. "Mommy! Someone's stolen all of our things. Our house is empty. Everything's gone!"

"What? What do you mean, everything's gone?" Emma's almost yelling in her panic. "Did you notice anyone, Theo?" She glances back at me as she takes all the porch steps in one leap.

"Uh, nope! But I've been busy." This reminds me of the conversation we had after I repaired those very porch steps. I follow, trying to contain my smirk.

Swinging open the front screen door, Emma storms inside. "Oh my gosh! Everything's gone!"

"That's what I said," Lachlan says in his matter-of-fact way.

She spins around, looking at me. "What am I gonna do? You're sure you didn't see anything?"

"Why don't you come home with me and we'll work out what to do?"

She ignores me as she races upstairs, moving quickly from room to room. "This can't be possible. Why would someone clean us out of everything? I don't understand." She comes back downstairs, stopping in front of me. "I don't believe you didn't see anything. This would have taken a significant amount of time to do." Her eyebrows are drawn down over her chameleon eyes.

I wrap my arm around her shoulders. "Kids, come on. Let's go home."

I guide my girl and her boys next door to their new home.

Opening the screen door, it only takes Em and the boys a second to realize that all of their furniture is here. With wide eyes, she turns to me. "So you didn't see anything?" She hits my stomach with the back of her hand. "Oh, my gawd! I was feeling sick to my stomach thinking all of our stuff was gone."

I wrap my arms around her, trapping her arms up between us. "Welcome home, Peaches." I press my lips to hers, licking across the seam, requesting entry. After a few seconds, she finally opens to me, letting me inside. In the far recesses of my mind, I hear the kids calling to each other from their bedrooms, but my sole focus in this moment is Emma. Emma's taste and the feel of her pressed against me.

Wholly and solely mine.

Pulling back slightly, I smile against her lips. "Surprise."

She smiles back, pressing her forehead to mine. "You must have worked so hard to get this all done. Thank you," she whispers.

"I had help. I couldn't have done it all on my own. I wanted you all here, in our new home sooner rather than later. I hope you don't mind." I kiss her again, only stopping when we're interrupted by the kids looking for their afternoon snack.

As the kids enjoy their snacks on the back deck, I take Em through our new addition to the house. "This is incredible, Theo. I'm so impressed by your skill," she comments as she runs her hand over the built-in shelving in her home office. I have a desk in here as well, for when I have to do the paperwork for my business. I have visions of us both working in here once the kids are in bed, her catching up on her planning, me doing my books, and ordering supplies online.

I can't see a future without Em and the boys in it. I know Kenny's completely in love with her and the boys. She's ecstatic that our living arrangement is going to be permanent. As she surveys our bedroom and the bifold doors that open out onto the deck, she steps into my body, wrapping me in her arms. My arms automatically come up to hold her tight. She looks up at me, with eyes a thousand different shades of green capturing mine. With a soft smile touching her lips, she whispers, "I love you, Theo. This is all so perfect."

I lean down, pressing my lips to hers. "You're the perfect one. Perfect for me. I love you, Peaches." I press my lips to her forehead, lingering for long seconds. Thinking how lucky I am that she gave me a second chance after I was such an asshole. "Thank you for giving me a second chance. I promise to work hard every day to be the man you deserve."

She looks up at me. "You already are the man I deserve, Theo. You already are." She presses her lips against my heart. "You have the best heart a girl could ever ask for."

*epilogue*

## CHAPTER 69

### —emma—

THEO AND KENNY HAVE THE BIGGEST MATCHING SMILES AS WE LEAVE the courthouse. I took a personal day off work so I could be with them at their adoption hearing. Even though Anna named Theo Kenny's legal guardian, he wanted to make their relationship more official. It was a reasonably straightforward process once Theo got all the paperwork in order.

"Let's go celebrate with lunch at the restaurant," Theo suggests.

My stomach grumbles in agreement with his suggestion. "Sounds perfect. You can tell your dad the good news. I think he was disappointed he couldn't make it to the courthouse today."

Theo leans across, laying a playful kiss on my lips. "Thanks for coming with us today."

"I wouldn't have missed it for the world. I'm so happy for you guys." I'm pretty sure my smile matches theirs.

"Thanks for all of your support throughout the entire process, Peaches." He winks at me, picking Kenny up to nuzzle her cheek.

"Daddy!" Kenny squeals in delight. "You're being silly."

"I can't help it. I'm so happy that I'm officially your daddy." He nuzzles her a little more. "Love you, Munchkin."

Theo opens the passenger door for me, then helps Kenny get situated in her booster seat.

"I hope you don't mind, but I need to make a quick stop."

"No problem."

After a few moments, he pulls into a parking lot, turns off his truck, then leans across to kiss me. "Back in a few minutes, ladies." He hops out of the truck, so I turn the radio up a little so Kenny and I can sing along to the songs to fill the time. Kenny and I often have dance-offs in the living room, much to the boys' amusement.

We're both dancing in our seats, singing at the top of our voices when Theo's door opens, and he hops in. "You girls having fun in here?" He smiles at us as he puts on his seatbelt.

"Yeah, Daddy! We've been dancing to all the best songs."

"That's great, Munchkin. Let's go get something to eat."

"Yeah, I'm hungry." Kenny rubs her tummy to make her point.

Walking into the restaurant, Theo's hand in mine, it takes a moment for my eyes to adjust to the dim lighting. When I can finally see properly, I'm surprised to find my boys and my entire family here. I guess Theo wanted everyone to join in the celebration.

"Congratulations!" everyone cheers at once.

Kenny jumps up and down before being engulfed by our families. Her pappoús picks her up, positioning her on his shoulders as though she's just hit a home run. Everyone takes turns congratulating the daddy and daughter of the moment, sharing in their ultimate happiness.

"Surprise, Mommy!" Austin cheers as he wraps his hands around my body, looking up at me with a huge smile on his face.

"I'm so surprised you guys aren't in school." I raise my brows.

"Nana and Poppa came and got us." He smiles mischievously.

Lachlan moves in to hug me. "You're not mad that we're not in school, are you, Mommy?"

I pull him close. "No way. I'm so happy you're here to celebrate with Theo and Kenny." And I am, but I'm mad at myself that I didn't think about organizing this for Theo and Kenny myself.

We all sit at the special table at the back of the restaurant, which Theo made when he was younger. Drinks are passed around and toasts are made around the table, honoring the guests of the moment. I look around the table and my heart swells. This is amazing. Our families get along like we've known each other forever, seamlessly joining together, sharing happy times.

The food is brought out, and it's as fabulous as usual. The smells and tastes delight my senses. Conversation ceases momentarily as we enjoy the first mouthfuls of deliciousness. Theo's dad has organized a variety of dishes, completely filling the table. After the initial quiet, the conversation starts again.

"I'm surprised you could make it," I say to Sarah across the table. "I know you're always busy at work."

She swallows down her food. "I started half an hour earlier today, so I could join you guys for lunch. I didn't want to miss out on the celebration."

"Hmmm. That's interesting. This seemed like a spur-of-the-moment idea when we left the courthouse."

She shakes her head in the negative. "Nope. Theo invited us last week."

Theo's hand covers mine on the table, and I look down at it. It's hard to see in the low light, but his ring finger looks different from the others. Lifting his hand in mine, closer to my face, I see there's a black mark, and it's a little red and puffy. Looking up at Theo, I ask, "What did you do here?" I don't want to touch it because it looks a little sore.

He kisses my lips tenderly. "Read it."

I pull it closer because it's tricky to see. My name, written in a cursive script, wraps across the top of his finger. My heart speeds up in my chest, and I'm worried it's going to thump its way right out of my body. Turning over his hand, I see an infinity symbol on the other side. I look up at him, completely puzzled. "What's this about?" I'm so completely confused. He doesn't have tattoos on any part of his body. Why on earth would he tattoo my name on his finger? Isn't that the worst possible thing you can get tattooed on your body? I watched a show once, where people were having to go to extreme lengths to remove an ex-lover's name they had tattooed permanently on their skin.

Raising my hand, he kisses the matching finger. Everyone's gone quiet now. Out of my periphery, I catch Mom's hands coming up to cover her mouth as Dad wraps his arm around her shoulder. "I wanted a permanent symbol of my commitment to you. I didn't want something I could slide on and off." He gently brushes my hair over my shoulder. "There's no going back for me, Em." He holds up his finger, pointing to the fresh ink. "This is forever, just like you're my forever. You and the boys."

He slides a beautiful oval diamond, surrounded by a halo of tiny diamonds, set in white gold down my finger until it can go no further. Even in the low light, it's stunning. My eyes must be as big as saucers as they meet his gorgeous oceanic irises.

*Is this what I think it means?*

It's completely out of the blue; I'm not sure if I'm making it up in my mind. He hasn't actually asked me the question, 'will you marry me?', so maybe I have this all wrong. Glancing around the table, everyone seems to be waiting. Waiting for what? I lean into my boyfriend. "I'm pretty sure you're supposed to ask me a question," I whisper for his ears only. I don't want to embarrass him in front of our family.

"Nope, I've said what I needed to say and I've put my ring on your finger." He's smug in his response.

I pull back, so I can study his face. "Are you asking me to marry you?"

"Nope. Asking allows you to say no. I'm not risking it. This is happening." He presses his lips to mine, sealing the deal, and all I can do is giggle. This man and the way he does things. This 'proposal' is Theo to the core. It reminds me of when he decided to sell his house so we could live together. There was no discussion then, either.

"Why don't you ask me and see what happens? It may just be your lucky day." I smirk at him. He glances between my mouth and my eyes for a few seconds, then nods to himself.

He pushes his chair away from the table, manhandling my chair to help me stand. Taking my hands in each of his, he looks down at me. Our eyes lock and hold. "Emma." He leans forward, landing a gentle kiss on my lips, just as he has a million times before. He loves stealing kisses at every available opportunity, but this one feels different. Against my lips, he whispers just for me, "Marry me, Peaches. Make me the happiest, luckiest man on the face of the earth."

He still hasn't asked me, but I have no other answer than the one that escapes freely. "Yes. Of course I'll marry you, Stud."

With matching smiles, our lips meet in a kiss to seal our future. As we wrap each other in our embrace, our families cheer, surrounding us with a giant family hug. Theo reaches down to pick up Kenny, and I step out to bring the boys into our family unit.

Five.

It's no longer just me and the boys. Theo and Kenny are now officially part of our family, and it feels amazing.

He moves back in close to whisper, "We'll have our own celebration later, Peaches." After a quick kiss, he pulls back, finishing with a wink.

Mmhm. I can't wait for later.

# CHAPTER 70

## —emma—

It's finally later—my heart rate picks up speed at the thought. The kids are all in bed, sound asleep, and I'm ready for my private celebration with my fiancé.

*My fiancé.*

I can't believe Theo and I are going to get married. Never in a million years would I have ever dreamed I'd be here like this with my sexy neighbor, but here I am. I never thought I'd be keen to get married again, but here I am, excited for a future with the man I've fallen madly in love with.

Stepping out of the shower, I notice my nipples are puckered from the temperature change—this is a good sign. My excitement's interrupted when a sharp knock sounds as the door handle turns. "You okay in here, Peaches?" Theo asks as his eyes trail my body from the top of my head to the tips of my toes and back again, pausing on my breasts. My nipples pebble further in response to his eyes on them. It's almost like they're showing off. His eyebrows rise as a slow smile graces his handsome face. His eyes move up to mine and it's my turn to smile at him. He wasn't expecting this development. "Oh yeah." He pinches one nipple between his rough fingers. "This *is* cause for celebration. Don't you think?"

"I agree. How are we going to celebrate? Any ideas?" My voice comes out soft, breathy.

"I have a few." He grabs me under my ass, picking me up as though I'm a size six, then carries me into our bedroom. Pressing me up against the nearest wall, he holds me there with his pelvis as I wrap my legs around his waist, locking him to me. Pulling back, he runs his nose up my neck until he reaches my ear. A sharp nip on the lobe is followed by a gentle kiss. His warm breath coats my skin, sending goosebumps skittering over my body, making me wetter. He kisses along my jawline, making his way to my lips, and I open with a sigh, inviting him in. This kiss is deep and full of emotion from the day. Knowing we've agreed to tie ourselves together for the rest of our days makes it more meaningful. Our tongues slide against each other in a way we've perfected over the time we've been together. It's practiced, yet it's not routine. Theo's kisses are anything but routine. He changes the pressure of our kiss from hard to light and back again, keeping me on edge.

Pulling back, he lifts me higher, pressing my body against the wall for purchase, my bare pussy resting against his firm stomach. Using his nose, he traces over my breast before licking around my nipples and carefully biting each one in turn. They bead further at the attention, and the utter relief I feel in this moment is overwhelming. It may seem silly to some, but I was worried that my breasts would never respond to stimulus again. I'm truly amazed at how well my body has recovered from the trauma it's been through.

Pulling away from the wall, he carefully lays me down on our bed. The softness of the bed covers a stark contrast to the hard wall I was pressed against. He comes down on top of me, his dick notching at my entrance. I'm so ready to have him inside me. "I need to be inside you, Em," he whispers against my lips, sliding into my body in one smooth glide. We both breathe out heavily at our connection, eyes locked together, mesmerized by the feeling that occurs every single time we're like this.

Leaning down, he continues our kiss—slow and languid. I attempt to move my hips to get things started, but he presses me down into the mattress. "Not yet. I just want to be inside you for a bit. I love the feel of your pussy around my dick."

He's so in control of himself, whereas I'm a wet, panting mess—ready to move things along. Realizing he's not going to give in, I relax into the moment, enjoying the sensations Theo creates in me with only his kiss. He's masterful with his tongue, whether it be in my mouth, trailing along my skin, or teasing my pussy along to climax.

Wrapping my legs around his waist, I pull us together as close as we can possibly be. Theo's heart pounds against my chest, just as mine pounds against his. I never want to be apart from him. I always want to be able to share moments like these with him. Even when our bodies are old and wrinkly, I want him to be the man I spend naked time with.

He finally begins a slow, gentle glide in and out of my pussy, sending delicious sparks skipping through my body.

Stealing my kisses, stealing my heart, and stealing my breath as he thrusts harder. Hitting that special secret spot I used to think was a myth until Theo came along. My hips move without thought, matching his—synchronizing our movements, our breaths.

"Oh, Theo. Don't stop," I whisper against his ear. "Don't stop."

"I've got you, Peaches. I'm not gonna stop." He leans forward, taking my mouth roughly, changing his position as he pushes my knees back toward my ears. He rears up, speeding up his thrusts; increasing his intensity. "I love watching your tits move when I fuck into you."

"Oooooo." His words cause my body to squeeze his shaft. Closing my eyes, I get lost in the rhythm. The push. The pull. The sheer beauty of him above me. The veins in his neck bulge with his exertion.

So hot!

So very masculine.

So very Theo.

"Open your eyes, Peaches. Look at me. Look at my cock sliding in and out of your pussy."

My walls flutter, squeezing tightly. My toes contract, the pressure moving up my legs as they tighten around Theo's hips until it reaches the apex between my thighs. "Ooooo, Theo!" Lights explode around the edge of my vision, my jaw dropping open in ecstasy. The tension spreads through my body as I come hard.

Theo gentles his thrusts through my orgasm, pressing back down over my body so he can kiss me. His tongue licks into my mouth in time with his hips, increasing the sensation inside of me. His hands cup my head reverently as his thumbs stroke my hair out of my face. "You're so beautiful when you come," he whispers, his eyes scanning over the entirety of my face. I can't stop my smile at his words, nor would I want to.

Once I recover a little, I move my hips slightly, tightening my legs around Theo and twist, managing to roll us over until he's under me. I push myself up, gradually stepping my hands down from his hard chest to his firm abs. Coveting that delicious v leading down to his impressive manhood nestled between my thighs. Gently, I score my fingernails across his nipples, then pinch them in much the same way he does mine. He pushes his pelvis up into mine. "Em, stop teasing me and move."

I'm the one in control now. I smile down at my man and swivel my hips slowly. Reaching one hand behind, I cup his heavy sac. His hands glide up my body, cupping my breasts before pinching my nipples. The sensations aren't quite one hundred percent, but there's something there and it'll only improve. I pick up my rhythm, sliding up and down the best I can. His thumb locates my clit, rubbing tight circles, and I begin to build again.

What is it with this man? He can *always* get me where I need to be multiple times. Sometimes I actually feel bad that he can't come again straight away, needing recovery time. I feel like he misses out a bit, but he swears he doesn't feel like he's missing anything. His prime goal is always my pleasure first.

My body tightens as I build again, my movements becoming irregular. He takes over, fucking up into me from below. Powerful, strong thrusts designed to break me quickly. His cock swells inside me and as he groans out his own release, I break apart for the second time. His groans and my moans fill the space of our bedroom. I'm so glad we're downstairs on the opposite side of the house, allowing us to be a little noisy. The rapid beat of my heart makes me dizzy and I remind myself to take a breath. Theo pulls me forward, so I'm lying on his chest. His heart beats a rapid tattoo against my cheek—proof of his vibrancy and vitality. His arms wrap around my back, holding me tight to him.

I tilt my head up so I can see his gorgeous face. "I love you, Theo. Thanks for telling me we're getting married." I giggle.

He groans. "Fuck, stop. You're pushing my dick out and I don't wanna leave yet." I chuckle again. I can't help it. The things he says. He holds my hips tight, pushing me back down as he pushes himself back inside. "That's better," he breathes.

Relaxing my body against his, I rest my head back down on his chest. His heartbeat has slowed a little, our breaths returning to normal. Goosebumps cover my skin as the sweat on my body begins to cool. Theo throws the other half of the cover over us, rubbing his hands soothingly up and down my back.

He kisses the top of my head. "I know it wasn't romantic, so thank you for not throwing my ring back at me."

I take hold of his hand, pulling it up to my face. Admiring the tattoo, I smile at Theo's dedication to show his commitment to me. I kiss the spot on the underside of his finger where he had the infinity symbol tattooed. "This means forever, you know."

"I know, Peaches. Because that's exactly what I want with you and your boys." He kisses me soundly, stealing my breath. "Forever. Em. I want forever."

KISSES
book one

bonus
epilogue

stolen
KISSES

DEBRA ST JAMES

# CHAPTER 1

## *-kenny-*

"HAPPY BIRTHDAY, KENNY," DAD SAYS AS HE TAKES THE CUP OF steaming hot coffee from my hands. Wrapping me securely in his arms, he kisses my forehead. "I can't believe you're twenty-one, Munchkin," his voice cracks as he whispers.

"Thanks, Dad." I return his hug, smiling into his chest. His familiar scent and embrace make me feel safe. I'm not sure why he still calls me Munchkin, but his silly nickname for me stuck—a little, secret part of me loves that he still uses it.

Mom wanders into the room, a huge smile on her gorgeous face. She pulls on Dad's arm. "Outta my way, I need to wish my girl happy birthday."

Dad releases me with a wink, stepping aside to give Mom space. She wraps me tight in her embrace. "Happy Birthday, Kenny. It feels like it was only yesterday that you scared the hell out of me while I was weeding my front garden."

"You mean spying on your new neighbor." I wink at her. She told me when I was old enough to understand about boys why she was weeding in the front garden the day we moved in—so she could get a glimpse of her new neighbors.

I don't really remember that day, but Mom and Dad enjoy reminding me about the time I gave Dad the shock of his life on the very first day I started living with him. Apparently, Mom wasn't much impressed with his parenting skills, not realizing we'd technically only just met.

"What time do you want to leave for breakfast?" Dad takes a sip of *my* coffee.

Checking the time on the oven, I calculate how long I'll need for a shower and to get dressed. "Maybe in an hour? Is that okay?"

He nods. "Yep. I'll let Dad and your brothers know what time to meet us." He kisses my forehead again as he leaves the room to make the calls.

Mom takes my hand, giving me a warm smile. She knows today is always an emotional one for me. Since I was old enough to understand what it meant to lose my mom, I've always felt her loss deeply on special days. "How are you feeling?"

I squeeze her back. "I'm okay. I'll always miss her, especially on these special days. But I'm okay. Thanks for checking in on me." She gives me a side hug, kissing my cheek. My memories of Mom are what I've pieced together from photos and stories Dad and Pappoús have shared with me. What I *do* know is that she would have been so incredibly happy that Emma came into our lives and that she became the mother I needed.

"Always." She steps back, making herself a coffee. "Mmmhm. That first sip in the morning is heaven, isn't it?" I nod in agreement. "Your mom would be so proud of the young woman you've grown to be. I know I'm proud of you and all that you've achieved." She gives me a bright smile. "I need to shower and dress so we can get to those delicious pancakes."

*Pancake Paradise* hasn't changed a single bit since we first started coming here when I turned five. It may seem silly and juvenile to still be coming here for my birthday breakfast, but I have the best memories of this place. Pappoús, Austin, and Lachlan are already in a booth waiting for us. These are my people and it fills my heart to bursting that they're all here with me this morning.

Pappoús is the first to greet me with one of his bear hugs. "Happy birthday, Kenny." He kisses both of my cheeks before cupping my face in his hands. "You're looking beautiful. Twenty-one looks good on you." He winks at me.

Austin wraps his arms around my waist from behind, lifting me off of my feet. "Happy birthday, Sis." I laugh at his typical antics.

"Put me down, you giant!" I giggle. He returns me to my feet. Turning around, I wrap my arms around him. It's been a while since I've seen him and I swear he's grown taller in that time.

"I'm far from a giant. It's not my fault you're so short." He rests his elbow on my shoulder to prove his point.

"Cut it out!" I push him away and he moves over to say hi to our parents.

"Uh, happy birthday, Kenny." Lachlan moves in to hug me, patting my back lightly before pulling away quickly. I see him more often because he comes to the house every day to work in Dad's workshop with him.

"Thanks, Lachlan." He steps to the side, hugging Mom and shaking hands with Dad. We all situate ourselves in the booth as Pappoús and Dad place our orders. We all have our standard orders each time we come here, so they know exactly what we want.

They return to the booth and slide in. "So, what did you get for your birthday?"

I look at Pappoús incredulously. He knows I never get gifts until we get home. "Nothing yet, Dad's probably been too busy to get to the store." I wink at him. It's a bit of a running joke since he pretended to forget to buy me a birthday present the first year I celebrated my birthday with him. Only he hadn't forgotten. He'd made me a gorgeous dollhouse, which I still have.

Dad scrapes his nails through his short beard which has more salt than pepper through it. "I knew there was something I was supposed to do last week."

Emma laughs. "Stop being so mean. You do this to her every year."

He leans across, kissing the side of her head. He's always kissing and touching her in some way. It's so incredibly sweet that after all of these years, they're still so affectionate with each other. Her eyes close as a serene smile touches her lips.

Our breakfast arrives and my unicorn pancakes are slid across the table to land in front of me. I'm the only one at the table with the kiddy pancakes and I don't even care. I love this dish and have done since I was five, so I don't see any point in changing it. After all, it's the reason we're still coming here for my birthday breakfast on my twenty-first.

As I look around the table at my family, my heart feels full and I can't hold back my smile. These people have given me so much love and support over the years. I'm extremely grateful for each and every one of them and what they give to me in their own special way. They've been constant in my life—all of my greatest memories include these people.

We finish our breakfast and leave the restaurant together. Mom kisses Dad and says goodbye to Pappoús, before coming up to me. "The boys and I will see you at home. Okay?"

"Okay. We won't be too long."

"Take as long as you need. We'll be waiting." She kisses my cheek and then steps away. Austin and Lachlan both hug me and then head for their cars, taking Mom with them.

Dad, Pappoús, and I climb into Dad's new truck so we can make our way to the cemetery. This is what we've always done and I'm certain it's what we'll always do. In the past, we've invited Mom and the guys to join us, but they wanted me to have this special time with my mother as our original family unit.

"You know, this is one of your last letters? The only ones left are the letters for your college graduation, when you marry, and when you have your first child." Pappoús twists slightly in his seat as he speaks to me.

My heart sinks. "I know."

I can't help but feel the loss of my mother as the last letters loom. Not that I'm even remotely close to getting married—I don't even have a boyfriend. So it's not going to happen anytime soon. It's the thought of never opening another letter from her. That final link that's keeping her alive in my mind will be gone. I've read over her letters time and again, committing each one to memory. As much as I look forward to receiving each one on my birthday, I can't fathom the toll it must have taken on her to write them for me in her last months. It was the most beautiful gift she could have ever given me.

We exit the truck and the three of us make our way toward Mom's final resting place. It's a tranquil spot, right beside Yaya beneath the shade of a beautiful Jacaranda tree. It's lovely here at the end of spring with the grass covered in a blanket of purple. The breeze is warm as I lower myself to the grass, while Dad busies himself cleaning around the headstones. He does this every time we come here. We place the peonies and gardenias Pappoús bought before breakfast in the vases on each grave, then we sit in quiet contemplation for a few moments.

Dad raises his butt from the grass, reaching around to his back pocket. He pulls out one of my final letters, holding it up in front of me. "Are you ready, Munchkin?"

I release a heavy sigh and nod. "Yeah."

"You want to read it this time?"

"Nope." My answer is always the same. I've never read my mother's letters until Dad reads them to me for the first time. I don't know why I still ask him to read them to me here, only that it feels like it's what Mom would have wanted.

He nods, already expecting my answer. Carefully, he runs his finger under the seal, opening the envelope before pulling out the letter. I swallow the lump in my throat and I notice Dad's doing the same. I know he still feels incredibly guilty that he wasn't here for Mom in her final months. That he let us all down. He looks at me with a half-smile, before dropping his eyes to the sheet of blue paper.

"Alright then …

*Happy Birthday, Gorgeous Girl*
*You're 21 today! 21!*
*I'm so excited for you to begin your life as an adult, to experience everything life has to offer a bright young woman such as yourself. If you're anything like me, you'll be ready to hit the bars and nightclubs and spread your wings, sharing fun times with girlfriends."*

Pappoús huffs out a laugh with a twinkle in his eye. "Your mom used to sneak out of the house to go to nightclubs *before* she turned twenty-one. She thinks I didn't know, but I knew a lot more about what went on than she thought."

"Did you ever ground her for it?"

He waves off my question. "What would have been the point? She'd have worked out another way to go out with her friends. She wasn't hurting anyone." He shrugs with a faraway look in his eyes.

I look back at Dad. "What would you have done if I'd done that?"

"I would have grounded your ass." He gives me a wink and I laugh at the fierceness in his tone.

"I do not doubt that you would have done that. Aren't you lucky I prefer to stay up late with my Kindle?"

He leans forward pressing a kiss to my forehead. "I consider myself extremely lucky to have you as my daughter, Kenny. You've made me proud every single day." My heart swells at his words. I've never had to wonder if I'm loved because I've felt it and been shown every day of my life. "You ready for me to keep reading?"

I nod. "Yeah."

*"I'm struggling with what I can possibly say to you that I haven't already said in previous letters. I wonder if we would have been close as you grew up, or would your teenage years have seen us grow apart as so many children and parents seem to do. I would like to think we would have been great friends at this point. That we would have stayed up late talking about boys and all of your plans for your future. I hope you've had that Kenny. That you've had a woman in your life that spent special time with you."*

Dad's eyes rise to mine and I know he's thinking about all the times Mom and I spent shopping or sitting on the back deck reading the latest book together. The times Mom consoled me after a boy broke my heart or I had a falling out with the girls at school. I've often wondered the very same thing. Would I have had all of those things with my mother? Dad gives me a half-smile, returning to the letter.

*"I don't know what you'll decide to do as your career, but I hope whatever it is fills your soul and puts a twinkle in your eye. I hope you wake each day looking forward to what's to come and that you feel excited to get out of bed. I hope you go to sleep each night, satisfied with your life."*

"Well, I certainly have that in spades. I love my job and the work I do. Working with people to help make their homes and workspace comfortable and stylish as well as practical." I get excited thinking about my current projects.

"Your mom would definitely be happy to know you landed on your feet with your job. You worked damn hard to get that position. You deserve it, Kenny." Pappoús pats my hand which is resting next to his on the grass.

"We're all proud of your hard work and determination to get the job of your dreams." Dad drops his eyes back to the letter.

*"As for love. I wonder if you've found that special person yet? I hope you find a man or woman who loves you for every beautiful part of you, inside and out. Don't accept anything less, Kenny, because you're worth everything and so much more.*
*If they don't love and respect you for the person you are, you need to walk*

*away—don't settle. Never settle for anything that doesn't make your heart pound and free the butterflies in your stomach. When you find it, grab it, fight for it, and never let it go. Because, Kenny, it's oh so rare and oh so magical.*

*I had it once, but I let it go thinking it wasn't what I wanted. But I did. I did want it. I was scared. Scared of what loving someone that much would do to me if something ever happened to them. I watched my father lose the love of his life and I couldn't bear to go through something like that, so I pushed my love away. Not once did I imagine that I would be the one to leave loved ones behind."*

I look at Dad and Pappoús with raised brows. Neither of them has ever mentioned any of this to me. "Did you guys know about this?"

They both shake their head in the negative. "Nope, but it probably happened after I moved east."

"I'm not aware of your mother falling that much in love with anyone." He almost looks sad. "It breaks my heart that losing her mother stole the opportunity she had to share a beautiful love with someone."

I wrap my arm around him as he gets lost in his head for long moments. He looks at me shaking his head, bringing his thoughts back to the present moment.

"You can't feel bad for her choices, Pappoús. She had her reasons and it sounds like she made a happy life for herself."

"You know the happiest time of her life was when she found out she was pregnant with you. She glowed throughout the pregnancy. And when you were born … well, she was ecstatic. She was a great mom to you. So devoted to your every need. You were what made her the happiest in her life."

My pappoús' words profoundly touch my heart. It feels like a warm blanket wrapping around me, filling me up with love and warmth. A tear slides down my cheek and he reaches up to wipe it away.

Dad clears his throat. "Maybe that's why she told me in her letter to me to be happy. Not to let past hurts stop me from future possibilities. She told me that if someone special were to capture my attention, I was to never let her go. It's why I pursued Emma for a second chance after I messed up the first time." He smiles, almost to himself.

"I'm so glad you did that. You know what my birthday wish was when I turned five?" I smile at him.

He shakes his head. "No. You're not supposed to share your wishes."

I laugh softly. "Well, I think it's okay to share now. I wished that Emma would be my mommy. I was so happy when we moved into their house and then they moved in with us. Even more so after you adopted me and asked her to marry you."

His eyebrows shoot up his forehead. "Really? Well, I'll tell you something. The day you called Emma, Mommy, for the first time meant the world to her. Neither of us was surprised because you loved her and her boys so much. It was like we were all meant to be one big family."

I smile, nodding. I don't remember deciding to call her Mommy, it just slipped out one day and I kept doing it.

"Should I keep going?"

"Yes, please."

His eyes drop back down to the paper, he sucks in a breath and continues.

*"I hope you live each day with love and hope in your heart. Make the most of each and every day. Value and appreciate the people in your life and let them know you love them. Fill your days with everything you love and make goals that fulfill your dreams.*

*Kenny. I don't want to bring you down on your birthday, but I need you to do something for me. I've already made your Uncle Theo promise that he will ensure this happens, but I want to implore you myself. Please, Kenny. Please get tested for the BRCA1 and BRCA2 genes. I was tested and found to be positive for BRCA1. I don't know if Yaya carried the gene, but obviously, breast cancer runs in our family. If you've never thought about it before, I beg you to think about it now. I don't want you to go through what Yaya and I have gone through. Please have the test and do whatever needs to be done as a result of that test to ensure you have a long and healthy life."*

Dad's oceanic eyes raise to mine. "I was going to speak with you about this next week. I didn't want to bring it up on your birthday. But I think it would be a good idea to do the test. It's a simple blood test and you get the results back within a few weeks. However, the decision is entirely yours."

I look at Pappoús. His eyes are glassy as he clasps my hands in his. "Please consider having the test."

I nod. "I will. I'll book an appointment when I have time next week. Promise."

They both blow out a heavy breath and thank me, Dad's eyes dropping back to the paper he holds in his shaky hands.

> *"I love you, Kennedy Olivia Drivas. Live your best life knowing that I'm*
> *watching over you. Always.*
> *Love you more than all the butterflies,*
> *Mom*
> *kiss, kiss, hug, kiss, kiss, hug"*

My nose tingles and I blink rapidly, trying to keep the tears burning at the back of my eyes at bay. The tears can't be stopped and they're too much to contain, dropping over my bottom lashes to roll down my cheeks. Two of my most favorite men in the world move in, wrapping me in their arms. They hold me until my tears settle. I dig into my purse looking for tissues, but Pappoús hands me his handkerchief before I can lay my hands on them, so I can clean myself up the best I can.

Dad holds out a small box. "Your mom wanted you to have this gift on your twenty-first birthday."

I take it from him with shaky hands and carefully open the sky-blue tissue paper. This is the second gift I've received from beyond the grave. Opening the box, I find a pair of earrings to match the necklace Mom gave me for my high school graduation. Gorgeous diamond studs with an elegant silver drop cage containing ruby hearts. The filigree work on the drop cage is stunning and I can't wait to put them on; I wish I was wearing my necklace today. I remove the earrings I'm wearing, so I can put my gift on straight away, then take a selfie on my phone to see what they look like.

"Oh my gosh, I love them so much." I hold my hair out of the way. "What do you think?"

"They look beautiful on you, Kenny."

# CHAPTER 2

## —kenny—

"HI, DR. PETERSON."

"Hello, Kennedy. It's nice to see you. How's the family?" The smile on Dr. Peterson's face is bright and welcoming as he gestures to one of the chairs opposite his desk.

Taking a seat, I get comfortable. "They're all doing great. Thanks."

"Good to hear. How can I help you today?" He folds his hands one on top of the other as he directs his full attention to me.

"Uh, well … you know how my mother passed when I was small." He nods. "I recently received a letter from her for my twenty-first birthday requesting I get tested for the BRCA1 and BRCA2 gene."

"Why did she request you do that?" His eyebrows draw down over his eyes.

"She died from breast cancer and so did my grandmother." His eyes widen as he nods. "My uh, Dad. Sorry, biologically he's my uncle, was tested for the gene some years ago and he came back negative."

"I'm pleased you've come to find out about the genetic testing. I would highly recommend you have it done considering your family history. I'm not practiced enough with the genetic counseling you'll require, so I'm going to recommend you see Dr. Starling. She's one of the best in the city." He types something on his computer and my phone vibrates. "I've sent her details to your phone. She gets very busy, so you may have to wait a little while for an appointment, but she's fantastic. Very thorough and knowledgeable in her field."

I swallow down the excess saliva pooling in my mouth. "Thanks,

Doctor. I'm honestly nervous about the whole process. I believe it's a blood test. Is that right?"

"Yes, that's right. But Dr. Starling will work through a series of questions with you first. She'll speak with you about the possible results and the next steps you can take depending on what the tests show. The actual test is painless. You don't need to worry about that. They'll take a sample of your blood and send it off for analysis."

I nod slowly. "That doesn't sound too bad, I guess."

He stands and comes around to sit on the front of his desk. "Having the test and arming yourself with this knowledge is powerful, Kennedy. It will allow you to make the necessary decisions for your health. It is much better to know so you can be prepared and proactive than it is to not know and maybe be underprepared for a possible issue."

"I know. The logical part of my brain tells me it's better to be informed." I wipe my sweaty palms on my jeans. "It's always been in the back of my mind. Mom's letter forced the issue, I guess."

He gives me a warm smile. "Moms have a habit of doing that, even from beyond the grave."

I chuckle. "Yeah. Crazy, huh?"

"Nope. She loved you so much, she's still looking out for you. A mother's love is such a strong and powerful thing. It's almost tangible."

I nod. I agree wholeheartedly, I've felt my mother's love every single day. Dad and Pappoús have made sure to keep her memory alive and well. It feels as though I've grown up with her. "Thank you, Dr. Peterson."

"You're most welcome, Kennedy. Please let me know how it goes. I'm happy to help you in any way I can." He presses away from his desk and I stand, dragging my purse strap over my shoulder.

"I will. Bye."

"Bye, Kennedy."

Mom's sitting in one of the rocking chairs on our front porch. I know she's waiting for me because that's what she does. She's always been there for me; I couldn't have asked for a better mom if I couldn't actually have my own. Taking a seat in the other chair, I sit for a little while absorbing her love for me.

"Dr. Peterson recommended I see a genetic counselor. He thinks it's a good idea to go ahead with the test."

"Did he recommend anyone in particular? You know your dad did the testing when you were young. You could always see the same lady." She places her coffee cup on the table between us.

I pull out my phone to check I have the right name. "Yeah, he suggested I see Dr. Starling." I look at Mom.

She smiles. "That's who your father saw. She's lovely and very supportive." Leaning forward in her chair, she places her hand over the top of mine. "Are you okay? This can be a *lot* to deal with."

I suck in a deep breath. "My mind's been spinning since my birthday." I look at the woman who's supported me, loved me, guided me when my own mother couldn't. The woman who had to fight her own battle with breast cancer. "It's always been at the back of my mind since I was old enough to understand the implications of Mom and Yaya both dying from breast cancer. In the past couple of years, I've done a little research, but I sort of brushed it off. You know?" Mom nods, giving me a tight smile. "I guess the letter dredged it all up and she was so insistent about getting tested that I'm now actually worried about it."

"Oh, Ken." Her smile drops, she opens her mouth, then closes it again. "It's tough to be in your situation. You don't have to have the test right now. You have time. What is it *you* would like to do?"

"That's the thing. I know it's better to have the test so I can be proactive. I'm scared that if it comes back positive, which let's face it, it probably will … I'm scared of the decisions I'll have to make then. Will I need to have a mastectomy, possibly have my ovaries removed?" Mom squeezes my hand, grounding me.

"You can't think that far ahead yet. Just take it one step at a time. The results may come back negative, and you'll have done all of this worrying for nothing." She stands, pulling me up with her, wrapping me in her motherly embrace.

I know she's right, but it's hard to switch my mind off. "I know. It's easier said than done, though. How did you manage, emotionally, when you found out about your cancer?" I was so young; I wasn't privy to any of the feelings or even how she dealt with the situation. I only remember her in the hospital and I was scared she was going to die, too. We both sit back in our rocking chairs.

I love these chairs. I used to sit for hours on this front porch doing my homework in these chairs.

Mom sighs, blowing her bangs out of her eyes. "I was a mess. It came so out of the blue and it wasn't something I was expecting. I was shell-shocked because nobody in my family had ever had breast cancer." She gives me a soft smile. "I cried a *lot* when I first found out. I felt as though the breasts I'd always loved had become the enemy and I wanted them gone." She looks out to the street and then back to me. "Your dad and I were on a 'break' when I found out, but once he was back in my life, he gave me an incredible amount of support and really helped me come to terms with the changes that my body had been through." She reaches across, squeezing my hand. Holding it in hers as she looks at me with compassion and understanding. "We're here for you, Kenny. Every single step of the way. I hope you know that?"

I smile at her. "I know that, Mom. It wasn't even a question in my mind."

We stand again, hugging. The screen door opens and closes behind me. "Everything okay out here?" Dad's concerned voice reaches me as his hand glides down the length of my hair.

Mom and I pull away, giving each other a wink, and holding onto each other's hands a little longer. "Yeah. Mom was helping me work through my feelings about having the genetic testing done."

Dad looks between the two of us, his eyebrows drawn tight, causing wrinkles to form between his brows. "I had the test not long after Emma went through her surgeries. When I was researching her form of breast cancer, I came across a website that talked about men getting breast cancer. It was never something I'd thought about. With Mom and Anna having had it, I thought I should get tested. It came back negative. You know, yours may come back negative, too." He strokes down my back in a soothing motion. "But no matter the result, we're here for you. Anything you need, Munchkin."

He pulls me into his arms. Wrapping himself around me, protecting me, and keeping me safe from everything. If only he could protect me from a possible future with cancer.

# CHAPTER 3

## *—kenny—*

Sitting in Dr. Starling's waiting room, I can't stop my hands from shaking no matter how hard I squeeze them together. I know I won't find out the results today, but tell that to my nerves.

"Kennedy Drivas." A smartly dressed woman with graying hair calls from the doorway. Dad and I stand at the same time to meet the doctor.

I smile as I step forward, though it probably comes out more like a grimace. "That's me."

"Hello, Kennedy. Please, follow me." She turns, walking down a short hallway and we follow quickly behind her. Stopping at a doorway, she stands to the side, gesturing us to step inside. I'm concerned she'll be able to hear my heart beating as I pass her.

Her eyes land on Dad. A smile crosses her lips as she closes the door and strides toward her large oak desk. "Mr. Drivas, it's so nice to see you again. How are you going?"

"It's nice to see you too, Doctor. I'm doing well, thank you."

She sits down in a comfortable-looking chair, then turns her focus to me. "Kennedy." She smiles, looking over the top of her glasses. "I believe you're thinking about undergoing genetic testing to see if you have inherited the BRCA1 or BRCA2 genes. Can I ask why?"

I look at Dad, swallowing down my nerves. He gives me a short nod and a wink to encourage me. I go on to tell her about my mother's letter and her request for me to be tested. I also explain about my mother and Yaya's breast cancer.

"Okay, so your mother ..." She points to me. "... is your sister?"

She points to Dad. "Do I have that right?" Dad nods to confirm. "Which means your Yaya, is your Dad's mother."

"That's right. Biologically, Dad is actually my uncle, but he adopted me after my mother gave him guardianship of me in her will."

Dr. Starling nods. "Okay. Now if I remember correctly, your mother and grandmother both had metastatic breast cancer. The most severe of all breast cancers. Your mother tested positive for the gene, but your grandmother was never tested." She looks at me. "Is that correct?"

"Yes, Doctor. That's the information I have." I nod, twisting my hands together.

"I can understand why you would like to undergo testing and I fully back your decision. However, I need to make some statistics clear. With your mom having the BRCA1 gene, there is a fifty percent chance that she passed it on to you. You need to remember that on the flip side, there's a fifty percent chance that she *didn't* pass it on. Without your father's genetic history, we don't know whether he was also a carrier of the gene." She leans forward across her desk. "Do you understand?"

On a shaky exhale, I nod. "Yes, Doctor. I understand."

She looks down at my file. "You're twenty-one, correct?" I nod. "I usually recommend waiting until you're closer to twenty-five as this is when things begin to change with your medical management."

"I understand that from my research, but I'd really like to know sooner rather than later if I can." I swallow around the lump in my throat.

"Of course. It's ultimately your body and your decision. If your test comes back positive for the gene, your chance of developing breast or ovarian cancer within the next ten years is zero point seven percent. This makes you seven times more likely to develop these cancers than women of the same age as you. Beyond that, your chances increase to 26.6%, which is approximately two and a half times higher than other women your age." My hearing becomes muffled with her statistics and she sounds more like a grown-up from a Charlie Brown cartoon, than the esteemed doctor she is. She leans back in her chair. "Before you make your final decision to have the test, you need to think about how these results may affect your mental health. Depending on your results, you may experience various emotions." Her voice softens. "For example, if your test comes back negative, you may feel terribly guilty that you *don't* carry the gene that your mother had and grandmother may have had. Emotions surrounding these results can be a strange and unpredictable beast. But we'll be here with you to help you navigate your way." We spend a significant amount of time discussing the pros and cons of going through the testing procedure.

I nod, trying to absorb all of the information.

"I want to be clear … if your test *does* come back positive, you *do* have options."

Dad reaches across and takes my hand, offering his silent support to me. I've asked him what he thinks I should do, but he's leaving the decision entirely up to me. "And if it comes back positive?" I swallow hard. "Is the recommendation to remove my breasts and ovaries straight away?"

"Not necessarily. And all of those decisions are entirely up to you. You can opt to begin annual breast screening from this point forward to keep an eye on your breasts. In terms of precautions against ovarian cancer, there are several things you can put in place there." She looks at Dad, giving him a soft smile. "I can take your blood today, or you can think about it some more and make another appointment. It's entirely up to you."

I look at Dad, hoping he'll give me some indication of what he wants me to do. "It's up to you, Munchkin. You have to do what's right for you. No one can make this decision on your behalf."

"I think I should get it done. It's going to always be on my mind. At least this way I'll have an answer and can make decisions based on the results."

Dad's shoulders drop, the relief of my decision written all over his face. "You wanted me to have the test?" I ask.

"Yeah, I did. But I wanted you to make the decision. I didn't want you to do it for me. I wanted you to do what was right for *you*." I lean across squeezing him tight. He's never swayed my decisions and I know there have been times when he hasn't necessarily agreed with some of them.

I look back at the doctor. "Okay. Let's do this." May as well get it over and done with so I can move forward with my life.

"Good. I think you've made the right choice." She stands, moving across to the cupboards at the side of the room, where she collects vials, a needle, and several other items. "Come and sit over in this chair, please."

I stand on shaky legs and take a seat. Dr. Starling sets about drawing numerous vials of blood. "We will be studying your DNA for

BRCA1 and BRCA2, as well as their associated genes in your blood-work." The blood slows as it fills the final vial, so she carefully removes the needle, placing cotton over the site. "Can you please hold this in place?"

I take over holding the cotton. "Sure."

While I keep pressure on the cotton, Dr. Starling records my information on the vials of my blood. "It'll take a few weeks before we have the results. Then I'll ask that you come back and we'll discuss what the investigation discovers and the steps we can take moving forward. How does that sound?" She gives me a compassionate smile.

"Okay. So, do I make the appointment today, or do I wait until I get the results?" I ask.

"We can make an appointment in four weeks to allow for any delays. You can do that at the front desk on your way out." She removes the cotton and replaces it with a band-aid.

"Thanks, Dr. Starling." I stand from the chair and grab my purse.

Dad joins me, shaking the doctor's hand. "Thank you. We'll see you in four weeks."

"Yes, you will." She looks at me. "Try to put this out of your mind. There is nothing you can do while you wait for the results and if you worry too much, you put your body under stress. Stress doesn't help anyone. Okay?"

"I'll do my best, but I can't make any promises." My voice comes out shaky, my nerves getting the better of me.

"That's fine. See you in four weeks, Kennedy. Bye."

"Bye."

Dad and I make our way to the front desk so I can make my follow-up appointment. As we step outside of the air-conditioned office, the heat from the pavement assaults us.

Dad wraps his arm around my shoulder, pulling me in close before landing a kiss on the top of my head. "How about a milkshake?" He raises his eyebrows as he waits for my answer.

"That'd be perfect. Thanks."

"You're welcome."

I look up at him. "No. I mean thanks for coming with me today. Having you there made it a little easier." The salt and pepper in his thick hair and scattered through his beard make him look wise and distinguished.

"Kenny. You never need to thank me for being where you are. It's been my honor, every single day, to be part of your life. To watch you grow into the lovely young woman you are." I squeeze him extra tight, to match the tightness in my chest at his words.

Stepping inside *Coffee and Cookies*, there have been several changes since the last time we were here, but it still feels familiar and comforting. Dad and I used to come here regularly after school for milkshakes and cookies. He always seemed to know when I needed to talk—just like today.

"The usual?" he asks as he steps toward the counter. I nod as I head straight for our usual booth near the window.

He slides into the booth opposite me and we both sit for a few minutes, watching people walk by outside. A young teenage waitress delivers our order to the table with a perky smile, she must be around fifteen if I were to guess. Dad and I both take a sip of our matching chocolate milkshakes. He takes a huge bite of his muffin, while I nibble my cookie. I have so much going around in my head, I don't know where to start.

"I was scared when I decided to have the testing done. I had never considered that men could get breast cancer. The idea that I had a greater possibility of getting any type of cancer really made me stop and think." He swallows, looking out of the window to the people on the street. "I felt incredibly guilty when my test came back negative. It should have been me, not your mom. I didn't have anyone and she … she had you. If anyone should have had the gene and ultimately lost the battle with cancer, it should have been me," he whispers.

I refuse to agree with him. I would have loved to have my mother still here. It's something I've wished for every single day of my life, but I wouldn't want to give up my time with him. "No." My voice comes out firm and strong, surprising even me. "Do I wish I hadn't lost Mom? Absolutely. I'd give anything to still have her here. But not at the expense of you." I reach across, wrapping my fingers around his forearm. "I wish cancer had never touched anyone in our family and I truly hope we've seen the last of it. Our family has already lost enough. We don't deserve to lose any more."

Quiet descends on us again for long moments as I digest what Dad said, my cookie becoming a mess of crumbs and chunks on my plate.

Dad reaches across the table, taking my hand in his, providing me with an anchor. "Talk to me, Munchkin. Let's work through some of the stuff going around in that head of yours."

I release a heavy breath, my shoulders dropping. "What if I can never have children? I always imagined myself with a couple of kids. If my tests come back positive, I want to have everything that could put me at risk removed from my body as soon as possible."

Dad's eyes become glassy as he gives me a sad smile. "Dr. Starling will help you make a plan if your test comes back positive. Mom and I will support you through any decisions you make, but there will always be a way for you to become a mother. It may not be conventional, but there are ways." He shrugs. "Whatever the result, we can work through it. The main thing is that we still have you, Kennedy." He rises from his side of the booth, coming around to mine. Sliding in, he wraps his arm around me, pulling me in tight. He kisses the top of my head and we sit quietly absorbing each other's love.

"Thanks, Dad. I guess I have to wait. Once I have the results, it'll be time to make some tough decisions." I shrug. "I need to try to put it out of my mind until then."

"It won't be easy to do, but I think you'll have a better chance if you keep yourself busy." He takes a drink of his milkshake. "What have you got going on at the moment?"

"I have summer exams coming up and I'm helping my manager with a new project at work." I still can't believe I managed to secure an internship at one of the most prestigious interior design companies in the state before I even finish my degree.

We finish up, me scraping together the crumbs on my plate, before heading home.

Sitting on the back deck, I contemplate what my future may look like, jotting down my thoughts. The first thing I'll need to do is have my breasts removed. That's a given. I circle it several times on my list of decisions to make.

The scraping of the chair next to mine drags me from my planning.

"How did your appointment go today?" Lachlan asks as he sits on the chair next to me.

I shrug. "I decided to go ahead with the test. I need to know so I can make a plan to mitigate any risk."

He studies me closely, then looks down at my notebook. "Why are you sitting here making notes? You can't make plans until you have the results."

"I know, but I want to be prepared." I look down at my breasts. They're not overly large, but they make me feel feminine.

"I think you are planning prematurely, Kenny. You should wait for the results." Always the logical one.

"What if I have to remove my breasts? They're what make me feel like a girl. I need to get myself used to the idea."

He looks at me as though I'm crazy, the skin between his eyebrows adorably crinkled. "Breasts don't make you a girl, Kenny. It's the estrogen and progesterone in your body that makes you feminine."

I huff out a laugh. Trust Lachlan to give me the facts. "I know."

"Besides, Mom still looks like a girl and she had her breasts removed." True.

"Maybe I should speak with her about that side of things?"

"I think that's a good idea. But I also think you are looking at the worst-case scenario, which isn't like you. Maybe wait for the results before you start planning surgeries which may not be necessary."

I use my toe to push at his thigh. "You're so wise, big brother."

His lips lift at my compliment. "Make sure you remember that."

I chuckle again. "Thanks."

He looks across at me, studying me like I'm a puzzle. "What for?"

"For reminding me that I'm not the girl who thinks of the worst-case scenario. For making me laugh a little."

"You're welcome."

# CHAPTER 4

## —kenny—

I WALK INTO DR. STARLING'S OFFICE WITH MOM ON ONE SIDE OF ME and Dad on the other. Today, I'll learn my fate. It's fitting that on the anniversary of my mother's death, I'll find out what my future holds.

I'm struggling to fill my lungs with air as I take one step after another. As much as I've tried over the last four weeks to put these results out of my mind, it was impossible. I announce myself to the receptionist and we take a seat together in the waiting room. It's hard to sit still or keep focused on anything in particular. My stomach's rolling—has been for days.

Mom leans in close as we sit. "No matter what the doctor says, we're here to support you. Remember that. You're not going through this alone. Okay?"

I try to smile, but I can't do it. "I know."

Silence falls around us and as I look around the waiting room, I wonder if the other people here are waiting for their results, too.

"Kennedy Drivas." Dr. Starling gives me a warm smile.

I swallow down the excess saliva in my mouth, wiping my sweaty palms on my jeans as I stand. I have to pull them up slightly because they've become loose with my lack of appetite. My heart's pounding as my shaky legs carry me forward. I can't help but compare this walk to one an inmate might make on the way to the gallows. The news I receive today is going to be life-changing.

I can feel it.

Mom takes my hand, squeezing it as we step forward, Dad joining us. "Dr. Starling."

"Hi, Kenny. Please come through."

We follow her down the same short hallway to her office. Filing into the stylishly decorated room, each of us takes a seat opposite her desk. It seems to take Dr. Starling an age to get comfortable and shuffle the papers she has on her desk to her liking. *Is it just me or does she seem to be dawdling?* She looks at each of us in turn. "Hello again, Emma. It's lovely to see you."

"Nice to see you too, Doctor." *I hope they're not planning on having a long reunion.*

She turns her gaze to me, a smile slowly forming on her lips. "How have you managed this past month, Kenny?"

Twisting my hands together in my lap, I try to string together enough words to make a sentence. "It's been … difficult."

She gives me a sad smile and my heart sinks to my feet. The look on her face telegraphs what I've been dreading. Why won't she just come out and tell me the results? The longer she takes, the more dread fills every inch of my body, from my toes all the way up to my head. She shuffles the papers on her desk some more, then looks from Dad to Mom to me. Her eyes light up and her lips spread, making her look younger. "Kennedy."

I roll the saliva around in my mouth before swallowing shakily. "Y-yes?"

"I have your results here." I nod. God, just tell me already. "They came back negative."

*Oh, God!*

This must be so hard for Dad to hear. To know that I'm probably going to follow in Mom and Yaya's footsteps. Dad and Mom jump up out of their chairs, pulling me up with them. Wide smiles fill their faces as they wrap me in their embrace.

Wait … why are they smiling? This is not the reaction I was expecting. I thought this would be a somber moment. Learning that I had the gene. I expected tears, not joy.

"Why aren't you happy?" Mom asks, realizing I'm not joining in with their celebration.

The emotions and tears which have been building for weeks break free, streaming over my bottom lashes, making their way down my cheeks, and dripping from my chin. Dad pulls me in tight, holding the back of my head as he sways our bodies from side to side.

"Shhh, Kenny. It's going to be okay. You're okay." I'm glad he's holding me up because my legs feel as though they're going to give out on me any minute.

Mom comes in behind me, rubbing her hand up and down my back in a calming motion. "Did you hear what Dr. Starling said?" I nod my head because words won't come. "Are you sure you *actually* heard and understood what she said?"

Turning my head to the side, I look at Mom. The creases between her brows show her concern for me. "You *don't* have the gene, Kenny. Did you hear that? You *don't* have it."

*Wait. What?*

I pull back from Dad. "What?"

Dr. Starling nods, her lips spread wide. "You don't have the gene, Kennedy. Your risk of developing breast cancer over your lifetime is the same as anyone else."

Looking between Mom and Dad, the doctor's words finally sink in. "I don't have it?"

"That's correct." She steps out from behind her desk, coming around to join us. "You don't have the BRCA1 or BRCA2 genes or any of the associated genes."

"Really?" My body sags. The utter and immediate relief is overwhelming and I'm suddenly exhausted. I sink into my chair and release a heavy breath. A breath filled with the angst and worry of the last few weeks. With each breath, I feel lighter, less burdened but equally guilty. Grateful that I've escaped the same fate as my mother. Guilty that I've escaped that fate.

Dad has always been able to read me so easily. "Stop those thoughts, Kenny. Your mother and Yaya would be incredibly happy that your results came back negative. It's exactly the result they would have wanted. Remember that."

I swallow down my emotions and give him a nod. Finally, a smile breaches my lips and I feel it's okay to celebrate. "I'm negative!"

Mom wraps her arm around my shoulders, pulling me in close. "This is the best news, Kenny. I'm so relieved and happy for you." She kisses my temple.

Wrapping my arm around her, I return her squeeze. "Thank you. Thank you for being here with me."

"I wouldn't be anywhere else. Ever." She pulls away, allowing Dad to move in. Wrapping both of his strong arms around me, he pulls me in tight, lifting me off of my feet.

"We need to celebrate!" He turns to Dr. Starling. "Thank you, Doctor."

She chuckles at Dad's excitement. "I didn't do anything. I just delivered the good news."

"So, is that it? I don't have to do anything else or be extra vigilant?"

"Nope. We consider you to have the same chance as any other woman of developing breast cancer. So, it's not zero. Around nine percent of women develop breast cancer at some point in their life. You still need to have regular checks, just like everyone else. Eat a healthy diet and look after yourself." She pats my arm. "I'm so happy to have been able to deliver such positive news for you, Kennedy."

I release a relieved breath. "Me, too. Doctor. Me, too. Thank you so much."

We say our goodbyes and head out into the sunshine. Tilting my head back, my face to the fluffy clouds, I close my eyes and smile for the first time in weeks. I feel lighter all the way to my soul and it's a wonderful feeling. Now to move forward with my life.

# pinterest

I put together a Pinterest board for Emma and Theo's story. If you're interested, you can check it out here:

*https://tinyurl.com/stolenkisses-pinterest*

KISSES
*book Two*

*moonlit*
KISSES

DEBRA ST JAMES

*inspiration*

This story was inspired by the lyrics ...

—> *I've Fallen in Love with You by Joss Stone* <—

# playlist

I've Fallen in Love with You ... *Joss Stone*
Push It ... *Salt-N-Pepa*
Love Junk ... *Diesel*
Don't Cha Wanna Ride ... *Joss Stone*
Picture of You ... *Diesel*
Put Your Hands on Me ... *Joss Stone*
Trouble Sleeping ... *Corinne Bailey Rae*
Super Duper Love ... *Joss Stone*
When I See You ... *Macy Gray*
Sweet Baby ... *Macy Gray feat. Erykah Badu*
Someone Like You ... *Van Morrison*
I Get to Love You ... *Ruelle*
Take My Name ... *Parmalee*

**You can check it out here:**
*https://tinyurl.com/moonlitkisses-spotify*

# CHAPTER 1

## —molly—

THE GRAY SKY MATCHES MY CURRENT MOOD AS I STAND OVER THE matching coffins being lowered into the icy ground side by side by side, the clay soil a stark contrast to the dirty snow. I can't believe they're all gone—just like that. Wrapping my arms tightly around my middle, I give myself the only comfort I can at this point. I have to be strong. I'm all I have left in this world.

As the service concludes, the few family friends we have—or is it had?—file past me, hugging me, giving me their condolences. It's okay for them, they'll go home, and their life will continue as normal. Sure, they'll miss Mom, Jack, and Ethan at social events, but my loss will affect me every single moment of every single day.

At twenty-six years of age, I'm an orphan.

Mom won't see her forty-fifth birthday. Jack won't ever share the crazy advertisements he finds in the newspaper or online with me, and Ethan will forever be thirteen years old.

I draw in a deep breath and then release a heavy sigh as yet more tears track down my cheeks. I didn't think I'd have any more tears left at this point. All I've done is cry since the police knocked on my door late that night, fourteen days ago. They said my family's car veered into the path of an oncoming truck and the coroner since found that Jack had suffered a heart attack at the wheel. It must have happened on the way home from checking out the Christmas lights. It was the first year I hadn't gone with them because I was volunteering at the shelter. I still don't understand. The guy was a fitness freak. He couldn't afford a gym membership, which meant he would run daily and use stuff around their trailer to keep in shape.

Trudging away from my family's ultimate resting place, I glance over my shoulder one last time. Everyone left as soon as the service was over, leaving me to my solitary grief.

*Solitary.*

Now there's a word for me, one I guess I'll have to get used to. Peering around the empty graveyard, I shiver. I'm not sure how long I was standing on my own, lost in my head. But it was long enough for a chill to seep through to my bones. I'm going to need to clear out their trailer, but I can't go there today. I'm too raw, too exposed, too shattered.

Pulling up in front of Mom and Jack's trailer I pause, my eyes scanning the outside. Even though they didn't have a lot, they always looked after their trailer. Mom believed you should always have pride in your home, no matter what type of home it was. Hell, she was grateful to have a home, as was I.

I can't believe that when I walk inside, it will be empty. Mom won't be baking chocolate chip muffins in the oven and Jack won't be pouring over the newspaper. Ethan won't have one leg slung over the arm of the couch as he watches cartoons, his bangs falling in his eyes. There'll be no more tight hugs, making me feel as though I'm the most important person in the world to the inhabitants.

I exit my car, full of dread. As I close the door, I catch sight of Ron, the park manager, striding toward me. He waves wildly in my direction as his steps hasten, bringing him right into my personal space. His eyes trail my body from the top of my head to the tips of my toes, pausing on my breasts and legs. Ron's always been a bit … I don't know … weird, I guess. He doesn't seem to understand personal boundaries and can be rather inappropriate. I've always felt uncomfortable whenever he's around.

"Hi, Molly. It's just tragic what happened to Nicole, Jack, and Ethan." The upbeat tone of his voice doesn't match his words and before I can say anything, he continues. "Any idea when you'll have the trailer cleaned out? I've got a waitlist of prospective tenants, and well, they only paid until the end of December and it's January eighth now, sooooo?" He leaves his statement hanging and all I can do is blink at him. "You know, I don't wanna be a dick or anything, but you know …" He shrugs. "It's business. You know."

As he stands looking at me with wide eyes, I realize he's waiting for an answer. "Uh, I'm here to sort through their things today. They don't have all that much. I can possibly have it all done by tomorrow night?" My last sentence comes out more like a question than a statement. I guess I can understand it from his side. The trailer is sitting unoccupied and not earning him any money. But he's speaking about my family as though it doesn't matter that they're no longer here. I hitch my thumb over my shoulder. "I'd better get started then." He nods, obviously happy with my answer, and then heads back the way he came.

It takes a bit of jiggling to get the key to slide into the lock, but I finally get the latch to release. When the door opens, I'm overwhelmed by the musty smell. I haven't been here since the day I had to collect an outfit for each member of my family to be buried in. The place is compact: two bedrooms; one bathroom, complete with a toilet; and the open plan living, dining, and kitchen. It's slightly larger than the one-bedroom apartment I live in not that far from here. I open the curtains and the dull light of winter makes its way into the room, highlighting the disturbed dust motes floating in the air.

With a heavy heart, I start in Ethan's room, making piles to keep, trash, and donate. I'll probably take the donations to the shelter I volunteer at. Often, women have to escape a shitty situation in a hurry and don't have time to pack, leaving with little to nothing but the clothes on her and her children's backs. As I move the last of his clothes out of the drawers, my fingers scrape across a scrapbook. A smile touches my lips unbidden at the memories flooding me. Dropping to my butt, I flip open the cover and run my finger over the lines on the page. Ethan loved to sketch muscle cars. Jack taught us both how to draw and while I'll draw whatever takes my fancy around me, Ethan was one hundred percent dedicated to drawing the great American muscle car. Page after page of sketches, gradually improving in skill and detail as he became more competent. Closing the last page, I hold it to my chest, deciding I'll keep it as a little piece of Ethan. I take it out to my car and place it on the passenger seat, then collect the boxes I brought with me and head back inside.

Throughout the weekend, I work like a Trojan, only stopping to eat the meager supply of snacks I brought with me. Memories trap me as I come across photo albums, scrapbooks, and special treasures that remind me of what I've lost. Mom was never just my mom. She was my best friend. She was only eighteen when she had me, and we spent the first eleven years of my life living in her car and occasionally staying in women's shelters. Our bond was unbreakable and now she's gone. An unbidden loud sob breaks the silence at the thought of never speaking with her again, never hearing her voice, or experiencing her hugs. I tilt my head up toward the ceiling, asking whatever force, *why*? It's not like we had a lot, only each other. Why take that away from me? I'm not sure I'll ever make sense of such a loss.

Darkness infiltrates the trailer, so I check the time. It's only five, but the storm rolling in has made it feel much later in the day. Looking around the space, I'm satisfied with what I've accomplished and decide to load as much as I can into my car to take to the shelter before it starts to rain, making sure I set the items I want to keep in a separate space. I don't want to get them mixed up. I'm not sure what to do with the furniture. There isn't much, only the basics. Mom and Jack never had a lot of money left over after paying all the bills and ensuring Ethan and I had everything we needed. They were never about collecting material stuff. It was more important to give us their time and love, to put nutritious food on the table, and to make sure we were happy and well cared for.

Loading the last bag into the back of my car, I give it a shove so I can close the door. I turn away from my car and Ron's right there, in my space, wearing the same clothes he had on yesterday.

"Just the person I needed to see." He claps his hands together, his smile stretching from ear to ear. "You nearly done? I've got a woman coming through in about ten minutes to look at the place."

Dumbfounded is the only word I can think of to describe how I feel about Ron and his enthusiasm. "Uh … uhm." I wrap my arms around my body to keep myself standing. Once I walk away from here, I won't ever be coming back. It will be final. I turn, my eyes canvassing the trailer, taking in every inch; the cute hanging baskets, the plastic table and chair set, and the neat curtains hanging over each window. "I've just finished, Ron. The only thing left is the furniture, and I'm not sure what to do with it."

He tucks his thumbs in the top of his jeans and rocks back on his heels, his smile returning to his face. "That can stay. No problem. I'll be able to charge more for a furnished trailer." My head spins at his lack of empathy for the situation.

"Uh, hello!" A young woman, maybe eighteen at the most, holding the hand of a little boy, calls out, interrupting our conversation.

Ron steps away from me immediately and heads toward the woman, his hand outstretched in welcome. "Hi. Mia?"

"Yes. Ron?"

"That's me." He turns toward me. "Thanks, Molly. You can go now."

My head flies back as though he slapped me. His dismissal is abrupt, and I don't know why, but it was also unexpected. Speechless, I climb into my car and drive out of the trailer park for what I *know* will be the last time.

# CHAPTER 2

## —max—

"Maaaax, phone for you!" Emma's voice startles me out from beneath the car I'm working on. Did I forget she was bringing the boys over this morning?

As I stand to my full height, I stretch out my back and stride toward my small office. I barely spend time here, choosing to do most of my paperwork at home. At the end of the day, I usually take whatever paperwork I need to complete home, then bring it back with me in the morning. I even bought a cheap laptop to make things easier to transport. My sister hands the phone to me, studying me from the top of my head to the tips of my steel cap work boots.

"Hello, Stanfield Auto Repairs, Max speaking."

"Hi, Max. I'm having car trouble again. Would I be able to trouble you to look at the old girl for me?"

"No problem, Mr. McNally. Would this afternoon be okay? Around three?"

"Perfect. Thanks, Max. I knew you wouldn't let me down."

"See you then."

"Great. See you at three. Bring your appetite. Jean will make you a snack." *Oh yeah,* Jean knows how to bake. This is my lucky day.

I laugh. "I definitely will." Ending the call, I glance at my sister, then around the small room. The boys are nowhere in sight. "Where're the boys?"

"Hanging out with Theo. I had to get some supplies for work and was passing by." She hands me a takeaway coffee. "I thought I'd stop in and have a quick coffee with my little brother."

I scoff. "Little brother!" I may be younger than her, but at six-foot-three inches, I tower over her five-foot-seven frame. I take the coffee from her, grateful for the warm beverage. Wrapping my hands around the paper cup, I take a sip and sigh with gratitude. "Thanks, Em." Leaning forward, I kiss her cheek in welcome. "Good to see you. How are the boys, and Kenny and Theo?"

She makes herself comfortable on my lone desk, her smile broadens, and a twinkle lightens her eyes. I've never seen my sister this happy. Theo and Kenny have been a great addition to Emma's family, and to our family. "They're great. They love hanging out with Theo and Kenny. Though, if Austin knew I was here, he'd be mad that I didn't bring him along." She chuckles.

"You should drop him over one afternoon. He can hang out here with me."

"You have enough going on. You don't need to be watching Austin when you have so much work to do. Speaking about how much work you have to do. When are you going to hire someone to help you with the office stuff?" she asks, as she studies the piles of papers on the corner of my desk.

I shrug. My family has been nagging me for ages to employ some staff, and while I could comfortably afford to pay some part-time wages, I don't have the time it would take to teach someone the job. It's a double-edged sword because I could use the help. It would free up my evenings and possibly give me some free time to … I don't know … maybe date. After seeing Emma find her happiness, I've realized how lonely I am and I want some of what she has. I want a family of my own. I take another sip of my coffee to delay my response.

Emma slides off of my desk and steps forward. She rests her hand on my forearm and tilts her head up. "We're worried about you, Max. You work too hard; you need to free up some of your time."

Sighing, I drop my voice. "I know. I just don't have the time to train new staff. Ya know?"

Her eyes soften and she gives me a small smile. "A little time upfront could save you a lot of time down the line. Think about it. Okay?"

I nod. "I have thought about it and I'll think about it some more. Promise." I finish with a smile to let her know I appreciate her concern.

"I'll leave you to your day in peace. See you at Mom and Dad's tomorrow?"

"Definitely. I wouldn't miss seeing my favorite people." I bend down to kiss my sister goodbye, careful to keep my greasy hands and body away from hers. "Thanks for stopping by, Em. Say hi to the family for me."

"I will." I follow her out to her car and watch her drive away. To her family. Something I don't think I'll have any time soon. Heading back inside the workshop, I mentally calculate how much longer I need on the job I'm working on, to ensure I leave on time for my house call this afternoon. I definitely need to consider hiring an office manager.

Aaron's hand lands heavily on my sweaty back as I bend over at the waist, trying to catch my breath. I'm getting too old for this shit. Not that thirty-six is old.

"You okay, old man?" he snickers.

"Fuck off. You're six months older than me. Cut the 'old man' bull-shit!" I stand to my full height, pushing him away playfully.

"You coming for a beer?"

"Yep. I'll meet you guys there." He heads off with Lincoln. They share a place, so it makes sense for them to share a ride to our pseudo-soccer matches. Lincoln's covered in tattoos and looks like he belongs in a biker club, but he's a decent guy who does beautiful tattoo work.

Turning around, I spot Gary walking toward me and I raise my chin. "Good game. You coming for a beer tonight?"

"Nah. Layla's sick. I need to get home. Maybe next week."

"Sure, man. Take good care of your girl." She's been sick a lot lately. I hope it's nothing too serious.

"I will. See ya next week." He jogs off toward his car and quickly climbs inside.

I think I'd prefer to be going home to a sick wife—well … not a *sick* wife, but a wife—rather than going to Brady's for beer and pizza. I thought I would be married by now, but I wasted a lot of years with Mona. When I think back now, I don't know what I ever saw in her. Sure, she was beautiful, but she was fucking shallow and superficial, not to mention rude as fuck to my family. I would always bite my tongue in front of my family so I didn't embarrass Mona, but when we got in the car, I would let her know I wasn't happy with her behavior. She'd always pout and start fake crying, apologizing profusely and promising to do better next time. Her behavior never improved. After the way she carried on about me wanting to help Emma during her cancer treatment, I couldn't take it any longer. My family was, *is*, more important to me than getting laid on the regular.

The bar's packed. It's always packed. And loud. When did this place get so fucking popular? We've been coming here for years. Back when the general population considered it a dive. Now every goddamn man and his mate seem to think this is the best place to be. I mean, it *is* a stellar pub. But c'mon, I just want to go back fifteen years to when it was quieter.

*Fuck, I'm sounding old.*

I spot the guys in our usual booths which Finn always keeps free for us—one benefit of being on his team. I slide in next to Aaron and opposite Finn.

"Is it busier than usual, or am I getting old?" I ask Finn as I glance around.

Aaron slides a pint in front of me. "It's busier than usual." He nods his head toward the opposite corner. "We have a celebrity here tonight."

Looking across the room, I spot Toby Summer. "I restored a car for him a couple of years back. He still brings her in for me to service a few times a year."

"Oh yeah? What is it?" Aaron asks.

"A sixty-seven Chevy Impala soft top. Beautiful car. Looked like brand new when I finished with her." I remember the expression on Toby's face when he came to pick her up. He was so fucking in love with that car.

The guys let out a collective whistle. "Nice."

I nod.

"How's the Sprint coming along? Surely, you're nearly done with her." Aaron asks before taking a long pull of his beer.

"It's slow. I don't get as much time to do the restoration side of the business. Too damn busy doing the auto repair work and office crap. Which is great and all, because that's what pays my bills, but man, I miss working on my cars." I sigh into my beer.

"Perhaps you should consider hiring some staff to take the pressure off. Give you more time for other things." He motions toward the bar. I glance across to see a group of women, who look to be in their early to mid-twenties, standing in their too-short skirts and too-low tops, reminding me of Mona. *Ugh. What the hell was I thinking?*

I dismiss the idea of hooking up with someone so young and return my focus to my table. "You're not telling me anything my family hasn't already suggested. Believe me, I've thought about it, but I don't have the fucking time to dedicate to training someone for the job. I'm too busy … maybe when things slow down." I hedge.

"Are you an idiot? Things never slow down for you. Your business has only grown busier and busier each year since you opened. You're a fucking outstanding mechanic and people know they can rely on you and that you won't rip them off," Aaron shoots back.

The guys around the table agree, nodding their heads like old men. "You guys sound like Em. She stopped in on Saturday and gave me the same lecture."

Lincoln sits up straighter at the mention of Em's name. "Yeah? How's Emma?"

"Married!" I snap. Fucking asshole knows this already.

"Still?"

"Yeah, fucking still. Probably will be for the rest of her life. Can't see Theo ever walking away from her and the boys." I smirk at the forlorn expression on Lincoln's face. He had his chance to make a move while she was single, but never grew the balls to do anything about it. His loss.

We shoot the shit for a couple of hours, eating pizza and drinking beer. I stop drinking early enough to ensure I'm still under the limit to drive home. It wouldn't be prudent for me to lose my driver's license in my line of work—it would cost me my fucking business. A business I've worked hard to build since I was twenty-four. There's no way I want to fuck it up.

I spot the clock on the wall. Eleven. Nearly closing time. "I'm out. See you guys next Monday." I rap my knuckles on the table as I stand.

Everyone waves goodbye around the table, and I make my way to the front door. A few people obviously have the same idea since it's almost closing time and I bump into a body. Turning my head to apologize, I catch the eyes of Toby. His eyes widen in recognition, a smile spreading his lips.

"Max. Great to see you, man." He takes my hand, shaking it with gusto. His bodyguard and friend, Shane, standing right behind them.

I nod to both of them. "Hey, guys. Great to see you. How's the car?"

We step out of the pub, where the cool air smacks me in the face. I pull my jacket around my body, offering a pitiful shield against the icy wind.

"The car's incredible. Absolutely incredible. Drives like a dream."

"Good, that's great."

"Actually, she's due for a service. When can I bring her in?"

I have a lot on my plate at the moment and I'm unsure when I have an available day. "Call me tomorrow when I have my calendar in front of me. You still got my number?"

"Yeah, sure. Talk tomorrow."

"Tomorrow." I tip my head goodbye and turn to walk in the opposite direction, toward my car.

Stepping inside my home, I toe off my shoes and throw my keys in the bowl on the hall table. The house is pitch black and silent. Coming from the noisy pub, the quiet seems overwhelming. I don't bother turning on any lights and make my way to the kitchen for a glass of water before heading to my room. Monday nights are probably the only nights I don't spend working on my books. The reprieve is welcome as I strip off and fall into bed.

# CHAPTER 3

## —molly—

MY ALARM BLARES AS IT DOES EVERY WORKDAY AT FIVE A.M. I HAVEN'T been for my morning run since ... well, since my life turned upside down. Today's the day I'm gonna get back to it. Running helps my mood and I need all the help I can get at the moment. It was emotionally tough cleaning everything out of the trailer on the weekend; I couldn't drag myself out of bed early enough yesterday morning, so I genuinely need this run to clear my mind.

The family photo from the last Christmas we spent together catches my eye. Picking it up, I trace the faces of my family. Every year, we would take a new photo together at Christmas. We'll never do that again and my family will be forever frozen in time.

No more family photos—*ever!*

The backs of my eyes sting and I work to swallow down my grief or I won't be running today either and I really need to do this. Placing the photo back on my nightstand, I climb out of bed and dress in my running gear, complete with the hot pink running shoes I got for my last birthday. I can't believe the stuff people get rid of. I don't think these shoes had ever been worn.

Grabbing what I need, I head out into the freezing morning. Careful to take smaller steps as I start slower than usual on the sidewalk, searching for patches of ice under the light dusting of snow. It doesn't take long before I find my rhythm and lose myself in my next step, my breaths forming small misty clouds in front of my face. My body heats as my muscles warm, and I unwrap the scarf from around my neck and tie it around my waist. It's quiet, not another runner in sight today. I don't blame them. It's freaking cold. If I didn't need to work through my emotions, I probably would have opted to stay in bed, too.

I shut down everything in my mind. Concentrating on the force of each foot hitting the pavement and keeping my breathing even. Gradually, my thoughts become completely focused on running, which is exactly what I need.

"Morning," a man calls out as he passes me with his teenage daughter. I've seen them before, though not usually until the temperatures warm up a little more.

"Morning," I respond as my heart constricts. Jack was pivotal in getting me into fitness. He trained me and helped me to build the length of time I could run comfortably daily. The emotional pain steals my breath and I falter. Slowing my strides, I rest my hands on my hips. My eyes burn and it's tough to swallow around the painful reminder. Coming to a stop in front of my apartment building, I bend at the waist to catch my breath. Silent tears track down my cheeks and I angrily swipe at them. Seeing that father with his daughter *should* be a happy memory, not one that makes me sad. I can picture Jack running with the widest of smiles. It was always something he loved to do, and he passed that love on to me. Because of that, I don't want to feel sad when I run.

Shaking off my melancholy, I use the climb up four flights of stairs to cool down, pausing at the top of the steps to stretch my calves on the last step. Releasing a heavy breath, I swipe away the sweat from my forehead with my forearm and notice a sheet of blue paper stuck underneath my door.

Unlocking my door, I bend down and swipe up the note. It's a reminder that my rent's past due. *Damn it!* I'll need to stop in to speak with the building manager before work to explain I need an extension.

Dressed for work, I knock on the door of the building manager. I've never paid my rent late. In fact, I always pay one week early to be sure I don't forget to pay.

Don finally answers the door, a cigarette hanging out of his mouth. Interesting that we're not allowed to smoke within the building, but he can do whatever he wants because he's the manager. He squints at me through the thick plume of smoke, scratching his armpit. "Yeah?"

I hold up the note I found under my door this morning. "Uhm, hi, Don." He has always insisted I call him Don. Not Mr. Ricci. Don. "I was hoping I could ask a favor."

He leans his shoulder against his door, crossing his arms in front of his gray-haired chest. "I don't do no favors." His old eyes scan me up and down, dragging like filthy fingers up my legs. "Not even for stunners like you."

I swallow down the bile his dirty perusal has caused. "It's only a small favor. You see, I'm always on time, if not a little early, with my rent. But, uh, I recently lost my entire family and I've had to use all of my savings for their funeral and burial." His face goes soft, and I think he may agree to give me an extension. "I was wondering if it was at all possible to have an extension. I can pay next month on time plus some of this month. Each month, I could pay a little extra until I'm caught up." I hold my breath, hoping for a little compassion.

He's silent and I'm hoping against hope he's seriously considering my proposal. He stands up straight. "Nope. You need to pay by Friday, or you need to find somewhere else to live. I'm not a fucking charity." Stepping back, he slams the door in my face.

*Shit!*

Now what am I going to do? I resist banging on his door until he opens it and agrees to my request. My shoulders slump and suddenly I feel … *tired*. Exhausted, in fact. Instead of climbing back upstairs and hiding beneath my blankets like I want to, I turn on my heel and head out of the building to scrape the ice from my car so I can get to work. Glancing up at the building, the sun shining behind it; I sigh. The apartment building isn't great. In fact, it's falling down around our ears, but it's home. The only home I have. It's where I've lived since moving out of the trailer park. I remember my excitement when I picked up the keys to move in; I felt like an actual adult. Thankfully, it came furnished because I had nothing to my name. I still don't have a lot, but I would miss this place if I had to leave.

Traffic isn't too heavy on the way to work, which is a godsend because I can barely focus. I'm more focused on running through what I need to say to Mr. Dunsley in the hopes he'll give me an advance. He was reluctant to give me time off work to deal with the funeral arrangements for my family. I think he only agreed because I couldn't stop crying and he wanted me out of the office because it was bad for business.

Unlocking the office door, I turn off the alarm and turn on the lights, then make my way to the small kitchen at the rear of the building. I set up the coffeepot and head back to my desk to switch on my computer. The bell above the door alerts me to someone entering the office. As I lift my head, I put on my best smile. "Good ..." My words dry up as my eyes land on Mrs. Dunsley. For some unknown reason, she's never liked me and it's made it difficult on my end to be friendly, but I'm careful to maintain my professionalism. "Good morning, Mrs. Dunsley."

She struts by me without a word. Shrugging, I make myself a coffee and get to work, replying to emails, booking viewings, and making appointments for rental inspections. Ironically, I work for a real estate agent, and yet I'm on the brink of losing my apartment. Day in, day out, I facilitate people finding their new homes while I'm not sure I'll be able to keep my own.

A pile of papers lands on my keyboard. "These need to be stapled again. The staples aren't exactly straight with the top of the paper. Do it now because I need them by nine." Mrs. Dunsley storms away without a please or thank you, which is usual for her. I pick up the papers that I stapled yesterday, studying the fasteners closely. She must have freaking measured them with a ruler because they all look parallel to the top of the page to me. Because I know how particular she is, I always take care to make sure I work to her exacting standards. Rolling my eyes, I pull out the staple remover and get to work, removing the staples carefully, because heaven forbid, I tear or bend the pages. She'd have me print the pages again and take the money for the additional expense out of my paycheck. She's done that before.

The bell rings above the door, and when I look up, a genuine smile spreads. "Good morning, Peter." I quickly stand as he comes around to me, his arms open wide. He wasn't in yesterday when I came back to work.

Embracing me tightly, he whispers, "How are you, Mols? We missed your smiling face around here. Are you okay?" He gives me a tight squeeze, then releases me and takes my hands in his. "I'm so sorry about everything you've been through. Is there anything you need?"

Tears flood my eyes, forming streams down my cheeks and dripping from my chin. My nose immediately turns into a snot factory, and it's taking everything within me to stay on my feet. With a hiccupping sob, I work to catch my breath and stifle my tears. With a watery smile, I finally respond, "You— You're the first person to hug me and ask me if I'm okay since I lost my family. I'm sor– … sorry I broke down like that." I'm mortified that my emotions overflowed so readily in front of one of the agents. Peter's always been like a second father to me. It shouldn't surprise me he was the first person to show his care and concern. I didn't realize how lonely and alone I've felt since that dreadful night until he hugged me.

He pulls me back into his large body, wrapping one hand around the back of my head and guiding it to his chest. "Oh, you poor girl. You've been through so much. Too much for someone as young as you." He pats my back, holding me close while I work to get myself under control.

"What the hell is going on out here? Is any work getting done?" Mrs. Dunsley's voice cracks like a bolt of lightning through the small front office. I immediately remove myself from Peter's kind embrace, keeping my eyes on the floor.

Peter's deep rumbling voice cuts through the quiet. "I was checking in on Molly. Making sure she's okay."

"Why wouldn't she be? We gave her time off to deal with her situation." She turns her body toward mine, addressing me directly. "You were supposed to deal with all this in your own time." She waves her hand around my face. "I expect you to be more professional when you're at work."

I feel Peter bristling beside me and place my hand gently on his arm to prevent him from speaking on my behalf. "I'm sorry, Mrs. Dunsley. It won't happen again."

She looks between me and Peter and gives a sharp nod before strutting away. I mouth 'thank you' to Peter and make my way to the bathroom to wash my face. I can't greet people at the front desk with snot running down my face and red, swollen eyes. It would be embarrassing, not to mention unprofessional.

I step into the kitchen to grab a glass of water. As I'm filling my glass, someone walks in behind me. I'm about to turn around to say hello when I hear a huff. My shoulders tense and I mentally prepare for her venom.

"My God, Molly. How many times have I told you the handle on the coffeepot needs to be on the left? I'm left-handed," she huffs as her eyes narrow at me. "Do you do it deliberately? Leave the handle on the right, knowing I have to twist the pot around?" I blink several times, unable to answer. "Well?" she snaps.

Shit. I never thought about it, but I guess if I wanted to annoy her, I could have purposely done that. "I'm sorry, Mrs. Dunsley. It won't happen again." I feel like it's all I ever do around here; apologize for being unable to meet the exacting standards she sets.

"Oh, I *know* it won't." She smirks as she pours her coffee and heads out of the kitchen. *What's that supposed to mean?*

I skip my lunch break with the hope I'll catch up on some of the work I've missed over the past week. It's difficult to focus with my thoughts scattered as I wait for Mr. Dunsley to arrive in the office so I can speak to him about an advance. If he doesn't agree, I don't know what I'll do. I'll be like the women I support every week at the shelter. I'll go back to living out of a car like I did when I was a child.

He finally breezes in at four p.m. "Don't disturb me. No phone calls," he barks at me as he hurriedly strides past my desk to his office, slamming his door behind him.

My smile drops and my shoulders slump. How am I going to ask him about my advance? *Shit!*

I power through the rest of the afternoon, working past my usual finish time. At six-thirty, I gather enough courage to knock on my boss's door.

"What?" Hmmm, he still sounds pissed. Maybe I should leave it for today and ask tomorrow? "You may as well come in now that you've disturbed me," he snaps out through the paper-thin barrier between us.

My hand shakes as I turn the knob and perspiration forms beneath my armpits. I'm going to have sweat stains on my good shirt at this rate. I poke my head inside as the space between the door and the jamb widens. "Uhm, sorry to interrupt."

He waves me in as he rolls his eyes. "Don't be timid, girl. You've interrupted me now. Sit down." He gestures to the chair opposite his large glass desk. "I need to speak with you, anyway."

"Do I need my notebook?"

"No. I'll be quick." He folds his hands, one on top of the other, on the glass table, and I can't help but notice his right leg twitching up and down. "The housing market has slowed considerably over the last two months and we're going to have to let go of some staff." I nod. I've noticed the drop in property numbers. I figured they would have to let a couple of agents go; I only hope it's not Peter. He's lovely and he has teenage boys that he's putting through college. He presses forward, leaning heavily on the glass, which I fear is going to crack underneath his weight. "I'm going to have to ask you to clean out your desk today. We're letting you go." He awkwardly spreads his lips in what I guess is supposed to be a reassuring smile and my mind blanks.

*Did he just fire me?*

I came in here to ask for an advance. I didn't even get the chance to open my mouth, and he's firing me. On the freaking spot with no notice! Is this a joke?

I scan the office, looking for cameras and for someone to shout out that I've been 'punked'. But nothing is hinting at a trick for a stupid television show.

How can this be happening? I've lost my family. Now I've lost my job and because of that, I'm going to lose my apartment!

Dropping my face into my hands, I shake my head, tears falling unbidden. Trying to suck in a full breath, I raise my head to the ceiling, attempting to stem my tears. "I can't believe you're firing me without notice."

He shrugs carelessly. "Sorry. It's nothing personal, you know. We can't keep hemorrhaging money. It's not like you bring in a commission. We're in business to make money, not lose it."

Mrs. Dunsley strolls into the office, taking up her position beside her husband, her head held up high as though she's better than everyone else. The gleam in her eyes tells me how happy she is that they've fired me.

I stand on shaky legs. He doesn't care that he's hammered the final nail in my coffin. "When will I get my paycheck?"

"You'll get paid as usual at the end of the month. I'm not in the business of changing procedures to suit individuals."

I don't remember leaving his office or packing my desk. I don't even remember the walk to my car and the drive home, but I find myself sitting on my small couch in the dark in my tiny one-bedroom apartment that I'm about to lose.

Numb.

Nothing. I feel nothing.

I wake to gray skies and snow flurries, still wearing the clothes from yesterday. Wiping the sleep and dried-up tears from my eyes, I jump up from my couch in alarm. Shit, have I slept in? I grab my phone to check the time, my heart beating double time. Seven-thirty!

Shit, shit, shit!

Running into my bedroom, I quickly grab a change of clothes and head to the bathroom to shower. My feet freeze as yesterday afternoon flashes like a movie clip. My shoulders slump in defeat. I can't believe how my life has turned to shit. I press my lips together to stifle the sob that wants to escape. The backs of my eyes burn from the tears I'm trying to hold at bay. Spinning around, I head back to my bedroom, drop my clothes on the floor, and climb into bed, sliding down deep under the covers. Maybe if I can shut out the world for a while, I can start over again when I come out. Curled up in a ball beneath my covers, I close my eyes tight and try to get my heartbeat and breathing under control. An anxiety attack is the last thing I need right now. I need to clear my head, get my thoughts in order so I can make a plan.

Maybe this is a sign.

Maybe I should use this opportunity to my advantage.

Maybe I could do something I've always wanted to do.

Maybe I could start over somewhere new.

Memories flood one after the other. When it was only Mom and me, she used to tell me all about her life on the west coast. It's where she grew up. I would ask her why she left if she loved it so much. She would always gently slide my bangs out of my eyes and tell me she moved because she loved me so much. Her boyfriend abandoned her when she told him she was pregnant, and her parents weren't happy with her teenage pregnancy. Her dad wanted her to have an abortion, so she ran as far as she could, ending up in Portland, Maine, where I was born. It's the only place I've ever lived. Her stories of life in the west always sounded magical to me as a young girl.

Leaving the safety of my cocoon, I grab my cheap laptop and make myself comfortable on my couch. A hiss leaves my lips as I check my bank account. If I'm super careful and sleep in my car, I may just make it. I'll need to get a job immediately, but I would have to do that here, anyway. I could pawn my television and laptop and possibly get a little more money. But I may need my laptop to apply for jobs and stuff like that—I guess I could always use the computers at the local library. I look around my small apartment, searching out more items I could sell—I have a couple of things.

Collecting them together, I place them near my front door, ready to take them to the pawn shop first thing in the morning. I load up one of my plastic tubs with Ethan's scrapbook, Mom's recipe books, and our family photo albums, plus all of my important papers. Next, I pack my clothes, toiletries, and linens. I debate what to do with the few kitchen items I have. If I don't take them with me, I'll have to buy new ones, anyway. I may as well take them and save myself some money. I have nothing else I can use to pack them into, so I'll have to get a box while I'm out tomorrow. Putting everything I'm taking with me into a neat pile in the middle of my living room, I wander around it a few times. It looks like a lot. I hope it's all gonna fit in my car.

I lay out my clothes for the morning, take a long look around my apartment, and head to bed to get a good night's sleep. I have a big few days ahead of me.

I doze off to images of west coast sunsets and a fresh start.

# CHAPTER 4

## —max—

Pulling in behind my workshop first thing, the sun barely peeking over the horizon, my eyes narrow as a low *what the fuck* escapes my mouth. Parked in my fucking spot is a navy two thousand and one Jetta sedan. Nobody ever parks behind here, because the bays are solely for the use of the business owners within this precinct. Each of the businesses here has an apartment above the workspace, so most of the other bays are already in use.

I used to live in mine until I started earning enough from the business to buy my home ten minutes down the road. As much as I love working with cars, I hated the smell of oil and other chemicals invading my home; I needed to have a separate space to live. Parking off to the side, I climb out of my car to inspect the unwelcome car parked in my space.

Looking around the backlot of my workshop, I notice nothing else out of place. I bend down enough to peer through the windows, which are slightly cracked open. My eyes widen as they land on a young woman asleep in the semi-reclined driver's seat. I glance in the back—there's too much stuff packed in the backseat to allow it to recline fully. As I scan the interior, it looks as though everything she owns is packed into the compact car. My eyes drop back to the woman, and I study her closely.

*She's fucking beautiful.*

She's young, really young, with clear pale skin and even paler hair. She's what I'd imagine an angel looks like. I watch her sleep for a few moments, her almost white hair fanned around her face, her thick lashes resting on the apples of her cheeks—*fucking stunning*. I wonder what color her eyes are. Not that I should care what color her eyes are. If she's *that* beautiful, she's probably a self-absorbed bitch, like my ex. I don't need another one like her in my life. She must be fucking uncomfortable because she looks tall, too tall for the space she's using as a bed.

It doesn't appear the interloper will wake up anytime soon.

"What the fuck?" I whisper.

I'm incredulous that my car pulling into the lot didn't wake her up. I have a mind to move my car, so it blocks this woman in. I don't want her sneaking off before I can have a word with her about her sleeping arrangements and parking where she's not welcome.

In fact, that's what I think I'll do.

Walking back to my car, I climb in and start the engine, which sounds deafening in the quiet of the morning. I move in behind her, meaning she'll have to come to find me when she wakes. Cutting the engine, I lock my car, then check on the sleeping beauty. She must be out of it because she hasn't stirred an inch.

Shrugging, I disarm the alarm in my workshop and slide open the heavy steel double door. Stepping inside, I turn on the overhead lights and unlock the front door on my way to my compact office to start the coffee machine. It was the one luxury I afforded myself when I was setting this place up. Why skimp on coffee if it's the thing that'll get me through my workday?

Toby's bringing his car in for a service today, but I need to finish working on the Lincoln before nine, so I drink my coffee as I turn on my laptop and then head into the workshop to get started. Lost in fitting the new radiator into place, I hit my head on the hood at the feminine voice calling out from the doorway. Glancing across, I find the young woman who was sleeping in her car out back. Stepping away from the car, I grab a nearby rag to wipe my hands as I walk across to her.

"Uh, hello. Is that your car blocking me in?" Her voice is sure, full of confidence, even though she must know that she shouldn't park where she is.

I was right. She is tall. I keep enough space between us to be polite. "Is that your Jetta?" I tip my head toward her car, parked in my space. I know full well it's hers because I watched her sleep like a creeper.

She swallows and turns her head in the direction I gestured as if to check I'm asking about her car, then back to me. "Yeah."

"You know that's a private parking space on private property reserved for the business owner? Right?" I ask, keeping my voice even. I cross my arms and her eyes drop, widening slightly as she watches the action.

"Uh, sorry. I've," she waves her arm out toward her car, "been driving solid for days, only stopping for gas and to nap. It was too late when I arrived last night to … uh … get a room somewhere. I pulled in here because it looked like a safe place to stop and get some sleep. I'm sorry if I've inconvenienced you. As soon as you move your car, I'll be outta your hair." She takes a step back from me.

"Where'd you come from?" Her accent suggests she's not from anywhere close by because I can't quite place it.

She tucks a lock of silky-looking hair behind her ear. *Gray.* Her eyes are gray. "Portland, Maine."

"What?" The word comes out harsher than I mean it to. "You," I point to her, "drove all that way on your own, in that fucking car?" I wave my arm out toward her car. Is she fucking crazy?

Her posture visibly changes.

Straightening.

Stiffening.

With her spine straight as a board, her shoulders drawn back tight pushing out her round tits—*stop noticing her tits, you perv!*—she snaps out, sharp as a whip, "Yeah, I did." Her gray eyes are blazing hot, her cheeks flushing. Fuck, she's gorgeous.

*No, she's not. She's too fucking young. Stop looking at her.*

I stride over to her car—even with her long legs, she almost has to run to keep up with me—and reach inside to release the hood. Stepping around to the front of the car, I set the hood on the prop and begin checking the connections, fluid levels, and hoses.

"What are you doing?" She follows every move I make with her eyes.

One of my pet peeves is people not treating their car right and expecting it to keep on running. "You barely have any water in your radiator. You could have blown up your engine."

She pushes in beside me, the top of her head coming to my chin, eyes wide. "Really? Thank goodness I made it then." She looks around. "Do you have a hose? I'll fill it up."

I'm shaking my head in disbelief before I can temper my response. "You can't fill a radiator with tap water. It contains minerals that'll damage your radiator over time. It has to be distilled water." I snap. "Did you even check your levels before you left Portland?"

I glance up from the engine bay to her face. Her bottom lip is wobbling, and her eyes are scarily glassy. I recognize a woman trying to hold back her tears. I have two sisters and I would do anything to ensure tears never fell because of something I said or did. But it appears I didn't offer the same courtesy to this stranger. She's wrapped her arms around her willowy body as if to protect herself from my wrath.

I sigh heavily with regret.

I had no right to be snappy with this young girl. She didn't deserve my Saturday morning grumpy ass. But I can't handle the mistreatment of cars. People seem to think they don't require care and maintenance.

She gives me a watery smile. "I'm sorry. I didn't know I was supposed to do that. My stepdad used to take care of my car for me. I honestly didn't know. I definitely don't need my car to blow up or to put myself at risk. But after the last few weeks I've had, it wouldn't surprise me." The defeat in her voice is heavy.

My eyes scan her face, noting the black smudges beneath her gorgeous eyes. She looks exhausted and her posture screams defeat. Her clothes are all creased and the slump to her shoulders is unmistakable. She needs a break. I can give her that. Pulling the rag out of my back pocket, I wipe my hands again. They're perpetually stained from grease and oil. I don't know why I bother anymore.

I soften my voice, regretting my heavy-handedness. "Come through to my office. I have a coffee machine. You can put your feet up while I give your car a quick check over and sort out your radiator. Okay?"

She studies me closely, her eyes cataloging every inch of my face. Wariness oozes from every single pore. "Uh, I don't have any money to pay you to do that. If you could just move your car, I'll be on my way and out of your hair." She glances up at my hair and I feel self-conscious about the few grays that have made a permanent home at the temples. The girl gestures to my car and raises her eyebrows at me.

A tentative smile touches my lips. I don't blame her for being wary. I was an asshole. "Did I say I was going to charge you?" I hold out my hand. "Give me your keys so I can move your car into the workshop." I get her reluctance, but I want to help her. My gut tells me she needs a helping hand. I wriggle my fingers in a 'give me' gesture and add, "Please."

She looks back at her car, deliberating my offer as she fidgets with her bracelet. I can tell the moment she relents as she huffs out a sigh and her shoulders drop from her ears. As she turns toward the driver's side, the sunlight catches a delicate ring I hadn't noticed in her nose. She retrieves her keys and drops them into the palm of my hand before looking up at me. Her stormy eyes, soft and appreciative. "Thank you."

"No problem. Let me show you to my office. You can make yourself a coffee, go to the bathroom, or whatever while I work on your car."

I brush past the young woman to head inside, assuming she'll follow, but she steps back to her car. I stop in my tracks to wait for her. She digs down into her car, giving me a sensational view of her ass. *Shit!* Don't stare at her ass. She's a fucking kid. When she straightens up, she's holding a backpack. As the girl steps closer to me, she looks down at her bright pink running shoes, then back up at me. "Uh, I have a lot of important stuff in my car. It'll be safe? Right?"

"Absolutely. I'm just gonna move it from there," I point to her car, "to there." I gesture inside.

She nods. "Okay. I just needed to be sure."

I guide her into my office. "There's the coffee machine. Do you need me to show you how to use it?" I gesture toward the poor excuse for a kitchenette, which takes up a small space in the corner.

She wanders over. Turning back to me, she smiles, showing off deep dimples. I'm a fucking sucker for dimples. "Nope. This is the same one my mom and stepdad used to have at home."

Hmmm. Don't think I haven't noticed the regular use of past tense. I don't think she's driven all the way from the other side of the country for a vacation. I wonder if she's a runaway? "Okay. There's cream and juice in the fridge." I nod toward a door on the other side. "The bathroom's through there. It has a shower and toilet. Though it's pretty small."

Her eyes light up. "Sir, uh …" She cuts off her words and shakes her head, but I can tell that whatever she was about to say was important to her.

"What were you gonna say?" I prod.

"Uh, would I be able to have … I mean, uh, would you mind if I had a quick shower? I've been on the road for days with only a quick wipe down in gas station restrooms." She's looking at me with pleading eyes and all I can picture is her wiping down those gorgeous long legs of hers.

How can I say 'no'?

"Sure thing. Make yourself at home. I'll need about an hour to work on your car, then you can be on your way." Realizing neither of us has introduced ourselves, I wipe my hand on the back of my overalls before holding it out. "Sorry. My name's Max."

The young woman chuckles, her cheeks flushing pink. "Sorry. Hi, Max." She slides her small smooth hand into mine. "I'm Molly."

*Molly*. I like that name. It suits her.

I nod my head as I squeeze lightly. "Nice to meet you, Molly. Make yourself comfortable." I gesture over my shoulder. "I'll get started on your car." Glancing down at the only available surface for her to sit and enjoy a coffee, I gather my strewn paperwork into a messy pile and situate it on top of my laptop to give her space.

I give Molly an embarrassed smile, then I turn to leave.

An hour later, I step into my office to find Molly on the phone while doing something on my laptop, a cute set of glasses perched on her button nose. "Yes, Mr. Barnes. I can see that your next service is due in two weeks. Would you like me to book you in?"

I glance at my desk, covered in neat piles of paper. I don't think it's ever been this organized.

"Sure thing, Mr. Barnes. That's all booked for you. Max will see you at eight a.m. on the twenty-eighth. Goodbye." She's smiling, creating deep dimples on both cheeks, as she hangs up the phone.

"Uh, what's going on in here?"

Molly's head snaps up, revealing wide eyes at my sudden intrusion. She glances around my desk, then up to me, shrugging. "I'm sorry. I thought I could help you out since you weren't charging me to check over my car. You don't mind, do you?"

"What exactly have you done here?" I ask, folding my arm across my body, using the nail of my thumb to drag across my bottom lip. Her eyes snag on the movement and follow my thumb as I pass back and forth across the pillow.

She looks back down at the desk and gestures across the surface like a TV show host. "I've sorted all of your invoices according to the type of expense and then I've ordered them further according to when the payment is due. Then there's been a couple of phone inquiries. I'm sorry, I didn't know your charges, so I've taken messages and told them you would call them back later today. I've booked a service and one tire change. I also noticed you have Thursdays blocked off, so I kept that day free."

She competently rattles off everything she's accomplished in the hour. I also notice her hair's wet and she's in different clothes than when I left, meaning she's grabbed a shower, too.

*What in the actual fuck?*

"Are you looking for a job?" The words fly out of my mouth before I can even think about them. But there's no way I'm taking them back. I need her here. Working with me. If she can do all of that in an hour, imagine what she can get done in a day. I'll never have to take work home again, nor be interrupted by the phone five thousand times a day.

# CHAPTER 5

## —molly—

*DID HE JUST OFFER ME A JOB?*

My first day in town and I thought I'd messed up in a major way, but now I already have the offer of a job. I'm certain my eyes are the widest they've ever been.

"Are you serious?" The pitch of my voice is higher than normal. Swallowing, I work to temper my shock and excitement. "I mean, are you really offering me a job?" I fidget with the leather cord of my special bracelet. Mom gave it to me when I turned twenty-one and I've never taken it off. She had a complementary one, which is now packed with all of my special treasures along with everything else I own in my car. I've found I rub the silver heart between my fingers more since I lost her; it makes me feel closer to her somehow.

Max seems to be schooling his own surprise. "Uhm, yeah." He laughs. A deep rich sound that sounds amazing after the way he reamed me out about my car. "I guess I am."

I jump up and down, squealing in delight. Running around to the other side of the desk, I throw myself at Max's tall body, wrapping my arms around him. Beneath the smell of grease and oil hides a masculine scent that's sexy as all hell. "Thank you so much. I can't believe how well today has turned out to be." I squeeze him again before releasing the man who's given me so much but doesn't realize. "It looks like everything's gonna work out!" I chuckle.

Max is frozen in place. He probably thinks I'm crazy. He doesn't know how much this means to me. How can he? I can't believe that on my first day in this new city, I've already landed myself a job. Things are looking up. Perhaps this was the right decision to make, after all.

The door opens and closes, so I step away from Max to greet the customer. My eyes almost pop out of my head when they land on the guy who's stepped through the door. He looks even better in real life than he does in pictures.

Toby Summer.

I can't believe I'm in the same room as a famous person. Not just *any* famous person. The hottest famous person on the planet. The greeting I should have dies on my tongue. He's followed by another equally hot guy. I've often seen him in the background of Toby's social media photos. He's his bodyguard. Finally, I gain my wits. "Good morning, I'm Molly. Welcome to Stanfield Auto Repairs. How may I help you?" *Look at me being all professional.*

He looks at me, smiling, then raises his eyes to Max, who's standing beside me. "Max, you finally got yourself some help around here!" He steps forward with his hand outstretched toward me! I'm worried I may faint as my hand connects with his. "Nice to meet you, Molly. I'm Toby. My car's booked in for a service this morning."

Max glances at me, his eyebrows scrunched together, making an adorable crease between them. "Thanks, Molly. I can take it from here."

I drop my hand and step back, realizing I've probably overstepped. I mean, he *only* offered me the position two minutes ago.

He turns to Toby. "Hey, Toby. Shane." He nods to the men. "Good to see you again. The girl needs a service, right?"

Toby nods. "Yeah. She's running like a kitten, but I want to make sure I look after her properly."

Max smiles. "That's what I like to hear. If you can give your keys to Molly. I'm running a little behind this morning, but your car should still be ready for collection at two."

"No problem. Shane followed me in his car. He'll take me home and bring me back later." He nods over his shoulder to the man behind him as he steps forward, handing me his car keys.

I'm holding Toby Summer's car keys in my hand. Oh. My. Gosh! I have the broadest smile as I study them as though they're precious gems.

Max points to a board next to the door, which leads out to the workshop. "You can hang them on there. On the booking sheet, you'll notice I give each car a bay number. Hang the client's keys on the corresponding bay hook. Okay? I've allocated bay one for Toby's car."

I nod. "Sure thing." I step over and hang the keys on the hook that says Bay 1.

"Molly will call you when your car's ready to be collected. Did you need me to check anything particular or are you happy with a general service and check?" Max asks Toby as the men walk back out through the front door.

I follow them, staying inside, but watching through the glass window in the door. I whistle quietly to myself as my eyes land on his nineteen sixty-seven Chevy Impala convertible. Wow! That's a nice ride. Ethan and Jack used to always be looking at muscle cars, making it easy for me to identify Toby's car, which is in great condition.

Max walks back into the small office, smiling. "Okay. Your car is ready, so if you want to head off, feel free."

"Oh, you don't need me to stay?" I'm confused. I thought he offered me a job, but now he's telling me I can go. "Aren't I supposed to phone Mr. Summer when his car is ready at two? Have you changed your mind about the position?" I hope not, I really need something to go right.

"Not at all. But you said you'd arrived in town early this morning. I figure you need to get to wherever you're planning to stay and settle in. You should do that. Come back on Monday. Eight a.m. You can start then."

"Oh, okay. Thank you." I guess he's being considerate. "See you Monday." I smile at him. With no money for a place to stay, I was planning to sleep in my car until I saved enough, but he doesn't know that. I guess I can use this time to familiarize myself with my new city and locate some safe places to sleep at night. Maybe even some public showers or something.

# CHAPTER 6

## —max—

Stepping onto the familiar porch, I head inside without knocking—there's no need to. The familiar smells of Mom's Sunday roast waft out of the kitchen to greet me, making my stomach grumble in response. This is possibly the best meal I get all week—not possibly, it *is* the best meal I get all week.

Austin and Kenny notice me first and sprint down the hallway, throwing themselves at my body with every faith that I'll catch them. And I will catch them. Every single time they need me.

I quickly drop Em's gift on the entry table to free both arms.

"Uncle Max! You're here!" cheers Austin.

"Uncle Max!" Kenny squeals at the same time.

I catch them both and lift them into my arms, land a kiss on each of their cheeks, and then place them back on their feet. There was a time, not too long ago, when I could throw Austin above my head, but he's getting too big for that. I mess his hair and relish in his little boy giggles before tickling Kenny under her chin, causing her to giggle too. One of the best sounds in the world is the laughter of little kids.

"I'm here. We can get this party started now!"

"Is that for Mommy?" Austin points to the gift I dropped onto the table.

"Yup, where's the birthday girl?"

"In the kitchen with Nana." The kids run to the kitchen, Austin calling out to Emma, "Uncle Max is here."

My long strides have me approaching the kitchen doorway quickly.

Even though it's Em's birthday, I head straight to Mom; if I don't hug her first, she gets all offended for some reason. Placing the gift for Emma on the counter, I wrap both arms around Mom and lift her off her feet.

She chuckles, playfully swatting my shoulder. "Oh, Max. Put me down."

"Hey, Mom." I kiss her cheek.

She brings her hand up to my bristly cheek, looking up at me with pure love in her eyes. That's the one thing I've never had to question. The depth of my family's love for me. "How has your week been, Love?"

"It's been great. Busy. Really busy," I respond as I steal a piece of cucumber from the chopping board.

I move over to Emma, who's busy taking the roast out of the oven for Mom. Once she's placed it down, I wrap my arms around her in a bear hug, lifting her off her feet. "Happy birthday, Em!" I rub my bristles across her cheek before landing a sloppy birthday kiss, causing her to giggle.

Her hands press against my shoulders. "Thanks, Max."

"How's your day been so far?"

She looks across to the kitchen table where Lachlan sits with Theo, a smile touching her lips. "It's been perfect." Contentment and happiness radiate from her, and I'm thrilled she's found that. The muscle in my chest tightens; I want that too. I'm not getting any younger and I want a family of my own.

I hand her the gift I brought. "Here you go. It's not huge, but I thought you'd like it."

She pulls the T-shirt out of the bag, holding it up so she can read it and a full-on belly laugh escapes.

"What's funny?" Sarah asks as she steps into the room, wrapping her arms around my waist in greeting. Wrapping my arm around her, I kiss the top of her head.

Emma turns the T-shirt around to show her the front. Sarah reads the text out for everyone, "I'm a proud sister of a freaking awesome brother (and yes, he brought me this shirt)." She promptly bursts out laughing, too.

"It's perfect, right?" I ask the room as Emma twists the shirt around for everyone to see.

Dad claps me on the shoulder and chuckles. "Only you, Max."

Sarah spins around, removing herself from me, pointing her finger. "Don't even think about getting me one of those." Her grin tells me it wouldn't bother her if I got her one, which I already did. I bought them at the same time, so I didn't have to think of another gift. I'm organized like that.

Everyone settles down, and we set the table ready for lunch. Theo serves Kenny and helps Emma with the boys, careful to ensure Lachlan's food isn't touching. I never thought I'd see Lachlan eating our roast dinner, but Theo's gradually been introducing him to new foods. Theo dishes Em's plate before serving himself and I nod my approval internally. It's fantastic to see Em and the boys being looked after so well. The first few moments are silent as we serve ourselves and take our first few bites of food.

The lamb is incredibly tender; falling apart in my mouth. I can't contain the moan that escapes me, and I refuse to try. "This is delicious, Mom."

She smiles at the praise. Mom loves feeding her family and we love to be fed by her. Being on my own and working the long hours that I do, I only ever make myself the basics for dinner and grab whatever I can from the deli over the road from the workshop for lunch. Which means I really look forward to our weekly family dinner. Maybe having Molly working in the office will afford me some more time and I can actually attempt to feed myself proper meals that take more than five minutes to put together.

"You said you've been busy at work. When are you going to employ someone to help?" Mom asks. At Mom's question, everyone's eyes land on me. They've been nagging me for quite some time to get help at the workshop.

I place my knife and fork down and wipe my mouth with my napkin, hiding my smile. "You'll be happy to know that I have an office manager starting at eight a.m. on Monday."

Cheers sound out around the table. "Finally!" Mom raises her voice to be heard above the din as Lachlan covers his ears. When he was younger, he probably would have cried at such a sudden noise, but as he's grown, he's dealing with the stuff we take for granted.

"How did you find this office manager and are you sure they're qualified?" Of course, Sarah would be the one to ask about Molly's qualifications since she's an office manager herself.

The thing is, I don't know if Molly has all the qualifications or even if she has any at all. She showed me how capable she was and after she left; I checked the work she'd done, and it was top-notch. For someone who wasn't familiar with my system, she did a good job. The only thing she hadn't done on the bookings was assign each vehicle to a bay. I can easily show her my specific requirements on Monday, knowing she has a good grasp of the overall system.

I must have taken too long to answer my sister. Her forehead creases as she asks, "She *is* qualified, right? You didn't just hire anyone off the street?"

Leaning my elbow on the table, I rub my thumbnail across my bottom lip in thought. That's exactly what I did. How do I break it to her?

"Oh my gawd! You did. Are you an idiot?" She rolls her eyes at me and Emma snickers.

"I'm not an idiot, Sarah," I snap, but then temper my tone. She's only looking out for my best interests. "She's highly competent or I wouldn't have hired her," I tell them how Molly came to be employed, leaving out the part about her sleeping in her car behind my workshop.

"Has she got somewhere to stay?" Mom asks, fidgeting with her necklace.

I shrug. "I didn't ask. I would assume she does."

Mom's worry increases. "If she's new to the city, she might need some help to get around and learn the area. Oh, my goodness, will she know which areas she should stay away from?"

My stomach drops. Shit, I didn't think about any of that. I assumed she knew where she was heading. What if she ends up renting a place in an unsavory area? I didn't get any contact details for her, so I can't check if she's okay. She'd be okay, right? I mean, she drove across the country on her own, for fuck's sake. Fuck. Now *I'm* worried about her. I check the time—only eighteen hours until I see for myself that she's okay.

"Now, when you leave work for the day, you can leave your work behind. That's great news, Son. It's been a long time coming for you." Dad pats my shoulder, drawing me back into the conversation, as he steps past me to place his dishes on the counter near the sink.

"How are things going at your office, Sarah? Any news on Eric's retirement?" Emma asks.

Sarah blows out a heavy sigh, her shoulders slumping forward. "Something happened and delayed Adam's move to the west coast. I'm not sure when things will change."

Emma gives Sarah a sympathetic smile. "Well, on the positive side of things, it means you get to work with Eric longer."

"That's true, and it's something I'm cherishing." She tucks a loose lock of hair behind her ear. "I love working with Eric and you guys know how I feel about change."

"Eric's grandson might be a lot like him. You never know, it might be a seamless transition." I do my best to put her at ease because I know how much Sarah dislikes change.

She nods as she places her silverware down, her expression serious. "I have something I wanted to talk with you guys about."

We all give Sarah one hundred percent of our attention. "What is it, Love?" Mom asks.

She blows out a breath. "Please don't judge me. I've thought long and hard about this and it's the right decision for me. I'm hoping you'll all be supportive."

Creases form between Dad's eyebrows. "Of course, we'll support you."

"Great." She blows out a long breath. "I've decided I want to have a baby." The silence in the room is loud. "I'm not getting any younger and it's impossible to meet someone decent. Someone I'd want to raise a family with."

Mom's hand rises to fidget with her necklace. "Oh. Well … uh … that's unexpected news. How will you make this happen?"

"There are agencies that help women like me. I complete a whole heap of paperwork, give them a whole wad of money, and they give me sperm from a baby-daddy of my choosing."

"My sister, Anna, did that." Theo looks across at Kenny with eyes full of love and adoration. "That's how we ended up with Kenny."

"Do you know which agency she used?"

Theo thinks for a moment. "I don't, sorry. Dad might know, though. I'll ask him and let you know."

Sarah smiles at him. "Thanks."

"This isn't the way we expected you to be having a baby, but we'll support you in any way we can." Dad reaches across, patting Sarah's hand with love and affection.

We all offer our support to Sarah in any way we can as she finds a baby-daddy and into the future, through her pregnancy, and then into motherhood. We clean up from dinner and then Sarah places a chocolate birthday cake on the table for Emma. I'm incredibly thankful we still have Emma with us to celebrate her birthday. I was worried we were going to lose her this time last year before she got her proper diagnosis, and we didn't quite know what was going to happen. We sing happy birthday in our usual terribly off-key fashion and then enjoy the delicious cake baked by my younger sister. She's been the designated birthday cake maker since she was old enough to bake.

# CHAPTER 7

## —max—

PULLING AROUND BEHIND MY WORKSHOP SOON AFTER DAWN, I HALF expect to find the blue Jetta parked in my space again. I'm not sure if I'm relieved or disappointed that it isn't there as I move through my usual morning routine. I try not to have any cars left over the weekend, leaving the workshop empty except for the Sprint.

Time becomes inconsequential as I get lost in the task of connecting the wiring for the rear lights of my restoration project. As I connect the last wire, I glance up to find Molly hovering inside the doorway to the workshop. Sucking in a sharp breath, I allow myself to release the worry I've been holding onto about Molly's safety since Mom brought up her concerns yesterday afternoon. She looks mighty different from the girl I met on Saturday. Dressed in office attire, I almost don't recognize her. A dark checkered skirt hugs her hips, sitting just below her knees and a white silky-looking blouse highlights her bust. Her almost-white hair is up in some sort of sexy knot on top of her head. She looks like a fucking hot secretary who works in a corporate office, not a mechanic's filthy workshop. *And I should not be fucking thinking about how hot she looks.* She's like twelve fucking years old. I run my hand through my hair as I make my way over to where she's standing, fidgeting with the bracelet on her slender wrist.

"Uh … hello, Mr. Stanfield. I'm ready to start work if the job is still available," she stammers; her eyes flitting around the workshop, avoiding me.

I cross my arms and rub my thumbnail across my bottom lip. "Morning. Why so formal today?"

She tilts her head to the side, not understanding my question. I wave my arm up and down her body, my eyes following. She has a sensational body—long legs, slim hips, not too much boobage—just enough. *Fuck, stop looking at her like that, you filthy pervert! You're her fucking boss.*

She looks down at herself as though to check what she's wearing. "Oh, this. This is what I wore for my last job. I wanted to be professional." She cracks those deep, deep dimples at me, her eyes wide. She looks too fucking professional for this place in that getup.

"You can probably wear jeans and a T-shirt here. I'm not sure what type of office you worked in before, but this is a more laid-back environment."

"Sure." She gestures over her shoulder. "I can change. I have my clothes in the car."

Spinning on her heel, I admire the shape of her calves in the black tights she's wearing. Then it registers that she said she had her clothes in the car.

*Why the fuck does she have her clothes in the car?*

My long strides catch me up to her quickly, and I'm directly behind her as she opens her trunk. It's not my business, but it looks as though she hasn't unpacked her car. I stroll to the side of the car, discreetly looking inside. Sure enough, the blankets she was using to sleep are folded neatly on the back seat, along with several small packing boxes.

"How come you still have all of your stuff in your car?"

Her head snaps up to me. I'm not sure she realized I was close by as she rummages through her bag, digging out a pair of jeans and a long-sleeve T-shirt. "I haven't found a long-term place to live yet. Most places were closed yesterday and by the time I left on Saturday, I'd already missed a couple of opportunities. I decided it was easier to leave my stuff in my car." I study her closely for a long moment. "You know, so I don't have to unpack and pack again." She widens her silver eyes with her explanation.

I guess that logic makes sense. "Fair enough. Is the place you're staying safe?"

She glances away from me. "Oh, yeah!" Nodding her head as if to confirm her answer, she adds, "Totally safe." She holds up an assortment of clothes. "Do you mind if I use your bathroom to change?"

"No problem. Go ahead. Then I'll run you through a couple of things before you get started. You'll need to fill out some employment paperwork, too." I close her trunk and we both make our way inside. "You want a coffee?"

"Yes, please. That'd be great. Cream, no sugar, thanks," she calls back through the closed bathroom door. I hear the shower turn on. *What the fuck?* I thought she was only changing clothes.

I hold back on making her coffee to ensure it's hot when she finally comes out, and deal with a client as they drop off their keys while she's in the bathroom. The door opens, and steam gushes out of the room into the small office space. "I thought you were just changing clothes?"

She glances back at the bathroom as she shrugs. "Sorry 'bout that. The place I showered this morning only had cold water. I couldn't resist. I hope you don't mind." *Too bad if I did.* I hope she doesn't expect to get away with whatever she wants while I'm waiting on her and making her coffee. From my experience, girls that look like her expect to always get their way.

Hmmm. I'm not used to being a boss, but she's on the clock. *My* clock. Should I cut her some slack? It's her first day, after all. Or should I be a hard ass? "Don't make a habit of it, okay? You're supposed to start work at eight. I had to deal with a client because you weren't ready for work." Hard ass it is, then.

Her cheeks flush prettily as she shifts on her feet. "Sorry, Mr. Stanfield. It won't happen again. I'll run these to my car and be ready to start." She holds up her fancy clothes and I nod.

She takes off and I make our coffee, ready to show her the system I have in place, although she had a pretty good grasp of it on Saturday without being shown. I spend the next thirty minutes leaning over Molly to show her the system. Each time I lean forward, I'm hit with her alluring scent; I can't quite place it, but it's a far cry from motor oil and grease. She's a quick study, even suggesting some ways to simplify the invoicing system, which I'm more than happy for her to do.

"Okay, I'm going to head out to work on the brake replacement in bay one. We need to get your employment forms sorted. Can you please fill them in?"

"Sure thing, Mr. Stanfield." She hits me with those fucking dimples as if they punctuate her sentence.

"Call me Max. Okay? Mr. Stanfield is my dad." I huff out a chuckle.

"Oh, okay, Max. I'll try to remember." I take one last glance at her with those cute glasses perched on her nose as she returns her focus to my laptop, then I step into the workshop to get to work.

"Shit, fuck!" My thumb instantly throbs from the impact of the mallet against it. Shoving it in my mouth, I realize my mistake immediately as the taste of grease coats my tongue. It's not the first time I've done it, and it certainly won't be the last.

Footsteps rush across the open space. "Are you okay? What happened?" My new assistant drops to her knees beside me.

I wrap my free hand around my thumb, attempting to reduce the throb. "Hit my thumb with the mallet. I do it at least once a week."

"Shit. That'd hurt." Molly stands and spins on her heel and runs back to the office. I'm guessing she doesn't like to see people injured. Shaking out my hand, I start back up where I left off, being more cautious of my own body parts. "Here. Wrap this around it." Molly grabs my hand and wraps a cold compress around my thumb, holding it in place.

Her concentration on the task is admirable, but I don't need to be this close to her this soon, especially when I can see right down her T-shirt. I quickly avert my eyes, but they snap back of their own accord to the creamy mounds restrained by a simple cotton bra. This morning was hard enough in my office. I was hoping the workshop would be a large enough space to ensure I didn't have to inhale her floral perfume. I'm not sure what type of magic it has, but it's affected me more than I want it to. At least I know she's not as young as I thought she was, but she's still too young for me.

Plus, I'm her fucking boss! I need to remember that.

I pull my hand away abruptly. "I'm okay."

Her delicate eyebrows drop over her steely eyes. "Are you sure? Your thumb is already swelling. I think it'd be a good idea if you iced it for a while."

I take the compress from her and hold it back on my thumb. "Sure. But I can hold it." I nod toward the office. "You have work to do. How did you go with sourcing those parts I wanted?"

"No luck at the first two suppliers, unless you're prepared to wait for four to six weeks. I was about to try the next one on the list." She fidgets with her bracelet, shifting on her feet. "I'm really sorry."

"What in the hell are you apologizing for? Sometimes I have to go through my entire list of suppliers before I find one who has the part I need in stock." I remove the compress from my thumb to inspect the damage. The ice seems to be helping. "Thanks for this." I hold up my thumb. "You'll get to know which suppliers are better for particular parts. If you're not sure, come and ask. No point wasting time." Molly nods, dropping her hands to her sides.

"Uh, do you want a coffee?"

I glance up at the large clock I have on the back wall of the workshop. It's after one already. "Nah, time to stop for lunch. You should take a break. You get thirty minutes for lunch each day."

"Oh, okay. Thanks."

We walk side-by-side back to my office, her floral scent invading my nose. "What is that perfume you're wearing?"

"I don't wear perfume. It's probably my shampoo and body wash you can smell." She smells her hand, then holds it out for me, and I draw in a deep breath. "Is that it?"

It's a subtle fragrance. "Yeah. What is it?"

"Rose. I'm sorry if it bothers you." What is with this girl apologizing for everything?

"No need to apologize. I was only asking. I … uh … I actually like it."

Her cheeks flush. "Thanks. My mom used to use the same products." Her voice has a shake to it and she drops her face toward the ground. Her mom used to use it. Does that mean she's lost her mom? I don't know her well enough to ask questions, but I make a note to get to know her a little better.

I collect my phone so I can grab my lunch from the deli across the road. Lawrence makes the best sub sandwiches. "I'm gonna head over the road to grab some lunch. Do you want anything?"

Her head snaps around to me, her eyes wide. "Oh. Thanks for the offer, but I'm okay."

I narrow my eyes. "You have lunch, right?"

She tucks a loose strand of silky white hair that's fallen from the top knot behind her ear. "Not today. I completely forgot about it. I'll have a coffee. That'll get me through."

I nod as I head out the door, pulling my jacket around me as I take my first steps. I don't like the cold weather and today's high of sixty-three degrees makes me shiver. The warmth is a welcome reprieve as I step inside *Lawrence's Diner*.

"Max. How's your morning been?" Lawrence calls out from the doorway to the kitchen.

"It was going pretty great until I hit my damn thumb with the mallet."

His face scrunches up with a pained grimace. "Ouch. You want your usual?"

"Yeah. Thanks. Could you make it two, though, please?"

"Sure. You extra hungry today?"

"Nah. I finally got myself an employee. I figured I'd buy her lunch to celebrate her first day." I stuff my hands in my pockets. "Her name's Molly. She might come over now and then to collect my lunch." I shrug.

He nods and goes about making two of my usual sub sandwiches. Turkey, cheddar, thick-cut bacon, and avocado in a ciabatta roll. Mmmm, my mouth's watering already. He wraps them in paper and slides them across the counter to me. "I'll add them to your account."

Grabbing the subs, I hold them up. "Thanks, Lawrence. I'll see you tomorrow." Waving over my shoulder, I head back out into the cold, rushing across the street back to my workshop.

"I got you a sub," I call out to Molly as I open the door to the office. Turning to face the room, I find it empty. I knock on the bathroom door. No answer. Hmph. I step into the workshop and scan the area. My eyes dart back to the woman sitting cross-legged on the floor near the Sprint, a coffee cup on the floor next to her. She reaches out distractedly to grab the cup, almost knocking it over. I wander over as quietly as I can to see what she's doing. She keeps looking down and then up again. Standing behind her like the creeper that I am, what she's doing comes into view.

"Did you sketch that just now?"

She jumps, her hand coming up to her chest. She looks up at me, looming behind her, with red puffy eyes. With her head tilted right back, she gives me a spectacular view of her elongated neck. If she wasn't so young and I weren't her boss, I would lean down, cup her chin, tease her lips with my tongue, and take them in a long, slow kiss to distract her from whatever's made her sad. I shake my head and take half a step to the side, squatting down to get a better look.

She flicks her eyes back down at her book as if to check what I'm talking about. "Yeah. I love to sketch different things. You know. The lines on this car sucked me right in. I couldn't help myself." She looks up at me. "I hope you don't mind. I won't do it while I'm supposed to be working. I'm sorry. I should have asked if it was okay first."

"I have no problem with what you do on your own time. Just be sure you're being safe when you're on the workshop floor." I hold up the sub. "I got you a sandwich for lunch." I hold it out to her, but she doesn't take it.

"Oh, uh, uhm. I'm happy to have a coffee for lunch. Thank you for the kind gesture."

I nudge it forward. "You need more than a coffee for lunch. Here, take it. Come and eat with me in the office."

She looks down at her sketch pad. "I really can't accept it."

"Why not? Are you gluten intolerant or something?"

She shakes her head in the negative. "No, I'm not allergic or intolerant of anything. Well, I don't think I am." She gives a small chuckle and wipes her fingers beneath her eyes.

"Then take it. Eat. C'mon." I stand and begin walking back toward the office, expecting her to follow. When I glance back, she's only just standing. Collecting her things, she slowly makes her way behind me.

Placing the subs on my clean desk, which is miraculous, I pull over an additional chair. I unwrap Molly's sandwich and then mine. Gesturing to the lunch I've laid out, I coax. "C'mon. I always have to eat lunch on my own." I give a false pout. Fuck. I didn't think I'd have to work this hard to feed her. "I was looking forward to eating with someone today."

She fiddles with her bracelet. I've noticed she does that a lot. "I'm on a tight budget. I can't afford to buy expensive lunches at the moment," she explains, without looking at me.

She mentioned money when I offered to look at her car, too. I press my lips together to temper my tone, careful not to respond too harshly. "Did I say you had to pay me for the sandwich?"

Her shoulders are up around her ears. "Uh, no. But ..."

I push her chair out with my foot and gesture toward it. "Sit. Eat with me." I grab my sandwich and take a bite. Softening my voice, I add, "Please."

Her shoulders drop and slight dimples form in her cheeks as she takes a seat. "Thank you. I am a little hungry." She takes a small bite. "This is delicious."

"Lawrence makes the best sandwiches around here." I gesture diagonally across the road. "He's over the road. If you ever want anything, head on over. He'll put it on my tab."

"Oh, I couldn't do that." She shakes her head in the negative, then takes another bite.

I finish my sub well before Molly does and as I ball up my paper, her sketch pad grabs my attention. Pointing with my chin, I ask, "Mind if I take a look?"

She freezes, her eyes widening. "Uh, sure?"

"If it's personal to you, you can say 'no'. You don't have to let me look if it's uncomfortable for you." I reassure her because I get the feeling she doesn't want me to look at her drawings.

"Oh, it's not that. It surprised me you wanted to look at them." She nudges it toward me, nodding toward her work. "Be my guest."

Opening the book, I study each sketch closely. Turning the pages, I'm mesmerized by the detail and variety of images I see. She clearly prefers drawing objects and nature: buildings, park benches, cars, a stained-glass window, bridges, trees, flowers, the river, the forest, and the beach. I raise my eyes to hers, finding her biting her bottom lip, eyes full of worry. "These are fantastic."

Her shoulders drop and a heavy breath leaves her lips. Her dimples make an appearance as her eyes smile at me. "Really? You think so?"

"Fuck yeah. You could sell these and make a fortune."

She laughs and I love the sound. "I don't know about that. It's only something I do for fun."

"You should think about it. My friend, Aaron, owns a café down by the river. He allows artists to display their work to sell. He takes a percentage of each sale, but the artist gets most of the money. I play soccer with him on Monday nights. I can show him this and ask what he thinks." My excitement builds at the prospect of helping Molly sell some of her work. Molly's face drops, a sheen glossing her eyes as they turn to silver. "You don't have to. It was only a suggestion." I close the book and slide it back in front of her.

She gives me a silent nod and a watery smile. "Thanks. I'll think about it."

# CHAPTER 8

## —molly—

THE SMELL OF SWEET TREATS GREETS ME AS I STEP INTO THE OFFICE. "Morning!" I call out. "What's all this?" I eye the white boxes stacked on the minuscule kitchen counter.

Max drops from the last step, carrying some type of bag over his shoulder, making his bicep bulge. "Morning! It's Thursday." As if that explains anything to me.

I open a couple of lids to check the contents inside. Tucked neatly inside are a variety of doughnuts and pastries. I can't remember the last time I could afford to splurge on some sugary goodness. Oblivious to my musings, Max unzips the bag and pulls out some type of contraption. As he works to open it, I discreetly enjoy the show he's unwittingly providing me as his muscles stretch and flex with his movements.

"Uhm, am I supposed to know what's special about Thursday?" There aren't any bookings for today. I assumed he kept the day free to catch up on office work, which he no longer needs to do now I'm here, but clearly, I'm mistaken.

He looks at me over his shoulder as he continues to set up whatever it is he's setting up. "Thursdays are dedicated to single parents. They can bring their vehicles in for a checkup, have me look at any issues they may have, or do a minor service. If I find anything major that needs further attention, I speak with the owner about it and work out a way to help them with the repairs for the lowest possible price. I don't charge them for my time, only the cost price of any parts I need to supply. It works out well for them." He stands upright after pushing the last strut into place.

A playpen. He has a playpen for the kids. Of course, he does. I'm guessing all the pastries are for the moms and dads, too. I rub the center of my chest to contain the flutters that erupt at his thoughtfulness. Not only is he providing a valuable service, but he's also making the experience special for the clients.

"If you don't mind, I'd appreciate it if you could look after the ladies and gents while they're waiting today. Normally, they mostly help themselves to the pastries and coffee, but since you're here, it would be great if they could relax a little while they wait for their car. Don't worry about doing too much office stuff. Just answer the phone when it rings." Creases form across his forehead as he waits for my answer.

"Of course. Anything you want me to do, I'll do. No problem." I gesture to the boxes of pastries. "How busy do you get?"

The tension releases from his face and he runs his fingers through his hair, drawing my eyes to the salt and pepper strands at his temple. "Pretty busy. Not everyone has their kids with them because some of them are at school, but some customers have young babies and/or toddlers, so it can get pretty noisy in here."

"How do I know if they're a single parent and not just a regular customer? Do they have some sort of token or something?"

He folds his arms across his chest and uses his thumbnail to rub back and forth across his bottom lip. I notice he does that often. I have to make a concerted effort to concentrate on his words and not get lost in thinking about what that lip would feel like against my skin. "There's a sign on the front door that says today is single parent day. No bookings required." He motions with his head toward the front door.

"But anyone could walk through the door and pretend they're a hard-up single parent. How do you monitor it?" This world is full of scammers, and I would hate to think someone would take advantage of Max's generosity.

He raises one shoulder in a careless shrug. "I work on honesty and hope my clients do the same. I've had no issues so far, and I've been doing this for a while." If it's worked this long, who am I to question it?

I nod. "Okay. Sure thing. I'll check the bathroom is clean." The cleaner came by Tuesday night, and I think he comes back on Saturday morning, so I don't think it'll hurt to give it a once over.

"Thanks, Molly. Can you please set up the changing table in there? It's upstairs. I'll run up and grab it." He makes his way up the stairs, two at a time, allowing me a superb view of his ass. To say I haven't enjoyed my man candy this past week would be an outright lie. But he's my boss and I can't go there. I desperately need to keep this job and falling for my hot boss would be a disaster. But there's no reason I can't enjoy the view. Right?

I grab the bucket of cleaning supplies and get to work cleaning the toilet, vanity, and basin. I check there are spare rolls of toilet paper close by and that the paper towel dispenser is full. It doesn't take long before it's pristine and I have the changing table set up in the corner, making the space tighter than it normally is.

I unlock the front door and our first client walks in with a toddler in tow. "Good morning, welcome to Stanfield Auto Repairs. How can we help you today?"

"I've been having trouble starting my car. I was hoping Max would have time this morning to take a look?" Max steps out of the bathroom in his overalls and the woman's eyes light up, raking over him in a not-so-subtle sweep. Her lips widen as her eyes sparkle. "Max!"

"Oh hey, Georgia. Car troubles?" He steps closer to her, reaching out for the toddler, who giggles wildly as Max tickles him. "Hey, Ryan."

"Yeah. I'm having trouble getting it started some mornings. I'm hoping it's not the battery."

He holds out his hand. "Let's take a look." She lowers her car keys into Max's hand, and he closes his fingers around them, her touch lingering beyond what would be deemed respectable. I resist, barely, rolling my eyes at her overt flirting. I bet it happens a lot on Thursdays. Max holds out his hand toward me. "Georgia, this is my new office manager, Molly. She'll take care of you while I work on your car."

From that point on, the day is a flurry of men, women, and children coming and going. I spend the day making cups of coffee and tea, handing out pastries, and playing with babies and toddlers of all shapes and sizes. It's crazy, but Max seems to be in his element. He's always happy when he's working on the cars and trucks he repairs, but today he has a pep in his step. Obviously, he likes that he's helping people who need a little extra. He reminds me of myself when I do my volunteer work. Something I want to get back to.

After the last client leaves, I lock the door and peer around the small office. It appears as though a storm has come through the small space. One lone box of pastries is left sitting on the counter. The chairs are all over the place after a game of musical chairs this afternoon; the bin is piled high with used paper cups and napkins, and I'm exhausted. I have no clue how Max must be feeling. He hasn't stopped since this morning, missing lunch altogether. I'm working up the energy to clean up the office when Max steps into the room. His overalls are filthy, and he has grease on his forehead. He looks tired but pleased. Genuinely pleased.

"Today was a great day. Thanks for all of your help. I got through more cars than usual because I didn't need to keep stopping to answer the phone and meet with the clients. That information sheet you made up this morning for each client to fill out helped streamline things."

My chest puffs up with pride. I'm thrilled I could help to make his job easier. "I figured if they quickly jotted down what the issue was, it would save you having to stop working to speak with the client. I'm glad it worked." Once I saw the time he was wasting this morning, I quickly drafted a check-in sheet and asked the clients to complete it. It just had some basic information and space for a brief explanation of the issues they were having with their vehicle. I then attached the sheet to a clipboard and hung it with the keys on the hooks.

Moving toward the bathroom, he undoes the fasteners of his overalls as he speaks with me, exposing his T-shirt. "It worked really well. I'm thinking maybe we can put it in place on our regular days too. What do you think?"

"I can do that. No problem at all. I noticed a couple of changes I'd like to make to it. If you have any suggestions, let me know and I'll add them to the form."

He nods. "Thanks. I'll take a closer look at it tonight." He closes the bathroom door behind him, and I get to work on rearranging the chairs back into position and cleaning up the small kitchen.

When he steps back out, he's wearing his jeans and T-shirt from this morning, his hair's wet and his forehead is now clear of grease. As he steps past me, his clean scent wafts behind him and I discreetly suck in a lungful of the delicious smell.

*Shameful, I know!*

He works to collapse the playpen I've already sterilized while I disinfect the changing table and bring it out for him to pack away.

"So, what made you start doing this?"

"What, fixing cars?"

"No, I mean helping single parents the way you do?"

He stops what he's doing to face me. "My sister was a single mom for a long time. I saw her struggle to make ends meet and figured if I could help one person, it would be worth it. In the beginning, people were wary of the offer, but it's grown over time and people in the local community have learned to trust that I'm not trying to rip them off or get them back in for more expensive work."

"Well, I think it's very noble of you. Each person who stepped through that door this morning was stressed." I wave my arm out toward the front door. "When they left, I could see the difference in their features and their posture. They were relieved that they had one less thing to worry about. Thanks to you."

He drops his head down, but not before I notice his cheeks flush, and a smile touch his lips. "Thanks. I like to help where I can."

The sun sits low on the horizon as I slow in front of the old brick building. It has great character and I'd love to sketch it some time. After finding a parking space just down the road, I draw in a deep breath and exit my car. The area doesn't look all that pleasant, so I double-check my locks are engaged. The last thing I need is for my car and all of my belongings to get stolen.

As I step through the large doors, an older lady greets me with a broad smile on her friendly face. She has a warm and welcoming demeanor about her, which instantly puts me at ease. I'm guessing it works well for her in this environment.

Appearances are obviously deceiving because the inside of the building is nothing like the outside. It's clean with simple but modern furnishings. The place has a welcoming vibe, much like the woman who greets me.

"Welcome to *Shelter*. My name is Simone. Come, sit." She gestures toward a couple of comfy chairs off to the side.

"Hi, Simone. I'm Molly."

"How's your day been, Molly?" She asks as she steps toward a counter along the side wall, complete with a coffee machine, kettle, and cups. "Would you like a cup of tea or coffee?"

"I wouldn't mind a coffee, thanks. No sugar, but I'll take cream." She smiles and nods at my preference, then directs her attention to making my drink. "Today's been great. Crazy busy, but awesome."

She turns toward me, her eyebrows raised. "You sound thoroughly pleased." Bringing our drinks over, she places them on the coffee table and then takes a seat in the chair opposite mine. "What brings you to *Shelter* today, Molly?"

I give her my best smile. "Well, I'm new to the area. Back home, I used to volunteer a couple of nights a week at the local women's shelter, and I wanted to do the same here." I take a sip of my drink, hoping there's some way I can help. "If the opportunity is available," I add.

Simone's smile widens, her eyes twinkling. "We can always do with volunteers. How wonderful of you to offer your time. Can I ask where you volunteered previously?"

"Sure. I moved here from Portland, Maine recently. I used to volunteer at *FemCity*. I would help with the sign-in registrations, chatting with the ladies, setting up the beds for the night, cleaning, and putting together the overnight toiletry kits. Oh, and I'd help in the kitchen if needed. Though, to be completely honest, I think I was more a hindrance than help in the kitchen." I chuckle.

"You sound like me. I'm terrible in the kitchen, too. When were you thinking of starting and how many evenings can you help?" Simone asks, leaning forward to collect her coffee.

"I'm happy to help maybe two or three nights a week and I can start anytime you want me."

"Sounds perfect. Would you mind completing some paperwork and then I'll give you the tour?" She takes a sip of her coffee. "I hope you don't mind, but we do need to run a background check. It only takes a few moments."

I nod, eagerly. This sounds promising. "That's not a problem at all. They had to do the same thing at *FemCity*, so I was expecting it."

Simone heads to another room and returns with a clipboard and a couple of pages of forms that I need to complete. "If you wouldn't mind completing these. Then I'll show you around. We'll start getting some ladies coming in soon, I expect."

I set to work filling out the paperwork but come up against a snag. I don't have an address. Shit! "Uhm, I don't have a permanent address yet. I only arrived on Saturday. Is it okay if I give you the address for where I work?"

Her eyes narrow ever so slightly. "Where are you staying?"

"Just couch surfing with some friends at the moment. As soon as I get a permanent spot, I'll let you know." I don't want to tell her I'm sleeping in my car because I have very little money. When I was young, Mom and I would only use the women's shelter on freezing nights. She never wanted to take a bed away from someone who was worse off than us. She always said that while we had our car, we weren't truly homeless. As an adult, I've learned that's not technically true, but I still don't want to take a bed from someone who needs it more than I do. Mom taught me all the tricks of the trade for surviving in a car and I'm managing okay so far.

"Sure. That shouldn't be a problem." She gives me a reassuring smile. "I quickly need to check that we're ready for registrations. Be back in a minute." I nod as Simone pats my arm on the way past me, then I continue to complete the forms.

I hand Simone my completed forms, and we begin the tour. "This is obviously where we meet with women as they come through the door. We like to have a quick chat first to find out how we can help. This facility has space for women who need short-term accommodation as well as overnight facilities to escape a night on the street. Unfortunately, we never seem to have enough beds, but we do our best. We find it best to offer our ladies the opportunity to have a warm drink during our initial chat. Like we just did." She smiles at me, then guides me around the corner. "We have a play area here for the little ones."

The area is well decked out with a playpen, similar to the one we used today at the workshop. There are toys that would suit different ages, from babies up to young children. There's a small table in the corner with a collection of writing and coloring pencils, as well as a pile of coloring and puzzle books. "Wow. This area looks great. I bet it's popular."

"Yeah. These kids have very little, most only have the clothes on their backs. Having this area set up gives them a sense of fun. It allows them to be kids for a little while, at least." I nod in agreement. As a kid, I thought it was the absolute best when Mom bought me a new coloring book. I always made it last as long as possible, only coloring a small amount each day.

We walk down a short hallway to a dining area. "This is the dining room. We have tea and coffee-making facilities that are accessible to our ladies. A microwave, fridge, stove, and toaster. We want the women that stop in here for any length of time to have a sense of independence. Often, they've lost that in their situation."

The tables are arranged as you would find in any restaurant. At the last shelter I volunteered, the dining room looked more like a mess hall.

Long stainless steel tables with chairs on either side. It didn't allow for this level of personal interaction.

"Are you available to stay and help tonight?"

"Absolutely. Put me to work."

"Great, I might get you to come back and restock the counter over here with tea and coffee." I nod. "Also, on the nights you volunteer, feel free to grab a meal and join the ladies. We find it a great way to interact with the women in a way that's non-threatening and less invasive. They tend to open up more about their situation when you share a meal with them."

I'm loving the sound of this place. "That sounds like a great approach."

Simone gives me one of her warm smiles. "We do our best to make our ladies feel comfortable and at home." She guides me out of the dining room and into the kitchen. "This is where the meal prep and cooking takes place." A small woman, probably in her fifties, with bright pink hair is checking something in the oven. "This is Rhonda, our cook."

"Hi, Rhonda." I give her a small wave.

"Rhonda. This is Molly. Molly is going to be volunteering with us. She recently moved all the way from Portland, Maine."

Rhonda wipes her hands on the side of her pants and holds out her hand. I shake it. "Wow. That's a long way away. What made you move over here?"

I shrug and swallow down the lump that always forms at the thought of why I've moved all the way to the opposite side of the country. "Wanted a fresh start, I guess."

"Well, it's great to have you on board. We can always do with more volunteers."

"I'm excited about getting started."

"I'm giving Molly the tour. Then she's going to come through to top up the tea and coffee center. If there's anything you need her to do, let her know."

Rhonda nods and waves us away. "Rhonda's been with us since we opened. She has quite the story to tell and will happily share it with you."

"I would imagine there are a lot of stories within these walls." Some of them may even be similar to Mom's.

"You bet." She waves her arm out as we enter a large dormitory. "This is one of our dormitories. We have three dormitories. Twelve beds in each. This dormitory doesn't have any cribs. It's for women who don't have children."

The room has twelve simple beds, divided by low panels to offer a semblance of privacy. There's a single lockable cabinet and a large drawer beneath each bed. The area is spotless—ready and waiting for tonight's guests. Simone shows me through the other two dorms and then takes me to the back of the building.

"Here we have ten small rooms which have two beds and cribs in each. We can have up to twenty women staying for up to six weeks at a time. It's enough time to help them get on their feet. As you're probably already aware, not all women are ready or at the point where they trust they can make the change toward a life away from the streets."

I nod. "Yeah. Some women don't have that trust in themselves that they're good enough to win and hold on to a job, which makes it difficult to gain the funds to create a home environment."

Simone hums her agreement.

The rooms are compact but offer greater privacy than the dorms we walked through earlier. Simple furniture of drawers and a wardrobe offering the feeling of permanency. We keep moving through the building to a couple of meeting rooms.

"We have Kelly, a counselor, who comes through each morning to eat breakfast with the ladies. She talks with them about their future. Any plans, dreams, and hopes they might have. Then she works with the ladies to help make things happen. We also have Jodie. She comes to us from Women's and Children's Services. She guides the women toward any assistance they're entitled to. Fortunately, we also have access to pro bono lawyers to help disentangle the women from toxic relationships when they're ready to do so."

"This place is amazing and the services you're providing for the women are incredible." I'm impressed by everything they have on offer for the women who come through this facility.

She tips her head, offering me a pleased smile. "We do our best. Our founder was once homeless, so she has a good understanding of what needed to be offered to the women."

That makes this place even more impressive. "Well, it shows. I can't wait to get started."

Simone laughs. "I love your enthusiasm. Let's get you back to the dining room. I know you said you're hopeless in the kitchen, but do you mind helping Rhonda tonight?"

"Of course not. I'm happy to help wherever you need."

We head back to the kitchen and Rhonda shows me where the stock is so that I can ensure the tea and coffee counter is well stocked. Women and children begin to trickle in, and I introduce myself throughout the evening.

Tonight's dinner is roast beef and vegetables, followed by chocolate pudding and custard, served buffet style. I learn Rhonda keeps the kitchen open until nine p.m. to ensure any late stragglers don't go to bed on an empty stomach. Even if women miss out on a bed for the night, they're encouraged to stay for a meal. The last place I volunteered closed the kitchen at seven-thirty and too bad if you came in late.

After dinner, I help Rhonda with the cleanup. Around ten, things have grown quiet. "We close the doors at ten. So, the women need to get here before then, or they don't get a bed for the night. Often the beds fill by six-thirty, anyway. It would be incredibly rare to still have a space available this late."

"Ah, there she is. I see Rhonda kept you busy for the entire evening." Simone breezes into the dining room a few minutes after ten. "How was your first day on the job?"

I blow out a tired but happy breath. After the busyness of today and then again tonight, I'm dead on my feet, but I feel amazing. "It was great. The women certainly appreciated the nutritious meal and a chance to sit and relax without having to watch over their shoulders."

Simone nods. "Yep. This is a safe place where they can let their guard down." She claps her hands together. "We close the doors at ten. We don't expect you to stay past that time. When do you think you'd like to come back?"

"Oh, uhm, maybe on Tuesday? Would it be okay if I volunteered on Tuesdays and Thursdays to start?" I shuffle on my feet, hopeful they'll be happy to have me.

"Absolutely. That'll be fantastic. You go home and get some rest and we'll see you on Tuesday."

A warm feeling fills my stomach, and I can't stop my smile. I've been in this city for less than a week and I have a job and now I have a place where I can give back to the community. Life's looking pretty great. Stepping toward Simone, I wrap my arms around her. I hope she doesn't mind, but I'm incredibly thankful for this opportunity. I need to hug her.

Simone chuckles. "It's like you're already part of the family. Right, Rhonda?"

My eyes sting and the lump in my throat feels more like a boulder at her use of the word 'family'. I guess I didn't realize how much I loved and needed my family until they were gone. I duck my head to hide the tears I'm fighting to keep at bay. "Thank you." I step over to Rhonda and embrace her too.

"It's been heaps of fun working with you. Thanks for being patient with me and showing me the ropes. Next week, I'll be an expert from the time I walk in the door."

Rhonda chuckles. "It was my pleasure. You're an easy study. I'll see you on Tuesday."

I grab my things, and Simone walks me out. "Where did you park your car?"

"Just across the street." I point in the direction I parked.

"When you come on Tuesday, there's parking around the back. Park out there, okay?" She points to a driveway at the side of the building, and I follow with my eyes.

What a relief to know I have a safer place to park my car in the future. "That's great. I was a little concerned about leaving my car on the street."

She nods. "Yeah. It's not the greatest area, but it's tough to find a building large enough to suit our needs at the right price. So, this is where we ended up."

"Okay. Well, bye. Thanks for everything."

"No. Thank you. It's been a pleasure and we'll see you on Tuesday."

I head down the steps as Simone locks the doors behind me. Even though I'm completely exhausted, I know I have a pep in my step and a smile on my face. It's been a great day. First, helping Max to help the single parents and then tonight, helping all the women who will spend tonight at *Shelter*.

I pause, looking up at the night sky. Tears sting the back of my eyes and I swallow past the lump in my throat. "It's such a great place, Mom. You'd love it here." A breeze blows a lock of hair across my forehead, and it reminds me of the times Mom would gently push my bangs out of my eyes as a child. The tears become too much to contain and fall at the memory. I scurry to my car, locking myself inside so I can have my moment in safety.

# CHAPTER 9

## —molly—

As I crouch down to collect the dirt I've swept together in the workshop, I smile to myself. Max was clearly shocked when I pulled out the broom to clean up at closing time. I've thoroughly enjoyed my first week at my new job. Max is a great boss and I think I'm going to be very happy here working with him. He works incredibly hard every single minute of every single day. I'm not sure when he had time to do his office work because he's always fully booked, with a minimum of two cars in the bays at a time. Even on Thursdays, the day he doesn't take any bookings, he's crazy busy if not busier.

I think I fell a little for my new boss last Thursday when I discovered the reason he doesn't take bookings. I mean, I'm pretty sure I developed an instant crush on him based on his looks alone, once I got past his gruff demeanor when we first met, but over the past week, he's been nothing but kind to me. He even bought lunch for me each day, which has helped me make my meager stash of food last longer.

"Are you ready to go home?" Max's deep voice reverberates through the workshop. Tilting my head back, I catch my breath as my eyes land on him in navy shorts and a white T-shirt, a bag slung over his shoulder. A navy logo of a knight's helmet surrounded by the words, *Monday Knights*, sits on his right pec. The T-shirt hugs his torso, showing the ridges of his stomach and the outline of his chest. Glancing down, I notice he has great thighs—powerful. For an older guy, he's in great shape. I wonder if he realizes how good-looking he is because he doesn't come across like he does. "Molly?" I realize I haven't answered him.

"Uh, I need to finish the cleanup for the day. Then I'll be on my way. Sorry if I'm holding you up."

"You don't need to apologize *or* clean. You know I have a cleaner come through to do it."

"I can do it as part of my job. To be honest, you don't have enough office work to keep me busy for the entire week. I'm happy to add this to my duties and save you some money."

He moves closer to me, towering over my crouched body. "I've been getting through a lot more work since you started because I don't have to keep stopping to answer calls or chase up parts. I don't want anything to distract you from doing that work."

I stand. We're only a couple of feet apart and the overhead light is highlighting the green flecks in his eyes. "It won't interfere. I'll do all of that and then do the cleaning before the shop opens and after it closes. No problem."

He studies me closely, thinning his lips, then nods slowly. "Okay. But that means I'll pay you what I would normally pay the cleaner. You don't need to clean every day either. I only have the cleaner come through twice a week."

I shuffle my feet, uncomfortable with the idea that he thinks I'm doing it to get more money. "I wasn't offering to do the cleaning for extra money. You're paying me enough to do both jobs already. I was hoping to save *you* some money."

He drops his bag, then turns on his heel to head back to the office. "We'll work it out." He calls over his shoulder as he disappears inside. I notice the number seven on the back of his shirt with STANFIELD in bold print across the top. I crouch back down to sweep up the mess and a couple of minutes later, he returns to me with a set of keys and the code for the alarm. "You may as well have a set of keys in case I'm late or need to leave before you." He shows me how to work the alarm system, which is similar to the one at my last job. "Make sure you lock everything up tight, okay? I have a lot of money tied up in the tools and equipment, not to mention the project car I'm working on." He nods his head to the farthest bay and the car I've been sketching.

"Don't worry. I get how important it is to keep this place secure. You can trust me." He studies me for a long moment and my body heats under his gaze. I'm going to need to shut down my reaction; a crush on my hot boss is not something I can afford. I need to sort myself out before I even think about getting involved with anyone, especially this sexy man.

Once I'm on my own, I turn up the music and dance around as I sweep. I've missed my morning run for a while now and I desperately need to move my body. I freeze in place when I realize I'm happy for the first time in weeks.

Mom would want me to move forward and be happy, but I'm quickly filling up with guilt. Mom never let anything stop her or slow her down, and she shared the importance of moving forward with me. She always said that it was okay to have my time for wallowing when something didn't work out, but then I had to pick myself up, make a plan, and move forward. She wouldn't want me to dwell on my losses, but it's tough when I've lost so much.

Without my family, I feel adrift; they were my anchor, my port that I knew I could always rely on. Now, I only have myself and it's a scary prospect. I think about Mom when she ran away from home: seventeen, pregnant, and completely alone. Living in her car and never knowing where she was going to get her next meal. She must have been terrified for her future, but she made it through. If she can do it with a baby on the way, I can do it too.

I wipe away the tears tracking down my cheeks and finish my task more somberly. Turning everything off, I secure the building, and head to the location I found close by on the weekend. It means I'm not using a lot of gas commuting to and from work, saving me some precious dollars until I get paid on Friday. The sports field comes into view as do the dozens and dozens of cars and trucks filling the parking lot. My lungs deflate in disappointment.

Teenagers are playing multiple games of soccer as grown men run laps around the perimeter of the field. I doubt I'm going to find a park while everyone's here. Driving past, a matte black Dodge Charger catches my eye. At lunchtime, Max said he was playing soccer tonight and he was dressed for sport when he left the workshop. I'm guessing this is where he is. The temptation to stop and watch him play is strong and after a few seconds of internal debate, I decide to do it. I'll stay away from the action, so he won't see me.

I eventually find a park at the far end of the lot and sit on the hood of my car to watch the action. Once everyone leaves, I can move my car to the spot behind the building where I normally park. It's mostly hidden from the road, and nobody's bothered me on the nights I've used it.

Watching the teenage kids playing brings a lump to my throat. Ethan loved playing soccer. He always moved with ease, maneuvering the ball away from their goal toward their strikers and the opposing team's goal. He would dodge left and right between his opponents with a bright smile because he was doing something that he truly loved. I wipe my cheeks as my emotions get the better of me yet again. Shaking my head mildly, I smile at the memory of him receiving a trophy last season for being the fairest and best player on his team. It's stashed away with all of my other treasures.

A group of men run past, laughing and pushing at each other, shirts tucked into the back of their shorts, leaving their torsos sweaty and bare.

*Oh, boy!*

This really was a good idea. I think this might become my favorite Monday night activity.

Another group follows behind and I notice they're wearing the same-colored shorts and T-shirts Max had on when he left. These guys are equally bare and equally sweaty. My eyes catch on a dark head of hair above everyone else in the group. My heartbeat picks up speed as he smiles at his friend. I duck my head at the last second, hoping he doesn't notice me. As they run past, I raise my eyes to find him staring directly at me over his shoulder. Shit, he's caught me. He raises his eyebrows at me, gifting me a gorgeous smile, then turns forward to continue his run with his teammates. He passes by once more before they stop to do some stretches and run some warm-up drills.

Three whistles blow, indicating the end of the teenage games. The boys leave the field after congratulating the winning team and the men make their way onto the field. I wish I had some snacks to enjoy while I watch Max play his game, but I need to be sparing with the food I have. He already knows I'm here; I may as well move closer to the field so I can enjoy the game properly. I rummage through my car to dig out a blanket to sit on and take up a spot on the sidelines. The guys get into position, and I'm pleased to see that Max takes up the same position Ethan used to play.

For forty-five minutes, I watch the guys run, dribble, and pass the ball from player to player. Max's team is getting hammered by the other team. My voice is becoming hoarse from all the cheering I'm doing, and it feels great to have a genuine smile and enjoy the moment. I'm not thinking about my worries or where I'm going to sleep tonight. I'm having fun, like any other woman my age. The guys move off the field during halftime, grabbing drinks and laughing amongst themselves. I figure, while they're taking a break, I'll use the bathroom facilities before they're locked for the night.

Max is leaning up against the wall as I step out of the building, his arms crossed over his chest, his legs crossed at the ankles. His posture looks casual, but his face is another matter. His eyebrows are drawn down low and his mouth is tight. Glancing across to the field, I see the game has already started. He notices me and stands straight, towering over me. "Are you okay?"

I look down at myself, my eyes scanning all around. "Yeah, why?" It's funny. I thought the first thing he would ask about is why I'm here watching him play soccer.

"You were in the bathroom for a long time. I got … worried." I'm stunned he noticed. It took me a while, because I brushed my teeth, and wiped myself down in all the important places since I won't get a shower tonight.

"I'm fine, truly. You don't need to miss your game for me." I wave my arm out toward the field. He studies me closely, then nods his head once.

"You sticking around 'til the end?" he asks as he jogs backward away from me.

I have nothing else to do or anywhere else to be, so I shrug. "Yeah, I figured I'd wait so I could congratulate the other team on hammering your ass into the ground." I snicker.

His eyebrows shoot up and a sexy half-smile touches his lips. "We'll see." He turns and jogs straight onto the field and I can't believe he left his teammates a man down while he was checking on me.

The last half of the game is intense. Max's team has upped the ante, scoring three goals in twenty-five minutes and not allowing any past their defense. They need to hold the other team until the end of the game, and they'll have the win.

In the last five minutes, the other team hits the back of the net, leveling the score. The excitement and energy are palpable on the field and off as Max wins the ball from the center pass and expertly dribbles it down the wing before passing it to their striker. I hold my breath as he lines the ball up and strikes the ball with a powerful force. Only seconds are left on the clock as the ball hits the back of the net. Max and the other guy go ballistic, running toward each other and falling over in an all-out hugfest.

The whistle blows three times, and their other teammates join in, piling on top of the pair, and jumping up and down as though they've won the World Cup. I'm cheering and celebrating on the sidelines as though they've won the Cup. It's crazy good!

I'm jumping around like a madwoman when a pair of muscular arms wrap around my body from behind, spinning me around, and lifting me off of my feet. My heart rate spikes until I realize it's only Max. His smile is wide and his eyes are sparkling with sheer elation. Sweat trickles down the side of his face, his hair sticking to his head, and he looks so freaking good. "I guess you won't need to congratulate the other team, hey?" He puts me down and I'm disappointed that I'm no longer trapped against his body.

I fake pout, shaking my head. "Very disappointing to see them come undone like that. They showed such promise."

"Oh yeah? Are you some kind of soccer expert?" My mood drops as I remember all the hours spent watching soccer games on television and attending practices and matches for Ethan. "Are you okay?"

I mustn't have hidden my thoughts well enough. Looking back up at Max, I nod. "Yeah." I clear my throat, putting a fake smile on my face. "You guys played a great second half and that last goal ..." I mime a chef's kiss. "Beautiful teamwork."

"You wanna come celebrate with me and the boys at Brady's Pub? It's close to here."

I brush off his offer with a flick of my wrist. I'm sure he didn't mean to ask. He's just excited about the win. "I didn't play, so there's no need for me to celebrate."

"You helped us win with your cheering and dancing along the sidelines. You had some sensational moves, by the way." *Is he flirting with me? My hot boss.* "You should celebrate with us." He winks.

"Nah. You go have fun with your teammates. I'll see you at work in the morning."

"You coming, Max?" A couple of the guys call out to Max from several feet away, then they tip their heads to me. "Thanks for the entertainment, Blondie!"

I was so caught up in the excitement of the game and cheering the guys on that I didn't stop to think that I might cause a scene. My cheeks heat and I drop my head to look at my shoes. How embarrassing. "I'm sorry if I caused a scene and embarrassed you."

"You didn't cause a scene, and you definitely didn't embarrass me. Maybe yourself though ..." He laughs, leaving the sentence hanging. He waves them off over his shoulder, calling out, "Meet you at Brady's." His friends walk toward the parking lot, leaving him behind, and I shuffle on my feet. How am I going to get out of this? "C'mon. See, the guys honestly appreciated your support. One drink and some pizza. My buy." When I take my time responding, he asks, "Do you have somewhere else you need to be?"

"No, it's … uh … I don't want to intrude." I don't want to tell him I have barely any money to get me by until payday, because he seems like the type of guy who would give me money and I don't want him to do that. It's important to me he doesn't know about my situation.

"You're not intruding. You can follow me." He runs back to collect his things, then drops to the grass at my feet to change out of his cleats. Standing, he pulls his T-shirt over his head, exposing his torso to me at close range. It's the first time I've seen him completely bare. My eyes scan the expanse of toned flesh, pausing above his heart where he has a tattoo. I step closer to get a better look at the inked design in the limited light. My fingers lift without permission to trace over the intricately designed mechanical heart which looks to be inside his chest; the skin having been torn open and pulled out of the way. The muscle in his chest flinches at my touch and I realize how inappropriate it is for me to touch him in this way, so I quickly snatch my fingers back.

My eyes snap up to his. "Sorry. I … I didn't realize I had touched you. I was engrossed in the detailed design."

He glances down at the tattoo. "It's okay. I guess I've become accustomed to it, I forget it's there half the time."

"It's beautifully detailed in its design. The artist is very talented." Dropping my eyes away from his, they catch on another tattoo on the opposite side of his body. On his flank, he has an open wound that is bleeding oil instead of blood. I smile as I look back up at his face. "I'm sensing a theme here." I wave my finger around in the general direction of his torso.

"Lincoln," he thumbs over his shoulder toward the parking lot, "did them for me. He owns a tattoo shop." He shrugs. "I've always loved cars. Looking at them, working with them. It's in my blood." He runs his hand over the heart tattoo and then down further across the wound.

I nod. "I can see that."

He pulls a fresh shirt over his head, stealing my view. "C'mon, let's go or there'll be nothing left by the time we get to the pub."

"Do other women join you guys after your game?"

"Hell, no. No women allowed."

My eyebrows jump up. "Then why are you inviting me?" I wave

my arm down my body and his eyes track the action. "In case you didn't notice, I'm a woman."

"Believe me, I noticed." His eyes slowly make their way back to mine. There's heat in them if I'm not mistaken. "I'm nominating you as head of our cheer squad, so you're part of the team now." He wraps his arm around my neck and drags me along with him toward the parking lot. "You wanna come with me? I can drop you back here afterward."

I push at him, wiggling from his hold. "Ewww, you smell." Not really, but he was making my stomach flip, and I needed some space to keep myself in check. It looks as though he's not going to take no for an answer and a slice of pizza and a pint of beer sounds awesome right about now. "Sure. That sounds good, but can I trust you not to drink and drive?"

"You have my word. I'll keep you safe. Promise." Even though I don't know him very well, I get the sense he's a man of his word.

# CHAPTER 10

## —max—

I HAVE TO ADMIT; I WAS COMPLETELY WRONG ABOUT MOLLY. I MADE assumptions about the girl sleeping in her car that were way off base. Yeah, she's fucking gorgeous, but she doesn't shove it in your face and her looks don't seem to be her priority. She's a hard worker who isn't afraid to get her hands dirty. Over the last three weeks, I've found her to be thoughtful, sweet, and friendly, if not a little guarded. Her capabilities in the office have helped to streamline some aspects that I never knew needed streamlining. And tonight, well, that was the icing on the cake. When I spotted her sitting on the hood of her car while I was warming up, I couldn't stop myself from showing off a little. I'm a decade older than her—not to mention I'm her boss—and have no business trying to attract her attention. But I wanted her to look at me and to like what she saw.

I grab her slender hand as we step over the threshold into Brady's. "The guys are usually in the back booths in the corner. Follow me." Not once on the way here did she worry about what she's wearing or the fact that she had no makeup on or that her hair is a mess. *It's fucking refreshing.*

Those dimples I love so much, make an appearance as she nods her head. She's still an enigma. She's shared very little about where she's from or what brought her to this city. It's not my business, but I sense she doesn't have many people around her—if any at all—and I wonder why that is. I guess I have to be patient and give her time to get used to me, to trust me enough to share her story. And I think she's going to have quite a story. Sometimes I catch her lost in thought, her eyes glassy and I wonder what's made her sad.

The boys spot us through the crowd, their faces lighting up at the sight of Molly. There was a fair amount of discussion about her during the half-time break until I announced she was my new office manager and told them to cut it out. For some reason, I didn't like them talking about her like she's just a hot body and pretty face. She's so much more than that.

Finn stands, allowing the two of us to slide in, then he takes his position at the end of the booth. He needs to sit on the end in case he needs to see to anything behind the bar. "Pizzas should be out in a minute."

The guys pat their stomachs, showing they're ready to demolish the dozen or so pizzas Finn supplies each week during soccer season. We try to make up for his generosity by buying drinks and eating here at other times during the week.

"Guys, this is Molly, my new office manager. Molly, this is Finn, Gary, Aaron, Lincoln, Brent, Rob, Sean, Matthew, Thomas, and Kevin." I point to each of my friends as I introduce them. "We'll have a quiz at the end of the night to see if you remember their names." Her eyes widen as I laugh. "Only joking."

She waves timidly at the group. "Hi, guys." She chuckles. "I don't think I'll remember all of your names, but I'll do my best."

Everyone says hello and offers her a free pass on remembering everyone's names. Gary stands. "Anyone want a drink while I'm at the bar?"

I pull out my wallet. "I'll take a beer." Turning toward Molly, I ask, "How about you, Dimples? What would you like to drink?"

She chuckles at my nickname but doesn't question it. I'm guessing she's probably been called it more than once. "I'll have the same as you, thanks."

Gary taps the table, takes my money, then heads up to the bar. He has to weave his way through the crowd. I swear it gets busier and busier every Monday night.

Aaron grabs Molly's attention. "So, Molly. What's it like working for this ogre?" He points his half-empty beer toward me.

"Fuck off! I'm a good boss, aren't I, Molly?" I nudge her arm with mine.

"Shut up! She can't answer honestly now that you've said that."

Aaron laughs. He gathers his composure, locking eyes with the girl next to me. "Seriously. Is he being good to you?"

She studies me for a few moments, her eyes scanning my face, then she turns her focus to Aaron. "He's been a great boss so far. I have no complaints and I'm not only saying that because he's sitting next to me." She bumps her shoulder against mine and gifts me with her dimples. I think I could grow addicted to her smiles.

The servers bring out the pizzas and Gary returns with our drinks. The talk around the tables dies down as we dig in. It's not until we've demolished almost all the pizzas that we slow down and chatter starts up again.

"How's Layla? Is she feeling any better?" I ask Gary.

He smiles at me, wiping his mouth. "She *is* feeling better. I was going to tell you guys something earlier, but we got sidetracked with our new cheerleader over there." He tips his head toward Molly, then stands. "Guys, if I can have your attention for a moment." Everyone quiets down, even the other patrons close by. "I've been wanting to tell you guys for a few weeks now, but Layla insisted we wait. Layla's pregnant. We're expecting our first baby!" His smile takes up his entire face as we all jump up to congratulate him. Even Molly congratulates him as though she's known him for years. Well, that explains Layla's sickness over the last few months.

Gary pulls out a square piece of paper to pass around. "Here's our first baby photo." He hands it to Molly first, and she studies it closely, then passes it to me. A pang of longing hits me out of the blue. I'm getting up there in age and I'm wondering if I'll ever meet someone and have a family of my own, or am I destined to always be the favorite uncle?

*Okay, I'm the only uncle, but I'm still the favorite!*

"If you ever need a babysitter, I'd be happy to help. I used to love looking after my baby brother." Molly offers. She never mentions much at all about her family or her life, so I'm surprised by the mention of a brother. I'm not sure she's mentioned him before. I'm dying to ask her about her family, but I sense it's not something she wants to talk about since she never brings them up. As much as I want to ask her more, delve into her history, this is not the time nor the place.

"Thanks. I'll let Layla know. It's been tough trying to get pregnant. I'm not sure she'll ever want to leave Junior behind." He huffs out a short laugh.

I feel like an asshole. I never knew they were even trying to conceive let alone that they were having trouble. "Well, congrats, man. I'm thrilled for you both. You're gonna make great parents," I tell him.

He glances down at the beer in his hands. "Thanks, man."

I spot Molly trying to hide a yawn. "You want me to drop you back to your car?"

She looks around the table. "You guys aren't done here, are you?"

I shrug. "We can leave whenever we're ready. I don't mind."

"If you're sure. Suddenly, I'm exhausted." She gives me an embarrassed smile.

I stand, then help her up. "See ya, guys. We're out."

Everyone says goodbye and I lead Molly out through the crowd, which doesn't seem to have thinned out any.

"I genuinely liked your friends. They seem like a great bunch of guys." She finishes her sentence with another yawn.

"Yeah. We've all known each other for a while now. Been playing as a team since we finished high school."

"I bet Gary and Layla are excited about their new baby."

I turn to glance at her in the limited light inside my car. She's genuinely excited for my friend. A man she's only just met. I hate to compare her to Mona, but she never gave my friends the time of day. She seemed to think she was better than them. Better than everyone.

"I didn't know they had been trying to have a baby. I felt like a real asshole to learn that tonight."

"It's probably not something they wanted people to know. You shouldn't feel bad about it." I pull into the parking lot at the sports field and stop behind Molly's car. "Thanks for tonight. It was heaps of fun. I'll see you at work tomorrow."

"Thanks for joining us. The boys enjoyed having you there." I lift my chin toward her car. "Get in. I'll follow you back to your motel to make sure you're safe."

Her head snaps up to mine. "Oh, you don't have to do that. I'm fine."

"I know I don't have to. I want to make sure you get home safe."

She gives me a tight smile but doesn't argue. Hopefully, she's learned that I don't back down easily on important things and that her safety is important to me. I reverse, giving her space to leave the parking lot, and then follow her fifteen minutes down the road to a dive motel. Slowing, I watch her drive into the central parking lot of the motel, which leads to the rooms. I don't like where she's staying; it looks too rundown.

I wonder if I should stop and walk her to her door. Perhaps that would be too much. I'll see her at work tomorrow. I don't think she'd appreciate my chivalry at this point, since I've already hijacked her evening.

# CHAPTER 11

## —max—

THE SUN IS ON THE RISE AS I MAKE MY WAY TO WORK. I CAN'T BELIEVE Molly's been working with me for a month already. The difference has been incredible. My home life has returned to being my break away from work and I'm able to work on more cars because I don't have to deal with as many interruptions. The Sprint is almost ready to sell because I've had my mornings free to focus on her. That woman has been a godsend. I'm grateful she decided to sleep behind my workshop all those weeks ago when she first arrived in town.

I glance across at the sports field where we lost our game last night. Even though we lost, I still feel energized by the challenge we gave the other team in the second half. It was a damn close game in the end. Turning back to face forward, a blue Jetta parked behind the building catches my eye. Changing lanes, I make my way into the parking lot and pull in behind the car that I'm pretty sure belongs to Molly.

Jumping out, I walk over to check it out.

*What in the actual fuck?*

She's fucking asleep in the front passenger seat, blankets up at the windows. I'm guessing to give her some semblance of privacy.

I don't want to scare her, so I gently tap the front window where the shade has slipped down to get her attention. She doesn't hear me, so I tap again, slightly louder. Meanwhile, my agitation at seeing her sleeping in a fucking parking lot is growing. I'm pissed that she's put herself at risk like this. What the fuck was wrong with the motel I followed her to last week? I tap louder and she finally stirs. Her eyes open slowly, and she looks around as if trying to locate the source of the noise. Her eyes widen and she bolts upright when her steely eyes finally connect with mine.

I gesture for her to open her door and it seems to take an age for her to do so. Moving around to her door once the lock disengages, I rip it open, surprised it doesn't come off from the hinges.

"Why in the fuck are you sleeping here in your car? What happened to the motel?" I snap.

She tosses her blanket away and climbs out of her car. Her hair's disheveled and her eyes are full of sleep, but she still looks stunning. Straightening her shoulders, her nipples press against the T-shirt she has on as she pulls her hair out of the tie and works her long hair into a fresh ponytail, making her tits jiggle.

"It's not your concern, Max. You're my boss. What I do with my time away from work is not your business," she firmly states, as though it doesn't fucking matter that she's sleeping in her car in a public parking lot.

I work to temper my anger. "Did something happen at the motel that you didn't feel safe there?" As if she would feel safe in a fucking parking lot.

She looks down at her socks, shuffling from foot to foot. "I'd rather not talk about it. I need to get ready for work. I'll see you there soon."

I try to soften further. Perhaps coming at her like a tyrant isn't the way to go. Running my fingers through my hair, I notice her eyes follow the action. "Look, I'm sorry. I was worried about you when I saw you sleeping in your car. I thought you were staying in a motel; that you were safe. I shouldn't have snapped at you like that." Stepping back, I give her space. "I'll, uh, see you at work. Feel free to use the shower in the office, if you need."

She nods, her posture softening. "Thank you." Molly's eyes have a suspicious sheen to them as she turns away from me and I take the hint, leaving her to do whatever she needs to do.

Footsteps sound across the workshop floor as I'm polishing the final panel on the Sprint. I'll be able to put her up for sale this week. It's been a long time coming. Glancing across, I see Molly carrying her things into the office, her head down low. I'm glad she's taken up my offer to use the bathroom. Heading across the road, I grab a breakfast sandwich for each of us. I have a proposition for my employee, and I want to make sure she can make a decision with a clear head, which means she needs food.

The shower turns off, and I set about making two cups of coffee. Her steps stall as she opens the bathroom door, her eyes locked on the office desk. I have two seats set at the desk and two sandwiches. I give her a smile as I carry our coffee to the desk and gesture for her to take a seat opposite me. Looking down at her feet, she slowly makes her way over to me and takes a seat, keeping her spine ramrod straight.

"Thank you," she whispers, eyeing the sandwich in front of her. She takes a sip of her coffee and then her first bite of the breakfast I bought for her. I keep my mouth shut for now, opting to eat in silence.

The atmosphere is stifling and uncomfortable. I've always found her company to be easy and relaxed but this morning is different. It's as though an immense brick wall has been built between us.

*I don't fucking like it.*

Halfway through my breakfast, I can't take it any longer. "I'm guessing you still haven't found somewhere permanent to live?" I keep my tone neutral, hoping we can have a conversation about her living arrangements.

Her shoulders rise and fall. She shakes her head in the negative, not making eye contact with me. "Uh, no."

"Do you have any family here?" I prod.

"No." Still, her eyes remain downcast.

"What about friends?"

She shakes her head. "No."

The situation is worse than I thought, and I can't believe the asshole that I am and that I didn't push sooner. "Can I ask why you moved here if you had nobody for support?" I know it's a fucking personal question and none of my business, but I can't suppress the questions running rampant in my head.

She shrugs, then slowly brings her silver gaze up to mine. "I don't know. It seemed like as good a place as any to start over. My mom grew up here and I wanted to see the place for myself." She's curled in on herself, trying to make herself as small as possible.

*I don't fucking like it.*

I want to know why she needed a place to start over, but I need to focus on the matter at hand. Getting her off the street. "If your mom grew up here, maybe you have some family that you've never met." I offer. "Have you thought to look them up?"

"I don't know, to be honest. My mom left when she was seventeen." She shrugs again like it doesn't matter, but I caught the hurt in her eyes.

"It might be worth a shot to look for your mom's family." I hedge, trying not to be too pushy, but I can't stand the thought that she has nobody. I mean, she has me, but I'm only her boss and maybe we have the early stages of a friendship but that's not enough.

She hums. "Maybe." Standing, she takes her wrapper to the trash and her cup to the sink before coming back to collect mine.

"I have something to show you. Come with me." I take hold of her hand and tug her toward the stairs. The smooth, unblemished skin of her hand is a stark contrast to my stained work-roughened one. The other thing I notice is how well our hands fit together. It makes me wonder how well other parts of us might fit together. My dick decides he likes that idea and I will him back to sleep.

"Oh-kay," she slowly says as we take the first step.

I open the door at the top of the stairs and move to the side to allow Molly space to enter, her rose scent tickling my nose as she passes me. "I was thinking you might like to move in here until you find a better place." I swing my arm out. With wide eyes, Molly steps into the small apartment. "It's not much, but it's better than that motel or your car. I can't believe I didn't think to tell you about this space sooner."

She's quiet for long moments as she walks around the space, bypassing the changing table and portable playpen I use on Thursdays, checking out the bedroom with its double bed and small bathroom-come-laundry. The apartment isn't anything special, but it was good enough for me until I could afford my home.

I move over to the exterior door. "This is another door, so you can come and go as you please without worrying about the alarm in the workshop. It has a separate alarm system from the workshop. You can set it here." I show her the panel near the door, and she steps out, orienting herself with where the stairs lead.

We move back inside. "How much would the rent be?" she asks as she opens and closes the kitchen cabinets, before checking out the small fridge and microwave.

I think this could make or break her accepting my offer. I shrug. "It's sitting here empty, gathering dust. You'd be doing me a favor if you moved in and looked after the place for me until I decide if I want to rent it out."

Her eyes narrow as she looks across at me. "What? You'd let me live here for free?"

"Yeah, sure. Unless you wanted to pay some rent. I honestly don't care." I tuck my hands in my pockets, trying to appear nonchalant as she looks around the space. "Maybe you could clean it up for me and make it presentable or something." She leans her hip against the kitchen cabinet, the sun streaming through the kitchen window creates a halo behind her almost-white hair. She peers around the space, as dust motes caused by our movement float in the air, and I feel I need to sweeten the pot to get her to agree. I sense she doesn't want a free ride. "What about this? How about you clean the workshop and office in exchange for living here, instead of me paying you the extra money? Would that work for you?" Holding my breath, I hope she accepts my offer. I don't want her fucking sleeping in that damn car another night. I'm certain that without her explicitly telling me, that's where she's been sleeping since she arrived in town. That's why she kept all her stuff in her car. It makes me feel like an asshole that I didn't know. "Just until you find your own place." I rush to add.

She looks at me, biting her lip and fidgeting with her bracelet. With a single nod, she says yes, and I take a breath. Stepping forward, I pick her up and spin her around, careful not to knock her into the two-seater couch. Smiles fill both of our faces and I feel the relief of her acceptance of my offer right down to my bones. Setting her back on her feet, I grab her hand. "C'mon, let's go get your stuff. You can move in now." I want to get her settled in before she can change her mind.

She tugs on my hand, and I turn toward her. "Hold on. It's almost time to open the workshop and I need to clean the downstairs bathroom. I can move some of my stuff during my lunch break and after work. There's no rush." She glances around the space again and tucks her hair behind her ear. "I actually wouldn't mind giving it a quick clean before I move my stuff in. Is that okay?"

I consider the space. "Of course. Do whatever you need to do to make this place yours. If you want to paint the walls and stuff, feel free. I'll even help on my day off," I offer.

"Oh, that's okay. It's already nicer than any place I've lived before." Molly slams her mouth shut; her lips closed tight as though she's said too much.

I need to move the moment forward, so she doesn't dwell on the fact she's let something from her previous life slip. "It *is* pretty nice." I lean against the doorjamb. "I lived here for a few years until I could afford to buy my house. The place isn't huge, but it's cozy." I smile and she gifts me those gorgeous dimples of hers. "It's pretty sparse. If you need any other furniture, just shout out. I'm sure we can source whatever you need."

She glances around again, cataloging the main area. "Nope. I think I'm good for now. I can add stuff slowly, but this is enough for me to be comfortable." Molly steps into my body, wrapping her scent and arms around me and pressing her tits against my torso. Her body fits perfectly against mine. "Thank you. Thank you so much for this. You have no idea what it means to me that you've offered me this apartment. I promise I'll look after it. I'll be the best tenant you've ever had."

I laugh. "That won't be hard to do. You're the only tenant I've ever had." She playfully slaps my chest. The agitation I was feeling this morning when I found her in the parking lot has vanished. Something inside me settles, knowing I've been able to help her in some small way and that she'll be safe from now on.

At three, I sent Molly to get herself sorted. During lunch, she said she has somewhere she needs to be after work, so I wanted to give her time to move her stuff in. I'm not sure where she needs to be; I didn't think she knew anyone else in the city, but maybe I was wrong.

Locking up the workshop, I clean up quickly, then head upstairs to check if she needs any help. The door's open, so I step into the apartment, noticing she's brought everything upstairs from her car. I wanted to help her with that. I run my fingers through my hair in frustration. I should have checked on her earlier, but I wanted to detail the inside of the Sprint so I can organize for buyers to look at her.

Music is coming from the bedroom, so I make my way to the doorway. The sight that greets me almost has me swallowing my tongue. She's making the bed, but while she's doing it, she's performing the actions of Salt 'n' Pepper's *Push it*. Her ass, wrapped in skintight jeans, thrusting in time to the music, waking up my cock. Adjusting my jeans to make more space, I try to distract my thoughts to calm myself down. I don't need my employee to turn around and find me with a damn pole in my pants. Once I'm under control, I knock on the doorjamb.

"Hey." She spins around, holding her chest, her eyes wide in alarm. "Sorry. Didn't mean to scare you." I gesture over my shoulder. "The door was open, and I wanted to check if you needed any help."

She catches her breath and giggles. "Sorry. I was in my own world." She waves her arm out around the bedroom. "What do ya think?"

It's pretty sparse, but she's full of pride as she waits for my response. "It looks great. This room's never had a feminine touch."

"I love it so much." She's beaming. "Oh shit! What's the time?" She snatches up her phone. "Shit! Shit! Shit! I need to go." She moves around the room on a mission as though I'm not even standing in the doorway.

She grabs a shirt out of the closet, pulls her T-shirt over her head and my eyes lock on her tits, encased in a simple white T-shirt bra like they're a heat-seeking missile. There's nothing sexy about it, and she's not even aware that she's exposed herself in front of me in her panic. As she pulls the fresh shirt over her head, her tits jiggle and my dick decides it likes the view, working its way to the waistband of my jeans. As her head pops through the top, her eyes connect with mine and widen. "Shit! Sorry." She quickly works the shirt down her body, sadly hiding herself from me. Her cheeks flush prettily as she collects her phone and slides her feet into her shoes.

"I'm not." I raise my eyebrows and lift one side of my lips, tucking my hands in the pockets of my jeans, attempting to disguise my hard-on.

She playfully hits my chest as she passes through the doorway. "Sorry. I need to get moving. I don't want to be late."

"Where are you headed tonight?" I've had this unexpected surge of irrational jealousy every time I thought about where she might be going tonight. Is she seeing someone?

Is it my fucking business?

No.

But did that stop me from ruminating over it all afternoon?

Also no.

She checks the outer door's locked and then makes her way to the internal door, waiting for me to follow. "I, uh, signed up to volunteer a couple of nights a week. Even though it's not paid work, I like to be professional. You know? Which means I don't want to be late." She widens her eyes, raises one eyebrow, and tilts her head toward the door, hinting that she wants to get going. "I really need to get moving."

I finally take the hint and step outside so she can lock up. "Sure. Sorry. Are you going to be okay getting back in tonight? Remember, you need to come in through the outer door." I point to the opposite side of the apartment.

We make our way down the stairs. Molly's almost running. "Yeah, no problem. See you tomorrow!" She waves over her shoulder, and I'm left admiring her ass as she climbs into her car.

# CHAPTER 12

## —molly—

MY LEGS ARE BURNING LIKE CRAZY. IT'S BEEN AGES SINCE I'VE RUN AND my muscles are reminding me of my laziness. The streets around here aren't all that flat either, adding to my misery.

I suck in lungfuls of air and remind myself that I love to run. It's the thing I love to do to start my day. It settles my mind and helps me to sleep better at night. I haven't had a decent night's sleep since the night of the accident. More nights than not, I wake with images I never saw stuck in my head and it takes ages to find sleep again.

Finally, the workshop comes into view, and I slow my pace until I'm out front. Walking in circles, my chest burns as my lungs attempt to get enough air. Bending at the waist, allowing my hands to drop to my toes, I slowly grasp my ankles, gently stretching my hamstrings, careful not to go overboard on my first day back. Now that I have a proper place to live, I can get back into my usual routine of running every day. The prospect is exciting—*how sad is that?* I work through my cool-down sequence, then climb the outside steps to my apartment.

A smile touches my lips at having my own space. No neighbors making obscene noises or listening to other people's arguments through the paper-thin walls. Mom would be happy with the way things are working out for me. My smile falls as thoughts of her drift through my head.

*I miss her.*

*I miss my brother, Ethan.*

*I miss Jack.*

Looking at my feet as I breach the last step, I wipe the escaping tears from my cheeks and softly smile at my bright pink runners. My last birthday present from my family. Perhaps I should pack them away for safekeeping?

Mom, Jack, and Ethan were so impatient with me as I slowly and carefully unwrapped the box. The sparkly purple paper was far too pretty to tear, and I wanted to save it to cover my newest sketch pad.

"C'mon, Molly. Just rip it for goodness' sake. It'll be your next birthday by the time you open your present," Mom coaxed.

A chuckle escapes at the memory. Jack was incredibly proud of the research he'd done to find the perfect running shoe for me. They were secondhand, but you'd never have known. They were like brand freaking new! I put them on straight away and went for a run with Jack and E. When we got back to the trailer, Mom had a birthday cake sitting on the table, decorated with twenty-six candles.

Unlocking the door, I step inside and toe off my favorite running shoes. Should I pack them away so I can keep them forever? Or should I use them the way my family intended? I ponder the thought as I strip down and head for the shower.

Turning on the faucet, I wait for the hot water to come through. And wait. And wait some more. I stick my hand beneath the flow and pull it back quickly. The water's still freezing. Damn it. I need to have a shower after my run. It's partly why I didn't run while I was living in my car. I couldn't always guarantee the ability to shower afterward. I remember the shower downstairs and decide to make my way down there.

Grabbing my phone, I check the time. Yep. I think I have time to whip downstairs to have a shower and be back up here before Max arrives. I collect my toiletries and make my way down the internal stairs, rush over to turn off the alarm, and then head for the bathroom. Closing myself in the small space, I turn on the hot water.

*Yes!*

I'm in luck.

I'll have to remember to tell Max about the situation with the hot water when he comes in later.

I work quickly, lathering up, shaving the essential areas, and scrubbing others. Climbing out of the shower, I grab my towel and dry myself, then use my favorite rose-scented moisturizer all over my body.

The door bursts open, and I freeze.

Max glances up, his eyes locking on me, and he freezes in the doorway.

Oh my God!

Neither of us moves and I don't understand why my body won't snap into action so I can hide behind my towel or something. Anything. I'm not the only one who's failing to act, though. He could close the damn door, but he's too busy trailing his eyes all over me. His Adam's Apple bobs up and down with his swallow, and I notice his eyes are darker than usual. Finally, my sensibilities return, and I grab my towel, trying to cover as much of my body as I can.

"Shit! Sorry." Max drops his eyes to the floor, away from me, but doesn't move to close the door to give me privacy. My body flushes at the thought of the man I'm currently crushing on seeing me completely naked.

*Did he like what he saw?*

Should I even be wondering if he likes my body?

Probably not.

I should tell him to close the door, but the words won't come. "That's okay. You didn't know I was in here and I didn't lock the door. I thought I had more time before you'd be in. It was my mistake." While his eyes are still averted, I move the towel away from my body to wrap it around myself properly. At that moment, he raises his head, his eyes locking on my nakedness *again*. My breathing picks up speed at the darkness in his eyes, and when I drop my eyes down his body, I can't miss the unmistakable bulge pressing behind his zipper. My tongue slips out without permission to lick my lips and my teeth latch onto the bottom pillow.

Max groans and runs his fingers through his hair, messing it up further. It's crazy hot the way he does that. "Fuck!" It's a harsh whispered word on a breath, but I feel its impact right in my solar plexus.

One side of my mouth tilts up at the knowledge that my hot boss is attracted to me. *Little old me.*

"I should … uh …" He thumbs over his shoulder. "I should close this fucking door before I do something stupid." He steps back and closes the door with a sharp snick.

He thinks it would be stupid to do anything with me. My heart cracks at the thought that I misinterpreted his reaction. *How stupid can I be?* Heavy disappointment floods me as all the air in my lungs escapes.

*Shit!* This is gonna be awkward now. I have to make the walk upstairs in my towel. My threadbare and too-small towel. Tucking the top of the towel in between my breasts to secure it in place, I collect my toiletries and open the bathroom door. When I poke my head out of the bathroom, he's nowhere to be seen. I hold my head up high and walk with a confidence I don't feel across the office toward the stairs. Closing myself inside my private space, I sag against the door.

I know he's older than me; the age difference doesn't bother me, but maybe it bothers him. Or is it the fact that he's my boss that's the issue? I swallow down my hurt pride and get myself ready for the day.

I chomp down on an apple; enjoying the crispness as the juice trickles down my chin. It's been great to have fresh fruit on the regular after being paid last month. I had to be careful not to go crazy in the grocery store and buy too much produce, reminding myself that I have money in my bank account now and I can go to the store whenever I need.

I can't delay the inevitable any longer. It's time to head downstairs and start work. Wandering to the far end of the workshop, I find Max working on the Sprint in his regular clothes.

"Hey. Sorry about earlier." I point over my shoulder. "You can get changed in the bathroom now." I know he hates working in his regular clothes. He prefers to keep the grease and oil stains on his overalls.

His head snaps up and his eyes skim my body, making it heat under his perusal. I'm fighting not to rub my thighs together to stem the ache he's creating between my legs. When his eyes finally make it back to my face, his eyebrows snap down, causing a crease to form between them, and I want to step forward to smooth it out with my fingers.

"Stop apologizing for everything. It wasn't your fault. It was an accident. I should have noticed the alarm was turned off and double-checked the bathroom before I entered." He tips his head toward the stairs to the apartment. "What's wrong with the shower upstairs?"

"Oh, uhm. The hot water wasn't working. I let it run for a few minutes and it wasn't even warming up a little. I just checked again, and it's still not working. Same with all the faucets upstairs."

His frown lines deepen, and he climbs out of the car, taking long strides toward the upstairs apartment. I almost have to run to keep up with him and I have freakishly long legs. "Lemme take a look." He walks straight to the bathroom-come-laundry and opens a panel on the outer wall, checking the switches.

I had wondered what that panel was for, and now I know. He flicks a switch and then moves to the basin to check the water. After a minute or so, a smile graces his lips. "There ya go. It used to happen to me sometimes. I'm not sure what causes the switch to turn off, but it's easy to flick it back on." He points to the switch in question, and I move in closer to get a proper look. His arm brushes against my boob as he tries to make space for me. He ignores it, but I can't. That simple touch sends fire scorching through my body.

Surely, I'm not the only one feeling this heat between us.

"I'd better get downstairs and open up. See ya down there whenever you're ready." He contorts himself around my body, careful not to touch me at all. My shoulders drop and I sigh.

I need to work on shutting down my crush. With a new resolve, I close the panel, push my shoulders back, and head downstairs. Moving through my regular morning routine, I quickly give the bathroom a once-over before our first client arrives for the day.

# CHAPTER 13

## —max—

*FUCK! I'M IN TROUBLE.*

I couldn't peel my eyes away from my office manager's stunning body. She's fucking perfect in every single way. Even the sanctuary between her legs is groomed exactly the way I like it. I don't think I'll ever be able to close my eyes again without seeing the image of her bent over, massaging that fucking addictive rose scent onto her long, smooth legs. I shake my head, trying to clear the image. I should have fucking closed the door. I don't know what came over me. Standing in the doorway like a letch, my eyes greedily soaking up the magnificence that is Molly.

Molly, my fucking *employee*.

Molly, who is a *full decade younger* than me.

Molly, the girl I can't seem to stop thinking about.

Girl. She's definitely not a girl. She's a fully grown, sexy ass woman. Those pink nipples. I groan as my dick expands in my overalls. At least it's not as obvious when I have a hard-on in these.

I need to shut this shit down. She's my employee. I broke all sorts of rules and regulations today. If she wanted to take me to task over what I did this morning, she'd fucking ruin me.

And you know what? I would fucking stand in that doorway and look my fill all over again.

*How fucking stupid is that?*

The woman who's never far from my thoughts steps into my peripheral vision. "I made you a coffee since you didn't get one earlier."

I don't raise my eyes. I can't. I'm embarrassed by my behavior this morning. She has a right to have a shower and get dressed in peace. Her boss should not be fucking ogling her in her place of work *or* residence. I groan internally at myself. "Thanks. Just leave it over on the bench, please."

"Sure. No problem." Her voice lacks its usual confident tone. She steps away and then comes back to stand right beside me, her rose scent playing havoc with my dick. I don't think I'll ever be able to smell it again without associating it with Molly. "What are you working on?"

Turning my head slightly, I look at her. Well, that was a fucking mistake. She's peering right at me. Those silver eyes of hers, bright and inquisitive. I return my focus to the cylinder head cover. "Just taking this off so I can replace the gasket." I drop the bolt I was removing down into the engine bay. "Fuck!" I whisper with a harsh breath.

"Oh, sorry. I'll get outta your way." Her thick eyelashes flutter and her cheeks flush. "What time is the guy coming to look at the car?" She tilts her chin across to the Sprint.

"Four-thirty."

"Okay. I'll leave you to it!" She spins on her heel and walks straight back to the office. Her long white-blond hair swishing behind her. I wonder if it's as soft and silky as it looks.

*Stop fucking thinking about her hair!*

Molly and I manage to get past the awkwardness of the morning and spend the rest of the day doing our respective work. Me in the workshop. Her in the office. Occasionally she comes out to check a serial number for a part, but we both maintain a professional manner.

*It feels forced and I don't fucking like it.*

When I glance up, Molly's walking toward me with Martin. He's a long-time client of mine. Martin's been watching me slowly restore the Sprint and, a couple of months back, asked me to keep him in mind when I finished the restoration and was ready to sell. He's studying Molly like a science experiment as she brings him over.

I don't like the way he's looking at her. I'm pretty sure he's married with a couple of kids and he's probably old enough to be her father.

I step between him and my girl, blocking his view. Holding out my hand, we shake in greeting. "Martin. How have you been? How's the family?" *Do you like what I did there? I reminded him he's a married family man.*

"Max. They're great. Holly's in her last year of high school. I can't believe how fast she's grown up." He turns his attention to Molly, holding his hand out to her. "And who do we have here?"

I pull her to my side, wrapping my arm around her waist and landing a kiss on the top of her head. Understandably, Molly stiffens in my hold. She's probably wondering what the hell's going on. "This is Molly. She runs the office for me."

Martin's eyebrows almost hit his hairline in surprise at my public display of affection toward my office manager. Fair enough because this would seem highly inappropriate.

Molly slides her hand into his, gifting him with her dimples. "Hi, Martin. Nice to meet you."

He holds her hand a little longer than what's socially acceptable. His eyes locked on hers.

*What in the actual fuck?*

I pull Molly back slightly, forcing them to disengage. He shakes his head as though he's waking up from a daze. Directing his attention toward the car, I ask, "What do you think of her?"

He tears his eyes away from Molly and looks at the Sprint. "She's gorgeous. Beautiful color!" He glides his hand over the surface. "Is this the original Rangoon Red?"

"Yeah. I wanted to keep her as original as possible." I follow behind him.

He dips down to peer inside. "Is that real leather on the seats and interior panels?"

"Yep. It's as soft as butter." I open the driver's door and gesture for him to take a seat. May as well put him behind the wheel. He runs his hand across the soft leather before situating himself inside. His eyes are taking in every feature and detail as he gets comfortable behind the wheel.

"This is magnificent. You've done a stellar job, Max." His hands glide over the dash and smooth their way around the steering wheel. He grasps the gearshift, and using the clutch, manipulates it through the gears.

"It has new wiring all the way through. Almost everything under the hood is new." I get out of the passenger side. "Come, take a look."

He peels himself away from his admiration of the interior and steps around to the front of the car. I raise the hood and his eyes light up as he releases a low whistle. "Man, this is incredible." He looks across at me. "You are a master."

"Thanks. Here, I'll raise her and you can see beneath the car." I close the doors and press a button to start the car lift, which raises the Sprint. I'm proud of the work I've done on this car. It was a heap of shit when I brought her in, but the body was in reasonable condition, so I knew I could bring her back to life.

Martin lets out another low whistle. Hands in pockets, he walks the length of the car, head tilted back, studying every single inch. "That exhaust system is beautiful. It's a shame it's hidden beneath the car and nobody can appreciate your work."

I laugh. "C'mon. Let's take her for a drive."

I start her up and the beauty purrs like a fucking kitten. Beautiful. I wave to Molly, and we cruise out of the workshop, making a left onto the street. As we're cruising, I fill Martin in on the specs of the car. It's not until we reach the highway that I can show him what she can do. The deep rumble as I change up through the gears, vibrates through the seats, warming my body. This. This is what it's all about. This is why I love working with cars. This feeling of freedom as you drive a beautiful machine along the highway. Just me, the car, and the road. It's my happy place.

Martin smiles across at me. "Noah's gonna love this. He's really into muscle cars."

"Oh yeah?" I grin back.

He hangs his arm out of the window, catching the wind. "So, how long has Molly been working for you?"

I glance across at him with narrowed eyes. "Just over a month," I answer cautiously.

He must sense my discomfort with the topic because he holds up his hands. "She reminds me of someone. That's all."

My shoulders relax. "She's new to the city. I doubt you know her."

We move away from the topic of Molly, and I run through what the Sprint is capable of. We make it to the coast, and I climb out of the driver's seat to allow Martin the opportunity to drive her back to the workshop.

If his expression is anything to go by, he's smitten. Exactly how I want him.

We make it back to the workshop and Martin carefully parks the car in bay three, where I've been working on her. He slowly turns to me, a smile as wide as anything on his face. "How much?"

I twist in my seat to face him, pulling out my phone. I took photos of the car before I started and then kept taking photos as the restoration progressed as a record.

"Before we talk about the price. Take a look." I hand him my phone. He's engrossed in the images as he flicks through dozens of photos. The first shows the wreck abandoned in a backyard, with grass and weeds growing almost to the top of the roof.

"That's this car?" His eyes are wide, his voice full of wonder.

I nod. "Yep. Looking at her there, though, I knew she would be a beauty."

"She sure is." He twists his body around, handing the phone back to me. "Okay. Hit me. How much?"

"Forty-nine K."

Martin's eyes widen, and his eyebrows shoot up. "Fuck."

I nod slowly. "Worth every penny, though."

"Oh, don't worry. I can see her worth." He glides his hand over the dashboard like any man would caress a woman's body. "Any room for negotiation?"

I tilt my head to the side. "A little."

"Might have to run it past the wife. When would you need an answer?"

"I'm not in any rush. I contacted you first like you asked. If you can't take her off my hands, I'll find another buyer. I'm not worried in the least. Talk to the wife. Bring her and the kids in to take a look, if you like," I suggest.

We climb out of the car and head back toward the office, so I can shut up the workshop behind him. Molly's sweeping the floor as we pass through. Martin's eyes draw to her like a magnet to metal, making my hackles rise again. I guide him straight through, aiming to get him out of the door, but he stops.

"See ya, Molly. It was nice to meet you." Deep divots bracket his mouth as he smiles at her.

She returns his dimples with her own as she responds. "Bye, Martin. Great to meet you, too."

Once I get Martin out of the shop, I lock up and head back to Molly.

"Is he gonna buy the car?" She asks, her eyes wide and hopeful.

"He has to speak with his wife. It's a lot of money to drop on a car that you don't actually need. But if I were a betting man, I'd say he'll buy the Sprint." She claps excitedly. "I need to get changed for soccer. Are you coming with me, or do you want to come later?"

She pauses her sweeping; her face snapping up toward me. "You want me to come with you?"

I shrug. "Makes sense. I can drop you back here after the pub."

She fidgets with the broom for a minute, and I wonder why the decision is so difficult. "Are you sure your friends would be happy if I come to the pub again? I feel like that's possibly time for the boys since you don't normally have women there."

"You're not a woman. You're our cheer squad."

Her shoulders drop, as does her face. With her eyes locked on her shoes, she takes a few moments. "I … uh … I'll meet you at the field if that's okay. I probably won't go to the pub after the game."

I understand she's allowed to make her own choices, and I'd never force her to do anything she didn't want to, but I thought she enjoyed hanging out with the boys. "Have you got something else to do?"

She shakes her head, her delicate eyebrows drawing down low over her eyes. "No. I don't have anything else to do. I'll be there to cheer you guys on the sidelines. Don't worry." She gives me a forced smile and focuses back on the sweeping, basically dismissing me.

The disappointment is strong. I wanted her with me. I've been looking forward to it since last Monday night. I feel like a kid who's been denied a play date with his best friend. I've grown used to her being at our games. Molly and I haven't known each other all that long, but I enjoy her company and was hoping she felt the same.

I collect my bag and move into the bathroom to get changed. When I come out, Molly's waiting at her desk, shifting nervously from foot to foot. "You okay?"

"Yeah, I wanted to ask you something." She's looking everywhere but at me, which is unusual for her.

"Sure. Ask away."

She collects a piece of paper from her desk, holding it close to her body so I can't see what's on it. "I was wondering what you thought about an idea I had." She turns the parchment around, allowing me to see what's on the paper. The air leaves my lungs in a gush, and I step forward to study it more closely. I'm torn between keeping my eyes on the sketch she's showing me and looking at her as she poses the question. "Do you think whoever buys the Sprint would like a framed sketch of it?"

"Are you serious?" She nods. "Fuck yeah! That's an incredible piece of work, Molly." I flick my eyes back up to her face. "Are you sure you want to give it away? You could sell this and earn some extra money."

"Oh no, I could never sell my work. It's not *that* good." She gives a self-deprecating chuckle.

I scoff. "That's bullshit. Your attention to detail and the fine lines are incredible. The shading that you do makes it appear almost like a photograph."

Her cheeks flush and her dimples make a shallow appearance. "You think so?" She sounds uncertain and I'm not sure why. Surely, she can see how good her work is.

"Why don't you bring it with you tonight and show Aaron? He has a pretty good eye for this stuff because he sells it in his café." I check the time. "I've gotta go," I tilt my head toward the paper, "bring it with you. See what he says."

"Oh, uh, I'll think about it." She waves me away. "You'd better get going. I'll see you at the field."

# CHAPTER 14

## —*max*—

I'M THINKING MOLLY MAY BE OUR LUCKY CHARM. WE WON AGAIN tonight. We've had more wins this season than last.

"We need to make sure Molly comes to every single game. She's like a good luck charm or something." Aaron pats me on the back as he makes his suggestion.

"As if I have any control over her coming to our games or not. I couldn't even get her to come out for a drink tonight."

His head pulls back an inch or two in surprise. "What do you mean, she's not coming out for drinks?" He steps away from me, then calls back over his shoulder. "Don't worry, I'll work my magic."

Oh shit! I don't want her to feel pressured to come to the pub. I only want her to come if she *wants* to be there with us.

"C'mon, Molly. You have to come to Brady's to celebrate with us tonight. We haven't won this many games in a season for a while. You're our lucky charm." He gives her his best smile. The one he uses to pick up when he's feeling like company.

*And I don't fucking like it.*

I don't like it aimed at my Molly. My gut tightens and I want to push my way between them and punch that smile off his face.

Molly looks down at her shoes, but I can see she's smiling. She tucks her hair behind her ear and then looks back up at him. She's slightly swiveling her body from side to side, like a coy schoolgirl.

*Does she fucking like him?*

I study my best friend. He can't take his eyes off her. I don't like the way he's fucking looking at her. He's too old for her. He has no business flirting with my Molly.

"Are you sure it's okay?"

"We all want you to come." He turns around to gesture to the guys, noticing I'm right behind him. "Don't we, Max?"

"I already invited her. She didn't want to come," I snap at my teammate while looking at Molly apologetically.

She glances at her shoes and I turn to give Aaron the filthiest look I can muster.

"Okay. I'll come for a little while." She flashes her sexy dimples at my friend.

What the hell just happened? I couldn't get her to join us tonight, but Aaron flashes her his pickup smile and suddenly she has a change of heart.

"Great. See you there." He backs away to collect his gear, tipping his chin to me.

I focus my attention back on Molly, placing my hands on my hips. "I thought you didn't want to come to drinks with us tonight? What's changed?"

"I'm allowed to change my mind if I want." She starts walking toward the parking lot, so I quickly grab my gear and follow behind, watching her ass and ponytail sway with each step. *Fuck! Stop looking at her ass.*

When we arrive at her car, we stop at her driver's door. "I get that you're allowed to change your mind. I'm glad you're coming." I wrap my arm around her neck, pulling her into my body.

She laughs and pushes at me. "Eww, you're all sweaty." Her hands feel electric on my body.

I release her and grasp my chest over my heart. "You don't like my sweat?"

"Nope." She pops the p like she's popping a bubble gum bubble.

I walk around to the passenger door. "You wanna drive and then drop me back here for my car?"

Her head snaps over to my car. "You're gonna leave your car here?"

"Or … we could take my car and I'll drop you back here to pick up your car. Either, or." I shrug, hoping that she chooses to come with me. She looks between my car and hers "You know how hard it is to find parking. If we take two cars, it's gonna be a problem."

She closes her door and locks her car. "We'll take your car. I'd hate to be responsible for something happening to your beautiful car if we left it here unattended. I doubt anyone will look twice at mine."

I smile inside. "Okay. Sure. Let's go." I pat the roof. "Your car's not that bad." I walk back around to her and guide her across to my car with my hand settled at the small of her back. "Be careful what you say. You don't want to hurt her feelings," I whisper low into her ear as we walk away, making Molly chuckle. I think her laugh is one of my new favorite sounds.

Before I climb into my car; I grasp the back of my T-shirt and pull it off. Searching through my bag, I pull out a clean T-shirt. When I tilt my head up, I catch Molly staring at my chest, and before I can help myself, I flex my pecs. "Did you enjoy the game?"

Her eyes snap up to my face, and I press my lips together to hold back my smile. *Yeah, I caught you checking me out!*

"Huh?"

I change out of my cleats into my running shoes. "Did you enjoy the game tonight?"

She grins at me. "You couldn't tell with all of my cheering and dance moves along the sideline?"

I chuckle. "You're pretty entertaining with your cheer moves."

She curtsies before climbing into the passenger side. "Why, thank you. I'll take that compliment."

We drive out of the parking lot and turn right toward Brady's. "It would have been easier if you'd come with me, instead of bringing two cars," I say as nonchalantly as possible. It's niggling at me that she agreed to come to the pub when Aaron asked, but not when I did.

"I was wondering how long it would take you to bring that up. Maybe, next week, I'll drive with you. Would that make you happy?"

Glancing across, I grin. "Ecstatic."

Brady's is packed as usual. I pull Molly against me to protect her as we work our way through the crowd, toward the guys.

Cheers go up around the tables when they spot us. Aaron, Brent, Gary, and Finn step out to hug Molly in greeting, pulling her away from me. She giggles but accepts each hug. The pit of my stomach sinks as I watch other men embrace her. I know she's not mine, but I don't fucking like the thought of some other asshole having their hands on her, even if I know they're good guys with the best of intentions.

We settle into the booth, and I work to school my features, but Aaron's already smirking at me. He knows me too well, and no matter how hard I try to hide the way I'm feeling, he always seems to read me.

"Pizzas are on their way. You two want a beer?" Finn asks as he glances around the tables.

"Nah, man. You sit. It's my buy." I turn toward Molly. "What can I get for you, Dimples?"

I catch Aaron's smirk out of the corner of my eye but make the conscious choice to ignore him.

"I can get my drink. You don't have to keep paying for me."

"You won't be paying while you're with me. I invited you, which makes you my guest. I'll grab you a beer." Scanning the table, I check the guys' drinks, but they're still looking healthy.

Aaron slides out of the booth. "I'll come with you. I need to speak with a friend of mine."

We make our way to the bar. The usual group of young women checks us out as we approach. They're probably about the same age as Molly, I guess, but the idea of going there with one of them has never appealed to me. Molly, on the other hand …

"What's going on with you and Molly? And don't give me any bull-shit. I can read you, man." Aaron slaps me on the back and squeezes my shoulder as he interrupts my musing.

"Nothing. She's my office manager."

He looks back at the table and I follow his line of sight. Molly's looking straight at us as she laughs at something Finn's saying. "You wouldn't mind if I asked her out then?"

"Yeah, I would fucking mind. There're plenty of other options available to you." I tilt my head toward the regular group of younger women close by. "No need to go after my employee."

"Is that the only reason I can't ask her out? Because she's your employee? 'Cause as her boss, you have no say in who she dates, right?" he hedges.

I order our drinks, buying myself some time before I answer my long-time friend, who I'm sure is fishing for information rather than being interested in dating my new employee. "I thought you had a friend you needed to chat with?"

"I *am* chatting with that friend." He chuckles. *Asshole.*

I pay for our drinks, then grab them, ready to head back to our booth, but Aaron stops me. "I can see the way you look at her and the way she looks at you. Are you going to do anything about it?"

My shoulders slump. "I can't. I'll admit, I find her attractive and as I'm getting to know her, I like her. I like her a lot. But I'm her boss, plus she's a decade younger than me."

Aaron sighs. "Sucks to be you."

I take a sip of my beer. "It most certainly fucking does."

We don't need to say anything else. Aaron gets where I'm coming from. That's what years of friendship and support give us.

When we arrive back at the booth, Gary is giving Molly a rundown of the baby's stage of development, and Molly's enthralled. I place the beer in front of her and she glances up to mouth 'thank you' and then returns her full attention to Gary. I can't help but note the difference again between Mona and Molly with my friends. Mona would never have shown any interest in Gary and Layla's pregnancy because Mona was all about Mona.

The pizzas arrive and everyone's quiet as they dig into the deliciously cheesy treat. Molly's oblivious to a piece of stretchy cheese that's landed on her chin as she chats with the guys. Reaching across, I pinch it between my fingers, pull it away and drop it into my mouth. When I glance back across the table, Aaron's studying me with a raised eyebrow, and I shrug in response. It would be different if Molly seemed offended, but she gave me a brief smile, then took another huge bite of her slice of pizza.

I love that she's not shy about eating her food in front of others. I guess her daily run allows her to eat whatever she wants without worrying about calories, like most women, or maybe she just enjoys food.

Gary makes a move to leave, and I check in with Molly. "Are you happy to stay, or are you ready to head home?"

"I wouldn't mind heading home if you don't mind. I have another late night tomorrow night and I want to get up early enough for my run in the morning." I still don't know where she volunteers. Maybe I'll ask her on the drive back to her car.

We say goodbye to everyone, Molly promising to be at next week's game. I can't stop my smirk, knowing she'll be back again next week. I nudge her shoulder with mine. "See, the guys really like having you around."

Her smile drops and her shoulders slump. "Yeah, I guess so." She turns her face away from me as we climb into my car.

"You okay?" I can't help but notice her mood's changed considerably since we stepped outside.

She shrugs. "Yeah. I'm okay."

I grew up with two sisters. I know for a fact that when a woman says she's okay, in that tone, that she's not fucking okay. It means I've done something wrong. I just don't know what it is.

I open the passenger door for her, then lean down after she situates herself to strap the safety belt on. I suck in a sharp breath as my arm brushes against her tit. That was a fucking mistake because her scent fills my lungs and wakes up my dick, which is becoming a perpetual problem the more time I spend with this woman. I turn my head to check she hasn't noticed, putting my lips close to hers. And that's my second fucking mistake. Her lips are right there. Slightly parted, as though she's waiting for me to kiss her. I glance away from her lips, catching on her molten eyes.

*Fucking stunning.*

I could lean forward ever so slightly, and my mouth could take hers. I could taste her. Would she taste as sweet as she fucking looks? I pull back slightly, saving myself from a possible lawsuit.

Is that disappointment marring her gorgeous features? Or is that wishful thinking on my part?

Closing her door, I use the opportunity as I make my way around to the driver's side to calm my dick down. She doesn't need her boss making inappropriate advances. I need a distraction. "You never told me where you've been volunteering."

She tucks a lock of hair behind her ear. "Oh, uhm, I volunteer over at *Shelter* on Tuesdays and Thursdays. It's a women's homeless shelter."

Of course, she does, because she isn't sweet enough already. "I know the one. Big red brick building."

She smiles. "Yeah, that's the one. I used to volunteer at a shelter back home." I'm struggling with the irony that she was sleeping in her car the whole time she's been here—well, I'm assuming that's what she was doing—and then she volunteers in her free time at a women's shelter.

"Any reason why you choose to spend your free time helping homeless women?" Her body stiffens and I can see her physically and emotionally shut down. I thought it would be a reasonable question. After all, she asked me a similar question about my Single Parent Thursdays. "Sorry. That was possibly too intrusive. You don't have to answer."

Her hand moves to fidget with the bracelet she wears. "Oh, uh, that's okay." She turns her head toward the passenger window, dropping her voice to barely above a whisper. "My mom and I were, uh … were homeless until I was eleven."

My head snaps toward her. Surely, I heard that wrong. Slowly she turns and our eyes connect, but not for long because I need to keep my eyes on the road. I swallow down the thousands of questions that battle for release. "That must have been tough." *What a fucking understatement.* No wonder she had no problem living in her car.

We pull into the parking lot and I don't want to let her go. I want to know what her life was like as she was growing up. My head can't even go there. It's so far removed from my childhood. The silence in the car sits heavy like Lachlan's weighted blanket. She turns in her seat, so her body is facing me and I want to scoop her up and sit her on my lap.

I want to grasp the back of her head under the fall of her silky hair and pull her into me, so I can kiss those plump lips of hers.

I want to give her a home that will always be hers.

But I can't do any of those things.

I turn forward, staring out of the windscreen, grinding my teeth to stop myself from asking her to stay awhile. To sit and chat. Out of my periphery, I see her lean closer to me and as I turn my head, my lips brush against hers. They're warm and soft and I want to press in deeper, take her mouth with mine.

I don't know where all of this is coming from. It's an impossible situation. I can't go there with her. I don't move, but she swiftly pulls away as though she's been scorched.

"Thanks for the ride." She jumps out of my car. "I'll see you in the morning." She closes the door carefully and jogs over to her car. I watch her climb in and I'm tempted to follow her back to her apartment to make sure she gets inside safely. She has nobody else to watch over her as far as I can tell.

I wait until she pulls out of the lot and then follow behind. I would never forgive myself if something happened to her. I slow to watch her get inside safely and then head home.

Her rose scent is trapped inside my car, playing with my senses and testing my resolve.

I strip off as I walk through my bedroom, my bed calling to me, but I desperately need a shower. Turning on the water as hot as I can bear it,

I step under the spray, hoping to release some of the tension that's built in my body during the car ride home.

I think back to Molly's lips skating lightly across mine accidentally and I close my eyes, picturing exactly how I'd like to take those pouty lips. My cock wakes at the thought of pressing my mouth against hers, teasing her lips apart, and taking the first swipe against her tongue with mine. I groan and my dick twitches as I imagine how soft and sweet she would be under my ministrations.

Wrapping my hand around my shaft, I give it a hard squeeze, followed by a quick tug. I picture Molly pressing her tits against my chest, rubbing her pelvis against my cock and my dick grows impossibly harder.

I'm going to have to deal with this.

I lather up some soap and grip myself firmly, using my other hand braced against the cold tile to hold myself up. The soap helps with the slide and pull of my dick, but I know this won't feel half as good as if I were inside what I imagine would be a phenomenally tight pussy. I groan as I picture delicate pink lips separating to reveal her pulsing clit and inviting wet heat.

My hand picks up the pace, sliding up to my crown to finish with a squeeze and a tug, before sliding back to the base with a twist. My breaths come faster and my heart pounds in my chest. Squeezing my butt cheeks together, I thrust forward into my hand, building a rhythm.

Too fast, tingles begin to form at the base of my spine and my balls draw up tight to my body. I throw my head back under the warm stream and shoot my load against the tiled surface, grunting out my release. Cum coats the tile and slides down as I catch my breath. Closing my eyes tight, I shake my head, full of disappointment.

*Fuck!*

I just came to thoughts of my office assistant.

I'm in so much fucking trouble.

# CHAPTER 15

## —molly—

Simone's sitting in the welcome chairs to the side of the entry, chatting with a stunning brunette. As she notices me, her eyes light up and that welcoming smile of hers graces her face. She waves me over. "Molly, come and meet Veronica. She's going to be staying with us tonight."

I step toward the two women with a genuine smile. I love coming here. Simone and the ladies have made me feel incredibly welcome from the get-go.

I hold out my hand to Veronica. "Hi, Veronica. It's lovely to meet you. I'm Molly. My friends call me Mols."

She warily slides her hand into mine and without making eye contact, she responds, "Hi. I prefer to be called Ronnie or Ron. If you don't mind?"

"No problem. Ronnie suits you."

She smiles at me and it's beautiful, though it doesn't quite reach her eyes, which catch me by surprise. Her left eye is a gorgeous blue, while her right eye is chocolate brown. I don't think I've ever seen anyone with two different colored eyes.

The door opens, and a woman walks in with a toddler in tow. She looks completely fried. "If you don't mind, I'll leave you two ladies to get acquainted while I meet our new friend."

We both nod at Simone and then I return my attention to Ronnie, who's busy studying her boots. She's dressed as most homeless women on the street do, as though she's trying to blend in, so she becomes invisible. I'm not sure how successful she'd be with those eyes of hers. They would make her rather memorable.

"I'm quite new to this city and I don't know my way around very well, but I love sitting by the beach and watching the sun go down. I used to live on the east coast and the sunsets were never as good," I say conversationally as I sit next to her.

Ronnie snaps her head up to me. "Really. I never gave much thought to the difference between here and there. Whereabouts did you live?"

"I grew up in Portland, Maine." Her eyebrows almost reach her hairline. "I decided to move here after I lost my family a few days before Christmas because this is where my mom grew up." I swallow down the lump that forms every time my family crosses my mind, but I've always found if I share something personal, the women are more likely to share their story in return.

She swallows and looks back down at her boots. "I'm sorry for your loss. Were they good people?" The fact she even asks that question tells me a lot.

I nod, fighting the sting behind my eyes. "Yeah." It comes out as a whisper, so I clear my throat. "Yeah, they were. The best."

Ronnie offers me a sad smile. "Why is it that the good people leave us too early and the assholes are left here to make our lives miserable?"

I shrug, shaking my head. "I dunno. I wish I knew the answer to that."

We're both quiet for a little while. "Have you always lived here?"

"Yeah." She studies her boots again. "I've never been brave like you to move somewhere new."

"I wouldn't say I was brave. I'd lost my family, my job, and my home in a matter of weeks. I had nothing left there, so I thought I'd quell my curiosity about the place where my mom grew up. Maybe if I were living here, I wouldn't have moved. From what I've seen so far, this is a pretty great city."

Ronnie shrugs, returning her gaze to her boots. She's quiet for long moments and I rack my brain, trying to come up with something else we could talk about, but maybe she's had enough for now.

"Uh, did you want me to show you to your bed and you can have a shower, then grab something to eat?"

She sighs and nods. "That'd be great."

Standing, I gesture for her to follow me, and I show her through to the dorm without cribs. She has a single backpack with her and she's holding it close to her body. If she's anything like me, it contains all of her most important possessions.

"It looks as though the two beds at the end are still vacant. You wanna take one of those?"

"Sure." We make our way between the beds until she arrives at her space for the night.

"There's a locked cupboard here." I show her how to use it. "We have some donated clothes if you want to check them out. They've all been freshly laundered."

Ronnie locks her backpack in the cupboard, and we make our way toward the room with the donated clothes for women and children. In another room, there are a few suits and fancier dresses the women can borrow when they go for job interviews. This place truly is impressive with its attention to detail, which helps women move forward with their lives when they're ready. On the way, I show Ronnie the bathrooms and then leave her with the offer to catch up in the dining room later if she wants to.

When I enter the kitchen, Rhonda greets me with her usual enthusiasm. "Mols, you're finally here! How are you, sweetie?" She wraps me in her tight embrace, almost knocking me over and we both giggle.

"I'm great, Rhonda! What have you been up to since I saw you on Tuesday?"

"Oh, you know, this and that. Catching up with all of my boyfriends." She winks at me and I chuckle. Anyone would assume she plays the field, but she's actually talking about book boyfriends. She talks about them as though they're real people.

"Oh yeah? Who are you dating this week?" I ask as I move toward the sink to wash my hands.

"Jake. Jake Normanton from the Leah Reynolds series." She fans herself. "That man brings everything to the table and I do mean ev-er-y-thing!" She finishes with an exaggerated wink.

Rhonda puts me to work and tells me all about Jake and Leah and their love story, which started back when they were kids. Leah's the daughter of a serial killer and Jake's the son of a drunk. It sounds like a fabulous read.

"Who's the author? I might check it out."

"Uh, hang on. I'll grab my Kindle and check. I'd hate to get her name wrong." She bustles off to the storeroom as I cut the bread rolls. "T. Maree. It's a series of five books. A real slow burn." She gets this smirk on her face. "But oh so worth it!" I chuckle. "How come you were late?"

"I wasn't late. I was chatting with a lady who's staying overnight. Veronica or Ronnie? Do you know her?"

"Oh yeah. Pretty girl with two different colored eyes. She comes in now and then. Haven't seen her for quite some time, though. I was hoping things had improved for her."

"I didn't know she'd been here before. She must think I'm an idiot. I was showing her where everything is."

Rhonda waves me off. "Nah. She's a sweetheart. Doesn't talk much and keeps to herself, but she's super polite. Not sure what her story is because she keeps everyone at arm's length."

The evening passes by in a blur. It's always crazy when I help Rhonda in the kitchen. I didn't even have time to step out and check that Ronnie grabbed something to eat. All the lights are out in the dorms as we close the kitchen down and put everything away. Rhonda's busy soaking a measured amount of chia seeds to add to the oats in the morning when Simone strolls in. She releases a heavy sigh and slouches against the counter.

"This is the first chance I've had to catch a breath. How are you ladies tonight?"

"Exhausted but good," I answer at the same time as Rhonda does.

"I'm ready to head home and soak my feet."

"Me too. Thanks for your help tonight, Molly. Did you manage to chat with Veronica at all?"

I lean back against the opposite counter. "A little. She said I could call her Ronnie or Ron. Told me she's always lived here. Something she said suggested that her family has hurt her." I shrug. "She didn't talk all that much."

Simone raises one eyebrow and one side of her mouth tips up slightly. "Well, you've managed to get more out of her than anyone else has."

I pull my head and shoulders back. "What? Really? I felt like I had failed. And then I got busy in the kitchen and I didn't get the chance to check back in with her after her shower."

Simone steps forward, placing her hand on mine and squeezing it. "You did well. Never feel that you've failed. You're here helping us help them. That's incredible, Molly." She gives my hand another squeeze before letting go. "Now go home. You've earned a good night's rest."

We all say our goodbyes and I promise to return next Tuesday.

I walk through my front door and head straight for the bathroom to take a quick shower, then drop into bed. I'm exhausted. After spending the day looking after the single parents and their kids, then tonight at *Shelter*, I'm dead on my feet. I glance across at the photo of Mom, Jack, and E I keep on my nightstand.

Reaching out, I pull it closer to me. I trace my finger over their faces and whisper, "I think I'm gonna be okay."

Their image becomes blurry, and I let the tears fall. They slide down the side of my face, landing in my hair. "I've met some genuinely good people. I'm pretty sure I made the right choice coming here, Mom. It's such a gorgeous city. You were lucky to grow up here. Thank you for sharing all of your stories with me. After all, they're what led me to my new life."

# CHAPTER 16

## —molly—

MAX HAS BEEN ACTING STRANGE SINCE TUESDAY MORNING, ALMOST like he's trying to avoid me. Whenever I speak with him, he's polite but short in his responses, then he makes an excuse to get away from me. I'm not sure what I've done to upset him, but I need to speak with him about my hot water. The stupid switch keeps turning off at the most inopportune times and I'm hoping he'll be happy to get an electrician to check it out. This morning it turned off while I was halfway through my shower, my hair lathered in shampoo. The freezing water forced me out of the shower before I had finished washing my hair. It was easy enough to flick the switch back on, but still, I think it needs to be fixed.

The only problem is that I don't want to seem like I'm ungrateful for a safe place to live. The apartment is amazing and I'm thankful that he's allowing me to live here. I don't want to be a pain in the ass and make things difficult. He might decide it's easier to kick me out and leave the place empty like it was before I moved in.

Making my way downstairs, I find the office empty, but the scent of coffee lingers. He must have made himself a coffee a few moments ago. I do the same and then make my way out to the workshop to say good morning, hoping he's returned to his usual friendly self. I don't think I can handle him being aloof toward me any longer. It's been really uncomfortable. I hope he hasn't changed his mind about me working and living here.

Only one way to find out. "Morning." I keep my voice as upbeat as I can.

Without looking up from whatever he's doing in the trunk of the Sprint, he responds. "Morning."

Moving next to him, I try to peer around his body to see what he's doing, but I can't. "I thought you'd finished working on this car. What are you doing?"

He glances up at me. "Martin's bringing his wife in this afternoon to look at her. I'm making sure all the wiring for the rear lights works properly."

"Oh, do you think he'll buy the car today?"

He stands to his full height, picking his coffee up from the floor to take a drink. He shrugs. "Maybe. He was pretty keen, but I guess it's important to him that his wife agrees. It's an expensive car, considering it won't be his everyday drive."

"If he buys it, will you buy another wreck straight away, or will you have a break in between?" I take a sip of my coffee.

"Depends if another car catches my attention straight away. I have my eye on a nineteen thirty-eight Ford pickup truck, so we'll see." He shrugs one shoulder and takes another sip of his coffee.

"Well, I hope Martin takes the Sprint off your hands so you can get the truck. I love the shape of those pickups." The lines are amazing on the vintage trucks, not like the models today. All square and bulky.

Max raises his eyebrows at me. "You know what they look like?"

"Yeah, my stepdad used to always be looking at the older cars. Muscle cars and pickups were his favorites. He was the one who taught me and my younger brother how to draw."

A smile forms at the memory of us sitting on our front porch in the trailer park and drawing our neighbor's truck. I'm pretty sure it was a late nineteen-thirties pickup, but it was in terrible shape. It always surprised me whenever it started. I chuckle at the memory of the time it backfired while we were drawing it. Ethan nearly pooped his pants.

"What's brought those dimples to life?" Max asks with a small smile of his own.

"Just remembering something funny. Our neighbor had a run-down pickup. One day, we were sitting on our front porch practicing our drawing skills when the old guy came out and climbed in. When he started it up, it backfired and scared my little brother. I think he was about five at the time. I've never seen him bolt inside so fast." Another chuckle escapes.

Max chuckles too. "Sounds like the engine was running too rich." I look at him in confusion. "It happens when there's too much fuel and not enough air."

"Oh, right." I take another sip of my coffee to hide my smile. I don't think he realizes he's actually looking at me as we have a conversation. The first we've had since he turned up at the workshop on Tuesday morning. I relax a little, feeling like we're back on even ground.

Remembering the sketch I've framed of the Sprint, I hold up my finger and take off back to the office to grab it. I haven't had a chance to show Max because he's been so distant. Jogging back, I hold the frame with the sketch facing me, hiding my surprise from him. I can't hold in my excitement. I hope he likes it. I stop next to him and make a big fuss about turning the frame around.

He chuckles until his eyes land on the framed drawing. The car looked great before, but framed with glass over the top, it looks professional. He steps forward, studying it closely and I hold my breath, waiting for him to share his thoughts. I don't need to wait for his words, because his expression shows everything he's thinking. He glances between me and the sketch. "Molly." His eyes drop back to the sketch, before rising to meet mine. "It's incredible." He holds his hand out toward the frame. "Do you mind?"

I hand it to him willingly. The look of awe and wonder on his face allows me to take a deep breath. I think he likes it a lot.

"It's a cheap frame from the discount store, but it makes a world of difference to the simple sketch."

"I wouldn't say this is a simple sketch. It's amazing." He looks back up at me. "As I've said before, you could easily sell this."

I wave off his comment. There's no way my sketches are good enough to sell. "I'm torn about what to do with it. Do you think Martin will want it if he buys the car? Or perhaps you could put it up in the office, like a wall of remembrance of the cars you restore and sell."

His eyes snap back to mine. "You'd let me keep this?"

"Of course." I shrug. "If you want it, you can keep it."

"I like the idea of starting a wall of sketches of the cars I restore. I mean, it's not like I restore that many. It always takes me a while, but I'd love to keep this as a record if you don't mind." He drops his eyes back to the sketch. "I'll pay you for it."

"You will not pay me for it. It's not like it cost me anything to do, besides the ten-dollar frame, and I'm pretty sure that won't break the bank." Well, it won't now that I have a regular job and a roof over my head to boot! I point my thumb over my shoulder toward the office. "It's time I set up for the day. I think you have three bookings this morning. What time are Martin and his wife coming to look at the car?"

"Somewhere around two. I should be finished by then." He hands the sketch back to me. "Can you put this in a safe place? I'll hang it later today."

"Sure." I take it from him and then get everything organized, and ready for our first client of the day.

It's funny, some people drop their car off and come back to pick it up, while others sit and wait for their car to be ready. Whenever I have someone sitting in the reception area waiting for their car, I feel I need to make conversation, which means I don't get my work done. But the guy waiting on his car this afternoon is giving me the creeps. I'm glad it's nearing two and Max should almost be finished with his car. I'm trying my best to ignore him, but he's not taking the hint. When I get up from my seat to file some paperwork, I catch him giving me yet another once-over. He's not discreet about it either, as his slimy eyes trail up and down my body.

"So, how tall are ya? Your legs seem like they go on forever. Wouldn't mind having them wrapped around my waist. If ya know what I mean." He finishes with a wink and I'm certain my face looks like I've chewed on a lemon.

He steps closer and I try to back away, but I'm blocked by the counter with nowhere to go. I press my body as far away from him as I possibly can, but I'm trapped.

# CHAPTER 17

## —max—

"WHAT THE FUCK IS GOING ON IN HERE?" I SNAP OUT AT THE SAME time as Martin slams the outer door closed. His face looks like thunder as he steps forward, his fists clenched tightly by his sides. His wife, standing to the side of the doorway.

Glen steps back from Molly and her body sags in obvious relief. "Just telling your new girl here how great her legs look." He says it like it's no big deal that he was making my employee uncomfortable. *Fucking loser.*

"I don't think I should have to tell you that my employee has a right to feel safe at work." *Yeah, good one.* Let's not mention to the room that you stood in the bathroom door and perved on said employee, while she was fucking naked. "Your car's ready. I'll send you the invoice," I snap. "And you can find yourself another mechanic. You're not welcome back here."

"But, I didn't do anything. You're overreacting, man." He folds his arms across his chest, standing to his full height.

I step forward. I still have a few inches on him and fold my own arms across my chest. "From what I saw, I don't think I'm overreacting at all. Your type isn't welcome in my shop. You can apologize to Molly and then you can get your sleazy ass out of my workshop."

He spits on the floor between us, and Martin takes a step forward, but I motion for him to stay where he is. This isn't his concern.

"I ain't apologizing for nothing. I didn't do anything wrong. It's not my fault if the bitch is an ice queen." He tips his head at Molly with an expression of distaste.

"You disrespectful little punk." Martin steps forward and grabs Glen's shirt, pulling his arm back, ready to lay him out.

Grabbing Martin's arm, I stop him from doing anything stupid. "Martin, take a breath. Don't do anything stupid. He's not worth it."

Glen raises his hand, knocking Martin's grip on his shirt loose. "I'm outta this shithole. There're better mechanics than you around." He looks around the room, knocking into my arm as he passes on the way out.

As the door slams behind him, we all take a collective breath. When I glance across at Molly, she's shaking and tears are filling those stunning orbs, making them appear stormy. I move into her space and wrap her in my arms, cradling the back of her head. Her hands come up to my flanks as she grasps the sides of my overalls. A heavy sob leaves her, and my heart cracks.

"I'm sorry, Dimples. He had no right to speak to you like that. He won't be back." Her sobs rack her body, so I pull her in tighter to me. "Shh, shh, shh. It's okay." I love how her body fits against mine, how she feels in my arms.

Martin steps closer. "Is she gonna be alright?" he whispers.

Molly stiffens in my embrace, attempting to pull her head away from me, but I keep her close. "She'll be okay. She just needs a minute. If you want to show Beth the Sprint, you can head through. I'll be there in a few."

He nods, then guides his wife through to the workshop, leaving me and Molly alone. It takes a few more moments, but eventually, Molly gets herself under control. I can feel the change in her, so as she tries to pull away, I let her go, but I miss her instantly. Her hands still rest lightly on my sides, and I love having them on me.

I need to remind myself that I'm her boss and she's ten years my junior. It's getting harder and harder to keep myself in check the more I get to know her. I've spent most of this week working my ass off to keep her at a distance after what I did on Monday night in my shower to images of her.

"Are you gonna be okay?" I whisper as I tuck a loose lock of silky hair behind her ear. Her hair *is* as silky as I imagined it to be. Her face is red and blotchy, her eyes puffy, and her nose is red, but she still looks gorgeous.

Her eyes skate past me, and as she bites her bottom lip, she nods her head once. Glancing back up at me, she finally whispers, "Yeah. I'm sorry about that."

Confusion colors my tone. "What are you sorry about?" I thumb over my shoulder toward the door. "That asshole?" She nods. "You have nothing to apologize for. He was the one in the wrong. He shouldn't have been speaking to you like that, and he certainly shouldn't have had you trapped against the counter with nowhere to go."

"Yeah, but now you've lost a client because of me and he probably won't pay the invoice for today's work. I feel like that was my fault."

"Have you seen how fucking busy I am? I won't miss that asshole one bit. Don't give it another thought. Clients come and go all the time." I smile at Molly, hopefully portraying that I'm not bothered. "How about you clean up and meet us in the workshop? You can join us when we take the Sprint out for a test drive. Help us convince Martin's missus that she should let him buy the car." I finish with a wink.

Molly returns my smile and nods. "Thanks, Max."

"No problem."

Martin's gaze switches to something behind me. His eyes turn soft as he takes a step away from me. "Are you okay, Molly?"

Molly forces a smile as an embarrassed flush stains her cheeks. "Yes, thank you. I'm sorry about the drama."

"It was no drama at all. That guy was an asshole who needs to be taught some manners." He guides her toward Beth. "I'd like you to meet my wife, Beth."

Beth sucks in a sharp breath as she gets her first proper look at Molly. Molly glances at me, her frown creating a crease between her eyebrows as she holds out her hand to greet Martin's wife. "Oh, Molly. It's lovely to finally meet you."

Okay, this behavior is fucking weird. Both Martin and his wife have their eyes locked on Molly; it's making me uncomfortable at this point. I can only imagine how it's making Molly feel, especially after what happened in the office with Glen. Molly glances over her shoulder at me with raised brows and I can only shrug. I have no idea what the fuck is going on.

"Alright, shall we take the Sprint out for a spin?" Pulling the keys out of my pocket, I open the front door and release the catch to move the front seat so the ladies can climb into the back. Once we're situated and the workshop is secure, we take off. "Where shall we go?"

"Where would you like to go, Molly?" Beth asks.

"Oh, um. I don't mind."

"Martin said you're new to the city," she says to Molly, then turns toward the front. "Perhaps we should show her the Pier?"

"Please don't go out of your way on my account. I'll slowly find my way around. You guys go wherever you need to get a good feel for the car."

"The Pier's a great idea. That okay with you, Max?" Martin asks.

I catch Molly's eyes in the rear-view mirror. Hers widen in confusion, and I mirror her but turn toward the Pier. It's as good a drive as any to give the Sprint a run and show Beth what the car can do. "Sounds like a plan. Maybe we can stop for a drink or something," I suggest.

Martin and I are quiet in the front, enjoying the drive.

"The interior of the car is like new," Beth comments from the back and I catch her gliding her hand over the interior panels in the rear-view mirror. "And the leather is so soft. It's gorgeous, Martin."

Martin turns to me with a smug smile on his face. "I told you how perfect it was."

A few moments pass before I hear Beth ask Molly, "Martin said you haven't lived here all that long. Where are you from?"

"I moved here from Portland, Maine."

"She drove all the way here by herself," I add from the front seat.

"Oh my gosh. What did your parents think of that?" Beth asks, clearly shocked.

Molly's quiet for long moments and I assume she's not going to answer. I glance up into the mirror because I'd also like to know the answer to that question. She's turned her head toward her window, and I see her throat move. She turns back toward Beth.

"Uh, I lost my family in a car accident before Christmas." *Fuck!*

The car is silent for long moments, nobody knowing what to say to that. If I weren't driving this damn car, I would wrap her up and pull her in tight. I had no fucking idea, and I didn't think it was my place to ask her such a personal question. I could kiss Beth right now for asking, and for providing me with such intimate information.

Once I discovered my first impression of Molly was way off base, and since spending almost every day with her, I've grown to admire her, to like her. I'm man enough to admit I'm attracted to her—who wouldn't be? She's fucking beautiful. But she has so much more to her than her looks. She's incredibly sweet and thoughtful. Kind and down to earth. She could easily be bitter, but I've seen none of that from her, which makes me admire her even more.

"I'm incredibly sorry, Molly." Beth's voice oozes compassion. "That's tragic. Please let us know if there's anything at all we can do to help you. You must be devastated. I can't imagine how much your life's changed."

Martin releases a heavy sigh next to me and stares out his window. The mood in the car is understandably heavy after Molly's confession. I catch the side of Molly's face in my mirror as she stares out her window. There's a sheen to her eyes as she reaches up to wipe her cheek. Turning back toward Beth, she nods. "Thanks, Beth. I'm doing okay."

Silence descends again and I think it would be fair to say that each of us is happy to keep it that way, lost in our thoughts.

I pull into the parking lot at Pier 7, searching for a park. It's reasonably busy since it's a nice day as we move into Spring. I find a spot a fair distance from the Pier, but nobody minds the walk.

I grab Molly's hand as soon as she climbs out of the car and pull her in close. Pressing a kiss on the top of her head, I whisper, "I'm so fucking sorry about your family. If I can help, let me know. Okay?" I catch her eyes and implore her to lean on me.

She gives me a fake smile. I know it's fake because it doesn't quite create her usual dimples. "You've already helped me a lot, Max. Thank you, but I'll be fine."

I squeeze her extra tight, then release her so we can make our way to the Pier. We stop at *Declan's Diner* and order cool drinks and hot fries to share. While we sit, enjoying the sunshine, I show Beth the same photos I showed Martin, giving her a sense of how much work I've done on the car.

She chuckles and waves off my spiel. "You don't need to impress me. I've already told Martin that if he wants the car, he should buy the car. He works damn hard and gives so much of himself to me and our family. He doesn't drink or smoke and he spends any free time he has with his kids." She looks across at him, her eyes full of love and admiration for her husband. "He deserves to have something special after working hard for as many years as he has to build his electrical company."

Molly gives me a genuine smile. She knows I have the sale. "Even though I haven't worked for Max for very long, I've learned he works incredibly hard on the cars to make sure they're running at their best. You won't be disappointed with the Sprint. He's worked hard on that car to make sure it's perfect."

My heart expands in my chest with her words, which are full of genuine pride in me and my work. My family has always been proud of me. Mona never gave a shit about my work, only ever complaining that it took too much time away from her and that my hands were perpetually stained. This feeling that Molly's given me with a few simple words—that she didn't have to say—makes me puff up with pride in myself. I place my hand on her thigh beneath the table and give it a gentle squeeze in gratitude.

I should move my hand away, but I casually leave it there and Molly seems happy enough for me to do so. The lines between us are becoming more and more blurred by the day.

# CHAPTER 18

## —max—

"C'MON, I'M TAKING YOU TO DINNER TO CELEBRATE THE SALE OF THE Sprint!" I clap my hands together in excitement as I step out of the office. She's crouched down low, collecting the dirt she's swept up from the workshop.

Molly stands, brushing her hands on her skin-tight jeans. "Congratulations." Her smile is wide and excited as she leans forward to hug me. "I'm truly happy for you. It was such a magnificent car."

"It certainly was, and I'm happy that she's gone to a suitable home where she'll be appreciated and looked after." Molly chuckles and I pull back to look at her. "What?"

"Nothing. Do you realize you talk about cars like they're people?"

"Well, duh. They *are* like people. They have quirks just like people and we need to look after them, make sure they're cared for, just as we would a loved one."

She bends over with an all-out belly laugh and I feel great that I could make her laugh like that after the heaviness of her confession. I don't suppose she has much to laugh about these days, not that I would have known if Beth hadn't asked about why she moved here. She keeps her private life to herself and generally only shows a bright, cheery demeanor, maintaining a high level of professionalism. There have been times when I've noticed her staring off into space, a distant look on her face as though she's lost in a memory, but she's never let it affect her work.

"Come on. I want to take you to this Mexican hole-in-the-wall place I found. I think you'll like it." She pauses for what feels like an eternity. "C'mon. Celebrate with me." I lift my eyebrows, waiting as patiently as I can for her answer. I never usually celebrate selling one of my project cars, but I wanted an excuse to spend more time with her. After today, I want to check in with her and learn more about her.

Her dimples make an appearance. "I love a good burrito."

"Great. Let's go." I grab her hand to pull her behind me to my car.

"Hang on. I haven't finished here, and I should probably get changed." My eyes skim over her. She looks perfect in her jeans, white T-shirt, and plaid shirt. "Don't worry about finishing up. We can sort it out on Monday morning. It's Saturday. Let's go have some fun."

She shrugs. "Okay, but will this be okay for where we're going?" She fidgets with her shirt.

"Yeah." I shrug. "You look great." I tug her with me and this time she follows.

I find street parking close to *Los Burritos*. Whenever I get the urge to have authentic Mexican, this is the place I come to. The outside isn't appealing in the least and I wait for Molly to arc up about eating here, but she doesn't say anything as I take her hand and guide her inside. It's still early, so it's busy, but not crazy, as we step up to the counter to place our order. The scent of spiced meat sits heavy in the air, reminding me how much I love the food here. Glancing around, I spot a clear booth toward the back that would be perfect for us.

"If you tell me what you want, I can place our order." I tip my head toward the empty booth. "You can take care of our booth."

"Sure." She studies the menu boards with careful consideration. "What do you normally have?"

"Honestly, anything you choose is gonna be amazing. I haven't been disappointed yet. I usually have something different every time I come here."

She nods and returns her attention to the board. "I think I'll have the super burrito with the spinach tortilla and chicken if that's okay?"

"Of course. Go take a seat and I'll be over once I've ordered." The guys working in the open kitchen are calling out order numbers and requests for more ingredients. Orders are taken swiftly and served quickly with fresh and tasty ingredients. I place our order with the friendly staff member and then head to the booth to join Molly as we wait for our number to be called.

"I would have walked right on past this place without a second glance. It doesn't stand out from the street, but judging by how busy it is, the food must be fantastic."

I glance around to see it through her eyes. "It's not even as busy as it usually gets. We're pretty early. By seven, there's a line down the street."

Her eyes widen. "That's crazy."

Our number's called, and I carry our burritos and drinks back to the table. Molly's eyes almost pop out of her head when she sees the size of the burritos. "Oh my gosh, that's huge!" she says with her eyes trained on the food.

"That's what she said," I respond without thinking. Her eyes snap up to my face and she bursts into laughter.

"Maybe you could show me sometime." I freeze and Molly snaps her mouth shut tight, a pretty blush rising from the base of her throat to her face. "Oh shit! I shouldn't have said that. How embarrassing." She covers her mouth with her hand and breaks out into silent giggles. I join in with her, shaking my head because I'm the one who shouldn't have said what I said. *What is it about this girl?*

We get stuck into our meals, enjoying the flavors as they touch our tongues. Molly moans in appreciation and my dick jolts in my jeans. *Calm the fuck down.* This is not the time nor the place. I need a distraction. "You wanna tell me about your family?" I want to swallow the words as soon as they fall out of my mouth. What a way to put a downer on the moment. I wanted a distraction, dickhead, not a fucking morbid reminder of what she's lost. "Sorry. You don't have to talk about them if you don't want to. I'm not sure what I was thinking." I give her an apologetic smile.

She finishes chewing the food in her mouth, and I watch her throat as she swallows it down. My dick bumps against my zipper, imagining what it would feel like if she swallowed around me. *Fuck!*

"That's okay. It'd be nice to talk about them. Uh, I haven't had anyone to talk to since it happened." She gives me a sad smile. "My mom was seventeen when she became pregnant with me and only eighteen when she became a mother. She actually grew up here. I think I already told you that."

I nod and she tells me that her father abandoned her mother, and her parents weren't happy with the situation. Apparently, her grandfather wanted her mom to have an abortion, and that's why she ran to the other side of the country.

"Anyway. Mom met my stepfather, Jack, when I was eleven and we moved into his trailer with him." A smile touches her lips and she looks far away. "We'd been living out of Mom's car before that, so it was incredible to have a bedroom of my own and a shower and kitchen." Jesus, the shit I've taken for granted my whole life is like a magical fairytale to her. "I think because of how things were, Mom and I were super close. She was my best friend." Her voice shakes on the last sentence, so I reach across and take her hand.

"I guess that means you were used to living out of a car, then." I raise my eyebrow. "You never stayed in that motel, did you?"

"No. I'm sorry I lied to you. I didn't want you to know I was homeless and think less of me. All of my money went toward paying for the burials and funerals for my family. Then I lost my job and my apart–"

I cut her off. "What do you mean, you lost your apartment and your job?"

She tells me everything that happened, which led to her deciding to start over here. I'm fucking furious that her boss and landlord didn't cut her any slack knowing what she'd endured. They'd better hope we never fucking cross paths. I take long, deep breaths to get my temper under control. She doesn't need me going off on a rant about the assholes. She carries on speaking about her family like everything that's happened to her isn't a big fucking deal.

"Jack was the best. He was the one who taught me how to draw and trained me to run. He treated me like I was his own daughter. Mom and I were incredibly lucky to have him come into our lives and open his heart and home to both of us." I can't imagine anyone not falling in love with her or her mother if she was anything like Molly. "Then Ethan came along." She chuckles. "He was the chubbiest baby I've ever seen. I fell in love with him the second I laid eyes on him." She pulls her hand from mine with a smile on her face. "Hang on, I have a photo I can show you."

She fiddles with her phone and then passes it across the table to me. My eyes land on Molly first, then scan the rest of her family. I use my fingers to enlarge the photo, studying Molly next to her mom. "Geez, you and your mom could almost be sisters. It's uncanny how similar you two are."

Molly's smile widens. "Yeah, it's crazy, right? Her eyes are blue, though, whereas mine are gray and she didn't have dimples. She says I got both of those features from my dad."

I move the photo around, allowing me to study Jack and Ethan. "Ethan's like a mini version of his dad."

"Yeah. He would always try to copy Jack in everything he did, too. Jack was such a great dad." Her smile drops and her eyes become glassy. "He would do anything to keep us happy and safe. He would have been beyond devastated that he was the cause of everything." She wipes away the tears tracking down her cheeks and offers me a shaky smile. "Sorry."

I climb out from my side of the booth and move in next to her and tug her body into mine. "Please don't ever apologize to me, Molly. You're allowed to be fucking sad."

"It's just been a lot. Ya know?" I nod. "And I'm trying my best to stay positive and be happy in the moment, but sometimes I slip." She shrugs, tilting her head down toward the table.

"You're allowed to grieve. I get the impression that you haven't had time to do that." I use my finger to tip her face back up. Our lips are so close I can feel her breath on mine, and I'm tempted to close the distance. Her eyes drop to my lips and I lick them instinctively. Just one taste. But that would be an asshole move when she's this vulnerable. I'd be worse than Glen. I pull back and she follows, moving forward, maintaining the hair's breadth distance between us. My eyes dart down to her lips, then back to her liquid silver eyes. "Molly," I whisper roughly.

Her eyes dart up to mine. "Yeah?"

"I don't want to be the asshole here."

"Then don't be."

She moves forward and the instant her soft lips meet mine, everything else ceases. My breath freezes in my lungs and in a split second, I make a decision. I press forward and she sighs, melting against me. My tongue licks out across her lips, and I can taste the barbecue sauce from her burrito.

*I should fucking stop.*

She parts her lips, and my tongue dips inside to slide against hers.

"Are you guys finished with the table? We're all waiting and you two are over here making out like teenagers," a disembodied voice douses us with its icy tone.

Reluctantly, I pull away and turn toward the stranger who interrupted our moment. I don't like confrontation for the sake of it, so I won't say what's actually on my mind in this situation because, in reality, Molly and I are in the wrong. This is not a fancy restaurant where you linger. It's a hole in the wall where you grab your food, you eat, and then you move on. Molly ducks her head in embarrassment and I decide the best approach is to apologize and move along. Our moment's broken now, anyway.

"Sorry about that. We got carried away."

I wrap Molly's left-over burrito and grab my trash and slide out of the booth. Holding my hand out for Molly, I tug her to her feet and nod our apology to the guy. On the way out, I throw my trash in the can and tuck Molly into my side. I guess we lost track of time because we step out into the darkness. I'm not ready to take Molly home when she's finally opened up to me about her family and the reasons that brought her to me. I want to keep her with me as long as possible tonight.

"Brady's often has a band playing on a Saturday night. You up for checking them out?"

She looks up at me; the stars reflecting in her eyes. "I think I'd like that."

With her tucked into my side and her arm wrapped around my waist, we make our way back to my Dodge. Unlocking the car, I step around to open her door for her, but instead find myself pressed against her, trapping her between my body and the car. My mind flashes back to earlier in the day when Glen did the exact same thing. The only difference is that Molly's eyes heat in response and she doesn't appear to be scared out of her wits. I collect a silky lock of her pale hair between my rough fingers and feel the soft strands, my eyes watching the motion. "You have the most gorgeous hair. I wondered if it would be as silky as it looks." I draw in a deep breath, inhaling the rose scent. "It's better than I could have imagined."

She smiles and reaches up to run her fingers through my short strands, tickling the sides where a few grays have snuck in, reminding me of my age. "I like these." She runs her hands down along my jaw, scratching her short nails through my five o'clock shadow. "I really like this." She presses up slightly and plants a gentle kiss on my cheek, then glides her lips toward my ear. "I'd really like to feel this in other places."

*Fuck me.*

I think my eyes must be as big as saucers with surprise at her sexy words. My dick wakes up and attempts to break through my zipper. He doesn't need to think twice about her offer, but my brain hasn't stopped functioning just yet.

She's young. Like, really young. And sure, she's been through a ton and she's incredibly mature for her age, but I can't forget that I have a decade on her. Does she realize what she's offering?

I lower my forehead to hers, kissing the tip of her nose. "I'm sorry. I got carried away inside and I shouldn't have kissed you. I'm your boss. I don't know what I was thinking." Her body stiffens as she brings her hands up to my chest and pushes. I step back, giving her the space she's silently requesting. Her gorgeous smile is nowhere to be seen and her eyes no longer meet mine. "Don't do that, Dimples. Don't look at me like that. I'm trying to do the right thing here."

"The right thing by who? Because I was giving all the signals that I'm okay with taking things further." She wraps her arms around her body, drawing my eyes to her peaked nipples.

It's fucking easy to get caught up in the moment … in my attraction to her, but what sort of guy would I be to pursue something with her when I know it's wrong?

I run through scenarios in my head, trying to find one that makes it okay for a boss to hook up with his employee, and I can't find a single one. Not that I'm looking for a hookup, because obviously, Molly is worth more than that. She's the type of woman you plan forever with, but what if it doesn't work out? I don't want her to be uncomfortable at work and she needs this job and the apartment upstairs. She has too much to lose.

She huffs out a sigh when I take too long to answer. "Look, forget it. Can you please take me home? I don't feel like going out now." Carefully, she maneuvers her body to open the door without touching me. Closing the door, I watch her secure her seatbelt, then face forward to stare out of the windscreen.

I huff out a sigh and link my hands behind my head. I fucked up tonight. I don't know how I'm going to make things right between us, but I'll need to do something.

Pulling my door closed, I turn in my seat to face the woman who has me so damn confused. "I'm sorry. I shouldn't have crossed the line. Please forgive me. I want us to be friends." I sigh when she doesn't respond. "At least don't hate me." Starting the car, I check the road and pull out safely.

"I could never hate you, Max," she whispers into the silence.

I release a heavy breath, my shoulders dropping in relief. Glancing across, she gifts me with a timid smile that doesn't reach her eyes, but it'll do for now. I want to reach across and take her hand, to offer her reassurance that things between us will be okay, but I don't know for sure, and I refuse to make a promise I can't keep.

We pull up to the rear of the workshop and Molly climbs out of the car silently. Perhaps some time apart will be a good thing for both of us.

# CHAPTER 19

## —molly—

I'M AS SWEATY AS ANYTHING AS I REACH IN TO TURN ON THE SHOWER. I have my fingers crossed that today's the day I can make it through my shower without the water turning freezing. Standing underneath the warm spray, my muscles relax after my run. I tried to outrun my constant thoughts about Max, but it didn't work. He's still in my head and I have to work out a way past them so I'm not awkward when I see him in the next half an hour. I can't believe I came onto my boss like that, but I'm reasonably certain I didn't misread his signals. *How could I get it so wrong?*

*Ah shit!*

Goosebumps dot along my skin as the water turns to ice. Again. I'm going to have to ask Max to call in an electrician. Which means I'm going to have to pull up my big girl panties and have a conversation with him. I was hoping to keep things strictly professional between us from now on to avoid crossing any more lines. I planned to go for a walk at lunchtime instead of eating with Max. It feels too friendly for a boss and employee to share lunch every day. I'm also planning to make up some excuse to avoid going to his soccer match tonight, which hurts my heart because it's something I love to do. Being at the game reminds me of some of the good times with my family and I'm reluctant to give that up, but what else can I do?

The more time I spend with my hot boss, the harder it is to remember he's my boss, and he's made it crystal clear that he doesn't want to cross that line with his employee. If I were thinking straight, I wouldn't want to cross that line either. I need this job and the apartment that comes with it. It would be crazy to attempt a relationship with Max for it to not work out.

It's not like I've been successful in relationships in the past. What makes me think a relationship with Max would be any different? Then where would I be? Out on the street, starting all over again. I'm only now beginning to feel settled and that my decision to come here was the right one. I don't want to mess it all up on a whim. I have too much to lose.

The smell of coffee entices me as I walk down the stairs, tying my hair into a loose knot on top of my head. I put on my best smile. Fake it 'til you make it, they say, and that's what I plan to do. I'm going to pretend Saturday night didn't happen.

"Morning," I say as brightly as I can when my foot reaches the last step.

Max looks up from his coffee, his eyes scanning my face. Is he looking for my fakery? Does he know me well enough to see through my bullshit? The crease between his brows suggests he's not completely buying my bright greeting this morning. "Hey. How was the rest of your weekend?"

"Not bad. It was such a beautiful day yesterday that I went down to the river to sketch. The location was beautiful. How about you?" *See, I can do this.*

The crease between his eyebrows disappears and a smile forms in its place. "Spent the afternoon with my crazy family. My niece and nephews …" His smile drops and he grasps the back of his neck, his bicep muscle bulging. "Sorry."

I glance around, confused by his apology. "What are you sorry about?"

"I shouldn't have mentioned my family." He shakes his head. "I can't believe how thoughtless I was."

My shoulders drop. Disappointment takes the place of the hope I felt that we could move past any awkwardness between us. "I lost my family. You didn't. You don't need to apologize for that, Max. It certainly wouldn't be fair or reasonable for me to expect people to never speak about their families while in my company. I can accept that life goes on. My experience isn't yours and I'm happy about that. Enjoy your family and talk about them. It makes me happy to hear about their antics and the fun you have when you're with them."

He nods to acknowledge me, then turns toward the coffee machine. "Do you want a cup of coffee?"

"Yes, thanks. I'd love one." I turn on the laptop, ready for the day, and Max hands me my cup of steaming goodness. "Thanks." I take a sip and close my eyes in appreciation. "I needed to talk with you about the hot water in the apartment. The switch keeps turning off all the time now, even when I'm in the middle of a shower. Would you mind calling an electrician?"

"Sure thing. I'll get someone to come out today. Sorry about that. I should have sorted it out sooner." He pulls his phone out of his pocket.

"I can pay for it. I don't want to cause you any extra expense. If I weren't living up there, the hot water wouldn't matter," I rush to offer.

"I'll pay for it because I'm the landlord and it falls under my responsibility. It's not a problem." He touches the screen on his phone. "Martin's an electrician. I'll see if he can come out today."

I gather my supplies to clean the bathroom while Max is on the phone with Martin. He steps into the room as I'm bending over the toilet, scrubbing it until it shines. "Martin needs to rearrange a couple of things, then he'll be over. He said he won't be too long."

"Oh, I didn't expect him to rearrange his day to fit me in. Now I feel terrible. I can always come down here to shower, but after last time …" I trail off as I remember how my body heated under Max's gaze. Pink stains his cheeks and he shifts on his feet. "Sorry. That was all my fault. I should have locked the door." I turn my back, returning to my task to hide my embarrassment.

"When Martin comes, make sure you come and get me. I don't want him going upstairs with you on your own."

I turn back around. "Why? Don't you trust him?" Why did he ask him to come and fix the fault if he doesn't trust the man?

"It's not that I don't trust him, it's that he acts weird whenever he's around you." He folds his arms across his chest, using his thumbnail to skim his bottom lip. It's freaking sexy when he does that. "In all the years I've known him, I've never seen him act the way he has the last couple of times he's been here. I don't know if you've noticed, but he watches you and it's fucking weird. But he's a great electrician and I trust him with the job. I just don't trust him with you."

"I'm glad it wasn't my imagination. I thought he was weird and when his wife knew that I'd recently moved to the city …" I shiver.

"That's probably my fault. I told him you'd only lived here a few weeks. He said you remind him of someone, and I said it would be impossible because you hadn't lived here for long. He must have spoken with his wife about you."

Another shiver runs down my spine. "Well, that's strange. Don't you think? Why is he talking with his wife about me? He doesn't know me."

"I agree. So, make sure you're not alone with him. Okay?" He raises his eyebrows, waiting for my response.

I nod. "Okay."

The outer door opens, and cool air from outside blows in.

"Hi, Molly. I believe you're having some issues with the wiring upstairs."

"Uh, hi, Martin. Yeah, I am. I'll grab Max and we can head up."

"That's okay. You can show me." He smiles, showing divots in his cheeks, which are mostly hidden by his beard.

I stand and make my way to the door to the workshop. "Oh, that's okay. Max wants to be there since he's the landlord and all." I call out to Max to let him know Martin's arrived.

He stops what he's doing, and I lock the outer door for now since I won't be in the office. Max steps into the office to meet us. "Hey, Martin. Thanks for coming out quickly. We appreciate it." They shake hands.

"No problem." Martin looks across at me. "I didn't want to leave you without hot water."

His concern for me seems a bit much considering we don't know each other. I'm glad Max insisted on being present while Martin's looking at the wiring. The three of us head upstairs to my small apartment. Max and I point across the room to show Martin where the bathroom is. I make it to the bathroom, assuming the guys are following me, but when I turn to speak to Martin, he's nowhere to be found.

Poking my head through the doorway, I find Martin staring at the family photo I have displayed on the wall in the living room. He's standing so close to the image I'm surprised he can see anything at all. His face has gone as white as the paint on the wall.

Max is standing behind him, his arm crossed over his chest, his thumbnail running across his plump bottom lip as he watches Martin closely. I'm puzzled about what could be so interesting in the photo.

"Are you okay, Martin? You look … pale."

He turns toward me, then glances back at the photo. "Nicole." He looks back at me, then points at the photo. "That woman is my Nicole."

Max looks between the photo, Martin, and me. His confusion matches mine. "Who's Nicole?"

"Nicole is my mom," I answer Max, then walk toward Martin. "What do you mean, '*your* Nicole'?" Martin opens his mouth and closes it again. Looks at me and then back to the photo.

"What the fuck is going on, Martin? You're acting fucking weird," Max snaps.

He looks between Max and me. "I knew you reminded me of someone. You look a lot like her, but I convinced myself I had to be wrong."

Max comes to stand beside me, offering his silent support without touching me. My gut's churning and I'm afraid to hear what Martin's about to say.

He takes one step closer to me, his posture softening. "I dated your mother in high school." He covers his mouth and turns away from me. His hand moves up to cover his eyes and a shudder racks his body.

I step toward him, wrapping my arm around his shoulders. I'm guessing he just made the connection that his old high school flame has passed away. I rub my hand up and down his back, attempting to offer him some form of comfort. Tears well in my eyes and I blink to hold them back. He doesn't need me to fall apart as he works through his grief. Even though it would have been a long time since he saw her, I guess it would be a shock to learn what he's discovered today.

His familiarity with me makes sense now. I *do* look a lot like Mom.

He takes in a deep breath and wipes away the tears from his eyes. "I was telling Beth how you reminded me of Nicole, but she didn't believe me until she met you on Saturday. Beth was one of your mom's friends in high school. We all used to hang out together. She's going to be devastated when I tell her this."

His body stiffens and he moves back to the photo. "So, uh, did Nicole have another child?" His hand shakily comes up to his mouth as he glances at me.

"Yeah." I move to stand next to Martin, pointing at Ethan. "My younger brother, Ethan." I point to Jack. "That's his dad, Jack."

Martin nods slowly. "Anyone older than you?"

I shake my head. "Nope. I'm the oldest. She had me when she was eighteen." I wonder if Martin knew my dad?

The little color that had returned to his face drains. He covers his mouth again as he staggers backward and drops onto my couch. His elbows rest on his knees and he drops his head, capturing it in his hands. He's clearly upset about something. He speaks without looking up. "I ... uh ... I was dating Nicole when she got pregnant." His head lifts and his steely-colored eyes lock onto mine. "She was seventeen, I was nineteen. We'd been together for nearly three years."

All the air is sucked out of the room and a haze forms around the edges of my vision. The rush of blood in my ears is deafening as my legs collapse out from under me. I don't hit the floor as I expect, instead strong arms scoop me up, but I can't make sense of what's happening around me. I'm underwater, moving through sludge, every-thing going in slow motion. My body connects with my soft mattress, and I can make out static mumbling, but can't decipher the words.

The mind is a tricky thing. It shuts down as a form of protection. It did it to me when the police officers knocked on my door to break the news about my family's accident. This is different, though. Instead of shutting down, it's like my mind is running on overdrive but is blank at the same time. It doesn't know what to process first. The whirling thoughts are moving faster and faster, and I can't make sense of anything.

Mom left here because she had no support when she found out she was pregnant.

Her father wanted her to have an abortion.

My father disappeared.

My grandmother didn't support Mom one way or the other.

She was alone, facing an unknown future.

Martin may not be my father. Maybe she was seeing someone else, and that's why he abandoned her.

I curl into a ball and pull the bedcovers over my head. I want to go to sleep and when I wake up; I want everything to make sense again because none of this is making sense to me at the moment. And I really need things to make sense.

# CHAPTER 20

## —molly—

I WAKE IN THE DARK, A FAINT LIGHT STREAKING ACROSS MY ROOM FROM the living room. I close my eyes again, remembering everything from this morning. I must have slept all day.

"You okay?" Max's deep rumble comes from the corner of the room.

Peeling the covers away from my face, I peer over at him sitting on the chair in the corner that I picked up from the second-hand market. I take stock for a few moments. "I think so. I'm sorry I let you down today."

He sits forward in the chair, his elbows resting on his knees. "Please don't apologize to me. You had a major bombshell dropped on you this morning." He moves across to sit on the edge of my bed. Carefully, he brushes what must be a rat's nest out of my face. "Martin's not doing much better than you. I had to call Beth to come and get him." Words won't come, so I nod. "Maybe give yourself some time to digest what you've learned today, then you probably need to have a chat." I lick my dry lips and nod again. "Do you want something to drink?"

I try to sit up, but with Max sitting on the bedcovers, I can't move properly. He lifts his butt and helps me to sit up, propping the pillow behind me. "Thank you. I could use a glass of water." I tuck my matted hair behind my ear. "What time is it?"

"Six."

"Shouldn't you be at your soccer game?" I can't believe I've screwed up Max's day so badly.

"Nope. This is where I needed to be." He leaves the room and returns quickly with a glass of cold water for me. I take a long drink, soothing my dry throat. When I've finished, Max takes the glass from my hand and places it on the nightstand for me. "You wanna talk about it?" I shrug. My mind is such a jumble. I'm not sure where to start. "Take your time. I'm not going anywhere."

Sounds from outside infiltrate my sleep and I slowly open my eyes. Something heavy across my middle makes it hard to move. I look down to see what it is and glance over my shoulder to confirm I'm not imagining what I'm seeing.

Nope!

Max is lying on top of the bedcovers curled around my body, his arm slung across me. I study his face. He looks different relaxed in sleep. The scruff on his cheeks is thick this morning, adding to his appeal. My stomach flips and I feel like a schoolgirl whose crush said 'hello' in the hall.

*He stayed.*

When I needed someone, he was there. Same as he's always been since we first met.

Maneuvering my body, I twist carefully in his hold. I don't want to wake him, but I want to study him more closely. He bands his arm around my body, pulling me in tight as I get comfortable.

"Stop moving, Dimples." My girly parts wake at the sound of his deep, raspy morning voice, and I freeze. His hand slides up my back, cupping the back of my head beneath the fall of my hair. "Your hair smells so fucking good." He kisses my forehead. I'm not sure if he's aware that he's being affectionate with me in his half-asleep state, but I'm not about to point out his behavior. I don't want him to stop. His fingers slip through the long strands, then he closes his fist around them. "So, goddamn silky." I doubt that. I'm certain it's a tangled mess at this point. He runs his lips down to the tip of my nose, landing another kiss. I smile to myself and snuggle in closer, wrapping one arm around his middle.

Lying like this, our bodies would touch at every available point if Max wasn't on top of the covers. I can't believe he isn't cold.

"How are you feeling this morning?"

Recalling yesterday, my mood drops. "Do you want my honest answer?"

He pulls away to study my face. "Always."

"I'm confused. I don't know what to think about any of it." Taking a deep breath, I take a few seconds to gather my thoughts. "At first, I felt bad for him finding out that his high school girlfriend had passed away. I imagine that would have been a shock. But then when he said he was dating Mom when she became pregnant … the world sort of fell away beneath my feet." My eyes sting and I have to glance away from Max's bright green gaze. I lose the battle and tears trickle down the side of my face, crawling over the bridge of my nose, and down into my hair. Max's deft fingers massage the base of my skull and I hide my face in his chest. I'm not sure why I'm crying again today. I should be happy that I may have found my father, but my thoughts won't stop spinning.

He abandoned Mom. Essentially, he abandoned me, too.

"I have too many thoughts running through my head at the moment. I'm finding it difficult to make sense of everything if I'm honest."

"It's completely understandable, Mols." He squeezes the back of my neck gently. "And you can take as long as you need to work things out."

I nod into his chest, then peer into Max's eyes. They're full of compassion and understanding. His breath tickles my face and I drop my eyes to his lips. He moves forward slightly, and I take the cue to meet him in the middle. At first, it's a simple press of lips against lips. Max's whiskers tease the skin around my mouth, adding to the sensation. He sighs, then presses in firmer and I meet his pressure. My tongue slips out to taste the soft pillows of his lips. Max tightens his hold and he glides his fingers up to grasp my hair close to my scalp. He tightens his hand into a fist, tugging my head back, and I peel my eyes open to find Max's heated gaze on me. He plants the softest of kisses down the side of my face, swiping my tears with his tongue. My breaths speed up and I press my boobs into him, silently begging for him to kiss me. To really kiss me. I fear he's going to come to his senses and stop.

He surges forward and I open willingly, allowing him to invade my mouth with his tongue, exploring and tasting me. I match him with an exploration of my own, bringing my hand up to run my fingers through the short strands of his hair. Our teeth clash as our tongues rut against each other. This kiss is hungry. No, it's more than that. It's like we've been starved for too long and we need this to survive. My lungs burn, but I don't want to break away. I don't want to lose this.

Max slows the kiss and I panic that he's going to stop. Reaching up, I press his head toward mine. His lips spread wide against mine. "Don't worry, Dimples. I'm not stopping." My lips match his in relief and he moves forward, nipping my bottom lip before sucking away the sting.

Using his body, he rolls me onto my back and then situates himself on top of me and I wish to all that's holy that we didn't have the bedcovers between us. What I would give to feel his naked skin against mine. My body heats at the thought and I lift my head from the pillow to steal another kiss. Our lips meld and move together as though we were always meant to kiss like this. It's a kiss that I'll remember forever as it sears an indelible mark on my soul.

He moans as I push my pelvis up to meet his. I need relief, but he presses his hips firmly against me, stopping my movements without losing an ounce of focus on what he's doing to me with his mouth.

I'm dizzy with lust.

My overloaded senses are begging for attention. My hands grasp his back, feeling the stretch and pull of his muscles. He pulls back, cupping my face in his large, calloused hands, and presses his forehead to mine. "This is wrong." His eyes drop to my nose ring as he toys with the blue ball.

My breath gushes out of me, replaced with disappointment. *Why is he fighting this so hard?*

His eyes move back up to mine. "But I don't want to stop. You need to be the strong one, Mols. Tell me to stop." He closes his eyes, blocking his forest gaze from me.

"I don't want you to stop. Don't ask me to be the strong one."

He tilts his head to the side and starts all over again. My breath whooshes out of my body in sheer relief. He pillages my mouth with rough strokes as he cups my face with a gentleness that doesn't match. My breaths are ragged and I don't care.

The buzz of my alarm steals the moment and we both pull away, panting. "Damn alarm," I mumble as I throw out my arm to mute the offending noise. Max rolls off me to allow me to twist further. Finally, my hand makes contact and I silence the stupid thing. It's five o'clock and I don't want to leave my bed to get my exercise today when I could have a perfectly good workout here.

With our moment gone, Max climbs out of bed and pulls me up. He tugs me forward and places a delicate kiss on my forehead, then spins me toward the bathroom. Smacking my ass, he laughs at my pout. "Go for your run. I'm gonna head home for a shower." He adjusts the obvious bulge in his jeans. "I'll see you back here for work."

"But I don't wanna run," I whine. "I wanna keep doing what we were doing." I'm close to stomping my foot on the ground to punctuate my sentence, but I fear that would remind him of our age difference. I'm certain it's one of the reasons he's been keeping himself in check around me.

"No arguments, Dimples. I have a busy day. I had to rearrange my schedule yesterday." He nudges me toward the door, but I stop and turn.

"I'm sorry, Max." I rest my hand over his heart. "My mess shouldn't impact you. I promise it won't happen again."

He reverently slides my hair behind my ear, his eyes locked on mine, as his fingers move to glide down along my jaw where he uses his knuckles to tilt my head back a little. "Yesterday was an anomaly, Molly. I would cancel everything all over again to be here with you when you needed me. I'll be here every step of the way as you navigate your way through this new information. That's if you want me to be here with you." His eyes dart back and forth between mine.

Raising my hand, I grasp the back of his neck and pull his face closer to mine. "Of course I want you here," I whisper against his lips before pressing a sweet kiss against them.

# CHAPTER 21

## —molly—

BENT OVER AT THE WAIST, I WORK TO CATCH MY BREATH AS I WALK slowly around the parking lot in front of the workshop. Tires crunch over gravel and I turn to see who's driving into the lot this early. My heart races as I read the sign on the side of the truck: *DeLuca Electrics*. He parks and turns off the engine. For long moments, he remains seated inside his truck as we watch each other.

I don't know if I'm ready for this conversation.

I was hoping the run would help me sort through my scattered thoughts. But I'm still as confused as ever. I suck in a deep breath and take a couple of steps toward the man who may well be my father. He takes that as his cue to exit his truck. We stand a few feet apart, silently studying each other. Mom always said I had my father's eye color and dimples, but it's weird to stand across from this man and see eyes that match my own. Something I hadn't noticed before. Probably because I wasn't looking. I swallow my nerves and give him a timid smile. "Martin."

"Hey, Molly." He tucks his hands into his pockets and rocks back on his heels. "I … uh … hope you don't mind me coming over. Beth said I should give you more time, but I think we've already lost enough."

I gesture over my shoulder with my thumb. "I can't talk long, because I need to get ready for work, but would you like to come upstairs for a coffee?"

His shoulders drop and a legitimate smile slowly spreads. "Yeah. I'd like that." He reaches inside his truck, pulling out a box the size of a shoebox. He locks the doors and then follows me upstairs silently. To say I feel awkward would be a gross understatement. I'm not sure where we go from here.

Unlocking the door, I gesture for Martin to follow me inside. "Please, take a seat." I gesture toward my two-seater dining setting. "How do you like your coffee?"

He pulls out a chair and sits, placing the box he brought on the table. "Cream, no sugar. Thanks."

Well, that's easy to remember, since it's how I have *my* coffee. I make our drinks and then carry them to the table. I pull out a chair and sit opposite him, looking at the box positioned in the middle of the table between us as though it contains poisonous spiders. We sit in silent contemplation; me studying the box; him studying me.

"This is awkward." I chuckle mildly, trying to break the ice.

He chuckles, too. "It is a bit." We both take a sip of our coffee.

He lets out a long, drawn-out breath, his posture softening. "I'm sorry, Molly."

Those three little words unlock the flood. Tears stream unbidden down my face, and I hide behind my hands as my body shudders from the onslaught. Martin's chair scrapes across the floor and then I'm engulfed in his arms. If my body was racked with sobs before, it's worse now. He rubs his hand up and down my back.

"Shh, shh, shh. It's okay. We'll work through this. I promise it will be okay." He kisses the top of my head, reminding me of the way Jack would soothe me when I was upset. It's such a fatherly action. He pulls away, tucking the hair that's fallen out of my ponytail behind both of my ears at the same time. Gray eyes to gray eyes, he gives me a tentative smile. I return it the best I can, but it's shaky.

"I'm gonna go wash my face. Be back in a minute." I close the bathroom door and study myself in the mirror, sucking in as much air as I can. After rinsing my face with cool water, I pat it dry, then take a couple of deep breaths, reminding myself I can do this. I'm strong, just like Mom.

I walk back to the table with my shoulders back and a new resolve to work through this. "Do you think we should do like a … paternity test or something?" I stammer. "You know, to make sure."

He opens his mouth and closes it again. "I guess so. If that's what you would like to do." He reaches across, covering my hand with his. "But I don't need it to know you're mine, Molly. I can see it in your eyes and the timeline matches." I can too, but I wanted to give him the option. It must be tough to suddenly meet the daughter you've never laid eyes on before. He grips the box and draws it close. "I brought some photos to show you. I thought it might be a good place to start."

I nod. "You have photos of Mom in high school?" Excitement bubbles in my stomach at the prospect of seeing photos of her when she was young. For obvious reasons, she had nothing to show me from her life back here.

"Yeah. You wanna see?" He smiles and his dimples, which match mine, pop.

He opens the lid with a flourish, and I can't wait to see what he has to show me. He pulls out a handful of photos and shuffles through them, then slides one across the table to me. It shows Mom, sitting on a picnic blanket beneath a giant tree. She looks tiny compared to the trunk behind her. "She's about fifteen in that photo. I thought Nicole was the prettiest girl in school and even though my friends gave me a hard time about dating a junior, I didn't care one bit."

Martin spends the next fifteen minutes showing me photos of Mom when she was a teenager. She looked so carefree and happy—a regular teenage girl, spending time with her boyfriend and her friends.

The rumbling of an engine reminds me I should be getting ready for work. I look at Martin with apology. "I'm sorry. I need to get ready for work. Max already had to rearrange his schedule yesterday because of me. I don't want to let him down again today."

Martin collects the photographs quickly. "Sure. I understand. I'll get out of your hair." He digs into his pocket and pulls out a card, sliding it across the table toward me. "Uhm, here's my number. Maybe when you're ready, we could … uh … meet for a coffee and a chat. I'd like to get to know you if that's okay with you?"

"Of course. I'll call you and we can work out a time."

He slides the box closer to me. "You can keep that if you want. Look through the photos at your own pace. If you have questions you want to ask me, I'm an open book. Really, I am." He holds out his hands.

The vibe between us is weird. We're both nervous and unsure of what to do. Should I hug him goodbye? I decide to go for it. He accepts the gesture and pulls me in tight, swaying from side to side.

It feels weird to hug a relative stranger this intimately.

A knock at my internal door disrupts the moment and we pull apart.

## CHAPTER 22

### —max—

MARTIN'S TRUCK IS PARKED IN FRONT OF THE WORKSHOP AS I PULL IN, making my temper flare. I can't believe he showed up this morning. It would have been better to give Molly some time to get her head around their relationship, rather than bombard her the very next day. I draw in a deep breath because ultimately, it's between the two of them to work out. It's none of my business.

As I climb the stairs, I prepare to lay eyes on the woman who's quickly overtaken my life. Sleeping next to her and waking with her in my arms is something I could easily become addicted to. I run my hand through my hair and sigh. I probably shouldn't have kissed her. She has enough going on in her life at the moment. But could I stop myself from tasting her? *Hell no.* And if it weren't for her alarm, I'm not sure I would have stopped at all. I wanted to strip her bare and taste every inch of her body, paying special attention to the haven between her thighs.

I knock on the door when all I want to do is storm inside and demand Martin gives her some space. It opens, revealing Molly still wearing her running gear. He must have been waiting here when she came back from her run and because she's a sweetheart, she didn't turn him away. Her smile is instant and genuine; their time together must have been okay, because she looks relaxed, which means I can calm down.

"Hey." She waves her arm out for me to come in and looks across at Martin. "Martin was about to leave so I could shower and get ready for work. I don't want to let you down again."

I step through the doorway and place my hand on her hip as I lean in to touch my lips to hers. Now that I've kissed her, I want to do it all the time. She sucks in a sharp breath but doesn't pull away.

"Hey," I whisper against her lips. I tip my chin toward Martin. "Martin." Clearing the door, I close it behind me. "Take your time. If you need today off, that's okay too. Yesterday took a toll on you." I glare pointedly at Martin.

"Thank you, but I'll be okay. It's better if I stay busy, anyway." She thumbs over her shoulder toward the bathroom. "You two can catch up if you like while I get ready." She glances between the two of us, then heads into the bathroom. Martin and I stay put until she closes the door, and we hear the water turn on.

I step toward him, my eyes narrowed. "Do you think it's a good idea to show up here today?" I wave my arm out. "You could have given her a couple of days to come to terms with what the two of you figured out yesterday." I'm proud of how well I temper my tone when, in reality, I want to punch this guy in the face and I'm not a confrontational person.

He steps toward me. "I appreciate your concern for Molly, but this is a family matter between the two of us." Martin raises his brows.

"I get that. But you didn't see how upset and confused she is about this." I run my hand through my hair in frustration that he's not considering Molly's well-being.

His shoulders drop. "Beth said I should give her more time, but when I think about everything," he shrugs, "I've already missed too much. I don't want to miss another second."

I blow out a heavy breath. There are no winners here. Both of them have a lot to work through. "I'm sorry. I didn't think about it from your point of view." A squeal sounds from the bathroom and the water shuts off.

"Shit. I never fixed the wiring yesterday. I'll go down and grab my tools and fix it now. The heating system's wiring is likely corroded. I'll take a look." He heads for the outer door.

"Thanks. I completely forgot about it yesterday." I move to the bathroom door to check on Molly. "You okay in there?"

"Yeah. The water turned freezing again." The door opens, exposing Molly wrapped in a threadbare towel. She peers around the apartment. "Has Martin left?"

"Not yet. He's gone downstairs to grab his tools. He'll fix the wiring today since we all forgot about it yesterday."

Molly blows out a breath. "Oh, thank goodness. Every time I have a shower, I cross my fingers that it won't go cold, but it doesn't work." She giggles. I'm not sure how she's still finding humor after everything she's been through. "I'll get dressed. Back in five."

Yeah right. I've never known a woman to be ready that fast. I openly admire her long legs until she closes her bedroom door. Sure enough, she comes out of her bedroom as Martin steps back inside to fix the hot water.

As Molly and I share lunch, I study her for any signs that she's still upset. But there's nothing. I shouldn't be surprised, because she gave no outward sign about her situation or how much she'd lost until the other night.

"Are you okay?" I'm not going to attempt to guess how she's feeling. Having two sisters, I know how difficult it can be to gauge a woman's emotions.

She raises her head, her eyebrows scrunched. "Yeah?" Her voice is unsure, the single word coming out more like a question.

"Are you okay after Martin showed up unannounced this morning?" I'm still pissed about it, and it had nothing to do with me.

"Oh right. It was a surprise, and I definitely wasn't ready. But I didn't have the heart to turn him away." She scrunches up her nose. "It was pretty awkward. He left some photos of my mom for me to look at, though, which is pretty cool. I never saw what she was like when she was young. When she left, she didn't take any of that sort of stuff with her." She shrugs and stays silent for a few moments, and I think that's all she's going to say. "I'm a bit confused, though."

"Yeah. What about?"

"I dunno. He … he basically abandoned Mom when she told him she was pregnant. But he seems incredibly upset about missing out on being in my life. His reaction doesn't add up." She shrugs and picks at her sandwich.

I run my thumbnail across my bottom lip as I collect my thoughts. "Maybe he's always regretted his decision. I don't want to make excuses for the guy, but he was *only* nineteen when he knocked up your mom."

She drops her sandwich back onto the desk and straightens. "My mom was *only* seventeen. But she took full responsibility. Made important decisions and stuck with them." Her eyes scan around the office like she's looking for something. "Mom had to grow up fast and face the reality of her situation. She didn't walk away—she couldn't. Her life was hard. Damn hard raising a baby on her own. Living in a car. Barely getting by. Working minimal jobs that allowed her to keep a baby in the back office for short periods of time." Her voice cracks and her eyes become glassy.

*Well, fuck.*

I move my chair closer to hers and wrap my arm around her shoulder to drag her in close. I gently press her head against my chest. "Your mom sounds like she was an incredible woman. She made tough choices and followed through. You're an amazing person as a result of her parenting." I stroke my hand down her soft hair. "The only way you'll get answers is if you ask Martin directly. Maybe there was some sort of misunderstanding? I dunno. I wish I had the answers and I could take away this pain for you."

She nods. "I know."

Molly peels away from me and heads to the bathroom to wash her face and gather her composure while I clean up from lunch. She opens the door, looking marginally more put together. "Are you gonna be okay? You can take the afternoon off if you need."

She waves away my concern. "I'll be okay. It's better if I keep busy. I promise I'm alright."

I hug her, place a gentle kiss on her forehead and then head back out to the workshop to get on with the tire change and wheel alignment I need to finish.

"Uncle Maaaaax!" Kenny's sweet voice shouts from the opposite side of the workshop.

Shit. I lost track of time and I forgot to let Molly know Emma was bringing the kids by this afternoon. Apparently, she needed to drop something off, but I think it's an excuse to check out my new office manager so she can report back to the rest of the family.

I drop the torque wrench and hurry to the office door before Kenny decides to run across my workshop to get to me. The kids know the rules. They're not allowed on the workshop floor unless they're right beside me or Emma, but Kenny gets excited and makes her own rules.

As I close in on the door, Kenny leaps at me—I love how much she trusts me. I catch her easily, throwing her into the air with a flourish. She giggles as I catch her and kiss her forehead. "How's my Kenny?" I press my forehead to hers. She's one of the sweetest kids I've ever met, and I don't think I'm biased because she's my niece.

"I'm good. We came to visit you." Her face is alight with joy, her body is practically vibrating with excitement.

"I can see that." I tap the tip of her nose, then place her back on her feet.

"Hi, Uncle Max. What are you working on over there?" Austin points in the direction I just came.

I muss his hair. "Hey, Buddy. I'm doing a tire change and wheel alignment."

His eyes light up. "Can I help?"

I glance at Emma for guidance but she's too busy smiling at her son's enthusiasm. "Probably not today. I can't stop for too long. The owner will be here to collect his car soon." His little face drops and his body sags. "Maybe next time I do the tires on the Dodge, okay? I'll have more time and we can do it together."

His eyes light with happiness. "Really?"

"Yeah. Really."

He runs to Emma. "Did you hear that? I can help Uncle Max change his tires one day. How cool is that?" My eyes catch on Molly. She's smiling as she watches my niece and nephews.

I move closer to Lachlan. "Hey, Lachlan. How are you doing today, Buddy?"

"I'm good. Thank you for asking, Uncle Max." Emma steps next to Lachlan.

"Show Uncle Max what you brought over for him." She leans into me. "Hey, little brother." I roll my eyes and Molly giggles. It's comical that she insists on calling me little brother.

He nods and then walks toward the door, picking up a square timber box. It looks a little heavy, so I move to help him. Molly makes room on the desk, and we place it down carefully. The workmanship is incredible. "What's this?"

Lachlan focuses on making eye contact with me and I smile inside at how far he's come over the past twelve months or so. "Theo helped me make this sorting box for you. You can put the different-size nuts and washers in here." He points to several of the compartments. Molly's hand comes up to cover her mouth and Emma's face is full of pride.

I crouch down to Lachlan's level. "This is incredible. It looks exactly like the one I was looking at buying last month. I keep mixing up all of my nuts, washers, and bolts and need something to help me keep them organized." His little chest puffs out with pride. "Thank you, Buddy. It's amazing."

"You're welcome, Uncle Max."

I lift my eyes to Emma. "This is incredible. Thank Theo for me, won't you?"

"I will. I'm pretty sure Lachlan did most of the work, though." She grins at her son.

I realize I haven't introduced Molly to my family. "I'm sorry. You guys haven't met Molly."

Kenny butts in. "Yes, we have. We already said hello before we saw you. She looks like Elsa, from *Frozen*. She's so pretty, Uncle Max."

Emma, Molly, and I all burst into laughter. Kenny's always comparing pretty ladies to her Disney princesses.

"We already introduced ourselves." Emma angles her body in such a way that she can raise her brows at me without Molly seeing. With wide eyes, she mouths, "She's beautiful."

I shake my head and huff out a laugh. Beautiful is an understatement, in my opinion.

"You should come to Lachlan's birthday party!" Kenny shouts as she spins around the room.

Molly's eyes snap to mine in confusion.

"Oh, you totally should. We'd love to have you come," Emma adds with glee. She knows exactly what she's doing. She's fucking stirring the pot. If she knew where I slept last night and what I was doing this morning, she'd be all over it and I'd never hear the end.

Molly's like a deer caught in headlights as her head swings between me and Em. "Oh, uhm, I wouldn't want to intrude on a family event."

"You wouldn't be intruding at all. The more, the merrier. Right, Lachlan?" Emma runs her fingers through Lachlan's hair.

He doesn't seem convinced. "Yes." He tilts his head up to Emma. "What does that mean? The more the merrier?"

I crouch down to Lachlan's level. "It means a party is more fun when there are lots of people."

His face scrunches up. "I don't like to be around a lot of people. It's too noisy."

"That's okay. I don't have to come, Lachlan," Molly offers. Sheer relief on her face that she has an excuse.

"Molly doesn't make all that much noise, Buddy." I smirk at Molly.

"Oh, okay then. But will she be mean like Mona?" he asks.

My grin drops and I shake my head. Mona was a fucking bitch to my family. I shouldn't have stayed with her as long as I did. I didn't realize the kids had noticed, but I shouldn't be surprised because Lachlan notices everything. "No, Lachlan. Molly wouldn't know how to be mean. She's incredibly kind."

He nods. "Okay then." He moves closer to Molly. "You can come." He turns to his mom. "Molly doesn't smell terrible like Mona did."

An embarrassed huff escapes from my sister and she mouths an apology to Molly, which she kindly waves off.

"Yay!" Kenny jumps up and down in excitement. "Can I braid your hair like Elsa?"

Molly's mouth opens and closes, her hand over her heart. "Thank you, Lachlan. I'd love to come to your party." Then she turns to Kenny. "I'd love to have you braid my hair like Elsa. I'm not sure it's as long as hers, though."

"That's okay. I'll make it work." Kenny nods to herself, then continues to spin.

"Okay. Well, that's settled. We really must be going." Em gathers the kids together. "It was nice meeting you, Molly." Then she turns toward me. "Do you mind helping me with the kids, Max?"

That's code for I need to speak with you about Molly. "Sure."

The door to the outside is barely closed when Emma nudges me. Hard. "Oh my gosh, Max. She's so gorgeous and incredibly sweet."

We walk toward her car, and I help buckle the kids into their seats. "Yeah, she's pretty great."

"Pretty great, huh?" Em raises her eyebrows. "She thought I was a single Mom, who had turned up on the wrong day to get my car repaired. She was so freaking apologetic."

Sounds like Molly. "She *is* an incredibly sweet girl. She's been through a lot."

Emma's face turns sad. "Oh, the poor thing. Well, make sure she comes to Lachlan's birthday. Everyone's gonna love her."

"Hang on a minute. You realize she's just my office assistant. The family doesn't need to 'love' her." As I say the words, I know I'm not fooling anyone, especially myself. She's already more than an office assistant to me.

"You keep telling yourself that, little brother." She presses up on her toes and kisses my cheek before climbing into her car. "Whatever makes it easier to work alongside her. But mark my words. She'll be part of our family soon enough." She winks, then closes her door, not allowing me to respond.

And I know. I know she's right. Damn it. This wasn't supposed to happen.

# CHAPTER 23

## —molly—

MAX LOCKS THE FRONT DOOR OF THE WORKSHOP, THEN TURNS TO ME. "I can come with you if you want?"

I think he's offered to come to dinner with Martin at least six times today. There hasn't been another kiss since Tuesday morning, but he's been checking on me at every opportunity. He's being incredibly sweet, even if he's not giving me what I really want.

It's comforting knowing he's concerned about me, and I don't have to deal with the fallout from Monday's revelation on my own. That he'll be available if I need him. I don't think he realizes the gift he's giving me.

I smile. "I promise I can do this. Thanks for offering your support, Max. It means a lot to me."

He searches for something in the top drawer of the desk, looking triumphant when he finds it. Placing the sticky note on the desk, he writes something and hands it to me. "My address." I look at him for clarification. "If you need someone to talk to after you finish with Martin, I'll be up late. Even if the lights are off, just knock. Okay?" He raises his eyebrows, waiting for my answer.

I take the paper from him as my heart expands to double its size at the gesture. "Okay. Thank you." I want to land a kiss on his cheek, but I'm not sure it'll be welcome since he hasn't kissed me since the other day.

He smiles. "Good girl." Flutters explode in my stomach with his praise. *Shit!* I had no idea I liked that so much. I can even feel my cheeks heating. "Where are you having dinner?"

"*Parable?*" I'm reasonably sure that's what it's called. "It has a heated outdoor patio area to sit."

He nods. "I know that place. It has great food. Do you know how to get there?"

"Yeah. I looked it up at lunchtime." He's being a mother hen and I love that he cares this much about me.

He steps closer, placing his hands on my hips. His touch sears through the fabric of my pants and sends my heart racing. *Will he finally kiss me?* I tilt my head up, locking eyes with his olive-green ones. "Good luck. I hope you get the answers you need and that the two of you work out a way to move forward from everything that's happened." He finishes with a lingering press of his lips to my fore-head, which isn't exactly the type of kiss I want from him, but I feel it all the way to my soul, like a brand. "I'm only a phone call away if you need me."

I swallow my emotions. I don't want to burst into tears. "Thank you," I whisper. "I promise if I need you, I'll call."

He nods and drops his hands from my hips. Leaving me cold. "I'd better let you get ready." He lingers, making no move to leave. I think this may be harder for him than it is for me. His care and concern for my well-being fill the parts of my heart that have felt empty for the past couple of months.

"Okay. I'll see you later." Our goodbye is awkward.

I want us to be more than two colleagues saying bye.

I want hugs and lingering kisses.

I want him to tuck my hair behind my ear.

I want his hands on me.

I want to feel his arms around me.

But I get none of that.

My legs are shaky as I walk into the restaurant. I thought I was doing okay until it was time to climb out of my car and walk inside. As I step inside, I'm worried I haven't chosen the right outfit. Perhaps I should have worn something a little dressier. I opted for the capris I used to wear for work and paired them with a white shirt and denim jacket to help dress them down a little.

Worrying about things that can't be changed right now filters through my mind as I wait for the hostess—*What if I disappoint him in some way? What if I'm not the type of daughter he expects me to be? What if I'm not good enough?*

A middle-aged woman with jet-black hair and striking features greets me at the podium. "Welcome to *Parable*. Do you have a reservation?"

I nervously tuck my hair behind my ear, my hand shaking. "Uh, yeah. I'm with Martin …" Shit! I can't remember his family name. I saw it on the side of his truck, but I'm drawing a blank right now. "Uhm, I'm sorry. I don't remember his surname."

She smiles at me with warmth. "That's okay. I have a booking here under the name of Martin DeLuca. He's the only Martin we have, so I'll assume he's your companion for the evening."

I fidget with my bracelet and give her a grateful smile. "Thanks. I'm incredibly nervous and I couldn't remember, but that's his name." I chuckle nervously.

"He's already here. If you'll follow me, I'll show you to your table."

We weave through the tables, and my eyes don't know what to take in first. The garden is lush. When Martin said it had a heated outdoor patio area, I didn't expect the restaurant to be like something I'd expect to find in a city like Palm Springs. Glancing up, thick vines grow over beams and hundreds, if not thousands, of fairy lights are strung up to add to the atmosphere. This place is gorgeous. By the time we arrive at the table, I've been distracted enough that I'm a little calmer and my legs feel less shaky. Thank goodness.

Martin stands abruptly, knocking his chair over as we stop at the table. A grimace forms on his face as he corrects his chair, and the hostess leaves us to our evening.

"Sorry about that. I'm a little nervous." He pulls out my chair for me to sit, but I awkwardly turn to hug him. I feel slightly better knowing he's feeling nervous, too. He squeezes me tight and then pushes my chair in as I sit, then takes his seat. "Uhm, I didn't order any wine because I wasn't sure if you drink wine or what you like to have."

"Oh, that's okay. I'll have a beer if that's alright?" *Am I supposed to drink wine? Will he think less of me because I drink beer?*

His shoulders drop and he gives me a shaky smile, running his fingers through his thick salt and pepper hair. "That's perfectly fine." He catches the eye of the waiter and orders two beers.

We're both silent.

I fidget with my bracelet and peer around the restaurant awkwardly. Martin's tearing the paper napkin to shreds as the waiter returns with our beers.

"Thank you." He nods to the man, and I give him what I'm sure comes across as more of a grimace. Martin holds his beer up toward me, so I pick up mine. "To new beginnings."

I tap the neck of my bottle against his. "To new beginnings." We both take a sip. Mine is small while Martin seems to finish almost half of his bottle in one go. A small smile touches my lips. "I'm nervous, too."

My words seem to put him somewhat at ease. "Did you go through the photos I left?"

"Yeah. It's amazing to see Mom when she was that young. I mean, we had a few photos from when I was a baby, so she was young in those, but these … I don't know. They seem like they're from a different time. She looked so carefree."

"I'd love to see those photos of you as a baby some time … uh … if you want to show them to me, that is."

"Of course. There aren't many, but I can show you next time. I didn't think to bring them with me tonight." I chuckle lightly. "It didn't even cross my mind to return your photos. I'm sorry." I hope he's not angry with me for keeping them this long.

He waves me off. "Keep them as long as you like. I can probably print you a set."

"That'd be great. If you don't mind." There were quite a few photos in the box. It wouldn't be cheap to print copies.

"Not at all. Tell me about your childhood." I guess it's a fair question, but what will he think about the way I grew up? *Will he think Mom did a terrible job?*

The waiter interrupts us. "Are you ready to order?"

We glance at each other and chuckle. "My apologies. We haven't looked at the menu. If you wouldn't mind giving us a few more minutes? We'll do that now."

"No problem." He leaves and we both study our menu.

The waiter returns after a few minutes, and we place our orders. I order the double cheeseburger with house-cut Kennebec fries, the cheapest thing on the menu. While Martin orders the grilled NY steak with potato leek gratin, rainbow chard, and pan jus, the second most expensive item on the menu. I get paid once a month, so I need to be careful with how I spend my money. This meal will mean I have to be more careful for the rest of the month.

Once the waiter's gone, Martin turns his attention back to me. "Tell me everything." He raises his eyebrows and offers a smile.

I rack my brain. Where do I start? What do I include? What do I leave out? I don't want him to judge Mom harshly or think poorly of us. Glancing around me, I try to think of what to say. I don't know why I didn't think about this before I came tonight. Of course, he was going to ask me about my childhood and growing up.

I can't pick a spot to look at, my eyes darting everywhere as I work to gather my thoughts, but there are too many to sort through. Maybe this was a bad idea?

Martin reaches across the table, laying his weathered hand over mine. "Perhaps that was too much. I only want to get to know you. I'm devastated I've missed so much of your life." He blows out a heavy breath. His eyes, so much like my own, are full of regret.

*Maybe I should ask a question of my own.*

I fidget with the cardboard coaster on the table. "Do you mind if I ask you a question?"

"Of course not. As I said the other day, I'm an open book." He gestures with his hands at the same time.

"Uhm … You … uh … seem really upset about not seeing me grow up." I swallow. "But after Mom told you she was pregnant. You disappeared and left her to deal with the aftermath on her own. Mom left because you abandoned her and then her dad wanted her to abort me. She didn't want to do that. She thought her only option was to run. I'm a little confused, to be honest." I lick my dry lips and take a shaky sip of my beer.

Martin's face falls and his shoulders slump. His eyes skate over the people around us and he runs his hands through his hair. It's become a mess with all of his nervous attention. "I was nineteen."

Not this. Anything but this. "She was seventeen," I toss back.

He nods slowly. "I know. When I say I was nineteen, I say it to point out that I was a dumb kid." He holds up his hand to stop me from interrupting. "Nicole was always too good for me. Even though she was two years younger than me, she was far more mature." He takes another drink of his beer, draining it. He draws in a deep breath and blows it out. "I did. I disappeared. I'm not proud of my behavior. She came to me crying that she'd missed her period, so she took a pregnancy test. When she showed me the white stick with two pink lines. Well … let's just say I didn't handle it well." He draws in a deep breath and rubs his hands down his face. "I blamed her. Shouted at her." He shakes his head. "I'm embarrassed to tell you I cussed her out. Told her she was ruining my life and walked away." He rests his elbow on the table and leans forward, rubbing his hand across his mouth. "It took me a few days to calm down and think through our situation. I loved Nicole. She was everything to me. Even though we were young, I couldn't see my future without her in it." I open my mouth to question his love, but he stops me with his palm facing me. "I know it doesn't sound like I did, but I did. And I'll circle back to the fact I was a dumb kid back then. Once I calmed down, I started thinking about what we could do. I was halfway through my apprenticeship to be an electrician, so I figured we could make it work. Things wouldn't be easy, but so long as we were together, we'd be okay."

The waiter interrupts with our meals. I'm not feeling all that hungry now. I want to leave. Hearing this is too difficult, and I don't like what he's told me so far. I don't like this man at all.

*I'm supposed to like him, right?*

He's my dad.

Neither of us touches our food. He draws in another deep breath. "I went back to see Nicole about a week after everything fell apart. She was gone. Her mother was devastated and her father beat the shit out of me. I ended up with fractured ribs and a broken collarbone, a smashed eye socket, and a broken nose." He points to the crooked bridge.

A gasp escapes and I cover my mouth in shock. Oh my God!

He shrugs. "I deserved it. And probably a lot worse. I left without any answers that day and staggered home. I gave it a few days and then went back when Mr. Lewis wasn't home. I hoped to have a better chance at getting information out of Nicole's mom. But she had no idea where Nicole had gone. She'd disappeared into thin air."

I nod. "I knew she'd left and not told anyone where she was going. She told me she didn't know herself. She didn't have a plan. She kept driving until she felt she was far enough away. Mom cleaned out the money she'd saved from birthdays over the years to get her to Portland."

Maybe if she'd held on a few more days, Martin and Mom would have sorted it all out.

Maybe things would have been different. But then I wouldn't have had Jack as my stepfather and there would never have been Ethan. I don't want to think about that. I loved Jack like a father and he loved me like a daughter. And Ethan. I loved my brother so much. It hurts thinking about them. About losing them.

I peer back up at Martin. His eyes appear glassy … and sad. Worry lines his forehead and he blows out a harsh breath. "I … I'm sorry. My immaturity back then has been my greatest regret. You probably hate me now, and I'm guessing I'll lose you all over again." He smiles, but it's sad and full of defeat. His posture is that of a man who's lost something he thought was guaranteed.

I return his sad smile and shrug. "I think I'm going to need a little time." As much as I don't like to waste food, because I know how hard it is to come by, I've lost my appetite and I don't want to be here anymore. My skin is itchy and too tight. I need space away to work through everything I've learned tonight. "I'm sorry." I point toward my plate of uneaten food. "I'm not usually wasteful, but I can't eat this and I'd like to leave if you don't mind."

He nods as though he was expecting me to walk away. "I understand. I'm truly sorry, Molly. For my actions back then and for everything we've both lost. If you give me the chance, I'll make it up to you. I'll be the man I should have always been for you. I'll spend the rest of my days making it up to you. If you'll allow me."

"I … I think I need some time to think. Can you give me that?" A storm is swirling in my stomach and I'm fighting to contain everything this conversation has stirred up inside me. I need to get out of here.

"I can try. Only if I know there's some possibility I haven't truly lost you when I've only just found you."

I give him a sad smile. "I can't make promises, Martin. This. It's … it's been a lot." I stand. "Bye, Martin." I can't bring myself to hug him. I don't want to touch the man who caused Mom so much pain. I was young when she told me why I didn't have a daddy, but I felt her pain. It rolled off of her in waves even though she tried to hide it from me. I spin and walk away quickly, unsure how my shaky legs will carry me.

# CHAPTER 24

## *—molly—*

As soon as I close myself inside my car, the storm I was holding inside breaks free, streaming down my face and dripping from my chin. I drop my head to my steering wheel and let the tears come. I need to purge this hurt out of me.

A warm hand slides around my back, underneath the fall of my hair, and I scream. I didn't even hear the door open. The hold tightens on me and I turn my head. Only my hair blocks my view.

"Shhh, it's only me, Dimples." Max pushes my hair away from my face, and I'm embarrassed at how I must look.

"Wha– … what are you doing here?"

One side of his mouth tips up and he shrugs carelessly. "I couldn't sit at home waiting and not knowing if you'd be okay. I've been sitting in the parking lot for the last thirty minutes, watching and waiting." His eyebrows scrunch low. "Do I need to kick Martin's ass?" His tone is deadly serious. Max is not a confrontational man, so for him to offer to kick Martin's ass means the world to me.

I drop my head to his shoulder and wrap my arm around him, pulling him close to me. A relieved smile touches my lips as I shake my head in the negative. Having him here settles the storm and calms my soul. I know I don't have to deal with this alone. Max has quickly become my new anchor, whether or not he realizes it. A sob breaks free, but it's full of relief knowing someone has my back. I've been missing the support since I lost my world.

"C'mon. Let me take you home. We can come back tomorrow to collect your car. Grab your purse."

I nod into his shoulder, hiding the mess that must be my face. Max helps me out of my car and into his. I spend the drive staring out of the window, not seeing anything, my mind running over everything Martin said. It's not until we pull into the driveway of an unfamiliar house that I turn to Max.

"Where are we?"

"My place. I don't think you should be alone tonight. You can have my bed. I'll sleep on the couch." He climbs out of the car and comes around to my side to collect me. Helping me out of the car, he carries me to the front door, only putting me on my feet to unlock the latch. As soon as it's open, he picks me up again.

"I can walk, you know." I chuckle. Secretly, I don't want him to put me down. His care is soothing.

"I know, but I want to care for you. You need some TLC." He plants a gentle kiss against my temple, melting my heart. The man who says he's *only* my boss and that we can't be anything more than that carries me across the living room, placing me on the chaise portion of his heather-gray sectional couch. He lays my legs out gently and props a large, red cushion behind my back. I remove my shoes and drop them onto the carpet next to the couch. I don't like having shoes on the couch. "Did you eat? You didn't seem like you were inside long enough to eat."

I shake my head. "I lost my appetite. To be honest, I'm not hungry."

"How about a hot chocolate, then? Mom taught me how to make the best hot chocolate for times like these." He looks hopeful, his hands tucked into his back pockets, tugging the denim tight across his firm thighs.

I smile. "That'd be nice. Do you mind if I use your bathroom? I wouldn't mind cleaning up a bit." I circle my fingers around my face, not that I want to draw his attention to the mess.

"Uh, sure." He rushes forward to help me up from the couch. "I'll show you where it is."

As he guides me through to the bathroom, I take in my surroundings. His house is bare but tidy. It has the essential items, but nothing more than that. I wonder if it's because he likes it this way, or maybe he hasn't been here all that long. He said it took a while for him to afford a house of his own away from the workshop.

The light turns on in the bathroom with a flick of the switch and Max leaves me alone, closing the door quietly behind him. Studying myself in the mirror above the sink, I cringe at my ruined mascara, smudged around my eyes with light black streaks down my cheeks. Oh my gosh, it's every bit as bad as I thought it'd be. I set about doing what I need to do, go to the toilet, and wash my hands. Max meets me back in the living room with a steaming cup of hot chocolate.

"Sorry, I don't have any snacks to go with the drinks," he says apologetically and passes me a cup once I'm situated to his satisfaction back where I was before. He's placed a tray on the couch next to me, so I don't have to reach forward for my drink.

"It's okay. I don't think I can stomach much, anyway." I draw in a deep breath of the steaming liquid. "This smells amazing. Thank you."

"You're welcome. If you want to talk about what happened, I'm here. If you would rather just watch a movie and forget for a while, we can do that too."

"Can we forget for a while?"

"Sure."

Max turns on the television and flicks through the channels. I catch a glimpse of a *Friends* episode. "Ooh, can we watch that episode? I think it's the one where Ross whitens his teeth."

He flicks back to the right channel, and we settle down, Max choosing the cushion next to mine. I rest my head on his shoulder and he takes my hand, placing it on his thigh, drawing circles on the back of my hand with his thumb. We both chuckle as Monica and Chandler lay eyes on Ross's teeth for the first time. The banter between them is so funny that Max and I chuckle. We giggle through episode after episode, my body sagging lower and lower until my head is resting in Max's lap and he's stroking my hair, lulling me into a sleepy state.

I wake slightly when Max's arms slide beneath my legs and shoulders. "Huh?"

He kisses my forehead. "You fell asleep so I'm putting you to bed."

"Mmm, 'kay." I snuggle into his warm body, too sleepy to offer to walk myself.

He lays me on the bed. "Uhm, do you want a T-shirt or something to sleep in so you're more comfortable?"

"Mmm, thank you." I give him a sleepy smile and begin unbuttoning my shirt, pulling it open to expose my cotton bra. Max's eyes widen and he rushes over to the drawers. Next thing I know, he's dragging a T-shirt over my head to cover me. He's already seen me naked, so I'm not sure why he's in such a hurry to cover me now. I undo my bra and pull it out through the sleeves, then take off my capris, leaving my clothes on the floor beside the bed. Lying down, I pull the bedcovers over my body. Max picks up my clothes and places them over the chair in the corner and then comes back to tuck me in.

Gently pushing my hair away from my face, he leans down and presses a soft kiss to my temple. "Good night, Dimples."

"Mmm, night." In my sleepy state, I realize he's not climbing into bed. I reach out my arm toward him. "Please stay." I open my eyes when he takes too long to respond. His face is full of indecision. "Please."

That seems to do the trick, and he undoes his jeans and removes his T-shirt. I wish I had my wits about me to appreciate my hot boss wearing only his jocks, but sleep is working hard to pull me under. He slides under the covers, keeping distance between our bodies, and turns out the lamp. I roll over and snuggle into his warm body, sighing at the feel of him beneath my hands and cheek. His steady heartbeat sends me into a deep sleep.

# CHAPTER 25

## —max—

I *WAS* TRYING TO BE A FUCKING GENTLEMAN. I HONESTLY WAS. I DON'T trust myself to share a bed with the woman who's taking up so much space in my head and, if I'm being completely honest, in my heart, too. I haven't slept properly since Monday night when I spent the night in her bed. Even though I spent the night on top of the covers, her scent surrounded me, and holding her close, felt … right.

With her body curled into me and her leg thrown over mine, I lay awake for what seemed like hours with a raging hard-on.

We fit perfectly together.

When she rested her head over my heart and released a contented sigh, I knew I would do anything for her. Anything to make this transition she's about to go through with Martin as pain-free as possible.

When I saw her drop her head to her steering wheel and her body heave in the parking lot outside of the restaurant, I knew she'd taken an emotional hit over dinner with her dad. I couldn't stop myself from going to her and outing the fact that I was following her. I didn't care.

I only wanted to be there for her.

To take away her pain.

Sitting with her snuggled into me on my couch and listening to her giggle at the TV eased some of the rage I'd been feeling toward Martin for upsetting Molly. She's already been through enough. She doesn't need this shit dredging up stuff that's gotta be tough for her. I wanted to ask her what he'd said, but I respect that she needs time to digest what she learned tonight. I blow out a long breath and work to relax my body. I wrap my arms around the woman I'm falling for and kiss the top of her head as she sleeps. She sighs contentedly, and my body relaxes further.

Before I even open my eyes, I know she's looking at me. I can feel her stare burning into the side of my face. Her hand scorches my lower abdomen and my cock thinks it's an invitation to rise for attention. I kept my boxer briefs on last night, so he's somewhat contained, but he's doing his best to escape the confines of the fabric.

I groan as her fingers trace the trail of hair that leads from my navel downward. I grasp her hand to stop her from reaching the elastic band and discovering the issue I'm trying to control but am failing. Her tits are pressed into the side of my body and every single inch of me is aware of every single inch of her. Every breath. Every beat of her heart.

"Morning," her whispered raspy voice reaches my ears and my cock jolts. He likes that just awake timbre. Fuck, she's sexy.

I crack my eyes open and turn my head slightly. "Morning." She's gifting me those dimples, and the idea that I want to see those dimples first thing every single morning for the rest of my life hits me hard.

"I didn't think you were going to wake up."

I reach up and tuck her loose hair behind her ear, sliding my fingers along the strands, admiring its silkiness. I've never felt hair so soft and silky. She leans forward a little, putting our lips a mere inch apart. Her breath fans across my lips and the urge to taste her builds.

I'm trying to be a fucking gentleman. *Remember that, asshole.*

Her eyes drop to my mouth and I swipe my tongue to moisten my lips. Suddenly, they feel as dry as an empty radiator, but my mouth is watering for a simple taste. Just one little taste. I tell myself it's only a taste—one little kiss. But it's a lie. I know it's a lie.

We both close the distance, meeting in the middle. The first press sets fire licking down my body, the second has me rolling her to her back so I can climb on top. Using my knees, I push her thighs apart, creating a space to cradle my cock against my girl's pussy; the heat radiating from her scorches my dick. She wraps her gorgeous long legs around me, locking them at the base of my spine and pulling me in tight to her core.

It's my fantasy come to life. I've dreamed about her legs wrapped around me, trapping my body to hers. The only thing that would make it better is if we were both naked.

Moving my hips slowly, I rub my shaft against her mound, drawing moans from both of us. My body is on fire for this woman as her hips rise to meet mine in a rhythm that could get me in trouble. She glides her hands down my back and scrapes her short nails along my spine on the way back up, sending goosebumps radiating across my flesh. I don't want to cum in my boxers like a sixteen-year-old virgin dry-humping his girlfriend in the back seat of his car. I tear my lips from hers and kiss my way behind her ear, continuing down the tendon in her neck, and across her collarbone, nudging the fabric of my T-shirt out of the way as I go. She arches her back, pressing her glorious tits into my chest. I want the fabric that's keeping her flesh from me, gone.

Her hands tickle down my spine to the top of my boxer briefs, where she follows the waistband to each side of my hips. "Can I take these off, Max?" she pants against my ear as she tilts her head to the side to allow me better access to her neck.

I pull back to check she's completely in the moment, and that I'm not pressuring her. Her irises have almost disappeared with desire, her cheeks flushed prettily, her lips swollen from my kisses. I nod and pull away to drag them off.

Her hands cover mine. "Can I do it?" Her eyes have dropped to my heavy cock, working to escape its confines.

I remove my hands and climb from the bed to stand. She crawls over to the side of the bed on her hands and knees, her tits swinging back and forth beneath the fabric covering them. The neck droops enough that I can watch them sway. My eyes zone in on the action and I almost miss that her cotton-covered ass is exposed as my T-shirt gathers in the middle of her back.

She rises in front of me, landing a kiss on the underside of my jaw and I drop my head back, relishing the touch of her lips. Her fingers tuck into the waistband of my briefs and she slides them down, pulling them forward slightly to work around the crown of my dick. Her eyes drop to watch what she's doing, and they widen. She licks her lips, then drops forward, swiping her tongue across my glistening slit. My heart pounds with a heavy rhythm to match my breaths.

"Fuck." My body jolts at the first swipe. She looks up at me with a satisfied grin. "You're a little minx, aren't you, Dimples?" She raises one perfectly sculpted eyebrow before leaning back in. I hold her shoulders still. "Uh, uh, uh. I need you naked. Now."

Her eyes sparkle as she pushes my underwear down further. They slip down my legs and I step out of them. I glide my hand beneath the fall of her hair and grasp the strands at the base, using my grip to pull her back up to my mouth. Her lips part in surprise and I swipe my tongue inside without warning. She gasps and I take advantage to thrust my tongue forward against hers. She presses her body against mine and I move one hand down to her silky thigh and slide it beneath the fabric of the T-shirt. I repeat the action on the other side, gliding my hands over her hips, to the dip of her waist, and along the side of her breasts.

"Lift up," I whisper against her lips, tapping against the side of her body.

She raises her arms and I slide the offending fabric from her stunning body and throw it over my shoulder, not caring where it lands. My eyes start at the top of her head and trail slowly over her face, noting her lustful gaze on my dick. She licks her lips, making them glisten. I need to have a taste. I lean forward, swiping my tongue along the same path.

Pulling away, I continue my perusal. The pulse point at the base of her throat is beating out a rapid rhythm. I grip her lightly around her throat, my palm against the pulse point, studying her heavy-lidded gaze. Molly whimpers, her eyes locked on my mouth. She generously drops her head back, allowing me to kiss the base of her throat and I smile against the rapid pulse, then suck on the flesh, drawing it into my mouth and tasting it with my tongue. She tastes fucking delicious and I'm looking forward to tasting her pussy. My dick throbs and taps against my abdomen at the thought. Molly's hands slide up my arms, along my shoulders, and up the back of my head. Her fingers glide through the strands of my hair and my eyes close in pleasure.

"Max," my name is whispered on a hot breath, her fingers tightening on the strands as she pushes my head lower, toward her tit. I lick my way down under her guidance, then lave the pink areola, before drawing the nipple into my mouth. Her hand pushes my face into the mound, and I suck hard. She presses her breasts forward and I cup her other tit, rolling the nipple between my fingers; it puckers beautifully under my touch, so I switch my mouth across to it.

Licking, sucking, teasing.

I pull back enough to praise her. "You've got beautiful tits. Full and perfect and pink. Look at how they're showing off for me." I pluck them both as I watch them harden further. "Fucking beautiful."

My eyes trail down her flat stomach and freeze on the silver jewelry decorating her navel. I drop, so I can investigate it further, then glance back up at her from my lowered position. Fingering the jewelry, I lean in to lick it with my tongue and then kiss my way to the top of her underwear. "You're full of surprises, Dimples. First the nose ring, now the navel piercing. Fucking sexy as hell."

She giggles, which morphs into a moan as I continue my path downward. Her fingers sift through my hair as I run my nose down her mound, sucking in a deep breath the lower I go. Her excitement is evident from the wet spot staining the cotton. I swipe my tongue over her clit, then nip it gently through the fabric. Her hips buck and she sucks in a sharp breath. I smile against the fabric, then look up at her. The view is fucking sensational. "Mind if I take these off?" She shakes her head, and my disappointment is swift and strong. "Okay." I can't believe I misread the situation so badly, but I pull back. I'm not the guy to force the girl beyond where she's willing to go.

"Why are you stopping?" Her eyebrows scrunch together, causing a crease between them.

"I figured you wanted me to when you didn't want me to take these off." I twist the elastic band of her underwear with my finger.

She chuckles. "I meant I didn't mind. Please. Take them off." She slides them down her athletic thighs, but I stop her.

"I want to do that. Lie down for me." She lies down like a good girl, resting on her elbows, still watching me.

"Good girl," I whisper. She bites her bottom lip as she watches me slowly tug the flimsy fabric down her long, smooth legs. I throw them over my shoulder to join the rest of the discarded items on the floor. Starting at the top of her foot, I glide my hands up the inside of her legs, toward the junction of her thighs, pushing them apart as I go. Goosebumps form under my touch, and her muscles quiver. "You have the most incredible legs. So long and sleek." Following the path of my hands, I place the softest of kisses on the silky skin until I reach the apex and my goal. I run my nose from the base of her slit to the top and back again, drawing in a deep breath and filling my lungs with her musky scent. "Hmmm." Meeting her eyes, I give her a wink and part her pussy lips, flatten my tongue, and take my first taste.

She's fucking luscious.

"Mmmm, Max," she moans as she presses her feet to the bed, bringing her hips up to meet my mouth. I smile against her mound and shake my head slightly.

"Don't be in such a hurry, Dimples. I've got you." I use my finger to slide up each side of her slit, gathering her essence before slipping into her opening. "Fuck!" The heat of her channel sears my skin, and my dick jumps in excitement for what's to come. I drop my mouth to lick and suck her clit in time with the movements of my finger. I slide the sole digit out and replace it with two. "Fuck. I can't wait to get inside you."

"Can you hurry and do that now?" she whispers as she tugs on my hair, attempting to drag me up her body.

My eyes snap up to hers. "What's the rush? Somewhere you need to be?"

"Nope. I just need to be filled with you. I feel like I've been waiting forever." I drop my head back down and return my focus to her delicious pussy. As I feast, I keep my eyes on her. Her tits shiver with each breath and the jewelry on her belly quivers as her muscles tense. "Max, I'm so close." She drops her head back like it's too much to hold up right now.

"While I'm busy down here, play with your tits for me." She brings her hands up, sliding them over her plump globes, pushing them together, and cupping them. I wish I could clone myself and have my mouth on them as well as on her pussy right now.

"That's a good girl," I whisper against her mound, moving my fingers inside her in a come-hither motion.

"I'm so close. Don't stop."

I shake my head in the negative because there's no way on this earth I would stop now. I keep my movements consistent—I don't move harder or faster. She needs to come so I can get inside her.

I fucking need to be inside her.

My balls are heavy as fuck and I need some relief, but not until she comes the first time. Her channel tightens around my fingers and the flutter of her muscles presses against them. She's getting close. The combination of her natural lubrication and the thrusting of my fingers creates a squelching sound as she tightens her legs around my head. I'm getting harder by the second. "Fuck, yeah. Just like that!" It's so sexy how into this she is.

Her entire body tightens and shakes as she moans long and low, her internal muscles strangling my fingers. She's gonna suffocate my dick and I'm gonna love every single second of it. I slow my movements and gentle my kisses, lapping up her cum.

She really should taste herself. I slide my fingers back inside to collect her cum and then move up her body to paint her lips. "Taste how fucking luscious you are," I demand before I kiss the hard peaks of her breasts. Her nipples have darkened from a pale rose to a dusty rose, looking amazing against the pale color of her flesh. A sheen of perspiration coats her skin, giving her an ethereal glow.

She licks her lips and moans. "I want to taste me on you." She slides her fingers into my hair to tug me up to her.

I don't hesitate.

I slam my mouth down on hers, pushing my tongue inside as she opens for me. Her eagerness to taste herself heats my blood and builds my excitement. Rolling on top of her, I notch my dick between her pussy lips and grind down. Long, slender legs wrap around my waist as the heels of her feet dig into my ass, urging me to keep moving. She tries to wedge her hips up as I slide downward, connecting with her entrance.

I tear my mouth from hers. "I need to grab a condom."

I hope I still have some here that haven't expired. Pushing up from Molly, I roll over to check the drawer. I have one left. I check the expiration date. My shoulders drop and disappointment fills my belly. I glance back at Molly, whose heavily lidded eyes are following me.

"What's wrong?"

"It's two months past its expiration. It would still be better than using nothing, but it's up to you." I smooth my hand up her leg. "I'll understand if you want to stop. I can grab some from the store and maybe we can pick this up again some other time."

She pushes herself upright and presses a gentle kiss against my mouth. Her eyes flick between mine. "I get the shot every three months. I have two weeks until I need my next one." She tucks a messy lock of hair behind her ear. "I'm clean."

"I'm clean too." I point over my shoulder toward the doorway. "I can show you if you like?"

She smiles, putting her dimples on full show. "I trust you."

I don't need any further encouragement. I dive straight back in, sucking on her nipple, cupping her breasts together, and massaging them. Her head drops back as she thrusts them forward into my face and hands.

Without wasting any more time, I shuffle her up the bed and spread her silky legs open wide, cradling my rock-hard shaft at their apex. Sliding down, I notch my head at her entrance, then hold my breath as I push inside, inch by inch, for the very first time. "Ah, fuck!"

I pause, pulling back to peer into my girl's eyes. The light gray of her irises has turned into molten mercury. They're begging me to move, but I want to enjoy the feel of her heat around me before I take us where we both want to go—heaven. Her lips part and I fill her mouth with my tongue.

Skin to skin, breath to breath, heartbeat to heartbeat. I can't be any closer without climbing inside her.

Sucking in a deep breath, I pull out, so the head of my dick sits just inside her entrance and then push in and up, making her tits jiggle. "I love your tits."

I don't know where to look. My eyes skate between her breasts and my cock sliding in and out of her body, her flushed pink pussy lips spread wide to accommodate me. Sliding one arm beneath her leg, I position it over my shoulder to open her wider to me.

"Ohhh, Max." Molly pushes her hips up, meeting each and every one of my strokes into her body, taking me deeper. My body's on fire and her moans make me hotter by the second. I'm going to self-combust at the rate I'm going. The flush climbing over Molly's body suggests she's feeling the same. It's incredible how in sync we are for our first time together.

She fits around me like a silken glove and when I lift her other leg over my opposite shoulder, my balls tighten up. Tingles race down my spine, collecting at the base. Urgency takes over and I can't maintain the steady rhythm I had before.

She needs to come.

"I need you to get there," I breathe heavily against her ear, between harsh pants. Her short fingernails dig into my back as she raises her hips. Her walls tighten around my shaft, making my eyes roll back in my head. "Be a good girl and come for me," I grit out between clenched teeth.

"I." Thrust. "I'm." Thrust. "Close." Thrust.

"Fuck. You feel incredible." I slide my hand between our bodies and press gently against her clit. It's gotta be sensitive after coming a short while ago. Massaging small circles around the bundle of nerves, her walls begin to flutter, tightening further. My shaft grows and the cum in my balls is close to the surface, but I've got to hold on ... *fuuuck!*

I couldn't do it. Streams of cum flood out of me and into my girl, my shaft pulsing as I coat her internal walls, filling her with my essence. Her channel contracts and we both moan; freezing in place as my orgasm sets off hers.

I suck in as much air as I can and drop my mouth back down to hers. This time, I kiss her slowly, reverently, carefully. I want to show her how much it meant to me that she allowed me the privilege of sharing her body. It's never something I take for granted, but for Molly to give this to me, it's special and meaningful. This isn't a quick fuck for either of us. It's not about just feeling good in the moment. It's about sharing a deep connection with another person, and we want to express that physically.

My eyes skate around her face as I pull back. Her eyelids have dropped closed, and she has a serene smile on her gorgeous face. She raises one eyebrow without opening her eyes. "You're staring at me." She giggles.

I press my hips forward, pushing my softening cock inside so she can't push me out. "Yes, I am. You're so fucking beautiful and you look stunning lying there all flushed and mussed up. I don't want to take my eyes off of you."

Her dimples deepen and I lean forward to lay a kiss on each one. "I probably look a mess."

"You definitely don't. Maybe I need to work harder to mess you up?" We both chuckle.

## CHAPTER 26

### *—molly—*

MAX INSISTED ON DRAGGING ME OUT OF BED, SO HE COULD CLEAN ME up, only to mess me up again as he was drying my body. I chuckle to myself at the expression he wore when he realized we'd need to have another shower.

"What's that chuckle about?" he asks as he slices fresh fruit for our breakfast. My favorite.

"Nothing." I pop a strawberry into my mouth and give him a wink.

I can't believe I had sex with my hot boss!

Awesome, life-altering sex.

With the man who's been diligently keeping everything professional between us, no less. The one who didn't see me as a woman and thought it was okay to invite me for drinks with the boys after soccer. I want to squeal with excitement, but I don't want to remind him I'm younger than him or that he's my boss—the sticking points that have been holding him back. I'm not sure what changed, but I'm glad it did.

Max carries the fruit to the small dining table, while I carry the juice. He grabs the yogurt, while I grab the bowls and spoons. We work silently to get breakfast set up as efficiently as we can. Max scoops fruit into both of our bowls and then I top them both with a healthy serving of yogurt.

"Damn. I forgot the honey," Max mumbles as he moves back to the kitchen. When he comes back, he holds up the container. "Would you like some?"

Honey's freaking expensive, and not something I've eaten very often. "Not normally. But I'll try some. Thanks." He dollops a small amount in each of our bowls, then sits. We both eat quietly for a few minutes, stealing glances at each other with satisfied smiles on our faces. I rub my toe up Max's leg over the top of his gray sweats. "I love these sweats." I wink at him. He brings out a cheeky side to me I'm enjoying.

His spoon stops halfway to his mouth, and he raises his eyebrows. "Yeah?" I nod and go back to eating. "I'll keep that in mind." After a few minutes, when we're both finished, Max rises and takes our dishes to the kitchen. "Would you like a coffee?"

"Thanks, I'd love one." I step beside him to wash the dishes as he makes us both a coffee. He glances at me with the strangest expression. "What's wrong?"

He shrugs. "Nothing."

Once the coffee's ready, we step out on the back deck to enjoy it. His backyard is low fuss. No garden, only grass with a decent-sized workshop I'm guessing he uses for car stuff. I take my first sip and close my eyes in appreciation, humming my delight.

"Did you want to talk about what happened with your ..." He runs his hands through his hair. "Uhm, your ... Martin?" I'm guessing he was going to call him my dad. Which is what he is, I guess. "You don't have to if you don't want to. I just want you to know I'm here."

I reach across the space between us and grasp his hand. "Thank you. He, uh, he told me his version of what happened when Mom told him she was pregnant. He didn't respond well. Cursed her out and told her she was ruining his life."

My stomach rolls as Max's eyebrows shoot up and if fire could shoot from his eyes, I'm certain it would. "He what?"

I shrug and give Max a pointed look. "He blamed it on being nineteen." I raise a brow.

"Sorry. Men ... no, boys are fucking dumb at that age. We have a toddler brain which is all about food and sex. Anything else doesn't compute."

I can't hold back my chuckle at his explanation, though it doesn't change how things unfolded all those years ago. "It sounded like he treated her terribly. I couldn't sit across from him any longer listening to his story. I get that he's regretful. But his actions had an enormous impact on our lives. I can't pretend it doesn't matter." Max laces his fingers with mine, squeezing them in silent support. "I told him I need time. I'm not sure how long, but it was a lot to digest." Max's gaze follows my tongue as I lick my dry lips. "I walked away, not liking the man who says he's my father. In fact, I'm not sure I have any respect for him."

Max tugs my hand, pulling me across to him. He situates me on his lap, stroking his hand along my spine. "I'm sorry, Mols." I sink into his warm body. "You were right to walk away if that's what you needed to do. You don't owe him anything at this point."

Silence surrounds us as I work my mind back to the night before. Then further back to when Mom explained to me why I didn't have a daddy who lived with us. I think she still loved him. Even after the way he hurt her.

"Do you want to come to lunch with my family?" Max breaks the silence. I turn my face to study his. Even though he seems surprised that he's invited me, his offer is genuine.

"Thanks for the invite, but I'm not in an emotional space today to meet the rest of your family." I kiss the scruff on his jaw. "I'll come to Lachlan's birthday, though." I hope he understands I feel too raw to be around people.

He returns my kiss, rubbing circles on my back. "Of course. I get it."

"I guess I should get out of your hair so you can get ready. Do you mind dropping me back at my car?"

"No problem. I'll put on a load of laundry and then we can head out."

The salty breeze off the ocean tickles the strands of hair across my face as the sun sets on another day of my new life. Resting my arms on my knees, I drop my chin down to rest on top. A smile touches my lips as I remember this morning. Was it only this morning? It certainly 'feels' like it happened this morning.

He's a generous lover who definitely knows his way around the female body. I guess that decade between us has given him the opportunity to gain extra experience. My stomach squeezes at the thought of Max with another woman, though I have no right to be jealous. We both have our pasts, which include previous lovers. A shiver runs down my spine as I remember how my body responded when he pushed inside me for the first time. The way he praised me and called me, 'good girl'. I chuckle quietly. *Who knew I'd like that so much?*

I focus on the waves lapping on the shore as the sun drops even lower on the horizon. I think this is my favorite thing to do. My chest tightens as I recall dinner last night with Martin. I'm unsure how to move forward. Blaming him won't change what happened or the path it led Mom down. He seemed genuinely remorseful and worried about the impact telling me his side of the story would have on our relationship now. It was confronting to hear his side of the story and the way he behaved to the news of Mom's pregnancy. I get it was probably a shock, and he was young, but shit, Mom was young too and I would imagine equally shocked. The situation would have been scary for her. Perhaps when it's not so raw, I'll be able to move past how I'm feeling at the moment.

Arriving home, my headlights land on a figure sitting on the bottom step leading up to my apartment in the dark. The closer I get, I recognize Martin's wife, Beth. My stomach sinks like a rock to the bottom of the ocean and dread fills me. I just need some freaking time.

Is that so hard?

I park around the back in my designated space, draw in a deep breath and remind myself that I'm a reasonable person and that my response to Martin last night was understandable. I was well within my rights to feel the way I felt as he shared his side of the story.

Beth rises from the bottom step, dusting off her pants as she stands to face me. Her face is drawn tight, and she gives me a smile that comes across as more of a grimace. "Uh, hi, Molly. I'm sorry to intrude, but I wanted to check on you and make sure you're alright after last night."

Well, that wasn't what I was expecting. I figured she was here to put Martin's case forward. "Hi, Beth. Thanks for stopping by. I guess Martin told you dinner didn't go so well."

She shakes her head. "Something like that. If I know Martin, I'm sure he blurted everything out without considering how it would be received or how distressing it may be for you to hear."

I huff out a breath. "Do you want to come upstairs?"

"Sure. Thanks." She runs back to her car, grabs her purse, and then follows me upstairs.

I unlock the door, turn on the light, and disarm the alarm before hanging my keys on the hook by the door and dropping my purse on the floor. I probably should buy an entry table, but money is still a little tight. "Make yourself at home. Would you like a glass of water? I don't have much else, sorry."

She waves me off. "A glass of water would be great. Thank you." Beth takes a seat on the small sofa and when I walk in with two glasses of water, I find her staring at the box of photographs Martin left behind. "There are some great memories in that box."

I nod. "I'm sure. It was nice to see some photos of Mom before she had to deal with the stresses of parenthood."

Beth nods. "We were all friends, you know." I got that impression when I looked through the photos and Martin said the same thing. There were several of Mom and a much younger Beth, as well as photos of the three of them. "I was devastated when Nicole disappeared. She was my best friend." She takes a sip of cold water, her hand shaking slightly. "It took months before Martin told me how he'd behaved toward her when she told him she was pregnant … and only after I'd got fed up with him being overly reckless. He turned to drink. One night, while he was drunk, he confessed everything. I didn't even know Nicole was pregnant until he blurted it out. She never said a thing. Just vanished." Tears are tracking down Beth's cheeks, so I grab the tissues and hand them to her. "Thanks." She takes a couple and wipes her eyes, then blows her nose. "Sorry. Whenever I reflect on that time, I get very emotional." This must be hard for her if they were as close as she says. Not only did she lose Mom back then, but she's also found out that Mom has passed away.

I nod. "I figured you were all friends from the photographs Martin left for me. How did it come about that you and Martin got together?" Oh, that was probably a little forward. "If you don't mind me asking."

"It was some time after. Martin and I remained friends and then I went through a terrible breakup. The guy I was with liked to communicate with his fists." She waves off the last part like it's inconsequential. "Martin stepped up and helped me get back on my feet physically and emotionally. One thing led to another …" she shrugs, "and here we are." Her eyes rise from studying her glass to meet mine. "I know I've always been his second choice. If Nicole had ever come back, I think he would have left me in a heartbeat."

I'm certain my head snaps back as though she's slapped me. "But you have kids together."

"I'm not sure that would have mattered. I don't know, and I guess I never will now." She reaches across, laying her hand over mine. "I'm truly sorry about your mom, Molly. When I picked Martin up from here last week and Max filled me in on what the two of you had discovered, I was devastated to learn that Nicole was gone. Even though I hadn't seen or heard from her in all these years, I still thought of her often and I missed our friendship."

Her pain is radiating from her in waves. But I have to wonder how she's lived in Mom's shadow all these years. Wondering if her husband would stay or leave if Mom ever returned. I don't think I could live that way.

"If I'm being completely honest, the more I'm learning about Martin, the less I want to get to know him. The way he reacted to Mom when she told him she was pregnant, to the way you're not even sure if he would have stayed with you had Mom returned. What I'm hearing is that he's a man who only thinks about himself. Not a quality I like."

Beth draws in a long breath. "Don't get me wrong. The man has his flaws, just as anyone does, but he is a *good* man. He's great with his kids; loves and adores them. He would do anything for them and for you … if you'll let him. He's been a fantastic husband. Attentive, supportive, and loving. What I mentioned before is my self-doubt." She brings her hand over her heart. "If I were to dig deep, I know he wouldn't walk away from me and the kids. He's too good a man for that." She pauses and nods her head slightly. "He would have done the right thing by you and Nicole if she hadn't left before he got himself together. I have no doubt about that."

We're both quiet for long moments. I'm not sure where we go from this point.

"Did he show you photos of our children?" Her voice is timid, as though she's unsure she should bring them up.

I shake my head. "No, he didn't. We mainly talked about Mom, and I needed to get ready for work. Then last night, I asked him to share his side of the events and, well … that didn't go down so well."

She digs out her phone, navigating to the photo album. "I think you may be surprised. You look a lot like Nicole but take a look."

She holds out her phone and I take it, preparing to see my half-siblings for the first time. Because out of all of this, I've learned I have a sister and a brother. I gasp as my eyes connect with my sister. Her hair is darker than mine, almost black like her mom's, but we are definitely sisters. I glance up at Beth with wide eyes. "How?"

"I don't know. I'm guessing that even though you have a lot of Nicole in you, you also have enough of Martin that you maybe didn't recognize because you weren't looking for it."

I guess so, but this is unreal. I flick to the next photo, which is of my brother. He looks like the male version of his sister, which means our resemblance is also strong.

"Noah doesn't have dimples," I comment and Beth shakes her head. I glance back at my brother. He looks about the same age as Ethan. "How old are they?"

"Holly is seventeen, while Noah is fourteen." The pride that fills Beth's face is unmistakable.

I raise my brows. "What are the chances that my name's Molly and your daughter's name is Holly?" I chuckle a little, because, well, that's just weird.

She lifts one shoulder and allows it to drop, shaking her head from side to side with a half-grin. "I dunno."

"I had a brother, Ethan. He was thirteen." My throat tightens as a lump forms, my heart beating double time like it has to beat for him too. I work hard to keep my tears at bay. Beth must sense my battle and moves closer, wrapping her arm around my shoulder and I can't fight the sadness any longer. "I miss them so much," I sob.

"Oh, sweet girl. I can't imagine what it's been like for you." She wraps her other arm around me and squeezes me in close.

I let go.

In this stranger's arms. I break down.

All the pent-up tears and emotions.

The heartache and the loss.

It all comes pouring out of me like a tsunami. She comforts me like a mother would as her hand cups the back of my head while the other one rubs up and down my back.

I burrow into her, deep into her shoulder, and release my misery.

My utter devastation.

When I eventually regain my control, I pull my head away from Beth, noting the large wet patch on her shirt. I want to hide away, embarrassment swamping me.

She cups my face, tucking the loose strands of sweaty hair behind my ears. Her face is full of compassion. "You know, I've been thinking about you coming back here. How you and Martin found each other. It feels as though you were brought to us, Molly." She smiles sadly. "Perhaps Nicole guided you home so you could be with us."

I nod. I've thought the same thing. Perhaps I was supposed to come here and find my family. Everything fell apart so spectacularly after the accident that I had no choice but to make a major life-changing decision. Maybe Mom wanted me here. Wiping my tears, I try to give Beth a smile of reassurance. "Perhaps."

She scrunches her eyebrows together and glances down at her lap, then draws in a deep breath before raising her eyes back to mine. "I know I'm not your mom and I could never fill her shoes. But I want you to know that I'm here for you. Whenever or whatever you need."

I lick my lips as a couple more tears escape. "Thank you, Beth."

"Maybe one day, we could be friends," she hedges.

I nod slowly. "Maybe."

The silence in the room has become stifling. "I'd better get home. The troops are probably wondering where I am."

We both stand and Beth collects her purse. "Thanks for stopping by." And I mean it. When I first saw her sitting on my steps, I didn't want to speak with her, and I was close to brushing her off. I'm glad I didn't.

She gives me a gentle smile. "Thanks for not sending me away. I hope we can chat again soon."

"I'd like that."

# CHAPTER 27

## —max—

I PULL THE TOW TRUCK IN BEHIND THE WORKSHOP, A SMILE OF satisfaction touching my lips. I can't wait to start work on this baby. It's going to be a huge project but I'm up to the task. I've been wanting to get my hands on one of these for a while now. Molly steps out through the back door of the workshop, her hand shielding her eyes from the early morning sun, the other resting on her hip. Her almost-white hair appears to be glowing in the morning light, and I can't wait to press my lips to hers. I would have been climbing into her bed last night if I didn't get the call yesterday afternoon to collect the truck I've had my eye on.

She's waiting at the open door for me when I drop down from the truck. I wrap my arms around her and drag her into me, loving how we fit together. I rub my nose alongside hers and then press my lips to hers. She opens for me without delay, and I sweep my tongue inside. My hands drop to grab her perfect ass and I press her closer, rubbing my cock against her lower belly. Remembering the jewelry she has dangling above her navel makes me even harder. She's so fucking sexy in the most unassuming ways. She wraps her arms around my neck, pulling me closer as she climbs my body like a fucking tree.

And isn't that the hottest thing?

This girl is as far gone for me as I am for her, and she's not shy about letting me know. Using one hand to hold her up, I use my other to guide her head the way I want, tilting my head so I can deepen the kiss. Our tongues move against each other as though we've been doing this for years, not days. Molly's heart pounds out a rapid beat to match my own as we reconnect.

We slow the kiss and shift back far enough to catch our breath and study each other. We're both breathing heavily as our matching smiles grow. I move in and lay a quick peck against her swollen lips, satisfaction filling me at the sight. "Morning, Dimples," I whisper against her lips.

She drops her forehead to mine. "Morning. I missed you last night."

I've never been with anyone before who hasn't played games with me. Molly's open heart and honesty are possibly one of her most attractive qualities.

"Me too." We've been spending most nights in her bed or mine. Once we crossed that line last Sunday morning, we haven't been able to stop. Taking every opportunity to spend time together—naked!

"How was the drive? I was worried about you driving so far, so late." She moves to drop her feet to the ground, and I reluctantly let her go.

"It was okay. I got to the guy's place around ten, bought it, and got back on the road. I ended up pulling over for a couple of hours of sleep." I tuck her silky hair behind her ear. "I have no idea how you slept in your car for all of those weeks." My admiration for her skyrocketed last night as I tried to get comfortable in the tow's cab, which has a ton more space than her compact car. "I'm tired, but a coffee, shower, and breakfast should get me going for the day."

"Show me this truck and I'll make you a coffee while you shower."

I take her hand and guide her toward my next project. I love that she's interested and understands the beauty I see when I look at the rust bucket. "The engine's frozen, and she has a lot of rust, but she's going to come up a treat." I drop my hands to her hips, rubbing my shaft against her. "Why don't you come in the shower with me?" I ask with my eyebrows raised in hope.

She laughs as she pushes me toward the bathroom. "Nope. We need to open soon, and you need to have breakfast. I'm going to run across the road and grab something for you. Get in the shower and I'll have everything ready when you come out." She briefly presses her lips to mine. As if that would ever be enough for me. I cup the back of her head and hold her in place while I take my time giving her a proper kiss. Since she won't join me in the shower, I'm going to have to rub one out—damn it.

I have one car on the books for today, which works out well unless someone brings their car in without a booking, which happens occasionally. Once I'm finished, I'll move the new project off the tow truck and clean her up a bit before I park her in my usual bay. Satisfied with my plan, I step out of the bathroom to be greeted by the delicious aroma of coffee and a breakfast sandwich.

"Thanks, Molly. How's Lawrence? I don't see him all that much now that you pick up our lunch."

"He's great. His daughter's coming home for a visit on the weekend, so he's excited about that."

"I don't think he sees her very often."

The bell at the front door rings. "I'll get that. You eat." She points to the desk as she lands a swift kiss on the top of my head on her way past and returns a few minutes later with a set of keys and her trusty clipboard. Molly's idea of asking clients to complete a simple questionnaire saves me a lot of time. I don't get caught up with the clients discussing basic information, which inevitably leads to talking about what's going on in the community or about whatever sporting team is at the top or bottom of their game this week.

After a hectic day, which included two callouts and an unexpected wheel alignment, I'm sliding the heavy front door closed when a young girl near the front gate catches my attention. Her hair's almost black and she's staring at the building. Something about her is familiar, but from this distance, I can't quite make out her features.

"Can I help you?" I call out to her. She's on foot, so I'm assuming she's not looking for a mechanic unless her car broke down and she walked here.

The girl steps forward, one slow step at a time. As she gets closer, I suck in a sharp breath. She looks a lot like Molly. A brunette version of my girl. The similarities are uncanny. I'm guessing this is one of Martin's kids.

"I'm looking for Molly." The girl seems a little nervous, a little unsure as she brushes her bangs out of her eyes.

"Yeah? Why are you looking for her?" I don't want this girl upsetting *my* girl.

She twists her fingers in front of her as she steps closer to me. "She's … uh …she's my sister."

"Max, I'm about to clo—" Molly freezes in place as her eyes land on the girl. "Holly?"

Holly swallows hard, her eyes wide. The two women stand, locked in place, their eyes scanning and cataloging each other. Seeing Holly next to my girl gives me an insight into how Molly must have looked during high school. Holly isn't as tall or willowy as her older sister. She's more petite, like her mother, but they definitely look like sisters. I bet the boys used to drool all over Molly. I rub the back of my neck. I don't like the thought of anyone drooling over Molly. *She's mine.*

"Did you. Uh, did you want to come inside?" Molly offers as she gestures over her shoulder.

The grace she's shown since finding out that Martin is her father is astounding. She told me all about Beth turning up unannounced and that she invited her in. Now she's doing the same with her sibling. She could have easily turned them away, and I would have completely understood.

"Yeah. Come inside." I wave my arm out to welcome her.

She steps forward, and the two women move toward the office. I wonder if I should give them their privacy. Perhaps I'll hang around for a little while until I know Molly's going to be okay. I need to get to soccer, but the guys will understand if I'm a little late.

*—molly—*

HOW BRAVE IS THIS GIRL? TURNING UP HERE, NOT KNOWING IF I would welcome or reject her. I show her into the office, but I think it might be better if I take her upstairs to my little apartment. "Do you mind waiting here for a sec?"

She nods. "Sure."

I don't need to search far to find Max. Realizing he can eavesdrop from here, I smile to myself as he sorts his workbench, which is adjacent to the office. He's been my greatest support as I navigate my new reality and come to terms with finding my father and his family, *my* family.

"Hey, you." Reaching up, I land a kiss on his cheek. "I'm going to take Holly upstairs to talk, and I'm not sure how long we'll be. I'll probably be late to your game, so I wanted to wish you good luck!"

He cups my cheek, his eyes studying me closely. "Are you gonna be okay? I can hang around down here in case you need me."

His offer eases my nerves and I realize that as much as I love having his support, I can do this on my own. Later, I know I can lean on him if I need to.

"Thank you." I turn my head and land a kiss on the palm of his hand. "Would it be okay if we catch up later?"

"Of course. Whatever you need, Dimples. If I don't see you at the game, I'll come straight back here after." I blow out a long breath. He didn't hesitate for one single second. God, I'm lucky.

"You don't need to do that. Have your drinks with the guys. I'll still be here." He pulls my face forward with care and kisses me. Stealing my breath and my heart. Now that I know how he can work my body, I react instantly to his kisses. My clit pulses and I squeeze my thighs together to temper my response.

We say our goodbyes and Max finally leaves for his weekly soccer game. I'm pretty sure the guys don't care if they win or lose. It's all a bit of fun and an excuse to catch up each week.

Holly and I head upstairs. "Can I get you anything? I have juice or I have water." I wave my arm out toward my tiny couch. That couch has been privy to some interesting conversations over the past couple of weeks.

"Juice, please." She sits and I prepare our drinks.

I hand her glass over and she takes a sip. "Do your parents know you're here?"

"Mom does. She dropped me off. She said I could text her and she'll come straight back to pick me up." I nod. "Is it weird for you how much we look alike? Because it's freaking weird sitting here, looking at you." She chuckles.

"Definitely weird. When your mom showed me photos of you and Noah, our similarities surprised me because I'm a lot like my mom." I point toward the photo I have on my wall. "Even though we all look similar, it seems Noah missed out on the dimples."

She nods as she gets up and moves closer to study the photo. "Yeah. He's happy about that, though. Says they're girly, which pisses Dad off something fierce. Wow! You really look like your mom." She comes back to sit on the couch beside me, not making eye contact with me. "It was pretty shocking to learn I had a big sister." She looks at me. "Not gonna lie. I was worried."

I tilt my head to the side, frowning. "Why would you be worried?"

She shrugs. "I've always been Daddy's girl."

We're both quiet for a long time as we contemplate how me being on the scene changes things. Whether or not we want it to, both of our lives have changed.

"Can I tell you a secret?" Holly nods, uncertainty written all over her face. "This has all been a huge shock for me and I'm still coming to terms with what it all means. I'm scared." Her eyes widen. "I'm twenty-six and I've only now met my father for the first time. What if I'm not a good enough daughter? I know I can be a great big sister to a brother, but I've never been a big sister to a sister before. What if I'm shit at it?" She laughs and the ice between us is shattered.

"Well, I've never been a little sister, so we can work it out together."

My shoulders drop and I know that we'll be able to muddle our way through this new relationship. Holly seems like a sweet girl, much like her mom.

"Your mom told me you're seventeen. How's your senior year going?"

She shrugs. "Okay, I guess. I don't like school. The kids are freaking annoying, and the boys are so immature." She rolls her eyes.

"I'm sorry to tell you they don't improve until their late twenties." I chuckle at the look of exasperation on her face.

"Thanks. That's something to look forward to. Not."

"What do you want to do when school's done?"

She flicks her hand down her body. "I want to be a fashion designer." She stands up. "I designed and made this."

Wow. I stand and make my way around her. "This is gorgeous. It looks like something I'd see in a fancy boutique."

Holly puffs up at my compliment. "You think?"

"I do."

"Mom and Dad always say stuff like that, but I figured they have to say that. You know?"

We talk for a while about her plans, and she tells me a little about Noah before her expression grows serious. "Dad is a genuinely great person, you know." I'm a little taken aback at her sudden declaration. "I overheard my parents talking about how you walked out on him when you guys met for dinner. He was crying and telling Mom that he was worried that he'd blown his chance to get to know you."

My heart sinks. I don't want her to hate me because I upset her dad. *My* dad. God, that's weird to get used to. "I'm sorry, Holly."

She shakes her head. "I didn't tell you to make you feel bad. I'm trying to put myself in your shoes. It must be weird to meet your dad for the first time. I don't exactly know the story or what happened between Dad and your mom, but I get the impression she was his first love. It grosses me out. Mom was … like … friends with them when they were dating." She grimaces and shivers. "I know my dad and I know it's important to him to have a relationship with you now he's found you." She shrugs. "I just want you to give him a chance. He's been the best dad a girl could ask for." She smiles and turns her head around, showing me her fancy braid. "He did this. Mom can't braid my hair if her life depended on it. Dad's always been the one to make my hair all fancy. I haven't bothered learning how to do this stuff, because I know he'll do it for me." She chuckles as she shrugs. "But it's more than fancy braids. I know if I need him for anything, he'll be there. He won't judge me or make me feel bad for making a mistake. He'll help me work things out so I can get back on track. Dad's never let me down. Like ever!"

I lay my hand over hers to settle her. She likes to fidget with her fingers like I fidget with my bracelet. "I'm thrilled to hear that. It's important for girls to have a great role model in their dad. I had a fabulous stepdad who always showed me exactly what I was worth. He taught me a lot about myself, and I only have happy, fond memories of him now." I shrug. "I think things with your dad, *our* dad, will settle down eventually. We just have to find our way."

Her eyes widen. "Does that mean you'll give him a chance?"

"Of course. I was always going to give him a chance. I just … I need some time, Holly."

Her smile reveals deep dimples to match mine, and her eyes light up. "I'm so happy to hear that. I'd better message Mom to come get me. It's getting close to dinner, and I still have homework to do." She drops her head back on her shoulders and groans. "I hate homework."

"We all do. Trust me, you're not alone. I can drop you home if you're not too far from here. I don't know my way around the city very well yet."

"I don't live that far from here. I could have walked, but Mom wanted to make sure I got here safely."

A few minutes later, I stop in front of a stunning three-story home. The lights are already on inside, giving it a welcoming feel. "You have a lovely home."

Holly looks up at it from her position in my car. "It's okay." She shrugs. "It's just a house." She has no idea how lucky she is to have a home, let alone one so beautiful. I'm glad that she takes it for granted because it means she's never gone without. Holly opens her door. "Thanks for the ride. Will I see you again?" she asks timidly.

"Of course. I have years of teasing to catch up on." I wink at her.

"Cool. Bye." She slams the door and takes the steps up to the front door, two at a time. Beth's waiting at the door for her. She waves at me, and I return it, then turn my car around so I can watch Max's soccer game.

# CHAPTER 29

## —molly—

WE STUMBLE THROUGH MY DOORWAY, MAX ALL SWEATY FROM HIS soccer game, his lips locked with mine as he disarms the alarm. He grabs my ass, hoisting me up, and I automatically wrap my legs around his hips as he kicks the door closed. He twists around and I lock the door. We work in tandem as though we've been together for years. I've never been with someone that I'm in sync with on so many levels.

He drags his mouth away from mine, kissing along my jawline to my ear. "I should have a shower."

"I don't want to let you go." I tilt my head to the side, giving him better access to my neck.

Tightening his muscular arms around me, he walks straight into the bathroom. Without hesitation, I drop to my feet and drag his shirt up his body, then toss it to the floor once it clears his head. I lean forward, placing kisses on his heart tattoo, and run my hands down his flanks until I reach the top of his shorts. His mossy eyes are quickly being overtaken by his dilating pupils and I give him a wink as I tuck my thumbs into the waistband, ensuring I have his boxer briefs and tug them down his legs in one swift action. I giggle. "I should have taken your shoes and socks off first."

His hand goes to my hair, and he pushes me down to my knees. Oh, I like this side of him. I drop willingly, unlacing his sneakers and removing each one along with his socks.

"You look so fucking good down there on your knees."

I tilt my head up; the tension across his shoulders and the intensity on his face steals my breath for a moment. His cock is only an inch from my mouth; without taking my eyes off my man, I lean forward to swipe the head with my tongue. He drops his head back on his shoulders with a groan and then drops his gaze back down to me. His stomach quivers as I take the next swipe from the root to the tip, then take the crown into my mouth. I bite down softly at the base of his crown and his hand tightens in my hair. The power that grows inside me while I do this to him is incredible. I feel like I could do anything right now.

"Good girl. Now take it deep."

I do my best to take him as far as I can and swallow around the head. I struggle to go as deep as I'd like because my gag reflex is a bitch. His stomach muscles tense and he uses his hold on my hair to move my head the way he wants.

"Mmmm," I hum around his shaft, stroking the underside with my tongue as he moves my mouth up and down his length. The base of his cock is exposed, so I wrap my hand around it firmly, stroking to match the movement of my mouth, and use my other hand to massage his balls, which are drawing up tight to his body. My pussy clenches around nothing as I press my thighs together. My blood thrums through my body as my heart pounds.

"I'm gonna cum down that sexy throat of yours and you're gonna take it all like the good girl you are."

I can only nod as I struggle to draw in enough oxygen into my lungs. They're on fire and saliva's dribbling down my chin. My eyes are watering and I'm certain I'm a mess, but when Max looks down at me, I feel beautiful. The heat and adoration in his eyes as his dick throbs and grows inside my mouth is clear to see.

"You ready?"

I nod again and moan around his shaft. It's all he needs to let loose. His cum coats the back of my throat and it seems like a lot of fluid as he pauses his movements. He groans long and low, creating a throb in my clit. I work hard to swallow all of his essence down because I don't want to disappoint him. He loosens his grip on my hair as he gradually pulls his dick from my mouth like it's the most painful thing to do. He swipes the head of his cock back and forth across my puffy lips, spreading what I'm sure is excess cum and saliva across them.

He releases my hair, massaging my scalp with tender strokes. "Such a good girl." He smiles at me, sliding his hands around to cup my face. He leans down, taking my lips in an uncontrolled kiss. It's messy with teeth and tongue, but it's full of gratitude and it's perfect. Using his hold on my face, he urges me to my feet and my hands find their place on his flanks, which are still trembling from his orgasm. He pulls back and uses his thumbs to rub the mess from around my mouth.

Resting his forehead against mine, his breath touches my lips as he whispers, "How did I get so fucking lucky?"

I press a kiss to his lips. "I'm the lucky one here."

His hands glide down each side of my neck, across my collarbones, and down my arms until he reaches my hands. He steps back toward the shower, taking me with him. He leans in, stretching and flexing his firm body as he turns on the water. "Let's get you naked, Dimples. I have plans for you."

The deep timbre of his voice and the dark promise sends shivers down my body, straight to my needy clit. We soap each other up, caressing the other with sensual strokes. We share plenty of steamy kisses, the shower space filled with pants and moans. I'm incredibly turned on at this point; I'm unsure how I'm still standing.

Max turns off the water and drags me out of the shower, drying my body with purpose. Whatever he has planned didn't involve the shower.

"I hope you're fucking ready, Dimples."

My stomach flips at the promise in his voice as he dips down, situating his shoulder into my middle before standing and striding to my bedroom. He drops me onto the bed without ceremony and I bounce slightly before settling in the middle of the mattress, resting on my elbows so I can watch him. He prowls toward me.

"Be a good girl and open your legs for me." His voice is commanding and I eagerly comply with his direction. He positions my feet flat on the bed to his liking, raising my knees. "Let them drop to the bed." Even though I'm incredibly exposed like this, I do as I'm told. He folds his arm across his chest, then rubs the thumbnail of his other hand across his bottom lip as he studies me. It's an action I've seen him do a thousand times, but it's goddamn sexy in this moment. I'm so exposed like this, but I'm panting in anticipation. His eyes rise to my breasts, which quiver with each rapid breath. "Fucking beautiful," he rasps on a heavy exhale.

He crawls onto the bed and drops his head between my legs, swiping his tongue from the bottom of my pussy to the top, sending a shiver through my body. A sigh escapes, and I drop my head back on my shoulders enjoying the sensations. Everything he does to my body makes me hotter and sends me higher.

Once he's teased me close to release, he stops and moves behind me, leaving me feeling empty. He rests his back against the headboard and pulls me into the cradle of his thighs, his erection pressing into my lower back. Taking each of my legs, he positions them on the outside of his, keeping me open wide. I wriggle against him.

"Stop it. It's my turn to play."

With one hand, he collects my hair and lays it over one shoulder, exposing my neck to his roughened cheek. He kisses behind my ear, dragging his lips in lazy kisses down my neck and across my collarbone. My blood vibrates through my body with arousal. He moves back and sucks on my neck as his hands move around to my quivering stomach. One work-roughened hand glides up to cup my breast, rolling and pinching my nipple as he continues to suck on my neck.

The sensations are overloading my senses and he hasn't done much yet. I don't know what I'm seeking, but I need something, so I push my hips forward. His other hand caresses down my stomach, flicking my navel piercing as he nips my neck. My pussy clenches the closer he gets to the tiny patch of hair right above my pubic bone.

"I fucking love this." He pinches the hair between his fingers and pulls firmly, making me gasp.

With a firm hand, he tilts my head and takes my mouth. Invading with his tongue, he strokes and tangles with mine as his fingers keep working over my breasts and then slide down through my soaked folds. I reach back to wrap my hand around his head, keeping his lips locked to mine as his deft fingers circle my clit before driving into my opening. My pussy clenches at the welcome intrusion. He moves two fingers in and out of me before returning to my clit to circle the bundle of sensitive nerves. Teasing me and sending my body higher. His other hand leaves my head and moves downward, teasing my breast before continuing down to my pussy. His fingers slide down my pussy lips, stretching me open wide.

"Good girl. You're so wet for me." He lands a kiss on my shoulder, dragging his roughened cheek along my neck. The feel of his bristles against my smooth skin adds to the overload of sensations, taking me closer to the edge.

I moan and push my pelvis up, hoping he'll breach my opening again. Instead, he taps my clit and glides his hands down and back up the inside of my thighs, leading back to my pussy lips, making my thighs tremble under his roughened touch. He drags his fingers through my folds; one hand tending my clit while he finger fucks me roughly. His long fingers find that special place inside which can send me flying. "Please, Max."

He withdraws his fingers, circling my clit, then caresses his way back up toward my breasts, leaving my pussy empty and throbbing. Frustration builds strong and swift, but he has plans and no amount of begging on my part will interfere. I've learned that he likes to be in charge and I trust him to give me the pleasure I need. He squeezes the mounds of my breasts together and plucks at my nipples until they're hard peaks.

"Look at your sexy body."

I glance down at my body and am surprised by how erotic it looks. My nipples are erect, and their soft pink color has become a ruddy rouge, my stomach's trembling, and my hips are moving without any guidance from me, my legs open wide and shaking. My skin's covered in a sheen of sweat and is flushed a pretty pink. I can't see my pussy, but I know it's throbbing.

"You're so fucking beautiful like this. Look at this greedy pussy, waiting for me to fill her up." I can only moan in response, words evading my brain.

His hand slides down my trembling body and I suck in a sharp breath as he thrust three fingers inside me. I'm so wet and ready to come. I raise my hips and turn my head to look up at him. "Max, stop teasing me. I need to come." I sound like a whiny brat.

"I want to play with you first. Now be a good girl and stop moving." He pushes my hips back onto the bed and continues his ministrations. Every time I get close to coming, he moves away and tends to another part of my body. Holding my throat, he kisses me deeply, tasting my desperation.

I've never been left on edge like this, especially not for this long. I'm terrified I'm going to rip in half when he finally lets me come. His tongue thrusts in and out of my mouth as his fingers mirror the action in my pussy, as his palm presses down on my clit. My internal muscles clench and I finally explode.

Blackness swamps my vision and the breath in my lungs seizes as my entire body convulses. My toes curl under, cramping at the extreme release of tension. I trap his hand between my thighs to prevent him from leaving me.

"That was fucking beautiful. You're gorgeous when you come," he rasps in my ear. His breaths heavy, his heart pounding against my back. I think I may have blacked out for a second or two.

He kisses me tenderly. Slowly. Reverently.

My body's a quivering, boneless mess of limbs and flesh. I'm mildly aware of him sliding down the bed and situating me over his cock, which is standing straight up from his body. He lowers me slowly, lining up my still throbbing pussy and easily sliding inside. I drop forward, resting my hands on his firm thighs, the hairs tickling my palms. Trying to catch my breath and regain my senses, Max lifts my hips, sliding me up and down his steely shaft. He's using me for his own pleasure now and it's so damn hot.

He groans and I answer him with a moan. "You feel so damn good," I whisper.

He thrusts in deeper, and I circle my hips on the downward stroke. "*We* feel so damn good, Dimples. You and me together."

I sigh internally. This man always seems to say the right things. But they're not empty words, he always follows up with actions.

Max and I work in tandem to build a solid rhythm. He thrusts up as I drop down, swiveling my hips each time to make sure he hits that special place inside of me. Dragging his cock out of my body, he swivels me around until I'm laying on my back. He rises over the top of me, sweat dripping down the side of his face, his muscles taut as he holds himself over me. I grip his shaft and guide it back into my body, sighing as he strokes in deep. The V leading down to his pelvis is stark and guides my eyes to where we're joined intimately.

"Be a good girl and watch me destroy your pussy."

I glance up at him, nodding that I heard his command, then drop my eyes back to where his penis draws out of me inch by glorious inch. The glistening shaft gradually revealed before he lunges back inside with a forceful thrust.

"Wrap those gorgeous legs around me," he grunts.

I do his bidding, locking my feet at the small of his back and bringing my pelvis up off the bed. We move together in time, working toward our mutual release. Every time he thrusts inside me, he releases a sexy grunt, his breath blowing across my face and I glance up at him. His veins are pulsing along his neck and sweat drips from his temples as he grits his teeth. The concentration and focus on me and his task are sexy as hell. This man is all about getting the best out of both of us, and he's doing a damn fine job.

"I … I'm so close. I … I nee–" I pant as my muscles draw tight, ready for release.

"I know what you need," he grunts, his voice rough, as he moves one hand down to pinch my clit.

And I'm gone.

I'm floating in the stratosphere. Untethered to the earth. It's beautiful in this place in between, as my body falls apart. Max's cock swells and pulses as he grunts out his orgasm. He throws his head back and I rise to lick the sweat from his Adam's Apple. His hot cum coats my walls as my muscles tighten and squeeze his pulsing shaft.

"Oh my God! I think I had an out-of-body experience."

"I *know* I had one. Fuck! That was incredible." He kisses me tenderly. "You're incredible," he whispers.

I drop my legs from around his hips as he pushes in and out slowly, gently. The aftershocks rattling through my body. Max rolls to the side, taking me with him, trapping me to him by throwing one leg over mine and pulling me close to his body, not leaving any space between us. He kisses my forehead and strokes my sweaty hair away from my face so I glance up at him. "That was amazing." Three little words want to escape, but I hold them in. I think it may be too soon, but I know I'm falling in love with him.

He hums in response, and I drop my head to rest over his heart, which is beating a furious rhythm to match mine. As my body cools, I shiver, and goosebumps cover my skin.

"Are you cold?"

"A little."

He taps my ass and releases me to climb out of bed, then he pulls the bedcovers out from beneath me and covers my body. "Back in a sec." I hear the faucet turn on and off in the bathroom and he returns with a washcloth. "Here, let me clean up my mess." He uncovers me and opens my thighs, wiping my entrance and paying special attention to the surrounding flesh and upper thighs. A smile slowly forms as he studies my pussy, dragging his fingers through the slit from bottom to top, causing me to wince slightly. His eyes glance up to mine before dropping back down, a furrow forming between his brows. "Did I hurt you?"

I shake my head. "No. It's a little tender, but it's a good tender." I smile at the relief that takes over his face. He steps out of the bedroom and returns a few moments later with a glass of water and some Tylenol. "I'll take the water, but I don't need the pain relief. I promise I'm okay." I wink at him. "You said you were going to destroy me. I think we can both agree that you succeeded."

He huffs out a laugh and shakes his head at me. "Only you, Molly. The fact you don't need the pain relief suggests I didn't destroy you at all." He turns off the bedroom light and climbs into bed, rearranging me to his liking as he curls his body around mine. Planting a kiss on my temple. I swoon internally at his gentle care. "Go to sleep, Dimples. You need your rest."

"Okay. Night, Max." I blow out a heavy breath of contentment. Lying in his arms and falling asleep here, with him wrapped around my body, I know I'm safe.

"Night, Dimples."

# CHAPTER 30

## —max—

I PULL MOLLY'S HAND INTO MY LAP TO STOP HER FROM FIDGETING WITH her bracelet. "I don't know why you're nervous. My family's not that scary."

Her head snaps around to me. "Oh, I'm sure they're not. Your sister's lovely, as are her kids. It's that I'm not used to extended family get-togethers." I squeeze her hand. "It was only Mom and me for so long and then Jack came along. Then, a few years later, they had Ethan. It was only ever the four of us for birthdays and special holidays."

I glance at her, then back to the road. My heart breaks for this woman and the things she's missed out on. "It's noisy, but it's always fun. If it gets too much, give me the signal and I'll get you out of there." I wink at her before settling my eyes back on the road.

She chuckles. "What sort of signal?"

"How about you tug on your left ear and give me a wink with your right eye?" We both burst out laughing and I think it was exactly what she needed to calm herself down.

"Thanks. I needed that." She shuffles the gift bag sitting between her feet on the floor, a crease forming between her sculpted eyebrows. "Do you think Lachlan will like his present?"

"He's going to love it. But I have to warn you. He won't be overly demonstrative about how much he likes the gift. It's just the way he is." I glance across at her. "He's on the Spectrum, which means he responds differently to things."

She waves away my warning. "That's okay. All kids are different.

Ethan never liked people making a fuss over him. When he was little, he would cry whenever we sang happy birthday." She chuckles a little at the memory. "I think we all have our idiosyncrasies; not everything has a label."

I love that view. Mona always had awful things to say about Lachlan whenever she spent time with my family and I would have to remind her to keep her opinions to herself. I can't, for the life of me, work out why in the hell I stayed with that woman.

"Tell me. What was it like having a younger brother that much younger than you?" She doesn't open up and talk that much about her family so I hope I haven't overstepped.

She takes a deep breath. "It was wonderful. I was old enough to appreciate him and his different stages. Though I remember it didn't impress me when he'd wake up during the night for a feed, I soon learned to sleep through the noise. I used to love it when Mom would let me sit on the couch and cuddle with him when he was a newborn. Even though he was tiny, he was a chubby baby. He'd look up at me with his big inquisitive eyes and wrap his fingers tight around my finger. When he was a little bigger, he would suck on my nose." Her eyes are full of love and her smile confirms it's a happy memory for her. "I remember when he first started eating solids. The stinky smell of his diaper." She scrunches up her nose as she giggles and my heart soars to hear her laughing as she remembers her brother. "Jack used to pretend to faint." Her dimples are deep, and her eyes are sparkling with joy. Jack sounds like he was a terrific stepdad to Molly. I only hope her biological dad can be equally terrific.

"Oh yeah, I remember Em's boys used to stink when they first switched over to solid food. It's not pleasant. I was never too keen to change their diapers once that happened." I take the turn into Emma and Theo's driveway and turn off the engine.

She turns to me with wide eyes. "We're here already?"

"C'mon. It'll be fine. I promise." Leaning across the console, I give her a chaste kiss, then climb out of my car. I know the second Mom lays eyes on me with Molly, she's going to know that I'm head over heels in love with this woman. My only hope is that she doesn't embarrass me too much.

With Molly's hand secure in mine, we make our way up to the porch. Sarah's standing inside the door when we enter and, knowing her, she saw my car pull up and made sure she would be the first one to greet us. She's probably annoyed that Emma has already met Molly.

"Max. It's great to see you." She wraps her arms around me, pulling me in close. I refuse to release Molly's hand, so I return her hug with my free arm, whacking her in the back with the gift bag I'm carrying for Lachlan. "Oh my gosh, she's so freaking pretty ... and tall," Sarah whispers in my ear before pulling back to greet Molly. "Hi, I'm Sarah. I'm Max's favorite sister." She leans forward to embrace Molly. "It's nice to meet you, finally." Molly gives Sarah her full smile, dimples and all. Sarah's eyes widen as she chuckles. "I can see why Kenny thinks you're a Disney princess."

Molly laughs. "Hi, Sarah. It's lovely to meet you."

"Uncle Maaaaax! Aunty Mollyyyyyy!" Kenny comes running from the back of the house, leaping at my body. "You came!" She squeezes my cheeks in her tiny hands and lands a kiss on my nose. "And you brought me a princess to play with." Molly, Sarah, and I chuckle at our niece, who stole our hearts from the minute we first met her.

Molly tickles Kenny under her arm. "Hi, Kenny. I washed my hair, especially this morning, so you could do a special braid for me."

Kenny reaches across, smoothing her hand down Molly's long hair. "It's so silky." Her eyes go wide. "I collected all of my best hair ties and ribbons together and I have my special brush and comb. It's gonna be so much fun." She wriggles her body, so I place her on her feet. Molly chuckles as Kenny runs back to where she came, shouting. "Mommy. Daddy. Uncle Max's princess is here!"

Molly's eyes widen and her cheeks flush prettily. "Oh my gosh. I'm so far from being a princess."

Sarah turns to her. "Are you sure about that? With your pretty eyes, gorgeous platinum hair, and dimples. Not to mention," she waves her hand up and down Molly's form, "your stunning figure. You're like a real-life Disney princess." She moves closer to Molly and motions for her to lean down. "Is my big bro being good to you?"

Molly smiles widely as she nods. She looks at me as she answers Sarah, "He absolutely is. He's the best."

My hand tightens around hers and my chest puffs out a little, knowing that I'm giving her what she needs. "Uh, Sis, do you think you can let us into the house?"

We're still standing inside the front door, for fuck's sake. She pokes her tongue out at me and spins on her heel, leading the way to the back of the house. I lean down slightly and steal a quick kiss from my girl.

"Ewwww, Uncle Max is kissing Aunty Molly." Austin's voice rings out, breaking the moment. I drop my forehead to Molly's and we share a laugh. When I pull back to study Molly's face, she's flushed, and her eyes are sparkling with happiness. I love this look on her. It's one I hope to keep on her face for a very long time. I love that the kids are already calling Molly, aunty. It's like they've been inside my mind.

It's all I can think about.

How I can make her mine forever.

We step into the kitchen, and I place my gift for Lachlan on the counter and drag Molly forward to meet Mom. I wrap my free arm around the woman who made me the man I am today and pull her in close, kissing the top of her head. "Hey, Mom." I pull Molly in beside me. "This is my girlfriend, Molly."

Molly freezes momentarily, her mouth partway open as she glances up at me. "Hi, Mrs. Stanfield. It's lovely to meet you." She holds out her hand for Mom, but Mom pushes through, wrapping her arms around Molly and drawing her in tight. Molly awkwardly returns the hug one-armed, Lachlan's gift bag dangling from her forearm, because I refuse to let go of her hand.

"Oh, my dear girl. Thank you for joining us today. It's all Kenny could talk about." She rolls her eyes light-heartedly. "But please, call me Sally. Or Mom." She smiles at Molly, then her face goes ashen, and her smile drops. Her hand rises to her necklace, and she fidgets with the chain. "Oh my, I'm so sorry. I didn't mean that ... I mean ... oh dear." Mom's flustered as she tries to recover, looking to me for guidance.

I wrap my arm around her shoulder. "It's okay, Mom."

Molly grins and waves her off. "Please don't feel you have to watch what you say with me, Mrs. ... I mean, Sally. I promise I won't break down."

Mom nods and I can tell she's holding back what she would like to say. Knowing Mom, she wants to wrap Molly up in a warm hug and tell her everything will be okay. That she has us now and that we'll take care of her. It's exactly what I want to do, but I know Molly's extremely independent and likes to stand on her own feet.

Dad comes in from the back deck, which Theo extended when Em and the boys moved in. It was already big, but now it's huge, with doors that open onto it, giving the impression that the kitchen and deck are one space.

"Son!" Dad walks straight toward me with a slight limp, and we embrace.

"Dad. How's your knee?" He was jumping on the trampoline with the kids last weekend and fell as he was climbing out, twisting his knee.

"Oh, it's fine. I'll be back to trampolining in no time." He pats my arm and finishes with a squeeze. "And who do we have here?" He turns to Molly.

"Hi, Mr. Stanfield. I'm Molly." She holds her hand out to shake and Dad treats her to the same fierce hug that Mom gave her. I've told my family a minimal amount about Molly, which included why she moved here. You can imagine how that went down with Mom and Dad. Mom was a sobbing mess and Dad wasn't too far behind her.

"Call me John. Mr. Stanfield is my father." He chuckles at his own joke.

Molly chuckles too, as she looks at me with a raised brow. "Sounds familiar."

"Can I do your hair now?" Kenny tugs on Molly's dress to gain her attention.

Emma steps inside. "Kenny. You need to wait until a little later. We're all gonna eat and have some cake, and maybe then you can braid Molly's beautiful hair." She looks at Molly for confirmation.

Molly crouches down to Kenny's height. "Oh yes. I'm too hungry to be able to sit still long enough for you to make my hair pretty. Do you mind waiting until after we've had the birthday cake?"

Kenny places her hands on her hips and tilts her head to the side. "Actually, come to think of it, I'm pretty hungry, too." She nods at Molly, then glances up at Em. "Are we gonna eat soon? I'm starving."

Em giggles. "Of course. I've come inside to grab what we need to set the table." She wraps an arm around Molly, squeezing her close. "Hey, Molly. I'm delighted you came today." Then she pats my arm on the way to the kitchen drawers and whispers, "You've done good, little brother."

Molly places Lachlan's gift on the counter alongside my gift and extricates her hand from mine, pressing up to land a chaste kiss on my cheek. "Can I help with anything? I'm happy to set the table." Everyone in the kitchen freezes, eyes on Molly. She flushes that pretty pink and her eyes widen. She looks across at me for guidance. "Did I say something wrong?"

I laugh and pull her into me, landing a kiss on her lips. "No, Dimples. You've said and done everything right." I turn to my family. "Stop making my girl feel uncomfortable."

Everyone returns to their chatter and whatever they were doing before and Molly fits in seamlessly, helping wherever she can. It's like she's always been part of this family and pride fills me that she's mine. We all carry the plates, dishes, silverware, and glasses out to the deck and work together to set everything ready for lunch.

I introduce Molly to Theo and his dad, Cristo, who takes both of Molly's hands in his. "You must come into my restaurant. I'll make an enormous feast for you both."

Theo chuckles. "Not everyone wants to be stuffed so full they can't move, Dad."

Cristo looks affronted. "What do you mean?"

They argue over the merits of eating until you can no longer breathe, and Molly and I collect our gifts to give them to Lachlan. I let Molly go first since she's been nervous about her gift for him.

"Happy birthday, Lachlan. I brought you a gift." She hands it to him.

He briefly glances at her, then his eyes settle over her shoulder. "Thank you." He's getting better at making eye contact with people, but it's still a work in progress with new people. He digs into the bag and pulls out a tool belt that should fit him perfectly. His eyes snap up to Molly's and one side of his mouth tips up. Dropping the gift bag, he tries to wrap it around his waist but isn't quite coordinated enough to pull it off.

"Would you like me to help you?" Molly asks. Lachlan nods, and Molly moves closer to assist him, settling the belt on his hips. I told her not to worry about the tools because he has that part covered with Theo's tools. "I wasn't sure if you already had one. Your Uncle Max told me how much you like to work with timber, and I hoped this would be a good idea."

His eyes snap up to hers and a full smile touches his lips. "I don't have one. Thank you very much." He steps away and heads straight for Theo. He runs his hands over the leather as he shows his stepdad his new belt. "This is the most useful gift I've been given today. I'll be like you now." He's standing tall, pride filling his little body.

Theo squeezes his shoulder and crouches down to inspect the belt more closely. "This is exceptional quality. I need a new one. I'll have to ask Molly where she got this one from."

I have to admit; I wasn't sure about Theo at first. He seemed like a total dick the day we all went to the beach, but the way he loves my sister and her boys, as well as how he stepped up for his niece, settled my concerns quickly. He's a genuinely good guy and I'm thrilled that he and Emma found their way to each other, even though the road was a little rocky for the two of them.

"Hey. I brought you a present too," I remind the birthday boy.

"Oh. Sorry, Uncle Max. I didn't mean to leave you out." He holds out his hand for the gift, which is probably lame compared to the tool belt. I hand him the gift bag and he dips his hand in, pulling out the Lego box. "Woah! You got me the Spider-Man Molten Man Battle set. This has two hundred and ninety-four pieces and shows the epic battle between Spider-Man and Molten Man from the movie, Far From Home." He looks down at the box with awe and I'm pretty happy that I chose a gift he'll enjoy. "Thanks, Uncle Max. I won't open it now because I don't want to lose any of the pieces."

"Fair enough. I'm glad you like it." He gives me a rare hug and runs inside to put his gift away for safekeeping.

Theo claps his hands together. "Okay, everyone. Let's eat. Kids first, then adults can sort themselves out."

The kids are served and set up to eat at the large table Theo built, quickly followed by the adults. At first, everyone's quiet as they enjoy the delicious barbecue Theo and his dad cooked, as well as the salads that Mom and Emma put together.

Gradually, everyone shares about their week. Theo puts down his knife and fork and asks me, "Did you get the truck you were after?"

I swallow the bite of food in my mouth. "Oh, yeah." I can't contain my smile. "She's fucking beautiful."

"Max!" Mom chastises. Molly elbows me at the same time, looking mortified.

I grimace at the kids. Inevitably, a fuck or two slips out at family gatherings. The kids mostly ignore it. I don't know why Mom still feels the need to pull me up on it. "Sorry."

Kenny giggles. "You're so funny, Uncle Max."

"Thanks, Munchkin."

Emma directs her focus to Molly. "The kids know Uncle Max has a potty mouth and they're not allowed to repeat the grown-up words he says."

"I don't know where you learned to talk like that." Mom shakes her head, pretending to be more upset than she actually is.

I sort of like that I'm the inappropriate uncle; it solidifies my place in the family. Molly leans in close and presses a kiss to my shoulder. Turning my head, I'm able to return the kiss on her cheek. When I glance back at the table, everyone's eyes are on us. Sarah and Emma have matching smirks, and I don't even care that they're going to give me shit later. I'm finally happy.

We all finish eating and Molly's the first to stand to collect everyone's dishes. Once again, my family is stunned into silence. I'll have to explain their reactions to her later. I get up to help, but Emma and Sarah tell me to sit back down. Mom jumps up too, and the three of them collect the dishes and silverware from the table and follow Molly inside. My gut tells me she's safe with them, but I don't trust them not to inadvertently drop me in the shit.

I prepare to stand, but Dad puts his hand on my shoulder, pushing me back into my seat. "Let them have their girl time. I'm sure Molly can handle it."

"I know she can handle it and I trust Mom and the girls implicitly to be kind to her. I don't trust that they won't tell Molly about stupid shit I did as a kid, though."

The guys laugh. "May as well find out if she'll stick around sooner rather than later." Theo offers with a shrug.

I huff. "I wanted to ask if you'd be interested in helping me redo the timber for the flatbed of the truck I picked up."

He scratches his fingers through his short beard. "Yeah. That'd be a great little project." He leans forward, resting his elbows on the table. "What sort of timber are you planning to use?"

"What would you recommend?"

He thinks for a moment. "Perhaps Asian Keruing or Apitong. It's commercially harvested and has the best strength-to-weight ratio." I nod. "It's reasonably dent and scratch resistant too, which would be an important feature. And it doesn't bend and flex easily, which helps to support heavier loads."

I'm impressed by his knowledge as he shares the pros for the timber. "Sounds good. I'll let you know when I get to that point."

He nods as the girls step onto the deck with fresh plates and Lachlan's birthday cake. Molly catches my eye and winks at me with a cheeky smile and a raised eyebrow. At least she didn't run away. That has to be a positive sign. Right?

The kids follow behind the girls and everyone takes their seat, with Lachlan at the head of the table. Sarah places the Spider-Man cake she made on the table directly in front of the birthday boy and he looks up at her with a smile. "Thank you, Aunty Sarah."

She ruffles his hair and leans down to press a kiss to his cheek. "You're welcome, Lachlan. I hope you like it."

"I love it. I don't want to cut into it and ruin it."

"That's okay. That's what cake is for, and I took heaps of photos." She winks at him.

Austin climbs into my lap as Emma lights the ten candles on the cake and we all sing happy birthday to my eldest nephew. I'm not sure where the time's gone. It seemed like yesterday I was holding him as a newborn. I miss those days.

I'm pretty sure I'm not supposed to feel my biological clock ticking, but I do. I want to be a dad. Like my dad, I want to be a great father. I study Molly and wonder if she'd think I was a psycho if I wanted to get her pregnant this soon into our relationship. I mean, I only referred to her as my girlfriend when I introduced her to Mom, otherwise, we haven't talked about our relationship or where we're heading.

We have amazing sex. Fuck me. The sex. She blows my fucking mind. But it's not only the sex. She blows my mind out of the bedroom, too. She's been through so much in her life, and nothing drags her down. I have an incredible amount of respect for the woman sitting beside me, something I've not felt for the women I've dated in the past. Our connection is deep on a fundamental level. I know she said her birth control shot was due, but I can't remember when that was. Maybe I could convince her to skip it.

The cake is cut and handed out and we all go silent except for the occasional moan. I hate that I notice Emma putting on a show for Theo as she moans around her fork and then slides the cake off in a long stroke. She glances up, noticing me watching her. I raise one eyebrow in a 'what the fuck are you doing?' look. My fucking sister smirks at me and shrugs. Typical.

As soon as Molly swallows her last bite of cake, Kenny cheers. "Yay! I can do your hair now." She hops down from her seat. "C'mon. Let's go inside. I have everything already set up."

"Ah, Munchkin. I think you'd better wash your hands first. I don't think Molly would like chocolate cake smeared through her hair." Theo rises ready to clean up his daughter. Well, niece, but that's neither here nor there since he adopted her.

Molly stands as Theo takes Kenny inside. "You don't have to let her braid your hair. You know." Emma clarifies.

"Oh no. I'm looking forward to it. Honestly." She gives my sisters the full dimple experience and I can tell my sisters think she's pretty great.

The girls move inside while I help Dad and Cristo clean up from dessert. Kenny runs into the living room excitedly. "I need *Frozen* on while I do Aunty Molly's hair."

Of course she does because the million times she's already watched it will never be enough. Lachlan and Austin groan. "Noooo. Not again." Austin drops his head back on his shoulders, looking up at the ceiling, adding to his dramatic response.

Molly chuckles. "She needs to make sure she's doing the braid correctly. Which means Kenny needs the movie on as a reference."

Lachlan latches onto Molly's explanation. "Yes. It's like when I build my Legos. I need the picture as a reference to know I'm building it correctly."

Molly smiles at my nephew. "That's right. We won't mind if she has the movie playing, right?"

"No. I guess that will be okay. But I'm gonna go play outside with Poppa and Pappoús," he responds.

"Me too," adds Austin.

The boys head out the back with Cristo and Dad, and Molly sits on the designated cushion on the floor, crossing her legs. I know she was worried about being around this many people, but she's coped like a champion. The opening scene of *Frozen* plays and Kenny attacks Molly's hair with a brush, dragging Molly's head back sharply.

Emma steps in, placing her hand over Kenny's, stopping her. "Kenny." She waits until Kenny looks at her. "You need to be gentle. You don't want to hurt Aunty Molly."

Kenny's bottom lip quivers. "I'm sorry. I didn't mean to hurt you, Aunty Molly."

Molly twists around and drags Kenny into her lap, snuggling her close. "You didn't hurt me, lovely girl. I wasn't quite ready. Long, smooth strokes work best with my hair." She winks at my niece, putting her at ease.

See, she's gonna be a great mom. I need her to have my babies.

Kenny brushes, combs, twists, and miraculously braids Molly's hair as she patiently sits for almost an hour. She has fancy hair clips sticking in and out of everywhere and it looks a total mess, but when Kenny asks Emma to take a photo to show Molly, she gushes over how fabulous her new hair-do looks.

Mom, Emma, and Sarah all look at me with *that* look on their face. The one that says they know I've found the one. The one that's perfect for me *and* perfect for our family.

*Trust me. I know.*

As the party winds down, we say our goodbyes. Each member of my family hugs Molly for long minutes, almost to the point it's a little uncomfortable. Even Lachlan gives her a brief hug, which is unheard of until he's known someone for a while. I remember he latched onto Theo quickly, too. Perhaps he has a sixth sense about whether someone is a decent person.

Mom hugs me extra tight as she whispers in my ear. "Molly's wonderful. She's definitely a keeper." When she pulls back, she pats my cheek. "I'm so proud of you."

I'm not sure what I've done to make her proud, but I'll take it. I'd rather she be proud of me than disappointed.

Molly and I climb into my car and as we pull out of the driveway, she releases a long breath, then giggles. "I don't know what I was worried about. Your family is amazing." She looks across at me. "I felt especially welcomed from the minute I walked in the door. You are incredibly lucky to be surrounded by such great people." She leans across, laying a chaste kiss on my bristly cheek. "Thank you for bringing me."

"You're welcome. I'm pretty sure my family's in love with you and will expect you at every Sunday lunch from this point forward."

Her head snaps toward me and her eyes widen. "Really? I'm glad I made a good impression. It meant a lot to me to be invited. I didn't want to mess it up."

I reach across and squeeze her thigh. "I don't think you could ever mess up after my last girlfriend." I tense my jaw and look out the passenger window before looking forward. "She, uh, she wasn't very nice to my family. You're the complete opposite."

"I wondered what those funny looks were about. I was worried I'd done something wrong." She fidgets with her bracelet.

"Nah. They were in shock that I brought home someone so sweet." She chuckles and I'm relieved that she's not going to dig any further about my previous girlfriends. I haven't had the best track record with the women I've brought home in the past. "Are you gonna tell me what you girls were talking about in the kitchen after lunch?"

"Are you nervous?" She raises one eyebrow and gives me a cheeky smile.

I shrug like I don't care one way or the other.

She pushes my shoulder playfully. "Sarah was fascinated with my nose ring. Then I showed them my navel piercing, and she started asking all sorts of questions about how the jewelry will go when I'm pregnant."

And doesn't that put the perfect visual in my head. "Oh yeah? How does it go when you're pregnant?"

"Once my stomach expands, I'll have to remove it. It's easy enough to do." I look across at her midsection, imagining it swollen with our baby. Maybe now would be the time to bring it up with her?

"Hang on. You're wearing a dress. How did you show them your stomach?"

Her cheeks flush pink. "Oh, uhm, it was only the ladies, so I lifted my dress. I have underwear on, so there was nothing to see."

I groan and readjust my position at the image of her innocently lifting her dress, and exposing her underwear. "Do you think you'll want to have kids?" I glance across at her.

She smiles. "Absolutely. I love kids." She pauses. "What about you?"

"I'd have kids tomorrow if I had my way."

Her smile widens. "Really?"

"Did you end up going back for your birth control shot last week?" I'm hoping she forgot, but I don't think Molly would do something like that.

"Yeah, I did. Why?" Creases have formed between her eyebrows and I want to smooth them away with my thumb. "I would never take the chance of getting pregnant unexpectedly. I saw what happened to Mom."

Of course. Fuck, I'm a stupid ass sometimes. I take her hand in mine and squeeze. "How about I take you to my favorite spot to watch the sunset and we can talk a bit more?"

"Okay." She pulls her hand from mine and fidgets with her bracelet. I've noticed she does that when she's uncomfortable or nervous.

I turn up the radio to combat the silence that's descended over us. I want to say something to put her mind at ease, but I don't know what to say. I figure it's best to keep my mouth shut for now.

## CHAPTER 31

### —molly—

I HOPE HE DOESN'T THINK I'M THE TYPE OF WOMAN WHO WOULD TRAP their boyfriend with a pregnancy or that I'm irresponsible with my birth control. I had hoped he knew me better than that. Now he wants to talk. About what? Have I done something wrong? Maybe he didn't like me showing my piercing to his family. I figured it would be okay. There weren't any men in the room. It's not like I have anything different compared to his mom and sisters. I didn't show them anything they wouldn't see down at the beach, but maybe he's weird about that stuff?

Actually, that reminds me. "Did you realize you introduced me to your family as your girlfriend?" I twist in my seat to face him fully. "Is that what I am?" I mean, we haven't given this thing between us a label.

He glances across at me with creases between his eyebrows. "Aren't you?" I watch his Adam's Apple bob up and down. "Did I misstep?"

"We haven't really spoken about our relationship." I hitch my shoulder. I'm not even sure if I should use the term 'relationship'.

He doesn't answer, which fills me with dread as he pulls the car into a quiet parking lot. There's only one other vehicle, which probably belongs to whoever's working in the food truck.

"Do you want something to eat before the guy closes up for the night?"

"I'm still full from lunch and cake, so I'm okay, thanks."

He gestures over his shoulder. "I'm gonna grab some wedges or something."

"Okay." We climb out of his car, and he takes my hand as we wander over to the food truck. Max orders a basket of sweet potato wedges and a couple of bottles of water, while I step closer to the beach and look out across the ocean, tugging my sweater around my body as the temperature drops with the sun.

I always find it peaceful watching the waves break on the shore. They never stop. No matter what. They remind me that you have to keep going. The salty breeze is cool, and I pull my sweater even tighter around my body. Warm arms wrap around me from behind and Max's body presses against mine, reducing the chill. He leans down, resting his chin on my shoulder.

"I love watching the sunset. I don't get down here nearly as often as I'd like," he quietly contemplates.

I turn my head and press a kiss to his temple; he turns, returning my kiss. Our lips touching sets fire licking through my body and my underwear quickly grows wet. It's difficult to keep it chaste, and neither of us tries to.

"Order's up!"

Max groans and pulls away, returning to the truck window to grab his food and our drinks.

"Come on. We can sit in the car and watch the sun sink below the horizon without you feeling cold." He places the wedges on the console between us and they smell so damn good I'm wishing I'd ordered some for myself. I glance across at the food truck, but he's closing everything down for the night. I don't blame him. It's not like anybody's here. Max nudges the basket closer. "Have some. I got the large serve in case you changed your mind."

Of course he did because he's always making sure I eat when I'm in his company. He still buys my lunch every day. We eat in silence for a few moments and I'm waiting for 'the talk' to start. He twists his body to face me directly and I mirror him.

"I'm not sure where to start or how to say what I want to say, so I'll just say it." I nod for him to continue and try to swallow down the food in my mouth, but my throat feels too constricted. "I don't know about you, but I'm in pretty deep with you already."

I breathe a sigh of relief and reach across for Max's hand. "I'm in the deep end with you."

He blows out a long breath and gifts me his gorgeous smile, which I return. "Fuck, that's a relief." We both chuckle. "I can't see a time when I won't feel this way about you. The more time I spend with you, the deeper I get, and I'm not even trying to swim for the shore."

"Me too," I whisper.

"It's happened really fast, but I know how I feel. I've fallen in love with you, Molly." A tear escapes, followed by another one and another one. "Dimples. Please don't cry. I never want to be the one to make you cry."

I swallow and smile at Max, shaking my head slightly. "They're not sad tears. They're happy tears." He rubs them away with his thumbs as he cups my face, pulling me forward for a kiss. After a moment, I pull away because I need to share my confession with him. "I think I fell a little in love with you the very first Thursday I started working for you. The kindness and care you showed the single parents that day. You've shown me the type of man you are time and again. I fell hard and fast for you. I love you, Max."

His smile is bright as he pulls me forward, taking my mouth in a searing kiss that marks me all the way to my soul. There's nothing teasing or delicate about our joining. It's all tongues and teeth, hot breaths, moans, and sighs. It's an epic confirmation of our mutual connection. He grips a handful of my hair and tugs my head back slightly; his eyes locking onto mine. "I need to be inside you."

I glance across, finding we're alone in the parking lot. There isn't a soul around. "I want that too."

We move the food to the dash, climb out, and adjust the front seats forward so we can climb into the back of his car like a couple of high schoolers. There's no preamble or foreplay. We're both ready to get to the main event. Max undoes his jeans and pulls them and his briefs out of the way, exposing his thick shaft. He's already weeping for me, as I am for him. He reaches for me, positioning me over his dick. His face is in shadow, but from experience, I know his pupils will have overtaken the mossy green I love. Hot puffs from his breaths hit the side of my neck as I balance on my knees and hold on to his shoulders, ducking my head to avoid the roof.

"Are you ready for me?" He swipes his knuckles over the panel of my panties, keeping my modesty for the moment. "Oh yeah. Your panties are fucking soaked already." He smirks up at me, then pulls the panel to the side and notches his head at my opening. I slide down easily, taking him all the way. We both groan at the sensation of being joined.

"I love having you inside me, Max," I whisper, then lean forward to swipe my tongue along his bottom lip. He opens for me, and I slide inside, tangling my tongue with his, enjoying the rasp of his five o'clock shadow on my skin.

He pulls back. "Be my good girl and show me your tits."

I raise my eyebrow at him. "Take your shirt off first." He smirks at me, then grabs his shirt from the back of the collar, pulling it off awkwardly in the confined space. As he tosses it to the side, I take off my sweater, undo the side zipper of my dress, and slide my arms out. Next to go is my bra as the cotton fabric pools at my waist. Max pushes the fabric down until he exposes my silver jewelry.

He flicks it with his finger and looks up at me. "I fucking love this." He pushes up into me. "Hold on, Dimples."

I comply, and he rewards me with a hard thrust and grind. His mouth drops to my breast, and he sucks as much of the globe into his mouth as he can. "Oh God. You're not messing around." I drop my heavy head back on my shoulders.

"I'm never just messing around with you. I hope you know that." Thrust. He uses his grip on my hips to guide me up and down his shaft as he repeatedly pushes up into me. I add a swivel to my hips, making sure to rub my clit against his pelvis.

Our bodies are slick. Our breaths come out in harsh pants and I'm sure if someone were to pull into the parking lot, they'd know exactly what's going on in here. The windows are fogging up with each labored breath and the car is rocking in time with our bodies. I can't find it in me to care. I want my release. My muscles are tensing and it's getting harder to keep up with Max's rhythm. My focus narrows to where we're joined and making sure I don't falter. I squeeze Max's dick.

"Fuck. Do that again and I'll come." I take the challenge and squeeze him again on the next stroke. He pinches my nipple with a frown marring his forehead, making me giggle.

He finds his way to my clit beneath the pooling fabric of my dress and circles it with deft fingers, returning his lips to my mouth. Hunching down, I use my legs to push myself up and down, bouncing over his cock as he takes me ever closer to my release.

Every thrust up pushes the air from my lungs and stars dance around the edge of my vision. His penis swells. He's as close as I am. Tingles spread all the way from my toes, up my legs, and down my spine. I drop one final time and break apart all over him. "Yeeees!" I gasp for air and lean down to kiss him. My kiss is sloppy as he comes undone, groaning into my mouth.

"Fuuck! You feel so damn good, Dimples." He returns my sloppy kiss. "I'm gonna fill you with my babies one day soon," he moans and my already racing heart picks up speed, thumping against my rib cage, trying to burst free. I pull back to study him. Guys say all sorts of stuff in the heat of the moment, and I wonder if he realizes what he's said. He opens his eyes to find me studying his face as if I can find the answer somehow. "I mean it. I want you to have my babies. I don't want you to get your next shot."

I blink at him. "You want to have a baby with me?"

"I sure as fuck do." His eyes move back and forth between mine. "Do you?" His Adam's Apple bobs. "Do you want to have a baby with me?"

"You don't think it's too soon to be talking about babies?"

His body stiffens and I place my hands on his shoulders, rubbing my thumbs along his collarbones. "You think it's too soon?"

I shrug. "We've only known each other for just over two months."

"I know it's fast, but I don't see the point of waiting when I know you're the one for me." He reaches up and tucks a lock of hair that's fallen across my face behind my ear. "I'm all in, Molly."

I nod, slowly at first, increasing in enthusiasm. "I'm all in too. I think you'd be the best daddy."

He smiles and moves in, taking my mouth. Our tongues entangle, and I feel him grow inside of me. Obviously, the idea of knocking me up has him excited. We move together, slower this time, languidly joined with our kisses as well as our sex. The interior of the car is filled with the scent of our coupling as Max takes over my body, my heart, and my soul. A sheen of sweat coats both of us as we climb higher and higher before we break apart. It's not as explosive as the first time, but it feels deeper, more meaningful somehow. We separate to draw in lungfuls of much-needed oxygen. Our eyes connect and I'm positive mine reflects his happiness.

"When can we start?" he asks with a cheeky grin. I giggle at his eagerness. "Fuck, don't do that. You nearly pushed me out." He pouts playfully and thrusts his hips up to push his half-soft dick back inside, making me giggle again. "Damn it, woman."

He slides out of me and the sensation of his cum trickling from my body moves me into action. Using the fabric of my dress, I rise higher and clean myself up as best I can in the limited light. I dread to think about the mess we've made on his leather seat. I shuffle slightly, pulling my underwear back into place, then rest my backside on his knees.

Resting my hands on his pecs, I lean forward and press my lips to his. Pulling back slightly, I break the news. "I definitely can't get pregnant within the next three months and it can take up to one year for my periods to regulate. But I could possibly get pregnant in as little as three months once the shot wears off."

Even in the limited light, I can see his face light up with his smile. "Well, that gives us time to practice our technique." He wriggles his eyebrows up and down.

I giggle. "That sounds good to me."

His hands squeeze my hips, and he drags me back in close to his body, my exposed breasts pressing against his chest. I sigh, deeply content to sit here like this all night. He rubs his hands up and down my spine in a soothing motion. With two orgasms under my belt, I close my eyes and enjoy the sensation, my breathing slowing down.

A rap on the window and a bright light shining inside startles both of us. We must have dozed off. "Everything okay in there?" Comes a muffled voice through the glass.

I look around, instantly alert. My eyes land on the police cruiser parked right next to us. I'm sure he can see my state of undress. *Shit!*

"Everything's fine, officer. Thanks. We were getting ready to leave," Max speaks for both of us.

"Okay. Just to remind you that public indecency is a fineable offense, and we'll leave it at that."

"Thank you, officer." I finally find my voice. The bright light disappears and the officer steps away from Max's car. "Shit!" I whisper-giggle.

"Damn. I felt like a kid again." He searches around on the seat for my bra but comes up empty. It's too dark to see anything. I pull the straps of my dress up and shiver as I do up the zipper. "You're cold. C'mon, let's go."

Max drags his underwear and jeans back up and we both climb out of the back seat and readjust the front seats. I grab my sweater and put it on as I situate myself. The officers give us a tilt of their heads as Max starts the engine and pulls out. Once we're on the road, we both break out into laughter.

When we settle down, Max takes my hand in his, resting it on his firm thigh, and rubs his thumb back and forth. "I think you should move in with me." He glances across at me.

"You're full of ideas tonight," I chuckle.

He shrugs. "It makes sense. I don't see the point of wasting time. As I said, I'm all in."

I bring his hand up to my mouth and kiss the palm. "I'd love to move in with you."

His smile is big and bright, and I know I've made the right decision.

# CHAPTER 32

## —max—

COULD LIFE GET ANY BETTER?

Nope. I don't think it can.

Molly's all moved in. Having her toothbrush in the holder with mine gave me a sense of satisfaction this morning that can't be explained.

Mona constantly hinted that we should move in together, but I didn't want her in my space. I needed time and space away from her and didn't want her in my home for more than the night. She'd always linger on a Sunday morning and I'd hate it. But with Molly, I wish we didn't have to leave the house to come to work. If I could stay home with her all day, it wouldn't be long enough. I huff out a chuckle to myself as I disconnect the muffler bracket from the worn rubber hanger.

My, how things have changed. I never thought I'd feel this way, but here I am. *And I fucking love it.*

I slide out from under the car I'm working on to be greeted by a pair of work boots. My eyes follow the path upward to identify the owner of the boots. Martin. I quickly glance across to the door that leads into the office.

Martin follows my path. "Hey, Max. Molly's not in the office." I push up from the trolley and stand. "I came to see her. I … uh … I've tried to give her some time, but I think we need to talk." He tucks his hands in his pockets, shuffling on his feet.

I nod. "Hey, Martin. She's probably grabbing our lunch." I wipe my hands with a rag. "You don't think it'd be better to wait for her to contact you when she's ready? She was pretty upset after your last chat." *That's an understatement.*

He glances down at the floor and shrugs. "It's been a month. I've already lost too much time. I want to get to know my daughter. I *need* to get to know my daughter." He runs his hand through his salt and pepper hair. "Beth and Holly have spoken with her and they said she was open and friendly. I'm hoping I can repair some of the damage I've caused with my carelessness."

"Maaax! Lunch is—" Molly freezes in the doorway of the office. I can tell from here that she's trying to decide what to do. She takes a tentative step forward—*so fucking brave*. "Hi, Martin." She stops a couple of feet away, then looks at me. "I didn't realize Martin had his car booked in today."

Martin steps closer to her. "Hey, Molly. I didn't. I … uh … I hope you don't mind me stopping by unannounced, but I wanted to see you." His shoulders drop. "I'm sorry. I probably should have called first. I keep messing this up." He takes a step back and spins on his heel to leave. "I'll leave you two to enjoy your lunch."

Molly glances at me, her eyes wide. "What should I do?" she whispers.

"It's up to you, Dimples. He just wants to talk." She blows out a breath and studies the floor as if the answer lies there somewhere. She spins around and runs after him. I follow along at a slower pace. Molly catches up to Martin as he's about to climb into his truck.

I can't hear what's being said from here, but Molly points toward me. He nods and she comes to me. She stops close and I use the loops of her jeans to pull her closer. I study her eyes carefully and she smiles at me. "I'm okay." I nod and kiss the tip of her nose. "Do you mind if I spend my lunch break with Martin?"

"Of course not. You don't need to ask my permission." I glance up at Martin. He's watching us closely and I want him to be aware that I'm watching out for Molly. I lean down and take her mouth in a heated kiss. It takes a beat for Molly to respond, but when her tongue strokes against mine, I wrap my arms around her and hold her tight. We pull apart slowly and I touch my forehead to hers. "I'll be here if you need me."

"Thank you." I don't understand how she fills two simple words with so much gratitude, but she does. "We're going to the park down the road." She thumbs over her shoulder.

"Take your lunch with you." I dash into the office to grab it for her.

She climbs into the cab of Martin's truck. With narrowed eyes, he lifts his chin at me, and I return the action. I watch the truck until they disappear, then return to the office to eat lunch on my own. I hope this chat goes well. Family's important to Molly and I want her to have family surrounding and supporting her. She deserves to have the world.

My phone lights up with Theo's number. "Hey, Brother. What's up?"

"Hiya, Max. I wanted to let you know I've sourced the timber you'll need for the truck. I'll keep it in my workshop to allow it time to dry out properly."

"Thanks, man. Appreciate it."

"No problem. How're things?"

"Damn good. Molly's moved in with me. Life's feeling pretty great."

He huffs out a laugh. "She's a keeper. Kenny hasn't stopped talking about her since Lachlan's party. Emma loves her, too."

"Don't worry. I'm never letting her go."

"Good to hear, man. I gotta go. See ya on Sunday."

"Sure. And thanks for sourcing the timber."

# CHAPTER 33

## —molly—

AS WE TURN ONTO THE STREET, MY FINGERS INSTANTLY FIND COMFORT in twisting my bracelet.

"So, you and Max, huh?"

I snap my head toward Martin and narrow my eyes. "What do you mean?"

He fidgets in his seat. "Are you together? More than boss and employee? More than friends?" He glances across at me. "I mean, it's none of my business, but I'm happier knowing you have someone and you're not completely alone." He clears his throat. "Not that you're alone. You *do* have us, we just need to find our feet."

"Uh yeah. It's pretty new. We started as boss and employee, then developed a friendship. It grew into more." I shrug. "I moved in with him on Sunday. It's pretty serious." Once I agreed to move in, Max drove straight to the apartment and we packed my stuff. He was a man on a mission.

Martin pulls into the parking lot and we climb out of his truck to stroll toward a vacant picnic table. "You don't think it's too fast?" Hmmm. My muscles tense. I'm not sure where he's going with this line of questioning, but I'm old enough to make my own decisions. It's not like he's been part of my life. He gives me a tight smile. "I'm sorry. I crossed a line, it's none of my business. It's hard to take off the dad hat sometimes. Max is a good guy. I'm sure he'll be good to you."

I shrug. "He's been nothing but fantastic to me so far. I can't see that changing. Ever." I take a bite of my sandwich as Martin opens a home-packed lunch box filled with vegetables, crackers, cheese, meat, and hummus. "I should make lunch for me and Max rather than him buying it for us every day."

"Beth insists on packing me a healthy lunch every day. She allows me to buy my lunch on Fridays." He smirks at me. "It's her love language to care for and feed her family." He dips a carrot into some hummus and chews thoughtfully. "She fell in love with you. Couldn't stop talking about you when she got home. That's why Holly wanted to meet you, too. She's steadfastly in the Molly fan club as well."

I blush. "They're both incredibly sweet. I thought it was coincidental that your daughter's name is Holly and mine is Molly." I chuckle.

"Yeah, it is, and it isn't. Nicole and I liked a lot of the same things. We often had the same thoughts at the same time. We were unquestionably in sync in that way." His body's still here, but his mind is somewhere else. He slowly comes back to the moment. "Look, Molly. I can apologize to you for the rest of my life, and I'll happily do so, but nothing is going to change how things happened all those years ago. I need you to know that I have regretted my response to Nicole's pregnancy every single day of my life. It wasn't my finest moment and it's not something I'm proud of. I lost so much because of my youthful stupidity. I only hope that one day you can forgive me and we can develop some sort of relationship."

I reach across the table and place my hand over his. "Thank you. I'm sorry I responded so badly at dinner."

He covers my hand with his. "You don't owe me an apology, Molly. I should have been more thoughtful in the way I shared the events of that time with you." He smiles sadly. "I would like the opportunity to get to know you, though."

"Me too." We both release a heavy breath. There's no point in holding a grudge. He genuinely wants to build a relationship with me, and I'd be stupid to turn down the opportunity to get to know my family. I think Mom would want me to put the past behind me and open my heart to Martin and his family. *My* family.

"So, uh, I can't believe I have to ask you this question, but when's your birthday?" He drops his eyes to his food.

"August thirty. I'll be—"

"Twenty-seven this year."

I smile. "Yeah."

"I figured you were born around there somewhere."

We study each other for long moments. It's comforting seeing my eyes staring back at me. "It surprised me how similar I am to Holly and Noah. I always thought I looked so much like Mom."

"Yeah. It's uncanny. The first time I laid eyes on you, I couldn't stop staring. The resemblance was remarkable to Nicole and your sister and brother. I went home and told Beth about you. She didn't believe me until she laid eyes on you the day we bought the car from Max." He glances away, then his eyes lock back on me. "When she had to come and pick me up from your place that day we worked out that you are my daughter. Beth wanted to pack you up and bring you home. We lost Nicole all of those years ago and then we lost her all over again that day."

The breath in my lungs seizes. I was so overwhelmed that day and I've been caught up in my own grief and loss as well as coming to terms with meeting my father, that I hadn't taken the time to consider his and Beth's loss. I've been so selfish. "I'm sorry you had to find out about Mom like that. It would have been tough."

He shrugs. "Is there anything you can share with me about yourself? What's your favorite thing to do?"

A genuine smile spreads. "I love to sketch. My stepdad, Jack, taught me and my brother, Ethan, how to draw. Ethan mostly drew cars, but I'll draw pretty much anything."

"Really? Holly's always sketching new designs for her clothes." The tension disappears between us as we find some common ground. Conversation flows more easily as we chat about Holly's passion for design.

I glance at the time. "Oh, my gosh. I need to get back. I only get thirty minutes for lunch."

"Sure." We quickly clean up our mess and head back to the workshop. Martin parks out front and then turns in his seat toward me. "Uh, would you like to come over for dinner one Saturday night?" I freeze. I'm not sure I'm ready to face his whole family at once. "You can bring Max with you."

"Do you mind if I think about it and let you know?"

He shakes his head. "Of course. No pressure."

"Thanks. And, uh, thanks for today. This was … nice." I open the door and climb down.

"Thank you for agreeing to have lunch with me. I hope we can move forward, Molly." I nod.

"Bye, Martin."

"Bye, Molly."

I close the door and head inside the workshop. A squeal escapes as I'm lifted off my feet from behind. Muscular arms wrapped around my waist tightening to keep me in place. Max's familiar scent swamps my senses. "You scared me." He places me back on my feet and I spin around. Immediately, I'm engulfed in his warm embrace as he studies my face closely, his brows scrunched together. I smile at him. "I'm okay. Lunch went well."

He blows out a breath and glances between my eyes and mouth, then leans in to kiss me. It's not a kiss to welcome me back, it's a kiss that fills me down to my toes. It makes me feel cherished and cared for. He's reminding me he's here for me and I don't have to deal with my new reality on my own. I return his kiss. Pouring my appreciation for his support into it. We separate slowly, gradually opening our eyes. "You're sure?"

I nod. "I'm positive. We even got invited to dinner one Saturday." His eyebrows shoot up. "I wanted to check that you would be able to come with me before I accepted."

"If you're there and you want me to be with you. Then that's where I'll be, Dimples." He presses his lips to my forehead, pulling me in tighter to his body, and I sigh. "Even if I had something on, I would cancel to be with you."

Luckily, he's holding me tight; I think my knees would have given out on me if he weren't. "Thank you. I'll let Martin know later. Now, what'd I miss?" With our arms wrapped around each other, we make our way into the office.

# CHAPTER 34

## —molly—

MAX STROLLS INTO THE KITCHEN AS I'M OPENING AND CLOSING EVERY cupboard. "What are you looking for? Maybe I can help."

"Do you have any lunch boxes?" I wave my hand in the general direction of the cupboards.

He glances around, then shakes his head. "I don't think so. Why?"

I fidget with my bracelet. "Today, at lunch, Martin had a lunch box that Beth had prepared for him. I wanted to start making our lunches. It's expensive to buy it every day. I can pack them the night before, and it'll be easy enough to keep them in the fridge at work." I hope he doesn't think it's a stupid idea.

He moves into my space, hooking his fingers through the belt loops of my jeans. He pulls me forward and smirks at me. "You wanna make lunch for me, for us?"

"Yeah. You don't think it's stupid, do you?"

He shakes his head. "Nah. Dad always made our lunches for us when we were living at home. But I buy our lunch every day to support Lawrence's business. I could have been taking lunch to work, but I'd rather help him out. He gives us a discount because we buy from him every day. But if it would make you fee—"

Of course, he does it to help his friend; that's Max all over. "Oh, I didn't realize that's why you did it. Forget I said anything." I press into him and lick his bottom lip. He opens and I slide my tongue inside to share a heated kiss. I love this man. "I love you."

Max's eyes widen and his lips spread wide to match. "Say that again, Dimples."

"I love you, Max. You're such a good man." I press a chaste kiss against his mouth.

"I'll never get tired of you saying those words. I love you, Molly. You're the sweetest, kindest woman I've ever met." His eyes are full of emotion, and I know the words are completely true. He's not saying them because I said them. He means them as much as I do.

He hoists me onto the kitchen counter, pressing his body into the space between my open legs. Our lips meet as his hands slide beneath my shirt, setting my skin on fire. I shuffle forward, making contact with his erection confined within the denim.

Suddenly, there's an urgency between us. Clothes go flying left and right until we're both naked, neither of us caring where they land.

His fingers slide through my slit as he kisses my breath from me. I'm already soaking and I want him inside me. Now! "I need you." I press my pelvis forward and reach for him, wrapping my hand around his long, hard shaft. "Please don't make me wait," I pant. My heart's hammering, swollen with love for the man who's about to fill my body, just as he's filled my life since I arrived.

"I need you. I promise we'll go slow later."

"Don't care. Just get inside me." I pant.

He thrusts in. Hard. Forcing all the air out of my lungs. My mouth drops open in bliss. "Fuck. You look so good with my dick in your pussy." I moan. God, I love his filthy mouth. "Look down, Dimples. I want you to see how beautiful your pussy looks stretched around my cock."

I tilt my head down. The sight is erotic as he slides out; his shaft glistening from my arousal. He slides back in with a groan and I press forward, meeting his push with my own. His lips drop to my breast, and he sucks the nipple into his mouth, sending shockwaves to my clit. I run my hands across his shoulders and down his back, feeling his muscles tense and move with his thrusts. I kiss the top of his head and he tips his face up to meet my mouth. His hands grasp my hips tight as he holds me in place to take his punishing pounding. My heart thumps hard against my ribcage as my breaths become choppy.

"Oh my God. That feels so good. I … I'm getting close. I … I need …" I whisper with harsh breaths.

One hand leaves my hip and he brings his fingers to my clit. He pinches the bundle of nerves, then rubs tight circles, building me higher. My toes curl as I run my hands through his sweaty hair, pulling his head in tighter to me. My breaths are short and sharp, matching the warm puffs of his against my neck. He pulls back, our eyes locking as I break apart and I feel his gaze drilling into me, all the way to my soul. My muscles clench around his shaft and Max grits his teeth. The veins in his neck are pronounced as he slows his thrusts through my orgasm, my cum coating his cock. His head drops and his mouth envelopes my other breast. I moan as my muscles continue to pulse.

Max looks up at me, one side of his mouth tilted up. "I fucking love making you come. The way your body flushes and your pussy strangles my cock. I'm never gonna get enough of this. Enough of you." We both lean forward, our tongues reaching for the other, sealing his words with a savage kiss.

He pulls out of my pussy partway and surges forward. He pounds into me, hammering my pussy. His shaft grows inside me, setting off a second, smaller orgasm I wasn't expecting. His dick pulses. "Fuuuuck! Your pussy is heaven." He throws his head back. "Fuck!" His cum streams out of him and into me and I wish this was the time we were making a baby.

Dropping his head back down, he roughly takes my mouth and I wrap my legs around him, keeping him locked inside me as long as possible as we share a prolonged kiss. Running my fingers through his hair, I grasp the strands at the base and keep him exactly where I want him. We're messy in this moment as our tongues twist around each other, our teeth clash, and I'm completely and utterly his.

No question about it.

We separate, dropping our foreheads together. Our eyes locked, our breaths combining. Gray eyes to mossy green. "I fucking love you, Molly."

I smile. And it's full and happy. "I fucking love you, Max." I chuckle.

We hold each other as our bodies cool, staring into each other's eyes. I can see right to his core, and I know what we have is rare and special. Not everyone is lucky enough to find this and I'm never going to let it go. And I know with certainty Max feels the same.

*—max—*

"DO YOU MIND IF WE GET SOME FRESH FRUIT?" MOLLY FIDGETS WITH her bracelet. I noticed how much she enjoyed the fresh fruit we had for breakfast the morning after the first night we slept together, and she always had some in her apartment.

I stop, pulling the cart to the side of the aisle, and turn Molly to face me. "Of course we can buy fresh fruit and vegetables and whatever else you need, Dimples. Why are you worried about asking?"

Her eyes skate around me, glancing everywhere but at me. "Fresh fruit was … still is a luxury for me. When I have money, it's one of the first things I buy. I wasn't sure if fruit was something you have on the regular and I didn't want to impose my preferences on you. I notice you don't seem to eat a lot of fruit and you don't have any in your fridge."

Such a simple thing. I've always eaten fruit. Mom always made sure we had fresh fruit every day with breakfast and Dad always packed fruit in our lunch box. As an adult, though, I can't remember the last time I took fruit to work that wasn't in a pie or muffin. I usually have a small amount of fresh fruit in the fridge at home for snacks or breakfast, but if I skip eating it for a day, I don't really think about it. Shit! It's not something I've thought about, which means I take it for granted. Here's Molly, who's always lived on the poverty line or close to it and she would never take something as simple as having fresh fruit every day for granted. She considers it a damn luxury.

I pull her in close and kiss her forehead. "If it will make you happy, we can have fresh fruit and vegetables for every single meal. I never want you to think you can't ask for what you want, for what you need. Being on my own, I didn't bother keeping much in the house. I'd make simple meals for dinner, and I was slack with breakfast. We can do better with two of us."

We make our way to the fruit and vegetables, and I watch as Molly carefully handpicks fruits and vegetables with glee written all over her face. Glancing at the prices, I note she's choosing the basic options that aren't too expensive.

I'm not having it. "Do you like berries?"

Her head snaps up to mine, then she glances across to the berry display. "I love raspberries, but they're a little expensive."

"I love raspberries too. Let's get some." I push the cart across and grab two containers of raspberries, two of strawberries, and one of blackberries. My girl will never go without the necessities of life again. Shit that we all take for granted.

Molly steps closer to the cart, studying the contents. Her gray eyes slowly creep up to mine and she tucks a lock of her silky hair behind her ear. "Oh, that's a lot. I don't know if we'll get through all of it before it goes bad."

I shrug. "I'm pretty sure I can eat a whole container in one sitting. I doubt it'll be a problem." I peck her forehead. "C'mon, we need to keep moving." I need to make sure my girl has everything she needs at her fingertips. We move down the aisles, filling the cart with groceries. More than I've ever bought before, but I'm not stopping until the cart is full. We have one more section to go. Ice cream. "What's your favorite ice cream flavor?"

She licks her lips and studies the freezer for long moments, then she glances at the cart. "I don't think we need anything else." She huffs out a laugh. "We already have more than we need."

"We need to have ice cream. C'mon, what's your favorite?"

She looks back at the freezer. "I am partial to vanilla caramel fudge. What's your favorite?" I grab a carton of her favorite and a tub of pistachio for me, holding it up so she can see. "I'll have pistachio. You don't need to grab two different cartons of ice cream. It's too much."

"Nah. As much as I love you, I don't share my ice cream." I press a kiss to the tip of her nose and dump the ice cream in the cart as Molly giggles.

We head to the front of the store to pay as Molly grumbles about how much food we bought. A couple of ladies have stopped in the aisle to have a chat and as we get closer, I realize one of them is Beth. She's speaking to an older woman. Neither of them has any groceries, so they must have just arrived. Molly hasn't noticed because she's still studying our cart with a frown. Beth's eyes catch on us and her mouth drops open slightly. She glances at the older lady and back to us several times. For some reason, she looks uncomfortable. Almost like we've caught her doing something she shouldn't.

Molly's feet lock in place as she notices Beth. "Hi, Beth," she greets, smiling.

"Molly. Max." I've only met Beth a couple of times and I don't know her all that well, but her usual friendliness is missing. Molly's smile drops and creases form between her brows; I'm not the only one who noticed the frosty greeting. Beth glances back at the older lady she's with as we all stand awkwardly. The lady turns around and her eyes widen, her mouth dropping open. Her hand rises to her chest as she grips her blouse. Beth gestures to the woman. "Uh, uhm. This is Joanna. Joanna *Lewis*." She raises her eyebrows at Molly.

*Lewis.* That's Molly's surname. My eyebrows shoot up. *Fuck!*

I move closer to Molly and wrap my arm around her. Her eyes skip between Beth and Joanna and I can see her putting one and one together. "Joanna Lewis?" Molly asks Beth.

Beth nods. "Joanna. This is Molly. She recently moved here from Portland."

Joanna steps into Molly's space, studying her closely. "Molly? That was my mother's name." She raises her hand, almost touching Molly's face before she realizes what she's doing and pulls back sharply. "I'm sorry. You look so much like …" She shakes her head as though she's trying to shift a memory.

Beth steps forward. "Joanna."

"How about we pay for our groceries and you can follow us home for a chat?" I cut her off. The ladies shouldn't have this conversation in the middle of the store. I'm not sure if Molly's come to the same conclusion I have, but if she's who I think she is, this conversation should happen in private.

Everyone agrees, and we pay for our groceries and load them into my car. Molly's been silent the entire time, fidgeting with her bracelet. Once we're on the road, I pull her hand across to rest on my thigh. "You okay?"

She tears her eyes away from her window and glances at me. "Do you think she's ... do you think she's my grandmother? I mean, her name is Lewis and the way she was looking at me and she said that her mom's name was Molly. Mom told me she named me after her grandmother." The words tumble out of Molly's mouth, each one coming faster than the last.

"I think she might be. How do you feel about that?" *What a fucking stupid question.* God, I'm an idiot sometimes.

"I don't know. I never even thought about finding Mom's parents. They didn't support her and her dad wanted the pregnancy aborted. Wanted *me* aborted. That's why she left." The despair in her voice is thick and I glance across to check on her. Storm clouds filled with rain look back at me. "Will she even care that Mom's gone?" She brings her hand up to wipe away the tears that have escaped. "I don't know if I'm ready for this."

"I can pull over right now and tell them we've changed our mind. We don't have to do this until you're ready, Molly." I squeeze her hand.

She's quiet for a long moment. "No, it's okay. I don't want to upset anyone." She straightens her shoulders as if she's preparing for battle.

"You're my priority. I don't give a fuck about upsetting anyone else. I don't want *you* upset. You've already had to deal with too much. I didn't think when we were in the grocery store. Before I invited them home, I should have checked with you. I was trying to keep the conversation that was about to happen private."

She flips her hand over, twining her fingers with mine. "Thank you. You're right, the grocery store wasn't the place for a family reunion." She draws in a deep breath. "May as well get it over and done with."

*Fuck, she's brave.*

"I want you to know that I have an incredible amount of respect for you. The way you deal with everything thrown at you with your head held high. You are a fucking queen." I lift her hand to my mouth to press a kiss to it.

We pull into our driveway and she draws in a deep breath. "Here we go!"

The ladies pull in behind us in two separate cars. Molly and I grab a couple of bags of groceries each and take them inside. Beth and Joanna grab some bags and help us, making quick work of unloading my trunk.

"My. How many people are you two feeding? This seems like a lot of food." Beth chuckles.

"Just the two of us. I didn't have much in the house and now that Molly's living here, we needed to stock the pantry."

Molly offers coffee and makes it while I put away the food that needs to be refrigerated or frozen. The rest can wait until later. Beth and Joanna stand awkwardly by the counter as Molly and I seamlessly work around each other in the kitchen. An uncomfortable silence filling the space.

Even though it's a nice day, I can feel a chill in the air as the sun drops lower. "How about we move into the living room?"

I show the ladies through and then head back to help Molly. "Do you want me with you or I can stay in here? Whatever you need."

She smiles at me, cupping my cheek. Her eyes are full of love and appreciation. "Do you mind sticking close by? I'm not sure how this is going to go."

Turning, I kiss the palm of her hand. "Of course." We grab the cups and head into the living room.

Beth and Joanna are standing in front of the same photo Martin saw in Molly's apartment. As we place the cups on the coffee table, Joanna turns around with tears in her eyes. "You– … you're my grand-daughter."

Molly stands up straight and sucks in a sharp breath, nodding slowly. I hate seeing her so unsure of herself. She's done absolutely nothing wrong in this whole fucked up situation. I don't care if the woman is elderly, if she fucking upsets my girl, I'm throwing her ass out on the street.

Joanna walks straight to Molly and engulfs her in a tight hug, sobbing loudly. Her whole body's shaking. Molly's hands slowly rise to comfort the woman, but she's holding her body stiff. Beth and I watch as the older woman breaks down, her body shuddering with her sobs. I glance at Beth and she looks lost. I go in search of some tissues and drop the box on the coffee table.

Joanna pulls back, holding Molly's upper arms. "You're so beauti-ful. And tall!" She looks Molly up and down. "You're so much like your mother." Joanna looks around suddenly as if she's looking for some-thing. "Is Nicole back home, too?"

I look at Beth. "You haven't told her?"

Beth's bottom lip shakes. "I … I didn't want to tell her in the grocery store. I was about to invite her to my home so I could tell her there. We lost touch and I haven't seen Joanna since I saw Molly. I didn't even think about it, to be honest. Now I feel terrible. It was sheer coincidence that I bumped into Joanna today."

"Tell me what?" Joanna asks as her eyes skate between the three of us.

I can read the dread on Molly's face, in her entire body. "Joanna, maybe you should sit down. I ... I need to tell you something."

Joanna nods and sits. "I can't believe I'm sitting with my grand-daughter. I never thought this would happen." She pats Molly's knee and leaves her hand resting in place. "Where's Nicole? Has she forgiven me? Can I see her?"

Molly glances at me, then at Beth before settling her eyes on Joanna. "Uhm. Mom's not here." She swallows and I know this is killing her. I can't let her do this on her own, so I take the cushion next to her and brush my hand in a soothing path up and down her delicate spine.

Molly takes Joanna's hand from her knee and holds it between both of hers. "Mom can't come home. She ... uh ... was in a ..." She turns and looks at me over her shoulder and I reach up to tuck a lock of her silky hair behind her ear and kiss her temple.

"You've got this, Dimples. I'm here." I press a kiss on her temple.

She turns back to Joanna and draws in a deep breath. "She was out with my stepdad and my brother, Ethan." Joanna's eyes widen at learning she has another grandchild. "They were looking at the Christmas lights. It was something we did every year. Last Christmas I was volunteering, which meant I couldn't go with them. On the way home, Jack, Mom's husband, had a heart attack at the wheel. They ... uh ... got into an accident with a truck."

Joanna raises her free hand to her mouth. Her wide eyes are locked on Molly as she breaks this devastating news to a stranger who happens to be her grandmother. "No!"

"No one is more sorry than I am to tell you she didn't ... she didn't survive. None of them did." Molly's voice cracks and I pull her back into my arms. This woman who looks so delicate on the outside is made of fucking steel.

Joanna folds in on herself, a loud wail escaping her. Beth moves over, wrapping her arms around Joanna in comfort, while I comfort my girl. I wish I could make all of this pain stop.

When will it fucking stop for her?

How much more is she supposed to endure?

Her body shakes in my arms with her silent tears and my heart splinters into a million pieces that I can't protect her from this pain.

The light in the room is fading with the sun. Our coffee sits cold on the coffee table and everyone's hearts are broken. This is not how I saw our day going.

# CHAPTER 36

## —molly—

GOD. I CAN'T BREATHE.

Everything feels like it's closing in on me.

I have to tell this woman that her daughter will never come home. I absorb Max's comforting touch as I recount the events that stole my family from me, sending Joanna's world crashing to the ground and mine spiraling downward as well.

The sadness in the room is stifling and if it weren't for Max holding me, I would do what I always do when everything gets too much. Curl up in my bed and hide under the covers. Try to block out the world with sleep and hope that when I wake, things are back to the way they should be. Mom would always let me have my time to wallow, then she would insist that I make a plan and move forward. It's what she always did.

"M– Molly." I turn toward Joanna. "I … I'm so sorry. Do you think you can find it in your heart to ever … forgive me?" Her eyes are swollen and red and I know that if I could see inside her chest, her heart would be in tiny pieces like mine. Her heartbreak is oozing from every pore. "I've missed Nicole and you every single day since she left us. I only hope you've had a good life."

"My life's been good. It's been hard at times, but I've had a great life." Max huffs behind me, mumbling something.

"Hard would be an understatement, Molly." He looks at me with disbelief in his eyes. He glances up at Joanna and Beth. "They lived out of Nicole's car until Molly was eleven." Joanna and Beth gasp and I stare at him in disbelief, trying to block them out.

Hurt fills me swiftly and I pull away from him to stand on shaky legs. "Max. I shared that with you in confidence. It wasn't your place to tell anyone. You had no right." I scan the room, seeing faces full of pity. I spin on my heel, grab my bag, and take off out the front door before anyone can stop me.

*Run.*

I need to run.

Even though I don't have my running gear on, I take off sprinting down the street, the sun sits heavy on the horizon as the streetlights turn on. I'm not sure where I'm going to go, but I can't be in that house with Beth and Joanna looking at me with eyes full of pity and guilt. I'm not sure why I'm hurt that Max told them about my living arrangements growing up, but I am.

My lungs burn and my feet hurt from pounding the concrete in the wrong shoes, but my mind won't switch off. What are they going to think of me? Will they think I'm less than because of the way I grew up? Will they blame Mom? I don't want them to. She did the best she could with what she had. She could have taken better-paying jobs, but she always put me first. She never wanted to leave me in care, and we had no family to look after me, to allow her to work longer hours.

I don't want them to judge her.

I don't want them to judge *me*.

Max's workshop comes into view, and I slow down. At the bottom of the steps, I kick out my feet with my hands resting on my hips to catch my breath. I'm tempted to go upstairs and curl up on the bed, but Max might come here looking for me and I can't face him right now.

Walking around to the back of the workshop, my car comes into view. I've been leaving it here most nights. It's easier for Max and me to share a ride to work now that I'm living with him. I climb in and drive.

It's not like I have anywhere to go. I drive aimlessly through the streets until I find myself at the beach. I'm not surprised I ended up here. There's something about the beach that calms and settles me. Reaching into the backseat, I grab the jacket that I left there and climb out of my car. I lock it and head down to the shoreline, my shoes sinking into the soft sand as I trek closer to the water's edge. Crossing my legs, I drop to my butt and watch the waves kiss the shore beneath the moonlight. I pull my jacket tighter around my body and drop my chin to my knees. I get lost in watching the waves roll in and out.

Max never gave me the impression he felt sorry for me, but maybe he does. I never want anyone's pity. I think that's part of the reason I enjoy volunteering at the women's shelter. I know the women don't want pity, and I'm able to interact with them on a level that doesn't include pity or shame or judgment. It's not something Mom or I ever wanted and I know it's not something they want.

I draw in deep breaths and release each one slowly, trying to untangle my thoughts.

# CHAPTER 37

## —max—

*FUCK!*

I fucked up badly.

She's right. I had no right to share that information with anyone and until then I hadn't told a soul. Even though none of it happened to me, I have a sense of protectiveness over Molly and I'm angry at Martin, Joanna, and her husband on her behalf. But I should have kept my fucking mouth shut.

Beth, Joanna, and I stand in my living room in stunned silence. Slowly, Beth turns to me. "I had no idea. I don't think she told Martin because he would have said something to me."

"Why didn't Nicole come home? I don't understand." Joanna mumbles in disbelief. "That poor girl. Living in a car for her child-hood. We could have helped her," she sobs.

"Look. I've already said too much, obviously. But I need you to leave. I need to find her and make sure she's okay. I need to apologize to Molly."

"Of course. Please let us know she's okay." Beth reaches into her purse and hands me a business card. "You can reach me on this number." She turns toward Joanna. "If you give me your number, I'll call you once Max calls me."

"Sure." I shuffle them toward the front door, stepping out with them and locking the house.

"Do you think she'll be okay?" Joanna asks.

I stop and study the two women. Creases across their foreheads display their worry. "Molly's been through a lot and she's as tough as steel beneath her delicate features. She'll be fine. She needs some time and space to deal with everything. It's been a lot for her. Losing her family," I raise my eyebrows at them, "finding her father, half-siblings, and now her grandmother. She's gone from having nobody to having a whole new family she never knew. She packed up her life over east and made her way here on her own. In my opinion, she's fucking amazing and she'll find her way through anything life throws at her. What I've learned about Molly is that she's proud and extremely independent. She won't want your pity and she doesn't want handouts." I stride toward my car. "I need to go."

I climb into my car and gun the engine, not allowing them to respond. They're not my priority right now. I need to find my girl. It's almost completely dark, and I don't want her out here on her own.

Where would she have gone? I know she's fit and can run for miles, but she didn't have her running shoes on. I have to assume that would limit her somewhat.

*Think.* Where would she go?

I drive to the park a couple of miles from home. Maybe she's there. It looks empty. Most families would be eating dinner now, leaving the park empty. I climb out to check the park on foot. The darkness makes it hard to see too far into the distance. I'll have a better chance of seeing her if I walk through the area.

"Molly!" My steps pick up speed when I don't get a response. "Molly!" I check in the tunnel kids often use to hide in. Empty. "Molly!" I call out as I wander around the entire space, becoming frantic.

Nothing. I don't think she's here.

I head back to my car. Maybe she went to the apartment at the workshop. She still has a key. As I pull in, I note the apartment is dark. If she's inside, she's sitting in the dark. I pull up around the back. Dammit, her car's gone. She could be anywhere. My mind races, trying to think of places she'd go.

Frustration bubbles up inside me and I slam my hands on the steering wheel. *Fuck!* I pull out my phone and press her number. The phone rings and rings. She doesn't have voicemail set up, so I can't even leave her a fucking message. I try again and again. Each time the phone rings out, my frustration builds. She has to know I'd worry about her. Why isn't she answering me?

Because she's pissed at me. That's why, asshole.

I drive for hours through the streets and along the riverfront. It's not until I'm driving along the coast that I finally spot her car in a parking lot at the beach. Relief fills me, then anger floods my system. I've been so fucking worried about her. She could have let me know she was okay. I park next to her car and jump out, glancing inside, but it's empty. Following the path down to the shore that I assume Molly would have taken, I use the flashlight on my phone to guide the way. As I get closer to the water, I see the lone silhouette of someone sitting close to the shore.

I take deep breaths to calm myself as I approach, then drop to the sand beside her. She doesn't even flinch, she simply draws in a deep breath.

I want to pull her into my body.

I want to wrap her up and never let anything hurt her ever again.

I want to protect her from all the awful shit.

"I've been worried about you," I whisper, "and with good reason. I could have been anyone coming up behind you, Molly."

Without lifting her head from her knees, she turns her head toward me, her eyes glistening in the moonlight. "I knew it was you. I heard your car pull in." She turns back toward the water. "I'm sorry I worried you." Her voice is small, sad. I put aside my frustration and move closer to wrap my arm around her. Pulling her in tight, I kiss the top of her head and she melts into me, heaving out a heavy sigh. "I shouldn't have run like that. I'm sorry, Max."

I blow out a heavy breath. "I'm sorry, too, Dimples. I shouldn't have said anything. It came out before I could think about it." I turn her chin with my fingers, making her look at me. "I can't help feeling protective of you and when you told me your story, I became pissed on your behalf. I know I have no right to be pissed at the people who let your mom down, but I do. When they were looking at you and your grandmother said she hoped you had a good life, I couldn't keep my frustration inside." I sigh. "I promise I haven't told anyone else. I know it's your story to tell." I lean forward and press my lips to hers; the taste of salty tears coating my lips. "Please forgive my stupidity."

Her shoulders relax and she offers me a sad smile, her dimples barely making an appearance. "Only if you can forgive me for worrying you."

"Now that I know you're safe, you're forgiven. But please don't run like that again. Go to another room in the house or something, but don't take off."

She nods and we both move forward to seal our apology with a kiss. Beyond the taste of tears is Molly.

My beautiful, sweet Molly.

My future. My world.

Cupping the back of her head, her silky hair fills my palm and I guide her mouth where I want it. Tilting it to suit and applying pressure to keep her lips locked with mine. Our tongues press forward, tangling with the other, apologizing with their own embrace. Without breaking our kiss, Molly climbs into my lap and straddles me. I drop back, taking her with me and we share scorching kisses which promise so much more. Stroking, licking, and sucking, our kiss goes on and on.

We separate to catch our breath. Molly presses her forehead to mine, our eyes locked on the other as our chests rise and fall with each new intake of oxygen. Her silken hair curtains us from the world, creating our own cocoon.

"Can I ask you something?" her whispered words blend with the breeze coming from the sea.

I scan her face, glancing between her eyes. "Of course. You can ask me anything."

"You promise to be completely honest with me?" I nod. "Knowing what you know about my life, do you pity me?"

She holds her body stiff as she waits for my answer, and I take a second or two to understand what she's asking me. I shake my head.

"There are many things I feel about you, Molly. Pity definitely isn't one of them." I reach up and tuck her hair behind her ears and give her a lazy smile. "Out of everything I feel for you, the biggest one is admiration. I fucking admire your strength of character so much. You are an incredible human being who handles life with courage and grace." She smiles at me, but it doesn't expose her dimples that I love. "The way you grew up doesn't factor into my feelings for you. It has no bearing on how I see you or how much I fucking love you. But it *does* factor into how much respect I have for you and your mom. Your life could have turned out so differently. *You* could have turned out so differently, but look at you. You are smart and determined. Strong and fiercely independent. I think you're one of the kindest, sweetest people I've ever met. You give your time to help others because you genuinely want to make their life better." I lower my head to rub my nose along hers.

"Wow. I wasn't expecting all of that."

"I'm not fucking finished," I snap and she giggles. "You inspire me to be a better man because I want to be worthy of you and your love. I want to be your equal in all ways, Molly." I rise to take her mouth.

Licking my tongue across her lips, I beg for entrance. She doesn't deny me, opening up and allowing me to swipe inside. She moans into my mouth and grinds her hot pussy down on my hard cock. I lift my hips to meet her and increase the pressure.

"I need you, Max. Please."

Fuck. How can I deny her?

I slide my hands beneath the stretchy fabric of her leggings and grasp her glorious ass, pulling the cheeks apart and squeezing the globes. Our breaths become pants as I rub her pussy along my engorged shaft, trapped behind the zipper of my jeans. I push the fabric of her panties and leggings down below her cheeks, exposing her pussy to the cool night air. My fingers are so close to her slit, and she tilts her hips up in need. "You want me to finger fuck your pussy?"

"Ye– yes, please. Please, Max." She moans against my ear, her hot breath burning my flesh.

I slide one hand between our bodies, seeking her clit, and circle it with firm strokes as I press my fingers inside her dripping heat. My body shivers at the sensation of her walls tight around my fingers. Pushing them in and sliding them out, I add another digit to open her up to me.

Fuck, I need to get my dick in here. "You're such a good girl, taking my fingers. Lift your shirt and let me suck on those beautiful tits of yours."

She moans and lifts her shirt and bra enough for me to capture her pretty nipple when she drops her body forward over my face. As she grinds down on my hand, her walls tighten around my fingers, creating a vacuum. My cock throbs and weeps in my jeans, fighting the constraints of the denim. Fucking her like this in the moonlight, sweat making her glisten under the stars, is perfect. I groan as she shatters on my fingers, her mouth dropping open in a silent scream.

*Fucking beautiful.*

I want to fuck her like this every single day for the rest of my life. Her limp body drops to press against mine and she takes my mouth in a messy kiss. She bites my bottom lip, then soothes it with her tongue, and I can taste the copper when she pushes her tongue inside my mouth. I slowly slide my fingers out of her channel and tap her thigh to lift up.

We wrangle one leg out of her leggings and release my cock from his confinement. Molly wraps her smooth hand around my shaft and gives it a firm stroke before notching it at her hot entrance. She teases her swollen opening with the crown, then pulls away.

"Don't fucking tease me," I grumble.

She giggles. "You tease me all the time. Turnabout is fair play. Don't you think?"

"No. I don't fucking think. Let me inside." I raise up and steal her mouth, kissing her until her breaths are labored. I take my cock in hand and notch it against her opening and press my hips up as she drops. Our joint moans are swallowed by the night air as our eyes lock together. I can't see her properly, but I know her skin is flushed, and her eyes will be mercury. I sit up and use my hold on her hips to guide her up and down my dick.

*Heaven.*

Fucking heaven.

Warm and tight and welcoming every single time I've been inside her.

"Be a good girl and ride my cock." She nods and with our eyes locked, she bounces up and down on my dick. Swiveling her hips, she creates a powerful rhythm. We sigh into each other's open mouths, exchanging breaths. "You fucking own me, Dimples."

She drops, throws her head back, and cries out, breaking apart beautifully over my cock. "So fucking beautiful."

Her elongated neck begs for my tongue and kisses so I lick up the side of her throat and nip her earlobe, then suck it into my mouth. She cries out again. Her long hair tickles my hands as I lock her hips in place and follow her into oblivion. I grit my teeth and my shaft grows inside her; my cum pouring out of me and into her. The same as my love for her. Our mouths join and our tongues dance slowly as our heartbeats gradually return to normal.

*Fuck! She owns me.*

Pulling away, I press my forehead to hers. "I know this isn't romantic and I should probably shut up and plan some way to ask you in a way you deserve. But I'm a selfish asshole and I wanna ask you now." She shivers, so I pull her top down to cover her and draw her in close to me. "Will you marry me?" Her eyes widen and her mouth drops open, but her head automatically nods. "Is that a 'yes', Dimples?"

She smiles, gifting me her dimples as she nods more vigorously. "Yes. I'll marry you, Max."

We move forward at the same time, sealing our commitment with another kiss. My heart beats wildly against Molly's and I tighten my arms around her body, holding her to me.

I'm never letting this woman go.

Tilting my head slightly, I deepen our connection, and my cock, which is still semi-hard inside her, grows. We both moan with the heat building between us again and move together in a slow, sensual dance under the moonlight, with the waves kissing the shore, and the salty breeze cooling our skin. This time, our joining is slow and measured. Our tongues match our hips, and we moan into each other as we surrender to our orgasm.

I bring my hands up to the side of Molly's face. Her heated skin sears the palms of my hands. I brush her sweaty hair away from her face. "I'm going to get down on one knee and ask you properly. I promise."

She giggles. "You don't need to do that. This was perfect." She leans forward and presses a gentle kiss to my lips. "Take me home?"

We peel apart and dress, cursing the sand. Holding hands, we run up the sand to our cars in the parking lot. After a lingering kiss, we make our way home.

I intend to make love to my fiancée all night long.

# CHAPTER 38

## —molly—

I'M STILL FLOATING WHEN I WALK INTO *SHELTER*. I CAN'T BELIEVE MAX proposed to me. It's all happened fabulously fast.

"Afternoon!" I wave and call out to Simone, who's at the desk assisting a young woman. The young woman turns around, her duo-colored gaze locking onto me. "Hey, Ronnie. It's nice to see you." I walk toward the young woman, noticing bruising up her arms. My eyes slide up to Simone and she subtly shakes her head. I take the hint and keep my mouth shut. "Once you've signed in, we can catch up. Do you wanna meet in the dining hall and we can have a juice or something?"

She smiles at me and gives me a wordless nod. I thumb over my shoulder. "I'll check the coffee buffet is stocked. Chat later?"

"Sure." She returns her attention to Simone. The door opens and a woman, balancing a baby on her hip while trying to wrangle a toddler, as well as struggling to carry what looks like their worldly possessions enters. I head straight for the woman and reach for her possessions. She twists her body away from me, blocking my help.

"Hey. I'm Molly. I volunteer here a couple of nights a week. Would you like me to help you with your things?" I give her my brightest smile and glance down at the little girl who's making life difficult for her mom. I drop to my haunches. "If we help your mom, we have some great toys and crafts you can play with." I drop my best smile on her, too, but she's not buying it at all.

The woman turns back to me, her posture relaxing. "Thanks." She gestures for me to take her belongings, a grateful smile on her tired and battered face.

Simone comes around to greet her. "Hi, I'm Simone. Welcome to *Shelter*. We're glad you found us." She gestures over to the same set of chairs we first chatted in and the woman sighs as she sits, her daughter climbing onto her lap. Simone glances up at me. "Would you mind taking those to room six? I think that will suit nicely."

"No problem." I wave at the little girl, and she gives me a pout in return. I get it. I truly do. Life is miserable when you're torn from your one safe place and everything's different. Ronnie notices my struggle to balance everything and rushes forward to help. She slings her backpack over her shoulder, then takes one of the ladies' bags, and we head through the building to room six. "How have you been, Ronnie? I haven't seen you around for a while."

She shrugs. "I only come in now and then when I want a proper shower and a decent night's sleep without worrying about perverts." She looks over her shoulder back at the new woman with her two small children. "Other people usually need the bed more than I do." She says it like it's no big deal.

But I know it *is* a big deal. Awful stuff happens to the homeless who live on the streets and have nowhere to go. We were fortunate to have our car. Mom kept me away from a lot of the stuff that happens on the street as a kid. She was always selective about where she parked, choosing locations that were in the nicer areas that she felt would be safer.

We stow the family's belongings in room six and close the door. "Do you want to come and chat with me while I stock the coffee buffet?"

Ronnie shrugs again. "I'd rather have a shower first. Is that okay?"

"Of course. I'll see you in a little while, then." We separate, her heading for the showers, and me to the dining room.

"Hey, Rhonda!" I call out as I step into the kitchen.

"Hey, gorgeous. You look particularly happy today." She studies me closely.

I'm bursting to tell someone my news. We told the guys after soccer last night, but they're Max's friends. I step closer to Rhonda, ready to burst. "I got engaged." My smile must be stupidly big.

She squeals and pulls my left hand up to her face. "Where's the ring?"

I pull my hand back. "I don't have one yet. It was an impromptu thing on Saturday night."

"Well, whoever he is, he's one lucky man. Congratulations, Molly.

I'm so happy for you, girl!" She leans in, wrapping me in a hug. Her hair smells like roast beef and her hug feels like a warm blanket.

"Thank you." I shake my head and smile at her. "I can't believe it, but I'm over the moon. He's a great guy, and he's been amazing to me since I moved here."

"Well, I'm glad. I'd love to stop and chat in-depth, but this dinner won't cook itself and it looks like we have a full house tonight."

I blow out a heavy breath and nod. "I'll quickly make sure the buffet's stocked, then I'll come and help in the kitchen." I'm not sure how I ended up in the kitchen every time I come here, because I'm pretty useless. But Rhonda's been teaching me some of her tips and tricks, and I've been enjoying her lessons. I'm finishing up when Ronnie steps through the doorway to the dining room. She glances around the room and when her magical eyes lock on me, she heads my way.

"Hey. Do you need any help?"

"Thanks for asking, but I'm almost finished. How was the shower?" Her chocolate-colored hair looks even darker now that it's wet.

She sighs and a slight smile touches her lips. "It was heavenly. It's the one thing I miss. Regular showers."

I nod. "I know, right? It gets tiresome doing the rough wipe down in public toilets." Her eyes widen. "I was homeless until I turned eleven when Mom met this fantastic guy." Her nose crinkles in disgust, but I ignore it. I gathered from our previous chat that she hasn't had the best experiences with men. "Then when I lost my family late last year, followed by my job and my home, I moved here. I didn't know anyone and had little money, so I was living in my car."

"Shit. You come across all sunshine and smiles. I figured you'd had it easy and were volunteering here out of some sense of duty because you're better off than the rest of us."

I'm not offended by her judgment call. I worked hard to portray that everything in my life was perfect. Too prideful to ask for help. "Yeah, well. You can't judge a book by its cover and all that." I shrug.

"I'm sorry."

"You don't need to be. How would you know what my life was like? Just like I don't know what your life is like." I turn my body to face her fully. "But I'm here because I want to give back. Mom and I would stay in shelters when it became too cold to sleep in the car. Especially when I was a baby. She was like you. She didn't want to take a bed away from someone who needed it more. She always said we had our car, which was more than other people had." I nod at her arm. "Do you need anything for that?"

She looks down at it as though she'd forgotten it's bruised. "Nah, I'm okay. A guy got a little handsy last night. I kicked him in the balls and made a run for it. Pretty sure he won't be adding to the population anytime soon." She snickers and I join her.

"Good for you."

"Molly! Could you help me in here for a minute?"

I look over my shoulder at Rhonda. "Sure." I turn back to Ronnie. "Sorry, gotta go." I touch her arm gently. "If you need anything, just shout."

She gives me a lopsided smile. "Thanks."

# CHAPTER 39

## —max—

WHILE MOLLY'S AT *SHELTER*, I THOUGHT IT WOULD BE THE PERFECT opportunity to visit the jewelry store. I step inside and wander around the store, studying the displays carefully. The cabinets are full of ostentatious rings, which I can't see Molly wearing. When I step up to the last cabinet, the perfect wedding set catches my eye. It must be white gold because I don't think they make wedding rings in silver. It has one medium-sized diamond in the middle which looks a little like a snowflake, with two diamonds on either side, becoming smaller. Small gaps between the diamonds are filled with some fancy design on the band. It reminds me of the delicate jewelry Molly wears and I think she'd really like this.

"Can I help you, Sir?" I startle at the woman's voice. She glances at the cabinet, her eyes catching on the ring I was admiring. She smiles at me. "That's a pretty ring. Would you like to see it properly?"

I nod. "Yes, please."

As she unlocks the cabinet, I step back to give the woman space. "I'm Stephanie. Did you want to look at the matching wedding ring, too?"

"Thanks." I lift my chin. "I'm Max."

She nods as she collects both rings and places them on a cushion on top of the counter. "These rings are eighteen-karat white gold. The largest diamond in the engagement ring is zero point five zero carats, the next two are zero point two five carats each, and the smallest ones are zero point one zero carats each. Giving the ring a total of one point two zero carats." She uses a pointer to indicate each diamond as she speaks. Then she picks up the wedding band. "The two outer bands are linked with alternating diamonds of zero point two zero and zero point one zero. There are seven of the larger diamonds and six of the smaller ones." She turns the ring over to show the underside is solid. "The diamonds total two carats." She places them on the cushion and slides it forward, along with a magnifying lens. "Take a look. It's a beautifully delicate piece."

I study both of the rings carefully and can imagine them on Molly's finger. Before I blurted out my proposal, I probably should have bought the ring. "I think my fiancée will love these. They're delicate like the jewelry she already wears."

Stephanie's eyes sparkle as her eyebrows shoot up. "You've already proposed?"

"Yeah. I blurted it out without being prepared."

She chuckles. "You'd be surprised how often that happens." Well, that makes me feel marginally better. "Do you know her size?"

I pull the string out of my pocket. When she was sleeping last night, I tied a piece of string around her finger to make sure I bought the correct size. "Will this work?"

Stephanie picks it up. "I think so. Let's see what we have." She grabs a cylindrical measuring tool and slides the string carefully down the shaft until it can't go any further. "I'd say we're looking at a five-point five." She searches through a set of bands until she comes to the one she's looking for. "Does this feel about right?"

I slide it on my pinkie. "Yeah, I'd say so. She's slender and has long, slim fingers." She smiles and nods at me. "Do you have her size in stock?"

"Let me check." She locks the display set back inside the cabinet. "I'll be back in a moment." Then she disappears through a doorway.

I tuck my hands in my pockets and rock back on my heels. Molly didn't hesitate to say yes when I asked her to marry me. And yes, it's quick, but it feels right. She's perfect for me and fits in seamlessly with my family. Even though the proposal slipped out, I had no thoughts about rescinding it.

Stephanie returns with a bright smile and two small ring boxes. "You're in luck! We only have a couple of sets in stock and her size was one of them." She places them on the counter and opens each box. "I think it was meant to be."

"I think so, too. Can I take them with me today?" I dig my wallet out of my back pocket, ready to pay.

"Certainly, Max. If you would like to come over to the register, we can get that sorted."

I pay for the rings and Stephanie tucks them into a small gift bag, wishing me congratulations. Choosing the ring didn't take long. I check my watch. I may still have time to grab some flowers.

When I arrive at *Blooms and Balloons*, the best florist in the city, the woman is locking up. "Damn," I mutter, then spin on my heel.

"Excuse me. Were you wanting some flowers?" the woman calls.

I spin back around to face her. "Yeah. But that's okay, I'm too late."

"You're not actually. I was sneaking out a little early because we were quiet. If you're happy to select a pre-made arrangement, I'd be happy to unlock the store for you." She turns back toward the door with her key in hand.

I quickly step closer. "I'd certainly appreciate it. I hope to propose properly to my fiancée tonight."

"Oh. How sweet. Well, I'm happy to unlock the store and help you out. I'll even make a fresh arrangement for you." She opens the door and ushers me inside, turning on the light as she goes. The fragrance as I enter the store is beautiful.

"My name's Cassia." She wraps an apron around her waist. "What type of arrangement were you thinking of?"

I'm blank. "Hi, Cassia. I'm Max. I hadn't thought about it. I was just gonna grab a bunch of flowers." I shrug.

She chuckles. "Fair enough. Do you know her favorite flower?"

I grimace and shake my head. Then it dawns on me. "She uses rose-scented body wash. I guess she probably likes roses." *See, I'm working this out.*

"Red roses would be the go then. I have these stunning black velvet roses." She holds up a finger and disappears through a side door and returns a few moments later with a stunning, deep red rose. The petals look like velvet.

My eyes snap up to her. "This is beautiful."

"I know, right?" She smiles at me and raises her brows. "Would you like the traditional dozen?"

"Yes, please." She disappears out the back again, returning with an arm full of roses.

"Because these roses are so stunning, I would recommend a simple arrangement containing only the roses. I'll remove all the thorns and excess leaves, wrapping some of this gorgeous gold ribbon around the stems." She holds up the ribbon. "How does that sound?"

I have no idea. I guess she knows what's best. "Sure. That sounds great."

She smiles at me and gets to work. "What's your fiancée's name?"

I smile. "Molly. We haven't been together very long, but it feels right. I don't want to let her go and I can't see a future without her in it."

"I don't think the time frame matters all that much. It's more about the connection you feel with that person. I get people in here who have been together for all different lengths of time before they get engaged." She shrugs and keeps working, tidying up the stems. Carefully, she bundles them together and wraps the gold ribbon around the stems several times, leaving the bottom open. She holds them up for my approval. "What do you think?"

"It looks stunning." I move my eyes back up to hers. "Thank you for opening up for me. I appreciate it."

"No problem. I'm always happy to help with matters of the heart."

I pay for the roses and I'm on my way. I can't wait for Molly to get home.

Smooth fingers glide down the side of my face and my lips tip up in a smile as I slowly slide into consciousness.

Shit. I must have fallen asleep.

The softest lips press against my forehead and the glide of a finger dances across my forehead, brushing my hair away. I reach up and grip the back of her neck and guide her mouth to mine. We open, our tongues dancing with each other in welcome. Using my other hand, I pull her down on top of me and she giggles as we kiss.

"Hey, handsome," she whispers against my lips.

"Hey. How were the ladies at *Shelter*?" I open my eyes, locking onto her silvery ones.

She pulls back slightly, her breath coating my cheek as she releases a heavy sigh. "I nearly offered my car to one of the semi-regular ladies tonight. She came in with bruises up her arms." She shakes her head. "Mom always kept us safe from that sort of stuff because we had our car. She would park in neighborhoods that were a little nicer. Not the fancy neighborhoods, because it would be hard to go unnoticed, but the sort of middle-class ones. You know? If Ronnie had a car, she wouldn't have to be on the streets."

That's my girl. She doesn't have much, but she would willingly give a stranger her car. "If you think that would help her, you should do it. We can manage with one car. I mean, we work and live together. I can drop you off and pick you up on the nights you go to *Shelter*, and you've been coming to my soccer games every week. Or, if you want to, you could offer her the apartment." I shrug.

Her eyes widen. "Really? You'd do that?" She grasps my face in both hands and kisses me with gratitude and heat. "You're truly a good man, Max." Her eyes slip away from mine and then return. "She doesn't strike me as someone who would accept a handout. She barely comes into the shelter because she doesn't want to take up precious space from other women who may need it more."

I press up and kiss the tip of Molly's nose. "Sounds like someone I know."

"I'll think about it. If I can work out a way to offer it to her without impinging on her pride, I'll do it. I'm not sure when I'll see her next, but I'll be ready with a plan."

"Good. Now speaking of plans. I have a plan of my own." I smirk at her as I sit up. Grabbing Molly's ass, I encourage her to wrap her legs around me and I stand. She wraps her arms around my neck with a chuckle, and I kiss her soft lips.

"Oh yeah?" She has that sexy, seductive quality to her voice that drives me wild. It always comes out when she's horny.

"Yep." We move through the house, locking the doors and turning off the lights. I place her on her feet outside our bedroom door. "I'm gonna need you to wait out here for a second."

I kiss the tip of her nose and slip inside the bedroom before she gets the chance to respond. Quickly, I turn on the fairy lights I strung up around the room and turn the overhead light off. I check the ring is in place and grab the roses I bought. Holding them behind my back, I swing open the door with a flourish and then bring the roses out to present to Molly.

Her mouth forms an O shape as her eyes widen. Her eyes flit between me and the roses and then around our bedroom. "Oh, Max. This is gorgeous." She takes the bouquet from me, bringing them up to her nose and then stroking a petal. "These are the most beautiful roses I've ever seen." Her eyes have become glassy as they make their way back up to mine. She reaches her hand around my neck and drags me in for a kiss. "Thank you so much. I love them."

My hands slide to her hips, and I use my hold on her to pull her further into the room, exactly where I want her positioned. Then I deepen our kiss. She holds on tighter with one arm banded around my neck and both of my arms banded around her middle, holding her tight to me. The heat between our bodies matches the fire building inside of me and I remember I want to get down on one knee, so I pull away slowly and drop down in front of the woman who has stolen my heart. Her gaze follows me as her lust switches to surprise. She brings her hand up to cover her mouth, and a tear falls from her bottom lash to land on her cheek.

"Molly, I know I've already asked you to marry me, but I wanted to do it properly." I draw in a deep breath. "The morning I arrived at work to find you asleep in your car has led to this moment." She giggles and I raise my brows and tip up one side of my mouth. "I had no idea that day that I would fall irrevocably in love with you. You were completely unexpected and such a beautiful surprise." I take her hand in mine. "And while you are one of the most beautiful women I've ever had the pleasure of laying eyes on, it's what's inside your beautiful heart and your character that brought me to my knees. Your kindness to others blows me away and your warmth and genuine desire to help anyone in need are like nothing I've come across before. The icing on the cake is the way you deal with whatever life throws at you with quiet strength, grace, and a steely determination to come out the other side stronger than you were before." I kiss her hand gently, smoothing my finger along her bare ring finger. I glance down at that finger, then flick my eyes back up to hers. "I can't imagine anyone else I would want to spend the rest of my life with. Raise a family with. Grow old with. Molly, will you do the honor of becoming my wife?"

She drops to her knees, her dimples on display as tears streak down her cheeks. "Of course I will, Max. I can't imagine a better man to spend the rest of my life with. You're the man I want my children to call Daddy and you're the only man I want to grow old with."

I breathe a sigh of relief and meet her in the middle for a kiss that's full of the promise of a long and happy future together. I pull back and grab the ring box. Opening it, I take her left hand and slide the delicate band onto her finger. Her eyes drop to watch. "Oh, Max. This is gorgeous." She holds it up in front of her face, twisting her hand this way and that. The twinkling of the lights strung around our room creates a sparkle.

"I thought it suited you. It's simply beautiful without being flashy. Just like you."

"You didn't need to go to this much trouble for me. I already said yes."

"Nothing was too much trouble for you, Dimples. You deserve the best. Always."

She wraps her arms around my neck and pulls me in for another kiss, which leads to clothes being discarded every which way and me sliding into heaven. I want to climb inside her and live there. She's my home, the one who holds my heart and soul in a way that feels eternal.

Drawing back, I lock my eyes with hers, dirty green to mercury. Her hold around my neck tightens as I move in and out of her heat, our mouths open and barely touching. Me breathing in her essence, taking her breaths as my own.

Resting my elbows on the floor, I cup her head, stroking her hair away from her beautifully flushed face. "I love you, Molly," I whisper breathlessly against the soft pillows of her lips. Our bodies move in sync as I enter and withdraw repeatedly from Molly's hot pussy. I make love to her mouth and her body, building us both to our mutual orgasm until we're both a mess of boneless limbs and sweaty flesh.

She smiles against my lips as we catch our breath. "I love you, Max. So much," she says with panting breaths. I rub my nose along hers and collect her to me, burrowing my face in the crook of her neck. I lick and suck the hammering pulse point, then move onto my knees and pull her up with me. With her arms and legs wrapped snugly around my body, I stand and walk us into the shower, where I tenderly wash her and then defile her all over again.

## CHAPTER 40

### —*max*—

I'M LOCKING THE FRONT DOOR TO THE OFFICE WHEN I SEE MARTIN pull in. He pulls to a stop and jumps out, heading straight for the door like a man on a mission, so I open it. "Hey, Martin."

"Hi, Max. I was hoping to see Molly." What is it with this family turning up unannounced all the time? I mean, my family does it, but this is a completely different situation.

"Molly's not here."

He looks around my body into the office as if to check for himself. "Where is she? Will she be back soon?"

"She's volunteering at *Shelter* tonight. It usually runs pretty late."

His shoulders drop, disappointment dripping from his features. "Beth told me about Molly's childhood."

I blow out a heavy breath. Me and my big mouth.

"Look, I shouldn't have said anything because it wasn't my place. Molly didn't want you guys to know. She's embarrassed that you know how she lived as she was growing up and she doesn't want any pity."

He huffs out a harsh breath, running his hands through his hair. His expression reminds me of Dad when he was pissed at Preston after he told Em he wanted a divorce. "I have a right to know how my daughter grew up," he snaps. His posture stiff, his attitude demanding.

Hang on a minute. "Uh, pretty sure you gave up that right when you turned your back on Molly's mom." Not that it's my business, but I don't like that he thinks he can waltz into my girl's life and be privy to things she would rather not share.

His eyes snap up to mine and narrow. "Look, Max. I know you're together and all that, but this is family business."

I shake my head. "See, that's where you're wrong, Martin. She's my family now. This *is* my business. I won't have you storming your way into her life when she's not fucking ready. Have some damn respect for what she's been through and dealt with on her own. She'll come to you when she's damn well good and ready." I step into his space, towering over him. "This shit." I point to the floor between us. "You turning up whenever you please, expecting to talk to her, is gonna stop. She needs time."

"What do you mean, she's your family now? You've only started dating recently." He steps back slightly, putting more space between us.

"I mean, she's wearing my ring and agreed to marry me. Which means I'm gonna watch out for her."

"But you don't need to protect her from me. I'm her father. I'm not here to hurt her or cause her harm." His posture's softened and his voice is full of sincerity.

I soften my voice and my posture to match. "Look. I know you won't intentionally hurt her, and I know you want to get to know her. I get it. I do. This is an impossible situation. But what you need to understand is that Molly and her mom only had each other for a long time, surviving through dire circumstances. Apparently, it took Nicole a long time to trust Jack. Can you imagine the bond between Nicole and Molly? Can you even fathom what she's lost? Her mom. Her brother. Her stepfather. All gone." I raise my eyebrows at him. "That sort of loss would be unimaginable. On top of that, she then lost her apartment *and* her job. Everything. Gone. Just like that. But she dealt with it all on her own." I huff out a harsh breath. "Storming in here, demanding to see her is unacceptable. You need to give her time."

He sighs and his eyes grow glassy. He drops his head, studying his boots and for long moments, we stand, silent. Blowing out a long breath, he raises his head. "I hear what you're saying, Max, and I appreciate you laying that all out for me. I've been caught up in my agenda to reconnect with my daughter and I hadn't considered any of that. Maybe I've been coming on a little too strong." He glances away, then back to me, his expression pained. "I don't want to lose her again. I only just found her."

I lift my hand and squeeze his shoulder. "Family's important to Molly. If you can give her some space, I know you won't lose her."

"I don't want her to think I've given up if I stop coming around.

What if she thinks I don't want her anymore because we know how she grew up?"

"I'm not saying to stop contact with her. I would never say that because I want Molly to have as much family around her as possible. What I'm saying is you need to check with her before you turn up. Shoot her a text. Ask her if she's available for a coffee or chat. Invite her to dinner. But don't just turn up; you're not at that stage yet. She needs to feel like it's her decision. That you're not taking the choice out of her hands. It will give her time to mentally and emotionally prepare. When you turn up unannounced the way you do, you put her on the back foot and that makes her uncomfortable." I hope he listens to what I'm saying.

He nods, seeming to accept my advice. "Thanks, Max. Beth and I would like to have you both over for dinner sometime. I'll be in touch."

He climbs back into his truck and pulls out of the parking lot. I drop my head, studying the pavement. I hope he takes my advice.

# CHAPTER 41

## —molly—

A VIBRATING SOUND BREAKS MY CONCENTRATION ON THE ORDER FORM I'm filling out. I peer around the office, trying to work out where the sound is coming from. It happens again and I remember I put my cell in the top drawer. I barely use the thing. It's not like I have anyone contacting me on the regular. I pull it out and read the screen to find a message from Martin. My heart beats faster and my hands become clammy. I haven't spoken to him since Max blurted out my history to Beth and Joanna.

> **MARTIN**
>
> Hi Molly. Beth and I were wondering if you would be free to come over for dinner on Saturday night?

I place the cell on the surface of the desk. Shit! I don't know if I'm ready to spend time with everyone at the same time. It's sort of been manageable one on one, not that it's always been easy, and after the last time I saw Beth and Joanna, I'm a little embarrassed.

> **MARTIN**
>
> Sorry, I forgot. You can bring Max along too

Max told me Martin stopped by last week while I was at *Shelter*. I don't want to use Max as a crutch, but he's been my rock through all of this. Does it make me weak that the offer is more appealing, knowing I can take Max with me? I'm normally independent and have no problem facing things head-on, but for some reason, I'm struggling with coming to terms with my new family.

MARTIN

> Beth reminded me to mention that the kids won't be here. Holly is staying at a friend's house for the weekend and Noah is going to camp. It'll just be the four of us

Warm lips meet the crook of my neck and I automatically tip my head to the side to give Max the freedom to kiss me however he wants. He nuzzles his roughened cheek against my sensitive skin, sending electricity shooting through my body. "Hey, Dimples. I missed you."

I chuckle. "I've been, like, fifty feet away from you."

"It's too fucking far," he argues.

My phone lights up with another message.

MARTIN

> Please say yes

Max moves around to face me. "Why does Martin want you to say yes?"

I unlock the phone and show Max the string of messages. He reads through them, then moves his eyes back up to me. "Do you wanna go?"

I drop my shoulders and blow out a breath. "I do and I don't."

"You want to talk it through? I can be a good sounding board."

I prop my elbow on the desk and drop my chin into my hand. "You're busy. Maybe after work."

"I've finished and it's almost closing time. How about I clean up and bring the car out ready for collection, then we can grab a bite to eat and talk this through?"

"Didn't you want to work on the truck this afternoon?" Why am I trying to find excuses to put off this discussion?

"It'll still be waiting for me tomorrow. This is important, Molly."

"Okay. Thank you, that sounds good." I force my lips to tilt up, but my attempt at a smile is half-hearted at best.

Max leans forward, pressing a kiss to my forehead, careful to not touch me with any other part of him because he's filthy. My smile grows at his care for me. The longer I spend with him, the more I come to realize what a good man he is. He has a golden heart hidden beneath that mechanical tattoo.

"Max! Molly! It's so good to see you. Come. Come. Let me find you a table." Cristo greets us enthusiastically, coming out from behind the podium to hug us both.

"Hi, Cristo," I say as he kisses my cheeks.

"We were walking by, deciding what to have for dinner, and thought we'd stop in to see if you had a table," Max explains. "We hope you don't mind."

"Of course. I'll always have a table for family. Follow me." He weaves his way through the tables toward the back corner of the restaurant to a private space, with us following diligently behind. "Here. This is my special table." He winks at us. "Allow me to select your meals, I have something special."

"Thank you, Cristo. You don't need to go to any trouble for us."

"It's no trouble at all, Molly. I'll bring some wine." He pulls out my chair and I sit. Max positions his chair closer to mine and sits next to me instead of opposite, as I expected. His thigh presses against mine and he rests his arm on the back of my chair, his warmth soaking through my clothes and searing my skin.

"Thanks, Cristo."

Max kisses my temple as Cristo makes his way toward the bar. "You don't think we're imposing, do you?"

Max looks across to the bar. "Nah. You saw how happy he was to see us."

Max's thumb creates patterns on my shoulder, sending goosebumps scattering across my body and heating me from the inside out.

*Maybe we should have stayed in?*

Cristo returns with our drinks, then bustles off to the kitchen. Max holds up his glass, gesturing for us to toast. "To the future. To loving together, living together, and working together. I can't wait to see what our future holds. Thank you for agreeing to be my wife."

My body heats further with his words, and my smile is wide. We clink our glasses together and take a sip. "I have a toast too. To the man who brought me back to life, has shown me nothing but kindness, and showers me with his love and support every single day. Thank you for asking me to be your wife, Max. I can't wait for our future." I'm dizzy thinking about what our life will be like. We lean forward, our lips meeting halfway in a soft kiss. His hand tightens on my shoulder, and he deepens our connection.

Pulling back slightly, he presses his forehead to mine. One of my favorite gestures. "I love you, Dimples."

I gift him with my dimples. "I love you, too, Max."

A plate slides onto the table in front of me, followed by another one in front of Max. Cristo stands like a proud father. "One of our most popular dishes. Pasticcio. This is the ultimate Greek comfort food. I'll go get the salad." He disappears and Max and I study the deliciously rich-smelling dish in front of us. With layers of pasta noodles, minced beef, and a thick, thick layer of béchamel sauce, I can't wait to dig in. Cristo returns with a mixed green salad which will complement the rich dish. "Enjoy."

"This looks and smells divine. Thank you, Cristo."

He bows slightly, his smile broad, and I can tell he gets a real kick out of feeding people good food. "You are most welcome. If you need anything else, please let me know." He bows again, then spins on his heel and heads back toward the front door.

Max and I glance at each other before digging in. The first mouthful is divine. Pure and simple. The food is more than something to fill your belly, it's soul food. "Mmmm, this is so good." I turn to Max with wide eyes.

He nods as he takes another forkful of food. "I came here once before when Theo proposed to Em. Cristo knows how to feed people."

We're both quiet, enjoying our meals for a few moments, the hum of other guests in the restaurant buzzing, wait staff weaving between the tables with delicious-looking meals. The surrounding aromas tantalize our senses. Max's leg presses against mine.

"Do you wanna work through how you're feeling about that invitation to dinner tomorrow night?"

I place my fork down and try to gather my thoughts. "When I saw the first message, my instant reaction was hell no, I'm not ready. The thought of joining them all for dinner was too much. Then the second message came through and I thought, well it will be more bearable if I have Max with me. But I don't want to use you as a crutch. That's not fair and it's not a partnership if one person always has to prop up the other. I also don't want to lose my independence. I used to deal with everything on my own, you know?"

Max nods thoughtfully, taking his time to respond. "But you realize we will have times where I support you through something and the roles will reverse at other times, where you'll need to support me when I'm having trouble. Leaning on someone when you need help doesn't mean you're going to lose your independence. It takes strength to recognize you need help and to ask for it when you need it."

"I know. But it's early in our relationship and I don't want to start out that way. I already feel as though you've done too much for me, that I've been too needy. I'm used to being independent and working my way through stuff on my own; only having Mom and then Jack to help me." I'm certain his steadfast support has been the one thing that's kept me going since I moved here.

He nods and tucks a loose lock of hair behind my ear. I love how he does that. It's such a tender gesture. "I know."

"But … if it's only going to be the four of us, that might work. I mean, it might be a good idea to get all the heavy stuff out of the way, so we can move forward." I take a sip of my wine. "What do you think?"

"I think it doesn't matter what I think. It matters what you need. What do you need to become comfortable with Martin? What will help you build a relationship with him? Because he's not going to let you go. You realize this?"

"Yeah, I know. And honestly … I don't want him to let me go. I want to get to know him and his family … *my* family. I guess … I guess I feel like I'm betraying Mom in a way. I can't explain it. He turned his back on her, on us, and now that the tough part's over, he wants in. I don't know what Mom would think of that." I drop my eyes to my plate. As I say this next part, I can't look at Max. I don't want him to think less of me. "He really hurt her, Max. I feel as though I shouldn't let him off the hook so easily," I whisper.

He takes my hand in his and uses his fingers to turn my head, ensuring I look at him. "Molly. Your loyalty to your mom is understandable. I get it. Even *I* feel a certain level of protectiveness over your mom where Martin's concerned. He made his choices, as stupid as they were, but … Molly … he's also deeply sorry for what he did all those years ago when he was young and dumb. You can't keep punishing the guy. That's not who you are. And, without knowing your mom, I don't think she'd want you to do that."

I nod because I agree with every word. "Thank you for understanding and for gently reminding me of the person I am." My throat is tight, and the back of my eyes are stinging with tears that want to burst free.

"I think your mom would want you to connect with him. I don't think she would want you to be without family. And I know how important family is to you." He kisses my temple and the tears I've been choking back escape, dropping over my lashes. Max wraps his arms around me and pulls me into his warm body, which now feels like home. I bury my head in his chest and quietly release my pain.

I catch my breath and wipe my tears as I pull away. "Thank you. Would you mind coming with me tomorrow night?"

"Anywhere you are is exactly where I want to be. Of course, I'll come with you." He kisses my temple with tenderness.

"Thank you." I give him a watery smile.

"Why don't you message him now? I bet he's stressing out that you're gonna say no."

I nod and pull out my phone.

> ME
>
> Hi Martin, Thank you for your invitation. Max and I would love to come to dinner tomorrow night

Within seconds, my phone lights up. It's like he had it in his hand and I suspect Max may have been right.

> MARTIN
>
> Thank you

> ME
>
> What time would you like us to come?

> MARTIN
>
> Seven?

> ME
>
> Okay. Can we bring anything?

> MARTIN
>
> Just yourselves. Thank you so much. You don't know how much this means to me

"Well, there ya go. I bet he's been pacing, waiting for your reply." Max glides his hand along my spine.

I blow out a breath and turn to him. "He *does* seem to want to build a relationship with me."

"Of course he does. Anyone who meets you falls in love with you." He presses his lips to mine and butterflies erupt in my stomach.

# CHAPTER 42

## —molly—

STANDING ON MARTIN'S FRONT PORCH, MY HAND SHAKES AS I REACH for the doorbell. Max grasps my hand and turns me to face him. With his hands gently cupping my cheeks, he peers into my eyes, mossy green to steel. "You have nothing to be nervous about."

"What if I'm not the daughter he was expecting to have? I mean, look at Holly. She's doing really well in school and wants to be a fashion designer. I did okay in school, but I'm not super smart or talented like she is. I don't even know what Noah's like. What if I'm not up to—"

He presses forward, stealing my words with his kiss. "Stop it. He should count himself lucky that he can call you his daughter. You *are* fucking talented, and you *are* smart. You picked up my system at the workshop without any guidance. Your sketches are incredible. You're a kind and generous person. He'll be proud of you. I promise."

The front door flies open, breaking the moment and both of our heads swivel toward the intrusion. Martin's standing in the doorway, glancing between the two of us. "Would you like to come in?"

Max chuckles. "That's why we're here."

I smooth down my dress and take the first step over the threshold into my father's home. "Uhm, hi." The three of us stand in silence, peering at each other.

Beth steps out from a room down the hallway, her face lighting up when she sees us in the entry. "Hi. I'm so happy you could join us for dinner." She comes toward us. "Martin, let them inside." She swipes at his arm, and he finally makes the move to guide us further into their home.

*Their beautiful home.*

The only other homes I've been to as nice as this were Emma and Theo's home and his parents' house. Max's house has the potential to be lovely, but it's still a bit of a bachelor pad.

"You have a beautiful home."

They glance around the space as if they don't realize they live in a gorgeous house. "Thank you. It wasn't much when we bought it, but we've renovated it over the years. Made it our own." Martin holds out his hand. "Come through. Would you like a drink?"

Martin prepares drinks while Beth collects a tray of pre-dinner snacks and guides us out to a covered deck with an outdoor heater for the cooler evening. Everything is immaculate, nothing is out of place, and nothing looks worn or misused. It's like one of the homes you see on TV.

My clothes feel cheap and uncomfortable and I suddenly feel itchy. Like I don't belong here. Max senses my discomfort and reaches across to lay his hand on my thigh, settling my nerves.

Beth leans forward in her chair. "I believe congratulations are in order." My eyebrows draw down low in confusion. Her eyes flick down to my left hand, then back up to me. "Your engagement." She holds her hand out, asking with her eyes to look at my ring. I lift my hand, allowing her to admire the gorgeous seal of our promise. "It's beautiful, Molly. Max made the perfect selection because it suits you."

"Oh, thank you." I look at Max. "It was a surprise. A really great surprise." Max lifts my hand and kisses my palm, easing some of my nerves.

"Any idea when you'll get married?" Beth asks.

I hadn't even thought about the actual wedding. Somehow, I skipped over that part and went straight to being married.

"As soon as possible." Max blurts and I stare at him in surprise. I'm certain I appear completely startled.

Beth giggles. "Well, if you need any help, I'm a wedding planner so it's kinda my thing."

Martin turns his head toward his wife, his face full of pride. "She's always booked out well in advance because she's one of the best in the city."

She waves him off. "It doesn't matter how busy I am, I can help you any way you need. Just shout out." She takes a sip of her wine and offers us a wink.

I tuck a loose lock of hair behind my ear. "Thank you. That's very kind of you to offer."

She stands from the table. "If you'll excuse me, I need to put the finishing touches to dinner. I hope you're hungry."

I stand to help, but she tells me to stay where I am, leaving Max and me with Martin, who has barely spoken since we arrived.

He clears his throat, now that it's only the three of us. "Uhm, Molly. I wanted to start with an apology." This is unexpected. He already apologized to me at lunch and I accepted it. "Actually, I have several apologies to make." He draws in a deep breath and releases it slowly. "I'm sorry for abandoning you and Nicole back when she told me she was pregnant. It's something I've always regretted and it's something I have no excuse for. I was young and stupid and selfish and I will go to my grave regretting my choice back then."

A boulder has formed in my throat and I'm having a tough time swallowing around it. Max reaches across and takes my hand, squeezing it in reassurance.

Martin glances at Max and then returns his apologetic gaze to me. "I'm also sorry for being pushy in my eagerness to insert myself into your life. I had no business bulldozing my way into your life and expecting that I could be your father, purely based on the fact that biology makes you mine. It takes more than sperm to make a man a father and I need to give you time to get to know me and for us to find our way forward in this new reality. I only hope you can open your heart to the possibility of a relationship with me. And with Holly, Noah, and Beth."

Saliva fills my mouth and that familiar stinging at the back of my eyes is becoming too much. I blink rapidly, doing my best to maintain my composure.

"The last thing I want to apologize for is how my choices impacted on your life." He gives me a sad smile and I glance up at his eyes, looking for his pity, but it's not there. All I see is hurt and sorrow. "Molly. I was devastated all over again when Beth told me about your childhood living arrangements. I can't help but feel responsible for all of it. If I'd been more mature … a better man … anything, your life would have turned out differently."

I lose the battle and the tears burst forth on a sob. It's like my heart's been split down the middle with an ax and I can't get enough oxygen into my lungs. Max's arms come around me, pulling me into his warm body. I rest my ear against his heart, listening to the steady rhythm as I work to calm myself. Thank God he's here.

"I … I'm sorry, Molly. I didn't mean to upset you," Martin whispers.

"It's okay, Martin." The vibration of Max's voice touches my ear as he calmly strokes my hair and reassures Martin.

How do I explain these tears aren't because I'm angry or hurt, it's because I needed him to acknowledge his mistakes so I could move forward? These tears are full of relief that he's owned up to his choices, and he's taken responsibility for them, even though some of them were technically out of his control.

"Oh, dear. What's going on out here?" Beth's voice breaks the silence.

I pull away from Max and wipe my eyes. "I promise I'm okay. Sorry about that. Do you have a bathroom where I can clean myself up?"

"Of course, follow me."

I clean up and when I come back out, Martin, Beth, and Max have moved to the table where dinner has been served. Roast chicken with all the trimmings. I love roast chicken. It was something we rarely had because it's so expensive, but Mom always made sure to have it for my birthday after we started living with Jack. As I sit, I promise myself that I'm going to enjoy this meal and I won't become swamped with memories—it's not fair to everyone else if I'm always breaking down into tears.

Martin and Beth serve us and the first few moments are quiet as we all dig into the delicious meal. The chicken tastes different from the way Mom cooked it. It has more of a smokey flavor to it. "This is delicious. Thank you for going to so much trouble."

Beth waves off my compliment. "It was no trouble. It's a family staple in this house. One of Holly's favorite meals."

I smile at her and it's genuine and full of hope. "It's my favorite, too." Beth smiles, appearing pleased at her choice of meal. These small connections are giving me hope that I'll be able to forge strong relationships with my new family.

As we eat dinner, Martin and Beth glance at each other, then their eyes land on me. "I have a funny story to share about Nicole, Beth, and me if you'd like to hear it?"

My eyes slide to Max and I swallow. Maybe hearing about some of their fun times will help. "I'd love you to share it with me." Max reaches across under the table and lays his hand on my thigh, squeezing it in support.

"Oh, no. Which story are you going to share?" Beth chuckles.

Martin looks at her with a sparkle in his eye. "Remember Mr. Fitzroy?"

Beth's eyes snap to mine, then back to her husband. "Oh. Do you think that's the best story to share?"

"Hell yeah. It was hilarious. Not that we thought it was funny at the time, but looking back." He sighs and glances away. "Good times." He nods to himself as he becomes lost in the memory.

Beth's eyes come back to me. "They were fun times. I think we were about sixteen. Well, you were eighteen." She swipes Martin's arm in jest. "Old enough to know better." She winks at me.

"Mr. Fitzroy was Nicole's neighbor. He had a swimming pool." I feel like I already know where this story might be heading.

"He was the only person with a swimming pool in the neighborhood," Beth adds.

"He was away on vacation and it was the hottest, muggiest night. We couldn't escape the heat. It had been days and days of the same stinking, hot, unbearable temperatures. The girls and I deci–"

Beth shoves her hands on her hips. "Hang on there. If I remember correctly, you coaxed Nicole and me to do it. We weren't so sure it was a good idea."

Martin tilts his hand from side to side as if Beth's recount isn't quite accurate. "Maybe, maybe not. Anyway, we took the opportunity of Mr. Fitzroy being away and decided to go for a swim late one night after we'd been at a party. The guy used to keep his gate locked, which meant we had to climb his fence to sneak around the back. The girls and I stripped down to our underwear and jumped in. It was heaven."

Beth nods. "I remember the sheer relief to finally have a reprieve from the heat. It was so good."

"Yeah. I'm not sure how long we swam, but we were having a great time. Suddenly, all the lights inside the house came on and before we could react, all the lights across the back of the house switched on and Mr. Fitzroy came storming out of the back door, yelling at us and threatening to call the police to report us for trespassing on his property." Beth and Martin chuckle.

"I don't think I've ever moved so fast. I jumped out of that pool, scooped up my clothes, and ran to the corner near the fence where it was still dark." Beth giggles. "Nicole, though …" she shakes her head, "she wasn't so keen on climbing out with Mr. Fitzroy watching because she had white underwear on."

A gasp escapes as I imagine Mom's embarrassment. "Oh, no."

Martin grimaces. "Yeah, I climbed out quickly, too, not realizing I left Nicole in the pool all on her own. Mr. Fitzroy was cursing up a storm something fierce. Lights came on next door and Mr. and Mrs. Lewis came out to investigate what was going on. Nicole was still in the pool, clinging to the edge, trying to hide her body while Mr. Fitzroy was shouting across the yard to her parents about what a terrible job they had done and that their daughter was a miscreant." Martin chuckles and Max joins in.

"Her parents were yelling at her to get out of the pool and she was yelling that she couldn't because her underwear was see-through. I was trying to put my clothes back on over my wet skin. Martin was hopping on one leg, trying to get his jeans back on and Nicole stayed in the pool, defiant."

"Oh my gosh, that sounds just like Mom," I add with a chuckle.

Martin nods. "Yeah. She was stubborn." I nod in agreement. "Anyway, eventually Nicole's mom came over with a towel and Nicole climbed out of the pool with most of her dignity intact."

"After that, Nicole was always careful to avoid Mr. Fitzroy," Beth finishes.

"I'm not surprised. Did she get into trouble with her parents?"

"Not really. They thought she'd learned her lesson. She was mad at me for days after that. Didn't speak to me because she blamed me." He shakes his head, but he has a twinkle in his eye. "Beth got her to come 'round, eventually." He smiles at her and she returns it. I wonder how difficult it is for Beth to remember those times when Martin's heart belonged to someone else. He kisses her temple and Beth's eyes flutter closed for a moment. "They were good times."

Beth nods. "Yes, they were."

"That sounds like something me and my sisters would have done when we were younger," Max adds.

Beth and Martin continue to share stories of the three of them throughout the meal, giving me an insight into Mom as a teenager. Before her life got heavy and complicated. She sounds like she was fun to be around, not that she wasn't fun. She would find ways for us to have fun at the park or the beach. Simple things that didn't cost money.

I help Beth clear the table and set up for dessert. As she rinses the dishes to stack in the dishwasher, I use the time while it's only the two of us. "Thank you for inviting us to dinner. This evening's been lovely."

"You are more than welcome. We hope this is just the beginning, Molly." I swallow down the lump that forms at her kindness and blink away the sting in my eyes. I refuse to cry again tonight.

*—max—*

BETH AND MOLLY carry out some type of creamy-looking dessert. "I hope you like Tiramisu." Beth proudly places the dessert in the middle of the table while Molly distributes the bowls.

"It looks great, Beth. Luckily, I have a bottomless pit for a stomach." I pat my stomach.

Martin and Beth chuckle. "Beth makes the best Tiramisu." His eyes are full of pride as he looks at his wife.

Beth dishes up and we're all quiet as we take our first spoonfuls. Molly moans in delight and it reminds me of the sounds she makes when I'm balls deep inside her. My cock swells in my jeans and I discreetly adjust my position and will him to behave. Molly glances across at me, then down at my lap. Her eyes widen and a half-smile touches her lips when she sees my predicament. She licks a smudge of cream from her bottom lip and raises a sculpted brow at me. Minx. She knows exactly what she does to me and I'll be sure to collect retribution when we get home.

Molly clears her throat, glances at me, then locks her sights on Martin. "Uh, Martin. I hope you don't mind, but I need to say something I think is important."

"Sure." He braces himself and Beth places her hand over the top of Martin's in a show of support. "Go ahead."

Molly tucks a lock of hair behind her ear and fidgets with her bracelet for a moment. Her eyes rise slowly, and she draws in a deep breath, then releases it. "I appreciate your apology. It meant a lot to me to know that you took responsibility for what happened all those years ago. But I think we all know Mom didn't necessarily need to run away to the other side of the country and leave everyone behind. I know she was doing what she thought was right and I don't pretend to know what she was going through or thinking at the time. In her mind, she wanted to protect me, and I'll be forever grateful for that. I'm not going to wish my life was different, because my life has been good. Great even. I had a loving stepfather who was the best dad a girl could ask for. He loved me as though I was his biological daughter."

Martin nods and his posture deflates a little.

"If Jack hadn't come into our lives, I would never have had Ethan. He was an awesome kid. I loved him with all of my heart." Her eyes are glassy, so I wrap my arm around Molly's shoulder and draw her in close. "And while I appreciate you feeling responsible for the way I grew up, none of that falls on your shoulders." She reaches across, taking Martin's hand, and a tear drops over her bottom lashes to coast down her cheek. "I don't blame you or hold you responsible. I'm happy, mostly, with how my life was as I grew up. I was loved and cared for. I knew I was the most important person in Mom's life and Jack's life when he came along. Mom always made sure I had nutritious food whenever she could, and she always made sure I was safe. I went to school and did all the things that I was supposed to do. So please, please let that go."

I'm fucking proud of my girl. I glance across at Martin as he stands, his eyes red, tears streaming down his cheeks. He moves around the table and drags Molly up into his arms, embracing her. They hold each other close. They hold each other in acceptance of a past that can't be changed, and for a future spread out in front of them. My eyes flick across at Beth. She's crying too, but her lips are tipped up slightly at the edges, her hand clutched in front of her heart.

She glances at me and nods. And I know we're thinking the same thing. Everything's going to be okay.

As soon as we get through the front door, I press Molly up against the wall and cup her face in my rough hands. "You are so fucking strong." I press the palm of my hand to her heart. "Your heart is pure and giving and kind. I feel privileged that I have even a small place in it."

I rub my nose along the side of hers, drawing her scent into my lungs. She smells like springtime; like a garden in bloom. I skate my lips across hers, swallowing her sigh. Dragging my hand down her body, I slide my fingers between hers and raise her arm above her head, trapping it against the wall. Repeating the process, I trap both of her hands above her head in one of mine.

Her breasts heave in time with her harsh pants as I leisurely drag my eyes down her lush body. "I love you, Molly." I lunge forward, taking her mouth in a harsh kiss. A kiss full of lust, love, and fucking gratitude.

Gratitude that this strong, sexy woman is mine.

She whimpers into the kiss, and I thrust my tongue inside to tangle with hers. I hold both her hands with one of mine and slide my other hand down her arm until I get to the side of her breast. She trembles beneath my touch and my internal caveman beats on his chest.

Me.

*I* get her this hot.

She presses her pelvis forward as our teeth gnash, our breaths coming in hard pants as we battle for oxygen. "Max. I need you to fuck me. Please."

I draw back, admiring the glazed look in her steely eyes. "Well, that's convenient, because I need to fuck you."

She gifts me her dimples and raises her eyebrows. "That sounds like a win-win situation."

"Absolutely," I whisper as I kiss my way down the side of her neck, nibbling the space where it meets her shoulder. I trace down her body, kissing over the top of the fabric of her dress. Dropping to my knees, I fulfill a fantasy and lift the skirt, dropping it over my head until I'm completely shrouded by the black material. I press my nose against her black cotton panties, inhaling her scent and nuzzling her clit. She presses her hips forward, creating more friction, and my tongue slips out to stroke the fabric, which is soaked with her arousal. "So fucking hot," I murmur.

"Mmm, Max," she mumbles.

I grasp her underwear and slide it down her legs to give me uninhibited access to her hot pussy. Without hesitation, I swipe my tongue through her lips. Her heat sears me and I moan. "Fucking delicious."

Actually, I decide I don't like being covered by her dress. I can't see her face as I taste her, and that won't fucking do. Standing, I make quick work of removing her sweater and dress, exposing her sublime body to me. I reach around behind her and flick the release on her bra.

As it loosens, Molly slides each strap down her arms and throws it to the floor. She's completely naked for my perusal. "You are goddamn beautiful." I reach forward to cup her breasts. "Perfect." Leaning forward, I take a rosy nipple into my mouth while I roll and pinch the other to a hard peak. I swap over, paying the other globe the same attention, then kiss and lick my way down her body. Her stomach trembles, making the jewelry there catch the moonlight streaming in through the entry window.

She moans as she grasps my hair, pushing me to where she wants me most and I chuckle, huffing a hot breath across her pretty pink clit which is swollen and begging for attention. I position one leg over my shoulder and lean forward to draw it into my mouth with a firm suck, then glide my tongue around the bundle of nerves. Molly's hips shoot forward with a gasp.

My eyes scrape up her body, flushed with arousal, a light sheen of perspiration coating her skin. Her head is tipped back in pleasure and her breasts tremble with anticipation. I glide my fingers through her lips and then thrust inside without warning, my eyes locked on the beauty of Molly's lust. Her mouth drops open and a mewl escapes. Her walls flutter around my fingers as her clit pulses on my tongue.

I pull out and away from her body.

She drops her head, opening her eyes. "Why … why'd you stop?"

I raise an eyebrow. "Remember what you did to me during dessert?"

Her eyes widen. "I … what?"

"You made me fucking hard with your little moans, and then you thought it would be funny to fucking lick your lips and tease me even more."

Her eyes narrow. "And … what does that have to do with this?"

"It's time for payback." I remove her leg from my shoulder and stand to my full height—I have roughly five inches on her—and I move in close. Our chests touch, her soft breasts pressing into my shirt. This is taking all of my willpower because I want to drop back to my knees and finish what I started, have her cum all over my fingers and tongue, but I have a dire situation in my jeans that needs attention. I press my cock against her pelvis. "Feel that?" She nods. "It needs your attention. Be a good girl and drop to your knees."

Without a word, she presses her hands against my body, putting space between us. She drops to her knees, keeping her eyes locked with mine. "Such a beautiful sight." I slide my fingers through her silky hair as her hands lift to my belt to release it and my jeans. I'm sure I hear my cock sigh. It pulses as she slides the denim from my hips, taking my boxers with them. They drop to my feet and Molly wastes no time, wrapping her hand around my heavy shaft and swiping it with her tongue, from base to tip, causing a shiver to climb up my spine.

I clench my hands at my sides, to allow her the freedom to do whatever she wants to me. Her mouth is what I imagine heaven to be like. Warm and inviting. She takes my cock to the back of her throat and hums around my shaft. My hips thrust forward without instruction. "Fuck." Her molten eyes snap up to mine and hold as she licks, sucks, and draws my orgasm forward like it's her goddamn job.

Fuck, that's hot. I slide my hand into her silky mane and clutch the strands at the base of her skull, dragging her mouth along my rock-hard length. She gently scrapes her teeth along my flesh, and it's almost my undoing. "You're such a fucking good girl."

She moans and draws her mouth from my shaft. "Only for you, Max." Her lips curl up and she winks before dropping back toward my dick. Using my grip on her hair, I hold her back because I never come first. It's one of the few rules I hold fast to. I bend down and pull my girl up, pressing her back against the wall. "Why'd you stop me?"

I run my nose along the side of hers. "Because that's not how I do things, Dimples." I roughly push my fingers back into her dripping center. Eliciting a long, beautiful moan. Dropping my head, I suck her nipple into my mouth and continue to thrust, ensuring I massage the spongy front wall as my thumb lightly circles her needy clit. I take her mouth in a hard kiss as her walls tighten around my intrusion, strangling me. Her short fingernails dig into my shoulders and I hope she leaves her fucking mark on me. Pushing my tongue inside her mouth to match the cadence of my fingers in her pussy, she rides out her orgasm through whimpers and gasps. Her arms wrap around my neck, her fingers sliding up into my hair to grasp it.

Removing my fingers, I line my cock up with her opening and slide slowly inside as her walls continue to pulse. My hands find Molly's ass and I lift her, pushing my cock in deeper as her long legs wind around my hips, and she tugs at my shirt to pull it off.

I press her harder into the wall and drag my shirt off by my collar, discarding the offending fabric to the floor. She wraps her arms around my neck, tightening her hold as my hands return to her gorgeous ass. Slipping my fingers down, I collect her cum and use it to ease a finger into her back entrance. Her eyes open wide and lock on mine as her mouth drops open with a silent moan.

Bracing my feet, I lift her as I slide out, then drop her down as I thrust up. She takes over the action, using her hold on me to bounce up and down on my cock while I drive into her over and over again. Molly and I have no problem creating a rhythm that builds us quickly.

"Ohh. I'm gonna come," she cries out as my dick thickens and pulses. Her walls tighten around me, strangling me, tightening on my finger and my cock. Our slick bodies slide against each other as we both chase our high.

Electricity races down my spine and my balls draw up close to my body. Molly's breaths are hot against my ear, and she leans forward to bite the lobe. Cum shoots out as my cock throbs and pulses, setting off Molly's orgasm.

We both moan as our bodies spiral into bliss.

Our chests heaving for air.

Eyes locked, mossy green to mercury.

I take her mouth in a searing kiss and then slow it down. Gently, I caress her mouth. Showing how much I adore her and appreciate her trust. How much I value her. I tenderly draw away, pressing light kisses to her lips. I drop my forehead to hers and our breaths mingle.

She scrapes her nails through my hair, then drags her hands around to cup my face. Her eyes flit between mine and my mouth. A smile grows, and she gifts me those gorgeous dimples. "Thank you," she whispers.

She fucking undoes me. "You never need to thank me for fucking you, Molly. It's a goddamn privilege that you share your heart and body with me."

Her eyes go soft. "I *do* need to thank you. Thank you for always taking care of me. Whether it's giving me your support as I navigate my new family or making sure that I have record-breaking orgasms every single time we come together. You've made my new life here truly remarkable."

She's the fucking remarkable one. Molly uses her hold on my face to draw me forward and presses her lips to mine. She swipes her tongue across the seam, and I open willingly. My semi-hard cock wakes up and I start slow, languid strokes in and out of heaven. I toe off my shoes and step out of my jeans, and carry my girl to bed, so I can take my time to love her the way she deserves.

# CHAPTER 44

## —molly—

My phone buzzes with a text from Martin. I'm not sure if I'll ever call him dad, but he doesn't seem to mind. We've been messaging regularly over the last two weeks, and he's even stopped in and had lunch with me a couple of times. He hasn't pressured me to share any more details about my life, but I've shown him my sketches and shared with him how much I enjoy running.

> **MARTIN**
>
> Would it be okay if I bring Noah around this afternoon?
> He's eager to meet you

> **ME**
>
> Sure. We close at 2. Come then

> **MARTIN**
>
> Great. See you then

I send him a thumbs up and then make my way out to Max. His body's twisted as he works on something underneath the dash of the car he has in the bay. "Hey."

He maneuvers his body out of the cramped space, a smile instantly brightening his face, which has a streak of grease down the side. He's so freaking handsome I can't stand it. I lean forward and swipe my lips against his and then lean on the open door.

"Hey. I'm gonna need your lips back here, Dimples. I wasn't finished." He gestures, flicking two fingers at me in a come here motion.

I chuckle. "Maybe later." I raise an eyebrow at him. "Martin messaged me. He asked if it was okay to bring Noah over. I hope you don't mind. I said they could come at two when we close."

"You know I don't mind." His eyebrows draw together, causing creases in between. "Are you gonna be okay? I know you've been anxious about meeting him." He stands, his eyes full of concern for me.

"I can't avoid him forever and I really do want to meet him." I shrug. Max wipes his hands with the rag he always seems to have handy and then glides his thumb down the side of my face in a barely there touch. His eyes bury themselves deep in mine as though he's searching all the way to the depths of my soul for my truth. "I promise I'll be okay. I'm going to do my best not to compare him to Ethan. Ethan was his own person, just as Noah is. I want to get to know him. By all accounts, he sounds like a sweet boy. There's no pressure if we meet here." I chuckle lightly. "He'll probably be more interested in your truck than he will be in me. He's crazy about cars."

"Yeah, I remember Martin telling me about that when we took the Sprint out for a test drive." Max glances across at the truck that he's started dismantling.

I follow his eyes. "I'm up-to-date in the office. Mind if I sketch the truck for a while?"

He turns back to me. "Go for it. I'm looking forward to seeing your sketches evolve as I restore the old girl."

I press a chaste kiss to his lips and skip back to the office to grab my sketch pad and pencils. Max gets back to work, and I get comfortable and start outlining.

"Woah!" The sudden intrusion breaks my focus and I peer up at the boy standing next to me. His eyes are wide as he studies my sketch. "Did you draw that?" He points at the page I'm working on.

I smile at him. "Sure did. You must be Noah."

Without hesitation, he drops to his butt beside me, crossing his legs to get comfortable on the cement floor. "Sure am. I wish I could draw. The best I can do is stick figures. My grade one teacher taught us how to look for shapes in things to help us draw, but I could never figure it out." His eyes drop back to my sketch.

"I could teach you if you like. It's not that hard."

His head starts nodding and his wide eyes rise to mine. "Really? You wouldn't mind?"

I chuckle. "Not at all."

"Holly can draw too, though she draws boring clothes. Your drawing is way cooler."

"I dunno about that. I saw the clothes Holly designed and they were pretty cool. I bet her sketches are amazing."

He scrunches his nose. "Yeah, I guess so. I'm not into clothes." His eyes widen. "But I *am* into cars. I want to be a race car driver one day."

"Really?" He nods like a bobble doll, and I glance over my shoulder, spotting Max and Martin talking several feet away from us. I wave over my shoulder. "Hi, Martin."

He smiles at me and moves closer. "Hey, Molly. Great to see you." He bends down and kisses the top of my head in a fatherly way. It's strange how our dynamic has changed in such a brief space of time. "Is this what you're working on at the moment?" He gestures toward my sketch pad.

"Yeah. I'm going to sketch the truck at different stages during the restoration as a record for Max." I smile up at Max.

"You should see the one of the Sprint in the office." Max gestures over his shoulder toward the office.

Noah stands. "Where is it? I wanna see."

I stand, too, and we all head into the office where Max proudly shows off my work.

"This is fantastic, Molly," Martin states without taking his eyes off my work.

Noah turns to me. "You know. I wasn't sure about having another big sister, because one is enough already. But I think I'm gonna like having you around, Molly."

We all chuckle lightheartedly, but my heart swells. I was worried about meeting Noah and how we'd get along, but I needn't have. He's a great kid. Even though I promised myself I wouldn't compare Noah and Ethan, they seem very similar in disposition.

As I walk Martin and Noah out to say goodbye, I decide to throw caution to the wind and invite them to Max's birthday barbecue tomorrow. Emma phoned me last week to ask if I had any plans for Max's birthday, which came as a surprise since I wasn't aware his birthday was coming up. I agreed to marry the man and I didn't even know when his birthday was. I felt like a terrible fiancée.

I've carried on the ruse that I don't know it's his birthday tomorrow, but I've planned a barbecue at a park down by the lake to celebrate with his family. Martin and Noah readily agree to come, promising that Beth and Holly will come along too. I can't wait to see the surprise on Max's face.

I spin on my heel and head back into the workshop, locking the door behind me, feeling lighter than I have in a long time. Max cleaned up and took off his overalls while I was outside.

He draws me in close, wrapping his arms around my lower back, resting his hands on my butt, locking us together. "How are you feeling, Dimples?"

I pause for a moment to assess how I'm feeling. Peering up into Max's caring eyes, which are almost brown today, I answer honestly. "I'm not gonna lie. I was nervous. He's the age that Ethan never got to be, and I wasn't sure if I'd be okay … emotionally. You know?" I draw in a sharp breath as Max nods. "I didn't want to be a sobbing mess in front of him and make things awkward."

Max presses his forehead to mine, kissing the tip of my nose. "You've lost so much and yet you're still thinking about everyone else. You're incredible. You know that, right?"

The heat that rises to my cheeks is embarrassing. "Not really. I didn't want to start with grief between us. He's just a kid and I'm a stranger. I'm glad we could connect with my drawings, though. I think having something we can do together will make it easier for us to get to know each other."

"He was impressed with your talent. But I feel sorry for the kid. He now has to deal with two sisters. I might have to give him some tips." I swat playfully at Max's arm, which he attempts to dodge, but I'm too quick and make contact with his muscular bicep. "C'mon, Dimples. Let's get outta here."

# CHAPTER 45

## —max—

I WAKE TO MOLLY'S MOUTH WRAPPED AROUND MY COCK, HER SILKY hair tickling my thighs. A moan escapes and I raise my head to look down my body at the gorgeous sight of my dick disappearing into her warm mouth. The sensations are incredible, and I prop one hand behind my head to watch. I sift my fingers through her silky strands to push them away from her face, to give me an unobstructed view.

Her eyes lift to find mine and she smiles around my cock at me. I gently massage her scalp, watching her saliva coat my cock as it slides out of her mouth. Her hand follows the movement while her other hand cups my balls. She squeezes gently and I moan, pressing my hips up.

"Take it deep," I grunt, as I push my pelvis up again. She swallows around the shaft, then uses her teeth to lightly graze my dick as she slides her mouth up. My body trembles, anticipating the downward stroke and hitting the back of her gorgeous throat.

Tight and hot.

She moans as she sinks back down, and I'm gone. "Good girl," I groan as my fingers clench in her hair, my balls draw up tight, and darkness flickers around the edge of my vision. I shatter, my heart tearing apart and gluing back together in one swift action. Cum streams down her throat and the eager lover that she is, she swallows it all down. I drop my head back, panting for breath as she cleans my shaft with her delicate tongue, and I finally release my harsh grip on her silky hair.

I peel my lids back open as I feel her sliding up beside me; her swollen lips caressing my torso on the way. Her slender fingers flick and pinch my nipples as she makes her way up my body.

"Happy birthday, Max."

I raise my eyebrow. I didn't think she knew. "How did you know?"

Her dimples make an appearance. "Emma." One word.

"Well, thank you for my birthday gift. I loved it. Feel free to give me gifts like that whenever the mood strikes." I gently brush her hair away from her face, raising my head to take her mouth in a grateful kiss, but she pulls back slightly.

"Why didn't you tell me it was your birthday today?" I'm not sure if she's hurt or not, her eyes glimmer with something, but I don't think it's hurt feelings. It feels more like … curiosity.

I glide my hand down her hair in a long stroke, moving down her slender back to rest on the cheek of her ass. "I didn't tell you because you've already given me so much. I didn't want you to feel obligated to buy me a gift or to make a fuss. You're enough. Until the end of my days. You're all I need. All I want." Her eyes go soft and she presses forward, touching her lips to mine in a slow exploration. "I fucking love kissing you," I whisper, my lips touching hers as I roll over.

As I line up my needy cock with her slick heat, I thrust my tongue inside to mirror the action of my hips. We both moan, closing our eyes momentarily as we're lost in the bliss. Every time I'm inside this woman, our bond grows, the tether between us tightening.

"I want us to get married soon. I don't want to wait." The words roll off my tongue. I don't know what it is, but when I'm inside her, it's like a truth serum explodes through my veins and I can't keep my thoughts inside.

Molly's eyes spring open. "Like how soon?"

"Like next month soon. Say you will."

She smiles, big and bright. "Of course. Can we get married on the beach, where you proposed to me?"

"Sounds perfect." I lean forward and press my lips against hers. "This is the best birthday ever."

I slide my hand down her slender thigh and pull her leg up high, opening her to me and return my mouth to hers as I slide my hips back. With lips barely touching, eyes locked tight, I drive into my girl over and over again. Our breaths blend and meld. The scent of sex fills the air, adding to the headiness of our lovemaking. Molly meets me thrust for thrust, building our pleasure.

She whimpers as I slide my hand under her ass and tilt her hips, changing the angle. Her short nails are sure to leave scratches on my shoulders as she grips me tight. The thought of seeing her marks on me makes my cock throb and pulse, my balls getting ready to shoot my load. One of these days, that cum is going to knock her up and I can't wait for that day. Until then, I'm happy to take us to completion as many times as possible until we get it just right.

Molly's walls spasm and I grunt as I work to hold back my release. I move closer to her ear. "Be a good girl and choke my cock." I suck and nip the lobe and she cries out as her walls squeeze around my shaft. Her body stiffens, and her breaths turn choppy. I grit my teeth to hold on to my release. "Don't fight it. Come," I demand, harshly.

Her release washes through her body like a wave as her pussy clamps down around my cock, choking it to oblivion, and I shatter. "Fuuuuck!" I press my hips in tight to Molly's. If I could fucking climb inside her right now, I would. I smooth her sweaty hair away from her face and smile at the serene look. I want to beat my chest in pride that I'm the man to put that look on her face. Her leg drops away from my hip to the bed and she squeezes her internal muscles. "Fuck. Stop." Shit. She chuckles. That almost hurt.

I drop my forehead to hers. "Happy fucking birthday to me," I whisper against her lips. Then I capture her mouth in a kiss that I hope she feels all the way to her toes.

Molly wanted to drive today. She said she wanted to give me the full treatment. After the spectacular way she woke me up, she cooked a full breakfast of bacon, eggs, hash browns, sausage, and roasted tomatoes. Now she's taking me somewhere before we head to Mom and Dad's for lunch.

"Where are you taking me?" I thought I had an idea where we were going, but she's turned down this long, winding, unpaved road and I'm not sure I know what's down this way.

She glances across at me with a half-smile. "You'll have to wait and see."

We drive around a wide bend and the road opens up to a parking lot alongside a wide grassed area with barbecues, picnic tables, and a wicked nature play area for kids, which overlooks a medium-sized lake with a small island in the middle. I'll have to bring Kenny and the boys here. They'll love it. "I can't believe I've lived in this city all my life and I didn't know about this place. How did you find it?"

"When I first moved here, I had nothing else to do on the weekends, so I would drive around to familiarize myself with the city. There's still a lot of the city I'm unfamiliar with, but I stumbled across this place and fell in love."

The parking lot is busy, but Molly finds a space and we climb out. Hand in hand, we make our way to the edge of the lake. I peer around at the people enjoying this sunny spring day and my eyes freeze on a group at a picnic bench by the edge of the water before the grass becomes a forest. I glance at Molly to find her dimples on full display. "Happy birthday, Max."

I pull her to a stop. "You did this for me?"

She nods. "With Emma's help." I drag her around to face me properly, then cup her gorgeous face in my hands. Her hands come up to hold onto my wrists, her eyes locked on mine. "I hope you don't mind."

"How did I get so lucky?" I touch her lips with mine. "Thank you, Dimples."

"You're welcome. Emma helped, though. I can't take all the credit." She presses her lips firmly to mine, then pulls away too quickly. "Come on. Everyone's waiting." Dragging me forward, we reach my family quickly.

Mom and Dad are the first to greet me. "Happy birthday, Max."

Mom reaches up to cup my bristly cheeks. Her eyes are full of love as she scans my face. "I can't believe my baby boy's thirty-seven." She glances at Dad. "When did that happen?"

I bend down and kiss her forehead. "It's been a long time since I've been a baby, Mom."

Emma interrupts, wrapping her arms around me. "Happy birthday, little brother." She smirks at me, knowing I hate to be called little.

I wrap my arm around her, pulling her in close. "Thanks, Em. And thanks for helping Molly with this today."

"I really like her. I'm so glad we get to keep her," she says with a softness in her eyes.

Mom and Dad nod in agreement. "Us too."

"You did good, brother." Em kisses my cheek.

Molly joins us with Kenny holding onto her back like a koala. "I'm gonna take the kids to the playground." She glances across at Emma. "Sorry, I probably should have asked first. Is it okay if I take the kids to the playground?"

Em waves her off. "Of course. Cristo will probably tag along." She points toward her father-in-law, who's busy setting up trays of food on the picnic table.

"I'll go too," I offer. I love that Molly's bonded so well with Em's kids. Every Sunday, she's become closer and closer to my sisters. She's well and truly one of the family.

Sarah joins us, wrapping her arms around me and squeezing tight. "Happy birthday, big brother."

I squeeze her back. "Thanks, Sare." Molly's smiling at our interaction and I raise my chin to her. "Do you wanna tell the girls the good news, or shall I?"

Everyone's eyes snap to Molly's stomach and she flushes pink. "Not that." She fidgets with her bracelet. "Max and I have decided to get married next month on the beach where he proposed to me."

The girls jump up and down, squealing in delight as Martin and his family approach our group. "Oh my God, next month. That doesn't give us a heap of time." Sarah's slightly panicked.

"It's only going to be family and probably some guys from soccer, maybe Molly's friends from *Shelter*, if they can make it. Don't get carried away."

Beth doesn't wait to be invited into the conversation. "Are you talking about your wedding?" Her eyes are wide, shimmering with excitement.

"Yeah." Molly steps forward, welcoming her family and introducing them to mine. I'm surprised they're here, but she must be feeling more comfortable with them. I know she speaks regularly with her sister, who occasionally drops by after school since the first time she turned up out of the blue. And dinner last month cleared the air between Molly and Martin. They still have awkward moments as they get to know each other, but they've come a long way.

"Come on, Molly. I wanna go play." Kenny reminds my girl.

Molly jiggles her. "Sure. Come on, Munchkin." She turns back to everyone. "Maybe we can talk about it later. I promised the kids I'd play with them and I always try to keep my promises."

"We can come too," the women offer. "The guys can organize the food."

Molly presses up to kiss my cheek. "See you in a while, Fiancé." She winks as she turns away with Kenny on her back and Lachlan, Austin, and Noah trailing behind, followed by five women all itching to help plan a wedding. She reminds me of the Pied Piper.

I chuckle to myself as I head over to Dad to see if I can help him with the barbecue. "Need any help?"

"You don't fancy talking about wedding planning?" He chuckles and Theo joins in.

"It's not that I don't want to." I glance across to the nature play area where the girls are chatting while the kids play. "I wanted to give Molly the opportunity to bond with the girls. I don't expect she's ever really had that because it was only her and her mom for such a long time."

Theo nods, but Dad's the one who responds, "Good thinking, Son."

"I know Em and Sarah will help wherever they can. Sarah was a great help to Em. Em probably still has her wedding folder somewhere. She was incredibly organized, she had little pockets for everything." Theo's eyes seek Emma out across the park.

Dad hands Martin, Cristo, Theo, and me a beer each and I take a drink, then respond. "Beth's a wedding planner. I'm assuming the girls will probably have everything sorted out quickly."

"Beth has all the contacts you two need. She loves planning a wedding, but I think this one will be special to her. She already thinks of Molly as her daughter," Martin adds, then takes a long drink.

"Family is incredibly important to Molly." I give Martin a meaningful look. I hope he doesn't hurt her.

Martin returns my look. "I know what you're thinking. I don't plan on hurting her. Ever. She's my daughter, whether or not I was with her while she grew up. I have a lot of time to makeup and I intend to do so." He steps closer to me. "I'll be talking to Molly about the wedding when I get the chance, but I'd like to give you a heads-up. I'd like to pay for everything, including your honeymoon. If the two of you will let me."

"That's a mighty generous offer, Martin. If you're doing it to win Molly over, you're going about it the wrong way. She's not about material stuff. She's about time, care, and commitment." I study him closely. "But that'll be between you and her. I'll go along with whatever she decides. It won't be an expensive event. We've already discussed keeping it small with little fuss."

He nods. "Fair enough. I'm not doing it to get in her good graces. I want to do it because I missed out on so much of her life."

The afternoon is great fun, and we all agree to come back in the summer to allow the kids to enjoy the lake.

# CHAPTER 46

## *—molly—*

DRIVING HOME FROM THE LAKE, I FILL MAX IN ON EVERYTHING THE girls told me. "Beth's going to work on getting the permits we need to have our wedding ceremony on the beach. We would normally need longer than five weeks, but because she deals with that sort of stuff all the time, she's pretty sure she can get it approved more quickly for us. She also has a celebrant that she uses regularly, so she's going to check if she's available." I draw a breath.

"Sounds good, Dimples."

"Yeah. And Emma told me about the florist she and Theo used." I rack my brain, trying to remember the name. "*Blooms and Balloons*, I think." I glance across at my groom-to-be. "I think we'll have everything organized quickly with everyone's help."

"That's where I bought your roses from. Cassia, the owner, is incredibly helpful." He lays his hand on my thigh. "Don't forget I can help too. Give me a list of tasks and I'll get them done." And there I go, falling in love a little more. "It's my wedding too. I don't expect you to do everything, especially since I'm the one who wants to get married quickly."

"I want to get married quickly, too. There's no point in waiting." I flick my eyes across to Max, then look back at the road. "Did Martin talk to you about paying for everything? He wants to cover the whole thing, including our honeymoon if we want one."

"He spoke to me about it and I said the decision would be yours. It's an incredibly generous offer."

"I know. He said it's the least he could do since he hadn't

contributed financially while I was growing up." Max's hand lands on my thigh and he squeezes it. "I didn't accept his offer because I wanted to speak about it with you. I hadn't realized the two of you had already spoken."

We pull into our driveway and head inside. Max pulls me into his arms. "It's up to you. It might help Martin with some of the guilt he's carrying about letting Nicole and you down." He shrugs and leans forward, pressing his lips tenderly against my forehead.

"I'll think about it, but not right now. I have a gift for you." His eyes widen as I pull away to collect his present. "Go sit in the living room. I'll bring it to you."

He's sitting on the couch when I return. I'm hoping he likes his gift because I struggled to figure out something at short notice. "Happy birthday, Max." I hand him the gift bag.

He accepts it with a curious smile. "You didn't need to get me anything. Organizing the barbecue at the lake with our families was more than I ever expected." He takes my hand, kissing the palm. "My favorite part was the way you woke me up this morning," he says as he wriggles his eyebrows.

Leaning forward, I chuckle as I taste his lips. "Open it."

He pulls out the large square gift to open first. I'm hoping he doesn't think it's a stupid idea. He peels away the paper, revealing the custom map I had made. He reads the inscription. "When Max asked and Molly said yes." He looks at me. "What is this exactly?"

"It's what the night sky at the beach looked like the night you proposed to me." I hold my breath, waiting for his response.

His eyes widen as he studies the map. "Fuck. This is incredible. We need to get one done for when we get married and every time one of our kids is born. We can make a wall of these babies." He leans forward, cupping the back of my head, and pulls me into him and we meet halfway. I open immediately, welcoming him eagerly.

I love kissing this man.

"I'm relieved you like it. I was worried you'd think it was pointless." I point my chin toward the bag. "You have something else in the bag."

He dips his hand in, pulling out the small box. He glances up at me and then tugs at the paper to open the box. He studies the contents for a long time, then glances up at me. Holding up the keyring I had specially made, he asks, "Are you serious? This is my car. How did you do this?"

"It's from a little store on Etsy. I managed to get a rush order at short notice."

He's wobbling his head from side to side as though he can't believe I bought him something for his birthday. "These gifts are really thoughtful. Thank you so much." He wiggles his eyebrows up and down and stands, holding his hand out to me. "Allow me to show you how much I love these gifts."

My lady parts flutter in delight. I'm about to get very lucky.

I wipe my sweaty hands down my jeans. My heart feels like it's going to beat right through my rib cage. Max wanted to come with me, but I needed to do this on my own. I needed to prove that I can still deal with things that may be difficult by myself. That I haven't become completely dependent on Max. I knock on the door and hear little claws scratching on the floor before tiny barks greet me through the door. Footsteps sound and then I hear, "Shhh, shhh, Christian."

The lock disengages as the dog continues to bark. Surprised blue eyes so much like Mom's greet me above a wiggling gray ball of fur. "Oh, Molly. This is a wonderful surprise." She steps away, then returns with a key to unlock the screen door. "Please come in. I'm thrilled to see you."

She steps to the side, allowing me inside her home. When Beth gave me Joanna's address and phone number, she also gave me some information which made my decision to visit easier. I want to get to know *all* of my family. Life's too short to miss out on opportunities. "I hope you don't mind me dropping by unannounced."

"Not at all. I'm just so happy that you have." She leads me through to a sitting room that overlooks a common area in the middle of the unit complex. My eyes catch on a large photo of Mom hanging in a prominent position on the wall. She notices me gawking and gives me a small smile. "Nicole was such a beautiful girl. So spirited and full of life." Her smile turns sad.

She offers me a drink and then sets about making it while the little gray fur ball acquaints himself with me. He's adorable. His name seems very formal, though. Joanna returns with cups of coffee on a tray and what appears to be homemade shortbread. "Would you like some?"

"Thank you." I point down at her little dog, which has finally settled on his bed, huffing out a sigh and dropping his head to his little paws, his ears still twitching. "Your dog is cute."

Her eyes drop to him, and she smiles. "I always wanted to have a dog, but my husband would never agree. The place I lived in when I first left him didn't allow pets. I finally saved up enough to buy this place fifteen years ago and one of the first things I did was get a rescue. Unfortunately, that dog passed away and then I got Christian. I named him after one of my favorite book characters." The connection dawns on me, and I'm certain my eyes are as wide as saucers. Does that mean my grandmother has read *Fifty Shades of Grey*? "Have you read the books?" she asks with eyes full of mischief, reminding me of Mom when she was sharing exciting news with me.

I shake my head, my voice mute for a moment. "Uh, no. Can't say I have." The awkwardness I felt earlier has increased tenfold, knowing my grandmother reads soft porn. I don't know whether to feel mortified or proud. I mean good on her, I guess. Perhaps I should introduce her to Rhonda. They could compare book boyfriends. I giggle internally at the idea of Rhonda with her bright pink hair swooning over book boyfriends with my grandmother, who appears to be as proper as a minister's wife.

I came here to apologize for my behavior when we first met. Once I calmed down, I was mortified at how I had run out of the house and left Max to deal with the aftermath. It was unfair and probably not the best first impression to give my grandmother. I take a sip of my coffee to soothe my dry throat and draw in a deep breath for fortitude. "Uh, I … I, uh, owe you an apology."

Her posture softens. "Oh, Molly. You don't owe me anything at all. It's *I* who owe *you* an apology. I should have fought harder and stood up to my husband. I never should have allowed him to speak to Nicole the way he did. I believe she ran away because of what he said to her. Because of his threats." A loud sob escapes. "I'm so sorry, Molly. I let my daughter down, and I let you down." She covers her face with both hands and the urge to comfort this stranger is strong.

I move to the cushion next to her, wrapping my arm around her shoulder. Beth told me that Joanna left her husband, my grandfather, not long after Mom ran away. She blamed him and his demand for an abortion for losing Mom. I'm not sure I'd be sitting here if she were still with him, because I don't think I could get past the way he spoke to Mom.

*He didn't want me.*

How could I possibly forge a relationship with the man?

The idea is impossible.

I'm not sure what I can say to make things better for Joanna. Do I accept her apology? But to me, that would mean I blame her. And deep down, I don't. I've been thinking about the whole situation a lot since I moved here. And I mean a lot!

I love Mom and I'll forever be on her side no matter what because ultimately, she thought she was doing the right thing. The choices she made were to protect me because she wanted me. But ... now I've heard the other side of the story and I've learned that maybe if Mom had taken a few days to let things settle instead of reacting so quickly, things probably would have turned out very differently. Which means some of the responsibility has to fall on her shoulders and it makes me wonder if she ever doubted the choices she made. Did she ever consider going home? Is it possible she realized her mistake but was too proud to return to her family and friends?

I understand being prideful. After all, I get that trait from her.

"Joanna." She removes her trembling hands from her face, revealing tear-stained cheeks and puffy red eyes. "The entire situation was unexpected and messy. Things were said and choices were made. Were they the best choices?" I shrug. "Maybe, maybe not. But they were the choices made at the time in the heat of the moment. We can't go back and change anything and, to be honest, I wouldn't want to. Was life difficult as a result? Yes, it was. I'm not gonna lie or sugarcoat things." I give my grandmother a small smile of reassurance. "But life was also great. Mom and I had a bond that not all mothers and daughters share." A boulder forms in my throat as I think about Mom and I have to swallow it down so I can continue.

"We were close, and our love for each other was unbreakable. Not once did I ever question how important I was to her or how much she loved me. She always, always put me and my needs first. Even though we couldn't afford a traditional home, she always made sure I had nutritious food, even if it meant going without herself. Then Mom met Jack." I smile as I remember meeting him for the first time.

"He was the best man you could hope your daughter and granddaughter to have in our lives. He was kind and generous to both of us. From the beginning, he treated me as if I were his flesh and blood. And then Ethan came along." And my heart cracks a little, as it does whenever I think of him, and a life cut too short. "I wouldn't wish for a life where I'd never had him. So, maybe things didn't turn out the way you maybe hoped they would, but we had a good life."

She takes my free hand in both of hers. "I hope you can forgive me, though."

I give her a small smile. "There's nothing to forgive."

She squeezes my hand. "Thank you, Molly. You're being very gracious. Perhaps someday you'll share stories about growing up and tell me all about my grandson."

I nod. "I'd be happy to." I fidget with my bracelet. "I don't know all that much about Mom's childhood or teenage years, so perhaps you can tell me more about her?"

She smiles at me. "Of course. I still have all of her photo albums. I think I even have some videos." She chuckles. "Though I may need to get them transferred into another format since I don't have a video player anymore." She pats my hand and climbs to her feet. "I'll grab the photo albums. We can look at them now."

Joanna comes back carrying several albums. When she opens to the first page of the first album, a gasp escapes me. "Oh my gosh. She was so cute. I'll have to bring the few baby photos I have so we can compare how much I looked like her."

She studies me. "You hold a remarkable resemblance to Nicole, even though you have some of Martin's prominent features. I'm sure you looked just like Nicole when you were a baby."

Joanna spends the afternoon showing me photos of Mom until the age of seventeen when the album abruptly remains starkly blank. We're both silent for long moments at the reminder of the years she's missed. Christian breaks the moment when he suddenly wakes and starts barking at nothing.

I remember I have some more recent photos on my phone, so I show them to her. Tears fill her eyes as she sees her daughter as a grown woman with the family she made for herself.

After long quiet moments, I decide now is the time to invite my grandmother to my wedding. "Uhm, Joanna. I have something I would like to ask you. Max asked me to marry him and I said yes." My stomach still flips when I think back to his proposal on the beach.

Her face lights up. "Oh, he seemed like such a lovely young man. He cares very much for you. I'm thrilled you've met such a wonderful man."

"Me too." My lips spread across my face, thinking about Max. "I was wondering if you'd like to come to our wedding? We don't have a date or time just yet, but it will be next month."

"Oh, I'd love to. Thank you for the invitation." She jumps up from her seat. "I'll be back in a moment."

I'm puzzled by her abrupt departure, but I stand to look out of the window at the shared gardens while I wait for her. My grandmother has a peaceful view out of this window. Perhaps I should call her grandma or something?

Joanna returns with a small box. She hands it to me with a timid smile. "This is something my mother gave me to wear at my wedding and I had hoped Nicole would wear it for hers." Her smile becomes somber. "I would be thrilled if you would consider wearing this on your special day."

I open the box and my mouth drops open. Inside is a beautiful sparkling pendant. I tip my eyes back up to Joanna. "This is beautiful. I would love to wear this, though I don't know what the design of my dress will be yet."

She raises her hands to her chest. "Oh, you've made me so happy. It's meant to represent the stars in the night sky."

"Max proposed to me under a moonlit sky, so we're planning to get married at sunset. This would be amazing. Thank you."

## CHAPTER 47

*—molly—*

MAX HAS HIS NEPHEW, AUSTIN, OVER FOR THE AFTERNOON TO 'HELP' him change the tires on his Dodge. Austin was almost exploding with excitement when he arrived to spend the afternoon working on his uncle's car. The day Max offered Austin the opportunity to help him in the future with his tire change, I figured it was lip service because Austin's so young. But I should have known better. Max is a man of his word and he didn't hesitate to include his nephew in his afternoon plans. It was so cute how Austin turned up in overalls, much like the ones Max wears. He's going to be such a great daddy one day.

I thought I'd leave them to their male bonding afternoon and spend the time getting to know my siblings. When I phoned to organize this afternoon, I half expected Noah and Holly to make up some excuse to avoid me. After all, I'm a complete stranger who happens to share their dad. I wouldn't blame them, but they were as keen as I am for us to get to know each other.

I've set up our afternoon snacks on the picnic blanket at the park near the workshop. I wasn't sure what type of snacks to bring, so I brought a little of everything. Whatever's left over, I'm sure Max will eat, but if I remember correctly, there won't be anything left with a teenage boy around. If Noah's anything like Ethan was, he'll have a bottomless pit for a stomach.

My breath catches in my lungs when I realize I thought about my brother without my heart splintering into a million pieces. Sure, the memory of him has pain attached, but I'm starting to feel less bogged down by it. I know my sense of loss associated with my family will never go away, but I hope that when I think about them, it won't always result in me breaking down in a sobbing fit. I need to remember there were a lot of good times, happy times. The only truly sad memory of my family is that they're no longer here.

I make a promise to myself to focus on the happy times as much as possible.

Dragging my backpack across to me, I check that I have what I need inside and pull out the sketch pads and pencils I brought. I promised Noah I would start teaching him how to sketch today. I figured Holly and I could show him some simple techniques to get him started. There are loads of sketching opportunities for Noah at this park.

When I glance up, I spot Noah and Holly walking toward me, matching smiles on their faces, one with dimples, one without.

I stand as they close the distance. "Hi, guys." I'm not sure if I should hug them in greeting or not. I always hugged my family and I hug Max's family too. I decide to do what I've always done. They can let me know if they don't like it. Stepping forward, I hug Holly. "Hey, Holly." Then Noah. "Hey, Noah. I'm glad you guys could make it today."

They each return my embrace. "We've been looking forward to spending some time with you. We were bummed we missed out on dinner with you and Max." Holly smiles at me, then glances at her brother. *Our* brother. Geez, that's hard to get used to. "Right, Noah?"

Noah nods. "Right. I can't wait for you to teach me how to draw as good as you."

Holly's brows tighten. "I could have taught you how to draw, you know. All you had to do was ask."

He huffs out a breath and toes the ground with his shoe. "You draw girly stuff." He flings his arm out in my direction. "Molly draws cool stuff like cars."

*Oh shit!* My eyes widen. I don't want to compete with my newly found sister. "I love Holly's clothing designs. The stuff she draws comes from her imagination. I just draw what I can see."

Holly's eyes snap up to mine and I gesture toward the picnic blanket for us to take a seat. Noah eyes off the array of snacks as he sits as close as possible to the food and I quickly open the containers for him. "Help yourself. I didn't know what you guys liked, so I packed a few different options."

"Thanks," Noah replies as he reaches for a chocolate cupcake.

"Holly, what would you like?"

She scans the food and then takes a carrot stick, dipping it into the hummus. "Thanks."

"You're welcome." I grab a couple of strawberries and enjoy their sweet juice on my tongue. Max always insists on having berries in the house because they're my favorite.

We enjoy the snacks in silence for a while, then Noah points toward the scrapbook and sketch pads I brought along. "Is that your book? The one with the car sketch I saw."

I chuckle at his enthusiasm. "Yeah." I glance between my new siblings. "I, uh, I also brought my brother's scrapbook to show you. I figured you'd like it because he only drew cars."

My heart pounds as I share something that's deeply precious to me.

Holly's eyes go soft and she glances over at her brother. Creases form between her brows and then she reaches across to smooth down Noah's unruly hair. He pulls away, giving her a puzzled look. Her gaze comes back to me and it's full of sorrow and I know she's thinking about what I've lost.

Noah breaks the moment with his excitement, completely oblivious to his sister's sadness. "Really. Can I see his drawings?"

"Of course." I select Ethan's book and shuffle closer to Noah, then open to the first page. "This book shows his progression clearly. You can see this first drawing is quite basic. But wait until you see his sketches at the end of the book." Holly balances on her knees behind us, studying E's drawings closely as I turn each page.

Her hand creeps between Noah and me, stopping me from turning to the next page. "This is where his skill leveled up." She traces her finger over the line of the roof of the car. "You can see the confidence in his lines." She snatches her finger from the page. "Sorry. I probably shouldn't have touched it."

"That's okay. And yes, you're right. This was the turning point." I flick to the next page.

"They all look really cool to me." Noah glances at me with wide eyes. "Do you think I could draw like Ethan?"

"I don't see why not. Shall we get started?"

"I'm ready." He reaches into his backpack and pulls out a sketch pad and some pencils. Holly and I chuckle at his excitement.

Holly and I spend the next couple of hours showing Noah some basic techniques, reminding him to draw what he sees, not what he *thinks* he sees. "That's the trick. Our mind wants to fill in the spaces, but we mustn't let it, or our drawing won't be accurate." He nods, his face full of concentration.

When I glance at Holly's sketch pad, I notice she's drawing a new outfit. I tip my head toward it. "That looks beautiful. You're incredibly talented." She glances up at me with a smile.

"She designed and made that outfit she has on," Noah states proudly.

"Yeah?" She flushes a pretty pink and tucks her dark hair behind her ear. "It's gorgeous. Did you apply for Art College?"

"Yeah. I got accepted and I'm excited to start!" Her eyes sparkle with delight. "At least I'll finally be doing something I enjoy."

I wrap my arm around her, pulling her in close for a hug. "Congratulations. I'm honestly not surprised you got accepted. They'd be crazy to reject your application." I lean back, releasing her.

I swallow down my nerves because I think now would be a good time to ask her to be part of my bridal party. "You know how Max asked me to marry him, and we're getting married soon?"

Noah and Holly nod. "Yeah. I really like Max. Well, I mostly like that he works with cars because I don't know him all that well, but he seems like a cool guy."

I chuckle at Noah. "He *is* pretty cool." Then turn my attention to Holly. "Well, Holly, I was … uh … wondering if you would be my bridesmaid?"

She squeals and leans forward, wrapping her slim arms around me. "I'd freaking love to. This is amazing. Thank you so much." We sway awkwardly from side to side, giggling with happiness. It feels fabulous to have a sister.

"God, you girls are weird!" Noah huffs out as he steals yet another cupcake.

Holly and I giggle. "Would you mind if I designed my bridesmaid dress?" Her eyes are filled with excitement.

Oh my gosh, I hadn't even thought of that, but what a fabulous idea. I nod, my eyes wide with joy that she wants to do something so amazing for someone she barely knows. "On one condition."

She freezes, looking unsure. "Uhm, okay?"

"You'll need to make a complementary dress for Kenny. She's going to be my flower girl, and I'd love for you two to match!"

Holly squeals. "Oh my God, yes. She's so freaking adorable. Thank you for trusting me with something so important."

I chuckle as she draws me back in to embrace me tight. "Of

course. I love your work. If it wasn't such a short time frame, I'd ask you to design and make my wedding dress, but it would be too much. It's less than three weeks away." My heart stalls when I realize how soon I'll become Mrs. Stanfield. "Will that be enough time for you to make two dresses? I don't want to put any pressure on you."

She waves off my concern. "I can definitely do them in three weeks. But I'll need to measure Kenny within the next few days."

I message Emma and we make plans to meet up with Kenny. I feel like I'm going to burst with happiness and excitement as I say goodbye to Noah and Holly. This afternoon worked out better than I could have hoped, and spending time with Noah wasn't anywhere near as difficult as I thought it was going to be.

I blow out a breath in relief and glance up at the cloudless sky. "I miss you," I whisper to the heavens. "But I think I'm gonna be okay."

A gentle, warm breeze rises, blowing my bangs out of my eyes, and I blink to keep the tears at bay because it reminds me so much of when Mom used to slide them out of my eyes. I don't want to cry today. It's been too perfect and I don't want to ruin it. I pack up my stuff and head home to my soon-to-be husband. *Eeek!*

# CHAPTER 48

## —max—

TODAY'S THE DAY I TIE MOLLY TO ME FOREVER.

*Thank fuck!*

I never want to lose this woman. I've missed her. After her volunteer shift at *Shelter* last night, she stayed with Martin and Beth, saying she wanted to follow tradition. I feel like I haven't been able to take a proper breath since she kissed me goodbye. Any minute now, I'll be able to lay eyes on her and I can't wait.

The late afternoon is perfect, the temperature is ideal, with a light warm breeze coming off the ocean, and the simple setup looks incredible. The circular timber ladder, which will frame the sun as it drops below the horizon, is decorated with Molly's favorite flowers—blush pink roses. It will act as a dais for Molly and me to exchange our promises. Simple wooden chairs for the small number of guests have been set up facing the wheel. Molly, Beth, and the girls have done an incredible job of pulling this together as quickly as they have.

Aaron stands beside me as I scan the small group of people gathered to witness our commitment to each other under a cloudless sky. Three chairs sit empty in the front row and my heart clenches as my eyes pause on each photograph of her family.

Today will be bittersweet for Molly.

In the second row on Molly's side, sits Beth, Joanna, and Noah, as well as her friends, Simone and Rhonda from *Shelter*. Molly was thrilled they could take a couple of hours out of their evening to share this special moment with us. On the opposite side of the aisle sits my family, and I spot Mom already wiping tears before we've even started the ceremony. Emma, Theo, and the boys sit with Sarah and Cristo, chatting quietly among themselves. The soccer boys are behind them, looking casual in shorts and T-shirts.

"Are you ready to lock yourself to one woman forever?" Aaron asks softly.

When I asked him to be my best man, he agreed without hesitation. We've been friends since elementary school, which means he's been witness to my failed relationships over the years. He saw the same thing in Molly as I did and that's why he gave me the nudge I needed to pursue her.

"Absolutely. I know it's been quick; just over five months. But when you know, *you know*. I'm not letting Molly get away." My heart's never been as full as it has since Molly came into my life. Knowing she feels the same for me is incredible.

"I would do exactly the same thing, man. She's an exceptional woman and I'm rapt that you came to your senses and pursued her." He sighs. "I have to admit, I'm a little envious."

I tear my eyes away from the direction Molly will come from to study my long-time friend. "It'll happen, man. When it does, it knocks you on your ass. So be ready."

He huffs out a laugh. "Oh, I will be."

The music changes to *I Get to Love You* by Ruelle and I snap my focus back to the crest of the pathway leading to me. Holly and Kenny are standing at the top of the sandy dune. They walk toward us, hand in hand, with bright smiles, wearing gorgeous blush pink dresses designed by Holly. When Holly asked Molly if it would be okay to design her dress, Molly jumped at the opportunity to support her creativity so long as she followed one request. To make Kenny a dress to match. Holly was rapt that Molly trusted her and dived straight into the project, designing and making both of their dresses in record time.

Kenny breaks away from Holly and runs straight for me with the widest of smiles. She leaps at me, and I catch her easily. "Uncle Max!" She squeezes my cheeks with her little hands. "Aunty Molly is a princess. Like a really real princess. She's so pretty."

I rub her nose with mine. "Is she as pretty as you?"

She chuckles. "You're funny, Uncle Max." I glance up, noticing movement on the dune. I kiss Kenny and place her on her feet next to Holly, all of my attention focused on my future wife.

Molly's revealed to me slowly as she crests the dune until she stands unobstructed at the top. I draw in a breath as my eyes devour her. With her platinum hair tied away from her face, her joyful smile is obvious, even from this distance.

I'm barely aware of Aaron patting me on the back and telling me how gorgeous she is. Her hand is carefully tucked into the crook of Martin's arm as he leads her to me; a proud expression on his face. My heart pounds the closer he brings her, and I can't believe I get to call this woman mine for the rest of our lives. Her top half is sheathed in lace, which fits her like a glove, accentuating her beautiful breasts until it meets a satin skirt that drags along the sand, making Molly appear to be floating across the surface. Occasionally, her toes peek out as she steps forward, giving me a glimpse of sexy jewelry on her feet instead of shoes.

Molly and Martin stop where the chairs for our guests begin, and I can't peel my eyes away from her. Martin whispers something in her ear, making her smile, and kisses her cheek, then takes the empty seat next to Beth. He's beaming broadly, showing the dimples that match his daughters'.

Molly moves forward on her own and I can't stand it. I want her to know that she's no longer on her own. I will walk any pathway with her from here on out, so I take long strides to meet her in the aisle between the small number of guests we invited today.

I reach forward, taking her smooth hand in my calloused one. "Hey," I whisper. I know I'm not supposed to kiss her yet, but she looks too divine to not lay my lips on hers.

She smiles at me, and I take my first full breath in the last twenty-five and a half hours. "Hey," she whispers back.

We stand with our eyes locked, silver to hazel, the warm salty breeze blowing the loose strands of Molly's hair around her gorgeous face. "You are stunning."

Her eyes skim down my body and then return to mine. "You're incredibly handsome, yourself, Max." She left it up to me to choose what I wanted to wear today. I chose a sandy-colored linen suit with a white shirt, leaving my feet bare. Aaron's wearing the same getup.

"Are you ready to become Mrs. Stanfield?"

Her smile widens further, deepening those dimples I love so much. Beneath the early evening sun, her eyes twinkle and she nods. "Absolutely, Mr. Stanfield."

I hold out my arm and Molly nestles her hand in the crook, holding her bouquet of blush pink roses in her other hand. We take the final few steps toward the celebrant together. Exactly how we're going to tackle everything from now on.

The celebrant, an older woman who is a friend of Beth's, smiles at both of us. "Are you two ready to make your lifelong promises to each other?"

I nod. "Yes, I am." Let's get this show on the road. The sooner she says those magical words and signs the formal paperwork, the sooner she's mine in every sense of the word.

Molly smiles. "Me too." She glances at me and then turns back to the celebrant, squeezing my hand in hers.

The celebrant raises her voice slightly. "Before we begin, I would like to thank you all for attending today's ceremony to bear witness to the joining of Molly Lewis and Max Stanfield. I am duly authorized by law to solemnize marriages according to the law. So, everything that happens here today will be legal and binding." She gives everyone a bright smile, her kind eyes glittering in the early evening sun. "We are here today because Max and Molly want to be bound together in the eyes of the law. A marriage is a joining of two souls who are complete and fulfilled in their own right but choose to tie themselves to a partner for life because they want to share their life's journey with that person. I've had the pleasure of spending time with Max and Molly, and I've gotten to know two highly capable, kind, and caring individuals who, on their own, could navigate their life's journey just fine. However, together, I believe they will lead a beautiful life rich in love, family, and togetherness. Marriage is about compromise and compassion, under-standing and unity. I see all of that between Max and Molly." She looks at me. "Max, would you like to share your promises with Molly?"

I turn toward Molly as I nod and lock my eyes on my future, taking her soft hands in mine. "Molly. When I first laid eyes on you, I was struck by your beauty. However, based on how you looked, I developed a preconceived notion of what you would be like as a person. You have spent the last few months destroying my incorrect assumptions and have surprised me at every turn, showing me that the beauty inside of you surpasses that which we can see. Which is spectacular." I wriggle my eyebrows at Molly, making her and our guests chuckle. "Since I first met you, you've shown me you're a compassionate, forgiving, resilient, and strong woman. You've shown courage and grace in situations that would break most people and my respect for you is only surpassed by my love.

"In you, I see the qualities I've always wanted in my life partner and the mother of my children. Because of this, I promise to spend my days working alongside you, building our business, raising our family, creating a home, and enjoying family time and vacations. I promise to spend my nights cuddled up on the couch with you, loving you, and lying beside you. I promise to care for you, support you, and love you through good times and bad, until the very end of time.

"Molly, I prayed for someone exactly like you and here you are. I am incredibly proud to have you as the woman who will be standing by my side for the rest of our days. I promise to be the best man I can be, the man you deserve. Because, Molly, I never want to let you down or disappoint you. I never want to make you sad. I want to give you the world and I look forward to building this life together." I lean in, swiping my lips against hers, and whisper, "And even though we're going to create our own family, I also give you mine." Her eyes become a little glassy as I touch my forehead to hers.

"Every day, I want to swim in the deepest part of the ocean with you. I love you, Molly. Today and every single day to come until my last breath." There's no way I can resist the temptation of her lips so close to mine as our breaths join in the shared space. I touch my lips to hers in a way I hope shows everything she means to me.

"That was lovely, Max. Molly, would you like to share your promises with Max?"

She nods and turns her gaze on me, making my heart pound. "Max. From our first interaction to now, you've always kept me safe and ensured that I have everything I need, whether it was making sure my car was running perfectly, or that I ate, or that I had a safe place to stay. You gave me sunshine during some of my darkest days and I will be forever thankful that you were brought into my life.

"As much as I love the way you look, it's what's inside that made me fall in love with you." She raises her hand, placing it over my heart. The heat from her touch burns through the fabric of my clothes into mine. "It was your kind and tender heart, your generous soul, and the way you care for your family and the people in the community, expecting nothing in return that made me fall for you. You're a good man. The very best, Max. And you're the man I want by my side as I navigate this life. Your patience, compassion, care, and understanding are the qualities I've always looked for in my partner because they are the qualities I consider most important for my children's happiness. You are the man I want to father my children, to nurture them, and to help them grow into the best possible people.

"I promise to always put you and our family first above all others and the busyness that life can become. I promise to always support you, encourage you, and cheer for you, as well as congratulate you and commiserate with you. I plan to be by your side through everything life throws our way, whether it be good, bad, or in between. I promise to give my all, every single day, to you and the family we create." She wriggles her eyebrows, making me chuckle. "Max, I look forward to falling in love with you every single day until I'm no longer here to fall." She presses her lips to mine. "I love you, Max. And I can't wait to swim in the deepest part of the ocean with you, unequivocally yours."

She leans forward, and I cup her face in my hands and meld our mouths together. This woman, who's had so little, gone through so much, gives so freely of herself to me and others. I pull back the smallest amount and whisper, "You slay me, Molly."

The celebrant clears her throat, reminding me we still have shit to get through before I can ravage my wife's mouth. "That was beautiful and very meaningful, Molly."

We complete our vows with the traditional promises to care for each other through sickness and health until death do us part. The muscles in my body seem to breathe a sigh of relief that Molly is now officially mine.

Finally, we exchange rings. As I slide Molly's diamond-studded band onto her delicate finger to join the engagement ring, I feel something settle deep inside. Seeing the physical token of her bound to me on her finger gives me a sense of peace I never anticipated. And when she slides my heavy-duty black tungsten band down my finger on my left hand, I see the same feeling of peace in Molly's eyes.

We both tilt our heads up, our eyes locking on the other as the sun sinks below the horizon. The golden glow on Molly's skin makes her appear to be an angel, reminding me of the first impression I ever had of her.

When the celebrant finally pronounces us husband and wife, our families and friends cheer as I seal my mouth to my wife's. My world narrows to this moment, to the sensation of her lips beneath mine, my tongue tasting her. Our shared breaths bind us together in a moment that transcends all others that have come before this.

She is my heart, the reason I'm here. She is my future, my life, my forever. Our bodies press against each other, molding together perfectly, our hearts beating in sync against each other's.

Aaron clears his throat, tearing us apart and stealing our moment so we can sign the formal papers. If he weren't my best friend, I would fucking lay him out for interrupting the best kiss I've ever had. We step forward, officially husband and wife, to be congratulated by each of our guests. I keep Molly's hand in mine because I'm never letting this woman go.

# CHAPTER 49

## —molly—

I can't wait to get my husband naked. It's been wonderful celebrating our marriage with our family and friends, but this is the part I've been looking forward to. I missed him terribly last night; I almost gave in and went home.

He hasn't let me go from the second he met me at the beginning of the aisle, and I haven't wanted him to. "I can't wait to see what you've got beneath this gorgeous dress, Dimples." My blood thrums through my veins and my body heats at his words. His hand tightens in mine and the hand at my waist pulls me in close to his body as we share a dance, his hard shaft pressing against my abdomen. I pull my hand out of his to wrap both arms around his neck and his hand drops to my waist, locking around me; making me feel secure, as though he's never going to let me go.

"Not long now, Husband."

He runs his nose along mine. "Say it again."

"Husband." I raise one eyebrow. He's been requesting the title since I said 'I do' as the sun settled on the horizon and subsequently set.

He pulls away, swiftly taking my hand in his. "That's it. I'm done. We're outta here." I giggle as he pulls me along. I'm glad I'm not the only one that's been feeling this way. He waves over his shoulder, calling out to our small number of guests. "Thank you for coming. We're heading out now."

I try to pull him to a stop because really, we need to thank everyone properly. Cheers rise, filling the intimate space. I guess they don't care if we skip out, but I still tug on his hand. "I'd like to say thank you properly before we leave."

Max sighs and we spin around to face our friends and family. He wraps his arm around my back, the heat from his hand searing my hip, and our guests quieten down.

"Thank you, everyone, for celebrating with us tonight. I especially want to thank all of my girls who helped put this beautiful day together with very short notice." I glance at Max and then back to the people who love and support us. "We didn't want to waste time. Life's far too short to wait and we appreciate that you could all make yourselves available to bear witness to our special promises with minimal notice." I swallow down the lump that's forming in my throat.

"To Max's family and friends. Thank you for openly welcoming me into your lives. I love you guys." Max's mom looks close to tears, and I don't want to cry, so I glance away, toward my family. My *new* family. "I know we haven't known each other long, but thank you for your patience with me as we navigated our new relationship."

Simone and Rhonda had to get back to *Shelter*, which meant they couldn't stay for the reception, but I was overjoyed they made it today. Everyone lines up to wish us goodbye, patiently waiting to hug us both.

Martin holds on extra tight as he whispers, "I'm so proud to have you as my daughter, Molly. I wish I could take credit for how you've grown into such an incredible young woman, but that's all you and Nicole. Thank you for allowing me to play a role today."

My throat clogs and I blink to keep the tears his words brought forth at bay. I return his squeeze, then pull back with a shaky smile. "Thanks, Dad." His eyes widen. "For everything. We appreciate it." He returns my shaky smile with one of his own.

"It's been my pleasure." He tips his chin over my shoulder. "I think your husband's growing impatient. You'd better go."

Twisting to glance over my shoulder, my husband's watching our exchange. "I'd better. See you soon." I give his hand one last squeeze and then turn toward my husband, my everything. "Ready, Husband?"

His grin is swift and full. "Absolutely, Wife."

We step out into the cool night air to make the short walk along the wooden boardwalk to our room for the weekend. We opted to spend tonight and the weekend in the hotel overlooking the ocean instead of going on a honeymoon. I didn't want to miss my volunteer evenings at *Shelter* and this way, Max only had to close his workshop for this afternoon and tomorrow. It seemed like an unnecessary expense to spend money on a lavish holiday when all we need is each other.

Max draws me to a stop halfway along the boardwalk, bringing me around to face him. Here, beneath the moonlight, he cups my face gently in his large hands and lays the gentlest kiss on my lips. "I love you so much, Molly. Today's been the second-best day of my life," he whispers, his lips brushing mine with each word. I pull back slightly, confused why today is the second-best day of his life. It's the best day of mine. He must read the question in my eyes because he explains, "The very best day of my life was the day I arrived at work to find you sleeping in your car. If not for *that* day, I wouldn't have *this* day."

My heart expands, sending warmth through my entire body. My smile is possibly the biggest it's ever been. "Well, that makes today the second-best day of my life, too."

Our lips meet in a heady kiss as our tongues explore and taste each other. I'm certain he can taste the champagne I enjoyed tonight, just as I can taste the whiskey he's been drinking. His hand slides beneath the fall of my hair to cup my head, using his hold to direct my mouth exactly where he wants it. I sigh into the kiss as he deepens it, pressing his thick cock against my pelvis. We draw back slightly, sucking in much-needed oxygen.

"As much as I could happily take you here, sex in the sand dunes doesn't appeal after spending days eradicating sand from my ass and jeans after our last time." He drops his forehead to mine as we chuckle.

"Well, we can't have that. Let's go." I collect his hand in mine and we hurry, side by side, to our room.

Max collected our keycard and dropped off our bags before the ceremony, meaning we don't need to check in and can head straight to our room without interruption. He opens the door, then lifts me into his arms to carry me across the threshold. As we enter the room, his kiss is passionate, just as it always is, but there's something more. A deeper connection and sense of belonging that wasn't there before today. "I need to make love to my wife," he whispers against my lips, his eyes especially dark and inviting.

Stepping further inside, the door latches closed behind him, and he flicks the lock, then carries me into the center of the stunning room. My gaze wanders around the space in amazement. Tiny candles cover every surface, shedding their flickering light across the walls, while rose petals cover the large rug centered over the teak wooden floor beneath the enormous bed. I'm pretty sure we won't need all that space because I won't want any space between my husband and me. "This looks beautiful." I glance back at Max. "Thank you for making this truly special."

"You're most welcome, Dimples." He brushes his nose along the side of mine, finishing with a lingering kiss. I tighten my hold around his neck, keeping his lips locked with mine until the need to take a breath becomes too much.

Max releases my legs and slowly slides me down his firm body and I enjoy the feel of every hard inch of his body against mine. He cups my face reverently and continues our kiss from before, licking into my mouth, sending fire to my belly, and making my beautiful lace panties soaked. His hands slowly trace down my neck, across my collarbones, and down over my puckered nipples, sending goosebumps skittering across my heated skin.

He draws back slightly and our eyes lock together. "You stole my breath when I saw you crest the dune. You are stunning on an ordinary day. Today ... today you are beyond spectacular." He takes a half-step back and his eyes lazily skate down my body. "This dress is incredible on you." His eyes slide up to my hair. "Your hair is gorgeous, your makeup ... everything is perfect." He glides his hands from my shoulders, down my arms, over the lace cuffs around my biceps, and threads his fingers through mine. He lifts my hands away from my body, holding them out as his eyes peruse me. "I've gotta be the luckiest man alive to have you by my side."

*Can a heart actually melt?*

Because I fear mine is going to end up in a puddle on the floor with his beautiful words and his genuine compliments. I move back into his space, pressing my body to his. "I'm the lucky one, Max. You're the best man a girl could ever ask for."

He looks completely different in his linen suit. I reach up, sliding my hands beneath the lapels of his jacket to slip it from his shoulders. The feel of his hard, defined pecs under my hands is heady.

This man is mine.

All mine.

Nobody else will ever get to touch him like this. I toss his jacket over the back of a nearby chair as I kiss his scruffy jaw, the bristles of his short beard tickling my lips. He sends my heart thumping against my ribs with the way he's studying me, the heat in his eyes, and the obvious bulge in his pants he hasn't bothered to hide.

"Dimples, tell me how to get you out of this beautiful dress."

I turn my back toward my husband and peer at him over my shoulder. "See these tiny pearl buttons?"

He glances down at the buttons, then back up to me with an incredulous look on his face. "Are you fucking with me? I thought these were for decoration and there would be a zipper magically hidden behind them. This has been designed to torture a man." He groans.

I chuckle. "It's designed to build the moment."

He's quiet for a long moment. "There are thirty-five buttons here. I don't have the patience for this. I just want my wife naked." He huffs out but raises his hands to carefully and methodically undo the tiny fasteners, kissing my shoulder as he works, sending goosebumps racing across my body. I step out of my slip-on sandals, leaving me with the simple silver and pearl strands decorating my feet.

The fabric of the bodice gradually loosens, and he slides it away, undoing the hidden zipper in the silk skirt. The gorgeous dress drops to the floor, pooling like snowflakes at my feet. Max steps carefully until he's in front of me, offering his hand to help me step out of the puddle of silk and lace. His heated gaze skims up and down my body, presented only in white lace panties, like a lover's caress, sending sparks shooting to my core.

"No bra." He drops his head back on his shoulders with a groan. I'm lucky my boobs aren't that big and are still perky enough that I could get away without a bra today, relying on the built-in cups in the bodice to keep the girls in place. His heated gaze returns to me. "You're so goddamn beautiful."

My body heats at his words, moisture pooling at the apex of my thighs. "I feel disadvantaged, Husband." Stepping forward, I undo the buttons of his shirt to expose his firm torso to my hungry eyes and slip it from his shoulders, tossing it aside carelessly. "I love these tattoos on you." As I stare into his eyes, I run my fingers across his abs and the muscles quiver in response to my delicate touch.

Dropping my eyes down, I work to open his belt and linen pants; his penis makes a notable bulge and I'm eager to get my hands on the steely shaft. His pants and boxer briefs drop to the floor, and he toes off his shoes to step out of the loose fabric. He removes his socks and then returns to stand at his full height in front of me. I admire his body; his muscular legs, his veiny forearms, his trim, firm body up to his scruff-covered jaw, and those incredible hazel eyes that change color depending on his mood. "Your body is perfection to me, but," I press my hand against his heart, feeling it beat steadily. "I meant what I said today. It's what's inside that made me fall in love with you."

Neither of us wastes another moment as we both step forward simultaneously, crashing our bodies and mouths together. Everywhere he touches me, he leaves a trail of heat and want, building my body to the point where I think I could explode before he even gets close to touching my pussy. His thumbs tuck into each side of my panties and he slides them down my legs and I step out of the flimsy lace. Max fingers the jewelry I wore in place of shoes for the ceremony.

"These are fucking sexy. They're staying on." His hands glide up the inside of my thighs, reaching their apex, his fingers sliding through my pussy lips and then pushing inside me hard and without warning, forcing the air from my lungs. I drop my head back on my shoulders as my mouth drops open in a silent moan. Spreading my legs open, I grasp his hair as he moves in to tease my clit with his talented tongue.

"Such a good girl," he whispers against the bundle of nerves. I love having his mouth on me. He nudges my clit with his nose, drawing in a deep breath. "I love your scent. Whether you're fresh from the shower, after your run, and most definitely when you're horny." His voice is gruff with need to match mine.

"You make me horny, Husband. Whenever I'm around you, I need you inside me," I whisper, gripping onto his hair as a shiver racks my body.

# CHAPTER 50

## —max—

I *NEED* TO BE INSIDE MY WIFE.

It's a desperation to consummate our marriage in the most primal way. As I fuck my fingers into her tight, hot pussy, my dick throbs to get inside her silky heat. "Be a good girl and come for me, Molly." I grit out roughly and then suck the bundle of nerves, hard. Her hands grip my hair tighter, and I'll be surprised if she hasn't pulled out half of the strands. Her legs tremble and I know I need to give my girl support, or she'll collapse. Wrapping my free arm around her tight ass, I maintain the speed and pressure of my fingers and tongue, feeling her walls flutter. Peering up her willowy frame, her stomach muscles quiver and her breasts heave with every panting breath she takes.

*Fucking beautiful.*

I grasp her ass cheek tightly in my hand and bite her clit and am rewarded with a long throaty groan and her muscles strangling my fingers as they tighten with her orgasm. Her cum coats my digits beautifully, dripping down my hand. Holding my fingers inside her, I lap at her orgasm and then slowly slide out of her pussy as her shudders lessen and climb to my feet.

"Oh my God. That was outstanding, Husband of mine," she sighs. Her dazed eyes slide to mine and a sex-drunk smile touches her lips. I love her like this and if I can keep her this way for the rest of my days, I'll consider myself a fortunate man.

Reaching for her ass, I lift her, positioning my cock at her entrance as she wraps her arms around my neck and her legs around my waist. Her tits press against my chest, our hearts both beating a heavy staccato. Locking my gaze on hers, I notch my cock at her center and slide into her welcoming heat. Her moan mingles with my groan as we join in the way nature intended a man and woman to join.

"I fucking love being inside you," my lips touch hers as I whisper. I lick inside her mouth as I lift her and thrust back inside, seating myself deep. Her mouth drops open on a mewl and her pussy tightens around my shaft. I drop my mouth to her neck and bite the tendon there, which rewards me with another squeeze around my cock. "Bounce on my cock, Dimples."

Gripping her fine ass, I help her rise and fall on my dick, our heavy breaths filling each other's mouths as the sound of skin slapping against skin fills the quiet of the room. "Max, I'm gonna come again," Molly whispers against my lips, pressing closer to take my mouth in a fierce kiss. I match her need with my own as our tongues tangle and taste, teeth clash and bite, and lips suck and soothe. She breaks apart in my arms, shattering into oblivion, while I grit my teeth to hold back my release. I don't want to come yet. I don't want this to be over so soon. For our first time as husband and wife, I need to stay inside her for as long as possible.

Holding still inside her as the aftershocks rack her body, I trace my hand up her delicate spine and grasp her gorgeous hair, dragging her head back to expose her throat to me. "Such a good girl. The way you come all over my cock," I whisper against her burning skin, followed by nips and sucks of her sweet flesh as her pussy tightens around me.

She fucking loves it when I praise her. This woman was made for me. "Hold on." I swivel and walk the few steps to the California King bed. Holding the back of her head, I carefully lower us both, keeping my cock buried deep inside my wife.

Cradled between Molly's thighs, my dick snugly wrapped in her heat, I rest on my elbows and peer down into her lust-filled gaze. She smiles at me full of love and sifts her fingers through the short strands of my hair.

"I love how you love me, Max." She presses up, landing a chaste kiss on my mouth. "I love you."

Goosebumps spread out across my burning flesh as my cock swells with her words. Words that are full of heart and honesty. Smoothing her hair away from her face, my eyes track her delicate features, eventually locking on her pewter-colored eyes. "I plan on loving you exactly like this until I take my last breath. You are everything to me, Molly. I love you, Dimples." Dropping my head, we kiss.

Tenderly, slowly. Caressing inside each other's mouth with loving strokes.

Her body arches into mine and I slowly slide out of heaven and then glide back in, pressing to the base of my shaft. My heavy balls slap against Molly's ass and she tightens her legs around my middle, her feet pressing into my ass. Her hands slide from around my neck, taking up their place wrapped around my back, her fingers tickling up my spine to rest on my shoulder blades. My muscles shift and flex with each measured thrust of my hips. Perspiration coats our skin and the scent of sex saturates the air.

In. Out. I grind, I push, I thrust.

Building us both higher, closer to release.

Skin against skin, Molly matches me stroke for stroke, her moans and pants building with my own. My heart hammers against my rib cage as though it's trying to break free and live inside her. She figuratively has my heart; she may as well literally have it, too. If I could reach inside my chest and give it to her, I would; knowing she would keep it safe and take tender care of it. Our tongues dance in time with our hips, our bodies moving in natural sync as we both build. "C'mon, Molly, choke my cock like a good girl."

She cries out, her pussy gripping my shaft like a vise. Her hands move up to pull on my hair. "Your filthy words make me so hot."

I reach between us, finding her needy clit and rubbing tight circles around it to push her over the edge. Her legs tighten around my hips as her body presses further into mine and she shatters beautifully. Her head pressed back into the mattress; her mouth dropped open seductively on a silent moan.

I grit my teeth through a couple more strokes. My balls draw up, my cock pulses, and my cum finally empties from my body to hers. I throw my head back with a long groan, the muscles in my neck tensing and straining as she shifts with me to kiss and lick my burning skin.

Sucking in lungfuls of necessary oxygen, I drop my head down to hers and kiss her. I give her everything I have from the deepest part of my soul, from the core of my very being. I desperately need to show her exactly what she means to me.

What her promises today mean to me.

Drawing back, my gaze searches her angelic face, finally stopping on her eyes. I bring her left hand to my mouth and kiss the rings that show everyone she's mine.

"Today's been incredible. The words we shared and the papers we signed locking us together in the eyes of our family and friends and the law. But this. What we shared just now. This is our true bond." Her eyes go soft as a tender smile touches her lips. "You generously taking me inside not only your body, but your mind, your heart, and your soul is what solidifies our connection today and for our future." I lay her hand on my heart and press the palm of mine to hers. "The love we share only grows stronger and more powerful, just as our bond does." I press my lips to hers and then whisper against the puffy pillows, "I love you with everything I have. Everything I am. Today and forevermore."

*epilogue*

# CHAPTER 51

## *—molly—*

I DON'T KNOW WHAT'S WRONG WITH ME. I HAD A GREAT SLEEP AND YET I'm exhausted down to my bones. My boobs are sore, and my stomach feels bloated. Everything smells disgusting, except for Max. I flop back onto the bed. Maybe I'm finally getting my period; it's been such a long time since I had one, I think I've forgotten what they're like. Excitement bubbles at the idea of getting my period, the first one since my birth control ran out just before our wedding because that will mean we can get pregnant.

With the way I'm feeling, there's no way I can peel myself away from this cocoon today. I roll over with a huff and snuggle into Max's warm body. He automatically welcomes me into his space, wrapping his arm around me and tugging me in close.

"You okay, Dimples?" Tears spring to my eyes. He's always asking if I'm okay. He cares deeply for me and reminds me every single day with every little thing he does for me. Moisture drips down the side of my face, landing on Max's bare chest. He pulls away slightly and tilts my chin up with his fingers so he can study me closely. "What's wrong?"

My bottom lip quivers. "Nothing. It's just really sweet how you love and care for me."

He chuckles. "Always, Molly. You know that. Why are you crying about it?" He looks thoroughly perplexed.

I shrug, awkwardly. "I'm just not feeling myself, I guess. It's coming up to the anniversary of the accident and I think I'm finally getting my period. So maybe that's why I'm feeling blah."

His eyes go soft, and he pulls me in tight, kissing the top of my head. I rest my ear over his beautiful heart, listening to its strong and steady beat. The heart he says beats only for me. I smooth my hand over his taut stomach and sigh.

"I'm here, Dimples. Whatever you need." He kisses the top of my head, tightening his hold.

My lips spread in a genuine smile, and I tilt my head back to look up at the man who is everything to me. "I know. Thank you. Have I told you lately how much I love you?"

He grins at me, raising his eyebrows. "Not today."

"I feel like my heart's going to explode with the amount of love I have for you. Like it's too big to fit inside my body." I push up to lay a kiss on my husband's tempting lips.

"That's a lot of love." He returns my kiss with interest, stroking his tongue into my mouth.

I lay my head back on his chest. "Can we just lie like this for a little while?"

"We can lie like this for however long you need." His hand comes up to stroke my hair slowly. He caresses me down my back, then starts back at the top of my head and repeats the process over and over. Long, gentle strokes.

I slowly come into wakefulness. I must have fallen back to sleep, which isn't a surprise. Max is gone, leaving me alone in bed.

He steps through the door from the bathroom, a towel wrapped around his slim hips, water droplets running down his smooth skin as he uses a second towel to dry his hair. He beams at me, then kneels on the edge of the bed, dropping to his hands to crawl toward me. Skimming his finger across my forehead, he pushes my bangs away from my eyes. "How are you feeling?"

I smile softly. "Better, thank you. Sorry about my mini-meltdown."

"You can have a mega meltdown if you need to. I'm here for all of it. You need to allow yourself some grace as you come up to the first anniversary. Take some time for yourself. Do what you need for your emotional health." He leans forward and presses a soft kiss to my temple. "Anything you need from me, just let me know."

I nod as I soak up his warmth and affection. "Thank you." I stretch out. "What time is it?"

"Almost twelve."

I fly into a panic, scooting out of bed quickly. "Oh my God. We're going to be late." I quickly grab some clothes. "I'll be quick, I promise."

Max chuckles at me as I run around our bedroom naked. "No need to rush, Dimples," he calls out as I jump into the shower.

I quickly wash my body, avoiding getting my hair wet, then climb out to dry off and get dressed. Max leans against the doorjamb with his arms crossed, watching me dress. His eyes singeing my flesh. Once I'm dressed, I step into his body and wrap my arms around him. "Come on. I'm ready." I land a kiss on his lips, planning to pull away quickly so we can get moving, but he wraps his arms around me and deepens the kiss.

I sigh.

My entire body sags against his and sighs. I don't know how I ever survived without Max's kisses. He gentles the kiss and pulls away slightly. I slowly open my eyes to find his affectionate smile.

"C'mon, let's go." He grasps my hand, and we make our way out of our bedroom.

Yesterday, I used my grandmother's recipe to make shortbread, so I collect it from the kitchen and meet Max at his car. It doesn't take long and we're arriving at Mom and Dad's house. "We're the last ones here."

"It's okay, Dimples. Stop worrying."

"I hate to be late. It's rude."

Max presses a tender kiss against my temple and rests his hand on the small of my back. "Mom sets a loose time for lunch. Any time around this time is fine." He slides his hand across to my opposite hip and drags me in close. "Come on."

We make our way inside. The front of the house is quiet, meaning everyone's already in the dining room at the back of the house, probably wondering where we are. Holding my hand, Max leads me through the neat home to the back room which overlooks the deck. It only takes a moment for his family to realize we're here. They've been incredible to me, and I love having pedicure afternoons with Sarah and Emma. They've taken me into the fold as if I've always been part of their tight-knit family. I even call Mr. and Mrs. Stanfield, Mom and Dad, which I know delights Max's mom to no end.

"I'm sorry we're late. It was completely my fault," I say to everyone as I place the shortbread on the sideboard.

"Oh, don't be silly. When you get here, you get here." Mom cups my face, studying me closely, then places the back of her hand against my forehead. "Are you feeling okay? You look a little peaked."

I hold on to her wrist and smile. "I'm feeling better than I was this morning." I glance at my husband. "Max let me sleep in a little, which helped."

"Come and take a seat," Emma calls out, patting the seat next to her. I move around the table, kissing everyone hello. Emma's boys must be with their father and Cristo must have Kenny this weekend because they're not here today. I miss them terribly on the weekends they're not with us, but today I'm in tears at their absence. *What the hell is wrong with me?* "Are you okay?" Emma asks as she tucks a lock of loose hair behind my ear, her worried eyes studying my face.

"Yeah, I just really miss the kids when they're not here and today, for some reason, I want to cry because I miss them so much." A small smile graces Emma's face as her eyes go soft.

Max sits next to me, and his hand smooths up and down my back in a soothing caress. He leans across and kisses my temple, then turns toward the table. "It's coming up to the anniversary of the accident and Molly's feeling emotional. I told her she needs to be gentle with herself." His family knows my story now. Everything. And all of my worry that people would pity me if they knew how I grew up and everything I lost was a waste of time. Not once did anyone in this family show me pity. They showed compassion and understanding. They showed kindness and care, just like Max did when he found out. Not once did I ever feel judged or pitied; not even for one single second.

"Well, then." Sarah breaks the silence. "I think we need a pedi afternoon. What do you think, Em?"

"Sounds perfect. How about Wednesday afternoon? Can you get off early?" she asks Sarah.

"Definitely. I'll start early and then we can take our girl here out for pedis, followed by coffee and cake."

Em turns to Theo. "Do you mind watching the kids on Wednesday afternoon?"

He leans forward, kissing her tenderly on the lips. "Of course not. I'll collect them from school so you can go straight there."

And plans are made without a second thought. Max's sisters knew I needed support, and they were more than happy to provide it, as usual. I love this incredible family, their warmth, their love, and their support for one another.

When I arrive at *R&R Nail Salon*, Sarah and Emma are waiting out front for me. I almost canceled at the last minute, because I feel so damn tired. The girls take one look at me as I drag my ass toward them and frown. "You look worse today. Maybe you should see a doctor," Sarah suggests.

My shoulders slump. "Thanks. I feel terrible."

Emma slides her arm through mine, and we stroll inside the salon for our appointment. "I only came because I knew I'd only have to sit. I don't think I can manage anything more than that."

Sarah opens the door, and we step inside, finding Phillipa waiting for us with a smile. "Hi, ladies. Come through. We're ready for you."

We follow her to our designated chairs, and she offers us our usual Mimosa. "Do you mind if I only have juice today? I don't think I can stomach any alcohol." Em and Sarah glance at each other.

Phillipa nods. "Of course." She turns on her heel to get our drinks and I settle into the comfortable chair.

Emma reaches across, laying her hand on my arm, her eyebrows drawn tight. "Tell me how else you're feeling, Molly."

I blow out a long breath. "I'm so freaking tired. Like I'm dragging myself through the day. Smells make me feel nauseous and my boobs are so goddamn tender, Max only has to brush against me, and I feel like crying. Talk about crying. I'm teary all the damn time." I gesture toward my stomach. "And see this. I've never been bloated like this. It's so freaking uncomfortable." I swallow back the tears that are welling in my eyes. I don't want to come across like a total nut job. "Today's the anniversary of the accident, and on top of that, I think I'm getting my period." The tears I was trying so hard to keep at bay drop over my bottom lashes.

"Oh, Molly." Sarah wraps her arms around me, stroking down my hair. "You poor thing."

"Uh … Mols." Sarah pulls away and we look across at Emma, who's watching us with a smile. "I don't think you'll be getting your period anytime soon."

"Why not?"

She glances at Sarah, raising her eyebrows. "I think you might be pregnant."

My heart races with her words. Could that be why I've been feeling this way? "Really? What makes you think that?"

"Everything you just said. I think we need to stop at the drugstore after we've finished here and get you a pregnancy test."

My lips stretch into a smile for the first time today and my wide eyes slide from Sarah to Emma and back again. "Shit. I didn't even think of that. The doctor said it could take a while to get pregnant after stopping the shot. I didn't expect it to happen this fast because I haven't had a period yet." My mind's racing a million miles a minute as thoughts rush in and out of my head. "Oh my God. What if I'm pregnant? Max will be over the moon."

The three of us squeal a little in excitement. I'm not sure I can sit here for the time we need for our pampering session; I want to race across to the drugstore immediately. It would certainly turn what's been an emotionally draining day into a happy one if I found out I was pregnant. And help balance out such a terrible memory with a great one.

With fresh polish on our toes, the three of us exit the salon and make our way across the street to the drugstore. Emma takes us straight to the aisle with the pregnancy tests. I shake my head at the logic of their placement. Fancy having them right next to the condoms.

"There's so many to choose from." The selection is overwhelming. The array of boxes with various calls to action. I look at Emma and Sarah. "Any you guys recommend?"

Emma deftly collects one from the shelf. "Here. This one is effective and straightforward. Pee on the stick and a minute later, voilà, you'll have an answer." She collects a couple more boxes from the shelf, handing them to me. "Here, it's a good idea to have extra, just in case."

We head to the counter so I can pay for my purchases, and I say my goodbyes to Max's sisters. "Thank you for listening to me and for this." I hold up my paper bag filled with pregnancy tests.

"You're welcome." Emma leans forward, hugging me tight.

"Make sure you let us know." Sarah also hugs me goodbye.

"I promise you ladies will be the first to know." I chuckle. "Well, after Max, of course."

## CHAPTER 52

### —*max*—

I HAVE A STUNNING ARRANGEMENT OF PINK ROSES, WINE, AND HER favorite ice cream ready for when my girl gets home. Cristo made Molly's favorite dish, Pasticcio, and dropped it over for our dinner tonight. I check my phone; I still have time. The girls' pedicures and coffee and cake always take a while.

I head through to our bedroom to shower and change before Molly gets home, then I'll put the dinner in the oven to reheat as per Cristo's instructions—he was very particular, which means I need to be careful not to mess it up. I hear the front door open and close as I'm pulling out a change of clothes, so I head toward the front of the house to investigate. Molly shouldn't be home yet.

"Hey, you're home early. Are you feeling okay?" She's been feeling like shit for a couple of weeks now, only admitting it to me on Sunday, but I've been watching her, and it's been going on for a while. I lean forward to kiss her.

She wraps her arms around my neck, pulling me into her, and deepens the kiss, something hitting me at the top of my back. "Hey. I … I needed to come home to do something." Her eyes are brighter than they were when she left the workshop to meet the girls, which is a good sign. Today, especially, has been tough for her.

I wrap my arm around her and lead her deeper into our home. "What do you need to do, Dimples? Can I help?"

Her shoulders drop and she smiles at me. God, I love this woman's smiles and they've been missing for the last week, which has been completely understandable, but I have missed them.

"You know I love you, right?" She presses her hand against my stomach and lays a chaste kiss on my jaw. Holding the paper bag up, she grins. "While I was out, I was telling your sisters how I've been feeling." I nod. I'm glad she has them to talk to. "Emma suggested that I'm probably not getting my period because I may already be pregnant." Her voice rises at the end of the sentence in excitement, her sculpted eyebrows rising.

My eyebrows must be almost touching my hairline as my heart picks up speed. I crouch down slightly, ensuring my eyes are at the same level as Molly's. "Do you think you could be pregnant?"

She holds up the paper bag. "Only one way to find out."

I run my hands through my hair. "Fuck. Wouldn't that be something?"

"Wouldn't it?" She shakes the bag. "I'm gonna go pee on a stick." She spins on her heel toward the bathroom and I follow directly behind her. She steps into the bathroom and closes the door, jamming it into my body and she chuckles. "What are you doing? I have to pee."

I take a step back. "Yeah, right. Sorry." I quickly kiss her. "Will you be able to pee on demand? Like, do you need to run the water or something?"

Molly giggles, pushing against my chest until I clear the doorway. "I'll work it out."

I quickly give her one more kiss, then step out of the bathroom so she can get down to business. I press my ear up against the bathroom door; I don't want to miss anything, just in case she calls out for help. It seems to take forever before I hear the toilet flush, then the water run as she washes her hands. I don't wait to be invited, I open the door and step inside. A small white stick rests on the vanity. My eyes snap up to Molly and we share a smile. I turn her around until she's facing me properly and clutch her hips to pull her in close.

"I want you to know I love you. No matter the result on that stick; whether it's positive or negative, my love for you isn't based on the lines that show or don't show." I press my forehead to hers, keeping my eyes locked with my wife's.

She wraps her arms around my neck. "I know, Max. I hadn't even considered that I might be pregnant until Emma suggested the possibility. I'm excited at the prospect of being pregnant already. Of changing today from one of my saddest to one of my happiest."

Her body's vibrating with the possibility of a positive result. I hope for her sake it's positive. She deserves to have every happiness. I swipe my lips against hers. Every time I do it, my entire body revels in the feel of her lips beneath mine. She opens for me with a sigh, and I slide inside, moving my hands to cup her gorgeous ass and drag her into my body. I pour my love for her into the kiss and give her yet another piece of my soul.

We pull apart slowly and catch each other's gaze. Without speaking, we agree it's time to check the result. Molly picks it up, holding it between us, and we both look down at the same time. Our eyes snap up, finding each other, matching smiles on our faces. I lift my girl off her feet and take off running through the house, cheering and hollering like we've won the World Cup. Molly giggles like crazy, holding on for dear life, as I run around our house like a maniac.

Then it dawns on me: I need to be fucking gentle with her.

I shouldn't be manhandling her like a fucking Neanderthal. I carefully put her on her feet and cup her face in my rough hands, feeling her silky skin. "We're gonna have a baby!" I exclaim against her lips, our noses touching.

Molly nods with a smile on her face. "We're gonna have a baby."

I press my mouth to hers, fierceness in my kiss. She meets my fierceness, and we kiss with teeth clashing and tongues tangling for long moments, our bodies pressed together as tight as they can be. This woman is my whole fucking world, and she's already given me so much. Now she's going to give me the ultimate gift of a child. "Thank you, Dimples. I don't know how I'll ever thank you for everything you've given to me."

*I kiss her again. My wife, my forever, the mother of my child.*

*moonlit*

# KISSES

## DEBRA ST JAMES

# CHAPTER 1

## —max—

"Fuck!" Goddamn Lego blocks will be the death of me. I swear I'd rather hit my thumb with a mallet repeatedly than step on fucking Lego blocks.

"Mommy! Daddy said fuck."

I spin around. "Shit!" Traitor. Doesn't he know us guys have to stick together? We're outnumbered in this house, and I'm convinced the baby Molly's carrying now will be yet another girl. You won't hear me complaining, though. I love that we have mostly girls in the house, though I'm not sure I'll feel that way when they're older.

"Mommy! Daddy said shit," he calls out, dropping me in it yet again.

I bend down so I can confront him man to man. "Nicholas. Shhhh." I hold my finger in front of my lips.

His eyes twinkle at me. He knows exactly what he's doing. "But you're not supposed to swear in front of us." He shrugs.

"I didn't see you there so it doesn't count."

My sexy wife steps into the living room with her delicate eyebrows raised as she shakes the swear jar. "Pay up."

I give my son the evil eye as I walk toward my heavily pregnant wife. "How are you feeling, Dimples?" I lean in to brush my lips against hers. Pulling back, I study her face, my eyes scanning her features. Her body sags slightly as she gifts me her dimples.

"I'm fine. Stop worrying about me."

"I'll never stop worrying about you. You and our kids. You're all too precious to me so don't ask me to stop."

Her eyes go soft and glassy, and I step in to cup her face in my hands. "Thank you, Max." Her expression changes to one of mischief. "But don't think you can distract me from collecting payment." She shakes the damn jar again. "Pay up, husband of mine."

A bundle of black fur comes careening around the corner, then rushes up the couch, leaping across to the curtain, which she swiftly climbs until she reaches the rod. She sits, peering down at us, her body balancing with ease.

"Come back, Licorice." Aurora calls out as she runs into the room, stopping inside the doorway to scan for her poor cat. She glances between me and her mother, then settles her gaze on me as she places her hands on her hips. "Daddy. Have you been saying naughty words again?"

I bend down to scoop her up. "Yes. I have. I'm sorry."

She holds my cheeks in her little hands. "That's okay, say the naughty words, Daddy. I want to go to Disneyland," my daughter says to me with a cheeky smile, showing off dimples to match her mother's. While Nicholas is a mini-me, Aurora is the spitting image of her mother.

And herein lies the problem. My kids love to catch me swearing because the swear jar is going to pay for our trip to Disneyland—Molly's idea. Any tiny indiscretion, the kids are ready to pounce, even if I whisper the words under my breath. I dig into my pocket, pull out a handful of notes, and hold them up to show the room. "How about I just put all of this in now and I'll be covered for the day?"

All three of them shake their heads. "Uh, uh. That's not how it works and you know it." Nicholas folds his arms across his chest, using his thumbnail to scrape his bottom lip. Molly glances at me with tight lips, trying to hold back her smile at his action. "You can put all of that in now if you like. But then when you swear again, I'm gonna have to ask you to pay up again."

I stare at my six-year-old son. Where the fuck did he come from? He's too damn smart for his own good. He's a master negotiator and doesn't miss a trick. Pride fills me with how clever he is for his age. I'm pretty certain I wasn't that switched on when I was six. I peel off one note. "Okay. I'll only put one note in this time."

"Make that two. You said fuck *and* shit," Nicholas smugly reminds me.

I point at him and turn to Molly. "Did you hear that? He swore!

He should have to pay up, too." I love messing around like this with my family. Molly shakes her head at us with a giggle.

Luna toddles in, making grabby hands at Molly. My wife reaches down and picks her up, resting her on her hip. "I hungy, Mommy." Luna is a mix of both of us. She has Molly's gray eyes and dimples, but my dark hair.

"Daddy, you're silly," Aurora says as she wriggles for me to let her down.

"I know. But only for you guys," I respond, mussing up her almost-white hair. "C'mon. I'll make us lunch and Mommy can sit and rest for a little while."

Molly gives me a grateful smile as she drops to the couch. I push the ottoman closer and lift her feet, then give her a quick kiss and herd the kids into the kitchen.

I clap my hands together. "Okay. Who wants what on their sandwich?" I already know what they're going to choose. They generally choose the same thing each time I'm making lunch because they don't trust me to make them anything else.

"Peanut butter and jelly!" calls Nicholas.

Luna raises her hands in the air, so I pick her up and place her in her high chair after blowing raspberries on her cheek, causing her to giggle and squirm. "Stop it, Daddy!" I strap her in, then press a kiss to the top of her hair, drawing in a deep breath of her baby smell.

"What do you want, Luna?"

"Jelly!" She shoots her little hands up in the air and kicks her feet.

"How about you, Rory?" Aurora loves her nickname, especially since she's more of a tomboy. She loves to help me when I do simple repairs on our cars.

"Cheese and butter, please, Daddy." So damn polite, this one. I lean across and kiss her temple.

"Alright. Let's go!" I wash my hands and then gather what I need.

I make the sandwiches, cut up some fruit, and give each of the kids a glass of cold water. I make cheese, pickle, and turkey sandwiches for Molly and me, rinse some raspberries for her, and pour a couple of glasses of iced water. As I'm about to put Molly's lunch on a tray for her, she waddles into the kitchen, holding her back. She gives me a tired smile. She's not getting a lot of sleep at this point. With only three weeks until our fourth child is born, she's struggling. I try to help her out as much as I can, but I can't help with the growing of a baby.

"Come and sit here, Dimples." I pull out her usual chair and guide her across to it, pushing it in as she sits. Kissing the top of her head, I quickly grab her lunch and place it in front of her.

"Thank you." She tilts her head back with a smile and I can't resist kissing my gorgeous wife. I swipe my tongue across her lips and she opens to welcome me. I slide my tongue inside to taste her. Her hand combs through my hair and a moan escapes. My dick instantly reacts, pressing against the zipper of my jeans. Molly's been insatiable through this entire pregnancy. *Lucky me!*

Little girl giggles break through the lust haze that I always fall into when I'm kissing, or anywhere near my wife. I give Molly a final chaste kiss and peer across at our daughters, who are giggling like crazy.

"Why you always kiss Mommy?" Luna says as she scrunches up her tiny nose.

"Because I love Mommy so much." I wink at Molly, then grab my lunch and join my family at the dining setting Theo made and gifted to us when we moved into this house. The place I bought was way too small for our growing family, so we found a bigger place not that far from the old one.

"Daddy, can I show you the new building I made?" Nicholas peers at me hopefully.

I nod as I chew my sandwich. "Of course. Eat up and you can show me once we've cleaned up from lunch."

We all finish our lunch and I set up Molly on the back deck with her sketch pad. The girls play in their cubby house, lovingly made by their cousin, Lachlan, and Uncle Theo, while Nicholas shows me his latest construction.

He points his little finger. "See that part there, Daddy?" I follow with my eyes and nod. "Watch this." He winds something around the back of the building and a bridge drops down, exposing two large doors.

My eyebrows shoot up to my hairline and I look at my son with admiration. "That's really cool. How did you make that happen?"

The smile that lights up his face is spectacular as he explains how he made the bridge. The way he creates stuff out of Lego blocks is so fucking clever. "You're really smart. You know that, right?"

"I want to build giant buildings when I grow up." He stands up as tall as possible, reaching for the sky to demonstrate how tall his buildings will be. "Do you think I'll be able to do that?" he asks with eyes full of dreams and a heart full of hope.

"I don't see why not." I wave my hand toward his latest construction. "Look at what you can do and you're only six. Imagine what you'll be able to do when you're a grownup. The sky's the limit, Nick."

"Do you really think so?"

"Absolutely. I can't wait for you to walk your mom and me through a building you make." I tug him in tight and hug him close, kissing the top of his head. I rest my cheek there for a moment, taking in his little boy smell.

# CHAPTER 2

## *—molly—*

"Okay, all the kids are in bed," Max reports as he sits on the couch and places my feet on his lap. He takes one aching foot and methodically massages and rubs every single inch until my eyes roll to the back of my head.

I moan, "Your fingers feel like heaven."

He smirks. "I've heard that before." Then he winks at me. God, I love him so much. He's the best husband a girl could ever want, not to mention he's the best daddy I could have ever asked for. His expression turns serious. "How are you feeling, Dimples? You're looking sore and tired."

I sigh. "It's to be expected at this point. I just want this little one to come out." I rub my enormous belly. "It's a struggle to sleep because I can't get comfortable. And even though I'm exhausted, my mind won't shut down." With my toe, I nudge his rock-hard stomach. "I know something that could help me, though." I give him a cheeky grin.

He adjusts himself and raises his eyebrows. "Oh yeah. What might that be?"

He already knows, but he wants to hear me say it. I drop my voice to almost a whisper, "I think you know."

"I think I need you to spell it out for me, Dimples." He glides his hand up my leg beneath my dress, stopping barely an inch from my panties. He has to feel the heat and if he were to run his fingers over the panel covering my most private part, he would feel how soaked my panties are for him already. Just having his hands on me is enough to get me going. I've been particularly horny with this pregnancy. I mean, I'm always horny when my husband's around and my sex drive always increases when I'm pregnant, but this time it's been explosive.

I awkwardly lean forward, running my nose up the side of his cheek, then whisper in his ear, "I need you to fuck me, husband of mine." I pull back enough to see his face. He has one eyebrow raised and his eyes are instantly full of heat for me as he draws in a sharp breath. Wasting no time, he stands from the couch and then leans down to collect me. I giggle. "I can walk, you know. There's no need for you to put your back out carrying a whale." I wrap my arms around his neck.

He stops in his tracks, glaring down at me. "Don't you dare speak about my hot wife like that. She's sexy as fuck and should never be compared to a whale."

I chuckle again, swinging my feet back and forth as he carries me through to our bedroom, his jaw tense. With gentle care, he places me on my feet, then undresses me, stitch by stitch, revealing every single inch of my body, including my extended belly.

I should feel exposed.

I should feel embarrassed by how big I look, but the heat in his gaze as he peruses my body from top to toe leaves no space for any of that. My thighs press together without instruction and judging by the tick in his jaw, he noticed.

"Get up on the bed, on your hands and knees."

I scurry into position as fast as my heavy girth will allow. He helps me get into position; my knees precariously balanced close to the edge of the mattress. I have every faith in my husband that he'll keep me safe and meet my needs at the same time.

The sound of fabric dropping to the floor has me turning my head to watch my hot husband reveal his still-perfect abs at the age of forty-four. I sigh and clench my internal muscles around nothing at the sight of him. He has a few more gray hairs and tattoos now which are completely unrelated to cars. Beneath the tattoo over his heart, he has a list of important dates which include the date he found me sleeping behind his workshop, the day he proposed to me as well as the date we got married, and each of our children's birthdays, all listed in chronological order. We have matching night sky prints for each date on display in the living room.

My eyes drop lower as his heavy dick springs free from his jocks, bobbing against his abdomen and almost reaching his navel. It's already glistening at the tip. I can always count on Max to be ready for me whenever I need.

I glance up at his face, my eyes fixed on his heated gaze, which is locked on my exposed pussy. I catch movement out of my peripheral vision and drop my eyes back down to his cock, which he's taken in hand. As he moves closer to me, he gives it a rough pull and I moan, my eyes dropping closed momentarily.

He's so damn hot.

His long fingers swipe through my folds, and he drops his head back with a groan. He captures my gaze again and holds up his glistening fingers. "Look at how fucking wet you are for me." He tucks the digits in his mouth and sucks on them like they're the tastiest lollipop ever. "So fucking delicious."

He lunges. Yes, lunges at my pussy. His tongue strokes through my folds from bottom to top as his thumbs open me up to him. When he reaches the top, he nips the sensitive bud and finishes with a tight swirl of his tongue.

I drop my head to the bed with a moan and push my hips back. I can't see anything with my enormous belly hanging down. His breath heats my skin as he chuckles at my eagerness.

"C'mon, Max. I need you." I push my hips back again, hoping he'll take the hint. "I'm not up for a long, drawn-out session. I just need you to fuck me hard so I can fall asleep."

Finally, he stops playing with me and notches the head of his cock at my entrance, dragging moisture from my pussy to my asshole and pressing his thumb past the ring of muscle as he pushes his cock in as far as he can go, his pelvis pressed tightly against my ass, his thighs touching mine at every available point. He drops down over me, nipping my shoulder as one hand lands near mine.

"That feel okay, Dimples?" He skates soft kisses along my shoulder and up my neck until he reaches my ear. I tilt my head to the side to give him better access. His hot breath sends goosebumps across my skin. "Because it feels fucking sensational to me," he whispers gruffly as he slides his thumb out slightly and pushes back in, causing me to moan.

I push my hips back as much as he'll allow, which isn't all that much. "So good." I turn my head to the side and Max knows exactly what I want after years of being together. He takes my mouth in a scorching kiss as he slides his thumb in and out of my back entrance, building the heat in my body. I whimper into the kiss, sloppily stroking his tongue with mine, finding it hard to concentrate with the pleasure he's bestowing on my body. Pulling away, he pushes himself up and grips my hip tightly.

"Now be a good girl and take my cock like you're built to do."

He draws out slowly and then slams back into my body. My heavy boobs swing and I shunt up the bed, my breath expelling from my lungs with force. I swing my head to look over my shoulder and the sight that greets me steals my breath. His body's drawn tight like a bow, his veins strained down his neck, his chest glistening with sweat as he drives into me repeatedly. My eyes roll into the back of my head as tingles race down my spine and I fear the orgasm that's building like a freight train is going to split me in half.

He groans, "Fuck! Your pussy's strangling my dick."

I don't even have time to prepare as a white light steals my vision and my body convulses, my toes curling so tight, a cramp explodes through my calf muscle and I cry out. Max stops his movements instantly and I snap my head around to him.

"Don't you dare stop," I order through gritted teeth.

Creases form between his brows and he looks between us as he slides out slowly and back in again. "You okay?"

"Uh-huh." I wiggle my ass back a little more.

He pulls out and then smirks at me as he removes his thumb from my ass, squeezing both of my cheeks, then grasps hold of my hips. He grips hard and then slams into me. If I thought he was pounding into me before, it was nothing compared to what he's doing to my body now.

Sweat coats my skin as my heavy breasts sway with every stroke of his body into mine. I whimper and moan with each thrust as he builds me back up into a second orgasm. He spoils me every time we come together. I've come to expect a minimum of two orgasms, and he's about to send me flying again. My panting breaths can't pull enough oxygen into my lungs and I'm becoming light-headed. Tingles spread out from my middle, reaching to the tips of my fingers and toes as I prepare to go off for a second time.

Max slams into me one last time as I fall apart. The only thing holding me up is his tight grip on my hips. He grunts out his release and his dick grows and pulses inside me, his cum filling me up. Somehow, his grip on me tightens as he presses firmly against my ass. My chest heaves as I work to catch my breath.

"You're squeezing my dick so damn good. I want to live inside your pussy." I chuckle. Only Max could say something like that and make it sound so hot. "Stop laughing, Dimples. It pushes my dick out and I'm not ready to leave."

I glance over my shoulder. "I never want you to leave."

He leans over me, pressing his chest to my back, and I sigh. I love having his body pressed to mine. We always fit together perfectly. He kisses down my spine and lightly smacks my butt cheek.

"I wish I never had to. But we need to get you cleaned up so you can get some sleep." He carefully slides out of my body and then lifts me to carry me into the bathroom.

Max carefully places me on my feet, keeping hold of me until he knows I'm steady, then takes my mouth in a scorching kiss that almost makes my knees buckle. When he pulls away, he winks at me and then leans into the shower.

Before long, steam rises and he guides me inside, where he washes me with care and gentle attention. He fucks me with his fingers until I come again and then leads me out of the shower before I can drop to my knees to reciprocate.

"C'mon, Dimples. Time for sleep. You've got a big day tomorrow, birthday girl." As I snuggle down into my pillow, I have a smile on my face.

*Could my life be any more perfect?*

My husband's arms wrap around me and he lays a soft kiss on my shoulder. "Night, Dimples."

"Mmm. Night, Max," I whisper with a smile.

# CHAPTER 3

## —max—

A LONG, LOW GROAN WAKES ME. I TAKE A MOMENT TO GET MY BEARINGS because it's still dark. The groan happens again and I turn my head toward Molly's side of the bed. Even before I lay my eyes on the empty pillow, I know she isn't there. I climb out of bed and head toward our bathroom, where Molly's bent over, her hands gripping the vanity as though her life depends on it. With my left hand stroking down the center of her spine, I lean down to kiss her shoulder.

"The baby's coming early," she whispers in between sucking in much-needed air.

"How long have you been like this?" I keep stroking her, massaging the dip in her lower back.

"What time is it?"

I step out of the bathroom quickly to grab my cell to check. Four fifteen. I place it on the vanity, so I can keep an eye on the time.

I return my hand to my wife because I need to touch her. I always feel fucking useless when it comes to this part. "It's quarter past four."

"About four and a half hours."

I see fucking red. "Why didn't you fucking wake me up?"

She waves off my question as her nose scrunches up and her back rolls with another wave. She pants through the contraction, taking in short sharp breaths like it's her job. The concentration on her beautiful face takes my breath away. This woman works so hard for this family, for each baby. As soon as she finds out she's pregnant, she only puts the best possible food into her body and makes sure she does everything that's recommended. Every single day, her life revolves around me and the kids. Making our home as comfortable as possible and ensuring we all know that we are the most important people in her world. I've always admired her because she's a beautiful soul, but my admiration for her as a mother is on a whole different level. Our kids are incredibly lucky to have her as their mom, and I'm the luckiest bastard that she agreed to be my wife.

"I thought I had time, but these contractions are out of this world. This little one is in a hurry."

*Fuck.* Maybe I was too rough last night? Guilt moves through me, thick and fast. Our eyes meet in the mirror and she smirks at me.

"I know what you're thinking, Husband. It wasn't your magic cock."

We both chuckle and hers turns into a grimace as she drops over again, her knuckles turning white. If I didn't know the strength of the granite counter of the vanity, I'd worry she was going to break a piece off. "You want me to call Martin and Beth to come over, so I can take you to the hospital?"

She lets out an almighty scream as she scrunches her body tight. Her panting resumes and I quickly press the number for Martin.

No answer.

I know he switches his phone to mute at night because often customers have no sense of time and he's often had people call in the early hours of the morning to fix their hot water or some shit. He wouldn't be expecting a call from us because this little tyke isn't due for another three weeks. Each of our babies has come right on time. I press Beth's number. It rings and rings, but still no answer.

*Fuck!* My parents are on a flight home, so I can't call them. I try calling Holly.

After several rings, her groggy voice comes across the line. "Hello."

"Uh, hey, Holly. I'm sorry to call in the middle of the night, but would you be able to come to watch the kids? Molly's gone int—"

Molly wails again. The cry ripping from her body is exactly the same as when she's pushing during the birth.

*Fuck!*

"I don't think I have time to get to the hospital. The baby's coming. I can feel the head. I know I'm not supposed to push, but I need to push!"

I move down to take a look, and sure enough, I can see the top of the baby's head.

*Fuck!*

"Shit. What should I do?"

She can't have the baby on the bathroom floor. I pick her up and carry her to our bed, placing her down carefully. I grab all the pillows and prop them behind her, then race into the bathroom and collect every towel I can find. Finally, I remember to wash my grease-stained hands, because I'm going to have to deliver this baby myself.

Molly has tears running down her ruddy cheeks, her eyes scrunched tight as she grips her thighs, gritting her teeth through another damn contraction.

"I'm here, Dimples. Hold on to me."

"Max. I can't have our baby here," she cries. "What if something goes wrong?" I pull her into me as best I can and try to soothe her. I've seen what they do and while I'm no expert, I have a rough idea of how to get her through this until help arrives. I remember I'd left Holly on the line and I need to call an ambulance.

"It'll be okay. I'll call an ambulance. They'll probably get here before the baby arrives. Everything will be okay. You'll see." I land a kiss on her dry lips. "I won't let anything happen to either of you. I promise."

I rush into the bathroom and grab my phone. "Holly. You still there?"

"Yeah. I'm on my way." She sounds out of breath and wide awake now. She must have heard everything that was happening.

"Thanks. Use your key to get in so I can stay with Molly." I disconnect the call before she can respond and dial nine-one-one. After I tell them everything they need to know, I focus on my girl, keeping the operator on speaker. I take another peek between her legs and can see more of our baby's head. This is happening faster than I expected.

Molly lets out another wail and scrunches her body tight, bearing down. I count her through, just like the midwives have done in the past, and help her push through the contraction. When it subsides, I kiss my wife and step back into the bathroom to get a wet washcloth to wipe her face. "You're doing great, Dimples."

Our bedroom door swings open to reveal a sleepy-eyed Nicholas rubbing his eyes. "What's happening? Is Mommy hurt? I can hear her crying out." His eyes land on his mother and widen. "Mommy?" A simple whispered word has Molly's head snapping toward her son. "Are you okay?" Tears glisten in his eyes and they snap up to mine. "What's wrong with Mommy?"

"Everything's okay, Nick. The baby's decided it wants to come out now, so I'm just helping Mommy until the ambulance gets here." His eyes drop back to Molly as she grunts, squeezing my hand tight. "Aunty Holly is on her way over to look after you and the girls. Okay?" Nick's eyes snap back up to mine. He's wide awake now.

"Now? The baby's coming now? Shit!"

I don't have time to chastise him for his language and I'm grateful Molly's too busy to have noticed as she pushes through another contraction. She always lays the blame solely at my feet whenever Nick swears and rightly so. He certainly didn't pick it up from her.

I turn my attention back to Molly. "You're doing fantastic, Molly. Such a good girl." I gently glide my fingers through her sweaty hair, pushing it away from her face. Her gorgeous gray eyes flick up to mine and she gives me a tired smile. "Nicholas. Can you go check if your sisters are still sleeping, then go downstairs and turn on the porch light for Aunty Holly?"

His expression changes from one of worry to very serious. "Okay, Daddy." He nods, then takes off and I know I can trust him to do the things I've asked of him.

Molly smiles up at me. "Thank you. I didn't want him to see this."

I kiss the top of her head. "No problem. I didn't want him to see you in pain, either." Another contraction, another push, and more of our baby's head is exposed. "I think I need to move down to the other end. The baby's head is almost all the way out." She whimpers but nods with frightened eyes. "It's okay. The ambulance is on its way. They'll get here in plenty of time."

Molly's eyebrows scrunch down, her eyes close tightly, and she bears down through another contraction. I gently grasp the top of our baby's head, supporting it as the entire head becomes exposed. I do as I've seen the doctors and midwives do before, checking there's nothing in the baby's mouth and making sure the umbilical cord isn't wrapped around the neck. My heart's beating a million miles a minute as I take in our baby's scrunched-up face. "Oh, Mols. The baby's beautiful. White hair, just like yours."

We work together, Molly pushing as I guide our baby out of the warm cocoon of its mother. I can't believe I'm delivering our baby. With one final push, our baby is completely free and I carefully cradle it in my shaky hands as it lets out a loud cry. I take a shaky breath in relief that everything seems to be okay and place the baby on Molly's chest. She instantly wraps her arms protectively around our new addition, kissing the top of its head. Her relief shows as her body relaxes and an exhausted smile settles on her lips. She glances up at me, gifting me her gorgeous dimples.

"You did so good, Dimples. I'm so fucking proud of you." I brush her sweaty hair away from her face and plant a kiss on her overheated skin. Moving the baby's leg slightly to check the sex of our little bundle, my breath gushes out with a chuckle and my eyes move back to my wife. "We have another girl!" I lean down and press a kiss on both of my girls as Molly chuckles. I place one of the towels I collected earlier over our little girl to keep her warm as she squints her eyes up at Molly.

"Poor Nicholas. Three sisters," she says to our baby while still chuckling, so I don't think she feels all that bad for him.

Movement in the doorway catches my eye and I glance up to find Holly standing there, her hands held over her heart, a soft look in her eyes. "Congratulations," she whispers, then thumbs over her shoulder. "The ambulance has just turned up."

I nod. "Thanks. Can you show them up?"

"Sure." She leaves us alone again and we glance at each other before focusing back on our brand-new daughter.

"Celeste was in a bit of a hurry," Molly whispers as she brushes her finger over the creases between our little girl's eyebrows. We already had our names picked out, wanting to make sure we were prepared either way. We've always opted to leave finding out the sex of our babies until we deliver. The surprise is something we love.

"She certainly was." I kiss my wife. "Happy birthday, Molly."

She grins up at me. "This is the best birthday present I've ever received." She chuckles.

I can't believe she can smile and laugh so easily after what her body's just been through. She's a fucking miracle.

# CHAPTER 4

## —molly—

THE AMBULANCE OFFICERS HELPED ME DELIVER THE PLACENTA AND made sure everything was fine with Celeste and me. They still offered to take me to the hospital for a more thorough check even though they said everything was perfect. Everything feels great, and we have an appointment with my obstetrician the day after tomorrow, so I'm happy to stay where I am for the time being.

Max finally got in touch with Martin and asked him and Beth to stop by the furniture store to buy us a new mattress because ours is ruined. Now I'm cuddled up on our new bed with our four kids and my favorite man in the entire world. This has got to be what heaven feels like.

"Mommy. When can I hold Celeste?" Aurora asks as she peers down at her new sister. She was most upset that she missed the event, but to say I was grateful the girls slept through the whole thing is a gross understatement. I'm still concerned about the long-term effects of Nicholas seeing me during labor; it had to have been traumatic for the poor boy. His little face was full of fear when he saw what was happening. I run my hand over his silky hair and he glances up at me with a small smile.

My eyes glide to Aurora. "In a little while. Celeste just had a drink, so we need to let that settle in her tummy first. Alright?"

She nods. "Okay."

We fall into a comfortable silence, all of our eyes glued to Celeste. I can faintly hear Holly, Martin, and Beth chatting downstairs. My eyes are feeling heavy and I can't hold in the yawn that forces its way out. I'm completely wrung out and exhausted after only getting a couple of hours of sleep last night.

"Okay, kids. Give Mommy and Celeste a kiss and cuddle, then you can go downstairs and play with Grandpa and Granny and Aunty Holly. Mommy needs to have a nap." Max rounds up the kids, holding them up to me so I can kiss each one in turn.

Luna's grabby hands accidentally catch Celeste's eye as she tries to hold her new sister's face for a kiss. Celeste gives a little whimper, her hand swiping in the vicinity of her eyes but not quite making it.

"I sorry, baby." Luna's little bottom lip trembles and her eyes rise to mine. "I didn't mean to hurted the baby."

I give her a gentle smile. "I know, Luna. It's alright. You just need to be careful. Okay?"

"Otay, Mommy."

Max draws Luna back to his chest, kissing her temple. "Celeste's okay, and I know it was an accident. Come on. Let's go downstairs."

I give him a grateful smile as he herds the kids out of our bedroom and downstairs, Luna on his hip, Aurora holding his hand, and Nicholas following behind. Nicholas pauses at the doorway. "Are you gonna be okay, Mommy?"

"I'm perfectly fine, Nick. I promise." I smile at him to reassure him that I'm fine.

He smiles in return, so much like his father, and follows his daddy and sisters downstairs. I know the kids will be in expert hands with Dad, Beth, and Holly, so I shimmy down further under the covers, ensuring Celeste is tucked safely by my side.

I release a heavy sigh and lay on my side to watch her sleep. Her little lips twitch and her eyes move back and forth behind her closed lids. I wonder what little babies dream of?

Max saunters back into our bedroom, quietly closing our door behind him, and climbs into bed on the other side of Celeste. He tucks his finger inside her hand and she tightens her hold around his digit. His finger looks so large, trapped in her tiny hand.

"She's beautiful, just like her mommy." He leans forward, pressing a kiss to the top of her head, just as he's done to me and the kids a thousand times before. It has no less effect on me today than it's always had since the first time he kissed my forehead. He captures my gaze. "I love you, Dimples. I'm so fucking proud of you."

"I couldn't have done it without you. Thank you for always being by my side." I press forward, being careful not to squish Celeste, and press a grateful kiss to my husband's lips.

# pinterest

I put together a Pinterest board for Max and Molly's story. If you're interested, you can check it out here:
*https://tinyurl.com/moonlitkisses-pinterest*

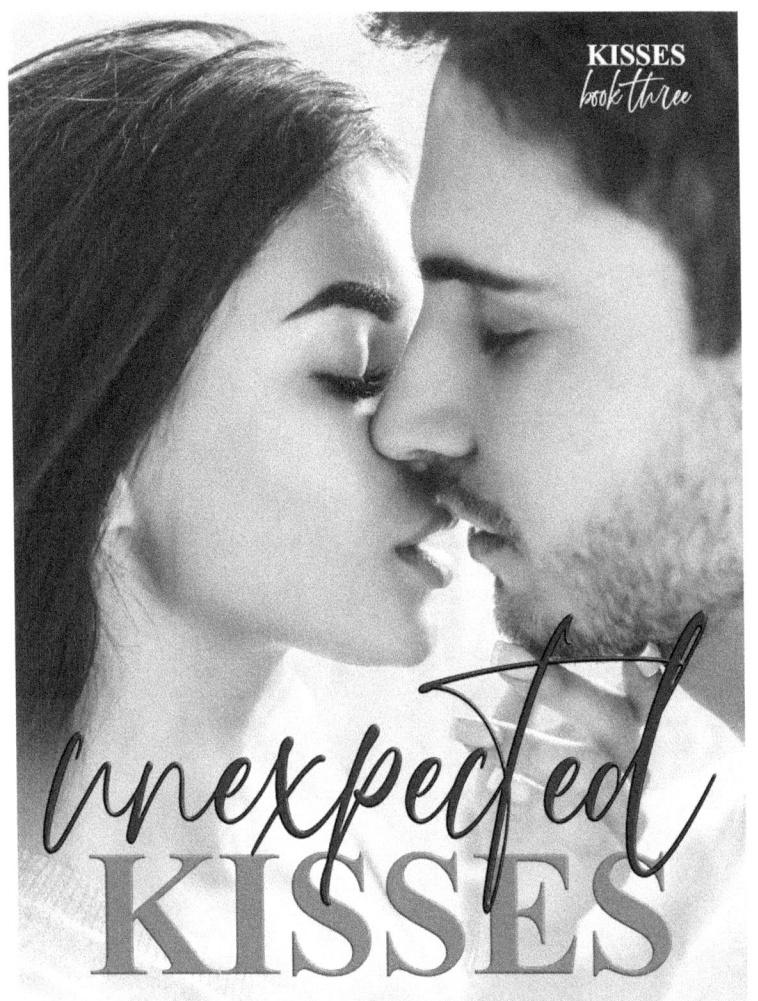

# unexpected
# KISSES

## DEBRA ST JAMES

*inspiration*

This story was inspired by the lyrics ...

—> *Adore You by Harry Styles* <—

# *playlist*

Adore You … *Harry Styles*
Slow Hands … *Niall Horan*
Terrified … *Katharine McPhee/Jason Reeves*
Everything Has Changed … *Jasmine Thompson/Gerald Ko*
Still Falling for You … *Ellie Goulding*
Once in a Lifetime … *Landon Austin*
Natural … *THE DRIVER ERA*
Beautiful Soul … *Boyce Avenue*
Like I'm Gonna Lose You … *Meghan Trainor/John Legend*
I Love You Always … *Betty Who*

**You can check it out here:**

*https://tinyurl.com/unexpectedkisses-spotify*

# —sarah—

## JANUARY

DRAWING IN A DEEP BREATH, I TAKE THE FINAL STEP UP THE PORCH OF my childhood home. I've promised myself that today I'm going to break the news of my plan to my family since I have my first interview with the fertility clinic this week. Actually, I think I'll refer to it as an agency. It doesn't sound so … so clinical. My family is always support-ive, and I know they always have my best interest at heart, so I'm not worried they'll disapprove of my decision.

Oh, what the hell? If I can't be honest with myself, who can I be honest with? I'm terrified they'll think I'm making the wrong decision. That they'll try to talk me out of it and encourage me to wait until I meet the love of my life. *Ha!* I thought I'd had that with Michael but I was sorely mistaken. Every time I think about the day he came home with his news about the promotion he'd accepted without considering me, I'm taken back to the years of misery when my heart was a pile of mush and barely functioning.

Balancing Emma's birthday cake with one hand, I open the screen and front door to step inside with a shiver. Warmth immediately greets me, wrapping me in a familiar embrace and taking me back to a simpler time. The house smells delicious—inviting me farther in. "I'm here!"

Mom steps out of the kitchen, drying her hands on her apron and wearing a wide smile. "Hiya, Honey. Oh, that cake looks amazing. Emma's gonna love it!"

"I figured she deserved a great cake for her last year in her thirties."
I step into the kitchen and place the cake in the middle of the counter.
Once my hands are free, I hug Mom. We're about the same height and
pretty much the same shape; I have her eyes, as do Em and Max. Apart
from the few grays that have snuck in, you wouldn't think Mom was old
enough to have an almost forty-year-old daughter. "Where's Dad?"

"He's drying Archie," she huffs. "That naughty dog rolled in mud
on his morning walk, so your dad thought he'd better give him a bath
before the kids arrive."

"He's always getting up to mischief." I chuckle and Mom rolls her
eyes. "Anything I can do to help?"

"Would you mind making the salad?" She points to the salad
vegetables sitting on the counter.

"Of course not." I set about doing as Mom asked and before long,
I have the salad ready to complement the feast I'm certain Mom's
prepared. She loves feeding us and always makes a big fuss about our
family's Sunday lunches.

Archie comes sprinting through the kitchen, bouncing around like
a gazelle. He's funny when he has a bath, it's like he gets a new lease
on life. "Oh, who's this handsome boy?" I crouch down to give him a
rub around the scruff of his neck. His back end wriggles like crazy
with the wagging of his tail.

Dad chuckles as his feet come into view, so I stand. "Dad."

He wraps his arms around me, pulling me in tight and landing a
kiss on top of my head. "Baby Girl. How are you?"

I draw back, still holding him. "I've had a good week. I hear you've
been rolling around in mud puddles."

We both chuckle, but he points down at the family dog. "That trou-
blemaker there, not me. I'm innocent." He holds his hands up in
surrender.

The front door opens, and the sound of little feet running on Mom
and Dad's hardwood floor, along with little girl giggles, fills the house.
Kenny bursts into the kitchen. "I'm here!"

Mom sweeps forward, collecting Kenny in her arms. She holds her
tight against her body while Kenny's little feet hang loosely. "Hello.
My, don't you look pretty today."

Kenny smiles wide at Mom's compliment then wriggles down to
greet Dad.

Em, Theo, and the boys follow close behind and we all greet each other with our usual boisterous happiness. I'm not sure if all families are this close or demonstrative in their affection for each other, but ours is, and I'm thankful for it. I love spending time with Mom and Dad, my brother and sister, and my niece and nephews.

I step out to go to the bathroom. While I'm here I may as well practice the news—*for the millionth time*—I'm going to share today. Butterflies erupt in my stomach as I study myself in the mirror, then I draw in a deep breath and head back to the kitchen, which is filled with loud laughter.

"What's funny?" I ask as I step into the room, moving straight to my brother to wrap my arms around his waist. He embraces me in return, kissing the top of my head. God, I love my brother; he's so steady and strong.

Emma turns the T-shirt she's holding around to show me the front. I read it out for everyone. "I'm a proud sister of a freaking awesome brother (and yes, he brought me this shirt)." I can't hold back my laughter. Only Max!

"It's perfect, right?" Max asks the room as Emma twists the shirt around for everyone to see.

Dad claps Max on the shoulder and chuckles. "Only you, Max." *Right!*

I spin around, pushing away from my brother, and point my finger at him. "Don't even think about getting me one of those." I can't hold in my grin, which probably gives away that I'm not all that serious. I honestly don't care what he gets me for my birthday, as long as I get to spend time with him.

Everyone settles, and we prepare the table for lunch. Theo helps Emma with the kids, careful to ensure Lachlan's food isn't touching. I don't think I've ever seen my sister so happy; Theo has been so good for her and the boys. The first few moments are silent as we serve ourselves and take our first few bites of food. *Mmm.* Mom's cooking is the best.

Our regular chatter strikes up once the eating slows, and Mom places her silverware down to study Max. "You said you've been busy at work. When are you going to employ someone to help?"

We've been nagging him for quite some time to get help at his workshop. He does too much on his own with the actual mechanical work and the restoration of old muscle cars and trucks, as well as the business management side of things. It takes up all of his time.

"You'll be happy to know that I have an office manager starting at eight a.m. on Monday," he proudly announces.

We all cheer. This has been a long time coming.

"Finally!" Mom raises her voice to be heard above the noise. I glance across to check if Lachlan is okay, but he's covering his ears. I smile inwardly at him, proud of how far he's come.

Hang on a minute. He's suddenly found an office manager? He never said he was advertising *or* interviewing. "How did you find this office manager, and are you sure they're qualified?"

I can see the cogs turning in Max's head, and I know my brother well enough to figure out he's hired some random person. "She *is* qualified, right? You didn't just hire anyone off the street?" He leans his elbow on the table and rubs his thumbnail across his bottom lip in thought. His action tells me that's exactly what he did. "Oh, my gawd! You did. Are you an idiot?" I roll my eyes at him and Emma snickers.

"I'm not an idiot, Sarah," he snaps. "She's highly competent or I wouldn't have hired her," he adds more calmly, then proceeds to tell us how Molly came to be employed and I have to admit, she does sound competent. Perhaps I'm worrying for nothing. We all tend to be a little overprotective of each other.

Discussion ensues regarding Molly's knowledge of the city since she's new here as well as where she's staying. I get the sense that Max hadn't given it much thought before now, but his concern for his new employee is obvious. This could be interesting.

"How are things going at your office, Sarah? Any news on Eric's retirement?" Emma asks.

I blow out a heavy sigh and slump in my chair. "Something happened and delayed Adam's move to the west coast. I'm not sure when things will change."

Emma gives me a sympathetic smile. "Well, on the positive side of things, it means you get to work with Eric longer." My mood improves at the thought.

"That's true, and it's something I'm cherishing." I tuck my hair behind my ear. "I love working with Eric, and you guys know how I feel about change."

"Eric's grandson might be a lot like him. You never know, it might be a seamless transition," Max adds.

I nod and place my silverware down. It's now or never. This is the perfect opportunity to talk with my family about my plans. I swallow the lump in my throat. "I have something I wanted to talk with you guys about."

Everyone gives me one hundred percent of their attention and my stomach rolls. Maybe I shouldn't have eaten. "What is it, Love?" Mom asks when I hesitate.

I blow out a breath, my nerves getting the better of me. "Please don't judge me. I've thought long and hard about this, and it's the right decision for me. I'm hoping you'll all be supportive."

Creases form between Dad's eyebrows. "Of course we'll support you."

*Well, that's a good start.* "Great." I blow out a long breath. Here goes. "I've decided I want to have a baby." The silence in the room is loud as I glance around the table. "I'm not getting any younger, and it's impossible to meet someone decent. Someone I'd want to raise a family with." I glance at Emma and the sympathy on her face tells me she understands what I'm saying.

Mom's hand rises to fidget with her necklace. "Oh. Well … uh … that's unexpected news. How will you make this happen?" I'm going to take this as a positive sign. She's asking for more details, not telling me I shouldn't do it.

"There are agencies that help women like me. I complete a whole heap of paperwork, give them a whole wad of money, and they give me sperm from a baby daddy of my choosing." A simplified explanation, but sometimes simple is the best approach.

"My sister, Anna, did that." Theo looks at Kenny with eyes full of love and adoration for his niece-slash-daughter. "That's how we ended up with Kenny."

That's right. I remember Emma telling me about it. Maybe that was the conversation that triggered my urgency to have a baby; knowing there was a way I could do it on my own. If things don't work out with the clinic I'm interviewing with this week, then maybe it would be a good idea to have a backup. Just in case.

"Do you know which agency she used?" I ask.

Theo thinks for a moment. "I don't, sorry. Dad might know, though. I'll ask him and let you know."

I smile gratefully at him. "Thanks."

"This isn't the way we expected you to be having a baby, but we'll support you in any way we can." Dad reaches across, patting my hand with love and support. Some of the tension I've been holding in my body releases, and I relax a little.

Everyone offers their support to me in any way they can as I find a baby daddy, through my pregnancy, and then into motherhood. I'm not sure why I was so worried. I should have known they would support me in any way they could. They always want the best for me.

We clean up from lunch, then I place the chocolate birthday cake I made for Emma on the table. We sing "Happy Birthday" in our usual, terribly off-key fashion and enjoy the delicious cake. I'm so thankful I got the chance to bake yet another birthday cake for my sister and that she's healthy after her brush with cancer.

Once things are quiet and the kids are playing with Archie in the backyard, Emma, Mom, and I have a few moments on our own. Emma slides her fingers through my hair and whispers, "You know I'll help you in any way I can once you have the baby." I smile and wrap my arms around her.

"Thanks, Sis. You're the best."

We separate and Em's eyes widen. "I still have the crib from the boys and some other stuff. Would you like it?"

Excitement fills me. "Absolutely. Thank you so much. I'll take whatever you have."

"I'll get everything out and bring it over. This is so exciting." She squeezes me tight, and I know she's genuinely happy and excited for me.

Mom catches our attention. "You're one hundred percent positive this is what you want to do?"

I nod. "I've thought about it a lot ever since Michael left. I know this must seem like it's come out of the blue, but I promise it hasn't. I've weighed up my options carefully, and I truly think this is what will work best for me."

Mom steps toward me, wrapping me in her motherly embrace. "I completely understand, Baby Girl." She smooths my bangs out of my eyes. "Once the baby's born, don't forget your father and I can help out with babysitting. That way you can go back to work at least part-time."

"Thanks, Mom. Your support means the world to me. I'll admit, I was nervous breaking the news to you guys."

Creases form between her eyebrows. "Why would you worry? You know your father and I try our best to support you kids however we can."

And now I feel like a shitty daughter because I *do* know that. "I'm sorry, Mom." I hug her close, attempting to show her how sorry I am.

# CHAPTER 1

## *—sarah—*

JUNE

MELANIE'S NAME LIGHTS UP MY SCREEN WITH A TEXT.

> MEL
>
> I'm waiting ...

Trust her to know my cycle. It only makes sense since we've known each other since kindergarten; we know most things about each other, and she knows how much I want this to work. The problem is that I'm not ready to tell anyone I failed again. Not even my best friend. After my second attempt to get pregnant, I'm still no closer to becoming a mom. The disappointment weighs heavily on my heart, and I'm terrified my dream may never become a reality. I blow out a heavy breath and pick up my phone.

> ME
>
> I got my period

I drop my phone back to the cushion beside me and take a sip of my wine. I'd been staying clear of the sweet goodness, but I needed something to help me commiserate my failure. Staring off into space, the doorway to the second bedroom mocks me. I don't know when it became essential to me that I needed to have a baby; I just know it's all I can think about. I've always wanted to be a mom. As a kid, I would always play mommies and daddies with my dolls, and watching Em with her kids makes me realize I have this gaping hole inside of me.

Sighing heavily, I blow out a long breath and sink into the plush cushion. My phone lights up again, and I read her messages without picking it up.

MEL

I'm sorry. I know how much you want this

My nose tingles and I swallow the lump in my throat.

MEL

I'm taking you out dancing tomorrow night. No arguments

I don't want to go out dancing. At thirty-four, I feel so old when we go to clubs. I grab my phone, ready to make up some excuse when it rings. I press the green button and hold it to my ear. "Mel—"

"Don't say it, Sare. No excuses. We're going dancing. There's a new club with an over-thirties crowd." Her tone is no-nonsense.

"I'm really not feeling it. I just want to wallow. Let me wallow. Just this once," I whine like a child.

She chuckles. "What sort of friend would I be if I let you wallow? Besides, you'll be a mom before you know it, and then you won't be able to go out and have fun with your bestie."

I know she won't relent, so I may as well save myself a whole lot of arguing and simply agree. "Okay. But I don't want to be out late. I have my shift at the hospital on Saturday morning."

"I know, I know. I have my shift too. I promise to get you home before you turn into a pauper!" My long-time friend giggles. "See you tomorrow night. Mwah!"

I can't help but chuckle too. She's infectious. "Tomorrow night, Mels Bells."

We end the call, and I take a long sip of my wine. I guess I should have dinner and finish crocheting the beanies I need to take with me on Saturday since I won't be able to finish them tomorrow night. Climbing to my feet, I head to my poky kitchen, pull out the container labeled Thursday, and pop it in the microwave. As I wait for the timer to go off, I check whether the cupcakes I baked as soon as I got home are cool enough to pack into Tupperware. They are, so I quickly transfer them, then top off my wineglass and grab a fork out of the drawer. With my butt leaning against the counter, I allow my gaze to wander around my small apartment. Even though the space is compact and it's not in the swanky part of town, I feel accomplished that I saved up enough money to buy it. I've always been great at saving money and working toward a goal. Even when I was a kid, I would save my birthday and pocket money until I had enough to buy something special. Which reminds me, I need to start saving again for more treatments. Not getting pregnant is going to set my plan back, but what else can I do?

The microwave dings so I grab my chicken masala and head back to the couch. I smile to myself, grateful that I didn't have to cook dinner tonight with the way I'm feeling. The hour of meal prep I do every Sunday morning saves me a heap of time and money because I'm not tempted to grab takeout when I'm tired or work late or just feel blah. A little planning goes a long way, and it helps me to keep on track with my financial goals, too.

I had saved enough money for two rounds with the clinic in the hopes I would get pregnant, but no dice. Now I need to start all over again—another eight grand for two more attempts. If I don't get pregnant by the end of those rounds, I'm not sure what my next step will be.

My tan patent heels clack across the stone floor as I make my way toward the elevator that'll take me up to the forty-fifth floor. I balance the two dozen cupcakes I baked last night as I walk toward Joe.

"Morning, Sarah," Joe calls across from his post near the elevator, ready to press the button for me.

I smile at him. Every day, he's here to greet me with his warm smile and a friendly hello. "Hi, Joe. How are things?"

"Never better." That's always his answer as he presses the button to my floor on my behalf.

I hold the container toward him and raise an eyebrow. "Would you like one before I take them upstairs?"

"I'll never say no to your baking." He reaches across, lifts the lid, and makes his selection. "Mmm, smell that lemon."

"There's a treat hidden inside." I wink at him. The lemon curd filling is always a hit.

"Nice. I'll look forward to it when I take my morning break. Thank you. Mr. Wainwright hasn't arrived yet."

That gives me pause. Eric is always in the office before me. Well, he used to always be in the office before me; now, not so much. "Thanks, Joe. Have a great day."

"You too," he says as I step inside the elevator with a stone-tiled floor and stainless-steel walls, which match the lobby. I don't have to share the space with anyone this early in the morning.

The building is incredibly stylish and classy, and I love that I work in one of the most iconic buildings in the city, *Stone Tower*. It doesn't hurt that, on occasion, I manage to lay eyes on the one and only owner of the building, Oliver Stone. That man is all sorts of hot! His wife is gorgeous too. I've met them both a couple of times over the years because Emma works with her and we crossed paths when Emma was in the hospital and again at her wedding. Even though I know Kate is really down to earth, I can't believe the wife of a billionaire businessman still works in an elementary school. I shake my head.

Using the polished stainless-steel walls as a mirror, I adjust the collar of the navy sleeveless dress I'm wearing today. Nobody would even guess the dress I'm wearing only cost thirty-nine ninety-five, including postage—such a steal. I love dressing up and finding outfits that accentuate my assets—which are on the curvier side—not that there's anyone to impress in the office, but I like to look nice.

The reception desk is empty when I step off the elevator, which is normal because Lucy doesn't usually get here until she's dropped her teenage kids off at school. I start her computer, then head toward my desk, located outside of Eric's office. As I pass by the research and development cubicles, I raise the Tupperware container of cupcakes so the guys know to grab one each before they all disappear. Evan and Jordan always start early on Fridays so they can leave early and hit the bars. Eric's always been generous with his staff, allowing us to start and finish whenever it suits us as long as we work our designated number of hours in the week. I was lucky to land this job over ten years ago.

I tuck my purse in the cupboard behind my desk and turn on my computer. Glancing at Eric's darkened office, I mentally run through his calendar, searching for an early appointment I've forgotten but come up blank. His behavior has been worrying and uncharacteristic as of late. He's been stressed about his grandson, Adam, taking over his position within the company. Eric's ready to retire, and it shows in the considerable decline of his enthusiasm over the last twelve months.

Adam's been reluctant, making Eric understandably upset. I consider the situation from Adam's point of view as I turn on the lights and computer in Eric's office. Glancing at the old black and white photograph of his daughter and her family he keeps on his desk, I study the little boy, Adam, closely. I guess it takes time to pack up your life and move across the country from New Jersey, but it's been over eighteen months and the delay is impacting Eric's health. Apparently, Adam moved there straight from college for a job and hasn't been home since, but surely he knew he'd have to take over from his grandfather one day. I'm not even sure he's capable of taking over such a large company; he's never even set foot in this building. Would he even know how to run *FutureTech*?

I drop the cupcakes off in the kitchen, turn on the coffee machine, then move through the rest of our floor, switching on the lights and printers. Once I've made myself a coffee, I pop my head in to say hello to Evan and Jordan. "Morning. Are you guys ready for your presentation with Eric this morning at ten?"

"Morning, Sarah. Yeah, we're ready, but where is he?" Jordan asks.

"I don't know. I'll give him thirty minutes, then I'll try calling him. Don't forget to grab a cupcake. I made the lemon ones this week."

They both nod. "Thanks, Sarah. Your cupcakes make Fridays bearable."

"You're welcome." I head back to my desk. Taking my seat, I work through the emails in my inbox, forwarding them where needed, and double-checking Eric's calendar for today. He leaves at lunchtime to play golf on Fridays; it's something he's always done. More often than not, by three p.m. on Friday afternoons, our office is almost completely empty. I love it because it affords me the quiet I need to prepare for the following work week.

Eric wanders toward me, looking a million miles away. "Good morning, Mr. Wainwright." I smile at him.

He glances up as though he's only now realized where he is. "Good morning, Sarah. Please cancel the presentation this morning. Move it to the first available time next week. I need to make an important call."

"Sure. Is everything okay?"

He waves over his shoulder as he disappears through the door to his office. "Of course."

Puzzled at Eric's uncharacteristic behavior, I check his calendar for next week and move the presentation, then head down the hallway to tell the guys. I'm sure they'll be disappointed. They seemed excited about showing Eric the new chip they've been working on.

I make Eric's pot of tea, pop a cupcake on a plate, and head back to his office, catching him before he makes his call. "I've changed the presentation to your earliest available time next Tuesday. Here's your tea, and I made lemon curd cupcakes this week."

His cloudy eyes meet mine, and he offers me a genuine smile. "What would I do without you, Sarah? Thank you."

"Oh, I'm sure you'd get by, but I'm glad I can help." I tip my lips up. "Do you need anything else?"

"No, thank you. Please ensure I'm not disturbed."

"Of course." I spin on my heel, closing Eric's door behind me.

# CHAPTER 2

I END THE CALL AND LEAN BACK IN MY LEATHER CHAIR, BEYOND PLEASED with the outcome. After my disastrous phone call this morning, I needed this. Dylan already knows the outcome is positive from listening to my side of the conversation, but he sits opposite me with his eyebrows raised and an expectant look.

"We got it!"

He jumps out of his chair, pumping his fist in the air. "Fuck yeah!" He wraps his hand around my bicep, pulling me to my feet, and we embrace in celebration. "I knew we had it in the bag, but I don't like to celebrate until the deal is sealed."

I chuckle at his enthusiasm. "This is an incredible opportunity for us. We'd better not fuck it up."

"We won't. We've got this. Everything we've done up until now has led us to this point. We're ready." He's always supremely confident in our abilities. I know he's right, but I hope we haven't taken on more than we can handle. It is only the two of us after all, and this is a big deal—it's the biggest contract we've ever had. The company, *booknow.com*, is listed in the top twenty tech companies in the US. If we can impress them, who knows where it might lead?

"Mr. Noble's going to send over the final contract for our lawyer to look at, then we can sign on the dotted line. This is huge for us." Excitement bubbles inside me. This is the break we've been working toward. Taking smaller jobs and edging our way closer to the bigger companies that will put us on the map has finally paid off. "He said he wants to keep the project between the three of us. He's even using his personal lawyer, so no one in the company knows what's going to happen. *He* doesn't even want to know when we're going to take the company down."

Dylan raises his eyebrows. "Makes sense to do a stealth attack." I nod in agreement as he claps his hands together. "This calls for a celebration."

"Yep, it sure does. Let's try out *Club Rumors*. It's a new club for the over-thirties crowd." I'm sick of the younger chicks. Most of them have nothing going on upstairs, relying solely on their looks. Dylan doesn't mind the lack of conversation because he's only looking to get laid, but I need more than a wet pussy.

He screws up his nose. "We're only thirty, man. I'm not sure I want to age up just yet."

I slap him on the back. "Haven't you heard how horny women are in their thirties?"

His eyes light up. "Oh yeah?" I knew that would pique his interest. "Okay. I'm down for that. Let's grab dinner first."

"Sure. We'll meet at *Cristo's* at seven-thirty. I'll book us a table."

"Cool. See you there."

The door closes behind him and I make a booking at our favorite Greek restaurant. As I end the call, my phone lights up with my sister's name.

"Unca AJ!" Colton, my three-year-old nephew, squeals down the line.

"Colton, my man." This isn't the first time he's picked up my sister's phone and called me. "How are you doing, buddy?"

"I good. I love you, Unca—" His words stop abruptly, and I'm guessing my sister's discovered him using her phone again.

"AJ? Is that you?"

I chuckle. "Yeah, it's me. I'm guessing you need to find a new hiding place for your phone?"

"Yeah. How'd you guess?" Hayley laughs. "I'm running out of places. I had it on top of the damn fridge! He pulled a chair over to the counter, climbed up, and then used a wooden spoon to drag the damn phone within his reach," she huffs out.

My heart races. "Shit! Lucky he didn't fall."

"I know. We can't take our eyes off him for a second. Lisa's not home from work yet, and I was in the bathroom." She sounds frustrated, and I can imagine her running her fingers through her dark-brown curls. I hear her draw in a deep breath. "Anyway, I was going to call you. How did your call go? Did you get the contract?"

"Yep!"

"Woohoo!" she sings across the line. "I knew you would. I'm so damn proud of you and Dylan! You've done incredible to build your reputation as quickly as you have."

Her praise means the world to me since she and Lisa run their own successful business creating and designing educational games. Lisa's an ex-teacher and Hayley is a game designer. That's how they met. Lisa had an idea for an educational game to help teach kids grammar, so she contacted Hayley. They started working together on the project and one thing led to another and they've been together ever since. From that initial project, the two have created a whole slew of educational resources which are being used worldwide. What they've built over a short period is truly inspiring. It also allows them the flexibility to work from home or in the office, which means they can take turns being home with their son.

I hear Colton squeal in the background. "Hey, I've gotta go. Lisa's home. Congratulations again. We'll have you over for dinner to celebrate."

"Sure. Bye, Sis." The call disconnects and I check the clock on the wall. I have time for a quick workout before I need to get ready for dinner.

"ID please." The woman at the door holds out her hand, a bored expression on her face.

I dig into my pocket. "We're over twenty-one."

She pops her bubblegum as her eyes scan us from head to toe. "I can see that. I need to check that you're at least thirty."

Fuck! I didn't think they'd be checking our ages. Dylan glances at me with a smirk. "Sure." I hand over my driver's license and so does Dylan. It was only two weeks ago that he turned thirty.

With a level of boredom I haven't seen since high school, the woman studies our licenses, then hands them back to us. "That'll be twenty-five each." I hand over my credit card and she scans it, then stamps our wrists. "Have a good night, boys." She winks at us, then directs her attention to the next people in line.

As soon as the doors open, a thumping bass beat hits me square in the chest. Oh yeah! I can't stop my body from moving as we make our way through the crowded space to the bar. We can't help but press up against women of all shapes and sizes who check us out in return as we pass by. I'm not being big-headed when I say that Dylan and I are good-looking guys. We generally don't have trouble gaining the attention of the ladies, particularly Dylan with his naturally flirtatious personality. He's the light to my darker features, with his blond hair, blue-eyed surfer look. He comes across as laid back, but he takes life seriously where it counts.

Skating my eyes around the darkened space, lit by random purple strobe lights, I'm already mentally patting myself on the back for my decision to come here tonight. The place is filled wall to wall with women who ooze confidence that younger girls just don't have. It would be great to finish the day by sharing a drink and interesting conversation with a beautiful woman. I mean, I wouldn't say no to getting naked with said woman, but I don't want to push my luck. My day's already been successful beyond my imagination.

Dylan leans in close to my ear. "You want a beer?"

I glance up at the drink menu, spotting my favorite craft beer. "Sure. I'll have a Crusoe." He nods and moves closer to the bar, which is three people deep in places, to order our drinks so it's going to take him a while. I tuck my hands into my pockets and step toward the dance floor to watch. It doesn't take long before a particular woman catches my attention. She has a banging body, all curves, dips, and valleys—just the way I like my women. Her black lace dress hugs her body as she shakes her delectable ass to the music. She spins around, finally facing me, and the front is as spectacular as the back. Her smile is contagious as her blonde friend grinds her ass against hers. They're too caught up having their own fun to be trying to impress anyone, and it's sexy as fuck.

Dylan steps beside me, handing me my beer. I take a drink and then tip my head toward the women. "They look like they're having a good time." He glances to where I'm pointing, then smiles at me with raised eyebrows. Where the brunette is everything I look for in a woman, her blonde friend is Dylan's perfect woman come to life.

"I think we're in for a good night, my friend." He taps his glass against my bottle and takes another drink.

I smile at my long-time friend, then take a drink. Both of us turn toward the dance floor to watch the women enjoying themselves. As many times as I tear my eyes away from the stunning brunette to peer around the room, they instinctually find their way back to her.

Six pillars topped with silver cages, rise out of the floor at random intervals around the room. Each has a woman inside wearing a barely there shimmering outfit. My eyes momentarily lock on the dancer closest to me as she moves her body to the music, but she can't hold my attention for long as my eyes fight to find the sexy brunette again. I snap my head around to seek her out but she's not where she was a moment earlier. Scanning the area, I come up empty. I shift my position to see if I can locate her, but she's vanished into thin air. *Fuck!*

Dylan leans into me. "Who are you looking for?"

I point to the spot where my girl was. "The brunette who was dancing with the blonde."

He nods, then lifts his chin in the direction of the large, raised booths facing the dance floor along the side. "They went that way."

I relax and Dylan leads the way, making a path through the crowd as purple lights strobe across the room in time with the music. Someone pinches my ass as I follow behind. I turn to lay eyes on the offender to be greeted with a wink and a wide smile surrounded by bristles. I raise my eyebrows and tip my head, but keep moving forward. He was decent looking if I swung that way, but I don't.

I spot the women in a circular booth toward the back, the farthest from the speakers. How fortuitous ... the other half of the booth is free. Walking directly toward them, I lean closer to the blonde, who's sitting closest to the edge. "Mind if we take the other half of the booth?"

Her eyes skate down my body and across to Dylan, then she returns her attention to me. "Be our guest." She waves her hand out toward the empty side.

"Thanks." I slide into the other end of the booth first, then Dylan follows in behind me. His eyes catch on the blonde and stay there for a long moment. I try to catch the eye of the brunette, but it's not happening; she's too busy watching the action on the dance floor. I press my back against the cushioned chair and stretch my legs out, playing with the coaster on the table.

"How are you feeling?" I look beside me, knowing full well the space is empty. The voice is as clear as if the woman it belongs to was sitting right beside me. I lift my gaze to the women at the other end of the booth.

The brunette blows out a breath. "Disappointed, but I'll survive."

The blonde rubs her friend's arm, her face full of compassion. "Have you got enough money to do another round?"

"Nope. I have to save again, which will put me behind schedule, but what else can I do? I want a baby."

*A baby.* I'm certain my eyebrows are touching my hairline and my eyes are as wide as saucers.

"I know." The blonde sighs. "Why don't you try picking up a hot guy and taking him home? There are plenty here to choose from," she suggests. "And it would be cheaper than going through the clinic."

"You know I can't do that, Mel."

"Why not? He would never have to know."

"Uhhh, because it's unethical. Plus, there's that little tidbit about my personality that you're forgetting."

The blonde pauses for a moment; her eyebrows scrunch down, then her eyes widen and her lips spread. "Oh, right. I forgot. You know, you can have sex for fun without being involved?" She nudges her shoulder playfully into her friend's.

"I know *you* can do that, but I've tried it. I wish I could do what you do, but I'm not built that way."

Thank fuck for that. The relief filling my body is swift, knowing she's not the type of woman who hooks up for the hell of it. I'm being completely unfair because God knows when I was in college, I hooked up with my fair share of women only for sex.

"I know you're not, Sare. So how long will it take you to save?"

"Another twelve months if I'm careful. This will have to be my last night out for a while."

Shit, she must really want a baby.

"Doesn't the clinic offer a payment plan or something?"

The brunette huffs out a breath. "I wish. Waiting another twelve months puts me on the cusp of needing to change to IVF, which is even more expensive."

"I wish I could help you." She rubs her hand along her friend's back in comfort. "How about I get us another drink?"

The brunette, Sare, maybe short for Sarah, smiles and nods at her friend. The blonde stands and heads to the bar, leaving Sare on her own. I glance down at my bottle, noticing it's empty.

"I'm gonna get us some refills. Be back in a minute," Dylan says and I nod, digging into my pocket for my card, but he waves me off.

I glance at the brunette and decide this is my moment to chat with her, so I close the four-foot distance between us.

# CHAPTER 3

## —sarah—

"Hi." I turn slightly to face the owner of the deep voice. It's the guy who asked to share our booth. "I'm sorry, I couldn't help but overhear your conversation with your friend." He gestures with a tilt of his chin toward Melanie as she heads to the bar.

I blush. Shit, I really should learn to keep my voice down. I thought our conversation would have been muffled somewhat by the music. How embarrassing that the guy I was checking out earlier overheard such a personal conversation.

He shrugs apologetically. "Sorry, I guess it's because the booth is curved; your conversation traveled. Honestly, I'm not a creeper or anything." He raises his hands in surrender. "I wanted to say how much I admire that you know what you want and you're going after it."

I blow out a relieved breath, and the tension across my shoulders disappears. I don't want people to think I'm some desperate woman. Well, I sort of am, but I don't want other people to think I am. I tuck a lock of hair behind my ear. "Thank you. I'm not getting any younger, and I really want to have a baby."

His eyebrows tilt down over his rich brown eyes surrounded by thick, dark lashes. What is it with guys always having the best lashes? "Which fertility clinic are you using?"

I swivel my body around so I'm facing the guy directly. "I'm using *Eastside Fertility*." He nods as if he's familiar with them. "They've been great, but it's a lot of paperwork and medical tests, not to mention expensive. But it will all be worth it if I have a baby. Though there are no guarantees, obviously. I've already had two rounds of the procedure with no luck." My stomach sinks at the verbal reminder as to the reason we're out tonight.

He twists his body so he's facing me, raising his knee onto the seat and pressing against my hip. His arm rests on the back of the curved booth, bringing his hand close to my head. "Is there a way you can do it without all the expense?"

"Afraid not. I haven't met the right person, and even if I met someone now, by the time I go through the dating process, get to know the guy, and figure out if the relationship will be successful ... it all takes time. Time I don't feel I have." I shrug. "It would be a little weird on the first or second date to say ... *oh, by the way, I want to have a baby. Would you mind knocking me up?*" We both chuckle. "I can't imagine it going down well. He'd probably run a mile. And with good reason." I take the last sip of my drink, then add, "And most guys don't stick around long-term anyway. They're generally not reliable so I'm happy to do it on my own." Well, that's what I tell people anyway.

"What if you found a guy who would be happy to help you?"

I wave my hand in front of me, brushing off his comment. "That's never gonna happen. If I want a baby, I have to take matters into my own hands."

He leans forward slightly, and his fresh citrus scent wafts around him. I move in slightly to inhale more of the fragrance. He smells so freaking good. "What if I said I'd be happy to help you?" The deep timbre of his voice vibrates through my body as he poses the question. He pulls back slightly with a smirk and my heart stops. *What?*

"Pardon?" Surely he didn't offer to get me pregnant.

He leans back in and I mirror him. My eyes lock on his and the warmth in his chocolate gaze invites me to get lost. I do love a bit of chocolate occasionally. "I said I would be happy to get you pregnant." He raises an eyebrow, and I swallow down the extra saliva that's suddenly pooling in my mouth.

I chuckle uncomfortably. "It's very kind of you to offer ... your ... uh ... services." Geez, Louise. This took an awkward turn. "But I don't know you and you don't know me. It's a little weird." Make that a lot weird.

"How much do you need to know? It's not like you know the donors from the clinic." He shrugs as if this is an ordinary conversation. He has a point, but at the clinic, I get to choose my baby daddy based on the extensive information they collect. "You only need my semen, right? You don't actually *want* a guy to stick around?" He raises his eyebrows as he waits for my answer.

Well, I *do* want a guy to stick around, but I've run out of options, and I feel my body's running out of time, so that was taken off the table. I want a family like the one I grew up with; a mom and dad working together to raise happy, healthy kids. I never imagined I'd be going down this route to have a family. The whole idea would have been preposterous to me in my twenties, but here I am. "I'd at least need to know your medical history and if your semen is viable, and that you're clean. Would you be prepared to do the necessary tests?" I can't believe I'm even entertaining this stranger's absurd offer.

"Of course. No point if I'm shooting blanks, right?" His answering smile is wide. He has beautiful teeth, straight and white. I scan the rest of his features. Tanned skin, thick dark hair. He looks healthy enough. He seems tall, but it's hard to tell while he's sitting down.

I shake my head. "No point." I ponder his offer for a few moments. He doesn't seem like a psycho, but I'm sure some psychos are good at hiding their true selves. Would it be any different from a hook-up? It's not like you know anything about the guy you take home for a night. But this is different. I *want* to get pregnant. This is a big freaking deal, and he's offering it to me like it's of no consequence. Who does that? "This is a big deal. You know that, right?" He nods and a grin slowly slides across his perfect lips. "I'd pay for all the tests. It wouldn't be fair to expect you to fork out money for my cause."

He waves off my offer. "I can afford to do all of that. Don't worry." Is he for real right now? He's incredibly nonchalant about his life-changing offer.

I drop my eyes to my glass and twist it by the stem. "I guess we'd need some kind of contract?"

He lifts one shoulder and drops it. "If it would make you feel better, but I don't think it's necessary. I'll give you my swimmers until you're pregnant, and then we'll go our separate ways, never to see each other again."

And why does my heart squeeze tight at the thought of that?

I tuck my hair behind my ear, glancing toward the bar, looking for Mel. Suddenly, I'm incredibly hot. His gaze is locked on my face, and I swallow my nerves. "Uhm, I'm not sure I feel comfortable. The clinic vets its donors. When I make my selection, I have a file I can read through to find the match that suits me best."

He shifts in his seat and taps his fingers on the table between us like he doesn't have a care in the world. "If you want to make up a questionnaire, I'll answer your questions. I don't have anything to hide."

I blow out a breath. This guy seems happy enough to do anything I ask. "Are you positive?"

"Yeah, I'd be happy to do whatever makes you comfortable." Even though his superficial body language is trying to portray this as no big deal, I can see the tightness around his eyes and across his shoulders. It's contradictory to his words and obvious actions.

"Why? Why would you help a complete stranger have a baby?" Why would someone offer to get a stranger pregnant? I can't help but question his motives.

He blows out a breath and glances around the club. When I follow his eyes, I notice Mel is still talking to his friend at the bar. Their conversation looks a lot lighter than ours as she throws her head back with laughter. "I like to help people where I can. It's not like you need a kidney, it's just sperm. I make new sperm every day." He chuckles, his eyes sparkling in the low light. He digs his hand into his pocket and pulls out a black business card, handing it to me.

*Jackson & Baker* is all it says on the front in stylish silver block letters. It gives no clue about what type of business it is. I flip it over to find an email and phone number.

"What type of work do you do?" Not that it's my business, it has nothing to do with his semen health or count.

"My friend and I"—he points his chin toward his friend at the bar, still chatting with Mel—"hack computer systems for companies to test out their security. Then we help them fix any issues they may have to secure their system."

"Oh … that … that sounds … uh … like you're very smart." Geez, Sarah, could you sound any more juvenile?

"We're pretty good at what we do." He doesn't come across as cocky or boastful as he says it, more like he's simply stating a fact.

"What made you get into that line of work?"

"It was fun. We met in college doing computer science, and in our spare time, we messed around to see if we could hack into big corporations. Then we would send them an email explaining the issues we found in their system. Once we worked out companies would pay us to test their system, we decided to start taking it more seriously and it sort of grew from there."

"Wow. That's incredible. Congratulations on making a fun hobby work out for you."

"Thanks." He pauses as if thinking about something as he glances around the club. "Would you like to dance?"

"Sure." I smile at him and then slide out of the booth, him following behind and before I can stop myself, I add extra sway to my hips. His warm hand takes up residence on my lower back, sending goosebumps racing over my body.

Don't get attached, Sarah. He's just gonna give you his sperm. No big deal.

We make it to the dance floor, the upbeat music fills my body, and I have no choice but to move. There's not a lot of room on the dance floor, so … shit, I don't even know this guy's name. I chuckle and he gives me a puzzled look. I lean in close so he can hear me, my breast grazing his arm. "I just realized I don't know your name. I'm Sarah, by the way."

He chuckles, then moves his mouth next to my ear. His hot breath hits the crook of my neck as I draw in a breath soaked with his citrus scent.

So sexy. *Stop it, Sarah!*

"My family and friends call me AJ. Since I'm going to be your donor, I'll consider you a friend." He draws back and winks at me. His soulful eyes melting my insides.

This is never going to work if I get attached to this guy. I've known him a whole thirty minutes and I'm already feeling things I shouldn't. Sure, he's attractive. Physically, he's everything I look for in a guy: tall, dark, *and* handsome. It seems unfair that I've met him under the circumstances I have. The song changes to a slower-than-usual version of "Slow Hands," the bass thumping heavily, pulsing through my body.

AJ moves in closer. Landing one hand on my hip, he spins me around. The front of his body molds to the back of mine, his strong thighs against my butt. Heat races up my spine, and I can't stop myself from pressing back into him. *What is wrong with me?*

Bodies press in on us from both sides, and his other hand comes around my front, holding me to him with firm pressure. Dragging my hair away from my neck, I reach up, moving my arms to the music. His hands slide up my body, trailing over my exposed flesh, sending flames licking through my blood as his hands tangle with mine above us. The chemistry between us is potent. Using his hips, he moves his body and mine in time with the sensual rhythm, and I get lost in the music—in the moment—with this handsome stranger who may well end up being the father of my baby.

# CHAPTER 4

I'M DOING EVERYTHING IN MY POWER TO KEEP MY HARD COCK AWAY from her delicious ass so she doesn't think I'm some kind of perverted asshole, but the way she moves her body is so damn sexy. She has a confidence about her that is rare, and it's sexy as fuck.

*Shit!* She presses back into my body, and she has to feel exactly what's happening in my pants. I try to pull back to put more space between us, but she drops her hand and grabs my hip, holding me in place. Well, if that's the way she wants to play it, I'm happy to oblige. I guess I'll be getting more intimate with her than this soon enough. Maybe she wants to start tonight? My cock expands at the thought. She turns her head to the side and glances up at me, a sexy smirk on her face.

I lean down. My mouth is so close to hers that her breaths cast lightly across my lips. I run my tongue across mine and glance up into her eyes. I can't quite tell their color in this low light, but they appear dark. I move closer still but am shoved to the side by a woman doing some type of crazy, over-the-top dance move. I tighten my hold to keep Sarah from falling, twisting my body to protect her from the crazy woman's moves. The lady is spinning around all over the place as though she has the entire dance floor to herself.

Sarah giggles and I turn her around to face me, her gorgeous smile brightening her face. "That was a close call." She swipes her hand across her forehead as if she's wiping away sweat.

Does she mean it was a close call that we were almost knocked over? Or does she mean it was a close call that we almost kissed? She grabs my hand and leads me from the dance floor, back to the booth we were sharing. Dylan and Mel are already there … making out. Sarah's steps pause momentarily.

"It looks as though our friends are getting along."

I drop my eyes to hers and nod. "It seems so." Not a surprise for me because Dylan gets along with anyone, particularly those of the female persuasion.

We drop into the booth, disrupting their moment. Sarah takes a sip of her wine, and I watch as her throat moves with her swallow. Peeling my eyes away from her, I take a drink of my beer. We spend the night talking over the music, drinking, and dancing. It's impossible to have any further meaningful conversation with Dylan and her friend sharing the booth with us.

"Well, I need to get home. I have an early start tomorrow," Sarah tells us, giving Mel a pointed look.

The girls climb out of the booth, and Dylan and I follow them through the club. I hold the door open for everyone and we step onto the sidewalk; I'm sad our night's come to an end. While Dylan and Mel lock lips again for a lengthy period, I study Sarah. What I would give to kiss her like that but I don't feel Sarah and I are at that stage. She's more reserved and I respect that about her.

I tuck my hands into my pockets and lean closer to Sarah's ear to keep our conversation private. "So, uh, about the baby thing. When did you want to get together about that?" I really want her to take me up on my offer. It'll give me an opportunity to spend time with her, to get to know her better, because the little time I spent with her tonight has made me want more.

She chuckles and tucks a lock of silky-looking hair behind her ear. "I figured you weren't serious."

I frown. "I thought I was pretty clear about my offer to help you. As I said, I'm happy to answer any questions and get any tests done. Just say the word."

She drops her gaze, looking at the dirty sidewalk beneath our feet, then raises her eyes to me. "Can I think about it? I have your number. I'll text you and let you know. Maybe we can catch up for a coffee and talk about it some more."

I'm not sure what she needs to think about. I'm offering my services, free of charge, so she can have a baby. I try to play off my enthusiasm with a shrug. "Sure." Leaning in, I place a chaste kiss on her soft cheek and her cheeks flush. I want to do so much more than that. I want to see her whole body flush. Out here, I can smell her subtle scent of spring flowers and I draw it into my lungs. "Do you mind texting me your decision either way?" That way I'll have her number and maybe I can at least coax her out on a date or something.

"Of course. And … thank you." She rests her hand on my forearm, her heat searing through the fabric of my shirt, and I flex the muscle. "I appreciate your offer to help." Sincerity shines in her eyes. She turns around and grabs her friend's arm, tugging her away. "Come on, Mel. Let's go."

Mel and Dylan mumble something to each other with matching grins, then Mel turns to Sarah. "Okay, okay. Let's go! See ya, AJ."

I raise my hand to wave goodbye to the girls, like the lame guy I am. "Yeah, see ya. Nice meeting you both." *Could I be any more pathetic?*

"What's up with you? You've checked your phone at least a dozen times in the last hour." With my mind a million miles from here, Dylan's voice seems loud in the quiet of our office.

"Nothing."

"Don't lie to me. I've known you for too long. What's up?"

Instead of answering and risking his judgment, I'll distract him with a question of my own. "What's up with you? You didn't take Melanie home on Friday night." I raise my brows and rest my ankle on my opposite knee, trying to appear relaxed.

"She shared a ride with Sarah and didn't want to leave her friend. I got her number, though. So we'll see." He taps his phone with two fingers. "How about you and Sarah? You seemed to be cozy."

"She's a cool chick. I … uh … actually offered to help her out with something. That's why I keep checking my phone. I'm expecting her to text me." He nods and turns back to the computer, his hands flying over the keys. "Do you want a coffee? I'm going to make a fresh one."

"Nah, I'm good. Thanks."

I grab my phone and head toward my kitchen; one of the perks of having our office in my home. I'm annoyed with myself that I didn't insist on grabbing Sarah's number. I would have followed up by now, but I have to wait for her. I'm unsure what it was about her that made me want to help her with her baby predicament, apart from the fact that my proposition means I'll have the opportunity to get to know her better. A nice side benefit will be that I'll be getting laid on the regular for the foreseeable future. And doesn't that bring a smile to my face. I can't wait to get my hands and mouth on her body. *Those curves!* I bring my fist up to my mouth and bite the knuckle. She's my dream woman come to life. Everything about her, from the color of her hair to her smile to her sweet, sweet curves, is utter perfection. Then, on top of all that, she's easy to talk with and kind to boot. When she told me how she crochets hats for premature babies in her spare time and how she loves spending time with her sister's kids, I think I fell a little in love with her. Her entire being almost vibrated with joy as she spoke about them.

I need to remember she only wants me as a donor. She wants a baby, not a partner. Cool your jets dickhead. Maybe with a bit of time, I can convince her I'm partner material. Fuck, the way her eyes lit up whenever she spoke about becoming a mom convinced me I'd made the right decision to help her.

As I pour coffee into my cup, my phone lights up with a text from an unknown number. I snatch it up and unlock the screen.

UNKNOWN

Hi, this is Sarah. I'm not sure if you remember me from Friday night at Club Rumors, but I'm the woman you offered to help

As if I wouldn't remember her, or our conversation. I roll my eyes at no one.

UNKNOWN

If your offer still stands, I was hoping we could meet and discuss it further

Fuck, yeah! I barely restrain fist bumping the air. I settle myself so I can respond. She's being formal in her messages, so I need to keep that in mind.

ME

Hi, how could I possibly forget you?

Of course my offer is still on the table. Happy to meet wherever and whenever you're free

Shit. Does that sound too eager? I mean, I am, even though my motives aren't purely altruistic—I want to give her more than my swimmers—but I don't want to sound desperate. I save her number in my phone.

SARAH

Would you be free Saturday morning? We could meet at The Bistro over on Fourth Avenue at 10

ME

Sounds great. See you then

It's gonna be a long week. I'll be counting down the days until I see the woman who consumed my thoughts all weekend. I blow out a breath, collect my coffee, and head back to work. The best thing I can do is get lost in our current projects.

"I'm getting close to breaching the firewall," Dylan informs me as I step back into the office.

"That was quick." I take my seat and a mouthful of coffee.

"Yep. Scarily so. I'm surprised hackers haven't sunk these guys already." He taps his keyboard a few more times. "I'm in!" He pushes away from the desk, rolling back a few feet in his chair, wearing a smug smile.

"Good job, man. Now we need to detail exactly what you did and what they need to do to secure their site."

"Yep. I made notes as I went. It won't take long to put my report together."

"Great." I turn back to my project and get to work. Saturday can't come soon enough.

# CHAPTER 5

## —sarah—

Nope, this outfit isn't any good either. Why is it so hard to choose a damn outfit to wear today? It's not like I need to impress the guy; we're not dating or anything. He's only giving me his semen, and then I'll never see him again. Simple. I sigh heavily. Just my luck to meet someone who seems to be perfect. Life is unfair sometimes. But looking on the bright side, I've hopefully found a solution to my problem, depending on how our chat works out today.

I huff as I pick up my jeans again. Maybe I can pair them with my off-the-shoulder top and my tan sandals. Yeah, that'll work. Glancing at the time, I fly into a panic. I don't want to be late, but at the rate I'm going, I will be. Dressing quickly, I apply a little makeup and tie my hair in a high ponytail. I check my appearance in the full-length mirror behind my bedroom door and smile—my butt always looks fabulous in these jeans.

Collecting the paperwork from my small dining table, I slide it carefully into my purse and check to make sure I have everything I need. Butterflies fill my stomach as I head toward the elevator. I have the distinct feeling that today is the beginning of a new chapter for me. I'm hoping he doesn't think I'm too neurotic and rescind his offer to help.

I finally find a parking space after driving around for fifteen minutes, my frustration growing by the minute, along with the sweat beneath my armpits. I'm definitely late now. It's a trait I don't like, so I get annoyed with myself when I'm late somewhere. If you say you're going to arrive at a certain time, then damn well be there on time.

Quickly, I climb out of my car, ready to race across the street when the handle from my purse gets trapped in the closed door, spilling the contents all over the street. Sheets of paper escape and I hastily stomp on them to prevent them from flying away. When I bend down to pick them up, they're all crinkled and imprinted with the dirty print of my shoe. Dammit, this is not how I wanted to present myself. Because as much as I'm looking at him and his genetics under the microscope, I want to make a good impression. I don't want him to think I'm not good enough to become a mom. He might change his mind about being my donor, and I don't want that. I scoop everything up and draw in several deep breaths, calming myself before I have a panic attack in the street. I drag my purse straps over my shoulder and take purposeful strides toward the café, fifteen minutes late. I can't do anything about it now, so I try to put the shit show of the last twenty minutes behind me.

Pausing outside the door, I calm my mind ready to meet with my possible baby daddy. The door opens and when I move to clear the doorway for whoever's exiting the café, I spot AJ holding it open with a warm smile.

Great. He probably saw everything.

His smiling eyes connect with mine and the last twenty minutes disappear. I don't know what's wrong with me. He has some magnetic force that draws me to him, which I'm trying hard to fight. He's only interested in sharing his semen, not his life. I must remember that but I always struggle to keep my heart locked away. It's why I could never risk Mel's suggestion of sleeping with some random guy to get pregnant. My heart doesn't know the difference between having hot sex and falling in love. It thinks sex means love. My brain knows that's not the case, but the damn muscle in my chest can't separate the two.

He leans forward to kiss my cheek, sending sparks shooting through my body. My heart tries to engage—nope, not happening—I push it down and pull away from his touch. His eyebrows sink low, but he quickly catches himself and smiles at me. "Hey, Sarah. It's great to see you." He waves his hand toward a table by the window. "I already have a table for us."

"Hey. Thanks for meeting me today. I'm sorry I'm late." He guides me forward with his hand at the base of my spine and those same sparks erupt again. I drop to the seat, placing my purse next to me and he sits opposite. "How's your week been?" Good one, Sarah. You're not here to make small talk and his week is none of your damn business.

"Pretty good, thanks. We cracked a couple of firewalls, which is always a great feeling. Did you want to order a coffee and then we can chat?" *See?* He just wants to get straight down to business.

We each order a coffee, and AJ quickly scans his card to pay for mine. "You don't need to pay for my coffee, I should be paying for yours since we're here because of me."

"Don't be ridiculous. A coffee and a slice of banana bread aren't going to break the bank. It's ingrained in me to pay for the lady. It's how I work." He shrugs and one side of his mouth rises. It's a half-smile but it looks oh-so-good on him. *Stop it, Sarah.*

We return to our booth and I drag out the paperwork I brought with me along with a pen. Placing them on the table, I press out the creases, giving AJ an embarrassed smile. He's watching me closely, and I think he's hiding his amusement behind his hand, but I can still see the crinkles around his eyes. "Sorry. I dropped them when I got out of my car."

"That's okay. What are all the papers for?"

"Uh, well, this is a questionnaire"—I hold up one set of papers— "for you to complete. And this one is a little information about me." I hold up the other set of papers.

His eyebrows rise. "Can't we just chat? Does it need to be so formal?"

I shift in my seat. I was worried he would say that. "We can do that, but would you mind completing some parts of the questionnaire? They're related to your genetic and health history. I tried to remember the information that was provided through the clinic, and I replicated it as best I could. I just want to be sure." I lick my suddenly dry lips.

God, has the temperature risen? Suddenly, it's incredibly hot and uncomfortable in here.

"I get that." He holds out his hand for the papers, and I place them in his palm.

His eyes drop to the document, and he holds out his hand for the pen, which I quickly hand over. I started with the most straightforward questions—age, blood type, height and weight, history of drug and alcohol use, and his level of fitness—so he's working quickly. His eyes rise to mine and a smirk lifts his lips.

A server delivers our food to the table and once he leaves, AJ asks, "Why do you need to know how many sexual partners I've had?"

Uh, I just added that one out of curiosity. I skate my gaze around the café and shift in my seat. "To make sure you won't be hooking up with other women while I'm trying to get pregnant. If you're used to taking home different women every weekend, then that would be unacceptable for me." It's not like we'll be having sex, but I don't want to worry about him contracting an STD while I'm trying to get pregnant.

Lines form across his forehead as he shakes his head. "I'm not like that. And while we're trying to get you pregnant, I won't see anyone else. I promise."

At his genuine answer, I blow out a relieved breath, and the tightness across my shoulders releases. I don't know why the idea of him giving me that level of commitment was so important to me. It's not like we're going to be in a relationship. I smile. "Thank you. That's ... that's a relief."

He drops his eyes back to the paperwork, and I take a shaky sip of my coffee. Even though I ordered a slice of banana bread, I'm not sure I can eat it. My leg bounces nervously beneath the table, and I drop my hands to my thighs to stop the action. While he quietly completes the form, I stare out the window watching people pass by. Pregnant women and women pushing strollers. Men and women holding hands and couples with babies. It's like that's all I ever see around me and I desperately want that.

AJ clears his throat. "I ... uh ... actually helped my sister and her wife get pregnant about four years ago and again about three months ago. So I guess, technically, I already have two kids ... well one, with another on the way."

My eyebrows rise with surprise. "How exactly did that work? That seems a little weird."

He chuckles. "Oh yeah, I guess it does. Hayley, my sister, and her wife, Lisa, went through a fertility clinic. Lisa's the one who carries the babies, and by using me as their donor it meant our family's genetics were passed on to their child."

Well, that makes sense. I had this weird vision of him impregnating his sister. "Oh, right. That's amazing. I would never have thought of doing something like that." I drop my eyes to my banana bread and break a piece off. "So does their child call you Daddy?"

"At the moment Colton calls me Uncle AJ because that's the role I play in his life. When he starts asking questions about where he came from, we'll sit down and explain to him that I'm his biological father in terms appropriate for his age. It's never going to be a secret. If he chooses to call me Dad from that point on, then so be it. It will be his choice at that time. The girls and I discussed it at great length before we went ahead with the donation." He rubs the back of his neck. "Is that going to be a problem?"

"No, not at all. Do you think your sister and her wife will want their children to have contact with this child?" I didn't really think about what would happen if he already had kids. I could still be tied to AJ and his family for life through this child—*if* it happens. "Actually, do you need to check with them if they're okay with you doing this?"

He leans back in his chair with a sigh and brushes his hand through his hair, messing up the strands, his bicep flexing. And what a bicep it is. *Stop looking at his bicep, Sarah.* I internally roll my eyes at myself. "I hadn't considered that. Maybe I should have a chat with them about all this before we move forward. Make sure they'll be okay with it and what their preference would be. I'm sorry. I hadn't really thought about this fully. I tend to be a little spontaneous sometimes." He releases a deprecating laugh.

Oh shit! Did he even think this through at all? He *was* very quick to offer his ... uh ... services to me last weekend. "Look. Maybe this is a bad idea." I place my hand on the papers to draw them back toward me but AJ places his warm hand over mine, stopping me in my tracks. His hand is so much bigger than mine with a tan that only comes from spending time outdoors. He squeezes gently and I lift my eyes to his.

"What did I say to upset you?"

His expression is open and genuine, curiosity evident. "I wondered if you'd thought this through. You were quick to offer to help me last weekend and maybe you should have taken time to consider all of the ramifications of such an offer." I swallow past the lump forming in my throat because if I walk away today, I'll have to go back to my original plan and it'll be at least twelve months before I can afford to try again. The backs of my eyes sting and I blink to keep my emotions in check. "I don't want you to rush into something that requires a significant amount of thought and consideration. You'll probably meet the woman of your dreams one day and want to start a family with her. This could end up being an issue for you."

He leaves his hand resting on top of mine, and I take comfort from his warmth, even though I shouldn't. He glances out of the window for a moment, then brings his eyes back to mine. "I know I was quick to offer my help, but that's because I've already gone through this process and I know how happy it's made Hayley and Lisa." The love for his sister is clear. "Had I ever thought I would do the same for a stranger? No. I can't say I had ever considered the possibility. After leaving you on Friday night, I went home and gave the whole idea some serious thought, and I decided to follow through with my offer if you reached out to me. The only aspect I hadn't considered was how my decision may impact my sister and her family. I'll talk with Hayley and Lisa, but I don't think there'll be a problem. Would you want this child to have regular contact with his or her half-siblings?" Creases form between his brows.

"To be honest, I hadn't considered this possibility. I knew when I was going through the fertility clinic that the possibility of half-siblings was inevitable, but it's a little different because I never met those donors face to face. There's a level of anonymity. The thought of family connections hadn't crossed my mind." Now I feel like a hypocrite for accusing him of not thinking it through when I've pretty much done the same thing. "If you don't mind me asking, how will it work for you when you eventually settle and want to start a family? How will you deal with the half-sibling issue?"

He shrugs. "I don't see it as an issue."

Hmmm. I'm not sure how I'd feel knowing a prospective partner offered to be a donor to a complete stranger. Hang on a minute. That's exactly what the guys who donate their semen to the clinic do. Why am I making such a big deal about AJ doing it?

"So, how did things work with your sister and her wife, exactly? Did you sign anything?"

"As I already told you, they went through a fertility clinic. They used my donation to do it, which reduced the cost somewhat, but they still had to pay the fees. I had to sign the documents the clinic requires a donor to sign." I nod as he explains. "I assumed we would skip the clinic, but is that how you want to do this?"

"I was hoping to do this without the clinic because it would mean I can try again sooner. But if you would feel more comfortable doing it that way, I can wait." Fingers crossed he's happy to skip the clinic.

He shakes his head. "Not at all. I'm happy to work it out between the two of us. I don't foresee any issues."

"Are you sure your sister and her wife will be okay with this? Their children will be related to this one," I remind him again.

He shakes his head. "I don't think they'll have any issues with it but I'll ask what level of involvement they would like, and we'll see if we can come to an agreement. You didn't answer me before, would *you* want the kids to know each other?"

I ponder his question for a moment. Since this will probably be the only child I'll have, it might be nice for him or her to know their half-siblings. My child wouldn't have this opportunity if I was using an anonymous donor through the clinic. I'd be crazy to refuse. I nod. "I think I would. But only if your family agrees."

He nods, then leans forward slightly, pulling something out of his back pocket. "I brought my paperwork. It's from six months ago when I went through the process with Hayley and Lisa for the second time, but if you want me to get a more up-to-date semen analysis and sexual health check done, I don't mind. I haven't … I haven't uh … been with anyone since these results." A slight blush stains his cheeks as his eyes drop away from mine. I'm not sure why he'd be embarrassed about that. I'm happy to know he doesn't sleep around on the regular.

He slides the results across the table, and I dig my glasses out of my purse to read them.

Concentration: 285 million. *I raise my eyebrows, that's fantastic.*

Motility: 85%. *Another fantastic result. This is promising.*

Morphology: 90%. *This guy's sperm is like the high achievers of sperm according to these results.*

I take off my glasses and glance up at AJ. He's sitting there like he got a perfect score on his SATs, and he *should* feel proud. These are outstanding results.

"Wow. Your sperm are real go-getters." I chuckle as I place my glasses on the table and slide the paper back to him. Did I think I would ever say a sentence like that in my life? Nope. But here I am sitting opposite a man who has one of the best semen analysis results I've seen.

He chuckles. "Thanks." He points at my glasses resting on the table. "You look cute with your glasses on."

I glance down at them and my cheeks heat at his compliment. "Thanks. I only need them for reading. Do you wear glasses at all?"

"Nope. I have twenty-twenty vision." He relaxes back in his seat. "About that last question." He points to the questionnaire.

I straighten. This is important. "Yeah."

"I'll stick with your pregnancy plan for as long as it takes, Sarah." He leans forward, placing his elbows on the table, looking intently at my face. "And I won't be seeing anyone during that time."

I blow out a relieved breath and my shoulders drop. "Thank you. But what if you meet someone?"

He shrugs. "I haven't met anyone yet, and I'm not actively looking at this point."

"Well, let me know if you do and we'll re-evaluate where things are at." He nods and I remember the paperwork I brought for him about me. I gather it together and hand it over. "Here's some information on my background. I figured it was only fair you had an idea of the type of person you're helping to get pregnant." I chuckle awkwardly. "Is this the weirdest conversation you've ever had?"

He tilts his flattened hand from side to side with a grin. "Maybe. How about you *tell* me a little about yourself? Like how did someone as gorgeous as you end up having to go down this path to have a baby?" My light mood slips a little and I drop my hands to my lap to fidget. I glance out of the window and watch the people passing by while I gather my thoughts. "If it's too personal, you don't have to tell me. It has no bearing on whether or not I give you my jizz."

I give him a grateful smile, but I feel as though he deserves an explanation since he's being so generous. I lick my dry lips and take a sip of my coffee. "I was dating my high school sweetheart. We did all the things you normally do in a long-term relationship, we moved in together, bought a dog, he proposed, and I said 'yes.' Then one day he came home from work and said he had accepted a promotion within his company. I was so excited for him until he told me it was in Perth, Australia." AJ's eyes widen and his mouth drops open a little. "I was settled and happy in my job, and I didn't want to leave my family and friends to travel to the other side of the world, so he left and I stayed. He took our dog and moved to Australia." AJ moves his hand to cover mine, and I soak up his kindness. "It all happened so fast. I couldn't believe he accepted the promotion without even discussing it with me. I thought our relationship was stronger than that … I thought I was more important to him, but I was wrong."

"I'm sorry, Sarah. That's tough and the guy's an asshole."

I shrug. "His dreams were different to mine, I guess. Anyway, I was thirty when that happened and by the time I recovered emotionally, I was thirty-two. Over the last two years, I've had some short relationships which were headed nowhere fast … and here I am." It sounds trivial when I lay it out in simple terms but my heart was shattered when Michael so easily chose the promotion over me.

"Thank you for sharing your story with me. Time moves fast, and I get that you feel like you're running out of time. I think you're incredible for taking matters into your own hands and going after what you want."

# CHAPTER 6

## *—aj—*

I REACH TOWARD THE NEXT PINCH HOLD, PUSHING UPWARD WITH MY legs, straining and pushing my body to the limit. Sweat trickles down my temples and my spine making my tank stick to my body. One more crimp and I'm at the top. My hand makes contact with the button to stop the clock and I glance down at Dylan with a grin.

"Zero point five seven seconds. That's gotta be your best time yet."

"Yep. I'm pretty happy with that." I glance up at the time, pride filling my chest. "Take," I call down to Dylan who's belaying for me today. I get myself into the seated position, my feet shoulder-width apart, ready to be lowered.

"Are you ready to lower?"

"Ready to lower."

I keep my feet high and push into the wall as I'm lowered to the pads below. I like coming to the gym a couple of times a week to maintain my muscle strength and endurance, so I'm climbing fit for whenever I decide to do an outdoor climb. When my feet connect with the pads, Dylan provides enough slack in the rope and then holds up his hand. I slap my palm against his, creating a puff of chalk dust and he pulls me in for a back slap-come-hug.

"Congrats, man."

"Thanks." I tilt my chin toward the wall. "Do you wanna see if you can beat my time?"

"Nah. I need to get going. I promised Mom I'd cut her grass this afternoon." He disengages from the belay rope, removing his harness, and I untie my knots to remove mine, then reach down for my hand towel to wipe away the sweat and remove the excess chalk from my fingers.

"Thanks for belaying for me today. Say hi to your mom for me."

"I will." He collects his bag. "See ya on Monday."

"Yep. Bye." He turns and heads out, and I decide to do some bouldering for a bit before heading to my sister's place. I need to chat with her about a possible half-sibling for Colton and the bubba. I hadn't really thought about the impact my decision would have on my sister's family.

I started climbing as a way to practice mindfulness. When I'm climbing, my thoughts and focus have to be solely on what I'm doing, planning my next hold, and my path up the rock face. I can't think about work, family, or anything else that's going on in my life. I've found since developing the skill, my work focus has also improved. I'm better at being focused on a singular task and planning the steps I need to take to see a job through to completion.

The lactic acid in my muscles is building, and they're beginning to shake, meaning it's time to call it quits for today. I do some cool-down stretches and head home to shower and get ready for dinner with my sister and her family.

"Knock, knock!" I call out through the screen door. The handle won't budge, which is a good thing. Hayley and Lisa started taking their safety seriously after a home invasion two doors down from them. Prior to that, they often left their doors and windows unlocked, even though I regularly lectured them about their personal safety.

Lisa walks toward me with a smile as she rests Colton on her hip, her very slight baby bump only now beginning to show. "Hey, favorite brother-in-law."

I huff out a chuckle as she unlocks the door to let me inside. Colton immediately reaches for me, climbing from Lisa to me. "I'm your only brother-in-law, so that doesn't make me feel special."

She waves off my comment and leans in to kiss my cheek. "You're still my favorite."

Colton presses his little hands on each of my bristly cheeks and rubs my nose with his. "Hello, Unca AJ!"

"Hey, little man." I kiss the tip of his nose. "Have you been a good boy for your mommy and mama?"

He nods vigorously. "I have."

I glance at Lisa and she nods at me, gently smoothing Colton's hair down with eyes full of love. "Mostly. You just need to stop climbing on everything."

"I want to be like Unca AJ!" He bounces up and down in my arms.

"Well, if you want to be like me, you have to stop climbing on the furniture and counters. I don't do stuff like that. I only climb where I'm supposed to." I make sure my tone is serious to ensure he understands the importance. If he keeps climbing the way he does, I'm worried Hayley or Lisa will suffer a heart attack.

His little eyebrows scrunch together over his brown eyes and his expression turns serious as he nods. "Okay, Unca AJ. I'll stop."

Maybe I should commission a climbing wall to make climbing safer. I'll talk to the girls about it when he's out of earshot. We head through the house to the backyard, where Hayley's standing at the grill. I place Colton down and go straight to her, wrapping my arms around her waist and lifting her off her feet.

She giggles and as I drop her to her feet, she spins around and engulfs me in her embrace. "AJ! It's so good to see you. It's been too long."

I kiss her cheek. "It has. I'm sorry. Work's been busy and Grandfather has been breathing down my neck." I roll my eyes at the last part of my sentence. "How have you guys been?"

"We're doing great. I don't know why Grandfather won't let it go when Mom's dying to step into the role."

I give my sister a pointed look. "You know exactly why."

"Yep. He's old-fashioned. As much as I love him, it's time he dragged himself into the twenty-first century." She huffs, rolling her eyes. She lifts the chicken from the grill to check it. "Dinner's nearly ready."

Lisa's setting the outdoor table, so I head over to help her. We work together to bring out the salads and drinks. "How are you feeling?"

She strokes her abdomen. "Still struggling to keep food down for most of the day. I'm hoping it will settle down for the second trimester like it did with Colton."

"Unca AJ. Look at me!" Colton calls out from his swing set as he climbs up the slide. I glance across at Lisa who's shaking her head at her son.

"Hold on with two hands!" I call back to him. While he's busy, I lower my voice. "How about I look at getting him a climbing wall for the backyard? I've seen them online. They don't look that hard to do. I could get a carpenter to build the frame and I can attach the holds."

"That'd be fantastic and maybe it would stop him from climbing everything in sight inside." Lisa sighs as Hayley places the tray of chicken onto the table.

"I'll get onto it."

Lisa and Hayley give me grateful smiles. "That'd be great. Thanks, AJ."

"No problem."

Lisa and Hayley lay out the food, placing small portions on Colton's plate while I retrieve him from the slide and take him inside to wash his hands, then he eagerly leads me back to the table. "Unca AJ, sit next to me."

He climbs into his booster chair, and I take the seat next to him. We all dig into the scrumptious barbecue. "This is delicious. Thanks for the invite."

"You're welcome. We meant to invite you last weekend but Lisa was too sick." Hayley smiles at her wife and tucks Lisa's hair behind her ear with affection. A pang strikes the muscle in my chest. I want what they have but I can't seem to find someone who wants the same thing. Even Sarah, whom I know I have a connection with, doesn't want a committed relationship. "What have you been up to?"

Even though the girls already know about the huge contract Dylan and I landed with *booknow.com*, I tell them a bit more detail about it. "This could put us on the map. It's a huge coup."

"Congratulations. I'm so proud of what you guys have built. You deserve all the success," Lisa says, mirroring Hayley's words when I initially told her about it.

"Thanks." I'm not sure why as a grown-ass man I need my family's approval, but it seems I still do as pride fills me with her praise. Maybe it's because everyone in my family runs a successful business, and as the baby of the family, I want to be considered successful in their eyes too.

"We had some good news this week too." Hayley glances at Lisa and matching smiles break across their faces. "My application to adopt Colton was approved. I'm officially his mama."

"Congratulations. I know how important it was to you." I stand from my seat to hug my sister and sister-in-law.

"Thanks. It was such a relief to have the official paperwork."

"I bet." I'm thrilled for them. Who knew that the non-biological parent would have to formally adopt her own child? It's ridiculous. We finish eating and I stand to collect the plates. "Why don't you two put your feet up and Colton and I will clean up." I give Colton a wink. "Are you ready to help me?"

He throws his little fist into the air. "Yeah, Unca AJ. Let's do this!" Colton climbs down from his chair and heads straight toward Lisa and Hayley. Taking each of their hands, he tugs. "Come on, Mommy. Come on, Mama." They both chuckle as they stand, following Colton's lead to the living room. I set about clearing the table, carrying everything inside to start the dishes as he ensures his moms are comfortable with enough cushions to sink a small boat. He lifts each of their feet onto the ottoman, then hands them the TV remote. He walks toward me with a look of accomplishment as his moms sink into the couch with matching grins as they watch him walk toward me.

After carefully packing away the leftovers, I wash all of the plastic cutlery and plates for him to dry. He stands proudly on the small step the girls have at the sink for him and he carefully dries each item, laying them on the counter. I notice the items aren't completely dry, so I'll have to wipe them over later so I can put them away. He's used to helping his moms, so we make quick work of the dishes.

I want to talk with Hayley and Lisa about my discussion with Sarah yesterday, but I need to have all of their attention when we discuss it, so I bathe Colton and offer to read him a bedtime story.

"This one, Unca AJ!" He waves a bright green book over his head as he runs back to his brand-new big-boy bed. He had been sleeping in his crib, minus one side but the girls decided to get him a bed so the crib was free for their next baby. He climbs into bed, handing me the book and I tuck him under the sheet. It's too warm for anything more than that; this summer has been unseasonably hot. I get comfortable beside him and scan the cover.

"By Crikey? What does that mean?" I look at my nephew.

"It's a book from Aus-tray-li-uh. It's something they say. It's really funny. Read it!" His little chocolate-colored eyes—exactly like mine and Hayley's—are sparkling with delight. "It's my fav-rite."

I chuckle. "Okay, okay." I read all about the sheep called Doug who lives on an Australian farm. He doesn't want to be shorn and his antics to avoid the experience at all costs are detailed with humorous illustrations. I take note of the author, Jodie Reeder, so I can check if she has any more books. I might have to get Colton the next book for his birthday.

"Can you please read it again? I promise to go to sleep if you read it again." How can I deny him when he gives me his puppy dog eyes? So I read it again, chuckling each time Doug the sheep manages to escape the shearer's clutches. When I close the book to place it on his nightstand and glance at my nephew's angelic face, his eyes are heavy with sleep. "Thank you, Unca AJ."

"You're welcome. Sweet dreams, little man." I dip down to kiss his forehead, brushing my fingers through his silky hair. I'm not sure if the strong bond I share with him is because I'm his biological father or if it's because we usually spend a lot of time together. I carefully climb from his bed and make my way to the living room where I find Lisa lying across the cushions with her head in Hayley's lap. Hayley's eyes are locked on the television as she strokes Lisa's hair, a look of contentment on her face.

They both notice me and Lisa pushes to sit up but I stop her. "Stay where you are. You look comfortable. I won't stay for long, but there was something I needed to speak with you both about."

Hayley responds, creases forming between her brows. "Sure. Sounds serious."

Now, where do I start? Suddenly, I'm nervous. What if they say no? I don't want to tell Sarah I can't help her. It wouldn't be fair but I need to consider my family first. I rub the back of my neck and start. I explain how I met Sarah and what she's hoping to achieve.

"Good for her." Hayley's quick to show her support. "Did she want to use the same fertility clinic we did? I have their details on my phone."

"Uh, no. She's already had two procedures without success with a clinic. She's going to do it independently or else she'll have to wait for another twelve months while she saves enough money." Both women nod. They understand the expense of trying to get pregnant. They were lucky that some of the costs were reduced because they had me as their donor.

"What's she going to do then?" My sister's eyes widen and a slow smile graces her face, which is so similar to mine and Colton's. "You're going to help her, right?" She wriggles her eyebrows up and down.

"Well …" I shrug. "Yeah."

"You're so sweet," Lisa chirps.

"More like he knows he'll get laid on the regular with this arrangement." Hayley chuckles. "Am I right?"

I get up to pace. "Well, a little of both. I wanted to help her out. I think what she's trying to do is admirable and I know my"—I wave my hand down around my groin area—"swimmers are viable. Plus, it won't hurt that I'll get to spend extended time with her. She's pretty cool."

"Good for you. Are you going to be able to do this without getting attached to her? I mean, you're going to have to spend a fair amount of time with her. It could take months for her to actually get pregnant." Hayley points out.

"Well, I can't get attached. She doesn't want a partner. Just a baby. I'm sure I can do it." I sit back down. "But I need to ask you two how you feel about it because her baby will be a half-sibling to your kids. She was wondering how the two of you would feel about it. If you would want the kids to know each other and spend time together?"

They glance at each other. They always seem to know what the other is thinking, it's quite weird. "We're fine with it. Honestly. I think it's great you're going to help her fulfill her dream of becoming a mother. It's the best thing. As for the kids being in contact, it would be nice, but it's up to her. We're absolutely open to the idea, but it's whatever Sarah feels most comfortable with."

I blow out a breath and a smile breaks across my lips. "Thanks. I knew you'd be cool with the whole thing." Lisa sits up and Hayley climbs to her feet to embrace me.

"Anytime." She lays her hand over my heart. "Just be careful, AJ. I don't want you to get hurt. You already seem to like her."

I brush off her concern. "I promise I'll be okay. She's really sweet and I think we'll be able to keep the lines of communication open if anything changes."

## —sarah—

"GOOD MORNING, MR. WAINWRIGHT," I SAY BRIGHTLY FROM MY PERCH behind my desk. It's weird being here before him because he's usually here long before anyone else.

Eric stops at my desk. "Morning, Sarah. How was your weekend?"

"Busy as usual. Got to hang out with the family yesterday." A smile tugs at my lips at the memory of Kenny and Austin chasing poor old Archie around Mom and Dad's backyard.

"Great," he says distractedly as he steps into his office, and I head to the kitchen to make his pot of tea.

It's obvious to everyone in the office he's lost his desire to be here. He's been passing more and more of his tasks over to Tony, the Vice President, who happens to be a dick. I only hope his grandson takes over sooner rather than later.

With Eric's tea in hand, I head back to his office with a smile, ready to go over his plans for the week. "Thank you, Sarah. I have a face-to-face call with Adam in ten minutes, so we'll do our planning after that. Please shut the door on your way out."

"Sure thing." I step out and quietly close the door behind me, returning to my desk to update the database. We changed to a new system and some of our information got lost in the transition, so I have the delightful task of cross-checking everything. It's an enormous job and tedious to boot.

Lost in the task, I jump at the sudden shout which bursts from Eric's office. I glance across, but he's closed his blinds, so I can't see inside. In all the time I've worked here, not once have I heard Eric raise his voice, and there have been times when the guys from development and testing have tried his patience. I strain to hear more of the conversation, my body leaning toward his office, but his words are muffled.

"Sarah. Can you let Eric know we're ready for the second round of testing for MicroE19?" Evan raps his knuckles once on my desk and heads back the way he came.

"Sure," I call to his retreating back and make a note in an email to Eric.

Eric's door opens and slams closed. With angry steps, he strides down the hallway carrying his briefcase. I quickly jump to my feet to follow him. "Mr. Wainwright. Is everything okay?"

He stops suddenly and I almost run into the back of him. He spins around, wearing a tight smile, his face flushed in anger. "No, Sarah. Everything is not okay. I've decided to go home for the day. I'll start fresh tomorrow." He spins on his heel and I struggle to come up with what to say. I've never seen him like this.

"Uh, okay. I'll see you tomorrow. Please take care."

He nods, waving over his shoulder, and the elevator doors close him inside the metal box. As I arrive back at my desk, my phone vibrates, so I quickly snatch it up.

AJ

Hi

I spoke with Hayley and Lisa and they don't have any issues with us moving forward

I'm ready to start when you are

I squeal inside, dropping my head back to gaze up at the ceiling in relief. I instantly feel lighter. I actually started ovulating yesterday, I wonder if it's too soon to ask him to start.

AJ

When do you start ovulating next?

Wow. He's perfect.

ME

Hey. That's awesome news

As good fortune would have it, I started ovulating yesterday

Straight away my phone lights up.

AJ

Perfect. I'm free tonight

My heart rate accelerates and my hand shakes. Tonight! I guess it's great he's eager, but am I ready? I mean, I know I'm ready, but this feels fast. I deliberate how to respond. I need to plan this. I didn't think he'd talk with his sister so soon. I thought I had time to work up the courage to do this with a complete stranger. Well, not a complete stranger, because we got to know each other a little more over coffee, but he's still a stranger compared to people I've known for a long time.

What if he's been luring me in with his nice guy act but he's really a creep? I didn't get that vibe from him, but I have been wrong in the past. Shit! Why is this so hard? He's offering me my dream and I still need to think it to death. I grasp my hair on either side of my head and tug on it in frustration.

My phone rings in my hand and I jump. Glancing at the screen, AJ's name is there clear as day. Shit! I don't know what to say to him. He's going to think I'm some crazy woman if I can't get myself together. It rings and rings while I try to gather my thoughts but they won't cooperate. My mind's a mess. This is everything I want. This man is offering to make my dream come true with no strings attached. But for some reason, I didn't think it would happen this month. I figured it would happen next month and I'd have time to plan things properly.

This is not following my plan! Ugh!

The device in my hand goes quiet, the screen going dark. Then the missed call message shows. I blow out a frustrated breath.

What the hell is wrong with me?

I drop into my chair and swivel around to stare out of the window, not really seeing the city skyline I normally adore. My phone buzzes again.

AJ

Sarah? Everything okay?

How do I tell him I had a momentary internal crisis? He's going to think I'm crazy. And I definitely don't want him to think that.

ME

Yeah. Everything's great, just overthinking everything as usual

I delete the last part of the message and change it.

ME

Yeah. Everything's great, just busy atm

AJ

Okay. Let me know if you want me tonight

Oh my, what an offer. Under any other circumstance, his offer would be totally hot. But for my overthinking brain, it's too much, too soon. But the sooner we get started, the sooner I'll get pregnant, right?

ME

Sure

I make myself a coffee and head back to my desk. Only I don't make it that far.

"Sarah," Tony calls from behind his desk, so I stop and poke my head in his doorway. "Where did Eric go? I need to speak with him about these figures."

"He didn't say. He was in a rush. Said he'll be back in the office tomorrow." I shrug, as though it's nothing out of the ordinary even though it really is.

"Tomorrow!" he bellows. "What the hell is going on with him?" he mumbles.

My eyes are going fuzzy and the slight pounding at the back of my head is warning enough for me to take a break from the screen. I glance at the time and notice it's past lunch. I may as well take a quick break and eat my lunch in the break room, something I rarely do. Collecting my phone and water bottle, I grab my lunch out of the fridge. Because it's past lunch, the room is empty, and the low hum of the fridge is the only noise in the room. I sigh and take the lid off my pre-prepared salad jar, tipping the contents into a bowl. Now that I'm not focused on the database, my mind spins back to AJ's offer to start on my pregnancy plan tonight.

Maybe it's best to jump in and get started. We're both clear on our arrangement, and he seems genuinely interested in helping me achieve my dream. I need someone to talk me through this. I don't want to call Emma and interrupt her day. I double-check the time. Mel may be available.

ME

Have you got time to talk?

I return to my salad, my mind churning over AJ's offer so I jolt when my phone rings. Quickly, I pick it up and accept the call. "Hey, Mel. Thanks for calling me back."

"Anytime, Sare. But this is unusual for you to be calling me in the middle of a workday. What's up?"

I blow out a heavy breath and spill everything about AJ and how I'm overthinking everything as usual. She listens to my rambling thoughts, as she always does. "It feels too fast."

"I hear what you're saying, but this is what you wanted. He's giving it to you on a silver platter. Book a hotel, it'll take you five minutes, and then text him the place and time. You don't need to overthink this, Sare. You've already thought of everything."

Thank God for my best friend. "Okay. I'll do it. Thank you."

"Have you got everything you need?"

"Yeah, I ordered everything I needed as soon as he offered when we first met. It arrived on Friday, so I'm ready."

"No excuses. Go forth and get knocked up, my friend." She chuckles. "If you need me, I'm off tonight."

"Thanks, Mels Bells. You're the best."

"I know. Mwah! Good luck."

We disconnect the call and I locate the number of a hotel not far from my place, make the damn booking, and message AJ.

ME

Hey, it's me

God, Sarah. He already knows it's you. Your name probably shows up on his damn screen.

AJ

Hey you

ME

Are you still available tonight?

AJ

Of course. My sperm is ready and waiting! I made a
fresh batch today

I chuckle. I'm glad he finds this whole thing funny.

ME

Would you be able to meet me at the Como after
dinner?

I hold my breath as I wait for his answer.

AJ

We could have dinner together

Shit! That would make it feel like a date and I'm not sure if I can
keep my emotional distance if we share a meal before doing what
needs to be done. I need to keep the lines clear and defined or my
heart may get confused.

AJ

Or we don't have to and I'll meet you at the hotel. Do
you have a room number?

ME

Thanks, I'm not sure what time I'll finish here and then I
need to get home. Room 743

See you after 7

Thank you

AJ

No problem

# CHAPTER 8

## —sarah—

I DON'T THINK I'VE EVER BEEN THIS NERVOUS BEFORE. MY LEGS ARE shaky, and I'm worried I'm going to tip over because I'm off-balance. I check in at the front counter and collect my key to the room. I didn't want to do this at my apartment, because well, I don't know AJ. I didn't think it was prudent to invite him into my home. I tighten my hold on the strap of my purse as I step into the elevator, pressing the button for my floor. As the doors are about to close, a couple enters and he whispers something to her. She glances across at me, then giggles. He pulls her incredibly close and nuzzles down into the crook of her neck and my chest tightens because I want that. I lock my eyes on the numbers above the door, so I'm not tempted to watch their interaction. Nothing good can come from wishing and hoping for something that's never going to happen for me. I have different priorities now and I need to remember that.

The doors finally open on my floor, and I scurry out after wishing the couple a mumbled good night. I'm sure their evening will be completely the opposite of mine. Though, if everything goes as planned, I'll be on my way to being pregnant! Yay me! Stopping outside my room, I scan the card with a shaky hand. Geez, Sarah, get yourself under control, girl. I'm a little early, but I wanted to set up before AJ arrives. He's been extremely accommodating, offering to meet with me at such short notice, so I don't want to waste his time.

The hotel isn't fancy and the room is basic, but it has everything I need. A clean bathroom and a bed. I drop my purse on the dresser, then fish out what I need. Bending down, I take off my shoes and pad into the bathroom, the tiles cold underfoot. I diligently wash my hands with soap and then lay out what I need on the vanity.

When I glance into the mirror, I pause, studying my reflection carefully. My life could possibly change tonight. I fiddle with my hair and smooth my hands down my clothes, twisting this way and that in the mirror.

Now, what do I do while I wait? Peering out of the glass doors to the small balcony, I think some fresh air is in order. The sounds of the city greet me as I step outside and draw in a deep breath. I love this city. I love the skyline at night, and I love the sunsets on the beach. I love spring walks along the river and hikes in the fall. This city has everything I need, which is one of the reasons I didn't want to leave when Michael got his promotion.

A knock sounds and I jump. *Shit! Calm down, girl.* My foot connects with the soft carpet as I step back inside to answer the door with a racing heart. I pause for a moment, my hand on the knob, and take breaths to calm my nerves. AJ's been cool and laid back throughout the entire process so far, and he's happily gone along with every request I've made. I shake out my hands while I draw in and blow out a long breath, put on my best smile, and open the door as though I'm not a nervous wreck.

My eyes connect with AJ's, and then dart around his face, taking in the five o'clock shadow he's had every time we've met. I then skim down his fit physique and the navy Henley, which hugs his torso like a second skin to the black ripped jeans, clinging to his defined thighs. He definitely has great genetics. Physically, he's my ultimate in every single way. I wonder how he stays in such great shape when his job keeps him tied to a desk. My eyes make it back to his face and the smirk he's wearing, his eyes crinkled in humor. My cheeks heat having been caught admiring him so blatantly.

"Hey." *Good one, Sarah.*

"Hi." He leans forward, laying a chaste kiss on my cheek and sending heat racing through my body, then bends down to collect a bag as if his kiss was of no consequence. When he steps over the threshold, I take a step back to allow him to pass through the doorway. I'm not sure why he needs an overnight bag, his part will be over and done with and he'll be able to go home shortly.

He places his bag on the luggage rack and glances around the room. AJ walks over to the bed and presses down on the mattress, then turns to me with a sparkle in his eye. "Are you nervous? Because I'm nervous and I really hope I'm not alone in my nerves." He chuckles, rubbing the back of his neck, and making his bicep bulge. My eyes follow the action with appreciation. "I've never had sex on demand before."

*Uhm, what?* His words jolt me out of my stupor and I snap my eyes back to his face.

What does he mean, he's never had sex on demand before? Does he think we're having sex tonight?

I can't have sex with him. Whenever someone sticks their dick in me, I fall in love with them. I can't separate my emotions from the act. My stupid hormones and heart think it's love. It's why I can't have one-night stands like Mel.

Well, this is awkward. I shuffle on my feet, glancing around the small space. Has the room shrunk? It suddenly feels too small. And hot. Is it hotter in here? My pulse pounds in my ears like a drumline.

AJ steps into my space, and this close I can smell his citrus after-shave. He smells so freaking good—his pheromones play havoc with my senses. I tip my head back, hoping he didn't notice me drawing in a deep breath of his scent. "Are you okay, Sarah?"

I nod, then bite my bottom lip, and his eyes drop to the action. His pupils dilate and his nostrils flare. I take half a step back, putting more space between us. "I, uh, think maybe there's been a ... a ... misunderstanding."

Creases form across his forehead and his eyes narrow. "In what way?"

"Well, uh, we don't actually need to have sex for me to get pregnant." I semi-chuckle awkwardly as I spin on my heel and head toward the bathroom. Collecting the sealed items I placed on the vanity earlier, I turn back toward AJ, bumping into him. "Uh, sorry. I didn't realize you were so close."

He glances down at the items in my hands, then up at my face. "What the hell is that for?" He waves his hand around the items I'm holding.

I hold one of the items up higher. "Well, you're going to collect your semen in this collection condom." I shake the pink packet in front of him. "Then you can go home. I'll use this syringe to get the sperm where it needs to go." I wave the plastic device around between us as I explain the process—I assumed he would be somewhat familiar with the collection process.

He studies the items as if he's never seen either of them before, then his eyes flick up to mine as his hands land on his hips. He opens and closes his mouth several times, then raises his hand to grasp the back of his neck, making his bicep bulge again. *Nice.* "You can't be serious."

"What do you mean? Of course I'm serious. I've never been more serious about anything in my life." I place the items back on the vanity.

"I figured we'd be doing this the old-fashioned way. You know … having sex." He paces away from me, shaking his head.

I cross my arms under my breasts and huff out a breath. Oh God, I hope he doesn't change his mind. I narrow my eyes and try to work out a way to keep him here. To ensure he follows through with our plan and our agreement. "You're not going to change your mind, are you?"

He spins around to face me, his eyes dropping to my breasts, then sliding back up to my face. "I said I'd give you my swimmers until you were pregnant. I don't go back on my word. Ever." He softens his voice, stepping closer to me. "Don't worry, I won't back out."

I blow out a long breath, my shoulders dropping from around my ears. "Oh, thank God. I was worried for a minute there. Well, if you want to get started"—I gesture with my head toward the bathroom— "I'll wait out here for you." I give him my best smile, trying to appear less frazzled than I feel.

He steps into the bathroom, studying me like he's investigating a science project and my body heats under his gaze. "So I wear this condom and do the deed in here, while you … you're on the other side of this door?" He points to the bathroom door.

"Uh, yeah. Do you need anything?" Maybe I should have brought some nudie magazines or something?

His eyes linger on me for several long moments before he shakes his head and begins to unbuckle his belt. I take the hint and pull the door closed. It's weird to be out here with a flimsy wall and door between us, knowing what he's doing in there. I glance at the door as I pace around the small room.

I can't believe he thought we'd be having sex. I *know* he didn't have sex with his sister-in-law to get her pregnant. I assumed he knew we wouldn't need to actually 'have sex.' I check my purse to make sure I have my handy dandy bullet and tuck it beneath the pillow.

I pace the room and I pace some more. Stepping closer to the bathroom door, I'm tempted to press my ear against it, but I resist— barely. As I'm pulling away, the door flies open and AJ is revealed. Shit, he nearly caught me about to eavesdrop. His hair is disheveled and his cheeks are adorably pink. He holds up the collection condom, the top pinched between his fingers. My heart gallops in my chest and I want to jump up and down on the spot with glee. He did it! My eyes snap to his and I hope he can see the gratitude I have for him.

"Thank you so much, AJ. You have no idea how much I appreciate this." I reach forward to take the condom from him but he drags it toward himself and away from me.

"You're welcome. What's the next step?" His voice is rough and slightly deeper than it was before.

"Well … uhm … I'm going to use that syringe"—I point toward the wrapped syringe on the vanity—"to draw up the fluid and then insert it inside me." My cheeks heat with embarrassment. It seems every conversation I have with this man is incredibly awkward.

He nods. "I guessed that much. Do you need any help?"

My head snaps up. "Uh, nope. I should be able to manage fine on my own. Thanks. Once you leave, I'll get straight to it to ensure your donation is as fresh as possible."

"Right." Only one word, but it comes out full of skepticism. "So …" He grips the back of his neck with his free hand. "I was reading up on all this and it says that you should *have sex*"—he raises his brows—"at least every second day while you're ovulating for your best chance." My heart pounds faster behind my ribs and my cheeks heat further. "Did you want to do this again on Wednesday?"

Could I be any more blessed to have found this guy? "You read up on the best practices for conception?" He simply nods as if it's not a big deal. "If you don't mind. I'd appreciate it."

He nods again. "Okay. Same time, same place on Wednesday. I'll uh … I'll leave you to it." He tips his head down to the condom he's still holding and passes it over.

I take it gratefully, swallowing my embarrassment, and give him an awkward side hug with my free hand. This stuff is as precious as gold, no it's even more precious, I don't want to spill a drop. "Thanks again, AJ. I'll see you on Wednesday."

I see him to the door and after a long pause, he presses the softest kiss to my cheek and leaves. My eyes drop to the condom I have pinched between my thumb and forefinger and my lips widen. This could be it! As I walk toward the bathroom to retrieve the cup and syringe, I squeal a little—giddy with excitement.

I grab the items and head toward the bed. Using the cup, I carefully balance the condom inside and remove my panties, hiking my skirt up past my hips. Reaching over to the nightstand, I unwrap the syringe and draw the plunger back, then press it all the way down as the website told me to do. I insert it into the condom, being careful not to touch the bottom. It's tricky keeping everything balanced but I manage and draw back the plunger, sucking up AJ's release. Lifting it closer to my face, I check for air bubbles and tap them out, careful not to let anything escape. I need every single one of those little suckers. Positioning a pillow in the middle of the bed I lay down with my hips tilted. The website said it wasn't essential to do this, but I want to give myself the best possible chance.

Dipping the syringe into my vagina, I position it where I think is best and slowly depress the plunger, hoping against hope I'm getting it in the right place. Then I grab my bullet. The website said it was best to have an orgasm to help push the semen where it needs to go. This whole situation feels so clinical, and I wonder how AJ managed to orgasm while standing in the bathroom with no stimulation. He's a guy, so it was probably no drama for him. I close my eyes and try to get in the zone but my mind won't quit. So many things have to go right for this to work. And I desperately want it to work.

With my eyes closed and my hips tilted, I try to clear my head and not think, just feel. Images of AJ in the bathroom stroking his cock come to the fore unbidden. My lids fly open as I try to push the images away.

I have no business thinking about him in that way.

He's helping me.

He's not in this for anything more than to give me his semen.

*Don't fucking get attached, Sarah.*

Think about someone else. Maybe Dean Winchester. Yeah, he's hot. That sexy smile of his and the shy way he tilts his head to the side. I relax into the moment, the buzz of the bullet against my clit beginning to work its magic when AJ's smile takes the place of Dean's.

*What the hell?*

My buzz wanes as I work to shoo him out of my mind, but he won't go. Damn it!

Dean's hazel eyes turn to warm brown and his light brown hair changes to dark brown in my mind. My clit pulses and I give up and go with it. AJ's handsome and has a body most men would die for. Every time he grasped the back of his neck tonight, his bicep bulged perfectly, and the obvious strength in his forearms is a real turn-on.

Even his fingers as he held the condom pinched between his thumb and forefinger looked strong and capable, and my mind can't help but go *there*!

What would it be like to have his fingers working me over right now instead of this silicone device? My body builds and an image of AJ pressing his perfect lips against mine blinds me along with my orgasm. I huff out a moan as shudders rack my body and my vagina pulses around nothing. As strong as the orgasm was, it wasn't satisfying in the least.

Once I calm down, embarrassment floods me. I can't believe it took thoughts and images of AJ—*my donor*—to make me come. Luckily we didn't actually have sex or I'd be asking the guy to move in with me, for God's sake.

Now to lie here in my mortification for the next thirty minutes and let gravity work its magic while I try not to let my shame overtake me.

# CHAPTER 9

To say I'm disappointed my evening turned out like this is an understatement. I figured I'd be getting lucky; that I'd be having sex all night. I walked into this hotel with a pep in my step, barely able to hold in my smile, knowing I was about to get laid. When Sarah broke the news that we weren't having sex and instead using sterilized equipment, I almost walked out the door. But I made a promise and I never break my promises. *Never.* I pride myself on following through, even if the task isn't something I want to do.

But what disappointed me more is the top-of-the-line firewall Sarah's built between us. I understand we're basically strangers, but she must trust me to some degree to meet me in this hotel on her own. I'm not sure how I'm going to break through the barrier she's built around herself, but I'll steadily crack her code until she lets me inside.

Shaking my head at myself, I sweep past the hotel bar, conversation and laughter trickling through the doorway. What the hell? I may as well have a drink before I go home. I have nothing to go home to anyway. Stepping inside, the place reminds me of a social club I imagine at the local lawn bowls center. It's nothing fancy, with basic furnishings and fans moving the stale air around the space.

I was surprised when Sarah chose this particular hotel; I assumed we'd go to her place to do the deed. I guess it makes sense to meet in a neutral place since she doesn't know me all that well. Smart really. The hotel certainly isn't anything flashy; I guess it would be on the cheaper side and if we have to do this a few times, she needs to consider her budget.

"What can I get for you, sir?"

I'm dragged from my thoughts, not even realizing I've taken a seat at the bar. Man, she has my head in a spin. I glance along the bar and notice several beers on tap. At least they have craft beers, which are always my preference. Tipping my chin toward them, I tell the bartender, "A craft beer, thanks."

He nods and sets to work pouring my beer. I dig into my back pocket, drag out my wallet, and hand the guy my card as he places my beer on a coaster with *Como* printed in block letters across the outline of a lake. I'm assuming this place is named after the city on the border between Italy and Switzerland. I always loved geography in high school and I still enjoy watching travel shows in my downtime.

Lifting the glass to my lips, I take a sip and lift my eyebrows at the familiar flavor. Raising my eyes, I meet those of the bartender, who's waiting for my approval. I raise my glass to him and tip my head. "Very nice. Local Honey?"

He grins and nods. "Good pick. What gave it away?"

"The lavender and eucalyptus flavors finished off with a tinge of honey. One of my favorite beers." I smile at him and take another sip. Nice. Just what I need to wind down.

Keeping my eyes on my drink, I run my fingers down the condensation that's formed on the glass and blow out a long breath. I can't believe I had to jack off in the bathroom when I had a perfectly sexy woman in the room next door. Though, seeing Sarah in her tight skirt and silky blouse was enough to get me hard. It didn't take much before I was filling the condom to images of the woman with the sexiest curves I think I've ever seen; images of peeling that tight skirt up her shapely thighs, tearing her panties away, and plunging my cock so deep into her tight, wet heat flooded my mind. I barely hold in my groan as the images flash through my mind again.

So damn sweet.

I was itching to get my hands and mouth on her body. To explore every single inch. I shake my head and adjust my position, willing my cock down. She never said we'd be having sex to get her pregnant. I made an assumption. I mean, it's a fair assumption to make. *Right?* I frown at my beer and think back over our conversations. No. We never talked about the mechanics of getting Sarah pregnant. Maybe I should have specified that's how I would participate. No. That wouldn't be fair. I agreed to give her my swimmers. Not orgasms.

I roll my eyes and take another drink. I can't help but feel I've missed out on an amazing experience, though. I would have made it good for her *while* helping her out. It would have been a win for both of us. Now neither of us will be feeling satisfied tonight. I guess Sarah will be, she got what she needs.

I finish my beer, decide to call it a night, and head for my car. Walking through the dark parking lot, I glance up and notice several of the lights aren't working. I don't like the thought of Sarah coming out here and walking to her car on her own; assuming she'll be coming out here tonight and not tomorrow morning. Stopping at my Jeep, I dig in my pocket for my keys only to come up empty. I know I didn't put them on the bar. Shit! I left my overnight bag in the room. I remember dropping my keys into the side pocket before going inside.

I glance up at the hotel and blow out a heavy breath. I'm going to have to go back up there to get my bag so I can go home. This works out well if Sarah's not staying the night, I can walk her to her car to make sure she's safe at the same time. Yeah, I like that idea. I'll feel better knowing she got to her car without incident. Striding back to the hotel doors, I head straight up to Sarah's room. As I come to a stop at the door, I pause. What if she's still doing whatever it is she's supposed to do? I don't want to interrupt the process.

Pressing my ear against the door, I feel like a total creeper and glance around me to make sure nobody's witnessing my shady behavior. Everything's silent. I can't hear any movement from inside. I hope she hasn't already checked out. I raise my hand to rap three times and wait. Shuffling sounds from inside and I breathe a sigh of relief that she's still here.

The door swings open and I'm greeted by a disheveled Sarah. "AJ," she squeaks. Her cheeks are flushed and her eyes are bright. She tucks some messy strands of hair behind her ear and drops her gaze, stealing her unique-colored eyes from me. They were quite a bright green when I arrived earlier, but now they're almost brown.

"Hey. Sorry to bother you, but I forgot my bag and it has my keys in it." I use my chin to point to where I left it.

"No problem." She opens the door wider and I step inside, my eyes tracing their way to the bed and the pillows resting in the middle. A pair of teal-colored lace panties sit on the bed covers, and I close my eyes, shifting my attention to my overnight bag.

"Did you, uh, did you manage everything okay?" I grab the handles of my bag.

She clears her throat. "Uh, yeah. Thanks. Easy as anything."

"Great. Are you staying the night?" This conversation is awkward, considering I just gave this woman my semen and she now has it inside her body.

"Uh, no. I'll head home."

"Good. Great. I can walk you down to your car. I noticed several lights are out in the parking lot. I'd feel happier knowing you got to your car safely."

Her eyes finally snap up to mine. "Oh, you don't need to do that. You've already done enough for me."

"I insist." I plant my feet, so she knows I'm not going anywhere until she's ready.

Sarah chuckles. "Okay. Okay. Just give me a minute to gather my stuff." She turns, heading toward the bed in a rush.

Then I remember what she's just done. She probably shouldn't be moving around so much. Dropping my bag, I move into her space. "Hey. How about you sit and I'll sort everything out? You should be taking it easy."

"Oh, you're sweet to offer. I think I should be okay, though."

"I insist." With my hand pressed to her lower back, I guide her to the bed and gently push her down to sit at the edge. I move around the room, collecting the used condom in the cup and the used syringe.

Sarah notices the items in my hand. "I have a plastic bag in my purse to put them in. I'll dispose of them at home."

I peek inside her purse and find the empty bag sitting on top, so I place the items inside and drop it back in her purse. Then I collect her lace panties and hand them to Sarah. She takes them with a pretty blush, her eyes dropping to the floor. "Thanks."

I nod and continue with my check. I drop her shoes on the floor next to her feet and double-check the bathroom to make sure there's nothing inside. When I step out, I spot Sarah tucking her panties inside her purse and raise my eyebrows in question.

"I can't put them on with you in the room. I'm driving straight home, so it doesn't matter." My pulse races with the visual of Sarah's bare pussy beneath that skin-tight skirt.

"Fair enough." I collect the pillow from the middle of the bed to toss it where it belongs and discover a small silicone bullet. I can't help the smile that tugs at my lips. I read online that an orgasm helps to move the sperm up to where they're needed, that's why I figured we'd be doing this the regular way. I wonder if we read the same article? With Sarah's back to me, she hasn't noticed my discovery so I pick it up, and before I know what I'm doing I take a whiff of the device, closing my eyes to get the full impact of her scent.

Mmmm.

*Shit, that probably makes me a creep!*

I hand it to her and the flush that spreads across her cheeks is sexy as hell. She quickly snatches it from me, hiding her eyes as she drops it into her purse. Clearing my throat I ask, "Are you ready to go? I think we have everything."

"Uh, sure. Thanks again." She still hasn't made eye contact. Interesting. I wonder what *or* who she was thinking about when she came.

I hold out my hand to help her stand, then place it just above her sexy ass to guide her to the door, collecting my bag on the way. The walk toward the elevator and the ride down to reception is made in silence. The air is thick with tension and I'm not sure how to break it or even whether I should. We approach the reception desk and the woman behind it widens her eyes as she smiles at us.

"Can I help you with anything?" she asks.

"No thanks. I'm just checking out," Sarah responds as she slides her keycard across the desk.

The woman's eyes skate between us and I can tell she's working to school her expression. It must look suspect that Sarah checked in a couple of hours ago and now she's checking out with a guy in tow.

"Was everything to your satisfaction?"

"Yes, everything was great. Would I be able to make a booking for Wednesday night, please?" Sarah glances at me, giving me a timid smile, then returns her attention to the woman behind the desk.

The woman glances between the two of us again. "Sure. Would you like the same room?"

"If I can. That would be great. Thanks."

She taps some keys and then smiles at Sarah. "All done. We'll see you on Wednesday." She finishes with raised brows at both of us.

I return my hand to her lower back, and guide Sarah to the double doors, the heat of her flesh searing my palm through the thin fabric of her blouse. Once we're outside and out of earshot of the receptionist, I burst out laughing and Sarah joins me. "I was waiting for her to tell you this establishment doesn't rent rooms by the hour."

Sarah's giggles increase and she snorts, making her even more attractive. "Me too. I was so embarrassed." She wipes tears from her eyes. "I never once considered how it would appear if I checked in and out on the same night."

"I'm sure she sees all sorts of people and situations. It's probably nothing out of the ordinary for her." I try to reassure her, because even though I don't know Sarah all that well yet, I know she's not the type of woman to hire a room by the hour and I don't want her to be uncomfortable.

We make our way toward Sarah's car through the dark parking lot, Sarah still chuckling now and then. "Sorry, once I get the giggles, I find it hard to stop sometimes."

"No need to apologize. You're beautiful when you let your worries go and laugh." Damn. I probably shouldn't have said that because she freezes in place.

"You think I'm beautiful?" Her voice is unsure, and I don't understand why.

"Hell yeah, you're beautiful. You're stunning." I shake my head. "Why are you asking as if you don't know?"

She shrugs. "It's been a long time since anyone outside of my family has told me that. It's nice to be told now and then."

If she were mine, I'd be telling and showing her exactly how beautiful I think she is every day. She would never have any doubts. But she's not mine and she's not looking to be anybody's, so I should keep my mouth shut—I don't want to make things any more awkward between us. It's the last thing I want to do.

*She wants to have a baby, dickhead, nothing more.*

# CHAPTER 10

## —sarah—

WELL, THAT WAS EMBARRASSING. THE RECEPTIONIST PROBABLY THINKS I'm a hooker, not that there's anything wrong with the profession, it just couldn't be further from the truth. Here I am trying to get pregnant and I'm not even having sex to do it. *Only me!* I barely refrain from palming my head.

When I opened the door to find AJ standing there after what I'd just done with thoughts of him invading every part of me, I couldn't look him square in the eye. And then he took care of me, cleaning up so he could walk me to my car to ensure my safety. Why couldn't I have met the guy under ordinary circumstances? Now we have this awkward connection between us, which I know can't go any further.

He doesn't want to be anything more than a donor. *I need to remember that.*

My car comes into view and my pulse speeds up. Sarah, get in your car and leave. You'll see the guy on Wednesday night. No need to prolong the evening and make things awkward. I'm sure he has plenty of other things he needs to do. "Uh, thank you for walking me to my car and for tonight." I tuck my loose hair behind my ear. "I guess I'll see you on Wednesday. Same place, same time." I do my best not to sound as awkward as I feel at this point.

He grasps the back of his neck, making his bicep bulge again. It seems to be something he does a lot, and I certainly won't be complaining about it. My eyes naturally drop to watch the action and I swear my mouth waters a little. For a computer guy, he has a great physique. "Yep. I'll come." He smirks at me and my cheeks heat.

"I see what you did there. Good one." I chuckle as I unlock and open the door, using the metal as a barrier so I don't do something stupid like kiss him goodbye. I mean I usually embrace my friends and kiss their cheeks, but we're not really friends. Are we? It's all so confusing. I throw my purse across to the passenger seat as AJ lingers. Is he feeling the same?

He winks and taps the top of my door frame. "See ya Wednesday, Sarah. Take it easy, okay?"

"I will. And … thanks. For everything."

"You're welcome." I close the door and he spins on his heel, walking toward his car. He tucks one hand in his pocket, pulling the denim across his tight ass. My forehead meets the steering wheel as I blow out a breath.

Stop staring at his ass. Stop noticing his muscles. *Just stop already.*

After a shower, I put on my most comfy pajamas and drop onto my couch to call my sister as promised. The phone rings twice, then her voice comes on the line. "How did it go?"

"Well, hello to you too, Sis." I chuckle.

"Sorry." She giggles. "Hey. How did it go?" she asks, impatience thick in her voice.

"As you know I won't know for a little while, but things went smoothly."

"Oh good. And the guy … he wasn't a creep? You felt safe?" Being the eldest, Emma always worries about us, even though she has her own family to worry about now. "You know Theo and Max would have happily stood outside the door to make sure you were safe."

"Oh, God. No way." I huff out a laugh. "Poor AJ. I can't imagine what his response would have been if he'd turned up to find my door guarded. I told you, he's a nice guy. He would have to be to help a stranger make her dream come true."

"I know you said he came across as a decent guy, but I worry. You know how many psychos there are out there."

"I know and I was careful. I promise. I wouldn't have taken things this far if I didn't feel completely comfortable with him." I pause. "Maybe too comfortable." My cheeks heat as my mind skips back to when I was lying on the bed trying to make myself come.

Her tone softens. "Sarah? What do you mean … too comfortable? You're not going to get attached to this guy are you?" Not that Emma would care if I did, so long as the feelings were mutual. She helped pick up the mess Michael left behind, and she never wants to see me hurt like that again.

"No. I won't. That's why I'm not actually having sex with him. You know what I'm like. I can't afford to catch feelings this time, and that's why I'm making it as clinical as I possibly can." I smile as I remember the look on his face when I showed him the collection condom and syringe.

I hear rustling in the background. "Oh yeah. Did he know that was the plan?"

"I assumed he did, but the look on his face suggested otherwise." He could have easily become upset and walked out when my plan was different from his, but he didn't. He's been completely accommodating from the beginning and I get the sense he'll always be that way.

"Oh God, Sarah. Was he okay with it all? He didn't try to change your mind, did he?"

"Nope. He was very amiable once he got over the surprise. He assumed we'd be having sex, so it was a bit of a shock to him. Honestly, it was a fair assumption."

"Well, I thought you'd be doing it that way when you told me about AJ." I can hear the smile in her voice. "So now you wait?"

I sink back farther into the couch, lifting my foot to rest on the cushion. "Actually. He did some research about trying to get pregnant and suggested we meet again in two days. We're going to repeat the process on Wednesday and maybe again on Friday but we didn't get that far yet." I can't keep the excitement out of my voice.

"Oh wow," she breathes. "He's serious about helping you."

"Yep. I can't believe how lucky I am."

"I'm so happy for you. I hope you're on your way to being pregnant as we speak."

"Me too." My heart twinges at the thought of not getting to spend more time with AJ. *Stupid heart!*

"You're going to be such a great mom. I'm proud of you, Sis."

Emotions clog my throat and I nod. "That means a lot coming from you, Em." I can only hope to be half the mom she is.

"I love you, Sare," she says, her voice soft.

"Love you, too. I'll let you get back to that sexy husband of yours. Talk soon. Mwah!"

"Mwah. Talk soon. Take it easy."

"I will." I press the red button, drop my phone to the cushion beside me, and stare at the doorway to the second bedroom. Maybe one day, sooner than I thought, I'll have a baby asleep in the gorgeous crib Emma passed on to me. I sigh at the thought. My phone buzzes.

MEL

I'm waiting

How did it go?

ME

It went really well. Everything was smooth and easy

MEL

He didn't mind that he had to use a condom *devil face*

ME

Not at all. He was great about everything. Even walked me to my car

MEL

Awww, he's so sweet. I have everything crossed that you're pregnant

ME

Me too

MEL

Chat later, just got paged x

ME

Okay x

I drop my eyes to my stomach and run my hand over the area. Wishing and hoping.

I almost bounce out of bed as soon as my alarm sounds. It's my Saturday to spend time with the babies in the neonatal intensive care unit where Mel works. Every second Saturday I get my fill of cuddling tiny babies, thanks to Mel. She's always known how much I love babies, so when she got the position there, she encouraged me to do the volunteer training to become a baby cuddler.

I move through my morning routine, ensuring I tie all of my hair out of the way and choose an outfit to help me stay cool while I'm there because the room is kept warm for the babies. Traffic is light this early and I make it to the hospital with time to spare. I grab the caps I crocheted over the last two weeks, toss the straps of my purse over my shoulder, and make my way inside the enormous building.

After I wash my hands thoroughly all the way up to my elbows, I put on the hospital gown provided over my clothes and secure it, then enter the NICU. The warmth of the room and the sound of machines buzzing and beeping greet me like an old friend, and I inhale the weird, but now familiar scent of antiseptic mixed with baby powder. I scan the room gauging how many babies are here this week. I look forward to my time here cuddling the babies when their families can't. As sad as it is that babies are born needing this additional care, I know they get the best possible attention here. I smile as my eyes land on Mel, and I head in her direction. I'm grateful she encouraged me to join this program, because as good as the cuddling program is for the babies, I get just as much out of it, if not more. In those moments when I'm sitting and cuddling a tiny baby, I'm quiet. My mind is quiet and so is my body. I'm calm and centered as I solely focus on the precious bundle in my arms while I give any comfort I can to the tiny human who needs a little extra love and warmth to flourish.

"Hey, Sare. How are you feeling?"

"Hey. I'm great and ready to get my cuddle on," I say enthusiastically.

She chuckles and leads me over to an incubator. "I'm glad to hear it. We have baby Robert. He has neonatal opioid withdrawal syndrome. His mom's struggling at the moment with her own issues, so she can't spend as much time with him as she'd like."

My eyes sting as my heart cracks right down the middle. "Oh no. Poor baby." Mel nods. She reaches in and carefully collects him along with all of his tubes and wires, nodding toward the chair off to the side. I take a seat and get comfortable for my cuddle session. She places Robert in my arms gently and his weight is barely negligible. "Oh my gosh, he's tiny."

She nods. "Yeah, it's common for these babies. You'll notice he's a little yellow too. He desperately needs this contact."

I tuck him in close to my body and get lost in studying his little face. His fair eyebrows, which are almost invisible because they're so pale, to his long eyelashes, and his little cheeks. When I finally glance up, Mel's busy dealing with a baby on the other side of the room.

Another nurse comes over, checking his chart and then her watch, ensuring he's comfortable and everything is still connected properly. The nurses are always incredibly vigilant. They must go home from their shift beyond exhausted, I know Mel does. This job takes such an incredible amount of concentration. I don't know how they do it and not get attached to each baby who spends time here.

I rock the chair back and forth slightly, rubbing his back gently with steady strokes, keeping him tucked in close to make sure he gets the maximum possible benefit from me. I chuckle as tiny creases form between his brows, his little eyes moving from side to side beneath closed lids. "What are you dreaming about, Robert?" I murmur.

At the end of my time, I reluctantly hand Robert back to Mel and she places him carefully back inside the incubator. "Thanks for coming today, Sare. And thanks for the new caps. They're so cute."

"Aww, it's always my pleasure. I love coming here, you know that."

"I know." She smiles at me.

I glance down at Robert—such a sweet baby—and wonder what his future holds.

I gently rub my finger over his soft downy hair, wishing him well with my whispered words. Then Mel closes the small window to help keep his environment stable, while my heart cracks as I say goodbye.

# CHAPTER 11

## —sarah—

I DON'T THINK I'VE EVER SEEN MY BROTHER SO HAPPY. IN FACT, I *KNOW* I've never seen him this happy. Molly has been the best thing to ever happen to him, and I'm thrilled they found each other. It's been so much fun helping Max and Molly prepare for today; everything looks simply stunning with the late afternoon sun shimmering on the ocean as a backdrop. I can't wait to see my brother's face when he lays eyes on his almost-wife in her wedding gown. Em and I were with her when she chose it and she looked spectacular. I can't imagine how gorgeous she looks with her hair and makeup done as well.

Cristo sits beside me, kissing each of my cheeks. "Geia sas ómorfi kopéla."

"Hi, Cristo." I chuckle. "I have no idea what you just said."

He gives me his cheeky smile. "Hello, beautiful lady."

Heat rises to my cheeks. "Thank you. You're looking handsome today."

He pretends to dust lint from his dark pants, a proud smirk on his face, so much like Theo's. "Why thank you." He tips his head.

"I bet Kenny was excited today."

"Oh"—he raises his thick brows—"she was. She'll be the prettiest flower girl."

"Yes, she will."

"Can I please sit next to you, Aunty Sarah?" Austin asks sweetly.

I pat the empty seat next to mine. "Of course. I was hoping you'd keep me company."

He makes himself comfortable and then takes my hand. "Thank you. I wanted to say hello to Uncle Max, but Mommy said he was busy right now."

I chuckle as the music changes and Max's head snaps toward the sand dune. Kenny and Holly are the first to crest the top, looking as pretty as ever in matching blush pink dresses. As the girls reach the chairs, Kenny breaks away and leaps for Max. He catches her easily, his smile as bright as I've ever seen. The muscle behind my ribs tightens with a sense of longing so strong, that it's almost crippling. I suck in a breath to gain control and look back toward the dune waiting for Molly. My breath freezes as she crests the dune. She's beyond stunning on an ordinary day, but she looks like a goddess today. I glance back at my brother and I'm surprised his tongue isn't dragging in the sand at his feet. His eyes are locked on her in a way I could only dream of having a man look at me.

"Wow," I whisper, and Cristo nods.

"Panemorfi," he whispers with a soft breath. "Gorgeous."

I can't peel my eyes away as Max leaves his spot to meet Molly. As I would expect, he kisses her, and with matching smiles, they walk toward the celebrant together. As they exchange their promises, I wipe away my tears. First Emma and Theo blew me away with their beautiful love and now my brother has found his. I'm happy for both of my siblings but I can't help the thoughts that whisper to me that I may never have what they have. I need to make peace with it and stop hoping for something that's unlikely to happen. I had my chance, but I chose my family, friends, and job over it. I guess that says it all.

If I wasn't prepared to walk away from everything for Michael, then maybe the relationship wasn't the right one. Surely if I felt more for him—that deep, deep connection—I would have moved to Australia with him.

Cheers erupt and I'm startled from my thoughts. Molly and Max are kissing, and I'm pretty sure if there weren't an audience my brother would be doing a lot more than that. I rise from my seat, lifting Austin with me so we can cheer along with everyone else.

"Ewwww, why does everyone have to kiss all the time?" Austin scrunches up his face.

I chuckle and tap his nose. "Because they love each other so much."

"I love you and Mommy and Theo and Kenny and Lachlan and

everyone else, but you don't see me kissing everyone like that. It's gross." He's quite appalled and I can't stop my laughter.

"One day, Austin, when you're big, you'll meet someone and you'll want to kiss them all the time."

He crosses his arms. "No I won't," he says.

"We'll see." I wink at him and place him on his feet. "Come on." I hope he does. I hope he finds a love as true as his mom has with Theo and Max has with Molly. Holding his hand I lead him forward so I can congratulate my brother and new sister. *New sister!* I'm ecstatic that we get to keep Molly in our family.

Austin and I join the line to congratulate the newly married couple. Max has Molly's hand in his, and I notice he's not letting go as each guest congratulates them. I chuckle as I reach my brother. "Are you going to let her go?"

He looks at me as if I've grown two heads. "Nope. Never."

"Okay." I wrap my arms around him, pulling him in as close as possible. "I'm so happy for you, Max. So happy you found your forever love." I lay a kiss on his cheek and pull back, wiping a stray tear—damn emotions.

"You know it'll happen for you, Sare." I nod, ensuring he sees my smile because I don't want to put a downer on his mood. I squeeze his arm and move across to Molly.

"Welcome to our family, Molly." I almost squeal as I embrace her, careful not to crush her gorgeous dress. "I'm so happy to be able to call you my sister." I lean in and kiss her cheek, her free hand wrapping around me, holding me close.

"I'm so blessed to have joined such a wonderful family. Thank you for always making me feel welcome." We squeeze each other before I move away and let Max's soccer friends have their turn to congratulate the pair.

My phone vibrates in my purse.

AJ

How are you feeling?

A smile touches my lips. Each evening, he's messaged to check on me. He knows I won't know if I'm pregnant yet, but he still checks on me. I can't believe the guy's still single, to be honest. He seems quite the catch.

> ME
>
> I'm feeling just fine
>
> Thank you for checking in with me but I won't have news for another 8 days

AJ

I know but I like to check on you

How's the wedding?

> ME
>
> Beautiful. My brother is so happy

The dots bounce, then stop. I wait and watch for a message but nothing comes, so I tuck my phone back inside my purse. It vibrates as I sit while Max and Molly sign the legal documents with Mom and Martin as witnesses.

AJ

Have fun

> ME
>
> Thanks. Enjoy your weekend

AJ

Are you doing anything over the weekend?

> ME
>
> Not really. Family lunch on Sunday

AJ

Did you want to catch up?

I almost drop my phone when I read his message. I already like him too much. If I spend time with him outside of trying to get pregnant, I'm not sure I'll be able to keep the distance I need to maintain between us. I'm already struggling and I haven't spent all that much time with him.

AJ

We could go to the beach or something. Let me know

I'll leave you alone to enjoy the wedding. Talk later

I blow out a breath. He generously gave me time to think it over.

"Is that the guy who's helping you?" Em's voice breaks into my thoughts.

I drag the phone to my chest to hide the screen, not that I need to, she already read the message. "Uh, yeah."

She raises her eyebrows. "He wants to catch up, huh?" She nudges me. "The beach." She wiggles her eyebrows and then spins around to Theo and the kids. "Who wants to go to the beach tomorrow?"

The kids cheer. "Yay. Me!"

She turns back to me, smiling. "Better text him back and invite him along." She finishes with an innocent look and spins on her heel to return to Theo's side. Damn Emma, stirring the pot.

"I'm not inviting him to the beach with the family." I rest my hands on my hips, I glance down at the kids. "He's just a *you-know-what* donor." I raise my brows at my sister.

She smiles at me. "If you say so. But I'd like to meet him. Invite him along."

I move closer to her and lower my voice. "Only if you promise not to invite Mom and Dad. You know how she gets, and I don't want to scare him off. I need his help. And you're not allowed to say anything either."

"I promise. Now text him. I want to lay eyes on him and make sure I get a good vibe." Her jaw is set in that stubborn line she gets when she's bound and determined to get her way.

I hold up my hands. "Okay, okay. I'll invite him to the beach tomorrow."

Emma smiles wide and claps her hands together as Theo watches on, shaking his head. He lays a kiss on top of her head and her lids drop closed for a second as he whispers something in her ear. She turns toward him, laying a chaste kiss on his lips and I return my attention to my phone.

"Usual beach, usual time?" I ask Em.

"Yep."

I nod and text AJ.

ME

> I'm going to the beach tomorrow afternoon with my sister and her family if you would like to join us

Immediately my phone vibrates.

AJ

Which beach and what time?

I tell him and he agrees to meet us there. I blow out a nervous breath and glance at my sister, who's watching me like a hawk. I nod and she smiles. She had better not embarrass me or I'll never forgive her.

# CHAPTER 12

I FINALLY PULL INTO A PARKING SPACE AFTER DRIVING AROUND IN THE heat for the last fifteen minutes. I glance at my watch. I'm late. I hate being late. It's one of the worst traits. I always aim to be early rather than late. When I left home, I didn't consider how busy it would be at the beach today. I shouldn't be surprised—it's damn hot. I don't know how I'm going to find Sarah and her family among the hordes of people down here.

I tug on my baseball cap, grab my cooler and towel, and head toward the beach. The pavement is hot as hell beneath my flip-flops and the sun is already burning my skin. I hope Sarah's wearing sunscreen because her pale skin must fry. Now to find the red umbrella she said they would have. As I reach the edge of the sand, I shield my eyes and scan the area for a red umbrella. There are at least a dozen red umbrellas scattered from one end of the crowded beach to the other.

I take off toward the first umbrella, studying the people underneath, no Sarah. I continue until I get to the sixth umbrella and finally lay eyes on the woman who always seems to be on my mind. I'm not sure if it's because I was with her every second evening last week and haven't laid eyes on her at all this week, but I can't get her off my mind.

She hasn't noticed me yet because she's busy building a sandcastle in the shade with a little girl, while two boys, which look to be a little older, eat apple slices. They look as though they've been here a while already. Sarah glances up, spotting me and preventing further observation, so I step forward. She stands, brushing sand from her butt and thick thighs as she steps forward to greet me, her eyes skating around her sister's family. She's told me a little about them, so I at least feel I know who each person is.

She smiles at me. "Hey. You found us."

"Yeah. I had no idea it would be so busy. I'm sorry I'm late. I had trouble finding a parking space and then …" I point to the red umbrella. "There are quite a few red umbrellas." I chuckle mildly.

She shields her eyes and peers around. "Oh. Sorry about that."

I step into her space and lean down to press a light kiss to her cheek in greeting, then glance around at her family. Her sister and brother-in-law are watching us closely. Emma's lips are tipped up slightly at the edges as she watches my interaction with Sarah, while Theo appears ready to land me on my ass. Shit, maybe I shouldn't have kissed her. Sarah pulls away abruptly, then turns toward her family.

"Uhm, this is AJ. This is my sister, Emma." I step forward to shake her hand, only she pulls me in for a hug while her husband continues to give me the evil eye.

"Hi, AJ. It's nice to meet you."

"You too. You and Sarah look a lot alike. I think I would pick you as sisters even if I didn't know you guys."

"Oh, you're so sweet! Obviously, Sarah's the beautiful one." She chuckles.

"Peaches," Theo growls, moving closer to us.

Sarah blushes but continues with the introductions. "This is her husband, Theo." I move to shake his hand. His roughened palm slides against mine and he squeezes—hard—as he tips his chin.

"Hi, Theo. Nice to meet you."

"We'll see." *Oh-kay* then.

Sarah clears her throat. "And these are their children, Lachlan, Austin, and Kenny." She points to each child as she introduces them.

The boys wave at me from their position, but Kenny jumps up and wraps her arms around my legs. "Hello, Uncle AJ!"

Sarah and Emma laugh while Theo glares at his little girl. I'm not quite sure what to do, so I pat the back of her head. She seems like a sweet kid. His glare moves up to me and then he glances at his wife, who smiles widely at him. He shakes his head and moves closer to her, landing a kiss on her forehead and I only wish I had the privilege to do the same with Sarah.

Kenny tugs my hand. "I want to go for a swim."

I place my cooler down and glance up at the others.

"We were about to head into the water. Boys, are you ready to get wet?" Emma asks.

"Yeah. Let's go!" The youngest boy, Austin, jumps up.

Theo grabs a pair of wings and heads straight for Kenny. "Not before you put on your water wings."

"I don't need them anymore, Daddy." His eyes go soft when she says his name, a marked difference from how he was just looking at me. "I'm a big girl now."

He turns toward Emma. "What do you think?"

"I think Kenny can go without, so long as she stays in the shallow part." She looks pointedly at the little girl. "There are four adults here to watch the kids."

Sarah and I nod as I drop my towel and remove my flip-flops.

"Okay." Theo relents, and Kenny jumps up and down with the glee of a young child who's managed to get her way. She grabs my hand, pulling me forward.

"Come on. Let's go."

"Hang on, Kenny. Mommy and I need to take off our coverups and you need to take off your shorts," Sarah tells the little dynamo.

Sarah pulls her coverup over her head, revealing a teal bikini. It's the most exposed I've seen her, and as amazing as she looks dressed, this may be my favorite. I grasp the back of my neck as I scan her curves. I can't stop the images of my hands gliding smoothly up those thick thighs of hers, across her soft stomach, to her luscious tits which are almost spilling out of the cups. She adjusts the straps, making them jiggle, and I struggle to tear my eyes away.

Glancing around the beach, I decide I don't want every asshole to see what will hopefully be mine one day. I drag my T-shirt over my head and hand it to her. "Here, you need to cover up out there." I point toward the water. Theo and Emma burst into laughter, and I feel I've missed out on some family joke.

"I don't need it. Thanks." She scowls at me, then turns her angry eyes toward her sister and brother-in-law.

Shit! I need to come up with a reason so she'll cover those damn curves. "You'll get sunburned. I felt as though I was getting burned just walking from my car."

"I'm wearing sunscreen. I don't need to cover up, thanks." She snips, grasping Kenny's hand and heading toward the water, leaving the rest of us behind. I admire her shapely ass as she makes her way across the sand. Austin jumps up to follow, and Theo shakes his head at me.

"I feel your pain, brother." He slaps me on the shoulder and takes Lachlan's hand to lead him to the water.

I grasp the back of my neck and look at Emma. "Did I say the wrong thing?"

She chuckles. "Not at all. You were being … *thoughtful*. Right?"

Well, I wouldn't call it that exactly. But I'll go with that so I don't sound like the asshole I seem to have become. "Yeah. It's not fun being sunburned."

"And I'm sure that's all you were worried about." She laughs and heads toward the water, so I follow close behind.

Austin and Kenny are having a blast, splashing each other and the adults in the process. I notice Lachlan is on the periphery, avoiding the splashes, but he's watching Austin and Kenny closely with a half-smile and I can tell they're being careful not to splash him. Theo wraps his arm around Emma and pulls her in close, not taking his eyes from the kids. They talk and chuckle quietly together and I move closer to Sarah.

"Uh, sorry about before. I didn't want your pale skin getting burned."

She glances across at me. "That's okay, but I can look after myself. I've been doing it for quite some time now."

"I get that. But I do consider us at the very least … friends. What sort of friend would I be if I didn't look out for you?"

She smiles at me then, and I take a full breath. I didn't like feeling as though things weren't right between us. "Friends? Is that what we are?"

"I'd like us to be friends at least." I point to her stomach. "Even once you're pregnant, I'd like to spend time together. I … uh …" I grasp the back of my neck and her eyes snap to my bicep. I tense it and smile internally when her tongue darts out to lick her lips. "I like spending time with you." Maybe she's not as unaffected by me as she portrays.

I drop my arm and her eyes slide back to my face. "I'd like that too." She glances around, tightness building around her eyes and mouth. "Does that mean you want to be part of the child's life?"

I'm hoping I'll be part of both of their lives, but she seems averse to a relationship, so I shrug, playing off the importance. "Whatever works best for you, Sarah. I'm not going back on our agreement or anything like that. You're the one in charge here." She nods thoughtfully and some of the tightness dissipates. I need to lighten the mood. I don't want her to change her mind and look elsewhere for a donor. "So, do you guys spend much time at the beach?"

She glides her hands through the water at her waist. "Oh yeah. We usually try to get down here as a family as many times as our schedules allow during the summer. How about you?"

"Yes and no. I like to climb, so I sometimes wake early and head out to some of my favorite climbing spots when the weather allows, then I tend to take a dip in whatever water's close by to cool off," I explain.

Her eyes skim my body, pausing on my abdomen, then traveling over my arms. "Well, that explains how defined you are considering you spend your days behind a computer."

I chuckle and glide my hand down my torso, her eyes following the path. "Thanks for noticing." I give her a wink and her cheeks turn pink. A splash of cold water against my back breaks our moment, and I spin around to catch the culprit trying to run away as she giggles. I chase after her, pretending to fight my way through huge waves to get to her. When I catch Kenny, I lift her out of the water as she giggles and wiggles, kicking her feet. I throw her up in the air and catch her, her giggles growing louder by the second as I drop her gently back into the water and splash a small amount of water at the sweet girl.

She squeals as she runs away, dropping down to paddle through the shallow water. "Ahhhh, Uncle AJ got me but I escaped. I'm a super-hero like Black Widow!"

"Well, that makes a change from her usual princesses." Sarah giggles, raising her eyebrows at her sister.

"Yeah, in the last week or so, she's been watching the Marvel movies with the boys. Normally, she leaves the room and plays with her dollhouse when the boys are watching the movies, but she's been staying. She's hooked!"

"I'm hungry, Mommy," Lachlan calls out to Emma, still keeping a safe distance from the action.

"Okay, let's get out and get something to eat."

We all head out of the water and back to our spot, Emma and Theo working together, along with Sarah to organize the kids. I read-just the umbrella to ensure the blanket and chairs are shaded, keeping up my ruse that I'm concerned about sunburn. As I watch Sarah with the kids; I know she's going to make a great mom. She obviously has a strong bond with her niece and nephews because there's a level of comfort between them that shows how much they love each other. Much like me and Colton.

After we've finished eating, the girls head to the bathroom with Austin and Kenny in tow, leaving me alone with Theo and Lachlan. As soon as the girls are out of sight, Theo's eyes snap to me.

"So, AJ, explain to me what sort of man offers to help a stranger in a club to get pregnant." His eyes bore into me and I swallow. The guy is freaking intimidating. I thought we had a moment before, but clearly, I was mistaken.

I glance around, then look him square in the eye. "Look, I'm going to be completely honest with you, but it has to stay between us. Do I have your word?"

He nods but keeps his lips sealed.

I grasp the back of my neck and then draw in a deep breath, hoping the guy doesn't think I'm some kind of psycho. "I saw her in the club and thought she was stunning. Not gonna lie, those curves drew me right in." He nods in agreement. Obviously, we have similar tastes because Emma has the same feminine body shape. "When I overheard her speaking with her friend about wanting a baby, I thought I'd take the opportunity to speak with her about it. Let's face it, the woman is way out of my league and I'm pretty sure she wouldn't look twice at me if it weren't for my …" I skate my eyes across to Lachlan and then down to my groin area, hoping he gets my meaning. "I helped my sister and her wife get pregnant, so I knew I could help her. And … well … I'm hoping if she spends enough time with me, she'll get to know me and want to stick around." I shrug as though my confession is no big deal.

Theo's entire body relaxes for the first time since I arrived and he nods. A slight tilt of his lips makes me relax too. "Just don't hurt her. Okay."

I hold up my hands in surrender. "Never. It's not even something I remotely want to do."

Emma, Sarah, and the kids return ending our chat and we spend the rest of the afternoon building sandcastles, getting wet, and having fun. It's possibly the most fun I've had in ages and as I get to know Emma and her family I think Hayley, Lisa, and Colton would like them too. I think our families would blend well together. Which reminds me.

"Theo, Sarah was telling me you're a carpenter."

He smiles. "Yeah. That's right."

I collect my phone and open the photo app. Turning it around, I show Theo the photo I have of the climbing wall I was looking at for Colton. "My nephew is three and he's a climber. He's driving my sister and her wife crazy, so I said I'd look into getting him a climbing wall for their backyard." He takes the device and studies the pic, showing it to Lachlan. "Do you think you could build the frame? I'll add the climbing holds."

He and Lachlan share a smile. "We sure can. This is an easy A-frame. We could use cedar and pine for this. What do you think, Lachlan?"

He nods. "Yeah, this looks pretty easy."

Theo returns my phone. "We should be able to build this for you. When did you want it? I have a couple of orders I'm working on at the moment."

"Whenever you can squeeze it in."

"No problem. I'll grab your number from Sarah when we're ready to start."

"Thanks. Appreciate it."

# CHAPTER 13

## —sarah—

A FAMILIAR, HEAVY FEELING FILLS ME WITH DISAPPOINTMENT. SLIGHT cramps and pain in my lower back deliver the news that I failed once again. That my body is still completely my own and I won't be sharing it with another life for at least another month. With already two failed attempts through the fertility clinic and now this one, I'm wondering if my dream will ever become a reality. I head straight to the bathroom to deal with it and mentally prepare myself for worsening cramps later this afternoon and tonight.

As I sort myself out, I remind myself it takes time to get pregnant, that it can take up to two years, but I'm worried I'm running out of time. My inner voice reminds me I can't decide one day I want a baby and it'll happen straight away, but that rational thought doesn't stop the sheer disappointment and anxiety. Running my fingers through my hair, I drag the elastic band from my wrist and tie it up in a ponytail, then grab the next load of washing.

If I can't get pregnant, is that a sign from the universe that I shouldn't be a mother? I know I want to be a mom. I know I love kids and the idea of a biological child, a child that's genetically part of me is a yearning so deep in my soul, it's something I can't ignore.

My phone vibrates with a text. It'll either be Emma or Mel checking to find out if I got my period and I'm not ready to admit my failure to anyone yet, so I ignore it. I know they mean well and I'm thankful for their support, but I need time to wrap my head around it before I share the news with anyone else, no matter how well-meaning they are. It vibrates again, so without looking at the screen I flip it over and tuck it beneath the couch cushion.

Cramping in my lower abdomen increases as the afternoon wears on, so I grab the heat pack and throw it in the microwave to heat, take a couple of Midol, and grab the bar of chocolate I allow myself for such an occasion. My phone vibrates again, but I ignore it.

Making myself comfortable on my couch, I grab my supplies and begin working on another cap to build up a fresh collection for my next volunteer shift. Choosing the super-soft pink yarn, I get lost in the stitches and rows, nibbling on my chocolate in between. Before I know it, the cap is finished and I'm ready to fasten off. I leave a six-inch tail, cut the yarn, and pull it through the final loop, tightening the end. Knowing I'm helping a tiny baby who's struggling in his or her first few weeks of life gives me a sense of satisfaction each time I complete a cap. I'm sure it seems trivial to some, but I love that I'm helping even the tiniest bit.

A knock sounds on my door, startling me. I frown as I run through my plans for this weekend. I'm not expecting anyone unless Emma got sick of waiting for me to return her text. Mel's working, so I know it's not her. As I swing the door open, I start with my excuse. "Em—" My words die on my tongue as I lay eyes on the one and only AJ. He's holding up a bag of takeout which smells delicious as he gives me a sexy smile.

"Sorry. Not Emma," he announces as he steps inside, pressing his soft lips to my cheek, his bristles a stark contrast against my skin. He wanders into my home as though he's my best friend and drops by all the time.

I shake myself out of my stupor to close the door and follow him in. "Uh, what are you doing here? More importantly, *how* do you know where I live?"

I narrow my eyes when I meet him in my kitchen as he opens and closes cupboards in search of something. "Where do you keep ... oh, here they are." He grabs two plates and places them on the counter. "I'm a hacker, Sarah. Or did you forget? It took me all of thirty seconds to find you." He reminds me as he raises a single brow while continuing with his quest to serve dinner for both of us, as if it's no big deal he's turned up at my apartment completely unannounced and unexpectedly. So far I haven't picked up on any psycho vibes, but maybe I missed them.

I cross my arms and clear my throat. "Please tell me how you being a hacker explains why you've turned up on my doorstep on a Saturday night with dinner?"

"You didn't answer my texts. The fact you didn't, suggests you started your period. I thought I'd come and keep you company since I figured you're probably feeling disappointed." My heart stutters at his thoughtfulness. He scoops equal amounts of food onto each plate as I watch the play of the muscles in his forearms. *Tasty*. And I'm not talking about the food.

As sweet as his gesture is, this wasn't part of the deal, and I can't afford to spend additional time with him outside of our arrangement. It was bad enough sharing the afternoon with him at the beach. Watching him play with my niece and nephews as though he'd known them all their lives. Having his eyes caressing every single inch of my body. Yes, I felt them. He thought he was being discreet behind those aviators of his, but I felt the burn of his gaze as though he'd traced my flesh with his fingers. It was too much. My heart's already trying to engage. Then I had to deal with Emma swooning over how handsome he is and maybe I should reconsider my methods for getting pregnant.

I'm baffled as to how he thought I'd be okay with him knowing where I live. I thought I'd made it clear I wasn't prepared to have him in my space by using a hotel each time we met. "AJ, can you stop for a minute and look at me." I try to soften my posture, so I uncross my arms, dropping them to my side.

He collects the loaded plates as he looks at me. "Do you mind grabbing the cutlery?"

I huff out a breath but grab the necessary cutlery and follow him to my small dining table. "AJ?"

"If you want me to apologize, I'm not going to. I promised I would support you with your pregnancy plan. This is me supporting you."

The stiffness in my body evaporates and my lips fight to spread in a grin. I think my ovaries are swooning. "Thank you. Even if this is a little … unexpected." Crazy is the word I actually want to use, but he's being thoughtful, sweet even.

"I hope you like Thai. Eat up." He points to my plate with his fork.

My stomach growls at the delicious smell of lemongrass and chili, mixed with the sweet scent of jasmine rice. "I do. Thanks for all this. You really didn't have to. It's not part of our deal." He raises his hand, flicking his wrist as if to erase my words and I take a forkful of the delicious chicken curry with rice, moaning at the flavors. "It's been such a long time since I've had Thai takeout. I'd forgotten how much I love it."

"Good. I figured most people like Thai, and if you didn't like it, I'd just order something different." He takes a bite of food, chews, and swallows; I watch as his Adam's apple bobs. "How are you feeling?"

My mood instantly drops and my shoulders sag forward. "Disappointed would probably be the first word to come to mind, along with a few others. I've spent the day reminding myself these things take time and I need to be patient. That it will all be worth it in the end." I shrug. "I'm also very aware that the longer this takes, the more I'm imposing on your valuable time."

"Well, there's no need to worry about that. None of this is an imposition at all. I told you I'm with you until you get the result you're looking for. I meant it, Sarah."

I nod. *See, Sarah. Remember, he's only in this to get you pregnant. Lock that heart away, girl.*

I need to change the subject before I drown in my thoughts. "Did you go climbing today?"

"Yeah. I have this place that's not too far out of the city; I visit whenever I can. It has a couple of different routes that vary in difficulty, so it's a favorite of mine."

Vivid images of AJ, shirtless and glistening with sweat fill my mind. His muscles straining and shifting as he scales a rock face; the sheer masculine strength required to pull your body weight upward against the forces of gravity. My eyes drop to his sexy forearms and hands, imagining his skilled fingers working over my body. Heat fills my face and I push back from the table. "Uh, did you want a glass of water?"

AJ chuckles. "Sure. Thanks."

Placing a glass of water in front of AJ and one in front of my dinner, I take my seat again and try to block out the images of him reaching for his next hold, instead concentrating on eating my meal.

"This is a nice place."

I lift my eyes, glancing at AJ while he studies my apartment. "Thank you. It's small but it's cozy and it's all mine. Well, it mostly belongs to the bank, but it'll be all mine one day."

He grins and tips his chin toward my couch. "Are you making another cap?"

I glance across and smile. "Yeah. I delivered my last batch this morning during my shift. So now I have to start all over again."

He tilts his head. "Your shift?"

"Yeah, at the NICU."

AJ's eyebrows shoot up. "Really? I thought you were a corporate secretary."

I chuckle. "Yeah, I am. But every second Saturday I volunteer at the NICU as a baby cuddler."

"I had no idea people could do that. I bet it's incredible. I used to love holding Colton when he was a newborn. Not that I don't love cuddling him now that he's bigger, but there was something so special about holding him when he was tiny and fragile. He needed the adults around him to keep him safe and to provide for all his needs. It was really special to be part of his inner circle."

I nod as he shares his experience, my heart expanding at the obvious love he has for his nephew. "Yeah, it's amazing. The babies are incredibly tiny and all they need is a little extra help to get to where they need to be. Parents can't be with their baby twenty-four-seven because they may already have other children at home, or they may still be recovering themselves. So the extra hands, or should I say warm bodies, is a big help."

"You sound like you really love it."

"I do. As much as I do it to help the babies, I find I get as much from the experience. While I'm there with the babies, I'm not thinking about anything else. I'm completely in the moment with them." AJ nods. "There's a certain quiet that settles over me when I'm cuddling the newborns."

"Climbing does that for me. It centers my mind and my body. I can only focus on what I'm doing, the next hold, staying safe, and moving forward. It takes all of my focus. I find it helps me with my work, too."

I tilt my head to the side. "How so?"

"Climbing has taught me to plan out my steps and stay focused on the task at hand."

"Interesting. So, how long have you been climbing?"

AJ stands, collecting our empty dishes. "Probably about five years or so. It was a little while after I finished my studies when Dylan and I were getting our business up and running. I used to find it hard to stay on track with my tasks, always getting distracted by some other unimportant task that could wait. A friend was getting married and as part of his bachelor party, we did a couple of hours of indoor rock climbing and I loved it. I started going once every few weeks and my interest grew from there. Once I noticed the difference in my work, I made it a habit and built it into my schedule." He fills the kitchen sink and proceeds to wash the dishes like it's the most natural thing in the world to do.

"I can do the dishes since you brought dinner." I try to nudge him out of the way so I can take over but he doesn't budge.

"It's no problem, Sarah. There are less than ten items." He elbows me out of the way, so I scoop up some of the bubbles from the sink and flick them at him. His eyes widen and a mischievous grin takes over his face and I know I'm in trouble. "Oh, it's on!" He scoops out some bubbles and flicks them at me, covering the front of my left boob. His eyes drop to where the bubbles are disintegrating, leaving a wet patch on my white tank and making my nipples pebble. "Shit! Sorry." His wide eyes glance up to my face, then drop back down when I wipe the spot, making my breast jiggle. It's only then I realize that by doing so, I've pressed the fabric against my flesh, making my peaked nipple visible through the flimsy fabric.

I chuckle, turning my back to him. "Don't worry, I totally started that. I'm just going to quickly change, so I'm not flashing you."

"I don't mind. You can flash me all you want." He winks and I head for my bedroom, chuckling. As I search through my drawers for a fresh bra and T-shirt, I can't help but wonder what it would be like to spend all of my Saturday nights like this.

I'M GLAD I COULD MAKE HER LAUGH WHEN SHE MUST BE FEELING crappy. I debated, for all of five minutes, whether it would be a good idea to turn up on her doorstep. I hoped she wouldn't think I was some creeper and that she'd let me inside. I figured it would be harder for her to refuse if I brought dinner with me and I was right.

I finish the dishes and make myself comfortable on her couch while I wait for her to change. I would like to say I'm a gentleman and I didn't take advantage of the view her see-through tank afforded me, but I'm not a liar. I pick up the pink yarn resting on the couch, running the strands through my fingers. It's so damn soft. I collect the cap she's left on the coffee table, fitting it over my fist. It's tight, reminding me how tiny a newborn is, and I would imagine the newborns in the NICU are even tinier than Colton was when he was born.

Movement out of my periphery has me glancing up. Sarah's standing just inside her bedroom door, watching me study the cap. "This is really something. How many of these do you make?"

"Depends on what I have going on and if I need to stay back late at work. But anywhere from five to eight every two weeks. Each one takes me around two hours to make from start to finish. I usually make a little pompom to go on top. They look so cute when they're done."

"Are they hard to make?"

"They were at first because I had to teach myself how to crochet. I had quite a few failures as I mastered the technique. And even now, I'm not the fastest, but it's a great way to wind down and relax while I'm watching TV."

"Could you teach me? I think Colton would like one of these. Maybe I could make one for Hayley and Lisa's new baby too." Her eyes widen and her mouth drops open a little.

"Uh, sure. If you like. Fair warning, I'm not an expert, though."

I pat the seat beside me, soaking in Sarah's fresh spring scent as she sits. She collects a hook thing and some yarn, then spends the next forty minutes trying to teach me how to start, but my fingers are too thick and I'm finding it difficult to get my hands to do what they need to do.

"Hmph, I don't think crochet is for me."

Sarah laughs. "Maybe not. What's Colton's favorite color? I could make him a cap easily enough."

"He loves orange. The brighter the orange, the better."

She chuckles. "I'm pretty sure I saw some fluorescent orange at the store the last time I stocked up on yarn. I'll grab some next time and make him one."

And just like that, Sarah's burrowed herself in a little deeper. Not that she needed to, I'm already so gone for this woman. When she didn't respond to my texts this afternoon, I grew worried. I know how much this means to her and she must be disappointed. This is her third attempt and still no baby. I was going to camp overnight and climb again tomorrow, but as it grew later and I hadn't heard from her, I couldn't stay away. Having her phone number made it easy enough to reverse search for her address. I've put measures in place to ensure others can't find the information so easily. If people knew how much information someone like me can access from only having a phone number, they would be shocked.

"Thanks. He'll love that. Let me know how much everything costs and I'll reimburse you."

"You will not. I'll happily make him one. After everything you're doing for me, it's the least I can do."

I sit forward. "I want to make one thing very clear. You don't owe me anything. Nothing at all. I'm happy to help you."

Her stunning smile falls from her face and her eyes drop to her lap. "I *do* owe you. I owe you so much for your time and your"—she waves her hand around the general area of my cock—"your generosity."

I chuckle. "I'm happy to help." I drop my voice. "I'm sorry it didn't happen this month. We'll start fresh next month. You let me know when we need to start again, and I'll be there."

"Thank you, AJ. I'm not sure what I did to get so lucky." She glances away. "Would you like a cup of hot chocolate? I'm craving chocolate today." She points toward an empty chocolate wrapper on the table.

"Sure."

Sarah makes our drinks and I turn on the television. She pops her head out of the kitchen. "Would you mind leaving it on that channel? It's the finale and I want to see what they bake."

I drop the remote to the couch and Sarah returns with our drinks, her eyes locked on the television screen. "I love baking cupcakes. I bake them for everyone in the office on Thursday nights and take them in on Friday. Sort of a celebration that we've made it through the week."

Is there anything this woman does for herself? She seems to give a lot of time and resources to those around her.

"Oh yeah. I don't mind a cupcake now and then. What's your favorite to bake?"

She ponders my question for a moment. "I love making lemon curd cupcakes if I had to choose one. The smooth lemon center is to die for, especially when they're freshly baked." She smiles. "Though, I try to limit myself to only one cupcake a week."

We get caught up watching the show. The level of comfort and ease between us makes me wonder what it would be like to share every Saturday night with Sarah. What would it be like to watch her make cupcakes every Thursday evening, cleaning up the mess for her while she decorates the tasty treats? The fantasy of living with her plays on a reel in my mind and the idea is wholly appealing. I can't see a downside to sharing a place with her, which is a concept I never imagined I would find attractive. Watching her while she watches the final minutes of the show, riveted to her seat as she waits for the winner to be announced, I decide I want to make it happen. I want to have Sarah living with me. Probably in my space. As nice as her apartment is, it would be too small for a family.

The show ends and Sarah turns to me. "I think I'm addicted to baking shows."

I shrug. "There are worse things you could be addicted to."

"That's what I tell myself."

I peek at my watch. It's getting late but I'm not ready to give up my time with Sarah yet. "Did you want to watch another episode?"

"You don't mind?"

"Not at all."

We spend the next hour watching the first episode of the next season and as fascinating as it is to watch, I would rather watch Sarah's interest in the program. She yawns for what must be the fifth time, letting me know that my time with her is coming to an end tonight.

As the credits roll, Sarah turns to me. "Thanks for indulging me."

"You're welcome. I've never seen the show before. I had no idea there were cupcake-making competitions." I chuckle as I stand, collecting our empty cups and heading toward the kitchen to clean up. Once I've rinsed the cups and placed them on the dish rack to dry, I step back into the living room as Sarah stands. She's rubbing across her stomach with a grimace. "Are you okay?"

"Yeah. Just cramps. They're always worse the first night. I'll take some more Midol and heat up the heat pack before I climb into bed." She moves closer to me. "Thanks for coming over and keeping me company."

"No problem. Are you doing anything for the Fourth?" Maybe I can see her at some point.

"I'll be spending tomorrow with my sister and her family to help set up for a party on Monday with friends and family. You?"

Damn. I tuck my hands in my pockets to stop myself from tucking the loose strands of hair that have fallen out of her ponytail behind her ear. "I'll be catching up with the family on Monday, too."

She walks me to the door and my mood drops considerably, knowing our time has come to an end and I won't see her until she's ovulating. "Have a great time with your family. Bye, AJ, and thanks again." She opens the door and I shuffle through, not wanting to leave. I lean forward, pressing my lips to her cheek, inhaling her subtle scent as I do.

"Enjoy the rest of your weekend. Bye, Sare." I tip my head and give her a final wave, disappointed I can't do more than that.

## CHAPTER 15

"AJ!" Mom gushes as she almost runs toward me with her arms outstretched. "It's so good to see you." I know I don't visit her as much as she'd like, but she's acting like she hasn't seen me all year, rather than the month since our last family dinner. I've been avoiding family events like this one because I'm tired of dealing with my grandfather.

"Mom." She pulls me in tight, kissing my cheeks.

"I've missed you so much." She pulls back, her hands on my biceps. "You're looking well. Healthy. Happy."

"Thanks, Mom. I'm making sure I eat better and the climbing helps me keep in shape." She nods, securing her hold on my arm and pulling me through my grandparents' home and out to the backyard which overlooks the bay. It's a stunning property, but Hayley and I could never just be kids and jump in the pool or run around the massive space inside. I mean they have a damn ballroom for God's sake. I'm not sure how my mother grew up here as an only child. I can't imagine she would have been allowed to have any fun. My earliest memories of spending time here always include the constant shushing and being told we weren't allowed to do this or touch that. We basically weren't allowed to be kids whenever we visited.

"Adam, look, AJ's here," Mom calls out to Dad as if he didn't already know I'd arrived, but Mom's being over the top today for some reason.

"Unca AJ!" Colton calls as he comes running for me. I crouch down to catch him before he's shushed or told to slow down.

"Hey, little man. How's my boy?"

Mom's hand flies up to her chest as she gives Colton a tight smile. "Oh, do you think it's appropriate to call him '*your* boy'?"

I frown at Mom. "What do you mean?"

"Well, he might get confused. You know with you being his biological f-a-t-h-e-r and all." She widens her eyes to make her point.

"It's just a phrase, Mom. Don't stress. But the girls will tell him who I am to him once he's old enough to understand. It's not going to be some big secret."

Colton claps his hands. "You're my bestest unca!"

I chuckle. "I'd better be your bestest! I'm your only uncle."

Mom chuckles nervously as Dad steps closer. I hold out my free hand to Dad. "Hey, Dad."

"Son. Good to see you. Life looks like it's been treating you well."

I readjust Colton, holding him more firmly. "Thanks. Life's pretty great at the moment."

"Oh yeah." He raises a dark eyebrow. "Why's that?"

"Dylan and I won the multi-million-dollar contract we were chasing." I desperately want to tell my family I've met the woman of my dreams, but I fear it's too soon—Sarah's still incredibly closed off. Who knows how long it'll take for me to break through her walls? But if I have the patience to hack into some of the world's most secure servers, I have the patience to break through Sarah's firewalls. I smirk at myself.

Dad's smile is swift. "Congratulations, AJ. I'm proud of you, Son."

"Thanks, Dad. We worked hard to position ourselves in such a way to even be considered a contender."

"Good planning is important. Congratulate Dylan for me, too."

"I will."

A hand drops heavily onto my shoulder and my muscles lock. "AJ. I'm happy you could make it. We need to talk."

"Grandfather. We do, but I'm sure it can wait until after lunch."

"No. I think it's best to get business out of the way. Join me in my study, please." I follow him with my eyes as he walks inside expecting me to follow.

I move my gaze back to my parents. Mom is chewing on her bottom lip, tightness pulling around her eyes. "I guess I've been summoned." I place Colton on his feet. "Why don't you go see if Mama will take you for a swim? I'll be back in a minute."

"Okay, Unca AJ!" He takes off toward Hayley, shouting, "Mama. I wanna go for a swim!"

Hayley waves to me and I return the gesture, then turn back to my parents. "What's going on? Has something been said?"

"Your grandfather is growing tired of waiting for you to make a decision."

I huff out a frustrated breath. "I've already given him my decision, but it doesn't stop him from harassing me about it at least once a week."

Dad sighs. "He's an old man, Son. Just humor him. Do what he asks and once he's gone, you can make your own choices."

"I don't want to do that. I have my own business with Dylan, which is growing by the week. I don't want to walk away from it. We've worked damn hard to build it up to where we are today." I wave my arm out toward Mom. "Mom is dying to get in there and take over. She's wanted to be part of it since she was a little girl—"

"It's his business, his decision," Mom says tightly. "Just go and get the conversation out of the way, so we can enjoy a pleasant afternoon as a family. Okay?" I don't know why she's happy to continue being overlooked for the position.

I roll my eyes heavenward. "Okay. But I doubt it will be a pleasant afternoon when I say what needs to be said."

I walk away before Dad can try to convince me to do otherwise. I'm sick and tired of being bullied into a role I don't want. A role I have absolutely zero interest in. My heart pounds and I strengthen my resolve as I close the distance to Grandfather's study—a place that was always off-limits when I was a child.

I blow out a breath as my hand connects with the heavy door to push it open. I'm taken aback when I look at his grand desk to find the chair behind it empty. Skimming my eyes around the spacious room, they land on him standing in front of the window, hands in the pockets of his shorts. It's odd to see him dressed so casually. From my earliest memories, even on weekends, he always wore a suit.

"Grandfather." I step into the middle of the room after closing the door.

He keeps his gaze out of the window. "I'm not getting any younger, you know, boy."

"I know."

"Exactly how long do you intend to make me wait."

As much as my body wants to move, to leave the room, I stay glued to the spot. "I've already told you, Grandfather. I don't want the position. It's something Mom has wanted since she was young. Give it to her. Your company will be in safe hands with her. In fact, she's probably better equipped to manage it than I could ever dream to be."

He turns around to face me, his features drawn tight in anger. "And I've already told you she won't be given the position. It *has* to be you. Stop trying to shirk your responsibilities, boy!" he shouts.

I keep my tone calm. He's been getting progressively angrier each time we have this same discussion, but I'm not prepared to budge. I guess I get my stubbornness from him. "I'm not shirking my responsibilities. I have my own company to run. I've built it from nothing and I'm not prepared to walk away from it or from doing something I love. Especially now we're hitting our stride. I don't consider that shirking my responsibilities."

He moves toward me. "Your responsibility is taking over the family company."

"And Mom is more than happy to take the reins. Give the leadership position to her." I want him to realize this is the twenty-first century and to make decisions accordingly, but we keep having this same argument. I could easily take the company from him and give Mom the position, but I want it to come from *him*. I think it's important that *he* makes that decision. I've seen how hurt Mom is each time he overlooks her and insists I take over. He needs to make it better.

"No."

I blow out a breath and grasp the back of my neck. "We're not living in the nineteen-fifties anymore, Grandfather." Though sometimes I wonder, with the decisions being made by the government. "Women hold CEO positions all the time. It's not uncommon. She would do a fantastic job. You know she would. You're being stubborn."

"Watch your tongue, boy. It's my company, my decision and you'll do as I say or so help me … you'll be out of my will," he snaps at me, spittle flying out of his mouth, reminding me of my place.

He wants me to take over his company but he still treats me like a child. He won't let Mom take over, even though she's been dying to do so since she was young, because, in his eyes, women don't run corporations, they run homes or do menial type work. It's infuriating.

I'm not going to win this conversation today. "Look, I think it would be best to have this conversation another day. This is meant to be a casual family barbecue celebrating the Fourth of July. I'll make time to come into the office and we can have this discussion where it belongs."

"It had better happen sooner rather than later, boy. I'm all out of patience. I want to retire at the end of this year. Do you hear me?"

"Yes, Grandfather. I hear you loud and clear."

# CHAPTER 16

DYLAN AND I FREEZE AS WE STEP INSIDE THE *CARDINAL QUARRY CASINO and Resort* lobby, our overnight bags in hand. Polished brown and cream marble flooring gleams beneath our shoes and I'm pleased we decided to wear suits for this meeting with Mr. Mitchell, the owner. I can't believe we were even on this guy's radar, but this opportunity is beyond our wildest dreams. If we can land this contract, it could open up a whole new world for us because this resort casino is one of many that come under the family's umbrella.

The twenty-minute drive from the airport to here in the complimentary limo sent by Mr. Mitchell to collect us was an unexpected bonus. The air conditioning was a welcome reprieve as we made our way through the city of Las Vegas toward the outskirts. The Mitchell family seems to be pulling out all the stops to impress us when it really should be us working to impress them. They even offered us the opportunity to stay in the hotel overnight free of charge and provided us complimentary chips for the casino. Dylan and I couldn't pass up their offer and opted to return home in the morning, even though our meeting will be well and truly over and done with this afternoon.

A man, much younger than I expected, strides toward us with his arm outstretched and a warm smile. "You must be AJ and Dylan. I'm Charles." I raise my eyebrows and glance at Dylan. "You were probably expecting my father, but he's handing more responsibilities over to me. I hope that won't be an issue."

"No, not at all. Happy to meet you, Charles." I grip his hand.

He shakes hands with Dylan. "Nice to meet you."

"You too. This is a stunning building." Dylan smiles at Charles.

"Thank you. We pride ourselves on offering a luxurious experience from the moment you step foot on one of our properties." He waves his arm out toward the front desk. "Katie, please ensure Mr. Jackson and Mr. Baker's bags are situated in their room."

"Certainly, Mr. Mitchell."

"Please, follow me." We make our way toward the elevator and enter the glass car which has a magnificent view across the desert, showcasing craggy outcrops I'd love to climb one day. When the elevator comes to a stop, we're guided into an office that is equally as impressive as what we've seen so far. "I thought we could get business out of the way first, then I'll show you around before we have dinner."

Floor-to-ceiling windows across the entire office wall overlook the view we just enjoyed in the elevator and I don't want to tear my eyes away. "How do you get any work done with this view?" I ask.

Charles glances out of the window as if to check what I'm talking about. "You know what. I've grown up here and I guess I take it for granted." He shrugs. "I don't even notice it anymore." If I had this office, I'd never get any work done.

He offers us a drink and we get down to business. Three hours later we've signed contracts and set up a schedule of events we'll implement to test the security of the casino's servers. Charles is concerned about the threat of hackers taking over the machines on the floor and the internal banking system they have in place for purchasing and cashing in chips. I can certainly understand his concern because a breach of their security could cost them millions of dollars.

With business out of the way, Charles takes us on a tour of the casino and resort. I'd love to bring Sarah here one day, perhaps for a weekend getaway. The pool area alone is something I've never seen before. The entire facility is tastefully designed and artfully decorated, which is very different from what I was expecting. From what I'd seen of casinos in Vegas, they tend to fall on the gaudy side.

"Well, I'll leave you two to explore." He hands us a keycard each. "I'll meet you in *The Quarry Restaurant* at seven for dinner. Enjoy, gentlemen."

"Thanks, Charles." We both say as we shake his hand in turn.

"This place is incredible," I say, my voice full of awe.

Dylan looks at me. "It's spectacular."

Deciding we want to celebrate our success, we stop at the *Cardinal Bar* and order a couple of local craft beers.

"To us and our success!" Dylan raises his glass, tapping it against mine.

I chuckle at his excitement. "To us, man. Who knew a couple of teenagers could make a career out of breaching firewalls!" We both take a long drink and the balanced salty and tart flavor bursts across my tongue, drawing a moan from me. "That's a nice blend of orange and blackberry."

Dylan nods and we recap some of the most significant points from the meeting and formulate a rough plan to get started.

"So, how are things going with Sarah's plan?" Dylan asks.

I wipe my fingers down the condensation of my glass. "We were unsuccessful last month. We'll try again when she ovulates this month, which I think should be any day now."

"Are you sure this is a good idea?" I give him a what the fuck look and he holds up his hands in surrender. "You seem to be getting attached."

"Yep, I think it's a fantastic idea."

He takes a sip of his beer. "If you're sure."

"I am." I take another drink and turn my head to check out the people around us. My phone buzzes in my pocket, so I grab it.

SARAH

I started ovulating today. Any chance you can come over?

Without thought, I turn to Dylan. "I need to go home. Will you be okay here to handle dinner?" We've finished the actual business part of our meeting, tonight's more about socializing.

His eyebrows scrunch over his eyes. "Why? What's happened? Is everything okay?"

"Yeah, nothing serious but Sarah's ovulating. I need to get home so I can do my part." I stand and finish my beer. Actually, I should check to see if I can get on a flight before I tell her I'm on my way.

"Can't it wait 'til tomorrow?" He's completely confused. And yeah, I probably could tell her I'm out of town and I'll be back tomorrow, but I don't want to. I've missed her and I want to see her.

"Nah. We need to act quickly. There's only a limited window of opportunity." I dig out my phone and call the airline. There's a flight leaving in an hour, then it'll be an hour and a half home, plus the drive; I won't be home for three hours. I check the time—five-thirty.

That'll work. "All right. I'll see you when you get home. Have a good night."

"Good luck. What should I tell Charles?" Dylan asks.

"Tell him I had an emergency and I had to get home. It's not a lie," I tell him as I step away.

In the elevator up to our room, I message Sarah.

> ME
>
> I'm in a meeting, so I'll see you at 8:30

> SARAH
>
> If you're busy, it can wait until tomorrow

> ME
>
> I'll be finished by then, see you at 8:30

> SARAH
>
> Okay, thank you. Just come to my place

> ME
>
> Are you sure?

> SARAH
>
> You already know where I live. May as well

One side of my mouth tips up. Yes, I do.

> ME
>
> Okay

Arriving on Sarah's doorstep, I draw in a deep breath, then knock on her door. I hear shuffling inside before the door opens revealing Sarah in shorts and a tank, her feet bare with teal nail polish.

She's stunning.

Her smile is immediate when she sees me, so I lean forward and press my lips against her soft cheek, simultaneously dragging a bouquet of flowers from behind my back. As she pulls away from me, her eyes land on the peonies and her smile widens. Mine matches hers without delay.

"Oh, AJ, you didn't have to do this." She leans forward and pecks my cheek and it was worth every penny of the eighty dollars the arrangement cost me from the overpriced shop at the airport. "They're stunning." She drops her nose into the bouquet, drawing in a deep breath. "They smell gorgeous too. My apartment's going to smell fabulous! Thank you so much."

She steps to the side and I enter her cozy apartment, which already smells incredible. She has one of her cooking shows on the television and she was obviously crocheting while she was waiting for me.

"You're welcome."

"Have you had anything to eat?" Sarah asks as she steps into the kitchen, bending down to reach under the sink and giving me a spectacular view of her plump ass. She stands, holding a vase, and looks at me over her shoulder as she fills it with water. I snap my eyes up, but I'm not sure I've done it quickly enough to not get caught.

"Yeah. I had something on the plane," I tell her.

She spins to face me fully, tightness surrounding her eyes. "On the plane? Where were you?"

"Vegas."

"Oh. How come you were there?"

Full of pride, I tell her about our meeting with Charles and how we've secured him as a client, while she arranges the flowers to her liking. Sarah surprises me when she wraps her arms around me, tugging me into her lush body. My hands automatically rise to hold her waist, taking advantage of the opportunity to feel her curves.

"Congratulations! You should be out celebrating with Dylan, not here with me." She releases me and grabs the vase, placing it on her dining table, then turns toward me with a smile. "Thank you. They're so beautiful."

"I'm glad you like them. Dylan and I were having a drink in the bar when you messaged."

Her sculpted eyebrows draw together, creating creases between them. "I … I hope you didn't leave early to come here … for me." Her words are stilted.

This could go one of two ways if I tell her I left Dylan behind to deal with our client when I was supposed to be there. She's either going to think I'm great for dropping everything to come here when she needed me, or she's going to catch on as to how invested I am. I want to be completely honest with her, though.

"Uh, I left Dylan to finish up. He'll be okay. All of the business stuff had already been sorted. Tonight was more about socializing."

Her eyes widen and she licks her lips. "AJ," she whispers. "You didn't have to do that. We could have done this tomorrow night."

I shrug like it's no big deal. "We can't waste any opportunities. This is important."

"Yeah, but so is your contract." She steps in, wrapping her arms around me, her eyes glassy. "Thank you, AJ. I don't know how I can ever thank you enough for what you're giving me. You left an important meeting to be here for me. I can't believe it." She drops the top of her head against my chest for long moments and I rub soothing strokes down her back because I sense she's having a moment. Having her in my arms is exactly where I want her to be, not because she's overwhelmed with gratitude, but because she wants to be wrapped up in me as much as I want to be wrapped up in her. When she pulls away, she sniffles and steps across to the coffee table to grab a tissue and I miss her immediately. She dabs at her eyes and wipes beneath her nose as she walks back into the kitchen. "Well"—she gives me a shaky smile —"I have something for you. It isn't as grand a gesture, but I made you some cupcakes."

I smile widely and rub my hands together. "Oh yeah! This is my lucky day." This explains the delicious smell which greeted me the minute I stepped inside.

She steps toward me with a plate of incredible-looking cupcakes. "I remembered you said you love apple pie, so I made you apple pie cupcakes." I flick my eyes between the cupcakes and Sarah's face, which is full of expectation. Surely she's not worried I won't like them. "They're not true cupcakes because they have no cake, but how cute are these?" Her eyes widen and meet mine as she finishes.

"They smell incredible and they look fantastic. Do you mind if I have one now?"

"Of course. I made them for you. You can take what's left home with you."

She picks one from the plate and passes it to me. Instead of taking it, I lean forward to take a bite; careful of her fingers but manage to brush them with my lips. Her eyes widen and her pupils dilate. My eyes drop to the pulse point at the base of her throat and I'm pleased to see it hammering as quickly as mine. Good to know I have some impact on the woman.

The sweet but tart flavor explodes on my tongue as the spicy apple scent fills my nose, and I close my eyes to fully appreciate it. When I open them again, Sarah's watching me closely, her lips slightly parted.

"You are a master. This is so good! Have you ever considered going into business and opening a cupcake shop? People would be beating down your door to get their hands on these." I take the cake from Sarah and take another bite, holding my hand beneath my chin to catch the crumbs.

Sarah chuckles. "Nah, that would take the fun out of making them."

I finish the first one, then take another cupcake and make short work of that one too. "I don't know if I can stop at two, but I probably should." I pat my trim stomach. Sarah's eyes drop to watch the action, and I don't think she realizes but her breaths are shallow. It's good to know I have some effect on her because God knows I can't stop thinking about her.

We chat for a while. Superficial talk about how she's been and what I've been up to. I get the impression Sarah wants to keep things shallow between us, not wanting to delve into deeper, more meaningful conversations. I'm happy to play along for now, but I'll slowly work out her code.

There's a lull in the conversation, so Sarah stands. "I have everything set up in the bathroom ready for you. You may as well get started since we both need to get up for work in the morning."

I stand too. "Okay." I step past her and pause in the doorway to the bathroom. "Wish me luck."

"Good luck," she chirps.

I close the door and lean my back against it. I've given up trying not to think about Sarah when I do this. It seems to be my default setting and thinking about her and what she looks like naked is a sure-fire way to get things happening quickly. I move over to the vanity and grip the edge, studying myself in the mirror. I want her to get pregnant, I do, but once I do, I won't see her again. I'm certain of it. Her walls won't allow her to see the potential of the two of us in a relationship that's more than donor and recipient. I sigh and spin around, grabbing her shampoo out of the shower and flipping open the lid. It smells like Sarah; that gorgeous scent reminds me of a field of spring flowers. I inhale deeply, filling my lungs and my cock wakes.

I unzip my pants and drop them to the floor then remove my boxer briefs, my semi-hard cock dropping into my hand. I sigh. I'd much rather have Sarah's pussy tightening around my shaft … I'd even settle for her hand at this point.

Washing my hands, I open the package containing the collection condom. With my cock in hand, I stroke loosely, bringing him fully to life, then roll on the condom. Resting my hand on the vanity, I drop my head and close my eyes, bringing forth an image of Sarah in her teal bikini. Tightening my grip, I replay the image of her adjusting the straps, making her tits jiggle, and scan my eyes down her soft stomach, to the triangle of fabric between her legs, then down her thick thighs, which I can't wait to have wrapped around my head. I widen my stance and tug on my cock, using my other hand to massage my heavy balls, then slide my fist up and down my length in quick, smooth glides, rolling my fist over the head, careful not to dislodge the condom. I repeat the process several times, my breaths coming sharper, and do my best to hold in my moans.

Doing this myself certainly doesn't give me the level of satisfaction I enjoy when I'm inside a woman, but I'm here to get the job done, not for the enjoyment of the act. I keep stroking to thoughts of Sarah, feeling the fire building through my body until it can no longer be contained and I blow into the condom with a moan, which was probably louder than it should have been in this small apartment. It's not like she doesn't know what I'm doing in here anyway, so long as I don't call her name out loud and make it completely weird between us. My knees weaken and I reach out to support myself on the vanity as I regain my composure. My breathing slowly returns to normal and the haze across my vision clears.

Once I'm back to normal, I carefully remove the condom, balancing it in the sterilized cup Sarah always provides, ensuring I don't inadvertently lose any swimmers. If there's one thing I've learned about the woman is that she's thorough in her planning and extremely organized. I wash my hands and rinse my softening cock, then tuck myself away and redress. With a cursory check in the mirror, I make sure I look presentable, ensuring my zipper is done up, and step out of the bathroom. Sarah freezes and her head snaps up to my face, her eyes wide and waiting for me to speak.

"All done," I say, forcing brightness into my tone, raising my eyebrows to add to the excitement I don't feel. Don't get me wrong, I'm happy to help, but I would prefer the experience if we were actually getting naked … together.

Sarah's body softens and a smile touches her lips. "Thank you. I feel like those two words aren't enough."

"You don't have to thank me every time we do this. Let's hope we get you pregnant this month." Who am I kidding? I don't want her to get pregnant this month because that'll mean I won't get to see her anymore and I definitely don't want that. I didn't think my feelings would get so damn complicated. "Well, I guess I'll leave you to it." I head for the door.

"Hang on. Don't forget your cupcakes."

"Oh right. Thanks for these," I say as she hands me a Tupperware container full of mini apple pies, which taste like heaven.

We awkwardly say goodbye at the door, and I hear Sarah engage the locks, then I make my way home to my empty warehouse. As soon as I get in the door, I take a minute to download an app to help me track Sarah's cycle. That way I'll make sure I'm always available when she needs me.

ME

Did everything go smoothly?

I grab a beer out of the fridge while I wait for her response.

SARAH

I don't know how to tell you this, but I dropped the cup and lost everything on my hardwood floor

I read the message again and again, as I head back out of my front door. With almost zero traffic on the road, it doesn't take me long before I'm knocking on Sarah's front door for the second time tonight.

"Hello." Sarah's voice is unsure and muffled through the door.

"It's me." The locks immediately disengage and a wide-eyed Sarah stands before me in pajama shorts and a camisole, sans bra. My cock immediately wakes at the sight. Fuck! It looks as though she's been crying.

"You didn't have to come back," she whispers.

I can't console her because that will mean touching her and I'm barely holding onto my control, so I step past her. "I know, but you only have a limited window, and I didn't want to waste an opportunity. Do you have another condom?" I have to keep moving and not linger because if I look at her in her current state, I may throw caution to the wind and take her to bed.

It must finally register what I'm here to do because she closes the front door and walks into the bathroom. She efficiently sets everything up and then stops for a moment. "Thank you so much." She swallows and I can see her eyes becoming glassy. "I can't believe you came back." Her whispered words are heartfelt and I hope she's beginning to realize I would do anything for her.

I can't resist any longer and cup her face in my hands. "I'll always come when you need me, Sarah." Her bottom lip trembles and I press my thumb to it before I press my lips to it. "Now, let's get this done, so you can do your thing." I wink at her and press a light kiss on her forehead.

Stepping back, she nods and says, "Okay," as she closes the door behind her.

I blow out a long breath and drop my eyes down my body to the bulge behind my zipper. I sigh heavily and get down to business. I don't need to imagine Sarah in her bikini because I have new material to work with now. Those pajamas were something else. My cum fills the condom, and I carefully prop it up in the cup, then clean myself up. Stepping out, I'm disappointed to find Sarah's covered herself with a wrap thing that women wear.

"Done." She jumps up from the couch and wraps her arms around me, her soft breasts pressing against my body, thanking me again. I get that she's grateful, but the constant gratitude is unnecessary. Returning her embrace, I kiss the top of her head. "You're welcome. How about I stick around to make sure everything goes smoothly this time?"

She takes one step away from me and I'm left feeling bereft. I much prefer to have my arms around her, her scent filling my nose, and her hair tickling my chin. "Okay. Good idea." She thumbs over her shoulder. "I'll just grab the condom. Make yourself comfortable on the couch, I'll see you soon."

# CHAPTER 17

## —sarah—

AJ's been incredible each time he's come over this past week to donate his semen; twice the first night, after leaving an important meeting and jumping on a plane to get to me. Not gonna lie, he almost broke through my walls, but I remained strong—*barely*. It's been much more comfortable doing it in my home than in a hotel, not to mention it's saved me some money, which I can put toward expenses for when I get pregnant and have the baby.

We have the process down to a fine routine now. He comes over, I feed him dinner, we chat a little, he steps into the bathroom and does what he needs to do while I pace, then he leaves so I can do my thing. An hour later, I always get a text from him asking if I'm okay and if everything went well.

If I'm being completely honest, it's a certain kind of torture. He's patient and reliable and he's happy to support me through this process for as long as it takes. I think he would be perfect for me. That we'd be perfect together. I'm not sure when he plans to settle and start a family, but whomever he ends up with will be an extremely lucky woman.

*If only that could be me.*

Why couldn't I have met him under different circumstances instead of being some desperate woman who wants to have a baby? Life is so unfair sometimes.

Stop it, Sarah! Geez, I've avoided sex with AJ at all costs, and yet my heart is still fighting to be involved. I may as well have sex with him at this point.

No. I wave my arm in the air. Nope. Not going there. I don't think I would survive.

Now to finish decorating Kenny's birthday cake for tomorrow. I can't believe she's six. I was planning to make her a princess cake, but she insisted on a Black Widow cake. I study the image I saved on my phone and add the blue pin striping carefully, ensuring I keep my hand steady so the lines are straight. I lift the piping bag away once I've finished, admiring how it's coming together when there's a knock on my door. Glancing at the time on the microwave, I realize I've lost track of time. AJ's here.

Butterflies erupt in my stomach as I call out, "Coming!"

"I will be too," he immediately returns, making me giggle as I wash my hands.

I answer the door with a smile, shaking my head. "Anyone tell you that you should have been a comedian?"

He laughs as he steps inside, carrying a gift box, and lays a peck on my cheek. Something he started doing every time we meet. His citrus scent wafts around me and I draw in a deep breath. He looks incredible as always with a simple T-shirt showcasing the union jack and cargo shorts. "Not today," he shoots back. I close the door and follow him further into my apartment. "You've been baking."

"Yeah. Remember I told you it was Kenny's birthday the other day? We're having a family party for her tomorrow, and I'm the designated birthday cake maker of the family."

He wanders into my kitchen, studying the half-decorated cake on the counter. He raises his eyes to me as I stand opposite. "This is amazing. You made this?"

"Yeah. I love making fancy cakes for the kids."

"Do you have photos of other cakes you've made?"

"Yeah, hang on. I have photos on my phone." I grab my phone and open the folder where I keep photos of the cakes I've made over the years.

"Holy shit! These are incredible. That Spider-Man is awesome! He's, uh, he's actually my favorite Avenger." Oh my gosh, how cute is that? He has a favorite Avenger.

"Is it because he can climb?" I joke.

"Huh." He looks thoughtful. "I never really thought about why I like him the best, but maybe that's it." He shrugs and then hands me the gift box. "This is for Kenny. If you wouldn't mind giving it to her when you see her tomorrow, I'd appreciate it since I won't."

"Would you like to come?" The words tumble out of my mouth before I can even think to stop them. It's so unlike me to be spontaneous. I haven't even checked if it would be okay with Emma and Theo, but I'm sure they wouldn't mind; she was smitten with him and Kenny loved him too. "That's if you don't already have plans. I know I've already taken up a lot of your week." I rush to add.

"I don't have anything going on. Are you sure it would be okay?"

"Pretty sure. I can double-check with Em and Theo, but I don't see a problem with it."

"Well yeah, I'd love to." I mentally jump up and down on the inside that I get to spend more time with AJ, but then I remember I should be avoiding the guy at all costs except for our essential donation requirements. *Damn it!* "Or, I don't have to come. You look worried."

I give him my best smile and wave him off. He's going to think I'm some nut job if I tell him I've changed my mind. "It's all good. I'll message Emma."

ME

Hey, would it be okay if AJ came to Kenny's party tomorrow?

I place my phone on the counter and clean up some of the cake-decorating mess to make room for dinner. I frown. "I thought you were bringing dinner with you?"

AJ grasps the back of his neck, treating me to the visual feast that is his tensing bicep. "Uh, yeah. About that. I thought maybe we could go out and grab a bite to eat."

Huh.

"Or, we could order in if you don't want to go out," he offers.

Does that make it like a date if we go out? Or is it pretty much the same thing as eating in? I'm not dressed to go anywhere. Or should I say I don't want to go out?

His rough hands land on my shoulders, his heat searing my skin. I'll be surprised if he doesn't leave char marks behind. He bends at the knees, so his eyes are level with mine, trapping me in their warm gaze. "Talk to me, Sarah. What's going on in that busy mind of yours?"

My phone buzzes with a text, so I grab it, thankful for the distraction.

EM

> Of course AJ can come tomorrow, Kenny loved him. You know what she's like, she collects people. *laughing emoji* Theo and Lachlan also want to show him the progress they've made with the climbing frame, so it all works out perfectly

I glance up to find AJ looking at the screen, a smile lifting the corners of his perfect mouth. I wave my phone between us. "You can come to Kenny's party."

"Great. I'm looking forward to it. Now tell me what's going on up here?" He taps the side of my head, and I blow out a breath.

"Nothing. Everything's great. I was thinking I need to change if we're going out to dinner." I force an upbeat tone into my voice to cover my confused thoughts.

"You look great. Come on, let's go." His hand slides down my arm to grip my hand, sending goosebumps racing across my body.

I chuckle. "Hang on. I can't go out in these leggings and tank. I'll change. I'll be quick. I promise."

He releases my hand, and I head toward my bedroom. "Okay, but I think you look great as you are." I glance over my shoulder, to answer him, only to find him staring at my ass. I stop and raise my brows at him, waiting for his eyes to make their way back up to my face. "Sorry. As I said, you look great as you are."

I chuckle and step into my bedroom, closing the door between us. I lean my back against the cool surface and blow out a long breath. Can I do this? Can I go to dinner, then come back here and wait for him to do his thing in the bathroom so he can give me his swimmers? The thing that started all of this. I'm getting attached. As I pull out my denim shorts and a silky tank, I reinforce the walls around my heart. I need to make the damn thing impenetrable. Dressing quickly, I release my hair from my standard ponytail and slip my feet into my Roman sandals, zipping up the back of each one. "I'm ready."

AJ's eyes snap up from his phone, then trail down my body and I feel his gaze as though his fingers are slowly caressing their way down my curves. Grabbing my cross-body bag, I pick up my phone and keys and head straight for the door, trying my best to ignore the wetness in my panties. His hand finds its way to my lower back as we make our way to the elevator.

"Is there anywhere around here in walking distance that's good?"

"Yeah. Do you like Mexican?"

"I absolutely do."

I point down the street. "*Los Burritos* is a fifteen-minute walk that way."

"Perfect." He takes my hand in his and we head off to grab dinner. I glance between us, my heart pounding behind my ribs and tingles racing up my arm. He's holding my hand … and it feels … natural.

The heat from the sidewalk radiates up and I wish I'd left my hair up in a ponytail. I don't even have an elastic handy on my wrist. "The place doesn't look all that great, but the food is authentic and the guys get it to you fast."

AJ nods as we step inside and once my eyes adjust, I mentally pat myself on the back. The place is packed, but I notice there are two empty stools down the back. I point toward them and we make our way through the busy hole in the wall. I can't possibly confuse this with a date. It'll be just like me and Mel grabbing something to eat. I should be able to keep myself in check.

"What's good here?" AJ asks as he sits.

I tuck my hair behind my ear and sit. "Everything. I promise you can't go wrong. The serving sizes are generous too."

"What do you usually get?"

"I usually get the chicken burrito on the spinach wrap. If you want to order yours, I'll hold our seats, then I'll order when you get back." If I pay for my dinner, it's definitely not a date. Right?

He nods. "Sure." I watch him walk toward the counter, admiring his broad shoulders which taper into narrow hips. The man is certainly built without being bulky. He glances at me and I quickly look away, hoping he didn't catch me staring at him.

I feel him, rather than see him sit back down. "I've ordered for you, but I wasn't sure what you'd like to drink, so I grabbed you a Mountain Dew. Hope that's okay."

"That's fine. Thank you. I was going to order mine."

He studies me closely and I have to stop myself from squirming under his gaze. "It's not a problem. You've been feeding me this week. It's the least I could do."

"I'm feeding you because it's the least *I* can do since you're donating to the cause and all." I chuckle softly.

AJ's name is called over the speaker system and he collects our food and drinks, bringing them back to our seats. It smells delicious and my stomach growls in response. AJ peels away the foil, and I watch him closely as he takes his first bite. His eyes drop closed and a deep moan escapes as the flavors burst on his tongue. I watch him chew and swallow, paying close attention to the bobbing of his Adam's apple.

Why is a guy's Adam's apple so damn sexy? Actually, everything about AJ is sexy. I can't believe the guy's single. There has to be a catch.

"Sarah! This is incredible. The flavors …" He mimes a chef's kiss. "So damn good. Thank you for bringing me here."

I smile as I unwrap my burrito. "You're welcome. I come here with Max sometimes."

We both get stuck into our meals, barely speaking until we each take our last bite. "That was so good. I'm going to have to bring Dylan here. He'll love this place."

The place was busy when we arrived, but it's crazy now. "We should probably head out and let someone else have our seats."

"Sure." AJ helps me down from my stool and we make our way outside where it's slightly cooler after being crammed into the small restaurant.

I force myself to relax as we stroll back to my place hand in hand. This time I try not to think about how right it feels to be this close to him, holding his hand in mine, heading home so we can work on my dream. This will be our sixth time doing this and I don't think I feel any less awkward about it.

"You're quiet." AJ breaks into my thoughts.

I glance up at him, then quickly turn my eyes forward again. "Just mentally running through what we're going to do when we get back to my place." *Oh God, Sarah! Really?*

He squeezes my hand. "Hopefully, in a couple of weeks, you'll know if it's worked or not."

"Hopefully." Sadness swiftly fills my body with the thought of not seeing AJ again. He said he wanted to stay friends, but what does that mean? I'll be busy getting fat with a baby and then I'll be busy looking after said baby. I can't imagine an attractive, single guy wanting to 'be friends' then. I should be filled with happiness at the thought of our efforts coming to fruition this month, not sad. This is something I've wanted for what feels like my entire life.

When we approach my building, AJ releases my hand to open and hold the door for me, his hand then taking up residence on my lower back again as we make our way to the elevator. The butterflies in my stomach have taken flight and I remind myself to take proper breaths as we wait for it to arrive.

We're both quiet as we make our way upstairs, lost in our thoughts. When we get inside my apartment, AJ stiffly thumbs over his shoulder toward the bathroom. "I guess I'll get started. Are the collection condoms still under the vanity?"

"Uh, yeah."

He nods and backs away from me toward the bathroom and closes the door behind him without another word spoken between us. I wonder what he does to get himself worked up. Does he have Pornhub loaded on his phone ready to go? Or is there someone he thinks about? An ex-girlfriend who got away? My heart clenches at the thought of him pining for someone.

I need to keep busy, so I wash my hands and start where I left off with Kenny's cake. It's almost finished, I just need to work on Black Widow's cuffs and belt. She's looking great so far. The cuffs are easy enough to make, I roll the gray icing flat and cut the appropriate lengths, adding the detail and setting each one on her arms. This is good. I'm not thinking about AJ and his strong hand stroking his cock while I'm doing this. Good one, Sarah, now I'm thinking about it again. I drop my head back in frustration, rolling my eyes at the ceiling. I'm hopeless. Really, I am. I chuckle a little at myself.

"What's so funny?" I startle at AJ's voice right behind me. I didn't even hear the bathroom door open.

"Wow, you were quick." I blush when I realize how that sounded. "Sorry. I'm sure you last longer when you're doing the real thing." I snap my mouth closed because that was even worse.

AJ drops his head forward and chuckles as his hands land on his hips. "I promise, I'm not that quick when I'm doing the real thing." He opens his mouth to say something else, but I see the moment he changes his mind and closes it tight. I don't dare ask what he was about to add because I think it may be too much at this point. "Anyway, I'm all done."

"Thanks again, AJ. I don't know how I can properly thank you for all of this." I step into his body and wrap my arms around him in gratitude. I feel like all I do is say thank you to the guy and yet it never feels like it's enough.

His arms come around me and he pulls me in close. His warm breath touches the side of my face as he whispers, "It's my pleasure. No thanks necessary." He places a gentle kiss on my jawline slightly below where it meets my lobe and I shiver.

*Did he feel it? He had to feel it.*

Mortification fills me and I pull back, putting much-needed space between us. I suck in a deep breath to recalibrate and grab the gift he brought for Kenny to put something physical between us. "Here, you can bring this with you tomorrow."

He takes it. "Did you want me to pick you up?"

I mentally berate myself when I almost agree. That wouldn't be a good idea. If my family notices us arriving together, they'll think there's more going on than there really is. It's bad enough I've invited him. I wish I had a time machine to go back and keep my lips sealed. "I'll be going a little earlier to help set up, so maybe you can meet me there. I'll text you the address."

His smile drops and his eyes skate away from mine. "Sure. Whatever's easiest. See ya tomorrow." He leans forward to give me a brief kiss goodbye and then he's gone. I sag against the closed door and chastise myself for getting too caught up in him. He only wants to be a donor. He's not looking for a life partner. I'd do well to damn well remember that.

I head into the bathroom to wash my hands and collect the condom and syringe. Then I set about doing what needs to be done. After the first day where I battled with myself to not think of AJ when I came, I've given up and given in. He's now my go-to thought. Imagining his strong fingers working me over along with his tongue, pushes me over the edge quicker than I've ever known before. I figure I may as well go with it.

# CHAPTER 18

## *—aj—*

I COULDN'T BELIEVE MY LUCK WHEN SARAH INVITED ME TO KENNY'S party today. I was stunned but there was no way I was going to say no. Even though I had a group climb planned today, I begged off saying I had an urgent matter I needed to take care of. When I bought Kenny a birthday gift, I never imagined it would earn me an invitation. I could tell by Sarah's shocked expression she hadn't meant to invite me, but I wasn't about to give her the opportunity to change her mind.

I wipe my sweaty palms as I take my first steps toward Emma and Theo's home and I look around at the other homes on the street. Is this what Sarah will want once she has her baby? I could easily sell my renovated warehouse; Dylan and I can rent office space somewhere and then I'd be able to buy a house with a white picket fence, fancy porch, and a backyard for our kids to play.

The screen door flies open and out runs Kenny. "You're here! I thought you'd never get here. I've been waiting for ages. Why didn't you come with Aunty Sarah?"

Woah!

"Kenny! What have I told you—" Theo's voice booms as he flies onto the porch. "Oh, hi, AJ. Kenny, just because it's your birthday party, it doesn't mean you get to forget the rules. Okay?"

Sheepishly, Kenny turns back toward her dad. "Sorry, Daddy. I was excited and I forgot."

He steps down from the front porch and straightens her crown. "I know you're excited, Munchkin." They both walk toward me, Theo holding out his hand in greeting. He doesn't squeeze quite as tight as he did at the beach. I'll take that as progress.

"Is that for me?" Kenny's wide blue eyes snap up to my face.

"It sure is." I hand her the gift, though seeing her already wearing a crown, maybe I should have bought her something different.

"What do you say, Munchkin?" Theo reminds the little dynamo.

"Thank you, Uncle AJ." She gestures for me to bend down, so I do, then she shocks the hell out of me when she plants a gentle kiss on my cheek.

My stomach flips at her easy acceptance of me into her family unit. If only it was as easy to win over her aunt. "You're welcome. I hope you like it." She takes off inside, leaving Theo and me on the front sidewalk.

"We'd better get inside. Lachlan and I have been working on your nephew's climbing wall. We'll show it to you later."

"Thanks. Colton's gonna love having a designated space to climb where he won't get into trouble."

We climb the steps to the front porch and I freeze when I see Sarah standing with the screen door open, waiting for us. Theo steps past her, leaving the two of us in the doorway.

"Hey." It's the only word that will come out. She looks gorgeous in a red sundress that leaves her shoulders bare and hugs her magnificent tits. I tuck my hands into my pockets in a bid to disguise my rising cock.

She smiles at me, and I swear the world around me stops. I'm not usually such a sap, but when she's around, I don't see or hear anything else but her. "Hey. You found it okay?"

"Yeah." I take the steps up to her and I can't stop myself from swiping my lips across hers. She gasps lightly and I draw back. "It was easy enough to find. How are you feeling?" I study her face closely.

Her eyes grow soft and she gives me a tender smile. "I'm feeling okay."

"You're not overdoing things, are you?" I want to pull her into me and wrap her in my arms while we have this conversation, but I can't. It'll be too much for Sarah.

"It's really sweet how you keep checking on me, but you need to stop worrying so much." She chuckles. "Come in. Kenny's already announced you're here." She takes a step inside then stops abruptly, spinning around to face me as I close and lock the screen door. "A quick word of warning. Please ignore anything and everything my mom may say to you. She has no filter. And I mean that. She'll say whatever's on her mind."

I chuckle. "It's okay." I glide my fingers along Sarah's hairline, tucking the loose strands behind her ear because I can't resist touching her any longer. This close I see her hazel eyes have a touch of blue in them today. "I promise I don't scare so easily."

"Okay. Don't say I didn't warn you." She steps back but takes my hand in hers, and I feel as though I've just dragged my body over the topmost edge of El Capitan.

When we turn to head further into the gorgeous home, a woman is standing just inside the open doors which lead out to what looks like an amazing deck. She has her hand pressed against her chest and she's wearing a soft smile. She has to be Sarah's mom, the resemblance is impossible to miss—it's like I'm looking at my future. I smile at her as we come to a stop.

"Mom, this is AJ. The man who's helping me. AJ, this is my mom, Sally."

I hold out my hand to greet her, but she presses into me, wrapping me tightly in her embrace. She pulls back after a moment, holding onto my biceps as she looks at her daughter. "Oh my, he's so handsome." She squeezes my arms. "Fit and healthy, too."

"Mom!" Sarah scolds as an older gentleman steps inside and gives the woman a look borne from years of marriage. Sally releases her hold on me and smiles at Sarah.

"Sally. Leave the poor boy alone." He kisses her temple and then holds his hand out to me. "Hi. I'm John, Sarah's dad."

I shake his hand. "Hi, John. Nice to meet you both."

Sarah takes hold of my hand. "Come on, everyone's out back."

I nod to Sarah's parents and as my foot lands on the back deck, I hear Sally speak to John. "You should have seen how he was looking at her and stroking her face when he first arrived. There's more going on there than Sarah's told us."

"Leave them be. They'll work it out without you meddling," John says in a firm but kind manner.

"Hmph. You spoil all my fun." I glance over my shoulder to catch John wrapping his arms around his wife as he presses a kiss to her temple. Her arms come up around his back to hold him close as she smiles up at him. It's beautiful to see a couple who have obviously been together for a long time still so in love. My parents aren't demonstrative with their affection, so it's a little foreign to me.

Sarah pulls me toward a tall guy standing next to a blonde woman. He has the same eyes as Sarah and Emma, so he must be Max, her brother. "Max. Molly. I'd like you to meet AJ."

Max's hard gaze traces me up and down, a look of distrust obvious by the narrowed eyes and tick in his jaw. Molly smiles at me, showing off deep dimples. She reminds me of a princess with her almost-white hair, gray eyes, and dimpled smile. She's tall too. Only a few inches shorter than me. She holds out her hand. "Hi, AJ. It's so nice to meet you."

"Hi. Nice to meet you too. Congratulations on your marriage."

"Thanks."

I hold out my hand to Max and his eyes drop to it, then rise back to my face. "What type of guy offers to get a stranger pregnant with no commitment?"

Molly's head snaps up to her husband as Sarah slaps his arm. "I can't believe you asked him—"

I cut Sarah off with a shake of my head. "It's okay, Sarah. It's a fair question and I'll share my reasons with Max in private, so we don't spoil Kenny's party." I finish with a tight smile at my future brother-in-law. Lifting my hand, I hold it out to him again with a raised brow. "Nice to meet you, Max."

He eventually relents and slides his hand against mine. We shake, both holding firm. I feel as though I can't show any weakness with this guy. The handshake feels as though it's never-ending, neither of us wanting to be the first to give in.

"Hi, AJ." Lachlan breaks the tension. "You should see the climbing wall we're building for Colton."

Max's head snaps to his nephew and his eyes flick between me and Lachlan with interest.

"Hi, Lachlan. Yeah, Theo said it was coming along nicely. You'll have to show it to me."

"Sure." He looks at his uncle with a frown. "Why are you holding AJ's hand?"

Max glances down, only now realizing we're still shaking hands. He releases me abruptly, taking a step back. "We were saying hello."

Lachlan takes my hand. "Come on, I'll show you what we've done so far."

Sarah gasps as he pulls me forward, collecting Theo on the way, and we head toward the enormous workshop at the bottom of the backyard. Theo swings the door open and switches on the light.

"It's over there." Lachlan points to the opposite side of the space.

"We've done the frame, now we need to add the planks for the walls. Do you think it will be big enough?" Theo asks.

It's larger than I imagined, but it's amazing and will allow me to attach a range of different holds to give Colton a variety of climbing experiences. I run my hand over the smooth timber frame in awe. "This is incredible. It's bigger than I thought it would be. I think Colton will love it."

Lachlan smiles, his body seeming to expand with pride, as Theo responds. "We can make it smaller if you want."

I immediately shake my head. "No, this is great. I'll be able to attach more holds for him. It will make it more engaging and hopefully keep him out of trouble."

"How will a climbing wall keep Colton out of trouble?" Lachlan asks.

"Well, you see, he loves to climb, and he keeps climbing on stuff inside that he shouldn't be climbing on and it's a little dangerous. His moms are worried he's going to hurt himself or break something. They don't want him to stop climbing, but they want him to be able to do it safely," I explain.

Theo looks at me with approval. "We should be finished by the end of the week."

"Great. Then I'll have to work out how to get it to my sister's place."

"Not a problem. We'll deliver it on the back of my truck." Considering the guy didn't seem to like me when we first met, he's being very generous now.

"Thanks, man. I appreciate everything. Let me know how much it all costs and I'll transfer the cash for you."

"It'll just be for the materials. I'll work it out and let Sarah know."

"What about labor?"

He waves his arm through the air. "Don't worry about it. It's been a great summer vacation project for me and Lachlan." Wow.

"Thank you. I don't know what to say."

"You already said thank you. That's all you need to say." Lachlan looks up at Theo. "Right, Theo?"

Theo runs his hand over the top of Lachlan's head. "Right, buddy."

Sarah steps inside. "Are you guys coming out? Lunch is almost ready."

We move out of the workshop, Theo closing and latching the workshop door, then we head to the deck, my hand at the base of Sarah's back. An older gentleman is standing at the grill and another couple has arrived. The woman has the most amazing red hair I've ever seen and the guy beside her is intimidating as fuck.

Sarah clears her throat and introduces me to everybody. No wonder the guy looks intimidating, he's Oliver Stone, the billionaire. Grandfather rents a floor in his building in the city.

I reach out to shake the older gentleman's hand. "Cristo. One of my favorite places to eat is a Greek taverna named *Cristo's.*" I chuckle.

He laughs, loud and boisterous. "Ah, it's always good to meet a fan."

My eyes widen and I'm sure my mouth drops open a little. "You're Cristo?"

"Yes. Next time, you must come and say hello! I'll give you my best table," he offers.

I glance at Sarah. "Wait until I tell Dylan. That's our go-to restaurant."

Cristo chuckles. "Bring all your friends. Bring my pretty Sarah here. I do not get to see her enough."

"Oh, I definitely will."

"Here, Dad. You can put the meat on this tray." Emma slides in next to Cristo, handing him a large platter.

"Thank you." He takes it from her and begins to stack the barbecued meat and vegetables. It looks heavy, so I take it from him to hold it with two hands while he finishes placing the food, then I carry it to the table and place it in the middle.

"We'll serve the kids first and then the adults can dig in," Theo announces.

The spread of food looks amazing and I feel obliged to try a little of everything, so I take small scoops from each dish, loading up my plate. Sarah leans in and whispers, "You know you can go back for seconds." She chuckles close to my ear, her warm breath tickling my cheek.

I turn to look at her, our lips mere inches apart. Her eyes drop to my mouth and I'm tempted to lean forward and close the distance. But our first proper kiss will not be in front of her family at a child's birthday party, so I refrain. "I know. It all looks so delicious, and I couldn't decide where to start, so I figured I'd have everything."

Conversation flows easily around the table and I'm happy to sit back and observe the family dynamics. This is obviously a family who are close and enjoy being in each other's company. Not once have I heard anyone shush the kids or remind them of their place, which is a stark contrast to my upbringing and the expectations at our family get-togethers.

Once everyone's finished eating, Theo rises and collects the empty dishes. I stand to help and so does Max. We make several trips back and forth from the table to the kitchen until everything is cleared away. Theo works on packing away the leftovers and I decide to start washing the dishes. Max moves beside me to dry the dishes as I place them on the rack. My muscles tense as I wait for him to strike up the conversation he wanted to have earlier.

He clears his throat. "So, about my question. You want to explain to me why you would offer to get my sister pregnant?"

Theo laughs and I glance at him over my shoulder. "You had to expect this question from her brother." He focuses his attention on Max. "I asked him the same thing when we spent the afternoon at the beach."

"Where the fuck was our invitation to the beach?"

"It was the day after your wedding. I'm assuming you were occupied with your wife." Theo raises his brows in humor.

Max's body relaxes. "Oh right." A smirk tips up on one side of his mouth.

I turn back to my task. "I'll tell you what I told Theo, but it has to stay between us. I don't want to ruin what Sarah and I are only now beginning to build." He raises his eyebrows but gives me a stiff nod. "I saw her when a friend and I were at *Club Rumors*. Not gonna lie, I thought she was stunning." I think I'll leave out the part about her curves. No brother wants to know some guy finds his sister hot. "When I overheard her speaking with her friend about wanting a baby, I thought I'd take the opportunity to speak with her about it. I know she's way out of my league and I'm pretty sure she wouldn't look twice at me if it weren't for my…" I wave my hand in the general area of my dick. "I helped my sister and her wife get pregnant, so I knew I could help her." His body relaxes slightly and his eyes become softer, less like he wants to strangle the life out of me. "I'm hoping if Sarah spends enough time with me, she'll get to know me and want to stick around. I don't want to only get her pregnant, Max. I want to be around for all of it. But I'm having a hard time getting through her fortress. She keeps a damn wall between us." I stand stock still waiting for his response.

He glances at Theo for a long moment, seeming to have a silent discussion. Theo raises his eyebrows and tilts his head to the side without saying a word. Max's head begins to move up and down slowly, his eyes coming back to me.

"A word of warning. You have to move slowly with Sarah. She overthinks and over plans everything. She doesn't like change, so she doesn't generally deviate from her plan."

I blow out a breath and the tension releases from my body. "I figured that much out. That's why I'm not pushing her or trying to move forward at the pace I would prefer. I don't want her to bolt."

He nods again and smiles this time. "Second warning. Don't fucking hurt my sister."

I hold my hands up in surrender. "I have zero intention of hurting her. I promise. I would rather eat my own arm than hurt Sarah."

"Good to hear."

"How are you guys doing in here? Kenny's bursting to have her birthday cake," Sarah says as she steps inside. Thank God she didn't step through the doorway a couple of minutes earlier.

"We're almost done. If you want to take out the plates, we'll be ready in a minute," Theo tells her.

She glances between Max and me, silently asking me if I'm okay. I nod and she collects the plates, heading back out to the deck.

"You do realize you two are already holding conversations without words, right?" Max asks. "I think she might be coming around, brother." His hand lands heavily on my shoulder and he squeezes.

Well, at least I seem to have her family on my side. Now to get Sarah on the same page.

We're all sitting around the table outside when Sarah walks out carrying Kenny's birthday cake. Kenny squeals with delight as Sarah places it on the table in front of her niece. "Aunty Sarah, it's beautiful. Thank you so much!"

Cristo and Theo are watching her with loving eyes and clear adoration for the little dynamo. Sarah explained to me that Emma lived in the house next door and that's how she met Theo and Kenny. Theo's technically her uncle but became her guardian when he lost his sister to breast cancer. It made me stop and think about Hayley, Lisa, and Colton and how much I love them; how devastating it would be to lose either of them.

We all sing happy birthday to the girl of the moment and the cake is cut and distributed after Kenny is certain Emma took enough photos so she never forgets what the cake looked like. Sally and John make coffee and tea for the adults and bring them to the table and conversation resumes.

"AJ, what is it you do for work?" John asks.

I wipe my mouth with a napkin. "I'm actually a computer hacker. My friend, Dylan, and I started our company after we finished college. Companies engage us to test their systems for security. We investigate and report any flaws we find and work with them to improve and tighten up their security."

"Oh, wow. That's very impressive," John praises.

"I'm fucking terrible with computers," Max grumbles.

"Max!" Sally chastises.

"Shit! Sorry," he mumbles as his shoulders hunch forward, and everyone bursts out laughing.

"Uncle Max, you're so funny!" Kenny giggles.

"Thanks, Munchkin." He smiles at her and Molly kisses his cheek with a grin, chuckling silently.

I can't believe he swore in front of the kids. I find it impossible to imagine anyone in my family speaking like that, let alone in front of kids. I mean, I'm no angel, I swear but I temper my language in mixed company. It further highlights the differences between Sarah's family and mine. I'm sad to say that I prefer hers.

"Do you have a business card?" Oliver asks. Oliver *freaking* Stone wants my business card! "I wouldn't mind having you take a look at our system sometime."

I could kick my own butt right now. "Sorry. I don't carry them on me to events like this."

He leans forward, grabbing his wallet out of his pocket. He deftly pulls out a card and hands it to me. "Contact Jase, my assistant. He'll set up an appointment."

I take the card from him. "Uh, sure thing. Any particular time?"

"Call him sometime this week. I'll let him know to expect your call. Let's see what we can set up."

I can only nod, trying to contain my internal fist bump at gaining the attention of one of the richest men in America. Wait until I tell

Dylan. The accounts we're winning lately are really putting us on the map.

The kids move onto the grass to play and conversation is easy around the table. Max constantly has some part of him touching Molly and Theo and Emma are the same, as are Kate and Oliver. I hope there comes a time when I can openly show Sarah the affection I feel for her. For now, I'll settle with pressing my leg alongside hers beneath the table. She hasn't pulled away, so I'll take it as a win.

# CHAPTER 19

## —sarah—

I CAN'T BELIEVE HOW WELL AJ FITS IN WITH MY FAMILY. I THOUGHT MY brother was going to have a problem with him, but throughout the afternoon, they've been talking easily.

All of the guys have decided to play a game of soccer on the grass, leaving us girls enjoying a peaceful cup of coffee on the back deck. I'm surprised Max, Theo, and Oliver were able to tear themselves away from their ladies. I'm thrilled about my siblings' happiness even if I'm a little sad for myself.

"I have to say, Sarah, AJ is a lovely young man. And so handsome, too," Mom blurts.

The other three women hum in agreement. "Yeah, he's one of the good ones, that's for sure," Emma states.

"You think so?" I ask.

"Absolutely. And genetically blessed too. Your baby is going to be gorgeous," Molly adds.

"Well, so long as my baby is healthy. That's all that matters to me."

"Of course."

"Oh, are you two trying to have a baby?" Kate asks, her denim eyes sparkling in the late afternoon sun.

I glance around the table. It's one thing for my family and close friend to know about our arrangement, but it's another for someone I barely know. Emma helps me out. "Sarah's ready to start a family but she doesn't have a boyfriend. AJ's her donor." She says it as though it's a common everyday occurrence for women to hang out with their donors on the weekend.

"Oh right. Good for you. You definitely have yourself a fine specimen there," Kate says as she fans herself and I feel my cheeks heat. He *is* a fine specimen.

Mom leans across the table, her eyes scanning the area. "Have you noticed the way he looks at Sarah?" Mom whispers.

"Mom. He doesn't look at me like anything. Don't start with this. There is nothing between us other than maybe the start of a friendship."

"I wouldn't be so sure about that, Sis."

"Oh, I agree. I think he's in deep with you already, Sare," Molly adds.

I shake my head. "No, he's not. He said he considers us friends. He's helping me with my pregnancy plan *until* I get pregnant. Nothing more."

"We'll see," Emma states with a soft smile and a look in her eye like she knows something I don't.

"Yeah, I wouldn't be so sure about that," Kate whispers. "I had no idea he was only your donor. He seems like so much more than that."

We fall into silence and Emma watches Theo with her boys wearing a contented smile as he supports Lachlan.

Molly's eyes are glued to Max. "You know, if things don't work out with AJ, you should come down to Max's Monday night soccer games. Some of his friends are pretty good-looking."

I chuckle. "You don't think I didn't crush on some of his friends. Aaron, Finn, and Lincoln are h-o-t! But to them, I was always Max's annoying little sister. I soon grew out of my infatuation." I nudge Emma. "I always thought Lincoln had a crush on you."

She laughs. "I don't think so. Remember, I was single for a long time after my divorce. He never showed the slightest interest."

"Yeah. I guess." I sigh as I turn my gaze back to the men, particularly AJ. The way he moves so fluidly for a guy who spends hours behind a desk is impressive. I guess the climbing keeps him pretty agile and fit.

Kate sighs. "It's so good for Oliver to have fun like this with other guys. His life revolves around work ... and me. Which I am totally grateful for, don't get me wrong, but I love seeing him having fun like this."

"You guys should come over more often. We have regular family afternoons like this. You're more than welcome to join in," Mom says.

"Thanks, you're so sweet."

The afternoon wears on and the sun begins to drop below the horizon. The guys have cleaned up, so there's no excuse to linger any longer. I need to get home and plan my wardrobe for my work week and make my salad jars. I ran out of time this morning because I wanted to get here and help Emma set up everything. AJ and I say goodbye to everyone and walk out to our cars at the same time, his Jeep parked behind mine on the street. I guess he needs a Jeep when he goes out to climbing locations.

"Thanks for the invite. I had a great time." He glances at Em and Theo's house. "You have a great family, Sarah. Really close."

I follow his gaze and notice Em, Mom, Molly, and Kenny duck away from the living room window and roll my eyes. "Thanks for coming and yeah, I love my family and how close we are. Kenny loves to be surrounded by people, so the more people at her party the better."

"She's a little dynamo, that one." He tugs on the back of his neck. "I think Colton would really have fun with Em and Theo's kids. He doesn't get to spend much time with other children."

"Oh." I don't like the idea of Colton missing out on fun. "Maybe we could organize an outing with all of the kids. Molly found this great park near a lake on the outskirts of the city. Leave it with me and I'll see what I can do."

And there I go making plans to combine our families. We're not dating, Sarah! Get that through your thick skull.

"That'd be great. Thank you. He'll love that."

I widen my eyes and raise my brows. "So, Oliver Stone wants you to hack his company."

"Hell, yeah. Never in a million years did I ever imagine I'd have his business card in my pocket." He pats the pocket of his shorts. "Dylan's gonna be ecstatic when I tell him tomorrow. Actually, he probably won't believe me." AJ chuckles.

"Well, good luck with it. I guess … I'd better be going. I have stuff to do before work tomorrow."

"Uh, yeah, sure, of course. Thanks again. I had a great time." He leans forward and presses his lips to mine and I freeze. He usually pecks my cheek, but this is the second time he's gone straight for my lips.

Does that mean something? Could the girls be right with their idea there's more between us? He pulls back and opens my car door for me.

"Thanks. I'll let you know when we can take the kids to the park. Bye, AJ."

"Yeah, bye." He closes my car door and stands in place as I pull out and drive away. I lose sight of him as I turn the corner and my mood immediately sinks. I hate that my relationship with him is contingent on my cycle and me getting pregnant. I sigh heavily into the silent car and contemplate how things might have been different if I hadn't met AJ under the circumstances I did.

Would he even consider dating me if he wasn't helping me to have a child? And while he's helping me, he's missing out on the opportunity to meet the woman of his dreams. Will he resent me if this goes on for too long? Will he want out?

Mel drops into the seat opposite me with a sigh.

"Hey, Mels Bells, what's up?"

"Just tired. I worked a double yesterday and I was on nights last week. It always throws my body clock out of whack and my sleep schedule is all off." Her eyes are glassy as it all comes tumbling out.

I reach across the table and lay my hand on hers. "Why on earth did you agree to meet for coffee if you're so tired you're almost in tears." Mel has never coped well when she's sleep deprived. I'm not sure why she went into nursing when nurses are possibly the most sleep-deprived people on the planet.

She pouts adorably. "I miss my best friend, Sare Bear."

I giggle at her use of her childhood nickname for me. "Well, today is my treat. You deserve it." I raise my brows. "The usual?"

She lifts my hand and kisses the back of it. "You're an angel. Yes please."

"Okay. I'll go order."

She smiles at me and then lays her head on the table, closing her eyes. I'll bet anything she's asleep by the time I get back to the table. While I'm waiting in line to place our order, my phone buzzes and my smile is immediate. I bet it's AJ checking on me. He does it at random times of the day now, instead of in the evenings. He said he wants to keep me on my toes. I liked the predictability of his text arriving in the evening, but I have to admit the randomness of his messages makes things more interesting.

AJ

How are you feeling?

My smile widens. Even though he's mixed up the times he sends his message, the actual message remains the same.

ME

I'm fine. Nothing's changed since yesterday

AJ

That's great news

I'm not sure what he thinks is supposed to be happening at this point in my cycle. It's not like I'm going to know anything until I get or skip my period.

AJ

Have you spoken with your sister?

Shit! Is something wrong with Em? I know Theo and AJ exchanged numbers last weekend to organize the delivery of Colton's climbing wall but has something happened?

ME

Not today. Why what's happened?

AJ

Nothing. I'm going there this afternoon to attach the climbing holds to the wall

I was wondering if you were going to be there

Hmmm. Maybe I should message Em.

ME

Hey, what time is AJ coming over?

EM

Hey. I'll check with Theo, hang on

I move to the front of the line and place my order and then head back to my table while I wait for Em's text. Sure enough, my best friend in the entire world is sound asleep. Her cute little snores are a dead give away and I chuckle. I'll let her sleep until our order arrives.

EM

He's coming around 2. They have some stuff to attach to the wall, then they're going to take it to his sister's place

Thanks

Are you coming over?

ME

Maybe

EM

You should. It's pretty hot outside, the guys may have to remove their shirts while they work *winking emoji* *hot emoji*

I giggle.

ME

Okay, you've convinced me. I'll come over

EM

Great. See you then

I flick to AJ's messages.

ME

I'll see you at my sister's

AJ

How about I pick you up?

Oh God! I don't know how I'll manage being trapped in a confined space with the man and his sexy scent.

AJ

We could maybe grab some dinner after we drop off the climbing wall for Colton

It would be a good opportunity for you to meet Hayley and Lisa

Shit! Is this weird? Maybe it is, but I'd like to meet his family, especially now he's met mine.

ME

Okay. That sounds like a plan

AJ

Great. I'll pick you up at 1:30

ME

See you then

"Here's your order." The waitress gains my attention.

"Thanks." I clear my half of the table so she can place the items.

"Enjoy!" she says brightly, then spins on her heel and heads back to the counter.

I smile at her retreating back, then look at my friend. I feel bad I have to wake her, but she could probably do with this. She never gets a chance to eat properly when she's working, not that this is proper food. I don't know how she maintains her slim figure.

I reach across and gently push the mass of blonde curls away from her face. "Melly Belly. It's time to wake up."

She twitches her nose. "Just a little longer."

"Your food is here," I coax. Her head rises sleepily. "Oh my God, Mel. We could have caught up another time. Seriously, let's have this and then you need to go home to bed."

She flicks her wrist between us. "I'll be good to go now. I've had a power nap." She smirks as she drags her coffee and devil's chocolate mud cake toward herself. "I only seem to see you when my shift aligns with your volunteer shift lately and I miss you. There's no way I'm going to miss out!"

And that's exactly why we've been friends for most of our life. We love each other and genuinely miss each other when we can't catch up regularly. "I miss you, too."

I drag my decadent triple chocolate flake cake toward myself and lean down to take a long whiff of the rich chocolate scent. This is always my favorite cake when we come here. It starts with stunning flakes of chocolate on top of a white chocolate layer of cake, the next layer is milk chocolate, then finally dark chocolate at the base, because you can never have enough chocolate. We each take a bite of our treats and moan at the same time.

"So good!" Mel says as her eyes roll back inside her head.

"I know, right? It's been a long time since I indulged myself like this."

Mel nods and we're both silent except for the occasional moan as we dig in. The cake is so rich, that I have to slow down once I reach halfway, so I take a sip of my coffee. "Anything interesting happening in your life?"

She scoffs. "You're joking, right? I feel like all I do is work, go home, eat, sleep, repeat!"

"You need to get a work-life balance before you burn out."

"Yeah, I know. I'm not sure how to achieve it, though."

I slump my shoulders forward. "Yeah. I don't know how you can either. What do the other nurses and doctors do?"

She shrugs. "We're all in the same boat. Why do you think so many doctors end up hooking up with nurses." She smirks. "They're the only ones who understand the craziness that is our life." We both take another bite of our food. Mel looks at me pointedly as she chews her food. Once she swallows the cake, she asks, "So how are things going with the baby daddy?"

I choke and half of my drink comes out of my nose. Grabbing the napkin quickly, I wipe my face. "Oh God, Mel. Don't call him that." I snicker.

She shrugs and leans forward. "Tell me you've at least screwed him. You're not still using the collection condoms."

I shake my head. "Sorry, I can't tell you that."

She groans, dropping her head back. "You know, this could be your last opportunity to have hot sex for a while. Once you're a mom, you'll be too busy to date. You should be using this as an excuse to be jumping that guy's bones any chance you get."

I huff out an extended breath. "Oh, Mel." I sigh. "I already like him too much for that. I don't know what I'm gonna do when this is all over and he doesn't need to come over anymore. You know, he sends me a text every single day, without fail, to check on me."

Her eyes go soft and dreamy and she reaches across the table to brush my bangs out of my face. "Oh, Sare. Maybe you could try with this guy."

I take a moment to gaze around the coffee shop, giving myself time to collect my thoughts. "I'm too scared," I whisper as I bring my eyes back to my long-time friend.

"Oh, Sare."

"I thought Michael was the one. I thought we were meant to be together forever, but he chose his career over me and I guess I chose my career, family, and friends over him. But he was the one who left.

And then look at Preston. He didn't stay with Emma, and they had two kids together. If that couldn't make him stay, then what would?"

"You know they're not AJ, though, right? You don't know if he would do that. And you won't know if you never open yourself up to the chance. Maybe Michael wasn't your one. Maybe he had to leave to make way for someone so much better. Maybe AJ is your one."

My defense dies on my tongue. I'd never thought about it like that.

"And look at Emma now. She's so much happier with Theo, so Preston obviously wasn't her forever person."

Well, that's true too. Trust Mel to give it to me straight.

"Shit! Stop making sense, Mel. How are you making so much sense when you're sleeping on your feet?" I chuckle as does she.

"All I'm saying is that maybe you could relax a little and see how things go. Don't close your heart to the possibility of something amazing growing between you and AJ … and I don't just mean a baby. Maybe you could be a family." She squeezes my hand to punctuate her sentence. "I know that's what you truly want … deep down."

"I know. The problem is, though, he keeps referring to us as friends and saying he'll be around *until* I'm pregnant. I assume that means he'll move on and I don't want to fall on my own."

"I dunno, Sare. I got a distinct vibe that he was interested in more than getting you pregnant." She wiggles her eyebrows up and down. "Just promise me you'll think about it. Okay?" She raises one finely sculpted brow at me.

"I promise." Her smile is wide, showing her beautiful teeth as a result of two and a half years of braces from the time she was seventeen. "Thanks, Mels Bells."

"Any time, Sare Bear."

# CHAPTER 20

## —*aj*—

PULLING TO A STOP IN FRONT OF SARAH'S BUILDING, I FIND A PARKING space on the opposite side of the street easily enough and climb out of the Jeep. Sarah's voice stops me as I'm closing the car door.

"Sorry, I wanted to be down here waiting for you so you didn't need to park." She's slightly out of breath as she apologizes, her breasts rising and falling, capturing my attention.

A car speeds past us, and I pull Sarah in close to keep her safe. She lands against me, her hands resting on my pecs. With her this close, I can't resist greeting her with a kiss. I press my lips to hers and feel her lips spread in a smile. We both pull back, our eyes tracing each other's faces. Mine drop to her mouth, dying for a longer taste—a more *intimate* taste. Maybe one day soon. She didn't gasp or pull away from me this time. Bit by bit, I think I'm working my way around her defenses.

"That's okay, I'm a little early." I couldn't wait to lay eyes on her. I drop my hand to her hip and guide her around to the passenger side. Opening her door, I wait for her to climb in, then ensure she's safely tucked inside by pulling the seatbelt across her body. The strap settles between her breasts, accentuating them. I tear my eyes away from the soft pillows and smile at the woman I can't stop thinking about. "You look gorgeous."

"Thanks. I wanted to dress as cool as possible today because it's so hot."

"Fair enough." I close her door and make my way around the back of my Jeep, so she can't see me adjusting myself in my shorts and climb in, then pull onto the street swiftly. "I can't believe how quickly Theo and Lachlan finished building the climbing wall."

"Lachlan's on vacation, so they have plenty of time to do the work. Theo has all the specialty tools, so it means they can work quickly."

"Right. That makes sense. I forgot about school vacation. Colton's too young to go to school yet, so it's not something I think about."

"Yeah, I probably wouldn't be keeping track of it if it weren't for the fact my sister's a teacher and her kids make a big deal about being on vacation while I still have to work." She chuckles.

"I know I've been checking in on you each day, but seriously, how have you been feeling this week? You haven't been overdoing things?" I'm genuinely concerned that she's not resting enough.

She turns her head to look at me and I fight to keep my eyes on the road where they belong. "I promise, I'm feeling fine and I'm not over-doing things. Thank you for always checking on me, it certainly wasn't part of our arrangement."

"You're welcome. As I said before, at the very least, I consider us to be friends."

"Well, you're incredibly sweet. Your future wife will be very lucky to have you." Her voice drops on the last part and she gazes out of her window as she figuratively takes five steps back from me and slams the door in my face. Just when I think I'm getting somewhere, that we're moving forward, she retreats.

"I guess so."

The rest of the ride to Em and Theo's home is made in silence, the tension inside the Jeep stifling. I guess I have to keep showing up and showing her that I'm not going anywhere.

As soon as I pull into the driveway behind what must be Theo's truck, Sarah has her seatbelt off and she climbs out. Once I collect the holds I need to attach to the climbing frame, I catch up to her at the bottom of the porch steps, confused as fuck with her change in mood. She knocks once on the screen door and then tries the handle, but the door is locked. Emma comes to the door, unlocking it quickly with a smile.

"Hey, you two. Come in." She leans forward, embraces her sister, then kisses my cheek. "Theo's out back. He's ready to help you with the finishing touches."

"Thanks, Emma. I guess I'll leave you two to catch up."

I move through their quiet home and step onto the back deck. The completed wall is sitting in the middle of the backyard beneath the shade of a tree, but Theo's nowhere in sight. He must be in the workshop. Standing at the open door, I spot him wrapping his tool belt around his hips.

"Hey, Theo. The wall looks fantastic."

He spins around to face me. "Oh, hey. Yeah, it turned out pretty great. Lachlan and I are thinking of making a couple more to sell."

"Good idea." I hold up the box containing the holds. "I can show you how the holds work so you know how best to attach them."

"That'd be great."

We step out of the hot workshop and head over to the climbing wall. I place the holds out on the ground in what I think will be a good layout, explaining the different holds to Theo as I go. I make some final adjustments and Theo helps me attach them to the timber. It's so freaking hot, we've both taken off our shirts as Theo drills and I attach each hold where I want it to go.

The ladies are sitting on the back deck, enjoying a cool drink. Now and then, loud laughter fills the backyard, but still no kids. "Where are the kids?"

"Em's ex has the boys this weekend. He was supposed to have them last weekend but with Kenny's birthday, he didn't mind swapping it around. When the boys are with their dad, Kenny stays with my dad. It gives me and Em some time together on our own once a month. But boy do I miss the kids when they're not here."

"So, Sarah and I are intruding on your couple time. I'm sorry, man. I'm sure there are better things you could be doing with your wife than helping me. This could have waited another week. There's no rush."

He waves me off. "It's okay. This is only a couple of hours and then I'll have my girl all to myself." A smirk crosses his lips as he glances at Emma.

"All right. Well, let's get this finished, so you can get back to your lady."

We get back to the task, quietly working together and before I know it, the job's finished. "All right, let's load this bad boy onto the back of my truck. I'll grab the dolly."

Once we have it loaded onto the back of Theo's truck and secured, I grab Theo's bank details and transfer the funds across immediately, with some extra to account for the time he and Lachlan spent constructing the wall. Even though he said he didn't want to charge me for their time, I feel it's only fair. He can't do anything about it now the money's in his bank account. I smirk to myself.

"Come and have a cool drink before you guys head off," Emma calls out.

Theo comes out of the house holding a couple of small towels. "Here, this'll help you cool off." He tosses one over, and it's freezing cold, I look up at him in question. "I put them in the freezer before you got here."

I rub the icy towel across the back of my neck and down my torso. "Aww, man. This feels sooooo good."

Sarah steps outside with two large glasses of what looks to be iced tea. "Here ya go, boys. I think you've earned these." Her eyes rake up and down my body, following the towel as I wipe away the sweat, and she gives me a wink. Talk about mixed messages.

"Thanks." I take a long gulp, the cool liquid soothing my dry throat. "I needed that."

Emma steps out with a tray holding four glasses. "I figured one glass wouldn't be enough. Here ya go."

She places the tray on the table and Theo goes straight for his wife and kisses her forehead. "Thanks, Peaches."

We all sit around the large outdoor table, which I'm guessing was made by Theo, enjoying our cool drinks under the shade of the deck.

"The climbing wall looks great. Will your nephew be safe climbing it?" Emma asks.

"Yeah. I'll teach him the correct holds and I have a couple of padded mats to put at the base in case he falls. He's pretty agile, though. I organized this for him because he's climbing on everything inside the house and my sister and her wife are worried he'll get hurt."

Emma smiles brightly. "Austin could have done with one of those. That boy used to climb everything." She looks at Theo with a mischievous glint in her eye. "Remember when he climbed up the side of my house to rescue his parachute Avenger?"

Sarah gasps. "Oh my gosh. How could we ever forget? He sprained his wrist. Poor little man."

Theo chuckles. "Yeah, if I remember rightly, we had a few words that day." There's a certain nostalgia in his gaze as he reminisces.

"Oh my. Yes, we did." She shakes her head with a smile. Obviously, the event holds some good memories for these two.

I glance between them. "Does Austin still like to climb?"

"Yeah, I guess so. There isn't anywhere for him to climb unless we go to the park," Emma responds.

"I'd be happy to take him to my climbing gym sometime. I could show him the ropes, so to speak," I offer.

Emma flicks her eyes to Sarah and then back to me. "I think he'd love that. I'll ask him."

"Great. Let me know and we can set up a time."

"I will. Thanks, AJ."

I feel good that I may be able to give something back to this family since they've been more than welcoming toward me. I finish my drink, remembering I'm taking up valuable alone time. "Well, we should hit the road and get outta your hair so you can enjoy what's left of your afternoon."

Sarah climbs to her feet, collects the glasses, and places them on the tray. I take the tray from her and head inside to wash them. "You're very domesticated." Sarah chuckles behind me.

I shrug. "I guess it comes from living on my own. If I don't do the dishes straight away, I have to do them later. No one else is going to do them for me."

We work side by side, her wiping the glasses and putting them away where they belong. Emma and Theo step inside. "Am I following behind you two, or are we all going in my truck?"

I glance at Sarah. "You can follow behind. That way you can come straight home and I can spend some time showing Colton how to climb safely."

"That makes sense." He turns to his wife. "Did you want to come too? We shouldn't be that long."

"I'll stay here and get the laundry folded so we have no interruptions to our afternoon." She winks at him and Sarah groans.

"Okay, you two. Can you at least wait until we're out of here before you start?" She chuckles.

Em and Sarah hug goodbye. "Say hi to the kids. I'm bummed I missed them today, but it was nice having some sister time."

"I will. Bye, AJ. Great seeing you again. I'll let you know what Austin would like to do."

I wave over my shoulder as Sarah and I head to my Jeep and reverse out of the driveway. I wait until Theo's behind me and then lead the way to my sister's place, making sure I don't leave Theo behind.

# CHAPTER 21

## —sarah—

Nerves have taken over my body and even with the air conditioning in the Jeep, I'm sweating more than I should, and I can't stop my leg from jiggling up and down. I'm worried his sister and her wife won't like me and they'll tell AJ he shouldn't help me. Ultimately, the child I'll be bringing into the world will be Colton's half-sibling. What if they change AJ's mind? I don't think I'd be lucky enough to find someone else as amazing as him.

I glance across at him, watching the muscles of his forearm tense and flex as he rests his hand on the steering wheel. What is it about muscular forearms that's such a turn-on? I'd never really thought about it before I saw AJ's perfectly muscular arms. I'm not into guys who look like they go to the gym seven days a week and are bulky like the Hulk but AJ's muscles are perfect. Masculine. Sexy.

He *only* sees you as a friend, Sarah! Stop thinking about his damn muscles.

*Then why does he keep kissing you on the damn lips?*

Good point. Why does he do that? Does he kiss all his friends on the lips? Surely not.

"So, do you have many female friends?" *Oh shit!* I can't believe I just blurted that out. "Sorry. It's none of my business," I rush to add.

He grins at me. That sexy grin which causes crinkles around his eyes and deep lines to bracket his mouth. "Let me think about that for a sec." He puts on a big show about tilting his head this way and that. "Nope. Can't say I have any female friends."

My body deflates as I release the breath I was holding while I waited for his answer. "Oh." *Oh*, Sarah? Really? That's the best you've got.

Silence fills the cab of the Jeep as we make our way toward his sister's house. It's not long before we're parking in front of a quaint cottage-style home. The garden reminds me of a *Home Beautiful* spring garden spread. I'm not sure how they've managed to have so much greenery in the middle of summer. "Your sister's home is gorgeous."

He looks out of his window at the property as Theo pulls around us and into their driveway. "Yeah, it's really nice. Lisa has a green thumb. If it were up to my sister, everything would be dead." She sounds a lot like me. I struggle to keep plants alive. Living in an apartment suits me for that very reason.

We both climb out of the Jeep and AJ opens the back door, pulling out two canvas mats so I move closer to help him. "I've got this. You probably shouldn't be lifting heavy stuff."

I smile at him. "I don't even know if I'm pregnant yet. It won't hurt me to help you."

He studies my face closely and eventually nods. "Okay, but be careful."

We work together to lift the mats out of his car and carry them up the driveway as Theo releases the straps securing the climbing wall. Two gorgeous women step outside, one holding the hand of a gorgeous little boy. I can easily pick his sister with her dark curls and chocolate-colored eyes. She has the same coloring as her brother and her son.

The little boy breaks away with an enormous smile. "Unca AJ!" he squeals, with his arms held up. AJ crouches down and catches the little bundle of energy easily. "Is that my climbing wall?" He studies it closely with wide eyes.

AJ stands with Colton secured in his arms, walking him closer to Theo's truck. "It sure is. What do ya think?" They study it closely.

"It's so big!" Colton stretches his arms out wide.

AJ laughs and jiggles Colton in his arms. "Hey, Colton. This is my friend, Sarah." Colton looks at me, then tucks his face into AJ's neck, hiding from me. "Don't pretend you're shy because we know you're not." AJ chuckles, but Colton buries in further.

I move closer. "Hey, Colton."

"Hello," he whispers shyly, tilting his head toward me.

The women make it to us with chuckles. "He's always so happy to see you." His sister presses up on her toes to kiss AJ's cheek.

"And so he should be. I'm his favorite uncle."

Theo and I both laugh. "We've heard that before. My brother, Max, says the exact same thing."

Hayley steps toward me. "You must be Sarah. I'm Hayley." She thumbs over her shoulder at AJ. "I'm this one's sister, and this is my wife, Lisa."

Lisa steps closer. "Hey, Sarah. Great to meet you." She turns to AJ. "This looks … big!" Her eyes are wide as she studies the climbing wall on the back of the truck.

"Great to meet you, too. This is my brother-in-law, Theo. He and my nephew built the climbing wall."

"Hi, Theo." The women say at the same time. "This is incredible. Thank you so much, and please thank your son."

Theo wipes his hands on the back of his shorts and holds out his hand to shake hands with the two women. "I'll pass on your thanks to Lachlan. He'll be thrilled you were so happy with it."

AJ and Theo work together to get the climbing wall down off the truck and located under the shade of a tree in the backyard, which is as impressive as the front yard.

Colton reaches up for Hayley and she picks him up. "Mama, look at my climbing wall." He points across to where Theo and AJ are working.

"I know. You're a very lucky boy." He glances at me, then nods slowly as he buries his face into Hayley's shoulder.

"I'm not sure why he's being so shy today. He's not normally like this," Lisa tells me.

I chuckle. "It's probably because I'm a stranger."

Colton climbs down and races over to his uncle, leaving me with Hayley and Lisa.

"You have a gorgeous garden. My sister would be impressed." Emma's always prided herself on keeping her garden looking nice. It was tougher when she was a single mom and had to do everything for herself, but since she met Theo, she has more time to enjoy it.

"Thanks. It's all Lisa. She's the gardener." Hayley snickers.

"If it were up to her, everything would be dead." Lisa nudges Hayley good-naturedly.

I nod and grin. "Same. I live in an apartment, which means I don't need to worry about trying to keep plants alive. My sister's tried time and again to turn me into a gardener, but no dice." Shit! Maybe I shouldn't have told them I can't keep plants alive. They might think I won't be able to keep a human alive either. Oh, God. There go my chances.

Hayley laughs. "We could be sisters! Come inside, I'll get some drinks for everyone."

She tilts her head toward the back door and I follow her. They don't have a deck, but they have a really sweet outdoor table and chairs under a gazebo between the house and the tree.

"It looks like Colton enjoys playing outside." Between the swing set and the climbing wall, he's going to be a busy boy.

"Oh, he loves it. And that climbing wall couldn't come soon enough. Did AJ tell you about Colton's penchant for climbing?"

"Yeah, he did. He sounds like my nephew. He was always climbing everything too. Drove my sister crazy."

"Kids, huh?" Hayley comments as she pulls out glasses and a jug of juice to place on a tray.

"Yeah." My voice has a wistful quality to it as I think about life with a child in the picture. I can't wait. I glance around their home. It's nothing extraordinary, but it has a really lovely, homely feel about it. Their home reminds me of a cottage I'd find in a tiny beachside town.

When we step back outside, Theo and AJ have already placed the mats at the base of each side of the structure and Colton's already halfway to the top. AJ's behind him, guiding him with a careful explanation as to where to put his hand and foot next.

Theo spots me. "I'm gonna head home." He kisses the top of my head in much the same way Max does. "See you tomorrow?"

"Definitely."

He turns to Hayley and Lisa with a smile. "I'll see you both another time."

"Thank you, Theo. Colton loves it so much," says Lisa.

"Yeah, thanks, Theo." Hayley's eyes widen and she holds up a finger. "Hold on. Before you go, would you mind looking at something inside?" she asks as she places the tray of drinks on the table.

"Sure."

She gestures for Theo to follow her inside.

Lisa moves closer to me, leaving AJ with Colton. "I bet she's asking him about building her a new bookshelf. The woman buys paperbacks like they're going out of style."

"Oh, well, Theo does beautiful work and at a reasonable cost too."

"He did a fantastic job of the climbing wall." I nod in agreement and we watch AJ and Colton in comfortable silence.

Theo and Hayley return a few moments later. "I'll call you with a price on Monday."

"Thanks, Theo."

"Bye everyone," Theo calls as he waves over his shoulder, heading for the side gate with Lisa.

Lisa comes back around to us. "I'm just gonna grab some snacks. Colton will be looking for something to eat soon."

Hayley watches AJ and Colton with a smile on her face. "He's gonna make a great dad one day." I nod silently. I think my ovaries exploded when I watched him with Colton out the front when we first arrived, and again now, wow. He has such a lovely manner with the little boy, who is so much more than just a nephew to him. "I'm sure AJ's explained his true relationship with Colton, but he doesn't look at him as his son. Though, their bond is so much more than an uncle has with his nephew."

I turn my head toward Hayley. "Yeah, he explained the situation. I think it's amazing he could help you and Lisa to have your babies."

"Yeah. He's been incredibly supportive of me and Lisa. Unlike some family members." She mumbles the last part. "We're grateful he stepped up and suggested he be the donor for our baby when he didn't have to."

"Oh, I didn't know he suggested it. I figured you guys had asked him to do that for you."

She huffs out a quiet laugh. "Nope. Lisa and I hadn't even considered him a candidate." She smiles at me. "You'd think he would have been the first person we would have asked, but he wasn't even on our radar, and I'm not entirely sure why. We were signed up to use a stranger as our donor."

"It makes sense, though, right?"

"Oh, definitely. I love that Colton has some of me in him."

"Are you kidding? I don't think he has 'some of you' in him, he looks exactly like you," I tell her.

She smiles widely, her eyes twinkling. "And isn't that the kicker for Lisa? She carried him for nine months and had to go through the whole morning sickness thing and delivery and he comes out looking just like me!"

We both chuckle. "So unfair!"

"Lisa doesn't mind. She loves that he looks like me because she thinks I'm the most beautiful woman in the world." She flutters her eyelashes.

Awww. "That's so sweet."

"Mama! Look at me!" Colton calls out.

We both look over at the little ball of energy. He's straddling the peak of the climbing wall, both of his hands reaching high into the air.

"Colton. Remember you're supposed to have three points of contact at all times. You need to put one hand back on the wall." AJ explains calmly.

"Sorry, Unca AJ." He drops one hand, holding onto the top of the frame. "Mama! Look at me!"

Hayley moves closer to him. "Look at you! You're at the top of the mountain, looking oh so tall!"

Lisa comes back outside and moves next to Hayley, dropping her arm around her shoulders and pulling her back into her body as best she can with her baby bump. She kisses the top of her head, and Hayley glances up and smiles at her. I feel as though I'm surrounded by loved-up couples, and I should tear my eyes away from them to give them the courtesy of privacy but they're too sweet.

AJ coaches Colton as he carefully descends the other side of the wall, while his moms watch him with obvious pride. After a short while, Lisa turns to me. "Come and sit over here. AJ will keep Colton busy for a while."

I follow the women to the outdoor setting. My skin feels prickly as I realize I don't have anyone as a buffer while AJ's busy with his nephew. Lisa offers me a snack, while Hayley pours the juice.

I take a slice of apple and cheese for something to do, chewing slowly as I try to think of what to talk about.

"AJ was telling us you're trying to have a baby," Hayley's the first to break the silence.

I swallow the food in my mouth, but it gets stuck in my suddenly dry throat. Coughing, I try to dislodge the food as gracefully as I can. Lisa pats my back as Hayley hands me a glass of juice, both women watching me with worried eyes.

"Are you okay?" asks Lisa.

I manage to get myself under control so I can answer. "Yeah." My voice doesn't come out quite right, so I take another drink. "Sorry about that."

"That's okay. Hayley's not really known for her timing." Lisa smirks at her wife and Hayley lightly pushes her.

I look at Hayley, trying to portray confidence I'm sorely lacking.

"Yeah, I am. I had two attempts through the fertility clinic, but neither were successful."

"We know how disappointing that can be." The two women glance at each other.

I nod. "Yeah. It costs a lot of money, so it meant I had to put any further attempts on hold until I could save for another round."

Both Lisa and Hayley nod. "We hear ya. It's not cheap."

"It took us about six months to get pregnant with Colton. So don't give up," Lisa shares. "AJ was patient with us. Never missed a single appointment."

I glance over at AJ. "He's been amazing so far. I was incredibly lucky when he offered to help me."

Hayley nods. "He's a good guy." She glances at Lisa and takes a sip of her drink. "Can I ask you a personal question?"

Here we go. "Sure." I try not to let my nervousness show in my voice.

"We know AJ is a great guy, but you didn't when you first met him. Why would you take up the offer of help for something like this from a complete stranger you know nothing about?"

"I'm hungry, Mama!" Colton interrupts as he climbs up onto a chair.

"Hey. You need to wash your hands first, little man! Come on, let's go." AJ holds his hand out to his nephew, giving me a subtle nod, checking I'm okay. Once I respond, he takes Colton inside and the three of us resume our conversation.

The interruption gave me a second to gather my thoughts. "That's a fair question. I debated with myself before I contacted AJ after he offered to help me. He put me at ease straight away because he was happy to answer any of the questions I had for him and he seemed kind. The thing that sealed the deal for me, though, was that he'd already helped you guys." I take a small sip of my drink. "Did he——"

"My hands are all clean!" Colton barges out the back door waving his hands in the air as he runs for us.

"Great job," Hayley praises as Lisa gives him a plastic plate.

He situates himself on a seat and selects a few different items, then makes himself comfortable as he nibbles on a cracker. AJ joins us at the table, grabbing a slice of cheese as he sits in the chair next to mine. I'm not sure if he realizes his leg is pressing against mine; the same as it was at Kenny's birthday. He leans forward to grab his drink, pushing his thigh harder against mine. He winks at me as he sits back. He has to know he's touching me and I take another drink for something to do.

"Thanks so much for organizing that amazing climbing wall, AJ," Hayley says.

"It turned out so much better than I imagined. Theo and Lachlan did an incredible job."

Lisa nods. "How old is Lachlan?"

AJ looks at me. "He's ten," I tell them.

Hayley's eyes widen. "Oh, wow. I'm impressed."

"I'll be sure to let him know. He only discovered he has a talent for working with wood when Theo moved next door to my sister when Lachlan was eight. He loves it."

AJ's attention moves to Lisa. "How have you been feeling?" He looks at me. "Lisa's had trouble keeping food down."

"I'm slowly managing to eat small amounts and keep it down. So I'm improving."

AJ nods then drops his hand across the back of my chair and collects my ponytail, twisting it around his hand. "That's great. Hopefully, you'll get back to your usual self soon." He tugs on my ponytail. "What were you guys talking about?"

I glance at the girls. "Hayley and Lisa were asking me why I accepted your offer of help when we were complete strangers. I was about to tell them about our meeting in the café."

His head snaps to the other two and creases form between his brows. "Does it matter? I offered, and Sarah accepted."

Hayley's the one to answer. "We were just interested. It's our way of getting to know Sarah as a person. After all, we'll all be connected when she has her baby."

I drop my hand on top of AJ's firm thigh. "It's okay, I don't mind. As I was saying, AJ and I met in a café and he was happy to answer my questions."

AJ chuckles under his breath. "She had this long-ass list with a million questions on it."

I scoff. "There weren't a million questions. Less than twenty."

He shrugs. "Twenty. One million. There's not that much difference."

We all laugh. "I tried to replicate the questionnaire the fertility clinic used. Then AJ kindly offered his semen analysis, which was stellar, by the way." He puffs up with pride and waves his hand across the table between Lisa's stomach and Colton with eyebrows raised. "Yeah,

yeah, I get it," I say through my smile and gently push against him. He wraps his arm around me and pulls me back against him playfully as we both laugh.

I catch Lisa and Hayley giving each other a certain look and pull away, straightening up.

"What's semen?" Colton asks when his mouth is empty.

I glance at AJ. "It's the stuff that helps to make a baby," he tells Colton without missing a beat.

"Okay." Colton takes another cracker.

We spend the rest of the afternoon talking about lighter topics, which don't make me feel as though I'm tiptoeing through a minefield. Time passes quickly, and I grow more comfortable with AJ's family as the afternoon wears on.

AJ stands, collecting the dishes and loading them onto the tray. "I'll do these and then we can head off."

Lisa and Hayley glance at each other. "Did you want to stay for dinner? We were thinking of ordering Thai."

AJ looks at me. "I'm happy to stay, but it's up to Sarah."

Oh yeah, lay the decision at my feet. I mean, we were going to have dinner together anyway and I guess with his family present, it might help to have that barrier. The more time I spend on my own with AJ, the harder it is for me to remember we're only friends. He's generously offering me my dream on a platter, and I refuse to put it at risk by falling any further than I already have for the guy.

I shrug. "Sure. That sounds great."

"We usually order a variety of dishes and share them. Will that work for you, Sarah?" Lisa asks as she stands.

"That's perfect." AJ smiles and heads inside with the dishes. "I'll help AJ with the dishes." I thumb over my shoulder, then spin on my heel to follow him inside.

"I guess dinner's sorted."

AJ turns toward me, his posture a little stiff. "Are you okay with staying for dinner?"

"Of course. It was unexpected, so it took me a little by surprise." I don't feel comfortable when plans change at short notice, but since spending time with AJ, I'm beginning to learn to be a little more spontaneous.

AJ visibly relaxes and he smiles at me. "We don't do this very often. I would say they invited us to stay for dinner because they like you."

My cheeks heat and my stomach flips. "Really?"

"Yeah. Why are you so surprised?"

Should I tell him about my worries before we arrived?

Oh, what the hell, I decide to be honest. I drop my eyes to the floor between us, too embarrassed. "It was important to me that your sister and Lisa liked me. I didn't want them to think I wasn't good enough and I was worried they'd stop you from helping me. If I get pregnant—"

"Okay, I need to interrupt you there." He steps into my space, using his fingers to gently tip my chin up, so I can't hide. "I have a couple of issues with your thoughts. First, what's not to like? You're a great person, Sarah. Second, it's not up to anyone but me whether or not I help you." He raises an eyebrow and I try to interrupt, but he shakes his head. "Third, it's not *if*, it's *when* you get pregnant," AJ states firmly as if it's a sure thing I'll get pregnant. I hope he's right.

I smile and roll my eyes. "Okay. *When* I get pregnant, I imagine there will be times when we get together so the kids have regular contact with each other. I wanted those times to be comfortable, so it was important to me that Hayley and Lisa liked me."

He leans in close and kisses my forehead. "As I said. What's not to like? You're a great person, Sarah, and they would have worked that out very quickly."

# CHAPTER 22

I HAVEN'T SEEN NOR HEARD FROM SARAH SINCE WE SHARED DINNER with Hayley and Lisa, apart from her brief responses to my daily texts to check on her. Some days, all I get is a thumbs up, as though she can't even be bothered to type a few words. Every time I think I'm moving forward with the woman, she steps back inside her fortress and slams the damn door. I've constantly run over our conversation from that day and can't figure out what I said or did wrong to make her withdraw from me.

I check the app on my phone which tracks her cycle. She's due to get her period today if she's not pregnant. I'm tempted to skip the message and turn up on her doorstep after work. I huff out a breath.

"What's up, man?" Dylan asks as he leans around his monitor to look at me, creases across his forehead. "You've been huffing and puffing and checking your phone all morning. I don't think I've ever seen you this agitated."

"Nothing."

"If you say so. It doesn't seem like nothing to me, though." He stands. "I'm making a fresh coffee. You want one?"

"Yes, please."

I glance back at my phone and spin it around on the smooth surface of my desk. What to do? It's not like I haven't been to her place before. My lips lift at the corners as I remember her expression when I turned up unannounced after she didn't respond to my messages. She took it pretty well that I'd used my skills to find out where she lives.

I give in and unlock my phone.

ME

How are you feeling today?

Same message every single day. Let's see how long it takes for her to respond. I'm not sure how I'm expected to concentrate while I wait for her answer. Dylan steps back into the office with two cups, placing mine next to me.

"Here ya go." He takes a careful sip of his hot drink and sits at his desk. "So, how are things going with Sarah? I'm assuming she's why you're so bothered."

I blow out a long breath. If I can't talk to my best friend about her, who can I talk to? "I dunno, man. I feel like I take two steps forward with her and five steps back again."

"What do you mean? You're only trying to get her pregnant, right?" The confusion on his face would be comical if it didn't match mine.

"Yeah, that's how it started and what was supposed to happen, but … we've spent a bit of time together and I … well, I really like her. I'd maybe like to see where things could go between us."

"Right. Well, that's unexpected."

"I know. It wasn't the original plan. I thought I'd get a few months of guaranteed sex, but it hasn't been like that. I don't want to share too much because it's personal, but I've developed strong feelings for her … and we haven't actually … uh been intimate."

Dylan begins coughing; choking on the coffee he just swallowed. "Shit, man. Give a guy some warning." He wipes his mouth. "So, how in the hell are you supposed to knock her up?"

"We've been doing it like they would at the clinic. It's all been very clinical so far. And as much as I want to help her have a baby and fulfill her dream, I don't want her to be pregnant yet, because I need more time with her." I pause, shaking my head. "Fuck, I'm an asshole."

Dylan rolls his chair around to my side of the desk. "You like her that much?" I nod. "Have you told her?"

I shake my head. "I can't tell her. She has so many damn walls up, that it's almost impossible to break through. Every time I think I've made progress, she throws up another wall and I feel as though I'm back at the beginning."

"You know as well as I do, there's always a way in. You just have to find the weakness."

My phone vibrates and we both glance down. Dylan's eyes rise back to mine and a smile spreads. "Speaking of the woman of the moment."

I snatch up my phone like my life depends on it.

CUPCAKE

I'm sorry to tell you it didn't work again

I got my period *crying emoji*

My expression must give away my thoughts. "What's wrong?"

"She's not pregnant."

Dylan's expression turns somber. "Sorry. But I guess it means you'll still get to see her, right?" He widens his eyes and raises his eyebrows. "Just like you wanted."

I blow out a harsh breath, rubbing my hand across my mouth. "Yes and no. I want her to get pregnant, but I don't want to stop seeing her." My phone buzzes again.

CUPCAKE

I'm sorry. If you want to rescind your offer, I completely understand

I must have taken too long to respond and she's taking it as a lack of interest.

ME

I'm not going anywhere until you're pregnant

"That's where you're going wrong, AJ," Dylan states adamantly as he points to my screen.

"What do you mean?"

"You just told her you're not going anywhere *until* she's pregnant." He studies me closely, but I'm still lost. He shakes his head. "When you say it like that, it sounds like you only want to be involved *until* she's pregnant, and then you're done. No wonder she's as closed off as she is. She doesn't think there's a relationship between the two of you. Well, nothing beyond getting her pregnant."

Shit! "I thought I was doing the right thing because she doesn't seem to want a partner, only a donor."

"I think you might need to have a chat."

I nod. "Yeah. I think you might be right."

CUPCAKE

Thank you. I'll let you know when I'm ovulating again

ME

I have a tracker on my phone. I know when you're due to ovulate but I think we need to talk

The dots bounce up and down. They stop. And it takes so long for something to happen that my screen locks.

"Well, that's not good. I say we need to talk and she disappears."

"She probably thinks it's weird that you're tracking her cycle, man." He scoffs.

I frown. "What's weird about it? I needed to keep track if I'm going to help her properly. Last month I was out of town and had to fly back. I'm trying to avoid those situations."

"I guess so. But it's a bit weird."

# CHAPTER 23

## —sarah—

HE WANTS TO TALK. *SHIT!* I RUN MY HANDS THROUGH MY HAIR, grasping the strands tightly on either side of my head.

Does he want out of this arrangement?

Calm down, Sarah. He also said he wasn't going anywhere *until* I was pregnant. The muscle in my chest spasms at the thought of getting my dream but not seeing the man I spend way too much time thinking about.

The man I'm falling for.

But when your boyfriend, not that he's my boyfriend, says we need to talk, that never bodes well. I stand from my desk and pace down the hallway, making a loop around our floor. I can't sit still as I try to figure out why he suddenly needs to 'talk.'

"Hey, Sarah. Do you have a minute?" Lucy asks as I walk by her desk.

"Uh, sure. What is it?"

"Do you think I could take Friday off from work? I want to spend the day with the kids before they go back to school."

We always check with each other when taking planned leave because we usually step in and do the other's work when they're away. She'll divert her phone and emails to me for the day, so nothing gets missed. When I'm away, I do the same.

"It shouldn't be a problem. I'll be here Friday, and it's always quiet by the afternoon. Enjoy the day with your kids."

Her smile is instant, the relief obvious. "I feel as though I've hardly seen them."

"No problem. Just let Jeff or Frank know in HR." I tap my fingers on her desk and keep walking.

As I make my way down the other hallway back to my desk, I think about how I'm going to manage to work full-time with a baby. Obviously, I'll need to take some time off at first and I'm sure Eric would let me work part-time from home. Hang on. Eric won't be my boss by then. His grandson, Adam, will be. I wonder if he'll be as flexible as Eric. Shit. My plan to have a baby couldn't have come at a worse time with Eric retiring.

"What's that sigh for, Sarah?" Eric startles me as I take my seat back at my desk. He knows I'm trying to have a baby. Even though he thought it was unacceptable for a single woman to be trying to get pregnant on her own, he still gave me his blessing and promised to accommodate any changes I would need to make to my work schedule. There's a daycare center in the building I've looked at. I'll need to put my name down for a place the minute I know I'm pregnant.

"Nothing. Just thinking. Did you need something?"

His eyes soften. "You're worried about something. I can see it. We haven't worked together all these years for me to not recognize the signs." I slump my shoulders. I shouldn't put my concerns on Eric's shoulders. He's my boss and he has enough going on with getting the company ready to hand over. "Talk to me," he prompts.

"I'm a little worried about my plans to have a baby. What if your grandson isn't as accommodating as you?"

"Oh." He waves his hand through the air, swatting away my worries. "I'll have it written into the changeover documents. You don't need to worry about any of that. I promise he'll take good care of you."

"It seems a lot to ask a new boss when he'll need me to show him where everything is and help him get used to how this place runs."

"Don't worry about it, Sarah. It will all be okay. I know how much you worry when things change, but I'm hoping this transition will be seamless." He can hope all he likes, but that doesn't mean it'll be that way.

"Oh, Lucy asked for Friday off. I didn't think it would be an issue since there's barely anyone in on Fridays."

"Of course. The kids will be back at school soon, and she's barely had any time to spend with her children. They need to have their mother around more." His forehead wrinkles as he contemplates.

"Maybe we should introduce some kind of policy that allows mothers to have the ability to work from home during school vacation."

I widen my eyes. "You could make the policy to include fathers. I'm sure they'd like to spend time with their kids during their vacation too."

He slashes his hand through the air. "No. That sort of thing really should be left to the mother." He spins on his heel and heads back into his office mumbling something.

I love Eric. Working for him has been wonderful for me but he's a little old-fashioned in his views. Maybe his grandson will be more of a forward thinker in terms of gender roles. We only have two women on staff here and both of us hold secretarial positions. I remember there were a handful of women who applied for the Vice President position when it was available and Eric and Johnathon, the previous Vice President, dismissed them outright without even reading over their applications. Perhaps it'll be good to have a change in leadership around here, because I get the sense Tony likes to keep women in their place, too.

My phone catches my attention and I realize I haven't responded to AJ's message. What does he want to talk about? Is he not happy with the arrangement? He has a goddamn app tracking my cycle for goodness sake. He seems pretty serious about following through with my pregnancy plan. But things change. I did say we would reevaluate if he met someone he wanted to pursue. Oh my God. Has he met someone? Is that it?

I pick up my phone and unlock the screen, reading back over our chat thread. The words are typed as clear as day that he's not going anywhere until I'm pregnant.

*Until I'm pregnant.*

That doesn't mean he'll be around after. I know it was the original arrangement, but things have changed for me. I know I wasn't supposed to catch feelings for the guy, but how can I not? He's amazing. Any woman would be lucky to have him. *Just message the poor guy, Sarah.*

ME

Okay. When would you like to talk?

I place the phone back on my desk and try to concentrate on the email I'm supposed to be drafting, but my eyes won't stay on the computer screen, instead skipping back to my phone. It lights up and I almost jump out of my skin.

AJ

How about tonight? I can bring dinner

and chocolate

He remembered I crave chocolate when I get my period. My heart expands, thumping heavily in my chest.

ME

Okay, but I can cook and I have chocolate already

AJ

I insist. Save your food, my treat

ME

Thank you

As expected, this afternoon dragged and I couldn't concentrate for the rest of the day. I may as well have gone straight home after AJ's message. My mind kept running in circles of *what-ifs*—making me almost dizzy as I leave for the day. The humidity is shocking as I step from the air-conditioned building onto the sidewalk. I stop at the liquor store and grab a couple of craft beers I know AJ will enjoy. Even though I'm not drinking, there's no reason for him to miss out and even though I'm careful with my money, he deserves a treat.

I walk through the door of my apartment and immediately slip off my shoes; as cute as these shoes are, by the end of the day, they pinch my feet. I glance at the clock and decide I have time for a shower so long as I don't linger.

At six-thirty, there's a knock on the door. My stomach immediately rolls with anticipation for our 'talk,' and my palms are instantly damp. I draw in a deep breath in the hopes of calming myself and answer the damn door. My heart skips a beat as I lay eyes on AJ in a navy and white striped V-neck T-shirt and navy shorts. His warm brown eyes lock on me and his lips slowly tip up. He holds up the food, which is dangling from two fingers, making his bicep bulge. I drag my tongue across my bottom lip. *Stop it!*

His smile drops and I'm certain he moans low in his throat, but I can't be sure. He swallows and I watch his Adam's apple bob. So damn sexy. Everything about this man is like he was made to my exact specifications. Frown lines form above his brows. "Sarah?"

I realize I've been standing in the open doorway looking at him like he's a piece of meat. *Good one!* I quickly move into action, stepping out of the way so he can pass through. "Sorry."

He leans in, landing a kiss on my lips but doesn't linger. His scent surrounds me, overwhelming my senses like it always does. "Are you okay? And don't tell me you're fine if you're not. You can be honest with me."

"I'm fine. Honestly. Nothing a delicious dinner won't fix, followed by some chocolate, Midol, and a heat pack."

He places the food on the counter and steps back into my space. He gently cups the side of my face and I barely resist the temptation to press into his large hand. His eyes slowly trace every single inch of my face. "Your eyes are incredible. The way they're always changing color. I hope our baby has your eyes." I suck in a sharp breath. He said, *our baby*. Not *your* baby but *ours*. Does that mean something or am I getting carried away as usual?

"Th-thank you. I have the same eyes as Emma and Max, which we get from our mom." Great Sarah. He's paying you a compliment, not seeking a family genetics lesson.

He smiles. "Well, you're all very lucky." He points to his warm chocolate eyes. "Mine are boring. Always the same color, day in, day out."

"I don't know about boring. You have warm eyes, caring and inviting." I slam my mouth closed. Now I've said too much.

"You think so?" I nod. We stand silently, trapped in each other's gaze for I don't know how long. He swallows again and my eyes drop to watch the action and unbidden, I mirror him. He reaches up and slides a lock of my hair through his fingers, his eyes dropping to watch, then lift back to mine as he releases the strands. "I guess we should eat before the food gets cold."

I take a step back and chuckle nervously. We just had a moment, right? I wasn't imagining it. "Good idea." Trying to lighten the tone, I rub my hands together. "What delicious treat did you bring with you tonight?"

"Vietnamese. I hope you don't mind."

"Oh, I don't think I've eaten Vietnamese food before."

"Well, you're in for a treat. The freshness of the flavors is something else."

He moves around my kitchen with familiarity and busies himself dishing up plates of food, while I pull out a beer for him and pour myself a glass of filtered water. When he places our dinner on my small table, his eyes snap up to mine. "You didn't have to get me beer."

I shrug. "I figured it's the least I could do since you were bringing dinner. I bought a six-pack, so you can take home whatever you don't drink while you're here."

"I can leave it here for next time." He sits, not realizing the impact his words have on me. I guess that means he's not telling me he needs to stop helping me with my pregnancy plan.

I take my first bite of the rolls AJ put on my plate and the fresh flavors burst across my tongue. "Mmm, you weren't kidding. This is delicious."

He nods at me with a mouthful of food, his eyes smiling. He chews and swallows. "Right?"

We continue to eat as he fills me in on the meeting he had with Oliver over the phone today. He asked him and Dylan to test out the system for the *Parkerville Project*. Apparently, the *CornerStone Foundation* supports it by providing the majority of its funding. They had money stolen a couple of years ago, and Oliver wants to ensure their system is secure and there is no possibility of it happening again.

"So, if we do a good job on that project, securing their systems to prevent possible future fraud, he said the next job we do for him would be to check over *Stone Corporate Investments*." AJ's excitement is palpable, and I can't help but get caught up in it with him. "This is a huge coup for us. With the job we recently won, then the one from Vegas, and now this one, big business will be beating down our door."

I lean forward, awkwardly engulfing AJ in a hug. "Congratulations. I'm so happy for you guys."

"Thanks. Dylan and I couldn't be happier with how our business is growing. We may need to take on another team member, which would be incredible."

"Oh, wow. That *is* a big deal."

We finish eating and AJ collects the plates from the table. I beat him to the sink and fill it with soapy water, so I can clean up before he does. He's always cleaning up and I don't think it's fair since he provided the meal.

"I was going to do the dishes," he tells me as he tries to work his body into position in front of the sink.

I turn my head, not realizing how close our faces are, our lips only inches apart. I raise my eyes to his and wish we were in a place where it would be okay to steal a kiss whenever I pleased. His warm breath brushes across my cheek and I quickly snap my head forward and wash the dishes. "Nope. I'm doing them tonight. You're always cleaning up after everyone. It's my turn since you brought dinner."

"And you're probably beginning to feel uncomfortable and should sit. Come and put your feet up."

"I'm okay. I can manage." It astounds me how in tune AJ already is with me, considering we haven't lived together or spent all that much time together. Michael never knew when I was getting my period or considered I might be experiencing discomfort at this time of the month. He wouldn't have had a clue when I was ovulating or what was going on with my body. I glance at AJ out of the corner of my eye, checking to see if he's real.

We work in comfortable silence until the job is complete and my nerves start getting the best of me again. I'm guessing he'll want to have the 'talk' now. I pull up my big girl panties and ask, "Did you want to have that talk now?"

"Yeah, sure. Let's get you comfortable on the couch and I'll grab a beer." He takes over, guiding me to the couch, then returns with chocolate, Midol, and a heat pack as well as a fresh beer. It feels strange to be cared for in such a way but when I think back over every interaction I've had with AJ, I realize he's been doing it from the very beginning. He sits beside me on the couch, handing me my current project. I think he's figured out I'm better at communicating when my hands are busy.

"Thanks. So, what did you want to talk about?" Let's get started.

He twists his body so he's facing me directly. "I hope you know I would never share anything truly personal with anybody outside of our relationship."

*Relationship.* He used the word, relationship.

I scrunch my eyebrows together because I'm not sure where he's going with this. "Um, yeah?"

"In saying that, I was agitated at work this morning and Dylan was asking me what was wrong. Then in between, you and I were texting. He saw the texts as they came through."

My cheeks heat with embarrassment at Dylan knowing I got my period today, not that it's anything out of the ordinary, but it's not something I normally share. I only shared it with AJ so he knew I wasn't pregnant this month. "Oh." But then it registers he said he was agitated at work *before* my messages. "Is everything okay with you? Why were you upset at work?"

He blows out a heavy breath. "Yes and no. I … uh … I felt as though I said or did something which upset you on Saturday."

I rack my brain, running through our conversation from Saturday, and shake my head. "I can't remember being upset with you on Saturday."

"It sort of felt like we were getting along okay and then suddenly you pulled back from me, which made me think I'd done something to upset you. Then today, Dylan saw the messages and he thinks he knows what I may have said to upset you."

"Oh. And what does he think you've said?"

"He thinks when I say things like 'I'll be around *until* you're pregnant,' it may be upsetting to you. That I'm implying we won't see each other once you're pregnant." My eyes widen. Dylan must be incredibly intuitive to pick up on that type of thing. I don't know too many guys who would be so switched on. AJ smiles and tips his head down, then looks back at me. "That's it, isn't it?"

I nod slowly, embarrassed. "It's okay, AJ. That was our arrangement, remember? There won't be any need for us to see each other once I'm pregnant. You have your life, and I have mine and they'll be quite different once I have the baby. I won't have as much time to spend with friends, especially in the early months; having to get up for feedings and diaper changes throughout the night. I'm betting on the weekends, I'll be a zombie and won't be pleasant company." I chuckle.

"But you see, the thing is, Sarah, I've grown to really like you. I enjoy your company, and I would hope once you're pregnant, you'll still allow me to drop around occasionally with dinner. Or, you know, I could watch the baby while you have a nap or something. I don't want to lose the friendship we have."

*Friendship.* That dreaded word.

"Oh, well, we can definitely do that if I have the time. No expectations, though. I'm sure you'll be sick of seeing me by then, anyway." I try to make my voice as upbeat as possible because the thought of not seeing AJ regularly hurts my heart.

I've fallen for this guy and it was the last thing I was supposed to do.

"There was something else I wanted to talk with you about. I have an idea and I want you to hear me out before you shoot me down." He widens his eyes, waiting for my agreement, which I give. "I think we need to try a different approach to getting you pregnant. I don't think the collection condom/syringe combo is working."

Dread fills me but I turn my body to face him more directly. "What would you suggest we do?"

"Hear me out, okay?" I nod. "I think we should have sex. Old-fashioned, missionary position, with the cushion under your butt, sex. Or maybe doggy style. I read that's pretty good for what we're trying to do. Cut out the middle-man, so to speak."

I'm frozen. Paralyzed where I sit. All of the air has been sucked out of my apartment.

"Sarah? Cupcake? Are you okay?" He places his hand on my shoulder, squeezing firmly to gain my attention. "Sarah. Take a breath."

Oh, God! He wants to have sex to get me pregnant. I can't do that! I'm already halfway in love with the guy.

"Sarah! Take a breath."

He shakes me and I snap out of my shocked state with a gasp. "I … I … can't … breathe." I manage to get out. I flap my hand in front of my face.

"Jesus, what do I need to do?" He stands, pulls me to my feet, and drags me to the window, opening it and pushing the top half of my body outside. I draw in gasping breaths, filling my lungs with each suck in and blow out. "Shit! Are you okay?"

I turn to look at him for the first time since he dropped his helpful suggestion, but my vision is fuzzy. I think his eyebrows are furrowed over his eyes and even though I can't see him properly, his worry for me is radiating from him in waves. It's almost stifling. I draw in deep breaths and try to regain my composure. That was possibly the last thing I imagined when he said we needed to 'talk.' And I'm not sure why it wasn't something I even considered a possibility.

"Are you okay?" He helpfully rubs his hand up and down my back, sending my body haywire. He has zero idea of the impact his touch has on me. How his concern affects me, my heart.

Without making eye contact I nod. "Yeah. Sorry about that. I'm not sure what happened."

"I think you had a panic attack. You ever had those before?"

I shake my head. "No. I don't think so," I whisper. Well, not that severe, anyway.

"Was it the idea of having sex with me that set you off?" My eyes snap up to his, my cheeks heating in embarrassment. I want to lean forward and erase the frown lines between his eyebrows but I daren't.

I nervously laugh. "Uh, what … no … of course not," I scoff. My heart beats an erratic rhythm and I'm worried I'm having a heart attack now. I'm too young to have a heart attack, right?

"Then what set you off?"

Oh, God! I can't tell him I've fallen for him and if we actually have sex, I'll be asking him to marry me. He'll think I'm a fruit loop and run for the hills, never to be seen again. He only agreed to be my donor, not tie himself to me for life. I step away from him to get some space and air that's not filled with his citrus scent, which is an aphrodisiac for me. "It … it's just that was never part of my plan. I don't like it when plans change suddenly and I'm unprepared." There, that doesn't sound too crazy. I hope.

He chuckles mildly. "I've sort of picked up on that trait of yours. I'm not saying we should have sex right now. You have time to get your head around the idea." He digs his phone out of his pocket and checks something. "You have ten days to get used to the idea."

My mouth drops open. "You really do have an app to follow my cycle."

"Yeah. I told you I did."

The tension I'd been holding in my body releases a little. "I was worried you wanted to talk about ending our arrangement because maybe you'd met someone." I point toward his phone. "But you're taking this seriously." I step closer and lay my hand on his forearm. "Thank you. And I'll think about the next step."

He grabs the back of his neck and looks down at the floor between us. "I have … uh … met someone."

I remove my hand from his arm as though I've been burned. "Oh."

"I'm taking it slow. I'm not sure if she feels the same for me as I do for her, and I'm trying my best not to rush things because I don't want to scare her off."

Well, if anyone knows how that feels, it would be me. I smile at him, but I'm certain it looks forced. "Are you sure you want to move forward with my pregnancy plan? She might not appreciate you spending time with me, to uh … you know, get me pregnant."

*—aj—*

Damn it! I've screwed up. I shouldn't have told her I'd met someone. She's going to assume it's someone else, and I can't tell her it's *her*.

"Oh yeah. I made a promise, and I intend to keep it."

"Well, I definitely don't think we should have sex then. That's not fair to the woman you're seeing." She's pulling away again. Me and my stupid mouth, but I didn't know what else to say to throw her off.

"It's okay. Honestly. I think it's all one-sided. An infatuation. It's not like we're dating, or anything. I made a promise to you first and I always follow through with my promises." I step back into her space. "I think you should give my suggestion the consideration it deserves. It'll be more efficient. It's the method that's worked for thousands of years."

She chews on her bottom lip and drops her eyes to the floor. Uncertainty is written all over her face. "I don't know if it's such a good idea. I don't want feelings to get involved for either of us or your lady to get hurt."

She doesn't want feelings to get involved. See, dickhead, it's all one-sided. You're way over your head here. My heart constricts. How is it I find the perfect woman and she only wants me to be her donor? She's so determined to stick to her plan that she doesn't see me at all. But I made a promise, and it's not her fault I've fallen for her when it was never part of the plan. I lower my voice. "Don't worry. Feelings won't get involved. I promise."

She nods slowly, her eyes become glassy, but she blinks quickly, then turns her face away from mine as she swallows. "Okay."

My eyes widen in surprise. Okay? Did she just agree to try my idea? Or was it okay because there won't be feelings involved?

I run my tongue across my dry lips. "Great. You can come to my place next Thursday night." Sarah nods. I think I should leave before the conversation gets any more complicated and I say more shit I shouldn't say. "All right, I'll head off and leave you to your evening. Are you gonna be okay? Do you need anything?"

She smiles and her entire face changes. Gone is the worry, replaced by a lightness I'd like to always see. I don't like that I've upset her. "I'm okay. Stop worrying about me. I promise I've managed just fine on my own."

I want to tell her that she no longer has to manage on her own, that I'm here now and I can help her, but we've just gotten back onto steady footing and I don't want to mess that up again.

"Okay. Call or text if you need anything. I'll see you in ten days unless you're free to get together before then." I lean into her and lay a soft kiss on her jawline near her ear, and she sucks in a sharp breath. I know she's somewhat affected by me, but she's bound and determined to resist it every step of the way for some damn reason.

"Take," I call down to Dylan. I needed to climb today. The excess energy in my body is driving me crazy the closer the clock ticks down to our arranged dinner date.

Not a date.

Stop thinking of it as a date. For fuck's sake. It's an impregnation session. Yeah. That's what I'll refer to it as in my head so I don't get too carried away. I don't want to scare the woman away. I think I'll be walking a fine line tonight.

"Are you ready to lower?" he calls back.

"Ready to lower."

My feet land on the mat and Dylan loosens the rope. "You're climbing like a machine."

I'm distracted in my reply. "Yeah. Thanks."

His hand lands on my shoulder and I look up at my long-time friend. "Hey. You okay?"

I blow out a breath. "Yeah. Just have a lot of nervous energy I need to burn."

"What has you so nervous? Is it because of the inevitable phone call from your grandfather tomorrow morning?"

My grandfather. The current bane of my existence. I'm going to drag that man into the twenty-first century kicking and screaming if I have to. He'll give the damn job to Mom or Hayley by the time I'm finished with him. "Nah, I haven't really thought about him, but I am getting ready for a face-to-face meeting. I've put together a slideshow of all the women who fill CEO roles in big business as well as their achievements and what they bring to the table." Dylan snickers. "Sarah's coming over tonight." I don't need to say anything more. Understanding washes over his features.

"You've got this. Just keep doing what you're doing and she'll come around. How can she resist you? You're perfect boyfriend material." He squeezes my shoulder then we release our ropes.

"Thanks, man. And thanks for coming with me this afternoon. I needed this."

"No problem." We both collect our bags and go our separate ways in the parking lot.

I walk in the door and head straight to the shower with thoughts of what's going to happen in a few short hours. Not gonna lie, I've been dying to get my hands and mouth on her sweet body. I can't count the number of times I've rubbed one out in the shower to thoughts of touching that smooth skin, running my hands over her killer curves—and there I go again. My cock grows and throbs.

"You're gonna have to wait a little longer, buddy. I don't want to waste a single drop of my swimmers today. They're all for Sarah." My dick taps against my stomach at the thought of filling Sarah with my cum, seeing her round with my baby. I blow out a breath and turn the water to freezing, trying to think of something else that will help my body calm down. Ignoring my dick, I wash my hair and my body, then step out and dry off.

I've noticed Sarah seems to like it when I wear my Henleys, so I choose a black one and pair it with my favorite jeans. I make sure the bathroom's tidy and do the same with my bedroom. I don't live like a slob, but I don't want Sarah to step in here and see any mess. I need everything to go perfectly tonight. I give one last cursory look to make sure I haven't missed anything and then head downstairs to make sure the living room is tidy.

Once I'm happy with everything, I grab the ingredients I need and start preparing dinner. I can't cook it in advance, but I can have everything on hand ready to go. I slice the chicken and peel the shrimp, then prepare the vegetables according to the instructions. Glancing at the time, I still have twenty minutes and too much nervous energy, so I grab a beer and head upstairs to my outdoor deck. I watch the traffic in the street as I lean on the glass and try to settle my thoughts, but they land back on Sarah like they always seem to do.

I get that her high school boyfriend hurt her when he took the promotion and left for Australia without considering her, but I wonder why she's so determined to do this baby thing on her own. Am I hoping for something that'll never happen between us because she only sees me as a donor and nothing more? How can I make her see me as something more? Can I make her fall for me, the way I've fallen for her?

I take the last sip of my beer as I see her teal Yaris park in front of my place. It's showtime.

# CHAPTER 25

## —sarah—

OUR LACK OF SUCCESS FOR THE LAST TWO MONTHS HAS LANDED ME ON AJ's doorstep, promising him that I'll try this *his* way. I'm not so sure it's a good idea when he's interested in someone else. And wasn't that a stab to my already tender heart, finding out he's interested in someone. I don't know how I'm going to survive this experience with my heart intact.

I like the guy.

*Really* like him.

But he likes someone else. I need to remember that.

I *was* hoping it wouldn't come to this. My stomach rolls and my heart knocks rapidly against my ribs as I contemplate what's about to happen. Raising my shaky hand, I press the doorbell and try to draw enough oxygen into my lungs so I don't pass out. Imagine that, AJ opens the door to find me collapsed on his stoop. I spin on my heel to face the street as a distraction and focus on gaining my self-control while I wait for him to answer the door.

Within less than a minute, the sound of the door opening has me turning around to face the man who has infiltrated my thoughts at every turn. Starting at the floor, I take in his bare feet, torn jeans, and black Henley.

Shit! I'm in so much trouble. I'm a sucker for AJ in a Henley.

This is going to be tougher than anything I've ever done. But if this works and I get pregnant, then all of this discomfort will be worth it. With a bit of luck, I'll be pregnant this time next week and I can put all of this behind me and focus on the future. And he can work on building his relationship with someone that's not me. I could cry at the thought.

His lips spread in welcome and he steps back, making room for me to enter his home for the first time. "Hey, Sarah." He leans forward, his warm breath ghosting across my skin as he presses a tender kiss to my jaw near my ear, and my flesh burns at his touch. It's not the first time he's kissed me there, and my reaction this time is no less potent than it was then.

"Hey." I try to make my voice light so he doesn't pick up on my nerves. His place has an industrial feel to it with a combination of rough brick and smooth concrete walls, as well as large factory-style windows. It should feel cold and sterile, but it feels warm and inviting. I would never have guessed this was a home from the outside because it looks like a factory with a roller door at the side of the building. I was expecting it to be dark and dank on the inside. I couldn't be more wrong. Even though the space is large and open, it has a certain home-yness to it. My entire apartment could probably fit inside his living room space. "You have a beautiful home."

"Thank you. It took a bit of work to get it to where I wanted it to be, but I'm happy with the outcome." I nod as he leads me deeper into his home and across gorgeous hardwood floors. "This is the kitchen, which is probably obvious." He half chuckles. *Is he as nervous as I am?* "And the space at the back of the house is my office. Dylan and I work here." He slides open a huge barn door to reveal the most incredible computer setup I've ever seen outside of the office. "All of the bedrooms are upstairs." He points to the ceiling.

"Wow. This is impressive." I'm genuinely impressed as I'm sure he can tell by my wide eyes as I take in everything.

"Thanks. Would you like a drink or anything?"

Since my tongue is stuck to the top of my mouth, I figure it may be a good idea to have a drink. I swallow around the dryness. "I wouldn't mind a glass of water if you don't mind."

"Of course." He deftly reaches up to grab a couple of glasses, exposing toned ab muscles just above the top of his jeans. I quickly tear my eyes away and watch the play in the muscles of his forearms as he releases the lever on the filtered water tap to fill them. His hand is steady as he passes a glass to me, and I take it, trying to hide the tremble in mine. His eyes rise to mine and a comforting smile touches his lips. "Are you nervous, Sarah?"

I half-laugh with embarrassment. "Yeah. How could you tell?"

He moves into my space and his scent surrounds me, comforting me, making me feel safe. From the first instant I met AJ, I felt completely safe in his company. He takes my free hand in his and my eyes drop to watch his much larger hand surround mine. "Your hand is shaking and your voice has a slight tremor that would be unnoticeable to most people unless they were paying attention."

My eyes snap up to his. I swallow. Has he moved closer? The lighter flecks of caramel in his chocolate eyes are impossible to miss with him this close to me. His other hand rises and he tucks a lock of hair behind my ear, then strokes his knuckles gently down the side of my face to my chin. He raises my face to his and I swallow the excess saliva that's decided to multiply in my mouth. "You don't need to be. We'll do everything at your pace. If you feel uncomfortable at any time, just say so. Okay?" He crouches down so he's at eye level, raising his brows in question on the last word.

How can he be so calm about this? *We're about to have sex!* It's not a date, where one thing leads to another and we *may* end up in bed together. This is *planned* sex and it feels terribly awkward.

I nod silently and his eyes follow the movement. One side of his mouth tips up and he moves closer, pressing his lips to mine tenderly. They're warm and soft, and I would give anything to be able to return his kiss, but I can't.

I need to keep myself in check.

He's doing this to help me get pregnant.

He's not in love with me.

He doesn't want a future with me. He wants someone else.

The reminders run through my head on a loop and I draw back, putting much-needed space between us. If he's disappointed he doesn't show it. "I thought we could eat dinner upstairs on the deck. How does that sound?"

He's acting normal. Like tonight's no big deal, so I follow his lead. If he can do this, so can I.

"That sounds nice." I hold up my sweater. "I have this if it gets a little cool." I set my purse and sweater on a stool and wash my hands at the kitchen sink. "Anything I can do to help?"

"Nope. You sit there"—he points to a stool situated at the counter —"and look beautiful."

I get comfortable on the designated stool as my cheeks flush. While he cooks dinner for us, I take a sip of my water and run through every-thing I've seen so far of AJ. He helps clean up whenever he's at someone else's home. I look around his neat home and decide he must do a decent job with housework, and now I find he cooks. He's fantastic looking. Is sweet and thoughtful, as well as generous with his time and his … uh sperm. He runs his own successful business and defies gravity by climbing rock walls. I can't find any faults with the man.

He holds up a plate with shrimp, snapping me out of my head and back to his kitchen. "You okay with these? I can leave them out."

"No. I'm all good. I'm not allergic to anything that I know of. Are you?" Do allergies get passed down through the genes? I should probably look that up. I take another sip of water.

"No, nothing that I know of." He turns back to the wok and continues preparing the delicious-smelling meal.

"What are you cooking?"

"Char Kway Teow. It's a Malaysian noodle dish. I hope you like it."

"It smells divine, I'm pretty sure if it tastes half as good as it smells, I'm gonna love it."

He scoops out two healthy servings and holds the bowls up in front of him. "Would you mind bringing up the drinks and cutlery?"

"Sure." I grab them and follow him upstairs. A gasp leaves me at the unexpected space I would never have imagined when I looked at the building from the street. "This is gorgeous. What an amazing space. The view is spectacular."

"Thanks. I like it up here." He places the bowls on the low table and takes the glasses from my hands, his fingers making contact with mine.

We both take our first bites of food. "Mmm." With wide eyes, I look at AJ. "This is divine. Thank you for making me dinner."

"You're welcome. I enjoy cooking."

"Ugh. I do my cooking on Sunday mornings for the week. I try to do all my food prep then so I don't have to worry about it when I get home from work. Some days, I don't leave the office until six. If I didn't have my meals already prepared and waiting for me, I'd be too tempted to buy takeout."

"I'd noticed all of your labeled meals in your fridge. That's a practical approach."

We spend the meal chatting, but there are also comfortable moments of silence. I could imagine spending evenings on this deck, enjoying a glass of wine, and watching our toddler play in a kiddie pool. I freeze. What the hell, Sarah? Stop it already! What am I doing sitting here like we're on some kind of date, fantasizing about a future that will never be? I stand abruptly, stacking the dishes. "I'll clean up since you cooked dinner, then we can … we can, uh … get started. I'm sure you have plans and don't need me taking up your entire evening."

"I don't have any other plans but we can get started. I can do the dishes later." Those words have to be the sexiest form of foreplay on the planet but I need something to do.

"I insist." With everything in hand, I make my way downstairs to the kitchen and set about washing the dishes. AJ works alongside me, drying them and putting them away. The task doesn't take long and I'm now wishing I'd dragged it out a little since there's nothing else to do but have sex!

With AJ!

Oh my God.

How am I going to get through this? I'm pretty sure my panties are already wet after being in his company, and this isn't about pleasure. It's about getting pregnant. I blow out a long breath. "I guess I'm ready."

He chuckles softly. "Anyone would think you're being sent to the gallows. It's just sex, Sarah. People do it all the time. I promise it won't be so bad."

Embarrassment floods me and my palms sweat. I drop my gaze to the floor and discreetly wipe my hands on my dress. I'm such a fool. I'm acting like a thirty-four-year-old virgin who's never been touched by a man. I've had sex plenty of times. The problem is it means so much to me. It's personal and private and when I have sex with a partner, I'm giving them a personal, private part of me I don't give to anyone else. It's why I confuse sex with love, even though I know the two don't always go hand in hand. I'm terrified this experience with AJ is going to show him how much I already care for him. Finally, I nod and grab my purse. "I know."

He takes my hand and leads me through his home to the stairs, which lead to the bedrooms. His grip is sure and strong, confident. I don't sense any jitters or nerves from him. My pulse increases and I have to remind myself to take measured breaths. I made sure to wear a dress, so I don't have to get completely naked, using the clothing as the barrier I need between us. I'm certain he's going to think I'm a weirdo, but it's the only way I could think to reduce the intimacy of our situation and send the correct message to my heart.

We cross the threshold into AJ's masculine bedroom. Hardwood floors and concrete walls complete with enormous floor-to-ceiling windows provide an impressive space for the king-size bed which is quietly intimidating in this situation. Holding my purse against my body like a shield, AJ leads me further into the room, which has his personality all over it. That quiet masculinity he wears so easily which appeals to me on a fundamental level.

Tugging me around in front of him, he studies my face closely, then takes my purse from me and places it gently on the nightstand. He brings his hand up to cup my face, his fingers sliding into my hair and I desperately want to press into his warm touch. With his eyes locked on mine, he moves in closer, his breaths licking across my lips.

He's going to kiss me.

He's going to expect foreplay and while I know I need to get him aroused, I've brought lube for myself. Though, I don't expect I'll need it if he starts kissing me and paying attention to my body in a way I know, just know will be incredible. I don't think the chemistry between us is in my imagination but I wonder if he feels it too.

AJ presses his lips to mine and for a moment I allow myself to enjoy the pleasure—the feel of his soft lips against mine, his tongue tracing the seam. I open with a sigh and he surges in, his tongue stroking along mine with confidence. This is a man who knows how to kiss. My body sags into his and his fingers slide further around to the back of my head. He grasps the strands of my hair firmly, tilting my head where he wants it, then proceeds to deepen the kiss in a way that leaves me breathless and my legs trembling. My shallow breaths speed up and my heart pounds a fast rhythm against my breastbone. He presses his body tight against mine, squashing my boobs between us and I can't miss the hardness in his jeans.

A tiny moan escapes and AJ groans in response, pressing his pelvis further into my stomach. My panties are soaked.

This can't happen. It will be disastrous for me.

I pull back swiftly and AJ's hand drops from my hair, a puzzled expression taking over his face. "What's wrong?"

"Uh, nothing. I didn't want to get carried away." I step back and without showing all my business, I drag my panties down my legs, scrunch them into a ball, and tuck them in my purse—heaven forbid he sees my underwear. He's about to put his penis inside me—I internally roll my eyes at myself. I point to his bed. "Do you mind if we pop one of your pillows beneath my butt?" I glance around the room, noticing an ensuite. "Damn it, I should have brought a towel with me, so there isn't any mess."

He shakes his head with a smile. "You can put a pillow anywhere you need and don't worry about the mess, I'll aim to get everything inside you. We wouldn't want to waste any." He chuckles mildly as he winks at me.

"Oh, right. Of course." I move the pillow to where I need it, slip off my shoes, and lay down, positioning my hips on the pillow so they're raised. The websites say you don't need to do this, but I figure I may as well give myself the best possible chance of this working. "I'm ready," I tell AJ with a bright tone as I lie stiffly on top of his covers.

"You don't want to kiss or have foreplay? Or get naked?" He rests his hands on his hips, looking positively puzzled.

"Uh no. I don't think it's necessary." I glance down at his jeans which still show the outline of an impressive erection. "I'm wet and you're ready. I think we're good to go." He seems reluctant, but he pulls his shirt over his head in that sexy way that guys do, grasping the back collar. He's so defined and this close I can see the details of the tattoo around his bicep. A rope with some kind of intricate knot—makes sense since he loves to climb.

Hang on. He can't take his shirt off, I need the barrier of our clothes. "You can put your shirt back on if you like and keep your jeans on too."

"What?"

I wave my hand around the area of his groin. "We just need the essentials to be bare. That'll do the job."

"The job?"

"Yeah."

"I'm not sure I can … uh … perform under these circumstances, Sarah." I glance back down at his zipper. It still looks impressive, so I don't think he has performance issues. But I can help him out if needed.

"Oh. I can help you." I sit up and reach for him, ready to help him but he pulls back.

"So, you'll help get me hard, but I can't help get you ready for me?"

I chuckle nervously. "You don't need to worry about that. This is for reproductive purposes, not for enjoyment." His eyebrows shoot up.

# CHAPTER 26

## *—aj—*

I CAN'T BELIEVE THIS. I'VE NEVER HAD SEX UNDER THESE circumstances, and I'm not sure I'll be able to do what needs to be done. For some reason I have no hope of comprehending, she wants us both to stay almost fully clothed, but I refuse to put my shirt back on. I'll keep my jeans on and drop them just below my ass if it helps Sarah feel more comfortable, but that's my limit.

She spreads her legs wider and the skirt of her dress slides down her thick thighs. I climb onto the bed, kneeling between the thighs that have starred in many of my fantasies since I first met her, and get my first glimpse of her pussy. I want to dip down and taste the silky flesh, so I do.

As my tongue makes first contact with her lips, her thighs slam shut around my head.

"What are you doing?" she gasps and her hand presses against the top of my head, pushing me away.

"I need to get you ready for me." I tilt my head down to my cock, but she's too flustered to look for herself. "I'm not a small guy. I don't want to hurt you." My cock grows thicker, as though he's showing off.

Without glancing down, she gives me a tremulous smile. "I'll cope. Just go slow at first." She drops back to the pillow, tension still filling her body and creases marring her beautiful forehead.

I reach forward and gingerly swipe my fingers along her lips, finding them dry. I need to work her over and build her up. I dip my finger inside her tight opening and she tenses.

She raises her head. "What are you doing now?"

Surely she knows. "Getting you wet."

She pushes up on her elbows and points to her purse. "I brought lube with me. If you can just grab it out of my purse, I'll be good to go."

Lube. Of course, she brought lube. Because she planned to keep this as impersonal as possible. I climb from the bed and grab the lube from her purse. I dribble some on her pussy and spread it with my fingers in the least sexual way I can. I grit my teeth and try to focus on the job at hand, not that my fingers are gliding through Sarah's pussy. This certainly isn't how I imagined our first time together.

After applying lube, I slowly edge my way forward and push inside Sarah's silken sheath for the first time. Gritting my teeth as she holds her body stiff, I push her legs open wider to help open her up for my cock, then apply more lube to my shaft to help me slide in more easily. I've never had to use lube before because I've usually been able to engage in foreplay with my partner. Sarah's aversion to anything remotely personal is messing with my head, but sliding inside her feels so damn good.

I drop my head forward and open my eyes to check on her. Her eyes are squeezed closed and her lips are pressed together in a tight line. "Sarah. Cupcake," I murmur. "Look at me."

She shakes her head slightly, keeping her lids locked tight and I sigh as I pull out of her glorious heat, gritting my teeth. Her eyes fly open as I rest my ass on my heels.

"What are you doing? Why'd you stop?" Her words tumble out in a panicked rush as she pushes upward, pulling her skirt down to cover herself.

"This isn't going to work if you can't even look at me while we're having sex. What's the problem?" She looks everywhere around the room and I guide her face back to me with my fingers gently cupping her chin.

"What does it matter if I look at you or not? This is about impregnating me, not an emotional connection."

I sigh heavily. She's fighting this for some reason. Obviously, I need to go slower and make her forget about the process, so we can move forward. "Okay. Sorry." I guide her to lay back against the pillow and shuffle forward, nudging my cock at her entrance, and press inside her welcoming heat, her pussy walls tightening around my shaft. Her mind may be fighting whatever this is between us, but her body is certainly happy to have me inside as her walls grip me. With my hips pressed all the way forward, my shaft is buried deep inside Sarah's warm heat and I wrap my hands around her thighs, pulling out slowly only to thrust back inside.

"Hold your legs open wide for me," I tell her, then drop down over her when she complies. I press my lips against hers, needing intimate contact, but she draws her head back, breaking the connection. I huff out a breath, making the loose strands of hair across her face move. I gently stroke them out of the way so nothing is impeding my view of her stunning face. Sarah holds her body stiff as I drag my cock out of her welcoming heat.

"Are you ready," I whisper lowly against her ear, noticing the thrumming at her pulse point.

"Yeah. Ready whenever you are." Her voice is breathy.

I push in and Sarah opens her legs wider still, ensuring that my hips have clear access without touching them, so I glide my hand down her silky thigh and grasp her ass cheek in my hand, squeezing as I draw back out. Sarah's breaths coat the side of my face as I push my cock slowly inside and glide back out. It's fucking incredible to be inside the woman who has stolen all rational thought from me since the moment I laid eyes on her in that damn club. I scan her face, noticing the frown lines between her brows and the tightness around her eyes.

This certainly isn't the way I anticipated our first time together. I never imagined I'd be having sex with a partner whose body language is screaming that she doesn't want any part of this, but contrary to those thoughts, my body is building closer to release.

It feels wrong.

As much as it pains me to do, I stop and withdraw, resting my ass on my heels again. Her lids fly open and she pushes up. "I'm sorry. I can't do this," I whisper, dragging Sarah's skirt down to cover her modesty. "I'm not built to have sex with someone who's so obviously opposed."

A pink stain coats her cheeks and she reaches forward to grasp my hand. "I'm sorry. Please don't stop. I'm not opposed to this, I promise," she says, panicked. "I'm trying to keep myself in check," Sarah whispers.

With my free hand, I rub her thigh tenderly. "Why do you need to keep yourself in check? Why can't you relax and enjoy the experience?"

She shrugs. "It's how I'm built."

"What, so you don't enjoy sex?" I'm honestly puzzled.

Creases form between her brows. "Of course I do." She glances out of the darkened window. "When I'm in a relationship, I love having sex with my boyfriend. This is different." She squeezes my hand. "I'll try to relax a little more. I'm sorry I'm being difficult."

"You're not being difficult, but I feel as though I'm forcing you and that doesn't sit well with me."

"You're not." She lays back and tugs her skirt up, revealing her pussy, and gives me a timid smile. "Please, AJ," she whispers.

The 'please' does me in and I stroke my softening cock back to life. I want to kiss her. Desperately. Dropping over her, I rest on my elbows and cup my hands around her head, stroking her silky hair. Locking my eyes on hers, I lower my head until our lips are a mere inch apart. Her warm breath is coming in pants while her lips separate slightly. I close the distance and swipe my tongue across the supple pillows and moan at her taste. Her lips part with a sigh, and I push my tongue inside to tangle with hers. This. This is what it's all about. The connection, the intimacy. I probably sound like a chick, but guys need to feel this too. Angling my head, I kiss her deeply, stealing her breath as I notch my cock at her entrance.

Sarah raises her hips, signaling she's ready for me to move, so I do. Inch by magnificent inch, I slide inside her inviting heat, her walls tightening around my shaft as I suck her tongue into my mouth. It feels incredible. Her body arches and I drop lower, pressing my body into hers, flattening her gorgeous tits, which are sadly covered. Maybe next time she'll let us get naked, so we can do this properly. At this point, I'll take her kissing me back and moving rather than laying stiff as a win. It's progress I wasn't sure we'd make.

Moving her hips in time with my thrusts, we begin to build a solid rhythm. The sensations building in my body are explosive and I know if Sarah ever allows her walls down and lets go, we'll be dynamite together. My body heats, sweat forming down my spine, while I slide in and out of her heat, her walls fluttering and tightening, causing my entire focus to narrow to a singular point.

Sarah's hands wrap around my forearms and her short nails dig into my flesh, sending ribbons of my cum into her without warning. Fuck! I grunt through my release and hang my head in shame. She's going to think I'm a goddamn two-pump chump. She didn't have an orgasm, not even close.

"I'm sorry."

She releases her grip from my forearms, her eyes opening as she presses her hips into the mattress, disengaging from me. She immediately grabs the pillow next to her and I take it from her and place it on top of the first pillow as she lifts her hips. The second pillow ensures her hips are tilted higher. Sliding it beneath her ass, my eyes drop to her pussy and I notice some of my cum leaking out, so I scoop it up and push it inside.

Sarah's eyes widen. "What are you doing?"

"Trying not to waste any of my cum." I keep my eyes on her center as I push my fingers in and out of her opening under the pretense of pushing my release inside.

She attempts to close her legs, but she can't because I'm in the way. "I'm sorry I came before I could get you there," I whisper, ashamed of myself.

"Oh, that's okay. I'm not here for the orgasms, remember." I huff and move my thumb over her clit, making small, tight circles around the bundle. "I'm sure it's all inside. You can stop now."

I glance up at her rosy cheeks. "I need to give you an orgasm to help my swimmers get to where they need to go. Remember?"

Her cheeks flush further and she looks stunning. "I brought my bullet for that. If you wouldn't mind stepping out, I'll do what needs to be done, and then I'll be out of your way."

I shake my head and hold out my hand. "Give me the bullet."

"No. I can do it." Her voice is sure and strong. Stubborn.

"Why won't you let me help you? Look, I'm sorry I came before you did. That doesn't usually happen to me. My only excuse is that it's been a while and despite your obvious aversion to having sex with me, you felt so damn good. But I never leave my partner unsatisfied."

She pushes up, bringing her face closer to mine, her eyes finally making contact. "It's okay. Honestly. I don't expect orgasms out of this. You're helping me to get pregnant and it's more than I ever expected from anyone. Now, if you wouldn't mind stepping out of the room, I need to ..." her eyes widen. "And if you don't mind, I like to lie still for about half an hour. Then I'll be out of your space. I'm sure you have other things you need to do."

I study her eyes closely. This is genuinely how she wants, *or maybe needs*, things to be between us, so I relent—reluctantly because I respect her. I don't want to force her or make her feel uncomfortable or she might decide to go back to how we were doing things before. At least this way, I get to be inside her regularly over the next week and I can work on getting her to forget and loosen up a bit—make it enjoyable for her and hopefully make her fall for me. More importantly, make sure she comes before I do.

I nod and move out from between her legs. "Okay. Uh, take your time." I grasp the back of my neck and Sarah's eyes drop to my bicep as they usually do, so I tense it. "There's no rush. I don't have anywhere I need to be."

I tuck myself away and collecting my shirt, I back out of my bedroom slowly, keeping my eyes on Sarah as I do. Closing the door quietly, I lean against it and blow out a breath, feeling like a failure. She's bound and determined to keep distance between us and I'm not sure why that is, but *I'm* bound and determined to erase every single inch of that distance and make her mine.

She steps into the living room, her hair slightly mussed and her eyes glassy. I bet she looks fucking stunning when she comes. "Uh, thank you." She thumbs over her shoulder toward the front door. "I'll … uh … get outta your hair."

I quickly stand. "I ordered dessert. It should be here any min—" The doorbell rings at that exact moment, and I refrain from tipping my head back and thanking the heavens for their impeccable timing. I stroll past Sarah and open the door.

"*Japanese Dessert House* delivery for Jackson?"

"Yep, that's me. Thanks." He hands over the desserts and spins on his heel, returning to his car. Closing the door, I make my way past Sarah and toward the couch. "Come on, let's eat." I drop the dessert onto the coffee table and make my way to the kitchen as if it's a given that she'll stay. "What would you like to drink? I have soda, juice, sparkling water …" She's frozen to the spot, holding her purse to her body as though it's a life preserver and she's adrift in the deepest ocean. "Come on, Sarah. Don't make me eat this alone."

The indecision on her face is plain for anyone to see. Even if I didn't know her, I would be able to see how torn she is between staying and leaving. She takes a timid step toward the couch, her shoulders dropping slightly. "Okay."

I duck back behind the fridge door to hide my grin and blow out a breath. "Great. Now, what would you like to drink?"

"Water's fine. Thank you."

I grab a beer for myself and water for Sarah and head back to the couch. The coffee table is too far away, so I slide it forward and open the dessert containers. "I didn't know what you liked, so I ordered one Ferrero Crêpe Cake and one Hokkaido Crêpe Cake."

She smiles at me, picking up a fork. "I've never had either before, but they look delicious."

"We can share both."

"I don't often treat myself to stuff like this because of my saving plan," she tells me.

"Fair enough. I don't eat dessert often either, but I figure it's okay now and then." She nods. "So, how did it go in there?" Good one, dickhead, you just got her to relax and now she's going to be all stiff and distant again. "Sorry. None of my business." I take a bite of crêpe cake to keep my mouth busy so I don't say more stupid shit. I hold in a moan when the lightness of the crêpes melds with the sweet tartness of the strawberries on my tongue.

She chuckles, but it's awkward and stilted. "Good. I guess. Hopefully, it works this time. I'm sorry it's taking so long for me to get pregnant." Her cheeks flush and she drops her eyes to the table.

"No need to apologize, Sarah. It takes as long as it takes. We didn't put a time limit on this, remember." The longer it takes, the better my chances of winning her over. And doesn't that make me the biggest asshole around.

A tight smile forms on her delectable lips, the ones I desperately want to kiss again. The small taste I had earlier wasn't nearly enough. "I know," she whispers. "I … I just feel terrible that I'm taking up so much of your time, and now I'm also invading your home … and you've met a woman you'd like to date. This isn't conducive to starting a relationship with someone. You've been incredibly kind and generous." She glances away then back to me. "I'll be forever grateful to you, AJ. I hope you know that." I knew I'd fucked up when I mentioned I'd met someone, now it's like I have a guillotine waiting to be released on my neck.

"I do." The mood has grown heavy and it's the last thing we need. "You wanna watch this Discovery show I recorded? It's about the most extreme places in the US."

She shrugs and agrees. "Sure."

I pull up the program and settle back into the couch, inching closer to Sarah, and press play as she settles in, making herself comfortable. I scoop a forkful of cake and offer it to her and she distractedly opens for me. I slide the food into her mouth and she closes her lips around the fork, giving a small moan as the flavors burst on her tongue. I scoop myself a mouthful of cake as we get caught up in the program.

"Hmm. I always thought Chicago was the windiest city," Sarah speaks for the first time as we've learned about the deepest lake and the quietest place in the US.

"Yeah, I thought that too. I love watching shows like this. I always learn something new." I chuckle.

"I think I could become a convert. I'm enjoying this more than I thought I would." She turns back to the television and I watch her for a few more moments. She's enthralled by the information being shared and I'm thrilled she's still here. My eyes snap back to the television when she points toward the screen. "That looks amazing. I wonder if they do overnight camps there? Not that I camp, but that night sky looks incredible."

"I could find out if you like." A perfect opportunity to steal her away for a couple of days.

She spins her head toward me. "Oh, you don't have to do that. I've never camped. I'm sure I'd be terrible at it."

"You'll never know if you don't try. I happen to love camping so I could teach you. I sometimes do an overnight trip when I climb."

"Really? I just figured you climbed close by."

"I do, mostly. But sometimes I like to get away for a weekend. I can let you know next time I'm going and you could come along if you like."

"You don't need to go to any trouble for me."

"It's no trouble at all. It'll be fun."

We spend the rest of the program learning about the highest and lowest places in the US, the coldest and the hottest, the driest and the wettest. When the credits roll, my stomach sinks because I know it means the end of my time with Sarah for tonight. My spirits lift when I remember that she'll be back here in forty-eight hours.

"Thanks for tonight, AJ. For everything. Honestly, you've been amazing," she says as she stands, collecting the empty dessert boxes.

I force out a laugh and stand too. "I wouldn't say I was all that amazing in there." I tilt my head toward the stairs and my bedroom, taking the boxes from her.

"We got the job done, right? That's all that matters." *Job*. It's not meant to be a job.

I dump the boxes in the kitchen and come back to the living room, where Sarah's edging her way toward the front door. "I guess so, but I promise it'll be better next time."

"As I said, I'm not here for the orgasms." She gives me a tight smile. "You delivered what you promised, and that's the main thing." She tugs her purse straps over her shoulder.

Pressing my hand to her lower back, I guide her to the door. I'd dearly love to guide her back upstairs where I can show her I'm not a thirty-second lover. That I know how to please a woman, but I know she won't stay. I'll have to show her next time. "Let me know you got home safely."

She nods. "Well, anyway. Bye. Thanks again." She leans forward to peck my cheek and scurries toward the street and her car before I can respond. My lips tip up at the fact she laid a kiss on me … *willingly*.

CHAPTER 27

*sarah*

WHAT A DISASTER! WELL, NOT A COMPLETE DISASTER. I *DO* HAVE HIS semen inside me.

I climb into my car and pull onto the street, drive for a bit until I'm far enough away from AJ's place, and then pull over. Tears burst from my eyes and I drop my head into my hands.

That was the most difficult thing I've ever done and he probably thinks I'm some frigid touch-phobic crazy woman. My phone lights up on the passenger seat, Em's name on the screen. I press the green button because I selfishly need my sister right now.

"Em," I sob.

"What's wrong? Where are you? What happened? Why are you crying?" Her questions tumble out one after the other.

"We h-h-had s-s-ex, and it was awful, and now I'm a mess and I'm parked on the side of the road!"

"Sheet! Can you get home safely? I'll come to you." I nod, the tears streaming down my cheeks. "Sare? Can you get home?"

"Y-yeah."

"Okay. I'm on my way." She disconnects the call and I wipe my eyes and draw in some measured breaths.

I go to pull back onto the street when a horn blares and I slam my foot on the break—my heart pounds and my hands shake. "Shit! That was close." I pause and make sure I'm focused, then double-check the street is clear so I can pull out. Keeping my eyes trained on the road, I drive home cautiously, park, and make my way up to my apartment.

When I get inside, I drop my purse and head straight to the bathroom. Switching on the light, I step in front of the mirror and cringe at my swollen eyes, red nose, and blotchy cheeks. I wash my face, splashing cold water on it repeatedly, hoping it calms down before Em arrives. When I look up to check, my eyes catch on my sister leaning against the doorframe, a startled yelp escapes and I jump a little. I wasn't expecting her so soon. She must have walked straight out the door after our call. Her eyes are full of worry and I break down crying again, so I cover my face with my hands.

"Oh, Sare." Her arms wrap around me and she pulls me in tight and strokes my back soothingly. She's always taken her role as big sister seriously. Once I catch my breath, she leads me through to my bedroom. "How about you get changed? I'll make us some hot chocolate and we'll meet on the couch."

I nod. "Thanks."

We separate and a few minutes later I'm flopping onto my couch. Emma places two cups of hot chocolate on the table, then pulls my phone out of her pocket to hand it to me. "It's been buzzing. It's him."

I take it from her like it's a ticking time bomb. "He wanted me to let him know I got home safely."

"Well, you should let him know you're home." She sips her drink, watching me over the rim of her cup.

Glancing at my phone, I find three text messages.

> AJ
>
> Are you home safe?
>
> Sarah?
>
> I'll come over there if you don't answer me

Shit! That's all I need. I don't want him to see me like this, so I quickly respond.

> ME
>
> I'm home safe. You don't need to come here

> AJ
>
> You're lucky, I was about to walk out the door
>
> Are you okay?

> ME
>
> I'm fine. Thanks for tonight

I promise next time will be better

Ugh! Tonight was crappy because of me. Nothing he did. I can't even think about next time.

ME

We got the job done. That's what's important

I tuck the phone between the cushion and the arm while Em waits patiently for me to spill. I take a sip of my drink and try desperately to gather my thoughts.

"So you had sex with AJ?" she says slowly and I nod. "And it was terrible?" She widens her eyes and raises her eyebrows. I nod again. "What was so terrible about it?"

Where do I start? How do I explain?

"Talk to me, Sis."

I blow out a breath and start from our two months of failed attempts and AJ's suggestion that we try having *actual* sex.

"Oh no."

"Yeah. You know that's not gonna end well for me, Em. I already liked him more than I'm supposed to—"

"What do you mean…?" she asks gently.

"Well, he offered to be my donor, not my lover, not my boyfriend, not my life partner. And … and he told me he's met someone he really likes. How's that gonna work?"

"Oh, Sare."

Tears trickle down my cheeks. "It's so not fair. Why couldn't I have met him without all this donor stuff between us? He's perfect in every way." My tears increase and my sister becomes blurry.

I feel the couch move as she shuffles closer and wraps her arm around my shoulder. "Sometimes we don't get to choose when we get to meet our person. Sometimes it happens unexpectedly. You can't plan everything, you know that, right?"

I tip my head back and blow out a breath. "I know."

"What was so bad about the sex, apart from knowing he likes someone else?"

How do I explain the disaster to my sister? "Just to be clear, I find everything about AJ sexy." She nods. "And I'm desperately trying to not fall in love with him. Though, that's not working out so well for me."

"Mhm." She nods again.

"He kissed me, Em." She raises her eyebrows. "It was everything." The edges of her lips tip up. "Before I went there, I knew I was in trouble, but when he kissed me, I *knew* I was in trouble."

"Mhm."

"So, I refused to get naked and told him to keep his clothes on too. I figured if I had a physical barrier between us, it would help."

"Did it?"

"Not really. He took his shirt off."

"Oh my."

"Right? So there went that plan." I tell her how I held myself so stiff and still with my eyes and mouth squeezed shut tight to try and limit the overwhelming sensations. "I shut down so well that he had to use lube. Lube, Em!"

She squeezes me tight. "Oh, Sare."

Tears form again. "He wasn't going to go forward with the plan because he felt like he was forcing me. I convinced him and let him kiss me and worked on relaxing and engaged a little, but I had to focus on everything else, so I wouldn't come. I … I couldn't be that vulnerable with him, Em. Anyway, mercifully, it was all over and done with pretty quickly. I'm not sure I could have held out much longer. He felt amazing but I'm reasonably certain he thinks I hated every single moment of it." I sob. "Then he left me to do my thing and he ordered dessert! Dessert, Em. Who does that after the woman laid there like a dead fish? AJ does. Because he's so damn sweet. And now I can never see him again, which means my dream to become a mom is over!" Tears flood down my cheeks.

As I cry, Em tucks my head into her shoulder and strokes my hair while whispering soothing words like the amazing big sister she is. The silence is broken when Em's phone buzzes.

THEO

If he's hurt her, I'll grab Max and we'll pay the asshole a visit, just get his address from your sister

With wide eyes, I look up at Em. "Oh my God. I love your husband."

A slow smile spreads. "Me too." She looks at me. "He knew you were seeing AJ tonight because I told him earlier. Then when I called you, I told him I needed to get to you as I was grabbing my car keys because you were upset."

A giggle escapes which makes Em smile. "You can tell him he can put his white horse and sword away."

She chuckles as she texts him back.

THEO

Only if you're sure. I don't mind

Em shows me the screen before she responds, then tucks her phone away. "Now, what are you going to do? Because avoiding him isn't going to help you make your dream come true."

Sighing heavily, I comb my fingers through my hair. "I know."

"Maybe if you were honest with him about how you're feeling and your tendency to confuse sex with love it might help him to understand. He might surprise you."

"How awkward would that be? *Oh yeah, I know you're into someone but I'm into you. Oops.* Yeah. I don't think so."

"Hmmm, I guess so."

"I think I'm gonna have to skip the rest of our insemination plans this month and put some distance between us. I'll use the time to recalibrate and strengthen the walls around my heart. That should work."

Em nods thoughtfully. "I'm not convinced you can switch off your feelings like that, but it's worth a shot. Step away this month and see how you feel."

"Yeah. It's worth a shot." That's what I tell myself anyway.

"What are you gonna tell him?" I frown at Emma. "He'll need a damn good reason from you for not following through this month. You'll need to be convincing."

"Hmmm, true." I think for a moment, running through different scenarios. "I've got it." I go on to explain my plan.

Em looks impressed. "That should work."

"I'll text him tomorrow." We spend a little more time talking about the kids and then she leaves to head home to her hunky Greek husband and gorgeous kids. Sigh. One day, that'll be me. Well, the gorgeous kid, singular, and not the hunky Greek husband either.

# CHAPTER 28

## —*aj*—

I HOLD MY PHONE AWAY FROM MY EAR. THIS HAS BECOME MY REGULAR Friday morning, listening to my grandfather dictate my future with no regard for what I want. Or that we live in the twenty-first century where women run corporations all the damn time. A text lights up the screen.

> **CUPCAKE**
>
> I just found out I have to go to a conference
>
> Flying out this afternoon
>
> Won't be back until Wednesday. Raincheck?

I frown at the screen, my eyes narrowing. *What?*

"Grandfather. I need to go." I disconnect the call without waiting for a response and read Sarah's message again. My gut tells me this is a ruse. That she's not really going anywhere. That she's building her damn fortress after last night. Dylan's not here today, so I can't get his take on this latest development.

> **ME**
>
> Tell me where. I can book a ticket and meet you. I can work from anywhere while you're at the conference and we can work on your pregnancy plan at night

I press send, satisfaction filling my chest. Let's see what she comes back with. I stare at my phone, waiting for her response. Tapping my fingers on my desk, my phone remains dark. I push away from my desk and head upstairs to my deck for some fresh air while I wait for her answer. An hour later and I still haven't heard from her. I could hack into the airline servers to find her and meet her at her conference, but I feel like that's maybe taking things too far. Not to mention, if I get caught hacking into airline servers, which is highly likely, I'll probably end up behind bars, which doesn't suit my plans.

Finally, my phone buzzes.

CUPCAKE

You don't have to do that. You've already been so generous plus I'm away for work and I like to be professional

There are social expectations for the evenings anyway

See you in a month *smiling emoji*

*What the hell?* If she thinks she won't be seeing me between now and her next ovulation cycle, she's sorely mistaken. For one, I wouldn't be able to survive that long without seeing her. And two, she's not going to get rid of me that easily.

ME

No

CUPCAKE

What do you mean ... no?

ME

I mean I won't see you in a month. I'll see you when you get back from your work thing

CUPCAKE

There's no need. Spend the time with your new lady

My heart spasms. That damn mistake is going to keep biting me in the ass. After a few minutes, I reluctantly text back in defeat.

ME

Okay

CUPCAKE

Great. Good luck with your lady

ME

Thanks. I'm gonna need it

CUPCAKE

Nah. She'll love you

Well shit! If only she did.

ME

I'm not so sure about that

CUPCAKE

Sure she will. What's not to love?

Apparently, my semen is the only lovable part of me.

CUPCAKE

Sorry, gotta go

I can't shake the feeling she isn't going anywhere, that she's making an excuse to avoid me. I know my performance was shit last night, but I know I can do better. I've never, in my life, since becoming sexually active, left my lover unsatisfied. Last night was an anomaly and I want the chance to show her what it would be like between us if she just let down those damn walls of hers.

Standing outside the hospital doors, I'm trying my best to appear casual—I'm anything but. My pulse pounds in my ears as I repeatedly swallow the excess saliva being produced by my nerves. The more I thought about Sarah's sudden need to attend a conference, the more my gut told me she was putting up her walls again. So here I am, leaning against the garden wall opposite the doors to the maternity wing of the hospital. I know this is her Saturday to volunteer. Glancing down at my phone, I check the time. She should be out in another ten minutes. I got here early to ensure I didn't miss her. I can't wait to see her face and hear her excuses.

My phone lights up as I'm about to put it away.

HAYLEY

Hey, when are you bringing Sarah around again?

ME

I don't know. I'm working on it

HAYLEY

Well, don't take too long. Colton loved her

ME

He's not the only one

HAYLEY

Oh, do tell, little brother *winking emoji*

ME

Next time we catch up

HAYLEY

Okay. Have you heard from Grandfather?

I roll my eyes.

ME

Only every single Friday for the past year

HAYLEY

I'm sorry you have to deal with him

ME

Me too, but I'd rather take his anger than you or Mom having to deal with it

HAYLEY

Love you xx

ME

Love you too xx Give Colton and Lisa a hug from me

See you soon

HAYLEY

I will

I tuck my phone in my pocket and when I look up, my eyes instantly lock on Sarah. I feel vindicated that my gut was right, but I'm also devastated she felt the need to go to these lengths to avoid me. She hasn't noticed me yet because she's busy waving goodbye with a wide smile to the staff. Her gorgeous eyes are probably sparkling with happiness like they always do whenever she talks about her time cuddling the babies.

She pulls her purse strap higher over her shoulder and as she steps through the doors, she looks up. Her ever-changing eyes land on me and she freezes. The glass doors are stuck open because she's rooted to the spot in front of the sensor.

I step forward. "Sarah." She swallows but still doesn't move. "How's the conference going, Cupcake?" I take her hand in mine, linking our fingers together. "I think we need to talk."

She blinks at me and nods slowly. I tug on her hand gently, encouraging her to move out of the doorway and she comes with me. Without words, I guide her to my Jeep, open the passenger door and help her inside, ensuring she's safe by engaging the seatbelt. I climb in and start the engine.

"My car," she says vacantly as we pass it on the way out of the parking lot.

"It'll be okay here. We'll come back later and collect it."

She nods and we make the drive toward *The Riverside Café* through Saturday morning traffic in silence. Mom and Dad used to bring Hayley and me here now and then. It's one of the best places in the city to enjoy brunch while relaxing by the river. I thought it would be the perfect place to chat, so I booked a table.

"I'm sorry," Sarah whispers and I nod to let her know I heard her apology, but keep my eyes forward.

I pull the Jeep into the parking lot and climb out of the car. Sarah opens her door before I can make it around to her side. Linking my fingers through hers, we make our way inside the busy café and are promptly escorted to a table with the perfect view. We place our order and the waitress leaves us alone. Sarah fidgets in her seat, glancing around the café and out of the windows which overlook the river where several kayakers are paddling, avoiding my gaze at all costs.

She's not going to talk, so I draw in a breath, gather my thoughts, and start. I need to be soft with her. There's no point showing her how upset and hurt I am because she'll clam up. "Want to talk about it?"

Her eyes drop to the table where she's tracing the wood-grain pattern. "I needed some space."

I nod. "I figured as much."

"How did you know?" She finally looks at me, her eyes wary.

I reach across the table and take her hand, linking my fingers through hers. Her touch settles me somewhat. "I know you. Well, the parts you let me see and the parts I've observed." She nods. "Talk to me, Cupcake."

She slumps and blows out a breath as she glances out across the river. Keeping her head turned away from me. I decide it's best if I wait her out. "I ... I don't know where to start."

The waitress delivers our food and I release Sarah's hand so she can eat. She looks down at her plate but makes no move to pick up her cutlery. "Eat," I point to her food with my fork. We're quiet for a few minutes. She needs the time to gather her thoughts and I need to give her that even though every cell in my body is demanding answers. My need to understand wins out.

"Can you explain why you felt the need to lie to me?"

"I needed the space. It's a little embarrassing," she mumbles the last part as she scrunches up her face adorably.

"You don't need to be embarrassed with me. I won't judge you."

She's quiet for long moments and then she huffs, sadness oozing from her. "The thing is, I've broken our agreement. I know our arrangement is only meant to involve you being my donor to get me pregnant, but I've grown to like you." Well, this is a step forward. I work to keep my expression blank because I want her to keep talking. My eyes drop to her throat as she swallows. "I like you more than I should and there's something else," she rushes to add, so I nod for her to continue. She swallows again and licks her lips. The lips I want to taste properly; take my time with and devour repeatedly. I watch her closely as she drops her eyes to the table. "I ... uh ... have a habit of confusing sex with love," she whispers in a rush. I'm pretty sure my eyebrows jump to my hairline. "So you can see my dilemma. Especially now you have someone you're interested in pursuing."

"You're going to need to explain this dilemma to me, Sarah. Because I don't see the problem here."

"What don't you understand? I've fallen for you and you've fallen for someone else," she huffs, hiding her eyes from me.

I collect her hand in mine and squeeze lightly, taking a moment to absorb her confession, which was completely unexpected. "Cupcake, can you please look at me?" I wait for what seems an eternity, while my heart tries to beat its way out of my chest, for her eyes to meet mine. "The woman I said I was interested in ... she's you." Sarah's eyes widen. "I too have a confession. You see, I've also broken our agreement and fallen for you. As much as I want to help you get pregnant, each month that we've been unsuccessful I've been grateful I get to spend another month with you. I know it makes me an asshole, but I'm being honest with you here."

She smiles and blows out a breath, then proceeds to start chuckling. Slowly at first, then her chuckles turn into full-blown laughter. "Oh my God. What a pair we are."

It's amazing to see her demeanor change so drastically. She's always been so confident, but it was missing on Thursday night and this morning. At least now, I sort of understand these walls she's been working hard to keep in place. "So where do we go from here?" I ask.

She shrugs. "I don't know."

She's still holding back. Even though she knows I've fallen for her, she's still closed. "Would there be anything wrong with us seeing where this leads? I want to be with you." I can't be any clearer about my intentions.

"Uhm, I still want to have a baby. It doesn't seem like the best way to start a relationship."

I shrug. "It's worked for us so far. It may not be the norm, but who says we have to follow society's expectations? So what if that's how we start out? Why can't we do things the way that works for us?"

"I guess so."

She's not convinced. "What else is holding you back, Sarah?"

Creases form between her sculpted brows and I lean forward to stroke my finger over them, wanting to erase her concerns. If only it was as easy as erasing some creases.

"What makes you think something else is holding me back?" She swallows. Awkwardness has replaced the lightness which was there mere moments ago.

I tilt my lips up slightly. "As I said before. I've gotten to know you a little. I've felt the more time we've spent together, the higher you've built your walls. And even now that we both know we've fallen for each other, you're still throwing up barriers. I can sense them." She nods slowly, her eyes tracking around my face. I can see a war going on inside her; she's not sure if she wants to open up completely yet. "Come on. Let's lay it all on the table, so to speak. Then we can move forward."

She studies me closely as if trying to work out if I'm genuine. She must see what she needs. "If I'm going to be completely honest with you, my priority is starting my own family. I'm happy to do it on my own because it's not guaranteed the father will stick around. The number of relationships that fail outnumber the relationships that work and I'll need to make my child my number one priority. Their safety, happiness, and well-being are what will be most important to me and I can't risk starting a relationship only for it to fail."

Woah. I didn't realize her views on love and relationships were so negative. There's a lot of love in her family, so I'm not sure where this is coming from. "No relationship is guaranteed. You know that, right?"

I watch her cement another brick back in place. "Yeah, I know. I've watched more relationships fall apart than stay together. It's made me wary, I guess."

I frown. "But your parents are happily married, and so are your brother and sister." I don't get it.

"Yeah, but Em's first marriage fell apart. They had two kids together and that wasn't enough to make Preston stay. My ex, Michael, chose a promotion over our relationship and we'd been together since high school. Mel's dad walked out on them when she was five. Men don't stick around. Not generally."

And now we're finally at the crux of the issue. I choose my words carefully. "I understand what you're saying. I've also witnessed many failed marriages and I honestly wouldn't say my parent's marriage is a great example either. But when I say no relationship is guaranteed, those words are true to some extent. However, there are things that couples can put in place to ensure they have a better chance at success. Couples need to *choose* each other every single day. It must be a decision each and every day to stay with your partner, to show them how much you love them, appreciate them, and adore them. It's not always going to be easy and as I said, I, like you, have been witness to marriages and relationships falling apart. But when I think about them, when I pick apart their relationship, I don't think they chose each other every single day."

Sarah nods and after a long moment, she finally responds. "I guess so. That makes sense."

"I'm asking for a chance, Cupcake. Let me adore you." I hold out my hand, hoping she'll take it.

"You don't think it's too much that at the beginning of our relationship, I'm trying to have a baby?" she asks, still unsure.

"*We're*"—I widen my eyes and wave between us—"trying to have a baby, and no I don't." She still looks uncertain. "Share the day with me. Let's have some fun and spend time together that's not about getting pregnant, but just hanging out." I lift my eyebrows with a hopeful expression still waiting for her to place her hand in mine.

Her lips tip up at the corners and she begins to nod meekly, gradually increasing in confidence. "Okay." She finally places her hand in mine and I feel as though I've cracked the greatest firewall on the planet.

"Okay?"

She giggles. "Yeah, okay."

I throw my fist into the air. "All right!" I lean across the table and plant a light kiss on her smiling lips. "Let's get outta here!"

I pay for our meals, keeping Sarah's hand in mine. Not far from the café is a guy renting side-by-side tandem bikes, so I drag Sarah across to him. She giggles the entire way, making me feel lighter than I have in months. "Let's go for a ride."

She points to the yellow one. "On that?"

"Yeah. It'll be fun." I sign my life away, then hand over my credit card and we're free to climb onto the bright yellow bike with a white and yellow striped canopy. It's a gorgeous day, the ideal temperature, with the sun shining down on us. It's like today knows this is a new beginning for us; the start of something beautiful.

As we ride along, we take turns pointing out pelicans and various other birds soaring above the river or floating on its shimmering surface. Sarah shares her easy smiles with me and my mood soars with the birds. The breeze has caused some strands of hair to come loose from Sarah's ponytail and she's battling to keep them out of her face as her eyes sparkle in the sunshine.

She looks beautiful. I've thought she was beautiful from the get-go, but today, there's a lightness about her that's been missing. The weight of her self-imposed safety net has been lifted and she's more carefree than I've ever seen her.

With our legs working together, I take her hand and rest it on my thigh, keeping mine on top to hold hers in place. I like this. The simplicity of spending this time with her without any pressures or worries. I like it a lot. It gives me a glimpse into our future. I only hope Sarah's seeing the same as me.

"This is fun," Sarah says simply, mirroring my thoughts. "I should bring the kids down here and do this with them. They'd really like it."

"We should make a day of it and include Colton, too."

"Definitely."

Our designated time is almost up, so we make our way back to the bike rental place to hand over the bike. Heading back to the parking lot, holding my girl's hand in mine, I tug her around to face me once we arrive at my Jeep. I glance between her eyes, which are bright like springtime grass, and her mouth. She licks her lips and I move in slowly, waiting for her to pull away once she reads my intention, but she moves forward, meeting me halfway. My hope soars that this is the beginning of our forever.

Her warm breath brushes over my lips as we make first contact, my heart beating a heavy rhythm, and my breaths seizing in my lungs. Under the bright, warm sun, with the breeze blowing at my back, I kiss Sarah the way I've wanted to since the night I met her. I bring my hand up to cup her face with reverence, while I wrap my other around her waist, tugging her body snugly against mine. Her soft curves press against my hard muscle like we were always meant to be together in this way. One pass, then two, my tongue darts out for a taste; teasing and tempting. Delicious. My cupcake sighs against me and I take the opportunity to slide my tongue inside against hers. Blood rushes in my ears and to my cock. Sarah presses tighter against me, her fingers sliding into my hair as I deepen the kiss, trying to reach all the way to her soul. I need her to feel my unfettered desire for her, to understand how much I want her. That this kiss isn't about anything other than enjoying her, connecting with her, appreciating her. As our tongues tangle and explore, our bodies pressed tight, and our hearts pound in a rapid rhythm against the other.

"Yeah, baby! Stick it to her!" shouted from a passing car rudely tearing us apart.

I chuckle as I press my forehead to Sarah's, taking pride in the fierce flush on her face. "Sorry, I got carried away." I press a light kiss to her lips. "Actually, I'm all about honesty today. I'm not sorry I got carried away, at all."

Sarah chuckles, her body shaking against mine. "If I'm being honest, I'm not sorry either."

# CHAPTER 29

## —sarah—

AJ'S PHONE BUZZES AND WHEN HE ANSWERS IT, THE VOICE ON THE other end sounds panicked. He listens for a moment, then responds, "We're on our way." He tucks his phone away. "That was Hayley. Lisa's parents have been in an accident and are being taken to the hospital. I need to pick up Colton."

My heart races. "Of course."

He links his hand with mine and quickly helps me inside his Jeep and we head to the hospital. The cab is silent, filled with tension as AJ navigates early Saturday afternoon traffic through the city. Even though he's clearly upset and in a hurry to get to his sister and her family, he drives cautiously.

I lay my hand on his thigh. "I'm sure they'll be okay." I know they're empty words because I have no idea how serious the accident was, but I need to offer some comfort.

He glances at me, his jaw tight. "They're good people, so I hope they are."

We pull into the parking lot and we spot Hayley and Colton straight away. AJ parks and we both jump out quickly. Colton leaps for AJ as soon as he's close enough, with Hayley close behind. "Unca AJ!"

"Hey, little man." His voice is calm as he lands a kiss on Colton's nose. That's something I've noticed about AJ; he seems to keep his cool.

While they're busy, I hug Hayley. "Hey. You okay?"

"Yeah. I'm worried about Lisa. She was really upset. They're a close family, and she's an only child."

I nod. "Hopefully everything will be okay. Please tell her I'm thinking about her and her parents." Hayley nods gratefully, squeezing me close. "Is there anything you need? Anything I can do?"

"Thanks. I'll let you know if there's anything."

"Aunty Sarah!" Colton sings, reaching for me. I take him from AJ and he immediately wraps his little arms around my neck. I can't believe this is the same shy boy I met three weeks ago.

"Hey, little man." I squeeze him close and step away from AJ and Hayley so they can talk without little ears. "You're so lucky, you get to hang out with your uncle."

"Yeah." His cheeks split in a wide grin. "And you, too."

"Yeah, and me too." I smile at him, jigging him in my arms. I tell him all about our bike ride along the river and promise that we'll take him one day.

Colton's booster seat is switched to AJ's Jeep and his backpack is placed on the back seat. Hayley hugs and kisses Colton goodbye, then disappears into the hospital, leaving us in the parking lot. We work quickly to situate Colton in his booster seat, and I kiss him goodbye.

His bottom lip trembles. "I want to play with you."

Glancing over the door to AJ, he shrugs. "How about you come back to my place? We can order pizza for—"

"Yay, pizza!" Colton shouts.

AJ and I chuckle. "Dinner and hang out," AJ finishes.

"Please, Aunty Sarah," Colton pleads with puppy dog eyes and it's impossible to refuse his cute little face.

"Okay. But I'll follow you." I thumb over my shoulder toward my car on the opposite side of the lot.

"All right. See you at home," AJ whispers. Pulling me in close he drags his bristly cheek along mine to plant a kiss on my lips. His body presses against mine, reminding me of our kiss earlier, but this time we have little eyes watching, so I pull away.

I follow behind the guys, with Colton waving to me every so often, and when we pull up to AJ's home, he opens a garage door that has space for two cars. He points at the space, indicating I should park inside, so I do. While AJ's helping Colton out of his booster seat, I grab his backpack and we head inside with Colton holding my hand. It's hard not to skip ahead into the future and imagine us coming home from a day out as a family.

Geez, he kissed me and I already have our future mapped out. *Slow down, girl!*

AJ hands Colton his backpack. "How about you take this upstairs to your bedroom?"

He has his own bedroom here? I shouldn't be surprised since they're so close.

"Okay." Colton grabs the bag and heads upstairs.

"I usually have Colton overnight once a month to give Hayley and Lisa a break," he explains. "Though, it's probably been closer to six weeks since he's been here. I'm not sure how that happened." I can see AJ working through his memory trying to figure out why it's been so long.

He sets about washing his hands and preparing a healthy snack for his nephew, then rolls a cart full of Duplo blocks, books, and toys out from beneath the stairs. It's only now I notice there are several cupboards, each of which must pull out. What an ingenious use of space.

We spend the afternoon creating questionable buildings, reading stories, and playing hide and seek with Colton, who obviously adores his uncle. AJ's a natural with him. They share a level of comfort that is plain to see. Being fortunate enough to spend this time with them is giving me an insight into AJ as a father and my heart skips as I watch him with his nephew; he's going to make a great dad one day. Perhaps to a child we create together if what he confessed is true. I squeal a little on the inside as I think back to earlier. It was scary to open up to him and share my honest thoughts and feelings, but he didn't balk at all. He was open and willing to lay my fears to rest.

"Okay, little man. Time for me to order our pizza. Shall I get our usual?"

"Yeah!" Colton shouts excitedly.

"I should go and let you guys enjoy your evening."

"No, have pizza with us." Colton grips my hand, preventing my retreat and I glance up at AJ.

"Stay. Eat with us. Once he's in bed, we can take up where we left off earlier." He winks. Now that's an invitation too good to refuse. How things have changed in less than forty-eight hours.

I glance between the two and relent. "Okay."

Colton cheers loudly, jumping around the room as though his favorite TV characters have stopped in for a visit.

"What pizza do you like? We usually have Hawaiian because Colton loves picking off the pineapple."

"I love anything. But I especially love Hawaiian pizza. You might want to order double pineapple." I giggle.

AJ pulls me in close, his sexy scent surrounding me and sending my senses haywire. "You're made for me, Cupcake," he whispers and I chuckle. I guess he's happy I like pineapple on my pizza.

AJ makes the call to order the pizza, and we continue to play while we wait for it to be delivered. As soon as it arrives, we wash up for dinner and dig in.

"This is great. I have to admit, it's been a long time since I've indulged in pizza."

"Me too," says Colton, and I chuckle because he sounded like an old man.

The evening moves swiftly once dinner is finished and Colton's bathed and tucked into bed after two stories and several hugs, leaving AJ and me to our night. Anticipation for what's to come fills my body and the ache that AJ stoked in me earlier today, returns. I make a bathroom stop and when I return downstairs, soft music is playing over the speakers and the lights have been dimmed. AJ waits for me in the middle of his living room with his hand outstretched. Butterflies erupt in my stomach as I step toward him, appreciating his masculinity. He gives me one of his signature smiles and tugs me into him the second my hand connects with his, holding it between our bodies.

We dance to the soft music, his other hand on my ass, holding me firmly to him and scorching my skin through the flimsy fabric of my dress. "Thanks for helping me with Colton," he whispers against my ear, sending goosebumps cascading over my skin. I wrap my free hand around the back of his neck, sifting the soft strands at his nape through my fingers.

"You didn't need my help. It was so sweet watching you guys together. He idolizes you." AJ's warm breath coats the side of my neck with his chuckle.

"I idolize him too. He's such a smart kid." I nod in agreement, then rest my head on AJ's chest.

This is nice. Moving slowly together without an agenda and enjoying the moment rather than planning everything down to the smallest detail. Soft lips press against my temple and I breathe deeply, taking in AJ's addictive scent. His strong heartbeat increases in tempo and his hand glides up my spine to grasp the back of my neck. His grip is sure as he tugs my head back, our eyes instantly finding each other in the dim light. It's hard to tell, but I'm certain his pupils are dilated to match mine. The ache from before has returned in full force now, and I desperately want him to kiss me.

To touch me.

To make me his.

Everything falls away as we both move forward to meet midway.

The first press of his warm lips against the corner of my mouth has a sigh escaping.

The gentle swipe of his tongue across the soft pillows of my lips has me sinking into him.

His breath blending with mine has me opening to him eagerly.

He draws my bottom lip between his, then pulls away, returning moments later to tease me again. Finally, he delves his tongue into my mouth and we explore and taste, tempt and tease as I press into AJ's firm body, ensuring every inch of me is touching every inch of him. His hard cock presses against my soft stomach, promising things yet to come. I slide my other hand around AJ's torso, grasping the back of his T-shirt, then drag my short nails down the planes of his back. Our kiss deepens, heightening my senses and making my skin acutely sensitive to his roaming touch. Having his hands on me and being able to fully enjoy the experience is unreal and I relax.

Relax into AJ, into this moment, into his kiss.

He pulls away and places teasing kisses, biting my bottom lip before returning to a full-on assault. My temperature rises and my breaths are becoming labored, yet I need more. I need to feel his skin. Sliding my hands down his trim body, I locate the bottom of his T-shirt and slide my fingers beneath the fabric, making contact with his heated flesh. He moans and goosebumps erupt beneath my touch.

"Cupcake," he whispers against my lips with a pant, his eyes heavy with need. "I want you so bad."

"Me too." Our lips connect again, deeper, more insatiable. Months of built-up desire finally have an outlet. AJ smooths his hand up my back, twisting in my hair and tugging the strands, sending fire licking through my scalp. "Mmm," I moan into his mouth. He presses his impressive cock deeper into my stomach, making my clit pulse and I grasp the sides of his T-shirt to hold him to me.

He pulls his lips away, his eyes locked on mine as he slides his hands down my arms to collect both of my hands in his. "Let's take this upstairs."

I nod and follow him willingly—quite the turnabout from Thursday night. Was that only two nights ago? And while this may seem sudden, it's been a long time coming. After many self-induced orgasms to thoughts of the man currently leading me into his bedroom, I'm going to finally get to experience him firsthand. Thursday doesn't count because I was doing my best *not* to enjoy our time together—one of the most difficult things I've ever done. My nerves shoot through the roof when I finally realize the reality of what we're about to do.

I'm going to have sex with AJ.

For real.

And not because I'm trying to get pregnant—though, that would be a great side-benefit—but because we're hot for each other.

He closes the bedroom door and immediately pushes me up against it, where we resume our kiss. Our hands explore, gliding beneath fabric and roaming over heated flesh. His kisses make me dizzy with lust and I'm certain my panties are drenched. He slides his thigh between my legs and I use it to quell the ache in my pussy. His fingers trace their way up the zipper of my dress and he tugs the slider slowly downward, loosening the fabric. The straps fall from my shoulders, exposing the tops of my aching breasts. His eyes drop, quickly followed by his head as he kisses each mound in turn; lavishing my sensitive flesh with much-needed attention. I push my chest forward and his hands come up to cup each breast firmly, pushing them into his mouth.

"God, I love your body," he moans, laying kisses across from one boob to the other. "Every single curve and dip. And I plan to explore them all tonight." I sigh, holding his head to my heaving breast. His mouth feels amazing, the softness of his lips so different from the roughness of his end-of-day scruff. His tongue darts out, blazing a path across my flesh and I shiver. I wonder if I could come from this? His eyes dance up to mine from his position, and he gives me a devilish smirk as his thumbs rub back and forth across my peaked nipples. He knows exactly what he's doing to me as I grind down on his thigh again.

Raising his hands, he kisses each shoulder softly as he slides the straps of my dress down my arms, making the fabric fall to the floor, leaving me in my matching lace teal panties and bra. I thank the heavens above I wore my matching set this morning. I was feeling low, so I thought I'd wear my best underwear to improve my mood. It always works. Sexy underwear beneath my clothes will always give me the lift I need.

He takes a step back, breathing heavily while his eyes scorch a trail over every inch of my body. I'm on the curvier side, but unlike Emma who was always self-conscious of her curves, especially after Preston's constant put-downs, I'm proud of my shape. It's feminine and sexy. AJ bends his knees and tips his head back with a groan, then drops his eyes back to me.

"Fucking stunning. I knew you would be and when I saw you in your bikini, it only confirmed what I already knew to be true. I can't believe how lucky I am to have you standing in my bedroom like this." With the tip of his finger, he tilts my chin up and takes my lips in a searing kiss I feel all the way to the tips of my toes. I press up and wrap my arm around his neck, holding him in place while I devour him as much as he's devouring me. He walks backwards to the bed, his hands holding my wide hips, without breaking the seal of our lips.

Now that we've decided to try a relationship, I'm all in. I no longer need to fear the consequences of having sex with AJ, because I know we're on the same page. I *do* need to be careful not to blurt the 'L' word, though. That wouldn't be prudent the first time we have sex. *Really* have sex. I'm not counting Thursday night's fiasco. It's probably best to wipe that experience from the memory banks.

I feel the clasp of my bra release and the cups give way, so I scoot back and slide the bra from my arms. And yeah, the girls don't look so perky now because they're definitely on the voluptuous side, but I don't think AJ is going to complain about that with the way he's scooping them up and pressing them together. He nuzzles his face into my cleavage, then glances up at me with a sexy glint in his eyes. "I'm gonna fuck these beauties once you're filled with my cum." My entire body shivers.

*So hot!*

He lowers his mouth, taking one nipple inside and sucking—hard. It feels divine and a low moan escapes unbidden. He switches over, paying the same attention to my other nipple, while his fingers twist the nipple he just released, then he kisses his way down my soft stomach to my panties. Burying his nose in my pussy, he draws in a deep breath. "Mmhm." His tongue pokes out and he glides it around my clit through the lace. Unable to keep still, I squirm under his ministrations and drop my hands to his head as I press my pussy against his face. He kisses me thoroughly through the soaking lace, moaning with pleasure. He tucks his fingers into each side of my underwear and slides them down my legs, tapping each foot in turn so he can remove them completely. I'm totally and utterly bare to him, while he's still fully dressed.

So unfair.

"AJ," I murmur with a moan as his tongue circles my needy clit. My hands slide through the strands of his hair, pulling him away to allow me to see his eyes. "I need you naked, too," I pant.

He quickly stands and using one hand he drags his T-shirt over his head, discarding it carelessly to the floor. I reach forward to trace the trail of dark hair—so damn sexy—leading from his navel down to the waistband of his jeans and disappearing behind the denim. Unsnapping his button, I release his zipper, pushing his jeans past his hips. Gravity takes care of the rest for me, thank God. I press my hand against the significant bulge trapped behind his boxer briefs, noting the wet patch near the band. He groans at my touch and his cock throbs beneath my palm. When I seek out his eyes, they're half-mast, watching me rub his erection through the fabric. I drop my gaze down his strong thighs, appreciating the sheer masculinity of his form. He certainly is an impressive male specimen.

"Take it out, Cupcake." His voice is gruffer than I've ever heard and it sends heat flaring to my needy clit. I do as he asks, his briefs falling to the floor. He steps out of them while I wrap my hand around his hot length. Steel wrapped in velvet, the head red and throbbing, leaking precum. I drop to my knees so I can have my first taste. With the gentlest of touches, I touch the tip of my tongue to the very tip of his cock and it thumps against his defined abdomen. I swirl my tongue around the crown and then through the slit, ensuring I clean up every drop of his musky precum. He moans, sliding his fingers through my hair, but instead of holding me in place, as I anticipate, he pulls my head back roughly. "Nope. Every single drop of that needs to be inside your pussy, not down your throat." He tugs my hair. "Stand up and lie on the bed."

He helps me stand and while I position myself as he wants, I allow my eyes to roam his physique. "You have an amazing body, AJ." I glance up at his face to find his carnal gaze gliding over my curves.

"Ditto, Cupcake." I smile at his term of endearment. He strokes his cock several times, then climbs onto the bed between my legs, his muscles shifting and moving. "My turn for a taste."

He reaches for a pillow to prop under my ass, then pushes my legs wider apart, so I'm splayed open to his liking. His eyes drop to my pussy and his lips tip up in a delicious smile. "I've been waiting so long to do this," he whispers, then he dives in. Literally dives in, swiping his tongue up my seam without prelude. He's not messing around. My back arches and I suck in a sharp breath. He nips my clit and then repeats the process over and over. Each stroke is incrementally firmer than the last.

"Ohhhhh," I moan, my stomach muscles quivering.

He positions my legs over his shoulders, then his thumb connects with my clit and he draws tight circles around the bud as his tongue delves into my opening. I drop my arm over my mouth to stifle my cries. The last thing we need is to wake Colton and have him stroll in here wondering what's going on.

"Let go, Cupcake, give me your first one." He replaces his tongue with his capable fingers and rubs that magic spot inside of me, which sets off my body. Lights explode around my vision and my heart seems as though it wants to escape the confines of my chest with the way it's hammering against my ribs. My legs involuntarily tighten around his head and I'm worried I'm going to suffocate the poor guy. Death by oral fixation. *Ha!* No, that's not even funny, Sarah. I release my legs with a sigh as the tremors ease from my body, and a sense of satiation takes the place of the tight muscles from a moment ago.

## CHAPTER 30

*—aj—*

"Fucking stunning." I knew she would be. With flushed cheeks and her mouth dropped open in an O, she's so damn beautiful.

Keeping her legs draped over my shoulders, I slowly make my way up her body, kissing, nipping, and licking a path to her magnificent tits. Even though Sarah's voluptuous body shape is my ideal, I've never been fortunate enough to be with someone with her shape. It's like a playground designed just for me. Lavishing her breasts with the attention they deserve, I rub my bristly cheeks across them to add to the marks caused by my sucks and bites. When I shift back to study my handiwork, my inner caveman beats on his chest with pride. I line up my cock with her entrance and slowly slide inside her silken sheath.

Pure and utter decadence.

That's what this experience is. I groan as I bury myself to the hilt, pausing to absorb the moment.

Sarah moans and glides her fingers through my hair, gripping the strands and guiding my mouth up to hers. We hungrily connect, our tongues lashing against each other. She tilts her hips up. "Please move, AJ," she says with desperation.

With her legs over my shoulders, I slide out and back in slowly, teasing both of us to the brink. In this position, I can push in deep, which is perfect for what we're trying to achieve. With both of our bodies coated in a sheen of perspiration from our exertion, I change my position slightly to ensure I hit that special place inside. I wrap my arms around Sarah's shapely legs and draw out and then snap my hips back in, my eyes on her heavy tits as they move with the force of my thrust. Her back arches as her head tilts back with a low mewl and I repeat the action over and over until I'm not sure I can last much longer.

Sarah bites her bottom lip as our eyes remain connected, tethering us to each other. This is everything I've ever wanted with her. It's more than I ever imagined that night in the club.

Sarah's pussy walls tighten around my cock, and I almost see stars, pushing me closer to the point of no return. I refuse to come before her ever again so I use my thumb to circle her clit lightly, sending her flying. The top part of her body lifts off the bed, while high-pitched pants leave her gorgeous lips and her body shudders with her release. I lose my fight to hold on and it seems every cell in my body is focused to a singular point as my balls draw up tight and my release shoots into Sarah. I press my hips tight against her pelvis to ensure I'm as close to her cervix as possible, giving us the best chance of getting pregnant. We're each lost in our moment as we come together for the first time. It's a time I'll always remember because it means Sarah's finally dropped her defenses.

Keeping my dick inside Sarah's sweet pussy, I lower my head to take her lips in a slow, luxurious kiss. With panting breaths, our tongues slide against each other sensually, completing the intimate moment. I lower my chest to Sarah's, pressing every hot, sweaty inch together. Her heart hammers against my pecs and brings me a sense of satisfaction and pride I'm not sure I've felt before. It hasn't been easy getting Sarah to this point, but it was certainly worth every ounce of my patience. Slowing the kiss, I tease her lips with light pecks and nips, then pull back enough so I can scan her features. Flushed cheeks, a satiated grin, heavy lids, and sweaty hair indicate a job well done and I only hope I redeemed myself somewhat after Thursday's disaster.

Leaning closer, I rub my nose against Sarah's with affection and her lips widen as her arms wrap around my neck. "That was …"

"Incredible," I finish for her. "We were so in tune."

She nods, her eyes twinkling. "Yeah." The word almost comes out as a sigh.

Pushing up, I keep my cock inside as I rest my ass on my heels while Sarah's butt rests on the pillow and my thighs. I rearrange her legs, so I can hold them up against my chest, rubbing soothing strokes up and down her thighs. With her body elevated like this, I'm hoping my release can get to where it needs to go. My bedroom is silent since our breathing has returned to normal, neither of us feeling the need to fill it with noise. I'm happy to be in Sarah's company in silence, watching television, enjoying a meal, or defiling her body. As long as she allows me the privilege to be with her, I'm a happy man.

Sarah's shoulders shake. "You don't have to hold my legs up, you know."

"I know," I answer flippantly. "I like that I can do this for you. It gives me an excuse to keep touching you."

Sarah's body sinks further into the mattress. "You don't need an excuse," she whispers. "I'm pretty sure we're past all that now." Something inside me shifts with her words. A sense of relief fills the deepest parts of my body. Fuck, I hope we're past all of that. She wiggles her legs. "I think that's long enough. I carefully disengage from her and move out of the way to lay her legs down, then lie beside her so I can tug her in close and kiss her forehead. "Do you think it worked this time?" she asks, her voice small.

I move my head back slightly, so I can see her face better and gently stroke her hair away. "I hope so, but just in case, I think we should do it again." I nudge her with my hips. "I need a minute and then I'll be ready to go."

I feel her chuckle against my body, rather than hear it as she tucks her face into the crook of my neck. "Have I released a beast?" I glide my hand down the side of her body, following the dips, and make a path to her delicious ass, squeezing one lush cheek in my hand as I pull her forward to feel my growing erection. She throws her leg over my hip and her face snaps up to mine. "Oh."

I kiss the tip of her nose. "Yeah, 'oh.' Up on your hands and knees. You're gonna take it deep from behind, so I can watch my cock disappearing between these luscious ass cheeks of yours." I slap the cheek I was holding and then release her, so she can do as I said.

Sarah scampers to her hands and knees without question, her tits hanging low. They're gonna look fantastic swinging as I thrust into her from behind. I crawl in behind her and swipe my tongue from the top of her slit to her opening and press it inside. She tastes like a combination of me and her—my new favorite flavor. Sarah drops her head to the pillow with a gasp, drawing her pussy out of my reach, then looks over her shoulder at me, her eyes full of heat.

Gorgeous.

"Stay still." I grasp her hips firmly and pull her back to my face. Licking and stroking my tongue in and out of her soaked pussy; her legs quiver as she sighs, moans, and mewls. I love that she's not afraid to make a little noise as she pushes back into my face.

When her opening flutters around my tongue, I remove it and replace it with my cock in one hard thrust, pushing her up the bed. Sarah's back bows as she cries out. Her tits swing forward as I hoped they would. With my fingers digging harshly into her hips, I push in and draw out of her opening, each time going harder than the time before. She switches her hold, gaining better purchase on the head-board, her spine making a beautiful curve as I continue to fill her and retreat.

"That's it. Take my cock the way you were born to." The sound of skin slapping against skin and the view of my cock disappearing between her cheeks is erotic as hell and my cock swells and throbs, ready to release a second time. "Play with your clit, Cupcake," I demand between harsh pants, my voice low and gruff. The musky smell of sex fills the air as we both build closer to our release.

"Oh my God!" Sarah cries out, her back bowing while her walls strangle my dick. Working her through her orgasm, I incrementally slow my movements to prolong the experience. Reaching around, I grasp one of her tits, rolling her nipple between my fingers to heighten her orgasm. The rippling of her walls around my cock has me close to coming for the second time tonight, but I want to see if I can take her into another orgasm. Leaning over her body, I nibble on the lobe of her ear, then kiss my way down the column of her neck to suck on the pulse point, tasting the saltiness of her exertion while still holding my dick inside her body. I'm dying to come, barely balancing on the edge. Her breaths pick up again as I play with her nipple and suck on her neck, so I take that as a sign to start moving again. I rear up, balancing on my knees, and pull Sarah back on my cock.

"Use my dick, while I play with your pretty clit."

"I … I don't think I can come again," she whispers with a harsh pant.

"Of course you can. Ride my dick."

"Mmhm." She drops her head and pushes back, connecting her ass with my thighs, and slamming those delectable cheeks against me. Her cheeks jiggle as I massage her clit and grasp her tit. The sight is so fucking hot, my balls draw up tight to my body and that telltale tingle moves down my spine as what feels like electricity makes its way from my fingers and toes, through my limbs to my balls, and I shoot my load, my cum pulsing deep into Sarah's body.

Her walls flutter and contract around my dick with her orgasm, and we both moan in between panting breaths. "Fuuuck!" I grit my teeth and hold myself still, ensuring I spill every last drop inside her. I don't want to waste a single swimmer.

As sated as I feel right now, I know I'm going to need her again tonight. I'm never going to get enough of her.

Sarah flops forward onto her stomach, collapsing beneath me. I drop on top of her, keeping most of my weight on my arms, our sweaty bodies fighting to catch each breath. She must feel my heart hammering against her back as it fights to burst out of my body and climb into hers.

She chuckles. "Wow. I don't know why we didn't just start with that instead of my asinine approach to getting pregnant."

"I would have been on board with that." I kiss my way along her damp shoulder.

The shakes in her body increase and she turns her head to the side. "I'm sure you would have." The sparkle in her eyes is so damn sexy, I lean forward to take her lips in a fiery kiss, spearing my tongue inside. She welcomes me readily, giving me the same level of fire as I'm giving her.

I roll to the side taking Sarah with me, so she's tucked in as close as possible, and drag the covers over our cooling bodies. Our lips unite again and we lose ourselves in a lingering kiss; neither of us is in a hurry for it to end.

Eventually, we pull away and Sarah buries her face in the crook of my neck. "Thank you," she whispers, her hot breath brushing across my pec. She traces her finger around my nipple, causing it to bead, then leans forward to swipe it with her tongue.

I slide my fingers through the silky strands of her hair, a shiver racking my body. "Stop thanking me, Cupcake. We're in this together, both hoping and wishing for the same outcome." I use my fingers to gently guide her eyes to mine. "Okay?"

She nods slowly, a smile tipping up the corners of her mouth. "Okay."

And I feel as though I've demolished one of the most powerful firewalls on the planet. This is exactly what I was hoping for. My dream woman opening her heart to include me in her plans to have a family. A family we can make together. A family which will be happier than my own. The child we'll create will be allowed to be a child and have fun, just like Colton. Just like Kenny, Austin, and Lachlan.

# CHAPTER 31

## —sarah—

THE END OF THE MONTH IS ALWAYS BUSY. ERIC LIKES TO FINALIZE projects and insists on meeting with each staff member to ensure they're on target to achieve the company's short- and long-term goals, as well as to make sure everyone's still happy and experiencing job satisfaction. So work was crazy today and traffic coming home was even crazier. I close myself inside my apartment and blow out a breath as I lean back against the front door. A smile forms unbidden as I run my mind back over this past month. It's definitely been a whirlwind of emotions—from the lows of trying to keep my walls intact to the highs of letting AJ in. I still can't believe it.

I move further into my apartment, my smile widening when my eyes land on AJ's business shirt draped over the dining chair. Picking it up, I bring it to my nose to inhale his yummy scent, then run my fingers down the front, noting the missing buttons. When I saw him in his suit last night, I got carried away and tore his shirt away from his body in a bid to get him naked as quickly as possible. I felt it was only fair to offer to repair the damage.

My mind slides back to last night and the way he caressed my body, worshiping every single inch of me as though it would be the last time he got to put his hands on me. I rub my thighs together as the memories assault me and notice the wetness there. My heart drops to my toes and the lust I was feeling vanishes into thin air. Disappointment rushes in, filling every cell in my body. When I hadn't gotten my period by lunchtime today, I was … hopeful. God knows I've had enough sex this month that I should be pregnant. My eyes sting and as much as I blink to hold back the tears, they still fill my eyes and drop over my lashes. For fuck's sake, Sarah, don't be such a crybaby. Just because you want it to happen, doesn't mean it's going to happen on your timeline.

I drop AJ's shirt back onto the chair and semi-stomp my way into my bedroom to grab clean underwear and step into the bathroom. I may as well have a shower and get into my PJs. It's not like I'll be going anywhere tonight and I need to be comfortable. Standing under the warm stream of water, I permit myself to let go. With tears hidden by the spray, I rub soap across my stomach, wondering how I can feel as though I've lost something I've never had. Why do I feel so empty?

Maybe I'm not meant to be a mom? Maybe the universe is telling me I'd be terrible at it, so it's not giving me what I want? Maybe I'm not worthy? Maybe I've left it too late?

I stand under the spray until the water turns cold and then finally step out of the shower to dry off, feeling detached from my body. I work on autopilot as I dress and dry my hair. My mind remains blank and numbness settles over me. Grabbing what I need from the kitchen, I skip dinner and curl up in bed, hugging my pillow, tears soaking the fabric.

It's dark when I wake, and I immediately know I'm not alone.

"You okay?" My sister's voice whispers in the dark. With the light from the living room spilling into my bedroom, I can make out her silhouette but not the details of her face. But I don't need to see her face to feel her concern for me. The fact she's here, laying opposite me tells me everything.

"I got my period."

She lifts her hand and strokes my messy hair out of my face. "I'm sorry, Sare."

"Maybe the universe is telling me I'm not fit to be a mom," I murmur.

She blows out a breath. "To use your own words, that's the bullshit-tiest bullshit I've ever heard. You're gonna be a great mom." She kisses the top of my head. "The best."

I burst into tears at her heartfelt words, and I feel her move close, then her arms come around my body, tugging me in tight. I bury my face in her chest and let it all out. I'm not sure how long we lie together while I work to compose myself.

"How did you know to come over?"

"AJ called Theo when you wouldn't answer your phone or the door."

"Oh my God," I whisper.

"He's waiting on your couch."

"No."

I feel her head nod. "Yeah." She smooths her hand down my arm and squeezes my hand. "He's really worried about you."

I sit up, brush my hair away from my face, and lean over to turn on the lamp. Squinting in the brightness, I turn back to Emma. "I don't want him to see me like this."

She sits up, glancing over my shoulder as the bed dips behind me. AJ's scent surrounds me as his arm wraps around my middle and he pulls me back against his hard body. "Cupcake," he whispers, then places the softest of kisses on my shoulder. My lids drop closed with appreciation for his tenderness and I feel the bed move. When I open my eyes, Emma's standing.

"I'm gonna go and give you two some space. If you need anything, let me know, okay."

I nod, and as Emma passes by me, I reach out and grab her hand. "Thank you."

She bends down and kisses it. "Anytime." When she stands, she pats AJ on the shoulder. "Take care of her."

"I plan to." Em smiles and takes her leave. The front door opens and closes, leaving me alone with AJ. "Why didn't you call me, Cupcake?" I can't answer him, so I shrug. "We're in this together and I don't want you upset and alone. You fucking broke my heart when I saw you curled into a ball in the middle of your bed." He lands another gentle kiss on my shoulder and I shudder beneath his touch.

AJ moves into the middle of my bed and then pulls me into him until I'm cradled between his legs, facing him. He wraps his arms around me and I have no escape; not that I would want to leave the safe cocoon he's created for us. "I'm sorry." I drop my forehead to his chest in shame.

His arms tighten around me, banding around my middle and his hand strokes leisurely up and down my spine. I slide my arms around his waist, holding him close and we sit in silence. AJ kisses the top of my head now and then, reminding me he's here, and I soak in every touch, his warmth, every breath as it puffs across the top of my head, and every beat of his heart as it thumps against my cheek. He's quickly become my person.

"What time is it?" I ask without lifting my head from my favorite spot.

"After nine." His hand slides up my back, gripping the back of my neck. "Have you eaten?" I shake my head. "You need to eat. C'mon, I'll feed you."

I shake my head. "I don't wanna move." I band my arms tighter and a puff of air rushes across the top of my head from his chuckle.

"We can come back to bed once you're fed." He taps my ass and I grumble as I shuffle from his lap. He climbs off the bed and then helps me stand. "How're your cramps?"

I melt. Literally, melt. "They're not too bad. I took some Midol before."

He guides me to my couch and gently pushes me down, hands me my crochet and the remote for the TV, and leaves me with a kiss. I find the latest baking show and work on my latest project while he heats the dinner he brought with him. Once it's ready, he brings it over to the couch and we sit together to eat as though we've always been together. These last few weeks with AJ, since our relationship has moved from the donor/recipient mode to relationship mode, have given me an insight into my future with him. This thoughtful, kind, and caring man. The one that's put me and my needs first since we met. As usual, once we've finished, AJ cleans up, then returns to me. He props himself in the corner of the couch, then encourages me to sit so I'm leaning against him. His hand comes around the front of me, and he holds it on my stomach, his thumb rubbing back and forth in soothing strokes.

And I decide … *this is nice.*

Turning my head to the side, I press my lips to AJ's and he immediately returns my affection. His hand slides up my body to cup the front of my throat as we deepen our connection. The light pressure turns me on and I twist so I have better access. I moan when his hands cup and squeeze my ass, pressing me into him, his hard length unmissable. AJ uses his hold on my ass to rub my clit against his dick—it feels amazing and pressure quickly builds in my core.

"Are you gonna use my dick to make yourself come, Cupcake?" he whispers with harsh breaths against my ear. He drags his scruff down my neck and bites my collarbone, drawing a moan from me.

"Yeah," I tell him, softly. One hand slides inside my sleep shorts, heading straight for my clit and the move is enough to break the spell. Pulling my body away, I quickly sit back as though a bucket of iced water has been poured over me.

"What's wrong?"

*What's wrong?* I widen my eyes at him. "I have my period. You can't put your hands down there."

"Yes, I can. You know orgasms help with cramps, right?" He winks at me and shuffles closer and I shuffle back, but I can't go any further because the arm of the couch prevents my escape. "Don't be shy. Not with me."

"I've never done it before when I have my period. Isn't it messy?"

"Not as messy as you would think, but there are ways around it if you're interested." His expression is hopeful. Since we had sex the first time—for real—I haven't been able to get enough of him, nor him me. He must sense me wavering from my initial stance because he stands and holds his hand out to me. I slide my palm against his roughened fingers and he tugs me to my feet, presses a kiss to the corner of my mouth, then swipes his tongue across the seam. His hands come around me, linking behind me as he deepens the kiss. The man is a master kisser and he easily drags me out of my head and into the moment. My hands slide up his back, gaining purchase as I cup his shoulders, holding us together as he tangles his tongue with mine for long moments.

AJ slows the kiss and pulls away, stepping backward toward the bathroom, and tugging me with him. He strips out of his clothes and then helps me with mine. As he tucks his fingers into the waistband of my panties, I grasp his hands to stop him, imploring him to give me a moment. "Let me deal with this part, okay?"

He nods, then steps out of the bathroom in silence. I blow out a relieved breath that he let me do this part in private. I know it's silly since he's kissed and caressed every part of my body, but my head is overruling my lust. I take care of the tampon and start the water, then open the door. The sight that greets me has my lust returning like a tsunami. His hand is wrapped around his thick length, stroking it slowly. His breaths are choppy and his eyelids are at half-mast. A slow, devious smile tips his lips, creating those deep creases to bracket his mouth.

I reach out and drag him into me, wrapping my hand over his to help him work over his cock. His answering groan sends pulsing waves directly to my clit. Using my hold on his cock, I walk us backward and into the shower.

"Are you wet for me, Cupcake?" he whispers against my ear, his hot breath tickling my flesh and sending goosebumps radiating outward.

"Mmhm." I nod, biting my bottom lip in an attempt to be seductive.

He wastes no time pressing my back against the cold tile and dropping his mouth to my boob. He sucks the nipple into his warm mouth, swirling his tongue around the sensitive bud. I slide my fingers into his wet hair to hold him in place, while he lavishes attention on my breasts. I love having his attention on my boobs and he loves giving it. His hand slides up my thigh, tracing the crease where it meets my body toward my clit which is in desperate need of attention.

His kisses start moving lower, down over my soft stomach and the action jolts me out of the moment because I know exactly where he's heading. I'm not ready for it. This is already out of my comfort zone. I use my grip on his hair to stop him and he peers up at me, not removing his lips from my body. I shake my head, pleading with my eyes. "Please don't do that. I'm not ready." He must recognize my discomfort because he gives a simple nod and works his way back up to my breasts.

"Maybe another time." The relief filling me with his ready acceptance of my limits is instantaneous and I quickly drop back into the moment, knowing I'm always safe in his hands. He lifts his lips from my boob for a moment. "Spread your legs for me, Cupcake." Expecting me to do his bidding, he returns to his ministrations and I spread my legs. Closing my eyes, I lean my head back against the tile as his fingers connect with my sensitive bud, sending a shiver through my body. I can't hold back the moan his touch elicits. I feel his lips spread against my flesh and he increases the pressure of his touch, alternating between circling my clit and sliding his fingers through my pussy lips. He dips his fingers inside and I hold my breath as he fingers me with first one finger, then two. It feels unreal; more sensitive than usual.

"Mmhm. Don't stop. Please don't stop." I tighten my grip on his hair. My breaths are mere shallow pants and my heart pounds as though it's trying to escape its confines, my legs shake and my internal walls tighten around AJ's fingers—everything's happening at once, overwhelming me. "I'm so clo—aaaah!" I cry out, using my grip on his hair to pull him up to my mouth. I attack his lips with a fierceness that surprises me and as I come back into my body, I realize I've been holding his cock this entire time and haven't been paying it the attention it deserves.

After tearing my mouth away from AJ's, I smile at him. I'm sure it looks stupid because I'm drunk on my climax. With what I'm hoping is a sexy wink, I push him back and then switch positions so his back is against the same wall I was using to hold myself up. I kiss him again, then glide my hands down his ripped torso and drop to my knees on the hard tile, ensuring I keep my eyes locked on his.

His brows furrow and his Adam's apple bobs with his swallow. "Cupcake?"

I wink at him, then swallow his shaft in one long glide. "Oh, fuck!" He closes his eyes and drops his head back against the tile, and his Adam's apple bobs again. So sexy. I trace my finger down the trail of hair from his navel, around the base of his shaft, and cup his heavy sac. He won't let me do this to him during my ovulation period, using the excuse that he needs to save all his swimmers. Even when I'm not ovulating, he still won't let me do this. I'm surprised he's letting me suck him off now. "You're so good at sucking my cock." I moan around his shaft as I take it deep, massaging his balls. Slipping my finger back further, I locate his taint and rub it with tight circles. A long, low groan echoes in the shower stall and he drops his eyes to mine as he thrusts his hips gently. His nostrils flare as he watches his cock disappear into my mouth. "I don't want to cum down your sexy throat. I want to paint your tits."

Oh my God. His mouth is so damn hot. I swear he could talk me to an orgasm. My clit pulses and I double my efforts. AJ's hand tightens in my hair and his shaft pulses against my tongue. He drags my mouth from his dick, and I move back slightly, so he can cum over my breasts like he wants. A couple of firm strokes by his own hand and ribbons of cum shoot across my breasts. Using the palm of my hand, I spread his orgasm over my breasts, massaging them seductively, and AJ's eyes flare wide.

"Fuck, yeah! Spread my cum over those gorgeous tits." His voice is rough and raspy, and I happily oblige. He uses his grip on my hair to tug me to my feet, switching our positions again and pressing me against the tile. He dips his head and licks his cum from my breast and it's the dirtiest, most erotic thing I've ever seen. Pressing his semi-hard cock, which seems to be growing harder by the second, against my stomach, he moans against my breast and the vibrations echo through my body. Bending his knees, he notches the head of his cock against my entrance. "You ready for me, Cupcake?"

"Oh my God, y–" He thrusts into my body roughly before I can finish, stealing my breath. Our mouths lock, melding together as he builds a fast, rough rhythm. Fucking me into the tiled wall, our bodies slipping and sliding against each other. Sighs and moans echo off of the walls as the warm water cascades over us.

High-pitched moans escape each time AJ hits deep inside me, my walls tighten around him, trying to hold him inside. "Fuck, you feel so damn good."

"Not as good as you," I pant. My vision goes hazy and my legs shake as I edge closer to the precipice of my release.

AJ sucks on my lobe and then bites his way down the tendon in my neck, and it's enough to set off the fireworks which have been building. His talented cock throbs inside me and he groans through his release, holding himself deep inside me. Wrapping his arms tight around me, he buries his face in the crook of my neck, and I slide my hands soothingly up and down the muscular planes of his back, while we both work to catch our breath.

# CHAPTER 32

*—aj—*

"I haven't been to this lake for years," I comment as we pull into the parking lot. Now to find a parking space.

"Really? We only discovered this place in May when Molly organized a surprise birthday party for Max here. The kids loved the nature playground and I thought Colton would love it too." She was adamant about inviting Hayley and Lisa to her family's Labor Day get-together, so Colton could meet and play with Emma's kids.

I pull into a spot and turn off the engine, then angle my body toward Sarah. "Thank you for including my family." I take a lock of hair between my fingers, appreciating the silkiness of the strands, and tug her to my lips. I hope my kiss conveys exactly how grateful I am for her thoughtfulness.

We pull away, our lips only an inch apart. "You're welcome," Sarah murmurs, her breath skating across my lips. She lays another quick peck, then we climb out of my Jeep and collect our picnic stuff out of the back.

Heading toward the picnic tables, we locate the last empty one at the far end. Even though it's busy, it seems our plan to arrive early paid off. Working together, we set everything up and wander to the lake's edge to watch the kids playing in the water while we wait for our families to arrive. Sarah has her hands wrapped around her middle as she watches parents play with their children, the longing she has for a child of her own obvious. I move in behind her, wrap my arms around her and encourage her to lean back against me.

After laying a tender kiss on the top of her head, I murmur, "We'll have that soon. I promise." I'm not sure I can keep the promise but I damn well intend to do my best to make her—*our*—dream a reality.

She spins in my arms, looking up at me. "What if I can't? I mean all of the tests I had to do with the clinic showed there was physically no reason for me not to get pregnant, but what if I can't?"

I dip down and kiss the tip of her nose, squeezing her tighter to me. I skate my gaze between her mouth and her eyes. "If we can't do it this way, then we'll work out another way to make you a mom. Don't give up, Cupcake."

She smiles softly and drops her forehead against my chest. "How did I get so lucky?"

"I'm pretty sure I'm the lucky one here, Sarah." I finish with a kiss on the top of her head.

"Unca AJ!" A little voice shouts from behind me. Sarah steps out of my embrace and we turn to find Colton running toward us as fast as his little legs can carry him. He bypasses me and heads straight for Sarah, crashing into her legs with a force that makes her take a step back. She giggles as she bends down to scoop him up. "Aunty Sarah!"

"Colton, my little man." She rubs his nose with hers, her eyes sparkling in the warm sunlight. Her easy acceptance of him in her life makes me fall harder for her. Watching them together when Colton spent the night with us made me long for our own family—nights enjoying a movie and playing games together and mornings where we share sleepy smiles and breakfast.

Hayley and Lisa make it to us and after our usual greetings, I take their picnic stuff from them and set it up at the table we procured.

"Can I go for a swim, Mommy?"

"In a little while. Let's wait for everyone else to arrive first."

"Okay." He helps me lay out the blankets next to the table, while the girls set out their picnic.

"Aunty Sarah!" I lift my head to see Kenny running straight for us, her smile a mile wide. "Uncle AJ!" She throws herself at me in my crouched position and I fall backward, landing on my ass with a chuckle.

"Kenny!" Theo calls to her. "You can't run off like that, Munchkin." He turns to me. "Are you okay?"

"Yeah, I'm fine."

"Sorry, Daddy." Theo musses her hair, then holds out his hand to pull me up.

Emma arrives, chuckling. "Are you okay, AJ? That was quite a landing."

"Yeah. I should have prepared myself for the attack." I wipe the grass from my butt.

We introduce everyone and Austin and Kenny take Colton into the fold with ease. Lachlan stands a little away, something I've noticed he does. Sarah explained to me he's on the spectrum and he takes a little while to warm up to new people. Molly and Max arrive and the introductions start all over again.

"Okay, where should we start? On the playground or in the water?" Sarah asks the kids.

"In the water!" Kenny and Colton shout.

"On the playground!" Lachlan and Austin call out at the same time.

"Oh no! Okay, how about this? Let's start with the water because you won't be able to swim with full bellies after lunch. Then after lunch, we can play on the playground," Sarah offers.

"Yay!" Kenny pumps her little fists in the air.

"Yes, let's do that!" Lachlan says, nodding his head.

We get the kids ready for a swim and head toward the water. The water only comes to above our knees this close to the edge, so Sarah's tucked her dress up into her panties to keep it dry. We toss a ball around the group, keeping the kids entertained until Colton complains he's hungry. Piling out of the water, we set about unpacking the coolers and serving the kids their lunch, closely followed by the adults.

As we dig into the salads and sandwiches, chatter starts up. Emma and Lisa have common ground with their teaching backgrounds, so they talk about the areas lacking in the curriculum and how she and Hayley hope to fill some of the holes with their computer games. I think maybe they've won Emma over to incorporating the use of their games in her program. Hayley updates Theo and Lachlan on Colton's progress with the climbing wall they built and Lachlan and Theo share that they've built and sold another one and have another order to make. Considering Theo is Lachlan's stepfather, they are incredibly close.

The thing that becomes obvious to me as the day wears on is how well our families integrate and knit together. The picnic has been easy and comfortable. Kenny and Austin have spent the day fussing over Colton, ensuring he's not left out, and Colton has soaked up every minute of the attention from the older kids.

As we're packing up to head home, Hayley stops next to me. "Sarah has a lovely family."

"I know. Her parents couldn't make it today, but they're equally as warm. So different from ours."

"Yeah. It seems everyone's family is more loving than ours." Sadness fills Hayley's eyes. I know what she means. It's something I'm adamant to change in my family with Sarah.

"How are Lisa's parents recovering from their accident?"

"They're okay. Her dad was being stubborn, trying to do everything for himself. But a broken arm does slow you down. And her mom finally accepted our offer to pay for a food delivery service for her while her broken collarbone heals. Slowly but surely, they're improving."

"Give them my best. Do they need me to cut their grass or anything?"

"Oh, would you? That'd be great."

"Sure. No problem." I can't believe I didn't think to offer sooner. I've been so wrapped up in Sarah, I haven't been paying attention to anything outside of our bubble.

Emma comes to hug me goodbye after my family leaves. "How is she?" she asks as her eyes find her sister, talking to Molly and Max.

I glance at my future. "She's okay. She picked herself up and dusted herself off." I tuck my hands into my pockets. "We'll keep trying until she gets pregnant. And if that doesn't work, we'll find another way. There are plenty of ways to make Sarah a mom."

Emma reaches forward, squeezing my forearm. "Thank you for supporting her through this. It's been something she's wanted for such a long time and I'm glad she met you, AJ. You're one of the good ones."

"You don't have to thank me, Em. It's my privilege to be with Sarah." I look across to find her watching me. I raise an eyebrow and give her a smirk. "I don't plan on going anywhere. She's it for me."

The happiness in Emma's eyes tells me she liked my answer. She leans in to hug me goodbye, and we all make our way to the parking lot to head home.

# CHAPTER 33

## *—aj—*

THE MINUTE WE WALK THROUGH THE DOOR OF SARAH'S APARTMENT, I grab her hand and spin her around, then take her lips in a fierce kiss. When we eventually pull apart, Sarah looks dazed, and I decide it's my favorite look on her, apart from how she looks when she falls apart beneath me. That would be my most favorite.

"What was that for?"

"Thank you for organizing today." I kiss her again, keeping it light.

"You're welcome. Colton had such a great time with the kids and they loved having him to play with." Her eyes light up with happiness that the afternoon was such a success.

I press her back against the door, kissing her deeply, my tongue sliding against hers, making my breathing erratic. I slide my hands up the side of her thighs, drawing the skirt of her dress up as I go, then dip my fingers into each side of her panties to slide them down her legs. Releasing them, gravity takes over and they drop to the floor. Sarah sucks on my tongue in response, and I swipe my fingers through her folds, groaning at the wetness there. "You're always so ready for me, Cupcake."

"Mmhm," she responds, chasing my lips to resume our kiss. Her hands slide up my arms to tangle around my neck.

Dropping her skirt, I take her hands and raise them above her head, pressing them into the door. "Keep them there, okay?" I raise my brow while I wait for her to answer me.

"Okay," comes her breathy acquiescence. So fucking sexy.

Dropping my eyes from her face, they get caught on her breasts which are heaving with her panting breaths. She's so damned turned on. This woman was made for me. "That's a good girl."

Her eyes flare and her mouth drops open in an O. She likes that. Good to know.

Kissing my way down the side of her neck to her collarbone, I nip her pulse point, then move to kiss her tits over the top of her dress. Lowering to the floor, I gather the skirt of her dress in one hand and duck closer to swipe my tongue through her pussy lips and up to her clit, where I roll the sensitive bud with my tongue. Sarah moans, dropping her head to watch me. "AJ," she whispers. "Do it again. Please."

I don't need to be asked twice, so I press in, teasing and biting her clit in between licks and sucks. I push my fingers into her opening and massage her front wall; the area I know sends Sarah flying. Her legs shake as she takes panting breaths in between her cries of pleasure. Her hands drop to my head, grasping the short strands and I immediately stop what I'm doing.

Her head snaps down, her eyes narrowed at me. "Why'd you stop?"

"Put your hands back where I told you to keep them."

"Oh my God, so damn bossy," she huffs out.

I wink at her. "You'd better believe it, Cupcake." I tip my chin up. "Go on."

She pretends to be put out but returns her hands into position, and I get back to work. It doesn't take long before she breaks apart beautifully beneath my touch, chanting my name repeatedly. I think my favorite thing to do is to make her come. Watching her fall apart is equally as beautiful as watching any sunrise.

"You're so damn good at that."

I stand and hold my fingers to her lips, painting the soft pillows with her release. Her tongue darts out, following the path. My cock, which is already fighting for space in my shorts, grows further, pressing against the zipper. I wouldn't be surprised if I don't have zipper marks on the damn thing.

"Get naked, beautiful," I tell her as I pull my T-shirt over my head and drop my hands to the button and fly on my shorts. Biting her bottom lip, she does as I ask, never tearing her eyes away from my body.

"I love your body, AJ," she tells me, her voice dripping with lust.

"Ditto, Cupcake." I lift my chin toward her. "Now get naked." She moves into action, removing the dress, and leaving her in only her bra and sandals. Once I'm naked, I drop down and remove each sandal carefully, ensuring Sarah doesn't lose her balance and she removes her bra. I point to the table. "Bend over the table for me. I need to bury my cock in your pussy."

She bends over the table, her full breasts squishing against the surface, giving me a spectacular view of her swollen pussy. I swipe the head of my cock through the glistening slickness and Sarah pushes back against me. "Hurry up. I need you."

I grunt as I notch my head against her opening and push inside in one swift thrust. We both moan at the beauty of our joining. I throw my head back and press in as deep as I can, holding still until I'm in control. If I start moving straight away, I'm not gonna last, and I never want this to end.

Sarah turns her head, watching me over her shoulder. "Are you okay?"

"Yeah. Just need a minute," I grit through clenched teeth. Rubbing my hands up and down her smooth back, to her neck, and down to her ass cheeks, I leave a trail of goosebumps in my wake. Her body shivers beneath my touch, and I feel like the king of the world. Once I'm certain I won't come in two strokes, I separate her ass cheeks and slide out.

"Oooooh," Sarah moans.

I slide my hands around to her hips, gripping tight, and begin to pump steadily, ensuring I hit that special spot each time I push inside. Small grunts leave Sarah's lips every time I bottom out, making my cock infinitely harder. Dropping my eyes to Sarah's ass, I admire the movement every time my hips slap against her and groan at the sight of my glistening cock sliding out of her heat.

"This is quite the fucking sight. I wish you could see this." I wonder if she'd let me record this sometime? My phone is completely secure, so the videos and images would be one hundred percent safe.

As I pick up speed and power, the table edges across the room with each thrust, adding to the obscene sounds of skin slapping against skin and the squelching sound Sarah's pussy makes every time I push back in. A sheen of sweat is gathering down her spine, and I run my hand down the dip to the crack of her ass. Separating her ass cheeks, my cock pulses at the view of her oh-so-tempting tight hole. Dragging my fingers along her sensitive area, I wet my thumb and then trace circles around the hole. Sarah freezes. "It's okay. I promise it'll feel good, Cupcake. Trust me."

Her body relaxes and she nods. Her trust is a gift and shows me how far our relationship has come. Rubbing around the tight hole, I dip back down to collect more of her lubrication, then carefully breach the ring of muscle eliciting a gasp from Sarah. She pushes back against me, panting, her legs trembling.

"Oh, God. That feels so good. I … I'm so close." I slide my thumb out and back in, matching the action with my cock. The pressure feels incredible as her walls tighten like a wave around my length. "Aaaagh!" Sarah shouts.

Her release sets off mine, and stars dance around the edge of my vision, my lungs trap my breath, and electricity shoots from the furthest parts of my body to one singular point—my cock. My balls draw up and my cum explodes in ribbons into her. "Fuuuck!" I moan while I bury my cock as deep as I can—my dick pulses, emptying everything I have into the woman I love.

*Love!*

I'm pretty sure I fell in love with her the first night we met, and my feelings for her have only grown deeper, more complex.

Draping my torso over her body, I keep my dick inside her as I kiss my way down her spine, running the palms of my hands down each side, tracing the valleys and curves. We're both panting heavily, working to catch our breaths when Sarah turns her head to the side and smiles sleepily at me. I move so I can meet her lips with mine. We connect in a lazy kiss as we come down from our high. Sarah wiggles her ass, and I take the hint that she probably needs me to climb off of her. I help her up, then carry her into her bedroom and position her ass on my thighs so I can hold her legs up.

She chuckles. "I'm not ovulating yet, we don't need to do this."

"Don't care. We may as well get started. Just in case." I wink at her, rubbing my hands up and down her legs. It's then I notice the red marks where her hips were probably connecting with the table. I run my fingers over the redness. "I'm sorry. I got a little carried away."

"You never have to apologize to me for getting carried away when I'm on the receiving end of it." She wiggles her eyebrows up and down, smirking at me.

And just like that, I'm hard again. Still holding her legs upright, I open her to me and slide my cock into heaven and proceed to defile her all over again.

Lying on my back with Sarah draped across my chest, her leg thrown over both of mine, I trace patterns up her arms. The room is considerably darker than it was before as day turns to night. We've pretty much had a sex-a-thon since arriving home this afternoon. "I think you should move in with me."

Sarah's head snaps up. "What?" At least she hasn't gone into a panic attack like she did when I suggested we have sex to get her pregnant rather than using the collection condom and syringe method.

"Hear me out. If you move in with me, we can have sex every morning and night. Surely, that'll get you pregnant. None of this every other day stuff only when you're ovulating."

"I'm pretty sure we were doing it more than every second day during my ovulation period last month," she sasses back.

"I want you with me," I murmur. Gliding my fingers through her messy hair, I watch her closely as she runs through the pros and cons. My Sarah is an overthinker, which is probably good because she balances out my spontaneity. And while my suggestion for her to move in with me may seem out of the blue, it's something I've been thinking about since we first decided to see where this relationship could go. I don't expect her to make a decision tonight, but I'd be thrilled if she did so we can move her things straight away.

Her eyes come back to mine and her lips slowly spread, her eyes twinkling in happiness. She begins to nod slowly, gradually picking up speed while her smile grows wider. "Okay."

"Okay?" Surely it's not that easy.

She chuckles. "Okay."

# CHAPTER 34

## —sarah—

I WAKE TO BUTTERFLY KISSES BEING PRESSED ALONG MY SPINE, SENDING goosebumps radiating out from the middle of my back through my body in waves. A tiny moan leaves my throat and I feel AJ's lips smile against my flesh.

"Happy birthday, Cupcake," he says, his voice gruff from sleep.

"It certainly is." I turn my head toward the window, noting it's not quite morning, and sigh. This has been my life since I moved in with AJ. He wakes me before dawn to ensure we have plenty of time to start our day right before we need to get ready for work. I've had so much sex these past weeks, I'm surprised my pores don't ooze semen.

He moves up my body, using his forearms to balance over me, and kisses the corner of my mouth which immediately tips up. Using his tongue, he traces the seam of my lips, and I lean forward slightly to nip it and suck it into my mouth. He groans and uses his knee to push my leg upward, positioning his cock at my opening. I love having him inside me, filling me up, knowing I'm the last woman he'll ever be with like this. I push my hips back, encouraging him inside until he's deep and every thick inch of him is buried inside me. Without taking his lips from mine, he moves his hips slowly but surely, languidly making love to me, no dirty talk, just pure physical connection. The way he fills my body is the definition of divine. Deep moans resonate from AJ, sending my pulsing clit into overdrive. Panting breaths brush across my cheek as the tell-tale tremors of my impending orgasm barrel down on me. Pushing my hips back to take AJ's cock as deep as I can, I cry out as I break apart, every single atom which makes up my body flying into space.

"Happy birthday, Cupcake," AJ breathlessly repeats, pressing another scorching kiss against my lips as I piece myself back together. Without removing his still-hard dick from me, he hoists up my hips and starts all over again, this time, his talented fingers work over my clit, while his dick hits my G-spot in the most delicious of attacks. "Feel your pretty clit putting on a show just for me."

My panting breaths and AJ's groans fill the silence of the room as I quickly build toward my second release. I probably won't be able to walk today and I'm more than okay with that. AJ's cock pulses inside me as my walls clamp down on his length. A long, low "fuu-uck" leaves his gorgeous lips as he holds completely still inside of me. His harsh breaths carry through the room and mingle with my fast pants.

"This has to be the best start to a birthday I've ever had." My body shakes with my chuckle.

"Fuck. Don't do that when I'm still inside you," he grumbles harshly.

I turn my head to look at him. Adorable creases are prominent between his eyebrows as he pulls out and carefully rolls me over to my back. Resting my ass on his thighs so he can hold my legs up, his roughened fingers glide up and down my heated flesh in a smooth caress and I smile at him.

"I love how you do this for me every time we have sex."

"I want this to work as much as you do. You know that, right?"

I nod dreamily. "Yeah."

He kisses the back of my knee, sending a smattering of goose-bumps across my leg. Leaning back slightly, his eyes drop to my exposed pussy. The next thing I know, his fingers slide through my slit to my opening and push inside me. This is the other thing he always does. He scoops any cum that slides out of me back inside with an impressive level of diligence. At first, it was shocking and embarrassing, but now I'm used to it.

AJ has been the most unexpected surprise throughout this entire journey. His eagerness to comply with whatever I've needed from him from the very start has been ongoing. He's made me feel completely comfortable throughout the process, even through the bumps in the road caused by my insecurities. I couldn't have asked for a better boyfriend if I'd made a list of what I was searching for. I close my eyes and sigh, thanking whomever it is I need to thank that my self-sabotage didn't scare him away.

"That was a big sigh. What's going on in that head of yours?"

"Just thanking the higher powers that be for bringing you into my life. I'm incredibly thankful you sat in our booth that night and were brave enough to approach me."

Still holding my legs up, he moves out from beneath me, bringing his face close to mine. "I'm the one who's thankful, Sare," he whispers against my lips, soulful brown eyes locked on mine. God, I hope our child has his gorgeous eyes, so warm and inviting. When he presses his lips to mine gently, I raise my head to deepen the kiss. I need to show him how much he means to me. I'm not ready to say those three little words yet, but I can show him.

Our kiss builds quickly, as it always does, going from a spark to a full-on inferno in mere seconds. He ignites a passion in me that's foreign and has been out of reach until him. A sharp smack to my ass has me jolting away from him. "What was that for?"

He tilts his head to the side. "No reason. I just love your ass. And I'm gonna love seeing my handprint on it when you climb out of bed." He smacks me again, lightly this time. "Come on. I want to make you a decent breakfast before you go to work."

We climb out of bed, and shower together, which leads to me dropping to my knees and him returning the favor. Oh yeah, three orgasms before breakfast! I'll definitely be walking into the office with a spring in my step this morning.

AJ makes breakfast burritos while I dress and then tells me he booked a surprise for my birthday over the next long weekend. He's not giving me any hints either, taking great joy in my incessant guesses which he says are way off base.

I kiss him goodbye for the day, and he reminds me of the dinner reservations he made for tonight; we'll be headed to *Cristo's* with my family for my birthday.

The second the elevator doors open, I spot my best friend speaking with Joe, still wearing her scrubs with baby penguins decorating the pink fabric. I run toward her as fast as my fitted skirt and heels allow. When she spots me, she breaks away from Joe and runs toward me with her arms open wide, wearing a broad smile on her gorgeous face. God, I love her. We collide with giggles. Just like the gif with the two little boys running toward each other on a sidewalk.

"Happy birthday, Sare Bear!"

"Thanks, Mels Bells."

She grips my hand. "Let's grab lunch. There's no time to waste."

We walk, arm in arm, toward the sushi train not far from my building. Grabbing two seats facing the train, we both make our first selection.

"Oh my God, this is so good!" Mel exclaims after taking a bite of her California roll.

"So good. Thanks for meeting me for my birthday."

"Always." She drags an envelope out of her purse. "I got you something, too."

I love presents. I mean what girl doesn't? I open the envelope and slide out a gift card for a nail pampering session at my favorite salon, *R&R Nail Salon*. I lean across and hug my long-time friend. "Thank you so much. I hope you're coming with me."

She reaches back into her purse and pulls out a second envelope. "You betcha! We just need to coordinate our schedules."

I always love spending time with Mel, she's the best friend a girl could ask for. "You seem less tired today."

She chuckles. "I'm on days this week, so I'm getting proper sleep. It always helps." She scans me up and down. "You look as though you're glowing and I don't think it's just because it's your birthday." She wiggles her eyebrows up and down.

I sigh with what I'm sure is a dreamy look on my face.

"Oh yeah, clearly lover boy is doing a good job at keeping you sexed up!" Mel chuckles.

"Oh my God, Mel. I've never had so many orgasms in my entire life. The man is a master." I chuckle. "But that's all the information you're getting out of me on that front."

"Boo! What sort of friend are you if you're not gonna share the deets with your bestest friend in the whole entire world?" She nudges me with her shoulder. "Only kidding. I'm happy to see you happy, my friend. You deserve it."

"You deserve it, too, you know," I tell her and she shrugs.

"So, do you think you're pregnant yet?"

My mood drops like a lead balloon. "I don't know. I should be for the amount of sex I've had this month." I shrug. "But who knows."

Mel places her hand softly on my forearm. "It'll happen. The universe knows what a great mom you'll be, so you *will* have a baby. You'll see." She squeezes my arm gently.

I'm glad she's feeling so positive about the whole thing. I'm honestly beginning to doubt if I'll ever have my dream. And will AJ want to stick around if I can't get pregnant? Or will he decide it's best to move on with someone who *can* have a baby? Is our relationship wholly contingent on us getting pregnant and having a child together?

Thankfully, Mel senses the drop in my mood and changes the subject to lighter topics; sharing stories about the girls she works with. Some of them sound a little unhinged which is surprising since they always seem so put together whenever I've volunteered, but Mel says they're great girls. I'll take her word for it. And they can't be too bad, they spend their days and nights caring for incredibly sick babies.

"Shit, I need to get back." Mel stands, tossing her purse straps over her shoulder. I stand too and we head for the pay station. "My treat today, since it's your birthday." She gives me a side hug.

"Thanks, Mel, and thanks for meeting me today. I love seeing your face."

"Me too. I mean, I don't love seeing my face, I love seeing *your* face." We both chuckle as we leave the restaurant and walk back toward my building arm in arm. We hug goodbye and I head back upstairs.

"Honey, I'm home," I call as soon as I enter AJ's home. Even though he's made me feel completely welcome here, I still think of it as his home. Everything's quiet. AJ and Dylan must still be working. I head toward their office at the rear of the house.

"Okay, I'll see you on the seventeenth!" AJ snaps harshly. I've never heard him raise his voice.

Dylan steps out of their office and smiles at me. "Is everything all right?" I ask and his head tilts to the side in question. I point at the open barn door. "AJ sounds pissed at something."

"Oh that. It's nothing, just some family drama." He steps closer and wraps his arms around me, lifting me off of my feet. "Happy birthday, Sarah."

I chuckle. "Thanks."

When he places me back on my feet, we both walk inside their well-appointed office. AJ has his back to the doorway, his hands resting on his hips, and his head dropped toward the floor. His shoulders are rising and falling with heavy breaths. I don't think his call was 'nothing,' he seems upset.

"Look who's home!" Dylan calls.

AJ spins on the spot and his entire demeanor changes when his eyes land on me. In three long strides, he has his arms wrapped around me, repeating Dylan's action by lifting me off of my feet. "Hey, Cupcake." He presses his lips firmly against mine and we go from zero to one hundred in five seconds flat. His yummy scent wraps around me, making me feel calm and steady. That's what he does for me. He steadies me, calming my overactive mind.

"All right, I'm outta here. Enjoy the rest of your birthday, Sarah."

By the time I manage to tear my lips away from AJ's, Dylan's gone. I wrap my legs around AJ's hips and study his face closely. "Is everything okay?"

Creases form between his brows and his hold on me tightens. "Yeah, why?"

"I heard you on the phone. You sounded pissed." His body tenses. "I'm just checking on you. That's what girlfriends do, you know." A smile tilts up the corners of his mouth.

"Yeah, everything's fine. Just some family stuff I should have taken care of ages ago."

"If you need to talk about it, I'm here."

He kisses the tip of my nose. "I know, but I promise, it's nothing. It'll be sorted out in the next few weeks."

His grip drops to my ass and he grabs a cheek in each hand, squeezing. I grind against him, feeling him harden against me. "You want my dick?"

"Yeah," I respond breathily. *Is that even my voice?*

His lips crash onto mine and I kiss him back hungrily, and I realize I never seem to get enough of this man. I'm turned on as soon as I'm in his vicinity. He doesn't even need to do anything and when I stop to think about why that could be, I come back to the fact that apart from being utterly sexy, he steadies me. He gives me a safe place where I don't need to think of every single scenario because I know he's got me. That we'll figure out whatever it is, *together*. I deepen our kiss, grinding down on his cock. I feel us moving, and then my butt lands on the cold surface of the kitchen counter. I immediately drop my hands to his belt and drag the leather through the metal buckle, then release his button and zipper.

"You're so fucking perfect," he groans into my ear, his hot breath skating down my neck adding to my arousal. "I bet you're already soaking for me."

Moaning at his words, I push down his pants and boxer briefs and wrap my hand around his engorged length. Hot and silky to the touch, it's heavy in my hand as I stroke it, then I swipe my thumb across the top, collecting his precum which I lick from my thumb with a moan. At the same time, AJ pushes up my skirt and slides my panties to the side, stroking his fingers through my pussy. "You're so fucking ready for me and I haven't done anything."

"I'm always ready when you're in the room. I can't help it," I murmur.

He groans, dropping his head back, before returning his heated gaze to me. His dark eyes are intense as they skate around my face. I line up his cock with my opening, and he thrusts inside without preamble making us both groan. I'm worried I'm turning into an addict for his cock. The more he's inside me, the more I want him inside me. I can't get enough and AJ's the same.

All of my focus narrows to where we're intimately joined and it's no longer just about making a baby, it's also about connecting with a man who's grown to mean everything to me. The sex is incredible, but it feels more like making love and building our connection the more we come together. He sets my body and my soul ablaze with every thrust of his hips and swipe of his tongue.

The erotic sounds of our coupling fill the space, echoing through the large, open room as our heavy breaths mingle with grunts and moans. I use my hold around his neck to pull him tighter to me and he picks up speed, his panting breaths blowing across my sweaty cheek. "Harder," I cry out between thrusts. "Please, AJ."

"I'll get you there, Cupcake," he breathes harshly. His hands tighten on my hips and I know I'll have his marks there. I love seeing the evidence of our joining in the various shades of bruises that seem to be constantly on my hips. His movements become harder, deeper, reaching that special place inside of me.

AJ slides his hand around the front of my body, and his thumb circles my needy clit, setting off an explosion of light behind my eyes while tremors rack my body from the tips of my fingers to my core and everywhere in between. My grip on him tightens as I break apart, shattering into a million pieces.

"Aaaah," I cry out, dropping my head onto AJ's shoulder as he buries himself deep inside me, his cock growing and pulsing with his release.

"Fuuuck!" He shouts as his body locks tight. The room is suddenly quiet as we both fight to catch our breath.

My lips widen against his hammering pulse point and I nip it lightly, then lick the saltiness of AJ's exertion. "I've turned into a limp noodle." I slide my fingers through the short, sweat-slicked strands of dark hair resting at his nape.

AJ chuckles. "That means I did my job." He strokes his hand lovingly along my thighs to my hips, which he rubs soothingly. Using his fingers, he grips my chin tenderly and raises my face to his. Gently, reverently, he takes my lips in a slow, lazy kiss. It's deep and soul-stealing and it's everything. He strokes my tongue with his in such a way that tells me he feels the same for me as I do for him. His hips begin to mimic the action of his tongue and with leisurely movements, he slowly builds the inferno once again, taking us both to completion.

# CHAPTER 35

## ~aj~

I'VE BEEN FLOATING ON A HIGH ALL WEEK, AND IT'S NOT JUST BECAUSE of all the sex I'm having, though I'm sure it's a contributing factor. Dinner at *Cristo's* with Sarah's family on Monday night was incredible. It was the second time Sarah and I have spent time with them since we decided to build a relationship, and her family is genuinely happy for us. Apart from Theo and Max laying down the law, which I understood, the Stanfields have made me feel welcome from the beginning, but on Monday there was a deeper level of acceptance I'm certain I wasn't imagining. I felt as though I belonged.

Heading upstairs, I go in search of Sarah. I noticed her car in the garage, but she never came to say hello, which is something she always does. "Sarah," I call out as I enter our bedroom. Checking the walk-in closet, I find the space empty. She wasn't downstairs and I'm puzzled as to where she could be. Maybe she's on the deck. As I step around the bed on my way out to check, a sob catches my attention, and I backtrack to the ensuite. Another sob sounds.

My heart sinks. Breaking and bleeding.

I drop my forehead to the wooden door, closing my eyes as my heart drops to my toes, leaving a bloody mess. I listen to her sobs through the door, feeling my heart crack for her, for both of us. Because even though this started as her dream, it quickly became mine as well. Placing my open palm to the surface, I whisper, "Sarah? Cupcake?" The sobs stop but she doesn't answer me. "Can I come in?" Still no answer, so I try the door but it's locked. "C'mon, Cupcake. Let me in. You don't have to deal with this alone. Let me hold you."

Silence fills the room for long moments before I hear shuffling from the other side of the door and the lock disengage. The second the door opens, I step inside and gather my girl in my arms. No words are spoken; none are needed. I know she's devastated as am I. My cupcake buries her head in my chest, her hands gripping the side of my shirt, and she lets go, releasing her pain and disappointment. Her body shakes and I tighten my hold on her, laying kisses on the top of her head and stroking her silky locks in long, soothing strokes.

I feel so fucking helpless.

I desperately want to give her what she wants and for the number of times I've been inside her, I was sure we'd made a baby this month. Her hands slide around to my back and she presses tighter against me as her sobs slow. "I'm so sorry, Sarah."

She mumbles something against my pecs I can't understand so I bring my hands around to cup her face, tilting it up to mine. Red, swollen eyes and blotchy cheeks greet me, breaking my heart further. I kiss her forehead, nose, and each eyelid. "What did you say, Cupcake?"

"I'm the one who's sorry. You have these super sperm, so I must be faulty."

Her words are like a red cape to a bull. I tilt her head back further. "Don't ever, and I mean ever, call yourself faulty. You're fucking perfect in every way." As she opens her mouth to argue, I drop mine over hers and kiss her in a way I hope shows her how perfect I think she is. How much I love her. Not that I've said the words yet. Sarah likes to do things slowly and at her pace, so I'll hold onto those three words until I'm certain she's ready to hear them, and now's not the time. I kiss her like it's the last time I'll ever get to kiss her and I do my best to take away her pain and piece her back together.

When we pull away to catch our breath, I drop my forehead to hers. "What if I can't get pregnant, AJ?"

"Then we find another way to make our dream come true." Her eyes widen and her mouth drops open in a small O.

"Our dream?" she whispers.

"Yeah. *Our* dream. You know I'm in this as deep as you are." I rub my nose along hers.

She nods slowly. "Thank you."

She seems to forget we've had this conversation before. I gently brush her hair away from her face, tucking the silky locks behind her ears. My eyes dart between hers. "You don't need to thank me, Cupcake. I'd do anything for you."

She smiles at me and a portion of the crack in my heart repairs. I want to make her smile all the time. I don't want to see these tears— this sadness. Without words, I undress her and turn on the shower. Slowly, I guide her beneath the fall of the water and make love to her. No words are spoken, they're not needed as our bodies move with synchronicity. Hands stroking and mouths teasing, we come together beautifully, Sarah's cries and my grunts echoing off the tiled walls.

I kiss her slowly as we both come down from our high, my softening dick sliding out of heaven. Still keeping my hold on Sarah, I step back slightly and grab the soap to wash her body. With careful strokes, I wash every inch of her, then start on her hair. First with shampoo, then conditioner, just the way she showed me. I massage her scalp with firm fingers, eliciting moans from my girl. "If you keep making those noises, I'm going to have to fuck you again."

She chuckles. "Like that's a punishment." She pushes her ass back, connecting with my growing cock. It's always like this with her. I'm addicted to her pussy, but more than that, I'm addicted to her.

"Where are you taking me?" Sarah chuckles as I manhandle her out the door. I packed our stuff while she was at the hospital for her volunteer shift and now we need to get moving if we're going to make it to the airport on time.

"You'll see when we get there. It's your birthday surprise."

"But I didn't pack anything. How do I know if you packed everything I need?"

I smirk at her. "I've got you covered. I used to be in the Scouts."

Her feet lock in place and she looks at me. "Really?"

"Nah, just kidding. But I have everything you need. I promise." I kiss the tip of her nose and drag her to my Jeep.

On the way to the airport, Sarah's questions don't stop. "Can't you give me a hint?"

"Nope." I pop the p like a teenager with attitude and grin at her as she huffs.

"I don't feel like I can relax and enjoy the experience without knowing where we're going or what we're gonna be doing?" And there she is, my overthinking cupcake.

I figure I'll throw her a bone. "I'm taking you camping. Well, sort of."

Her head snaps toward me and with wide sparkling eyes, she asks, "Really?"

"Yeah."

Her smile is wide. "I've never been *sort of* camping before."

I collect her hand and place it on my thigh, leaving my hand resting on top of hers. "It'll be fun."

We pull into the airport parking lot and find a parking space, then make our way into the terminal. "Where on earth are we camping that we need to catch a plane to get there?" Sarah giggles.

Sarah spends the flight updating me on the babies in the NICU. She practically vibrates with joy when she shares her excitement at getting to meet the parents of a baby she cuddled last time and how grateful they were she was there to love on their baby when they couldn't.

The off-road RV I organized is waiting out front of the terminal when we arrive and we waste no time in getting on the road to our final destination for the next two nights. Sarah's eyes almost pop out of her head when she realizes where we're headed. "I've never been here before. Have you?"

"I haven't, so it will be a first for both of us." I glance across at her.

Her answering grin and whispered words, "I like that" make me feel as though I'm standing atop El Capitan.

Once we arrive at Stovepipe Wells, we grab our camping site, and I make us a bite to eat from the supplies in the fully stocked kitchen. Because it's almost late afternoon, we decide to check out the nearby Mesquite Sand Dunes for some fun and then we'll have a picnic dinner to watch the sunset. I specifically brought Sarah here because, while it's not considered the darkest area in the United States, it's rated pretty high by the International Dark Sky Places Program. And I remembered her saying she would like to experience this when we watched the documentary about the most extreme places in the US.

We climb out of the RV, and as Sarah and I scan the area, the vastness of the dunes steals our breath. "Oh my. It's gorgeous," Sarah whispers reverently.

"Yeah." I grab our sand boards, which were kindly supplied, and hand in hand, Sarah and I begin our trek through the dunes. The number of footprints in the soft sand is incredible, but what's surprising is that some parts are dry and cracked like a dried-up lake bed. Obviously, it hasn't been too windy the last couple of days to erase the footprints covering the dunes.

Sarah points far off into the distance. "Look at that one. It must be enormous, it juts out so much higher than the others."

"Shall we check it out?"

"Yeah. But let me carry one of the boards."

"I'm okay. If they start to get heavy, you can carry one."

We climb over each dune, past dead gnarly trees, taking the time to snap some shots of the magnificent backdrop with our phones. Sarah photobombs some of my shots so I make sure to return the favor, pulling funny faces as I leap across in front of the lens.

As the sun crosses the sky, we finally reach the highest dune we were aiming for. We must have walked about a mile. Nobody else is here and we're both hot and sweaty from the workout of climbing dunes in soft sand. Panting, we both drop to our asses.

"Shit, that was quite a workout!" Sarah exclaims through panting breaths.

Sitting beside her, I raise my knees and clasp my hands around them loosely. "I'm gonna need a minute before we take these bad boys to the bottom." I tip my chin to the boards beside me.

"I can't believe I was sitting in the NICU this morning and this afternoon I'm sitting atop the tallest dune here." Her eyes are full of wonder as she takes in the incredible landscape, and I take the opportunity to sneak in a photo. Her skin looks golden with the reflection of the late-afternoon sun casting across the dunes.

"Are you ready to ride the dune?" I ask, wiggling my eyebrows.

Sarah chuckles. "Of course. Let's go."

We situate ourselves on our boards and push off at the same time, ensuring we're a safe distance apart. Sarah screams on the way down, holding onto her board for dear life, while I laugh at her, ensuring I don't fall off my board. When we get to the bottom of the dune, my board stops, but the momentum of the slide means I keep going forward, rolling in the deep sand. I manage to close my eyes, but my mouth fills with sand. Once I come to a stop, I spit out as much sand as I can as Sarah comes running over to me and drops to her knees.

"Are you okay?" I can't make out her face with the sun shining behind her, but I can tell by her tone that she's worried.

I begin to laugh and reach forward to pull her down on top of me. "I'm fine," I tell her through the grit stuck to my tongue. Our water bottles are at the top of the dune along with our shoes, so I'll have to wait until I'm at the top before I can rinse out my mouth. "That was so much fun. I wanna do it again and again and again."

She chuckles as she props herself up on my pecs. "Me too!" I push up and press my lips to hers chastely, then we climb to our feet and begin the trek back to the top. The afternoon passes by as we slide, climb, and slide again until our legs won't carry us any further. "I think my legs are gonna fall off. I don't think I can climb it again *and* have enough energy to walk all the way back to the parking lot."

"Let's head back then. I have a picnic dinner waiting for us and we can watch the sunset."

"You've thought of everything." I hope I thought of everything. I wanted to make this getaway memorable for her.

I pull her into me, holding her hands behind my back, making her body flush with mine. Lowering my head, Sarah presses up on her toes to meet me halfway and our lips collide. Our kiss is deep and bruising. Rough and explorative as we connect. I love how we can go from laughing our asses off, sliding down a dune, to sharing passionate kisses which leave me breathless.

Sarah pulls her lips away, her eyes glistening in the low light. "I felt like a kid again. Sliding down the dune was exhilarating." She squeezes my hands. "Thank you for planning this. It's the best birthday present I've ever been given."

"Anything for you, Cupcake."

Sarah sets up the outdoor camping chairs while I collect our picnic dinner and we both put our feet up while enjoying the feast as the sun disappears below the horizon. She points toward the dunes. "Look at how the colors are changing with the waning light." She takes a drink of her soda. "Stunning," she whispers.

"Yeah." I couldn't care less about the colors of the dunes because I can't tear my eyes away from my girl.

She notices I'm not looking at the dunes. "Look. You don't want to miss it, we only have a sliver of sunlight left."

At her insistence, I turn my head and my eyes catch on the almost glowing amber dunes under the waning light. I reach my hand out to grasp Sarah's, and I picture us doing this when we're much older and we've lived a long and happy life together. The way her face lights up with an appreciation of the spectacular show nature is putting on for us is something I'll file away and remember for the rest of my days.

We clean up from dinner and lock our RV, then head back into the dunes with a blanket tucked beneath my arm. "Thank goodness for the full moon. It's making it easy to see where we're going."

"Yeah, it worked out pretty well for my plan." When we're far enough away from the parking lot, I lay out the blanket and invite Sarah to join me. Lying on our backs, we look up at the night sky. At first, the stars aren't all that clear. I turn my head toward Sarah. "It'll take about twenty minutes for our eyes to adjust from the light of the RV to the darkness, so we can see the stars clearly."

She turns her head toward me with a smile. "Whatever shall we do to fill the time?" she asks all innocent-like. We're the only ones out here tonight, so I roll on top of her.

# CHAPTER 36

## —sarah—

When AJ rolls on top of me I can't contain my giggle, until he drops his lips to mine. That shuts me up quickly. I adore the way he kisses me. I sigh as he places a soft kiss on my bottom lip, then traces his tongue along the seam where my lips meet. "You're so beautiful, Sarah. And I'm not just talking about how you look. You have a beautiful heart," he murmurs against my lips, sending my heart somersaulting.

My hands grip his sides as I press up to capture his lips. He opens and slides his tongue into my mouth without hesitation. As our tongues dance with each other, I slide my hands along the hard planes of AJ's back, feeling the play of his muscles as he holds his body weight off me. I press down, encouraging him to close the distance between us. I want to feel him on top of me, be trapped beneath his strong, hard body. He takes the hint and drops so his chest is pressing against mine, his pelvis cradled between my thighs. I wrap my legs around him, locking him to me, and push up against his steely shaft trapped behind his zipper. He grinds down and it's amazing, sending sparks flying through my body. Gliding my hands to his shoulders, I trace his muscles down his arms and back again, finally sliding my fingers through the short strands of hair at his nape.

My heart pounds in a fast rhythm, as our kiss continues, deepening, becoming more intense. He's making love to my mouth under the full moon in the middle of the sand dunes and I want this moment to last forever. I want to burn it into my memory banks and remember it when I'm old and gray. With confident movements, AJ removes every stitch of clothing from my body and his and makes love to me beneath the starry night sky.

With glistening skin, we lay on the blanket catching our breath, wrapped in each other's embrace. I gasp when my eyes land on the night sky and the billions of stars twinkling above us. "This is gorgeous, AJ." I turn my head to look at him. "Thank you for bringing me here."

He presses a kiss on my lips. "You're welcome, Cupcake. Happy birthday." I shiver. "Are you cold?"

"A little."

"Let's get dressed, then." We both quickly dress, curling back around each other to enjoy the starry night for a while longer. As our eyes grow heavy, we decide to make our way back to the RV in the dark. "I thought we could sleep here tonight." AJ presses a button and the roof shade slides back, exposing the night sky through a moon roof. The perfect name since we now have a spectacular view of the night sky while laying on our soft bed.

"Oh my God, this is amazing!"

AJ locks the door and climbs into bed beside me, he places his hands beneath his head, and a proud smile fills his face. "I'm glad you like it."

"*Like* it? I freaking love it. It's incredible." I snuggle into his side, and he wraps his arm around me, tugging me in tight to his body where I know I'll always be safe.

I wake to the early rays of dawn streaming down on me, wrapped in AJ's big spoon. I press back into him, enjoying his warmth and he kisses the back of my head. "Morning." His voice is gruff from sleep, and my body immediately responds. "I should have closed the roof last night," he grumbles.

I turn over within his embrace. "I'm glad you didn't. I want to watch the sunrise with you."

His lips tip up and he kisses the end of my nose. "We could make that a thing you know. Watching the sunrise together. We're both early risers."

"I like the sound of that," I whisper. AJ's fingers glide lazily up and down my spine, following the curve from the base of my neck to the top of my ass as the cabin fills with golden light to start a brand-new day. We lay in silence, my mind quiet while I soak up this moment, both of us happy to absorb each other and our uninterrupted time together. "We should get up and watch the sun touch the dunes."

AJ taps his fingers on my hip and climbs out of bed, helping me up. I throw on one of his T-shirts, and he pulls on a pair of gray sweats, leaving his magnificent torso bare. My breath gushes out of me as my feet touch the cold gravel and my eyes land on the golden dunes. AJ's arms wrap around me from behind and he walks me forward, his breath warm against my neck. He rests his chin on my shoulder, and I bring my hands up to cover his, tucked beneath my breasts.

My gaze skates across the dunes, appreciating their beauty, so different from yesterday. "How is it that the same landscape can look so different in a new light? This has to be one of my most memorable moments," I breathe.

Cataloging the changes to the landscape, I have a sudden epiphany. I think Mel was right. Michael and I had to fall apart to make room for AJ to come into my life. When I think back to the years I spent mourning the loss of that relationship, I wish I could go back and change my perspective now I can see things in a new light.

I feel AJ nodding. "Definitely. I know I'll never forget it."

Once the sun rises, we get dressed and eat breakfast, then AJ proceeds to spoil me with adventure after adventure. I can't believe he planned all of this for me. When we weren't doing the touristy thing, AJ was inside me, blowing my mind and loving on my body. The memories we've created during this trip will stay with me forever and I let a future with AJ wash over me. Trips together, exploring, growing together, and raising a family ... *together.*

As I place Eric's morning pot of tea on his desk, he smiles at me. His demeanor has been more relaxed over the last couple of weeks. He tips his chin toward the seat opposite his desk. "Please sit, we need to discuss a few things."

"Do I need my tablet to take notes?"

"No, you'll be fine." I take a seat, ready to listen. It's been great to have the old Eric back, the office is back to its usual relaxed atmosphere. Eric straightens and folds his hands one on top of the other on his desk. A smile forms and his eyes glisten. "My grandson will be coming in next Monday."

My heart skips a beat. I know this is what Eric wants, what he needs, but I can't help the selfish side of me that doesn't like change. I squeeze my hands together to stop myself from fidgeting. "That's wonderful, Mr. Wainwright. I can't wait to meet him." Hopefully, my smile looks genuine and I make a mental note to prepare a special batch of cupcakes in an attempt to impress my new boss.

"Yes, it's been a long time coming. He's moving from New Jersey as we speak, and I couldn't be happier to have my grandson home." He blinks his eyes rapidly and moves his gaze over my shoulder. I barely resist turning around to see what's caught his attention.

"I bet the entire family will be happy to be reunited with him. I can't imagine my mom being too happy if one of us moved that far away from home." Another reason why I let Michael go all those years ago.

"Well, yes." He tugs his collar away from his neck and smooths down his tie. "We need to ensure all of our handover documents and the updated policy handbook are completed. Can you make them into those fancy books you do?"

I nod. "Of course. I noted a couple of things you need to take a closer look at, then I can make those adjustments and print it. Did you want copies for all staff, or only for Adam?"

"Since it's been updated, let's make enough policy handbooks for each staff member, but only Adam needs the handover documents. Book a staff meeting on Friday morning, so I can deliver the updated policy handbook and let everyone know Adam will be in first thing Monday morning. I don't want people poking their heads out of offices wondering what's going on."

"Okay. Will that be all?"

"For now. Thank you, Sarah."

"No problem. I'll work on the documents today and tomorrow and get them printed and bound, ready for Friday."

Collecting the handover document with my notes, I take it to Eric and explain my thoughts. He agrees with my suggestions and I return to my desk to make the necessary changes. I spend the rest of the day formatting the files, which requires minimal concentration on my part. Exactly the sort of work I need. My mind won't stop racing, imagining how things around here might change under the new boss. Will he be as good to the staff as Eric is? Will he still allow for flexible working hours? I know a lot of people here rely on that flexibility to work around school drop-offs and pick-ups for their kids. How will it impact the leave I was hoping to take if I ever get pregnant?

Eric seems to have a lot of faith in Adam, so I should trust his judgment, but my anxiety is growing by the minute. My stomach rolls at the thought of not seeing my long-time boss every day. I glance across at the window between my space and Eric's office. Someone else will be sitting behind that desk, and it doesn't feel right.

# CHAPTER 37

## *—sarah—*

"Joe! Hold the elevator, please." I quicken my steps to make it to him as fast as possible, nausea making it difficult—damn anxiety. He smiles at me and presses the button to hold it. "Thanks, Joe. I can't believe I'm running late. Of all the days."

"You're welcome, Miss Sarah."

I hold up the Tupperware container of cupcakes. "I'll save you one."

"Thank you. I'll look forward to it!" Joe smiles as he pats his stomach.

I quickly step inside, then glance at the other occupants, my eyes landing on AJ. The surprise of seeing him makes the nerves that were overwhelming me moments ago dissipate and I smile as I move closer. He hasn't noticed me because he's frowning at something on his phone. He said he had an important meeting this morning. One that was going to be difficult but I had no idea it was in this building. I bump my shoulder into his arm to catch his attention. His eyes snap away from his screen to me and his entire face relaxes; a smile immediately forming.

"Sarah," he breathes. That single word makes my heart pound faster and my stomach flip.

"Hey." He leans down, pressing a kiss to my lips and I melt. I was naked with this guy yesterday morning, yet that simple kiss has butterflies filling my stomach. "I missed you last night. How are your parents?"

"They're slightly better today. I can't believe they were both so sick at the same time. I don't think it's ever happened before. I was up most of the night checking on them. Molly's spending the day looking after them, so I could come to work."

"You work in this building?" I guess I've never told him where I work, only that I worked in the city.

"Yeah. Is this where your meeting is today?"

"Yeah."

The elevator stops and people step out, while others step in.

"I'm running late. I think I dozed off in the early hours of this morning and slept through my alarm after not getting a lot of sleep during the night. I hate being late." I huff. "But I have cupcakes!" I raise the container for him to see.

He reaches toward the container with a cheeky grin. "Can I have one?"

I snatch it back. "Nope, they're to impress my new boss. I'll make you some when I get home."

AJ's eyebrows dip causing creases between them. "That's today?"

I nod and draw in a shaky breath. "Yeah. And I'm feeling so crappy."

He places the back of his hand against my forehead. "You don't feel warm, but you look pale. Should you even be at work today? Maybe you caught the virus your mom and dad have?"

The elevator comes to a stop and more people step in.

"I don't think so. I've been anxious about meeting my new boss, and it's causing an upset stomach. I'll be okay."

He gives me a soft smile, tucking my hair behind my ear. "Your new boss will love you. You don't need to be nervous."

The elevator stops at my floor. His meeting must be with Oliver Stone. His floors are the only ones above ours. "Anyway, this is my stop. Good luck with your meeting. I hope it's not too tough." I press up on my toes and peck his cheek.

AJ glances up at the floor number, a puzzled expression on his face. "This is my floor, too."

We both step out of the elevator and the doors close, leaving us standing near the front reception desk of *FutureTech*—the only company on this floor—and Lucy.

"Really? Are you here to check our systems? I didn't have anything about it on my calendar for today?" I'm confused. I keep track of everything that goes on because I have to keep abreast of everything for Eric. But maybe it slipped my attention because I've been so stressed about today. "Who are you meeting with?"

"My grandfather. Eric Wainwright."

*No.* My legs shake and the room spins. Suddenly, there's no air and I can't seem to catch my breath.

"Morning, Sarah. Are you okay?" Lucy steps from behind her desk. "You look pale."

AJ takes the container of cakes from me and grasps my bicep, leading me to the nearby chairs. "Would you mind getting Sarah a glass of water?"

"Sure." Lucy disappears down the hallway and I'm left alone with AJ.

My gut rolls and I have a sinking feeling. "Adam?" I whisper.

"Yeah."

*Shit!*

Only me. This shit can only happen to me.

The stranger who offered to help me have a baby.

The man I've fallen for even though I wasn't supposed to.

The guy I'm living with is going to be my new boss.

This is the crappiest of crappy situations ever. AJ pushes my head down between my legs as my breaths grow choppier.

"Are you my new boss?" I ask from my position between my legs.

"Fuck!" I hear him shuffling. "I'm hoping I won't be. I haven't agreed to take the position. I'm trying to convince my grandfather to give the company to Mom. She wants to run the company and she'd be damn good at it. But he's an old-fashioned misogynist and he doesn't believe women can be successful in high-level positions."

I sit up and twist in my chair, facing him directly. "But Eric said you lived in New Jersey. He said you only moved here last week, that you had to finish your work and it had taken longer than expected. I don't understand. You said you've always lived here." He couldn't have lived in New Jersey, because I met him back in June and have been living with him since September.

AJ takes my hand in his as Lucy returns with a glass of water for me. I take it gratefully, my hand shaking. "Thanks, Luce."

"You're welcome." Her forehead creases in confusion as her eyes dance between me and AJ. I tip my head to the side and pointedly look at her desk, hoping she gets the hint to leave us alone. Thankfully she does and steps away.

"I *have always* lived here. Look, I don't understand why my grandfather told you I lived in New Jersey. I've never lived anywhere but here. I've never lied to you; I promise. My relationship with my grandfather is"—he glances away from me, grasping the back of his neck—"complicated. It's a long story, and I'll be happy to fill you in later, just not here." He huffs out a breath and shakes his head, tension and anger emanating from him.

"Adam!" Eric's voice booms from down the hallway and I carefully slide my hand out of AJ's hold, shifting in my seat to put as much distance between us as possible. Eric's eyes catch on me as he steps closer. "Sarah, are you feeling okay? You don't look well, my dear."

"Uh, yeah, I'm okay. I just met"—I glance at AJ with a tight smile —"Adam in the elevator and felt a little dizzy. He was kind enough to help me sit so I can catch my breath." I hold up the glass of water. "I feel better now." I force myself to make eye contact with AJ ... *Adam.* "Thank you for your help." I climb to my feet, hoping my shaky legs hold me. AJ stands too, his hand reaching out to support me, but I take a step away and force a smile to my lips. "I'm sorry I was late this morning, Mr. Wainwright. I'll go and set up for the day. Let me know when you're ready for me to join your meeting."

Smoothing down my skirt, I step away from the man who's been like a grandfather to me and the man I was beginning to believe I could have a future with. I don't know how I make it to my work area, but I do. I tuck my purse in the cupboard behind my desk and turn on my computer as usual, then head straight to the bathroom. In my need to escape, I push the door open too hard and it bangs loudly against the wall. Trying to catch it, so I can close it quietly, I push it shut with a quiet snick. Leaning against the vanity, I look up at the ceiling. "Why?" I roll my eyes and huff out a breath, then study myself in the mirror. Everyone's right. I do look pale. I don't feel so good and the connection I've just discovered isn't making my anxiety and nausea any better. Dipping down, I splash some cool water on my face and take measured breaths to regain my composure. I need to get to work and act like the professional I am. I've already got off on the wrong foot with my new boss!

Ugh! Boss.

Fuck my life.

I blow out a heavy breath and head to the kitchen to make a pot of tea for Eric and coffee for ... Adam. God, it's going to be so hard getting used to calling him that.

As I'm making the drinks, I work through my memory for signs I must have missed that AJ is Adam. But I don't think there were any to miss. AJ and I hadn't talked about work very much and not once did he mention he was expected to take over the family business. Plus, Eric said his grandson lived in New Jersey. How would I have possibly thought AJ was Adam? None of it makes sense. AJ's been here the entire time I've known him whereas Eric said Adam only moved here last week. My head hurts trying to piece it all together.

Lucy steps into the kitchen with my container of cupcakes. "Here ya go. I thought I'd bring them down before I ate them all." She chuckles and leans her hip against the counter. Raising her eyebrows, she fans her face. "The new boss is pretty hot. Too young for me, but ideal for you."

Saliva pools in my mouth and I choke on air. I snap my head around, checking there's no one in earshot. "You can't talk about our new boss like that, Luce," I whisper-shout at her. "Plus, do you remember the updates to the handbook? No fraternization between employees."

She shrugs with a smirk. "At least we'll finally have some eye candy in the office." She chuckles as she walks toward the door to leave.

"Stop it!" I hiss and then hear her chuckle from the other side of the wall.

I blow out a breath and add some cupcakes to a plate, then place everything on a tray with shaky hands. I guess AJ will get a cupcake after all. I fortify my shaky legs and carry the drinks and food to Eric's office. The door's closed, so I place the tray on my desk and raise my knuckles to knock, only to be startled by Eric's shout.

"She's a woman! And not fit to run this company." My eyebrows almost shoot to my hairline. I had never heard Eric raise his voice, but over the past few months, he's done it a lot. I glance through the gap in the closed blinds to see a red-faced Eric leaning over his desk in a most intimidating way. AJ is still seated, looking as calm as anything.

Since there's a lull, I knock on the door and open it, pasting on my best smile. "I brought you both a drink and some cupcakes. Do you need anything else?" I look at Eric, then glance at AJ to check if he's all right after his grandfather's outburst. He nods his head slightly and I turn my attention back to my current boss.

He smiles at me, straightening his tie and returning to a seated position. "That will be all for now. Thank you. I'll let you know when we're ready for you."

"No problem, Mr. Wainwright." I tip my head and escape, closing the door behind me. I quickly make myself a cup of decaf coffee and get to work checking emails and updating the database—it's hard to maintain my concentration, though. Now and then Eric raises his voice, but never AJ. I'm not sure what's going on, but clearly, Eric isn't happy.

I grab my phone and shoot Mel a message.

ME

Guess who my new boss is

Forget it, you'll never guess

MEL

Is he a super stud hot model that poses in Calvin Klein underwear?

Of course, Mel has her mind in the gutter and ordinarily, I would laugh at her message, but not today. I'm too wound up at the prospect that I've lost AJ, and I've totally ruined my career by sleeping with my future boss. I drop my head to my hands. How could I mess up this epically?

ME

Nope. I wish it were some super-hot model. That would be a hell of a lot simpler than the real answer

MEL

He can't be that bad

ME

Yes, yes he can

MEL

Well, don't keep me in suspenders. Who is it?

ME

AJ *crying emoji* *crying emoji* *crying emoji* *crying emoji* *crying emoji*

My phone instantly rings, so I jump up from my desk and head toward the reception area, the farthest distance from Eric's office as I can possibly be and remain on the same floor.

"You have to be shitting me."

I blow out a heavy breath. "Nope. I wish I was. God, Mel. How is this possible?" I pull my hair back and hold it away from my face as I pace. Lucy gives me a weird look so I lower my voice. "Why? Mel.

Why does this shit happen to me? Just when I thought I could have something real and meaningful with AJ, this happens. I'm going to lose him now and I could lose my damn job."

"Calm down. You met him *before* he became your boss, surely that means it won't impact your job and you don't know if you'll lose him. Is there anything in the company policy about dating colleagues?"

I glance over, noticing Lucy leaning forward. I would take the call in the stairwell, but it's a dead zone and I can't get reception in there. I move further away and soften my voice. "Not in the original employee handbook, but he included it in the updates. What am I gonna do?"

"You're going to do your damn job because you're good at it, and then you're going to speak with AJ when you get the chance and find out what the hell's going on. I thought Adam lived in New Jersey and only moved back here last week?"

"I know, right? I'm totally confused. I know AJ hasn't lied to me about where he lives, that would be impossible. But why would Eric lie about where his grandson lives? I don't understand."

*–aj–*

FUCK! FUCK! FUCK!

I felt it. I felt her shut down on me. This is the worst possible scenario. The situation with Grandfather and his company is bad enough, but now I find out Sarah's his assistant and I had no damn clue. And how would I? Grandfather never refers to her by name, it's always 'my assistant' because he doesn't deem her important. I've never called his office, so I've never spoken to his 'assistant.' Now I'm wishing I had because I wouldn't have been blindsided. She let her last boyfriend go because she loved her job ... and her family ... so much that she couldn't bear to leave.

*What if she chooses her job over me?*

Sarah steps into the room with a fake smile plastered on her face. I know it's fake because her lips are too tight. Normally, she smiles so big her lips separate and she shows her perfectly straight teeth. Her hand shakes as she places a tray of cupcakes and drinks on Grandfather's desk.

"I brought you both a drink and some cupcakes. Do you need anything else?" She looks at Eric, then glances at me. I can see the question in her eyes. She had to hear Grandfather's outburst. I nod my head discreetly to let her know I'm okay, and she returns her attention to my grandfather.

He softens his posture and smiles at her, straightening his tie and returning to his seat. "That will be all for now. Thank you. I'll let you know if we need you." He's different with her. Softer, kinder.

"No problem, Mr. Wainwright." She tips her head and escapes without giving me a second glance, closing the door behind her.

Grandfather pushes the plate of cupcakes toward me. "Sarah makes these every Friday. She made these, especially for you." He nods to the plate and I blow out a breath, then take a cupcake. I love her cupcakes, so I'm not about to say no. I'll take anything to make this situation more bearable.

"Thanks."

Grandfather takes a sip of his tea, then places the cup on its saucer. "Women don't belong in CEO roles, Adam. As much as you want to be progressive, it's not appropriate. They don't have the same level of success as men do."

"Only because they're not given the opportunity because of men like—"

"Watch your mouth, boy." Spittle flies across the desk and I'm glad it's as wide as it is or I'd be wiping it from my face.

I sit forward on the edge of my chair. "What about Diane Hendricks? Huh." I raise my brows. "She took over sole ownership of the company she had with her husband and then went on to buy out her two biggest rivals. She made history."

His face turns red. "One. One successful woman doesn't mean that all women are cut out for this role, Adam."

I pull the thumb drive from my pocket and hold it up. "I have an entire presentation I can show you, with all the facts and figures you could possibly need to be convinced to give the company to Mom."

He scoffs, rolling his eyes. "This is *my* damn company, and it's my decision whom I hand it over to. A woman will run this company over my dead body." His face is red and splotchy, his breaths becoming harsh.

I feel as though I'm going in circles and getting absolutely nowhere. This is the same conversation we've had since he got it into his head that I was the only suitable candidate to take over the company, our family legacy, so he could retire. He's always treated me like a child, so I'm not sure why he's so adamant I run things. Oh, that's right, I'm the only direct relative with a penis instead of a vagina.

He presses a button on his phone. "Please join me in my office." He lifts his finger, cutting off the call without waiting for a response. I sit back further into my seat, savoring the final bite of my cupcake while I wait for Sarah to join us.

The door opens and in strides a man I've never met. I peer behind him, hoping to spot Sarah, but he closes the door quickly and moves to take the seat next to mine. "Tony. This is my grandson, Adam. Adam. Tony, my Vice President."

I hold my hand out to greet the man. "Nice to meet you, Tony." He tips his head to me, with no move to take my proffered hand, so I drop it back onto my lap. There's a level of frostiness radiating from him that has my hackles rising.

"Adam here is still trying to convince me to give the company to his mother instead of him," Grandfather scoffs at Tony as though I'm no longer in the room, making me feel small. Anger blooms inside me, and I know I'm going to struggle to keep it contained.

Tony studies me with clear disdain. "As I've said to you before, Eric. I'll be happy to step in and run the company with you still at the helm. There's no place for a woman in the leadership role here."

Jesus! I glance around the office. Standing, I stride to the windows and peer down at the cars on the street. Finally, I check the date on my phone.

"What the hell are you doing, boy?"

"Just checking that I'm living in the twenty-first century and not the damn nineteen-fifties," I snap. "No wonder you won't budge. Your Vice President thinks exactly the way you do." I turn to Tony. "I was hoping you would help me drag him into the current century, but you're as entrenched in the old ways as he is." I refuse to allow this idiot to have any more control in this company. I turn back to Grandfather. "I'll take the damn position *and* the damn company." I glance between the two men, frustration and anger filling my body. I'm surprised the top of my head hasn't blown off. "But let me make this clear." I move back in front of Grandfather's desk and poke my finger angrily at the surface. "You will not interfere with how I run it. Once it's in my hands, I'll fill the leadership roles with whomever I see fit, whether that person is a man or a woman." I rarely lose my cool, but as I stand here with these two dinosaurs, I can no longer contain my anger.

I spin on my heel, and storm out of the office, slamming the door behind me. Sarah's head snaps up from her computer and frown lines form between her brows as she studies me closely. "Are you okay? That all sounded very intense in there."

I step closer to her desk. "I don't know how you've managed to work here as long as you have."

She leans forward, glancing behind her at Grandfather's door. "What do you mean?"

"I mean, my grandfather is a damn misogynist still living in the nineteen-fifties." I blow out a breath.

She chuckles and waves her hand in the air like she's dismissing my comment. "He's not that bad. A little old-fashioned maybe."

"You know I never knew the name of his assistant because he always referred to you as his 'assistant.'" Her eyes widen. "Yeah." I nod and hold out my hand to Sarah. She studies it but makes no move to take it. "We need to talk."

She glances back at the door as boisterous laughter comes from Grandfather's office. "Not now, I'm working," she hisses.

"When you get home, then."

Her shoulders jump up to her ears. "About that." She glances at the door again, then leans closer, dropping the volume of her voice. "I'll need to pick up my things."

"No!" I shout, then lower my voice. "I know what you're gonna do and I won't let you."

"This is my job, AJ."

The muscle in my chest pounds heavily and I search for something to say. "And I'm your boyfriend."

She shakes her head. "You can't be. You're gonna be my boss," she whispers, her shaky hand coming up to push a lock of hair roughly behind her ear.

I lean over her desk, closer, locking my eyes with Sarah's, imploring her to listen to me. "I don't give a fuck if I'm going to be your boss. I'm not letting you go. Not now. Not ever. Don't throw away what we have for this." I drill my finger into her desk.

She presses forward and my eyes drop to her cleavage as her top gapes open. "It's okay for you to expect me to give up this job, you have your own company and then you'll have this one," she hisses. "How will I support myself? This is one of the best-paying assistant jobs around."

"I can support you, Sarah. You and our baby when we have one. You won't need to work."

She huffs out a sarcastic chuckle. "So, you're like your grandfather then. You think women should be at home with the children, not in the workplace."

*What the fuck?*

I draw my head back as though she slapped me. "No. Of course not. How can you say that? All I'm saying is you don't need *this* job. You've got me." I jab my thumb into my chest. "But maybe you don't want me. This only ever started with you wanting a donor. Is that all I'm good for, Sarah?" Her eyes widen and her mouth drops open. I snap my mouth closed and hold my hands up in surrender. "I'm sorry. I shouldn't have said any of that." My anger at the situation and fear of losing Sarah has crumbled my usual control.

Grandfather's door opens, catching Sarah and me staring at each other in disbelief that we've just fought. If I was worried I'd lose her before, then I'm pretty sure I just hammered the nail in our coffin. "I thought you'd left." He steps to the side of the door, waving his arm inside. "Come back inside, we'll hammer out some of the details."

My eyes bounce between Sarah and Grandfather, and I grasp the back of my neck and squeeze it tight. "No. I can't. I have a project I need to get done today." Without another word, I spin on my heel.

"Are you okay, Sarah? You don't look so well," I hear Grandfather say. Every molecule in my body is telling me to stop. To go back. To make things right. To check she's okay. But I can't. I've said too much and crossed too many lines today. I need to regroup.

I climb into my Jeep and slam the door, then thump the steering wheel. I start the car and drive. I need to think and I need to calm the fuck down. I never lose my cool like that, but the fear of losing Sarah was overriding my common sense and I couldn't seem to shut my damn mouth. It felt as though a knife stabbed me in the chest when Sarah chose her job over me. I knew it was coming the second I realized she worked for my grandfather, but I had hoped that she loved … no, cared for me enough that she would choose our future together over her position in the company. A company that doesn't even respect or value her.

Glancing at the back seat, I check if I have my climbing bag in the car and I do. I turn right instead of left and head toward the gym. I can't sit in an office with this pent-up frustration inside of me. I need to burn some of it off.

Grant does a double-take when he spots me walking through the door. "You're not usually here at this time of day."

"Need to expend some energy. Is it okay if I climb?"

"Go for it. You know you're always welcome here. I can come and belay for you in a minute, once I finish updating my books."

"Thanks, Grant. Appreciate it, man." I head to the locker room to change and start with some basic bouldering while I wait for Grant.

Taking a few deep breaths, I focus my attention, pushing this morning to the far recesses of my mind. It won't do me any good to be unfocused while I'm climbing. Grant's changed the holds since I was here last, something he does regularly to keep the climbs fresh, making it easier to narrow my focus from one hold to the next.

"Looking strong there, AJ."

"Thanks." I make my way to the other end of the wall easily and climb down to the mat. Grant's waiting ready to give me a high-five. Chalkdust flies in the air and we make our way over to the rope section.

I spend most of the day climbing, using the ropes when Grant's available, and bouldering when he's not. I direct all of my focus toward climbing the route better than the previous time, using faster more efficient moves. My muscles burn and cramp and my stomach feels as though it's going to revolt. I've experienced this before when I've pushed myself too hard—I need to stop.

I climb down carefully and drop onto the mat, exhaustion taking over my body. Sucking air into my lungs, I shake out my arms and legs. Dipping down to my bag, I grab my water bottle, coming up empty. Damn it. I didn't have one with me. I spot the water fountain and make my way over there slowly. Pressing the button, I gulp the cool water like my life depends on it and this is the last of the available water on the planet. Lowering to a nearby bench, I drop my head into my hands. I could climb all the way to the top of Mount Everest, but it won't help me keep Sarah. I should be devising a plan to make her see reason, rather than escaping up a damn wall.

Collecting my bag, I check my phone. Missed calls and messages from Hayley and Dylan fill the screen. Nothing from Sarah. I blow out a breath, my heart feeling heavy in my chest. I wave at Grant on my way out and make the drive home.

The instant I open the door, I know something's not right. "Where the hell have you been?" Dylan barks at me.

"I need to have a shower." I walk past him and head straight for the stairs up to my bedroom.

"Sarah was here." He pauses. "She packed her stuff and left in tears."

My feet freeze on the step and that heavy feeling in my chest implodes and shatters. My nose tingles and eyes prickle and I keep my back to my long-time friend. Nodding my head a couple of times, I take the stairs slowly, leaving shattered pieces of my heart behind, and close myself in our bedroom, leaning my back against the door. I squeeze my eyes tight because I can't bear to see the room without her things in it, but it's futile because her springtime scent still fills the space. I kick the heel of my foot against the door and run my hands through my hair. "Fuck!" I was hoping she would at least talk this through and try to work out a solution. I'm not a violent man, but I have an overwhelming desire to punch something.

I had no idea Saturday night would be the last night I got to spend with the woman of my dreams. If I'd known I would have never let her leave this room and then we wouldn't be in the mess we're in. I head for the shower, noting the shelf is void of Sarah's stuff, except for the pink razor she uses to shave her legs.

Dylan's waiting outside my bedroom door with two beers when I open it. He nods his head toward my deck and makes his way outside. I follow behind because I need someone to talk to right now and it may as well be him.

"Did Sarah say anything to you before she left?"

He shakes his head, his lips pressed tight.

I blow out a breath, then start at the beginning, telling him about seeing Sarah in the elevator, finding out she's Grandfather's assistant, to our argument at her desk.

"Fuck, man," he whispers. "What are you gonna do?"

I shrug. "I was hoping we could talk it through and work out a way forward, but it makes it damn hard if she's running in the opposite direction." I take a drink of my beer. "She chose her job ... and her family and friends ... over her boyfriend four years ago, and they had been together since high school."

"Shit, man. I don't like your chances."

Yeah, thanks for the vote of confidence. "Me neither."

# CHAPTER 39

## —sarah—

"THANKS FOR LETTING ME STAY, MEL. I DIDN'T HAVE ANYWHERE ELSE to go," I sob as I wipe the tears that won't stop away from my cheeks. I could have gone to my sister's but he knows where she lives and I wouldn't put it past him to turn up there. I needed somewhere he didn't know and couldn't find.

"You know you're always welcome here, Sare." She wraps her arm around me and tugs me inside her apartment which is even smaller than mine. "Even though I only have a pull-out sofa." She steps back into the hall and grabs my suitcase, bringing it inside and putting it next to the other one. I drop my overnight bag from my shoulder and it thumps as it lands heavily on the carpeted floor.

Mel guides me to the couch and sits me down, then heads for her tiny kitchen. I grab a tissue from the coffee table while she fusses for a few minutes, before returning with two steaming cups of hot chocolate. Ordinarily, this would be wine or something stronger, but she knows I've been avoiding alcohol since I started trying to get pregnant. Though, maybe I could have a drink. It's not like I'm pregnant or have any prospect of getting pregnant in the near future. She drops to the cushion beside me, curling one foot beneath her butt, and resting her drink on her raised knee. "So … AJ is Adam."

With gut-wrenching sadness, I nod. "I can't believe it. Of all the people."

"It was certainly unexpected. I can't imagine the shock you're feeling. What are you gonna do now?"

"I can't afford to lose my job, Mel." I explain how AJ … *Adam* …

expected me to give up my job and said he would take care of me and our baby. Not that there's a baby.

"I don't see the problem with that, to be honest. It'll give you time with the baby when it's born and during the early formative years."

I nod because deep down I love the idea of having that time with my baby in the early years. It's something I can't afford to do if I'm on my own. "I'm not even pregnant." More tears stream down my cheeks at the reminder that I got my period again this month, though it was lighter than usual. I've been stressed about meeting my new boss and my body's trying to cope with my sky-high anxiety. It's probably why I'm having trouble getting pregnant—too much stress.

Mel places her cup on the coffee table and moves in closer to embrace me, letting me sob into her shoulder. My tears are filled with pain for the loss of AJ and my dream of a baby. A baby with him. Creating a *real* family with the man of my dreams.

"I don't understand why it has to be an either-or situation. Why can't you stay with AJ *and* keep your job?" She rubs her hand up and down my arm in a soothing motion.

"How would that look?"

Mel's face scrunches up. "Who the fuck cares how it would look, Sare? You were with him *before* either of you knew … he didn't know you worked there, right?"

I shake my head. "No. Apparently, Eric always referred to me as his assistant, never by name."

"What?"

"AJ said he's a misogynist and doesn't deem me worthy of using my name. Which was completely shocking to me because I've never found Eric to be like that. He's a great boss. Fair and flexible with the staff. Admittedly, there are only two women in the company and both hold secretarial-type positions."

"Sounds like he might be to me."

"But then AJ wanted me to give up my job to raise our baby, doesn't that make him the same?"

Mel shrugs. "Depends what his reasons are and why he said it. To me, it sounded like he was saying it to give you options. He probably knows you well enough and realized you'd break things off with him to keep your job. But think about this, Sare. If you break things off with AJ to keep your job and he becomes your boss, you'll have to work with him every single day. Will you be able to do that? Knowing what the two of you share and what you've given up, could you be happy seeing him every day and not be able to touch him?" She chews on her bottom lip. "How will you feel if he starts dating someone else?"

I drag my hair around to one side and fiddle with it, feeling sick to my stomach at the thought of AJ with someone else, while I think about Mel's questions. She's right, dammit. This is why I love her. She knows me so well that she knows exactly how and why I respond to things the way I do. "It'll kill me," I finally whisper.

"Then why can't you have the man *and* the job?" She squeezes my arm. "He obviously adores you, Sare. Why would you give that up? Jobs come and go, but love … true, deep, lasting love, that's not so easy to find."

Tears burst forth again, pouring over my lashes and down my cheeks. "Oh my God, I've made a terrible mistake, Mel." I press my face into my hands. God, I'm stupid. As if a job is worth more than AJ. "It was a knee-jerk reaction to hold onto my job. I'm so used to having to take care of myself and plan for my future."

I'm not sure how long we sit in silence on Mel's couch before her stomach growls loudly, breaking through my haze. I look at my best friend: sitting beside me, comforting me, giving up her sleep for me. I have to be the luckiest girl in the world to have Mel as my best friend. I pat her leg and climb to my feet, shaking out the pins and needles in my left foot so I can put it on the floor without tipping over. "How about I make us something to eat and you can shower and get ready for work?"

She shows me her gorgeous straight teeth and nods. "Sure, that'd be great."

She heads off to her bedroom, and I step into her kitchen, ready to look after my best friend. Opening her fridge leaves me scratching my head. It's pretty bare, but I think I can make us both an omelet. By the time she comes out, dressed in her cute pink scrubs with baby elephants on them, I have two omelets plated and ready to eat. I quickly pour Mel a coffee and we sit at her two-seater dining table pushed against the window to eat.

Mel moans around a forkful of food. "Delicious, Sare. I always love your cooking."

I chuckle. "Only because you don't cook. Your fridge looks like it belongs in a bachelor pad."

She shrugs. "I'm not here all that much. The food spoils if I have too much stuff." She takes another bite and then swallows, locking her gaze on me. "What are you going to do?"

"I'm going to sleep on it tonight because I need to plan how I'm going to apologize properly to AJ. I need to be clear about what I'm going to say. I'll talk with him after work tomorrow. Hopefully, he's the forgiving type and won't hate me too much for my behavior today. I only wish I respond better when I'm blindsided like I was. I'm not proud of my actions, Mel. I'm ashamed of myself. He's been nothing but supportive and caring toward me."

"We all make mistakes, Sare. You're not the first and you definitely won't be the last. It's how you take responsibility for it that matters."

"Thanks, Mel." I lean across and hug my girl, then shoo her out the door for her shift. "I'm sorry you didn't get your sleep today."

"That's okay. I'm glad I could be there for you. I probably won't see you tomorrow. So, good luck."

"Thanks." We hug goodbye. She heads to work and I clean up from our meal.

After minimal sleep last night because I was missing AJ so much, work was awful today. It felt like it was never going to end, and all I wanted to do was get to AJ. I'm so churned up about seeing him, that I couldn't bear to eat anything for fear it would make a reappearance. This whole situation has me questioning everything. AJ hasn't messaged me and I'm second-guessing my plan to go over to his house to apologize. Maybe he's thankful he's finally free of me. After all, I was just a stranger he offered to help.

I take a deep breath and reach up a shaky hand to press AJ's doorbell. The sound is empty, reminding me of how I feel knowing I've hurt AJ. I spin on my heel to peer down the street while I wait for an answer. I can't hear anyone making their way to the door, so I ring again and wait.

No answer.

I have a key I could use, but it feels all kinds of wrong to walk inside his home after the way we left things and I packed up and moved out. I'm kicking myself for my overreaction yesterday. If I'd only taken a moment to think things through properly. He must think I value my job more than I value him and the relationship we were building.

When there's still no answer, I wander around to the side entrance, the one he uses for the business. I knock on the door and I don't have to wait long before I hear footsteps moving close. It swings inward, revealing Dylan. He tips his chin at me and steps back inside, leaving the door open, I assume so I can follow him.

"Hi." My voice comes out shaky.

"Hey. AJ's not here." Dylan's frosty greeting adds to my anxiety about speaking with AJ. He leans against a desk, crossing his arms over his chest and his feet at his ankles. His stance is one of careless relaxation, but there's an undertone of annoyance.

"Oh. Any idea when he'll be back?"

He shrugs. "Nope. He said he needed some space, so he's gone camping to climb."

Shit! That's not good. I was hoping to sort this out today. "Do you know where he went?"

"Nope. And I've tried to call him, but he's out of range."

Panic quickly fills my body. "Is that safe? What if he has an accident or something? How will he get help?"

"He knows what he's doing, and it's really none of your concern anymore, is it?"

I prickle at his tone. "What do you mean? I still care about him. I don't want him to get hurt."

He chuckles, but it's completely fake. "You already hurt him, Sarah. That's why he took off."

My eyes prickle and a boulder quickly forms in my throat knowing I've hurt AJ. I try to swallow, but it's stuck. I glance around the room, trying to fight off what's happening inside my body, but I can't catch my breath. I bring my palm up to my throat and pat the base, trying to dislodge whatever's trapped in there, but nothing happens. I can't breathe and my heart races. Panic overwhelms me and the more I try to suck in air, the less air I'm getting. Everything's starting to spin when strong hands grasp my biceps.

"Sarah!" I'm shaken, but nothing helps, I can't get any oxygen into my lungs. My legs tremble and I'm sure Dylan's grip on my arms is the only thing keeping me standing. "Sarah!" he shouts, shaking me more vigorously. "Fuck!"

I feel him push me into a chair and fold me almost in half so my head is down between my legs. This keeps happening to me and I'm sick of it. I need to learn to manage my emotions better.

"Sarah, I want you to take deep breaths with me. Okay? Breathe in, one, two, three. Hold it. Breathe out, one, two, three." I focus on his deep, calming voice and follow his instructions. He repeats the process several times, kindly stroking his hand soothingly up and down my spine.

When I feel I'm finally back in control, I sit up and wipe my face with shaky hands. Finally, my heart feels like it's slowing to normal speed and my lungs don't feel as though they're on fire. "Thank you," I murmur. I'm so damn embarrassed. I push my sweaty hair away from my face and give Dylan a timid but grateful smile. "Sorry about that."

He leaves the office and comes back with a glass of water. Handing it to me, he studies me closely, creases between his blond eyebrows. "Does that happen often?"

"Uh, when I'm super anxious about something it can sometimes happen." I shrug and take a sip of the cool water. It seems to be happening a lot lately.

"Are you gonna be all right?"

"Yeah. But could I ask you a favor? I know I have no right, but if you hear from AJ, can you please let me know. I need to know he's okay. I'm sorry I hurt him, and I came here to apologize and ask his forgiveness. I was hoping we could put it behind us."

He nods, studying me like I'm some sort of alien being. "Sure. Give me your number and if I hear from him, I'll let you know."

I smile gratefully. "Thank you." I give him my number and stand to leave.

"You're not gonna stay here?"

I tuck my still-damp hair behind my ear. "No. I don't think it's right for me to stay until I know he's forgiven me." Dylan nods. "Thanks for taking care of me."

"No problem. Take care, bye."

# CHAPTER 40

## *—aj—*

WITHOUT SARAH BESIDE ME, SLEEP WAS IMPOSSIBLE TO COME BY LAST night, so I decided to pack and come to one of my favorite climbing spots for a few days. It's not too far from the city, but far enough away that I can leave everything behind. Dylan understood my need to take a few days when I told him I'd be back by Friday. I just needed enough time to clear my head and work out if there's any way I can move forward with Sarah. She made it pretty clear her job is more important than me or a relationship with me. Not gonna lie, that fucking stung. I thought we were building something real, but clearly, I was wrong.

I look up at the rock face, studying it and planning my route. There's a buttress to the right, but it's a little off the path that looks safest. The climb isn't that high, only about thirty feet, but I'll be free climbing it on my own, so I need to ensure I take the safest path possible. Attaching my chalk bag, I rub the ball of chalk between my hands ensuring I have decent coverage. Testing the rock, I make my first hold and follow with my feet, testing the stability. I'm only a foot off the ground, but it feels great to have the sandstone beneath my fingers and the sun on my back. I work my way up carefully, following the path I mapped out visually before I started.

When I'm about fifteen feet from the ground, a bird swoops low, landing on a ledge just above me. It peeks over the edge like it's watching what I'm doing. I smile at it, contemplating how brave it must be to come so close to a human. Returning my focus to the rock face, I grumble when I notice the distance to my next suitable hold. It didn't look that far from the ground but I'll need to stretch wide and push hard with my legs if I have any chance of reaching it. I take a deep breath and push up with my legs and stretch out with my arm, but miss and at the same time, the rock beneath my other hold gives way.

"Oh shit!"

My heart falters as I begin to free fall. My head connects with something hard and pain shoots through my skull.

Everything goes black.

Pain radiates through my body and I try to open my eyes. The heaviness of my body is foreign to me like my limbs are weighed down by heavy boulders. A woman's voice sounds far in the distance and I'm cold all the way to my bones. Shivering hurts. *Everything fucking hurts.* I groan. Well, I think I do.

"Sir. Sir." Hands squeeze my shoulders. "My name's Violet. Help is on the way. We've got you. You're going to be okay." I think I nod if the throbbing in my head is anything to go by. I've never felt agony like this before. It's too much so I stop moving, hoping this is a bad dream.

Blackness infiltrates from the outer edges of my mind, swamping me, taking me under again.

Jostling and pain. I think I'm moving. Levitating over the ground.

Voices fade in and out.

Pain. So much pain.

The throbbing in my head pounds like a jackhammer and my need to vomit is strong. Bile moves up from my stomach, burning through my body.

Tight. Everything's so tight. I can't move. I'm trapped. The contents of my stomach explode out of my mouth.

I'm swimming in blackness.

Loud noise. Jostling. Voices. Throbbing. Cold air. Agony. Darkness.

## —sarah—

IT'S MID-AFTERNOON AND MY PHONE RINGS WITH AN UNKNOWN NUMBER. I'm always reluctant to answer calls I don't recognize but I'm hoping this is Dylan with an update on AJ. I need to see him and tell him how sorry I am. I need his forgiveness. The whole thing's been eating away at me. I need to tell him I'm prepared to find a job somewhere else, so we can be together. I've already applied for a couple of positions this morning on the other side of town. It's just a matter of time before the applications close and I'll know if I have an interview.

With trembling fingers, I press the green button and hold the phone to my ear. "Hello, this is—"

"Sarah." The male voice is panicked, sending my pulse skyrocketing. "It's Dylan." Blood rushes to my ears because I know from his tone that something terrible has happened.

"Wh-where is he?" I stammer.

"Mercy Vale."

"Oh my God. This is all my fault. I'm on my way." My legs shake as I stand, my breaths coming fast, and grab my purse, heading straight for the elevator.

"Sarah!" Dylan almost shouts down the line. I forgot I still had him on the phone. "Don't drive. I don't want you having an attack like you did yesterday while you're driving. Fuck, I should have come and picked you up. Stay on the line with me. I've already called AJ's family."

"O-okay." I get to the reception desk. "Lucy." She snaps her eyes to me. The tone of my voice has her eyes widening in alarm. "C-can you please call me an Uber? I n-need to get to Mercy Vale Hospital. I'll wait downstairs." I can't believe my shaky legs are holding me up and my heart is still inside my chest.

"Is everything okay?" Her eyebrows are scrunched low over her worried eyes.

"I do-don't know." Shit, I should probably tell Eric.

I take my first step toward Eric's office when he comes barreling toward me. "I need to go. My grandson's been in an accident." He tosses at me as he passes.

I pick up my pace and follow him. "Can I come with you?"

"What's going on, Sarah?" Dylan's voice calls out and I remember I still have him on the phone.

"AJ's grandfather is on his way to the hospital and I'm asking if I can go wi—"

"Who are you speaking with, Sarah?" Eric interrupts.

"Dylan, AJ's best friend." Creases form between his brows momentarily but waves me forward to follow him. As I pass Lucy, I tell her to cancel the Uber and follow Eric into the elevator. His driver is waiting out front and we climb straight in. "Dylan. I'm in the car with AJ's grandfather. We're on our way. Where can we find you?"

"Emergency. Come straight to the Emergency Room. We're all here."

"Okay." Ending the call, I turn toward Eric. "We need to go to the Emergency Room." We make our way toward the hospital in silence, both of us lost in our thoughts. My leg bounces involuntarily and the nausea I haven't been able to shake since Monday morning threatens to escape. Squeezing my hands together in my lap, I try to keep my thoughts positive and in the moment, so I don't have another panic attack—it won't do me any good to fall apart. I monitor my breathing carefully, making sure I take measured breaths in and out. I need to keep it together.

For AJ.

God, I hope he's going to be okay. I can't lose him.

Glancing at Eric, I find him gazing out of the window, but I doubt he's seeing the traffic. He looks vacant. "He'll be okay," I tell Eric, but the affirmation is more for myself than for him.

Eric huffs. "Why was Dylan calling you?"

I squeeze my hands together, twisting my fingers. "Uhm …"

Eric turns his head toward me, his eyes searing into the side of my face. "Sarah?"

"Uhm ... I ..." I swallow the sudden build-up of saliva that's pooled in my mouth. "We ... uh ..." Damn it, just spit it out, Sarah. "AJ and I were living together."

"What?" He spins in his seat, facing me properly and I drop my gaze to my lap, so I don't have to meet his narrowed eyes and down-turned mouth. "Explain."

We're probably another fifteen minutes away from the hospital at this point. I start at the beginning when I met AJ at *Club Rumors* at the beginning of June. I explain how he offered to be my donor and how our relationship changed and grew into more. I mean, I leave out the intimate details because he doesn't need to know all that. The expression on his face filters through various emotions, the last one being guilt. He must know that I know he lied about his grandson.

"If you want me to resign from my position, I'm happy to do that." I rush to add.

He swipes his hand through the air. "There's no need to make rash decisions."

Finally, we pull into the hospital parking lot and I jump out of the car and head straight to the emergency doors, barreling through like my life depends on it. I head straight to administration. "Hello. I'm here for—"

"Sarah!"

I spin on the spot at the sound of my name to find Hayley hurrying toward me. I race to her, embracing her tightly. "Do you know anything?"

She shakes her head, tears gliding down her cheeks, her nose red. "Nothing yet." She pulls away and takes my hand, leading me toward Lisa, Dylan, and an older couple I'm guessing are AJ's parents. They look exactly the same as they do in the photograph on Eric's desk, only older. "Sarah, this is our mom and dad, Elaine and Adam. Mom. Dad. This is Sarah. AJ's girlfriend." Hayley mustn't know about our argument.

Their eyes widen, obviously unaware that AJ had a girlfriend. Not that I'm certain if we're still a couple or not. AJ's dad is the first to reach his hand forward. "Nice to meet you, Sarah."

His mom steps forward with a shaky smile. She's obviously been crying if her red-rimmed eyes are any indication. "It's lovely to meet you, Sarah. I only wish it were under better circumstances."

I swallow the lump in my throat carefully—so I don't choke—and take her hand in my shaky one. This is not how I imagined I'd meet

AJ's parents. Thank goodness I've already met Hayley, Lisa, and Dylan. "Nice to meet you both."

Dylan comes over and embraces me, then steps back, holding my shoulders. I read the unspoken question in his eyes and give him a shaky smile. "I'm okay. Holding it together the best I can."

"Father." Elaine walks with quick steps toward Eric.

"How is he? Any news?"

She shakes her head. "Nothing."

"Well, that's not good enough." He stomps over to the registrar, demanding answers. The woman behind the desk remains calm, obviously used to dealing with anxious family members. He steps away from the counter, shaking his head, his face red.

"Mr. Wainwright, why don't you come and sit with your family? We may have to wait for a while. I'll go and get you a cup of tea from the cafeteria." Look at me being all cool, calm, and collected. If I stay busy, I have a better chance of holding myself together. He smiles softly at me, nodding as he takes a seat next to his daughter, who is looking at me as if she's trying to solve a puzzle.

Hayley flicks her eyes between me and her grandfather. "Do you know each other?"

I glance at Eric and before I can open my mouth to answer, he does. "Sarah's my assistant."

Everyone's eyes widen; everyone except Dylan. I'm assuming AJ told him who I was before he went climbing. Hayley's mouth drops open and she comes to stand next to me, leaning in close. "Oh my God, how have you managed to work with him? He's intolerable," she whispers. She links her arm through mine and then turns to her family. "I'll go with Sarah to get drinks for everyone. I think we're gonna be here a while."

We head off in search of the cafeteria, leaving everyone behind, and weaving down hallways until we find it. All the while my heart hammers wildly in my chest and I'm concentrating hard to control my shakes. I need to know AJ is going to be okay. I need to apologize, beg for his forgiveness, and then I need to tell him I love him. I was holding back before. Too scared we were moving too fast and worried things wouldn't work out. But I might not get the chance and that thought devastates me. I don't want to lose the best thing that's happened to me in a long while—if ever. I can't believe I thought it would be better to hold onto my job instead of him. I must be the world's biggest idiot.

While we're waiting for our order to be filled, Hayley turns to me.

"Did you know Grandfather and AJ were related? AJ never mentioned anything and I had no idea you were Grandfather's assistant. He's never even mentioned your name." AJ said something similar and it doesn't sting any less, considering I've worked for Eric for more than ten years and I thought we were close.

I shake my head. "No. Neither of us had any idea and Mr. Wainwright only just found out on the way here that AJ and I are in a relationship." Or should that be past tense? I shake my head. "We didn't have time to unpack the situation properly."

"This is crazy. Did you know Grandfather wants AJ to take over *FutureTech*?"

I nod, feeling like a bobble doll. "I've known for a while that Mr. Wainwright wanted his grandson, Adam, to take over, but I never put two and two together because I've always called him AJ. I didn't know AJ's name was Adam." I raise my eyebrows at Hayley.

"Yeah, it reduces the confusion with Dad and AJ having the same name." She shrugs.

"Also, Mr. Wainwright told me that Adam moved here last week after living in New Jersey since college."

"What?"

I nod. "Yep. There was no way I'd ever connect the two being the same person or that I was dating him."

"Yeah, I can see how you wouldn't make the connection. I wonder why Grandfather lied about AJ living in New Jersey? Maybe he was trying to save face because AJ kept holding off on taking the position. He doesn't want it."

"Maybe. I don't know." We collect our order and make our way back to the waiting room. Hayley and I distribute the drinks and sit. I lock my gaze on the doors which I assume a doctor or nurse will come through to tell us any news. We each sit in silence, the hard plastic of the chairs uncomfortable even for my padded butt. One would think the damn chairs would be more comfortable since people have to sit in them for hours on end. People come and go as the light outside the windows wanes.

"What the hell is taking so long?" Eric huffs as he climbs to his feet to pace.

His wife, who arrived not long after we were all settled with warm drinks, stands. "Eric. Calm down and have some patience. Come and sit back down." She coaxes him back to his seat and I smile at how sweet they are together.

A woman in scrubs steps through the doors and I straighten. Waiting. "The Jackson family." *Finally.*

We all jump to our feet, quickly making our way over to the woman. "We're Adam's parents."

She directs her attention to Elaine and Adam. "Mr. and Mrs. Jackson." She smiles. "Your son had a nasty fall, and from what we were told, rock debris also landed on him. He's currently in recovery. He hasn't woken since he arrived and from reports, he was in and out of consciousness during his rescue this morning."

Why is it taking her so long to tell us if he's all right? "Is he going to be okay?" Shit, it's not my place to ask, so I slam my lips closed.

She smiles at me. "He's going to be okay."

We breathe a collective sigh of instant relief and Dylan's arm comes around my shoulders, squeezing me to him. I glance up and give him a relieved smile.

"He's not out of the woods yet, though. As I said, he hasn't regained consciousness since arriving here. We've done a scan of his head, which shows swelling indicative of a concussion." Elaine gasps and my heart lurches. "He has a contusion and fifteen stitches where he hit his head. He was possibly unconscious before he hit the ground. He has an open fracture of the lower leg, both the tibia and fibula were broken, and we've realigned them with screws and plates which will remain permanently in place. He will need a cast for several weeks, followed by physical therapy. As one would expect, he also has lacerations, bruising, and swelling."

"Can we see him?" Elaine asks.

"Soon. A volunteer will come through to collect you once he's settled in his room."

"Thank you. And thank you for taking care of our boy." Adam reaches forward to shake the doctor's hand.

"You're welcome. We have another scan scheduled for the morning to keep an eye on the swelling and concussion." She spins on her heel and disappears back the way she came.

Elaine and Adam hug as do Lisa and Hayley and Eric and Anne. The relief is palpable among our little group. I turn into Dylan, holding onto him like a lifeline. "Thank you for calling me. I know AJ and I hadn't left things on great terms, so I appreciate you including me."

He scans my face. "He would want you here." I nod, giving him a shaky smile. "And, Sarah. This wasn't your fault. None of it. I shouldn't have said you're the reason he took off. That was part of it, but it was also because of his grandfather." My eyes sting and I blink to hold back my tears. I've kept it together this long, I can keep it together a little longer. Dylan tightens his hold, squeezing me, then lets me go, taking my hand to keep me steady.

"Thank God he's going to be okay, Adam." Elaine sobs and Adam rubs her back soothingly. I can see why AJ's family calls him AJ instead of Adam. Things could easily get confusing.

"Of course, he's going to be okay. That boy is as stubborn as they come." Eric states.

Elaine pulls away from her husband giving Eric a pointed look. "He gets that from you, Father."

Anne chuckles while Eric sputters his denial. We all move back to our seats, slightly more relaxed than we were before, knowing he's going to be okay. Lisa says her goodbyes to everyone so she can collect Colton from their neighbor, who kindly offered to watch their little one at short notice. They've been messaging back and forth, checking on him, but it's late and way past his bedtime.

This afternoon has felt as though it's been the longest of my life. Every minute has dragged beyond belief. My feet are aching and so is my back and as my anxiety settles marginally, the come down from the burst of adrenaline has left me exhausted. Finally, a volunteer steps through the doors. "The family of Adam Jackson?"

We all stand. "We're his family," Adam informs the woman.

She smiles at us. "Please follow me." She heads back through the doors with the seven of us hot on her heels. The hospital smell of disinfectant and sterile rooms hits me as we stride through the halls, into an elevator, and down a few more hallways. She stops outside of a room and waves her hand out. "He's in here but he's not awake from his surgery yet. You're welcome to have short visits, only two at a time, though. There's a family lounge at the end of the hall where you can wait."

My heart rate picks up at the news he's still not awake. AJ's parents go in first while the rest of us make our way to the end of the ward. It seems to take forever for them to come out so AJ's grandparents can see him. I stand to pace, unable to keep still while I less than patiently wait for my turn. When they finally return, Hayley turns to me and Dylan.

"Do you two want to go in next?"

I glance at Dylan. "If you don't mind, I plan on staying. So you and Dylan can go in next."

Hayley nods and I notice out of my periphery that AJ's parents and grandparents are speaking quietly between themselves. Dylan and Hayley head toward AJ's room and I take the few steps over to the window. It's dark out, and the streetlights are on, shining the way for people to head home.

When Hayley and Dylan return to the family, Hayley steps into her mom's arms and they both break down in tears. My heart thumps heavily in my chest and my worry increases exponentially as I fear what I'm about to see.

Dylan wraps his arm around my shoulder. "Are you going to be okay going in there on your own?"

I nod slowly, building my resolve. AJ needs me to be strong for him and that's exactly what I'm going to be. "Is he awake yet?"

He shakes his head. "Nope and he's pretty banged up. You need to prepare yourself."

I swallow, my mouth suddenly as dry as the dunes AJ and I climbed. My heart pounds and blood rushes to my ears, but I refuse to allow my body to shut down on me. I draw in measured breaths and push my shoulders back. I've got this. I say my goodbyes to AJ's family and Dylan and head down the hallway alone to AJ's room on rubber legs. The hallway seems longer than before, each step filled with dread as I imagine AJ's broken body lying still on a hospital bed. The man who is so full of life and vitality.

As I reach the doorway, I pause and suck in much-needed air. You can do this Sarah. He needs you. It's your fault he's lying in the damn bed, broken and battered. I cover my mouth to hold in my sob and steady my shaky legs, then push open the door to his room. Machines beep a steady rhythm in the low-lit room and I urge my feet to move me forward. Air gushes out of my lungs as I lay eyes on the man who's only ever been kind, generous, and patient with me.

His head, wrapped in a bandage, is the first thing my eyes latch onto, before slowly cataloging the rest of his face, noting every scratch and bruise. A gasp escapes and my eyes well as I take in his bruised and battered features. "I'm so sorry, AJ," I whisper to nobody.

Pulling over one of the two chairs in the room, I gently take his hand in mine, keeping my eyes firmly locked on him for any change or movement.

*-sarah-*

Soft touches glide through my hair, waking me from a fitful sleep. It takes me a moment to figure out where I am, and when I sit up, a pinched pain in my neck pulls me up short. Rubbing the area, I glance around the hospital room, memories of yesterday afternoon and last night assaulting me. I'm unsure how I managed to sleep with the constant sound of beeping machines and the dim light the nurses kept on so they could see what they were doing each time they came to check on AJ. I made myself as comfortable as I could on the plastic chair, leaning my head on the side of AJ's hospital bed because I couldn't bear to leave him.

The guilt swamping me about his accident and how I responded on Monday were eating at me, making me feel like throwing up. He's lying in this bed, broken, because of me and my shitty response to our new reality. I wish I could go back in time and change everything that happened.

"Sarah." AJ's raspy voice captures my attention and I snap my gaze to his face.

His eyebrows are scrunched low and there's tightness around his eyes. "AJ," I breathe. "Do you need me to get a nurse?"

He nods, then winces. "Please."

I stand, smoothing down the skirt I wore to work yesterday—*was that only yesterday?*—then head out to look for someone to help. I find a nurse stepping out from behind the desk. "Hi, my boy— ... uh, Mr. Jackson in room five two seven is awake and in pain."

"Sure. I'll be there shortly. I just need to give these to another patient." She holds up a tiny cup with some tablets.

"Thank you." I spin around and rush back to AJ.

A glass of water with a straw rests on the side cupboard, so I offer him a drink while we wait for the nurse. I stroke my fingers down the side of his face, cataloging each cut and bruise so I don't hurt him worse than he already is. His usual five o'clock shadow has become more of a fuzz since I saw him on Monday. I lower my face to his and kiss his temple with the lightest of touches, cupping the opposite side of his face gently. "I've been so worried about you."

He presses into my touch. "Sorry."

"You don't need to apologize. I'm the one who's sorry." I draw in a deep breath of hospital air. "I'm so sorry. I'm just glad you're okay. I couldn't bear to think of a world without you in it. That I never got the chance to tell you I love you." One of my tears lands on his cheek and he reaches up slowly, wiping beneath my eye with his thumb.

He slides his fingers through my hair, cupping the back of my head and bringing me down to his mouth, pressing his cracked lips to mine. "I love you, too. So much." His warm breath brushes my lips, and I lightly press my palm against his heart, reminding myself he's here and he's going to be okay, if not a bit banged up for a while. My eyes dance between his, noting his sincerity and exhaustion.

*He loves me. He said he loves me.*

His words bathe me from head to toe in warmth and lightness that's been missing since Monday. I could float on the clouds with relief.

Squeaky footsteps break our moment, and I look up to see the nurse I spoke with in the hallway. "Nice to see you awake, Mr. Jackson. I'm Adele, and I'll be your nurse. I believe you're in pain." She presses her fingers to his wrist and watches her fob watch. "On a scale of zero to ten, zero being no pain and ten being the worst pain you can imagine, what would you rate your pain level?"

"Maybe a seven or eight."

I wince. Here I am confessing my love for him, and he's in terrible pain. He probably won't even remember this conversation or that he told me he loves me. Maybe it's the drugs in his system doing the talking?

"Okay. I'll grab your meds." She records information on her tablet after checking over the machines, then leaves us alone again.

"Do you remember what happened?" He nods and groans. "Stay still."

"I remember looking up for my next hold and realizing it was farther away than I originally thought it would be. I knew I'd have to push hard and stretch long to reach it but I don't remember doing it." His eyebrows slash low over his eyes and I watch him as he works through his memories. "Or falling." The beeps on the heart monitor change; increasing in frequency. "I can't believe I fell."

I take his hand in mine and slowly stroke my thumb back and forth across his knuckles. "Don't worry about that now. You're going to be okay." He shakes his head and groans. "Stay still, AJ. You're going to hurt yourself and getting upset won't help anything. You're going to be back to your usual self in no time." I lift his hand to my lips and lay a soft kiss against the back of it, trying to settle him.

His eyes skate around my face, drifting down to my clothes. "You're in your work clothes."

I glance down at my creased skirt and blouse. "Yeah. I came straight from the office yesterday when Dylan called. I haven't been home to change. I didn't want to leave you here on your own."

His body visibly relaxes and he melts into the mattress. "Thanks for being here."

I squeeze his hand, careful of his grazes. "I wouldn't be anywhere else, AJ. I needed to be here with you. I needed to know you were okay. I needed to tell you I love you," I tell him softly, hoping he realizes how important he is to me. "I've done a terrible job so far of showing you how much I value you and how much I love you. My dismissal of you on Monday was awful and hurtful, and completely unacceptable. I'm so sorry. I only hope you can forgive me." I bring his hand to my lips and press another kiss to his knuckles. The need to kiss him and make him feel better is overwhelming. "I promise to do better."

"Good morning." AJ and I turn toward the woman's voice. "I'm Doctor Fieldman. I believe you're experiencing a fair amount of pain. Let's take a look." She checks AJ over from head to toe, explaining his injuries to him as she works. "Do you know what day it is?"

He looks at me. "Uh, Tuesday"—he glances out of the darkened window—"night?"

Doctor Fieldman glances at me. "It's actually very early Thursday morning. You were found and rescued mid-morning yesterday by Parks and Wildlife and brought here immediately. We operated on your leg and head wound yesterday afternoon."

AJ's eyes widen. "But I was climbing on Tuesday. That's when I fell." He shakes his head and groans. "I can't believe I fell. I never fall."

Shit! That means he was lying unconscious exposed to the elements overnight before he was found. I snap my head back to the doctor, waiting to hear her thoughts on that.

Doctor Fieldman purses her lips and makes some notes. "You were very lucky then, Mr. Jackson. The temperature was fifty-nine on Tuesday night. I'm surprised your condition wasn't worse when they brought you in."

I glance at AJ, thanking whoever above that he was brought back to us. "He's going to be okay, though, right?" I'm doing my best not to panic.

"Oh, absolutely. His leg and head will heal nicely, and he'll be as good as new with some physical therapy." She turns her attention back to AJ. "You'll have a nasty headache, bouts of confusion, and extreme fatigue for a few days as a result of the concussion. Make sure you rest and don't put pressure on yourself to be at full capacity right away. We'll keep a close eye on you while you're here." She raises an eyebrow at AJ and he nods slowly.

"I'll make sure he rests."

She turns her focus to me. "Good. I'll leave you to it and send a nurse in with some pain medicine."

"Knock, knock." The three of us turn toward the door, finding Hayley standing on the threshold. I'm not surprised she's here at the crack of dawn, she was reluctant to leave the hospital last night. Hayley makes a beeline for her brother, and I step out of the way so they can reunite. Her body shakes and AJ does his best to stroke his hand up and down her back, but the angle is awkward.

I thank Doctor Fieldman, while AJ and Hayley embrace, stepping off to the side to give them some privacy. Maybe I should leave? I'm sure his family will be coming to visit and they don't need me hanging around. Eric gave me the day off to be with AJ, but perhaps I shouldn't intrude on family time.

Hayley takes the chair I slept in as I stand beside the window to give them space. "Sarah," AJ calls my name, snapping me out of my thoughts and I turn to him. He's holding out his hand for me. "Come here, Cupcake. I want you next to me." The rigidness I was holding in my body dissipates instantly. He wants me next to him which means I'm not going anywhere, even if I have to live in these clothes for the entire time he's in the hospital. I step forward quickly to slide my hand into his roughened one and he pulls me forward. When I try to sit on the second visitor's chair next to his bed, he tugs me forward. "Sit here."

I smile at him and perch my butt on the edge of his hospital bed, careful not to bump him. "Okay." I lean down and peck his lips. He explains to Hayley about his fall, coming to the end of his story when his mom and dad walk in, closely followed by the nurse.

"Oh, you have a full house. I have your medicine here." Everyone says hello and she administers AJ's medicine through his IV. "You'll probably feel sleepy in a little while. It's the best thing you can do for your body's healing." After she checks the monitors again, she leaves the room and AJ's parents fuss over him, his mom sobbing.

My phone buzzes in my purse, which is on the floor beside Hayley. "Would you mind passing my purse?"

She hands it over and I dig around with my free hand to find it. Mel's face flashes on my screen. "I'm just gonna step out and take this." Reluctantly, AJ releases my hand and I step into the hallway to accept the call. "Hey, Mel."

"Hiya. I wanted to check how you were doing. I'm sorry I'm on nights this week and haven't been around much." I burst into tears at the sound of my best friend's voice. "Hey, hey, hey. Sarah." Her voice is panicked. "Do you need me to come home?"

"I … I'm okay. I'm not at your place, I'm at the ho-hospital," I manage to say through my tears.

"Why are you at the hospital? Are you okay?" Her words tumble out quickly.

"It's AJ. He f-fell when he was cli-climbing."

"Oh shit! Is he going to be okay?"

I calm down enough to tell Mel everything, and when she offers to grab me a change of clothes from her apartment and bring them to me after her shift, I thank her profusely. When I step back inside AJ's room and return to my spot on the edge of his bed, he smiles at me sleepily, so I take his hand in mine and kiss him gently. "Sleep. I'll be here when you wake," I whisper against his lips, noting the dullness in his eyes.

"Promise?"

"Promise. I'm not going anywhere." He closes his eyes, leaving me with his family, who stay for a short while, then leave with promises of returning tomorrow.

# CHAPTER 43

## —aj—

Sounds of machines infiltrate my consciousness and I slowly wake. I don't know what they gave me, but whatever it was knocked me out. Sluggishly, I open my eyes. Squinting, I peer around the small, sterile room. When I look to my left where Sarah was when I fell asleep, my heart rate spikes to find the chair empty.

She promised she would stay.

The disappointment of finding her gone is overwhelming. I was sure she told me she loved me, but maybe the drugs in my system had me hallucinating the whole thing because that's what I want. Maybe she was never here at all. I turn my head and stare up at the ceiling, working through everything that's happened.

I can't believe I fell. I've never fallen, even when I was starting out. I run through the last moments before I knew I was going down. I was holding on and then I had to push up and across to reach my next hold, then … A retching sound comes from the bathroom, breaking into my thoughts and startling me. It continues for a few minutes and I would prefer to investigate, rather than lie here on the uncomfortable hospital bed, but with my leg in a cast and the pounding in my head, I'm reluctant to move so I call out, "Hello. Are you okay in there?" The retching happens again and the need to know who's being sick in my bathroom outweighs my need to remain still.

Pushing myself into a seated position, I ignore the aches and pains in my body, then twist so my legs are dangling over the side of my bed. Fighting the pounding in my head, I inch my butt closer to the edge and place the foot of my good leg on the floor to test my balance, then using the furniture, I collect my bag of fluids in one hand and drag the IV pole with me as I hop slowly to the bathroom—it's tough to balance with all the shit I'm carrying. My head spins while the pounding in my brain feels like the drummer from AC/DC is practicing a solo.

I knock on the bathroom door. "Are you okay in there? Do you need me to call a nurse?"

"I'm okay. I'll be out in a sec." That's Sarah's voice.

She *did* stay. Relief swiftly replaces the disappointment I was feeling.

But why is she sick? If she's sick, she shouldn't be here watching over me. She should be home resting. Has she even been home?

*Ah, fuck!* Grayness pulls at the edge of my vision and my head spins. The floor comes up to meet me and I barely get my hand out in time to stop my face from smashing into the linoleum. Shit, that fucking hurts. I grunt as I try to push up but before I can move, the door swings inward and Sarah stands in the doorway. Her face is blotchy and the loose hairs around her face are stuck to her cheeks. I can see she's been crying.

"Shit, AJ, are you okay? What on earth are you doing out of bed?" She immediately crouches down, hooking her arm around my waist to help me back to my feet. She awkwardly guides me back to bed, permanent creases marring her normally smooth forehead. She helps me sit on the edge of the hard mattress, then carefully lifts my broken leg, followed by my good leg onto the bed. "I don't think you're supposed to be up yet. And I definitely don't think you should be putting any weight on your leg," she chastises me as she covers me with the starchy sheet and thin blanket, efficiently ensuring the tubes going into and out of my body aren't twisted. I lie back on the pillow and close my eyes to catch my breath. I feel as though I've run a damn marathon with that short trip to the bathroom.

"Are you okay? You were sick." I study her closely. She looks pale beneath the blotchiness.

She waves me off. "Yeah. I've been feeling off all week. I think the anxiety of all this"—she waves her hand in my general vicinity—"tipped me over the edge. I'm sure I'll start to feel better now I know you're going to be okay." I take her hand to pull her closer, but she resists. "I need to brush my teeth. Back in a sec." She pulls her hand free and steps back into the bathroom, returning a couple of minutes later. "I hope you don't mind. I used your bathroom to have a quick shower while you were sleeping."

"Be my guest. I'm just happy you're still here, but if you need to go, don't feel obliged to stay. Shouldn't you be at work?" I figure I should give her the option since work is so important to her. Maybe she only said she loved me out of worry and she doesn't really mean it.

She frowns at me. "Are you trying to get rid of me?" I shake my head, ignoring the thumping. "Good. Because this is exactly where I need and want to be. I'm not going anywhere, AJ."

I blow out a relieved breath and hold out my hand to her. When she puts her hand in mine, I tug her forward, cupping the back of her head to pull her down to me. Our lips are mere inches apart and this close I can see the residual tears in her dull eyes. She must have been genuinely worried about me. "Trust me, Cupcake. I don't want to be away from you either, but if you need to go and rest, you should do that." I press up, ignoring the pounding in my head, to swipe my lips across hers. Closing my eyes, I remind myself she's here. She's with me and she's not going anywhere. "I missed you," I whisper on a breath, then press more firmly against the soft pillows of her lips. My arms shake as I try to hold my body up, but I'm not about to stop what I'm doing, so I hold her to me as I lower my head back to the starchy hospital pillow. I kiss her soft bottom lip, followed by the top. Sarah opens, willingly inviting me inside and I don't waste a moment, plunging my tongue into her mouth to reunite with hers, tasting the minty toothpaste. Our kiss is slow and sensual, full of apology and forgiveness, of love and passion, knitting the cracks in my heart back together.

This woman is it for me. I knew it from the second I overheard her talking about wanting to have a baby and my feelings for her have only deepened the more time I've spent with her. I've been in deep from very early on, waiting for her to join me. Even while we've been living together, I still felt as though she wasn't in as deep as I was. But this kiss is showing me she's finally caught up.

Maybe it wasn't such a bad thing that I fell after all? I always like to find the positives out of a negative situation.

"Ahem."

Damn it, between the doctors, nurses, and my family, I can't catch a break. We separate, and the dazed expression on Sarah's face makes my day. She goes to step away from me, but I grip her hand to keep her close. She'll be lucky if I ever let her go.

"It seems you're feeling much better this evening, Mr. Jackson." The doctor steps further into the room, checking the machines. I'm pretty sure it's the same doctor from before, but I can't be sure. I've been finding it difficult to keep track of things since I woke up. They said it was normal to experience some confusion and disorientation after a concussion, so I'm not too worried.

"I am, thank you."

"And your head? How are you doing?"

"Still have a bit of hammering if I move too fast, but I'm okay."

"And how's the pain level for your leg?" She asks as she squeezes each of my toes. "Can you feel that?" I nod. "Good."

"The pain isn't unbearable."

"Excellent. That'll be the pain meds doing their job."

# CHAPTER 44

## —aj—

"Okay, Mr. Jackson," Doctor Fieldman starts as soon as she crosses the threshold into my room. "Your head scan and bloodwork have come back clear. You're managing to shower and go to the bathroom yourself, so I have your discharge papers here." She smiles at us, clearly delighted to be giving us good news. She'll probably be glad to see the back of me because I've been begging to go home.

"Already?" Sarah asks, her brow furrowing. She's in no hurry for me to leave the care of the nurses and doctors, though she must be exhausted.

"Yes. Mr. Jackson is making good progress. There's nothing more we can do for him here. There will be follow-up appointments required, and he'll need assistance at home for a while, but he's on the road to a full recovery."

After what felt like the longest week of my life, we finally leave the hospital and the fresh air feels amazing. Sarah stayed with me the entire time, only stepping out on Saturday morning for her volunteer session at my insistence. I draw in deep breaths, exchanging the stale hospital air for fresh air and Sarah pushes me toward our Uber and then helps me get in.

"*Stone Tower*, please."

"I don't want to see my grandfather," I grumble as my muscles draw tight. I'm not ready to deal with him yet.

She takes my hand in hers. "I need to collect my car. It's still parked at work."

My muscles relax and I nod. "We also need to get your stuff. You're moving back home."

Sarah grins at me. "Oh, am I now?"

"Yep." I lean across and touch my forehead to hers. "No arguing with the invalid." I may as well use this to my advantage if it gives Sarah the excuse she needs to move back in.

"Even if you weren't all broken to pieces, I'd be moving back in. I don't want to be away from you any more than I have to."

Finally.

Fucking finally she's with me.

To be fair, her sleeping in that uncomfortable chair for the duration of my hospital stay showed me all I needed to know. I did my best to convince her to join me on the bed, but she was stubborn. If she thinks we won't be sharing my bed tonight, she's gonna be sorely mistaken. I refuse to allow her to sleep anywhere else but with me.

We switch cars, stop at the drugstore for my medication and the other stuff I need, and then make a final stop at Mel's place to collect Sarah's things. Sarah kisses my cheek, then climbs out of her car. I feel like I've handed in my man card when I have to wait while she carries her things downstairs on her own, loading them in the trunk. As soon as I'm back on my feet, she won't have to lift a damn finger. I'll make sure of it.

We arrive home and Dylan comes out to meet us. "Hey. It's good to have you back." He embraces me carefully. "I'm fucking glad you're okay, man," he whispers next to my ear. When he pulls back, I can see the worry in his eyes.

"It's good to be back." He tries to help me inside, but I brush him off. "Can you please take Sarah's bags up to our bedroom? I can get inside on my own."

"Are you sure?"

"I'm okay. I can manage." Sarah grumbles as she drags one suitcase out of the trunk of her car.

I nod. "Yep. I don't want her doing the heavy lifting on her own." I lock my eyes with Sarah's, so she gets my point. "It's bad enough she had to carry them downstairs from Mel's place."

She chuckles, holding up her hands in surrender. "Okay, okay."

Good. I'm glad she's listening to me without an argument. Dylan grabs the bags and lugs them upstairs while Sarah helps me inside, settling me on the couch with my injured leg resting on the ottoman. Exhaustion is quickly taking over now that I'm settled back home.

She blows out a heavy breath. "I'm going to make us all a coffee."

Sarah disappears into the kitchen, and I rest my head on the back of the couch and close my eyes as I listen to her work. A sense of peace and calm washes over me, knowing she's home for good.

"You okay?" Dylan's voice breaks my quiet moment. Damn, I think I could sleep for a week. I'm completely shattered. Not that I'll admit it to anyone.

I open my eyes slowly and without lifting my head, turn in his direction. "Yeah. I was just listening to Sarah in the kitchen and appreciating her being back where she belongs."

"Where? In the kitchen?" Dylan jokes. "You're becoming more and more like your grandfather every day."

"Piss off." I huff. "As if. No, I mean home."

"I knew what you meant. Hopefully, she's here to stay, right?"

"Hopefully."

# CHAPTER 45

## —sarah—

My anxiety is finally quiet since being home with AJ and knowing he's going to be okay. It's all I need—well, I wouldn't mind if my upset stomach finally disappeared—because nothing else is as important as him being safe.

After helping AJ bathe away his hospital stay, I help him to bed. He looks drained after the effort it took to get him upstairs and then showered. I'm also feeling exhausted after a week of the shittiest of shit sleep in the hospital. I'm grateful Eric allowed me to work on a laptop from the hospital and has told me there's no need to rush back to work. I quickly shower and clean up the bathroom. As I open the bathroom door, my gaze catches on my man, so I lean against the door frame to watch him for a few moments while his eyes are closed. He's probably already passed out.

"Are you gonna stand there and watch me like a creeper all night?" He smirks and I walk toward him.

"Maybe," I sass.

"Come here, Cupcake. I need to hold you properly." A sigh escapes as I climb into bed. God, I've missed him. I'm not sure how I thought I'd be able to live without this man. He holds his arm out and I snuggle as close as I can without touching him. We had to swap sleeping sides so I won't accidentally knock his broken leg during the night. He sighs and drags me closer. "You can touch me."

"I don't want to hurt you. You've just had a major fall."

"You won't hurt me, Cupcake. Not being able to touch you hurts far worse than any of my injuries. Plus, I'm feeling okay." I lay my hand on his abs and settle my body so it's touching every available inch of his. His muscles relax beneath my palm and when I glance up at his face, his lips are raised in a serene smile.

I press a light kiss to his bristly jaw. "Goodnight. I'm so glad you're home safe. I love you."

He turns his head, kissing my forehead with a lingering press of his lips. "I love you. Night, Cupcake. Thanks for taking care of me."

I leap out of bed before I'm fully awake, careful not to bump AJ, and race into the bathroom to empty the contents of my stomach. I drop to my knees, the tiles digging into my flesh, retching into the toilet over and over. A never-ending, gut-wrenching purge that seems to have no end. The room spins when I finally finish, and I flush away the evidence. Closing the lid of the toilet, I fold my arms on top and rest my head on them to catch my breath, noticing some of my hair is covered in vomit—yuck. Geez, that was close. I almost didn't make it. The sound of the bathroom door opening has me looking up through bleary eyes. God! I don't want him to see me like this. His worried gaze locks on me.

"Sarah? How can I help you?" He lumbers into the bathroom balancing on his crutches, coming closer and I hold up my hand. He's getting better at moving around, even though we've only been home five days. Tomorrow marks two weeks since his fall and I'm still not over the shock of it all—ugh!

"Please stay away. I'm revolting and I don't want you to come any closer."

"Cupcake," he breathes. "Let me help you."

"No. I'm okay. I'll … uh … just have a quick shower. You shouldn't be up on your feet. Remember. You need to stay off that leg as much as possible." I point to his cast. "I can manage. Promise." I implore him with my eyes and he takes a reluctant step back, leaving me in the bathroom with a nod.

"If you need anything, just shout. I'll help however I can."

"Thanks. I won't be long."

I brush my teeth, then climb into the shower. I let the warm water beat down on me, rinsing the vomit from my hair. With my eyes closed, I let the spray rinse away the past two weeks—a time I'll never forget. The regret I'm holding onto about my reaction to AJ being my new boss, which sent him out climbing to clear his head and subsequently falling is overwhelming. A sob leaves my throat with the guilt I'm holding on to. Even though Dylan tried to make me feel better and remove some of the blame from my shoulders, it's the only place the blame belongs.

The sound of shuffling captures my attention and I open my eyes to find AJ standing naked on the other side of the glass, wearing the waterproof cast we picked up from the drugstore. I open the door and help him inside. As much as I know he shouldn't be standing unnecessarily, I selfishly want him with me. He pulls me into his body, cupping the back of my head, and my sobbing resumes.

"Shhhh, shhh. It's okay. Let it out, Cupcake." His roughened hand glides from the top of my head, down my back, and then starts back at the top, repeating the process. The action is soothing and makes me feel cherished. Something I'm not sure I deserve after my behavior. I don't think I'll ever forgive myself.

I catch my breath and wipe my eyes, then look up into AJ's soulful brown orbs. "I'm sorry I've kept you at a distance. I was scared and wrong, and I promise I won't do it anymore. If you'll still have me, I would like the opportunity to make things right."

His eyes flick between mine as he brushes my wet hair out of my face. "I'm not sure how you missed the signs, but there's never been a question in my mind about us. I've wanted to be with you since the moment I laid eyes on you. I've just been waiting for you to catch up."

My lips tip up in relief. Somewhere deep inside, I've known it all along, but my stupid fear stopped me from seeing it for what it was. I press up on my toes and touch my lips to AJ's tenderly, aiming to keep it light but AJ wraps his hand around my hair, holding me in place, our lips a hairsbreadth apart.

His eyes dart between mine and a sensual smile forms on his face. "I need more than that, Cupcake."

I eagerly move forward, careful of his leg, and wrap my arms around his torso to cup his shoulders, as I show him how much I love him. Expressing my sorrow and begging for his forgiveness. Our tongues tangle while our teeth clash, and I whimper into his mouth when I feel his cock growing between us, pressing against my soft stomach. I can't believe that after all he's been through, he's getting hard. I pull far enough away to study his face, my eyes cataloging his features. "How are you feeling today?"

I watch him closely as he takes a moment. "I feel fine. Still have a bit of a headache, but Doctor Fieldman warned me about that. My leg aches, but not enough to stop me from coming to you when you need me." His voice has dropped low as he strokes my hair away from my face.

My heart pounds in a heavy rhythm at his subtle seduction. I carefully guide him to sit on the ledge at the end of the shower and then lower to my knees in front of him, ensuring I don't bump his broken leg. His hands automatically cup each breast and his thumbs swipe across the sensitive nubs, his carnal gaze watching the movement.

"You have the most gorgeous breasts." His gaze flicks up to mine momentarily before dropping back. "So full and lush." He lowers his head, sucking one nipple into his mouth, while he plucks and rolls the other between his deft fingers. I moan. The feel of his warm tongue swirling around the hard bud sends an electrical pulse straight to my clit. My boobs are always sensitive to attention, but this is unreal. Not having AJ's hands on me for the last two weeks has made me more sensitive than normal. I hum my pleasure, reaching up to slide my fingers through the short strands of his hair, avoiding his stitches. He switches over, paying the same attention to my other boob, and I finally come to my senses enough to remember why I'm on my knees in front of him.

Using my hold on his hair, I pull his head away and meet his lustful gaze. "There's something I wanted to do." I press my lips to his roughly and then kiss my way along his jawline to his ear. "You make me feel so good, let me do this for you." I nip his lobe and then trail my fingers down his torso, following with my mouth. Kissing, sucking, and licking my way to his gorgeous thick cock. "I love your body. But mostly, I love *you*."

"Ditto, Cupcake."

He squeezes my left breast and I tease the tip of his cock, swirling my tongue around it like I'm licking my favorite lollipop before wrapping my hand around the engorged length to stroke him.

I move closer until AJ's shaft is flush between my breasts, then press them together, surrounding his length. When I look up at AJ's face, the heat in his lidded gaze steals my breath. I slide up and down the length, squeezing my breasts tight and when the tip of his cock slides out from between the tight space, I dip down to press a kiss to the crown. AJ's harsh whispered, "fuck" makes me smile.

He reverently cups my face, tilting it up to his. "You're so damn beautiful." He crushes his mouth to mine in a rough, messy kiss, and I lose my momentum for a moment. When we pull away, I release my boobs and wrap my hand around his hot length and slide it partway into my mouth, swirling around the tip with my tongue.

His hands find my hair and he grasps a handful at the roots, pulling me away from his dick. "You don't have to do this, Cupcake."

I smile at him. "I know. I want to. I *need* to." I implore him with my eyes and as his eyes dart between mine, he nods slowly.

"Okay." He guides my mouth back to his shaft and this time I don't mess around. I take him to the back of my throat and his hips jolt upward. "Fuuuck!" he groans. "You're so good at taking my cock. Do you like having my thick cock in your mouth? Does it make you wet?" It's my turn to moan at his filthy words. "Fuck. Do that again." He raises his hips as I moan around his shaft and I relish in the tiny bit of pain he causes as he tightens his hold on my hair.

Rubbing my thighs together, I bob up and down his length, wrapping my hand around the base to ensure I have as much of him covered as I can. The hand that's not holding onto my hair returns to my breast as he massages the globe and pays attention to my nipple —pinching and plucking it until it's sharp enough to cut glass. AJ's hips thrust gently into my mouth as he uses his hold on my hair to move me how he wants. I lift my gaze to his face and the sheer masculinity that greets me is breathtaking. The veins in his neck are protruding as his heated gaze watches his cock slide in and out of my mouth. My heart hammers sending my blood thrumming through my veins.

"Take it deeper, Cupcake, and swallow when you can't go any further. I fucking love watching my dick disappear between your sweet lips." I drop my hand between my legs and circle my fingers around my aching clit needing relief. Nothing's as good as AJ's touch, though, but this will have to do. His eyes drop lower, watching me work myself over and he groans, tugging on my hair to speed up my movements. He presses his pelvis closer to my face and pauses as his thickness grows in my mouth. "Do you want to taste it?"

I nod the best I can with a mouth full of his dick. He throbs in my mouth, growing to take up all of the available space. His mouth drops open with a groan and his release hits the back of my throat. My clit pulses and my body tingles as I detonate, sending me skyrocketing into bliss.

AJ's head bangs against the tiled wall and I quickly snap my focus back to him. Sliding his softening cock out of my mouth, I swallow his orgasm. "Are you okay? You shouldn't be banging your head against the tile; you have stitches and the tail end of a concussion." I shake my head and stand on jelly legs, feeling slightly dizzy with the rush of blood that just went to my clit. "I can't believe I did that in the shower. How damn stupid am I? I put you at risk." My drunken lust haze dissipates quickly.

Spinning to turn off the faucets, I help AJ stand and climb out of the shower. "Calm down, Cupcake. I'm thinking that was exactly what the doctor ordered. I feel great."

I playfully hit his pec as I return to him with a towel to dry him off. "I bet. But that probably wasn't a good idea for your head injury."

"I dunno. While all the blood was rushing to my cock, my head wasn't pounding so much."

I furrow my brows and narrow my eyes. "How bad is your headache?"

He softens his voice, regarding my face closely. "I'm okay. Stop worrying. That blow job made me feel amazing." AJ's lips tip up cheekily and I relax a little. "Now let's go back to bed so you can sit on my face."

"That's not even funny." I can't believe this guy.

"Remember, you're not supposed to argue with the invalid," he taunts.

I roll my eyes heavenward. "I'm not sitting on your face when you have fifteen stitches in your head and you're recovering from a concussion."

"That sounded like you said you don't love me." He pouts. He's genuinely pouting at me like a five-year-old child.

"What the hell? No, I didn't. I'm not sitting on your face *because* I love you. You're supposed to be taking it easy." I bend down to remove the waterproof cast carefully as he holds onto the vanity, his semi-hard cock right in my face. I kiss it, then stand.

"You can't tease me like that, Sarah."

"Of course I can." I lead him into the bedroom and sit him on the edge of the bed and then do my best to help him dress. He's not helping at all. "Can you help me out a little here? Please."

"Nope. I don't wanna get dressed. I want you to fuck my face."

"No." I step into the walk-in closet and dress out of his line of sight, returning to find him still as he was when I left him. "C'mon, AJ. Help me out. I promise I'll sit on your face when the doctor gives you the all-clear." I can't believe this is the conversation we're having.

His eyes light up. "Promise?"

I shake my head at him and huff out a laugh. "Promise."

# CHAPTER 46

AFTER A LINGERING KISS, SARAH climbs into her car and heads off to work. Having her here with me, living with me, still feels unreal. If I could walk without crutches, I'm certain I'd have a bounce in my step. It took a bit of convincing to get Sarah to return to the office, but there wasn't anything more she could do for me at home. I can manage everything and Dylan's here during the day anyway.

I pour myself a coffee and lean against the kitchen counter to enjoy the first sip of steaming goodness. Nothing beats a good cup of coffee in the morning. Well ... maybe that's not quite true. I can think of several things, all of which involve my sexy girlfriend, that trump coffee. My phone vibrates in my pocket and I dig it out.

> GRANDFATHER
>
> My office. 9:30 a.m. sharp.

My eyes widen, then I frown at the message. I've been home for a week and have an appointment at one for a follow-up with my doctor. It's one of the reasons Sarah didn't want to go back to work but Dylan promised to take me and report every single detail back to her.

The large barn door to our office slides open. "Morning," Dylan calls as his footsteps get louder the closer he comes to me. I glance up at him to say hi. "What's going on?"

I hold up my phone to show him the screen. "I've been summoned by the almighty to his tower."

Dylan grabs a cup and makes himself a coffee. "Shit. What do you think it's about?"

"Really? You have to ask."

He turns, leaning his ass against the opposite counter. "You'd think he'd give you a little time to recover after your accident."

I nod. "One would think so but we are talking about my grandfather here."

"I can drive you in."

"Thanks." I tuck my phone back into my pocket and take another sip of my coffee. "Let's get some work done first."

We make our way into our office and as I'm about to sit my phone rings and Hayley's face lights up the screen. "Hey, Sis. What's up?"

"I got summoned into the office for a nine-thirty meeting."

"Shit. So did I." Dylan spins in his chair, listening to my side of the conversation.

"What do you think it's about?"

Who the fuck knows if Hayley's gonna be there? He's never deemed her worthy to talk with about business.

"I assumed he was calling me in to finalize the details of me taking over the company, but maybe that's not it if you're going to be there too."

"Hmm. I've never been to his office before." No kidding. Neither had I until the day everything went to shit.

"You want me to pick you up? I mean Dylan will pick you up since he's gonna be driving."

"How about I come and get you? Seems more efficient."

"Sure. See you at nine." We disconnect the call and I spin my chair toward my best friend, who's waiting for information. "Hayley's gonna pick me up since she's been summoned as well."

Dylan whistles long and low. "Man, I wonder what's going on?"

"Me too."

We reach the glass doors to the magnificent building, which is owned by one of our new clients, Oliver Stone. Hayley holds the door open for me and I lumber through, then we make our way toward the elevator. The same guy from last time is waiting to press the button like people aren't capable of pressing it for themselves. The elevator is as busy today as it was two and a half weeks ago.

Hayley chews on her bottom lip, fidgeting with her fingers. "Stop worrying. I'm sure it's nothing."

My phone vibrates in my pocket and I pull it out to read the message.

CUPCAKE

Your mom's just arrived

Before I can respond, the doors open to *FutureTech*. I hadn't told Sarah I had been summoned to the office, I figured she'd already know. As we step out of the elevator I tell Hayley, "Apparently Mom's here."

Her head snaps toward me. "What? This is strange."

I nod. "It's very unlike Grandfather. I wonder what's going on?"

We announce ourselves to Lucy, and she buzzes Sarah to let her know we're here. Within moments, Sarah comes into view from the hallway leading to Grandfather's office, wearing creases between her brows I want to smooth out with kisses. She glances across at Lucy, then puts on a more professional expression.

"Good morning, Mr. Jackson. Ms. Jackson."

Hayley totally breaks protocol, not reading Sarah's tension, and moves in to hug her. "Sarah. It's so great to see you."

Sarah stutters, "Y-you too." Her wide eyes catch my gaze over my sister's shoulder as she awkwardly returns Hayley's enthusiastic embrace.

Lucy's watching it all go down as though she's at the movies. All she needs is a tub of popcorn. I know Sarah's uncomfortable about the office knowing about our relationship, but they're gonna find out sooner or later. It may as well be sooner. That's if they haven't already worked it out after Sarah left with my grandfather to race to the hospital. Sarah told me all about sharing a ride with him and having to tell him about our relationship. I felt sick to my stomach that she was put in that position.

I glance across to make sure Lucy's still watching, then I clear my throat. "Uh, Sis. You mind letting me hug my girlfriend?" I smirk at Lucy's widened eyes, then focus on moving closer to my girl.

"Uh, yeah, sure. Sorry." Hayley releases Sarah and steps out of the way, brushing her curls away from her face.

"Come here, Cupcake." Coughing sounds from behind the front desk and Sarah shakes her head at me as a slow smile forms.

She moves into me, wrapping her arms around my torso. "I know what you're doing and I'll get my revenge later," she whispers, her warm breath fanning across my ear. Between that and her words, a shiver makes its way down my spine.

"I'll look forward to it," I whisper, then pull back to wink at her.

She steps away. "Thanks, Lucy." Looking at Hayley and me, she asks us to follow her and we make our way down the hallway to our grandfather's office. My eyes drop to Sarah's ass, wrapped in a tight dark gray pencil skirt; her calves look sensational in the heels she's wearing. She knocks on Grandfather's door, then promptly opens it when he tells her to come in. "Mr. Wainwright. Mr. and Ms. Jackson are here to see you."

"Thank you, Sarah. Please show them in."

"Certainly, Sir." Maybe I *should* take the position, then she can call me 'sir.' The thought makes my dick hard. She turns back to us and we step across the threshold into Grandfather's office. "I'll bring in some drinks."

"Thank you, Sarah."

The door closes with a click and my eyes land on Mom, sitting ramrod straight opposite her father, her face pinched tight. I never wanted Mom and Hayley on the receiving end of Grandfather's chauvinistic ways; it's bad enough we have to deal with him at family events. I didn't want them to have to deal with him when he's in business mode and his misogynistic beliefs are at an all-time high.

I lean down the best I can to kiss Mom's cheek. "Hi, Mom."

She cups my cheek. She's been different since my accident. More openly affectionate and even though I'm thirty, I'm loving this side of her. It's something that's always been missing in our household. "AJ. How are you feeling?"

"I'm doing okay. I'm getting around a lot easier, even if I am a little slow with these things." I balance on my good leg and hold out my crutches to the side.

"You're looking much better. If you need anything, your father and I are only a phone call away."

"I know. Thanks, Mom." I turn my attention to my grandfather as Hayley says hello to Mom and we both take a seat. "What's going on?" I ask. Let's get this meeting underway.

He leans forward in his chair, folding one hand on top of the other on his massive desk. "Your grandmother and I have been talking. Well, she's been talking and I've been ... uh ... listening. She said she'd been holding her tongue for too long and it was time she told me some home truths."

Hayley, Mom, and I glance at each other, and I know we're all thinking the same thing: since when does Grandfather listen to anyone besides himself?

There's a quiet knock on the door and all eyes turn toward it. Sarah steps in with a tray of drinks, which she distributes efficiently and we each thank her. As she turns to leave, Grandfather stops her. "Please take a seat, Sarah. This meeting involves you too."

Her brows furrow, and to say I'm confused as to what's going on would be a gross understatement. "Sure. Do I need my tablet?"

"No. Just take a seat, please."

Sarah takes the seat next to mine, and I want to reach out and take her hand to calm her obvious nerves, but I know she wouldn't appreciate the gesture. I'm already going to be in trouble for what I did in front of Lucy. This would be far worse in her eyes.

The silence in the room builds and I've never seen my grandfather look more uncomfortable. He stands and walks over to his floor-to-ceiling windows, tucking his hands in his pockets with his back to us for several moments, then he heaves a loud sigh. We all look at each other. I wish he'd start talking and put us all out of our misery.

"Grandfather?"

"Give me a moment, Adam, would you?"

I lean back in my chair. And wait.

He finally spins on his heel to face us. "Adam. You've made it very clear you don't want to take over *FutureTech*. For the life of me, I can't understand why, but recent events and discussions with your grandmother have opened my eyes a little."

I nod and blow out a breath. Finally. I glance at Mom and Hayley, noticing them sitting forward slightly in their seats. I know they want to get their hands on *FutureTech*. They've discussed the possibility of bringing Hayley and Lisa's software company under the *FutureTech* umbrella, allowing them a greater reach.

Grandfather walks toward us, gripping the back of his leather chair. "Elaine."

"Yes, Father." It's easy to hear the note of excitement in her voice. I hope he's made the only choice he can make. The *right* choice.

"After careful consideration, I would like to offer you the CEO position of *FutureTech*. Along with that position you will become a fifty percent shareholder in the company."

Mom rises from her chair and I'm certain she wants to jump up and down on the spot, but years of social conditioning have her controlling her reaction. She steps around to Grandfather and wraps him in a stiff hug. "This means the world to me. Thank you for putting your trust in me. I won't let you down, Father."

He pats her back as if he's patting an acquaintance. "I hope not." And there we have it, folks. The lack of faith and acknowledgment of Mom's talents. He forgets—or fails to recognize—she was a CEO of a Fortune 500 company until eighteen months ago when she decided to retire with the hope she would eventually take over *FutureTech*.

I glance at Sarah. Her mouth is dropped open slightly and her eyes are wide as she watches their interaction. She had a taste of how cold my family is when she met them while I was recovering in the hospital. They stopped by regularly to visit, but there were no warm embraces or the general love and affection Sarah is used to from her family.

Mom returns to her seat, wearing a slight smile. I know she's holding back her joy at this new development. Grandfather turns his attention to my sister. "Hayley."

"Yes, Grandfather." She sits a little straighter.

"I know it's roughly six weeks until your little one will be born, but I would like to offer you the position of Vice President. You and Lisa can work out a system that will work best for you in terms of looking after your children and balancing work. With the role, you will receive a twenty-five percent share in the company."

She jumps out of her seat, squealing in delight. Obviously, she doesn't care for the years of conditioning. And I can understand her excitement. This means big things for her and Lisa's software company. Running around the desk, she flings herself at our grandfather, and finally, he cracks a smile as he returns her affection. "Thank you, Grandfather. I won't let you down. We're going to take *FutureTech* to the next level. You wait and see."

"We have more to discuss."

Hayley moves back to her chair, but not before embracing Mom in an excited hug. When they separate, both of their eyes are twinkling in happiness and their nervous disposition from earlier has completely vanished.

"Congratulations, Mom. Congrats, Hayley. I'm happy for you both." I look at my grandfather. "Thank you."

He tips his chin. "You're not completely off the hook, Adam. I may not have given you a role as such, but I want you involved as a silent partner. You will take the position of the second Vice President and hold the final twenty-five percent of the company's shares. Your skills and talents could be very useful here." He scans the three of us. "No arguments."

Damn it. That doesn't seem fair since I won't be as involved in the day-to-day operational side of things. I'll have to speak with Mom and Hayley about it once Grandfather steps down. I don't want to upset his good mood and bring it up now because this is the outcome I've always wanted for Mom and Hayley.

"Now, Sarah. It is entirely up to you, my dear, but I'm hoping you'll stay on to help Elaine and Hayley during the transition period and beyond. You know as much about the running of this place as I do and you will be an invaluable asset to them."

Sarah blinks a few times. She told me she offered to resign from her position because of our relationship. "I would love to stay, Mr. Wainwright. It would be an honor to assist Mrs. Jackson and Ms. Jackson as they transition into their new roles."

"Please, call me Elaine while we're in the office." Mom smiles at Sarah. "You can call me Mom the rest of the time." She winks. My mother winks at my girlfriend. Well, soon-to-be fiancée if I have anything to do with it. I feel like aliens have taken over my family.

"Same goes for me. Hayley will do just fine."

"Okay." Sarah's still trying to maintain her professionalism, but I can see the excitement vibrating beneath the surface. She turns back to my grandfather. "What about Mr. Booth?" Ah, the asshole who supported Grandfather with his outdated views. "Will he be staying on?" Sarah's stiff as she waits for an answer.

"Uh, no. I'll be informing Tony, when the time is right, that he will need to seek other employment. It's recently been brought to my attention how old-fashioned we both are"—he pointedly looks at me—"and I think it would be a good opportunity for a clean sweep. I believe these changes are exactly what *FutureTech* needs to carry it forward." He sits and places his hands on his desk. "I would like this transition to begin as soon as possible."

We all nod in agreement, the room feeling more relaxed than it was forty minutes ago.

# CHAPTER 47

Since I've been home from the hospital, Sarah's thrown up as soon as her eyes open every single morning. I feel helpless and she refuses to see the doctor about it. She says it's because of her anxiety, but I don't think it's that at all. The tracking app on my phone says she should have finished her period yesterday, but Sarah hasn't mentioned anything about getting her period this month, and I didn't find her crying in the bathroom as she has before.

I wonder if she's given up. Or maybe she doesn't want to mention it because she's trying to cope with her devastation on her own?

"Hey, Dylan. Can you help me with something?"

"Sure. What do you need?"

"I need to get some flowers for my girl and I can't drive yet. She's been through a lot of stress with trying to get pregnant, then finding out I was supposed to be her new boss, and then the fall." Fuck, that's a lot of stress in a short period. Maybe it *is* stress making her sick.

"No problem. Let's go."

I'm getting around much easier with the crutches, so it's not long before we're on our way. We stop by one of the best florists in the city, *Blooms and Balloons*, to get an arrangement of spring flowers for Sarah. As soon as I saw the bright colors and smelled the springtime scent, I knew they'd be perfect for my girl. We stop at the drugstore to pick up a couple of items, then hit the grocery store so I can cook a meal for us tonight, instead of Sarah having to do everything when she gets home. I'm steadier on my feet, and I can sit at the counter to cut up the ingredients.

Stopping in front of my place, I turn to Dylan. "Thanks, man. If you can help me get all this inside, then we may as well call it a day."

"No problem. I might take up being an Uber driver if our business ever tanks."

"As if that's ever gonna happen. We're busier than ever with the accounts we've secured lately. Mr. Mitchell's happy with our work for *The Cardinal* and Oliver's impressed with our work for *The Parkerville Project*, he wants us to look at his business. Don't forget how happy Mr. Noble was with our work for him. These are huge fucking contracts. We won't be going out of business anytime soon." If anything, we need to seriously look at employing another member to join our team.

"Yeah, I know. I was joking around. Let's get all this shit inside. I might go for a ride since the afternoon is nice."

We make quick work of unloading Dylan's car and then he takes off. I clean up a little: wash the breakfast dishes, tidy the living room, set up the upstairs deck for dinner, and take a seat at the counter to start preparing our meal.

I'm about to set the timer on the oven for the chicken casserole when Sarah walks in the door. "Honey, I'm home!" She calls out with a smile in her voice. My lips tip up in a matching grin. Her brows furrow when she steps into the kitchen and scans the counters to see the mess I've made. "What on earth are you doing? You shouldn't be making dinner. You're not supposed to be on your feet."

My smile widens as I step toward her, wrapping one arm around her waist as soon as I'm close enough. I love how much she worries about me. I press my lips against hers without preamble. Her body softens against mine and her hands find their place in my hair at the nape of my neck. Once I've given her a proper welcome-home kiss, I draw back slowly, keeping my lips close to hers. "Welcome home, Cupcake," I whisper, then bite her bottom lip gently because I can't resist the puffy pillow.

One side of her lips tip up and I glance at her sparkling eyes. "I missed you today."

"Not as much as I missed you." We have thirty-five minutes to kill and I have just the thing to keep us busy. I tug her hand. "Come with me, I have something to show you."

She drops her purse on the sideboard where she usually keeps it and I grab my second crutch. Sarah follows me slowly up the stairs— though I am getting faster at climbing them—and into our bedroom. A gasp escapes her and her eyes widen when they land on the flowers and gift bag. She tears her eyes away from them and steps carefully into me, wrapping her arms around my torso. I can't embrace her the way I want while I'm holding both crutches, so I drop one and wrap my arm tightly around her.

"Thank you. They're gorgeous but you didn't have to get me anything."

I kiss her forehead. "I wanted to thank you for looking after me since my accident. The flowers don't seem enough for all you've done for me."

She presses her lips together and creases form between her sculpted brows. "You don't have to thank me for anything. Helping you has given me the chance to show you how much I love you. I wouldn't be anywhere else." She rises on tiptoes and swipes her lips across mine. I slide my tongue between her lips to deepen our connection. Every time I kiss Sarah, I fall for her all over again.

She's my life, the very breath that fills my lungs, the reason my heart beats faster—*the reason it beats at all*. I'm sure it was thoughts of her that pulled me through the night I was partially buried by rockfall in low temperatures.

I soften our kiss slowly and nudge her nose with mine. "Open your present."

Her smile spreads across her lust-drunk lips. "Okay. I love presents, so I won't say no."

I chuckle. "Of course, who doesn't love getting presents? It's not much, so don't get too excited."

She smells the flowers first. "These are gorgeous."

"They reminded me of you," I tell her as I step closer.

Sarah opens the gift bag and peers inside, finding the rectangular box. Her eyes narrow as she studies it closely. "What's this about?"

I step into her body and take the box from her. "Do you know what day it is?"

"Well, of course. Do you?"

"Yep. It's Friday. I'm all good with my days now." I was getting confused there for a while.

She lifts her hand to my cheek, cupping it gently, her eyes going soft. I lean into her touch before turning to press a kiss on her palm. "Do you realize that you should have finished your period yesterday?"

Her eyes dart back and forth and I can practically see the wheel's turning in her head. She lifts her wide eyes to mine. "Do you think …"

I raise my brows and nod. "Yeah, I do."

"Holy shit." She looks at the box, covering her mouth with her palm. "What if … No, I can't say it. I probably skipped my period because of all the stuff that's been going on and my anxiety." She pushes the box back toward me. "I'm too scared to take the test. What if it's negative?"

I transfer the box to the hand holding my crutch and slide my fingers through her soft hair, tucking it carefully behind her ear. "But what if it's positive?" I whisper around the lump in my throat.

She bites her bottom lip, taking a moment to think about it. "I *have* been sick and my boobs have been super sensitive." She reaches down to take the box from me, pushing her shoulders back and her beautiful tits out. "I'll take the test. Will you take it with me?"

"I wouldn't be anywhere else." She spins on her heel and rushes toward our bathroom, and I follow behind as quickly as I can. "Hang on. I'll need to pee on the stick first. Wait out there." She points at our bedroom.

"I was wondering how long it would take you to realize you needed to pee first." I chuckle and then sit on the edge of our bed to wait.

After a few moments, I hear the toilet flush and the water run, so I climb to my feet to join Sarah in the bathroom. She spins as I open the door. "Our lives could change in a couple of minutes," she whispers with eyes full of hope. God, I hope the test is positive. I'll feel so shitty if I've given her hope where there is none.

With my heart pounding, I lean my hip against the vanity, using only one crutch to hold me up and pull Sarah in close. "My life changed the night we shared a booth in the club." Her body softens against mine. "There was no going back for me once you agreed to let me be your donor. I just had to wait patiently for you to catch up."

Sarah brings her hands up to my pecs, resting them there as her eyes flick between mine. "I'm sorry I was so blinded by my plans and I was too scared to take the leap. I wasted so much time. I love you so much, AJ."

"Love you, too, Cupcake. And it doesn't matter because we're together now." I press a kiss to her lips and drop my eyes to the white stick. My heart bursts with happiness as my smile instantly spreads and I look back at Sarah's face. "And you're stuck with me forever."

Her eyes widen and snap down to the test and the two pink lines. "Holy shit! We're pregnant." She jumps up and down, then realizes she's jostling me and freezes in place. "Shit, sorry. Oh my God! We're pregnant." She slams her lips onto mine and I bring my hand to the back of her head, grasping the silky strands at the base of her scalp to tilt her where I want her, deepening our kiss. Our tongues unite and dance with one another in celebration. Tasting and teasing. Teeth clashing and breaths mingling. I want to share these moments endlessly with her.

With the need to draw breath, we reluctantly pull apart, and I press a few soft kisses to her swollen lips. I drop my forehead to Sarah's. Our dazed eyes find each other, our smiles matching. "We're gonna be parents, Cupcake." She nods against me with an enormous grin and I drop my hands to cup her stomach with affection. I can't wait until she's round with our baby. *Our baby.*

We did it. We fucking did it!

"We are." She covers my hands and gives me the biggest smile I've ever seen. Her eyes are sparkling with delight, and she's never looked more beautiful to me than in this moment.

# CHAPTER 48

## —sarah—

I'M LITERALLY FLOATING ON A CLOUD AS I CARRY OUR DINNER UPSTAIRS to the deck. With only a month until winter, the evenings are cool, so AJ has turned on the outdoor heater and drawn the clear blinds to keep the area cozy. His smile is instant the moment I breach the doorway with a delicious-smelling dish in each hand. I love this space up here, but what I love more is that AJ comes with it.

"This smells divine. I think I'll keep you around since you're such a good cook."

"Yeah? And here I thought it was because of my super sperm." He winks as he takes his plate of chicken casserole from me, placing it in front of him, while I chuckle.

"Well, that too." I press my lips to his cheek as I sit beside him and take my first bite. Flavors explode on my tongue, matching the deliciousness of the aroma. "Mmmhm. So good." I quickly scoop up some more, ready to shovel it in as soon as I swallow the first forkful.

AJ nods. "Not too bad." He swallows his food. "You have your volunteer shift tomorrow. Will Mel be working?"

"Yeah."

"You gonna tell her?" Mel's been incredibly supportive through all of this, she should be the first person I share our news with, but it feels wrong not to share it with my family first.

"We probably need to get it confirmed officially first. It could be a false positive." I still can't believe the tests were positive. Yeah, tests. I had to do both of the tests that came in the box. I didn't trust the first one was accurate. After all of these months. If I am pregnant, I'd only be barely pregnant because I got my period last month, even though it was light. I shrug. "I want to be sure."

AJ reaches across and takes my hand. His warm grip is sure and strong, soothing as he rubs his thumb across my knuckles. "I understand. But I'm convinced the tests are accurate. Let's book a doctor's appointment as soon as possible so we can share the news."

I love how excited he is. When I thought I'd be going through this on my own, the unexpected happened and the perfect guy came into my life. I get to create a family with the man I love. A man whose focus is always to fulfill my needs above his own. The man who has the biggest heart and kindest nature I've ever been lucky enough to call mine. I think if I gave him the okay, he'd be on the phone sharing the news with his sister and Dylan straight away.

Squeezing his hand, I agree. "I'll call first thing and see if I can get in to see my GP after my shift tomorrow. Then we can tell everyone over the weekend."

His eyes light up. "I'm coming to your appointment. I don't want to miss a single thing."

Leaning closer, I put my mouth as close to AJ's ear as possible. "I love you," I murmur.

He rubs his scruff against my cheek, his warm breath coating my sensitive flesh. "Good." His fingers slide through my loose hair, pushing it gently away from my face, then he grasps the strands making a fist. "Because I'm never letting you go, Cupcake." He caresses my cheek with open-mouthed kisses until he arrives at the corner of my mouth.

I sigh, knowing exactly what's to come. When AJ kisses me, it's the only thing that takes up space in my mind for those moments. His kisses are all consuming and I think—not think, *know*—I'm addicted to them, addicted to him. Using his grip on my hair, he tilts my head to his liking as his tongue traces my bottom lip. I dart my tongue out to meet his softly, teasing him. The vibration of his groan resonates through my hand resting on his pecs and satisfaction fills me at the effect I have on him. I swallow it greedily and his tongue delves inside my mouth. AJ presses me closer using his grip on my hair, tightening his hold as he ravages my mouth. Heavy breaths and soft sighs escape as our tongues mingle and teeth clash.

Sliding my hand down his defined abs, I reach the waistband of his gray sweats and slip my hand inside, palming his hard cock. He increases the intensity of our kiss, so I squeeze his shaft. Suddenly he pulls away, his hands falling to the waistband of my leggings. "Take these off and climb on." He stretches out the fabric and tries to pull it over my hip one-handed.

I stand with panting breaths, willing to do as he asks because it's exactly what I want. I step back from him to give him a show, dragging my sweater over my head and revealing the cups of my lacy bra which do nothing to hide my beaded nipples. The heat in his eyes burns my skin as he reaches behind his neck, dragging his Henley off and displaying his phenomenal abs and my favorite part, the dusting of dark hair which trails from his navel to beneath the waistband of his sweats.

"As sexy as that bra is, lose it. I want those pretty nipples bare for my mouth while you bounce on my cock." I rub my thighs together at his rasped words. I quickly unlatch it and let it fall down my arms, then toss it on top of my sweater.

He raises his butt and hooks his thumbs into the waistband of his sweats, sliding the fabric down his muscular thighs. His thick cock springs free, bouncing against that sexy trail of hair I was admiring. "I love your body. It's so sexy."

"Ditto, Cupcake." I lick my lips and bend down to taste the tip of his dick, my sensitive nipples brushing the hairs on his thighs. His hand grasps the back of my neck and he drags me up for another scorching kiss. Once he's stolen all of my breath, he pulls back. "Lose the leggings, Cupcake. I need your pussy."

On shaky legs, I stand and hook my thumbs into the waistband of my leggings and panties, taking my time to drag them down my legs. All the while, I keep my eyes locked on AJ as he fists his cock and strokes it seductively. A moan leaves my lips, and I quickly remove my clothes the rest of the way. AJ crooks his finger at me, motioning me forward. As soon as I'm within reach, that same finger slides through my slit and into my opening without preamble. Not that I need any. "Fuck, you're drenched."

"Mmhm." I sweep my tongue across my bottom lip, dropping my chin to my chest so I can watch the corded muscles in his forearm flex as he teases me with his talented fingers. He applies pressure, using the finger he has inside me to tug me closer until my shins hit the edge of the outdoor lounge.

"Come and straddle me." He holds his dick straight up and there's something inherently delicious watching him handle his shaft. His fingers wrapped around the thick length, inviting me to use it for my pleasure and his.

"How can I refuse?" *And why would I want to?* I position myself, careful not to knock his injured leg, with my knees on either side of his thighs. Holding the back of the lounge, I rise ready to slide down onto AJ's shaft, but he releases his cock and grasps my hips firmly. He pulls me down on top of him and leans forward, claiming my mouth. As he fucks my mouth with his tongue, he uses his hold on my hips to rub my pussy along his length in delicious strokes. "Oh, AJ. That feels so damn good," I pant, then return to his lips.

"Hell, yeah it does. You're perfect for me, Cupcake." With his grip on my hips, he lifts me away from his body and he drops his eyes to watch. "Look how wet my cock is from your juices." His volcanic gaze lifts to mine. "Watch as I slide into your perfect pussy."

I nod, my eyes dropping to where we're about to be joined. I take my weight when he releases his grip to grasp his dick, rubbing it through my swollen lips before notching it at my needy opening. I want to drop down and swallow his shaft until I'm completely full, but he squeezes my hip to stop me. "Not so fast. Let's do this nice and slow."

"You really know how to torture a girl. You know that, right?"

His hot breath brushes my lips with his chuckle. "Only in the best possible way." He winks, giving me a sexy smirk. "Watch."

I can't argue with that, so I don't even bother. I drop my eyes to watch his dick disappear inside me, inch by fabulous inch, stretching me wide, until my pelvis is resting against his. He brings his hands up to cup my face and I drop mine to grip his shoulders. With him buried to the hilt, his eyes dance between mine. "If I could live with my cock buried inside your pussy, I would." He presses up, then winces. "I'm afraid you're gonna have to do all the work, Cupcake." He kisses my lips with a tenderness that surprises me and I press into him, my breasts crushing against his pecs. His hands glide down each side of my neck, to my collarbones, around my breasts, and trail to my hips. Grasping them, he lifts me slowly.

A moan escapes me as I take the hint and press away from AJ's body, then I use my thighs to push myself up, feeling the slide of every ridge of his shaft massaging my muscles until just the tip of his crown is still inside. I pause, peering down between us to see his shaft coated with my lubrication, and snap my eyes to his face. "That's so hot. Seeing your dick so wet from me." Using my thigh muscles, I control the drop, making sure I slide down slowly, swallowing his thick length as I take him back inside. I repeat the teasing process over and over, getting hotter with each stroke.

AJ's eyes dance between my bouncing tits and his cock, his breaths hot on my skin—sending goosebumps scattering across my heated flesh. One hand leaves my hip and reaches for my breast. He palms the mound, then scoops the peak into his warm mouth. I cry out as his tongue circles my nipple and lose my focus for a moment, remaining seated pelvis to pelvis with AJ deep inside. He tears his mouth away from my breast. "If you stop, I stop and I know how much you love it when I suck on these pretty nipples."

I'm scandalized. "You wouldn't."

He simply raises an eyebrow and it's enough to move me back into action. He resumes his ministrations, this time working over my other breast as I bounce up and down on him, building us both ever closer to our completion. High-pitched pants leave my lips on puffs of air as his other hand finds its way to my clit. Using his thumb, AJ makes tight circles around the pulsing bud, and sparks quickly form around the edge of my vision while my hair sticks to my face. My thighs are burning and my toes cramp as I grow ever closer to what I know is going to be an explosive orgasm. AJ groans when the wetness from my pussy makes squelching sounds every time I drop down his shaft.

I've never been this free and uninhibited with a lover before and I know it's because AJ makes me feel safe and cherished. Safe to be exactly who I am, flaws and all. There's nothing more freeing than that. It's a gift I'll never take for granted.

"Fuck. You know how hot it is that you get so wet for me?" He grips the back of my neck, pulling my lips to his, smashing the pillows together. His tongue invades with rough strokes and with everything that's happening to my body, I can't hold back my orgasm. I moan into his mouth as my body tightens from the tips of my toes to the very end of each strand of my hair. "Ah, shit! Feel your pussy." He bites my neck and his cock swells inside me, a hot burst of his cum filling me up as he throbs.

On a long moan, I use my pelvic muscles to tighten around him, keeping us locked together. My breaths are choppy and my vision swims with the lack of oxygen filling my lungs. I drop against him, our sweaty bodies pressed together everywhere. He brings his arms around me, caressing his fingers up and down my spine in a calming motion. Our chests rise and fall rapidly as we try to catch our breath and our hearts do their best to beat their way out of our bodies. With the cooler evening air, despite the outdoor heater, it doesn't take long for our heated skin to cool and a shiver to slide through my body. AJ squeezes me tight, then drags the blanket we keep on the back of the lounge around me, wrapping us within its cocoon.

I bury my face in his neck and my lips naturally spread. His citrusy scent is more pronounced after our strenuous activity. It's a smell I'll always associate with AJ. With home. "I love you," I murmur against his hammering pulse point.

His hands tighten around me. "I love you, Cupcake. Thanks for letting me share your booth."

I chuckle and tip my head back to look at him properly. "Thanks for volunteering to get me pregnant."

*epilogue*

# CHAPTER 49

## —sarah—

With our hands entwined, AJ carries a stunning flower arrangement while I carry balloons and a gift for Colton as we make our way down the hallways toward the maternity ward. We're both excited to meet the newest addition to the Jackson family. Lisa gave birth to their second son, Braden, late last night and AJ was determined to be one of the first to visit and wish them well. My thoughts race forward to the day when we finally get to meet our baby and I drop my hand to rub over my very slight bump. If you didn't know I was pregnant, you'd think I ate a big meal. I still have to pinch myself that I'm finally living my dream with my dream fiancé. That's right. Once my doctor confirmed my pregnancy, we invited everyone over to share our good news, and AJ surprised me by dropping to one knee to propose.

Our steps slow as we come to Lisa's room. Glancing at each other with matching smiles, we step through the door. The sight that greets us makes my heart sing. Hayley and Lisa are both sitting on the bed, with their new son resting across Colton's lap. The girls lift their gazes to us but Colton is too focused on his new baby brother to notice we've arrived.

"Hey," I whisper as I carefully lean down to kiss Lisa and Hayley's cheeks. "Congratulations." I glance down at Braden. "He's so handsome."

They both swell with pride. "Thank you. We're just a little in love with him. He's been so good."

"Looks like Colton loves him already."

"Yeah. He hasn't taken his eyes off him since Lisa's Mom dropped him off a little while ago."

I chuckle then move out of the way so AJ can pass on his congratulations. I place the balloons on the side cupboard, then bend down and place a soft kiss on top of Colton's head. "Hey, little man." His eyes skip up to me quickly then return to his little brother.

"Have you met my brother?" he asks.

"Not yet. You wanna introduce us?"

He nods. "This is Braden. He's my baby brother, and I'm gonna look after him and make sure he's always safe."

My heart melts. How adorable. I loved Colton already, but he's just burrowed himself deeper into my heart. "I bet you will. You're gonna be the best big brother." I smooth my hand over his dark hair.

His eyes snap to his uncle. "Unca AJ. You're here."

AJ chuckles. "I wouldn't be anywhere else. I had to meet the new guy. Is he being a good boy?"

Colton nods enthusiastically. "Yep."

"Colt, you wanna let Aunty Sarah and Uncle AJ have a cuddle?" Hayley coaxes. "They brought you a present."

His little eyebrows dip over his gorgeous brown eyes, and I can see him working through his options. He finally nods slowly. "Okay."

"Who wants the first hold?" Lisa asks.

AJ tips his chin toward me. "Sarah can have the first hold because once I have him I won't want to give him up."

I chuckle. "Okay. If I have to." I hold out my arms and wiggle my fingers. Carefully, I lift him from Colton's lap and cradle him close to my body as I did with the baby I cuddled in the NICU this morning. I take a deep breath, drawing his newborn smell into my lungs. I love that new baby smell. "He's so tiny." I automatically sway my body gently from side to side as I kiss the top of his head.

Colton climbs across to AJ and lifts him into his arms. "Hey, Colt. How's it feel to be a big brother?"

He thinks about it for a moment. "Good so far." We all chuckle at the serious tone of his voice. AJ hands him his gift and sits him back on the bed so he can open it. He tears into the paper and reveals the gift AJ found for him. "It's Doug from my book!" he exclaims, holding the plush sheep above his head.

Braden jolts in my arms and lets out a whimper at the sudden noise.

"Sorry, Braden." Colton rises to his knees to check on his little brother, and I lean closer so he can see he's okay.

"He's okay. See?"

Once he's satisfied, he returns to his sheep, snuggling it tight and studying it closely. "Thank you, Unca AJ."

AJ musses his hair. "You're welcome. It's from Aunty Sarah too."

"Thank you, Aunty Sarah."

"You're welcome. I'm glad you love him."

We chat quietly with Lisa and Hayley, and AJ tells them about the dinner service we ordered for them for the next two months so they don't need to worry about cooking dinner.

"Thanks for such an awesome gift." Hayley climbs from Lisa's bed to hug AJ and when they've finished, I pass him the baby, so I can hug her too. "That'll be one less thing we need to worry about."

We chat for a while longer, AJ hogging the baby, and when Braden starts fussing, Lisa tells us it's time for his next feeding, so we take our cue to leave.

"All right, Colton. You wanna hug Braden? It's time for us to go." We had already made plans with Colton that he'd stay with us for a few days when the baby was born, and he was excited about it. He's been asking when it's going to happen for weeks.

"I don't wanna leave Braden. I'm s'posed to look after him." AJ glances at me. This is new. He's always eager to spend time with us. Lisa and Hayley weren't sure how he'd respond to the new baby. They were worried he'd be jealous or feel left out. We thought if he stayed with us for a day or two, we could make a fuss over him while the girls settle their new addition at home. I don't think any of us predicted that Colton would be so infatuated and protective of his new sibling. It's endearing.

AJ crouches down so he's at Colton's level. "I understand. But Aunty Sarah and I were hoping you'd hang out with us for a little while." He glances up at his sister. "We'll only be a little while and then we'll bring you back to Braden."

Hayley nods, recognizing Colton's need to stay close. "Uncle AJ and Aunty Sarah have a surprise for you, then they'll bring you back to the hospital."

His eyes widen. "A surprise?"

I nod. "Yep. It's really cool, too. I think you'll love it."

He finally relents and we head in the direction of AJ's climbing gym. This will be his first time back at the gym since his accident.

When we arrive, Theo and Austin are already waiting out front for us. Theo offered to meet us here so we didn't have to drive to the opposite side of town to pick up Austin.

The boys greet each other like they're best buddies and Colton excitedly shares how he's now a big brother.

Austin listens carefully. "You're lucky he's a boy. Little sisters can be a bit annoying sometimes." It's the first time I've ever heard him say anything negative about Kenny. "They talk a lot and they always wanna hug you. Even when you're in the middle of jumping on the trampoline." He rolls his eyes and we all laugh. He's not wrong there, Kenny's always very affectionate.

Theo rests his hand on Austin's shoulder. "If she annoys you, just tell her to stop."

Austin shrugs. "It's okay. I love her mostly and her hugs are pretty good." Theo catches my eyes, raising his eyebrows.

When we step inside the gym, Colton and Austin's eyes almost pop out of their heads. They turn this way and that, taking in the array of climbing walls, but AJ guides them straight to a section designed especially for kids.

"Can I climb?" Colton asks, his voice full of excitement.

"Absolutely. That's why we're here."

"This is the best," Austin chirps.

"It really is. I love hanging out here. So let's do some climbing." AJ claps his hands together and we make our way over to two empty spaces on the beginner's wall.

The boys cheer and AJ sets them up, explaining everything with just enough detail. Colton has a fairly good idea about the holds because of his climbing wall, but he's never used a rope before. Theo and I listen closely so we can help. Standing side by side, AJ and Theo support the boys as they climb the wall, then come back down to them only to do it all over again.

Throughout the afternoon, the boys' skills and speed increase as well as their confidence. I love that AJ wanted to include Austin. I love watching him interact with the boys as he patiently coaxes and encourages them every step of the way. He's going to be such a great dad. The afternoon flies by, and the boys are beginning to look a little tired.

"Uncle AJ, I wanna see you climb."

"Yeah, show us how you climb," Colton encourages.

"Go on. I'd love to see you in action." I wink at him. I know he's a little nervous since he's only had two physiotherapy appointments so far, but this place is completely safe. It would be good for him.

I can see the internal argument he's having with himself but he finally agrees. The boys cheer as we move to the climbing area for adults. The array of colored holds scattered across the walls is mind-boggling. It's incredible to think that a little piece of plastic can support an adult. My eyes scan the numerous climbers in various positions up the wall. There's even a woman hanging upside down from the roof. My heart pounds as I watch her go for her next hold, and I blow out a relieved breath when she makes it successfully.

"Would you mind belaying for me? I'll only do a couple of quick climbs, then we'll get out of here."

"You would trust me to do that for you?"

He pauses and scans my face. "Of course. I trust you to be the mother of my child." He cups my small bump. "That's the most trust I could put in anyone, Cupcake." And there goes my heart, melting in a puddle at my feet. He slides his fingers through my hair and draws my face closer to his. "You're the person I trust with my heart and soul. Of course, I trust you with this." He swipes his lips across mine.

"What is it with the grownups always kissing?" Austin moans, breaking the moment and making us giggle.

Before I know it, AJ and I are connected to the ropes, and he's making his way up the wall at a steady pace but I can tell he's favoring his recently healed leg. When he makes it to the top, Colton, Austin, and Theo cheer while relief swamps me. I'm proud of him and glad he did this today while the kids were with us. I think having his personal cheer squad helped his confidence. When he makes it back to the mat, the boys race to him. Colton wraps his arms around his legs, looking up at his uncle with pride. Theo gives me a side hug and then shakes AJ's chalk-covered hand.

"You were awesome. You could be Spider-Man!" Austin tells AJ.

"That'd be pretty cool. He's my favorite Avenger," AJ tells him.

I raise my eyebrows. "You were amazing. You looked really strong, considering you've only had your cast off for a little while."

"Thanks. It felt good to be back on the wall." He leans closer and presses a chaste kiss to my lips. "When we get home, I'll thank you properly." He winks at me, giving me his signature grin.

# CHAPTER 50

Sarah's smooth tongue licking up the underside of my cock drags me into consciousness. I press my hips up and a moan escapes from the deepest part of me. When I open my eyes and trace them down the length of my body, the sight that greets me makes my cock throb. Sarah's tits hang heavy as she balances on her knees to work me over. Her eyes glance up, then pause on mine. She smiles at me, her eyes glittering in the early morning sunlight.

"Happy birthday."

I slip my hand into her hair and return her smile. "It's pretty happy so far." I raise a brow and she snickers. Raising my head, I drop my voice. "Happy Valentine's Day, Cupcake." I tug her up to my face and drag my morning scruff across her cheek until I reach her ear. "Now get on your hands and knees." She opens her mouth and I'm certain it's to argue, so I press the pad of my thumb to her lips and shake my head. "No arguments. I'm the birthday boy and I get what I want."

Her delectable mouth slams closed and she moves to the middle of the bed, holding onto the headboard, her back bows beautifully, and her fantastic ass juts out. I move in behind her, running my hand along her spine and around her waist until I can caress her expanded belly. "How's our baby today?"

She turns her head to look at me over her shoulder. "He's great."

I raise my eyebrow at her. She insists we're having a boy since Hayley and Lisa have two boys now, but I want us to have a little girl with hazel eyes and a beautiful heart like her mother. I lower myself until my front is touching the length of Sarah's back, then kiss my way down her spine, rubbing my morning scruff before sucking and licking over the redness. Her back rises and falls with her sighs, then she pushes her ass into my dick.

"Give me your big cock," she moans breathily.

My lips widen. I love how she tells me exactly what she wants, so different from how she was the first time we came together. Gliding my roughened palms up the outside of her thighs, I grasp each ass cheek and squeeze, then skim my fingertips through her pussy. "Fucking drenched," I groan.

She was made for me. Her beautiful heart, perfect curves, ever-changing eyes, and lust for my cock are everything. Not to mention how damn hot she looks carrying my baby.

She rocks back on my fingers, adjusting her angle. "AJ," she whimpers.

I kiss her ass cheek and swipe my fingers up to her already pulsing clit; so damn responsive; more so since she became pregnant. Making delicate circles around the bud, I slide one finger into her hole and pump it in and out, exchanging one finger for two, two for three; the sounds of her wet pussy make me hotter for her. She rocks her body in time with my fingers, a sheen of perspiration building along the dip of her spine. My cock juts out toward Sarah's pussy, begging to get inside her.

"Stop teasing me," she growls and I chuckle.

"So bossy." She pushes back hard, her frustration getting the better of her. She's been so damn horny, which is perfect for me because I can't get enough of her.

I drag my fingers out and slap her ass, making her jump and cry out. My pink handprint looks fantastic on the lush cheek. I shuffle forward, notching my cock at her opening and before I can push inside her slick heat, she lunges back, taking me deep. "Fuck!" I groan with a harsh breath. Gripping her hips, I stop her from moving anymore until I'm ready. "Don't move. Not yet."

She smirks at me over her shoulder, knowing exactly what she does to me. "Fuck me, AJ. Please."

Tightening my grip on her hips, I nod and drag my cock out of her warm sheath, relishing every single perfect inch. I snap my hips forward, slapping my thighs against hers, making her ass jiggle and shunting her up the bed. "Are you ready for me, Cupcake?"

"Oh yeah." She sighs and I watch her knuckles turn white as she tightens her grip on the headboard.

Withdrawing slowly and torturing both of us, I drop my gaze to my glistening cock. "You should see how wet my cock is." I grab her ass cheeks, separate them, and snap my hips forward, filling Sarah deep. Her walls flutter around my shaft and I groan. "You feel so damn good. I think you should let me stay inside you all day as my birthday present."

She chuckles with a moan as I swivel my hips, hitting that special spot inside her. "I have to go to work."

"Call in sick."

"I'm thinking your mom might catch onto the fact it's your birthday and that I'm not actually sick." She raises one eyebrow at me over her shoulder—so damn sassy.

I groan. "Don't talk about my mom while I'm inside you." She giggles again. "Your pussy feels incredible when you laugh, but you'll make me come too fast if you keep that up," I groan again.

Enough talking. I pull out and snap my hips forward repeatedly, directing all of my focus to my cock. Her panting mewls and the tightening of her walls tell me she's getting close to her release so I move my fingers to her clit, rubbing delicate circles around the tight bud. When I pinch it, she explodes, strangling my dick and sucking me inside so I can't even see the root of my cock. It's enough to have fireworks exploding throughout my body and tension locking up my muscles. My dick swells and I quickly pull out of Sarah's heat to finish off on her ass. Stroking my cock, I watch the ribbons of creamy fluid coat her ass. Stars dance around the edge of my vision and I have to close my eyes as the tension in my body finally relents. When I open my eyes again, they instantly drop to Sarah's ass and I lay my palms over the smooth globes, spreading my release across her flesh.

"Mmhm. I love it when you decorate my skin," she rasps in between panting breaths.

See. Perfect for me.

I lean over her, wrap my arms around her middle and kiss my way across the curve of her shoulder until I reach the nape of her neck. "I think you should skip your shower this morning. That way you can smell like me all day."

I roll carefully to my side, taking Sarah with me. She snuggles her body back into mine until we're spooning. "You know, if it were the weekend, and it was just you and me, I'd totally do that." I nuzzle into her neck with a smile because I know she would. She's done it for me before. "I have a birthday present for you." She smiles, turning her head and pressing her lips to mine.

Cupping her face, I deepen the kiss and tangle my tongue with hers. I'll never tire of kissing the woman. Softening the kiss and pressing smaller kisses to her lips, I pull back slightly. "You just gave me the best birthday present ever."

Her grin is big and beautiful. She tries to wriggle out of my hold, but I tighten my grip, making her laugh, and her tits jiggle. Oh yeah! "You might have to let me go so I can get it for you."

"Don't wanna." I pout like a toddler.

She slides her fingers through my hair and presses a hard kiss to my lips. "I promise you'll love it."

I loosen my hold. "Okay then."

She climbs out of bed and heads to the bathroom to do her normal morning stuff, and I take pride in the fact that she's wearing my hand-print on her ass. When she comes out, she heads to her nightstand and pulls out an envelope then climbs back on the bed. Her eyes remain focused on the white paper as she runs her fingers around the edges repeatedly.

"I had no idea what to get you for your birthday, so I hope this is okay." Her eyes lift to mine and she hands it to me with a swipe of her lips across mine. "Happy birthday, Husband" she whispers, her breath touching the place she just kissed.

That's right, *husband*. I whisked us off to *Cardinal Quarry Casino and Resort* along with our friends and family for a New Year's Day dawn wedding. I take the envelope from her and peel it open. Inside is a slip of paper. As I tuck my fingers inside to pull out the paper, she lays her hand on mine, stilling me. "This is totally for you. Don't show me or tell me what it says."

My eyes narrow, drawing my eyebrows down. Now I'm intrigued. I nod my agreement and she removes her hand. I pull out the slip of paper and open it, careful to angle it in such a way that Sarah can't see it. The word 'boy' is written across it in an unfamiliar scrawl. I snap my eyes back to Sarah. "What's this?"

"I know you wanted to know what we're having and you've been going along with my need for a surprise, so I thought I'd ask our obstetrician to write it down for you. I have no idea what it says and I still don't want to know so don't spoil the surprise for me."

My heart swells with the trust she's giving me. I tuck the slip of paper back inside and roll over to my nightstand to put it out of sight, then I pull my girl into me. Wrapping my arms around her, I drag her in tight to me and take her lips in a fierce kiss full of gratitude. Sarah's always thinking about everyone else's needs above her own. It's one of the reasons I fell in love with her so easily. Softening my mouth and slowing our kiss, I press my forehead to hers. Our eyes lock and hold, Sarah's eyes twinkling with delight. "Thank you, Wife." I'll never tire of calling her that. I press a kiss to the tip of her nose and raise a brow. "Sure you don't want me to tell you?"

She uses the hand resting on my pec to push at me playfully. "No. And you're not allowed to tease me either. That's not fair."

"But I love teasing you, and you love it when I do."

She wraps her arm around my neck with a chuckle, her stomach trapped between us. "I just love *you*."

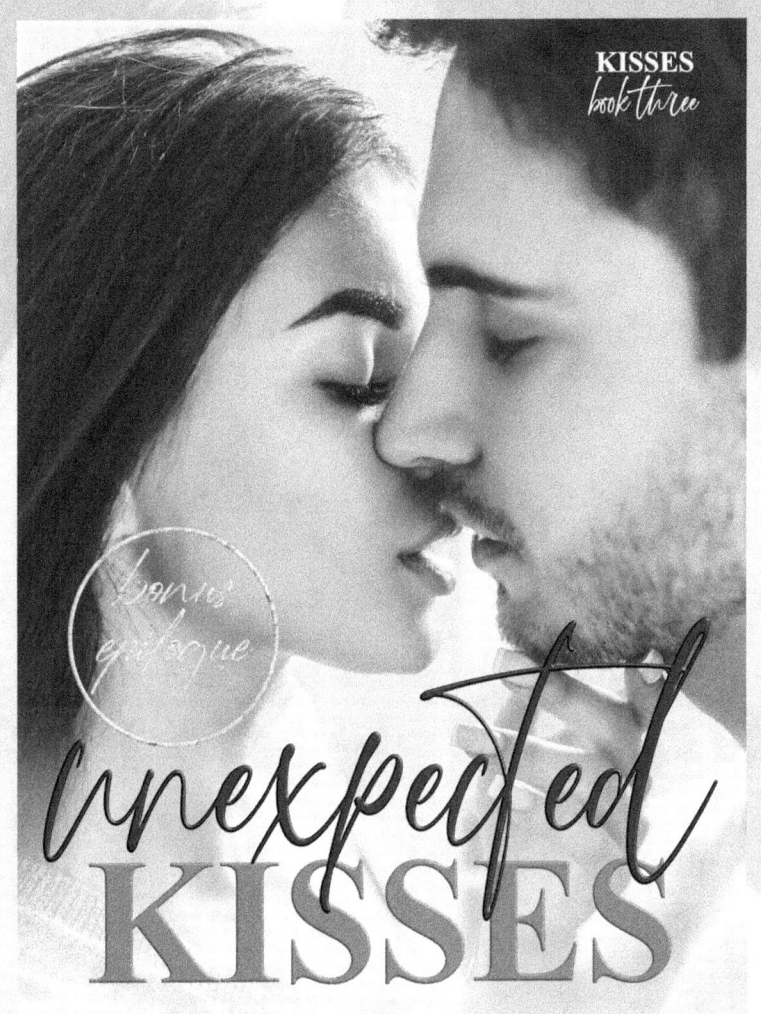

KISSES
*book three*

*bonus epilogue*

*unexpected*
KISSES

# DEBRA ST JAMES

# CHAPTER 1

## *-aj-*

I wake with a dull ache in my lower leg. The one that was broken one year ago when I stupidly went free climbing on my own. *Idiot!* I shake my head and roll my eyes at myself. I know it's all in my head because I haven't had any aches or pains since it healed and I finished my physiotherapy. I've heard of this sort of thing where the body remembers trauma, so that must be what's happening.

Immediately, I know I'm alone, and turning my head to Sarah's side of the bed confirms it. As much as I love our son, I miss waking up next to my wife. I scrub my hands down my face and climb out of bed to see my two favorite people in the world. I quickly drag a pair of basketball shorts up my legs, make a brief stop in the bathroom, and pad down the hallway to Adam's room. Pausing in the doorway, I take a moment to lean against the frame to watch Sarah feeding our son.

I can't believe how lucky I am.

Sarah's eyes are glued to Adam as he suckles on her breast, while her feet move slightly to maintain the steady movement of the rocking chair she loves to use when feeding him during the night and in the early morning.

She must feel my eyes on her because she looks up at me, her lips slowly tipping up. "Hey."

"Hey," I answer as I step into the room. Stroking the soft, downy hair on Adam's head, I bend down and capture Sarah's lips. "I could have brought him to you. Nudge me next time," I murmur.

She glances down at our son; her smile still in place. "I didn't mind. You did the two a.m. feeding."

Adam's dozed off and stopped suckling, so I rub his soft cheek to get him started again. "You need a glass of water?"

She nods. "Please." I press a kiss on Adam's head, followed by Sarah's lips, then head downstairs to get a glass of water. We learned early on that Sarah needs to keep up her water intake while she's breastfeeding or she gets dehydrated. As I step back inside the nursery, Sarah's closing the clasp of her maternity bra, so I place the water on the nightstand and take Adam from her to burp him and change his diaper.

"You go back to bed, get naked, and wait for me."

Her shoulders shake as her eyes twinkle in the dim light. "So bossy," she says with a smile. She's not bothered, she likes it when I'm bossy.

"Damn right. Watching you nourish our child turns me the fuck on. So be ready for me, Cupcake."

"Okay, I'm not about to argue with you." She presses her lips to the top of Adam's head, stroking his dark hair, then presses a chaste kiss to my lips. Sauntering out of the room, she winks at me over her shoulder, kicking her leg up behind her as she disappears out of sight.

God, I love her.

I amble around the nursery with Adam's head resting on my shoulder as I gently pat his back. Sometimes it can take him a while before he burps, but we've learned not to give up or he ends up with pains in his tummy and screams the house down. That's never fun. After several minutes, he releases a burp that sounds loud in the quiet of the early morning. He swivels his head to the opposite side and shoves his tiny fist in his mouth, scrunching up his little face. Without disturbing him too much, I change his diaper and then lay him back in his crib. I gently apply a little pressure to his butt until I know he's out and then leave him to sleep, stopping to clean my hands with sanitizer before I leave his room. I should have enough time to make love to my wife and then squeeze in a quick nap before we start our day.

Rounding the door into our bedroom, I find my gorgeous wife spread out on top of the bedcovers. Her feet press into the mattress while her knees are raised. Her glistening pussy is on display as her fingers circle her clit. My dick immediately hardens at the sight.

Perfect.

I take a few steps toward our bed and prop my knee on the edge, my eyes skimming over Sarah's curves. She bites her bottom lip as her eyes trail over my body. I'm glad she likes what she sees because I'm rewarded every time she's naked. "You started without me," I murmur.

"Just getting warmed up for you."

Dropping my hand to her knee, I glide the palm down her silky thigh, then kiss the top of her knee before reaching for her pussy. I stroke my fingers through her soaking folds. "Always so ready for me, Cupcake," I groan.

She raises her hips, and I slide a single finger inside her silken sheath. "Mmm." Her lids drop low with lust, and her tongue glides across her bottom lip. So damn sexy.

Exchanging one finger for two, I angle them upward to rub the special spot that sets her off and lick my way down her delicious thigh to circle her needy bud with my tongue. She pushes her pelvis into my face and I smile against her clit, giving it a sharp nip with my teeth. "So needy," I whisper.

Her fingers slide into the short strands of my hair, and she presses me in tight. "You make me needy. Make me come, AJ. Stop teasing me."

I move my eyes up her body, watching her massage her breast before locking my eyes on hers. "Always in such a rush, Cupcake." I wish I could clone myself so I can have my mouth on her breasts *and* her clit at the same time. Her hips move in time with my fingers and tongue, and her thighs tighten around my head. As my eyes rove her body, her stomach quivers, and her internal walls tighten around my digits. She's close already, and I've barely started. The sound of her wetness fills our quiet bedroom, along with our heavy breaths and Sarah's whispers of praise for me. I press my groin into the mattress to stave off my orgasm because I refuse to give my cum to the damn bedcovers and suck her pulsing bud between my teeth, biting lightly. I'm rewarded with a long moan and another press of Sarah's hips against my face.

When she's this close, I need to keep everything the same. She doesn't like it if I increase the pressure or change the speed, so I concentrate on tipping her over the edge. Making sure my eyes are locked on her face, her pussy walls rhythmically tighten around my fingers, her mouth drops open with a reverently whispered, "AJ, oh my God," and her body shudders. She presses her body into the mattress, her fingers desperately clasping the strands of my hair.

And I absently wonder if that's how men go bald. Shit, that's not a good thought to have, since my father is balding. *Blech!*

Sarah's sigh and the smile that spreads across her delicious lips bring my mind back to her. She's so damn beautiful when she breaks apart for me, and knowing I'm the last man to ever bear witness to it satiates a deep-seated need in me I'd never experienced before her. Using her grip on my hair, she pulls my face away from her pussy, tugging me upward. I oblige, climbing over her to capture her lips with mine. Over the last almost eighteen months together, I've discovered Sarah likes to taste herself on me after I go down on her, and it's sexy as hell. I'm not sure if it started because it's what I like to do or if she always liked to do it.

And now I'm in a bad mood thinking about her sharing her body with other men. God, I'm an asshole. I push the thoughts aside and kiss my wife the way she deserves to be kissed—with everything that I am. I tell her how much I love her every day, but it's in these moments that I get to *show* her properly.

Her hands push at my pecs, and she uses her body to roll me to my back. I don't offer any resistance because I know what's coming and there's no way in hell I'm gonna delay it. I'll let her play for a bit, but I want to cum in her pussy this morning. I'm not one hundred percent sure of the chances of knocking her up while she's breastfeeding a four-month-old, but there's no use wasting the opportunity—just in case. Her warm mouth closes around the head of my cock and my hips jolt upward, pushing my shaft deeper. She takes my dick further, swallowing around the length as her hand wraps around the base, ensuring every inch is wrapped snugly.

"Fuck!" I breathe, sliding my fingers through her soft hair to push it out of her face so I can watch her swallow me without obstruction. She swallows again as my cock hits the back of her throat. Sarah doesn't have a gag reflex—just another way she's perfect for me. "Do that again." My voice is harsh, my breaths labored as she slides my cock to the back of her throat again and swallows. "Fuck yeah! You're so damn perfect."

Even with a mouth full of cock, I can feel her smile at my praise. I lay my free hand on her backside and slide my fingers between her ass cheeks until I reach her opening. I press my thumb inside and Sarah pushes her body back into my hand. I fuck her with my thumb while she treats my dick to a fantastic blow job.

"I'm not coming in your mouth, Cupcake." Removing my thumb, I drag her mouth from my cock and shuffle my way up the bed so my back's resting against the headboard. Holding my cock upright, I tell Sarah, "Climb on."

Her eyes sparkle as she mumbles, "So damn bossy." But she shuffles closer, throwing one leg across my body so she's straddling me. I take her mouth in a heated kiss while I notch my dick against her opening, then grasp her hips and push her down. We moan against each other's lips as we fit together the way we were meant to. Wrapping my arms around her gorgeous body, I press her tight to me, appreciating the heavy staccato of her heartbeat against my chest.

"Do you feel what you do to me, Sarah?" I shift my face back enough and stroke her hair out of her face so I can see her properly. "I'm not just talking about my dick," I press up into her, then place her hand on my heart between us, "but my heart. This heavy thrum?" She nods, her gorgeous hazel eyes locked on mine. "It beats for you and for Adam."

She curls her fingers against my heated flesh, and her eyes go soft. She flips our hands around, pressing my hand against her breast. "Same. Only for you and Adam."

We meet in the middle for a desperate kiss and she begins to move over me, sliding up and down my cock in measured strokes, our eyes locked together. With slick skin and heavy pants, we move in sync, expressing our love for each other through our bodies in a way we've practiced but feels new every single time. Sarah's movements become erratic the closer she builds, so I hold on to her hips and help her. Black spots dance around the edge of my vision and that telltale electricity builds from my fingers and toes, moving through my body and directing all of my focus to one singular point. Her walls squeeze around me as she cries out, and I shoot my release. I groan as my cock pulses endlessly, emptying everything I have into Sarah, while I hold her still and push my hips up so I'm buried as deep as I can possibly be.

Our lips unite, and our tongues tangle while we hold on to each other tight. Every part of my torso is in contact with every part of Sarah's, our lungs fighting for air but our mouths refusing to separate.

# CHAPTER 2

## *—sarah—*

I WAKE SLOWLY. MY MUSCLES FEEL DELICIOUSLY STRETCHED AFTER OUR early morning romp. When I turn my head, AJ's side of the bed is empty and when I slide my hand across the sheets, I find them cold. He's been gone for a while. My lips tip up. I must be the luckiest woman on the face of the earth to have AJ as my husband and the father of our son. He always insists on letting me sleep as much as possible. He says he couldn't do any of the work while I was carrying Adam and now that he can, he wants to do his share. Honestly, I'm pretty sure he does more than his share. I can't believe this is my life. I pinch my thigh to check I'm not dreaming. "Ouch."

Quickly moving through my morning routine, I go in search of my two favorite guys—I'm not even a little sad that I'm the only woman in the house for now. I wouldn't mind if we had a little sister for Adam. I hear AJ's voice coming from the kitchen and when I round the corner, what I see steals my breath. AJ's shirtless—always my preference—flipping pancakes while Adam's enjoying tummy time on his play mat a safe distance away. AJ's speaking to him about the latest firewall he and Dylan managed to break through and what they did to make sure it would never happen again. Adam's pushing up on his forearms and holding his head up toward AJ's voice, and it's the sweetest thing ever.

I step into the room fully, kissing my hunky husband before scooping Adam into my arms and snuggling him. Drawing in a deep breath, I inhale his baby smell—one of my favorite smells in the world behind AJ's citrus scent—then press a kiss to his chubby little cheek.

He's quite the chubby baby, complete with little rolls of fat on his thighs. "Good morning, mister." I rub my nose back and forth across his in a sweet kiss. His eyes light up and his hands come up quick as lightning, wrapping his little fingers in the strands of my hair.

AJ removes the pan from the heat and wraps his fingers gently around Adam's, peeling each one open. "We have to be gentle with Mommy. No hair pulling." He winks at me, then raises an eyebrow in that sexy way he does and I chuckle. "Unless daddy's doing the pulling," he murmurs against my lips, sending my heart racing. "You want to sit at the table? Breakfast is ready, Cupcake."

I take my seat, turning Adam forward so he faces the table, and AJ places a plate of pancakes and bacon in front of me. "You spoil me."

He bends down, pressing a kiss to my lips. "I need to keep you fed. You only keep me around for my cooking skills." He winks, then takes the seat next to me. "You want me to take him so you can eat?"

"I'm okay. I need my morning snuggles." I take another whiff of his baby scent, then use my fork to cut a piece of pancake, closing my eyes when the fluffiness makes contact with my tongue. "So good."

"Mom didn't mind you taking the day off today?"

"Nope. She was fine. She understood what today means to both of us." AJ nods. "How are you feeling about going back?"

"I'm okay. I can't believe it's taken me this long to do it. But I'm looking forward to it."

"I'll pack us a picnic after we finish breakfast."

AJ parks the car in the empty parking lot. "I've never been here before." I spin slowly, taking in the spectacular scenery. "This is beautiful." I can see why he would use this place as an escape when everything was feeling too much. I still have bouts of feeling guilty about his accident.

"Yeah, I like it here. I've missed it, but I wasn't ready to come back." He grips the back of his neck, treating me to a tempting display of his bulging bicep. "In my mind, I promised myself I'd come back today whether I was ready or not."

I make my way around the Jeep to my husband, my heart breaking for him. I knew the accident had impacted him, but I didn't realize how much. It tainted climbing for him, so I'm hoping this excursion today will help him put it behind him and allow him to get back to something he loves to do. He's done a little climbing in the gym but hasn't done anything outdoors, and now I understand why. Wrapping my arms around him, I peer up at his handsome face. "I'm sorry. I didn't completely understand how deeply you were affected by your accident. How can I help you?"

He smiles down at me. "You and Adam being here with me today is everything I need."

I press up on my toes, meeting AJ halfway for a soft press of lips. We separate and work together to grab the stuff we need for this part of our adventure. AJ helps situate Adam against me using our wrap—it's adorable when AJ uses this to carry Adam when we're out and about—and throws our backpack on. Today's the perfect day for us to revisit the fall site and turn a negative memory for AJ into a positive one. I've spent the last week psyching myself up to see the place where AJ was hurt and needed to be rescued after spending the night trapped beneath a rock fall. With Adam secured to my front, AJ takes my hand and leads me toward a path that will take us to the rocks AJ was climbing when he fell. Being a weekday, we're the only ones on the trail, and I realize it would have been exactly like this a year ago.

"I can see why you came here when you needed space to think. It's incredibly peaceful."

He squeezes my hand and glances around us. "Yeah. It's always been one of my favorite places to climb. I'm hoping that by coming back here, I can put the accident behind me and return to outdoor climbing."

"I know it shook your confidence, but I've watched you climbing in the gym and I can see the way you carefully choose each hand and foothold. I think it was a freak accident. I don't think it was anything you did that day." I hope he can hear the confidence I have in him and his ability.

We reach the location and my heart speeds up as we come to a stop. Dropping my gaze to the ground, I imagine AJ lying unconscious with rocks on his legs, and I close my eyes to block out the unwelcome image. Opening them again, I glance around noticing a pile of rocks alongside the path. "I can understand how you weren't found straight away, especially on a weekday. This part is a little away from the pathway and you wouldn't have been visible to anyone walking the track." I stand on my tiptoes to see the main path. With him lying on the ground, he would have been impossible to see.

AJ's busy studying the rock face I assume he was climbing that day. "I still can't believe I fell." He shakes his head and takes the backpack off, placing it on the ground. He digs out his chalk bag and applies it to his hands, then he steps closer to the wall. AJ then grasps a tiny lip and finds his footholds, taking him off the ground. When I look up, I can see a patch of rock that looks lighter than the rest. That must have been the part that crumbled beneath his hold, causing him to fall.

I have every confidence in him, but my heartbeat increases a little as I watch him in action. I take comfort from Adam, wrapping my arms around him as I watch AJ deftly climb until his feet are higher than my head.

He didn't hesitate. Not for a minute. I wonder if he realizes how brave he is.

I stand, watching the play of muscles across his back and arms beneath his fitted Henley. When he looks down at me and Adam, his expression steals my breath for a moment. I shield my eyes from the sun as I watch him take himself higher without fear. I know it's something he was worried about. Whether he'd be able to put the accident behind him and climb again. Obviously, he needn't have worried. "Look at your daddy," I whisper to our sleeping son.

Once he reaches a certain spot, he pauses and looks back down at us with an enormous smile on his face. "I did it!" he shouts.

"You did. Congratulations!" I rub my hand down Adam's back as pride fills me and a red-tailed hawk swoops overhead, causing a shadow over us. I shade my eyes to watch him soar through the air.

AJ carefully makes his way back to us, wipes his hands on his shorts, and wraps me and Adam in his happy embrace. "I wasn't sure I could do it. That's why I started climbing straight away. I figured it would be best if I just did it. Sorry, I took off without saying anything."

I cup his face with my free hand. "It's okay. I understood why you did it. How are you feeling?" I study him closely, waiting for his answer.

He takes a moment as he flicks his eyes between mine. "Good. Great, actually. I'm glad we came back here and did this." His smile is easy and bright as he glides the palm of his hand over our son's soft, dark hair. "Thanks for swapping your work days to come with me." I'm grateful I work with a boss who understands the idea of putting family first. Though from what AJ has told me, she never did that for her family; it's more a concept she's learned.

"I wouldn't be anywhere else. Your mom understood how important this was." I reach up and AJ bends down to meet me in the middle and I press my lips to his. "I'm so proud of you," I murmur. AJ deepens the kiss, and we get lost in each other; Adam squished between us.

Footsteps sound along the pathway, and we break apart to see who's approaching. A woman in a ranger uniform is walking in our direction with a tablet in her hand. When she notices us, she smiles. "Morning. It's a great day for a hike."

"Morning."

Her gaze dances between us. "Oh, how precious. How old is your baby?" She steps closer, and I smile.

"He's four and a half months." I glance up at AJ as the woman gazes down at our boy.

"He's adorable. I'm sorry to intrude on your time. I'm doing my quarterly inspection for *Centaurea solstitialis*." She points to an area close by with some straggly-looking bushes sporting dying yellow flowers. "I promise to be as quick as possible, then I'll be out of your hair."

I'm about to tell her we won't be here much longer when I glance at AJ and note the creases between his brows. "You said quarterly. Did you happen to be here this time last year?"

She turns her attention toward AJ, and her gaze traces his face. Her eyes widen and a broad smile splits her face. "Yeah, I was. You're the guy who had an accident here last year." She steps closer and throws her arms around him without warning. "Oh my God. I'm so glad you're okay." Still holding his forearm, she pulls back. "I've thought about you often since that day. Wondering if you were okay." She releases him and steps away; her cheeks flushing. "Sorry. I'm just so happy to see you're okay."

AJ steps forward, embracing her this time. "Thank you so much … I don't even know your name to thank you properly."

She chuckles. "Sorry, I'm Violet."

AJ introduces us to Violet, then his voice drops, and I watch his Adam's apple bob, tears forming at the tender moment. "You saved my life that day." He looks at me. "Sarah …" His words die and he releases her to come to me. "What's wrong, Cupcake?" He cups my face, his thumbs wiping the tears from my cheeks.

I shake my head. "Nothing. It just hit me how lucky we were that you were found in time." I turn to Violet. "Thank you so much. I don't know what we would have done if you hadn't found and helped AJ." Stepping away from AJ, I wrap her in my arms the best I can with Adam strapped to me.

"Oh, you don't have to thank me. I'm just glad I was able to get help to him in time." She turns back toward AJ. "How are you, anyway? Any long-lasting effects?"

"Nah, I'm all good. I had a broken leg and a concussion, but I fully recovered … physically." He taps his head. "The mind was another matter. I needed to come back and climb it again to prove to myself I could do it."

She nods. "I get that. Experiences can certainly have long-lasting impacts on mental health." Violet shifts on her feet. "Well, I'd better get to work. It was great to meet you guys. I'm glad you're okay, AJ."

I'm thinking now that we know who helped AJ, we should organize to have some flowers delivered as a thank you. I glance around. "So, do you, uh … work in this park in particular, or do you travel?" There's nothing on her uniform to give me a hint.

"I'm based at the North Gate Entrance." She tilts her chin in the direction, which I'm assuming is north—I'm terrible with direction. "My work is solely focused within this park, so I'm very familiar with it. This particular area is always popular with climbers."

Adam begins to move around, his little eyes squinting open. I shield him the best I can from the bright sunlight and turn my back to create a shadow for him. He's due for a feeding. Glancing around, I spot a rock that could pass as a seat under the shade of a large bush, so I take a seat and release Adam from the wrap and position him at my breast. Violet heads off to do her work, and AJ steps closer to me and Adam, a broad smile splitting his cheeks.

"I can't believe I got to meet the woman who helped save me." He lowers to sit beside me, stroking Adam's head softly.

"I know, right? Now that we know where she works, we shou—"

"Send a thank you gift." We both chuckle.

"Exactly!"

He studies me thoughtfully. "What do you get someone who had such a profound impact on your life? If she hadn't come along, I may not have made it."

My heart skips a beat, and I swallow the lump in my throat. I hate thinking about him not coming back to us, and I refuse to even enter-tain the idea. I reach across and lay my hand on AJ's knee, squeezing it in reassurance. "You were always meant to come back to us. I refuse to think of a different outcome." My throat squeezes tight at the thought of him not being discovered in time. I push it away because it has no place here with us.

We pack up our stuff, say goodbye to Violet, and head back to the Jeep. We need to drive to a different location within the park to have our picnic.

# CHAPTER 3

## —aj—

I STILL CAN'T BELIEVE I FELL. THE CLIMB IS EASY AS ANYTHING AND I can't work out what went wrong. My nerves almost got the best of me as I began to ascend today, but I took a deep breath and started anyway. I didn't want to leave the park without having made an attempt. I'm proud of myself for pushing through my doubts and making it to the point I was aiming for last year.

Today's been a gift. Having Sarah and Adam with me as I confronted my demons helped me to follow through with the promise I made to myself. I feel as though I can do anything with them by my side. And it was a bonus to meet the woman who helped get me to safety. If not for her …

Sarah lays her hand on my thigh and I drop my hand on top. "How are you doing? You've been quiet."

I smile at her, then return my eyes to the road. "I'm okay. I was thinking how lucky I am to have you and Adam with me today while I slay my demons." I raise her hand and kiss her knuckles.

"We'll always be here for you, AJ. I hope you know that."

"Of course I do." And I do. Sarah has stood by me, sure and strong from the moment we recovered from our bump in the road. Not once have I doubted her commitment to me or our relationship. We fall quiet again as we make it back to the city limits. "Did you have a good day?"

"Yeah. It was nice to get out into the fresh air, and it was fantastic to see you climb. I'm so proud of the way you confronted your demons." She sighs. "And the views from the picnic spot were beautiful. Thank you for sharing it with us."

I kiss the back of her hand again. "You're welcome. I'm glad you liked it. We'll go again sometime. Do you mind if we stop and order the flowers for Violet?"

"Great idea. Let's do that and then we'll pick up some takeout for dinner. After all the hiking we did today, I'm worn out." She glances into the back seat and a smile touches her lips. "Wish I could sleep as easily as he does."

"After dinner, I'll run you a bath and put you to bed early."

"That sounds divine. I won't say no to your offer, but only if you'll join me."

I like the sound of that. "Pretty sure that can be arranged."

We pull into the parking lot closest to the florist I prefer and we climb out. Sarah helps to strap Adam to my chest, and we make our way inside. The bell over the door tinkles and the scent of hundreds of flowers overwhelms my senses as we enter.

Sarah gasps beside me. "This little shop is gorgeous. How did you find this place?"

I quickly scan my memory. "I'm not sure. Maybe Hayley or Lisa told me about it. It's where I got your flowers from when I thought you might be pregnant and again when Braden was born." This reminds me, I rarely buy Sarah flowers. I tend to buy foodie-type treats instead of flowers. I wonder if she would like to receive flowers more often.

The woman who's helped me each time I've come here steps out from a door that looks like it goes to the back of the store. "Hello, I'm Cassia. How may I help you?" She studies me closely.

"Hi. I'm AJ. This is my wife, Sarah, and our son, Adam." I point to Adam resting against my chest. "We're hoping to have some flowers delivered. Do you deliver?"

"Sure do. I can deliver locally, statewide, nationwide, or internationally."

"Great."

"Any special occasion?"

I glance at Sarah, and she gives me a subtle nod. "I just met the woman who played a major role in saving my life last year and I want to send her flowers as a thank you."

Cassia raises her hand to her heart as her eyes dance between the three of us. "Oh! I'm so glad everything worked out."

"Me too." Sarah steps closer to the counter.

"Any ideas what type of flowers or arrangement you'd like?"

I shake my head. I have no clue. Flowers don't seem nearly enough for what she did for me.

Sarah looks at me. "She works in a state park, so maybe wildflowers or something along those lines." I'm glad I brought Sarah with me, or I'd look like a total dumbass.

"Sure. Give me a sec, and I'll grab some examples to show you."

Cassia returns through the door which she came and I turn to Sarah with gratitude. "Thanks. I had no clue where to start." I press my lips against her forehead and she strokes her hand down my bicep, squeezing it in support.

We spend the next couple of minutes looking through photo books showing various arrangements and chatting with Cassia. "My sister works in one of the state parks. Which state park does your rescuer work in?" We tell her and her eyes widen. "My sister works there. Her name's Violet."

"No kidding! Your sister was the person who found me and organized my rescue a year ago today. Well, tomorrow, really." I can't believe the coincidence.

Sarah's equally surprised. "What are the chances?"

Cassia shakes her finger at me, her eyes narrowed. "I think I remember you. You came in here on crutches looking as though you'd been beaten up." She shakes her head. "I remember when it happened. Violet was dying to know if the guy she helped was okay, but she was left out of the loop once search and rescue stepped in. She was worried about you. If only I'd known you were the guy. I could have set her mind at ease." Her eyes widen. "This is gonna sound weird, but Violet doesn't like to receive flowers. She believes they should be left to grow. It's always been a bit of a sticking point since this was originally our gramma's florist shop. Violet's never really liked cut flowers."

Oh shit! Now, what do I do? "Okay, so flowers are out." I look at Sarah. "Any ideas?"

"If you don't mind a suggestion, I know she wouldn't want you to make a fuss. But, if you're determined to thank her, you could get her a pamper package. She's a single mom and rarely treats herself. I can look after her daughter, so you don't have to worry about any of that. It's completely up to you, though."

"Thanks. You obviously know her better than we do. What do you think, Cupcake?"

"I love the sound of a pamper package. I bet all the work she does in the park would take its toll on her body. A nice relaxing massage would probably be appreciated now and then."

"Done." I turn to Cassia. "Thanks for your help."

"You're welcome."

We say our goodbyes and make our way to a day spa that Sarah and Emma use occasionally, then we grab takeout and head home.

Sarah's tucking Adam in for the night after his last feeding—well, his last one until he wakes at two a.m.—while I prepare our bath. Switching off the faucet, I add some of Sarah's favorite bath oil and light a couple of candles to add to the ambiance. Today was a big day for all of us and I want to show Sarah how much I appreciated having her with me—that I didn't have to face something that had been bothering me alone.

Without looking up from where I'm swirling the oil in the tub, I know Sarah's entered the room. My heart is fundamentally tethered to hers, and I inherently know when she's close by. I can *feel* her. Turning my head, my breath seizes when my eyes land on her completely bare body. I'll never tire of seeing my wife naked. If we could live naked, I would.

Hang on, that would mean everyone else would see her spectacular curves and they're only for me. We'd have to stay home all the time for that to work. My cock grows behind my zipper at the thought of having Sarah walk around our home naked all day. Yeah, I *really* like that idea.

Standing from the edge of the tub, I hold out my hand. "Come here, Cupcake." She smiles at me, placing her hand in mine, and I tug her against me. Her hands land on my pecs, then snake up around my neck to play with the strands of hair at my nape. "I love having you naked. I was thinking about how I could make it so you were naked all the time."

She chuckles. "Only you would spend time thinking of ways to keep me naked."

I run my nose down the side of hers and press a light kiss to her lips. "Of course. What else am I meant to be thinking about when I have you for my wife?" I press kisses along her jawline, up to her ear, and whisper, "I'd have to be naked, too."

She shivers in my arms and I love that she's equally affected by me as I am by her. "Now that's an idea I could get behind."

I nip her lobe and make my way down to her collarbone, licking and biting my way across to her shoulder, where I lay a kiss. As much as I want to ravage her body, I can see she's tired, so I take her hand in mine. "Come on, Cupcake. Let's get you into the bath."

She sighs as she places first one foot and then the other into the warm, soothing water. "Thank you for taking care of me." She lowers herself to sit, then smiles up at me. "You promised to join me, so …" she waves her hand up and down my body, "get naked, Husband."

"I'm gonna kiss Adam goodnight. I'll be back."

Stepping quietly into our son's bedroom, I can't believe this is my life. The best decision I ever made was suggesting to Dylan that we celebrate our success at *Club Rumors*. It led me to meet Sarah and have what I have now. Without disturbing Adam, I bend over the side of the crib and lay a gentle kiss on his temple, then run my finger gently down his smooth, chubby cheek. The love I have for Adam and Sarah fills my heart to the brim.

Leaving him to sleep, I make my way back to my wife. As soon as I step over the threshold to our bedroom, I strip, ensuring I walk into our bathroom naked, the same way Sarah did.

Her gaze snaps to me and heats as she skims her eyes up and down my body, pausing on my growing cock. She shuffles forward in the bath, making room for me. Her eyes follow my every move as I step forward, and her head tilts up so as not to break contact as I slip in behind her. I snake my hand around her, cupping her chin so I can taste her lips, my cock jutting straight out, trying to get in on the action, but he'll have to wait a little longer. She sighs into the kiss and we linger for a moment before I slowly lower into the tub, my legs on the outside of hers. Guiding her until she presses her back against my front, I wrap one hand around her middle and use my other to trace a line down the curve of her neck and across her shoulder, where I place a soft kiss. "I love you, Sarah. So much."

She turns her head to look at me over her shoulder. "You were so unexpected, AJ, but I love you so much, too."

*Would you like to spend Mother's Day with the Stanfield siblings? Sign up for my newsletter to share their special day.*
*https://tinyurl.com/kisses-bonus*

*Emma's friend, Kate, finds her HEA in* **Loving Summer**.
*A grumpy/sunshine billionaire romance*
A steamy, low-angst, stand-alone contemporary romance about a grumpy, determined hidden billionaire and a penny-pinching, tenderhearted teacher doing her best to protect her heart.
*https://books2read.com/dsj-lovingsummer*

*Max's soccer friend and the owner of Brady's Pub, Finn Brady, meets his match in*
**Enemy Kisses**.
*An enemies to lovers romance novella*

A steam-filled, angsty, stand-alone contemporary romance about a misunderstood pub owner who has no problem working for the affections of his brand-new neighbor and the baker who tries her best to guard her heart but isn't able to fight the tempting pull of her enemy.

*https://books2read.com/dsj-enemykisses*

# pinterest

I put together a Pinterest board for Sarah and AJ's story. If you're interested, you can check it out here:

*https://tinyurl.com/unexpectedkisses-pinterest*

# debra's books

### The Summer Twins
Loving Summer | *Kate Summer & Oliver Stone*
Second Chance Summer | *Toby Summer & Cassia Phillips*
The Summer Twins | Complete Series
Spin-off Novella
Loving Roman | *Roman Armstrong & Alice Reed*

### Kisses
Stolen Kisses | *Emma Miller & Theo Drivas*
Moonlit Kisses | *Max Stanfield & Molly Lewis*
Unexpected Kisses | *Sarah Stanfield & AJ*
Kisses | Complete Series

### Monday Knights | *novellas*
Enemy Kisses | *Finn Brady & Harriet Dubois*
Wicked Kisses | *Lincoln Kingsley & Sophie Chalmers*

### Everlasting
Everlasting Love | *Shane Sutton & Violet Jamison*
Everlasting Promises | *Hope Sullivan & Benjamin Taylor*
Everlasting Vows | *Nixon Steele & Abigail Steele*

Debra has a list of her books available on her website.

### You can find them here:
*https://debrastjamesbooks.com*

# connect with debra

## stalk me

### You can stalk me pretty much everywhere!
*https://debrastjamesbooks.com/connect/*

### How about joining my Facebook group?
*https://www.facebook.com/groups/DebsBibliomaniacs*

## newsletter

Join Debra's newsletter to receive important updates before anyone else. Newsletters will be sent once a month unless something exciting is happening.
*https://debrastjamesbooks.com/newsletter/*

# thank you

A book doesn't just happen. It's been hours upon hours spent researching, typing one word after another, creating a sentence, building a paragraph, molding a chapter, and eventually, weaving an entire story.

Thank you, Di, for sharing your particular experience with me as I was working to ensure Emma's story reflected the reality of *Ductal Carcinoma In Situ*. I appreciate the candor with which you answered my numerous and personally invasive questions. You're the best, lady!

Moonlit Kisses wasn't the story I was supposed to write. Shane's story was supposed to be next, but after discovering a hidden truth about my paternity, I wasn't in the right mindset for his story. Last August, I learned the man I grew up believing to be my biological father, is, in fact, not my biological father at all. It turns out I've never met my biological father and I'll probably never know who he is. As you can imagine, my mind was muddled, so I decided to write Max's story, thinking it would be a little lighter than what I anticipate Shane's story to be. Perhaps this is why I wanted Molly to meet her father.

Thank you so much for reading Sarah and AJ's story and making it through the slowest burn I've written to date. When Sarah's story came to me, I imagined her and AJ having sex almost from the first chapter since she wanted to have a baby. However, the woman had a plan and she was bound and determined to stick to it. But we got them there in the end and that's the most important thing.

As always, I would like to thank Mr. St James and our two sons for their support and patience with me when dinner was late, or I didn't listen as attentively as I should have, or I didn't want to leave my cave because I was working on this baby.

To my beta readers, Kelly, Debbie, Wendy, Rita, Tanya, Julia, and Di thank you for your invaluable feedback. Andrea, thank you for your invaluable information regarding AJ's injuries and treatment. Your medical knowledge and advice really helped to make that part of the story realistic. And finally, Tiffany. Thank you for sharing your experience in the NICU to help make Sarah's volunteer shifts as a baby cuddler as accurate as possible.

To my online support network, you were there for me on the days when I doubted myself. Ladies, you are so very important to me. I'm grateful we connected and I can call you my friends.

To you, the reader. Thank you for taking a chance on me; for reading my book. I truly do appreciate your time. If you've enjoyed reading about the Stanfield family, I'd love to hear from you.

# *about the author*

Debra St James is an author of spicy, slow-burn contemporary romance that features cinnamon roll heroes who listen to their women's hearts and their words. She takes her time to weave a detailed tapestry of genuine characters, real-life struggles, love, and romance to create engaging stories that will have you so immersed in the story that you'll never want to leave. Her stories are always guaranteed to take you on an emotional journey that ultimately ends with a HEA!

Debra loves to read romance. Her family often finds her with her nose stuck in her iPad, swooning over her latest book boyfriend. She writes part-time from her Perth home, which she shares with Mr St James and their two sons, whose antics often make her roll her eyes and laugh in equal measure.

Writing a novel had never been on her radar. One morning, she was enjoying a coffee by the river and a story sprouted, seemingly from nowhere. At 51, she pulled up the Pages app on her phone and began to type, giving life to her debut, *Loving Summer*.

The rest, as they say, is history!

amazon.com/author/debrastjames

facebook.com/debra.stjames.books

instagram.com/debrastjames_books

bookbub.com/authors/debra-st-james

goodreads.com/debrastjames

pinterest.com/debrastjamesbooks